D0131049

Reader's Digest

ILLUSTRATED GUIDE TO THE

Treasures of America

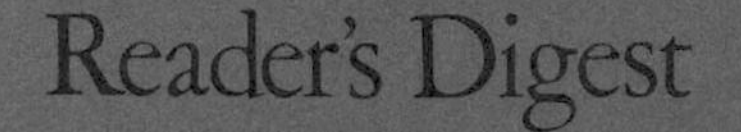

Illustrated Guide to the

TREASURES OF AMERICA

E PLURIBUS UNUM

The Reader's Digest Association, Inc.,
Pleasantville, New York

The Reader's Digest Association, Ltd.,
Montreal, Canada

The editors of Reader's Digest General Books wish to express their gratitude for the invaluable contributions of the following individuals:

JOHN ELY BURCHARD
Dean Emeritus, School of Humanities and Social Science
Massachusetts Institute of Technology
Cambridge, Massachusetts

DR. VICTOR J. DANILOV
Director, Museum of Science and Industry
Chicago, Illinois

MILO M. NAEVE
Director, Colorado Springs Fine Arts Center
Colorado Springs, Colorado

DR. JOSHUA C. TAYLOR
Director, National Collection of Fine Arts,
Smithsonian Institution, Washington, D.C.

Without the conscientious cooperation of state officials, curators, directors, managers and ministers as well as selected regional authorities—more than 5000 in all—a project of this magnitude would have been impossible. We extend sincerest thanks to all of these people, who were so generous with their time and interest.

A Vigorous People in a New Land Produced an Amazing Array of Treasures.

Many are the marvels in America and many are unrecognized: this lady, for example. The 19½-foot bronze Statue of Freedom *is little known although she graces the dome of the U.S. Capitol, one of the most looked-at buildings in all of Washington, D.C.*

Treasures, in the time-honored tradition of Europe and the Orient, are the jewels, paintings and palaces created for the rich, for royalty and for the Church. The treasures of America have a wider compass. There are, to be sure, the great works commissioned by the rich, but there is also the work of carpenters, mechanics and craftsmen who made objects for everyday use but made them with such exquisite care and sensitivity that they have since become museum pieces. The treasures described in this book include mills and meetinghouses, humble dwellings, bridges and dams, marvelous trains and automobiles, buildings made for commerce, great parks and gardens and places that are steeped in the history of our land.

The treasures of America have a character and quality unlike those of any other place: they are a direct expression of the vitality derived from the blending of many peoples from many different countries and cultures. One of the strengths of the American way has been our ability to work together with the materials at hand and to learn from one another.

Among the more than 5000 treasured places described in this book, you will find the familiar and expected such as Mount Vernon, the collections of the Smithsonian Institution and San Simeon. You will also find hundreds of fascinating small museums, out-of-the-way historic houses and special displays of artifacts and other objects—and many of these may be closer to your home than you think.

If you wish to get on with the pleasure of seeing what is to be found in your area, or locate a place you plan to visit, simply turn this page and check the contents of the book. You will see that we have divided the country into nine regions, each with its own treasure map.

If you are intrigued by a particular subject, such as sculpture, early American painting, automobiles, silver or clocks, turn to the Topical Directory starting on page 592.

The treasures are here and the book is yours to use.

Contents

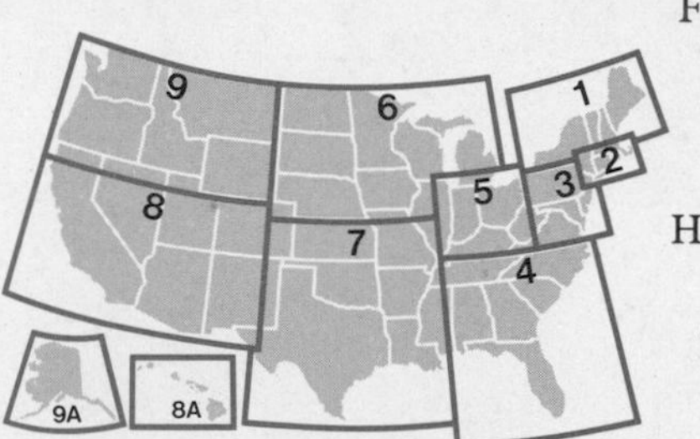

1
2
3
4
5
6
7
8
9
9A
8A

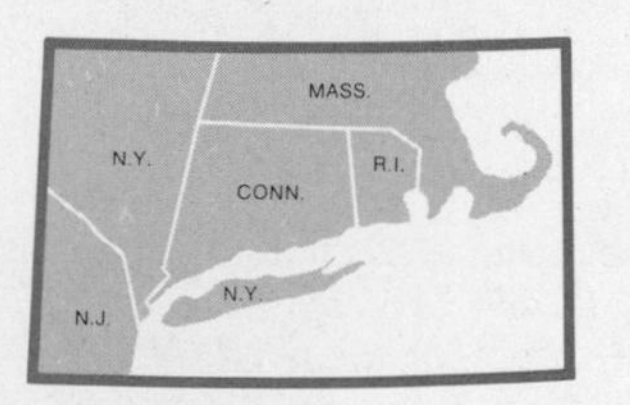

MASS.
N.Y.
CONN.
R.I.
N.Y.
N.J.

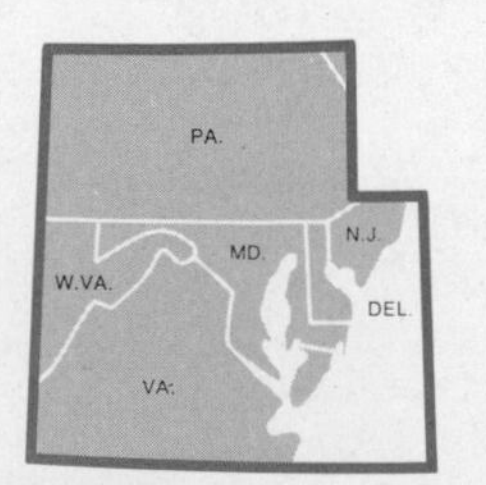

PA.
N.J.
MD.
W.VA.
DEL.
VA.

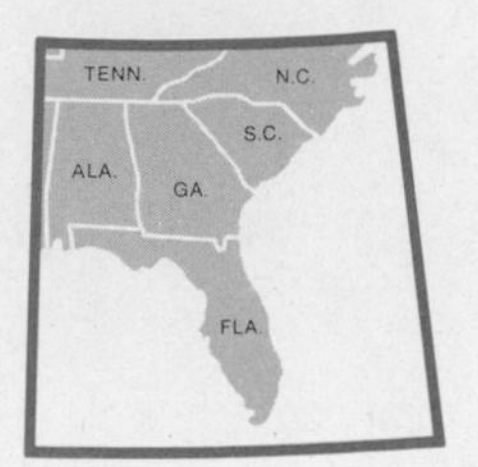

TENN.
N.C.
S.C.
ALA.
GA.
FLA.

How the Treasures Came to Be

Most of the buildings, the decorative and mechanical marvels and, to a lesser degree, the painting and sculpture that comprise the treasures described in this book were created by Americans. There are, of course, overtones of our European heritage and great displays of European, Oriental, African and Oceanic art all across the country—much of it brought here by vigorous collectors such as Henry Frick, Andrew Mellon and Samuel Kress. But in the following overview of how the treasures came to be, we are primarily concerned with American artists, architects, craftsmen and inventors. In each category, mostly in chronological order, the important names and influential schools and movements are explained and evaluated. A thoughtful reading of these essays should give more insight into the treasures of America; it should encourage one to seek further afield for new interests and to appreciate them more fully.

Evolution of the Fine Arts

Our restless search for insight and beauty by means of painting and sculpture

Unlike the first settlers in the Americas who brought with them from Spain and Portugal the trappings of an aristocratic tradition encompassing a flamboyant taste in both civil and religious art and architecture, most of the Colonists who settled in what is now the United States had little reason to consider the fine arts an essential part of their culture. What art there was served as a symbolic tie with the Old World tradition they had left behind them. The sensitively designed but candid portraits they hung in their houses kept alive a sense of family lineage, as well as a fascination with a rendering of material facts.

Mrs. Elizabeth Freake and Baby Mary *was painted around 1674 by an unknown Colonial portrait artist.*

A few names of these earliest American artists, such as Thomas Smith, the Gerret Duyckinck family, Henrietta Johnston and Justus Engelhardt Kuhn, have come down to us, but most of those who painted before the middle of the 18th century are now known to us only by their individual styles. They are usually distinguished by the names of their best-known sitters; hence we have the Freake Limner, who painted *Mrs. Elizabeth Freake and Baby Mary,* the Gansevoort Limner, the Patroon Painter and others.

Artists Begin to Arrive

During the second quarter of the 18th century, artists of modest talent came from Europe to paint for wealthy families in New England, the Middle Colonies and the South. A more sophisticated approach to representation, characterized by shimmering lights and shadows and fully modeled forms, took precedence over the flat, lively patterning of the early limners.

The most influential of these new arrivals was John Smibert, a thoroughly trained, Scottish-born painter from London, who brought with him copies of old masters he made in Italy, intending to establish a college with Bishop

Berkeley in Bermuda. Smibert's studio in Boston was an inspiration to many young artists eager to carry on the great tradition of painting.

The young Benjamin West from Pennsylvania left for Rome in 1760 to make direct contact with that tradition. Settling in London a few years later, he helped to found the Royal Academy of Art and succeeded (1792) Sir Joshua Reynolds as its president; he became the favorite painter of George III. West painted both portraits and vast historical canvases. Although he never returned to America, his influence was great, for his London studio became the center for the growing number of young American artists who saw art as a noble calling.

Portrait of Paul Revere *is by John Singleton Copley, one of the earliest American painters to consider portraiture a matter of rendering personality as well as physical likeness.*

One of these, John Singleton Copley of Boston, developed his own extraordinary style, translating the candid observation of the limner into the rounded, illusionistic forms of the more recently arrived painters. Yet he did not sacrifice the sharp, analytic vision that made the objects of his immediate world a continuous fascination to him. A poised hand, the reflection in a mahogany table, or the subtle shape of a silver vessel in the hands of craftsman Paul Revere were all treated with such care that simply seeing with precision becomes a wonder and delight. But Copley also wanted to be a painter in the tradition of Raphael and Titian, and after an encouraging correspondence with West, Copley left in 1774 to follow in West's footsteps, going first to Rome and then to England. The transformation that then took place in his painting dramatically exemplifies a change in the concept of art that was also to prevail in the young republic. Copley turned the viewer's attention from the object depicted to the artist himself—that is, the evident manner in which the artist painted an image became a major element in a picture. His broad, rhythmical brushstrokes, following a current London manner, and his dramatically constructed compositions elevated the homely features and heroic activities of his contemporaries into a generalized, timeless world of art.

Conscious style, as in the works of the Englishmen Thomas Gainsborough, Joshua Reynolds or Thomas Lawrence, made art an elevating, idealizing force that could raise the local champion to the realm of hero or place local womanhood on a par with classical beauty. John Trumbull, who also studied with West, set out to do just this in a series of paintings on the American Revolution, now at Yale University. The paintings in the Rotunda of the Capitol in Washington, four of which are by Trumbull, reflect this aim. In portraiture, Gilbert Stuart, who also had established himself in England, had the greatest impact, creating paintings with an extraordinary ease and subtlety of brushwork that almost magically equates a refinement of artistic style with the sitter's individual character.

Still another of West's pupils, Charles Willson Peale, a remarkable Philadelphian who was an inventor, naturalist and devoted public educator, established a museum in the 1780s and tried unsuccessfully to found the first academy of art in the United States. But the high concept that art should depict noble actions that elevate the viewer beyond local circumstances finally led to the establishment of academies in Philadelphia, New York and Boston. These provided plaster casts of ancient masterpieces and regular exhibitions of past and modern works to guide the artist and educate public taste. Yet few patrons could be found for any paintings other than portraits, and it was eventually the suave and elegant style of portrait painter Thomas

Portraitist Thomas Sully came to the U.S. at nine but later studied in his native Britain, where he acquired his elegant yet relaxed style. Captain J. David *is among his many paintings—some 2600 in all.*

Sully, refined in color and rhythmically ideal in form, that ruled the day.

Not content with this dashing English style, John Vanderlyn of Kingston, New York, studied the more austere classical style of Jacques Louis David in France, where he enjoyed considerable success. But his nude *Ariadne,* praised in Paris, shocked Americans, who, when in mixed company, still preferred not even to look at casts of Greek sculpture.

Equally disenchanted with artistic facility, Washington Allston, who came from Charleston and graduated from Harvard in 1800, set out to create an art that brought to the modern world the quiet, mysterious beauty found in the mellowed works of 16th-century Italian masters such as Titian. For him a painting, whether a portrait or literary scene, was an invitation to meditate, to make contact with an inner spirit pervading nature and man. When he settled in Cambridge, Massachusetts, after a successful beginning in Italy and England, he became a living symbol of the artist as the soul of the community, a contact with permanent spiritual values that the growing mercantile society was beginning to threaten. This rather idealized concept was in sympathy with the New England Transcendentalists, with the writings of Ralph Waldo Emerson and even Henry Thoreau. It can be detected as well in the highly personal works of the doctor turned artist, William Rimmer, who went his own way in the creation of his haunting sculpture, paintings and drawings.

A long line of American artists, most of them from New England, now began to set up shop in Italy, usually in Rome, where, Nathaniel Hawthorne said, they went ". . . chiefly for the warmth of each other." They wished to live their art in a sympathetic environment. Samuel F. B. Morse, Henry Peters Gray and William Page all brought back the glow of Old World ideality in their paintings. Those who stayed longest were the sculptors.

The Beginnings of Sculpture

For nine years Horatio Greenough worked on this godlike Washington *in his Florence studio. Its nakedness scandalized Victorian America.*

Sculpture began late in the United States. Though the carvers of ship figureheads, tombstones and architectural ornament plied their trade from the mid-18th century—and many of their works show great vigor and imagination—monumental sculpture was hardly known until the 1830s and '40s. Earlier works were by Europeans such as Jean Antoine Houdon, Giuseppe Ceracchi and Antonio Canova, who made likenesses of George Washington and other statesmen. When the Capitol was begun in Washington, most of its sculpture was produced by Italian sculptors brought for the purpose because no Americans were considered capable.

William Rush of Philadelphia was an exception, producing bold and vigorous portraits and figures in wood, and Samuel McIntire, Hezekiah Augur, John Browere and various sculptors combined "heads" and occasional figure sculpture with other craft activity. But Horatio Greenough, who went to Italy in 1824, Thomas Crawford, who set up his studio in Rome in 1835, and Hiram Powers, who settled in Florence in 1837, established a new tradition. The public was hardly prepared for Greenough's monumental, Zeus-like *Washington,* only partially draped, when he brought it to the capital in 1842, but shortly thereafter Hiram Powers's nude white marble *Greek Slave* was heralded as high moral art, and Crawford's sculptural decoration for the Capitol, including *Freedom* surmounting the dome, won him acclaim. Erastus Dow Palmer, who stayed in New York, rather domesticated the high classical style in works such as *White Captive,* but most American sculptors preferred the artistic atmosphere of Rome, where, among other things, skilled Italian craftsmen could cut their works in marble.

An American Consciousness

Directly opposed to the sympathies for the past that drew artists together in Rome was a growing interest through the 1830s in an art based on directly observed nature rather than on the established images of art. Since this required no European study and seemed to be free of established tradition, it was considered a peculiarly American taste, even though it was shared by many contemporaries abroad. For the first time paintings of popular subject matter became common, as in the expertly depicted rural scenes of William Sidney Mount in New York, the classically composed but sharply observed riverboatmen of George Caleb Bingham in Missouri or the anecdotal tableaux of Richard Catton Woodville in Maryland. The extraordinary John Quidor gave his special animation to scenes of Rip Van Winkle and other American stories, and David Blythe of Pittsburgh painted humorous situations in a style that was pointedly anti-ideal. Many of these images were translated into engravings, and the newly developed process of lithography eventually permitted such timely and familiar scenes to reach an enormous public. Nathaniel Currier and James Merritt Ives joined forces in 1857 to produce their popular lithographs, and the firm continued until 1907.

George Caleb Bingham depicted a variety of common people at work and leisure in Missouri where he lived most of his life. Boatmen like these in Raftsmen Playing Cards *were a favorite subject.*

Many of the artists committed to precisely drawn illustrations and homely scenes went to study in Düsseldorf, Germany, where the central American painter was Emanuel Leutze. He executed his famous *Washington Crossing the Delaware* there in 1851. The "Düsseldorf manner" was as matter of fact and sharp in outline as the Italianate manner was soft in color and ideal in form. Later, the Düsseldorf style gave way to new interests in perception. Eastman Johnson, whose best-known work is *Old Kentucky Home,* set out to capture the total effect of an object or a scene before adding detail. Light was of infinite fascination as it revealed the form of things. Winslow Homer, who began by recording activities during the Civil War for *Harper's Weekly,* became a master of luminous renderings in which everything seems to be caught in a breathless moment of perfect composition, yet exists in a wholly natural environment. This extraordinary combination of compositional poise and acute observation of light and atmosphere is especially remarkable in the watercolors which Homer made after he settled on the Maine coast and visited the Bahamas.

In both Johnson and Homer, the subject is less important than the pleasure of seeing, yet other artists such as John George Brown carried on the anecdotal tradition, but with sharpened vision, well through the century. Sculpture, too, had its story-telling side. After the Civil War, John Rogers sold castings of his small, expertly modeled narrative "Rogers groups" throughout the country by catalog. Their charm comes from their minute accuracy and convincing narration, rather than beauty of form.

The Inspiring Challenge of a Vast Continent

While some painters turned to domestic scenes, others moved westward to study the new continent. John James Audubon traveled through the South and Midwest making studies for his superb illustrations of the birds and marvels of the New World. George Catlin and Karl Bodmer painted the Western landscape and Indians, starting a tradition that continued through the century in the works of John Mix Stanley, Charles Deas, Frederic

Remington and Charles Marion Russell. Catlin's sympathetic Indian portraits were acclaimed in Europe as well as America, and Alfred Jacob Miller recorded scenery and Indian life as far west as the Rocky Mountains for an expedition led by the Scotsman Captain William Drummond Stewart.

But there was another aspect of the new concentration on nature that began in the 1830s. According to the philosophies of William Cullen Bryant and Ralph Waldo Emerson, in nature man could escape the limits of his own thoughts and make contact with God. Nature's way was God's way, and any departure from the exact face of nature in all its complexity was sacrilege. The first landscape paintings in America had been either interior decorations, simple records of estates and cities as done by Ralph Earle or Francis Guy or intellectually organized "classical" landscapes such as those of young Washington Allston. Yet it had been recognized for a long time that in a painted landscape, as in a landscaped garden, the jagged forms of rocks and caves and straggling trees could evoke emotions contrary to those aroused by open, peaceful fields and regular clumps of foliage. Thomas Cole, painting in the Catskills, the White Mountains and the Hudson River Valley, carried this natural expressiveness to its furthest point, finding special spiritual meaning in the phenomena with which he identified himself. His twisting trees, bursting light and panoramic views were meant to overwhelm human complacency, as were his series on the course of life or the course of empire. Most of those who worked in the Hudson River area, such as Thomas Doughty, Asher Brown Durand, Worthington Wittridge and John Kensett, admired Cole but were less concerned with dramatically expressive form. They eventually concluded that nature itself, accurately transcribed, carried its own spiritual meaning. For the first time America, because of its abundant wild, unspoiled countryside and its freedom from tradition, could consider itself superior in artistic potential to Europe.

Asher B. Durand painted Kindred Spirits *in memory of Thomas Cole, one of the first of the Hudson River school of painters. While Cole and poet-editor William Cullen Bryant occupy a central position in the composition, the beauty of the place is the main subject. Like his friends, Durand celebrated the wonder of unspoiled nature.*

After mid-century, however, some landscape painters felt the need to search in far places to keep alive their fascination with the mystery of nature. Frederick Edwin Church staggered the eye with great vistas of the Andes. Martin Johnson Heade, with the interest of both landscape painter and naturalist, caught the strangeness of impending storms, exotic plants and birds and tropical jungles. Albert Bierstadt, fresh from studies abroad, went west to explore the Yellowstone River and devoted the rest of his life to depicting the grandeur of areas that would later become national parks. Thomas Moran carried the tradition into the 20th century. It was largely this fascination with the grandeur of landscape as the country pushed west that helped to establish the first national park (Yellowstone) in 1872.

The Barbizon Mood

Some artists who were devoted to the study of nature, however, took a direction quite opposite to those who sought the wild and the overwhelming. George Inness, who began like the Hudson River painters, developed increasingly hazy, richly colored and suggestive landscapes on a domestic scale. These paintings recall a bit the works being done in France at mid-century by artists living with the peasants in the forest of Barbizon.

William Morris Hunt, one of the early admirers of the Barbizon painters, encouraged Boston collectors to buy works of Théodore Rousseau, Camille Corot and especially Jean François Millet. In the second half of the century, American painters, imbued with the humble Barbizon view of nature, flocked

Still life of Old Models *by William Harnett emphasizes the color and texture of objects. After the Civil War when Harnett worked, no one painter or school of painting dominated art in America.*

to the rural areas of France as they had earlier to the city of Rome. Their simplified paintings of unspectacular landscapes that capture a mood, usually of twilight, were an antidote to the exciting and grandiose panoramas of the American West painted by artists such as Bierstadt, Thomas Hill and Thomas Moran; they were different as well from the clear, luminous works of Winslow Homer.

By the 1870s the American public was prepared to accept a wide range of art, from the "fool-the-eye" still life paintings of William Harnett to the misty evocations of George Fuller; from the neighborly sculptures of John Rogers to the classical purity of William Henry Rinehart's work and the heroic figures of the Paris-trained Augustus Saint-Gaudens and Daniel Chester French. Art, in fact, had a new place in society, and art museums were founded in various cities to carry the image of art in all its diversity to a wide public.

A group of American painters who studied in Munich, chiefly centered on Frank Duveneck, developed a bold, direct way of painting based to a degree on the 17th-century Franz Hals and the Spanish master Velázquez. Like Edouard Manet in France, the Munich group's interest was in capturing the bold effect in a few direct, full brushstrokes, but unlike the French painters, they preferred the dark tones of old masters. Some, like William Merrit Chase, eventually developed a much lighter palette, especially after working in Venice. Duveneck settled in Cincinnati, where his school made a great impact; Chase became an influential teacher in New York. In a somewhat similar fashion, John Singer Sargent, who was much in demand as a fashionable portrait painter, gave his literally observed images a grace and verve through dashing brushwork.

The White Girl *by James McNeill Whistler, exhibited in 1863, plays on subtleties of perception by showing a white figure against a white drapery standing on a white rug. This interest in form and color relationships would dominate Whistler's later work.*

The works of these artists are vastly different from those by J. Alden Weir, Theodore Robinson, John H. Twachtman, Edmund C. Tarbell, Willard L. Metcalf, Childe Hassam and others who, like the French artists Claude Monet and Alfred Sisley, wished to savor the nice complexities of color and light. Often called American Impressionists, they worked in France and shared sympathy with these French painters but retained their own sense of evocation and sentiment. (Only Mary Cassatt of Philadelphia remained in France as an actual member of the French group.) Thomas Dewing, for example, found in the sensibility of Impressionism a kind of twilight nostalgia of extraordinary refinement. In contrast to the bold execution of the Munich painters and the preciosity of painters such as Dewing stands the isolated figure of Thomas Eakins.

Like many American artists in the second half of the century, Eakins studied with the academic painters of Paris. From the 1850s L'École des Beaux Arts and other studios in Paris drew a large American contingent. Eakins's master was Jean Léon Gérôme, who painted in a precise, calculated style. Taking this precision to a direct study of nature, spurred by a fascination with scientific truth, Eakins produced his extraordinary paintings of boxers, silent oarsmen and candidly scrutinized personalities. His candor earned him few friends. Such intensive observation was acceptable in the still lifes of William Harnett or John Peto, but not as applied to humankind!

In 1885 James McNeill Whistler announced that to tell the painter he should paint the whole of nature was like telling a musician he might simply sit on all the keys of the piano. He had been showing his simplified, deliberately patterned paintings for over 20 years and by now his "arrangements" and "nocturnes"—he called the portrait of his mother *Arrangement in Grey and Black, No. 1*—appealed to those who also found refreshing values in Japanese prints and blue and white porcelain. This awareness of formal values created interest in a wide range of world art that did not fit the recent Western tradition. Whistler understood that art was nurtured by art.

The rhythmically modeled surfaces and heroic pose of Augustus Saint-Gaudens's The Puritan *reflect the artistic idealism of many turn-of-the-century artists and architects.*

John LaFarge began his studies in Paris, but, unlike Whistler, developed a sentiment for history. Whether inspired by nature or a Byzantine mosaic, his works live in a realm of historical memory. It is not that his murals for Boston's Trinity Church or his colorful stained glass actually look like past works; they simply persuade the viewer to look at them much as he would old churches in France and paintings in Florence.

This historical sentiment, however, was only one aspect of an art drawn from personal feeling and distilled in evocative form. The strange, luminous landscapes of Ralph Blakelock reach into the mind, not into the past. Even more, the mysterious canvases of Albert Pinkham Ryder, with their overtones of Wagner, Shakespeare and the Old Testament, prod the mind and sensibilities to become among the most memorable paintings created by an American.

But it was historical sentiment that dominated much public art at the end of the century. The Columbian Exposition of 1893 in Chicago was a tribute to a new merging of the arts in which mural painters teamed with French-trained architects working in historical styles and with Paris-trained sculptors such as Augustus Saint-Gaudens, Daniel Chester French and Frederick MacMonnies to create monuments to connoisseur taste—among them the Boston Public Library and the Library of Congress.

The Ashcan School

The identification of art with wealthy collectors and refined taste was bound to find opponents, and so it did in the work of a group of young painters centered on Robert Henri. They found their subjects in the city streets and painted with directness and verve. When Henri organized a New York exhibition of works by himself, John Sloan, William J. Glackens, George Luks, Everett Shinn, Ernest Lawson, Maurice Prendergast and Arthur Davies, the show was considered a threat to accepted standards. The group was referred to as the Eight, and those around Henri, including young George Bellows, were derisively called the ashcan painters.

With a clear but never cold eye, John Sloan observed the life of New York City. Here are two women at Three A.M.

While these vigorous paintings of teeming city life broke through the accepted limits of art by opening up the world upon which the artist drew, another revolution was at hand. Some painters in Paris became aware of tendencies that offered new expressiveness of form. Alfred Maurer, H. Lyman Saÿen and Max Weber responded, as did his younger French contemporaries, to Henri Matisse's extraordinary paintings of 1905—in which color, released from the restriction of likeness or scheme, became part of a freely evocative game. These painters responded also to the work of Cézanne when his paintings found a new public after his death in 1906.

The venturesome photographer Alfred Stieglitz opened a gallery in New York in 1905, and it was there that Maurer and his Paris colleague, John Marin, showed their new work in 1906. The group that formed around Stieglitz and exhibited in his modest gallery included his wife Georgia O'Keeffe, Marin, Marsden Hartley, Arthur Dove and photographers Edward

Steichen and Paul Strand. The gallery, which also showed new European art, became a bridge between Paris and New York, in contact with Cubism by 1909 and Futurism in its turn.

The Famous Armory Show

Stieglitz reached a very small public. Most Americans knew of the rebellious European currents only through sensational Sunday supplement articles. But an exhibition organized by a group of artists in 1913 was calculated to confront the public at large with the full range of modern works. The Armory Show (so-called because it opened in New York's 69th Regiment Armory before moving on to Chicago and Boston) was an education in the history of modern painting and sculpture, from Ingres and Delacroix through Cézanne, van Gogh and Gauguin to contemporary artists. It included a broad selection of American works, both conservative and new. The public's reaction was unfriendly and sometimes violent, but from this moment new forms in art could not be ignored in America.

Marcel Duchamp's Nude Descending a Staircase, *shown at the 1913 Armory Show, was used by critics to condemn new tendencies in art but served as inspiration to many artists.*

Henceforth, art that followed earlier traditions coexisted with the new tendencies springing up in Europe. The canvases of Eugene Speicher, Bernard Karfiol and Alexander Brook carried the sense of painterly craftsmanship through the 1930s and beyond, particularly in portrait painting. Even today the closely observed paintings of Andrew Wyeth reach back into tradition. Meanwhile Marin, Marsden Hartley, Abraham Walkowitz and Charles Demuth, to name but a few, became the pioneers of a new tradition which emphasized personal ways of painting made possible by the new concepts.

Directions varied. There were improvisations on the interplay of forms, as in the early works of Max Weber and Joseph Stella and, eventually, in the precise, refined images of Charles Sheeler and the sparkling abstractions of Stuart Davis; but there were also a free, expressive use of form and imagery by Maurer and O'Keeffe, for example, and the lyrical, organic forms created by Dove. Aspects of this kind of painting seemed in sympathy with Surrealism later, although relatively few Americans other than Man Ray were actively engaged in either the New York branch of the Dada movement or doctrinaire Surrealism. The mystery of Mark Tobey's entanglements of white writing from the 1930s and Morris Graves's birds lost in the universe reflect Eastern philosophy, not modern psychology.

Changing Concepts in Sculpture

Sculpture underwent changes similar to those that affected painting. The tradition of the Paris studios established in the late 1800s by the sensitively modeled bronzes of Saint-Gaudens, French and MacMonnies, as well as by the Rodinesque marbles of Lorado Taft and the rugged figures of George Grey Barnard, was countered by young sculptors such as William Zorach and John Flannagan who insisted that sculpture must be drawn forth from the stone by the artist himself. They believed that the material and process should never be obscured by representational details. A sculpture was a discourse between a creative mind and the material.

Gaston Lachaise and Elie Nadelman were less concerned with process than with giving an astonishing buoyancy and life to the simple, polished forms in which they built their figures. Ukrainian-born Alexander Archipenko, who settled in the United States in 1923, had a major impact with his elegant, polished forms and new attitudes toward modern materials. The free play of imaginative forms characterized both the strange and evocative sculptures of Isamu Noguchi and the constructions of Alexander Calder. To the interrelationship of forms, Calder eventually added the complication of actual motion in his mobiles, which totally revolutionized the idea of sculpture as static mass.

The New Tie With Europe

With the founding of the Museum of Modern Art in New York in 1929 and the activity of other groups such as the *Société Anonyme* and the Whitney Museum, any gap in communication between European tendencies and America was closed, and during the next two decades many established European artists settled or stayed for periods of time in the United States. The first group included Hans Hofmann and László Moholy-Nagy in the 1930s, and later such others as Piet Mondrian, Fernand Léger, Marc Chagall and, of particular importance, Marcel Duchamp.

But it was also during the 1930s that there arose, both in Europe and America, a new concern for the local scene as subject for the arts. Grant Wood, John Steuart Curry and Thomas Hart Benton, in their different ways, turned to the life and legends of the Middle West. The New England townscapes of Charles Burchfield and the silent glimpses of the city and isolated houses at the shore by Edward Hopper found new audiences. Reginald Marsh, Isabel Bishop and the youthful Paul Cadmus reflected on aspects of crowded urban life. W. H. Johnson, Jacob Lawrence and Romare Bearden recorded in the 1940s the black's experience in society. The role of art as a social force was much discussed, with full consciousness of the Mexican mural painters, particularly José Orozco and Diego Rivera, who worked in the United States.

This new social awareness coincided with the projects devised by the government to aid artists during the Great Depression of the 1930s and is reflected in some of the murals executed under federal sponsorship by painters such as Ben Shahn, William Gropper, Henry Varnum Poor and Nicolas Biddle. But artists of all kinds were given the opportunity to develop their work under the WPA. Easel paintings as well as murals were produced by the thousands for public places. Almost all of the artists who emerged as leaders in the 1940s, regardless of style, had been sustained by this extraordinary government-supported project.

American Modern

Mahoning *exemplifies the sweeping, vaguely Oriental, black and white canvases of Franz Kline.*

Just after World War II a fresh creative energy infused American art, and the accumulated ideas from local tradition or abroad were brought together in a new expressive confidence. From the beginnings of this movement in which form was a personal symbol, as in the remarkable paintings of Arshile Gorky, a kind of painting developed which was closely allied with human activity and feeling. In the very different canvases of Jackson Pollock, Willem de Kooning, Franz Kline or Mark Rothko, often so large as to engulf the spectator, an active process demands the attention, supplanting any concern for static compositional form. Generally called Abstract Expressionism, the tendency had many facets: the more evocative paintings of Adolph Gottlieb and Robert Motherwell; the tense, simplified canvases of Barnett Newman; and the dynamic, vivid paintings of Hofmann whose teaching had great impact. Now, for the first time, American art became a world influence.

Once set on a vital course, artists began freely to explore many ranges of experience. Unexpected and surprising uses of common objects and commercial imagery by Andy Warhol, Robert Rauschenberg, Roy Lichtenstein, Jasper Johns, Tom Wesselmann and others, loosely dubbed Pop Art, brought into the realm of art the entire spectrum of contemporary urban experience, nicely entangling association and formal play. The huge, soft renderings of common objects by Claes Oldenburg were both comic and obsessive. Both in Chicago and San Francisco, a consistent preoccupation with provocative contemporary imagery, as in Leon Golub, June Leaf and James Nutt, and in Nathan Oliveira and Richard Diebenkorn, created a sense of local school.

David Smith pioneered in using welded steel forms in sculpture. The work shown here is called Becca.

In contrast both to the free forms of Abstract Expressionism and the involvement with urban imagery during the 1960s an interest developed in the interplay of forms so precisely defined that they excluded all outside association. Sometimes optical phenomena were exploited, as in the subtle color adjustments in Joseph Albers's interrelated squares or the hypnotic color combinations of Richard Anuszkiewicz. Sometimes the painting depended on the arresting quality of simple forms, as in the work of Ad Reinhardt and Ellsworth Kelly. Beginning with the canvas itself as the object, its proportion and shape became factors for painters such as Jules Olitski and Frank Stella. The tendency was to reduce the importance of the material substance so as to intensify the mind's commitment. It was this fascination with minimal form that dominated much sculpture, beginning with the extraordinarily live works of David Smith and extending to the strict simplicity of the rectangular forms of Robert Morris or Tony Smith. Allied with this taste was the use of prefabricated, or seemingly prefabricated, forms by Alexander Lieberman, Mark di Suvero and others.

The Expansion of Art

Possibly as a consequence of this emphasis on the mind rather than on form in art, some artists turned wholly to activity, as in Allan Kaprow's happenings, or as in Richard Serra's chance exhibitions or Robert Morris's post-hard edge forms. There was no limit to the range of media used. Communications became a theme, drawing on technological apparatus, computers, television and copying devices. Artists such as Robert Smithson carried out projects in the actual landscape that could be known chiefly by report, and some artists presented plans for projects that had their being only in the realm of possibility. Conceptual art was opposed to perceptual art, on the assumption that it was most significantly allied with the modern world. At the core of this new approach was the conviction that art is not looking at, but participating in; that it provides a stimulating process that has neither beginning nor end.

While in the past critics spoke of advanced tendencies and stylistic breakthroughs, it is characteristic of art today that it is not reduced to a single direction or even a few opposing directions. The context of present art is broad, recognizing barriers neither of means nor subject. The exacting, almost photographic images of Philip Pearlstein and Richard Estes coexist with the geometric plastic forms of Ron Davis or the draped canvases of Sam Gilliam; the meticulous, traditional paintings of Andrew Wyeth have their place, as do the haunting plaster figures of George Segal. All can find a place in the modern consciousness. Art now is measured not by form or manifesto, but by a shared sense of value between the individual artist and a perceptive public.

Architecture: From Survival to Elegance

Dramatic response to the challenge of building in a vast, varied and ever-changing land

The Europeans who came to North America in the 16th and 17th centuries found only one type of native Indian construction that influenced what they built: the terraced and multistoried pueblos of the Southwest. All the other native American types—the tepees, wigwams and long houses—were far more primitive than the medieval and Renaissance buildings the colonists had known in Europe.

The Spaniards came first, seeking treasure and the conversion of the Indians to Christianity. They built flimsy log forts which were sacked frequently by English raiders and sometimes by Indians. But after the English occupied St. Augustine in 1668, the Spanish regents ordered a great stone fort, the Castillo de San Marcos, to be built. One of the most impressive Spanish structures in North America, it is the best example in the United States of the type of fort found in Europe after the advent of gunpowder, a modification of the medieval castle providing lower, sloping walls and projections to deflect artillery fire. The design was a success. Between 1702 and 1740 the Castillo withstood repeated attacks by English colonists.

A Blending of Spanish and Indian Forms

Even before the founding of St. Augustine in 1565, other Spaniards were busy exploring the Southwest. In what is now New Mexico they encountered the Indian pueblo, a type of building dating from the period 900–1200. Pueblos were communal houses, sometimes of stone but more often of adobe made from sun-dried clay. The walls were spanned by logs that the Spanish called *vigas* (beams or rafters). These were crossed by smaller poles overlaid with rushes or branches to support the layer of clay that made the flat roof. The *vigas* were thick and long and often had to be brought long distances. They were so hard to cut that when they turned out to be too long their ends were allowed to project beyond the wall, creating the picturesque but essentially nonfunctional hallmark of Southwest Indian design.

Elements of pueblo architecture are evident in the Governor's Palace at Santa Fe. Begun by the governor of the Spanish province of New Mexico, Don Pedro de Peralta, soon after he founded the capital at Santa Fe in 1609, the palace is probably the oldest surviving non-Indian building in the United States.

Moorish influence shows in the arches of San Xavier del Bac. Why one tower was never finished is unknown.

The pueblo influence is more explicit in New Mexican mission churches such as those at Taos and Acoma. To build them, each friar came with ten axes, three adzes, three spades, ten hoes, one medium-size saw, one chisel, two augers, one plane, a few latches, hinges, locks and 6000 nails. With these few implements and the crude skills of Indian workmen, the friars could not aspire to the ornate; they could not build vaults or domes. They did, however, use their tools to square up the *vigas,* carve modestly elaborate details and make wooden doors and window frames.

The finest mission structures remaining today are all in the vicinity of San Antonio. They include the Alamo (about 1744), San José y San Miguel de Aguayo (1720–31) and Mission Nuestra Senora de la Purisima Concepcion de Acuna (1731–55). Of the dozen or so missions built in the 17th and 18th centuries in the region now known as Arizona, only one is now intact, San Xavier del Bac at Tucson (1784–97). It rivals San José in San Antonio as the finest Spanish church in the Southwest.

The last of the Spanish mission-building provinces, California, has by far the largest number of well-preserved and restored examples. The California chain of missions was built with remarkable speed. Begun in 1769 at San Diego by the great friar Junípero Serra, who died in 1784, the chain was completed in 1823 and comprised 21 missions stretching more than 500 miles over the old Camino Real (King's Highway) from San Diego to San Rafael, north of San Francisco.

The Influence of the French

At its peak in the early 18th century the French Colonial empire was larger than the Spanish, but it left fewer architectural remains. Interested primarily in exploration and fur trading, the French generally built forts rather than towns. There were few French settlements other than New Orleans and some plantations along the lower Mississippi.

New Orleans, founded in 1718 as Nouvelle Orléans, was one of the early planned towns in North America. Although it had some architectural distinction, as can still be seen in the French Quarter, or Vieux Carré (old square), the city was largely wiped out by disastrous fires in 1788 and 1794. But a few, usually decaying or altered, fragments of French houses can be found in the Vieux Carré. One of the oldest houses, now being restored, is Madame John's Legacy (1788), an urban version of the plantation house in which the ground floor, fronting the street, has abandoned the *galerie* in favor of a solid plastered wall and several doors.

Dutch Colonial

Though it was for less than half a century that the Dutch governed the Hudson River and parts of Long Island and New Jersey, the Dutch Colonial style, with Dutch and Flemish elements, influenced this area's architecture for 200 years. The Dutch immigrated with the intention of staying as working settlers and they meant to make New Netherland as much as possible like the motherland. Many of their colonists were expert craftsmen, including Europe's most skilled brickmakers and bricklayers.

Even after the British took over New Amsterdam in 1664, the architecture remained predominantly Dutch. But most of the old city was destroyed in the fire of 1776, and even the remnants have disappeared. The best surviving examples of the Dutch Colonial style are to be found in towns up the Hudson from Manhattan, particularly West Coxsackie and Rensselaer.

New England Colonial

New England is outstanding for its preserved 17th-century buildings; nearly 80 still exist. There were three almost standard New England house plans. The simplest had one principal room. The entrance door opened into a vestibule that had a steep staircase against the immense wall of the chimney. There was a main room, usually about 16 by 18 feet, for living, dining and cooking; the fireplace staircase led to one large sleeping room, either under a sloping roof or in a full-height second story. This plan was used in the early cottages of Plymouth and Salem, Massachusetts, and was common in smaller dwellings throughout the century.

More usual with the passage of time was a house with two principal rooms on the first floor. There was a vestibule and staircase in the middle and flanking rooms on each side, one called the hall, the other the parlor; in each was a large fireplace back to back with the other. The bedrooms above were called the hall and parlor chambers, respectively.

Larger than either of the others was the lean-to house, generally called the saltbox. The lean-to section of the two-story house had rafters that leaned from one-story eaves against the back of the house. The middle room of this addition was a kitchen, with fireplace and oven using the same chimney. On the cold north side was a pantry; on the warmer side, facing south, was a downstairs sleeping room, the only one called a bedroom in Colonial times. Narrow stairs from the kitchen led to a garret or two small chambers used for sleeping.

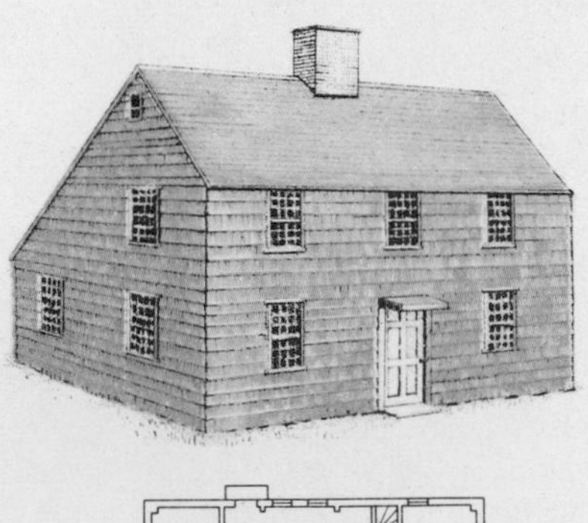

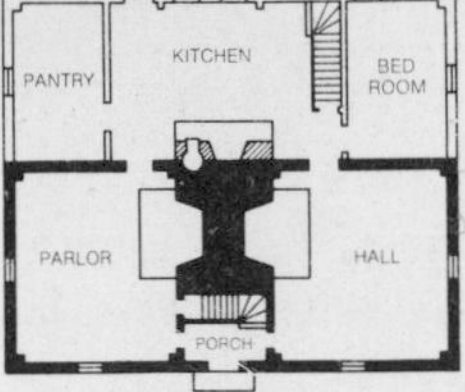

Rather than growing room by room as needed, a saltbox was usually completely built when a family moved in. The design for the house came from England; there the plaster and framing were left exposed. In the New World, clapboards were used to cover the exterior.

The dominant interior element of the New England Colonial house was its exposed wood framing. Nor could the eye escape the massive fireplace that served for both heating and cooking. Many of these were eight feet wide and more than four feet high. The lintel spanning the smaller fireplaces was stone, but for the wider ones it was a squared oak timber high enough above the hearth so as not to burn, although it was often charred. With the swinging iron crane and other practical cooking accouterments, the fireplace was an important aspect of the New England Colonial style.

The communities, few of which, save Boston, could claim to be cities, were compact, primarily for protection from Indians and for nearness to the meetinghouse. The topography caused layout variations, but all were centered on the meetinghouse and the fenced-in common, or village green, around which the houses were clustered. Near the frontier the villages were stockaded. Although we now think of these villages as white, paint was not used until after 1700, and the village color was that of exposed wood siding—silvery near the coast and chocolate brown inland.

The other important New England Colonial building type was the meetinghouse. It was very plain and barnlike; the architectural form was adapted from the Elizabethan Gothic. The early meetinghouses had no tower, spire, cross or embellishment. The altar of the Gothic style was abandoned for a side pulpit for the sermon, which became the focus of the service. Benches lengthwise of the church, far from comfortable, faced the pulpit, and the entrance doors opened in the middle of the other long side. Such an arrangement gave little reason for an oblong floor plan, and soon a square plan, usually 40 to 45 feet on a side, replaced it. An aisle down the center separated the men from the women. The roofs were hipped or pyramidal, and a small square platform at the top carried the belfry. The oldest surviving church in the English Colonies—and the only one remaining from the 17th century in New England—is the Old Ship Meetinghouse at Hingham, Massachusetts, dating from 1681.

The Southern Colonists

The other great area of English settlement lay between the Delaware and Savannah Rivers, from the coast to the hilly Piedmont. Unlike the New England settlers, who were generally humble folk and religious dissenters, most of the Southern colonists were loyal to the Anglican Church, the king and, in almost every respect, to the mother country. The atmosphere was distinctly less plebeian than that of New England.

The terrain was different, too. The South was cut into segments by strong rivers: Susquehanna, Potomac, James, York, Rappahannock, Santee, Ashley and Savannah. To move north or south by land was extremely difficult, so the plantations spread along the rivers. Most of the plantations were highly self-contained, and towns and villages were much less common than in New England. With its one-crop economy and large land holdings, the South seemed destined to develop an aristocratic, manorial society and a corresponding architecture. This trend was reinforced by local hospitality, intermarriage and frequent visits to the mother country from which the latest English fashions in dress, manners and architecture were imported.

The Southern houses differed from those of New England in two respects: the chimneys were at the ends of the house instead of the center, and the ceilings were much higher, for cooling and ventilation.

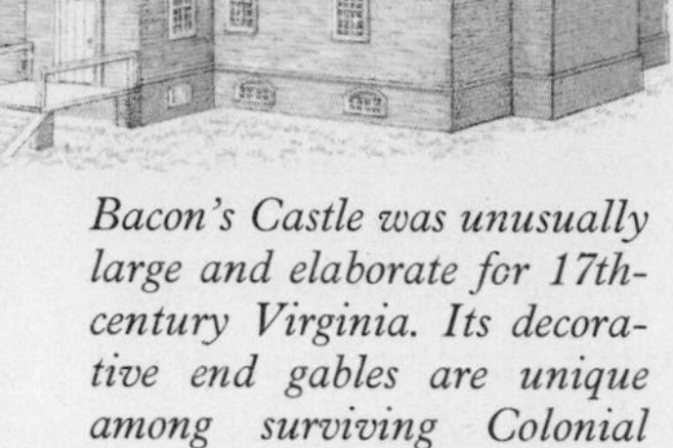

Bacon's Castle was unusually large and elaborate for 17th-century Virginia. Its decorative end gables are unique among surviving Colonial houses. The name derives from its occupation by followers of Nathaniel Bacon in his rebellion of 1676.

The central hall, desirable for cross ventilation and possible because of the end placement of the chimneys, became characteristic of Southern architecture. A hallway containing the staircase and with doors at the front and back separated the two main rooms (hall and parlor). The hall started as a narrow convenient passage, and the staircase was steep and unimpressive; but gradually this area was made larger and more elegant until it became a spacious room suitable for living, especially in the summer.

The most elaborate development in Southern Colonial architecture was known as the cross plan. In the front was a two-story projection with a porch on the ground floor and a bedroom above. At the rear was another projecting element, usually containing an open stairway; if the stairway remained enclosed in the central hall, the rear projection was used as a parlor or omitted altogether. This cross plan was employed in Maryland and Virginia and also in Bermuda.

The Adam Thoroughgood House near Norfolk (built 1636–50) is the oldest brick house in Virginia and one of the oldest in the English Colonies. Bacon's Castle in Surry County (built about 1655) is the earliest Virginia example of a cross-plan house and one of the most remarkable architectural achievements of the American Colonial period; it has been well restored.

An Emerging Need for Elegance

By 1700 the times were ripe for a change. Parts of the eastern seaboard had been settled for three-quarters of a century. It was mostly under English rule, even though many citizens were not of English descent. Class distinctions were becoming increasingly important, and a social aristocracy was clearly forming. It was a time of prosperity; society was looking more and more to England for culture, manners, taste and architecture. In England Sir Christopher Wren had set new standards in the new garden front of Hampton Court Palace (1682–94) and in his 53 London churches. The spires of many were directly copied in North America. Of equal influence was James Gibbs, who built St. Martin's-in-the-Fields (1721–6) on Trafalgar Square, a direct inspiration for a number of American Georgian churches.

Many upper-class Americans traveled to England and saw these works. But of perhaps greater importance were the books. There were the Renaissance classics, from Vitruvius and Alberti to Serlio and Palladio. Less theoretical and probably more useful were such popular books as Gibbs himself published in 1728 and 1732, containing building and architectural ornament designs.

In America there were few professional architects. But there were plenty of gifted amateurs who were almost the equal of the good professionals and

REGINA VIRTUS

THE FOUR BOOKS

ANDREA PALLADIO's

ARCHITECTURE

After a short Treatise of the Five Orders,

BUILDING

LONDON,

Published by

ISAAC WARE,

Anno MDCCXXXVIII.

British and American builders used Palladio's four books as texts during most of the 1700s.

superior to the poor ones. These were such men as Andrew Hamilton, a Philadelphian who, while studying law in the English Inns of Court, also observed enough to enable him later to design Independence Hall; William Byrd, whose education in London and his later visits there helped him to imagine Westover in Charles City County, Virginia; Richard Munday of Newport, Rhode Island, an innkeeper and later a master carpenter; Joseph Brown of Providence, a manufacturer; Dr. John Kearsley, who with Hamilton and Samuel Rhoads, a builder, provided many of the best buildings in Philadelphia; and Richard Taliaferro of Williamsburg.

Peter Harrison, whose architectural career extended from 1748 to 1763, is usually regarded as America's first distinguished architect. Among his greatest works are the Touro Synagogue and Brick Market in Newport, Rhode Island, and Lang's Chapel in Boston. There were painters like John Smibert and John Trumbull, who designed Faneuil Hall in Boston; and, foremost, there was Thomas Jefferson. Most of the houses were planned by their owners, assisted by the books and a master carpenter.

Evolution of the Georgian Style

In the Georgian period (1714–1820) there were some stone dwellings in Pennsylvania and clapboard types in New England and South Carolina, but the typical Georgian house in North America was brick. The bricks were of many textures, glazes and colors, but they were almost always laid in the Flemish bond. Stone trim was the ideal for the Georgian in England, but it was so expensive to carve into the desired classic moldings that in America most of the pilasters, capitals and cornices were carved of wood and painted white.

Windows were located rhythmically and symmetrically on the facade, often at the expense of sensible partitions, light or even stairs on the inside. The Colonial casement windows were rapidly superseded by double-hung windows, and the trisection Palladian window became a favorite accent in the middle of a facade.

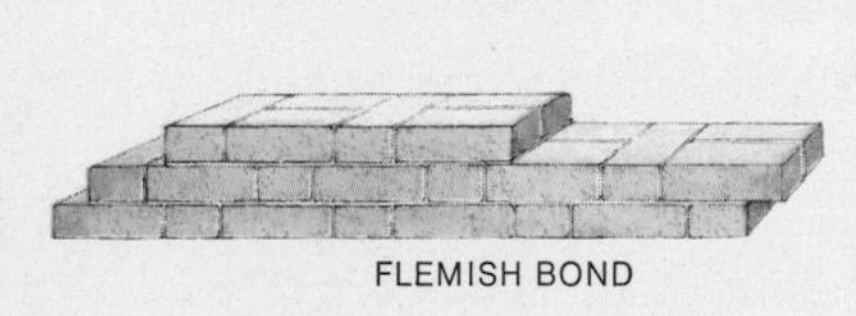

FLEMISH BOND

ENGLISH BOND

Each layer of Flemish bond has stretchers (bricks whose lengths parallel the wall face) alternating with headers (bricks whose ends are toward the wall face). English bond has layers of stretchers alternating with layers of headers.

Georgian roofs were pitched lower than those of earlier styles, producing a gable shaped essentially like the pediment of a classic temple. The ridge was usually cut off to allow a narrow, flat roof deck which was enclosed by a balustrade and called a widow's walk. It is legendary that the walk was invented in Salem or some other seaport town so that the shipowners or the captains' wives might watch for returning vessels. The widow's walk may have been put to such use, but its design had actually appeared long before in English Stuart houses located far from the sea.

It was in Virginia that the American Georgian style reached its greatest refinement. In the first place there was Williamsburg, one of the earliest of the planned towns, now restored and containing such outstanding buildings as those of the College of William and Mary (1695–1702), the old Capitol (1701–5), the Governor's Palace (1706–20) and Bruton Parish Church (1710–15). The great plantation houses included Westover (about 1730–4), perhaps the most famous; Mount Airy (1758–62), Richmond County; Mount Vernon (remodeled 1757–87), Fairfax County; and of course Thomas Jefferson's Monticello (1768–75), near Charlottesville. Jefferson eventually became disenchanted with the Georgian style and between 1793 and 1809 ordered extensive alterations to Monticello that portended a transition from Georgian to Classic Revival.

Transition to Federal Style

The popularity of the Georgian in America died away and by 1825 was almost totally extinguished. Since Revolutionary days many Americans had called for expressions in the arts that would repudiate the past and Europe as the symbol of it. For lack of any other, the Federal style (1780–1820) might be considered typically American.

This style reflects three notable influences: a revived Roman classicism, which Jefferson and others thought most suitable for a republic; French architecture of the time of Louis XVI; and a continuation of the Georgian tradition which was modified by the latest English influence of the Scottish architect Robert Adam and his brother James.

The styles of the columns used in the classic Greek and Roman ages are called architectural orders. Above are the three most common types.

The facades of the Federal style were quiet and dignified and the decorative detail restrained, but there were, nevertheless, changes from the Georgian. The Federal style evidenced an increased desire for classical correctness in the use of the architectural orders. The walls were smooth and white; the exterior, as well as the board or plastered interior, was painted. Circular, oval or octagonal rooms appeared and were designed with care for their geometry. There was often a grand portico. But the most distinctive property was the Federal doorway, with its narrow sidelights and elliptical fanlight overhead. A good example of the style is Samuel McIntire's Gardner-Pingree House (1804) in Salem, Massachusetts.

Greek Revival

Greek neoclassicism swept the country from the East Coast to San Francisco after 1820. It arose from an idealization and an oversimplification of the past. Greek motifs were taken to symbolize democracy, Roman to stand for stern republican virtue, Gothic for religious faith. Such associations might have been based on false premises, but they dominated architectural thinking until well after the Civil War.

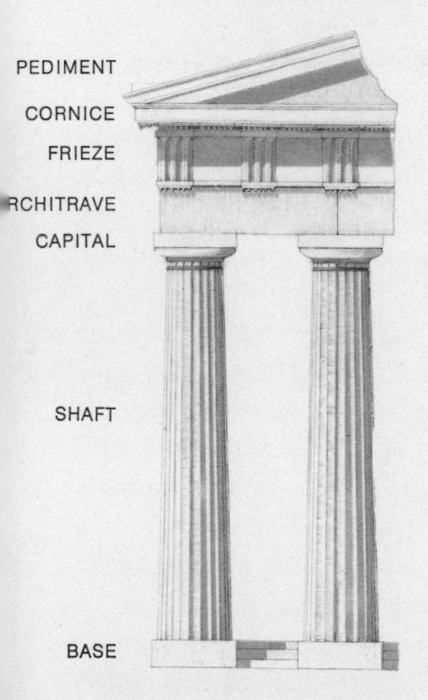

The Greek Revival portico, an open, roofed space, usually had a pediment over the entablature and columns, as here.

Greek Revival buildings were constructed from Maine to Georgia, from the Atlantic to the Northwest and all over the lower Mississippi area. The architectural basis of the style was the classic portico, usually Doric or Ionic. The portico fronted churches, commercial buildings, small and large houses —everything but factories and barns. Although the porticos imitated the facades of the great Greek temples, the whole result was actually not very Grecian. Some of the columns were indeed of stone, but more were of brick painted white, and most were of wood. Moreover, few buildings tried to imitate the whole temple, with a peristyle, or colonnade, all around it.

Nonetheless, when professional architects applied Greek elements to contemporary plans with sensitivity to scale and good craftmanship, the results vied with the Georgian as the best architecture the United States has produced, at least until modern times. Entire Greek Revival towns—such as Nantucket, Massachusetts; Saratoga Springs, New York; Marietta and Newark, Ohio; Frankfort, Kentucky; Madison, Indiana; and Athens, Georgia—achieved a noble serenity of appearance.

Gothic Revival

By the time the Greek Revival was at its height, the Gothic style was a strong competitor, especially in the building of churches where the argument against "pagan" architecture was most telling. In England Augustus Welby Pugin built, drew and wrote to prove that Gothic churches would inspire better moral behavior.

Important engineering changes were taking place in America in the mid-1800s, but their results in big buildings would not emerge in serious architecture until near the end of the century. In dwelling houses heavy timbered structures gave way to light "balloon" frames with 2 by 4 studs on 16-inch centers, which became almost universal after 1833. In commercial buildings, for reasons of economy and fire resistance, an interior framework of cast-iron columns and beams was adopted.

At first the practical metal skeletons were hidden behind masonry facades, but soon there were cast-iron fronts to match. The cast-iron front was short-lived and carried the seeds of its own destruction. It was too easily cast into complex ugly forms, and in the hands of eccentric eclectics led to ridiculous facades. It also turned out not to be so fireproof as anticipated.

A Rampant Eclecticism

The freedom of architectural choice grew even wider after the Civil War. There were Roman villas, Tuscan villas, Lombard churches, Regency Moorish castles, Byzantine cottages, Chinese pavilions and even a Moorish synagogue in Cincinnati. These became popular despite the outcries of intellectuals such as Ralph Waldo Emerson, Horatio Greenough and Joseph Henry, the first director of the Smithsonian Institution. Other voices were more persuasive: for example, the designers Andrew Jackson Downing and Alexander Jackson Davis, who wrote books that praised eclectic houses and provided ready-made designs for many types.

The designs in Andrew Jackson Downing's influential book on country houses ranged from a laborer's cottage to this "Norman-style" villa.

From the end of the Civil War to the end of World War II, eclectic styles continued to dominate American architecture. But for a while Victorian Gothic was so popular that it seriously threatened to become the American "national" style, though it never quite made it. The style started in England with John Ruskin's ideas of the relation of great architecture to moral and social improvement. Actually, Victorian Gothic was not particularly Gothic. Although it used many Gothic elements (rib-vaulted ceilings, pinnacles and towers), often in wood instead of stone, the overall effect was sometimes French, sometimes Venetian and usually not quite either.

Richardson and Hunt

In the socially pretentious East there developed a contest for acclaim between Richard Morris Hunt and Henry Hobson Richardson, champions respectively of French Renaissance and Romanesque styles. Both Hunt and Richardson were upper middle class and well educated; both studied at Harvard and L'École des Beaux Arts in Paris.

Hunt's sojourn in France sealed his understanding of and affection for the French chateau architecture with its varied asymmetrical plan, tall steep roof and rich outline made by carved ornament. It was in this style that he did his best work, far more faithful to the details and even the spirit of historical work than any American had been previously. His clients were the rich who wanted palatial mansions—men such as the Vanderbilts, who were his most noteworthy patrons and who deferred to his taste. Three examples of his most important work are in Newport, Rhode Island: Chateau-sur-Mer (1852), the Marble House (1892) for William K. Vanderbilt and the Breakers (1895) for Cornelius Vanderbilt. In Asheville, North Carolina, he designed Biltmore (1895) for George Washington Vanderbilt, the largest, most palatial and chateaulike of all his work.

On the other hand, Richardson explicitly disclaimed any interest in reproducing French chateaus for rich Americans, although he said he was competent to do so. He left the field to Hunt, from which we have all gained since Richardson was the more creative architect. He designed powerful stone buildings in a style so distinctive and widespread that it became known as Richardson Romanesque. His outstanding large buildings include Trinity Church (1872-7) in Boston and the Allegheny County Court House and Jail in Pittsburgh, a masterpiece.

The Chicago School

The intimations of the revolution in architecture occurred in Chicago, where the disastrous fire of 1871 created building needs that required years to fill. The most interesting of all the Chicago designers was Louis Henri Sullivan. An erratic and wayward genius, he grew up in Boston, dropped out from both the Massachusetts Institute of Technology and L'École des Beaux Arts, and then worked for a time in the office of Frank Furness, the imaginative but eccentric Philadelphia designer. In addition to practicing architecture, Sullivan wrote extensively and provocatively.

The best examples of his work in Chicago are the Carson Pirie Scott department store (1899-1904) and the Chicago Auditorium (1887)—the latter a brilliant combination of his talents with those of the architect and engineer Dankmar Adler and the first public building to use electric lights profusely; it has been fully restored.

An important aspect of Sullivan's talents was his unusual flair for the design of architectural ornament, manifestly Celtic in inspiration but in the vein of Art Nouveau, most of which it preceded. Ultimately far more influential, however, was his approach to the design of tall buildings, as epitomized by his Wainwright Building (1890-1) in St. Louis. It was here that Sullivan stated his belief that the overriding aesthetic feature of a tall building is that it must *look* tall. It is one assertion of the principle that form follows function, but the function is here aesthetic. Thus Sullivan had no hesitation about increasing the number of vertical components by interposing between the load-bearing elements others that had no load to carry. He recognized also that a building needs a clearly apparent base and top and a substantial section between them (the principle of the classic column), and he made each of these serve specific functions.

The 1891 Wainwright Building has been compared to a classic column: the first two stories are the base; the next seven, the shaft; the frieze and cornice, the capital. Its tall look was heightened by the visible verticality of Sullivan's uninterrupted columns.

Despite these new stirrings, beaux-arts classicism prevailed at the World Columbian Exposition in Chicago in 1893. The commission formed for the Exposition included Daniel Burnham, John Root and the firm of Adler & Sullivan; but the Chicagoans were dominated by the more famous New Yorkers, Richard Morris Hunt and Charles Follen McKim. McKim was the architect who designed the Boston Public Library (1888-95), an Italian Renaissance palace that is still one of the handsomest buildings in this country. Sullivan, who frequently deprecated McKim's work as "imperial," later complained bitterly that the exposition had set American architecture back 50 years. He may have been right.

When Did "Modern" Start?

Precisely when the Modern movement began in America is still in question. An important year in Europe was 1919, when Walter Gropius established the Bauhaus school of design at Weimar, Germany. The beginning could perhaps be traced to the Berlin studio of Peter Behrens, where a few years earlier Le Corbusier, Mies van der Rohe and Gropius were all briefly associated. There were intimations of a trend, however, in London's Crystal

Palace (1851) and the still earlier work of Henri Labrouste in Paris.

In 1933 the Nazis dissolved the Bauhaus, and a number of leading European architects emigrated to America. Richard Neutra and Rudolph Schindler were among the first. Gropius and Mies followed. In the early 1930s the Museum of Modern Art in New York mounted an important show, organized by the architect Philip Johnson, offering a comprehensive display of work by Le Corbusier, Mies, Gropius, J. J. P. Oud and Frank Lloyd Wright. In 1939 the museum moved into a striking new building designed by Philip L. Goodwin and Edward Durell Stone.

The Skyscraper Arrives

But the set of American opinion was still conservative and firmly opposed to "chicken coop" architecture. Skyscrapers dominated the nation's interest, and by 1929 the country had almost 400 buildings more than 20 stories high, half of them in New York.

The nature of American taste in skyscrapers was clearly revealed in the Chicago Tribune Tower Competition of 1922. This was the world's first international competition for the design of a building and was entered by many eminent modern-minded Europeans, including Gropius, Adolph Meyer, Max Taut, K. Lonberg-Holm and Adolf Loos. None of their designs came close to being selected. Most Americans were thrilled by the Gothic winner designed by Raymond Mathewson Hood. The Tribune Tower is still a sculptural landmark in Chicago.

Following his Chicago victory, Hood, who was not wedded to the Gothic, went on, frequently in association with J. Audré Fouilhoux, to be the most experimental and probably the best designer of tall buildings until his death in 1934. Outstanding among his designs were the McGraw-Hill (1930) and New York Daily News Buildings in Manhattan. His greatest contribution —also claimed for William K. Harrison, Fouilhoux and Reinhart, among other collaborators—was the planning of Rockefeller Center in New York. The original grouping combined tall slab buildings and lower detached pavilions, plazas, walk-throughs, resting places, plantings and fountains. The concept was much praised but not often emulated, and the recent additions to the Rockefeller Center complex are generally a denial of the important urban principles announced in the proposals for the original complex.

The last of the imperial mansions was designed in 1932 by Reginald Johnson as the Montecito, California, residence of Senator David W. Clark of Idaho. It is still impressive, especially the fine wood panels of the interior, although some of the Italianate outdoor terraces and balustrades are deteriorating. It is better architecture, though smaller and less interesting, than the extraordinary castle, San Simeon (begun in 1919), which Julia Morgan designed for William Randolph Hearst.

In the 1940s it became harder and harder, regardless of cost, to maintain and service large urban mansions. The wealthy then took to living in luxury apartments such as those on Lake Shore Drive in Chicago and Park Avenue in New York or in enclaves such as River Oaks in Houston.

Architects as Planners

Much more important as a portent of the future were the efforts of a few American architects to create modern middle-class suburbs. Among the early examples was Forest Hills Gardens in New York, designed by Grosvenor Atterbury and Frederick Law Olmsted, Jr., in 1911. This complex attempted to recapture the charm of an English village for people who would commute to work in the inner city. Far more significant was Sunnyside Gardens, also in New York, with its cul-de-sac streets, built (the first units in 1924) by Henry Wright, Clarence S. Stein and others. The more advanced Radburn, New Jersey (1928-9), by the same team separated vehicular and pedestrian traffic and also employed cul-de-sacs and connected gardens.

Ideas used here were a considerable step forward in providing a new social pattern for a town; but Wright and Stein were more planners than architects, and the buildings designed by others were traditional. There was no marriage between good neighborhood planning and good architecture. Much can be admired in the planning of such "new towns" as Columbia, Maryland, and Reston, Virginia, but there is still a long way to go.

To the Americans who were thronging to the suburbs, romantic revivals of earlier regional styles were all the rage: Cape Cod or saltbox houses in New England, stone houses in Pennsylvania and New Jersey, "adobe" houses in New Mexico and Arizona, Spanish-style houses in California.

But since the beginning of the 20th century a different sort of regionalism had been developing in California and the Middle West, a regionalism that scorned revivalism but sought nonetheless for a result uniquely suitable to the area. In California the architects most associated with this aspiration were the brothers Charles S. and Henry M. Greene, Irving Gill and Bernard Maybeck; in the Middle West were William Gray Purcell, George Elmslie and the greatest of them all, Frank Lloyd Wright.

In California the Greene brothers built picturesque, Japanese-influenced wooden houses with interesting interior spaces. Typical, and one of their best, is the David B. Gamble House (1908) in Pasadena, which has been respectfully and completely restored. Irving Gill worked in concrete and stucco, providing unsentimental, even cubistic, forms that were much nearer to being prototypes of the modern work that was to follow.

The beloved great man of this time in California was Bernard Maybeck. His houses, though often quite dark inside, used redwood in attractive ways, provided large picture windows where there was a view, and outside married the wood to the surrounding vegetation. This was his best style, and it is revealed at its height in the Christian Science Church in Berkeley.

Frank Lloyd Wright

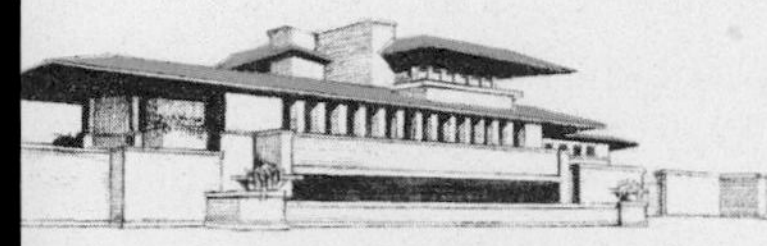

Although it appears low, the Robie House actually has three stories. Wright set the living-dining area on the second floor for light and view and extended it onto the porch. The free-flowing spaces were a departure from the prevalent boxlike rooms. Another innovation was the first house-connected garage.

In the Middle West even more important work was being done by Frank Lloyd Wright, an authentically American architectural genius. His early prairie-style houses demonstrated his belief that a building's form should grow naturally out of its environment. The houses hugged the ground and had prominent verandas and sweeping roof overhangs, creating an effect that was low and broad like the prairie itself.

Wright's best existing houses of this style (open to the public) include the Robie House (1909) in Chicago, his own house-studio Taliesin East (1911) in Spring Green, Wisconsin, and the Little House (1912) in Wayzata, Minnesota. New York's Metropolitan Museum of Art has purchased the Little House and intends to dismantle it, put the spacious living room on display in Manhattan and make the remainder of the rooms available to other museums.

The greatest of Wright's early buildings, however, and the most influential, was not a house but the Unity Temple (1906-8) in Oak Park, Illinois, which he often referred to as his best work. Its spaces flowed into each other; the concrete floor planes interpenetrated the spaces. Of all American buildings, it was the most prophetic as to the future of modern architecture.

Aside from Taliesin West (1938) at Scottsdale, Arizona, the best of Wright's later houses, and one that was nearer to being a prediction of the future of concrete, is Fallingwater (1936–9), built as a summer retreat at Mill Run, Pennsylvania. It is a marvelous combination of cantilevered concrete terraces, open spaces and areas through which the stream runs.

The best examples of Wright's large work are the Johnson Wax Administration Building (1936–9) and the Research Tower (1944–50) in Racine, Wisconsin. Near the end of his life, Wright designed the H. C. Price Tower (1956) in Bartlesville, Oklahoma, the Theater Center (1959) in Dallas, Texas, and the Guggenheim Museum (1959) in New York City.

Enter the Engineers

Americans have provided splendid engineering aesthetics in some moving objects with which this essay does not deal and in static structures for other than building purposes, such as bridges, dams and highways. American contributions have been particularly notable in suspension bridges, of which we boast the four longest in the world: Verrazano-Narrows, New York (4260 feet); Golden Gate, San Francisco (4200 feet); Mackinac Straits, Michigan (3800 feet); and George Washington, New York (3500 feet). Shorter but important are the pioneering Brooklyn Bridge (1595 feet), Bronx-Whitestone, New York (2300 feet), and the very slender Tacoma Narrows II (2800 feet). The newer bridges are handsomer than the earlier ones because they are simpler and their towers do not have architectural embellishments.

The first innovations in cast-iron and wrought-iron construction were by Europeans. But when steel became the major structural material, Americans used it most creatively. Later developments, such as arc welding, use of elevators and air conditioning, which made high-rise buildings possible, can be credited to American engineers.

Mies van der Rohe championed impersonality. With his insistence on perfection for even the smallest detail, he created many outstanding structures. Here is the Seagram Building.

At the end of World War II there was a remarkable shift in architectural values. Eclectic opposition lacked vitality, and within a few years "contemporary" architecture was taken for granted. But what was contemporary architecture? Having won a victory, the victors split into many camps.

For about a decade the pattern seemed to follow the dictum of Mies van der Rohe, "Less is more." The metal frame structure should be hung with sheets of glass, without any distraction by ornamental details in the frame or the glass, and with only the simplest color schemes. Introduced in the 860 Lake Shore Drive apartments in Chicago by Mies in 1949–51, the mode was popularized by Skidmore, Owings & Merrill's Lever House in New York (1951–2). The style was brought to a climax by Mies himself in S. R. Crown Hall at Chicago's Illinois Institute of Technology (1952–5) and the Seagram Building in New York (1955–8, with Philip Johnson).

Concrete—and Tomorrow

In time another material emerged to rival Miesian steel. The material was concrete, the favorite of France's great modern architectural genius Le Corbusier. The development of precast modular elements and of ingenious powerful cranes soon enabled concrete to challenge steel in all buildings at least up to 24 stories.

By providing a module, precast concrete made possible elegant repetitive design in the hands of men capable of good proportioning. This was demonstrated by I. M. Pei in the Green Building at the Massachusetts Institute of Technology in Cambridge, Massachusetts. American architects also turned to concrete because they saw that it could be cast in all sorts of textures and shapes and could be used to restore deep shadow-forming elements—a very important restoration of plasticity to an architecture suffering from too much flat surface and too much reflection of light from its acres of glass.

Finally, concrete offered new structural opportunities for long cantilevers, wide spanning arches and especially thin shells, making possible such buildings as Minoru Yamasaki's barrel-vaulted air terminal in St. Louis (1954) and three outstanding structures of Eero Saarinen: the Kresge Auditorium at the Massachusetts Institute of Technology, the TWA Terminal Building at Kennedy International Airport in New York and the Dulles International Airport near Washington, D.C., which may be his masterpiece.

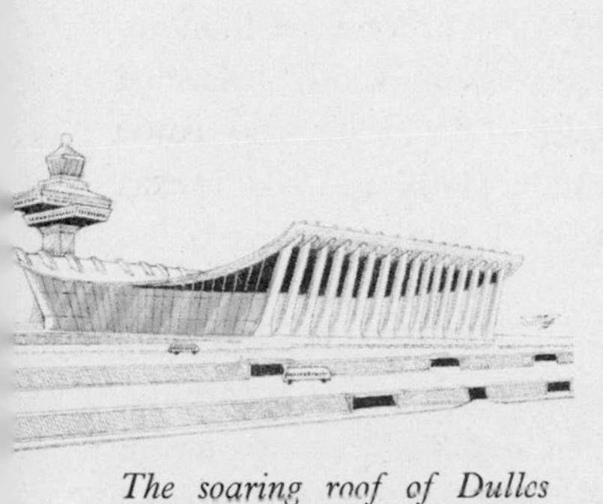

The soaring roof of Dulles International Airport is made of concrete panels fitted between suspension bridge cables. The architect, Eero Saarinen, combined a Miesian attention to detail and function with a sculptor's feeling for form.

Many other distinguished Americans did fine work in concrete, such men as Gerhardt Kallmann, Paul Rudolph, John Johansen, The Architects Collaborative (TAC) and Louis Kahn. But the unquestioned genius of them all was Marcel Breuer, whose masterpiece is the rough, hard-edged bell tower and church at St. John's Abbey, Collegeville, Minnesota.

One could not say that concrete had swept the field nor that there was a "Concrete style." Miesian buildings were still being made while at the same time much more extreme structures were being built. Noteworthy among these were Buckminster Fuller's geodesic dome for the U.S. Pavilion and Moshe Safdie's Habitat, both for Montreal's Expo '67. Equally extreme are Paolo Soleri's visionary cities of the future.

It is evident that there is no consensus even among the best American architects as to a common style for our times and no basis for predicting what it might be tomorrow. We can only assume that the changes will continue and hope that the architects will be worthy of the challenge.

The Art of Mechanics and Inventors

Unexpected beauty: the by-product of our native genius for making useful tools and machines

The mechanical arts were slow to develop in the Colonies. The English discouraged manufacturing and scientific investigation because they were more interested in having the colonists supply England with lumber, iron and other raw materials.

The early American mechanical emphasis was on the making of tools and equipment for carpentry, tanning and milling and on making glass, shoes, cloth, bricks, rope and barrels. These ordinary implements, and the products of their use, are now recognized for their beauty and can be seen in many museums devoted to Americana. The gunsmith, too, was not only a skilled mechanic but, often, a master of wood carving and metal engraving.

The first person to receive a patent for machinery in the Colonies was Joseph Jenks, an English ironworker who came to Massachusetts to help build a foundry and forge to make tools and utensils. In 1646 the colony's

General Court gave Jenks a 14-year monopoly on water mills for "speedy dispatch of much worke with few hands." The water mills, too, are now recognized for their beauty of form as well as for efficiency.

The Coming of Steel

It was also in 1646 that the American steel industry was born at the Saugus Ironworks at a site along the Saugus River about 10 miles north of Boston, Massachusetts. The ironworks, now rebuilt and open to the public, illustrate the ingenuity of our forebears as well as their dedication to hard work.

Ironmaking remained a primitive process until 1832, when the first high-quality crucible steel was made in the United States by William Garrard of Cincinnati, Ohio. Even then it was too expensive (at 25 cents a pound) to substitute for wrought iron in bars, rails, plates, sheets and pipes.

Waterwheels pumped the furnace bellows, and a rare rolling and slitting machine made iron for nails at the Saugus Ironworks. However, most of the power still came from men's muscles.

In 1851 William Kelly, an Eddyville, Kentucky, kettle maker, perfected a blast furnace in which steel was made by burning carbon out of molten iron by intensifying the fire with blasts of air. About the same time Henry Bessemer, an Englishman, developed a similar furnace, and Robert Mushet, a Scot, discovered how to add manganese to strengthen steel made in the Bessemer converter. These three discoveries were combined—and called the Bessemer process—to establish the first method of producing steel cheaply in large quantities.

In 1868 the open-hearth furnace was introduced in the United States by Abram S. Hewitt at Trenton, New Jersey. Steel soon began to replace wrought iron and to find new uses. American agriculture was greatly influenced by the developments in iron and steel. Among the first tools to be improved was the plow. Thomas Jefferson had designed the first American model to gain wide acceptance. This was superseded by Charles Newbold's cast-iron plow; then Jethro Wood changed the shape for better cutting. James Oliver developed a chilled-iron plow that broke the tough sod of the prairies. And finally John Deere's "singing" plow of saw-steel further helped to open the West by solving the problem of cutting straight furrows without the soil sticking to the plow. It "sang" as the soil peeled away from the blade. Pioneer museums across the country have examples of this basic tool.

With the availability of malleable steel wire at low cost came an invention that was to change the face of the prairie and alter the course of history. In 1873 an Illinois farmer named Joseph F. Glidden developed and patented the first machine to twist sharp steel spurs into the strands and make barbed wire. He could not have imagined the impact of his idea. The wire was efficient and lightweight and could be shipped anywhere. It brought an end to the open range and is still the standard fencing in cattle country. There are approximately 400 patterns of barbed wire, and they are widely collected. The best collection—some 100 samples—is at the Smithsonian Institution's National Museum of History and Technology in Washington, D.C.

John Deere, an Illinois blacksmith, made his first "singing" plow from a circular steel blade discarded by a sawmill.

New and improved iron and steel were also factors in the evolution of the windmill, which brought water to Western farms. Until the mail-order windmill made water available to everyone, the man who controlled the waterholes controlled the stock on the range. Steel also made possible important inventions by Cyrus H. McCormick. The McCormick reaper, patented in 1834, substituted a number of shears for the scythe's swinging blade and was the first of a series of major mechanical innovations that continued the revolution in farming.

The Factory System Starts

From the earliest days nearly every Colonial home had a spinning wheel and hand loom. As the demand for fabrics outstripped the capacity of hand production, textile mills and the necessary machinery were developed.

The first true factory in America was a cotton-yarn mill built in 1793 by Samuel Slater in Pawtucket, Rhode Island. (It is now a museum.) In the same year Eli Whitney invented the cotton gin, which vastly accelerated the separation of the seeds from the fiber of cotton and changed the face of the industry. Two replicas of Whitney's revolutionary invention can be seen at the National Museum of History and Technology—the original model burned in a Patent Office fire.

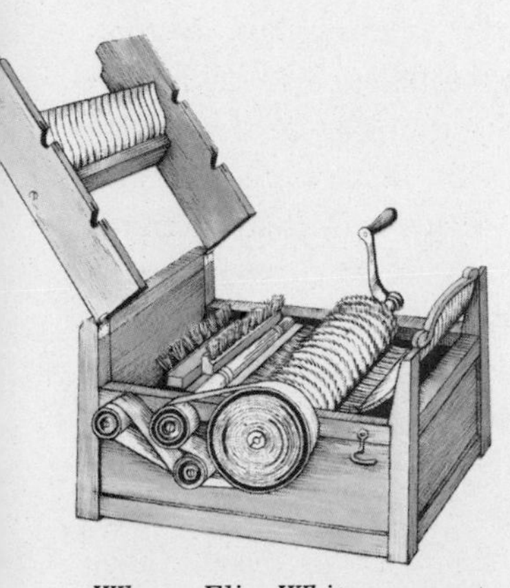

When Eli Whitney went South, cotton and slavery were declining. His cotton gin made both profitable. The uncomplicated machine was easily pirated, and Whitney spent years trying unsuccessfully to get payment.

Mechanized textile mills followed. And in Waltham, Massachusetts, in 1814 Francis Cabot Lowell opened the world's first factory capable of converting raw cotton into cloth by power machinery housed within a single building. The success of the venture resulted eight years later in the founding of Lowell, Massachusetts, the first American mill city, which was a thriving textile center until the early 1920s.

With plenty of fabric at hand, faster ways to stitch it together were needed. Walter Hunt of New York City invented the first true sewing machine in 1832, but he withdrew the machine and refused to apply for a patent because of his fear of throwing seamstresses out of work and "injuring society."

Elias Howe of Boston had no such fears. He took out the first patent for a sewing machine in 1846 and was the first to sell a practical machine to the public. As has proved to be the case with most labor-saving inventions, it ultimately created more jobs than it eliminated. Howe's double-thread, lock-stitch principle remains the basis for most of today's sewing machines. But it was an innovator and promotional genius named Isaac Merritt Singer who added a score of other improvements, including the treadle, the presser foot and, later, the electric motor, to make the machine a household necessity.

Eli Whitney's Marvelous Machines

After Eli Whitney returned to New Haven, Connecticut, from Savannah, Georgia, where he was visiting when he invented the cotton gin, he perfected a system of manufacture that involved the use of interchangeable parts so that unskilled workers could regularly turn out a product worthy of skilled craftsmen. This concept brought about drastic changes in Northern industry.

He first applied the system to the manufacture of 10,000 rifles for the U.S. Government in 1798. Because of start-up and mechanical difficulties, it took eight years to deliver on the two-year contract. But in 1812 Whitney took an order for 15,000 guns and turned them out within two years.

What is called the American system of manufacture evolved from Whitney's interchangeable-parts concept and the invention of new machine tools. Henry Ford's assembly-line production of cars, introduced in 1913, was a direct descendant of the Whitney system.

America Puts to Sea

The first major industry in America was shipbuilding. There was a plentiful supply of timber, England needed ships, and they could be built more cheaply in American ports. By the time of the Revolution a third of all British vessels were being built in America.

Boston became the hub of a vast shipbuilding, fishing, whaling and foreign trade complex that stretched along the New England coastline. Trade with China and the East Indies transformed Salem, Massachusetts, from a small codfish and trading port into one of the most affluent maritime centers in the Western world. The masters of Yankee ships brought back fabulous works of art from the Orient. The museums (and antique shops) in the Boston area still show the results of this bounty. New London and Mystic, Connecticut, prospered as major whaling and shipbuilding ports until the discovery of crude oil in 1859 slashed the market for whale oil. Mystic, of course, still survives as a museum village that recaptures the days of sail.

Requiring only a small crew, the schooner successfully rivaled steam for many years. Originally two- or three-masted vessels, they were later built with six and even seven.

This early involvement with the sea led to experimentation with new types of vessels. The first American nautical invention was the schooner—a fast, easily handled vessel that was more suitable to American waters and weather than the English ketch, which was designed for stormy channels.

The U.S.S. *Constitution* ("Old Ironsides") was built at a Boston shipyard between 1794 and 1797 for use as a frigate by the U.S. Navy. She saw action against the Barbary pirates and against the British in the War of 1812. The nickname came from a sailors' tale that British bombs bounced off as if her sides were made of iron.

Five Americans built and operated steam-powered vessels before 1790, but it was Robert Fulton who developed the first commercially successful steamboat, the *Clermont,* in 1807. It made the 150-mile run from New York to Albany in 32 hours and the return trip in 30.

The greatest sailing ships in the history of the world—the Yankee clippers—were built in great numbers in New England and New York between 1840 and 1860. The most famous were the work of Donald McKay at his East Boston yards. His best-known clipper was the *Flying Cloud,* which sailed in 1851 from New York around Cape Horn to San Francisco in 89 days. This was her maiden voyage, and the record still stands. The original *Flying Cloud* no longer exists; the best model of this noted ship is exhibited at the Museum of Fine Arts in Boston.

The clipper ships had long, narrow hulls and sharp, gracefully curved bows. They carried rectangular sails on three masts that slanted slightly backward. The handsome narrow hulls that were built for speed eventually led to the clippers' demise. Their limited cargo space and high operating costs could not compete with the newly built railroads that carried goods across the continent.

Long before steam was used at sea, the calmer inland waterways had been plied by luxurious steam-driven riverboats.

As good wood for shipbuilding became more scarce and iron and steel became more readily available, metal ships gradually replaced wooden ones and steam turbines took the place of sails. With the steam engine and the paddle wheel came the most romantic of the American maritime innovations—the riverboat. A few originals still remain, and there are a number of replicas afloat. The greatest of the originals is the *Delta Queen,* which still plies the Mississippi between St. Paul and New Orleans.

The Age of Steam

The groundwork for the age of steam was laid in 1769 when James Watt, a Scot, patented improvements on the steam engine that had been patented by Thomas Savery in 1698 and improved upon by Thomas Newcomen in the early 1700s. Additional improvements came rapidly in the early 1800s. When the International Centennial Exposition was held in Philadelphia in 1876, the theme was "Power," and the principal exhibit was a huge Corliss steam engine that generated 1600 horsepower. Steam engines were used throughout the country in sawmills and factories of every kind. They

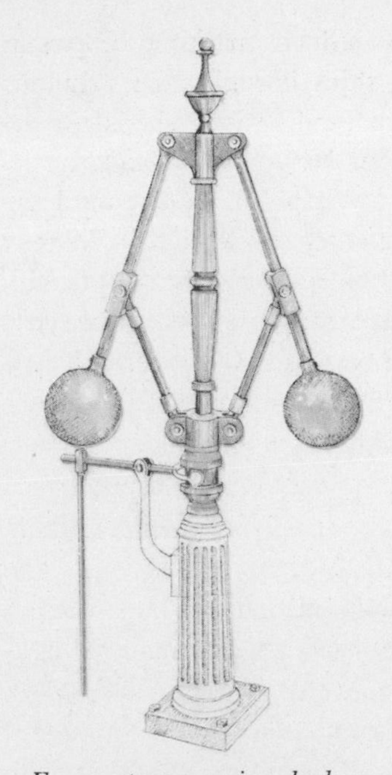

Every steam engine had a governor (speed regulator). This one, with its fluted column and turned finial, typifies the decorative detail proudly lavished on machines.

generated electricity and powered tractors, reapers and harvesters on farms. The workmanship and engraved and engine-turned decorations on these early machines were remarkable and are still a source of pleasure wherever they are to be seen, particularly in the Henry Ford Museum at the Edison Institute in Dearborn, Michigan.

The first known application of steam locomotion to railway track in the United States was made by Colonel John Stevens in 1825. He built a small locomotive with an upright boiler and ran it on a circular track on his Hoboken, New Jersey, estate. Stevens's son Robert later invented the now-universal T-rail track.

The first full-sized locomotive to run on rails in America was an import from England. The "Stourbridge Lion" was one of three locomotives acquired by the Delaware & Hudson Canal Company of Pennsylvania, which planned to start a railroad. It was the only one of the three that worked, and then just briefly. The six-ton locomotive moved down the track in a cloud of dust and steam at the amazing speed of 10 miles per hour on Aug. 8, 1829. After a few miles it was decided that the locomotive was too heavy for the track. It was then removed from the rails and used as a stationary power engine. Years later the remains of "Stourbridge Lion" were transported to the Smithsonian Institution, where the original boiler and cylinder can be seen today in the National Museum of History and Technology.

In 1830 the first of a series of races between a locomotive and a horse took place near Baltimore. Peter Cooper, a New York ironmaster, had built a one-ton, one-cylinder, one-and-a-half horsepower locomotive called "Tom Thumb"; it was so small that its boiler tubes were made of gun barrels. The operator of a stagecoach line challenged Cooper to race the locomotive against one of his horses, and Cooper accepted. "Tom Thumb" built up a big lead; then its drive belt slipped, the steam engine came to a stop, and the live horse beat the iron horse in their first race. But the little locomotive still bears the distinction of being the first engine to pull a load of rail passengers in America. On Christmas Day in 1830, a few months after that race, the locomotive "Best Friend of Charleston" was put into service by the South Carolina Railroad. It was the first locomotive built in this country for regular service on a railway, and the South Carolina company was the first to offer scheduled railway passenger service using a steam locomotive.

Because their four wheels were on two fixed-position axles, the heavy English locomotives like the "Stourbridge Lion" often derailed on sharp curves.

The National Museum of History and Technology has a model of the "Tom Thumb," and the Baltimore & Ohio Transportation Museum in Baltimore has a slightly oversized replica. An operating model of the "Best Friend of Charleston" is exhibited at the Wings and Wheels Museum in Santee, South Carolina.

The iron horse soon caught the imagination of the public, and within five years of that first race there were more than 1000 miles of railroad track in operation in the United States. By 1840 there were 2800 miles of track in this country and by 1860 more than 30,000.

However, it was the Erie Canal in New York State that provided the engineering knowledge and manpower to implement the railroads' westward push. The 363-mile waterway from Albany and Troy on the Hudson to Buffalo on Lake Erie was completed in 1825 and effectively joined the entire Great Lakes system with the Atlantic Ocean. There had been few engineers in America when the canal was started in 1817, but the complex job was a good training ground. By the time the trains were ready to roll, there were men with the knowledge to lay the track.

Two Tracks of Steel from Coast to Coast

The greatest example of engineering skill was the completion of a transcontinental railroad route along the 42nd parallel in 1869. The Union Pacific Railroad built westward from what is now Omaha, Nebraska, and the Central Pacific built eastward from Sacramento, California. When the two lines met at Promontory Point in Utah on May 10, 1869, a golden spike was driven into a special crosstie of polished laurel to celebrate the achievement. That original golden spike is at the Stanford University Museum near Palo Alto, California, and the National Museum of History and Technology has a replica and a major exhibit on the subject. Golden Spike National Monument at Promontory Summit, Utah, commemorates the historic completion of the transcontinental link.

Railroads in the early days were not as safe as they should have been. Many accidents were caused by the lack of adequate signaling and braking systems. Both problems were solved by George Westinghouse, who developed the compressed air brake in 1868 and an automatic signaling system in 1880 in Pittsburgh. Westinghouse was a man of many talents and made important contributions to the development of natural gas and a new power source, electricity.

Something New in the World

This strange force, which was next to catch the imagination of the tinkers, mechanics and inventors, is not fully understood to this day. Benjamin Franklin became interested in electricity about 1750 and developed the theory that it consists of a single fluid. He was also the first to apply the terms "positive" and "negative," and he proved that a spark generates heat. Franklin's most famous experiment—the flying of a kite in a storm to show that lightning is electricity—was conducted in 1752.

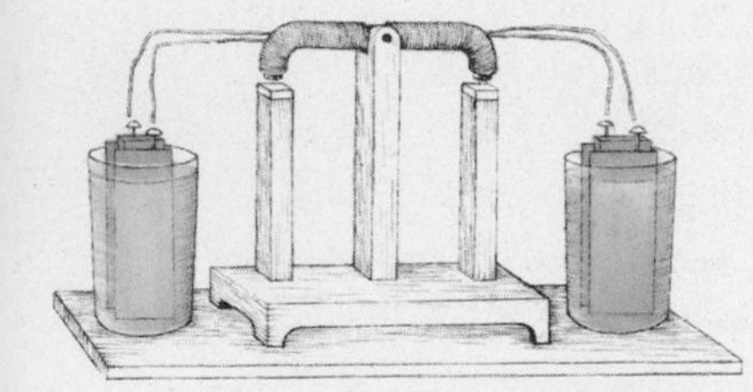

This first electric motor consisted of a wire-wrapped iron rod rocking on a central pivot, connecting and disconnecting with two primitive batteries.

Compared to Franklin, physicist Joseph Henry is little known, and was even less appreciated in his time. He was, however, one of America's great experimental scientists, and his principle of electromagnetic induction formed the basis for developing generators, motors and transformers. Because of Henry's reticence and his reluctance to patent his inventions, his English counterpart, Michael Faraday, beat him in announcing the discovery of current induced by magnetism and became much better known.

Henry built the first electric motor and the first electromagnetic telegraph in 1831. He served as the first secretary and director of the Smithsonian Institution and helped to organize the American Association for the Advancement of Science and the National Academy of Sciences.

Henry's experiences also called attention to the need for patent reform. In 1836 the Patent Office was reorganized and the first full-time Commissioner of Patents was appointed. The number of patents granted rose from 436 in 1837 to 4778 in 1860. In 1972, 83,661 patents were issued.

Thomas Alva Edison

In a span of 60 years Thomas A. Edison, sometimes called the world's greatest inventor, patented 1093 inventions—more than any other person in American history. He defined genius as "one percent inspiration and 99 percent perspiration." All problems interested him, and he would try everything to find a solution. When involved in a project, he would work for days at a time, stopping only for short naps. He is also credited with establishing the team concept of specialists working together to solve problems and develop ideas. This is now a standard practice in developmental laboratories.

Fascinating evidence of Edison's inventions and his ways of working can be seen at the Edison National Historic Site in West Orange, New Jersey. The first profitable invention of "The Wizard of Menlo Park" (so called for the site of his New Jersey laboratory), was an improved ticker used to telegraph stock prices to brokers' offices. Much to his surprise, he received $40,000 for his patent. The money enabled him to open his first workshop, where he developed an improved typewriter in 1874. Edison substituted metal for wooden parts, corrected the alignment of the letters and improved the distribution of ink. Until he made these changes, it had been faster to write by hand than by machine.

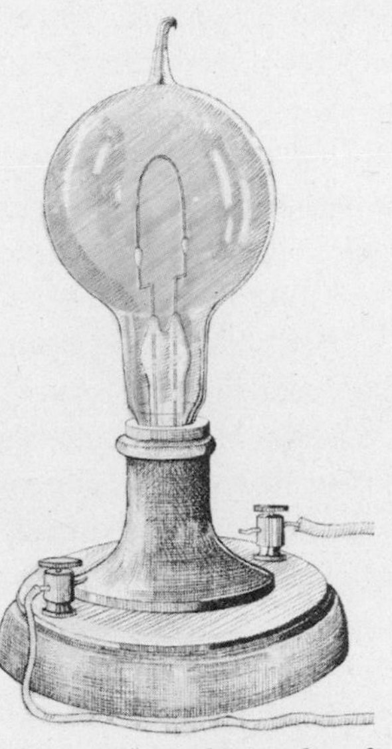

After testing thousands of fibers, Thomas Edison used carbonized sewing threads in his first incandescent light bulb, which lasted 40 hours. He continued working on his invention to make the bulb burn longer and to reduce its cost to under 40 cents.

Edison also improved the telephone in 1876 by adding the carbon transmitter, which made it possible to be heard without shouting. His favorite invention was the phonograph, which he developed in 1877. He was a former telegrapher, and the idea came while he was attempting to find a means for recording messages automatically.

In 1879 Edison made the incandescent lamp commercially practicable. This development brought electricity into the home. In 1882 the first important commercial electric power station, designed by Edison to transmit direct current electricity, went into operation in New York City. Because Edison was committed to the use of direct current, he clashed with George Westinghouse, who had acquired foreign alternating current patents and improved on the designs. Westinghouse set out to popularize alternating current; but Edison and his supporters, claiming that high-voltage transmission was more dangerous, were temporarily successful in forestalling its widespread acceptance. In the end, however, the proponents of alternating current prevailed, and this is the mode that most of us now use.

A primitive form of motion picture projector—the kinetiscope—was invented by Edison in 1893, and he developed an early version of talking motion pictures in 1913. Among his other inventions and improvements were the storage battery, a cement mixer, the dictaphone, a duplicating machine and synthetic rubber made from goldenrod plants.

Edison had little time for social life, but he occasionally got together and exchanged ideas with the electrical engineering genius Charles P. Steinmetz, industrialists Henry Ford and Harvey Firestone and naturalist John Burroughs. He entertained at his comfortable home in Sarasota, Florida. This house, its extensive garden and his laboratory there are open to the public. On the golden anniversary of the electric light in 1929 and as a memorial to Edison, Ford moved Edison's original Menlo Park laboratory complex to the Edison Institute, named after his friend, in Dearborn, Michigan.

The Telephone and Telegraph

Edison's career touched on at least three other major developments during the 19th century—the telegraph, the telephone and photography. Joseph Henry had done some early experiments with the electromagnetic telegraph, but it was Samuel F. B. Morse who perfected the "lightning wire" in 1837. A painter, Morse became interested in developing a practical telegraph after hearing about Henry's experiments.

Morse secured his patent in 1840 and attempted to interest wealthy men in his invention, but there was an economic depression at the time and he could not find backing. He was almost destitute in 1844 when Congress appropriated $30,000 for him to construct a test line between Washington and Baltimore. From a sending device in the Supreme Court chamber, Morse tapped out the scriptural message, "What hath God wrought?" The test worked, and the telegraph was here to stay. It proved its usefulness in the Civil War, and without it the West could not have been so quickly settled.

Like Edison, Alexander Graham Bell was involved in working with the telegraph. A Scottish teacher of the deaf, he came to Boston in 1871 and sought to develop a harmonic telegraph in which electric current would vibrate metallic reeds to produce different sounds. He accidentally discovered that one of the plucked springs would change its vibrations into variations of electric current. These variations produced the same vibrations in a receiver at the other end of the connection. Bell then placed a diaphragm over the end of his spring to make a mouthpiece, and the basis for the telephone was established. While testing a crude transmitter in 1876, and with his assistant Thomas A. Watson waiting at the other end of the line, Bell upset a battery and spilled the chemicals on his clothes. Impulsively he shouted: "Mr. Watson, come here. I want you!" Watson's prompt arrival was proof enough that the instrument worked.

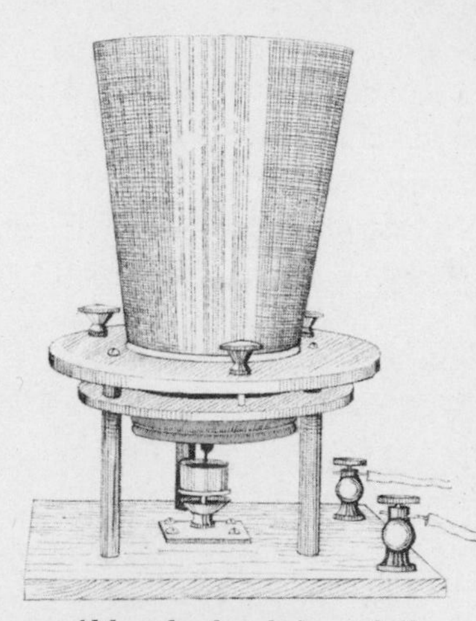

Although the design of the telephone has changed greatly, the basic principles have remained the same since Alexander Graham Bell exhibited a transmitter like this in 1876.

Bell exhibited his invention—which had a receiver and a transmitter that could be used interchangeably—at the 1876 Centennial Exposition in Philadelphia. The public seemed unimpressed, although the development was hailed by scientists. Some of the best replicas of Bell's early telephones can be seen at the National Museum of History and Technology and at the Museum of Science and Industry in Chicago.

Photography Begins

Considering the impact of photography on our culture, its early history has been given little attention. Morse, for example, made a small but important contribution to the art in 1838 when he opened one of the first photographic portrait studios in the United States. But the studio failed because too much time was required to sit for a portrait.

The following year John W. Draper, professor of chemistry and physiology at the College of the City of New York, took the first photographic portrait in the modern sense of a reasonable exposure time. In 1840 he photographed the moon for the first time. It was a small image and not very sharp, but it was the forerunner of astronomical photography.

The value of the camera for reporting was first dramatically demonstrated by Mathew Brady, who captured the reality of the Civil War in photographs. The Library of Congress in Washington has the largest collection of Brady's monumental work, more than 3000 plates and prints. The National Archives in Washington also has a significant collection.

In Brady's day the photographer had to coat his own glass plates with a light-sensitive emulsion, make the exposure and develop the plates immediately. But in 1879 George Eastman, working in Rochester, New York, invented a machine for coating the glass plates. This was the big breakthrough that made possible the photographs we take and see today. In 1884 Eastman perfected flexible film and a roll holder to wind it on. Soon afterward he produced the simple box camera, which he called the

Kodak, and by 1900 he was able to sell a workable camera for $1.00 and start millions of amateur photographers on their way.

The first Kodak had a fixed focus lens and took fairly sharp, circular snapshots of anything more than eight feet away. It was about seven by four inches and had a shutter speed of 1/25th of a second.

In the years that followed, Eastman's company contributed to the development of the camera, improved processing, color photography, slides, motion pictures and other aspects of photography. The early developments and many later improvements can be seen in his former home in Rochester, which now houses the International Museum of Photography.

The next major photographic breakthrough for amateurs did not come until 1947, when Edwin H. Land invented a camera that would develop its own film. He founded the Polaroid Company, and today's Land camera can make good color prints in less than a minute.

As the inventions made in the early 1900s became vastly profitable, companies later began to set up sophisticated research centers that attracted and supported the most creative minds they could find. Teams of scientists and researchers accelerated the pace of improvements and new inventions. From the General Electric laboratories, for example, came the work of Charles P. Steinmetz and Irving Langmuir.

Steinmetz is best known for his development of the theory of alternating current and his experiments with man-made lightning. During Langmuir's half century with GE, he improved the ordinary light bulb, invented the high-vacuum pump and experimented with cloud seeding to make rain. With Gilbert Lewis he developed the Lewis-Langmuir theory of atomic structure and in 1932 was awarded the Nobel Prize in chemistry for his work on chemical reactions.

Despite the trend toward collective investigation and innovation, a few individualists—such as Henry Ford, the Wright brothers and Lee De Forest—had a profound effect on the development of the automotive, aircraft and electronic industries early in the 20th century.

Taking to the Road

The first motor vehicle in the United States was Oliver Evans's steam-powered *Orukter Amphibolos,* or amphibious digger, that operated on both land and water in Philadelphia in 1805. In 1836 Thomas Davenport developed a working model of an electric-powered vehicle in Brandon, Vermont. There are many early steam and electric cars on display in our museums, but in most instances their practicality was not adequately proved. The concepts, however, are still intriguing, and inventors have not given up hope of an alternative to the internal-combustion engine.

Between 1890 and 1900 hundreds of people built automobiles. The 500-pound "gas buggy" devised by Henry Ford was the lightest of the gasoline-powered cars.

The first gasoline-powered American car was made in Springfield, Massachusetts, in 1893 by Charles E. and J. Frank Duryea. Henry Ford came along with his "gas buggy" in 1896. It was about this time that Ransom E. Olds began preaching and practicing the idea of a cheap car for the masses, and automobile manufacturers soon realized the importance of making interchangeable parts that could be used on any car of the same model.

Ford was neither the first to manufacture an automobile powered by an internal-combustion engine nor the first to mass-produce one. However, he did develop a durable, practical and inexpensive vehicle (the Model T, introduced in 1908) that was the forerunner of the modern mass-produced car. In doing so, he did more than anyone else to put the nation on wheels and to promote the spread of assembly-line production. The mass production of automobiles in this country has probably had a greater impact on the face of the land and ways of the people than any other single development. Most of the early-day models of Ford cars can be seen at the Henry Ford Museum at the Edison Institute.

The design of the early cars had an awkward charm that slowly evolved into a sleek and exuberant expression of speed as new techniques were developed for shaping metal. Some of the world's most beautiful cars—such as the Mercer Raceabout, Stutz Bearcat, Duesenberg, early Packard, Pierce Arrow, Auburn and Cord—were made in America and can be seen in various automotive museums.

The Flying Machines

The story of American flight and rocketry began in Europe in 1785. It was that winter that a Boston-born physician, John Jeffries, and a Frenchman, François Blanchard, made the first aerial crossing of the English Channel in a balloon. The interest in balloons and other lighter-than-air craft for specialized uses has persisted. Their most important American role has been a means of observation during the Civil War and in World War I.

After learning how to fly their machines, the Wright brothers were able to fly for 38 minutes in this 1905 plane.

One of the first men to experiment successfully with heavier-than-air, power-driven flight was Samuel P. Langley, secretary of the Smithsonian Institution. In 1896 his 16-foot, steam-driven model airplane, Aerodrome No. 5, flew a distance of 3200 feet over the Potomac River. In 1903 he twice tried unsuccessfully to launch a full-scale, man-carrying, radial gasoline-powered version of the Aerodrome from a houseboat on the Potomac. The second attempt took place only two weeks before the historic flight by Wilbur and Orville Wright.

It was a cold day on the 17th of December in 1903 that the Wright brothers made the first sustained flight with a motor-driven, heavier-than-air machine. Orville was at the controls and Wilbur ran alongside for that first epoch-making excursion of 120 feet. Three more flights were made that day; the longest was 852 feet. The original plane is in the Smithsonian's Arts and Industries Building, but there is a replica in the museum at Kitty Hawk, North Carolina, where the first flights were made.

The Wright brothers returned to their home in Dayton, Ohio, and built a new machine that they flew 105 times from a rented cow pasture. In 1905 they made a flight of nearly 25 miles in 38 minutes. The air age was definitely at hand. More evidence of the Wrights' pioneering efforts can be seen at the Edison Institute and at Wright-Patterson Air Force Base in Dayton. The Wrights' bicycle shop, where their first plane was made, and some of their early engines are also exhibited at Edison Institute.

Charles Lindbergh stands in front of The Spirit of St. Louis *at Curtiss Field where he worked on the plane before his historic flight to Paris.*

Many early airplanes, especially those of the World War I era, are displayed in museums throughout the country. These pioneer aircraft exemplify the remarkable beauty that evolves when form is established purely by function. Every part of the early planes was required to make them fly; anything extra would defeat the purpose. The ingenuity of the early models is there to see—in the wooden frame, the canvas covering, the supporting struts and wires.

Perhaps the most famous aircraft in the world, *The Spirit of St. Louis,* hangs high overhead in the Arts and Industries Building. In this airplane Charles A. Lindbergh took off from Roosevelt Field, Long Island, New York, on May 20, 1927, and landed at Le Bourget Airport near Paris just $33\frac{1}{2}$ hours later. This first nonstop solo flight of about 3610 miles across the Atlantic captured the world's imagination and ushered in an era of aeronautic exploration that would venture to the moon and beyond.

Rockets and Computers

For centuries man has aspired to rocket flight and space exploration. But the development of rockets as we know them today is based on the work of American space pioneer Robert H. Goddard, a physics professor at Clark University in Worcester, Massachusetts.

In 1926, after years of investigation, Goddard successfully launched a small, liquid-propellant rocket that climbed 184 feet in two-and-a-half seconds. By 1935 he had fired an 11-foot rocket that reached a height of 7500 feet. Goddard's 1926 rocket no longer exists, but his second version (1928), which contains some parts from the first rocket, is on exhibition at the National Museum of History and Technology; the museum also has a 1940 version. Goddard rockets of 1938-9 are displayed at the Roswell Museum and Art Center in Roswell, New Mexico.

Dr. Robert Goddard posed by the first rocket fueled with gasoline and liquid oxygen just before it was ignited.

German rocketry during World War II and the Soviet Union's orbiting of the Sputnik I satellite in 1957 gave impetus to the American space program. Tangible evidence of the success of this monumental effort can be seen in the Smithsonian Institution, where the largest moon rock brought to earth from man's first lunar landing by the crew of Apollo 11 is displayed. Other moon rocks are sometimes exhibited at NASA installations in Houston, Texas; Cape Kennedy, Florida; and Huntsville, Alabama.

The computer has a history traceable to the Jacquard loom and the player piano, both of which are based on the concept of holes punched in paper to differentiate and record bits of information. The holes in the early punch card computing and tabulating systems have, in the last 80 years, evolved into electrical impulses recorded on magnetic tape. But the purpose of the computer is still to screen and store information.

The invention in 1948 at the Bell Telephone Laboratories of the tiny transistor to replace the bulky vacuum tube made miniaturization possible. Today's computer is equaling the motor car in its impact on society.

While the purpose of industry and the mechanical arts is not to create beauty, there is remarkable aesthetic appeal in the tools, the engines and the vehicles that have come to be. Good evidence of this fortunate circumstance can be seen in museums of every size all across the country.

The Decorative Arts

A fruitful blend of many cultures in American ceramics, silver, textiles and wood

Americans for centuries have fostered diversity in furnishings and decorative objects. We came from many different countries and a wide range of social, economic and religious backgrounds. Differences in climate and the availability of materials, plus the blending of the tastes of people of varied backgrounds, have further increased diversity. So it is not surprising that our heritage in the decorative arts is the most interesting, imaginative and varied in the world.

Colonists in the 17th century looked homeward to England and the rest of Europe for standards in beauty and comfort. This custom has bound succeeding generations to the Old World and has linked our decorative arts to those of every epoch in the East and West. This is not to say that early Americans made no contributions to the decorative arts. Although styles and techniques were rooted in the Old World, the creative freedom in America soon expressed itself in such original concepts as the rocking chair, invented here before the Revolutionary War, and in the unadorned elegance of our earliest work in silver, pewter, ceramics and glass.

For centuries nearly every home had at least one decorative silver porringer for porridge or soup. This one was made in Boston in 1655.

We have also consistently modified European objects both in scale and in the use of ornamentation. For one thing, our rooms were smaller than those in European mansions and called for smaller furnishings. Nor did we have so broad a range of craftsmen. As a result our artisans were forced to achieve decorative effects by emphasizing other qualities, such as crispness of line, vitality of form, emphasis on overall proportion and the use of materials specifically for decoration. The shortage of skilled labor also encouraged standardization of parts and so further influenced design.

Although colonists such as the Dutch in New York and New Jersey and the Spanish in the Southwest all brought decorative traditions from their homelands, these national influences have largely given way to the stronger force of English traditions. Beginning with the early 17th century, most of the colonists in New England and the South came from central England. In this conservative area, a lingering medieval tradition mingled with northern European courtly fashions which, in turn, were influenced by the 15th-century Florentine revival of ancient Roman traditions. The early colonists may not have known the source, but this was essentially the background they brought to their chosen land.

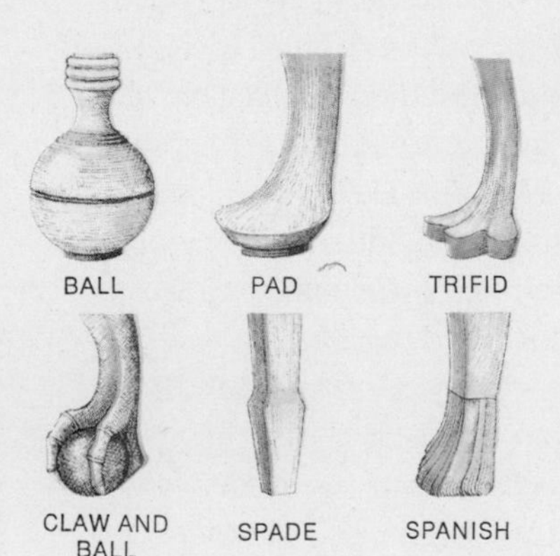

The legs of furniture often give an indication of the period in which the piece was made. Shown here are major styles that can be seen in the period rooms of museums around the country. The ball and Spanish feet are found on William and Mary furniture. The pad and the trifid are typical of Queen Anne style; the claw-and-ball foot was featured by Chippendale. The spade foot was often used in American Federal designs.

In the last 100 years Americans have become increasingly aware of the quantity, variety and quality of our remarkable heritage in the decorative arts and have seriously preserved, collected and documented them. The best that has been produced here can be studied in depth through collections in eight American cities: in New York at the Metropolitan and Brooklyn Museums; in Philadelphia at the Museum of Art; in Wilmington at the Winterthur Museum; in Boston at the Museum of Fine Arts; in Winston-Salem at Old Salem and the Museum of Early Southern Decorative Arts; in Detroit at the Institute of Arts and the nearby Edison Institute with its Henry Ford Museum and Greenfield Village; in Chicago at the Art Institute; and in Los Angeles at the County Museum. Period rooms and galleries in these institutions offer an unexcelled foundation for understanding the American decorative arts and their relation to painting, sculpture and interior and exterior architecture. In addition, craftsmen continue to demonstrate and maintain many of the nearly vanished colonial skills at Williamsburg, Virginia; Shelburne, Vermont; Old Sturbridge Village, Massachusetts; and other reconstructed communities.

Potters and Silversmiths

Silversmithing and pottery-making have been important crafts in this country from the very beginning. By the time of the Revolution, Boston, Newport, New York and Philadelphia supported dozens of silversmiths, and every community of moderate size claimed at least one. Beauty and function were but two reasons for the abundance of plate, as it was called. Banks

For their pottery the Pennsylvania Germans used traditional or humorous sayings and folk motifs like the double-headed eagle on this fine plate made for Cadarina Raeder in 1786.

did not exist before the Revolution, and coins accumulating from trade presented problems of storage and of identification if stolen. For the meager cost of the labor, coins could be converted into objects easily identified by form, decoration, craftsman's marks and owner's arms or initials. Plate thus represented wealth and often served in place of money.

Every community of consequence also had at least one resident potter. With a potter's wheel and kiln he could produce more than was needed locally, and so most were also farmers or fishermen. Only German potters in the Middle Colonies exploited the plastic qualities of their material. Using the locally abundant red clays, they followed traditions of their homeland in modeling and in drawing naïve inscriptions, tulips and figures on their wares. Additional decoration in slip and colored glazes made their achievements comparable to the folk arts of central Europe.

English ceramics and other materials for kitchen equipment replaced redware after the Revolution, although rural potters continued making it until the mid-1800s. At the same time pottery production expanded and the potter frequently marked his work with his name and community. These wares, often decorated in the blue of cobalt, found their greatest use in kitchens and as industrial containers.

The Early Furniture

In the early 17th century furniture was limited both in quantity and form. Chests served as storage areas, benches and tables. Stools doubled as tables and for seating until assigned a decorative role in the 1730s. Chairs, though expensive, included high chairs for children. With increasing wealth came the luxury of true tables. Some, for dining, had trestle bases and removable tops, while others served for dining and writing. And, late in the century, there appeared the type with folding leaves and hinged legs known today as gate-leg tables. Low-post beds provided inexpensive counterparts to those with high posts and curtains, although simple pallets served many children and servants.

*This carved Jacobean cupboard gets its name from James I (*Jacobus *in Latin), king of England from 1603 to 1625. Colonists continued to make massive, straight furniture of this kind for nearly a century after James's death.*

Craftsmen in the first years of settlement practiced most of the basic techniques of construction and decoration. They turned ash and maple on lathes to form furniture parts. Oak, also favored in England, was joined for chests, cabinets and other case pieces. For decoration they sometimes split spindles and stained them black to imitate the ebony used in European furniture. Carved motifs included the ancient Roman guilloche and the Greek triglyph dancing in classically incorrect partnership with the lozenges, spirals and strapwork of northern Europe, or with stylized leaves, flowers and whorls from medieval England. Time and skill were of such little value that for over two centuries raw materials were more expensive than labor.

Late in the 17th century a growing and prospering population, now better adjusted to its new environment, was lacking in sympathy for the religion and society of Stuart England. One result, especially in New England, was an increased interest in the provincial English style combining medieval and Renaissance elements. Objects surviving from this period by silversmiths such as John Hull and Robert Sanderson and furniture associated with Thomas Dennis are as elaborate in design and as skilled in workmanship as those produced in central England.

More sophisticated colonials in the late 17th and early 18th centuries brought a new era to the arts. Their trade, society and privileges rested with

London. These ties shifted standards from the tradition of the English countryside to the taste of the British professional and mercantile class prospering under the Glorious Revolution of 1688, which had placed the progressive Dutch Prince William III on the throne along with his consort Mary and brought England firmly into the age of empire. New styles now spread from London to the major colonial cities and finally into smaller communities and the countryside. In each community elements of design mingled with previous styles to form a different mixture. It took about a century for a style introduced in the courtly houses of England to appear in remote American farmhouses.

William and Mary Style

The fashion opening this era in the late 17th century and lasting through the first quarter of the 18th is identified today as the William and Mary style. Features of the style had appeared in England and reached America before the reign of William and Mary, but their rule particularly encouraged it. Known as the Baroque on the Continent, it had originated a century earlier in Rome and gradually spread through France, Holland and England. In America, New England craftsmen gained the greatest facility with the style, as can be seen in the work of such men as the Boston silversmith Edward Winslow.

Typical William and Mary designs suggest movement within large, clearly defined shapes by the use of bold curves and extreme contrasts of light and dark values. Vertical lines predominate over horizontal and many decorative details suggest the Renaissance style.

Windsor chairs became a speciality of Philadelphia craftsmen. Also known as stick chairs, they were made in several variations of high and low backs, all with thin rod back supports, stick legs and contour seats.

As a result of trade with China, Oriental influences also were introduced into design about this time and extended the variety of forms of household furnishings. Equally important, new Oriental motifs, processes and materials were introduced to craftsmen here.

With the William and Mary style came new furniture forms. The increased use of drawers accounts for the appearance of desks, secretaries and the sets of high chests and dressing tables popular until the Revolution. A greater variety of chairs, including corner chairs and easy chairs that doubled as commodes, appeared on the scene, and replaced the earlier simple stools and benches. Other innovations were daybeds, tall clocks and looking glasses. And with the introduction of tea, a new form of table—the tea table—evolved.

Decorative techniques also changed. As lathes became more common, turnings were finer and more numerous. Carving was more limited and was used mainly for shaping such forms as the Spanish foot, which resembled a paint brush. Veneers of honey-colored maple burl were used on elaborate New England case pieces. Gesso and varnish also were employed to copy the Oriental lacquer technique known as japanning and appeared on furniture of various colors painted with designs.

At the same time, skilled turners working with lathes developed contemporary Windsor furniture beyond that produced in Windsor, England. The variety of plentiful woods encouraged selection by function, with paint of various colors disguising the combinations. Windsor-style side, arm and high chairs, settees, stools and stands were common in all rooms of the average house, in secondary rooms of the wealthy and in gardens. Specialists in the craft standardized parts to increase production and lower cost.

These are two fine examples of Queen Anne furniture. Both pieces have sweeping cabriole legs and typical cushioned-pad feet. The highboy has the characteristic scallop-shell motif. Tea-drinking, and therefore tea tables, were an innovation of the late 1600s.

Queen Anne Style

A second phase of Baroque design revealing greater influence from the Orient is known today as the Queen Anne style. It evolved during the general period of Queen Anne's reign, but became popular in America during the second quarter of the 18th century. Simplicity, undulating curves and the favored motif of the scallop shell marked the shift in taste.

The need for strength and the English dictates of the Queen Anne style encouraged the use of walnut throughout the Colonies. Despite standard design and material, there were interesting regional variations such as the delicacy of pad shapes among feet in New England, trifid shapes in the Middle Colonies, and heavy pads and trifids in the South. Until about 1800 the furniture of New England maintained a more delicate and vertical character than that of other areas.

The apple form of this teapot, made by Jacob Hurd in Boston around 1735, is one of the many shapes popular in the early 18th century.

The Queen Anne style served as the basis for the Rococo style, a new trend in taste introduced to this country in the late 1750s and prominent throughout the 1780s. It came to England from France and then spread to America.

In contrast to the formal balance and sweeping curves of the Queen Anne style, Rococo forms relied on delicate designs in staccato, asymmetrical arrangements. S-shaped and C-shaped scrolls locked flowers, leaves, fluttering ribbons, musical instruments, shells, ruffles and classical motifs into intricate patterns. In England, and later in America, the style also incorporated medieval and Chinese elements. All these varied designs mingled and covered surfaces in rich profusion and high relief. The Mid-Atlantic Colonies produced the highest expressions of the style as the crafts flourished there in the Pennsylvania glass factories of Henry William Stiegel, the silversmithing of Joseph Richardson, Sr., of Philadelphia and Myer Meyers of New York, and the work of carvers and the other specialists who turned out fine furniture.

Queen Anne forms overlaid with Rococo, Gothic and Chinese ornament remained dominant to the 1780s. Three innovations—the claw-and-ball foot reflecting an earlier vogue in England, the straight leg and the shaped top of a chair called the cresting rail—may have been further influences from the Orient. Furniture designs based on these sources and published by the London cabinetmaker Thomas Chippendale gained such influence that today his name has been given to pieces of that period.

The cut-out and carved back, cabriole legs and claw-and-ball feet on this armchair are Chippendale characteristics.

English fashion introduced mahogany and encouraged development of carvers among other specialists making chairs and cabinet furniture. These craftsmen trained others in three to six years of apprenticeship and, with the encouragement of patrons accustomed to their approach, increased regional variations in design. Philadelphia became the largest and wealthiest of American cities and produced the most elaborate furniture in this period. Shops, such as that of Benjamin Randolph, offered custom- as well as ready-made products.

During the years the Rococo ruled in America, a new style based on ancient Roman and Grecian art arose in England and introduced a half-century of classical revivals. Each took a different form and all eventually appeared in the United States, where English culture had idealized the ancient world for a century and the ancient republics served as models for the new society.

Robert Adam and Neoclassicism

Revolution and depression in America delayed introduction of the first Neoclassical style until the 1790s. It had originated in England in the workshop of a Scottish architect, Robert Adam, who opened his practice about 1758. Adam designed every architectural and furnishing detail in structures he built or remodeled, which resulted in remarkable aesthetic unity in his creations. He worked with his brother James in a large firm, but remained the chief innovator and creative force in the style they created.

This Neoclassical sauceboat, made in Philadelphia around 1810, is noteworthy for the mixture of motifs. This one piece is decorated with an asp, a ram's head and sphinxlike figures on the paw feet.

Books published in London in the 1790s popularized Robert Adam's Neoclassicism and introduced his new form of the sideboard and great variety in tables and seating furniture. George Hepplewhite's designs followed Adam's earliest style of mahogany veneer inlaid with plain or decorated bands and classical motifs of urns, swags and bellflowers. Hepplewhite's models were soon followed by those of Thomas Sheraton, which featured complex forms and three-dimensional surface treatments of carving, reeding and fluting. Individual craftsmen's personal interpretations of these and other designs in turn resulted in a variety of local styles.

Many craftsmen from the 1790s to the 1840s specialized in delicate painted furniture of every type and price decorated with Neoclassical designs. Examples are rare, because the fragile forms and surfaces did not hold up as well as the earlier pieces of sturdy mahogany. Late interpretations of the style are largely confined to chairs with stencil decorations, such as those by Lambert Hitchcock and his competitors.

The Neoclassical style was a direct reaction to the complexities of the Baroque and Rococo. It is characterized by extreme simplicity based on straight lines and oval and round motifs. This simplicity, combined with delicate ornament in low relief, created an airy lightness of form and decoration in an atmosphere of order and stability. Silversmiths such as Paul Revere of Boston also adopted this new approach in preference to the earlier Rococo style.

Classical forms were copied with greater accuracy by the late 1790s and were occasionally mixed with motifs from India, China, Egypt or medieval

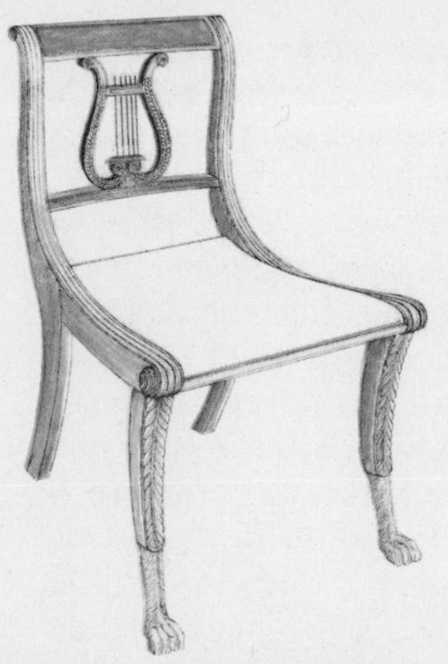

The lyre-back chair, one of Duncan Phyfe's most popular designs, is still copied today, though without his masterly carving of acanthus leaves around the frame of the lyre.

England. Shortly before the War of 1812 these were modified with the accents of extravagant ornamentation that became characteristic of the Empire style.

Hepplewhite and Sheraton influences prevailed in the new nation, while innovations in style and production accompanied the commercial success of enterprises in New York City. Before the War of 1812 the Scottish immigrant Duncan Phyfe pioneered in the early phase of the Empire style. Phyfe's control of quality in a shop of 100 workmen secured his success in the later phases of Neoclassicism. Thrifty interpretations by Phyfe and others of French gilt mounts accenting mahogany veneers made gild stencil decoration a specialty of New York.

Simplified classical styles of the 1830s were well suited to mass production and increased use of this technique. Joseph Meeks and Sons of New York City, for example, used power saws to cut flat, curved elements which they combined in various forms. John Hall of Baltimore further established this approach. His furniture pattern book of 1840, the first in America, was widely distributed. It popularized the use of bold outlines with curved or flat surfaces veneered in mahogany and adorned with machined bands of ripple decoration. Styles of the following decades led to the use of jigs, devices that guided equipment to repeat turnings mechanically. These developments and other uses of power tools helped found the commercial furniture industry and make inexpensive pieces available to ordinary people.

Revivals of classical art were the first of many short-lived fashions inspired by the past. Technology supported these revivals by accelerating communication, reducing cost and increasing production. Styles once delayed a generation or more in reaching America now were introduced within a few seasons.

From the 1840s through the 1860s four main stylistic themes reigned. The simplified Classical style emphasized Grecian forms and continued the regeneration of classical taste launched by Robert Adam. The Gothic style, which reached full development in the 1840s, employed pointed arches, crockets (resembling curved foliage), finials, rosettes (circular designs based on the rose) and tracery gleaned from English architecture of the Middle Ages. The Naturalistic style in turn featured curving tendrils, leaves and flowers. It was evident throughout the period and commonly merged with the most popular taste at mid-century, the Rococo Revival. Known also as the Louis XV or Antique French style, the Rococo Revival relied basically on curves, C-scrolls and S-scrolls that were more loosely formed than their 18th-century forerunners.

Practicality became increasingly important as simple machines were more often employed to make basic patterns like this table of John Hall's design. Heavier than the preceding styles, the furniture was still graceful enough to fit into the Classic Revival houses prevalent in America.

The delicate tracery and strength required by the Rococo Revival stimulated craftsmen in New York and elsewhere to perfect an early form of plywood for use in their quality furniture. John Henry Belter of New York led in this style and technique after receiving patents for his version of the process. It included several layers of wood and glue laminated under pressure and steamed to shape for the sinuous backs of chairs, love seats and sofas in the new forms he produced.

Despite improving technology, however, relatively few American products were able to meet foreign competition until the Civil War. Up to that time American prices were high, and we lacked skills in manufacturing and design to equal the Chinese porcelains, English cottons, European wallpaper and

Delicate woodwork made possible by the laminating process of John Henry Belter can be seen in this ornate upholstered Belter armchair.

Near Eastern carpets. There was also a feeling of status associated with owning fine foreign furnishings that has persisted to this day.

In the latter half of the 19th century designers continued to adapt various styles from the history of design. A Renaissance style emerged during the 1850s and survived for 30 years in various interpretations of 14th- and 15th-century Italian sculpture, architectural elements and decorative arts. From free interpretations some styles turned to actual imitations. English Queen Anne, Rococo and Adamesque designs reappeared in rapid succession in the 1880s and 1890s, while French Rococo and Empire gained popularity at the turn of the century. All have continued to hold their appeal.

With the Centennial of the Revolution, Americans also began turning to their own past for inspiration. As a result of the new enthusiasm for American history, both simple and sophisticated versions of 17th-century styles reappeared and have remained a popular source of designs for factory furniture to this day. Now they are generally known as Early American.

Traditional European styles that have persisted include those of the Germans in Pennsylvania, the Scandinavians in the Midwest and the Spanish in the Southwest. The simple lines, plain surfaces and elegant proportions of the handiwork produced by the English Shaker sect were eventually absorbed into the American mainstream.

The Arts and Crafts Movement

Not every one was interested in reviving styles from the past, however. A revolt against historical approaches to style and mechanized interpretations of handcraftmanship arose late in the 19th century and continued to World War I. Known as the Arts and Crafts movement, it was inspired by the Arts and Crafts Society in England. William Morris, the English poet, designer, craftsman and reformer, personified the new trend for Americans. Art and handicrafts, he believed, should be a part of daily life. Leaders in American society, intellectuals and professional as well as amateur craftsmen joined forces to establish this principle. Prominent among them was Elbert Hubbard, whose Roycroft Shop at East Aurora, New York, published artistically designed books and magazines propounding these beliefs.

Charles Eastlake's publication *Hints on Household Taste,* issued first in London and then in America in 1872, marked the beginning of this revolt against industrial trends and historical styles. Furniture of the Arts and Crafts movement was inspired by his appeal for handcraftmanship and use of oak in simple forms. Gustav Stickley also promoted designs from his own workshops and franchises and made the hinged-back chair, associated with William Morris, a symbol of reform.

At the root of the Arts and Crafts movement was an emphasis on fine, individual workmanship which fostered highly original interpretations of its three major sources: the arts of the Gothic period, those of Japan and motifs from nature such as flowers and trees. Several other characteristics are evident. Features of handicraft such as irregularities and toolmarks were integral parts of form and surface decoration. Textures and colors of materials in their natural or crafted state appeared in many combinations on a single object. Rectilinear forms predominated and patterns were linear, two-dimensional accents. Comfort, function and durability influenced the selection of materials for furniture.

In the first two decades of the 20th century, French interpretation of the

Arts and Crafts movement combined with influences from Germany and Japan to bring yet another important style to the American decorative arts. The new art, which featured elongated plant and flower forms combined with sinuous curves, got its name, "Art Nouveau," through association with S. Bing's Paris shop, L'Art Nouveau, where he sold furnishings and Japanese art. Displays in the Paris Exposition of 1900 gave Art Nouveau immediate popularity. In America it both gained a separate treatment and mingled with the later stages of the Arts and Crafts movement. Its limited appearance in American furniture was mainly as decorative elements in the Mission style. This sturdy furniture produced in midwestern factories before World War I also derived design elements from the Arts and Crafts movement and was noted for its simplicity of form.

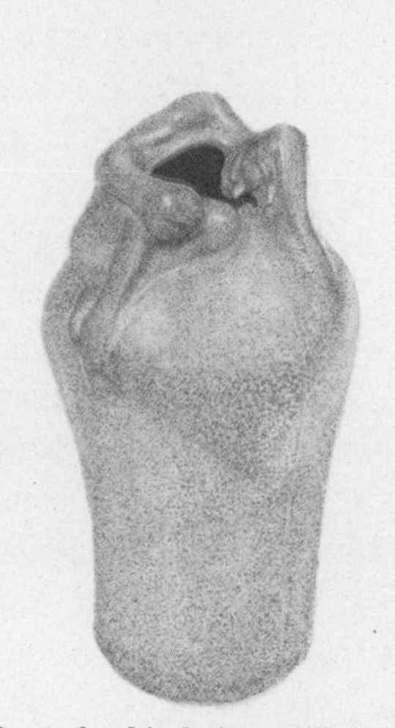

One-of-a-kind pieces, like this vase, produced by the Rookwood Pottery were noted for their rich colors and had a wide influence.

The Arts and Crafts movement also helped to keep many good individual potters from being absorbed into the ceramics industry. Maria Longworth Nichols produced fine examples of the new-art pottery in her Rookwood firm in Cincinnati. The Grueby works in Boston and the Van Briggle Pottery of Colorado Springs were two more of a number of firms that won international reputations for technical and aesthetic excellence.

Louis Comfort Tiffany's formation of the Tiffany Glass Company in 1883 was the beginning of experimentation and production influential in the new wave of art glass in the United States and abroad. He introduced Favrile glass among other new types and shapes influenced by designs from the Near East, nature and Art Nouveau.

Even before World War I the French Art Deco style was evolving in reaction to Art Nouveau, and in 1925 it gained international celebrity when it was featured in an exhibition. The new style's name was derived from a shortened version of the official title of the Paris show, *Exposition Internationale des Arts Decoratifs et Industriels Modernes.*

Art Deco adapted tradition to Cubism, one of the contemporary Parisian movements in painting and sculpture. Geometric shapes predominated, with surface designs in angular and circular forms. Many decorative motifs were inspired by the definite shapes and bold colors of Cubist painters. Indian art of the American Southwest also was sympathetic to the style and frequently appeared in American interpretations.

Carefully crafted exotic materials distinguished Art Deco in its early phase, and simulation of these materials remained characteristic in popularized versions of the late 1920s and the 1930s. Art Deco furniture favored exotic grained veneers on rounded and angled forms. After the panic of 1929, however, economy dictated simplification and flat, reflective surfaces became more common. Through the 1930s furniture continued to be more bulky and massive in form.

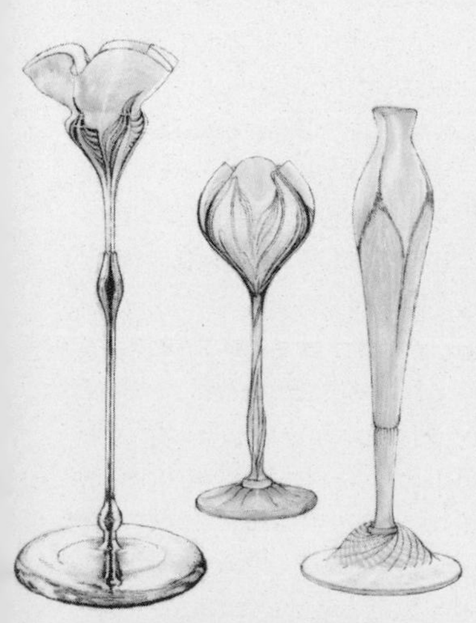

Louis Tiffany blended colors and shapes into the texture of Favrile glass. Shown above are examples of his flower-form and bottle-shaped vases.

In the meantime Americans had made significant contributions to glassmaking. After a number of short-lived attempts, the glass industry successfully developed on a production basis in the 1820s. At first craftsmen blew glass into hinged molds, a Roman technique that may have been revived or invented anew in the United States. It served for the production of inexpensive imitations of cut-glass tableware in a wide range of forms. In the late 1820s Deming Jarvis of Sandwich, Massachusetts, and other factory owners turned from this method to pressing glass in every current design.

By the mid-19th century further experiments in the chemistry of glass made a variety of types and colors available and encouraged fanciful shapes and decoration in blown and molded glass. Improvements in lathes for cutting led to the revival of cut glass late in the 19th century. The quality wares manufactured by Steuben Glass, founded in 1933 as a division of the Corning Glass Works, ranked American glassmakers high among international competitors. In recent years Harvey Littleton has led a movement encouraging a new school of artists in the United States and abroad to use glass as an expressive sculptural medium.

A New Direction

Household furnishing identified today as Modern Design developed from the experimental atmosphere of the early 20th century. Modern Design was more an approach than a style. Design was based on the intended use of an object—form followed function. Modular elements and interchangeable parts were used to lower costs.

Architects creating the International style in France, Holland and Germany during the 1920s fostered the new concepts. German disciples of the new ideas, centering in the Bauhaus that had moved to Dessau in 1925, influenced the international scene when the conservative Nazi regime forced their emigration. Many came to the United States, but World War II delayed full development of their principles here until the postwar period.

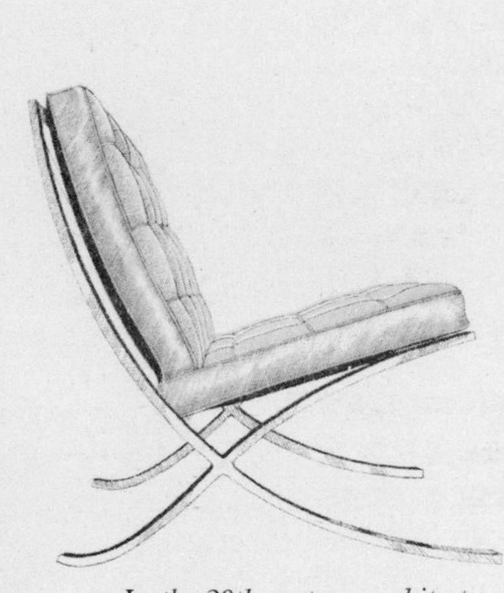

In the 20th century architects have taken a hand in designing furniture appropriate to their buildings. This is one of the most famous pieces of furniture created by the architect Mies van der Rohe. He designed the chair of chrome-plated steel bars and leather for the German Pavilion that he built for the 1929 Barcelona Exhibition.

Because of their views on the needs of society, these men were deeply concerned with the domestic scene and so encouraged industrial designers capable of applying the new principles. Austerity marked the first phase of Modern Design. Objects without decoration presented a series of planes influenced by Cubism. Spare lines and precise edges have continued with relaxed curves and abstract forms since the late 1930s.

Rapid technological progress during the war opened a reservoir of new materials and manufacturing processes for the principles of Modern Design. Charles Eames and Eero Saarinen were among the first Americans to use the new approach successfully. Their designs and those of their contemporaries strove to be practical while meeting aesthetic and commercial demands. Despite its variety, furniture expressing these themes generally has been austerely shaped in either geometric or abstract forms.

Few furniture craftsmen have survived the competition of contemporary mass production. George Nakashima is among them and has successfully continued the traditional processes of woodworking. Others concerned with individualized production have recently turned to anthropomorphic shapes. Their creations are expensive and have all but closed the age of personalized design and handcraftmanship in the production of furniture in America.

Reaction to the austerity of Modern Design, however, re-established the potter as a craftsman during the 1950s. Tableware and decorative objects again revealed the potter's skill and imagination. Revival of the craft opened a new avenue for sculptors, painters and other artists of the 1960s. A vase may serve its traditional purpose and also deserve consideration for surface design and sculptural form. Ceramics, then, is the most vital handicraft in America today.

Furnishings now available in America are more varied than those in any other country. Almost every style from the American, European and Oriental past is collected, reproduced or interpreted. Never before has the individual had such freedom to pursue the pleasures of personal taste.

The Treasures of America Where They Are, How to Find Them

Wherever people congregate to live, as soon as they find the necessary time and money, the human need for order and beauty will be expressed. Churches and monuments, the beautiful homes and museums where treasures are stored, are the dramatic manifestation of this need. These are found all across America, sometimes in the most unexpected places.

Every state is rich in treasure, and the most interesting and rewarding places are included in this book. In our initial nationwide survey, more than 8000 potential entries were indexed. To make a book of manageable size and to do justice to the places we included, this number was reduced to 5000. Among the 3000 that were considered and not included there are sure to be many that are locally thought to be superior to some that were included. Such disappointments are inevitable in a book as subjective as this must be. As editors we can only say that we have done our level best to make the book as interesting, varied and balanced as we were able.

Every entry is based on material submitted by the place itself. The entries were written and returned to the source for verification.

"Open daily" means open every day, including Sunday; "except holidays" does not necessarily mean every legal holiday, but does indicate that the treasure is closed more than two holidays.

When there is no information given on the days open, this means that the place is not open to the public or can be visited only by appointment. Most such places were eliminated except for a few with attractions so compelling as to be worth seeing for the beauty of the exterior alone, or to justify the extra effort to gain admission.

If there is no mention of a charge, there is none. The term "small charge" means one dollar or less; if the charge is more than that, the amount is given.

Every date, name and verifiable event has been double-checked by experienced *Reader's Digest* researchers. Even so, there are bound to be some inaccuracies. Times of opening and prices may have changed since publication, and some places may have closed. This happened while we were compiling the book, and adjustments were made right up until the time it went to press. We believe, however, that you now have in your hands the most thorough, colorful, interesting and informative book on the subject of America's treasures ever produced. We sincerely hope and trust that you will find this to be true.

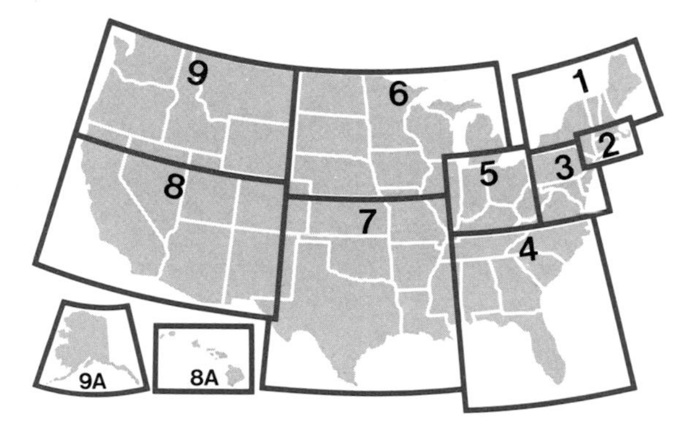

A Note About the Maps

The large map on the following two pages (reproduced in miniature above) shows how the book is divided into nine self-contained regions. All the treasures included are indicated on each regional map with a special dark brown color. Each major entry is identified with a symbol and a number that corresponds to its listing in the text. The symbols are explained in the key accompanying each map. Numbers for each treasure are arranged as logically as possible along roads and highways, progressing from north to south and west to east. The lower numbers, therefore, are always in the upper left area of the map and the higher numbers are in the lower right. Other entries, which are listed alphabetically by state in the back of the book, are indicated with a solid brown dot. Page references to these other treasures are given on the regional maps. All interstate highways are included on the maps to help in selecting the fastest and most convenient routes from region to region and treasure to treasure.

How the Regions Are Divided

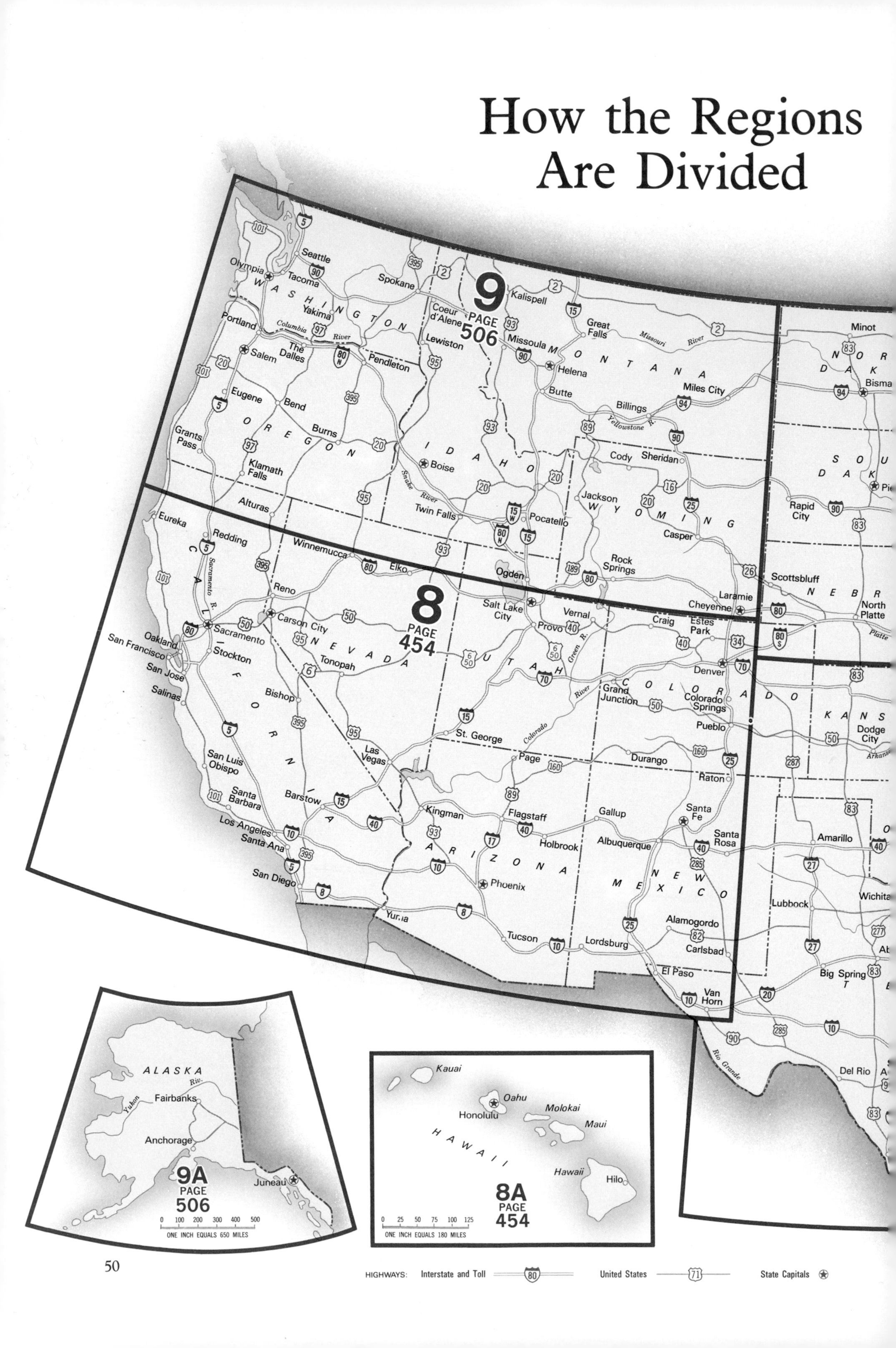

In each of the nine regions shown below there is an average of 500 treasures. At the beginning of the chapter for each region there is a large colored map on the pages indicated. These maps are essentially the same size but, as shown here, the size of the area covered by each is different because in some regions the treasures are closer together than in others.

Note that the State of Hawaii, shown separately here, is included with the Region 8 map, and the State of Alaska is included with the Region 9 map.

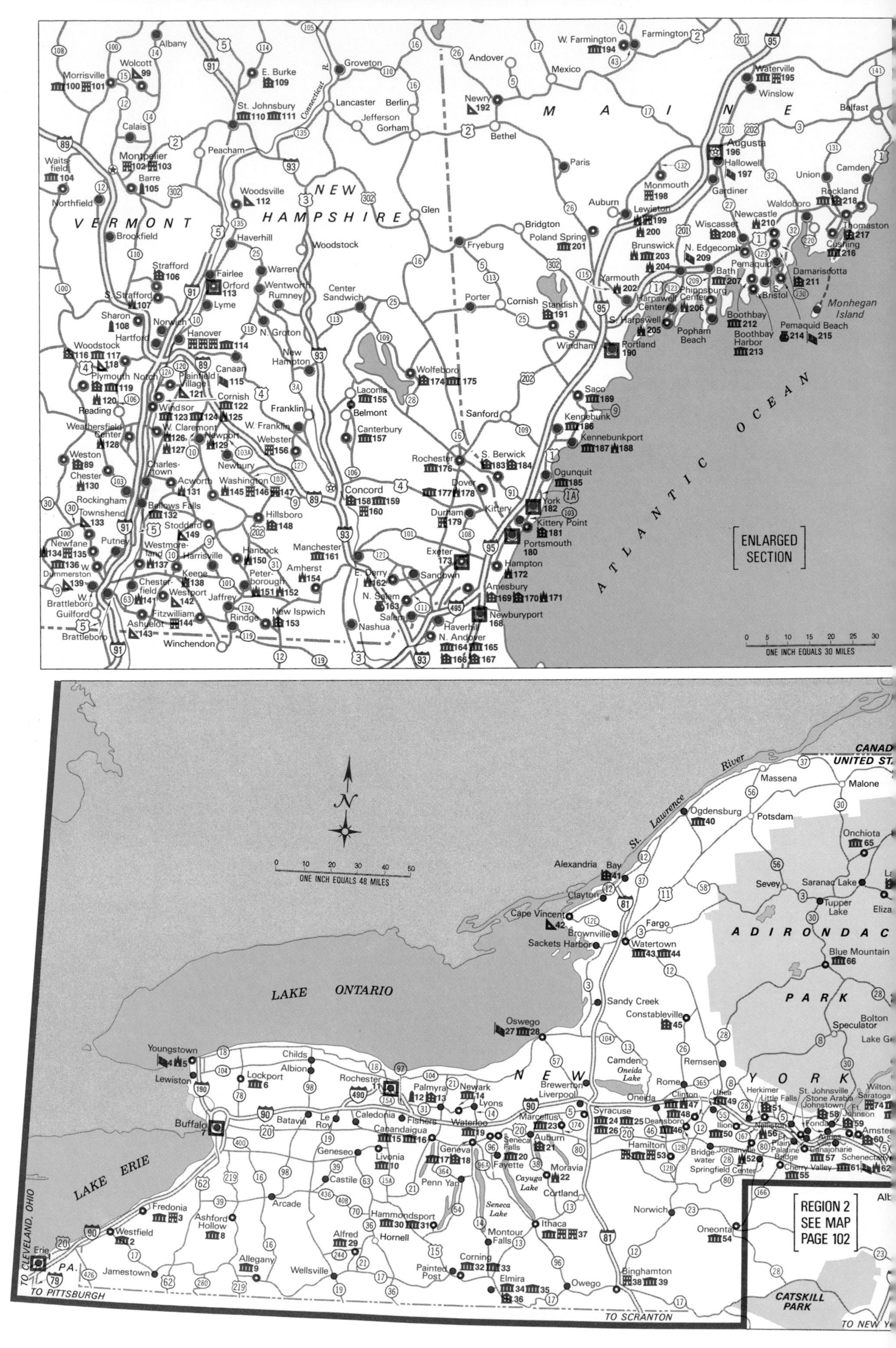
VERMONT
NEW HAMPSHIRE
MAINE
ATLANTIC OCEAN
ENLARGED SECTION
ONE INCH EQUALS 30 MILES
Albany
Wolcott 99
Morrisville 100 101
E. Burke 109
Groveton
Connecticut R.
Lancaster
Berlin
Jefferson
Gorham
Andover
Newry 192
Bethel
W. Farmington 194
Farmington
Mexico
Waterville 195
Winslow
Belfast
Augusta 196
Hallowell 197
Gardiner
Camden
Union
Rockland 218
Waldoboro
Thomaston 217
Cushing 216
St. Johnsbury 110 111
Calais
Montpelier 102 103
Barre 105
Waitsfield 104
Northfield
Peacham
Woodsville 112
Brookfield
Haverhill
Woodstock
Glen
Paris
Monmouth 198
Auburn
Lewiston 199 200
Bridgton
Poland Spring 201
Fryeburg
Wiscasset 208
Newcastle 210
Brunswick 203 204
N. Edgecomb 209
Pemaquid
Damariscotta 211
Bath 207
Yarmouth 202
Phippsburg
Harpswell Center
S. Bristol
Monhegan Island
Strafford 106
Fairlee
Orford 113
Lyme
Warren
Wentworth
Rumney
Center Sandwich
Porter
Cornish
Standish 191
S. Harpswell 205
Popham Beach
Boothbay 212
Boothbay Harbor 213
Pemaquid Beach 214 215
S. Strafford 107
Sharon 108
Norwich
Hartford
Hanover 114
N. Groton
New Hampton
Woodstock 116 117 118
Plymouth Notch
Plainfield Village 121
Canaan 115
Cornish 122
Wolfeboro 174 175
S. Windham
Portland 190
Reading 119 120
Windsor 123 124 125
Laconia 155
Belmont
Franklin
Sanford
Saco 189
Kennebunk 186
Kennebunkport 187 188
Weathersfield Center 128
W. Claremont 126 127
Newport 129
W. Franklin
Webster 156
Canterbury 157
Weston 89
Charlestown
Newbury
Rochester 176
S. Berwick 183 184
Ogunquit 185
Chester 130
Acworth 131
Washington 145 146 147
Concord 158 159 160
Dover 177 178
Rockingham
Bellows Falls 132
Townshend 133
Hillsboro 148
Durham 179
Kittery
York 182
Kittery Point 181
Portsmouth 180
Newfane 134 135 136
Putney
Stoddard 149
Westmoreland 137
Harrisville
Hancock 150
Manchester 161
Exeter 173
Hampton 172
W. Dummerston 139
Keene 138
Peterborough 151 152
Amherst 154
E. Derry 162
Sandown
Amesbury 169 170 171
W. Brattleboro
Chesterfield 141
Westport 142
Jaffrey
N. Salem 163
Salem
Newburyport 168
Guilford
Fitzwilliam 144
Rindge
New Ipswich 153
Nashua
Haverhill
N. Andover 164 165 166 167
Brattleboro
Ashuelot 143
Winchendon
CANADA
UNITED STATES
St. Lawrence River
Massena
Malone
Ogdensburg 40
Potsdam
Onchiota 65
ONE INCH EQUALS 48 MILES
Alexandria Bay 41
Clayton
Cape Vincent 42
Brownville
Sackets Harbor
Fargo
Watertown 43 44
Sevey
Saranac Lake
Tupper Lake
ADIRONDACK PARK
Blue Mountain 66
LAKE ONTARIO
Sandy Creek
Constableville 45
Oswego 27 28
Bolton
Speculator
Youngstown 4 5
Childs
Albion
Lockport 6
Lewiston
Rochester 11
Palmyra 12 13
Newark 14
Lyons
Camden
Oneida Lake
Brewerton
Liverpool
Remsen
Rome
NEW YORK
Herkimer
Little Falls 51
St. Johnsville
Stone Arabia
Johnstown 58
Johnson 59
Wilton
Saratoga 74
Buffalo 7
Batavia
Le Roy
Caledonia
Canandaigua 15 16
Fishers
Waterloo 19
Marcellus
Syracuse 24 25 26
Oneida
Clinton 47 48
Utica 49
Ilion 50
Deansboro 46
Auburn 21
Seneca Falls 20
Geneva 17 18
Fayette
Geneseo
Livonia 10
Hamilton 53
Bridgewater
Jordanville 56
Springfield Center 52
Palatine Bridge
Canajoharie 57
Cherry Valley 55
Fonda
Amsterdam 60
Schenectady 61 62
Castile
Penn Yan
Moravia 22
Cayuga Lake
Cortland
LAKE ERIE
Fredonia 3
Arcade
Ashford Hollow 8
Hammondsport 30 31
Seneca Lake
Ithaca 37
Norwich
Oneonta 54
REGION 2 SEE MAP PAGE 102
Westfield 2
Alfred 29
Hornell
Montour Falls
Erie 1
Jamestown
Allegany 9
Wellsville
Painted Post
Corning 32 33
Elmira 34 35 36
Owego
Binghamton 38 39
CATSKILL PARK
TO CLEVELAND, OHIO
TO PITTSBURGH
PA.
TO SCRANTON
TO NEW Y

Considering the overall impact of three centuries of civilization on the American landscape, this northeastern corner is little changed. A Colonial farmer returning today would find such familiar landmarks as wooden churches and barns, stone fences, covered bridges and saltbox houses.

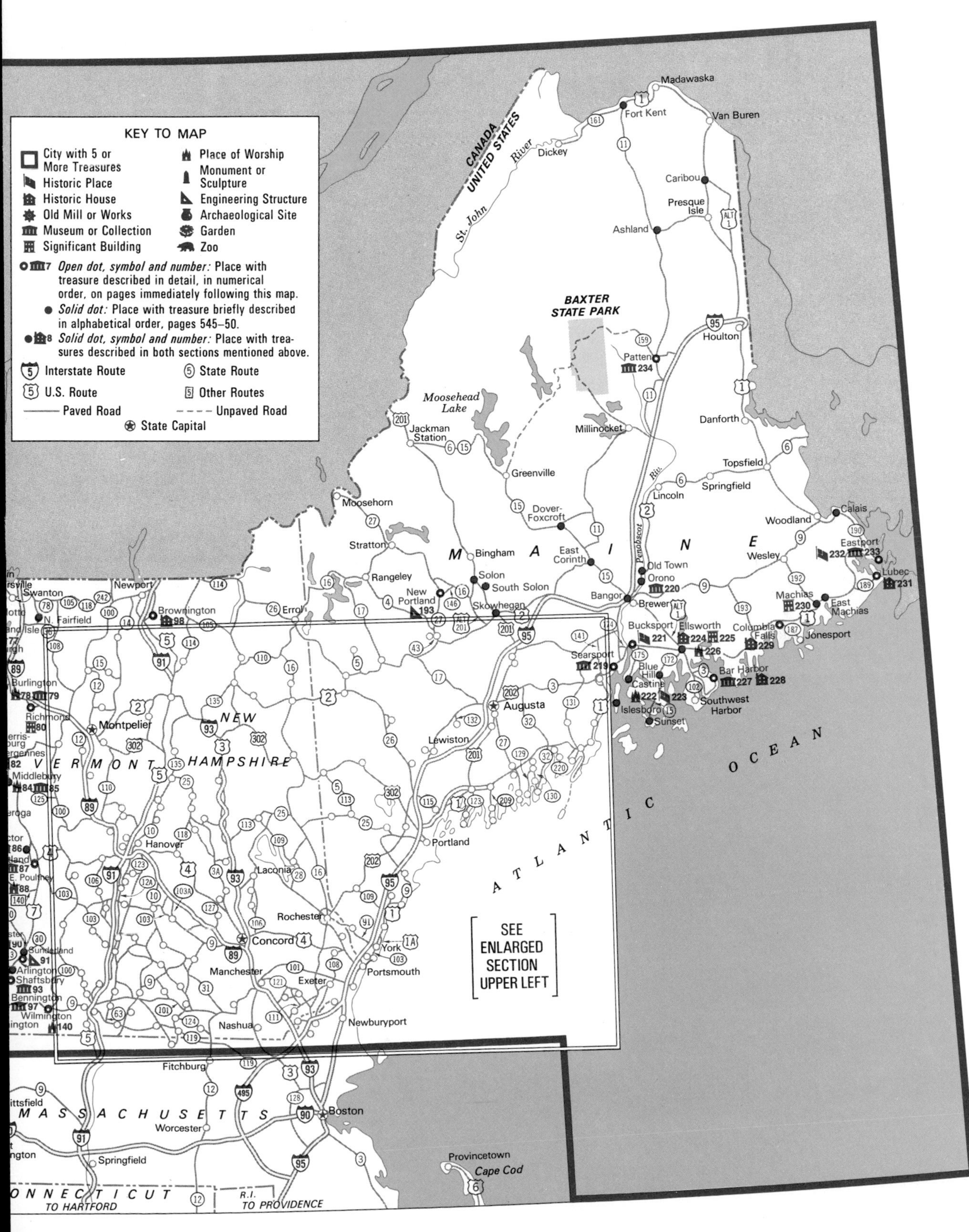

1. Erie, Pa.

Named for the Eriez Indian nation and first settled by Americans in 1794–95, Erie's early commercial and industrial development was largely due to its favored location on Lake Erie.

Brig "Niagara" *Lower State St.* In September of 1813, the nation's future looked bleak when a British fleet sank Commodore Oliver Hazard Perry's flagship on Lake Erie. Undaunted, Perry boarded the brig *Niagara,* defeated his stronger foe and sent the famous message: "We have met the enemy and they are ours." The ship was built in Erie under difficult conditions involving a shortage of materials and labor, and was later allowed to decay and sink. The remains were raised and reconstruction begun in 1913, and today this square-rigged, two-masted ship carries a 100-foot mainmast and a number of reconstructed cannons. Quarters for the captain and crew, storerooms, a sail bin and other space below decks can be seen. *Open daily.*

Erie Public Library *3 S. Perry Sq.* In addition to the standard services, the library has considerable genealogical material and an art gallery as well as circulating collections of art reproductions, including sculpture. *Open Mon.-Sat.*

Erie Public Museum *356 W. Sixth St.* This brownstone home of an Erie industrialist was completed in 1895; since 1944 it has served its current purpose. The original library with hand-carved woodwork is still intact, and 14 rooms are used for permanent exhibits connected with natural science, local history and the arts. Temporary exhibits and a wide range of programs are also offered. *Open Tues.-Sun. except holidays.*

[1. *Brig Niagara*] *Behind the open "windows" on the sides of this warship which won the Battle of Lake Erie under Commodore Perry in the War of 1812 are 32-pound guns used for close-in naval battles.*

Old Custom House *407 State St.* Following the failure of two banks, this 1839 Doric-style building was sold in 1849 for use as a post office and custom house. It was the first building in the country to use native marble and has six fluted columns in front of the portico. Owned by the State of Pennsylvania and headquarters of the Erie County Historical Society, it now has a museum devoted to the history of northwestern Pennsylvania. *Open Tues.-Sat. May-Nov.*

Perry Memorial House and Dickson Tavern *Second and French Sts.* The famous naval hero is believed to have been a guest at this 1809 tavern during the completion of the U.S. fleet he successfully led against the British. Originally known as Dickson Tavern, it is a typical saltbox design with several secret passageways used to assist slaves escaping on the "Underground Railroad" before the Civil War. The building was acquired by the City of Erie in 1924. A number of interesting rooms, including the commodore's, have furnishings from several periods and items of local historic significance.

Perry Monument *Presque Isle Peninsula* This 101-foot limestone-sheathed shaft was erected in 1926 to mark Perry's decisive victory over the British on Sept. 10, 1813. It stands on the peninsula's Crystal Point. *Open daily.*

St. Peter's Cathedral *Tenth and Sassafras Sts.* Begun in 1873 and completed 20 years later, this French Gothic structure of red sandstone trimmed with white cut stone is the cathedral church for the Roman Catholic Diocese of Erie. Among the most beautiful features of its interior, which was redecorated in 1951, are the hand-painted Stations of the Cross in wood frames, the many stained-glass windows and the three white marble altars. The organ, built in 1893 for the World's Columbian Exposition in Chicago, was installed in 1916. Each day the clock-tower chimes play a special copyrighted selection believed by some to have inspired Gershwin's *Rhapsody in Blue. Open daily.*

2. Chautauqua County Historical Society History Center and Museum *Village Park, Westfield, N.Y.* James McClurg, a Scotch-Irish trader and merchant, completed this house in 1820. It was built in the midst of the wilderness by bricklayers from Pittsburgh in the style of an Irish manor house. It was so ornate for that time and place that settlers in the area christened it McClurg's Folly. In 1950 the Chautauqua County Historical Society acquired the building to display their collection of regional items, including Indian tools and weapons, period furniture, kitchen equipment, old farm implements and a library devoted to county history. *Open Tues.-Sat. mid-Apr.-June, Tues.-Sun. July-Aug., Tues.-Sat. Sept.-Oct. Small charge.*

3. Academic Center *State University College, Fredonia, N.Y.* Designed by the well-known architectural firm of I. M. Pei and Partners, this striking group of buildings includes, in addition to the two described below, Houghton Hall (a science center), Maytum Hall (offices and a computer), and McEwen Hall (classrooms

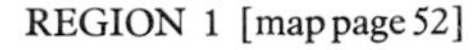

[**4.** *French Castle*] *The plain facade is deceptive of the structure's real purpose, and it was meant to be. The so-called castle at Old Fort Niagara was built in 1726 as an outpost and trading center by the French who then laid claim to territory from Quebec to Louisiana, and it is camouflaged in order to deceive the local Iroquois tribes. They wanted only a "house of peace" built in their midst. The main floor where the Iroquois traded their beaver pelts looks innocent enough, though there are musket loopholes in the heavy oak shutters. The third floor was outfitted as a gun deck, the dormer windows serving as platforms for six-pound cannon. To the left is the original bake house.*

and lecture halls). The center was dedicated in 1969.

MICHAEL C. ROCKEFELLER ARTS CENTER This multilevel building contains two theaters, a 1200-seat concert hall and an art gallery as well as classrooms and studios. *Open daily, gallery open Mon.-Sat.*

REED LIBRARY The size of a football field, this building houses more than 175,000 books and thousands of research items. It is a center for governmental studies and also contains local historical documents and artifacts. *Open daily.*

4. Old Fort Niagara *Rte. 18, N. of Youngstown, N.Y.* Originally constructed of wood in 1679, this French fort was rebuilt of stone and renamed Fort Niagara in 1726. It was twice captured by the British. Visitors can now see a moat, drawbridge, blockhouse, parade ground and ramparts. Restoration was completed in 1934. A Flag Day ceremony takes place annually in early June. *Open daily. Small charge includes French Castle.*

FRENCH CASTLE This three-story stone building was the 1726 fortification which served as an Indian trading center and barracks. The Jesuit chapel, prison and top-floor gun deck are of particular interest. In the restored building are Louis XIV furnishings.

5. Our Lady of Fatima Shrine *Swann Rd., Youngstown, N.Y.* Located on 15 acres, the chapels, outdoor statuary and plantings that comprise this shrine together form the shape of a cathedral. Dominating the setting is the main chapel, with a unique transparent dome bearing an outline of the Northern Hemisphere. On top of the dome is a 13-foot granite statue of Our Lady of Fatima, accessible by two exterior stairways. Two smaller chapels are attached to the main structure. Wide paved walks lead to the large heart-shaped Rosary pool and the Avenue of Saints, which has more than 100 life-sized statues carved from Italian marble. The shrine is directed by Barnabite Fathers, a Catholic teaching order founded in Italy in the 16th century. Each summer youth groups organized by the shrine stage pageants of the Fatima story. *Open daily.*

6. Niagara County Historical Center *215 Niagara St., Lockport, N.Y.* This complex of buildings includes the 1860 Dr. Samuel Outwater House, which serves as headquarters for the Niagara County Historical Society. The house has an ornate Victorian parlor and an American Empire dining room. It contains an early medical collection and examples of old toys, glassware and china. The adjoining brick structure served in 1835 as the law office of Washington Hunt, governor of New York (1851-53). The Pioneer Building shows artifacts from prehistoric Indian tribes, a diorama of an Iroquois village and a collection of military relics from several U.S. wars. In the Red Barn are carriages and various 19th-century farm implements. The Niagara Fire Company Building contains some of Lockport's earliest fire-fighting equipment. The grounds include a delightful herb garden. *Open Tues.-Sun.*

7. Buffalo, N.Y.

The second largest city in the state, Buffalo is the largest flour- and feed-milling center in the world and one of the most active of the Great Lakes ports. Millard Fillmore and Grover Cleveland were citizens of Buffalo. President William McKinley was assassinated here in 1901 while attending the Pan-American Exposition.

Albright-Knox Art Gallery *1285 Elmwood Ave.* An outstanding painting and sculpture collection is shown to great advantage in two fine buildings of interesting architectural contrast. The original Albright Gallery, built in 1905 in Greek Revival style, is connected by a sculpture court to the modern dark-glass auditorium and gallery, designed in 1962 by award-winning architect Gordon Bunshaft. The sculpture collection, of great variety and depth, ranges from 3000 B.C. to the present, with works by Daumier, Degas, Rodin, Brancusi, Matisse and Picasso. Almost every

International Museum of Photography
900 East Ave., Rochester, N.Y.

This collection devoted to the art and science of photography has grown, mainly through private donations, into one of the most comprehensive in the world. The museum itself is in the former home of George Eastman, father of modern photography. In 1888 Eastman introduced an inexpensive, easy to use camera ("You press the button, we do the rest") that used roll film rather than plates. Anyone could take snapshots with a Kodak, and amateur photographers around the world have been doing so ever since. The front of the museum is furnished, much as it was when Eastman lived there (1905–1932), with antiques, books and paintings from his collection of old masters. Galleries in the rest of the house are filled with photographs and apparatus from the early daguerreotype era (1840s) to the present as well as a number of well-mounted exhibits on the technology of photography. *Open Tues.–Sun. except Jan. 1 and Dec. 25. Small charge except Wed.*

People in this 1855 daguerreotype of Niagara Falls are posed for comfort (very long exposures were required) and painterly composition. Only gradually did photographers realize the potential of the camera to create a new art form and to explore details the naked eye does not always perceive.

All these objects are 19th-century still cameras in the museum collection. A casual glance might lead one to suspect that they include a telescope, a revolver and weird binoculars, among other things.

contemporary sculptor of note is represented, including Moore, Giacometti, Epstein, Smith and Caro. The painting collection boasts major works by most of the important 19th-century French artists, such as van Gogh (*The Old Mill*), Gauguin (*The Yellow Christ*), Corot, Pissaro and Toulouse-Lautrec. Contemporary paintings include European and American works. Represented among the latter are Pollack, Kline, Motherwell, Still, Johns, Warhol, Stella and Noland. A major donor, Seymour H. Knox, has given over 500 works of art to this magnificent collection. *Open Tues.–Sun.*

Buffalo and Erie County Historical Society Museum *25 Nottingham Ct.* Constructed of white Vermont marble, this imposing Doric structure is the only remaining building from the 1901 Pan-American Exposition. The museum includes a reconstruction of an 1870 street with a drugstore, jewelry shop, music store, bank, newspaper office and dry-goods stores. Also of interest are a handsome apostolic clock built by Myles Hughes, tableware from 1600 to today, pioneer crafts and a reconstructed pilothouse. The library contains most of the papers of the 13th President of the U.S., Millard Fillmore, who was the first president of the Buffalo Historical Society and a founder of the University of Buffalo and the Museum of Natural Sciences. *Open daily.*

Buffalo Museum of Science *Humboldt Pk.* Many of the major arts and sciences are represented on three floors in changing exhibits. Of particular note are masterpieces of ancient Chinese ceramics, examples of African art, Marchand flower models, an Allosaurus dinosaur skeleton, Egyptian mummies and artifacts and a hall of local bird and animal specimens. There is also a special children's room where exhibits can be touched and used. *Open daily.*

Our Lady of Victory Basilica *Rtes. 62 and 18 at Lackawanna* In 1926 this ornate Renaissance shrine opened its great doors to an interior of beautifully carved marble, statuary, paintings and ceilings decorated in rich designs. A nine-foot statue of Our Lady of Victory carved from a single block of Carrara marble graces the main altar. *Open daily.*

Theodore Roosevelt Inaugural National Historic Site *641 Delaware Ave.* Known as the Ansley Wilcox House, this painted brick Greek Revival home has been reconstructed as it was in 1901 when Theodore Roosevelt took his oath of office here as 26th President of the U.S. The library where the oath was administered has been restored with furnishings and fixtures of the period. *Open daily. Small charge.*

8. Griffis Sculpture Park *Ahrens Rd. (off Rte. 219), Ashford Hollow, N.Y.* Sponsored by the Ashford Hollow Foundation of Buffalo, this park occupies a 400-acre tract of woods and meadowland at an elevation of 2000 feet. More than 70 naturalistic and abstract works by the sculptor Larry W. Griffis are on display. Constructed of bronze, steel or aluminum, many are of heroic size, 25 feet or more in height and weighing as much as two tons. Here at the park, among nature trails and picnic

sites, music festivals, poetry readings and ballet performances are held on an outdoor stage. *Open daily. Adults small charge. Parking fee.*

9. St. Bonaventure University Library *Rte. 17, Allegany, N.Y.* Donated by Colonel Michael Friedsam, a New York businessman, this brick building completed in 1938 houses a large and important collection of rare volumes and manuscripts, plus art works by Rembrandt, Rubens, Giovanni Bellini and Velázquez. A number of canvases by 19th-century and contemporary artists are also displayed. Among the most valuable books is the oldest manuscript Bible in the U.S. Completed on vellum in the early 1200s, it comprises 90,000 lines written and illuminated by hand. The collection also holds a Latin Vulgate Bible produced by Franciscan friars in England in 1368. *Open daily.*

10. Livonia, Avon and Lakeville Railroad Depot and Steam Engine *Livonia, N.Y.* This depot, built in 1860, holds maps, paintings and photographs of interest to railroad buffs. The 1927 Baldwin steam locomotive hauls passenger coaches dating from the 1920s along the 23-mile scenic route. Once destined for the scrap heap, this portion of the old Erie Railroad was saved by steam-engine enthusiasts from all over the country, and it is still kept in service for transporting freight. *Open Sat.-Sun. end of May-June, Tues.-Sun. early July-Aug., Sat.-Sun. early Sept.-early Nov. Trips: adults $2.25, children over 3 $1.25.*

11. Rochester, N.Y.

This industrial city, home of Eastman Kodak and the Xerox Corporation, also has the University of Rochester and the Eastman School of Music. Its lovely parks and gardens have given it the name of Flower City.

Campbell-Whittlesey House *123 S. Fitzhugh St.* This imposing Greek Revival brick house was completed in 1836 for Benjamin Campbell, a miller and merchant. It was purchased in 1852 by Frederick Whittlesey, vice-chancellor of the New York State Court of Chancery, and remained in his family for 85 years. Exterior features include four Ionic portico pillars and an overhanging cornice embellished by a Roman bracket. Inside are a handsome marble dining-room fireplace and Grecian doorway carvings where paints blended from old formulas are used on the trim. There is also a rare collection of stenciled Empire furniture. *Open Tues.-Sun. Jan.-Nov. Small charge.*

Hervey Ely House *11 Livingston Park.* This dignified two-wing Greek Revival mansion was built in 1837 for a wealthy miller by architect Hugh Hastings. Among its attractions are marble fireplaces, front and back parlors opening onto a central room with a patterned ceiling, a winding staircase and furniture from the 1830s. A sideboard once used by Washington can be seen here. The house is owned and operated by a chapter of the Daughters of the American Revolution. *Open Wed. Small charge.*

International Museum of Photography *900 East Ave.* See feature display above.

[**11.** *Memorial Art Gallery*] *Once the figures in this 12th-century limestone capital looked down on the faithful in a French church. Peter and two others watch as Christ shows his wound to doubting Thomas (minus head).*

Memorial Art Gallery of the University of Rochester *490 University Ave.* Works from all the main periods and cultures of world art can be seen in this 1914 Italian Renaissance-style building and its adjoining wing, which was opened in 1968. It is one of the best-balanced art collections in the country and is especially rich in medieval art. A small but impressive collection of pottery, stone sculpture and metalwork includes pieces from Middle and South America and the Near and Far East. On display are canvases by Tintoretto, Rubens, Hals, Rembrandt, El Greco (*Vision of St. Hyacinth*), Degas, Cézanne and Monet (*Waterloo Bridge*). American artists represented include Copley, Cassatt, Homer and Sloan. The gallery's programs include changing exhibitions, lectures, films and concerts from October through May, and sponsorship of the annual Clothesline Art Show and Sale. A library holds 10,000 art books and periodicals. Art classes and an art-lending service are also provided. *Open Tues.-Sun. Small charge except Tues. and Sat. eves.*

Rochester Museum and Science Center *657 East Ave.* Natural science, archaeology and cultural history are featured here as are reminders of Indian, pioneer and 19th-century life of the area. The material on the North American Indian from earliest times is especially valuable. Dioramas, scale models and reconstructions of rooms, shops, places of business and the like are used to dramatize the collection. The Strasenburgh Planetarium adjoins the museum, as does a garden of fragrance featuring Colonial herbs and roses. *Open daily.*

Susan B. Anthony House *17 Madison St.* From 1866 to 1906, this modest brick house was the home of the famous leader of the Women's Suffrage movement and a center of suffragette activity. Containing much original furniture, it also displays material related to the ratification in 1920 of the 19th Amendment to the Constitution. *Open Thurs.-Sun. Small charge.*

Woodside *485 East Ave.* This three-story brick home of an early Rochester merchant, now the headquarters of the Rochester Historical Society, represents a blending of the Federal and Greek Revival styles. Completed in 1840, it is noted for its spiral staircase that rises to the "peppermill" cupola, and an 1890s smoking room paneled in wood and leather. Displayed here are mid-19th-century Upstate New York paintings and a collection of guns, costumes and objects of local significance. *Open Mon.-Fri.*

12. Angel Moroni Monument *Hill Cumorah, Rte. 21, S. of Palmyra, N.Y.* According to Mormon lore, gold plates were buried in this hill in the fifth century by a prophet named Moroni. They were retrieved 1400 years later in 1827 by Joseph Smith, who founded the Mormon faith. Inscribed with the history of an ancient people, they were translated into the Book of Mormon and became scripture. In 1928 the Church of Jesus Christ of Latter-Day Saints erected a monument honoring this event. In the Visitor Center are displays relating this story. A religious pageant is presented the last week of July. *Visitor Center open daily.*

13. Joseph Smith Home *Stafford Rd., Palmyra, N.Y.* The founder of the Mormon faith spent several boyhood years in this frame house which he helped his father and brothers complete about 1825. It was here, the Mormons say, that he brought the gold plates received from the Angel Moroni. The rooms contain period furnishings and interesting original floorboards. Located on the property is the Sacred Grove where Smith had his first vision as a boy of 14. *Open daily.*

14. Hoffman Clock Museum *Newark Public Library, Newark, N.Y.* Almost 100 American and foreign clocks displayed here trace the fascinating history of timepieces from the first examples made by hand to the introduction of the inexpensive factory-made article. *Open Mon.-Sat. Sept.-June, Mon.-Fri. July-Aug.*

15. Granger Homestead *295 N. Main St., Canandaigua, N.Y.* Gideon Granger, a Cabinet member in the administrations of Jefferson and Madison, built this handsome Federal house in 1814. It is filled with period furniture and contains much fine woodwork. A carriage museum occupies three barns near the house; it includes an early hearse, a three-seater break and an ointment wagon used for delivering patent cures. A small law office is also on the grounds. *House open Tues.-Sun.; museum open daily late June-early Sept. Small charge for each, $1.50 both.*

16. Ontario County Historical Society Museum *55 N. Main St., Canandaigua, N.Y.* On display in this 1914 Greek Revival building are original maps and deeds of the Phelps and Gorham Purchase of most of western New York from the state of Massachusetts (1778). The Indians' copy of the 1794 Pickering Treaty granting settlement of western New York can be seen here. A full set of presidential autographs can be viewed along with a collection of rare Indian signatures and relics. The first piano brought to the county (1825), an early-19th-century dulcimer and a rosewood melodion are among the various interesting musical instruments included in the furnishings of the museum. *Open Tues.-Sat. except holidays.*

17. Prouty-Chew House *543 S. Main St., Geneva, N.Y.* Charles Butler, a Geneva attorney, built this handsome Federal brick house in 1825. His inlaid Dutch cupboard forms the nucleus of the furniture collection displayed here. Restored in 1960, the building is operated as a museum, art gallery and research library by the Geneva Historical Society. The Victorian parlor, the costume room and the antique-toys room are popular attractions. Art exhibits and displays of local historic significance are regularly scheduled. *Open Tues.-Sat.*

18. Rose Hill Mansion *Rte. 96A, E. of Geneva, N.Y.* This Greek Revival house achieves a balanced design with its large central portico supported by six fluted Ionic columns, and smaller columns in front of matched wings on either side. Built in 1839 and restored in 1968, its spiral staircase, wallpaper and fabrics typify the lavish Empire style. The 16 rooms open to the public contain much of the original period furniture. Concerts, antiques shows and art exhibits are frequently held on the grounds. A candlelight tour of the mansion, featuring period music, is offered on the first Sunday in May. *Open daily May-Oct. Small charge.*

19. Waterloo Memorial Day Museum *35 E. Main St., Waterloo, N.Y.* In 1966 the U.S. Congress officially recognized Waterloo as the site of the first Memorial Day, held in 1866. This commemorative museum is a 16-room, partially restored brick structure built between 1836 and 1870. It houses a collection of mementos from the first Memorial Day and its founders and the centennial celebration, as well as Civil War material. *Open Tues.-Fri. mid-May-mid-Sept.*

[14] *Clocks have long been valued as decorative objects. Here, left to right, top to bottom: A Dutch hood clock (1730-50), German wall clock (1800), French domestic clock (1700-50), American mantel clock (1868-70).*

20. Seneca Falls Historical Society Museum *55 Cayuga St., Seneca Falls, N.Y.* Local historical material is housed in this three-story building, also known as the Becker House, which has been a museum since 1961. Dating from 1823 but substantially enlarged in the 1850s and 1870s, its 22 rooms hold interesting displays of textile-industry machinery, period clothing, toys, objects associated with the Women's Rights movement and relics from several U.S. wars. A library specializes in the early history of the state and Seneca County. *Open Mon., Tues., Thurs., Fri. Apr.-Dec.*

21. Historic Seward House *33 South St., Auburn, N.Y.* Some great moments in American history are recalled in this home of William H. Seward, who was Lincoln's Secretary of State, governor of New York and one of the early influential leaders of the Republican Party. Fourteen rooms containing the original Seward furnishings, books, paintings and memorabilia are open to the public. Of particular interest are a Mongolian armored jacket from Alaska, handwritten Lincoln letters, a catalogued library of 7500 books, and paintings by well-known artists of the period, including the famous *Signing the Alaska Treaty* by Emanuel Leutze. A 15-year-old apprentice carpenter named Brigham Young helped carve the fireplace. *Open Mon.-Sat. Mar.-Dec. Small charge.*

22. St. Matthew's Church *16 Church St., Moravia, N.Y.* Built in 1823, this Episcopal church is notable for the outstanding Oberammergau carvings throughout its interior done by Hans Mayer in 1914-18. Also of interest are two plaques, one commemorating the wedding of Millard Fillmore, which was held here Feb. 5, 1826, and one bearing the signature of Abraham Lincoln. *Open daily.*

23. Martisco Railroad Station Museum *Martisco Rd., Marcellus, N.Y.* Constructed in 1870, this brick building stands on the earliest (1838) section of the old New York Central System. In 1966 it was purchased by a chapter of the National Railway Historical Society. Currently undergoing restoration, it houses a library, an early telegraph key and other items of railroadiana. *Open Sun. May-Oct.*

24. Canal Museum *Weighlock Bldg., Erie Blvd. E., Syracuse, N.Y.* The 1850 Greek Revival building housing this collection is the last surviving structure related to the operation of the state's 19th-century canal system. Boats were weighed and their cargo tolls determined here. Exhibits explain the story of the Erie Canal and its influence on those living along it; many prints, photographs, paintings and models are also displayed. A library is available for research, and guided tours along the old towpath are regularly scheduled. *Open Tues.-Sun. except holidays.*

25. Everson Museum of Art *401 Harrison St., Syracuse, N.Y.* Opened in 1968, this three-story modern stone building provides an attractive setting for an excellent collection of American art, ranging from two anonymous 1742 portraits to contemporary works. Included are paintings by Eastman Johnson, Robert Henri and Grandma Moses. There are also outstanding collections of early Chinese art and contemporary ceramics as well as a sculpture court and an auditorium. *Open Tues.-Sun.*

26. Lowe Art Center of Syracuse University *309 University Pl., Syracuse, N.Y.* The paintings, sculptures, drawings and prints in the university collection are here in the Lowe Art Center. Although the emphasis falls on 20th-century painters and sculptors including Dufy, Epstein, Bourdelle and Meštrović, such earlier artists as Dürer, Cranach, Dosso Dossi and Reynolds are also represented. There is a fine display of Chinese bronzes. *Open Mon.-Fri.*

27. Fort Ontario *Foot of E. Seventh St., Oswego, N.Y.* This outpost was built in 1755 as part of a chain of fortifications guarding England's vital trade and military route from the mouth of the Oswego River to the Hudson Valley. The scene of several engagements during the French and Indian Wars, the Revolution and the War of 1812, the fort has flown the flags of England, France and the U.S. Fear of a British invasion from Canada during the Civil War led to a strengthening of the garrison, which continued to serve as a U.S. Army post until after World War II. Restored to resemble an 1860s military base, Fort Ontario is staffed from July through Labor Day by guards dressed in period uniforms. Demonstrations of sentry posting, marching and artillery drill are given. Reconstructed quarters and a military museum are open to visitors. *Open daily Apr.-Oct.*

28. Richardson-Bates House *135 E. Third St., Oswego, N.Y.* This elaborate Victorian structure, built in 1850, was presented in 1946 to the Oswego County Historical Society by members of the Bates family. It contains decorative hand-carved interior woodwork, original furniture, china, paintings and books. The second floor is largely a local-history museum, displaying items that link Oswego with the Civil War and World Wars I and II. Portraits of Civil War officers and 19th-century mayors are on view, along with old toys and costumes, a rare Louis XV commemorative medal for the French victory at Oswego in 1756 and a display of old silver. *Open Sun., Wed., Sat. May-June., Tues.-Sun. July-early Sept.*

29. Binns-Merrill Hall, State University College of Ceramics *Alfred University Campus, Alfred, N.Y.* Several important collections of glass and porcelain are displayed here. The Alexander Silverman glass collection includes some older pieces but concentrates on glass made in the past 100 years. It contains examples from many countries as well as specimens of Professor Silverman's own work, which includes alabaster glass—a lost art until his rediscovery of the technique. The Wesp Collection of porcelain has some 400 examples of European dinnerware and various decorative pieces. The firms of Rosenthal, Thun and Tettau are among those represented. Many of the designs were created by George Wesp, to whose memory the collection is dedicated. *Open daily.*

30. Glenn H. Curtiss Museum of Local History *Lake and Main Sts., Hammondsport, N.Y.* Many of the achievements of one of the nation's best-remembered aviation pioneers are displayed here. It contains several Curtiss aircraft and engines built from 1904 to 1927, including a famous Jenny trainer from World War I and many photographs tracing the history of aviation at Hammondsport. *Open daily mid-May-Oct. Small charge.*

31. Greyton H. Taylor Wine Museum *Bully Hill Rd., Hammondsport, N.Y.* Opened in 1967 in a building that housed the original Taylor Wine Co., this is the first museum of its kind in the U.S. It displays early wine-making equipment, interesting old labels, and bottles and glasses used in the White House by several Presidents. The library has the nation's largest collection of books on wine making. Vineyards planted in 1887 surround the museum. *Open daily May-Oct. Small charge.*

32. Corning Glass Center *Centerway, Corning, N.Y.* This impressive structure was built in 1951 to house three main areas devoted to various aspects of glass-

[32] *In the Steuben glass factory at the Corning Glass Center, visitors may watch as craftsmen create pieces of blown and cut glass. An elaborate work can take a team of 10 or so several months to produce. Here an engraver uses a copper wheel to grind the intaglio design into "Hawaii," part of a limited edition. "The Butterfly" is a crystal prism. Only one wing is engraved; the prismatic effect produces the illusion of a second wing.*

making. The Corning Museum of Glass traces the history of glass with exhibits arranged chronologically from Egyptian containers of about 1500 B.C. to art glass of today. Special displays are also scheduled. Exhibits in the Hall of Science and Industry show modern manufacturing techniques and uses of glass, and include push-button displays demonstrating how it is used. From a large gallery in the Steuben factory, visitors can watch Steuben crystal being shaped and finished by skilled craftsmen. *Open daily June-Oct., Tues.-Sun. Nov.-May. Summer parking fee.*

33. Rockwell Gallery *Rockwell's Department Store, W. Market St., Corning, N.Y.* In this department store gallery paintings, drawings and pastels by Remington, Russell, Sharp, Bierstadt and other artists convey the spirit of the Old West. Several Remington bronzes are exhibited along with some Winchester rifles, Colt pistols and Navajo Indian rugs. An extensive glass collection traces the career of Frederick Carder, a gifted Steuben glass designer. *Open Mon.-Sat.*

34. Arnot Art Museum *235 Lake St., Elmira, N.Y.* The 19th-century industrialist Matthias Arnot collected more than 70 European paintings, including *Ulysses Discovering Himself to Nausicaa* by Claude Lorrain, *Flemish Fair* by Jan Brueghel and other works ranging from the Old Masters to contemporary French academicians. These and some 200 later acquisitions, mostly American, make up the permanent collection. The museum is in the Arnot home, built in the 1830s in Greek Revival style. *Open Tues.-Sun.*

35. Chemung County Historical Center Museum *304 William St., Elmira, N.Y.* An Indian civilization of 5000 years ago is represented here by findings from Lamoka Lake. The museum also contains many other Indian artifacts, plus early household items displayed in 10 Colonial rooms, relics of the Revolutionary and Civil Wars, an apothecary shop and a Mark Twain collection. *Open Tues., Wed., Fri., Sun.*

36. Mark Twain Study *Elmira College, Elmira, N.Y.* Mark Twain wrote most of *Tom Sawyer* and parts of other books in this charming octagonal study built for him by his sister-in-law in 1874 and designed as a replica of a steamboat pilothouse. It was moved here in 1952. Twain's original furnishings and writing equipment can be seen. *Open Mon.-Sat. July-Aug.*

37. Cornell University *Ithaca, N.Y.* A land-grant college chartered in 1865, the university was named in honor of its founder, philanthropist Ezra Cornell. The campus of 423 acres is beautifully sited on a hill overlooking the town of Ithaca and Cayuga Lake.

HERBERT F. JOHNSON MUSEUM OF ART This collection is housed in a monumental reinforced-concrete building designed by I. M. Pei and Partners. The collection features several hundred paintings by 17th-century Dutch, mid-19th-century French and American artists, as well as works by contemporary painters and sculptors. The graphics collection includes more than 7000 prints and drawings by outstanding European and American artists. Ceramics, painting and sculpture of China, Japan and Southeast Asia are on display. *Open Tues.-Sun.*

[**37.** *McGraw Tower*] *The 173-foot-high tower affords a spectacular view of Cayuga Lake and the sprawling Cornell University Campus. The set of chimes in the belfry is one of the largest and best known in the country.*

MCGRAW TOWER Known until 1961 as the Library Tower, this structure has been a university landmark since its completion as part of the old undergraduate library in 1891. It houses the 18 cast-bronze bells of the Cornell chimes, ranging from $2\frac{1}{2}$ tons to 250 pounds. During the academic year three 15-minute concerts are played daily on the chimes. Visitors can climb the 163 steps to watch the chimesmasters ring the bells by hand. *Open daily.*

MORRILL HALL This was the first building to be completed when the college was opened in 1868. It is now a National Historic Landmark. The hall was named for Justin S. Morrill, author of the Morrill Land Grant Act. It is an adaptation of French late-Renaissance style. *Open daily.*

38. Binghamton City Hall *Binghamton, N. Y.* Built in 1897 by one of the most famous architects of the period, Francis Almirall, this is an excellent example of the Hôtel de Ville style of French Renaissance architecture, with mansard roof and cupola. *Open daily.*

39. Roberson Center for the Arts and Sciences *30 Front St., Binghamton, N.Y.* Four buildings here accommodate a wide range of exhibitions, workshops, lectures and performances. The handsome Roberson Mansion was completed in 1906. Its rooms contain period furniture; Indian dioramas, costumes, ceremonial masks and archaeological finds; a fine collection of Royal Worcester birds; and historical objects and manuscripts. In the Carriage House are galleries, studios and a crafts shop. The Two Rivers Gallery, at 22 Front Street, features work by local artists and craftsmen. The New Building, designed by Richard J. Neutra, houses art galleries, a planetarium and a small theater. Among the exhibits is the Link Collection of undersea archaeology. *Open daily except holidays.*

Remington's painting of the Spanish-American War, The Charge of the Rough Riders at San Juan Hill, *is his best-known oil (1898). He also did on-the-scene sketches of the war for William Randolph Hearst's newspapers.*

Coming Through the Rye *is a 1902 bronze of carousing, hard-riding cowboys.*

The Howl of the Weather (*oil, 1906*). *Chippewas ride out a river storm.*

Cabin in the Woods (*oil, 1890*). *The contented man lighting his pipe is a self-portrait of the artist.*

The Sentinel (*oil, 1909*) *was painted at the end of Remington's short life.*

The Rattlesnake (*1905, bronze*). *A horse and rider rear in fright at the coiled snake on the ground.*

40. Remington Art Museum

303 Washington St., Ogdensburg, N.Y.

The artist who has left the best record of the American frontier lived most of his life on the East Coast. Frederic Remington grew up in Ogdensburg, N.Y., studied for a while at Yale Art School and then in 1880 at the age of 19 abandoned collegiate life to explore the West. He worked as a cowboy, prospector, sheep rancher and saloon owner, rode the cattle trails and wagon train routes from Canada to Mexico and became known as a man to be reckoned with in a fistfight. Settled once again in New York in 1885, Remington began to re-create in art the life he had experienced, a life fast vanishing under the inevitable civilizing influences of the newly completed cross-country railroads. Magazine sketches quickly earned him praise—and money—as an illustrator, and he was also highly regarded as a painter and sculptor. As may be seen in the works shown here, attention to detail and a distinctive sense of gesture and movement typify his work. Remington died in 1909. The most comprehensive collection of his work in the country is displayed in this museum. It was in this house that Remington's wife lived for a number of years after his death. *Open Mon.-Sat. Oct.-June, daily June-Sept. Adults small charge.*

[**47.** *Chapel*] *The chapel, completed in 1828, is notable for bold proportion and detail. Like so many Colonial buildings, the style of the exterior and interior is derivative of English 17th- and 18th-century architecture.*

41. Boldt Castle *Heart Island, Alexandria Bay, N.Y.* An impressive imitation of German Rhineland castles, this turreted, marble-halled, 100-room complex stands on one of the Thousand Islands which George C. Boldt, the builder, ordered shaped in the form of a heart. Having intended the castle as a tribute to his wife, Boldt left the structure unfinished after her sudden death in 1903 and an expenditure of $2,000,000. *Open daily early May-mid-Oct. Small charge.*

42. Tibbets Point Light House *Tibbets Point, Cape Vincent, N.Y.* First built in 1827 and reconstructed in 1834, this handsome 67-foot light marks the entrance to the St. Lawrence River and Seaway from Lake Ontario. *Open Sat., Sun. May-Oct.*

43. Jefferson County Historical Society Museum *228 Washington St., Watertown, N.Y.* Built as a private dwelling in 1876, this museum contains furniture of the Victorian and earlier periods, Indian artifacts and clothing once worn by residents of the county as well as relics from the War of 1812 and the Civil War. Works of art and objects related to commerce on Lake Ontario and the St. Lawrence River are also displayed, and there is a replica of an Early American kitchen in the basement. A small gallery is reserved for temporary exhibits. *Open Mon., Tues., Sat., Sun. except holidays.*

44. Roswell P. Flower Memorial Library *229 Washington St., Watertown, N.Y.* This impressive marble building was presented to the city by the daughter of a prominent Wall Street broker who was governor of New York between 1892 and 1895. It is especially noted for the Napoleon Room, with its collection of Empire pieces and other items from the early French settlement in this area. An extensive doll collection, an exhibit of miniature furniture and a number of murals depicting episodes in the history of Jefferson County are also on view. *Open Mon.-Sat. except holidays.*

45. Constable Hall *Off Rte. 26, E. of Constableville, N.Y.* William Constable, Jr., one-time owner of 4 million acres ($^1/_{10}$th of the land) in New York State, completed this 10-room Georgian home of cut limestone in 1819; the Constable family continued to live here until 1948. Among the displays are correspondence from General Lafayette to William Constable, Sr., some pieces of Napoleon's china, a mahogany wine cooler built by Duncan Phyfe, an ornate canopied Chippendale bed and a chess set once owned by Clement Moore. *Open Tues.-Sun. June-Oct. Small charge.*

46. Musical Museum *Rte. 12B, Deansboro, N.Y.* Restored musical antiques are displayed so that visitors can operate them. Fifteen grind organs are on view as are Swiss music boxes, barrel and pipe organs, player pianos, early phonographs and a mechanical bird that flaps its wings and chirps. Many of the instruments are labeled with their individual histories. *Open daily. Adults and children over 10 $1.50.*

47. Hamilton College *Clinton, N.Y.* Hamilton was first chartered as a college for men in 1812.

EDWARD W. ROOT ART CENTER Exhibits of painting and sculpture as well as works collected by E. W. Root are shown in the informal atmosphere of his homestead. *Open daily Sept.-May except college vacations.*

HAMILTON COLLEGE CHAPEL Organ concerts are occasionally performed here in one of the few three-story churches remaining in America. *Open daily.*

48. Kirkland Art Center *On the Park, Clinton, N.Y.* Local paintings, sculpture, photography, graphics and crafts are shown here both in permanent and temporary exhibitions. The annual Spring Art Fair is held at the end of May. *Open daily.*

49. Munson-Williams-Proctor Institute *310 Genesee St., Utica, N.Y.* Art and architecture at their finest are represented here by two buildings and collections widely divergent in style: the Museum of Art and Fountain Elms. Also located on the grounds are the School of Art, housed in two converted carriage houses, and the Meetinghouse, which contains paintings from the institute's collection.

FOUNTAIN ELMS Adjacent to the museum (see below), this beautifully restored Tuscan-style villa built in 1850 has four period rooms of Victorian furniture and art. Some of the fine, signed pieces include a silver tea set by John Osborn, Wittingham brass andirons and a secretary by Anthony Querville. *Open daily.*

MUSEUM OF ART This dramatic, dark-granite cube, sliced by bronze crossbeams, was designed by Philip Johnson. Much of the institute's collection of contemporary American works is exhibited in the museum, illuminated by natural overhead lighting. Displays feature paintings by Cole, Hopper, Gorky, Mondrian, Pollock, Dali and Picasso and, in the sunken sculpture court, works of Calder, Moore, Baskin, Duchamp, Vil-

lon and Marini. An extensive art library and nearly half of the 4000 art works, including a collection of Japanese woodcuts, were contributed by Edward W. Root. There is also a supervised toy-filled room where children can stay. *Open daily.*

50. Remington Gun Museum *14 Hoefler Ave., Ilion, N.Y.* This well-organized and well-identified collection encompasses an example of every firearm manufactured by the Remington Arms Company since its formation near Ilion in 1816. Over 300 rifles, shotguns and pistols are displayed here, including military weapons used as early as 1846 in the Mexican War. *Open daily.*

51. Herkimer Home *Rte. 5S, Little Falls, N.Y.* This two-story Dutch Colonial brick mansion, notable for its gambrel roof, is located in a 135-acre park maintained by the state. It was built in 1764 by General Nicholas Herkimer, the Revolutionary War hero, and the furnishings include some of his original Chippendale pieces. *Open daily Apr.-Oct.*

52. Holy Trinity Monastery *Rte. 167, Jordanville, N.Y.* Operated entirely by monks of the Orthodox church, this religious community was founded in 1930 by two Russian monks. The distinctive cathedral, with gold-leaf "onion" domes, derives from 12th-century Russian church architecture. Consecrated in 1950, its interior contains elaborate frescos and ceiling paintings of saints and angels, as well as icons of Christ and relics of various saints. *Open daily.*

53. Colgate University *Hamilton, N.Y.* Founded in 1819 by the Baptist Education Society, Hamilton Literary and Theological Institution had its name changed to Colgate University in 1890.

ALUMNI HALL Completed in 1861, the building is made of stone from the university's own quarries. With the interior remodeled it now houses archaeological and ethnological displays relating primarily to the American Indian.

CHARLES A. DANA CREATIVE ARTS CENTER Designed by Paul Rudolph and opened in 1965, the center, of reinforced concrete and ribbed concrete blocks, is an impressive sculptural form on the landscape. It contains the Picker Gallery, where a wide diversity of art forms are exhibited, the University Theatre and the departments of art, music and drama. *Open daily except college vacations.*

EVERETT NEEDHAM CASE LIBRARY Named for a former president of the university, the library was opened in 1958. It presently holds more than 250,000 volumes. The rare book collection, which may be seen on request, includes four Shakespeare folios and the Gospel of Saint Matthew from the 1450 Gutenberg Bible. In the lobby are display cases and a colorful Italian mosaic column that depicts the 13 persons who founded the university in 1819. *Open daily except college vacations.*

54. Yager Museum *Hartwick College, Oneonta, N.Y.* The fourth and fifth floors of the museum-library building contain a fascinating collection of Indian artifacts. Based largely on the vast private collection willed to the college by Willard E. Yager, an Oneonta resident, it encompasses his surface finds of arrowheads, axes, beads, hatchets and other items, mainly of upper Susquehanna Indians. Several other collections include objects from various Central and South American Indian cultures from 1000 B.C. to A.D. 1500. The Early Man Exhibit on the fifth floor contains crude stone tools from the Oneonta region that are believed to date from about 20,000 B.C. Reproductions of Iroquois false faces used in healing ceremonies, dolls and musical instruments are on display. *Open Mon.-Fri.*

55. Cherry Valley Museum *Main St., Cherry Valley, N.Y.* This 15-room museum house was built in 1832 facing the Great Western Turnpike, the route used by stagecoaches and freight wagons traveling west. Of interest are block-printed wallpaper, Swan organs, Belknap guns, a display of old fire engines and relics of the Cherry Valley Massacre. *Open daily end of May-Sept. Adults small charge.*

56. Palatine Church *Rte. 5, N. of Nelliston, N.Y.* This limestone church was built in 1770 by Evangelical Lutheran Palatines who came to this country from Germany by way of England. It is one of the Mohawk Valley's few surviving pre-Revolutionary structures, and has been owned by the Palatine Society since 1938. *Open in summer for special services.*

57. Canajoharie Library and Art Gallery *Erie Blvd., Canajoharie, N.Y.* This small gallery owns outstanding examples of American art from Colonial times to the present. Its collection of Winslow Homer oils and watercolors is the third largest in the country. Other featured artists include the 18th-century portrait paint-

[52] *True to Russian Orthodox style, the rich interior of Holy Trinity Cathedral is designed to imbue a sense of the glory of heaven. The altar screen, frescos and most of the construction work were done by the Holy Trinity monks.*

ers Gilbert Stuart and John Singleton Copley, Edward Hopper and Andrew Wyeth. There are also representative works of the Hudson River and Ashcan schools. A group of sculptures is also exhibited here. *Open Mon.-Sat.*

58. Johnson Hall *Hall Ave., Johnstown, N.Y.* This handsome two-story Georgian structure was built in 1763 by Sir William Johnson, superintendent of Indian affairs for the northern colonies during the French and Indian Wars. His home was the scene of important Indian negotiations, and his control over the Six Iroquois Nations helped end French influence east of the Mississippi. Restored and administered by the New York State Historic Trust, the building's two large drawing rooms contain period furniture, including some of Johnson's own possessions. A stone blockhouse adjoining the mansion houses a diorama showing life on Johnson's baronial acres. *Open daily.*

59. Old Fort Johnson *Fort Johnson, N.Y.* Substantially built of gray fieldstone, this Colonial mansion was completed in 1749 by Sir William Johnson. Fortified and palisaded in 1755, the house was confiscated in 1777 by a group of patriots who removed the lead roof and melted it down into bullets for the Continental army. Several rooms have been furnished with period furniture, some of which belonged to Sir William and to his son Sir John, who lived here from 1763 to 1774. Included among the exhibits are the Richmond and Frey collections of Indian artifacts and relics. There is also a miller's house (1742) on the property. *Open daily May-Oct. Adults small charge.*

60. Guy Park House *366 W. Main St., Amsterdam, N.Y.* Sir William Johnson, founder of Amsterdam, built this house in 1766 for his daughter and her husband, Guy Johnson, his nephew. The two-story Georgian mansion was destroyed by fire but was rebuilt shortly afterward. Although two wings were added in 1858, it still maintains its handsome pre-Revolutionary appearance, with 18th-century furniture in six of its rooms. The house was confiscated by the State of New York during the Revolution when Guy Johnson, a Tory, fled to Montreal with his family. *Open Mon.-Fri.*

61. Schenectady County Historical Society Headquarters *32 Washington Ave., Schenectady, N.Y.* The society is housed in a turn-of-the-century Georgian-style building with a handsome doorway and an elaborate pediment and pilasters. The latter are repeated at the corners and between the front windows. Inside are a number of displays of scientific materials, including several of Thomas Edison's inventions. A collection of manuscripts, Indian and military relics and items from Schenectady's past are also on exhibit, along with monthly shows of local significance. A library is maintained for public use. *Open daily.*

62. Stockade *Schenectady, N.Y.* Encompassing 12 city blocks bounded by State, Washington, Front and Ferry Streets, this unique group of privately restored structures stands on land originally surrounded by a log stockade built by the Dutch in 1662. The scene of a massacre in 1690, when the French and Indians burned the settlement, the area was rebuilt and fortified in 1704. Although the houses are privately owned and not open to the public, visitors can admire the many handsome exteriors that include several excellent examples of Dutch, Colonial and Federal architecture dating from 1700 to 1840. Each year the interiors of six homes can be seen during a walkabout tour; an annual outdoor art show is also held.

ST. GEORGE'S EPISCOPAL CHURCH *30 North Ferry St.* This is the oldest church of any denomination in the Mohawk Valley. Built between 1759 and 1766, it was used as a barracks when services were suspended during the Revolution. Constructed of brown limestone, it was

[57] On the Cliff, *one of the Homer watercolors in the Canajoharie Art Gallery, was painted in 1881. The women, each wrapped in solitude, seem to await an answer from the sea.*

[59] *This Georgian house, fortified during the French and Indian War, was one of the first large homes built in the Colonies. Except for the outside walls, all the materials used were imported.*

[**66**] Lake Lucerne, *an oil by William B. Baker (1859-86) a little known painter of the Hudson River School, is an elegant scene of urban ladies and gentlemen on a country outing in the Adirondacks. Lucerne is one of many lakes near Saratoga Springs, N.Y., a fashionable resort in the late 19th century. The wilderness of the Adirondacks was a natural theme for Hudson River painters, as it is here that the source waters of the mighty river are found.*

enlarged in 1840 and 1881 and completely renovated in 1953 when two chapels and a sanctuary were added. The unusual tower was originally made of wood, then rebuilt of stone in 1870. Washington is known to have attended services here. *Open Sun.-Fri.*

63. Waterford Historical Museum and Cultural Center *2 Museum Lane, Waterford, N.Y.* A blending of Federal and Greek Revival architecture is evident in this wooden structure, which was built in 1830 and later enlarged. Once the home of Hugh White, a Waterford businessman and Whig congressman, its 24 rooms contain some fine Empire and Victorian furnishings. Facing demolition, it was moved 400 feet to its present location in 1964 and dedicated as a museum two years later. It offers displays of early Americana and lectures on local and world history, fine arts, crafts and music. There are changing displays of ceramics, sculpture, glassware and other objects. *Open Sat., Sun.*

64. Kent-Delord House Museum *17 Cumberland Ave., Plattsburgh, N.Y.* In 1814 occupying British officers hastily escaped from this frame house after the Battle of Plattsburgh, leaving behind a mess chest and some pieces of regimental silver. These, as well as fine period furnishings and portraits, including a Copley pastel, are on display. The house was built in 1797 by Captain John Bailey, inherited by his daughter, the wife of James Kent, chief justice of the Supreme Court of New York, and sold in 1810 to Henry Delord, whose family owned it for over a century. It became a museum in 1924. *Open Mon.-Sat. mid-Jan.-mid-Dec.*

65. Six Nations Indian Museum *Off Rte. 3, E. of Onchiota, N.Y.* Elements from past and present cultures of this famous Indian confederation are featured in the collection. Costumes, early artifacts and relics are on display, including a 75-foot beaded record belt that portrays the story of the founding of the Iroquois Confederation. Miniature Indian villages, food storage techniques and different types of fires can be seen outdoors. *Open daily late May-Nov. Small charge.*

66. Adirondack Museum *Blue Mountain Lake, N.Y.* More than 50 horse-drawn vehicles, Adirondack guide boats, dioramas and some 300 photographs help unfold the development of this region during the 19th century. August Belmont's private Pullman car is on display, as are an original log hotel and tools used for logging, ice cutting and maple sugaring. Exhibits of prints and paintings are changed regularly. *Open daily mid-June-mid-Oct. Adults $2.00, children small charge.*

67. John Brown Farm *John Brown Rd., Lake Placid, N.Y.* The famous abolitionist moved his family into this frame farmhouse in 1855, and lived here occasionally until he was executed in 1859 for his abortive raid on Harper's Ferry, Virginia. He was buried here. A bronze statue of Brown and a black boy, representing those he died to free, stands near the entrance to the restored house. Some of the period furnishings belonged to the Brown family. The site is registered by the New York State Historic Trust. *Open daily.*

68. Adirondack Center Museum and Colonial Garden *Rte. 9, Elizabethtown, N.Y.* The formal beauty of these gardens is created by reproducing many of the features of the Williamsburg, Virginia, gardens and others of Colonial times. Brilliant blooms appear in July and August among patterned brick walks, iron benches and a white-picketed summerhouse. There are nature walks and a picnic area on the grounds. The adjoining museum shows life as it was lived many years ago in the Adirondack area. It contains a push-button map, a room of antique dolls and toys, tools, a transportation display and a schoolroom. Regional 19th-century photographs are also on view. *Open daily mid-May-mid-Oct., Fri. eves. only mid-Oct.-mid-May. Small charge.*

69. Champlain Memorial Lighthouse *Rte. 8, N.E. of Crown Point, N.Y.* Built jointly by New York and Vermont, this lighthouse was dedicated in 1912 to mark Samuel de Champlain's discovery in 1609 of the lake now bearing his name. Designed as a monumental structure, it consists of a granite base, Doric columns and a lantern 50 feet above ground. A bronze bas-relief by Rodin set into the base was a gift from France. Above it stands a statue of Champlain flanked by an Indian and a French voyageur. Marble steps descend from the base toward the lake.

[70] *Fort Ticonderoga, built by the French in 1755, was taken and retaken by the British and French in their struggle for control of the strategic valley beside Lake Champlain, and by the Americans and British during the Revolutionary War. The fort was built to hold 400 men; reinforcements camped on the flats. Vaulted rooms below the bastions (the pointed sections) were used for refuge and storage of water, food, horses, guns and gunpowder.*

70. Fort Ticonderoga *Rte. 22, S. of Ticonderoga, N.Y.* Located directly north of the once strategic junction of Lakes Champlain and George, this elaborate four-sided structure was built in 1755 by the French, who called it Fort Carillon. Originally constructed of timber and earth, the walls were later faced with stone. In 1759 the British under General Amherst captured the fort and renamed it Ticonderoga. Garrisoned for 16 years by a small British detachment, it fell to Ethan Allen's Green Mountain Boys in 1775. The British captured the fort again in 1777, but burned and abandoned it the same year. Gradually falling to ruin as settlers took materials for houses, the site was purchased in 1820 by William Pell, whose great-great-grandson began restorations in 1908. Almost entirely rebuilt according to the original French design, the superb reconstruction includes ramparts, a central parade ground, bastions and barracks. The large number of English, French, Spanish and a few U.S. cannons form the finest collection of its kind in the country. The museum contains an excellent selection of muskets, swords, historical documents and Indian artifacts as well as some possessions of George Washington, General Philip Schuyler, Sir William Johnson and other important Colonial figures. The immediate surroundings include many well-marked vestiges of British entrenchments dug during an unsuccessful assault on the fort in 1758. *Open daily mid-May-mid-Oct. Adults $1.50, children 10-14 small charge.*

71. Fort William Henry *Canada St., Lake George, N.Y.* This reconstructed log fort, named after two grandsons of King George II, was originally built in 1755 by the British as a springboard for raids against the French and as a defense of the vital portage linking Lake George with the Hudson River. The garrison withstood a French assault in 1757 but was forced to surrender later that year to General Montcalm, who burned the fort. Its ruins lay undisturbed until restoration began in 1953. Visitors can see replicas of barracks and a stockade as well as a museum with old swords, muskets, maps, dioramas and many Colonial artifacts from the vicinity. Most of the displays are explained by "heritage phones." A 25-minute program recounts the rich history of Lake George, and a movie theater shows a shortened version of *The Last of the Mohicans.* There are special activities in July and August with guides in period British army uniforms who lead tours, perform drills and fire muskets, cannons and rockets. *Open daily May-Nov. Adults $2.25, children small charge.*

72. Hyde Collection *161 Warren St., Glens Falls, N.Y.* An unusually excellent collection of art objects from the 5th century B.C. to the 20th century can be seen throughout the former home of Mr. and Mrs. Louis F. Hyde. Built in 1906 in the Italian Renaissance style that was popular then and established as a museum in 1952, the house preserves the aura of a gracious private residence of a more leisurely time. It serves as an ideal setting for the Hydes' collection of furniture, sculpture, paintings and drawings by many of the world's most renowned masters, including da Vinci, Rubens, Rembrandt, El Greco, Degas, Cézanne, Matisse and Picasso. Works by several of our most distinguished American artists such as Whistler, Bellows and Eakins are also on display. *Open Tues., Wed., Fri., Sun.*

73. General Philip Schuyler House *Schuylerville, N.Y.* Six days before his surrender at Saratoga in 1777, the British general John Burgoyne ordered the burning of the original Schuyler residence and this frame structure was built to replace it. The work was completed in 17 days with materials furnished by Schuyler's sawmills and his forge, which also produced gun carriages during the Revolution. Simple but elegant in design, the building along with 25 acres was acquired in 1950 by the Saratoga National Historical Park, and restoration was completed by the National Park Service. The rooms contain Colonial furniture. During the summer volunteers in period costumes demonstrate spinning, candlemaking and other crafts. *Open Sat., Sun. end of May-mid-June, daily mid-June-early Sept., Sat., Sun. early Sept.-mid-Oct. Small charge.*

74. Casino *Congress Park, Saratoga Springs, N.Y.* A reminder of the splendor of the world-renowned resort and spa, this American Victorian brownstone casino was constructed in 1867 by John Morrissey, one-time U.S. heavyweight champion, congressman and state senator. Opened in 1869, it was soon labeled Morrissey's Elegant Hell. Among its guests were the nation's most formidable and flamboyant figures, including J. P. Morgan, Lillian Russell and "Diamond Jim" Brady. In 1894 the property was sold to Richard Canfield, a connoisseur of the arts. Under his guidance the casino and adjoining restaurant were transformed into the epitome of elegance. Huge mirrors, unusual "High Victorian" furniture and bronze statues remain to tell of the former grandeur of the complex. A magnificent Tiffany glass window on the ground floor of the casino is one of the nation's finest examples of work from this famous studio. *Open daily May-Nov.*

HISTORICAL SOCIETY OF SARATOGA SPRINGS MUSEUM A museum on the second floor of the casino displays mementos of the two owners and some of their guests plus a collection of Indian artifacts, war relics and prints and photographs from the era of the great resort hotels.

WALWORTH MEMORIAL MUSEUM Several rooms on the casino's third floor contain furnishings and documents from the home of Reuben Hyde Walworth, a Saratoga Springs resident who served until 1848 as New York State's last chancellor. *Both museums open daily mid-May-Oct. Adults small charge.*

75. Hathorn Gallery *Skidmore College, Saratoga Springs, N.Y.* A small but well chosen permanent collection of prints, paintings, photographs, ceramics and sculpture is on view here. The collection includes one of the last paintings completed by I. Rice Pereira and a Joan Mitchell abstract oil painted in 1958. Among the gallery's programs are invitational exhibits. *Open daily Sept.-May except holidays.*

76. National Museum of Racing *Union Ave., Saratoga Springs, N.Y.* This modern Georgian-style building stands directly across from the Saratoga Race Course. Within, the history of thoroughbred racing is traced in paintings (including two by Remington) and sculptures of early and contemporary champions; racing colors, trophies and other memorabilia relating to the sport are exhibited. Famous horses, trainers and jockeys have been commemorated in the Hall of Fame at the rear of the building. *Open daily.*

77. Hyde Log Cabin *Rte. 2, Grand Isle, Vt.* Captain Jedediah Hyde, Jr., a Revolutionary War veteran and surveyor, built this crude cedar-log cabin in 1783; its survival makes it the oldest log cabin in the U.S. Inside are period furnishings. During restoration in the 1950s, its roof was replaced and the stone fireplace was rebuilt. *Open daily end of May-early Sept.*

78. First Unitarian-Universalist Church *141 Pearl St., Burlington, Vt.* This solid brick structure was built in 1816 from plans drawn by Peter Banner, the designer of Boston's Park Street Church, and approved by Charles Bulfinch, the senior architect. Its square, balustraded tower supports a porch, octagonal belfry and lantern. The spire is a copy of the original, which was damaged in 1945. The original Communion silver, which predates the completion of the church, is on display. *Open Mon.-Fri., Sun.*

79. Robert Hull Fleming Museum *University of Vermont, Burlington, Vt.* Named for an 1862 graduate, this decorative building was dedicated in 1931. Its collections contain the art of many American, European and Asian cultures. Works from Pre-Columbian South America, Africa and the South Pacific are also on view. An Egyptian mummy and Chief Sitting Bull's scalping regalia are popular attractions. Monthly exhibits, usually of contemporary sculpture and painting, are held in the main galleries. *Open daily.*

80. Old Round Church *Richmond, Vt.* This unique 16-sided structure was built by William Rhodes in 1812-14 for worshipers of five denominations. The interior, almost the same now as it was then, has a center aisle flanked by the original high box pews, with more pews around the sides. In 1880 religious services were discontinued in the church and it was taken over by the town of Richmond. It now is used for town meetings and an occasional wedding. *Open daily June-Sept.*

[76] Man O'War *by Franklin B. Voss is one of some 250 paintings concerning the sport of kings in the National Museum of Racing. The famous stallion set five world records and won 20 of his 21 races.*

Two reminders at Shelburne of once-common sights on America's inland waterways: the more-than-100-year-old Colchester

81. Shelburne Museum

Rte. 7, Shelburne, Vt.

Shelburne is a 45-acre museum village that was developed largely because of one woman's lifelong passion for the American past. As a young girl of 16, Electra Havemeyer decided to buy a cigar-store Indian, much to the surprise of her parents, the Henry O. Havemeyers, noted collectors of European art. She married J. Watson Webb, a native of Vermont, who was also fascinated with Americana and interested as well in American architecture. After some 40 years of collecting, the Webbs had amassed 125,000 objects. They bought land in Shelburne, restored an 1835 house for use as a museum, built a barn from old timbers for the display of Mr. Webb's carriages, sleighs and coaches, and went on collecting. Today Shelburne consists of 35 18th- and 19th-century American buildings including homes, barns, a jail, railroad station, schoolhouse, stagecoach inn and meetinghouse, all carefully moved from their original sites and painstakingly restored. Some are furnished as homes: an 1840 stone cottage in the modest style of a farmhouse and a 1790 Vermont home with furnishings appropriate to a wealthy sea captain. Others contain the rest of the collection, remarkable in its overall quality and diversity: toys, rugs, glass, pewter, ships' figureheads, weather vanes, clocks, snuffboxes, maps, blacksmith tools and music boxes, for example. In the Webb Art Gallery is an excellent collection of works by 18th- and 19th-century American artists and in the Memorial Building are Georgian paneled rooms and furnishings and European paintings from the Webb's New York apartment. *Open daily mid-May–mid-Oct. Adults $3.50, students $1.50.*

Well-furnished Vermont House has American items (Queen Anne chairs, New England table) and imported goods (Oriental rug, decanters—probably Irish).

Lighthouse from Lake Champlain and the sidewheeler S.S. Ticonderoga, *one of the last passenger steamers on the lake.*

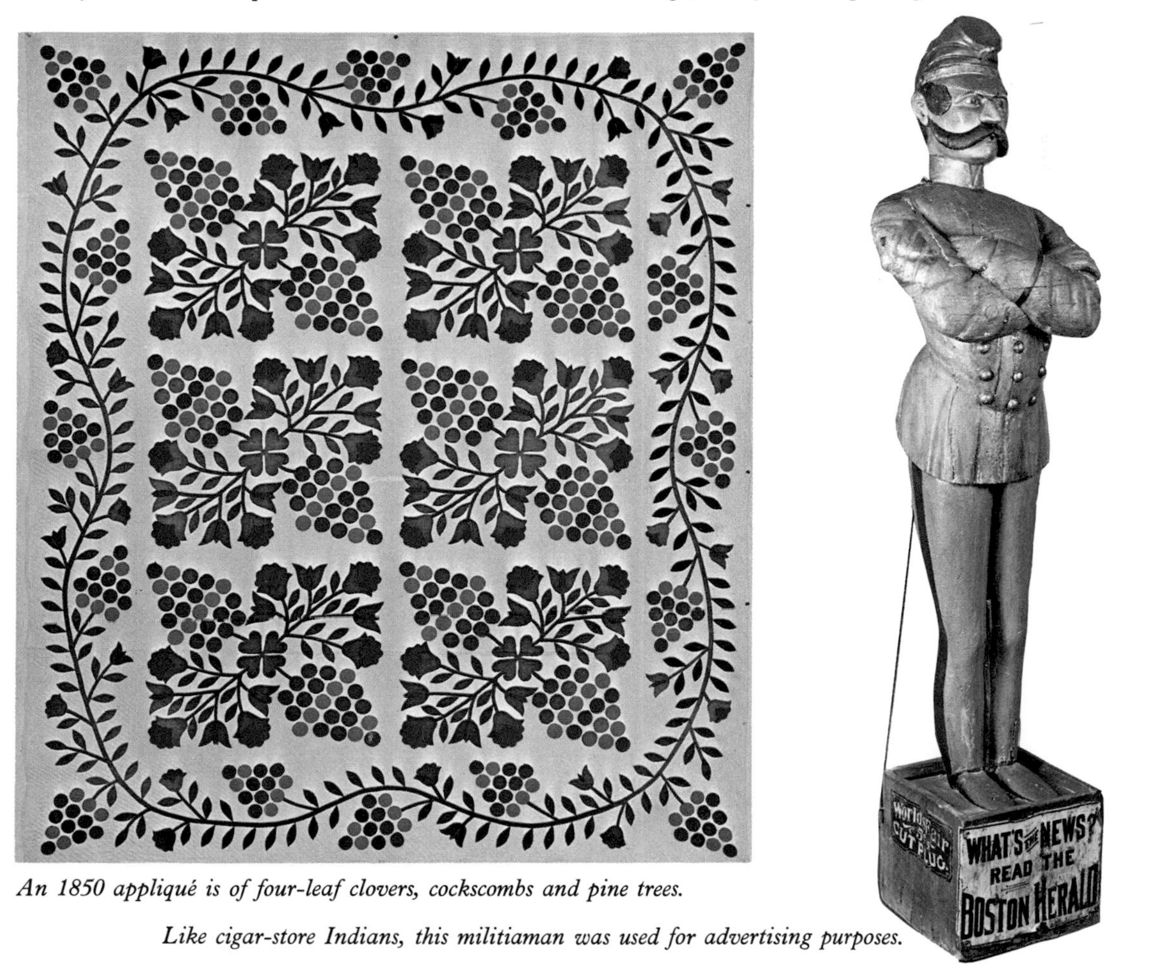

An 1850 appliqué is of four-leaf clovers, cockscombs and pine trees.

Like cigar-store Indians, this militiaman was used for advertising purposes.

81. **Shelburne Museum** *(continued)*

The 1840 general store and apothecary shop are well stocked with period items.

A dramatic wooden Indian this, with a whole eagle's head on his headdress and bear claws around his neck.

This graceful hand-pegged pleasure wagon carried President James Monroe on a Vermont tour in 1817.

A fearsome tiger is one of a menagerie of carrousel figures from Gustav Dentzel's Philadelphia woodwork shop.

Kitchen of the Salmon Dutton house, a 1782 Vermont saltbox, is fully equipped as it would have been then. The pulley suspended from the mechanism on the wall above the fireplace, called a clock jack, eased the housewife's cooking chores by turning the spit. The small open square in the brick was used as an oven.

Grandma Moses remembered a kitchen scene from her 1870s childhood in this painting, Tramp on Christmas Day.

[86] *The drawing room of Wilson Castle is furnished in a French Renaissance manner with French antiques and some Oriental objects. The three stained-glass windows depict "Music," "The River Thames" and "Thought."*

82. Bixby Memorial Library *258 Main St., Vergennes, Vt.* This classic yellow-brick building with imposing white pillars was designed by Frederick Frost in 1911. Considered by many to be one of our finest examples of Greek Revival architecture, it houses collections of rare stamps, paperweights, Indian artifacts and cup plates of china and Sandwich glass. *Open Mon.-Fri. June-Sept., Mon.-Sat. Oct.-May.*

83. General John Strong Mansion *Rte. 17, Addison, Vt.* About 1795, on the shores of Lake Champlain, this two-story dwelling was built of bricks made on the farm of General Strong of the Vermont Revolutionary militia. Purchased in 1934, restored and still maintained by the Vermont State Society, Daughters of the American Revolution, it contains period furniture and many belongings of the Strong family. The front hall is especially attractive with its grandfather clock and graceful stairway, and in the upper hall there is a handsome Palladian window. The wide floor planks in the kitchen are the originals as are all the fireplaces, the big bake oven and most of the hardware. The house provides a good picture of a prosperous 19th-century farmer's life. *Open daily mid-May-mid-Oct. Small charge.*

84. Congregational Church *Pleasant and Main Sts., Middlebury, Vt.* Lavius Fillmore, a cousin of President Millard Fillmore, designed this lovely church in 1806-9, and gave it a most unusual steeple: a spire and two octagonal stages set on top of three square stages. Palladian windows at the front and back, and graceful rounded windows along the sides, are other distinctive features. *Open daily June-mid-Oct., Sun. mid-Oct.-May.*

85. Sheldon Museum *1 Park St., Middlebury, Vt.* This three-story 1829 brick house is named for a one-time village storekeeper who occupied it in 1875 and established a museum here seven years later. The oldest village museum in New England, its period furnishings include portraits in the primitive style, pewter, china and pianos. A nursery with toys and a faithful restoration of an old-time country store and taproom are other features of interest in the 17 rooms. In the library are many documents and papers of local interest, including a collection of 30,000 handwritten personal letters. *Open Mon.-Sat. June-mid-Oct., Tues., Thurs. mid-Oct.-May. Small charge.*

86. Wilson Castle *W. Proctor Rd., Proctor, Vt.* This three-story brick and marble mansion and its furnishings are a monument to the opulence of Victorian design. Built in 1867 with many stained-glass windows, ornate paneling and 13 fireplaces, the 32-room house is decorated with intricately worked furniture and Oriental rugs. Artists and photographers frequently exhibit their work in the art gallery, with its 34-foot-high ceiling and stippled skylight. Sunday afternoon chapel services are also held here. Staff members are outfitted in uniforms of the Swiss Guard. *Open daily mid-May-late Oct. Adults $1.50, students small charge.*

87. Chaffee Art Gallery *16 S. Main St., Rutland, Vt.* Sponsored by the Rutland Area Art Association, this gallery is housed in a late-Victorian mansion, once the home of George Chaffee, a civic-minded businessman, and still owned by his family. There are one-man shows by regional artists and special exhibitions dealing with all aspects of the arts. Classes, lectures and musical and dramatic performances also take place here. An art festival is held annually in the adjoining park. *Open Mon.-Sat. mid-May-Sept. except Labor Day.*

88. Baptist Meeting House *Rte. 140, East Poultney, Vt.* Among the notable features of this 1805 Federal-style church are the carvings on the cornice, window frames and bell deck. Inside, the original pulpit, pews and collection boxes can be seen. A second floor was added in 1839 and the lantern tower replaced in 1937. The elaborate weathervane that tops the steeple is a copy of the original. *Open Sun.*

[88] *The gracefully simple design of the Baptist Meeting House embodies ideas compiled by American architect Asher Benjamin in his book* The Country Builder's Assistant, *which greatly influenced Colonial styles.*

89. Farrar-Mansur House *On the Common, Weston, Vt.* Captain Oliver Farrar built this combination tavern and family house in 1797. Largely unchanged, it has an L-shaped kitchen, taproom, ballroom, council room and bedchambers. Furnished with many local heirlooms, the house retains a lived-in atmosphere. *Open Tues.-Sun. July-mid-Oct. Small charge.*

90. Southern Vermont Art Center *Off West Rd., Manchester, Vt.* This Colonial-style mansion was purchased by the Southern Vermont Artists, Inc., in 1950, and 11 of its 28 rooms now serve as art galleries. In the music pavilion programs of ballet, concerts and films as well as art classes and exhibits of the work of painters, sculptors and photographers are offered each summer. The art center sponsors events in the Village Gallery and elsewhere during the winter. A sculpture garden is located on the spacious grounds. *Open Tues.-Sun. June-mid-Oct. Small charge except Tues.*

91. Chiselville Bridge *Sunderland, Vt.* This 117-foot covered bridge, built in 1870, crosses Roaring Branch. The latticework side windows reveal an exciting view of the water 140 feet below.

92. Green Bridge *West Arlington, Vt.* Built in 1851, this picturesque wooden bridge is set in rolling New England countryside. Its lattice-truss construction was designed by the architect Ithiel Town.

93. Topping Tavern Museum *East Rd., Shaftsbury, Vt.* In 1777 Peter Matteson built this stagecoach tavern as a stopping place for weary travelers. As stage travel declined, it became the Matteson family homestead. It has now been fully restored, complete with taproom, ballroom with rare swinging partition, country bedrooms, musicians' gallery and musty blacksmith shop. Furnished with fine American antiques, it also offers an invigorating view of the Green Mountains. *Open Tues.-Sun. May-Oct. Small charge.*

94. Burt Henry Covered Bridge *S. of Rte. 68A, North Bennington, Vt.* This picturesque covered span measuring 125 feet in length was built in 1832. Designed in the once-familiar Town lattice-truss style, it crosses the Walloomsac River.

95. Governor McCullough Mansion *Park and West Sts., North Bennington, Vt.* In 1865 T. W. Park, a Bennington lawyer, built this flamboyant Victorian frame house, which was occupied by John G. McCullough, governor of Vermont (1902–4), following his marriage to Park's daughter, and by members of the McCullough family until 1965. The furnished interior is American Victorian, with inlaid floors, carved woodwork, 16-foot ceilings and several Italian marble fireplaces. Within a 200-foot radius of the house stand 30 varieties of trees. Events here include art exhibits, concerts, craft demonstrations and a children's film program. *Open Tues.-Fri., Sun. July-Oct. Small charge.*

96. Old First Church *Monument Ave., Old Bennington, Vt.* Serving the oldest Protestant parish (1762) in the state, this fine frame structure was designed in 1805 by Lavius Fillmore, whose style is especially evident in the intricate detail of the arched belfry. Several remodelings, including a major alteration in 1865, eliminated many handsome original aspects of the interior. In 1937 funds were raised for restoration. The high pulpit and box pews were accurately rebuilt, those in the galleries at the back and sides of the church with wood from the original pews. A number of plaques honoring famous state figures from all walks of life hang inside the church. The poet Robert Frost is buried in the cemetery, as are American and Hessian soldiers who fell during the nearby Battle of Bennington in 1777. *Open daily end of May-mid-Oct., Sun. mid-Oct.-end of May.*

[**97**] Standing Stag (*1852*), *a piece of Victoriana in the Bennington Museum, is made of flint enamel, one of several kinds of decorative and utilitarian pottery that was produced by a local Bennington family during the 1800s.*

97. Bennington Museum *W. Main St., Bennington, Vt.* Antique furniture and household utensils, old military relics, Bennington pottery and a very fine collection of Early American glass combine to make this one of the nation's most impressive regional museums. Among the most popular exhibits are the Bennington '76 Flag, the oldest Stars and Stripes flag in the U.S., and a large collection of paintings by and memorabilia of Grandma Moses, which is on display in the Grandma Moses Schoolhouse. *Open daily Mar.-Nov. Small charge.*

98. Old Stone House *Off Rte. 5, Brownington, Vt.* Built in 1836 as a dormitory for a school established 13 years earlier, this four-story granite building was saved from demolition in 1916 and converted into a museum by the Orleans County Historical Society. Its 26 rooms contain period furniture, tools, farm equipment, clothing and war relics. Old books, newspapers and magazines can be seen in the library. *Open daily mid-May-mid-Oct. Small charge.*

99. Fisher Covered Bridge *Off Rte. 15, Wolcott, Vt.* This covered railroad bridge over the Lamoille River is one of the last in use in the U.S. Built in 1908, its cupola, running the full length of the span, provides for the smoke escape of the big locomotives of the period. The bridge has since been reinforced with steel beams.

100. Morristown Historical Society Museum *1 Main St., Morrisville, Vt.* Restored and furnished with antiques, this two-story brick building, known as the Noyes House, was built in 1830 with six fireplaces, one of which contains a bake oven. On display are a large collection of old porcelain pitchers and glassware, clocks, various Civil War relics and items from the early days of settlement in 1790. *Open Mon.-Fri. July-Sept.*

101. Welch Farm *Elmore Rd., Rte. 12, Morrisville, Vt.* Located on this private farm is a large barn with 20 narrow sides, making it seem almost round. Built in 1916 by local carpenters, it measures 240 feet in circumference. In the center is a silo that rises 40 feet, giving the roof line a cupola effect.

102. Pavilion Building *109 State St., Montpelier, Vt.* The 1875 "Steamboat Gothic" Pavilion Hotel, a five-story brick and wood building, stood on this site, but it was torn down and completely rebuilt in 1971. The reconstruction has a mansard roof and is flanked on two sides by wooden porches with ornate pillars and railings. The spindles of the railings along the veranda and balcony are original, as are the granite window keystones and the sills. The stenciled ceiling and marble floor in the lobby have been restored to their former elegance. Four floors are now devoted to state offices, while the museum and library of the Vermont Historical Society occupy most of the ground floor. *Open Mon.-Fri.*

103. Vermont State House *State St., Montpelier, Vt.* Dedicated in 1859, the third statehouse on the site resembles the Temple of Theseus in Greece and is constructed of Vermont granite. The huge wooden dome is sheathed with copper, covered with gold leaf and topped by a 14-foot wood statue of Ceres, the Roman goddess of grain. The impressive Doric portico was part of the second building, destroyed by fire in 1857. On the porch is a statue of Ethan Allen, leader of Vermont's Green Mountain Boys during the Revolution, and a brass cannon captured from the Hessians at the Battle of Bennington in 1777. The lobby contains a fine marble floor, Ionic capitals supported by fluted wooden shafts and decorative iron stairs to the second floor. A strong Corinthian influence is evident in the oval senate chamber where a handsome ceiling, with a magnificent chandelier, and black walnut desks and chairs dating from 1858 can be seen. Arranged in cabinets in the lobby outside are many Vermont battle flags from major wars. In the governor's office is an oak chair carved from timbers taken from the U.S.S. *Constitution* and a large painting of the Battle of Cedar Creek, Virginia, in 1864, in which Vermont troops distinguished themselves. *Open daily July-early Sept., Mon.-Fri. early Sept.-June.*

104. Bundy Art Gallery *Rte. 100, Waitsfield, Vt.* This striking Norman-brick, copper and glass building is surrounded by 80 acres of lawns and woodlands where works by contemporary sculptors, including Aschenbach, Minguzzi and Fortier are shown. Home of the Bundy Gallery School, it has a fine collection of modern paintings, including works by European and Central and South American artists. *Open Wed.-Mon. July-Aug.*

105. Robert Burns Statue *Spaulding Graded School, Washington St., Barre, Vt.* Dedicated in 1899, this memorial to the famous Scottish poet combines the work of Barre artisan Samuel Novelli, who cut the statue, and Elia Corti, who carved the relief panels in the base that depict scenes from four of Burns's best-known poems. Standing more than 22 feet high on the school lawn, this is considered one of the finest granite statues in the world.

[102] *In the 19th and early 20th centuries the social life of Montpelier, Vt., centered around the Pavilion, a rambling "Steamboat Gothic" hotel, which was too costly to renovate and so was torn down in 1970. In an effort to preserve the architectural integrity of old Montpelier, a new Pavilion, basically the same in appearance as the old, was built. It is used as an office building and a museum with exhibits of Indian relics, Vermont history and artifacts.*

106. Justin Smith Morrill Homestead *Strafford, Vt.* This is an interesting Gothic Revival house with a variety of attractive Victorian touches and 19th-century furnishings. It was the home of Senator Justin Morrill, who proposed the act for land-grant colleges. *Open Tues.-Sun. mid-May-Oct.*

107. Universalist Church *South Strafford, Vt.* The first Universalist church in the country, this remains just as it was when it was built in 1868. The brass lamps have since been wired for electricity, and its square steeple with clock is as graceful now as the day it was erected. *Open Sun. July-Aug.*

108. Sculptures on the Highway *Along Rtes. 89 and 91, Vt.* This unique program of roadside beautification displays 18 abstract marble and concrete sculptures in established roadside rest areas. The sculptures, many specifically designed for their location, are placed away from the highway, encouraging viewers to leave their cars to enjoy them. Created during the University of Vermont's International Sculpture Symposiums in the summers of 1968 and 1971, the impressive pieces represent the work of artists from the U.S. and eight foreign countries.

109. Burklyn Hall *Bemis Hill Rd., East Burke, Vt.* This stately 35-room neo-Georgian mansion was completed in 1908 for Elmer Darling, a native Vermonter and New York hotelier. Crowning 86 acres, it is noted for its lavish interior, which includes a copy of the staircase in the Longfellow House in Cambridge, Massachusetts; nine fireplaces with carved mantels; and outstanding paneling in several of the rooms. From the porches and grounds of this three-story house visitors may enjoy a spectacular view of the Green and White Mountains. Burklyn is open to the public for lectures, demonstrations, fairs and concerts as announced.

110. Fairbanks Museum of Natural Science *83 Main St., St. Johnsbury, Vt.* This handsome Romanesque red sandstone building was dedicated in 1890. Part of the turreted structure has been recently transformed into a planetarium. The museum houses an excellent collection of mounted birds, fossils, minerals and shells. There are displays related to the American Indian and to the people of Africa, the South Pacific and the Orient. The Hall of Science features exhibits of the physical sciences. *Open daily except holidays.*

111. St. Johnsbury Athenaeum *30 Main St., St. Johnsbury, Vt.* One of the nation's oldest art galleries, the Athenaeum was given to St. Johnsbury in 1873 by Horace Fairbanks. It contains works by Hudson River school painters, including William and James Hart, Cropsey and Moran. By far its most impressive work is *Domes of the Yosemite,* Bierstadt's 10-by-15-foot masterpiece. *Open Mon.-Sat. except holidays.*

112. Haverhill-Bath Covered Bridge *Rte. 135, Woodsville, N.H.* Because of the walkway on one side of this Town lattice-truss bridge, the roof line resembles the slope of a typical saltbox house. The state's oldest authenticated covered bridge (1827), its two spans crossing the Ammonoosuc River total 278 feet in length.

WHEELER HOUSE

113. Orford, N.H.: The Federal Style

(*See feature display on pages 78-9.*)

The Federal Style, purely American in character, is an adaptation of Robert Adam's style in England and the Romantic style of continental Europe. These, in turn, derived from the domestic architecture of Rome, rediscovered in the mid-1700s in archaeological diggings at such places as Pompeii and Spalato in Yugoslavia. The light, classical detail of Roman homes became the ideal of European architecture. This graceful trend took hold in America in a simplified manner just after the Revolutionary War. Characterized by delicate balustrades, thin columns and pilasters, traceried fanlights and sidelights and low roofs, it is evident in such decorative motifs in houses built between 1780 and 1820. The finest group of Federal houses in America span a ridge in the small town of Orford, New Hampshire, which was at the height of its prosperity when the Federal style became popular. In two cases the ells at the rear of these houses were earlier structures already in existence. The houses were designed by local builders, usually with the help of Asher Benjamin's handbooks and their own ingenuity. The facades of the neatly aligned houses, all privately owned, are an impressive sight. (See following pages.)

Samuel Morey House Inventor Samuel Morey owned all the land on the ridge. He built the first Federal house there, an addition to a Colonial structure, then sold lots to other builders. The house is authentically furnished throughout in early American style. It may be visited by arrangement with John H. Hodgson, the present owner.

Wheeler House A merchant bought the first lot from Morey. His Bulfinch-style house with a facade of matched board sheathing is the finest example here of the Federal period.

Lane House A lawyer built the house adjacent to Wheeler's and copied its facade; originally it also had a balustrade.

Beale House and Vanderbilt-Dillon House The two northernmost houses were built next, and they are the only ones made of brick.

Wilcox House Morey built part of this house for his daughter, who died young. Leonard Wilcox, her husband, added the front section when he married the second time.

Warren-Fifield House The last house built on the ridge is closer in style to Greek Revival (gable front, heavier proportions), which supplanted the Federal style around 1830.

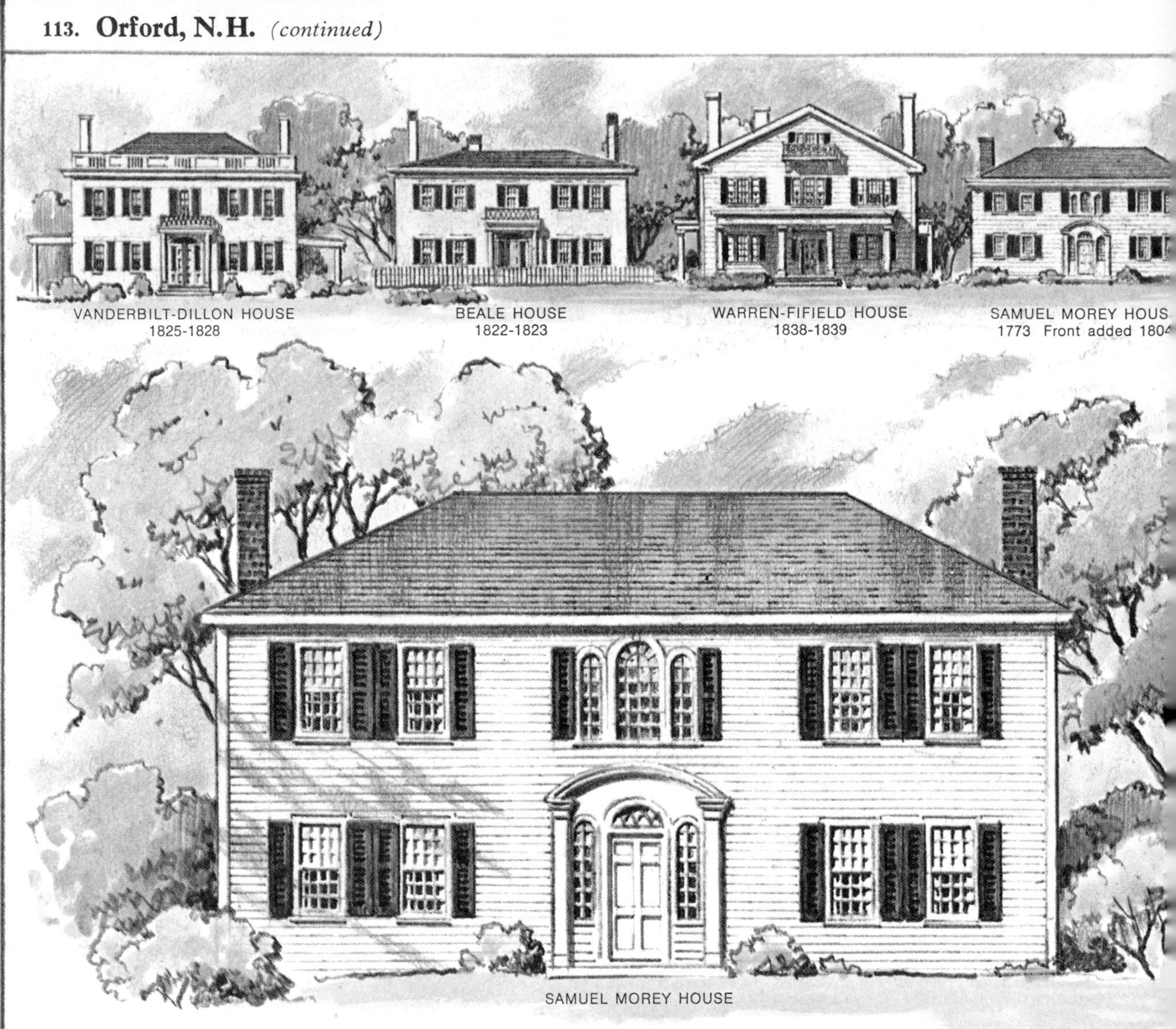

VANDERBILT-DILLON HOUSE
1825-1828

BEALE HOUSE
1822-1823

WARREN-FIFIELD HOUSE
1838-1839

SAMUEL MOREY HOUS
1773 Front added 180

SAMUEL MOREY HOUSE

The Elements of Federal Style

Federal architecture is characterized by good proportion and a number of specific decorative details. It is a fluid style, remarkable for its simple grace. The architectural elements at right, from the Wheeler House, are particularly fine examples of Federal decoration. The eaves balustrade on the hip roof is pure ornament, whereas a balustrade on a Colonial house usually encloses a real porch higher up on a steeply pitched roof. The entry is typically Federal with traceried sidelights, an elliptical, traceried fanlight and a six-paneled door with the two small panels at the top. A plain Doric entablature is used for the portico, a common feature of later Federal houses. Comparison of the Wheeler House with the Morey House, 10 years older, shows the evolution of Federal style. The Morey House has less detail—no portico or balustrade, paned sidelights—and is heavier looking because it is lower. It has a set of double windows on either side and, in the center, a Palladian window—a form more often seen in earlier Georgian houses than in the Federal.

EAVES BALUSTRADE

WILCOX HOUSE
1806
LANE HOUSE
1817-1821
WHEELER HOUSE
1814-1815
WHEELER HOUSE
RAHILL
ENTRY
DORIC
ENTABLATURE

[**114.** *Dartmouth Row*] *Four college buildings originally built in the late 18th and early 19th centuries on a rise on the Dartmouth campus are an architectural reflection of the discipline and simplicity of academic life. While the design of each building is outstanding, the graceful site and elegant grouping heighten the overall effect.*

114. Dartmouth College *Hanover, N.H.* Home of the Dartmouth College Library, the Dartmouth Skiway and the Hopkins Center for the Creative and Performing Arts, this private college is now in its third century of undergraduate liberal education and graduate study.

BAKER MEMORIAL LIBRARY *N. Main St.* This large Colonial-style brick building with its imposing clock tower was completed in 1928. Its most impressive interior features are the striking frescos painted by Mexican artist José Clemente Orozco (1883–1949) between 1932 and 1934, while he was teaching at the college. Fresco, an ancient and demanding technique of wall painting, requires a good eye and sure hand because the colors are applied directly to wet plaster. This Orozco work, largest of its kind in the U.S., covers 3000 square feet of wall space and is known collectively as *An Epic of American Civilization. Open daily Sept.–June, Mon.–Fri. during college vacations.*

DARTMOUTH COLLEGE MUSEUM *E. Wheelock St.* The emphasis here is on natural history and biology. Fine displays of rocks, fossils, animal heads and birds are shown. On exhibit are African and Oceanic artifacts, as well as archaeological findings of several North, Central and South American Indian cultures, including a collection of 9th-century southwestern pottery. *Open daily.*

DARTMOUTH ROW *E. side of College Green* There are four buildings in this complex of classrooms and faculty offices; all are three stories high with white painted-brick exteriors and black-shuttered windows. The largest is Dartmouth Hall, which replaced the 1791 wooden structure destroyed by fire in 1904. Reflecting the simplicity and balance common to many buildings constructed in Colonial times, its only adornment is a cupola containing a bell. Smaller but equally impressive are Thornton, Wentworth and Reed Halls, all of which are handsome examples of the Greek Revival style. The first two were completed in 1828 and the third in 1840 from designs by A. B. Young, an eminent Boston architect whose work includes the Boston Custom House and the Vermont State Capitol. Dartmouth Row is handsomely sited at one end of the large lawn known as College Green, or the Town Common.

HOPKINS CENTER FOR THE CREATIVE AND PERFORMING ARTS *E. Wheelock St.* Opened in 1962, this large building is named for Ernest Martin Hopkins, president of Dartmouth College from 1916 to 1945. Devoted to all aspects of the arts, it includes two theaters, two stage shops, a rehearsal hall and related rooms where every facet of the theater, from directing and lighting to stage managing and acting, can be studied and practiced. A broad visual arts program encompasses study in painting, drawing, sculpture, ceramics and film-making, while student workshops offer outlets in jewelry-making as well as wood- and metal-work. Three art galleries organize about 40 shows every year of works drawn from public and private collections. Exhibits from a permanent collection include many fine examples of European, Asian and American paintings, sculptures and drawings from the 17th to the 20th centuries. Concerts by visiting artists and lectures on a wide range of the arts are regularly featured. The Top of the Hop, the social center of the college, is also located here. *Open daily.*

115. Canaan Historic District *Canaan St., Canaan, N.H.* A sample of early community living is preserved along this $1\frac{1}{8}$-mile street bordered by many 18th- and 19th-century structures. Among the more noteworthy are a 1793 meetinghouse which still serves for town gatherings, two churches completed prior to 1845 and four former inns and taverns, the earliest dating from 1786. The Canaan Library and the Canaan Historical Museum share a building designed originally as a school in 1839. It now houses many items pertaining to the town and its development over the years. (The Stillson wrench, a plumbing tool in wide use today, is said to have been invented by a Canaan resident about 1850.) An annual Art of Northern New England exhibit helps raise funds for the museum's maintenance. Double rows of old sugar maples and a large, unspoiled lake (at one time used for baptismal services) add to the beauty of the setting, which also offers a number of fine views of distant mountains. A member of the National Trust for Historic Preservation, this is the first historic district in the state to be established outside the framework of town zoning. *Library open Wed., Sat., museum open Sat. July-Aug.*

116. Dana House *26 Elm St., Woodstock, Vt.* This nine-room, three-story house built in 1807 is maintained by the Woodstock Historical Society and contains a variety of furnishings, portraits, tools and other historic articles. Especially notable are the collections of old costumes, dolls and silver. *Open daily. Small charge.*

117. Norman Williams Public Library Museum *10 The Green, Woodstock, Vt.* The museum in the basement of this noteworthy, triple-arched, stone edifice contains an engrossing collection of Japanese artifacts that include swords, bronze, jade, crystal and ivory pieces, Satsuma ware and cloisonné. The objects were collected in Japan in the late 19th century by Dr. Edward Williams, who built and endowed the library. *Open Mon.-Sat. Small charge.*

118. Three Covered Bridges over the Ottauquechee River *Rte. 4, Woodstock, Vt.* The New Middle Bridge, built in 1969 near the Woodstock Village Green, is the first Town lattice-truss span to be constructed in New England since 1889. It closely resembles an earlier bridge on this site. Four miles upstream is the 1865 Lincoln Bridge. The 1836 Taftsville Bridge, three miles downstream, is a combination of Long- and Burr-truss design.

119. Calvin Coolidge Homestead *Plymouth Notch, Vt.* In the early morning of Aug. 3, 1923, word reached this hamlet that President Warren Harding had died. Vice President Calvin Coolidge, here visiting his family, dressed hurriedly and was sworn in as the 30th President of the U.S. by his father, acting in his capacity of notary public. The interior of this simple frame farmhouse with its attached shed and barn is virtually the same as it was on that occasion. Coolidge lived here from the time he was four until his departure for college, and many of the furnishings and effects of his family can be seen. In 1956 the property was given to the State of Vermont by the Coolidge family. Next door to the Homestead is the Wilder House, the early home of Coolidge's mother, and across the road is his birthplace, which adjoins the general store.

FARMERS' MUSEUM In a large barn that once belonged to the Wilder family is an informal display of farm tools and equipment, as well as an early hearse and doctor's gig. *Open daily end of May-mid-Oct. Small charge includes all buildings.*

120. Union Christian Church *Plymouth Notch, Vt.* Completed in 1840, this nondenominational church is handsomely proportioned, and sparsely ornamented with four pilasters on the front facade. The interior, renovated in 1890 in provincial Gothic style, is finished in natural pine. President Coolidge attended services here during his boyhood; a flag marks the pew he occupied. *Open daily mid-May-mid-Oct.*

121. Cornish, N.H.-Windsor, Vt., Covered Bridge *5 mi. S. of Plainfield Village, N.H.* Declared a National Historic Engineering Landmark in 1970, this is now the longest covered bridge in the U.S. The two-span Town lattice-truss, built in 1866 and renovated by the state in 1954, is 460 feet long. It crosses the Connecticut River.

122. Saint-Gaudens National Historic Site *Off Rte. 12A, Cornish, N.H.* The house and gardens of the famous sculptor Augustus Saint-Gaudens (1848–1907) stand on 82 acres, and many of his works can be seen on the grounds and in his two studios. Each summer exhibitions of American art are held in the gallery and a series of concerts is offered. *Open Mon.-Fri. mid-May-late Oct. Adults small charge.*

123. American Precision Museum *196 Main St., Windsor, Vt.* This building and its contents have great relevance to the history of the Industrial Revolution. In 1846 it housed the Robbins, Kendall and Lawrence Armory and Machine Shop, which was the birthplace of the "American system" of manufacture using completely interchangeable parts. It is this principle that makes mass production possible. The rifles manufactured here were later duplicated in England and known as Enfield rifles. Also produced here were Jennings breech-loading repeating rifles, and sewing machines. The museum has examples of these products and exhibits dramatizing the importance of tools and machines. *Open daily end of May-mid-Oct. Small charge.*

[119] *In this simply furnished Vermont farmhouse Calvin Coolidge was raised in the puritanical tradition of hard work and public service, attitudes which led him into a political career capped by five years as President.*

Steamtown visitors wait to board a steam-driven train. They will hear the rhythmic pulse and whistles of steam-power on a short trip in the Vermont mountains. Locomotive No. 15 was built by Baldwin in 1916.

124. Old Constitution House *16 N. Main St., Windsor, Vt.* In 1777 the constitution of the Republic of Vermont was adopted in this former tavern. The first percolator and cookstove made in the state are on display, together with a rare doll collection and old clocks, bells, guns and tools. *Open daily late May–mid-Oct.*

125. Old South Church *Main St., Windsor, Vt.* Built in 1798, this beautiful Congregational church with its unique louvered belfry was probably designed by Asher Benjamin. The steeple is four-staged; tall columns rise majestically from the front steps. *Open Sun.*

126. Old St. Mary's Church *West Claremont, N.H.* This brick building was constructed between 1823 and 1824 by Father Virgil Barber, son of the minister of the West Claremont Union Episcopal Church. (Both father and son converted to Roman Catholicism.) The first Catholic church in New Hampshire, a schoolroom over its nave housed the first Catholic school in the state. The church was restored in 1964–65.

127. Union Church *Old Church Rd., West Claremont, N.H.* Begun in 1771, this is the oldest standing Episcopal church in New Hampshire. The Revolution interfered with its construction, and it was not completed until 1789. Many Tory members of the parish, including the first rector, were mistreated and imprisoned during the years of conflict with England. The tower and belfry were added in 1801, and the building was enlarged in 1821. The original box pews with doors made from single boards are still in use. *Open daily.*

128. Weathersfield Meeting House *Weathersfield Center, Vt.* Dedicated in 1822, this brick building with its wooden steeple is now the home of the First Congregational Church of Weathersfield. It was remodeled in 1861 to accommodate church services on the upper floor and town meetings below. *Open Sun. June–Sept.*

129. South Congregational Church (United Church of Christ) *58 S. Main St., Newport, N.H.* A magnificent four-stage tower rises above this fine-looking 1823 brick church. Windows set into slight recesses are distinctive of the Isaac Damon design that has been changed very little. The interior, however, has been considerably modified. *Open daily July–mid-Oct., Sun. mid-Oct.–June.*

130. Congregational Church *Chester, Vt.* This wood structure built in 1828 is noteworthy for its handsome sanctuary. The steeple is remarkably similar to that of the 1826 Unitarian Church in Peterborough, New Hampshire, suggesting that the builder was influenced by the fine lines of the earlier church. *Open daily.*

131. Church on the Hill *Acworth, N.H.* This Congregational church was built between 1821 and 1824 to serve a parish founded some 50 years earlier. Its hilltop site faces the common of this unspoiled town.

132. Steamtown

Rte. 5, N. of Bellows Falls, Vt.

Steamtown is a collection of steam machines—locomotives, fire engines, a steamboat, steam shovel, pumping engine and many, many more. A walk around the 84-acre site evokes Steam Age America, perhaps the most flamboyant and freewheeling era in our history. Between 1830 and 1930 the steam engine was the chief means of generating power for trains, boats and industrial machinery, and as such was largely responsible for the growth of America from a fledgling nation to a continent-spanning world power. During these 100 years pioneers pushed the frontier to the Pacific Ocean (slaughtering Indians and buffalo in the process) to make way for farms, ranches, cities and, most important, the railroad. New industries were developed by men like Rockefeller (oil), Vanderbilt (railroads) and Carnegie (steel). It was a period of prolific invention. The steam engine was perfected for use in locomotives (less efficient steam engines had been utilized since 1711 when the Englishman Thomas Newcomen built a practical water-pump engine), and the electric light, glass-melting furnace, telegraph, telephone and skyscraper were introduced. Of all the attractions at Steamtown, the most illustrative of life in Steam Age America is the 22-mile trip on a steam-driven train through the picturesque Vermont countryside. *Open daily May-Oct. Adults $3.95, children 5-11 $2.50, for all activities.*

Between 1880 and 1920 steam traction engines like this were used to run threshing machines and sawmills.

A bell cast in the famous foundry of Paul Revere and his son is mounted in the five-stage steeple.

132. Steamtown *Rte. 5, N. of Bellows Falls, Vt.* See feature display above.

133. Scott Covered Bridge *Off Rte. 30, Townshend, Vt.* The three spans of this 1870 bridge across the West River total 276 feet in length. The center span, of Town lattice-design, measures 165.7 feet and is the longest in the state. The other two have king-post trusses.

134. First Congregational Church of Newfane *West St., Newfane, Vt.* The exterior of this 1839 frame structure is distinctive for its winged shutters designed to close over second-story windows with pointed tops. Since a remodeling in 1865, when the gallery was reduced and the pulpit modified, the upstairs has been used for services and the ground floor for meetings. The slate roof dates from 1897, when new pews were also installed. *Open daily.*

135. Windham County Court House *Rte. 30, Newfane, Vt.* An imposing Greek Revival building on the village green, the court house is noteworthy for its pilasters between windows, decorative cornices and columns supporting the portico. Completed in 1825, it brings a marked dignity to its surroundings. Inside are pictures of judges who have presided over the court. *Open early March-June, early Sept.-Nov.*

136. Windham County Historical Society Headquarters *Newfane, Vt.* A substantial collection of furnishings, farm implements, musical instruments, costumes and other items displayed here trace the history of the community, beginning with its establishment on Newfane Hill in 1774 and including its removal to the present site in the valley in 1824. Special evening programs are scheduled throughout the summer, and the museum is the focus for the Heritage Festival the first weekend in October, which features arts and crafts exhibits and demonstrations. *Open Sun. May-Oct.*

137. Park Hill Meeting House *Park Hill, Westmoreland, N.H.* This Congregational church dates from 1763. In 1826 it was moved 90 feet to its present site, after which a steeple was added. A bell, the 366th of almost 400 cast by Revere and Son, was installed in 1827; it cracked and was recast in 1847. The works of local artists are exhibited during July and August, and a rare 1791 pewter Communion set owned by the church is occasionally displayed. *Open Sat.-Sun. July-Aug.*

138. United Church of Christ *Central Square, Keene, N.H.* Originally a simple meetinghouse, built on another spot on Central Square in 1760, this church was moved to its present site at the head of the square about 70 years later. In 1860 the building was extensively remodeled and enlarged. Victorian refinements were added, as were Corinthian pilasters and columns, the gallery and the attractively detailed steeple. *Open daily.*

[139] *The covered bridge was a design devised to protect a wooden span from the elements, thereby increasing its life, and was a common sight in 19th-century America. The West River Bridge seen here was built with the lattice-truss method patented by businessman-architect Ithiel Town, who sold rights for its use to local builders.*

139. West River Bridge *Off Rte. 30, West Dummerston, Vt.* This handsome covered bridge was built in 1879 in Town lattice-truss style. At 280 feet in length, it is the longest covered span in Windham County.

140. Our Lady of Fatima Church *Rte. 9, Wilmington, Vt.* The entire face of this award-winning contemporary structure, completed in 1965, is a sweep of stained glass. The stark simplicity of the design is enhanced by a tall cross on the roof and by the oaks and maples that surround the church. *Open daily.*

141. Asbury United Methodist Church *Rte. 63, Chesterfield, N.H.* Completed in 1844, this handsome and well-preserved structure continues to serve a parish that has been active here since 1795.

142. Swanzey-Slate Covered Bridge *E. of Rte. 10, Westport N.H.* This span crossing the Ashuelot River is over 142 feet long. A Town lattice-truss design reinforced with iron turnbuckle rods, it was completed in 1862 to replace a bridge built here about 1800.

143. Winchester-Ashuelot Covered Bridge *S. of Rte. 119, Ashuelot, N.H.* This 160-foot bridge over the Ashuelot River was constructed in 1864 in the Town lattice-truss style. It is flanked by pedestrian walks.

144. Fitzwilliam Town Hall *Fitzwilliam, N.H.* A true example of expert Colonial handcrafting, this onetime Unitarian church was built in 1817. Its beautiful three-stage spire winds around a mast set in place by Boston ship riggers; the square belfry tower beneath houses a Revere bell. Flanking the entrance are four pine pillars, all finished by hand. A second floor was completed and a clock installed in 1861 when the structure was converted into a town hall. *Open Mon.-Sat.*

145. Seventh-day Adventist Church *3½ mi. S.W. of Washington, N.H.* The Seventh-day Adventist denomination developed from a movement led by Baptist preacher William Miller, who prophesied that the Second Coming of Christ would occur on Oct. 22, 1844. Ridicule ensued when the day passed uneventfully. A group of Miller's followers became the nucleus of the present Seventh-day Adventist church. The simple frame structure, built in 1843, is said to be the first Adventist church and is the scene of annual meetings of members from around the world. *Open Sat. June-Oct.*

146. Shedd Free Library *On the Village Green, Washington, N.H.* This stone and brick building was built in 1881 to house a growing town library. Boasting 292 books at first, it now has over 3300. *Open Wed.*

147. Washington Town Hall *On the Village Green, Washington, N.H.* This building was the religious center of Washington from the time it was completed in 1789 until 1840, when the high interior was divided into two stories and it became the town hall. Its large windows have 40 panels of glass which are believed to be original, but the steeple was added later, probably in the early 1800s.

148. Franklin Pierce Homestead *Rte. 31, W. of Hillsboro, N.H.* The 14th President of the U.S. was born in this two-story Federal house in the year of its completion, 1804, and lived here for 30 years. Inside are rare examples of early wall stenciling. *Open Tues.-Sun. late June-early Sept. Adults small charge.*

149. Stone Arch Bridge *Rte. 9, Stoddard, N.H.* The style of this open, stone bridge is typical of the Contoocook River Valley. Constructed without the use of mortar during the first half of the 19th century, its two arches stand as a tribute to the exceptional skill of the early New England stonemasons.

150. Congregational Church and Town House *Main St., Hancock, N.H.* This handsome church, with an elaborate spire and Revere bell, was erected nearby in 1820 and was moved to its present location in 1851. The arrangement of a church auditorium on the second floor and a town hall on the first was once widespread in New Hampshire, but today this building is one of only three in the state where church and state coexist in a single structure. *Open Sun.*

151. All Saints' Parish Church *Concord Street, Peterborough, N.H.* A classic example of the transitional phase from Norman to early English architecture, this unique Norman Episcopal church was built between 1916 and 1920 of native granite. The interior contains many rare objects, including copies of the Old and New Testaments published in 1837. There are 11 stained-glass windows. A carillon of 10 bells was donated to the church in 1923. *Open daily.*

152. Unitarian Church *Main St., Peterborough, N.H.* This brick church, completed in 1826, has a wooden steeple which houses the town clock. The building is believed to be a Bulfinch design. The three arched doorways and fan-shaped blind in the gable are among the details typical of his work. Between 1827 and 1848, the minister, Abiel Abbot, was responsible for establishing the first free library in the U.S. Several art exhibits, concerts and a lecture program by noted speakers are held here in the summer. *Open daily Sept.-June, Sun. July-Aug.*

153. Barrett House *Main St., New Ipswich, N.H.* This elegant 1800 mansion with its unusual third-floor ballroom contains furniture and portraits that belonged to the original family, owners of the first cotton mills in New Hampshire. A collection of spinning and weaving equipment is on display in the adjoining carriage house. *Open Tues.-Sat. June-Nov. Small charge.*

154. Congregational Church *Amherst, N.H.* Although this church has had many modifications since it was completed in 1774 and moved to its present site in 1836, a few old pews, sections of paneling and parts of the early gallery still remain. The original steeple is the oldest in the state. *Open daily.*

155. Million Dollar Show-Schuller Museum *On Rte. 106, midway Belmont-Laconia, N.H.* Joachim Schuller amassed this collection of ancient English arms, armor, heraldic plaques and palace furniture during his career as a concert pianist in Europe. The museum is organized into three separate halls which include the Hall of Knights, the Hall of Medieval Arms, and the Palace Hall, which displays French, Italian and Spanish royal furniture as well as royal clocks by famous makers. *Open mid-Mar.-early Nov. Small charge each hall.*

156. Old Meeting House *Rte. 127, Webster, N.H.* Built in 1791 on the bank of the Blackwater River, in 1941 this structure was moved up a steep hill to the center of town by means of a horse and capstan. The wide unpainted floor planks, pews and hand-hewn beams are of particular interest. Each window contains 28 panes of glass, almost all of which are original. The meeting house is now operated as a museum. Occasional summer exhibits feature collections of local memorabilia. *Open Sat., Sun. early July-early Sept.*

157. Shaker Village *Off Rte. 106, Canterbury, N.H.* One of the two still-active Shaker communities, this village consists of several interesting buildings. The original (1792) meetinghouse has separate entrances for women and men. Now a museum, it contains a number of inventions and other attractive and practical items manufactured and used by former village inhabitants. The 1856 barn, 250 feet long, is said to be New Hampshire's largest. *Open Tues.-Sat. end of May-early Sept. Adults $1.50, children small charge.*

[155] *The display of suits of armor in the Medieval Hall of the Million Dollar Show-Schuller Museum makes clear that these tempered-steel garments were designed with sartorial style in mind as well as protection.*

[157] *The importance in Shaker life of simplicity and careful workmanship is reflected in everything they did, including the furniture. The emphasis is on clean, functional design and pleasing proportions.*

158. Franklin Pierce House *52 South Main St., Concord, N.H.* Pierce helped to build this French-style Victorian house while serving as President of the U.S. He lived here from his retirement in 1857 until his death in 1869. Much of his furniture, including his bed, can be seen along with 19th-century glassware, china, pictures and a library of private and official letters and other papers as well as some of his favorite books. *Open daily May–Nov.*

159. New Hampshire Historical Society Headquarters *30 Park St., Concord, N.H.* The society, which was founded in 1823, moved into this large granite building in 1912. Many lovely examples of old New Hampshire furniture, silver, ceramics and glassware are shown in changing exhibits. The Prentis Collection, comprising four 18th-century facsimile rooms, has displays of authentic New England antiques and portraits that recreate the domestic surroundings of a typical wealthy merchant. In the rotunda, built of imported marble, there is a restored Concord stagecoach, made in 1856 by the Abbot-Downing Company, the firm that supplied Wells Fargo & Company in the Civil War period. The library of more than 75,000 volumes features New England history and genealogy. Many of the papers of Daniel Webster, Franklin Pierce and other public figures from New Hampshire's past are kept in a manuscript section that includes 500,000 items. The society offers a series of lectures on historical subjects each year, and its publications include the quarterly magazine *Historical New Hampshire* and a newsletter. *Open Mon.–Sat. except holidays.*

160. New Hampshire State House *Main St., Concord, N.H.* Built of native granite, this impressive building was completed in 1819. Between 1864 and 1866 the structure was remodeled after the Hôtel des Invalides in Paris. A third story was added and the old dome replaced with the present elaborate one. An addition was completed in 1910 and an annex in 1939. The copper eagle on top of the dome is more than six feet high. It was installed in 1957 when the original eagle, dating from the building's first year, was removed to the adjacent New Hampshire Historical Society building. The state house currently accommodates about 400 members of the legislature, the largest body of its kind in the U.S. Inside, the senate chambers are decorated with murals depicting historical episodes relating to the state. They were painted in 1942 by New Hampshire artist Barry Faulkner. A collection of portraits of figures in state history can be seen in the corridors and larger offices. In the rotunda of the main building is a Hall of Flags where a number of old provincial and state regimental banners are displayed. In the basement is an exhibit of birds and wildlife found within the state. On the two acres of lawn stand statues of some of New Hampshire's most famous sons, including Daniel Webster, the brilliant lawyer, statesman and orator, and Franklin Pierce, the 14th President of the U.S. *Open Mon.–Fri.*

161. Currier Gallery of Art *192 Orange St., Manchester, N.H.* Named for a former governor of the state, this Renaissance-style limestone and marble building lends dignity to the fine collection it houses. Ground-

[159] *In the 19th century the Concord Coach gained a worldwide reputation because of its superior suspension system and durability. Thousands were sold throughout the United States and in Australia and Africa.*

floor displays are devoted mainly to the decorative arts and include a number of excellent examples of 18th- and 19th-century New Hampshire furniture. Works by the elder and younger Reveres as well as Samuel Edwards, Jacob Hurd and other Colonial silversmiths are represented along with Early American pewter and glassware; there are also several outstanding American paintings of the 19th and 20th centuries. On the upper floor are European painting and sculpture, ranging from the 14th to the 20th centuries. Included in the painting collection are canvases by Jacob van Ruisdael, Monet, Homer, Hopper, Andrew Wyeth and Picasso. *Open daily except holidays.*

162. First Parish Congregational Church *Hampstead Rd., East Derry, N.H.* Extensive changes have been made to this church since it was built in 1769. The steeple, which shows the influence of Wren, was added in the 1800s. Six fine stained-glass windows distinguish it from most other Colonial churches. Dr. Matthew Thornton, a signer of the Declaration of Independence, helped erect the original building. *Open Sun.*

163. Mystery Hill *Rte. 111, North Salem, N.H.* Archaeological investigations are still going on at this 15-acre site, where strange stone buildings, walls, wells and underground chambers suggest that a form of religious activity may have been practiced here about 2000 B.C. Among the many curiosities located on this hilltop are a 4½-ton sacrificial table, and a large winter solstice monolith upon which the sun sets each December 21 when viewed from the center of the site. The stone writings discovered here are thought to look like Phoenician symbols, while excavated crude stone tools and pottery bear a strong resemblance to late Neolithic artifacts unearthed in parts of Europe. *Open Sat.-Sun. Apr.-mid-June, daily mid-June-Oct. Adults $1.50, students 13-17 $1.25, children 6-12 small charge.*

164. Merrimack Valley Textile Museum *Massachusetts Ave., North Andover, Mass.* Three galleries in this brick building contain displays of carding engines, wool and flax wheels, spinning jennys, looms and other equipment once used in the manufacture of textiles. An exhibit, Wool Technology and the Industrial Revolution, traces the progress of cloth-making from the Revolution to 1876. Spinning and weaving are demonstrated on Sundays. *Open daily. Small charge Sun.*

165. North Andover Historical Society Headquarters *153 Academy Rd., North Andover, Mass.* The society maintains a two-building complex consisting of the Samuel Dale Stevens Memorial Building, built in 1932, and the Johnson Cottage of about 1795. The Memorial Building contains changing displays of Early American furniture from the Stevens collection of fine Chippendale, Queen Anne, Hepplewhite and Sheraton pieces. In the three-room cottage interesting examples of Colonial pewter, tools, cooking utensils and lighting devices are shown. *Open Sun. Small charge.*

166. Parson Barnard House *179 Osgood St., North Andover, Mass.* This house is a rare example of the architectural transition from 17th-century Elizabethan to 18th-century Georgian influences. Built about 1715 by the Reverend Thomas Barnard, the house with its period furnishings is preserved by the North Andover Historical Society. Among its attributes are the original staircase, delicate trim on the fireplace wall in the east chamber and the ornate pilastered chimney. *Open Sun. Small charge.*

[**161**] The Bootleggers, *a 1925 oil painting by Edward Hopper, shows a common sight on East Coast waters during Prohibition; chances were that an unknown boat running close to shore at night carried contraband.*

167. Stevens-Coolidge Place *137 Andover St., North Andover, Mass.* Set in 89 acres of woodland, lawns and formal gardens, this Colonial Revival house contains the furnishings of the last owner, Mrs. Helen Coolidge, who died in the 1950s. A barn and greenhouse are also located on the property. *Open Sun. Small charge.*

168. Newburyport, Mass.

In 1764, having become totally involved in maritime pursuits, Newburyport, at the mouth of the Merrimack River, broke away from the more rural town of Newbury. Most of its impressive buildings, and there are many throughout the Yankee City, were constructed during the 18th and 19th centuries.

Central Congregational Church *Titcomb and Pleasant Sts.* Built in 1861, this Italianate edifice stands on the same land as the original 1768 church. The steeple clock is known as Old Betsy, after its donor, Miss Betsy Gerrish from nearby Salisbury, who used to listen for its daily striking to set her watch. *Open daily.*

First Presbyterian Church *Federal and School Sts.* Known for years as the Old South Meetinghouse, this church dates from 1756 and is noted for its whispering gallery and an original slave pew. It contains a Revere bell purchased in 1803 and a tower clock installed in 1895. It is believed that in 1775, after the Battle of Lexington, the first company of volunteers to enlist in the Continental army was formed here, and

that later in the same year Benedict Arnold and his army worshiped in the church on their way to the unsuccessful attack on Quebec. The Reverend George Whitefield, a noted English evangelist, founded the congregation and was buried in 1770 in a crypt beneath the pulpit. The church contains some of his possessions, including two Bibles and a desk. *Open daily.*

High Street This historic thoroughfare, dating from the 1600s, runs between Atkinson Common, Newburyport, and Newbury where it is known as High Road. Outstanding examples of Early American and Federal architecture can be seen along its entire length.

KNAPP-HEALY HOUSE *47 High St.* The considerable talents of local shipbuilders are evident in this house, which has an intricately worked roof-balustrade design repeated in the front fence. Built in 1810 for Captain Benjamin Peirce, this is an imposing example of maritime Federal architecture.

CUSHING HOUSE *98 High St.* Maintained by the Historical Society of Old Newbury, this beautiful 1808 Federal brick house later became the home of young Caleb Cushing, a Massachusetts statesman. Cushing's friends included Franklin Pierce and Jefferson Davis, both of whom were guests here. Adjacent to a formal garden, the 17-room house contains fine collections of silver, china, portraits and marine items. The society holds special monthly exhibits. *Open Tues.-Sun. May-Oct. Small charge.*

LORD TIMOTHY DEXTER HOUSE *201 High St.* Built in 1771, this elegant combination of Georgian and Federal architecture was owned between 1796 and 1806 by an eccentric resident of the town who assumed noble rank. At one time, the grounds were filled with 45 statues, standing on high pedestals. The subjects varied from Adam and Eve to George Washington. The elaborate octagonal cupola is surrounded by a captain's walk.

LOWELL-TRACY-JOHNSON HOUSE *203 High St.* Built between 1772 and 1775 by John Lowell, this outstanding early-Federal-style house has been owned by the Johnson family since 1809. The exterior is typically symmetrical, but the rounded window tops are unusual.

HALE-KINSMAN-LEARY HOUSE *348 High St.* Thomas Hale built this frame structure in 1800; today it remains as an excellent example of a Federal town house. The painted wood fences with graceful urns topping the entrance posts are part of the original design.

SWETT-ILSLEY HOUSE *4 High Rd. (Newbury)* When this house served as the Blue Anchor Tavern, Washington, Adams, Lafayette and other public figures of Colonial times were entertained here. It was begun as a two-room cottage by Stephen Swett, a shoemaker, in 1670 and later enlarged by ship's carpenters. There are such interesting structural details as beveled ceiling beams and doors with distinctive locks and hand-wrought hinges. The former taproom contains a 10-foot fireplace, said to be the largest in New England. *Open Tues., Thurs., Sat. June-Sept. Small charge.*

DR. PETER TOPPAN HOUSE *5 High Rd.* Named for its builder, a physician who was an early graduate of Harvard, this handsome house was completed in 1697. The gambrel roof and double overhang are notable features of the brown-shingled building.

TRISTRAM COFFIN HOUSE *16 High Rd.* Eight generations of the Coffin family have lived in this frame house begun in 1651 by Tristram, a selectman and court representative. Fortunately, few changes were made in the structural details, which can still be admired along with the family furnishings. The house is owned by the Society for the Preservation of New England Antiquities. *Open Tues., Thurs., Sat. June-Sept. Small charge.*

SHORT HOUSE *39 High Rd.* Nathaniel Knight built this brick-ended clapboard house in 1717. Its exterior features include a beautiful central doorway, "12-over-12" windowpanes and old red trim. Large fireplaces and pine paneling in the rooms make an attractive setting for the period furniture. *Open Tues., Thurs., Sat. mid-June-mid-Sept. Small charge.*

MARKET SQUARE HISTORIC DISTRICT Actually the streets leading into the triangular area of Market Square, this is one of the last early-19th-century marketplaces where the original brick Federal buildings remain almost unaltered. The uniform three-story attached commercial row buildings, most of which had ground-floor shops, were built to conform with a building code enacted after a disastrous fire in 1811. The impact of the regulations can be seen in the exposed fire walls, which extend from basement to a point above rooftop between attached buildings. The two-story brick Market House (1823) contained grocers' and butchers' stalls until 1864 when it was permanently converted into the city's fire station. The hip roof and the pleasing balance achieved by the placement of windows lend a distinct dignity to this substantial structure. At the eastern end of the district stands the gray-granite Greek Revival Custom House built during 1834 and 1835. It was designed by Robert Mills, the first native-born architect to be trained in this country. Mills also designed several structures in Washington, D.C., including the Treasury Building and the Washington Monument. Almost all the buildings are now being sold by the Newburyport Redevelopment Authority, which is carrying out an extensive preservation and restoration program here.

Unitarian Church of the First Religious Society *26 Pleasant St.* Admired for its window frames, delicate cornice and elaborate steeple with a Revere bell, this 1801 church also has a superb fanlight over the main entrance. Inside are railed box pews, some of which contain drawers for the family meals that were eaten between morning and afternoon services. In front of the skillfully carved organ is a large 1797 English "Act of Parliament" clock, so called because of the short-lived tax levied on all clocks when William Pitt was prime minister. Exhibits by local artists are shown each month. *Open Sun. and early Aug.*

169. John Greenleaf Whittier Home *86 Friend St., Amesbury, Mass.* Eight rooms are open in this house where the famous poet lived from 1836 until his death in 1892. Of special interest is the Garden Room, where Whittier wrote "Snowbound" and other works in surroundings that remain unchanged. The house is owned by the Whittier Home Association, and is a National Historic Landmark. Children must be accompanied by an adult. *Open Tues.-Sat.*

170. Mary Baker Eddy Historic House *277 Main St., Amesbury, Mass.* The founder of Christian Science was a guest here for two short periods in 1868 and 1870. The house, with its unusual bowed roof, was built in the late 18th or early 19th century. Many of the original

[174] *Typical of early Colonial homes, the Clark House kitchen was the center of family life, serving as dining and living room as well as kitchen. Folding and collapsible furniture, in designs dating back to medieval times, was used to save space. The trestle table, for instance, may be easily dismantled, and when needed the oval back of the chair beside the settee can be dropped to become a table top. The stick-leg, or Windsor, furniture seen here was most popular in the Colonies. The design originated in 17th-century England (near the town of Windsor) and was used at first in gardens and on verandas.*

furnishings still decorate the rooms. *Open Tues.-Sun. May-Oct. Adults small charge.*

171. Rocky Hill Meetinghouse *4 Portsmouth Rd., Amesbury, Mass.* Considered one of the two best examples of a Colonial meetinghouse, this structure served a Congregational parish from 1785 to the late 19th century. Beautiful in its simplicity, it remains unchanged and is much admired for the interior woodwork and hardware. The pulpit and gallery are particularly interesting. Two or three services are held here in summer. *Open Wed.-Sat. June-Oct. Small charge.*

172. First Congregational Church of Hampton *127 Winnacunnet Rd., Hampton, N.H.* A unique pulpit associated with this parish since 1799 was rescued after many years of exposure outdoors and installed in this simply designed church, built in 1843. The church has been in continuous existence longer than any other in the state. *Open Sun.*

173. Exeter, N.H.

One industrial innovation after another brought the wealth that is reflected in the town's fine Colonial and Federal buildings. Although Exeter is still one of New Hampshire's manufacturing centers, it has retained the quiet beauty of another era.

Cincinnati Hall *Governor's Lane* This rambling frame home overlooking the Squamscott River was built by Nathaniel Ladd in 1721. Originally it was a two-story brick house, with two rooms on each side of a central entry. In 1747 it was enlarged by Ladd's cousin Daniel Gilman, who added a more elaborate porch and two great fireplaces, and covered the brick walls with clapboard. The house remained in the same family, except for a short time, until 1902 when it was purchased by the Society of the Cincinnati. On display are a table made in 1752 of two boards and Gilman family possessions such as a sampler, a coat of arms and a draft copy of the proposed Federal Constitution. A portrait of Washington attributed to Stuart can also be seen. *Open Tues., Thurs. May-Oct.*

Congregational Church *21 Front St.* This meetinghouse, completed in 1801, was the first in New Hampshire to blend Georgian refinements with the usual meetinghouse styling. The hip roof, cornices and Doric pilasters and entablatures are all noteworthy, and a tower over the entrance supports a fine octagonal belfry and dome. A Palladian window can be seen at the rear of the second story. *Open daily.*

Exeter Historical Society Headquarters *27 Front St.* The society's home, an 1831 brick building, was originally a bank but was later put to other uses. (A town member, now in his 90s, recalls attending kindergarten here in 1882.) Well-proportioned with its arched, recessed doorway balancing two Dutch-style gables and chimneys at either end, the structure appears now very much as it did when it was completed. The society maintains a small library and local history museum. *Open Thurs.*

Gilman Garrison House *12 Water St.* The original section of this interesting house was built near the end of the 17th century as a fortification against Indian attack. In 1772 John Gilman's grandson added a new wing. The sumptuous paneling and classic woodwork of the addition contrasts with the rough-hewn log walls and puncheon floors of the original structure. The rooms in the new wing are furnished as they were in the late 18th century. Among the original pieces is the crude desk that Daniel Webster used when he stayed here as a student at Phillips Exeter Academy.

Library of the Phillips Exeter Academy *Front St.* Opened in 1971, this building is destined to take its place as one of the world's best secondary school libraries. It can accommodate 250,000 volumes and seat 500 students. *Open Sept.-June except holidays.*

174. Clark House *South Main St., Wolfeboro, N.H.* Wide hemlock floor boards, massive hand-hewn oak beams and gunstock corner posts are notable features in this 1778 Cape Cod-style house with five fireplaces, period furniture and a fine pewter collection. Special exhibits of paintings, glass and pottery are sometimes held. *Open Mon.-Sat. July-Aug.*

[**180.** *Moffat-Ladd House*] *An exquisite example of Georgian architecture, the house, like most of that period, was designed by its owner and built by local carpenters. It remains essentially the same as when it was built in 1763.*

175. Libby Museum *N. Main St., Wolfeboro, N.H.* The late Henry Forrest Libby, a Boston dentist, established this museum in 1912 to house his impressive collection of minerals, fish, birds, mammals and Indian artifacts native to the Lake Winnipesaukee region. An amateur sculptor, painter and taxidermist, he designed and mounted many of the displays, including several interesting miniature landscapes. The Wolfe Room is devoted to the campaigns fought by Generals Wolfe and Montcalm during the French and Indian Wars. The museum frequently displays the work of local artists. *Open Tues.-Sun. late June-early Sept.*

176. New English Art Gallery and Studio *Charles and Liberty Sts., Rochester, N.H.* This Tudor-style, ivy-covered brick structure was built early in the 20th century and once served as an Episcopal church. It is currently the gallery and studio of a German-born expressionist artist, Frederick Solomon, internationally noted for his religious paintings as well as for landscapes and portraits. Exhibits are occasionally given by other professional artists from New England and New York. *Open daily June-Sept., Tues., Thurs., Sat., Sun. Oct.-May. Small charge.*

177. Annie E. Woodman Institute Museum *182-192 Central Ave., Dover, N.H.* This museum consists of three buildings, the oldest being the Damm Garrison House, which initially stood about three miles from its present location. The house was erected about 1682, and its original 14-inch squared timbers with musket ports are still intact; a northern section was added in 1712. Inside, displays include many old kitchen utensils, clothing, tools and an unusual twin cradle. The Woodman House, an 1818 brick building and former residence of the museum's donor, contains a collection of fossils, minerals, birds, mammals, marine life and other interesting aspects of natural history. In the Senator John P. Hale House, built in 1813 and once the home of the outspoken abolitionist who served in the U.S. Senate from the 1840s to 1865, there are many items of local historical importance, including pieces of pewter, navigational instruments and old furniture. Many Civil War weapons can be seen on the top floor. A "Napoleon" cannon is on the grounds. *Museum open Tues.-Sun., house open Tues.-Sun. May-Oct.*

178. First Parish Church *218 Central Ave., Dover, N.H.* This 1829 brick Congregational church has three lovely front windows with rounded tops, and an ornamental wooden steeple in which an octagonal lantern sits above a similarly shaped belfry. A tower clock was installed in 1835 and stone steps running the breadth of the facade were added in 1913. *Open daily.*

179. Ezekiel W. Dimond Library *University of New Hampshire, Durham, N.H.* This brick building was named for the university's first professor. Open to the general public, it contains more than half a million volumes, including a number of rare books and special collections. Displays are presented in the lobby and on the main floor. *Open daily.*

180. Portsmouth, N.H.

The atmosphere of New Hampshire's only seaport is reminiscent of Colonial times. Its winding streets and fine old houses hark back to the 1600s, when Portsmouth was called Strawbery Banke.

Governor John Langdon Mansion Memorial *143 Pleasant St.* This beautiful example of Georgian architecture was built in 1784 by John Langdon, patriot, governor of New Hampshire and first president of the U.S. Senate. The mansion is noted for its elegant interior; the hand-carved chimneypieces and stairway are especially impressive. The captain's walk on the hip roof is surrounded by an ornate wood railing, and the front portico is graced with four Corinthian columns. George Washington, John Hancock, General Lafayette and James Monroe are known to have been visitors here. An attractive garden is located on the grounds. *Open Tues.-Sat. June-Oct. Small charge.*

Jackson House *Northwest St.* Believed to be the oldest surviving house in New Hampshire, this clapboard saltbox was completed about 1664 by Richard Jackson, a shipbuilder, whose descendants lived here for over 250 years. Special features of the window frames are of interest, such as the sills, which project into the rooms. A collection of simple, functional furniture can be seen throughout the house. *Open Tues.-Sat. June-Sept. Small charge.*

John Paul Jones House *Middle and State Sts.* America's first naval hero did not own this house, but he lived here in 1777 while the sloop-of-war *Ranger* was being completed. He returned here once more in 1781 to await the launching of the 74-gun *America*. This elegant frame house built in 1758 by Captain Gregory Purcell, a prominent mariner, contains period furniture, china and silver. Tours are led by guides in Colonial costumes. *Open Mon.-Sat. mid-May-Sept. Small charge.*

Moffat-Ladd House *154 Market St.* In 1763 Captain John Moffat built this outstanding Georgian mansion for his son; it was later the home of General William Whipple, Moffat's son-in-law and a signer of

[**180.** *Strawbery Banke-Clark House*] *This house is a good example of how the colonists adapted the Georgian style—so popular in England during the 18th century—to their simple four-square dwellings. The exterior is classicized by the addition of pediments over the windows and a pilaster-supported pediment at the doorway. Beautifully restrained wainscoting has been added to make the formerly plain interior walls more interesting.*

the Declaration of Independence. It is now maintained by the National Society of the Colonial Dames in America. One of the first three-story houses in Portsmouth, its roof is crowned by a captain's walk. The central hallway, superb staircase and original wallpaper imported from Paris and a good collection of period furniture are among the attractions. A countinghouse (1800) and coach house are on the property, as is a 19th-century formal garden. *Open daily mid-May-mid-Oct. Small charge.*

North Congregational Church *Market Sq.* This example of early Victorian church architecture was built in 1854 on land occupied by an earlier church dating from 1712. Its massive white steeple carries considerable ornamentation and holds a clock. *Open Sun.*

Peirce Mansion *18 Court St.* This is one of the finest early Federal houses to survive the several fires that swept Portsmouth in the early 1800s. Built in 1799 by John Peirce, a merchant, its facade combines flamboyance with simplicity. A spiral staircase is among its typical Federal features. The house is owned by the Middle Street Baptist Church, to which it is adjoined, and is used as an educational center by the church.

Portsmouth Athenaeum *9 Market Sq.* This handsome Federal-style building is maintained by private membership. Its 26,000-volume library includes many rare books, pamphlets and manuscripts. Paintings of early Portsmouth days decorate the walls of the Adam-style reading room, whose collection of ship models includes the *Clovis,* carved in full rig from whalebone by French prisoners of war, and a 1749 Admiralty model of the H.M.S. *America. Open Thurs.*

St. John's Church *Chapel St.* This is one of the earliest Episcopal churches and the first brick church of any faith in the state. Built in 1808, it holds many unusual objects, including a mahogany chair believed to have been used by George Washington at a service in an earlier meetinghouse that served this parish. A 1717 Vinegar Bible, one of about 12 such volumes known to exist and so named for a misprint of "vineyard," can also be seen here. The rare Brattle pipe organ, imported from England prior to 1708, is the oldest such instrument in the U.S. The tower holds a French bell brought back by the captors of Louisbourg, Nova Scotia, in 1745. *Open daily.*

Sheafe Warehouse *Off Marcy St.* When John Paul Jones was equipping the *Ranger* here for service at sea in 1777, this building was already 72 years old. Carefully restored, it contains a fine collection of ship models and folk art relating to Portsmouth's marine heritage. The building is of structural interest because of its exposed frames. *Open daily June-mid-Sept.*

Strawbery Banke This is the original name for Portsmouth. Settled in 1630 by English colonists, this 10-acre area at the southern end of Portsmouth includes more than 30 late-17th-century-to-early-19th-century buildings in various stages of restoration. The Visitor Center regularly offers a color film on the settlement as well as occasional art and architectural exhibits. Demonstrations of spinning, weaving, smithing, boatbuilding and other crafts are a high point of tours. The following are some of the most interesting structures. *Open May-Oct. Adults $2.00, children under 12 small charge.*

CAPTAIN JOHN CLARK HOUSE *Jefferson St.* Built about 1750, this restored house exemplifies a restrained application of the generally elaborate Georgian style. The understatement is especially noticeable in the exterior cornices, while inside it is revealed in the plain though plentiful paneling, which includes folding window shutters. The front staircase features paneling that is more elaborate in detail.

CAPTAIN KEYRAN WALSH HOUSE *Washington St.* Workmanship is the outstanding characteristic of this Federal "double house," (one dwelling having two chimneys and a central hall). Wood is the material to which skilled craftsmen applied detailed carvings and paints. The hall stairway is a fine example, exhibiting both the restored marbleized paint and delicately turned wood balusters. *Open daily May-Oct. Adults $2.00, children small charge.*

CHASE HOUSE *Court St.* Recent work on this 1762 house eliminated many changes made in 1884 and restored to it the look of an affluent merchant's dwelling of the early 19th century. A handsome mid-Georgian structure with unusual exterior lines, its quoined corners, ornate doorways and the woodwork in several rooms are particularly impressive. Washington visited here in 1789 during a tour made shortly after his election to the Presidency.

DANIEL WEBSTER HOUSE *Hancock St.* The great lawyer and statesman rented this 1785 house from 1814 to 1816. Small and unpretentious, it has four rooms, a center chimney and four fireplaces. The roof is unusual, hipped at one end and gabled at the other where a two-story addition was once attached. Moved here in 1961, restoration of the house was supported partly with funds contributed by the state's schoolchildren.

GOVERNOR GOODWIN MANSION *Hancock St.* This early-19th-century mansion escaped destruction in 1963 when it was brought here from its original site in another part of town. It was sold in 1832 to Ichabod Goodwin, a local businessman and politician who served in the state legislature and as a Republican governor from 1859 to 1861. The mansion is of Federal design, but the portico with its Ionic columns is one of several later additions in the Greek Revival style. Other modifications include marble fireplace mantels and iron grates for coal which are distinctly Victorian. So also are Goodwin's former office and many of the furnishings throughout the house. Among the many original Federal elements are the front hall with its fine cornice, a spiral staircase and a lovely fanlight over the front door.

KINGSBURY HOUSE *93 State St.* Built at an intersection in about 1815, this house has two facades, one facing each street. Owned by expert carpenters Sam Kingsbury and Sam Kingsbury, Jr., it exhibits the quality of life enjoyed by Portsmouth's skilled craftsmen. Handmade items are sold here. *Open Mon.-Sat.*

[180. *Warner House*] *Elaborate Early American and English furniture in the upstairs parlor is an indication of the wealth of the owner. Compare this for example, with the simplicity of the John Clark House interior, p. 91.*

SHERBURNE HOUSE *Puddle Lane* The oldest house in Strawbery Banke, this interesting dwelling was begun about 1695 by Captain John Sherburne, a seaman, and completed a few years later by his son. The western half is earliest and consists of two rooms and an attic where exposed beams with decorative chamfers and "lambs' tongues" can be seen. The eastern section presents a different face with a lighter, less embellished frame, but with considerable ornamentation elsewhere, as exemplified by a decorative cornice over one of the fireplaces. The steep roof is typical of houses of this period, and small casement windows with triangular panes reflect a style popular until the early 1700s.

Thomas Bailey Aldrich Memorial *380 Court St.* Readers of Aldrich's *The Story of a Bad Boy* (1870) will remember this as the Nutter House, where many an escapade was planned by the book's young hero. Built in 1790 and owned by the author's grandfather, it contains Victorian furnishings and an interesting collection of signed letters, first editions and silver. *Open Mon.-Fri. June-Sept. Small charge.*

Warner House *150 Daniel St.* Believed to have been completed in 1716, this is one of the most magnificent 18th-century brick town houses in the U.S. Its superb early Georgian exterior and rich interior reveal the enormous wealth and impeccable taste of its original owner, the Scottish merchant Archibald Macpheadris. The woodwork is outstanding, particularly the marbleized paneling in the dining room. The house is furnished with authentic period pieces, including fine portraits of Warner family members by Joseph Blackburn. On the stair landing are murals depicting two of the Indian sachems presented to Queen Anne in 1710. In the mid-18th century, Governor Benning Wentworth conducted state affairs here during a short occupancy; General Lafayette was among many entertained here. The house is a Registered National Historic Landmark. *Open mid-May-mid-Oct. Small charge.*

Wentworth-Coolidge Mansion *Little Harbor Rd.* Originally a fisherman's house built in 1695, this mansion was enlarged in 1730 and 1750, assuming an H shape, and now consists of 40 rooms. It was once the official residence of Benning Wentworth, royal governor of New Hampshire from 1741 to 1766, and his large ground-floor council chamber can be seen. Presented to the state in 1954 by Mrs. Templeman Coolidge, it was restored in 1966 but is not furnished. Lilacs on the grounds are thought to be among the first brought from England to this country. *Open late June-early Sept. Small charge.*

Wentworth-Gardner House *140 Mechanic St.* Considered one of the finest examples of Georgian architecture in the nation, this frame structure was presented in 1761 to Thomas Wentworth (nephew of Governor Wentworth) as a wedding present from his mother. Three master carvers are said to have labored for 18 months on the interior trim alone, and outstanding cornices and medallions and fluted pilasters and Corinthian capitals can be seen throughout the halls and in the rooms. There are 10 fireplaces, some with ornate mantels and original inlaid Dutch tiles. The scenic wallpaper in the dining room is especially decorative. Carefully restored and fully furnished, this National Historic Landmark has had several owners, including Major William Gardner who bought it in

[**180.** *Wentworth-Gardner House*] *The symmetric simplicity of the facade, long windows, the quoins and wide clapboard rusticated to imitate stone—the chief material used in 18th-century English houses—are marks of the Georgian style at its height.*

1796 and the Metropolitan Museum of Art, which once considered moving it to Central Park in New York City. *Open Tues.-Sun. May-Oct. Small charge.*

181. Lady Pepperrell House *Rte. 103, Kittery Point, Me.* The widow of Sir William Pepperrell, who captured Louisbourg from the French in 1745, built this outstanding Georgian frame house in 1760. Noteworthy are the hip roof, handsome interior woodwork and fine Colonial furniture. The front door is flanked by a pair of two-story Ionic pilasters and is topped with two intricately carved dolphins, representing the sea on which the Pepperrell fortune in salt fish was based. The house is owned by the Society for the Preservation of New England Antiquities. *Open Tues.-Sat. mid-June-mid-Sept. Small charge.*

182. York, Me.

Dating back to the 1600s, York still retains much of the peaceful character of Colonial days. The picturesque village is unique among Colonial museums because its buildings are in their original surroundings.

Elizabeth Perkins House *South Side Rd.* The central portion of this Colonial house on the York River was built in 1686 and survived an Indian raid in 1692 when most of the dwellings in this area were burned. The front section added in 1732 includes a doorframe with well-executed Ionic pilasters. The windows throughout the house are interesting for their protective "Indian shutters," which slide closed from the inside. Other handsome interior details include wall stenciling in the drawing room, and wood paneling in the bedroom. The Victorian furniture throughout the house belonged to the last owner, Elizabeth Perkins, who bequeathed the house to the Society for the Preservation of Historic Landmarks, which she had founded. *Open daily July-mid-Sept. Small charge.*

Emerson-Wilcox House *Rte. 1A* This restored house has served at various times since 1740 as a private dwelling, tavern and post office. Period furnishings are on display in all the rooms. The center chimney contains an unusual passageway formed by flues from six fireplaces. *Open late May-Sept. Small charge.*

First Parish Congregational Church *York St.* A steep roof line is one of the few original details of this 1747 church on the village green. Substantial alterations were made in 1882, and further remodeling was completed in 1951. A handsome old weathercock still adorns the top of the spire.

Jefferds Tavern *Lindsay Rd.* Built about 1750 by Captain Samuel Jefferds in nearby Wells, this stagecoach stop served refreshments to passengers traveling between Kennebunk and York. It was systematically dismantled in 1939, reconstructed in its present location, facing the Old Burying Ground, and restored. Some of the interior paint and paneling is original. *Open daily end of May-mid-Sept. Adults small charge.*

Old Gaol Museum *Rte. 1A* The building consists of a stone cell built in 1720, and several additions completed by 1806, making it the oldest English civic building in the U.S. Its living quarters contain antique furniture and 1745 Bulman crewelwork bedhangings, the only complete American set known. A special exhibit is given for one month each summer. *Open daily end of May-Sept. Small charge.*

[**182.** *Old Gaol*] *Shown here is the bedroom occupied by the resident turnkey. The gaoler's quarters are quite luxurious, with fine furniture, pewter, pottery and porcelain. (The dungeons are considerably sparser.)*

183. Hamilton House *Vaughan's Lane, South Berwick, Me.* This Georgian frame mansion was built about 1785 by Colonel Jonathan Hamilton, a West India trader, whose wharves once lay below the house on the Salmon Falls River. Rose and scroll pediments above dormer windows, a handsome hip roof and four tall chimneys are among the architectural attractions. John Paul Jones occasionally visited this house, which is now a National Historic Landmark. A garden is maintained here. *Open Wed.-Sat. June-Sept. Small charge.*

184. Jewett Memorial *Portland St., South Berwick, Me.* Built about 1774, this frame house is an interesting example of Colonial architecture. The staircase, interior paneling and early wallpapers are especially handsome. The house was owned by Captain Theodore Jewett, grandfather of the writer Sarah Orne Jewett, born here in 1849. She wrote most of her books here, and her bedroom-sitting room has been kept just as she left it. The memorial is administered by the Society for the Preservation of New England Antiquities. *Open Wed.-Sat. June-Sept. Small charge.*

185. Barn Gallery of the Ogunquit Art Association *Shore Rd. and Bournes Lane, Ogunquit, Me.* In addition to the permanent display of the Hamilton Easter Field collection of modern art, the works of many contemporary northeastern New England artists of the Ogunquit Art Association can be seen in monthly exhibits here. Next to the gallery is an outdoor sculpture court. Lectures, workshops, demonstrations, concerts and films on art are offered by the association as part of a diversified program. *Open daily mid-June-mid-Sept.*

186. Brick Store Museum *105-117 Main St., Kennebunk, Me.* Dating from 1824, the main building, originally a store, contains an outstanding collection of ship models, kitchen utensils and other features of local historic import. The remaining buildings serve as art galleries and provide space for lectures, auctions and workshops in painting, embroidery and weaving. *Open Tues.-Sat. Jan.-Feb., Apr.-Dec. Small charge.*

[187] *This 1905 open-car electric trolley, made of wood, used to carry New Haven crowds to the Yale football games. Restored, it now takes visitors seated on the crosswise benches on a scenic mile-and-a-half ride.*

187. Seashore Trolley Museum *Log Cabin Rd., Kennebunkport, Me.* More than 70 U.S., Canadian and foreign electric trolleys are assembled here. Weather permitting, visitors can enjoy rides on cross-bench open-air trolleys. *Open daily mid-June-early Sept., Sat.-Sun. early Sept.-mid-June. Small charge for rides.*

188. South Congregational Church *Temple St., Kennebunkport, Me.* Built in 1824, this church has a handsome multifaced clock in an elaborate bell tower. Services are held on the second floor. The ground floor is now a gallery for the work of the established local artists. *Open daily.*

189. York Institute Museum *375 Main Street, Saco, Me.* Incorporated in 1867, this museum has a fine collection of 18th- and 19th-century furniture, silver, paintings and manuscripts. Among its furnishings are a Hepplewhite sideboard, Sheraton chest of drawers and 98-piece set of 1810 Spode china. *Open Tues.-Sat.*

190. Portland, Me.

On this site in 1775 the town of Falmouth was burned by the British. Here in the sheltered harbor the seaport of Portland developed and became Maine's first capital. The fine old Federal houses were built by prosperous merchants and manufacturers in the following century.

Cape Elizabeth Lighthouse *Two Lights Rd. (Off Rte. 77), Cape Elizabeth* This lighthouse dates from 1828 when its first keeper was appointed by President John Quincy Adams. Consisting originally of two rubblestone towers and known as Two Lights, it was modified in the 1920s to a single beacon that rises 67 feet high and is visible at sea for 17 miles.

Cathedral Church of St. Luke *143 State St.* This was the first Episcopal church in the U.S. to serve as a cathedral from the time of its completion. Built of stone in 1868 in Gothic Revival style, it features a carved-oak reredos. The octagonal Emmanuel Chapel, built in 1905 with a handsome interior of mahogany, has as its alterpiece *The American Madonna,* painted by John La Farge. *Open daily.*

Cathedral of the Immaculate Conception *190 Cumberland Ave.* Completed in 1869, this red-brick cathedral's exterior reflects ornate Victorian tastes. An 18-section Munich stained-glass window depicts episodes in the life of the Virgin Mary. *Open daily.*

First Parish Church *425 Congress St.* The oldest stone building in Maine, this Unitarian meetinghouse was planned without the assistance of architects and dedicated in 1826. The parish itself was founded in 1674. The main entrance opens directly into the base of the tower. A solid carved mahogany pulpit and a superb crystal chandelier were installed in 1826. The American poet Henry Wadsworth Longfellow worshiped here. *Open Tues. July-Aug., daily Sept.-June.*

Portland Head Light *Off Shore Rd., Portland Harbor* In 1787 George Washington ordered the construction of this rubblestone lighthouse, one of four Colonial lighthouse towers built so well that they have never required any rebuilding. It measures 89 feet above the ground and 120 feet above the water. First lighted in 1791, this is one of the oldest beacons on the Atlantic coast. It served as the inspiration for many poems by Longfellow. *Open daily.*

Portland Museum of Art *111 High St.* Excellent collections of paintings, drawings, prints and sculpture, primarily by 19th and 20th century Americans, are shown on two floors of the Sweat Memorial Building. The collection includes works by Marsh, Steichen, Davies and Higgins, along with Andrew Wyeth's *Broad Cove Farm* and Gaston Lachaise's *Standing Nude.* An impressive group of paintings done between 1820 and 1920 by local artists known as the Portland Painters are also on exhibit.

MCLELLAN-SWEAT MANSION The adjoining Federal-style McLellan-Sweat mansion was completed in 1801 for Hugh McLellan, a shipping magnate, and in 1908 was willed to the Portland Society of Art. Outstanding interior details include a flying staircase and a second-story Palladian window. Although little of the furniture is original to the restored brick mansion, there are many handsome Queen Anne, Hepplewhite, Chippendale and other early pieces. There is a collection of 19th-century glass with examples of the rare Portland glass, a local product produced for only 10 years (1863-73). *Open Tues.-Sun. except holidays. Small charge for mansion.*

Victoria Mansion (Morse-Libby House) *109 Danforth St.* This outstanding example of opulent Victorian architecture was completed in 1863 for Ruggles Morse, a New Orleans hotel owner. A two-story brownstone dwelling, topped by a three-story tower, it reflects an unusual blending of Greek, Italian Renaissance and Romanesque styling. Its well-preserved interior displays much decorative woodwork, including a handsome mahogany flying staircase with more than 300 hand-carved balusters. The painted wall and ceiling medallions and the seven carved Italian marble fireplace mantelpieces are of particular interest. *Open Tues.-Sat. mid-June-mid-Oct. Small charge.*

Wadsworth-Longfellow House *487 Congress St.* Longfellow spent his early life in this house, which was built in 1785 of bricks shipped from Philadelphia by his grandfather, General Peleg Wadsworth. It was Portland's first brick house; its plain design is embellished only by a Doric portico over the front entrance. The third floor and hip roof were added in 1815 following a fire. The original furnishings reflect the tastes of several generations of the poet's family, which occupied the house from the time it was built until it was willed to the Maine Historical Society in 1901 by Longfellow's sister. On display are possessions and documents of the family. *Open Mon.-Fri. June-Sept. Small charge.*

191. Daniel Marrett House *Standish, Me.* This large two-and-a-half-story house, built in 1789, is a well-preserved homestead typical of the region and period, with early furniture and interesting family portraits. It takes its name from the Reverend Mr. Marrett, who bought the house in 1796. During the War of 1812, coin from Portland banks was stored in the basement of the house when it was feared that the British might take the city. *Open Sun., Mon. June-Sept.*

192. Sunday River Bridge *Off Rtes. 5 and 26, Newry, Me. (4 mi N.W. of Bethel)* Completed in 1872, this covered bridge was constructed in two halves. Also known as the Artist's Bridge, it is Maine's most frequently painted and photographed covered span.

[**190.** *Cape Elizabeth Lighthouse*] *The 25 or so lighthouse stations that existed in the U.S. when this one was built in 1828 used oil lamps. Today some 10,000 lighthouses dot our shores; most now use electric lights.*

[**190.** *Victoria Mansion*] *The flying staircase in the reception hall manages to dominate the eclectic decor. Each of the 337 balusters supporting the railing required one man one week to complete.*

[**190.** *Wadsworth-Longfellow House*] *In 1841 the poet Longfellow sat at this old schoolmaster's desk to write "The Rainy Day," a poem most remembered for the line "Into each life some rain must fall."*

193. Wire Bridge *Off Rte. 146, New Portland, Me.* Steel cables imported from England in 1842 still support traffic on what is believed to be the first suspension bridge built in the U.S. Once referred to as Maine's Fool Bridge, it sways uniquely when crossed.

194. Red Schoolhouse Museum *Rtes. 2 and 4, West Farmington, Me.* A vanished aspect of rural education is preserved in this restored 1852 building, which served as a one-room schoolhouse for more than 100 years. Visitors can observe the original "punkin'" pine wainscoting, an unusual arched ceiling, wood desks, old schoolbooks and other items associated with the three Rs. The vestibule serves as a county information center. *Open July-early Sept.*

195. Colby College *Mayflower Hill, Waterville, Me.* Maine's second oldest college occupies 600 acres.

BIXLER ART AND MUSIC CENTER This building houses an art museum and studio facilities. The art museum has a fine permanent collection which includes works by Renoir, as well as Copley, Stuart, Homer and Andrew Wyeth. The Montague Sculpture Court displays William Zorach's impressive *Mother and Child. Open daily Sept.-May, Mon.-Sat. June-Aug.*

COLBY COLLEGE LIBRARY This imposing brick building contains over 300,000 volumes. The library's Edward Arlington Robinson Room, named for Maine's greatest poet, holds his personal books and papers as well as one of the best Thomas Hardy collections in the U.S. The modern Irish collection includes letters and signed works by Yeats, O'Casey and Joyce. *Open Mon.-Fri. June-Aug., daily Sept.-May.*

196. Augusta, Me.

Located on the Kennebec River, Augusta has been the capital of Maine since 1832. John Alden and Captain Miles Standish, immortalized by Longfellow, were among the original settlers of the colony founded here in 1628.

Fort Western Museum *Bowman St.* Benedict Arnold, Aaron Burr, Paul Revere and other Colonial notables stopped at this fort built in 1754 on the east bank of the Kennebec as an armed trading post. The last remaining pre-Revolutionary fort in Maine, its original building was augmented in 1921 by reproduction of the blockhouses and a stockade. The museum shows military and naval items, Indian relics and early tools and features 18th-century period rooms. *Open daily mid-May-early Sept. Small charge.*

[**196.** *Fort Western*] *The first Pilgrims at Plymouth, deeply in debt to a London company, built a trading post here around 1625 in order to barter with the Indians. Their descendants built Fort Western on the same site in 1754.*

[**196.** *Maine State Capitol*] *A proponent of classic style, architect Charles Bulfinch made use of ancient forms (cupola, round arch, Greek columns) in the many public buildings he designed throughout New England.*

James G. Blaine House *Capitol and State Sts.* This 1830 frame house, in the Classic Revival style, was the home of the Speaker of the House of Representatives (1869-75), Secretary of State (1889-92) and unsuccessful Republican candidate for the Presidency (1884). In 1919 it was presented to the state and has served ever since as the governor's mansion. The library has been restored to its original appearance, and there is a fine collection of paintings and 19th-century furniture. Among the mementos is a pass issued to Blaine in Lincoln's handwriting. *Open Mon.-Fri.*

Maine State Capitol *Capitol and State Sts.* Set on 34 acres, this massive building of native Hallowell granite was completed in 1832. Designed by the Boston architect Charles Bulfinch, it was twice remodeled and enlarged, each time retaining the impressive Bulfinch facade. The original cupola was replaced in the early 1900s by the present dome, which supports a gilt-copper figure of Wisdom. Battle flags from Maine regiments that have served in several wars are displayed in the rotunda, and portraits of many of the state's most distinguished citizens, including a number of former governors, are shown in the corridors and halls. The building overlooks the State Park. *Open Mon.-Fri.*

STATE OF MAINE LIBRARY-MUSEUM-ARCHIVES BUILDING This modern granite structure on the grounds of the State Capitol was dedicated in 1971. Much of its space is devoted to public exhibits associated with Maine's past and present. A library, including a large reading room and a separate State of Maine room, provides space for almost half a million volumes. The museum's extensive collections, formerly housed in the

State Capitol, include a broad range of wildlife, birds, fish and minerals native to Maine. *Open Mon.-Fri.*

St. Mary's Church *41 Western Ave.* An English Gothic architectural style is evident in this granite Catholic church built in 1927. An impressive spire rises to the right of the main entrance. A granite tablet on the grounds perpetuates the memory of 21 priests who served in this area from 1611 to the present. *Open daily.*

197. Hallowell Historic District *Hallowell, Me.* Situated below Augusta on the Kennebec River and encompassing more than 200 acres, this is a fine example of a 19th-century river port from which ships once sailed for the West Indies. The city of Hallowell, first settled in 1754, is still a place where people live and work while many of the buildings are being restored by private citizens. An interesting example of adaptive-use preservation is Row House, on Second Street, consisting of five identical attached dwellings. Also called the Antique Center of Maine, Hallowell is known for its large number of waterfront antique shops. The historic district is listed in the National Register of Historic Places. *Open daily.*

198. Cumston Hall *Main St., Monmouth, Me.* Designed and principally decorated by Harry H. Cochrane, a talented man with limited architectural training, Cumston Hall was built as a community hall in 1900. The building houses the Cumston Public Library and town offices, as well as a small theater remarkable for its flawless acoustics and elaborate frescos. Shakespearean plays have been presented in it since 1970. The exterior is distinctive for the ornamented tower and rhythmic groupings of Romanesque windows. *Library open Wed., Sat.; theater open daily July-Aug.*

199. Bates College *Lewiston, Me.* Originally Maine State Seminary, Bates College was chartered in 1864.

BATES COLLEGE CHAPEL *College St.* Built of granite in soft shades of tan and amber, the details of this English Gothic-style church were influenced by King's College Chapel in England. The intellectual tradition of the West is represented in stained-glass windows by the figures of Aristotle, Erasmus, Shakespeare, Goethe and Marie Curie. *Open daily Sept.-June.*

HATHORN HALL *Andrews Rd.* This brick building was opened in 1857; today its handsome classical exterior remains almost unchanged. The original bell still rings for classes. *Open Mon.-Fri. Sept.-June.*

200. Ss. Peter and Paul Church *27 Bartlett St., Lewiston, Me.* Of modified French Gothic design, this Catholic church is 230 feet long, with twin towers that rise 180 feet above the ground. It is the largest parish church in Maine. *Open daily.*

201. Shaker Village *Rte. 26, Poland Spring, Me.* This is one of the last surviving communities of its kind in America. Four of its 17 buildings are open for guided tours, including a 1794 meetinghouse with the original wood intact and the only remaining Shaker herb house. The Shakers are renowned for the elegant proportions, clean lines and functional beauty of the tools, furniture and buildings they designed and made. A library holds a large collection of manuscripts and photographs relating to this religious sect. *Open Tues.-Sat. end of May-Sept. Small charge.*

202. Old Meeting House on the Hill *Hillside St., Yarmouth, Me.* This outstanding example of early meetinghouse architecture was built in 1796. The unusual front windows have bluntly pointed tops and delicately interlaced sash bars. Above the square belfry is an octagonal stage with the same interesting windows. The 100-foot spire served as a landmark to ships entering the harbor. *Open Wed. July-Aug.*

[201] *Shakers believed that beauty derives from order and function. They strove in their work to make this definition visible and they succeeded, as may be seen in this study room. Every item of furniture—designed and handmade by Shakers—serves a specific purpose and each is devoid of superficial detail. For this reason the plaster walls are bare (pictures were specifically forbidden) and there is nothing to be seen that does not meet their high standards.*

203. Bowdoin College *Brunswick, Me.* Longfellow, Hawthorne and President Pierce were graduates of this private college, which was founded in 1794.

BOWDOIN COLLEGE CHAPEL The Romanesque structure of undressed granite, completed in 1855, has twin towers and spires that rise 120 feet. One of these towers contains a bell; 11 chimes were installed in the other in 1924. The interior, which follows the plan of English college chapels, has black walnut woodwork, and on the walls are displayed 12 large paintings depicting scenes from the Old and New Testaments.

BOWDOIN COLLEGE MUSEUM OF ART *Walker Art Building* The 1891 building is based on the designs of two Renaissance structures in Florence, Italy. Among the interior details completed especially for the museum are a bronze relief by Daniel Chester French plus murals by four 19th-century American artists: Elihu Vedder, Abbot Thayer, John La Farge and Kenyon Cox. An important group of portraits by Copley, Stuart, Trumbull and other early American artists, as well as major works by Eakins, Homer and Andrew Wyeth are on display. *Open daily.*

[208] *An unknown builder designed this fine Federal house, using drawings from Asher Benjamin's* American Builder's Companion *for the entry and cornice and his own ideas for the Palladian window and fanlight.*

204. First Parish Church *Maine and Bath Sts., Brunswick, Me.* This early Gothic Revival structure, designed by Richard Upjohn, was built in 1846. During a service here in 1851 Harriet Beecher Stowe was inspired to write *Uncle Tom's Cabin,* and in 1875 Longfellow read from the pulpit a poem to commemorate the 50th anniversary of his graduation from nearby Bowdoin College. From 1806 until 1966, except during World War II, all the Bowdoin Baccalaureate and Commencement services were held here or in the earlier building on the same site. *Open Sun.*

205. Elijah Kellogg Congregational Church *Rte. 1, South Harpswell, Me.* Named for its first minister, this church with its arched doorway reveals the skills of the local shipbuilders who completed it in 1843. The steeple, soaring more than 100 feet high, still serves as a landmark for yachtsmen. *Open daily.*

206. Phippsburg Congregational Church *Parker Head Rd., Phippsburg Center, Me.* Scarcely altered since its completion in 1802, with white raised pews trimmed in mahogany, this is one of New England's most beautiful Colonial-style churches. It is located on a knoll above the Kennebec River and adjacent to a massive linden planted before the Revolution. *Open Sun. Jan.-May, daily June-Sept., Sun. Oct.-Dec.*

207. Bath Marine Museum *963 Washington St., Bath, Me.* An 1844 classical-style mansion houses a nautical museum where the history of southern Maine shipbuilding is recalled. Featuring the 19th-century age of sail, many models, paintings, photographs, dioramas and related displays explain the area's contributions to an industry that began here in 1607. Among the 32 exhibit rooms is an imaginative children's room with items labeled "Please Touch." *Open daily end of May-mid-Oct. Small charge for mansion and shipyard.*

PERCY & SMALL SHIPYARD *263 Washington St.* The shipyard has been restored by the Marine Research Society of Bath to its appearance during the period 1894-1920, when seven of the 12 six-masted schooners launched in the U.S. were built there. This is the only surviving American yard where large wooden sailing vessels were built. Five of the original buildings are intact. The indoor exhibits show period machinery and tools and 15 small craft once active off the Maine coast. *Open daily end of May-early Sept.*

208. Nickels-Sortwell House *Maine and Federal Sts., Wiscasset, Me.* The imposing facade of this three-story 1807 mansion includes delicate Corinthian portico pilasters that frame an elaborate front door. A Palladian window and furnishings of the period complement the Federal styling of this house, which belongs to the Society for the Preservation of New England Antiquities. *Open Tues.-Sat., June-Sept. Small charge.*

209. Fort Edgecomb Memorial *Off Rte. 1, North Edgecomb, Me.* One of the few remaining blockhouses in the state, this weathered timber structure was built in 1808 to protect Wiscasset Harbor, then the most important shipping center north of Boston. Patterned after old English forts, Edgecomb has the distinction of never having had a shot fired from its octagonal tower. *Open daily end of May-early Sept. Small charge.*

210. St. Patrick's Church *Academy Rd., Newcastle, Me.* Constructed of native brick in 1808, this is the oldest surviving Catholic church in New England. It has a Revere bell, the original altar and much of the original woodwork. *Open daily.*

211. Chapman-Hall House *Main St., Damariscotta, Me.* A fragrant herb garden adjoins this village farmhouse, whose high windows meet the eave of a sloping roof. Built in 1754, the kitchen still has its original whitewashed walls. Notable wainscoting and paneling can be seen along with antique furnishings and exhibits of early craft tools. Exhibitions change yearly. *Open Tues.-Sat. mid-June-mid-Sept. Small charge.*

212. Boothbay Theater Museum *Rte. 27 (Wiscasset Rd.), Boothbay, Me.* This is one of the few theater museums in the U.S. Its collection encompasses playbills, autographs, costumes and other memorabilia associated with great stage performers from the 18th century on, including Sarah Bernhardt, Edwin and John Wilkes Booth and Katharine Cornell. Special exhibits are presented each year. The museum is next to the Boothbay Playhouse. *Open Mon.-Sat. June-Sept.*

213. Grand Banks Schooner Museum *100 Commercial St., Boothbay Harbor, Me.* Grand Banks fishing equipment is displayed here. Guided tours can be taken on the *Sherman Zwicker,* a 142-foot dory schooner, and the 88-foot *Seguin,* the nation's oldest wooden steam tugboat. *Open Sat., Sun. end of May-mid-June, daily mid-June-mid-Sept., Sat., Sun. mid-Sept.-mid-Oct. Small charge.*

214. Ancient Pemaquid Restoration *Pemaquid Beach, Me.* Recovery of fragments of English and European artifacts such as pottery, coins and tableware, plus the unearthing of several building foundations, tell a story of the settlement established on this peninsula in the early 17th century. A deed indicates that the Indian chief Samoset was paid 50 beaver skins for the Pemaquid Peninsula in 1625. The Pemaquid colony occupied an important strategic position, and it is known that wood forts constructed here in 1630 and 1677 were burned by the Indians and replaced in 1692 by the first stone fort built in New England (see below). Visitors can observe archaeologists still at work or browse through the small museum which contains more than 30,000 of the items found in the vicinity. *Open daily end of May-early Sept. Small charge for museum.*

215. Fort William Henry Memorial *Pemaquid Beach, Me.* This circular stone fort, a reconstruction, was originally built in 1692 by the first royal governor of Massachusetts, Sir William Phipps. Although it was the largest and strongest stone fort of its day, the French and Indians captured and destroyed it in 1696. Various artifacts excavated from the remains of the nearby 17th-century English settlement can be seen here. *Open daily end of May-early Sept. Small charge.*

216. Olson House Museum *Pleasant Point, Cushing, Me.* Andrew Wyeth used this 1800 seacoast farmhouse as a studio from 1940 until 1968 and created more than 200 major works here. During that time it was occupied by the owner, Christina Olson, who was the subject for one of Wyeth's best-known paintings, *Christina's World.* Displayed are some 70 Wyeth paintings, drawings and sketches, all of which relate to the house. *Open Tues.-Sat. mid-June-mid-Oct.*

217. Montpelier *Rte. 1, Thomaston, Me.* This is a faithful reconstruction of the mansion built in 1794 by General Henry Knox, the first Secretary of War and founder of West Point. Its 17 rooms are filled with fine furniture, most of which belonged to Knox. Among the many impressive interior details is an arched flying staircase with intricate balusters accurately copied from the French originals. There are a mirrored bookcase believed to have belonged to Marie Antoinette, a traveling chest presented by Lafayette, silverware, rugs, china and three excellent grandfather clocks. The imposing two-story mansion is crowned by a decorative balustrade on the roof, and steps rise to an elliptical front-entrance facade. *Open daily end of May-Sept. Small charge.*

218. William A. Farnsworth Library and Art Museum *Elm Street, Rockland, Me.* Completed in 1948, this three-story brick building houses an impressive collection of 19th- and 20-century American paintings, prints, drawings and sculpture. Art relating to Maine and the sea is represented by the works of several artists, including Homer and three generations of Wyeths. *Her Room* is one of 12 original Andrew Wyeth paintings displayed here. The first-floor library features volumes on Maine and its people. *Open daily June-Aug., Tues.-Sun. Sept.-May.*

FARNSWORTH HOMESTEAD The donor of the museum, Lucy C. Farnsworth, spent her life in this Greek Revival mansion built about 1840. Its appointments all belonged to the original family and include marble-faced fireplaces and black-walnut Victorian furniture. *Open daily June-mid-Sept.*

219. Penobscot Marine Museum *Main and Church Sts., Searsport, Me.* Three 19th-century homes and the Old Town Hall now house superb collections of shipping and whaling memorabilia. Among the many displays are those of ship models, a variety of interesting small boats, navigational instruments, harpoons and ship-building tools. A research library, with charts and log books, reflects Maine's maritime history. There is also a remarkable collection of pressed glass. *Open daily June-Sept. Small charge.*

[219] *Sailors often spent their leisure time carving pieces like the ivory scrimshaw above. All the displays in this museum evoke the era when Maine was the center of shipping in this country and there was enough business for eight shipyards in Searsport alone.*

220. University of Maine Art Collection *Carnegie Hall, College Ave., Orono, Me.* This collection of more than 1500 original works of art in all media is displayed throughout the public areas of some 90 buildings on the Orono campus. The emphasis is on American artists, including Whistler, Cassatt, Benton and Hopper, and on Maine artists in particular, such as Homer, Hartley, Marin and Zorach. Among the European artists represented are Chagall, Goya, Cézanne, Degas and Picasso. Located in Gallery Two of Carnegie Hall is the Artists of Maine exhibition, a continuous but constantly changing multimedia display of a single work by each of 75 artists currently active in the state. Seven exhibits are given each month during the academic year; a summer arts festival takes place in July and August. *Open Mon.-Fri.*

221. Fort Knox Memorial *Rte. 174, S.W. of Bucksport, Me.* A northeastern boundary dispute between the U.S. and Britain was the reason for starting this granite fort on the Penobscot River in 1844. Work was halted in 1864, and the building was never completed, but existing underground stairways, circular stairs and curved brick arches reveal considerable skill in masonry. Named for Henry Knox, the Revolutionary War general, this is one of the largest forts of its kind in the nation. *Open daily May-Oct. Small charge.*

222. First Parish Church *Castine, Me.* This church, begun in 1790, is the oldest church building in eastern Maine. It stands in a beautiful setting by the town Common. It has a Bulfinch-type tower and a bell cast by Joseph Revere, which replaced the Paul Revere original. *Open daily July-Aug.*

223. Fort George Memorial *Castine, Me.* The British built this fort in 1779 to protect their Canadian interests during the American Revolution, and it was the last fort they abandoned at its close. In the War of 1812 they repaired and reoccupied the fortification, but in 1815 they were forced to blow it up. The original moat and earthworks can be seen as can the 1962 reconstruction of ramparts, barracks and a magazine. *Open daily end of May-early Sept.*

224. Colonel Black House *W. Main St., Ellsworth, Me.* Colonel John Black, a land agent, built this mansion in 1802, and three generations of his family have lived here. Period furniture and a graceful spiral staircase can be seen on guided tours of the two-story brick house. Standing on 300 acres with many old trees and a formal garden, the property includes a carriage house with a collection of old sleighs and carriages. *Open Mon.-Sat. June-mid-Oct. Small charge.*

225. Ellsworth City Library *46 State St., Ellsworth, Me.* Known as the Tisdale house, this 1817 building has served as a library since 1898. It is a classic example of the Federal style and has Palladian windows and a cupola. *Open Tues.-Sat.*

226. First Congregational Church *Church St., Ellsworth, Me.* Widely considered Maine's best example of Greek Revival church architecture, the building has a handsome portico supported by six Ionic columns. The original steeple was replaced in 1971 by an exact copy in steel and fiber glass. The pipe organ was presented by Washington's aide-de-camp, Colonel John Black, who worshiped here. *Open daily.*

227. Robert Abbe Museum of Stone Age Antiquities *Sieur de Monts Spring, Bar Harbor, Me.* Established in the 1920s, this interesting one-room museum stands in a wooded section of Acadia National Park. It holds Indian artifacts which include intricate beadwork, baskets and ancient stone tools of such local tribes as the Penobscot and the Passamoquoddy. Several well-designed dioramas illustrate the seasonal activities of Stone Age Indians. Informative talks are given several times each day. *Open daily June-Sept.*

228. Sonogee Mansion *Eden St., Bar Harbor, Me.* Patterned after an Italian villa, this tile-roofed, stucco, 40-room mansion echoes the wealth and grandeur once associated with the summer resort. Built in 1903, its opulent interior features a staircase of solid marble and hand-painted French wallpaper. One of its owners was A. Atwater Kent, the radio magnate of the 1920s, and many of his Oriental rugs, antiques and paintings are

[220] The Elms *is a large (3 by 4½ foot) oil painting by George Inness (1825-94), one of the most important landscape painters in 19th-century America. It is typical of his work in that a central tree divides foreground from background, and there are no people in the scene. Inness was a member of the Hudson River School; this view is probably a reminiscence of rural New York or Pennsylvania.*

[231] *Roosevelt's Dutch Colonial summer "cottage" on Campobello Island was a wedding gift from his mother. FDR spent boyhood summers on the island and returned with his own family before and during his Presidency. The house, spacious but unpretentious, is maintained as it was when the Roosevelts enjoyed its casual atmosphere.*

still here. Six acres surround this house, and several formal gardens are maintained. *Open daily June–mid-Oct. Adults $1.50, students small charge.*

229. Ruggles House *Main St., Columbia Falls, Me.* One of New England's most beautiful flying staircases (attached only at top and bottom) is among the interesting features in this house built in 1818. Elegant and graceful handcarvings done with a penknife by an English craftsman include intricate rope beading over the fireplaces. The period furnishings and detailing of the exterior trim show the same delicacy of design. *Open daily June–mid-Oct. Small charge.*

230. Burnham Tavern *Main and Free Sts., Machias, Me.* Here in 1775 a band of volunteers planned the capture of the H.M.S. *Margaretta* in what is called the "Lexington of the Sea." Built five years earlier, this charming gambrel-roofed building contains documents, clothing, weapons and furniture of the periods from 1770 to 1830. The tavern has been maintained by the Daughters of the American Revolution since 1910. *Open Mon.–Sat. June–Sept. Small charge.*

231. Roosevelt Campobello International Park *Campobello Island, N. of Lubec, Me.* The beloved summer home of Franklin D. Roosevelt is preserved almost exactly as it was during the years he vacationed here. Built in Dutch Colonial style, the 34-room red clapboard house contains many articles and pieces of furniture closely related to Roosevelt's private and political life. In his study can be seen the leather chair he sat in at Cabinet meetings, china from the White House and a breakfront holding several volumes from his unusual collection of miniature books. The rest of the house is furnished as it was when the Roosevelt family lived here, including the furniture in the master bedroom where Roosevelt lay in 1921 after he contracted polio. Although the property originally included about nine acres, it now consists of a 2700-acre tract on the southern end of Campobello Island, which is part of New Brunswick, Canada. Several trails, lookouts and picnic areas have been developed by the park commission, a unique body consisting of three American and three Canadian members. A short film entitled *Beloved Island* is shown every half hour at the reception center. *Open daily mid-May–mid-Oct.*

232. Eastport, Me.
Champlain made contact with an Algonquin tribe here in 1604, more than 150 years before Eastport was settled. Located on Moose Island, this is the easternmost city in the U.S. Homes here are mostly of wood and form an engaging miscellany of styles, ranging from Colonial to Victorian. A good sampling can be found on Washington, Water, High and Ray Streets.

233. Barracks Museum *Washington St., Eastport, Me.* This frame building was part of Fort Sullivan, built in 1809 for coastal defense and vitally strategic during the War of 1812. It served as quarters for U.S. troops and, at one time, for the surgeon general; from 1814 to 1818 it was occupied by the British. After the Civil War it was moved to its present site for use as a private dwelling. Now owned by the Border Historical Society, the building houses items of regional historic significance. *Open Mon.–Sat. late June–early Sept.*

234. Patten Lumberman's Museum *Rte. 159, Patten, Me.* Artifacts from the earliest days of Maine lumbering are on display in six buildings. Among the best exhibits are models of lumber camps and sawmills, a 20-ton steam loghauler, a relief map with a model of the tramway used to transfer logs from Allagash waters to the Penobscot River, dioramas and bateaux. *Open Tues.–Sun. end of May–Oct.*

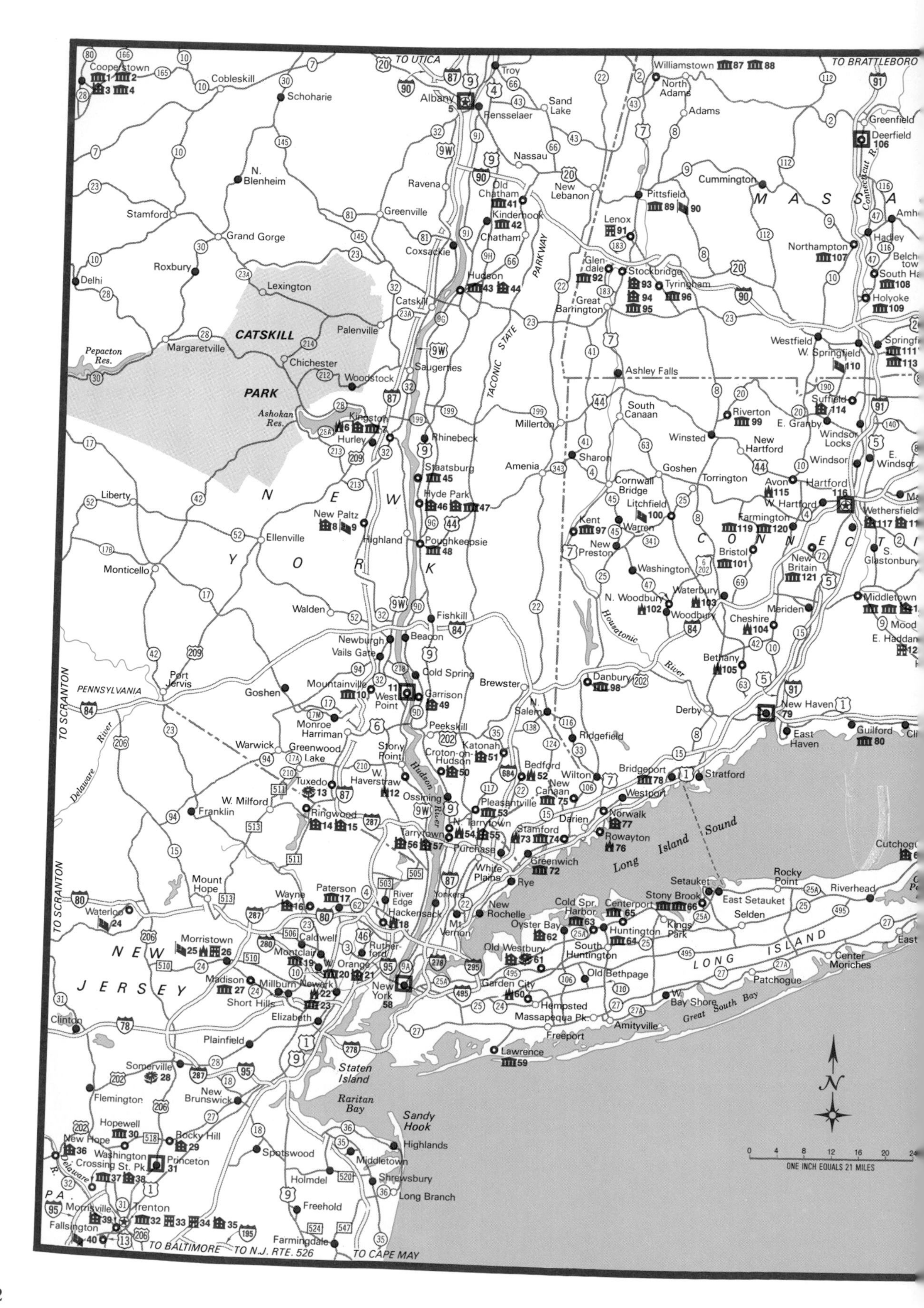
TO UTICA
TO BRATTLEBORO
Cooperstown 1 2 3 4
Cobleskill
Schoharie
Albany 5
Troy
Rensselaer
Sand Lake
Nassau
Williamstown 87 88
North Adams
Adams
Greenfield
Deerfield 106
N. Blenheim
Ravena
Old Chatham 41
New Lebanon
Pittsfield 89 90
Cummington
M A S S A
Stamford
Greenville
Kinderhook 42
Chatham
Lenox 91
Grand Gorge
Coxsackie
Northampton 107
Hadley
Roxbury
Lexington
Hudson 43 44
PARKWAY
Glendale 92
Stockbridge 93 94 95
Tyringham 96
South Hadley 108
Holyoke 109
Delhi
Catskill
Great Barrington
CATSKILL
Palenville
Margaretville
Pepacton Res.
Chichester
TACONIC STATE
Westfield
W. Springfield 110
Springfield 111 113
Saugerties
Ashley Falls
Woodstock
PARK
Ashokan Res.
Kingston 6 7
Hurley
Rhinebeck
Millerton
South Canaan
Riverton 99
E. Granby
Suffield 114
Winsted
New Hartford
Windsor Locks
Windsor
E. Windsor
Staatsburg 45
Amenia
Sharon
Goshen
Torrington
Avon 115
Hartford 116
Liberty
N
E
W
Hyde Park 46 47
Cornwall Bridge
Litchfield 100
W. Hartford
Wethersfield 117
New Paltz 8 9
Kent 97
Warren
Farmington 119 120
Ellenville
Highland
Poughkeepsie 48
New Preston
Bristol 101
New Britain 121
S. Glastonbury
Monticello
Y
O
R
K
Washington
C O N N E C T I
Walden
N. Woodbury 102
Waterbury 103
Woodbury
Middletown
Meriden
Fishkill
Cheshire 104
Moodus
E. Haddam
Newburgh
Beacon
Vails Gate
Housatonic River
Bethany 105
Port Jervis
PENNSYLVANIA
TO SCRANTON
Delaware River
Goshen
Mountainville 10
West Point 11
Cold Spring
Garrison 49
Brewster
Danbury 98
Derby
New Haven 79
Monroe
Harriman
N. Salem
Peekskill
Ridgefield
East Haven
Guilford 80
Warwick
Greenwood Lake
Stony Point
Katonah 51
Croton-on-Hudson 50
Hudson River
Bedford 52
Wilton
Bridgeport 78
Stratford
Tuxedo 13
W. Haverstraw 12
Ossining
New Canaan 75
Westport
W. Milford
Franklin
Ringwood 14 15
Pleasantville 53
Darien
Norwalk 77
Rowayton 76
N. Tarrytown 54 55
Stamford 73 74
Tarrytown 56 57
Purchase
Long Island Sound
Cutchogue
Greenwich 72
White Plains
Rye
Mount Hope
Wayne 16
Paterson 17
River Edge
Hackensack 18
Yonkers
Rocky Point
Setauket
Stony Brook 66
East Setauket
Riverhead
Waterloo 24
New Rochelle
Cold Spr. Harbor 63
Centerport 65
Selden
TO SCRANTON
Morristown 25 26
Caldwell
Mt. Vernon
Oyster Bay 62
Huntington 64
Kings Park
N E W
Montclair 19
W. Orange 20 21
Rutherford
Old Westbury 61
South Huntington
L O N G
I S L A N D
East
Center Moriches
J E R S E Y
Madison 27
Millburn
Newark 22
New York 58
Garden City 60
Old Bethpage
Patchogue
Short Hills 23
Hempsted
W. Bay Shore
Great South Bay
Clinton
Elizabeth
Massapequa Pk.
Amityville
Plainfield
Freeport
Lawrence 59
Somerville 28
Staten Island
N
Flemington
New Brunswick
Raritan Bay
Sandy Hook
Hopewell
Rocky Hill 29
New Hope 36
Highlands
Washington Crossing St. Pk. 37 38
Princeton 31
Spotswood
Middletown
Shrewsbury
Holmdel
Long Branch
Delaware R.
PA.
Morrisville 39
Trenton 32 33 34 35
Freehold
Fallsington 40
Farmingdale
TO BALTIMORE
TO N.J. RTE. 526
TO CAPE MAY
0 4 8 12 16 20 24
ONE INCH EQUALS 21 MILES

Through the ports of this seacoast region came the first great waves of trade with the rest of the world. The legacy, still, is rich beyond measure. Boston and New York City alone have more museums, churches, historic houses and famous buildings than any other two cities in America.

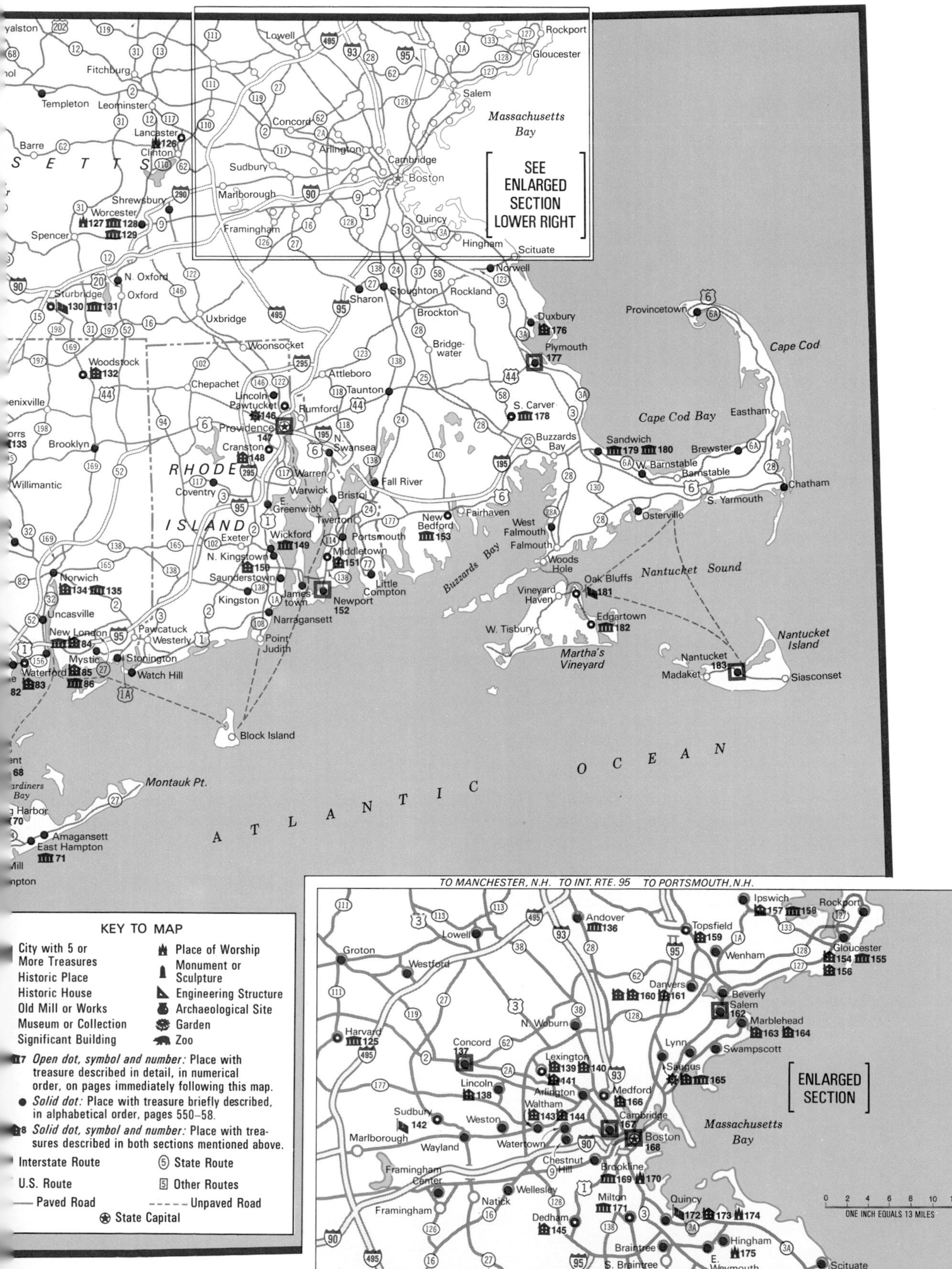

[4] *Baseball fans who step up to this re-creation of Babe Ruth's locker can almost hear the crack of the bat as the great Sultan of Swat belts out another home run. In fact, one of the objects displayed here is the ball Ruth hit for his 60th home run.*

[3] *The 32 stars on the shield of this pilothouse figure once mounted on a Great Lakes vessel date it around 1858.*

1. Carriage and Harness Museum *Elk St., Cooperstown, N.Y.* Built in 1901, this was the private stable and coach house of F. Ambrose Clark, avid Cooperstown horse fancier and sport driver. Much of his elegant collection of tandems, gigs, phaetons, Bronson Wagons and harness equipment is on view. *Open daily May-Nov., Mon.-Sat. Dec.-Apr. Small charge.*

2. Farmer's Museum and Village Crossroads *Rte. 80, Cooperstown, N.Y.* Across the road from Fenimore House there are exhibits which bring to life rural America of the late 18th and early 19th centuries. A barn built in 1918 and subsequently enlarged holds a collection of early farming tools and equipment and kitchen implements. Working craftsmen can be seen here as they spin and weave, manufacture brooms and fashion iron objects at a forge. Here also lies the Cardiff Giant, a 10-foot gypsum figure of a man that was secretly buried in a barnyard south of Syracuse, "discovered" and promoted as an early fossil in an elaborate 1869 hoax. At the Village Crossroads nearby, a dozen buildings have been assembled from a 100-mile area to form a typical early rural community. Among the restored and completely equipped structures are a lawyer's and a doctor's office, a country store, printing shop, schoolhouse, tavern and church. *Open daily June-Aug., Tues.-Sat. Sept.-May except holidays. Adults $1.75.*

3. Fenimore House *Rte. 80, Cooperstown, N.Y.* This imposing house was built in 1932 as a private residence on a tract of land overlooking Otsego Lake, where James Fenimore Cooper's cottage once stood. It serves as headquarters for the New York State Historical Association, whose new library building is close by. An outstanding collection of folk art is on display here, including paintings, wood carvings and examples of needlework. Painters of the Hudson River school are represented with canvases by Durand, Cole and Thomas Doughty, and a number of excellent early portraits can also be admired, most notably Stuart's outstanding work of Colonel Joseph Brant, the famous Mohawk Indian chief, and a likeness of Robert Fulton by Benjamin West. The Hall of Life Masks contains 18 bronze busts of early U.S. Presidents and other public figures; in the Cooper Room are manuscripts, paintings and other objects relating to the 19th-century novelist. *Open daily except holidays. Adults $1.25.*

4. National Baseball Hall of Fame and Museum *Main St., Cooperstown, N.Y.* Dedicated in 1939, this attractive brick building stands in the town where Abner Doubleday is believed to have invented the national sport in 1839. In addition to the plaques of baseball players enshrined in the Hall of Fame, there are bats, gloves, balls and personal belongings associated with Babe Ruth, Honus Wagner, Ty Cobb, Lou Gehrig and other past and present players. The recorded voices of former stars and descriptions of memorable events can be heard here, and many paintings—including the well-known *Three Umpires* by Norman Rockwell—photographs and a display of baseball equipment through the years are exhibited. An excellent library is available to researchers. *Open daily except holidays. Adults $1.50, children small charge.*

5. Albany, N.Y.

Founded in 1614 as a Dutch fort and trading post, Albany has maintained its status as a major center down through the years. The state capital since 1797, it is today not only a hub for rail, air and highway traffic, but a port for overseas boats via the Hudson River.

Albany Institute of History and Art *125 Washington Ave.* History of the Albany area and the Hudson Valley are the main themes represented here by Patroon Portraits and paintings by Thomas Cole and other members of the Hudson River school. Exhibits also include furniture, pewter, silver and china, a replica of a late-17th-century chamber and a completely furnished 18th-century London drawing room. Egyptian, Etruscan, Greek and Roman art objects are effectively displayed. The building housing this collection dates from 1907, but the institute itself is the fourth oldest museum (1791) in the U.S. *Open Tues.-Sun.*

All Saints' Cathedral *62 S. Swan St.* Constructed between 1884 and 1904 of red Potsdam sandstone, the exterior of this modified Gothic-type Episco-

pal church still remains unfinished. The beautiful interior contains 17th- and 18th-century hand-carved Belgian choir stalls. There is a fine rose window by John La Farge above the entrance and the window over the high altar is one of the nation's largest. *Open daily.*

New York State Capitol *State St.* The Romanesque style predominates in this huge five-story building, but Gothic, French Renaissance and Moorish influences are also present. Built mainly of granite and completed in 1899 after 32 years, it includes a vast array of elaborate and often lovely stonework. It took five years to complete the stone Million Dollar Staircase, where sculptured heads of 77 famous state and national figures are grouped with imps and angels. Outside the assembly chamber, a stained-glass window with the state seal illuminates the lobby; the interior of the chamber is designed in Gothic style. The senate, planned under the guidance of Henry Richardson, is considered one of the world's most beautiful legislative chambers. In the Hall of Governors is a collection of portraits, including a fine likeness of Cleveland by Johnson. The Red Room (executive chamber), paneled in mahogany, displays portraits of Washington, Lafayette and state governors. On the second floor a military museum exhibits relics from past wars. *Open daily July-Aug., Mon.-Sat. Sept.-June.*

New York State Museum *State Education Building, Washington Ave.* On the top floor of this huge Classic Revival structure is the natural history museum established in 1870. Major exhibits include specimens of rocks, fossils, minerals, mammals and birds of New York. It is also a center for the study of the state's native inhabitants, the Iroquois Indians. An important collection of artifacts and six life-like dioramas trace the early culture of the tribe. *Open daily except holidays.*

St. Peter's Episcopal Church *107 State St.* This fine example of French Gothic architecture was built in 1859 and its memorial tower added 17 years later. Among the many interesting features and accouterments are a Caen stone altar, stained-glass windows and an inscribed silver Communion service commissioned by Queen Anne for an earlier church on the site and delivered in 1712. Lord Howe, the French and Indian War British general, is buried here. *Open daily.*

Schuyler Mansion *27 Clinton St.* Also known as The Pastures, this house was built in 1762 by Philip Schuyler. Its unusual hip, gambrel roof has gabled dormers and a Chinese Chippendale balustrade. Inside are handsome period furnishings, a decorative stairway and fine paneling. In 1780 Alexander Hamilton was married to Schuyler's daughter here. Among many famous visitors were Washington, Franklin, Lafayette and the British general Burgoyne after his surrender at Saratoga. *Open Tues.-Sun. except holidays.*

South Mall This ambitious complex of 10 marble state government buildings occupies more than 64 acres. It is built on and around a five-level Main Platform whose first three stories provide parking, service and mechanical support facilities. Situated on the top level is the 25-acre Mall Plaza with three reflecting pools, fountains, playgrounds and a winter ice-skating rink, plus attractive promenades situated among lawns, trees and sculptures. The Grand Concourse, on the fourth level, has a quarter-mile-long corridor which gives access to a wide range of shops, conference rooms and restaurants. Connected with the Main Platform at all levels is the striking 44-story Office Tower. Four identical 23-story Agency Building Towers stand on the west rim of the Main Platform, and flanking one end are the impressive Legislative Building and the smaller Justice Building. The Swan Street Building, a long, narrow structure parallel to the long axis of the Main Platform, houses the Department of Motor Vehicles, and the unique bowl-shaped Meeting Center holds two large auditoriums sharing a huge center stage. The Library-Museum Center has wide entrance steps that can serve as seats for the outdoor amphitheater. Scheduled for completion in 1975, this four-tiered building will house an enlarged State Museum. Imaginative displays will feature "Man and Nature in New York State," tracing the area's history from the time of the earth's formation to the present, and a science facility where anthropological and geological surveys can be seen. The library is expected to provide space for 15 million volumes and periodicals, and the Archives Center will hold historical documents including the Federalist Papers, the New York State Constitution, a number of letters written by Washington and Lincoln's preliminary draft for the Emancipation Proclamation. *Open daily.*

6. Old Dutch Church *272 Wall St., Kingston, N.Y.* Known officially as the Reformed Protestant Dutch Church at Kingston, this Greek Revival structure was built in 1852 and serves the oldest church body (founded in 1659) in the U.S. Among its interesting elements are a bell cast in Amsterdam in 1794 and an 1891 Tiffany window. A letter from Washington, who visited an earlier church in 1782, is kept in the museum room along with other items of historic interest, including a silver beaker presented to the church by Queen Anne in 1683. In the churchyard is the grave

[**5.** *N.Y. Capitol*] *It is said that Teddy Roosevelt used to charge up the front steps of the building just to wear out the reporters who were following him. This magnificent interior staircase is decorated with handsome carvings.*

[**9.** *Jean Hasbrouck House*] *Begun as a one-room dwelling in 1692, the house was later enlarged. Beams over 40 feet long support the wooden ceiling. Indian artifacts, pewter and guns are displayed in the front room.*

of George Clinton, first governor of New York, and graves of 68 Revolutionary War patriots. *Open daily.*

7. Senate House *312 Fair St., Kingston, N.Y.* The brick and stone house, built in 1676 by Wessel Ten Broeck, was the meeting place of the first New York State Senate in 1777, which adjourned hastily when it learned that a British force was approaching to burn Kingston. The building was gutted, but its walls survived and the structure was soon rebuilt. It remained a private residence until it was purchased by the state in 1887. In the house are many 18th-century furnishings from the area.

SENATE HOUSE MUSEUM The adjoining museum, built by the state in 1927, houses a collection of Hudson River marine art, portraits of early political figures and a library. An outstanding collection of portraits and drawings by John Vanderlyn (1775-1852), a native of Kingston, is also displayed. *Open Wed.-Sun.*

8. Colonel Josiah Hasbrouck House *Rte. 32 S. of New Paltz, N.Y.* Colonel Hasbrouck built this spacious Federal dwelling, also known as Locust Lawn, in the Southern style with large rooms around a central hall. The original furnishings cover the period from 1790 to 1860, and fine china as well as the colonel's papers when he was a member of the U.S. House of Representatives are on display. There is also a farm museum on the grounds. *Open Tues.-Sun. late May-Sept. Small charge.*

9. Huguenot Historical Society Houses *Huguenot St., New Paltz, N.Y.* New Paltz was settled in 1677 by Huguenot religious refugees from France. In 1692 they began erecting the stone houses seen today on one of the oldest streets in the U.S. that still has its original dwellings. Several of these houses are virtually unaltered and have period furnishings from the 17th century to the early Victorian era.

ABRAHAM HASBROUCK HOUSE A secret attic room, many legends and the elegant proportions of the architecture attract visitors to this house. The first of its three sections was built in 1692 and the last was completed in 1712. It has 18th-century furnishings. *Open Tues.-Sun. mid-May-mid-Oct. Small charge.*

BEVIER-ELTING HOUSE Built in 1698 with only one room, an attic, cellar and wine subcellar, this structure was considerably modified and enlarged in 1755. *Open Tues.-Sun. mid-May-mid-Oct. Small charge.*

DEYO HOUSE Originally a simple stone house, this was the first (1692) built in New Paltz. It was extensively enlarged and redesigned in the Victorian style in 1890 and now serves as headquarters for the society *Open Tues.-Sun. mid-May-mid-Oct. Small charge.*

FREER-LOW HOUSE The north end of the house was built in 1694 and the south section added about 1735. The building was restored in 1943 and contains interesting furniture. *Open Tues.-Sun. mid-May-mid-Oct. Small charge.*

JEAN HASBROUCK MEMORIAL HOUSE This is the only house of its kind in the U.S. It originally consisted of one room, built in 1692; additions were made in 1712 that reflect Flemish styling. It has been used as a museum since 1899. *Open Tues.-Sun. mid-May-mid-Oct. Small charge.*

LEFEVRE HOUSE Also known as the 1799 House, this handsome Federal dwelling has a brick facade that demonstrates the beginning of an architectural trend away from stone. The library here is devoted to Huguenot history and is sometimes used for social events. *Open Tues.-Sun. mid-May-mid-Oct.*

10. Storm King Art Center *Old Pleasant Hill Rd., Mountainville, N.Y.* This collection of contemporary art includes paintings, prints and drawings. The emphasis, however, is on sculpture in various media which can be seen in the gardens, including 13 impressive works by the late David Smith. Changing exhibits are presented in the galleries. *Open Tues.-Sun. Apr.-Dec.*

11. West Point, N.Y.

This historic military reservation is situated in an area of great natural beauty overlooking the Hudson River. During the Revolutionary War it was a strategic key to the defense of the Hudson River Valley; General Washington made his headquarters here in 1779.

United States Military Academy Established at West Point by Congressional action in 1802, the academy has played a great role in the nation's history. Many of its buildings are open to visitors, who also enjoy such cadet activities as parades and football games.

BATTLE MONUMENT *Trophy Pt.* Dedicated on May 31, 1897, the monument was erected in memory of the officers and enlisted men of the Regular Army who were killed during the Civil War. *Open daily.*

CADET CHAPEL One of the largest church organs in the world, with over 15,000 pipes, may be heard in this massive building. The church itself, a classic example of military Gothic architecture, is made of native granite. The beautiful stained-glass windows memorialize each graduating class. *Open daily.*

CHAPEL OF THE MOST HOLY TRINITY The striking Norman Gothic church is a replica of St. Ethelreda Carthusian Abbey Church in Essex, England. It seats 550 and is operated for Catholic personnel of the academy by the Archdiocese of New York. *Open daily.*

OLD CADET CHAPEL The chapel was built in 1837 and moved to its present location in the post cemetery in 1921. Throughout the building there are memorial plaques honoring military men who died for their country in the Revolutionary War, the War of 1812, and the Spanish-American War. Of particular historical interest is the plaque with only rank—major general—and a birthdate—1740—which was to have been inscribed for Benedict Arnold, before he betrayed his country. *Open Wed.-Sun.*

VISITORS INFORMATION CENTER Displays that depict various aspects of West Point history and cadet life can be seen here. A model cadet room is exhibited, and a brief movie about West Point is shown. Personnel on duty provide tour information to visitors. *Open daily mid-Apr.-mid-Nov.*

WARNER HOUSE *Constitution Is.* A short boat trip arranged through the Constitution Island Association will take you to this quaint 18th-century house on this government-owned island, the site of a major defense location during the Revolution. Because of its strategic importance, many famous names are associated with the island: George Washington, Benjamin Franklin, Tadeusz Kościuszko. The house is named after two sisters, Susan and Anna Warner, both writers, who owned the property from 1836 to 1908. Anna Warner was musically inclined and the author of the familiar children's hymn "Jesus Loves Me."

WEST POINT MUSEUM One of the world's largest collections of military arms and accouterments is housed here along with exhibits and displays depicting every aspect of military history and the art of war—logistics, tactical developments, medals and decorations, great military leaders and the everyday life of the soldier. Other exhibits, often making use of dioramas and full scale models, acquaint the visitor with great battles of the Western world, from Cynoscephalae to Gettysburg, or illustrate how warfare has changed. All of these are designed to support the museum's primary function of supplementing the academic and military education of the cadets. There is also a large collection of paintings, many of which deal with warfare in Europe and America. *Open daily except Jan. 1 and Dec. 25.*

12. Marian Shrine *Filors Lane, W. Haverstraw, N.Y.* Set on 250 tranquil acres overlooking the Hudson River, this shrine depicts the Fifteen Mysteries of the Rosary in life-size statues by Arrighini. An impressive outdoor altar of marble, mosaic and bronze and some fine examples of Florentine religious art can be seen here. *Open daily May-Oct.*

13. Sterling Forest Gardens *Rte. 210, Tuxedo, N.Y.* Since the first tulip bulb was planted here in 1959 by Princess Beatrix of the Netherlands, these gardens have become among the most luxuriant in the country. The curving paths and beds, both formal and informal, are set on 125 acres of land surrounded by the 22,000-acre Sterling Forest. Tulips predominate in the spring and are followed through the season by brilliant displays of annuals, perennials, shrubs and flowering trees. *Open daily. Adults $2.95, children $1.00.*

14. Ringwood Manor House *Sloatsburg Rd., Ringwood, N.J.* Begun in 1810 by the ironmaster Martin Ryerson, this 51-room, ornately filigreed, gabled early Victorian mansion is set on 579 acres of parkland that include a nature trail and formal gardens. For two centuries Ringwood was the home of a succession of ironmasters, among them, Robert Erskine, Surveyor General to the U.S. Army during the American Revolution, and Martin Ryerson, who produced iron for the War of 1812. The foremost ironmaster in the U.S. in the 19th century, Abram S. Hewitt, made Ringwood his summer home. The house contains many of the original furnishings; a hammer and anvil used in one of the old forges, a huge mortar and a deck gun from "Old Ironsides" can be seen on the property. *Open Tues.-Sun. May-Oct. Small charge.*

15. Skylands Manor *Sloatsburg Rd., Ringwood, N.J.* Although built in 1924, this 44-room mansion is a perfect example of an English manor house of the Jacobean style. The architect, John Russell Pope, designed it for millionaire Clarence McKenzie Lewis as a summer house and deliberately gave it the look of age, with sagging roof, weathered stone and Monel Metal drainpipes made to look like aged copper. Leaded stained-glass windows add to the effect. The 1110 acres of the Skylands section of Ringwood State Park include a variety of formal garden settings and rare trees and shrubs. *Mansion open Tues.-Sun. and Mon. holidays May-Oct. Small charge. Parking fee.*

[11] *This aerial view shows the strategic location of West Point, overlooking a sharp bend in the Hudson River. During the Revolutionary War the Americans stretched heavy iron chains across the river to keep the British from sailing north and cutting off the New England colonies. The grounds of West Point cover some 15,000 acres; perhaps the most interesting time to visit is during the football season, when the breeze is brisk off the Hudson, the trees have turned, and the campus bustles with excitement.*

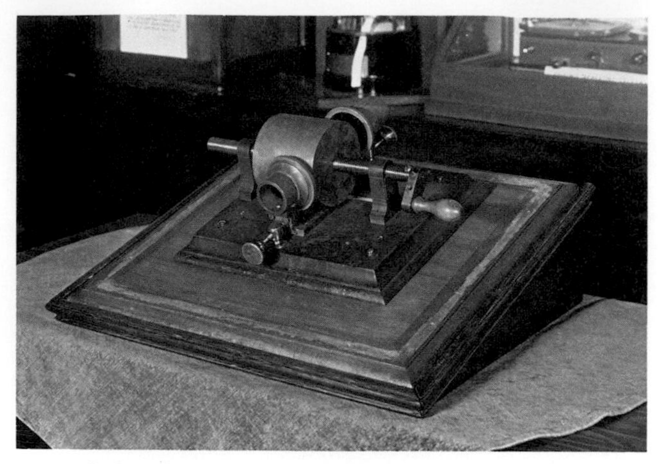

[20] *Edison's original phonograph consisted of a hand-turned, tinfoil-wrapped cylinder. A needle etched the cylinder while Edison cranked and shouted out history's first recorded words: "Mary had a little lamb."*

16. Dey Mansion *199 Totowa Rd., Wayne, N.J.* This stone and brick Georgian manor house, completed in 1740 for Dirck Dey and his son Colonel Theunis Dey, was used as General Washington's headquarters in 1780. In 1934 the house was restored and furnished in an 18th-century manner. There is a third-floor museum with displays of Colonial artifacts and documents. On the grounds are formal and kitchen gardens and a barnyard with live animals. *Open Tues.-Thurs., Sat., Sun. Small charge.*

17. Passaic County Historical Society Museum *5 Valley Rd., Paterson, N.J.* Five rooms in the elaborate Lambert Castle serve as a museum for the Passaic County Historical Society. Visitors will see a large collection of souvenir spoons, a library with a gold-leaf ceiling and exhibits relating to native son Garret Hobart, McKinley's Vice President. The stone castle was built in 1892 and is named for its first owner, a prominent Paterson manufacturer.*Open Wed.-Sun.*

18. First Reformed Dutch Church *42 Court St., Hackensack, N.J.* Commonly called the Old Church on the Green, this sturdy stone Gothic Colonial building was erected in 1696 and rebuilt in 1728. Its walls hold 24 engraved stones, each bearing the name of a Dutch family that once belonged to the congregation.

19. Montclair Art Museum *3 S. Mountain Ave., Montclair, N.J.* This collection of American paintings from the 18th to the early 20th centuries includes works by Inness, Durand, Hopper, Sargent and Arshile Gorki. Various exhibitions on loan from other museums are shown throughout the year. Of special interest are the American Indian art gallery and the Whitney silver collection. *Open Tues.-Sun. Sept.-June.*

20. Edison National Historic Site Laboratory Unit *Main St. and Lakeside Ave., West Orange, N.J.* In these buildings where Thomas Alva Edison worked for 44 years, many of his major inventions and scientific ideas were developed. The unit includes his chemical laboratory, physics laboratory, machine shop and library. Edison's notebooks and many original models of his inventions, including the tinfoil phonograph invented in 1877, are on display. *Open daily except holidays. Adults small charge.*

21. Glenmont *Llewellyn Park, West Orange, N.J.* Edison purchased this 23-room Victorian house in 1886 and lived there until his death in 1931. The house contains almost all the original furnishings, including paintings, books and much Edison memorabilia. Of particular interest is the paneled dining room, with displays of Venetian glass, the oak-paneled entrance hall and the upstairs library containing Edison's desk, which he called his thought bench. *Open Mon.-Sat. except holidays. Adults small charge.*

22. Cathedral of the Sacred Heart *89 Ridge St., Newark, N.J.* Consisting of a green granite exterior and a limestone interior, this is a fine example of French Gothic architecture. Among the many elaborate appointments are the mosaic and gold vaulted ceiling in the Baptistry, the mosaic Stations of the Cross and 200 stained-glass windows, including a superb rose window in the west transept. In the two towers there are 14 perfectly pitched bells which were made in Padua, Italy. The organ built with 150 ranks is used for concerts given each week except in the summer. *Open daily.*

23. Newark Museum *49 Washington St., Newark, N.J.* This museum of art, science and industry was founded in 1909. Among its wide range of exhibits are a large collection of Tibetan religious art, 15th- to 19th-century European clocks and American painting and sculpture of the 18th to 20th centuries. Especially impressive are the portraits by Stuart, Vanderlyn and Charles Willson Peale; *The Bridge* by Stella; *The Sheridan Theatre* by Hopper; *Parking Garage* by Segal, and the stainless steel *Untitled* by the sculptor David Smith. Among the French painters represented are Gauguin and Toulouse-Lautrec. The Schaefer Collection of ancient glassware is considered one of the nation's best; visitors can also see many examples of early pottery, silver and 18th- and 19th-century American furniture, including a number of New Jersey pieces. In a one-acre garden behind the museum are Newark's Old Stone Schoolhouse (1784) and the Newark Fire Museum. *Open daily except holidays.*

24. Waterloo Village Restoration *Rte. 206, Waterloo, N.J.* Once known as Andover Forge when the town supplied iron cannonballs and musket barrels for the Continental army, the original pre-Revolutionary village dates from 1760. Its buildings are all of the Colonial period except for three built in the 1850s. Visitors can enter the houses, church, gristmill, inn and shops and view the nearly 90 rooms of antique furniture. Each summer there is a musical festival in which many well-known musicians perform. *Open Tues.-Sun. Adults $2.50, children $1.50.*

25. Morristown National Historical Park *Morristown, N.J.* The courage and tenacity of General Washington and his troops first showed itself at this stark headquarters site during the winter of 1779-80. Here, only 30 miles from British-occupied New York, the Continental Army was reorganized.

FORD MANSION *230 Morris St.* In the winter of

1779-80 George and Martha Washington used this stately Colonial mansion, built about 1774 by Colonel Jacob Ford, as headquarters. The house features a fine Palladian doorway and two large chimneys. Most of the furnishings are excellent examples of the Chippendale and Queen Anne periods. Some of the pieces, such as the secretary-dish in the living room, were actually used by Washington. The kitchen is a particularly well-equipped example of the Colonial style. *Open daily. Small charge includes Historical Museum.*

FORT NONSENSE *S. Court St.* This hilltop, now overlooking Morristown, was a key vantage point during the Revolution. The name is derived from the legend that the fort was built merely to keep the soldiers from getting restless *Open daily.*

HISTORICAL MUSEUM *Behind Ford Mansion* There is much here to recall life during the Revolutionary War: arms and other military equipment, old prints and manuscripts, glass, pewter, silver, pottery and dioramas. *Open daily. Small charge includes Ford Mansion.*

JOCKEY HOLLOW *4 mi. S. of Morristown* Reconstructed log cabins with wooden pegs and clay chinks that were built to house 10 to 12 soldiers can be seen here, as well as a camp hospital and other vestiges of the winter encampment of some 10,000 troops. The rural setting has a wildlife sanctuary. *Open daily.*

WICK HOUSE *Jockey Hollow* In 1750 Henry Wick built this New England-style shingled farmhouse, where, it is said, his daughter Temperance hid her horse in her bedroom to protect it from mutinous soldiers. The house served as the military headquarters of Major General Arthur St. Clair during the Revolutionary War, and is well-furnished with typical country pieces of the period. Behind the kitchen is an interesting 18th-century herb garden. *Open daily Feb.-Nov.*

26. Saint Mary's Abbey *Mendham Rd., Morristown, N.J.* Designed by Victor Christ-Janer Associates, this modern Benedictine church is distinguished by a dramatic arrangement of cubes and walls punctuated by tall narrow windows. The brick, concrete-block and steel walls contrast nicely with the terrazzo, marble and mahogany of the nave. There are a Blessed Sacrament Chapel of elegant proportions and a Lady Chapel. Monthly organ and choral recitals take place from September to June. *Open daily.*

DELBARTON SCHOOL The school, maintained by Benedictine monks and laymen, has its administrative offices in a large, three-story stone structure originally designed as a private home by Stanford White. Surrounding it are formal gardens, statues and a pool.

27. Museum of Early Trades and Crafts *Main St. and Green Village Rd., Madison, N.J.* The trades and crafts that supported life from Colonial times through 1850 are represented by materials, equipment and products shown in room settings, workshops and working displays. There are implements used by blacksmiths, coopers, potters, harvesters and housewives. The building was formerly a library. It is a handsome granite structure with Tiffany stained-glass windows and handwrought bronze hardware. *Open daily except holidays.*

28. Duke Gardens *Rte. 206 S., Somerville, N.J.* Unique greenhouse gardens designed to resemble outdoor plantings of different countries can be seen on the estate of Doris Duke. Beneath one acre of glass are a formal Louis XVI-style parterre garden on two levels, an Edwardian arrangement of palms, ferns and orchids, and a superb English setting with examples of topiary and spring and summer wildflowers. A knot garden of herbs plus succulents in the shape of a sundial can also be seen. The Chinese garden utilizes a bamboo grove and an arched stone bridge; in addition there are the styled naturalism of a Japanese garden, the lushness of a tropical jungle and the stark beauty of an Arizona desert. Displays are frequently changed. *Open daily Sept.-June. except Jan. 1 and Dec. 25.* $1.75.

29. Rockingham *Rte. 518, Rocky Hill, N.J.* From August to November of 1783 George Washington used this clapboard farmhouse with its unusual second-story balcony as his last headquarters. It was here that he wrote his farewell address to the troops. The house, also called the Berrien Mansion, has excellent and authentic examples of William and Mary and Chippendale period furniture. *Open Tues.-Sun. Small charge.*

30. Hopewell Museum *28 E. Broad St., Hopewell, N.J.* The homey atmosphere of this charming gray Victorian house built in 1877 is appropriate for the displays of local furnishings, kitchen utensils and costumes from Colonial, Federal and Victorian times. The Indian room contains stone artifacts and basketry and hand-weaving exhibits; there are fine pieces of early needlework throughout the house as well as changing exhibits. *Open Mon., Wed., Sat. except holidays.*

[28] *A latticework canopy lends an air of mystery to the formal French Gardens, based on a style in vogue at the time of Louis XVI. Beds of spring flowers, bordered by holly, are planted in the shape of fleur-de-lis.*

31. Princeton, N.J.

First settled by Quakers in the late 1600s, the Princeton area is now the site of many lovely homes and several scholarly institutions.

Princeton University The 2500-acre campus of this outstanding university founded in 1746 offers a broad spectrum of architectural styles and materials. Lawns, dozens of varieties of trees, many miles of walks and a diversity of modern sculpture welcome visitors to the college whose alumni include such outstanding figures in American life as James Madison, Woodrow Wilson and F. Scott Fitzgerald.

ART MUSEUM In a new building since 1966, this wide-ranging, long-established museum exhibits works from ancient to modern times, representing most areas of the world. It is a teaching museum with noteworthy holdings in the Oriental, medieval and early American fields. In the sculpture court are small reproductions by the artists of large works scattered around the campus. *Open Tues.-Sun.*

HARVEY S. FIRESTONE MEMORIAL LIBRARY Opened in 1948 and expanded some 20 years later, this Collegiate Gothic building is the largest open-stack library in the U.S. and houses collections on the humanities and social sciences. Its holdings range from Babylonian cylinder seals, Egyptian papyri and the earliest printed books to the papers of F. Scott Fitzgerald, Bernard Baruch, Adlai E. Stevenson and James V. Forrestal. The John Foster Dulles Library of Diplomatic History was added in 1962. Exhibits of rare books, manuscripts and graphic arts are regularly displayed. *Open daily.*

NASSAU HALL Completed in 1756, this building was designed by Robert Smith, architect of Independence Hall in Philadelphia, and Dr. William Shippen. British and Colonial troops used it as a barracks and hospital during the Revolutionary War, and the Continental Congress sat here in 1783. In the center of the building is Memorial Hall, where the names of the 650 Princeton men who lost their lives in the country's wars are inscribed on the marble walls. Off Memorial Hall is the Faculty Room, once the campus prayer hall. *Open daily.*

[**31.** *Harvey S. Firestone Library*] *Princeton's handsome library is the scene of changing exhibitions drawn from its collections, such as part of the manuscript of* This Side of Paradise *by F. Scott Fitzgerald, class of 1917.*

PRINCETON UNIVERSITY CHAPEL Designed in 1925 by Ralph Adams Cram, a leading Gothic Revival architect, this chapel is built in the shape of a Latin cross, and its pinnacled turrets resemble those of a great cathedral. Elaborate carvings decorate the choir stalls and benches, fashioned from Sherwood Forest oak. The stained-glass windows depict the life and teachings of Jesus Christ and culminate in four great windows at the ends of the cruciform shape. The carved pulpit is French and probably dates from the 16th century. The great Baroque organ is played every evening during the school term as well as at Sunday services. *Open daily.*

WOODROW WILSON SCHOOL OF PUBLIC AND INTERNATIONAL AFFAIRS Completed in 1965, this is a notable example of the work of the architect Minoru Yamasaki. The building has 58 graceful, white-quartz-covered columns with Italian travertine and gray glass walls. Sculptor James Fitzgerald's *Fountain of Freedom* in the plaza memorializes Wilson, who graduated from Princeton in 1879 and served as the president of the university from 1902 to 1910. *Open daily.*

32. New Jersey State Museum *205 W. State St., Trenton, N.J.* Built in 1964 as part of a new cultural center, the museum comprises three buildings: the Museum, the Planetarium and the Auditorium. The fourth building in the complex is the State Library. The fine arts collection in the museum galleries features 20th-century painting, sculpture and prints, including works by Kandinsky, Picasso, Calder and Segal, and the most complete collection of Ben Shahn graphics in existence. There is also an excellent selection of 19th-century New Jersey decorative art including pottery, porcelain, glass, silver and furniture. The science section has natural history, geology and paleontology collections. There is an outdoor sculpture garden with works by Calder, Hunt and Rickey among others. *Museum open daily, planetarium and auditorium open Sat., Sun.*

33. Old Barracks *S. Willow and Front Sts., Trenton, N.J.* In 1758 the citizens of New Jersey petitioned for the building of winter barracks to billet the British soldiers serving in the French and Indian War. Of the five built, this two-story structure of native stone is the only one that remains. It once housed 300 men and was used at various times by British, Hessian and American troops. The building has been completely restored; its rooms now display china, silver, furniture, firearms of the Colonial and Federal periods and some George Washington mementos. There is a reconstructed soldier's room, and dioramas show "The Ten Days That Changed the World." *Open daily. Small charge.*

34. State House *W. State St., Trenton, N.J.* The original part of the capitol was built in 1790. Fire damaged the building in 1885, and by 1889 it had been rebuilt into today's imposing gray limestone Renaissance structure. Visitors may tour the legislative chambers and governor's reception room and see the push-button voting system in the assembly chamber. *Open daily.*

[**37**] Washington Crossing the Delaware *captures one of the most crucial moments in American history: Christmas night, 1776, when Washington led his weary, relatively ill-equipped troops across the ice-filled Delaware River to a decisive victory over the British. The British troops were mostly Hessian mercenaries, and many were recovering from celebrating the holiday. Not one of the 2400 Americans died. The Battle of Trenton, won in about two hours, was a turning point in the war.*

35. William Trent House *539 S. Warren St., Trenton, N.J.* This two-story red brick Georgian structure, believed to be the city's oldest, was built in 1719 by William Trent, for whom the city of Trenton was named. Refurnished according to an inventory of the original contents made in 1726, it contains excellent Queen Anne and William and Mary pieces. Governors Lewis Morris, Philemon Dickerson and Rodman Price resided here, and both Washington and Lafayette were guests. Especially notable are the magnificent hand-loomed draperies throughout, a 1760 mahogany grandfather's clock and rare 17th- and 18th-century British pieces. *Open daily. Small charge.*

36. Parry Mansion *S. Main St., New Hope, Pa.* Five generations of the Parry family have lived in this stone mansion. It was recently restored by the New Hope Historical Society to illustrate the evolution of upper-middle-class taste in interior design from 1775 to 1900. The different periods of furnishings represented in the various rooms of the mansion include Georgian Colonial, Hepplewhite-Sheraton, Empire, Victorian and Eastlake. On the rear of the house is a handsome Victorian Gothic porch flanked by a garden. *Open daily Mar.-Oct. Small charge.*

37. Memorial Building *Washington Crossing State Park, Pa.* This building stands near the spot where Washington crossed the Delaware River on Christmas night, 1776. It features memorabilia of the crossing and a full-size, exact copy of Leutze's *Washington Crossing the Delaware* by Robert B. Williams. *Open daily.*

38. Thompson-Neely House of Decision *Washington Crossing State Park, Pa.* It was here that Washington and his officers laid plans for their famous Delaware River crossing and the ensuing attack on the Hessian mercenaries quartered at Trenton. The simple 1702 house was requisitioned from the Thompson and Neely families for use as river headquarters. Made of fieldstone, it is a fine example of early Pennsylvania architecture and masonry. *Open daily.*

39. Pennsbury Manor *Off Rte. 13, Morrisville, Pa.* Quaker William Penn gave his name to Pennsylvania and dedicated his life to the idea that peace and prosperity are attainable goals. This is a re-creation of his country estate, originally built in 1683 on the banks of the Delaware River. The manor house contains a large collection of 17th-century furniture typical of that owned by Penn. Also on the 40-acre site are a bake and brewhouse, smokehouse, icehouse, stable, plantation office and English garden. *Open daily. Small charge.*

40. Historic Fallsington *Fallsington, Pa.* William Penn worshiped in this village near the Delaware River. Among the most interesting of the 25 early American buildings here are the restored 1685 Moon-Williamson House, a log cabin flanked by two ancient sycamores; the stone Stage Coach Tavern dating from the late 18th century; and the 1789 Burges-Lippincott House, which has a handsome doorway, a fine carved mantel in the living room and period furniture. Its one-story wing added in the mid-1800s once served as a doctor's office. *Open Wed.-Sun. mid-Mar.-mid-Nov. Adults small charge.*

41. Shaker Museum *Shaker Museum Rd., Old Chatham, N.Y.* In the late 18th century, what was to become the nation's largest Shaker colony was established nearby at Mt. Lebanon. The museum's several buildings house items from there as well as from other Shaker communities. Tools used in carpentry, ironwork, spinning and other crafts are displayed along with the uniquely simple and beautiful end products. Everything the Shakers put their hands to reveals their infallible eye for line and proportion. A library holds many Shaker books and documents. *Open daily May-Oct. Adults $1.50, children over 6 small charge.*

42. House of History *16 Broad St., Kinderhook, N.Y.* This 1810 house of Hudson River brick has a handsome facade with a fine second-story Palladian window which repeats the outline of the front door. Now maintained as a museum and reference library by the Columbia County Historical Society, it is beautifully furnished with period pieces and contains a graceful flying staircase. *Open Tues.-Sun. June-early Sept., Sat., Sun. early Sept.-late Sept. Small charge.*

43. American Museum of Fire Fighting *Firemen's Home, Harry Howard Ave., Hudson, N.Y.* Founded in

1925, this museum contains one of the oldest and most comprehensive collections of fire-fighting equipment and memorabilia in the country. Among the displays are fire-fighting apparatus from 1731 to 1926, banners, badges, hats and models. There is also a large art gallery featuring oil paintings, photographs and the memorable folk art carving, *The Statue of a Fire Chief.* *Open daily.*

44. Olana *Rte. 9G, Hudson, N.Y.* Frederick E. Church, prominent member of the Hudson River school of artists, completed this opulent summer residence in 1874, adding a studio wing in 1890. Essentially Victorian, the impressive brick and stone structure shows Persian and Moorish influences as well as Italian and East Indian characteristics. U.S. and foreign furniture from several periods as well as landscapes by Church and other artists of the Hudson River school are on display. *Open daily mid-Apr.-mid-Nov.*

45. Mills Museum *Ogden and Ruth Livingston Mills Memorial State Park, Staatsburg, N.Y.* The furnishings and decorations of this 65-room French Renaissance mansion built in 1832 include antique Louis XV and Louis XVI furniture; paintings by Reynolds and other great artists; rugs from India, Turkey and Scotland; rare tapestries; Etruscan pottery and Chinese pieces. Many of the furnishings were owned by the original builder, Morgan Lewis, the third governor of New York State. The last occupant was Ogden Mills, Secretary of the Treasury during President Hoover's administration. *Open daily mid-Apr.-mid-Nov., Sat., Sun., holidays mid-Nov.-mid-Dec., early Jan.-mid-Apr. Small charge.*

46. Vanderbilt Mansion *Rte. 9, Hyde Park, N.Y.* This 54-room Indiana limestone structure was built in Italian Renaissance style in 1896-98 for Frederick W. Vanderbilt, grandson of Cornelius Vanderbilt on an estate of some 200 acres. The furnishings include pieces in Louis XIV style, Russian walnut and Santo Domingo mahogany paneling and 16th- to 18th-century tapestries. A dining room running the full width of the building has a ceiling brought from Italy. A National Historic Site, the mansion cost over $2,000,000 to decorate and furnish. *Open daily. Small charge.*

[**46**] *Mrs. Vanderbilt's bedroom is one of the most lavish in the Vanderbilt mansion, fit for a queen in the time of Louis XV. Every piece of furniture is an exact copy of a French original. Gilded paintings decorate the walls.*

47. Franklin D. Roosevelt National Historic Site *Rte. 9, S. of Hyde Park, N.Y.* Comprising 187 acres of gardens, trees and lawns, this memorial to the 32nd President of the U.S. includes the two structures described below in addition to the simple grave where he and Eleanor Roosevelt lie buried. *Open daily.*

FRANKLIN D. ROOSEVELT HOME Roosevelt spent much of his life in this comfortable 30-room house where he was born in 1882 and it clearly reveals his wide-ranging interests. Visitors can listen to a "tape talk" by Mrs. Roosevelt describing the bedrooms, the living room, Dresden Room, dining room, private office and other parts of the house open to the public. *Open daily. Small charge.*

FRANKLIN D. ROOSEVELT LIBRARY More than 36,000 books, papers, letters and objects associated with President and Mrs. Roosevelt can be seen here. There are also many ship models, naval prints and paintings. The desk and chair he used in the White House and gifts from world leaders are displayed. The President's Room, which he arranged and furnished, was the scene of radio broadcasts and wartime talks with famous Allied leaders. Wings added in 1972 in memory of Mrs. Roosevelt contain exhibits pertaining to her many activities before, during and after the White House years. *Open daily. Small charge.*

48. Vassar College Art Gallery *Taylor Hall, Raymond Ave., Poughkeepsie, N.Y.* Built in 1915, Taylor Hall houses a good collection of Baroque art in several media. Impressively displayed in the Warburg Print Room are more than 140 works, including 75 Rembrandts and 45 Dürers. Examples of 15th- to 17th-century Italian and 19th-century French art can also be viewed, plus many Oriental jade objects, ceramics and scrolls. The sculpture collection, although small, is outstanding. Works by members of the Hudson River school form part of the 19th-century American holdings, while Nicholson, Hartley, Tomlin and Rothko are among artists represented in the collection of 20th-century paintings. *Open daily mid-Sept.-May.*

49. Boscobel *Rte. 9D, Garrison, N.Y.* See feature display on page 113.

50. Van Cortlandt Manor *Off Rte. 9, Croton-on-Hudson, N.Y.* Begun in the 1680s with upper floors added later, this handsome Dutch manor house was once the center of a huge estate owned by one of New York's most influential families. This is an authentic restoration and contains many of the beautiful, original furnishings and a number of interesting family portraits. There is also a kitchen and ferry-house on the grounds. Special annual events include the re-enacting of a military muster and a program tracing the making of cloth from sheep to shawl. *Open daily except holidays. Adults $1.75, children over 6 small charge.*

Boscobel's facade of elegant proportions and classic architectural detail typifies the Adam style.

49. Boscobel

Rte. 9D, Garrison, N.Y.

Boscobel, a 12-room mansion above the Hudson River completed in 1806, embodies the neoclassic ideas of Scottish architect Robert Adam, the man who contributed so much to the development of architecture in England and to the Federal style in America. Heirs of the original owner lived in the house for a century, but some 150 years after it was built Boscobel was unoccupied and slated for destruction. Fortunately it was saved, moved to its present splendid site 15 miles from the original location and furnished mainly with English and American antiques. The below-ground kitchen is totally equipped as it would have been in the 19th century. The grounds too are kept in an early 19th-century manner with herb, vegetable and flower gardens, brick paths, an orangerie, a necessary (privy), spring house (used to keep dairy products cool) and a gate house. *Open Wed.-Mon. Mar.-Dec. except Thanksgiving Day and Dec. 25. Adults $2.00, children small charge.*

Interior design was as important to Adam as architecture. The fanlight, furniture, drapery, molding, plaster ceiling ornament and mantel (detail at left) in the drawing room at Boscobel reflect his refined taste.

51. John Jay Homestead *Jay St. (Rte. 22 S.), Katonah, N.Y.* The first Chief Justice of the U.S. lived in this handsome stone and frame house from 1801 until his death in 1829. Since its acquisition by the state in 1958, most of the rooms have been restored to their original appearance in the 1780s. Many of Jay's original possessions can be viewed throughout the house; a wing completed in 1925 contains portraits by Stuart, Trumbull and Sargent. *Open Wed.-Sun. except holidays.*

52. Bedford Presbyterian Church *Village Green, Bedford, N.Y.* An excellent example of Carpenter's Gothic architecture, this frame structure was dedicated in 1872 as the fourth church of a congregation founded in 1681. It has stained-glass windows and an Angell pipe organ. A silver Communion service presented in 1810 by John Jay is still used regularly. *Open daily.*

53. Reader's Digest *Rte. 117, Pleasantville, N.Y.* This huge Georgian-style brick office building stands in the midst of beautifully landscaped grounds with lovely formal and informal gardens. The interior contains many fine antique furnishings, and an outstanding collection of Impressionist and Post-Impressionist paintings. They include works by Cézanne, Monet, Renoir, van Gogh, Braque, Picasso and many other well-known artists. *Open Mon.-Fri.*

54. Old Dutch Church of Sleepy Hollow *North Tarrytown, N.Y.* This gambrel-roofed church was built in 1685 by Frederick Philipse, a Dutch settler who became Lord of the Manor of Philipsburg. Its walls, more than two-feet thick, are made of rubblestone and flat yellow bricks brought from Holland. The octagonal belfry houses the original bell, cast to order in Holland. Washington Irving is buried in the adjacent cemetery. *Open daily May-Oct.*

55. Philipsburg Manor *Rte. 9, North Tarrytown, N.Y.* In the early 1680s Philipse, one of the richest men in the province, constructed this northern trading center for his holdings, which encompassed about 90,000 acres. Now a 20-acre site, it includes a two-story manor house with period furniture, a working gristmill with huge millstones and a waterwheel, an oak and stone dam and an early barn where craft demonstrations are given. These structures have been restored to reflect the early 1700s. Tours include a showing of the award-winning film on the history and restoration of Philipsburg Manor. *Open daily except holidays. Adults $1.75, children over 6 small charge.*

[53] *Two paintings from the* Digest's *outstanding fine art collection, a van Gogh and a Modigliani, grace the walls of this reception room. The Sheraton sofa and crystal chandelier add to the elegant atmosphere.*

56. Lyndhurst *635 S. Broadway, Tarrytown, N.Y.* Located above the Hudson River on 67 acres of sweeping lawns and fine old trees, this mansion of more than 30 rooms is a stunning example of the Gothic Revival styling that enjoyed great popularity during the post-Civil War "Gilded Age." Built in 1838 for William Paulding, mayor of New York City, Lyndhurst was constructed of marble and wood made to look like stone. Jay Gould, the railroad magnate, financier and arch-rival of Cornelius Vanderbilt, purchased it in 1880, and its restored interior reflects the opulent taste of its owners. Intricately carved woodwork and marble fireplaces and columns decorate the rooms; the large number of mullioned stained-glass windows are believed to be the work of Louis C. Tiffany. Many of the paintings, statuary and bric-a-brac collected by the families who occupied the mansion are on display, as well as furnishings and other possessions from different periods. Among the 15 buildings on the grounds are a gardener's cottage and a superintendent's house, both in Gothic style; a 400-foot greenhouse rebuilt by Gould in 1881 and an 1865 coach house. The estate is now owned by the National Trust for Historic Preservation. *Open daily. Adults $1.50, children small charge.*

57. Sunnyside *Off Rte. 9, Tarrytown, N.Y.* Washington Irving once described Sunnyside as "a little old-fashioned stone mansion, all made up of gable ends, and as full of angles and corners as an old crocked hat." Designed mostly by Irving, this delightful little house contains much of his original furniture and personal possessions. Of particular interest is Irving's study, filled with his books and mementos. The huge desk was a gift from his publisher, George P. Putnam. The room has been restored and faithfully reflects the descriptions of it by many who visited Irving here. *Open daily except holidays. Adults $1.75, children over 6 small charge.*

58. New York City, N.Y.

New York was first visited by Verrazano in 1524. In 1609 Hudson sailed up the picturesque river that now bears his name. Seventeen years later Dutch administrator Peter Minuit bought Manhattan Island from the Indians for the equivalent of $24. Washington was inaugurated here as first President of the U.S. in 1789. The Stock Exchange began its rich history operating on a Wall Street green in 1792. Until 1898 New York City was composed only of Manhattan Island. Today it is made up of five interdependent boroughs. This vast and diversified center is the focal point of one of the largest metropolitan areas in the world. The total population is about 8 million; another million persons commute here from as far away as 80 miles each working day.

BRONX

The Bronx was named after Danish settler Jonas

[**58.** *N.Y. Zoo*] *One of the exciting aspects of the World of Birds is the freedom with which birds can fly about. Visitors to the South American rain forest, shown here, have the feeling of being in the middle of a lush, bird-haunted jungle. The birds are adapting well and even breeding in their new environments.*

Bronck, the first European to settle beyond the Harlem River, in 1639. The site of several college campuses, the borough also has the world-renowned Bronx Zoo and the New York Botanical Gardens.

Bartow-Pell Mansion *Shore Rd., Pelham Bay Pk.* Overlooking Long Island Sound, this outstanding Greek Revival mansion is surrounded by beautifully landscaped grounds and a well-tended garden. Interior details include an elliptical staircase, fine woodwork and period furnishings loaned by New York City museums. Built between 1836 and 1842 by Robert Bartow, a descendant of the original landowner, Thomas Pell, it was restored and the grounds were developed by the International Garden Club, which uses it as headquarters. *Open Tues., Fri., Sun. Small charge.*

New York Botanical Garden *Southern Blvd. and 200th St.* Spacious lawns, attractive flower beds, wooded areas and a waterfall contribute to the natural beauty of the garden's 230 acres, while its impressive buildings house a botanical and horticultural museum, laboratories and the largest botanical library in the U.S. Among the attractions are two Dawn Redwoods, an ancient Chinese Empress tree brought to New York by Dutch colonists, a 40-acre hemlock forest and changing exhibits of rare plants. *Open daily. Small parking fee.*

New York Zoological Park *Southern Blvd. and 185th St.* Commonly called the Bronx Zoo, this 252-acre tract, opened in 1899, is one of the largest zoos in the U.S. Its wide collection of mammals, birds, reptiles and amphibians ranges from the commonplace to the nearly extinct. Its many naturalistic displays rely on deep moats and fenced-in plots instead of barred cages. The attractions include the Reptile House, the Bison Range and the African Plains site where antelopes, deer and birds can be viewed alongside lions. The Elephant House also contains rhinoceroses and hippopotamuses. The Children's Zoo has many animals that can be petted, and the remarkable World of Darkness building exhibits nocturnal animals in a simulated nighttime environment. Herons, flamingos, ibises, terns and spoonbills are among the specimens to be seen in the Aquatic Birds Building, while the recently opened World of Birds features 25 replicated natural habitats, including excellent desert and jungle settings and a 40-foot waterfall. The Rockefeller Fountain and Rainey Gate, the sculptured metal main entrance, are Historic Landmarks. *Open daily. Small charge Fri.–Mon.*

Van Cortlandt House Museum *Broadway and 246th St.* Built in 1748 by Frederick Van Cortlandt, this Georgian stone dwelling has brick window trim and a mansard roof. A mixture of Dutch and English styles is evident inside, where period furnishings, Delftware, handsome paneling and a number of old toys can be seen. At successive times during the Revolution the house served Washington as headquarters. *Open Tues.–Sun. Adults small charge, Tues.–Thurs., Sun.*

BROOKLYN

The Dutch founded Brooklyn in 1636 and called it Breuckelen, or "broken land," after a small town in the province of Utrecht. Although it is a part of New York City, if considered as a city in itself, it ranks fifth in U.S. industry and first in foreign trade.

Brooklyn Botanic Garden *1000 Washington Ave.* There are more than 10,000 trees, shrubs and other plants to be enjoyed here. Major attractions are the spectacular Cranford Rose Garden, the Shakespeare Garden for children and the flowering cherries, magnolias and rhododendrons. The Japanese Garden has some of the most realistic and beautiful interpretive plantings in the U.S., and the Ryoanji Temple Stone Garden is a faithful replica of the famous 15th-century one in Kyoto, Japan. The Fragrance Garden for the Blind has each plant labeled in Braille. Bonsai and tropical plants are grown in the conservatories. *Open daily. Conservatories and Japanese Garden small charge Sat., Sun. and holidays; Ryoanji Garden small charge.*

Brooklyn Bridge *Cadman Plaza* See page 117.

Brooklyn Museum *188 Eastern Pkwy.* Opened in 1897, this museum has an unusually wide range of possessions. There is an excellent collection of African sculpture and masks, plus art objects of Oceanic, American Indian and other primitive cultures. The Egyptian galleries are considered to be among the finest in the country, with reliefs, statues, jewelry, woven fabrics and paintings. Oriental arts are well represented by items from the Han, T'ang, Ming and other dynasties. Effective groupings of ancient Middle East, Islamic and East Indian art are also displayed. Many examples of American and European pewter, silver, ceramics and furniture are shown, while almost 30 fully furnished replicas of American interiors represent periods from 1675 to the 1930s. A fine collection of Colonial American paintings is highlighted by Stuart's 1796 portrait of George Washington, and works by Eakins, Bingham, Ryder, Church, Sargent, Homer and the Eight are prominently exhibited. Examples selected from more than 20,000 prints and drawings from the late 14th century to the present can also be viewed. A sculpture garden holds

[Museum of Natural History] The African elephant group in Akeley Hall typifies the realism with which museum taxidermists portray animals, down to the muscle structure under the skin.

[Statue of Liberty] The new American Museum of Immigration circles the base of the statue. Exhibits include enormous blow-ups of historic newspaper photographs and models of immigrants in native dress.

an unusual collection of architectural ornaments salvaged from demolished New York City buildings. *Open Wed.-Sun.*

New York Aquarium *Boardwalk and W. Eighth St.* Almost 3000 creatures of the sea can be observed here, including Beluga whales, sharks, seals, penguins and an electric eel. Among the popular attractions are the whale and dolphin training sessions and the Touch-It tank where children can handle live starfish, horseshoe crabs, sea urchins and other marine life. *Open daily. Small charge.*

Verrazano-Narrows Bridge *86th St. and The Narrows* Designed by O. H. Ammann, who built the George Washington Bridge, this 4260-foot span is the world's longest suspension bridge. Its twin towers soar almost 700 feet above the water, and traffic moves between Brooklyn and Staten Island on double-decker roadways. The bridge is named for Giovanni da Verrazano, the Florentine navigator who discovered New York Harbor in 1524. A monument at the Brooklyn end commemorates the event. *Small toll.*

LIBERTY ISLAND

Located in Upper New York Bay, the island lies partly in New York State and partly in New Jersey. It is reached by regular ferry service from the Battery.

Statue of Liberty The 152-foot statue rises more than 300 feet above the harbor. Created by the Alsatian sculptor Frédéric Auguste Bartholdi, it realized a French historian's proposal to commemorate the alliance between France and America during the American Revolution and the reverence shared by both peoples for the concept of liberty. Bartholdi applied more than 300 hammered-copper plates to an iron framework designed by Gustave Eiffel. The statue was shipped to its present site and dedicated by President Grover Cleveland in 1886. In the right hand is a torch held high above the sea and in the left a book representing the Declaration of Independence. A spiral staircase leads to a windowed 10-by-17-foot chamber in the head, which offers a magnificent view of the city. The two-tiered granite American Museum of Immigration at the base of the statue was formally opened by President Nixon in September 1972. *Open daily. Small charge for elevator.*

MANHATTAN

The borough of Manhattan, covering only 22 square miles, is the smallest of New York City's five boroughs. It is a center for the arts, communications, finance, industry and transportation, and the dynamic hub of the East Coast.

American Museum of Natural History *79th St. and Central Park W.* The first section of this huge complex was opened in 1877; it now comprises 20 connected buildings containing almost 60 exhibition areas. Throughout the 23 acres of floor space are displays encompassing the entire world of nature, with halls devoted to the biology of man, primates and fish and to Eskimos, early mammals, Indians, earth history and other subjects. Reconstructed early and late dinosaur skeletons and a 91-foot model of a blue whale are among the most popular exhibits; more than 200 display cases showing birds and mammals in superb re-creations of their natural habitats can be seen. As the world's largest natural history museum, its collections include over 21 million minerals, jewels, insects, mammals, birds, reptiles, fish and fossils plus an extensive number of artifacts that trace the development of man. Occupying three city blocks, the buildings themselves are of considerable architectural interest, representing the important elements of Romanesque and neo-classic styles. *Open daily. Small charge.*

Brooklyn Bridge *City Hall Park and East River* When it was completed in 1883, this was the first bridge connecting Manhattan and Brooklyn and the longest suspension bridge in the world. It was a product of the engineering and construction genius of John A. Roebling and his son Washington. Soon after approval of his design in 1869, John Roebling died, and the construction was carried on by his son. The elder Roebling developed an improved method which set the pattern for all great suspension bridges. Galvanized steel wire is spun by pulley and reel into the steel cables and holds the bridge's clear span of 1595 feet; its stone towers and Gothic arches contrast with the graceful sweep of the cables.

Cathedral Church of St. John the Divine *Amsterdam Ave. and 112th St.* It takes time to build a great cathedral, and this one is no exception. The cornerstone was laid in 1892, and it may be a hundred years or more before the building is finished. But as it stands today, it is the largest Gothic cathedral in the world. Because the front towers and central spire are still to be built, its size is not so apparent from the street. Step through the sculptured bronze doors into the interior, and the grandeur of the space is undeniable. In the nave to the right of the entry are colorful stained-glass windows depicting a variety of games and sports; on the left are the All Souls windows showing works of mercy; and above the entry is a rose window, 40 feet across. The tiled dome above the cathedral crossing creates the most impressive space in the building. Beyond the dome is the sanctuary and choir surrounded by eight gigantic columns of polished Maine granite. The baptistry is considered to be the finest single example of Gothic-style architecture in America and houses the 15-foot baptismal font ornately carved from French marble. The seven adjacent chapels are designed to represent the various nationalities most prevalent in New York in 1892. Among the many outstanding works of art are the Mortlake tapestries based on designs by Raphael; paintings by Veronese, Sabbatini and di Paolo; and an exceptional collection of icons. *Open daily.*

Central Park *5th to 8th Aves. between 59th and 110th Sts.* The nation's first formally designed park was laid out by Frederick Law Olmsted and Calvert Vaux. It was a masterwork and still stands as one of the great parks of the world. Begun in 1857, it occupies 840 acres and its irregular topography includes attractive plantings, much statuary and a variety of lakes. There are bridle paths, walks for pedestrians and cyclists, athletic fields, a skating rink-swimming pool and also a conservatory garden. The zoo, including a children's zoo, and an old carrousel are especially popular with youngsters. In the summer, concerts and plays are regularly presented throughout the park. *Open daily.*

Central Synagogue *123 E. 55th St.* This well-executed blend of Moorish and Gothic architecture is the oldest continuously used Jewish house of worship in the state and the second oldest in the nation. Built of brownstone in 1872 with minarets and ornate "onion" domes, its interior pillars provide separate bays for the naves, choir and organ loft. There are several fine stained-glass windows and an exhibit of ritual silver in the lobby. *Open Mon.-Fri.*

Chrysler Building *405 Lexington Ave.* Completed in 1930, this was the highest structure in the world (its 77 stories reach 1046 feet) prior to the completion of the Empire State Building in 1931. It was one of the first skyscrapers to carry stainless steel on its exterior. Some of the building's architectural details derive from the Chrysler automobile of the period, for example the Chrysler eagle appears at the four exterior corners of the tower floors. The lobby ceiling bears a huge mural of man's progress in mechanical invention through the ages. *Open daily.*

Church of the Transfiguration *1 E. 29th St.* Widely known as The Little Church Around the Corner, this Episcopal brick church, built in 1849, was given its popular name in 1870 when the minister of another church refused to conduct funeral services for an actor, suggesting the actor's friends try "the little church around the corner," where the services were subsequently held. Noted for its stained-glass windows dedicated to New York actors of the past, memorial carvings, paintings and a delightful garden, this is a fine Victorian Gothic structure. *Open daily.*

Cloisters *Fort Tryon Park* See feature display on pages 118-9.

Columbia University *Morningside Heights, W. 114th-121st Sts. between Broadway and Morningside Dr.* Columbia was founded as King's College in 1754 with a charter granted by George II. It includes Columbia College for men, Barnard College for women, Teachers College and a number of graduate schools. Among its famous graduates were Alexander Hamilton and John Jay. Periodic tours start at Low Library. *Open daily.*

AVERY HALL This 1912 brick and stone building houses the School of Architecture. Its architectural library is considered one of the best in the world. In the paneled 18th-century English-style Lenygon Room are a number of rare drawings, documents, a bookcase designed by Samuel Pepys and a Queen Anne chair. *Open daily.*

BUTLER LIBRARY Opened in 1934, this Italian Renaissance structure houses the fifth largest university library collection in the world with over 4 million volumes and one million manuscripts. Its collections include cuneiform tablets, papyri and rare first editions. *Open daily.*

LOW MEMORIAL LIBRARY The first building to be erected here (1897), this New York City landmark was selected by a panel of architects in 1913 as one of the nation's 10 most beautiful buildings. Once the university's working library, it now houses the Columbia archives and administrative offices. *Open Mon.-Fri.*

ST. PAUL'S CHAPEL An Italian Renaissance exterior and a Byzantine interior mark this brick church. Designed in the shape of a short Latin cross, the plan of this New York City landmark includes a vaulted portico and semi-circular apse. *Open Mon.-Fri.*

[Brooklyn Bridge] The bridge, soaring 133 feet above the East River, has a surprisingly airy quality; it seems almost to float from the delicate-looking cables. Walt Whitman was one of the poets who praised its beauty.

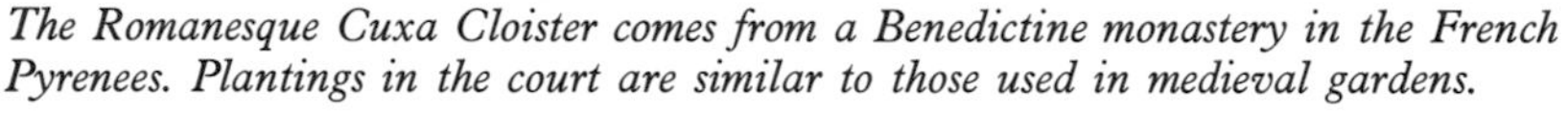

The Romanesque Cuxa Cloister comes from a Benedictine monastery in the French Pyrenees. Plantings in the court are similar to those used in medieval gardens.

A French 14th-century stained-glass window portrays the prophet Isaiah in a typical medieval manner. He holds a Latin scroll that says "Ecce Virgo" (*Behold the Virgin*).

The Virgin in this 14th-century statue glows with the tender love of a mother for her child. Earlier medieval statues often show her in a more stylized, less human way.

Cloisters

Fort Tryon Park, Manhattan, New York, N.Y.

The Cloisters is an extraordinary museum of medieval art situated on a bluff above the Hudson River on the northern fringe of Manhattan. A series of authentic medieval rooms from France and Spain—chapels, cloisters, a chapter house and halls—are interconnected to create a monastery-like environment. Within these cool stone rooms are statuary, stained glass, frescoed walls, metalwork, illuminated manuscripts, tomb effigies, altarpieces and magnificent tapestries. The collection is arranged in chronological order so that visitors may trace the growth of medieval art and architecture from its sturdy Romanesque roots to the flowering of the delicate Gothic style that preceded the Renaissance. Throughout the Cloisters, medieval man's calm devotion to God is evident. There are also delightful glimpses of the lesser known, altogether earthy side of his temperament, especially in the various cloisters. Here, nameless stonecutters uninhibited by religious restraints decorated pillars to suit their fancy. Close inspection of their carvings reveals fantastic animals, lush vegetation, intricate geometric designs, grotesque figures, sinners and lovers. *Open Tues.–Sun.*

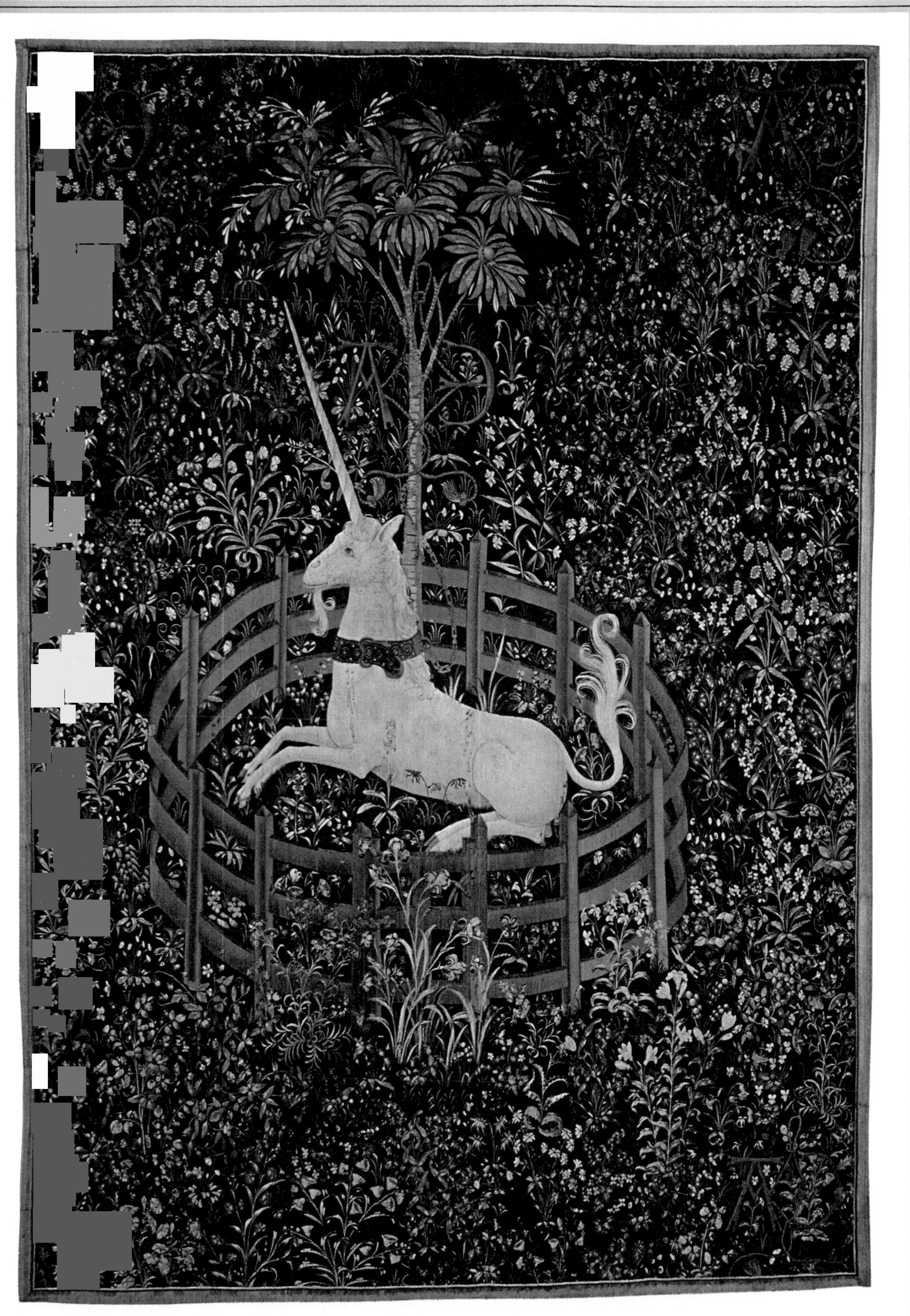

Seven "Hunt of the Unicorn" tapestries, French or Flemish masterpieces woven about 1500, hang in the Cloisters.

[*Empire State Building*] *Many daytime visitors return for the totally different experience of a nighttime view of New York City. The building is open until midnight every night. The upper 30 stories are lit with high-intensity floodlights, and the lighting is visible for 50 miles. The lights are turned off during the spring and fall bird migrations to prevent great flocks of birds from being attracted by the lights and dashing themselves to death against the building. During a thunderstorm the building may be struck by lightning as many as 20 times. It is so high that visitors sometimes see rain beginning to fall below them while they remain dry.*

Cooper-Hewitt Museum of Design *9 E. 90th St.* This 64-room mansion was built in 1901 for Andrew Carnegie. Devoted entirely to historical and contemporary design, it contains an impressive collection of textiles, wallpaper, glass, ceramics, furniture, metalwork and related objects. An important collection of drawings from the 16th century to the present includes over 300 works by Winslow Homer and some 2000 sketches by Frederick E. Church. This is a private museum of the Smithsonian Institution that may be visited by appointment, but it is planned to open it up to the public soon.

Empire State Building *350 Fifth Ave.* Spectacular views of New York City and its surroundings for a radius of 80 miles can be enjoyed on clear days from the 86th- and 102nd-floor observatories here. Opened in 1931, the building rises 1472 feet from the street to the top of its TV tower. Its claim to being the tallest building in the world has been challenged by New York's World Trade Center and Chicago's Sears Tower. It has 60,000 tons of steel beams, 5 acres of windows and 2 million square feet of office space. *Open daily. Adults $1.66, children small charge.*

Federal Hall National Memorial *26 Wall St.* This Greek Revival marble structure was built in 1842 for use as the New York Custom House. Remodeled in 1862, it became the U.S. Subtreasury and later served other official purposes. A superb statue of Washington by John Quincy Adams Ward stands in front of the main entrance. The museum here contains many historic items, including a section of railing and balcony from the original Federal Hall which stood on this site where Washington was inaugurated in 1789. *Open daily.*

Frick Collection *1 E. 70th St.* The home of the late steel magnate Henry Clay Frick was built in 1913-14 largely to provide an appropriate setting for his carefully chosen art collection. Strong in 16th- to 19th-century European paintings, it includes works by Titian, Bellini, Rembrandt and Goya as well as Velázquez and El Greco. Superb 18th-century French furniture in the Fragonard Room complements the panels depicting *The Progress of Love* which were painted for Madame du Barry. The Boucher Room contains additional period furniture, Sèvres porcelains and eight panels on *The Arts and Sciences* which were once owned by Madame de Pompadour. In the library a number of canvases by Gainsborough, Constable and Turner can be seen along with outstanding paintings by other 18th- and 19th-century English artists and fine Renaissance bronze. The mansion encompasses a handsome colonnade court with benches, sculpture and a fountain. *Open Tues.-Sun. Sept.-May, Wed.-Sun. June-Aug. except holidays.*

General Grant National Memorial *Riverside Drive and W. 122nd St.* This 150-foot domed granite monument was dedicated in 1897 to the memory of Ulysses S. Grant, Civil War general and 18th President of the U.S. Popularly called Grant's Tomb, its wide stone steps lead to a portico supported by 10 fluted Doric columns. In the open crypt that dominates the interior are the sarcophagi of Grant and his wife surrounded by busts of Union Army leaders. Three mosaics of Civil War events top the white-marble-lined rotunda. Two exhibit rooms contain trophies of Grant's career. *Open daily.*

George Washington Bridge *W. 178th St. and Hudson River* Designed by Othmar Ammann and dedicated in 1931 by New York Governor Franklin D. Roosevelt, this handsome structure spans the Hudson River between West 178th Street in Manhattan and Fort Lee, N.J. At its opening it was the world's longest suspension bridge and an unprecedented engineering feat; today it ranks fourth in length. It is supported by two towers that rise 604 feet above the water and by four great cables each 36 inches in diameter. In 1962 the opening of a lower level made this the only suspension bridge in the world with 14 lanes. The bridge is dramatically illuminated at night by mercury-vapor lights, and on holidays a huge U.S. flag—said to be the world's largest free-flying flag—is flown over the upper roadway. *Small toll for eastbound cars.*

Greenacre Park *217 E. 51st St.* Opened in 1971, this "vestpocket" park was designed by Hideo Sasaki and donated to the city by Abby Rockefeller Mauze. The artistic blending of shrubbery, decorative brick paving and water creates a restful setting. A brook along the east side of the park flows to the rear where a 25-foot waterfall cascades over large granite blocks. Chairs, tables and stone benches are located beside trees and flower-filled urns. A raised terrace is covered with a roof that radiates heat in cool weather. The park is illuminated at night. *Open daily.*

Jewish Museum *1109 Fifth Ave.* The museum in this 1908 mansion, once the home of Felix M. Warburg, has a dual focus. Through its permanent collection, it illustrates the continuity of the past and the present; and through its changing art exhibits featuring contemporary works, it shows the spirit and quality of Jewish life through the ages. Thousands of elaborate Jewish ceremonial and ritual items as well as textiles, ceramics, paintings and photographs are displayed here. Highlights of the collection include a 1600 gold Kiddush cup, an early 18th-century silver Hanukkah menorah and the oldest known spice container (about 1550). *Open Sun.-Fri. except Jewish holidays. Small charge.*

Lever House *390 Park Ave.* This slim rectangle of blue-green glass and stainless steel soars 24 stories above Park Avenue. Designed by Skidmore, Owings & Merrill, the striking building, opened in 1952, set the style for many contemporary office buildings in New York; it is still considered to be among the best designed, most functional and most attractive in the city. Exhibits of professional painters and sculptors are displayed in the lobby throughout the year on a regularly changing basis. *Open daily.*

Lincoln Center for the Performing Arts *62nd to 66th Sts., between Columbus and Amsterdam Aves.* This vast complex of artistic and educational institutions is among the most distinctive cultural centers in the world and is certainly the most ambitious and costly (about $185,000,000). It includes a central plaza and six buildings—where opera, plays, ballet, concerts and other activities are offered simultaneously. The buildings, which together make a strong sculptural enclave, were designed by a group of distinguished American and European architects headed by Wallace K. Harrison, and paid for largely by private contributions. Guided tours of the buildings are available at frequent intervals.

GUGGENHEIM BANDSHELL The New York City Parks, Recreation and Cultural Affairs Administration presents a series of free outdoor concerts here during the summer months. The bandshell seats 2500 and is located in Damrosch Park south of the main plaza. It was a gift of the Daniel and Florence Guggenheim Foundation.

HENRY MOORE'S SCULPTURE This is the largest work ever executed by the noted British sculptor, and his first to be installed publicly in New York. *Lincoln Center Reclining Figure* stands in the reflecting pool of the North Plaza.

JUILLIARD SCHOOL Linked to the rest of Lincoln Center by a footbridge, the Juilliard School offers courses in music, dance and drama. The building, the newest of the complex, has classrooms, studios, practice facilities and workshops. There are four performance halls, the largest of which is Alice Tully Hall.

LIBRARY AND MUSEUM OF THE PERFORMING ARTS The New York Public Library's extensive collection of the literature of the theater, music and dance is housed here, as well as a large collection of recordings. In addition to the research collections, more than 60,000 volumes and 12,000 albums are available in the circulating library. There is also a small auditorium for concerts, films and dance demonstrations and four galleries for exhibits. *Open Mon.-Sat. except holidays.*

METROPOLITAN OPERA HOUSE Designed by Harrison in 1966, this is one of the largest opera houses in the world. The auditorium, with a seating capacity of 3784, is decorated in red, gold and ivory and is faced with African rosewood. From the burnished gold ceiling hang great crystal chandeliers, a gift of the Austrian government. At the head of the red-carpeted grand staircase is the famous sculpture *Die Kniende* by Lehmbrück, a gift of the West German government. The foyer contains two magnificent large murals, 30 by 36 feet each, by Marc Chagall.

NEW YORK STATE THEATER Five balconies ring the horseshoe-shaped auditorium which seats 2729 people. Designed by Philip Johnson and opened in 1964, the theater is the home of the New York City Opera and the New York City Ballet. The hall is decorated in garnet and gold, and from the ceiling, which is covered with 22-carat goldleaf, hangs a chandelier 16 feet in diameter. The Promenade, a popular strolling area during intermissions, is almost a city block long.

PHILHARMONIC HALL This is the home of America's oldest symphony orchestra, the New York Philharmonic. Designed by Max Abramovitz, it was the first building to open at Lincoln Center, on Sept. 23, 1962, and towers nine stories in glass and travertine marble. It contains three outstanding sculptures: Lipton's *Archangel,* a nine-foot high construction in bronze and Monel Metal; Hadzi's *K. 458 The Hunt,* a bronze inspired by a Mozart Quartet; and *Orpheus and Apollo,* Lippold's bronze space-sculpture, which weighs five tons and extends for 190 feet above the Grand Promenade.

VIVIAN BEAUMONT THEATER Designed by Eero Saarinen and opened in 1965, this building is the home of the Repertory Theater of Lincoln Center. The building contains a main theater, which has a seating capacity of 1140, and a small auditorium, The Forum, which is used for experimental drama.

[Lincoln Center-Philharmonic Hall] One of the great pleasures of concert-going in New York is the opportunity to promenade along the corridors of Philharmonic Hall. Huge windows look out over Lincoln Center Plaza. Music lovers can also look across at each other on the several levels of this Greek temple-style concert hall. Orpheus and Apollo, *Richard Lippold's space sculpture, extends the whole length of the Grand Promenade, hanging from stainless steel cables.*

The Plantation, *an 1825 oil-on-wood painting by an unknown artist, is a delightful example of the American primitive style. Some 300 paintings on display in the American section, from the museum's collection of 3000, survey American art from Colonial days to the present.*

Young Woman with a Water Jug, *Johannes Vermeer (1632–1675). Vermeer's realistic depiction of the play of light and shade on objects was unsurpassed until the camera was invented in the last half of the 19th century.*

Irises, *Vincent van Gogh (1853–1890). Van Gogh, a Dutch painter, was influenced by the French Impressionists, as may be seen in the coloring of these flowers. They seem, too, to be infused with powerful emotion and vigorous movement, two other distinctive characteristics of his work.*

Metropolitan Museum of Art

Fifth Ave. and 82nd St., Manhattan New York, N.Y.

Ranked today as the fourth largest museum in the world, the Metropolitan opened in 1871 with a collection of 174 European paintings hung, temporarily, on the walls of a dancing school. Several years later, when the museum moved into the first wing of its permanent home—an elegant Greek Revival building now four blocks long—it had already acquired its famous collection of Greek, Phoenician, Assyrian and Egyptian antiquities, and since then has continued to seek the best examples of available art. Within this 20-acre treasure house are thousands of paintings, drawings and prints, magnificent period rooms, sculpture, an Egyptian tomb, 18th- and 19th-century clothes, ancient jewelry and many other forms of decorative art as well as arms, armor, musical instruments and mummies and a museum for children. Judging by the weekend crowds, European period rooms and European paintings—34 galleries of work from early Renaissance to the present—are the most popular collections. The American collections include period rooms arranged chronologically to illustrate changes in American interiors through the centuries, silver, ceramics, glass and the most comprehensive collection of 17th- through 18th-century American paintings in the world. In the galleries of modern art, 20th-century American paintings are shown together with those from Europe. Major visiting exhibits are frequent. To help visitors decide what to see, free floor plans are available in the Great Hall, and acoustiguides can be rented for a small fee. *Open Tues.–Sun. except Jan. 1 and Dec. 25. Small contribution.*

Aristotle Contemplating the Bust of Homer, *Rembrandt van Rijn (1606–1669). The communicative power of this most expensive painting ($2,300,000) enthralls, as does that of the 31 other Rembrandts in the gallery.*

Metropolitan Museum of Art *(continued)*

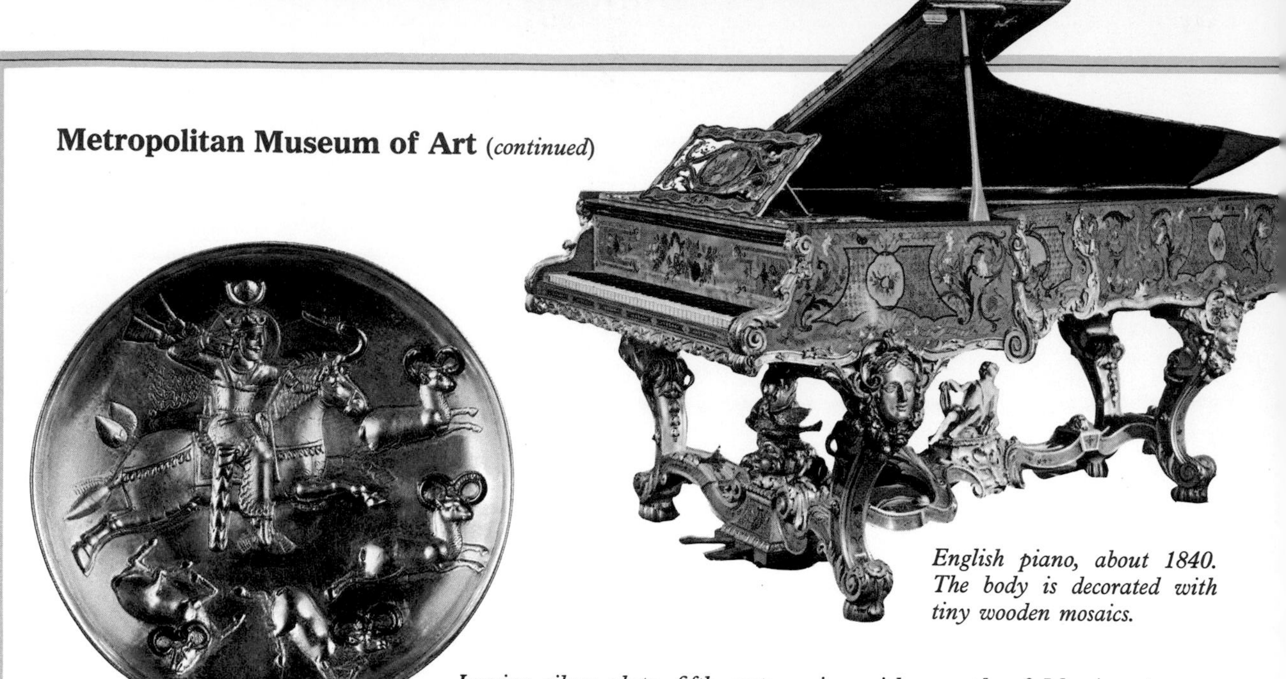

English piano, about 1840. The body is decorated with tiny wooden mosaics.

Iranian silver plate, fifth century, is a rich example of Islamic art.

Gold statue of the Egyptian God Amun (about 900 B.C.) was found in the excavation of his temple at Karnak.

Suits of armor. The Earl of Cumberland (1558–1605) owned the etched steel suit overlaid with gold and probably used it more for jousting than for battle. The Japanese armor, about 1550, looks much more fragile, but is actually made of lacquered steel plates linked with silk ribbons.

Tiffany glass. Louis Comfort Tiffany (1848–1933) is best known for his glass objects but he was also a painter and worked in other decorative arts, such as tapestry and pottery.

18th-century dining room from the Lansdowne House, Berkeley Square, London. This interior was designed by Robert Adam (1728–1792), the man whose neoclassic style so influenced Georgian architecture and design in England and America.

[*Museum of Modern Art*] Three Musicians (*1921*) *shows Picasso's mastery of form and color. He managed to blend all the elements of the composition into a single abstract design with no one figure predominating.*

Morris-Jumel Mansion *Edgecombe Ave. and 160th St.* Captain Roger Morris, a British Loyalist, built this frame-covered brick house in 1765. Considered one of the nation's most handsome Georgian dwellings, it contains much late 18th- and early 19th-century furniture. During the American Revolution the house served at separate times as headquarters for George Washington and British General Sir Henry Clinton. It was purchased in 1810 by the wealthy French merchant Stephen Jumel, whose widow married Aaron Burr in the Tea Room in 1833. Several of Burr's possessions are displayed. Among the notables who visited the mansion were Jefferson, Franklin, Hale and Joseph and Louis Napoleon. *Open Tues.-Sun.*

Museum of the American Indian *Broadway and 155th St.* The largest collection of North and South American Indian artifacts in the world is housed in this Renaissance-style building operated by the Heye Foundation—some 4 million objects in all. The arts, crafts and technology of North American Indians of all periods and areas is effectively displayed in well-lighted exhibits on the first two floors; the third floor shows the cultures of Central and South American Indians from pre-Columbian times to the present. The displays are changed frequently to show more of the vast collection. *Open Tues.-Sun. Sept.-July except holidays.*

Museum of the City of New York *Fifth Ave. and 103rd St.* The city's development from an early Dutch town to a modern metropolis can be traced on the five floors of this attractive Colonial-style stone building. Dioramas, fire engines and an excellent marine collection focus on events in New York City's history. There are impressive displays of early silver, furniture, costumes and toys. Of special interest to adults are the two rooms from John D. Rockefeller's home. Children can handle 17th- and 18th-century household items in the "Please Touch" collection. *Open Tues.-Sun.*

Museum of The Hispanic Society of America *Broadway between 155th and 156th Sts.* Limestone lions by Anna Hyatt Huntington, wife of the museum's founder, Archer M. Huntington, flank the entrance of the first of two impressive buildings. Devoted to all phases of Spanish art from the prehistoric to the 20th century, the collection includes religious paintings by El Greco and portraits by Velázquez and Goya (the latter's famed *Duchess of Alba* is hung here). The large library contains works on Spanish and Portuguese history, art and literature, including early books and manuscripts. *Museum open Tues.-Sun. except holidays; library open Tues.-Sat. Jan.-July, Sept.-late Dec. except holidays.*

Museum of Modern Art *11 W. 53rd St.* Considered to be one of the finest museums of its kind in the world, the museum was opened in 1939 by President Franklin D. Roosevelt. Dedicated to all the visual arts, this museum houses many displays devoted to graphic arts and industrial design as well as to painting and sculpture. Major works by Rodin, Cézanne, Matisse, Monet, Dali and Pollock can be seen here plus photographs by Steichen. The Picasso collection is among the best in the world and includes *Guernica* and *Les Demoiselles d'Avignon.* The attractive sculpture garden, opened in 1953, and the films shown daily in the auditorium are popular attractions. Since its inception the museum has been a major force in encouraging new directions in art. *Open daily. Adults $1.75, children small charge. Donation required Wed.*

New York City Hall *City Hall Pk.* Completed in 1811, this beautiful marble structure is still the seat of city government. Two stories high, it has an attic floor surmounted by a domed cupola in the central section. The exterior and the central rotunda, with its double staircases, are Federal in design but show French influence. The impressive interior rooms are purely Federal. The portraits of past mayors in the Governor's Room are particularly interesting. *Open Mon.-Fri.*

New York Historical Society *170 Central Park W.* Founded in 1804, the Society has been in its present location since 1908. The five-floor museum emphasizes the art and industry of New York from its earliest days. Included are a fine collection of early silver, furniture, toys, fire-fighting equipment and horse-drawn carriages, as well as a large number of maps, lithographs and drawings. An excellent exhibit of weapons ranges from flintlocks to late-19th-century pieces. There is also a large collection of 18th- and 19th-century American paintings, including portraits by Charles Willson Peale, Rembrandt Peale and Trumbull, landscapes from the Hudson River school and hundreds of Audubon watercolors of birds. *Open Tues.-Sun.*

New York Jazz Museum *125 W. 55 St.* Housed in a bright blue former carriage house, the New York Hot Jazz Society's museum is the only center in the world covering the entire scope of jazz, from its African origins to the music of today. The permanent exhibit includes posters, sheet music, photos and instruments played by famous jazz musicians. Changing exhibits focus on a single musician, era or place significant in jazz history. The Jazz Panorama—an audio-visual history—is shown daily, along with a collection of short films in the 50-seat viewing room. Films, live bands and lecturers are part of the extensive touring program. *Open Tues.-Sun. Small charge for films.*

New York Public Library *Fifth Avenue and W. 42nd St.* Almost 4½ million volumes plus a vast collection of engravings, maps, documents, manuscripts and photographs make the Central Research Library here the nation's second largest surpassed only by the Library of Congress. Completed in 1911, the structure's imposing Renaissance architectural style is embellished by three arches and Corinthian columns on the facade; two stone lions flank the wide front steps. Many permanent and temporary exhibits are shown throughout the building, including a collection of American stamps dating from 1845, portraits by Trumbull, Stuart and Reynolds and many Currier & Ives prints of fire fighting. Among the rare holdings are a letter written by Columbus, a Gutenberg Bible and a draft of the Declaration of Independence as it was written by Jefferson. The circulating library also housed here is one of 82 branches in Manhattan, the Bronx and Staten Island. *Open Mon.-Sat.*

New York University When the university was founded in 1831 by Albert Gallatin, the first hundred students occupied rented quarters; in 1837 the first building was purchased on Washington Square. Today the university has 15 schools and colleges at six centers in New York City and over 45,000 students.

80 WASHINGTON SQUARE EAST Constructed in 1879 as New York City's first bachelor apartment building, this six-story, painted-brick structure features multi-storied bay windows. It is now used by the university's School of Education. *Open Mon.-Fri.*

JUDSON HALL AND TOWER *51-54 Washington Sq. S.* This structure, designed by Stanford White, is a fine example of Italian Renaissance architecture. The American artists George Inness, Jr. and John Sloan once worked in the studio comprising the top two floors of this building, which is now a student residence hall.

LOEB STUDENT CENTER *Washington Sq. S. and La Guardia Pl.* This contemporary building is used for student activities and as a recreational and cultural center. Monthly exhibits are held in the Contemporary Arts Gallery, and sculpture displays can be seen in the north lobby. *Open Mon.-Fri.*

SYLVETTE *University Plaza and La Guardia Pl.* This 60-ton, 36-foot sculpture has a background on three sides of tall apartment towers designed by I. M. Pei. The abstract rendering of a woman's bust has been etched by sandblasting to show a patina on the off-white surface of the black Norwegian basalt underneath. The Norwegian artist Carl Nesjar executed the sculpture on site from the prototype designed by Picasso.

WASHINGTON MEWS *Off Fifth Ave., N. of Washington Sq.* This cluster of charming buildings consists of converted stables that predate 1850 and several houses of uniformly low height built in 1939. They are used as private residences and university offices. The street is cobblestoned and closed to traffic; a fine arched brick-and-iron gate can be seen at its east end.

WASHINGTON SQUARE NORTH ROW HOUSES *1-13 Washington Sq. N.* This group of Greek Revival town houses was developed in 1833, and still has the original railing. All the buildings remain in excellent condition. Number Three, remodeled in 1884 in Queen Anne style, has been occupied by famous painters, including Rockwell Kent and Walter Pach. Edward Hopper died in his top-floor studio here in 1967.

Paley Park *3 E. 53rd St.* In a small (1/10 acre) open space between two buildings, ivy-covered walls, locust trees and flower-filled urns offer a restful interlude in an urban setting. A 20-foot waterwall stands at the far end, and chairs and tables on the Belgian-block paving stones attract the passerby. The park, designed by landscape architects Zion and Breen, is a memorial to Samuel Paley, the father of CBS Board Chairman William S. Paley. *Open daily.*

Pierpont Morgan Library *29 E. 36th St.* Designed by the noted firm of McKim, Mead and White and completed in 1906, this Renaissance-style, pink marble structure houses the remarkable library assembled by the famous financier. His son, J. P. Morgan, gave it the status of a public reference library in 1924. An annex more than doubling the available space was added in 1928, and further additions were made in 1962. Each year many outstanding exhibits drawn largely from Morgan's collections of manuscripts, incunabula, prints, drawings and art objects are held. *Open Mon.-Fri. June-July, Mon.-Sat. Sept.-May.*

Riverside Church *490 Riverside Dr.* The nave and tower of this limestone, Gothic-style, interdenominational church were opened in 1930; the south wing was added in 1959. The tower, rising 400 feet, houses a 74-bell carillon. Carved into the impressive West Portal, and forming a frame for the seated figure of Christ, are likenesses of scientists, philosophers and religious leaders of the ancient and modern world. In the nave is a lovely chancel screen of Caen stone bearing 80 carved figures of famous persons, including Luther, Lincoln, Milton and Booker T. Washington. Among the many stained-glass windows are four made for Bruges Cathedral in the 16th century. *Open daily. Small charge for bell tower.*

[*Pierpont Morgan Library*] *Even the borders of illuminated medieval manuscripts are full of life and interest. This scene of St. George slaying the dragon is from the* Book of Hours *made for Catherine of Cleves.*

Rockefeller Center *Fifth Ave.-Ave. of the Americas, 47th-52nd Sts.* Begun in the early 1930's and still being expanded, this complex of office buildings occupies 24 acres of land. In addition to the attractions described below, there is an extensive underground concourse with many shops and restaurants. Guided tours include the 70-story-high Observation Roof of the RCA Building and backstage at Radio City Music Hall. *Open daily. Tours: adults $1.95, children $1.25.*

CHANNEL GARDENS *Fifth Ave. between W. 49th and 50th Sts.* These formal gardens, with fountains and shallow pools, feature spectacular seasonal floral displays. Named because they are flanked by the French and British buildings, they lead to the Lower Plaza.

RADIO CITY MUSIC HALL *Ave. of the Americas and 50th St.* Opened in 1932, this is the world's largest indoor theater, seating 6200 people. Famous for its first-run movies and spectacular stage shows, it features a symphony orchestra, ballet company, choral group and the world-renowned Rockettes. The building is noteworthy for its richly decorated interior. *Open daily.*

RCA BUILDING *30 Rockefeller Plaza* This 70-story building is the "flagship" of Rockefeller Center. Several impressive murals and panels, mostly installed in the 1930s, can be seen throughout the lobby. Guided tours take visitors to the NBC studios. *Open Daily. Tours: adults $1.85, children small charge.*

STATUE OF ATLAS *Outside 630 Fifth Ave.* This 45-foot-high, seven-ton bronze statue by Lee Lawrie was installed in 1937. The figure supports a huge armillary sphere, an ancient instrument used in astronomy, which carries the twelve signs of the Zodiac.

STATUE OF PROMETHEUS *Lower Plaza* This 18-foot-high sculpture by Paul Manship, cast in bronze and covered with gold leaf, has been on display since 1934. It represents Prometheus bringing man the gift of fire. An illuminated fountain serves as a backdrop.

St. Bartholomew's Episcopal Church *Park Ave. and 50th St.* Opened for worship in 1918, this imposing structure is a fine example of Byzantine and Romanesque influences. Particularly outstanding is the triple-arched portal unified by sculptured friezes, which was designed by Stanford White for an earlier church and incorporated into the present building. The five domes of the narthex are lined with intricate mosaics depicting the story of the Creation. Unusually beautiful is a white marble font in the Baptistry in the form of a kneeling angel holding a shell, the work of the Danish sculptor Bertel Thorvaldsen. The pulpit is constructed of intricately worked yellow Siena marble. *Open daily.*

[*Rockefeller Center-Prometheus*] *Fire in his hand, the signs of the zodiac carved into the ring around his waist, he looks down on skaters in winter and patrons of the French and English restaurants the rest of the year.*

[*St. Patrick's Cathedral*] *St. Patrick's, reminiscent of Cologne Cathedral, has long been a cynosure for New Yorkers of all faiths. Stained-glass windows, dominated by a heavenly blue, illuminate the gilded high altar.*

St. Mary's Catholic Church *246 E. 15th St.* Built in 1963, this Byzantine rite church is an interesting example of modern Greek architecture. Its impressive stained-glass walls and abstract bell tower are particularly effective. Inside is a handsome screen with mosaics and a variety of hand-painted icons. *Open Sat., Sun. and religious holidays.*

St. Patrick's Cathedral *Fifth Ave. at 50th St.* Begun in 1858 and consecrated in 1910, this is one of the nation's largest churches, with a seating capacity of about 2500. Designed in the Gothic style by James Renwick, it has twin spires that rise 330 feet. The interior includes 15 side altars dedicated to different saints, a magnificent 9000-pipe organ and 70 stained-glass windows from England, France and the U.S. In the Lady Chapel is an especially graceful white marble figure of the Virgin. *Open daily.*

St. Paul's Chapel *Broadway and Fulton St.* This native stone Georgian structure, completed in 1766, is the oldest public building in Manhattan. Resembling St. Martin in the Fields, a London church designed by James Gibbs, it remains one of the loveliest Anglican Colonial churches in the U.S. The woodwork and hardware are handwrought; most of the ornamentation was done by Pierre Charles L'Enfant, who laid out the original city plan for Washington, D.C. The 14 chandeliers are made of Waterford cut glass. Washington at-

tended services after his inauguration in 1789, and continued to worship here regularly for two years. His pew is marked by Continental Army flags. *Open daily.*

St. Thomas Church *Fifth Ave. and 53rd St.* In 1913 services were first held in this imposing Gothic-style Episcopal church which boasts exceptional carvings in stone and wood. Most outstanding is the superb stone reredos with intricately carved pinnacles and some 60 sculptured figures of saints and church leaders. Rising 80 feet from the altar to the vaulted ceiling, the screen is one of the world's largest. Beautiful stained-glass windows and a delicately carved oak pulpit displaying figures in relief of 19 distinguished ministers further enrich the interior. There are chancel carvings and decorative panels behind the baptismal font with representations of the eight virtues. *Open daily.*

Seagram Building *375 Park Ave.* This 38-story structure was the first bronze building in the world. Designed by Mies van der Rohe, in collaboration with Philip Johnson, it heralded the beginning of a new age in modern architecture. Its greenish-gold hue and amber-shaded windows, the grand plaza, the fountains and the superb scale of the whole endow it with a character that many buildings have emulated but none have equaled. A fine art collection, including works by Miró, Braque and Picasso, can be seen throughout the building. There is also a collection of antique European and U.S. glassware and a replica of an 18th-century Scottish inn with original furnishings. Special exhibits are frequently presented in the lobby and on the plaza. *Open Mon.-Fri. except holidays.*

Solomon R. Guggenheim Museum *Fifth Ave. and 89th St.* Named for the mining magnate who commissioned it, this unusual cone-shaped structure, completed in 1959, is the only building in New York City designed by Frank Lloyd Wright. Within is a quarter-mile spiraling ramp with gently curved spaces where paintings and art objects are displayed. The soaring interior space is, on its own, a work of art. Temporary exhibits augment its permanent collection of almost 3500 19th- and 20th-century works, including paintings by Kandinsky, Léger, Delaunay and Klee, and sculpture by Brancusi, Calder, Maillol, Moore and Giacometti. The Thannhauser Collection of Impressionist and Post-Impressionist paintings is also on permanent display. *Open Tues.-Sun. except July 4 and Dec. 25. Small charge.*

South Street Seaport Museum *16 Fulton St.* This 5-block area and pier on the East River were part of a bustling port in the 19th century. The Georgian buildings and the boats moored here recreate the atmosphere of the original "Street of Ships." Among the vessels are the 1885 Delaware River schooner *Pioneer,* the lightship *Ambrose,* an old Fulton ferry and the steam tug *Mat Mathilda.* The square-rigged *Wavertree,* an 1885 British merchantman, is the flagship of the South Street fleet. *Open daily. Small charge for* Wavertree.

Temple Emanu-El *Fifth Ave. and 65th St.* Dedicated in 1930, this basilica-style Reform temple is one of the nation's largest and most distinctive synagogues. Its three entrance doors stand in a recessed arch highlighted by a superb rose window. The interior, which seats 2500, includes side galleries with marble columns in several colors, a fine Ark of the Testimony flanked by two seven-branch menorahs and much mosaic work.

[United Nations] This nighttime view of the striking buildings making up the U.N. complex looks north along the East River. In the mid-1940s this was an area of deteriorating apartments, slaughterhouses and breweries.

The Byzantine, two-domed, Beth-El Chapel contains handsome marble and two large silver and enamel chandeliers. *Open daily.*

Theodore Roosevelt Birthplace *28 E. 20th St.* Reconstructed in 1922, this is an exact replica of the four-story brownstone house where the 26th President of the U.S. spent the first 15 years of his life. There are five rooms with ornate Victorian furniture, marble fireplaces and patterned wallpaper, and two museum rooms with family pictures, wild animal heads, personal diaries and items that trace Roosevelt's career. *Open Mon.-Fri. Small charge.*

Trinity Church *Broadway and Wall St.* The site with its tree-shaded churchyard, now in the heart of the financial district, has been occupied by Trinity Church since 1697. The present Gothic-style church was dedicated in 1846. Its tower with a handsome spire holds three 18th-century English bells. The white marble altar was installed in 1845 and the bronze doors added 50 years later. Alexander Hamilton, Albert Gallatin and Robert Fulton are buried in the churchyard. *Open daily.*

United Nations *First Ave., E. 42nd-48th Sts.* Dominated by the 39-story glass and marble Secretariat, the 18-acre landscaped area on the East River also includes the General Assembly Building, the Conference Building with its famous Security Council Chamber, and the Hammarskjöld Library. The library, available to graduate students and scholars, specializes in international law and relations, sociology and economics. Among the more interesting art objects is the Marc Chagall stained-glass window in the Conference Building, dedicated in 1964 to Dag Hammarskjöld. On the grounds are several sculptures, including the statue of *Peace* and a work by Barbara Hepworth in front of the Secretariat. One-hour guided tours are conducted in more than 20 languages. *Open daily. Tours: adults $2.00, children and students small charge.*

[Whitney Museum of American Art] Edward Hopper captured the feeling of loneliness and isolation in the American landscape. Early Sunday Morning *shows a deserted street in Nyack, New York, the artist's hometown.*

Whitney Museum of American Art *945 Madison Ave.* Founded in 1930 by Gertrude Vanderbilt Whitney, the museum moved to its present location in 1966. Marcel Breuer's architectural design is an ideal arrangement for exhibiting art. Each of the three gallery floors projects beyond the one below it, providing some 30,000 square feet of unobstructed exhibition space. The severe exterior is relieved by the sculptured form of the projecting windows. Inside, flanking the large galleries, are more intimate, carpeted exhibition areas. The Whitney can lay claim to the most comprehensive permanent collection of 20th-century American painting and sculpture in the U.S., although 18th- and 19th-century works are also displayed. The Ashcan school and the Eight are well-represented, as are the abstract expressionists and the younger avant-garde artists of today. *Open daily. Small charge.*

Woolworth Building *233 Broadway* With its 60 stories rising 792 feet, this was the world's tallest building from its completion in 1913 until 1930. It was built for the founder of the famous five-and-dime-store chain in a Gothic style exemplified by the spire, flying buttresses, statuary, lacy stonework, terrazzo floors, marble wainscoting and the glass mosaic ceiling in the lobby. From the Greek marble entrance arcade to the lobby's fine marble staircases and whimsical gargoyles (including Frank Woolworth, who is seen counting his nickels and dimes), this structure fits its sobriquet of Cathedral of Commerce. *Open daily.*

World Trade Center *1-6 World Trade Center* Construction of the remarkable and ambitious $700,000,000 complex of five buildings along the Hudson River in lower Manhattan was begun in 1966 and is expected to be completed in 1974. These buildings include two of the tallest structures in the world, the 1350-foot (110 stories) North and South Tower buildings, plus the eight-story U.S. Customs Building and the nine-story Northeast and Southeast Plaza buildings. An observation deck and a visitors' escalator that travels the three floors to the building's top are planned for the South Tower; both will provide extraordinary views over lower Manhattan and New York harbor.

QUEENS

Located on Long Island, Queens covers almost 120 square miles and is the largest of all the boroughs. It is the home of John F. Kennedy International Airport and the Forest Hills Tennis Club, where major professional and amateur tournaments are held.

Bowne House *37-01 Bowne St., Flushing* Believed to be the oldest house in New York City, this frame dwelling was built in 1661 by John Bowne, an English Quaker whose descendants occupied it until 1945. For permitting Quaker meetings in his house he was imprisoned in 1662 and finally banished. With the help of Quakers, he made his way to Holland where he appeared before the Council of the Dutch West India Company. They sent a letter to Governor Peter Stuyvesant pressing for religious freedom for everyone. The house is a fine example of the Colonial period and contains original 17th- to 19th-century furniture. *Open Sun., Tues., Sat. except Easter Day and Dec. 25.*

RICHMOND (STATEN ISLAND)

Commonly known as Staten Island, Richmond lies at the outer edge of New York harbor. Still relatively rural, the island is linked to Manhattan by the venerable Staten Island Ferry and the Verrazano-Narrows Bridge.

Conference House *Hylan Blvd., Tottenville* On Sept. 11, 1776, just two months after the signing of the Declaration of Independence, British general Lord Howe offered peace terms unacceptable to Benjamin Franklin, John Adams and other delegates of the Continental Congress in the dining room of this stone house. Built in 1680 by Captain Christopher Billopp of the British navy, this two-story dwelling contains Colonial furnishings, a collection of arrowheads found on the property and remembrances of Franklin. The cellar has a brick floor and a huge fireplace. *Open Tues.-Sun. Small charge.*

Richmondtown Restoration *302 Center St., Richmondtown* Restoration continues at the site of a community, once known as Cocclestown, that was first settled in the 1600s. It thrived as the county seat until 1898, when Staten Island became part of New York City. On its 96 acres are 40 main buildings, several of which have been moved from other parts of the island. The restoration will eventually reflect its interesting history in furnishings and equipment.

LAKE-TYSEN HOUSE *Richmond Rd. and Court St.* This 1740 dwelling with its gambrel roof and open fireplace in the kitchen is a fine example of a Dutch Colonial farmhouse. It was moved here in 1962 and is now restored and partially furnished in the style of the period. *Open Sun. May-June, Tues.-Fri., Sun. July-Aug., Sun. Sept.-Oct. Small charge.*

STATEN ISLAND HISTORICAL SOCIETY MUSEUM *302 Center St.* Built in 1848, this brick building served as headquarters for the surrogate and county clerk until 1919. Most of the museum's items relate to Staten Island and include antique furniture, farm equipment, paintings, old photographs, toys and maps. A library holds genealogical data. *Open Tues.-Sun. Small charge.*

THIRD COUNTY COURT HOUSE *302 Center St.* This Greek Revival structure was built in 1837 and now houses the offices of the Staten Island Historical Society.

TREASURE HOUSE *Arthur Kill and Richmond Rds.* Samuel Grosset, a Huguenot tanner, built this 1700 frame house with a raised fieldstone foundation. It takes its name from the discovery of $7000 in gold coins in the walls. The sum is believed to have been left behind by a British army paymaster during the American Revolution. When fully restored, the building will be used for leather-making demonstrations.

VOORLEZER'S HOUSE *63 Arthur Kill Rd.* A 1695 frame building said to be the oldest elementary schoolhouse in the U.S., it also served as a Dutch Reformed church and home for Hendrick Kroesen, the *voorlezer* (lay preacher). In 1701 it became the home and office of the county clerk. *Open Sun. May-June, Tues.-Fri., Sun. July-Aug., Sun. Sept.-Oct. Small charge.*

59. Rock Hall Museum *199 Broadway, Lawrence, N.Y.* Administered as the Town of Hempstead Museum by the Society for the Preservation of Long Island Antiquities, this 1767 frame dwelling is considered one of the nation's most beautiful Georgian Colonial houses. Owned by the Hewlett family from 1824 to 1948, it bears a delicate balustrade around its gambrel roof and has period furnishings, including several fine Chippendale pieces. *Open Wed.-Mon. Apr.-Nov.*

60. Cathedral of the Incarnation *Cathedral Ave., Garden City, N.Y.* Consecrated in 1885, this 13th-century Gothic-style Episcopal church is beautifully designed in stone. Its soaring tower holds 13 bells originally cast in 1876 for the U.S. Centennial Exhibition in Philadelphia. There are many superb stained-glass windows, intricate hand-carved woodwork and examples of rare marble. *Open daily.*

61. Westbury House *Old Westbury Rd., Old Westbury, N.Y.* The former estate of the financier and sportsman John S. Phipps includes a massive Georgian-style brick and limestone mansion surrounded by acres of lawns, tall trees and gardens. The interior of the 1906 house contains many English art objects and 18th-century furnishings, including pieces by Chippendale, Hepplewhite and the Adams brothers, plus Waterford crystal chandeliers and oak paneling. Its grand rooms have gilded mirrors, handsome old brocades and paintings by Reynolds, Gainsborough and Raeburn as well as family portraits by Sargent. *Open Wed.-Sun. May-Oct. Small charge.*

OLD WESTBURY GARDENS The influence of the 18th-century Great Parks of England is evident in the beech and linden allées and the well-designed and maintained plantings of the 100-acre estate. Visitors can wander through a circular rose garden, a terraced and walled garden and four demonstration gardens for small homeowners. There are fine seasonal showings and, in the summer, a superb perennial garden. Children enjoy the Cottage Garden with its thatched cottage and three log cabins. *Open Wed.-Sun. May-Oct. Adults $1.50, children over 6 small charge.*

62. Sagamore Hill *Cove Neck Rd., Oyster Bay, N.Y.* This informal three-story Victorian house was completed for Theodore Roosevelt in 1885 and served as the summer White House during his two terms as U.S. President between 1901 and 1909. Standing on 83 acres, the 22-room structure contains the original furnishings, including TR's hunting trophies and gun collection and bronzes by Remington and Saint-Gaudens. The large North Room, paneled with Philippine and American woods, is a warm personal room with an amazing assortment of furnishings, mementos and hunting trophies. *Open daily except holidays. Small charge.*

63. Whaling Museum *Main St., Cold Spring Harbor, N.Y.* The town was once a whaling port, and the museum displays a fully equipped whaleboat from a New Bedford whaling ship. There is also a large collection of scrimshaw (carved whalebone and ivory), 700 sailor's knots and other exhibits. *Open Sat., Sun. mid-Apr.-mid-June, daily mid-June-early Sept., Sat., Sun. early Sept.-mid-Oct. Small charge.*

64. Heckscher Museum *Prime Ave., Huntington, N.Y.* Founded in 1920 by financier August Heckscher, this museum is rich in 19th-century American paintings. Eakins, Inness, Blakelock, Church and Moran are among the artists represented; works by European artists such as Cranach, Murillo and Courbet can also be seen. *Eclipse of the Sun* by Grosz is particularly outstanding. An average of six special exhibits are given annually. *Open Tues.-Sun.*

65. Vanderbilt Museum *Little Neck Rd., Centerport, N.Y.* Bequeathed in 1949 as a public museum by William K. Vanderbilt, Jr., this 24-room Spanish-Moroccan mansion set on 43 acres reflects the flamboyant life-style of its former owner. It is filled with rare and unusual furnishings and anthropological items gathered during Vanderbilt's many excursions around the world. More than 17,000 marine and wildlife specimens are exhibited; a vintage car collection is highlighted by a 1906 Reo roadster. There is also a planetarium on the grounds. *Open Tues.-Sun. May-Oct. Small charge for museum; adults $1.50, children over 6 small charge for planetarium.*

[62] *Gutzon Borglum's bronze cast for his sculpture of Theodore Roosevelt at Mount Rushmore dominates this view of the Trophy Room. Here are some of Roosevelt's treasures, including his Rough Riders hat and sword.*

66. Suffolk Museum *Stony Brook, N.Y.* Housed in this attractive native-stone building is the world's largest collection of paintings by William Sidney Mount (1807–1868), a distinguished American artist who lived nearby. The building, nicknamed the Stone Jug, is a former village hall where Mount played the fiddle for local dances. Other exhibits include an old country store, a cobbler's shop, a millinery shop, antique dolls and an Indian diorama. *Open daily except Thanksgiving Day and Dec. 25. Combination ticket Museum and Carriage House adults $1.75, children small charge.*

CARRIAGE HOUSE OF THE SUFFOLK MUSEUM An extensive collection of horse-drawn vehicles, featuring both commercial and private coaches, is shown here. There are two carriages once owned by King Ludwig of Bavaria. Other exhibits include harnesses and a harness shop, tools, and prints and paintings of horse-drawn vehicles. A blacksmith shop, print shop, schoolhouse and the last steam locomotive of the Long Island Railroad are on display. *Open daily Apr.–Nov.*

67. Old House *Rte. 25, Cutchogue, N.Y.* Many intricate structural features can be seen in this restored 1649 frame dwelling which was moved to its present location in 1659. Furnished with period pieces, it has two enormous fireplaces and a handsome chimney. Some of the rare triple-mullioned leaded-glass windows on one wall are original. *Open Sat.–Sun. June, daily July–Aug., Sat.–Sun. Sept. Small charge.*

68. Oysterponds Historical Society *Village Lane, Orient, N.Y.* Orient, Long Island, which dates from 1661, is unique among early American towns—more than half of its present population are descendants of the original settlers. Six buildings have been restored by the society: a village inn, containing exhibits of tools, toys and Indian artifacts; a 19th-century home, with marine exhibits, farm implements and a carpenter's shop; the Old Orient Point Schoolhouse, including a library on crafts and Americana; a combination carriage house and general store; an 1830 dames school which is used to teach craft skills; and a 19th-century homestead, used for temporary exhibits and children's activities. *Open daily July–Oct. Small charge.*

[73] *In this striking church architect Wallace Harrison achieved his goal of combining the atmosphere of a Gothic cathedral—soaring buttresses, diffused light, enclosed space—with a totally modern use of materials.*

69. Parrish Art Museum *25 Job's Lane, Southampton, N.Y.* Samuel Parrish, who founded this museum in 1897, intended his passion for Italian Renaissance and early Roman art to be shared. The museum's permanent collection now numbers more than 1500 works, including Renaissance and modern American paintings, classical sculpture and Renaissance bas reliefs. The museum also has an excellent library. *Open Tues.–Sun.*

PARRISH ARBORETUM This adjunct to the Parrish Art Museum includes a sculpture garden with several marble busts of the Caesars. The landscaped grounds form an attractive setting for the arboretum's many rare and exotic trees. *Open Tues.–Sun.*

70. Suffolk County Whaling Museum *Main St., Sag Harbor, N.Y.* The museum was established in 1936 in the former home of whaler Benjamin Huntting. An outstanding example of Greek Revival architecture, the home was built in 1845. In addition to many whaling relics, harpoons, tools and logbooks, it contains a superb collection of scrimshaw. There is also an early gun collection and a children's room featuring dolls and toys of the period. Outside, an authentic whaling ship is on display. *Open daily May–Sept. Small charge.*

71. Guild Hall *158 Main St., East Hampton, N.Y.* Supported by local artists, writers, musicians, actors and scholars, this cultural center has art classes, films, concerts and lectures. There are galleries and a crafts area which offer exhibitions from the permanent collection of more than 500 paintings, prints and photographs. In summer a regional exhibition is presented. The John Drew Theater, named for the late actor, who was a local resident, is in part of the building and is the oldest continuous summer playhouse on Long Island. *Galleries open Mon., Wed.–Sat. Sept.–May, Mon.–Sat. June–Aug.; theater open for scheduled performances.*

72. Bruce Museum *Steamboat Rd., Greenwich, Conn.* Built in 1856, this granite Victorian mansion now holds natural history and art collections. There are 53 large dioramas representing subjects from Connecticut Valley dinosaurs to an imaginary moonscape. Dioramas also serve as backdrops for displays of the world's birds, mammals, reptiles and insects. There are Indian artifacts from North and South America, the West Indies and Mexico. Two galleries contain African, Etruscan and Chinese art as well as European and American paintings. There is a small zoo in the building. *Open Sun.–Fri. except holidays.*

73. First Presbyterian Church *1101 Bedford St., Stamford, Conn.* Completed in 1958, this church is unique in its aesthetic motif, contemporary structural design and interior appointments. The church was designed by Wallace K. Harrison, one of the architects of Rockefeller Center, Lincoln Center and the United Nations. The sanctuary floor plan and elevations are in the shape of a fish, an Early Christian symbol. Huge reinforced-concrete panels act as walls and frames for more than 20,000 pieces of stained glass that abstractly

[**75.** *Hanford-Silliman House*] *The 18th century is reflected in the keeping room and tavern, while the early 19th century is more apparent in the parlor, dining room and bedrooms. Many pewter pieces are displayed.*

depict episodes from the teachings, crucifixion and resurrection of Christ. These translucent sections, extending to a roof that tilts at 10 different angles, create constantly changing light values. Connected to the sanctuary by a long glass corridor is the education complex. This wing includes a chapel with a beautiful stained-glass window that fills the wall behind the altar with the story of the creation, and a wall mounted with more than 100 stones from at least 30 countries that trace the progress of Christianity. Outside the church, a 260-foot tower supported by four narrow shafts holds a 56-bell carillon, the largest in New England. *Open daily.*

74. Stamford Museum and Nature Center *39 Scofieldtown Rd., Stamford, Conn.* Situated on 100 acres of woodland, this educational complex includes a library, a weather station, collections of Indian artifacts and dioramas showing activities of various early tribes throughout the U.S. An art, drama and dance studio, a planetarium and an observatory with a 22-inch telescope provide instruction for a small fee. The Heckscher Farm and Zoo cares for a wide range of wildlife native to the area as well as for a variety of farm animals. A Junior Curator Program teaches children how to care for the various animals. Each May Farm Day features displays of early crafts and tools plus demonstrations of horseshoeing and sheepshearing. In addition, there are miles of nature trails and an active outdoor theater. *Open daily except holidays. Parking fee.*

75. New Canaan Historical Society Complex *13 Oenoke Ridge, New Canaan, Conn.* Since its founding in 1889, the society has worked to perpetuate the history of the community. Its interesting collections are displayed in the buildings described below. *Small charge includes all buildings.*

HANFORD-SILLIMAN HOUSE Stephen Hanford, a weaver and tavern keeper, built this frame house in 1764. It was later acquired by Joseph Silliman, whose descendants lived in it until 1924. It now contains 18th- and 19th-century antique furniture, early pewter and some antique toys. *Open Tues.-Fri., Sun.*

JOHN ROGERS STUDIO This small frame structure served as the studio of the famous 19th-century American sculptor from 1878 to the time of his death in 1904. A National Historic Landmark, it contains more than 30 of his "Rogers groups" plus many personal belongings. *Open Tues.-Fri., Sun.*

OLD TOWN HOUSE Constructed in 1825, this charming Colonial house serves as society headquarters and also contains a library with books and documents on state and local history. On the second floor is a costume museum with 600 garments dating from post-Revolutionary days through the early 20th century, some of which are used in special exhibitions. In the annex is a replica of a 19th-century New Canaan drugstore, with original fixtures and merchandise. *Open Tues.-Sat.*

TOOL MUSEUM Over 400 early tools used in shoemaking, carpentry and farming are displayed in this small building. A reconstruction of a 19th-century printing office contains a rare handpress. *Open Tues.-Fri., Sun.*

76. United Church of Rowayton *210 Rowayton Ave., Rowayton, Conn.* Dedicated in 1962, this distinctive, contemporary church received the American Institute of Architects' first-honor design award a year later. In its unique sanctuary is a redwood communion table supported by a huge rock unearthed during the excavating. The shingle roof, containing vertical colored-glass panels, twists upward like a billowing sail. *Open daily.*

77. Lockwood-Mathews Mansion *295 West Ave., Norwalk, Conn.* This fortress-like, granite, Victorian mansion was built in 1864–68 by financier LeGrand Lockwood, Norwalk's first millionaire, at a cost of $1,500,000. The 63-room interior is dominated by an octagonal rotunda with a 45-foot skylighted ceiling. Designed by Detlef Lineau, a charter member of the American Institute of Architects, the mansion is noted for the magnificent craftsmanship of its many inlays (both marquetry and parquetry) and carvings in wood and marble. It is now a National Historic Landmark and a museum of Victorian arts, maintained by the Lockwood-Mathews Mansion Museum of Norwalk, Inc. *Open Sun.*

[77] *Even 100 years ago the Lockwood-Mathews Mansion cost $1,500,000—and to heat it in winter took more than a ton of coal a day. Inside, it has notable frescos in blue and green and exquisite wood inlays.*

[**79.** *Winchester Gun Museum*] *This deluxe Winchester 1873 cost $100; the standard model was $60. The gun could fire 15 shots without reloading and was known as the gun that won the West.*

78. Housatonic Museum of Art *Housatonic Community College, 510 Barnum Ave., Bridgeport, Conn.* Established in 1970, this museum boasts one of the largest collections of contemporary art at any junior college. Believing that original works of art should be part of the academic environment, the college began collecting 19th- and 20th-century drawings, paintings, sculpture and graphics in 1967. Picasso, Matisse, Warhol, DeChirico, Dine and Lichtenstein are among the artists represented. *Open Mon.-Fri.*

79. New Haven, Conn.

New Haven has a long history of urban planning which began when the Puritans laid it out in nine equal squares, reserving the central square as a public green. Today its downtown area is involved in one of the most ambitious and successful urban revitalization projects in the country.

Center Church on the Green *250 Temple St.* The British allowed structural timbers for this massive brick building to be floated through their blockade during the War of 1812, thus ensuring its completion in 1814. Based on the design of a London church and built by Ithiel Town, it was designated the First Church of Christ in New Haven. It has an ornate roof balustrade decorated with urns, an elaborate pediment carving and a superb spire. Inside, a Tiffany window depicts a scene of the colony's founding. The crypt holds over 130 17th- and 18th-century gravestones. *Open Tues.-Sun.*

Trinity Church-on-the-Green *Temple and Chapel Sts.* This Gothic Revival stone church, one of the first of its kind in America, was designed by Ithiel Town and completed in 1815. The tower, the long, pointed Tiffany stained-glass windows and the Aeolian-Skinner organ are among its distinctive features. The dark wood interior has a vaulted ceiling and impressive stone piers. The Choir of Men and Boys of Trinity Church, formed in 1885, is well-known for its concerts and recordings. *Open daily.*

United Church on the Green *Temple and Elm Sts.* Built by the noted architect David Hoadley in 1815, this Federal-style brick building with its richly embellished steeple and octagonal lantern-tower is considered to be his masterpiece. In 1855 the Reverend Henry Ward Beecher preached here to a group of abolitionists before their departure for Kansas to join John Brown. The party had earlier been furnished with Bibles and "Beecher's Bibles" (rifles) purchased with money raised by the congregation. *Open Tues.-Thurs.*

Winchester Gun Museum *275 Winchester Ave.* One of the nation's oldest and the world's finest collections of guns and related equipment is displayed here on the street floor of the Olin Mathieson Research Building. Of the approximately 5000 items in this collection, almost 1000 can be seen, ranging from Chinese weapons of 25 B.C. to modern firearms and including examples of all Winchesters manufactured since the late 19th century. *Open Mon.-Sat. except holidays.*

Yale University One of the oldest universities in the country (1701), Yale has occupied its present campus since 1716. The old ivy-covered buildings and Gothic-style dormitories present an interesting contrast to some striking modern architecture. Free guided tours are offered when the college is in session.

ART AND ARCHITECTURE BUILDING *180 York St.* There are nine stories divided into more than 30 different levels which give strong sculptural qualities to this rough-concrete building. It was designed by Paul Rudolph when he was chairman of the Yale department of architecture. Exhibits by art students are shown regularly. *Open daily Sept.-June.*

BEINECKE RARE BOOK AND MANUSCRIPT LIBRARY *Wall and High Sts.* This elegant structure combines granite, bronze, glass and thin, translucent marble walls through which softly glows an amber light that changes with the sun. Outstanding collections include American, English and German literature, Western Americana, medieval manuscripts, early printed books and 18th-century newspapers. The permanent display of a Gutenberg Bible and Audubon's *Birds of America* is augmented by several temporary exhibits each year. The white marble courtyard sculptures by Isamu Noguchi are a modern interpretation of Japanese Zen temple gardens. *Open Mon.-Fri. Aug., daily Sept.-July.*

CONNECTICUT HALL *Old Campus* This is Yale's only surviving pre-Revolutionary building. Built of brick and designed in the Georgian style, it was completed in 1752; the fourth floor and gambrel roof were added later. It is presently used for a faculty room and freshman reading and refreshment rooms.

DAVID S. INGALLS SKATING RINK *Sachem and Prospect Sts.* Designed by Eero Saarinen and completed in 1958, this unusual structure has a huge reinforced-concrete arch which is connected to the low walls with steel cables that support the roof. It is built without interior piers so that there are no obstructions to spectators' views. *Open daily Sept.-Apr.*

HARKNESS MEMORIAL TOWER *High St.* The unique Gothic-style building is the center of Memorial Quadrangle. The 221-foot tower contains a 54-bell carillon, and at its base is a Memorial Room decorated with woodcarvings of scenes from college history.

MARSH HALL *360 Prospect St.* Originally the home of Othniel C. Marsh, the first professor of paleontology in the U.S., the four-story brownstone house is an interesting amalgam of Victorian and Gothic elements. It is a National Historic Landmark. Now used for college offices, its unusual exterior and the adjacent botanical garden continue to attract interest.

PEABODY MUSEUM OF NATURAL HISTORY *170 Whitney Ave.* This 1925 Gothic building houses one of the most famous museums in the world. The outstanding natural history collection includes dinosaur skeletons, an exhibit of Pre-Columbian cultures, birds of Connecticut and dioramas of North American mammals. The life of prehistoric local Indians is traced in photographs, drawings and artifacts. *Open daily. Small charge Tues., Thurs., Sat., Sun.*

YALE COLLECTION OF MUSICAL INSTRUMENTS *15 Hillhouse Ave.* Consisting of a large number of fine keyboard string instruments, many of which are antiques, this is one of the largest and best collections of its kind. Each year free concerts are performed on restored old

[**79.** *Yale University Art Gallery*] *Yale owns over 100 paintings by Colonel John Trumbull. His* Declaration of Independence *here is far livelier than the larger version he did for the Capitol in Washington, D.C.*

instruments. *Open Tues., Thurs., Sun. Sept.-June except college vacations.*

YALE UNIVERSITY ART GALLERY *1111 Chapel St.* The outstanding collection includes Italian Renaissance paintings, Pre-Columbian art, African sculpture, American painting and decorative arts of the 17th through 19th centuries and 20th-century painting and sculpture. Among the best-known works are van Gogh's *Night Café;* Stella's *Brooklyn Bridge;* Revolutionary paintings and miniatures by Trumbull; sculptures by Moore and Maillol and excavations from Dura-Europos. *Open Tues.-Sun.*

80. Henry Whitfield State Historical Museum *Whitfield St., Guilford, Conn.* The Reverend Henry Whitfield, a Puritan leader and the founder of Guilford, built this house in 1639 with stone quarried a quarter of a mile away. The building served the early settlers as a fort, church and meeting hall. A fine example of English domestic architecture, it is believed to be the oldest stone dwelling in New England. The home was restored to its original state in 1936 and furnished in the style of the mid-17th century. *Open Wed.-Sun. mid-Jan.-mid-Dec. except holidays.*

81. First Congregational Church of Old Lyme *Lyme St., Old Lyme, Conn.* One of the most photographed of New England churches, this beautiful building is a replica of another church built on the same site in 1816 and destroyed by fire in 1907. The original was built by Colonel Samuel Belcher, who, it is believed, used plans of a London church designed by Wren. At the portico four Ionic columns support a pediment topped by a square clock-tower, a square belfry, an octagonal stage with engaged columns and finally a spire ornamented with a finial. *Open daily.*

82. Lyme Historical Society Museum *Lyme St., Old Lyme, Conn.* From 1900 to 1920 the American Barbizon Impressionist painters gathered each summer at this 1817 Federal house as guests of Florence Griswold. Canvases and door panels painted by Hassam, Metcalf, Wiggins and Bricknell can be seen. The house also contains a collection of 17th- and 18th-century china and a toy museum. *Open Tues.-Sun. mid-June-mid-Sept. Small charge.*

83. Harkness Mansion *Harkness Memorial State Park, Waterford, Conn.* This 42-room Italian-style mansion, built just after the turn of the century, was the home of philanthropist Edward Stephen Harkness and his wife Mary Stillman. Its rooms are now galleries for one of the foremost collections of bird studies by naturalist-artist Rex Brasher. The luxurious 235-acre Harkness estate overlooks Long Island Sound, and part of the beautifully planted grounds are reserved as a private recreation area for Connecticut's handicapped. *Open daily late May-mid-Oct. Small charge.*

84. Lyman Allyn Museum *100 Mohegan Ave., New London, Conn.* Early New England furniture, silver and toys as well as Oriental, Greek and Roman art objects are displayed in this building which was opened in 1932 as a memorial to a local whaling captain. There are paintings by Degas, Utrillo, Matisse, Gris, Braque, Johnson, Andrew Wyeth and other established artists. There is an art library, and art classes and lectures are offered. *Open Tues.-Sun. except holidays.*

DESHON-ALLYN HOUSE Located on the museum grounds, this 1829 granite dwelling is a fine example of Federal-style architecture. Completely restored, it has many furnishings that belonged to the first owner.

85. Denison Homestead *Pequotsepos Rd., Mystic, Conn.* This frame dwelling was occupied by 11 generations of the Denison family from the time it was built by Captain George Denison III, in 1717, until 1941, when it was willed to the Denison Society. It has several unusual structural details, such as summer beams that run north and south and a trimmer arch supporting a fireplace hearthstone. The house has been restored to show the life of five different periods, including a Revolutionary and a Civil War bedroom, a Federal parlor, an early-20th-century living room, and a Colonial kitchen complete with cooking utensils, pewterware and wooden plates. Furnishings throughout are original family pieces. *Open Tues.-Sun. mid-May-mid-Oct. Small charge.*

[**80**] *The austerity of the Great Hall in the Whitfield House gives visitors an idea of what life was like for the Puritans who had left Surrey, England for the wilds of America in pursuit of religious freedom.*

Fierce eagle holding the American flag is from Mystic Seaport's collection of ship carvings. This traditional American art is still practiced, and visitors may watch craftsmen at work in the carving shop.

Seaport Street resembles many a New England quay of 100 years ago. Beside this stretch of the Mystic River are (left to right): a cooperage, a sailor's home and a working printing press.

Proud figureheads arch out from the walls in the Stillman Building. Glass cases contain fully rigged models of 19th-century and earlier sailing vessels; attached to the ceiling beams are carved ship nameboards.

86. Mystic Seaport

Rte. 27, Mystic, Conn.

The history of Mystic, one of the oldest shipbuilding ports in the country, mirrors the maritime past of cities all along the Eastern seaboard. In the 17th century Mystic-built ships developed a lucrative West Indies trade; in the early 1800s, when sealing became profitable, they sailed to Cape Horn. They plied whaling waters several decades later (whale oil had superseded sealskin in demand) and made for California during the gold rush. Mystic shipyards built transports for the Union Army during the Civil War and, from the 1860s to 1890s, large, fast sailing yachts. Since then shipbuilding has slowed considerably in Mystic, but the port is still well known. For 44 years it has been the site of the Marine Historical Association's 40-acre museum dedicated to the preservation of America's maritime heritage. Seaport Street, on the waterfront, is lined with 19th-century shops: a shipsmith's workshop where whaling implements are forged, a loft where sails are cut and sewn, a carving shop, cooperage and chandler stocked with goods to outfit ships and sailors for long voyages. There is also an authentic waterfront tavern. Moored across the way are a square-rigged whaler, training ship and fishing schooner, some of which can be explored to see what life was once like below decks. Exhibit buildings house displays of figureheads, scrimshaw, ship models, marine paintings, navigation aids, shells and China Trade objects. Nineteenth-century homes, furnished as they might have been by seafaring families, can be visited. The whole atmosphere at Mystic is of complete dedication to the sea. *Open daily except Jan. 1 and Dec. 25. Adults $3.50, children $1.50 Apr.-Nov., adults $3.00, children $1.25 Dec.-Mar.*

The Nellie, *a 30-foot-long wooden steam launch, was built in Boston in 1872 for use on small lakes and bays. Steam generated in the black boiler (center) by a coal fire turned the long driveshaft and propeller. Until the 1900s only the wealthy could afford such a pleasure boat. Aboard the* Nellie *passengers under the fringed canopy could travel as fast as seven knots.*

Most treasured ship at Mystic is the Charles W. Morgan, *a whaler built in 1841 in New Bedford, Mass.*

[92] *The range of Daniel French's talent is impressive. Here in his studio are displayed casts for many famous works, including the* Seated Lincoln. *At the far left is the cast for the bronze doors to the Boston Public Library.*

87. Sterling and Francine Clark Art Institute *South St., Williamstown, Mass.* This white marble building opened in 1955 contains paintings, sculpture, drawings, silver, china and furniture collected by the Clarks. European painters from the 14th to 17th centuries are represented, as are the Americans Sargent, Remington and Homer, but the emphasis is on the work of 19th-century French artists, and the scope of the collections is excellent. Included are many excellent paintings by Renoir, Corot, Degas, Monet, Toulouse-Lautrec and others. There is also French sculpture and a fine collection of old English and American silver. *Open Tues.-Sun.*

88. Williams College Museum of Art *Lawrence Hall, Williamstown, Mass.* This octagonal museum building, completed in 1846, was donated by Amos Lawrence of Boston. Exhibits encompass Roman glass; Greek, Etruscan, Peruvian and Mayan pottery; medieval, Renaissance and Baroque art; and an especially good collection of Spanish painting. Early American furniture is on display, as are English and American portraits of the 18th and 19th centuries and sculpture from the time of ancient Egypt to the present. *Open daily during academic year.*

89. Berkshire Museum *39 South St., Pittsfield, Mass.* Founded in 1903, this museum of art, science and history includes an impressive art collection ranging from early Egyptian through modern American. Among the works of art are canvases by Rubens and Vandyke, and a strong Hudson River and early American collection. *The Flight into Egypt* by Patinir and Bierstadt's *Giant Redwoods of California* can be seen here along with much fine silver, Chinese pottery and sculpture and 15 excellent dioramas of animals in miniature. The historical room contains a life mask of Lincoln. *Open Tues.-Sun. Small charge for historical room.*

90. Hancock Shaker Village *Rte. 20, W. of Pittsfield, Mass.* Settled in 1780, and active for 180 years, this one-time religious community contains 19 buildings, 11 of which can be visited. One of the most interesting structures is the restored 1826 Round Stone Barn which has a diameter of 95 feet and was ingeniously designed to allow entry from three levels. Other attractions include the 1790 Laundry and Machine Shop and the 1820s Sisters Shop with medical, dairy, weaving and herb displays. Throughout the buildings are examples of the labor-saving tools, stoves, furniture and household items of the exquisite, elegantly simple designs for which the Shakers have become famous. There is a Kitchen Festival each August. *Open daily June-mid-Oct. Adults $1.50, children small charge.*

91. Lenox Library *Main St., Lenox, Mass.* Originally the county courthouse, this striking example of Federal architecture was designed by Isaac Damon in 1815 and became a library in 1874. Exhibits feature work by local artists and displays from a permanent collection of autographs, rare books and bookplates. Each summer art shows are given in the library's gallery. *Open Mon.-Sat.*

92. Chesterwood *Off Rte. 183, Glendale, Mass.* The famed American sculptor Daniel Chester French (1850-1931), creator of the bronze *Minute Man* at Concord, Massachusetts, and the marble *Seated Lincoln* in the Lincoln Memorial, Washington, D.C., lived and worked in this summer home. His studio and gallery contain plaster casts and drawings of several of his more famous works, including the two above. A revolving modeling-table, set on railroad tracks in the studio, enabled French to wheel his work outdoors to study the effect of natural lighting. The property, which belongs to the National Trust for Historic Preservation, includes a sculpture area where visitors can try modeling with plastelene, plus a garden and nature trails decorated with statues. *Open daily June-Sept., Sat., Sun. Oct. Small charge.*

93. Mission House *Main St., Stockbridge, Mass.* The simplicity of this 1739 frame house is interrupted only by a lovely pedimented doorway flanked by pilasters. Designed by Mrs. John Sergeant, whose husband was the first missionary to the Stockbridge Indians, it contains fine paneling and period furniture. Also displayed are two huge volumes of the Old and New Testaments which were given to the Indians in 1749 and carefully carried by them to Wisconsin. The house, a Massachusetts Historic Landmark, was moved to its present site in 1928. There is a fine example of an old English garden on the grounds. *Open Tues.-Sun. and Mon. holidays. Small charge.*

94. Naumkeag *Prospect Hill, Stockbridge, Mass.* This 26-room Norman-style mansion was once the summer home of J. H. Choate, U.S. ambassador to England. Designed by the noted architect Stanford White in 1885, the house is marked by turrets, soaring chimneys and gabled windows. It contains many antiques, Chinese porcelains and other art objects. The terraced gardens include formal flower-beds, fountains, pools, sculpture and tree-lined walks. There is also an authentic Chinese temple and garden with stone lions and Buddhas. *Open Tues.-Sun. and Mon. holidays July-early Sept. Small charge for house, grounds; $1.50 for both.*

95. Old Corner House *Main and Elm Sts., Stockbridge, Mass.* This late-18th-century Georgian structure, once the home of writer Rachel Field, is now operated by the Stockbridge Historical Society. It houses a local-history museum and the only public collection of paintings by Norman Rockwell, a longtime Stockbridge resident. His most popular works, such as *The Four Freedoms, The Golden Rule* and *Self Portrait,* are on permanent display, while others are displayed on a rotating basis. *Open daily. Small charge.*

96. Tyringham Galleries *Tyringham Rd., Tyringham, Mass.* This unique building, often referred to as The Gingerbread House, has a contoured roof designed to represent the rolling Berkshire Hills. In the 1930s it was converted from a 19th-century farmhouse into the sculpture studio of Sir Henry Kitson, creator of *The Minute Man* statue in Lexington and *The Plymouth Maiden* in Plymouth. Displays include examples of Kitson's work and other sculpture, paintings and ceramics. *Open daily mid-May-Oct. Small charge.*

97. Sloane-Stanley Museum *Rte. 7, Kent, Conn.* This unique museum contains the Eric Sloane collection of more than 500 early American hand tools and implements. Sloane, a distinguished artist and writer, donated his collection and arranged the displays to serve both artistic and educational functions. The building, a gift of Stanley Tool Works, is a replica of a Colonial barn and is on the site of the Kent Furnace, which produced pig iron for some 70 years in the 1800s. Ruins of the works still stand. Displays in the museum show the original ironworks and explain the smelting process. *Open Wed.-Sun. late May-Oct. Small charge.*

98. Danbury Scott-Fanton Museum and Historical Society Headquarters *43 Main St., Danbury, Conn.* In 1947 the Scott-Fanton Museum and the Danbury Historical Museum and Arts Center merged to better foster interest in Danbury's history and achievements in arts and crafts. *Open Wed.-Sun.*

CHARLES IVES HOMESTEAD Built about 1780, the house was acquired by the Historical Society as a memorial to the distinguished composer, born here in 1874. It was moved to its present site in 1966 and is now undergoing restoration. The home contains Ives' family furniture, heirlooms and memorabilia.

DAVID TAYLOR HOUSE This 1770 shingled house displays Connecticut furniture, costumes and uniforms, children's clothing and toys, Chinese porcelains, Lowestoft and Canton china and needlework.

DODD HOUSE AND HAT SHOP For two centuries Danbury was a major hat-manufacturing center, and this house was the first retail hat shop in the city. It has a unique collection of hats of all periods, machinery, tools and other related materials.

HUNTINGTON HALL This neighboring modern building is the administrative headquarters of the Danbury Historical Society. In addition to offices and lecture rooms, it features changing displays of regional arts, crafts, science and industry.

[**99**] *The subtly blended colors of the fruit and flower designs stenciled on these painted, rush-bottomed wooden chairs gave them a luxurious look, but back in the early 19th century they retailed for as little as $1.50 each.*

99. Hitchcock Chair Company *Rte. 20, Riverton, Conn.* Reproductions of the famous early American Hitchcock furniture are made here in the restored, original factory. From windows in the showroom workmen can be seen milling wooden parts, handweaving chair seats of cattail rushes and stenciling tables, chairs and cabinetry. In an adjacent church which Lambert Hitchcock helped build in the early 1800s is a museum with an extensive collection of 18th- and 19th-century Hitchcock furniture and other decorated pieces of that interesting period. There is also a good collection of early woodworking tools. *Museum open Tues.-Sat. May-Nov., Sat. only Dec.-Apr.*

100. Litchfield Historic District *Litchfield, Conn.* This is one of the best-preserved 18th-century areas in New England. Founded in 1719, Litchfield served as a frontier outpost and trading center and, during the Revolutionary War, as an important military supply depot. The streets of the historic district (around the Green and along North and South Streets) have changed since the early days, but they are still lined with houses of historic interest, many dating from the 1700s. The oldest, built in 1753, was the home of Oliver Wolcott, a signer of the Declaration of Independence. Ethan Allen, Revolutionary leader of the Green Mountain Boys was born here, as were Henry Ward Beecher and his sister, Harriet Beecher Stowe, the author of *Uncle Tom's Cabin.*

FIRST CONGREGATIONAL CHURCH *On the Green* This church is a fine example of the double-octagon steeple design. Built in 1829, it was moved in the 1870s to make way for a new, more fashionable Victorian Gothic shingle church. With the steeple removed, the old church served as a meeting place and movie theater until 1929, when it was moved again to its original site on the Green and was completely restored to its former beauty. *Open daily.*

LITCHFIELD HISTORICAL SOCIETY MUSEUM *On the Green* A collection of 18th-century paintings, including several by Ralph Earl, can be seen here. On display are many beautiful examples of 19th-century American lace, some pieces of American marked pewter and Indian artifacts, as well as the furniture, china and costumes of early Litchfield families. *Open Tues.-Sun.*

TAPPING REEVE HOUSE AND LAW SCHOOL *South St.* The Reeve house is the only residence open to the public. It has a comfortable, wood-paneled room with stenciled walls which came from an early Suffield home and furnishings typical of the early 18th century. On the same property is the one-room law office in which Judge Tapping Reeve started the Litchfield Law School—the first in America—in 1784. Seldom has a building of such modest proportions had such an array of distinguished graduates, including two Vice Presidents, Aaron Burr and John C. Calhoun; three U.S. supreme court justices; many state governors; and well over 100 U.S. senators and representatives. *Open mid-May-mid-Oct. Small charge.*

101. American Clock and Watch Museum *100 Maple St., Bristol, Conn.* More than 600 clocks and watches are displayed here in the Miles Lewis House, a frame building constructed about 1802 and now restored to its original condition. The Ebenezer Barnes Wing was added in 1955. The diversified collection includes some early-18th-century British examples, but mainly illustrates the development of the U.S. clock industry, begun in Bristol and nearby Plymouth in 1790. The timepieces are as interesting for the craftsmanship and beauty of their cases as they are for the ingenuity and precision of their mechanisms. The exhibits include clockmakers' instruments and antique furnishings. *Open Tues.-Sun. Apr.-Oct. Small charge.*

102. North Congregational Church *Main St., North Woodbury, Conn.* Built between 1814 and 1816 in the classic tradition of the New England meetinghouse, this frame church has three handsome fanlights over its front entrances. The tower supports a beautifully executed belfry with eight columns, and a weather vane rises above the lantern dome. *Open Sun.*

103. Church of the Immaculate Conception *74 W. Main St., Waterbury, Conn.* This large Italian-Renaissance-style basilica was completed in 1928. The limestone exterior reveals a richly ornate facade with three sets of double bronze doors. Seating 1500, the interior has a nave with Brescia marble columns and a semicircular apse lined with Siena marble. The fine bronze pulpit and the Stations of the Cross painted on wood are particularly beautiful. *Open daily.*

104. First Congregational Church *Church Dr., Cheshire, Conn.* Situated on a small village green, this attractive church was built in 1826-27 from a design by David Hoadley. It was the third edifice to be built by the Congregational Society, which had been organized in 1724. The portico is supported by Ionic columns; atop the building is an unusual conical spire. The interior has recently been stripped of its Victorian additions and restored to the condition of its original Colonial simplicity. *Open daily.*

105. Christ Episcopal Church *Amity Rd., Rte. 63, Bethany, Conn.* David Hoadley designed and built this small white-pine clapboard church in 1809. The Federal-style exterior has a classical entrance with a semicircular fanlight and Palladian window, a square tower with three black wooden windows in place of glass and a belfry topped with a red, tinned spire and a weather vane. The church survived a fire in 1915. In 1970 it was restored to its original appearance. *Open daily.*

106. Deerfield, Mass.

When this town was laid out in the 1660s, it stood on the western fringe of the colony, and its early settlers suffered from Indian raids. Although most of the original structures were destroyed in an attack in 1704 by Frenchmen and Indians, they were soon rebuilt, and buildings from the early 18th to the 20th centuries can be seen beneath stately old elms and maples. Among the many fine old structures here, the following are open to the public.

Asa Stebbins House An aura of elegance pervades this handsome brick house completed in the 1790s for the son of a wealthy landowner. Portraits by Stuart and Greenwood are displayed with Hepplewhite and Sheraton furniture plus ceramics, glassware and a number of fine rugs. Handpainted wall decorations can be seen in the pantry and dining room, and the south parlor has a handsomely molded plaster ceiling. *Open daily. Small charge.*

Ashley House This unpainted clapboard house was occupied by the Reverend Jonathan Ashley from 1732 to 1780 and later used as a tobacco barn. It has been restored and furnished with period pieces. The front parlor is considered one of the most handsome 18th-century rooms in the U.S. *Open daily. Small charge.*

Dwight-Barnard House Similar in exterior design to many of Deerfield's houses, this 1754 structure was built in Springfield, Massachusetts, by Josiah Dwight. Its unusual kitchen includes the comforts of a living room, and distinctive grained paneling can be seen in the south bedroom. One room is furnished as an 18th-century doctor's office. Early clothing and portraits are displayed. *Open daily. Small charge.*

First Church of Deerfield This nondenominational church built of brick in 1824 still serves the community. Its windows are recessed in narrow round-top arches, and the facade has three doors. The simple square bell tower supports blind octagonal stages, a dome and a weather vane. *Open daily.*

Frary House Parts of this frame house are of undetermined date, but most of it was built in the mid-18th century. The south wing, which contains a fine ballroom, was added in the 1760s when the house was remodeled to become a tavern. Whig meetings were held here during the Revolution, and Benedict Arnold stopped here in 1775 on his way to participate in the attack on Fort Ticonderoga. *Open daily. Small charge.*

Hall Tavern Built about 1760 in Charlemont, Massachusetts, this tavern once served travelers journeying along the Mohawk Trail between Boston and the Hudson Valley. It is furnished with 17th- and 18th-century pieces and also has a pewter collection and century-old tools used to make pewter and tinware. *Open daily. Small charge.*

[**106.** *Ashley House*] *Period furnishings, 18th-century crewelwork, English and Oriental ceramics and old prints and portraits await the visitor who steps through the handsome doorway of this solidly built wooden house.*

Helen Geier Flynt Fabric Hall This converted barn is named for the woman who in the 1940s began with her husband what is now Historic Deerfield, Inc., the organization that restored and now maintains many of these buildings. The building contains a fine textile collection that includes early American and European spreads, carpets, needlework and clothing plus period furnishings. *Open daily. Small charge.*

Indian House Memorial This central-chimney, garrison-type Colonial house is a reproduction of one that was built in 1698 by Ensign John Sheldon and survived the 1704 French and Indian attack. It did not, however, survive a wrecking crew in the mid-1800s. The original door with the hole chopped through by a tomahawk is displayed in Memorial Hall. *Open daily mid-May-Oct. Small charge.*

Memorial Hall The earliest of these connected brick structures was designed by Asher Benjamin in 1797 for Deerfield Academy, founded in the same year. The extensive collection includes Indian artifacts, early American furniture, metalware, tools, tavern signs, textiles and musical instruments. A replica of a Colonial kitchen, installed in 1880, is believed to be one of the oldest period-room reproductions in the U.S. *Open daily Apr.-Nov. Small charge.*

Parker and Russell Silver Shop Named for Isaac Parker and John Russell, 18th-century Deerfield silversmiths, this 1814 frame building contains the workshop of a modern silversmith and a display of early American silver. *Open daily. Small charge.*

Sheldon-Hawks House Owned for two centuries by the Sheldon family, this 1743 frame house contains many family pieces and other early furnishings. Its original paneling and rear staircase with a double approach are interesting; a sewing room exhibits period dresses and fabrics. *Open daily. Small charge.*

U.S. Post Office Reflecting the distinctive architecture of the Third Meetinghouse of Deerfield, which served the village between 1696 and 1728, this modern square frame building now contains the post office for the Deerfield area. *Open Mon.-Sat. except holidays.*

Wells-Thorn House The central part of this restored clapboard dwelling was built about 1717 by Ebenezer Wells, a farmer and tavern keeper, who added the front section some 35 years later. The south rooms contain original paneling and furnishings of the period. A lawyer's office of about 1800 has been fitted out and contains some belongings of Caleb Strong, an early governor of Massachusetts. *Open daily. Small charge.*

Wilson Printing House Returned to its original location after five moves, this 1816 frame structure has served a grocer and cabinetmaker as well as a printer. A working hand press and printed material of the last two centuries are on display plus a number of early furnishings. *Open daily. Small charge.*

Wright House This is one of Deerfield's two brick houses, built by Asa Stebbins in 1824. There is an excellent loan collection of mostly Federal-period furniture with pieces by Phyfe, Sheraton and Frothingham, and there are fine examples of porcelain, including early China Trade tea sets. *Open daily. Small charge.*

107. Smith College Museum of Art *Elm St. and Bedford Terr., Northampton, Mass.* Nineteenth- and 20th-century French and American painting is emphasized in this highly selective collection. The museum is also known for its fine examples of drawings and prints from the early 1600s to the present. *Open daily Sept.-June except holidays.*

108. Mount Holyoke College Art Building *Rte. 116, South Hadley, Mass.* Completed in 1971, this attractive contemporary building houses five art galleries, an auditorium, studios, offices and a library. The Norah McCarter Warbeke Gallery has an unusual collection of Far Eastern art; a number of Greek vases and bronzes are in the Ancient Art Gallery; and the Medieval Gallery specializes in Sienese art. Among the 19th-century American paintings are Bierstadt's *Hetch Hetchie Canyon,* Inness' *Conway Meadows* and Prendergast's *Festival Day, Venice.* Special exhibits are given from time to time. *Open daily Sept.-June.*

109. Holyoke Museum *238 Cabot St., Holyoke, Mass.* Moved to its present site in 1874, this Victorian mansion was the home of William Skinner, a prominent silk manufacturer and philanthropist. It has long been called Wistariahurst for the vigorous flowering vine that clings to its walls. The house itself is a museum. Its staircase with an English wrought-iron banister, a room with leather-covered walls, much hand carving and parquet floors with different designs in every room form a handsome setting for a collection of fine art, antiques and nine dioramas showing the early days of Holyoke. *Open daily Aug.-June except holidays.*

110. Storrowton Village *Eastern States Exposition Grounds, Memorial Ave., West Springfield, Mass.* All the old buildings in this typical early community were donated in 1929 by Mrs. James Storrow, a Boston philanthropist. The structures, built between 1767 and 1834, were dismantled, moved to their present site, put up around a village green and carefully restored. There are volunteer guides in period costumes for tours of the buildings, some of which offer craft demonstrations. Each September during the Eastern States Exposition, a weeklong creative crafts exhibit is held. *Open Mon.-Sat. mid-June-early Sept., daily 3rd week in Sept. Adults small charge.*

CHESTERFIELD BLACKSMITH SHOP The small seam-faced granite structure was constructed in 1825 and originally stood in Chesterfield, New Hampshire.

EDDY LAW OFFICE Zachariah Eddy practiced law from 1806 to 1860 in Middleborough, Massachusetts. In 1810 the building was completed there for use as his office on land that had been owned by the Eddy family since 1640.

GILBERT HOMESTEAD The 1794 farmhouse was built by Levi and Peletiah Gilbert in West Brookfield. Many of its hand-hewn timbers are 30 feet long, and the entire structure is held together with wooden pegs and hand-wrought nails.

LITTLE RED SCHOOLHOUSE Five generations of Whatley children were taught the three Rs in this brick building, constructed in 1810.

PHILLIPS HOUSE Beams and sills of hand-hewn oak plus graduated clapboard widths are among the features of this 1767 gambrel-roofed house. Built by Edward Phillips in Taunton, it is the oldest building in the reconstructed area.

POTTER MANSION Except for the plastering, the entire frame house was built by Captain John Potter, who made the nails and hardware and cut the elaborate wood ornamentation. Begun before the American Revolution and completed afterward, it was moved here from North Brookfield.

SALISBURY MEETING HOUSE Built in 1834, the structure was formerly located at Smith's Corner in Salisbury, New Hampshire. It contains an 1824 Pratt organ, and in the tower is an 1851 Howard and Davis clock.

STORROWTON TAVERN The present tavern comprises two old buildings which have been restored and joined together. One of them, formerly known as the Atkinson Tavern, was originally built in Prescott, Massachusetts, and served also as a store and dwelling. The other section, built in Southwick, Massachusetts, served first as a Baptist meetinghouse and later was used for large town meetings.

111. Connecticut Valley Historical Museum *Rear 220 State St., Springfield, Mass.* The William Pynchon Memorial Building in which the museum is located is one of four in the Springfield Library and Museums Association complex. A fine manuscript collection here traces the economic history of the Connecticut Valley, and seven period rooms show original furnishings from the 17th to 20th centuries. *Open Tues.-Sat. July-Aug., Tues.-Sun. Sept.-June.*

112. Museum of Fine Arts *49 Chestnut St., Springfield, Mass.* Located on the Museum Quadrangle, this building, opened in 1933, holds a number of well-organized collections. There are, among many others, galleries devoted to Gothic, Renaissance, Venetian, 17th-century Dutch and 18th-century French, English and American art. The most impressive displays are the Oriental collections, including Chinese ceramics and bronzes—some dating from the Neolithic period—Tang Dynasty statuettes and Japanese prints. Portraits by Blackburn, Earl and other late-18th-century American artists hang here, as well as works by Gauguin, Millet, Courbet, Monet and Pissarro. The museum also has a good collection of comtemporary American art. A tapestry and armor court in the center of the building is used for concerts and lectures. *Open Tues.-Sat. July, Tues.-Sun. Sept.-June except holidays.*

113. Springfield Armory Museum *Federal St., Springfield, Mass.* Built of brick in 1847, the main arsenal houses over 15,000 military items, ranging from a 14th-century hand cannon to modern automatic weapons. In addition to the permanent displays of arms used in a number of U.S. wars, the museum contains the nation's largest collection of toy soldiers. A popular

[112] *The Springfield Museum of Fine Arts is noted for its collection of late-19th-century American paintings. Prominent among the so-called primitive works is the enormous* Historical Monument of the American Republic *by Erastus Salisbury Field. It is a fantasy of multiple images, with colonnaded towers advancing and retreating into infinity. It is 12 feet by 9, and dominates the collection of pictures by this remarkable artist.*

attraction is the "Organ of Rifles" which Longfellow mentioned in his poem "The Arsenal at Springfield." Once the location of a military installation, the grounds include the commanding officer's quarters, constructed of brick in 1847 in Greek Revival style. *Open daily. Small charge.*

114. Hatheway House *Main St., Suffield, Conn.* This large restored clapboard house was built about 1760 and purchased in 1806 by Asahel Hatheway, an affluent local merchant. Its rooms are elegantly furnished in styles reflecting the whole range of 18th-century decor. The wing added in 1795 is dated and signed and contains four original French Réveillon wallpapers from the 1780s and superb Adamesque plasterwork decoration. *Open daily mid-May–mid-Oct. Small charge.*

115. Avon Congregational Church *6 W. Main St., Avon, Conn.* Designed by Hoadley in 1818, this graceful church is a fine example of the Federal style and the break from the traditional New England meetinghouse. Notable are its Roman Ionic capitals, rare in Connecticut. The original bell cracked while ringing out Lee's surrender at Appomattox at the end of the Civil War and was later recast. *Open Sun.–Fri. Sept.–June.*

[**116.** *Mark Twain Memorial*] *The many-windowed, top-floor study was one of the author's favorite retreats. That it was the scene of great productivity is clearly shown by the author's cluttered desk.*

116. Hartford, Conn.

The capital of Connecticut since 1662, Hartford has recently undergone extensive urban renewal. City planners have won praise for the way they have integrated older historic buildings with the new additions.

Cathedral of St. Joseph *150 Farmington Ave.* This impressive modern cathedral is sheathed with Alabama limestone. Especially notable are 26 magnificent stained-glass windows; and three bronze doors surmounted by a dramatic travertine frieze. *Open daily.*

Connecticut Historical Society Headquarters *1 Elizabeth St.* Founded in 1825, the society's research library and record museum have been housed in the former Curtis Veeder residence since 1950. In addition to the large book, manuscript and genealogy collection, there are nine galleries with changing exhibits. The assemblage of 17th- and 18th-century Connecticut furniture is particularly noteworthy, as are the prints and paintings, including portraits by Trumbull and Morse. *Open Mon.–Fri. June–early Sept., Mon.–Sat. early Sept.–May except holidays.*

Connecticut State Capitol *Capitol Ave.* A great golden dome rises above this marble and granite building designed in 1878 by Richard Upjohn. Bas-reliefs and statues of historic scenes and figures adorn the exterior. Of special interest are the legislative chambers and the Hall of Flags. *Open Mon.–Fri. except holidays.*

Connecticut State Library *231 Capitol Ave.* The Italian-Renaissance-style building is the repository of state archives and books and manuscripts pertaining to Connecticut history. Among the documents on display are the original Charles II charter and the state constitutions. The famous Colt Collection of Firearms is exhibited here, as are the Newcomb Clock Collection and the Mitchelson Coin Collection. A full-length portrait of George Washington by Stuart hangs in Memorial Hall. The State Supreme Court occupies the west wing of the building. *Open Mon.–Sat. except holidays.*

Constitution Plaza *Between Columbus Blvd. and Market St.* This 12-acre urban-renewal complex comprises eight modern office and commercial buildings of glass and concrete, intermingled with raised walkways and attractive landscaped plazas.

Harriet Beecher Stowe House *77 Forest St.* The famous author of *Uncle Tom's Cabin* lived in this simple Victorian house with her family from 1873 to 1896. Fully restored, with many of the original furnishings, it has a number of interesting rooms, such as the small sitting room in which Mrs. Stowe did much of her writing. Nearby is the Day House, containing a research library devoted to the period from 1840 to 1900. *Open Wed.–Sun. Jan.–Feb., Tues.–Sun. Mar.–mid-June, daily mid-June–Aug., Tues.–Sun. Sept.–Dec. and Mon. holidays; closed other holidays. Small charge. Combination ticket with Mark Twain Memorial, adults $2.00.*

Mark Twain Memorial *351 Farmington Ave.* American author Samuel Clemens, whose pseudonym was Mark Twain, wrote *Tom Sawyer, Huckleberry Finn* and *Life on the Mississippi* in this three-story Victorian Gothic house. Completed in 1874, the red brick house contains 20 rooms and has a porch resembling the deck of a Mississippi River steamboat. Many Clemens family belongings can be seen here, and there is a handsome Tiffany window above the fireplace. *Open Wed.–Sun. Jan.–Feb., Tues.–Sun. Mar.–mid-June, daily mid-June Aug., Tues.–Sun. Sept.–Dec. and Mon. holidays; closed other holidays. Adults $1.25, children small charge.*

Old State House *800 Main St.* Completed in 1796, this is one of Charles Bulfinch's masterpieces. The cupola was added in 1826—two years after Lafayette was entertained here. The building served as the State Capitol until 1879 and then as the Hartford City Hall until 1915. The authentic 18th-century restoration of the senate chamber has been widely admired. Exhibits of early Connecticut life and Indian artifacts can be seen. *Open Tues.–Sat. except holidays. Small charge.*

In his oil Gossiping Women, *Francisco de Goya (1746–1828) moved away from the classical themes so popular in 18th-century art and used techniques—flat surfaces, large areas of black—which had a tremendous influence on early modern painters such as Manet and Courbet. His later works became increasingly nightmarish.*

Death of General Montgomery *(oil, 1832) is one of a series of Revolutionary War paintings by John Trumbull (a relative of Wadsworth's by marriage) that were part of the museum's opening exhibit. Trumbull concentrated on American historical scenes; several of them are in the rotunda of the U.S. Capitol.*

Presentation Urn *by Philadelphia silversmith Joseph Lownes (about 1780) shows the influence of the classical style that had recently been revived by English architect Robert Adam.*

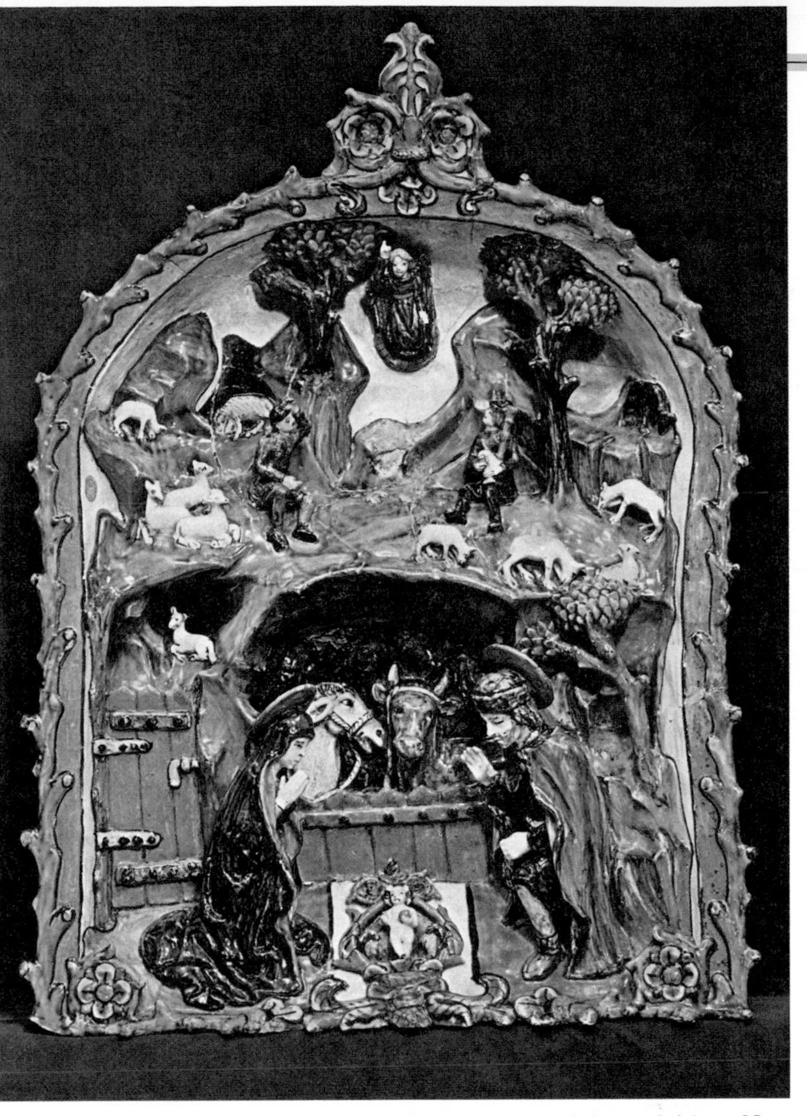

This Italian 15th-century Nativity *is majolica (tin-enameled porcelain), a Near East process introduced to Italy by Majorcan traders. The painting technique was superior to any used in European porcelain decoration since ancient times.*

Wadsworth Atheneum

600 Main St., Hartford, Conn.

The state capital of Connecticut, widely known as the insurance capital of the world, is also the home of one of the finest museums in the country. In 1841, when Hartford was a small town of 13,000, Daniel Wadsworth interested a group of citizens in founding the first public art gallery in America and donated property for the site. The museum, built by Ithiel Town and Alexander Davis in Neo-Gothic style, opened in 1844 with a display of 82 objects, the most important of which were paintings by the American John Trumbull. Over the years the Atheneum has grown in size and importance through gifts and the acquisitions of perspicacious curators. National prominence came to the museum in 1917 when the financier J. P. Morgan (who was born in Hartford) presented it with exquisite Greek and Roman bronzes and 18th-century porcelain from his collection; nearly 10 years later the Wallace Nutting Collection of Furniture of the Pilgrim Century (1620–1720) was donated. Soon after, the Atheneum began to expand under the leadership of A. Everett Austin, a man of eclectic and advanced taste. Before 17th-century Baroque painting was highly regarded, Austin bought works by Caravaggio, Poussin, Murillo and Lorrain. He acquired Italian Renaissance and 19th-century French paintings (Boudin, Gauguin, Daumier, Géricault, Monet), and added to the already impressive American group works by Hopper, Shahn, the Peales, Copley and West. Austin's interest in theater led him to buy the Lifar collection of stage and costume designs created for the famous Diaghilev Ballet. It includes drawings by Picasso, Matisse, Derain, Gris, Rouault and de Chirico—artists whose talents Diaghilev recognized long before they became world famous. While the museum is primarily interested in European and North American art, it also has galleries devoted to the artistic products of Asia and Central and South America. In the past few years the Atheneum has maintained its forward-looking reputation by acquiring works by such contemporary artists as Albers, Andrew Wyeth, Calder, Pollock, and Rauschenberg. *Open Tues.–Sun. except holidays.*

117. Buttolph-Williams House *249 Broad St., Wethersfield, Conn.* The oldest restored house in Wethersfield, this 1692 Colonial frame mansion with an overhang is perhaps one of the finest 17th-century structures in New England. It boasts the most completely furnished kitchen typical of that period. The early wooden and wrought ironware and the rare half-circle settle in the kitchen, along with the fine collections of ceramics and antique furniture in the other rooms, make it an interesting museum-house. *Open daily mid-May-mid-Oct. Small charge.*

118. Joseph Webb House *211 Main St., Wethersfield, Conn.* In 1781, General George Washington and the Count de Rochambeau stayed in this Georgian frame house for five days while they planned the Yorktown campaign that would bring an end to the American Revolution. The bedchamber where Washington slept still has its original dark red flock wallpaper. The exhibits of Colonial silver, rare books, textiles and period furnishings are noteworthy. *Open Tues.-Sun. May-Oct., Tues.-Sat. Nov.-Apr. Small charge.*

119. Farmington Museum *37 High St., Farmington, Conn.* Also known as the Stanley-Whitman House, this oak clapboard structure of the central-chimney type was built about 1660. Now a National Historic Landmark, it has a steeply pitched roof, hand-carved pendants on the framed overhang and diamond-shaped, lead-casement windows. A lean-to was added onto the back of the original four-room house about 1760. At the rear of the house is a carriage shed containing an old sleigh and early farm tools, and a Colonial garden with 30 varieties of herbs and scented geraniums. Early American furniture, household items and manuscripts are on display throughout the house. *Open Tues.-Sun. Apr.-Nov., Fri.-Sun. Dec.-Mar. Small charge.*

[123] *The Goodspeed Opera House presents a 15-week summer season of musicals (it premiered* Man of La Mancha *in 1965) and a variety of programs for members from silent films to children's theater, the rest of the year.*

120. Hill-Stead Museum *Mountain Rd., Farmington, Conn.* This elegantly furnished Colonial mansion, built about 1900 for Mr. and Mrs. Alfred A. Pope, was designed by their daughter Theodate and the famous architect Stanford White. Impressionist paintings collected by the former owners, and including Manet, Monet and Degas, hang on the walls; and various art objects, such as an ivory chess set, Ming Dynasty porcelains and fine bronzes are on display. *Open Wed., Thurs., Sat., Sun. Small charge.*

121. New Britain Museum of American Art *56 Lexington St., New Britain, Conn.* A magnificent collection of American art from the Revolutionary period to the 1920s is on view in this small converted mansion, donated to the New Britain Institute in 1937. Its 16 galleries display almost 1500 watercolors, oils, prints, sculpture and antiques, with strong emphasis on the early 20th century. Among the artists represented are Copley, Cole, Eakins, Johnson, Harnett and the "Eight," the group that included Sloan, Henri and Prendergast. Works by three members of the Wyeth family, Andrew, his father N. C. Wyeth and sister Henriette, are on exhibit as are Benton's famous murals *The Arts of Life in America.* Special exhibits by guest artists are held from October through June, and many lectures, films, concerts and demonstrations are scheduled each year. *Open Tues.-Sun.*

122. Wesleyan University *Middletown, Conn.* Founded in 1831 as a men's college, this small private institution recently became coeducational.

ALSOP HOUSE *301 High St.* The 1838 Greek Revival mansion built by Richard Alsop IV has trompe l'oeil figures on the exterior and interior oil-on-plaster wall paintings that are unique in this country. The beautifully furnished house contains the extensive print collection of the Davison Art Center which covers the history of printmaking from the early 15th century, including most of the great masters. *Open daily Sept.-June except Fri., Sat. during college vacations.*

OLIN LIBRARY *Church St.* This Georgian-style building was named for two former presidents of Wesleyan. Completed in 1927, it was designed by McKim, Mead and White from sketches by Henry Bacon. The building contains over 650,000 volumes as well as valuable collections of publications, manuscripts and papers of John and Charles Wesley, Yeats, Einstein, Camus, Pound and Kazan. *Open daily except holidays.*

RUSSELL HOUSE *350 High St.* This outstanding Greek Revival home was completed in 1828 for Samuel Russell, a China trader. Constructed of brick with an imposing portico supported by six Corinthian columns, it contains 42 rooms. In 1936 the mansion was presented to the university. It now provides offices for the honors committee, the philosophy department and some faculty members. *Open Mon.-Fri. Sept.-June.*

123. Goodspeed Opera House *East Haddam, Conn.* Rising six stories at the river's edge, this beautifully restored Victorian theater, built by William H. Goodspeed in 1876, is the tallest structure on the Connecticut River for several hundred miles. The interior is lavishly decorated in the style of the steamboat saloons of the day and boasts a hand-painted backdrop of a river

[126] *The noted architect Mies van der Rohe ranks Bulfinch's Fifth Meetinghouse among the 14 most beautiful structures in the country. The church was built of Lancaster bricks and slates in the record time of 151 days.*

steamer. The building has been used as a legitimate theater since its restoration in 1963. *Open for scheduled performances early June–mid-Sept.*

124. Gillette Castle *Hadlyme, Conn.* American actor William Gillette, who portrayed Sherlock Holmes on the stage for more than 30 years, designed this unique medieval-style castle overlooking the Connecticut River. Construction was begun in 1914 and completed five years later at a cost of more than $1,000,000. Built of granite and southern white-oak, the castle contains 24 rooms on three floors. All the interior woodwork is hand-carved oak, and each of the heavy doors has a hand-carved wooden lock designed by the owner. The castle with its 122 acres of land became a state park in 1943, six years after Gillette's death. *Open daily late May–mid-Oct. Small charge.*

125. Fruitlands Museums *Prospect Hill, Harvard, Mass.* Author Louisa May Alcott's father made an unsuccessful attempt to found a new religious and social colony here in 1843. Fruitlands, the 18th-century farmhouse on this site, is now a museum of Amos Alcott's Transcendental movement and contains objects belonging to his family as well as to Emerson and Thoreau. The farmstead also has household objects displayed in a Colonial kitchen. On the same site stands the 1790s Shaker House, which features Shaker handicrafts; the American Indian museum with dioramas of early Indian life and prehistoric implements; and the Picture Gallery with a good collection of primitive American art and Hudson River school landscapes. *Open Tues.–Sun. and Mon. holidays late May–Sept. Small charge.*

126. Fifth Meetinghouse *Town Common, Lancaster, Mass.* This National Historic Landmark is popularly called the Bulfinch Church and is widely considered one of the finest examples of this designer's genius. Built of brick in 1816, it reveals details innovative for their day, such as the square tower with its large, round cupola and the arched portico openings. Owned by the First Church of Christ, it contains a superb pulpit and a Paul Revere bell. Displays of church belongings and organ concerts are regularly scheduled. *Open Sun.*

127. Cathedral Church of St. Paul *38 High St., Worcester, Mass.* Built in 1874 in the Gothic style, this dark granite structure has a 145-foot tower which was completed in 1889. Dominating the contemporary interior is a huge, red Resurrection Cross. A modernistic tabernacle flanked by medieval German woodcarvings of the Virgin and the apostles stands in front of a sunburst tapestry. The extraordinary stained-glass windows designed by Clare Leighton trace the life of St. Paul. A Vandyke painting of the head of St. Paul can be seen in the rectory. *Open daily.*

128. John Woodman Higgins Armory Museum *100 Barber Ave., Worcester, Mass.* The collection of arms and armor encompasses examples from the Stone, Bronze and early Iron Ages through medieval and Renaissance periods and the 19th century. More than 100 suits of armor and mail, including boys' and even a dog's, are exhibited in the great hall. Paintings, wood carvings, tapestries and contemporary weapons are also displayed. *Open Mon.–Sat. except holidays. Small charge.*

129. Worcester Art Museum *55 Salisbury St., Worcester, Mass.* A 5000-year-old Sumerian figure and paintings by contemporary artists indicate the range of the permanent collection at this excellent museum. More than 30 galleries, chronologically arranged, hold examples of Roman mosaics from Antioch, 13th-century Italian frescos and paintings by Raphael, Rembrandt, Goya, El Greco, Hogarth, Rouault, Savage, Copley and Stuart. A reassembled Romanesque chapter house from France is one of the major features of the collection. In 1921 and again in 1933, the growth of the collection necessitated expansion of the original 1898 building. The latest addition, the Higgins Education Wing (1970), houses the School of the Worcester Art Museum and public education programs, including children's art classes. A full schedule of films, lectures, seminars and concerts is provided, and special exhibits of paintings, sculpture and photographs are held regularly. *Open Tues.–Sun. except holidays.*

[129] *This exquisite silver teapot in the Worcester Art Museum shows Paul Revere's skill as a silversmith. He was also an engraver; his* Boston Massacre *furnished powerful propaganda for the Revolutionary cause.*

130. Old Sturbridge Village

Sturbridge, Mass.

After the Revolutionary War the job of creating a new nation began. During this period of change from colonial to independent existence, farming communities were the backbone of the country. These villages, spread all along the East Coast, were inhabited by hardworking, public-spirited people. European visitors in the early 1800s were amazed that so many American farmers could read and write, were interested in political affairs and worked at other trades such as law, carpentry or printing in addition to tending their farms. Old Sturbridge Village is a re-creation of one of these self-sufficient American towns and, like them, its center is the village common, graced by a white-steepled meetinghouse. The nearly 40 buildings at Sturbridge Village include farmhouses, barns, a bank, cabinet shop, printing office, grist mill and tavern. All are authentic early New England structures, faithfully restored and in use either as they were originally intended or for demonstrations of early-19th-century arts and crafts, such as candle dipping and barrel making. Sturbridge Village is a working community; the daily routines and chores needed to keep it going are carried out by men and women in period dress. *Open daily except Jan. 1 and Dec. 25. Adults $3.50, children small charge.*

Using a wooden plow and muzzled oxen, a farm worker plows a village field in preparation for planting.

The modes of transportation in the village are limited to those typical of the era—one or two horsepower.

Woodenware, ceramics, New England art and old tavern signs are exhibited in the village tavern.

The meetinghouse on the common is Greek Revival. The style of homes ranges from Colonial to Federal.

The cooper's trade is one of the many demonstrations of early American crafts at Sturbridge Village. In the 18th and 19th centuries staved wooden containers such as these were used for storage of all kinds of goods.

131. Sturbridge Auto Museum *Rte. 20, Sturbridge, Mass.* This is a tour through automotive history, covering the formative stages of the industry from 1897 to 1939, with antique, classic and special-interest cars on display. Among the vehicles are a 1912 Model T Ford Torpedo Roadster; a 1937 car with front-wheel drive and retractible headlights; a 1906 Cadillac Roadster which was driven up the Capitol steps to show its low-gear ability; and a 1900 car with the acceleration of a present-day automobile. *Open daily Apr.-Nov. Small charge.*

132. Henry C. Bowen House *Rte. 169, Woodstock, Conn.* This pink dwelling, called Roseland Cottage, was built in 1846 for a New York publisher, whose guests here included Presidents Grant, Harrison, Cleveland and McKinley. An interesting example of Gothic Revival architecture, it holds many of its original furnishings. The grounds are attractively landscaped and include an outbuilding with one of the country's first privately owned bowling alleys. *Open Tues., Thurs., Sat. June-Oct. State residents $1.00, others $2.00.*

133. William Benton Museum of Art *University of Connecticut, Storrs, Conn.* This fine art museum, established in 1966, is one of the state's newest museums. Housed in a renovated Gothic building constructed in 1920, its broad collections include the Landauer Collection of Kathe Killwitz prints and drawings, one of the country's largest, and the Beach Collection of American and European painting endowed for purchase by former university president Charles L. Beach. *Open daily except holidays.*

134. Leffingwell Inn *348 Washington St., Norwich, Conn.* This fine frame house was built in 1675 and purchased 25 years later by Ensign Thomas Leffingwell, who turned it into a public house. The inn became the site of many meetings by advocates of independence from England. In 1776 George Washington enjoyed a meal in the north parlor, which is still furnished with the original Queen Anne and Chippendale pieces. The furniture in the fully paneled tavern room contains a good collection of late-17th- to mid-18th-century objects made locally. The inn was moved to its present location and restored in 1956. *Open Tues.-Sun. mid-May-mid-Oct., Sat., Sun. mid-Oct.-mid-May. Adults small charge.*

135. Slater Memorial Museum *108 Crescent St., Norwich, Conn.* This large three-story Romanesque structure on the grounds of the Norwich Free Academy displays a broad range of art objects from Oriental metalwork and temple carvings to Greek sculpture to early American furniture. Fine collections of American Indian artifacts, Greek figurines and Egyptian pottery are displayed in the spacious exhibit areas. The Converse Art Gallery offers changing monthly exhibitions. *Open Tues.-Sun. June-Aug., daily Sept.-May.*

136. Addison Gallery of American Art *Phillips Academy, Andover, Mass.* The permanent collection of this attractive gallery is generally recognized as one of the outstanding of American art of the 18th-20th centuries in this country. The original gift of American paintings that initiated the gallery's growing collection was made in 1928 in honor of the 150th anniversary of the founding of the school. Now exhibits include notable selections of Early American silver, glass, furniture and scaled ship models. *Open daily except holidays.*

137. Concord, Mass.

Founded in 1635, Concord was the site of the Provincial Congress and the birthplace of the minutemen. Many famous writers, including Hawthorne and the Transcendentalists Alcott and Emerson, made their homes here, and Thoreau's Walden Pond is nearby.

Concord Antiquarian Museum *200 Lexington Rd.* Period rooms here display authentic furniture dating from 1690 to 1840. Ralph Waldo Emerson's study, removed from his home across the street, and items from Thoreau's Walden Pond cabin can be seen. Among the most interesting displays are relics from the 1775 battle at Concord's North Bridge and the lantern that hung in Boston's Old North Church on the night of Paul Revere's famous ride. *Open daily Feb.-Nov. Adults $1.50, children over 14 small charge.*

Minute Man National Historical Park This historic 750-acre site encompasses the scene of the momentous clash in 1775 between British regulars and American militia which began with the firing of "the shot heard round the world." Besides the points of great national significance detailed below, the site is interesting for its many Colonial houses and part of the route taken by the British on their march on Apr. 19, 1775. On weekends from mid-June to mid-October, musket firing demonstrations are given by latter-day minutemen in costume. *Open daily except holidays.*

MINUTE MAN STATUE This fine bronze work by Daniel Chester French was installed in 1875 to mark the position held by American forces prior to the exchange of fire with the British on Apr. 19, 1775.

NORTH BRIDGE Advancing toward this timbered and plank-decked bridge which spans the Concord River, the minutemen answered the fire of the Redcoats on the opposite bank and forced them to withdraw to Concord. The bridge was reconstructed in 1956.

WAYSIDE This 17th-century house was used to conceal patriot arms at the time British troops sent from Boston passed it on their way through Concord. It was redesigned by the Alcotts in 1842, and in 1860 Nathaniel Hawthorne added the tower as a writing room. Margaret Sidney, author of *The Five Little Peppers,* built the piazzas in the 1880s. *Open Thurs.-Mon. Apr.-May, daily June-Aug., Thurs.-Mon. Sept.-Oct. Small charge.*

Old Manse *Monument St.* The philosopher Ralph Waldo Emerson spent much of his boyhood in this clapboard dwelling, and it was in the study here that he wrote *Nature,* his first book of essays. Built in 1769 by his grandfather, the Reverend William Emerson, a Continental army chaplain, the house is noted for its handsome gambrel roof, the pediments over two doorways and the furniture, much of which is original. Nathaniel Hawthorne lived here from 1842 to 1846, and inscriptions which he and his wife scratched onto window panes with her diamond ring can still be seen. In 1846 Hawthorne wrote *Mosses from an Old Manse* in the same room where Emerson had worked. A Massachusetts Historic Landmark, the house has been owned by the Massachusetts Trustees of Reservations since

 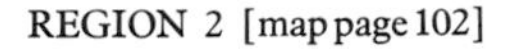 

[**137** and **140**] *Some time after midnight of April 18, 1775, Paul Revere reached Lexington and warned John Hancock and Sam Adams, who were staying at the Hancock-Clarke House (the bedroom of which is shown below left) that the British were preparing to attack by sea. Two days earlier Paul Revere had made a ride to Concord to tell the patriots about the British intention to destroy their supply of arms. On the morning of April 19 the minutemen, alerted by Revere as he galloped toward Lexington, assembled on the Lexington Common, summoned there by the roll of this drum (left) beaten by a 16-year-old youth. The patriots had sufficient arms and luck to hold their own at Concord's North Bridge (below right), and the British were forced back to Boston.*

1939. *Open Sat., Sun., holidays Apr.-May, daily June-mid-Oct., Sat., Sun., holidays mid-Oct.-Nov. Small charge.*

Orchard House *399 Lexington Rd.* Also known as the Alcott House, this Victorian frame dwelling was the home of the Alcott family from 1858 to 1868. Louisa May Alcott wrote a number of her stories here. Originally there were two structures, built in 1650 and 1730, which were later joined and remodeled. The house contains Alcott family furnishings and memorabilia as well as dioramas of scenes from *Little Women. Open daily mid-Apr.-mid-Nov. Small charge.*

Ralph Waldo Emerson Memorial House *28 Cambridge Tpke.* This 1828 frame house was the home of the great philosopher from 1835 to the time of his death in 1882. Still owned by his descendants, it remains intact except for his library and study, which have been moved to the Antiquarian Museum across the street. *Open Tues.-Sun. and Mon. holidays mid-Apr.-Nov. Small charge.*

138. Codman House *Codman Rd., Lincoln, Mass.* Built in the 1730s, this three-story Federal-style house assumed its present exterior appearance in the 1790s. Occupied almost continuously until 1969 by members of the Codman family, the house contains many of their furnishings in several period styles. The Elizabethan dining room dates from an 1860s remodeling. *Open Tues., Thurs., Sat. June-Oct. Lincoln residents small charge, others $2.00.*

139. Buckman Tavern *1 Bedford St., Lexington, Mass.* John Buckman, a member of Captain John Parker's company of minutemen, was landlord here when the British arrived on Apr. 19, 1775. And it was in his taproom that the minutemen waited prior to the Battle of Lexington. Built about 1710, and one of the most popular of the 12 taverns that once prospered in the town, the hostelry appears almost exactly as it did on that famous day in 1775. Original hearths may be seen in both the taproom and the kitchen, along with period furniture and utensils. *Open daily mid-Apr.-Oct. Adults small charge; $1.25 includes Hancock-Clarke House and Munroe Tavern.*

140. Hancock-Clarke House *35 Hancock St., Lexington, Mass.* Originally a parsonage for the Reverend John Hancock, grandfather of the signer of the Declaration of Independence, this hand-hewn oak frame house was constructed in 1698. On Apr. 18, 1775, Samuel Adams and John Hancock, guests of the Reverend Jonas Clarke, were sleeping here under guard for fear of capture by the approaching British, until Paul Revere, according to the popular legend, roused them with his famous cry of warning. *Open daily mid-Apr.-Oct. Adults small charge; $1.25 includes Buckman Tavern and Munroe Tavern.*

141. Munroe Tavern *1332 Massachusetts Ave., Lexington, Mass.* The Munroe family lived in this inn, built (according to tradition) about 1695 by William Munroe, for more than 140 years. Many of their furnishings remain here, including a flintlock musket used by John Munroe against the British on Lexington Common. Lord Percy and his British troops made this inn their hospital and headquarters on Apr. 19, 1775. Washington, a more welcome guest, dined and entertained here in 1789. *Open daily mid-Apr.-Oct. Adults small charge; $1.25 includes Buckman Tavern and Hancock-Clarke House.*

142. Longfellow's Wayside Inn *Wayside Inn Rd., Sudbury, Mass.* Built about 1702 by Samuel Howe, this is said to be the oldest operating inn in the U.S. Formerly known as Howe Tavern and the Red Horse, it acquired its present name after being referred to in Longfellow's *Tales of a Wayside Inn* (published 1863). After a fire in 1955, it was restored by the Ford Foundation and contains much authentic 18th-century furniture. A chapel, one-room schoolhouse and gristmill are on the grounds. *Open daily. Small charge.*

143. Gore Place *52 Gore St., Waltham, Mass.* This unique brick mansion is one of the most beautiful examples of Federal architecture in the U.S. Built in 1805 for Christopher Gore, governor of Massachusetts, from designs conceived by his wife, its 22 rooms contain many fine period furnishings, including pieces once owned by the Gores. On the 40-acre site are gardens and a restored pre-Revolutionary stable. *Open Tues.-Sun. except holidays. Small charge.*

144. The Vale *Lyman St., Waltham, Mass.* Although remodeled and enlarged in the 1880s, this fine 1793 country house still reveals the genius of its designer, Samuel McIntire. His style is especially apparent in the impressive ballroom and bow parlor, the latter displaying two pieces created by him. The stable is also McIntire's work, and the outstanding landscaped grounds include old greenhouses and gardens. *Open daily July-Aug. Small charge.*

145. Fairbanks House *511 East St., Dedham, Mass.* Built in 1636, this ancient lean-to-style structure is said to be the oldest wooden frame house in America. The huge central chimney was made from bricks that served as ship's ballast; the two wings were added later as the family grew. The low ceilings, hand-planed paneling, oaken beams and old wallpaper add interest to the interior. A family home for eight generations, it still has many of the early furnishings. *Open Tues.-Sun. May-Oct. Adults $1.50, children small charge.*

146. Old Slater Mill Museum *Roosevelt Ave., Pawtucket, R.I.* Built in 1793 by Samuel Slater and two partners, the mill was the first successful cotton mill and one of the first factories in America. It contains exhibits of early industrial machinery which is demonstrated for visitors, as well as hand tools and implements. Also open is the Sylvanus Brown House, an early-18th-century urban dwelling, and parts of the Oziel Wilkinson Mill, which dates from 1810. *Open Tues.-Sun. Feb.-Dec. Small charge.*

[145] *Few modern houses blend so well into their surroundings as the old Fairbanks House. The weathered shingles of the sloping central roof seem to rise out of the earth itself. The additions testify to family growth.*

[146] *One function of this restoration of the Old Slater Mill in downtown Pawtucket is that of reducing urban blight and stabilizing the central city by emphasizing its historic role as a cultural and economic center.*

147. Providence, R.I.

Founded in 1636 by Roger Williams, Providence was a noted seaport in Colonial days. After the Revolutionary War it grew to be one of the most prosperous cities in New England. Now the second largest city in the region, it is the capital of Rhode Island.

Arcade *Westminster St.* This unique three-story shopping complex was completed in 1828 in the Greek Revival style. Built of granite with a rose-tinted glass roof, its 12 stone columns are among the largest in the country. The interior contains attractive iron staircases and balustrades. *Open daily.*

Benefit Street This roadway, Providence's second street, was built in the 1750s for the "common benefit" of people who wanted a street farther from the river. Today Benefit Street and the streets nearby are lined with lovely late-18th- and early-19th-century buildings. Below are three of the street's finest homes.

GOV. STEPHEN HOPKINS HOUSE *12 Benefit St.* The rear wing of this house was built in 1707 in another Providence location. Additions were made in 1743 by Stephen Hopkins, ten times governor of Rhode Island and signer of the Declaration of Independence. George Washington was a guest here on two occasions. Lovely period furniture and an 18th-century garden complement the house. *Open Wed., Sat.*

NIGHTINGALE-BROWN HOUSE *357 Benefit St.* This three-story frame Colonial house was built in 1791 for Colonel Joseph Nightingale and is one of the largest of its type still in existence. Some 20 years later it was purchased by Nicholas Brown, member of a prominent shipping family.

SULLIVAN DORR HOUSE *109 Benefit St.* Designed by John Holden Greene, who planned many of the houses on Benefit Street, this fine 1810 Gothic dwelling has a three-story central section between two two-story wings. Thomas W. Dorr, Sullivan's son, led the Dorr Rebellion for universal manhood suffrage in 1842.

Brown University The oldest university in the state, Brown was founded in 1764 as Rhode Island College. In 1804 the name was changed in honor of an early benefactor. Brown was one of the first universities to endorse complete religious freedom.

ALBERT AND VERA LIST ART BUILDING *64 College St.* As would be expected of a building designed by architect Philip Johnson, this one, dedicated in 1971, is modern and functional, with a reinforced concrete exterior, cantilevered sunscreens and a jagged roofline of skylights. Inside are facilities for the university's art department and the David Winston Bell Gallery open for special exhibits. *Building open daily.*

ANNMARY BROWN MEMORIAL *21 Brown St.* This memorial, built by General Rush C. Hawkins in memory of his wife Annmary, comprises a mausoleum, art museum and library. The Hawkins Collection of Incunabula, one of the world's finest, is of particular interest to book fanciers. The memorial is now one of the university libraries. *Open Mon.-Fri. June-Sept., Mon.-Sat. Oct.-May.*

JOHN CARTER BROWN LIBRARY The library's collection of Americana printed during the Colonial period is perhaps the finest one available. Contained here are more than 40,000 items, many of which are regularly displayed. *Open Mon.-Fri. June-Sept., Mon.-Sat. Oct.-May.*

JOHN D. ROCKEFELLER, JR., LIBRARY This building houses the humanities and social-studies collections as well as the central order and cataloging services for the library system. Here also are the Gardner Chinese Collection on the Ch'ing Dynasty (1644-1912) and the Chambers Dante Collection of scholarly editions and commentaries, mostly in Italian. *Open daily.*

JOHN HAY LIBRARY The university library's rare books and special collections are housed here. Among them are the McClellan Lincoln Collection, one of the finest collections of Lincoln books and manuscripts; a nearly complete collection of the writings of John Hay, who served as Lincoln's assistant private secretary; and the Harris Collection of American Poetry and Drama, the largest such collection in existence. The Webster Knight Collection of cancelled U.S. stamps in blocks is also here. *Open Mon.-Fri. June-Sept., Mon.-Sat. Oct.-May.*

UNIVERSITY HALL The building served as a barracks and a hospital for French and American forces during the Revolutionary War and is a National Historic Landmark. Built in 1770, it was the first building on the college campus. An event of great local popularity is "The Illumination" which takes place on Independence Day, Christmas and other special occasions. Lighted candles are placed in all the windows of the darkened building, producing a striking effect. The tradition began when George Washington received an honorary degree here in 1790. *Open daily.*

Church of the Blessed Sacrament *165 Academy Ave.* John La Farge created the stained-glass windows and campanile in this Italian Romanesque Catholic church, and his son did the outstanding frescos. Dedicated in 1904, its red granite and marble exterior and Byzantine interior make it one of New England's most beautiful churches. The marble columns and gold-leaf paintings are especially noteworthy. *Open daily.*

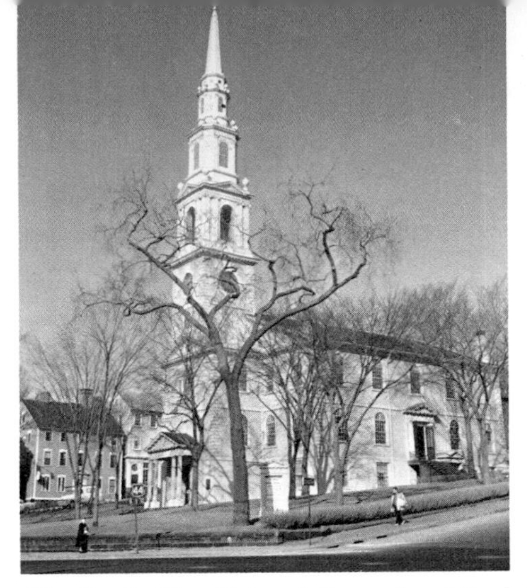

[**147.** *First Baptist Church*] *Joseph Brown found the design for this many-staged spire in a book of architectural drawings. It was one of many studies for the tower of the Church of St. Martin in the Fields in London.*

First Baptist Church in America *75 N. Main St.* The first Baptist church in this country was founded in 1638 by the great champion of religious freedom, Roger Williams; it is one of the two oldest churches in Rhode Island. An excellent example of 18th-century Georgian architecture, the present meetinghouse was completed in 1775. The impressive church steeple, one of the tallest in New England, towers 185 feet above the city, and is considered among the finest of its type. *Open Sun.-Fri. except holidays.*

First Unitarian Church of Providence *Benefit and Benevolent Sts.* One of the largest bells ever cast in the foundry of Paul Revere and Son rings out from the steeple of this Federal-style church, designed in white granite by John Holden Greene. Although organized in 1720 as the First Congregational Church, the present building was not completed until 1816. The focal points are four huge columns which support the pediment of the portico and the great two-story windows which enhance the interior height. The delicate carving and decoration on the ceiling and woodwork are done in the Adamesque style that was so popular at the time. *Open daily.*

John Brown House *52 Power St.* John Brown, a wealthy 18th-century merchant, built this impressive Georgian mansion in 1786. An unusual exhibit here is his chariot, constructed in Philadelphia in 1782 and believed to be the oldest existing carriage made in America. The building, now the home of the Rhode Island Historical Society, contains a fine collection of Rhode Island furniture, paintings, silver and pewter. *Open Tues.-Sun. except holidays. Small charge.*

Museum of Art *Rhode Island School of Design, 224 Benefit St.* Founded in 1877, the museum is noted for its outstanding collections of classical art, 19th-century French and American paintings, European decorative arts and Oriental costumes. An integral part of the museum is Pendleton House, a reproduction of an 18th-century Georgian dwelling. The house contains the Charles L. Pendleton Collection of American Furniture and Decorative Arts. *Open Tues.-Sun. Sept.-July except holidays. Small charge.*

Old State House *150 Benefit St.* This early brick building, erected in 1762, has brownstone trimming, a hip roof and a tower belfry that was added in 1851. On May 4, 1776, the General Assembly passed an act here proclaiming Rhode Island to be the first free republic in the New World. Visited by Washington, Jefferson and Adams, it has served as both a Colonial and a state capitol and is now the home of the Sixth District Court. *Open Mon.-Fri. during court sessions.*

Rhode Island State Capitol *Smith St.* The dome of this impressive building is second in size only to that of St. Peter's in Rome. Built in the early 1900s and designed by the famous architect Stanford White, the capitol is set on a hill overlooking the city. The Senate, House of Representatives and the State Library are housed here. Historic documents and paintings, including a Stuart portrait of George Washington, are on display. *Open Mon.-Fri. except holidays.*

148. Governor Sprague Mansion *1351 Cranston St., Cranston, R.I.* Two state governors who became U.S. senators occupied this house originally owned by a prominent family in the textile industry. Built about 1795, it has Oriental art objects and family memorabilia. The brick carriage house contains a display of sleighs and carriages. *Open Tues., Sun. mid-May-mid-Sept. Small charge.*

149. Smith's Castle *Post Rd., Wickford, R.I.* Smith's Castle was built in 1678 on the site of a trading post owned by Roger Williams, the founder of Rhode Island. In excellent condition, the building is carefully maintained by the Cocumscussoc Association. The furnishings are all authentic, and, in addition to many priceless 17th- and 18th-century antiques, it contains a beautiful collection of dolls in Colonial costume. *Open daily mid-Mar.-mid-Dec. Small charge.*

150. Casey Farm *Rte. 1A, North Kingstown, R.I.* This interesting group of farm buildings, erected about 1750 and still in operation, was once owned by General Thomas Lincoln Casey, supervising engineer for the Washington Monument, Library of Congress and other structures in the nation's capital. Set in a lovely rural location overlooking Narragansett Bay, the farm is maintained by the Society for the Preservation of New England Antiquities. *Open Tues., Thurs., Sat. June-Oct. Small charge.*

151. Whitehall *Berkeley Ave., Middletown, R.I.* The renowned Irish philosopher George Berkeley, later Bishop of Cloyne, built this hip roof house in 1729 on 96 acres of farmland near Newport. He lived here during his brief stay in America while awaiting funds for a college in Bermuda that never materialized. He gave his farm to Yale in 1733 after he returned to England. The National Society of Colonial Dames in Rhode Island has restored and furnished Whitehall as a memorial to Bishop Berkeley. *Open daily July-early Sept. Small charge.*

152. Newport, R.I.

Few cities of its size in the country can claim a more colorful and interesting history. From its beginnings in 1639, Newport was a haven for pirates and privateers of Colonial days, a major port for the trade in rum, molasses and slaves, and an important fishing and ship-building center. In the late 1800s it became the opulent summer playground and social capital of the Gilded Age where the rich came to summer in their sumptuous 70-room "cottages." The records, relics, art and artifacts of its history are well preserved in the city's museums, mansions and landmarks.

Art Association of Newport *76 Bellevue Ave.* Changing exhibits of paintings, sculpture, graphics, crafts and photographs are shown here. The main building was completed as a private residence in 1863, its design based on the English half-timbered home. There are fine carved paneling and different floor patterns in each room. The adjoining Cushing Memorial Gallery, added in 1920, also schedules exhibits. *Open daily Jan. 2-Dec. 24.*

Belcourt Castle *Bellevue Ave.* Designed as a summer residence for O. H. P. Belmont, son of financier August Belmont, this 60-room castle was modeled after Louis XIII's palace in France. Now owned by the

[**152.** *Elms*] *Built and furnished as a unit, the mansion has changed little since its golden days. Crystal chandeliers sparkle on the mahogany walls and gold-coffered ceiling of the Venetian dining room, where eight footmen used to serve the formal dinners. The fireplace is agate and onyx marble. Some of the furniture was sold at auction around 1961, but the interior has never been modified. In 1962 the Preservation Society of Newport County raised the money to save the mansion from demolition.*

[**152.** *Touro Synagogue*] *Peter Harrison used the Georgian style in designing this interior, but adapted it to the requirements of Sephardic ritual. The synagogue's first permanent rabbi was Isaac Touro, hence its name.*

Harold B. Tinney family, it houses their famous antique collection of furniture, paintings, rugs, armor and other works of art from 32 countries. Other highlights include the Royal Arts Foundation exhibition of early French furniture, a replica of an 18th-century Portuguese coronation coach and many fine stained-glass windows. *Open daily Apr.-Nov., Sat., Sun. Dec.-Mar. Adults $2.00, children over 6 small charge.*

Breakers *Ochre Point Ave.* One of Newport's most magnificent residences, this 70-room mansion was built in 1895 for Cornelius Vanderbilt. It was designed by the well-known architect Richard Morris Hunt in the style of the northern Italian Renaissance palaces. All rooms retain their original elegant furnishings, and lavish marble, mosaics, paneling and tapestries can be seen throughout. The wrought-iron fence around the property is an outstanding example of ornamental ironwork. *Open Sat., Sun. Apr.-late May, daily late May-Nov. Adults $2.00, children small charge.*

Chateau-sur-Mer *Bellevue Ave.* Considered one of the finest examples of Victorian architecture in the U.S., this home was originally built in 1852 by William S. Wetmore, a wealthy China trader. In 1872 his son, George P. Wetmore, hired Richard Morris Hunt to expand the house. Hunt's additions included a French ballroom, a library and an Italian dining room decorated by Luigi Frullini of Florence. Many of the furnishings are original. *Open Sat., Sun. Apr.-late May, daily late May-Nov. Adults $1.75, children small charge.*

Elms *Bellevue Ave.* Built in 1901 for Edward Berwind, Philadelphia coal magnate, this stately mansion is an unusually fine example of the 18th-century French chateau in America. Many of its furnishings come from museums; others are original pieces that were commissioned to suit the opulent materials and design of the interior. The grounds include bronze and marble statues, fountains, formal French sunken gardens and a rare collection of trees and shrubs. *Open Sat., Sun. Apr.-Nov. Adults $1.75, children small charge.*

Hunter House *54 Washington St.* This three-story clapboard house dates from 1748 and ranks among the best examples of Colonial architecture. A National Historic Landmark, the interior is notable for its fine carving, paneling, marble pilasters and Dutch-tiled fireplaces. Now completely restored, it features 18th-century Newport furniture, including a number of pieces by Townsend and Goddard, the distinguished Newport cabinetmakers. *Open daily late May-Sept. Small charge.*

Marble House *Bellevue Ave.* This superb mansion was built in 1892 as the summer residence of William K. Vanderbilt. Designed by Hunt, it is styled after the palace of Versailles and was named for the many kinds of marble used in its construction. The highlight of the lavish interior is the ballroom with extensive gold ornamentation and huge mirrors. The home contains all the original furnishings, many of which were designed expressly for the room in which they are used. *Open daily late May-Oct., Sat., Sun. Nov.-late May. Adults $1.75, children small charge.*

Old Colony House *Washington Sq.* Now a National Historic Landmark, Old Colony House is the original capitol of Rhode Island and the second oldest statehouse in the U.S. The Declaration of Independence was read from the balcony on May 4, 1776, two months before it was read in Philadelphia. Completed in 1742, the building is one of the few remaining brick structures of pre-Revolutionary Newport. *Open daily June-Aug., Mon.-Sat. Sept.-May.*

Rosecliff *Bellevue Ave.* The Trianon of Versailles was the model for this lovely French mansion. Completed in 1902, it was designed by the noted architect Stanford White for Hermann Oelrichs. *Open Sat., Sun. Apr.-late May, daily late May-Nov. Adults $1.75, children small charge.*

Salve Regina College *Ochre Point Ave.* Ochre Court, now the main building of this Catholic women's college, was built in 1890 by Ogden Goelet. It was designed by Hunt, the architect of Newport's most luxurious residences, who modeled it after the French châteaus of the Middle Ages. The superb ironwork first seen at the entrance gates is continued inside the house. The wall paneling, the elaborately carved marble and woodwork, and some of the original furnishings are also of exceptional quality. *Open Mon.-Fri.*

Touro Synagogue *85 Touro St.* An architectural gem, this synagogue is the oldest in the U.S., and its interior is considered by many to be the most beautiful. Built in 1763, it was declared a National Historic Site in 1946. The synagogue was designed by Peter Harrison, the most noted American architect of the mid-18th century, and it is still in active use. *Open Sun.-Fri. late June-early Sept., Sun. only early Sept.-late June.*

Trinity Church *Church and Spring Sts.* This lovely Georgian frame church was built in 1726 for the first Anglican parish in Rhode Island. Considered to be one of the most outstanding Colonial churches, the building was designed by Richard Munday and was modeled after the London churches of Christopher Wren. It is noted for its delicate wooden spire topped with a gold bishop's miter. The triple-decked wineglass pulpit is most unusual. *Open daily mid-June-Aug.*

153. Whaling Museum *18 Johnny Cake Hill, New Bedford, Mass.* Scrimshaw, figureheads, sternboard carvings and a large collection of whaling and navigational equipment are among the many interesting items in this unique museum. The main attraction is the half-scale replica of the 1850 whaler *Lagoda.* Over 60 feet long, it is the world's largest ship model and can be boarded by visitors. There are also a doll room and displays of early china and glassware. *Open Mon.-Sat. June-Aug., Tues.-Sat. Sept.-May. Small charge.*

154. Beauport *Eastern Point Blvd., Gloucester, Mass.* Built between 1903 and 1934, this large house has a distinctive exterior, incorporating stone towers, eight different chimneys, various rooflines, terraces and lead-casement windows. The interior is no less unusual with its 40 replica rooms, containing furnishings collected from all parts of New England. Emphasizing the 18th century and reflecting various architectural styles, they include the Paul Revere Room, Benjamin Franklin Room and an interesting Chinese parlor. The house is owned by the Society for the Preservation of New England Antiquities. *Open Mon.-Fri. June-Sept. Adults $2.00.*

155. Hammond Museum *80 Hesperus Ave., Gloucester, Mass.* Overlooking the Atlantic Ocean, this distinctive stone castle was the home of John Hays Hammond, Jr. (1888-1965), famous electronics inventor and devotee of the arts. Built in the Gothic-Renaissance manner between 1926 and 1928, it simulates in its details and furnishings the many period influences seen in Europe. Among the most impressive attractions are a 15th-century courtyard and pool; a magnificent dining room with an intricate 15th-century Spanish ceiling; and a Gothic room displaying a 14th-century Italian wrought-iron bed and floor tiles from the palazzo of Christopher Columbus' son. The Great Hall, extending for 100 feet with a 60-foot domed ceiling and a stone floor, contains a superb Hammond organ with 10,000 pipes, 4 manuals and 144 stops. Many concerts by world-famous organists are given each year on this instrument, which took 20 years to construct at a cost of $250,000. *Open daily, weather permitting. Adults $1.25, children under 12 small charge.*

156. Sargent-Murray-Gilman-Hough House *49 Middle St., Gloucester, Mass.* A terraced lawn with a series of stone steps leads up to this gambrel-roofed Georgian house built by Winthrop Sargent in 1768. The frame structure with much interior carving and paneling was the home during the late 1780s of the father of American Universalism, the Reverend John Murray, who was married to Sargent's daughter. John Singer Sargent, noted late-19th-century portrait painter, is among the artists whose work hangs here. The house also contains antiques and early glassware. *Open Tues.-Sat. June-Sept. Small charge.*

157. John Whipple House *53 S. Main St., Ipswich, Mass.* Exposed joists, chamfered beams and huge fireplaces characterize this house built in 1640 by John Fawn. Occupied by Elder John Whipple two years later, it remained in his family until 1833. Additions were made in 1670 and the early 1700s. It was purchased and restored in 1898 by the Ipswich Historical Society. A lovely 17th-century garden with clamshell walks is open to visitors. *Open Tues.-Sun. mid-Apr.-Oct. Small charge; $1.50 includes Waters Memorial.*

158. Thomas Franklin Waters Memorial *40 S. Main St., Ipswich, Mass.* Built by John Heard in 1795, this Federal-style home and its adjoining formal garden are now owned and operated by the Ipswich Historical Society and named for the society's founder. Over the entrance is a Palladian window; inside is a wide central hall and a Chippendale staircase. The Heard family, in residence here until 1936, acquired their wealth through the China trade, and the house is full of furniture and other treasures from the Far East. There is a museum displaying china, costumes and children's toys. *Open Tues.-Sun. mid-Apr.-mid-Oct. Small charge.*

159. Parson Capen House *1 Howlett St., Topsfield, Mass.* Joseph Capen, a Topsfield minister, lived in this 1683 oak-frame clapboard house. Noteworthy exterior details include carved wooden pendants at the corners, a decorative chimney and an overhanging second story. Inside, large fireplaces, exposed timbers, wide floorboards and 17th-century furnishings can be seen. *Open daily mid-June-mid-Sept. Small charge.*

160. Glen Magna Estate *57 Forest St., Danvers, Mass.* Originally built as a simple farmhouse in 1692 and transformed into a stylish country house two centuries later, this estate is now owned by the Danvers

[**153**] *"A dead whale or a stove boat" was a well-known motto on New Bedford whaling ships in the 19th century. The artist who painted* Stove Boat *shows an unhappy but not uncommon event. Most whalers carried three or four whaleboats, each with a crew of six; the men would race to be first to strike a whale. Some whales attacked boats and men, crushing boats in their jaws or destroying them with a wallop of their tails.*

Historical Society. The 20-room house, with a front-entrance portico and covered porch, is surrounded by 11 acres containing gardens laid out by Frederick Law Olmsted, the designer of Central Park in New York City, and Joseph Chamberlain, the famous 19th-century British statesman. *Open daily May–Sept. Small charge.*

DERBY SUMMER HOUSE About 1793 the Salem designer Samuel McIntire was commissioned to build this charming two-story gazebo at the summer residence of Elias Derby, the wealthy Salem merchant. Moved to the garden here in 1901, the three-room, Federal-style structure has a handsome roof decorated with an urn at each corner and two hand-carved wood figures. A National Historic Landmark, its facade features pilasters and carved swags between the upstairs windows.

161. Samuel Fowler House *166 High St., Danvers, Mass.* In 1810 Samuel Fowler, a leading industrialist, built this fine Federal brick mansion to be near the ships important to his business. Now owned by the Society for the Preservation of New England Antiquities, it is superbly furnished with articles of the period and is also notable for the hand-carved woodwork and 1829 wallpapers by Jean Zuber of France. *Open Tues., Thurs., Sat. June–Sept. Small charge.*

162. Salem, Mass.

Nathaniel Hawthorne wrote *The Scarlet Letter* in Salem, one of the oldest cities in the country. Founded in 1626, it became a prosperous shipping center by 1800.

Assembly House *138 Federal St.* In 1796, 14 years after it was constructed as a hall for social gatherings, Samuel McIntire remodeled this structure into a private dwelling. The pediment with a half-round lunette and the graceful Ionic pilasters on the facade are outstanding. In the Victorian parlor is 19th-century Oriental and Indian teakwood furniture. *Open Tues.–Sat. Small charge.*

Essex Institute *132–134 Essex St.* The history of Essex County through the 19th century is perpetuated in this group of handsome structures. The main building, Plummer Hall (1857), houses a museum where changing displays can be seen along with early Massachusetts furniture arranged in period rooms. Included are collections of silver, pewter, costumes, paintings and redware pottery. A research library in the Daland House (1851) contains many rare books and documents of local significance. The complex includes the Crowninshield-Bentley House (shown on page 159) and the four houses described below. *Open Tues.–Sun. except holidays.*

JOHN WARD HOUSE Domestic life in the 17th century is shown in this 1684 house, moved here in 1910. *Open Tues.–Sat. June–mid-Oct. Small charge.*

GARDNER-PINGREE HOUSE Designed in 1804 for John Gardner by Samuel McIntire, this dignified brick Federal structure contains fine McIntire carvings plus period furniture and early china. *Open Tues.–Sun. June–mid-Oct., Tues.–Sat. mid-Oct.–May. Small charge.*

LYE-TAPLEY SHOE SHOP Believed to have been built in 1830, this small building displays the evolution of shoemaking from 1750 to 1850. It was moved to its present site from Lynn in 1910. *Open Tues.–Sun. June–mid-Oct.*

VAUGHAN DOLL HOUSE The extensive Elizabeth R. Vaughan collection of dolls and other toys can be seen

[**162.** *Peabody Museum*] *The first American ship that sailed for China brought back 137 chests of porcelain. Patriotic and commercial themes, like this painting of the Salem ship* Friendship, *were highly prized. Porcelain, since it also served as ballast, virtually paid its own way.*

in this house, which was built around 1688 to serve as a Quaker meetinghouse. It was moved here in 1865. *Open Tues.–Sun. June–mid-Oct.*

Hamilton Hall *9 Chestnut St.* The famous Colonial designer and master carver Samuel McIntire utilized Palladian windows and ornate swags to add distinction to this social hall which he completed in 1805. Considered one of his most successful designs, it is now a National Historic Landmark. The interior includes a large elegant ballroom where lectures, parties and other social events are still held. *Open Mon.–Sat.*

Peabody Museum of Salem *161 Essex St.* The East India Marine Society of Salem, organized in 1799, built this structure for a meeting hall in 1824. It was enlarged from time to time to hold the growing collection of objects from the Far East, Pacific, Africa and North and South America, as well as memorabilia of the society. In addition to ethnological and maritime displays, the natural history of Essex County is represented with dioramas and bird and fish exhibits. The library has a valuable collection relating to the museum's interests. *Museum open daily, library open Mon.–Fri. except holidays. Small charge.*

Peirce-Nichols House *80 Federal St.* This handsome three-story Georgian clapboard house built in 1782 is one of Samuel McIntire's earliest and most successful designs. The interior reveals both Georgian and Federal details and contains authentic furnishings of the period. *Open Tues.–Sat. Small charge.*

Ropes Mansion *318 Essex St.* This typical home of a wealthy merchant and sea captain, built in 1719, was occupied by Judge Nathaniel Ropes and three generations of his descendants. The house is furnished with original family pieces and also contains a fine collection of Chinese porcelain and early Irish glass. Handsome formal gardens are on the grounds. *Open Mon.–Sat. May–Oct. Small charge.*

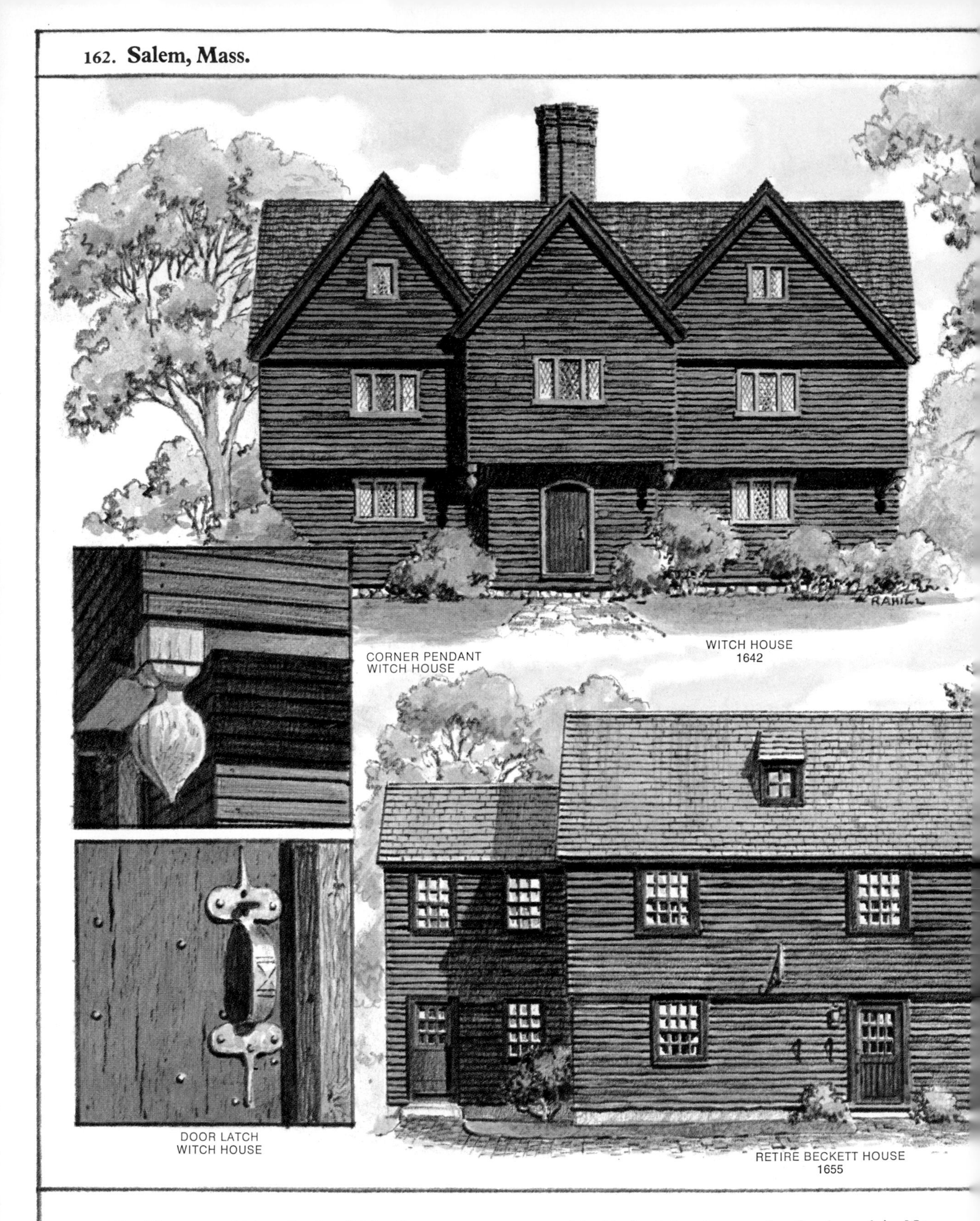

CORNER PENDANT
WITCH HOUSE

WITCH HOUSE
1642

DOOR LATCH
WITCH HOUSE

RETIRE BECKETT HOUSE
1655

The Elements of New England Wood Colonial Style

Seventeenth-century New England houses reflect the character and background of the Puritans who built them. They are solid and direct, similar to the Puritans' former homes in England. Wood, abundantly available to them, is the basic material, with chimneys of brick and steep pitched roofs of shingles. (Thatch had been used in England but it proved a fire hazard in New England and gave too little protection from the cold.) Windows were small—no more than two feet square—with leaded glazing or oiled paper, since glass was expensive and hard to replace. It is not too widely recognized that the Puritans were, in the main, well educated and highly cultivated. They did not frown on beauty for its own sake, and they liked to employ decorative architectural elements, as can be seen in the drop

HOUSE OF SEVEN GABLES
1668

CROWNINSHIELD-BENTLEY HOUSE
1727

ENTRY DETAIL
CROWNINSHIELD-BENTLEY HOUSE

pendant and iron door handle of the Witch House and the fancy brickwork of its chimney. The second-story overhang, a space-gaining device in crowded English towns, was copied literally at first, later used mainly for decorative effect (see the Retire Beckett facade). As Salem residents prospered through shipbuilding and foreign trade and many of the families became quite wealthy, sizable additions were made to existing houses. The House of Seven Gables, for instance, was originally a two-room, one-chimney house. Prosperity brought a desire for the latest, so-called English style, as well as the money to acquire it. In the Crowninshield-Bentley House, the symmetry, pedimented Doric-columned doorway and four-paneled door, gambrel roof, large windows and painted facade are all elements of the Georgian style that superseded wood Colonial—first in East Coast towns and later farther west. The Puritans' architectural style, though functional, was short-lived.

(*continued next page*)

162. Salem, Mass.: New England Wood Colonial Style

(*See feature display on pages 158–9*)

Salem was settled in 1626 when an adventurous band of Puritans left Plymouth to establish a new outpost at what was then the Indian fishing village of Naumkeag. Evidence indicates that their first dwellings were temporary shelters of two kinds—timber-lined, thatched-roofed dugouts and wigwams patterned after those of the local Indians. Salem was a thriving community of several thousand people by 1692, the year the witchcraft hysteria spread through the town as the result of the false accusations of a few young girls. When Salem residents began to build permanent homes for themselves in the 1630s and '40s, they modeled them on the sturdy Elizabethan houses they had abandoned in their native land. The most important room was the combination kitchen-dining-living room, dominated by a large fireplace which provided cooking and baking facilities as well as heat. In the main, daily life was carried on in this large all-purpose room. Privacy was not an important concern to people in the 17th century and, besides, upstairs rooms were hard to heat. Most New England adaptations of this basic plan were made to provide better insulation from the harsher climate and protection from Indians. The inside walls of the half-timbered structures were daubed with clay, later plastered and paneled. Clapboard was added onto the outside. Iron hinges and frames were used both on the double-thick doors and the small-sized windows. Salem has outstanding examples of the few houses of this type left in New England. The following are among the most interesting from an architectural and historical point of view.

Crowninshield-Bentley House *132 Essex St.* The wealthy Crowninshield shipping family designed its early 18th-century home in the Georgian style, first used in England. Later additions and furnishings were added and the house now reflects the taste of an entire century. *Open Tues.–Sun. June–mid-Oct. except July 4. Small charge.*

House of Seven Gables *54 Turner St.* Nathaniel Hawthorne immortalized this house in his famous novel of the same name. When Captain John Turner built it in 1668, it consisted of only two rooms. *Open daily except holidays. Adults $1.25 early Sept.–June, $2.00 July–early Sept.; children small charge.*

Retire Beckett House *54 Turner St.* Larger square-paned, up-and-down sash windows, the paned door and narrower overhang make this 1655 house appear more modern than nearby Hathaway House (1682). *Beckett House open daily Apr.–Nov.; Hathaway House open daily July–Aug.*

Witch House *310½ Essex St.* The home of Judge Jonathan Corwin, dating from 1642, is so called because witch pre-trial examinations were held here in 1692. The house is typical of the early 17th-century style with its steep roof, gables, central chimney, overhang and small windows. *Open daily mid-March–Nov. Small charge.*

Salem Maritime National Historic Site *Derby St.* Salem's rich heritage as a once-important seaport is reflected in this interesting preservation. Encompassing one mile of waterfront and several buildings, it is administered by the National Park Service. *Open daily.*

CUSTOM HOUSE A fine Palladian window and a large gilded eagle perched on the roof balustrade mark this 1819 Federal brick structure. Nathaniel Hawthorne worked here for three years as surveyor of the port, and referred to it in *The Scarlet Letter.* The cupola and bonded warehouse are open to visitors, and exhibits of Salem's link with the sea are presented.

DERBY HOUSE Completed in 1762, this is Salem's oldest brick house. It was built for Elias Derby by his father, a wealthy merchant and shipowner, whose business he later inherited. Inside the Georgian structure is much outstanding woodwork, including a beautiful staircase; some of the original wall paint can still be seen. *Small charge.*

DERBY WHARF This is a reconstruction of docking facilities built in the 1760s by Captain Richard Derby, whose son Elias later used them for fitting out Revolutionary War privateers. Jutting almost 2000 feet into the harbor with an 1871 lighthouse at its head, the wharf was a center for merchant-shipping activity.

HAWKES HOUSE Designed about 1780 by Samuel McIntire as a second home for Elias Derby, this frame house was purchased and remodeled in 1801 by Captain Benjamin Hawkes, a merchant and shipbuilder.

SCALE HOUSE The weighing and measuring instruments displayed here were moved onto the nearby wharves when a ship came in so that custom duties on coffee, spices, rum and other goods could be estimated. The building dates from 1829.

WEST INDIA GOODS STORE Built about 1800 as an outlet for sugar, molasses, rum, oranges and other goods brought from the West Indies, this structure is now an antiques shop.

163. Jeremiah Lee Mansion *161 Washington St., Marblehead, Mass.* Completed in 1768 for a prominent merchant and patriot, this superb Georgian frame dwelling gives the appearance of being built of stone. The illusion was created by adding sand to the original exterior paint. Fully restored, its handsome details include a front entrance portico, fanlight and cupola, interior paneling, an elaborate solid-mahogany stairway, original hand-painted English wallpaper and fine examples of period furniture. Primitive paintings, original letters and documents of local historic interest are displayed. Among the distinguished guests here were George Washington, General Lafayette, James Monroe and Andrew Jackson. From 1804 the house was used as a bank for more than 100 years; it was acquired in 1909 by the Marblehead Historical Society. *Open Mon.–Sat. mid-May–mid-Oct. Small charge.*

164. King Hooper Mansion *8 Hooper St., Marblehead, Mass.* Robert Hooper, fondly called King by sailors on his merchant ships, lived in this 1728 frame dwelling. In 1747 he added the Georgian front section with a simulated stone facade. Attractions include an ornate stairway, superb paneling, early furniture and a third-story ballroom; the grounds are beautifully planted. *Open Tues.–Sun. Small charge.*

165. Saugus Iron Works National Historic Site *244 Central St., Saugus, Mass.* Consisting of a blast furnace, forge, hammer, bellows and several waterwheels, this is a working reproduction of a plant established on this site in 1646 through the efforts of John Winthrop, Jr., son of the governor of the Massachusetts Bay Colony. For almost 25 years, bars and rods of iron were produced for a fledgling nation in need of hoes, hinges, shovels, scythes, nails and other tools and hardware. Constructed in 1954, the site enables visitors to observe 17th-century techniques used in the production of iron. *Open daily.*

IRONMASTER'S HOUSE This multigabled frame house is a fine example of 17th-century architecture, with leaded windows and carved pendants at the corners. Built in 1648 by the company of undertakers for the ironworks in New England, it contains 10-foot fireplaces, hand-hewn beams and period furniture.

IRONWORKS MUSEUM Many relics discovered during excavations made in this early industrial area can be seen as can paintings, slides and charts that show how iron was made here 300 years ago.

166. Royall House *15 George St., Medford, Mass.* Considered one of the most beautiful Georgian houses in New England, this large three-story structure was originally built of brick in 1637. It was redesigned between 1732 and 1737 by Colonel Isaac Royall, an affluent Antigua merchant. During the siege of Boston in 1775-76, it was occupied by General John Stark and troops from New Hampshire. Among the exterior charms is the west facade, with its fluted Doric pilasters at the corners and wood blocks resembling Georgian stonework. Inside, furnishings ranging from 1700 to 1800 include a number of excellent Queen Anne, Chippendale and Hepplewhite pieces. *Open Tues.-Thurs., Sat., Sun. May-mid-Oct. Small charge.*

167. Cambridge, Mass.

Founded in 1630 as New City, Cambridge received its present name in 1636 when Harvard College was started. Although the city has developed as an important industrial site and a historic residential area, it remains predominantly a university town with Harvard University, Radcliffe College and the Massachusetts Institute of Technology located within its boundaries.

[167. *Christ Church*] *This light, airy and graceful interior reveals the skill of architect Peter Harrison. Among the church's memories of the past are the days when Theodore Roosevelt taught Sunday School here.*

[167. *Harvard University-Holden Chapel*] *The chapel is easily recognizable with its bright blue gable and coat of arms. General Washington's Revolutionary troops were quartered here during the siege of Boston.*

Christ Church *Zero Garden St.* Opened in 1761, this frame Episcopal church is distinguished by a flat tower supporting a belfry but no spire. It was closed during the Revolution because of feelings against its Tory congregation, although it was used to house Connecticut troops after the Battle of Lexington in 1775, and a service which was attended by George and Martha Washington was held there on the last day of that year. The spot where their pew once stood is marked. A bullet hole near the entrance serves as a reminder of a melee that followed the funeral of a British officer in 1778 when an enraged Yankee mob wrecked the interior. The styling of the present interior is Victorian. *Open daily.*

Harvard University Founded in 1636, this is America's oldest institution of higher learning. In the 18th century Washington quartered his troops in the buildings of Harvard Yard during the siege of Boston. Visitors enjoy the many museums, and the air of a venerable academic establishment.

BUSCH-REISINGER MUSEUM *29 Kirkland St.* Known especially for its 20th-century holdings, this museum houses the most comprehensive collection of German art outside of Germany. The building, dedicated in 1921, is derived from 18th-century German architecture. *Open Mon.-Sat. Sept.-May, Mon.-Fri. June-Aug.*

CARPENTER CENTER FOR THE VISUAL ARTS *19 Prescott St.* Le Corbusier's rough concrete-and-glass structure is the only project of his design built in the U.S. and, many believe, one of the most significant of his later period. Its five floors contain open design studios, film and photography workshops, and exhibition galleries. *Open daily except holidays.*

HOLDEN CHAPEL James Otis delivered a fiery oration to the provincial house of representatives here, and for a while the medical school used this building for dissections. The third oldest structure in Harvard Yard, this 1744 Georgian edifice has been used for everything but a chapel since 1766. It is now headquarters for the Harvard Glee Club.

MASSACHUSETTS HALL Originally built as a dormitory, the three-story brick Colonial hall is Harvard's oldest remaining building. Built in 1720, it now houses administrative offices and dormitory space.

SEVER HALL The massive brick Romanesque classroom building, designed in 1880 by Henry Hobson Richardson, became a model for classroom architecture in the late 19th century.

UNIVERSITY HALL Bulfinch designed this Federal structure of Chelmsford granite in 1815. The building is now used by the administration, and the beautiful second-floor chapel is the main faculty meeting room.

UNIVERSITY MUSEUM *Oxford St.* Here are five museums in one, with extensive exhibits in the field of botany, geology, zoology, mineralogy, archaeology and ethnology. Especially notable is the unique Ware Collection of Blaschka glass flowers in the botany museum. *Open daily except holidays. Small charge.*

WILLIAM HAYES FOGG ART MUSEUM *Quincy St.* The collections here illustrate the evolution of the art of East and West from ancient to modern times. Especially noteworthy are the collections of Chinese sculpture and bronzes, the Romanesque sculpture, the Italian primitives, the French 19th-century paintings and the European prints and drawings. *Open Mon.-Fri. July-Aug., daily Sept.-June.*

Longfellow House *105 Brattle St.* Built in 1759, this two-story frame house with a hip roof and Ionic pilasters is a fine example of Georgian Colonial architecture. George and Martha Washington lived here during the siege of Boston, and Longfellow made it his home from 1837-1882. Much of his best-known poetry was written here, and the 18-room house remains today just as it was at the time of the poet's death *Open daily. Small charge.*

Massachusetts Institute of Technology *77 Massachusetts Ave.* This well-known institution is not only a center of technological study and research but also a center of the arts, exemplified in the contemporary architecture and outdoor sculpture around the campus.

CHAPEL Called one of the most extraordinary religious buildings of our time, this circular, windowless structure was designed by Eero Saarinen in 1955. Daylight, reflected from a water-filled moat, enters the chapel through irregularly shaped arches in the floor. Behind the altar is a floor-to-ceiling metal screen designed by the noted sculptor Harry Bertoia. *Open daily.*

FRANCIS RUSSELL HART NAUTICAL MUSEUM Part of MIT's department of ocean engineering, this museum boasts a large collection of ship models from 1000 A.D. to the present as well as nautical paintings, photographs and ship plans. *Open daily.*

HAYDEN GALLERY Although the bulk of MIT's art collection hangs in offices, dormitories and other public areas, this is the focal point for the visual arts at the university. The gallery hosts eight major exhibitions each year, including painting, sculpture, architecture, photography, graphics and other multimedia forms. *Open Mon.-Sat. mid-June-mid-Sept., daily mid-Sept.-mid-June except holidays.*

KRESGE AUDITORIUM A second example of Saarinen's work on the MIT campus, this arching glass structure was also built in 1955. The three-cornered spherical roof is a single concrete dome only $3\frac{1}{2}$-inches thick at the top.

"SAIL" *McDermott Ct., East Campus* The largest Calder sculpture in America, this enormous steel stabile of curved sail-like shapes was cast in France and shipped in 35 separate pieces.

168. Boston, Mass.

Boston was foremost in protesting the tyranny of the British Crown, and in 1775 Paul Revere carried the call to action that began the American Revolution. Since then, the city has grown to be a major financial, insurance and maritime center for the U.S., as well as a world center of education, medicine, research, electronics and the arts.

Boston Public Library *Copley Sq.* Chosen as one of the 50 most important buildings in the history of American architecture, this 1895 library of Italian Renaissance style was designed by Charles Follen McKim. Besides the traditional research and reading material, there are murals, paintings and sculpture by leading masters, along with a wide collection of rare books and manuscripts. *Open Mon.-Sat. June-Sept., daily Oct.-May except holidays.*

Cathedral of the Holy Cross *1400 Washington St.* This is the titular church of the Archbishop of Boston, and is the largest church building in North America. Built in 1875, it has a length of 354 feet, and a transept width of 170 feet. The church contains shrines to Pope Saint Pius X and the Blessed Maria Assunta. *Open daily.*

Faneuil Hall *Merchant's Row* Originally built as a public market in 1742 and then used for Boston town meetings, this three-story brick edifice with the grass-

[**168.** *Faneuil Hall*] *Peter Faneuil, a leading Boston merchant, was a generous host who felt the need for a central food market quite directly. He had Faneuil Hall built as his gift to the people of Boston.*

hopper weather vane became known as the Cradle of Liberty. From the rostrum in the hall above the market came many of the greatest orations of the American Revolution, including those of Samuel Adams and James Otis. In the 19th century the building was the center of the abolitionist movement, and Wendell Phillips delivered his famous anti-slavery speech here. On the third floor is a military museum, maintained by the Ancient and Honorable Artillery Company of Massachusetts, containing relics of U.S. wars. *Open daily except holidays.*

First Baptist Church *110 Commonwealth Ave.* This 1882 church of Roxbury stone is considered the classic Henry H. Richardson Southern Romanesque edifice. It is especially renowned for its 176-foot tower, topped by a frieze of the sacraments and four gilded trumpeting angels. This frieze was designed by Bartholdi, known best for the Statue of Liberty. The rose windows on three sides of the church are particularly beautiful. *Open daily.*

First Church of Christ, Scientist *Christian Science Center* The world headquarters of the Christian Science movement includes the original 1894 Romanesque church, seating 900, the 1906 Byzantine-Renaissance extension, which seats 4000, and administrative and publishing offices. I. M. Pei and Partners designed the new Church Center, with three monumental modern buildings beautifully related to a 700-foot-long reflecting pool and a spacious plaza with inviting benches and plantings. *Open daily.*

Government Center In what was once a rundown section not far from the Common, this boldly conceived complex brings together several branches of government in such structures as the 22-story Leverett Saltonstall State Office Building, the vast State Service Center for Health, Welfare and Education, the curved Center Plaza Office Building and the two buildings described below. The dramatic ranks of steps, fountains and sculptural forms about the area create an impressive urban landscape.

JOHN FITZGERALD KENNEDY FEDERAL BUILDING This building demonstrates a harmonious blend of brick, concrete, granite and aluminum. It is divided into two sections consisting of a 26-story twin tower and a four-story building; it holds 19 agencies and 4000 U.S. government employees. *Open Mon.-Fri.*

NEW BOSTON CITY HALL This massive, low-level structure has the strong architectural features of Aztec designs. Built at a cost of $26,000,000, the different departments within it are arranged floor by floor according to the number of visitors: those receiving the most visitors are located on the ground floors, those receiving the least on the top floors. *Open Mon.-Fri.*

Harrison Gray Otis House *141 Cambridge St.* Designed by Charles Bulfinch, this dignified 1796 Federal mansion with Adamesque details was built for the prominent attorney who also served as a U.S. representative and senator and as mayor of Boston. Today the carefully restored three-story building serves as headquarters of the Society for the Preservation of New England Antiquities. Attached to it is the society's museum which contains an interesting architectural fragment display, an architectural library and photographic archives as well as toys, glass, pewter, ceramics and furniture. The wallpaper and textile collections are among the nation's best. *House and museum open Mon.-Fri. Small charge.*

[**168.** *First Church of Christ*] *The magnificent organ in the church extension is about eight stories high, has more than 13,000 pipes ranging from 32 feet to three quarters of an inch in length, and covers nine octaves.*

Isabella Stewart Gardner Museum *280 The Fenway* The building, built by Mrs. Gardner as a private residence and museum in 1902, reflects a 15th-century Venetian style of architecture that successfully blends Gothic, early Italian, Chinese and Spanish influences in many of its rooms. It provides an excellent setting for the Italian Renaissance paintings plus works by Vermeer, Raphael, Rembrandt and Rubens. Among the 19th-century artists represented are Sargent, Manet, Degas and Whistler. The 30 displays on three floors also include sculpture, textiles, furniture and rare books. There is a central courtyard garden with a visual impact that words cannot fully describe. *Open Tues.-Sat. July-Aug., Tues.-Sun. Sept.-June except holidays.*

King's Chapel *58 Tremont St.* Built during 1749-54 on the site of the first Anglican church in New England, the chapel later became the first Unitarian church in America. It was designed by the distinguished architect Peter Harrison. The old English interior is particularly fine. *Open daily.*

Museum of Fine Arts *Huntington Ave. and The Fenway* See feature display on pages 164-5.

Museum of Science *Science Pk.* This Boston institution is a pioneer in the concept of a teaching museum. The exhibits here try to involve the observer, inviting him to "push," "pull" or "listen." There are frequent lectures, courses and panel discussions with the aim of helping the layman keep up with all branches of science. The remarkable museum, now over 140 years old, has recently opened a new wing which more than triples the former exhibit space. *Open daily except holidays. Adults $2.00, children 5-16 small charge. Fri. nights half-price.*

Porcelain Japanese jar, Edo period (1615–1868).

George Washington as painted in 1796 by Gilbert Stuart.

View of Medieval Sculpture gallery. Objects from the 10th through the 15th centuries are on display here.

Paul Revere, who was a silversmith as well as a libertarian, made this bowl in 1768 in honor of 92 House of Representatives members who openly defied George III.

Museum of Fine Arts

Huntington Ave. and The Fenway, Boston, Mass.

Ever since Revolutionary days Bostonians have been noted for their civic pride, and there is perhaps no better example of it than Boston's Museum of Fine Arts (founded in 1870), one of the most important museums in this country. Bostonians financed the museum building, a massive Greek Revival structure, without the help of millionaire sponsors or municipal funds. Bostonians have also contributed generously to many of the collections here. Starting in the 1870s, a number of local merchants and scholars began to visit Japan, and bring back art objects—paintings, ceramics, prints, sculpture, lacquer work—to display in the museum. The MFA acquired many of these treasures with the aid of citizens' contributions as permanent loans and gifts. Today the Oriental collection, which includes Chinese, Indian, Korean and Central and Southeast Asian works, is one of the most extensive in the world. The museum's collection of Colonial and Federal furniture and 18th- and 19th-century American paintings, comprehensive and of excellent quality, was recently enriched by the gift of two noted Boston collectors, M. and M. Karolik. The Egyptian government elevated the museum's already eminent Egyptian collection with gifts of Old Kingdom sculpture in return for Boston-financed excavations at the Geza Pyramids. Other outstanding collections here are those of European Old Masters, French Impressionists, Greek and Roman art, costumes from Europe and the Far East, Colonial and English silver (including Paul Revere's Liberty Bowl), prints and drawings from the 15th century to the present, an extensive collection of textiles—early French and Flemish tapestries, ancient Peruvian and Coptic weavings, European and Near East embroideries, lace and printed fabrics—and the Leslie Lindsey Mason Collection of musical instruments. This is the second largest comprehensive art museum in the U.S. (the Metropolitan in New York City is larger): it is much too big and too interesting to see in just one visit. *Open Tues.-Sun. except holidays. Adults small charge.*

Detail of Poor Man's Store *by American artist John Frederick Peto (1854–1907). A shadowy figure minds the tiny shop, well stocked with penny candy for children.*

Bal à Bougival *by Auguste Renoir. The MFA has a fine collection of French Impressionists, many of them gifts from turn-of-the-century Bostonians.*

This 1950 B.C. *Egyptian statue of Lady Sennuwy was found in 1912* A.D. *as a result of MFA-Harvard University-sponsored excavations which lasted 40 years.*

[Old North Church] Twice the tower has been toppled by a hurricane and twice rebuilt, in 1804 and 1954. After the latter storm, people from all over the country donated money to restore the tower. During the British occupation of Boston many officers, including General Gage, attended services at the church. Major Pitcairn, leader of the Royal Marines at Lexington, who died at Bunker Hill, is buried here. Every year on April 18, at an evening memorial service, a descendant of one of the three who spread the alarm on that famous night in 1775—Paul Revere, William Dawes and Robert Newman—hangs the two lanterns from the highest window.

Nichols House Museum *55 Mt. Vernon St.* Believed to have been designed by Charles Bulfinch, this early-19th-century, four-story brick town house was the home of landscape architect Rose Standish Nichols. Bequeathed as a museum in 1961, its notable features are a handsome spiral staircase, a console table in the front hall that belonged to John Hancock and other examples of Colonial and Victorian furniture. This is the only private house on Beacon Hill that is open to the public, and its library serves as headquarters of the Boston Council for International Visitors. *Open Wed., Sat. except holidays. Small charge.*

Old City Hall *45 School St.* One of the few remaining examples of French Second Empire architecture in Boston, this building's design was based on one of the pavilions of the Louvre. Construction was begun in 1862 by architects Gridley J. F. Bryant and Arthur Gilman and was completed in 1865. In 1970 the exterior was restored to its original elegance.

Old North Church (Christ Church) *193 Salem St.* Two lanterns shone forth from the steeple in this church the night of Apr. 18, 1775, to warn the people across the Charles River that the British were marching to Lexington and Concord. The beautifully proportioned church was designed in the tradition of Sir Christopher Wren, architect of London's St. Paul's Cathedral. Completed in 1723, it is Boston's oldest existing church building. The gracefully simple interior still contains the original high box pews, brass chandeliers, Avery-Bennett clock and wineglass pulpit. A chalice designed by Paul Revere is used at Communion services. *Open daily.*

Old South Church in Boston *645 Boylston St.* Many historic events are associated with this church, founded in 1669. It was in the first church building on this site that Judge Samuel Sewall publicly confessed his error in presiding over the witchcraft trials in Salem. This was the church of Mary Chilton, one of the Pilgrims of the *Mayflower;* Benjamin Franklin was baptized here. The original cedar building was replaced in 1729. The present church, erected in 1885, has stained-glass windows of the 15th-century English type, a carved Caen stone screen in the rear and elaborate mosaics over the front doors. One of the gravestones near the front entrance bears the name of John Alden, son of John and Priscilla Alden of the Plymouth Colony. *Open daily.*

Old South Meeting House *Washington and Milk Sts.* On Dec. 16, 1773, over 4700 indignant citizens gathered in and around this building to protest the unloading from ships of tea on which the British had imposed a tax. At a word from Samuel Adams, men disguised as Indians, followed by those inside the building, rushed down to Griffin's wharf, boarded the ships and dumped the tea into the harbor. Built as a Congregational Church in 1729 by Joshua Blanchard, the meetinghouse was used for religious worship from 1739 to 1872. It is now a museum of Revolutionary history. *Open Mon.-Sat. except holidays. Small charge.*

Old State House *206 Washington St.* One of the oldest public buildings in the country, this fine Georgian structure was constructed in 1713. First the seat of British, then of town government, it was the site of many of the great political events in Massachusetts' history. Here in the Council Chamber, in 1761, James Otis fought against the Writs of Assistance before Governor Hutchinson, resulting in the law that no one can search a house without a warrant. In 1776 the Declaration of Independence was read from the eastern balcony to the crowds below, while everything pertaining to English sovereignty was burned in Dock Square. *Open Mon.-Sat. except holidays. Small charge.*

Park Street Church *Park and Tremont Sts.* Built in 1809 on a knoll overlooking the Boston Common, the 217-foot-high spire of this church still dominates the landscape. During the War of 1812, powder was stored in the church crypt, and since then the site of this church has been known as Brimstone Corner. In 1826 the American Temperance Society was founded here, and, in 1831, *My Country 'Tis of Thee* was sung here for the first time. *Open daily.*

Paul Revere House *19 North Sq.* Built in 1667, this house is the oldest frame house in Boston and the only remaining example of a 17th-century dwelling in that city. On Apr. 18, 1775, the famous patriot and silversmith rushed from here to begin his wild midnight ride to warn the Revolutionary patriots in Lexington. Revere lived here from 1770 to 1800, and the interior and furnishings have been restored to the style of the period. *Open Mon.-Sat. except holidays. Small charge.*

St. Stephen's Church *401 Hanover St.* This Italian Renaissance brick church with an original Paul Revere bell was designed in 1802 by Charles Bulfinch. Twice gutted by fires, the church was completely restored in 1965 to its original Bulfinch design. The simple white interior contains two handsome pewter chandeliers, each eight feet in diameter. *Open daily.*

[*State House*] *Boston, home of the bean and the cod, honors the latter with an effigy of a codfish in the lobby of the dignified Bulfinch State House. The gilded dome rising over Beacon Hill is a popular landmark.*

State House *Beacon St.* The original colonnaded structure with the golden dome was completed in 1798, and is considered one of Charles Bulfinch's architectural masterpieces. Another wing was added in the 19th century and one at each side in the 20th. The building is situated high on Beacon Hill overlooking the Boston Common, on land which was originally owned by John Hancock. The Archives Museum contains many historic documents, including the Mayflower Compact. Also in the building are two guns both of which are alleged to have fired the first shot of the American Revolution at Concord. *Open Mon.-Fri. except holidays.*

Trinity Church *Copley Sq.* Designed by the distinguished architect Henry Hobson Richardson, this architectural milestone was completed in 1877. It was styled after a French Romanesque church—a style later nicknamed Richardson Romanesque. The church is noted for the murals on the interior walls and for the opalescent glass windows, both designed by the eminent painter John La Farge. This was the church of the great preacher Phillips Brooks, who wrote the hymn "O Little Town of Bethlehem." *Open daily.*

U.S.S. "Constitution" *Boston Naval Shipyard, Charlestown* *Old Ironsides,* as she is known in Oliver Wendell Holmes' poem, is one of the most noted ships in the Navy's history. Launched in 1797, this wooden square-rigger fought against the French, the Barbary pirates and in the War of 1812. When the *Constitution* was condemned as unseaworthy in 1830, public outcry was so great that she was rebuilt and made a National Historic Landmark. To keep rigging and spars weathered equally on both sides, the historic ship makes an annual turn-around cruise in the harbor. *Open daily.*

Women's City Club of Boston *39 and 40 Beacon St.* Built in 1819 for Daniel Parker and Nathan Appleton, wealthy Boston industrialists, these superb brick Greek Revival twin buildings were designed with unusual curved mahogany doors, bay windows, circular stairways and domed skylights. The early wallpaper and Federal furniture are especially handsome. Daniel Webster and Edgar Allen Poe were guests here, and Longfellow was married at Number 39 in 1843. *Open Wed. Small charge.*

169. Mary Baker Eddy Museum *120 Seaver St., Brookline, Mass.* This 100-room brownstone mansion was moved stone by stone from Marquette, Michigan, by the Longyear family in 1903. In 1926 the Longyears endowed a foundation to preserve the memory of Mary Baker Eddy, the founder of Christian Science. The home contains a large collection of manuscripts, books, photographs and memorabilia of the renowned religious leader. The turn-of-the-century decor and eight acres of lawn and formal gardens provide an ideal setting for the exhibits. *Open Tues.-Sun. Small charge.*

170. Temple Ohabei Shalom *1187 Beacon St., Brookline, Mass.* This great domed edifice, built in the 1920s, is a remarkable example of Baroque-Romanesque architecture. Especially notable are the 20 impressionistic stained-glass windows in the chapel and the annex. The oldest Reform congregation in New England, the group began meeting in 1842. *Open daily.*

171. Museum of the American China Trade *215 Adams St., Milton, Mass.* This 1833 Greek Revival home of a China trader is an appropriate setting for the many Chinese porcelains, textiles, silver and teas that trace the interesting history of this commercial venture. Paintings of ships and harbors and personalities in the trade are shown as is a fully furnished Chinese room. Lectures and classes are offered on art and diplomatic and commercial history; the archives can be used by scholars. *Open Tues.-Sat. except holidays. Adults $1.50, children small charge.*

[*U.S.S.* Constitution] *"Old Ironsides" was one of the first fighting ships built for the new navy ordered by President John Adams, alarmed at the depredations of American merchant ships by foreign privateers.*

172. Adams National Historic Site *135 Adams St., Quincy, Mass.* Occupied for 139 consecutive years by four generations of the famous Adams family, this Georgian frame dwelling was the home of two U.S. Presidents, John Adams and his son John Quincy Adams; an ambassador, Charles Francis Adams; and a distinguished historian, Henry Adams. The earliest section, built in 1731 by a West India sugar planter, was purchased by mail in 1787 by John Adams while he was serving as ambassador to England. The house was first enlarged under the direction of his wife, Abigail. Further enlargements were completed in 1836 and 1869, and a large stone carriage house was built in 1873. A National Historic Site since 1946, the house remains as it was when the Adamses left it in 1927. It still contains original family furnishings, documents and books. Of special interest are the Louis XV furniture in the Long Room and the upstairs study which John Adams and John Quincy Adams used as a library. A fine 18th-century garden on the grounds still boasts a number of plants brought from England. At the corner of the garden stands the stone library where books belonging to John Quincy Adams can be seen. *Open daily mid-Apr.-mid-Nov. Small charge.*

173. Quincy Homestead *34 Butler Rd., Quincy, Mass.* In 1706 enlargements transformed the original 1685 farmhouse into the historic hip-roofed mansion where four generations of Edmund Quincys have resided, including Dorothy Quincy, who married John Hancock in 1775. The exterior is decorated with a delicate roof balustrade, while the largely restored interior includes furniture from the 18th century and French Réveillon wallpaper dating from 1790. On display in the carriage house is a "Bobby-hut" coach which belonged to John Hancock. The homestead is operated by the National Society of Colonial Dames of America in the Commonwealth of Massachusetts. *Open Tues.-Sun. mid-Apr.-Oct. Small charge.*

174. United First Parish Church (Unitarian) *1306 Hancock St., Quincy, Mass.* Designed by Parris, this handsome church was built in 1828 in the Greek Revival style. It resembles a temple, with a pitched roof on a granite portico that is supported by massive Doric columns and six columns holding up the cupola of the steeple. The granite of which the building is constructed was donated by John Quincy Adams. Both he and his father, John Adams, are buried with their wives in a crypt underneath the church. *Open Mon.-Fri. July-Aug., daily Sept.-June.*

175. Old Ship Meetinghouse *90 Main St., Hingham, Mass.* This is the oldest frame church and the oldest church in continuous use in the U.S. Originally Elizabethan Gothic in design, it was erected in 1681 with hand-hewn roof beams that resemble an inverted ship's hull. The framework, plus the compass painted on the ceiling beneath the cupola, undoubtedly gave this Unitarian church its popular name. It was enlarged in 1730 and 1755 and carefully restored in 1930. *Open Tues.-Sun. July-Aug.*

176. King Caesar House *King Caesar Rd., Duxbury, Mass.* Ezra Weston II, once one of the most prominent shipbuilders on the Atlantic coast, built this handsome frame house in 1809. Fully furnished, it contains a collection of Cable china and glassware commemorating the first transatlantic cable from Duxbury to France. *Open Tues.-Sun. June-early Sept. Small charge.*

[183] *Joseph Starbuck, a prosperous Nantucket whale oil merchant and shipbuilder, had three handsome brick Georgian mansions built on Main Street for his three sons, beginning around 1833. This is West Brick.*

177. Plymouth, Mass.

A group of courageous Pilgrims seeking religious freedom and a new life set out across the Atlantic Ocean in the good ship *Mayflower* and landed in Plymouth in 1620. Much of the spirit of these early years has been preserved or recreated in this historic town.

Antiquarian House *126 Water St.* The famous orator Daniel Webster was a frequent guest in this Federal-style house, built in 1809 and enlarged in 1830. Operated by the Plymouth Antiquarian Society, it contains an unusual three-story ell, creating a "split-level" arrangement, plus three octagonal front rooms. Old toys, china, authentic local furniture and period clothing on mannequins can also be seen. *Open daily June-Sept. Small charge.*

Howland House *33 Sandwich St.* This is the only surviving Plymouth house where Pilgrims (John and Elizabeth Howland) lived. Built in 1667 by Jacob Mitchell and later sold to the Howlands' son Jabez, it was enlarged in 1740. Owned and restored by the Pilgrim John Howland Society, it contains interesting furniture of the day. *Open daily mid-May-mid-Oct. Small charge.*

Mayflower Society House *4 Winslow St.* Edward Winslow, great grandson of the third governor of Plymouth Colony, began this harbor-view home in 1754. Restored in 1890, it has fine interior woodwork and 18th- and 19th-century furniture. Dr. Charles Thomas Jackson is thought to have conducted his early experiments in anesthetics here. *Open daily June-mid-Oct. Small charge.*

Pilgrim Hall Museum *75 Court St.* Designed in 1824 by Alexander Parris, this Greek Revival building owned by the Pilgrim Society is the oldest public museum in North America. It houses many items that belonged to passengers of the *Mayflower,* including Myles Standish's swords and Governor William Bradford's chair. Early examples of silver and Delftware and a number of portraits are displayed. A library emphasizes the history of the Pilgrims and New England. *Open daily. Small charge.*

Plymouth Rock *Water St.* Costumed guides tell of the Pilgrims' first step ashore onto this rock in 1620 to found a new nation. Sometimes called the Cornerstone of the Nation, the rock is quite probably the very one the *Mayflower* passengers used. *Open daily. Guides available Apr.-Oct.*

Spooner House *27 North St.* Built before 1750, this frame house was occupied by members of the Spooner family from 1763 to 1954. Furnished entirely with their possessions, it is maintained by the Plymouth Antiquarian Society. Emerson and Thoreau were guests here. *Open daily June-Sept. Small charge.*

178. Edaville Railroad *Rte. 58, South Carver, Mass.* Authentic steam engines and coaches that once served rural Maine carry passengers on this two-foot-gauge railroad. A fire museum with the largest fire engine collection in New England can also be seen plus 150 toy trains, many Kentucky rifles, antique cars and reproductions of several 19th-century shops. *Open Sun. early Apr.-early June, daily mid-June-mid-Oct., Dec. Adults $2.00, children small charge for museum and train; adults $1.75, children small charge for train only.*

179. Heritage Plantation of Sandwich *Grove and Pine Sts., Sandwich, Mass.* Opened to the public in 1969, this beautifully landscaped 76-acre estate displays an outstanding collection of Americana. The plantation includes the Round Barn, which houses the extensive antique automobile collection of Josiah K. Lilly III; the Military Museum—modeled after a 1783 Publick Building—which contains collections of miniature soldiers, antique firearms and military flags; the Old East Mill, a restored windmill dating from 1800; and the new Arts and Crafts Building, including a 1912 working carrousel. *Open daily May-Oct. Adults $2.00, children over 5 small charge.*

180. Sandwich Glass Museum *Town Hall Sq. and Rte. 130, Sandwich, Mass.* The Boston and Sandwich Glass Company produced in its long career (1825-1888) some of the most beautiful art forms in glass created in America. The museum has a large collection of memorabilia and products of this renowned manufactory. Samples of the popular pressed lacy glass made before 1840 and other rare examples of pressed glass and blown glass are on exhibit. *Open daily Apr.-Nov. Small charge.*

181. Camp Grounds *Oak Bluffs, Mass.* Oak Bluffs, on Martha's Vineyard, has been the scene of annual Methodist summer camp meetings since the 1830s. Originally a cluster of tents around a speaker's platform, by the 1870s the camp grounds consisted of a conical ironwork tabernacle and more than 300 charming tiny cottages along curving streets. The jigsaw, a recent invention at the time, was used to make elaborate decorations—scrollwork, flowers, birds and animals—for porches, cornices and windows, creating the fantasy of Victoriana that attracts visitors today.

182. Thomas Cooke House *Cooke and School Sts., Edgartown, Mass.* Thomas Cooke, a customs officer and justice of the peace, was the first owner of this frame house built in 1765 by ships' carpenters. Maintained by the Dukes County Historical Society, its 12 rooms have distinctive slanted beams, floors and paneling. There is a choice collection of Martha's Vineyard period furniture and costumes, scrimshaw, ship models, whaling items, old china and glassware. A boat shed displays a whale boat, whaling apparatus and fire engine. There is also the original Fresnel lens from Gay Head Lighthouse. *Open Tues.-Sun. June-Sept.*

183. Nantucket, Mass.

The seafaring men of Nantucket, for 200 years the world's leading whaling port, brought the island wealth and commerce. It still recalls the atmosphere of a whaling center. Among the interesting old buildings are the following:

Christian House *Liberty St.* This lean-to house built in the mid-18th century typifies the sturdy construction methods used by the early inhabitants of the island. The heavy timber of the corner posts, girders and summer beams have lasted intact through the centuries. *Open daily June-Oct. Small charge.*

1800 House *Mill St.* A fieldstone foundation, rough-hewn floor beams and wide pine paneling are some of the more interesting architectural features of this early Nantucket home. American Empire furniture, a spinning room and a borning room are typical of domestic life in the early whaling period. *Open daily June-Oct. Small charge.*

Hadwen House-Satler Memorial *Main St.* In contrast to the Quaker austerity pervading much Nantucket architecture, this wooden 1845 mansion is a 19th-century version of a Roman temple with Ionic columns. Within is a variety of Empire and Victorian furniture. *Open daily June-Oct. Small charge.*

Jethro Coffin House (Oldest House) *Off W. Chester St.* This lean-to-style building was considered a mansion when built in 1686. The huge central chimney is the most interesting feature, with the initials "J. C." on a raised brick horseshoe. A prevalent belief is that this was a good luck charm to guard against witches. *Open daily June-Oct. Small charge.*

Peter Foulger Museum *Broad St.* Shown here are ship models; Indian artifacts; Quaker toys, including an egg-shell tea set; whale oil lamps; and the Walter Folger astronomical clock, telescope and compass. *Open daily June-Oct. Small charge.*

Whaling Museum *Steamboat Wharf* Displays here include an 18-foot sperm whale's jaw, an exact reproduction of a brick tryworks on the deck of a whale ship and a collection of scrimshaw. Among the interesting items in the library is an 1808 entry in the log of the ship *Topaz,* navigated by Captain Mayhew Folger of Nantucket, reporting the discovery of Pitcairn Island and the remaining survivors of the *Bounty* mutiny. *Open daily June-Oct. Small charge.*

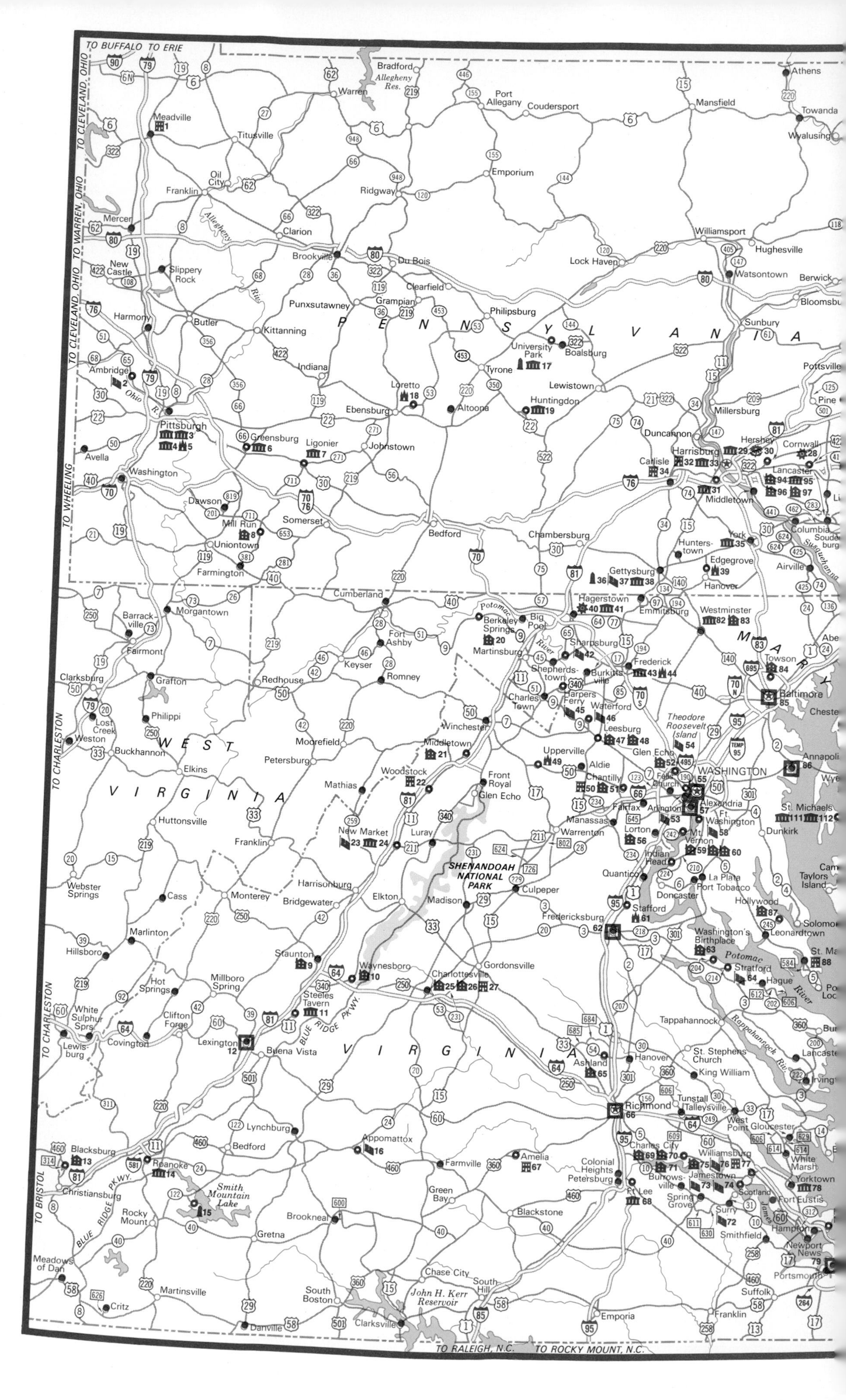
TO BUFFALO
TO ERIE
TO CLEVELAND, OHIO
TO WARREN, OHIO
TO CLEVELAND, OHIO
TO WHEELING
TO CHARLESTON
TO CHARLESTON
TO BRISTOL
TO RALEIGH, N.C.
TO ROCKY MOUNT, N.C.
P E N N S Y L V A N I A
W E S T
V I R G I N I A
V I R G I N I A
M A R Y
Bradford
Allegheny Res.
Warren
Port Allegany
Coudersport
Mansfield
Athens
Towanda
Wyalusing
Meadville
Titusville
Emporium
Oil City
Franklin
Ridgway
Mercer
Allegheny
Clarion
Williamsport
Hughesville
New Castle
Slippery Rock
Brookville
Du Bois
Lock Haven
Watsontown
Berwick
Bloomsburg
Clearfield
Grampian
Punxsutawney
Philipsburg
Sunbury
Harmony
Butler
Kittanning
University Park
Boalsburg
Indiana
Tyrone
Pottsville
Ambridge
Ohio R.
Loretto
Lewistown
Pine
Huntingdon
Millersburg
Pittsburgh
Ebensburg
Altoona
Duncannon
Hershey
Cornwall
Greensburg
Ligonier
Johnstown
Harrisburg
Avella
Washington
Carlisle
Lancaster
Middletown
Dawson
Mill Run
Somerset
York
Columbia
Uniontown
Bedford
Chambersburg
Hunters-town
Edgegrove
Farmington
Gettysburg
Airville
Hanover
Cumberland
Hagerstown
Emmitsburg
Westminster
Barrack-ville
Morgantown
Potomac
Berkeley Springs
Big Pool
Fort Ashby
Sharpsburg
Fairmont
Martinsburg
River
Keyser
Frederick
Towson
Clarksburg
Grafton
Redhouse
Romney
Shepherds-town
Burkitts-ville
Baltimore
Charles Town
Harpers Ferry
Waterford
Lost Creek
Philippi
Winchester
Leesburg
Theodore Roosevelt Island
Weston
Buckhannon
Moorefield
Middletown
Annapolis
Elkins
Petersburg
Upperville
Aldie
Glen Echo
Woodstock
Front Royal
Chantilly
Falls Church
WASHINGTON
Mathias
Glen Echo
Fairfax
Arlington
Alexandria
St. Michaels
Huttonsville
New Market
Luray
Manassas
Ft. Washington
Dunkirk
Franklin
Warrenton
Lorton
Mt. Vernon
Indian Head
SHENANDOAH NATIONAL PARK
Webster Springs
Harrisonburg
Quantico
La Plata
Taylors Island
Cass
Monterey
Bridgewater
Elkton
Madison
Culpeper
Port Tobacco
Doncaster
Stafford
Hollywood
Fredericksburg
Solomons
Marlinton
Leonardtown
Washington's Birthplace
Hillsboro
Staunton
Gordonsville
Stratford
Millboro Spring
Waynesboro
Charlottesville
Hague
Hot Springs
Steeles Tavern
BLUE RIDGE PKWY.
White Sulphur Sprs
Clifton Forge
Tappahannock
Rappahannock Riv.
Covington
Lewis-burg
Lexington
Buena Vista
Hanover
St. Stephens Church
Ashland
Lancaster
King William
Irvington
Richmond
Tunstall
Talleysville
West Point
Gloucester
Lynchburg
Appomattox
Blacksburg
Bedford
Charles City
Williamsburg
White Marsh
Roanoke
Farmville
Amelia
Colonial Heights
Jamestown
Yorktown
Christiansburg
Petersburg
Burrows-ville
Scotland
Fort Eustis
Smith Mountain Lake
Green Bay
Ft. Lee
Spring Grove
Rocky Mount
Brookneal
Blackstone
Surry
Hampton
Gretna
Smithfield
Newport News
Meadows of Dan
Chase City
Portsmouth
Martinsville
South Boston
South Hill
Suffolk
Critz
John H. Kerr Reservoir
Emporia
Franklin
Danville
Clarksville

REGION 3

Pages 170–243

The social and political life of 18th- and 19th-century America is richly represented in the Colonial and Federal houses, great plantations, Pennsylvania Dutch barns and pioneer log cabins in this part of the country. Times of trouble and strife are memorialized in the many Revolutionary and Civil War monuments, memorials, museums and battlefields.

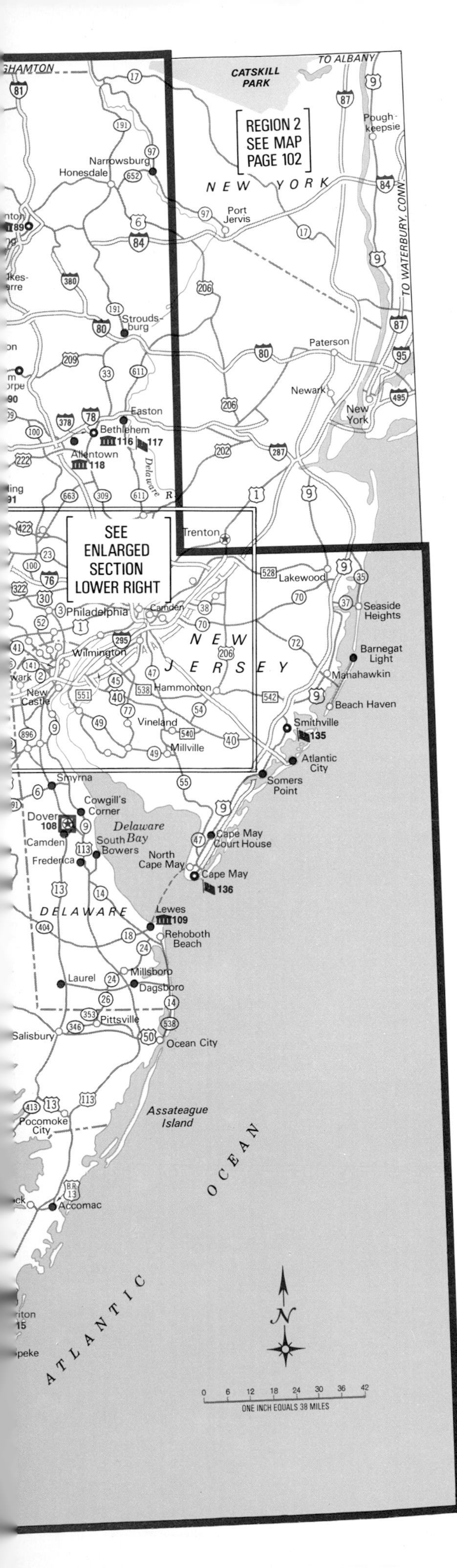

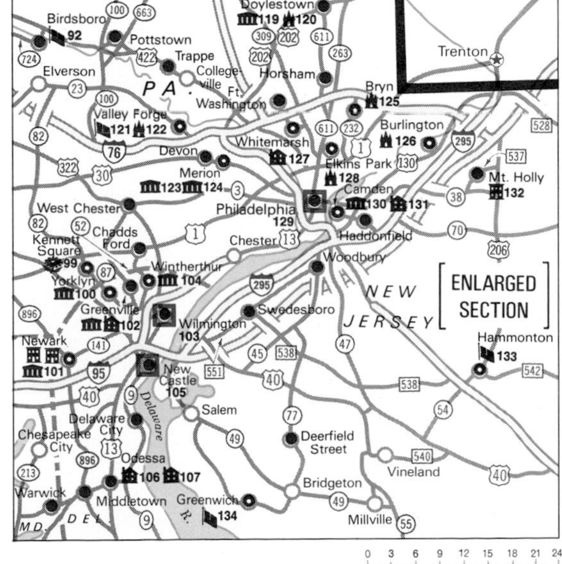

1. Bentley Hall *Allegheny College, N. Main St., Meadville, Pa.* The Reverend Timothy Alden, founder and first president of Allegheny, also designed its first building (finished in 1824), one of the best examples of Colonial-style architecture in the country. The center portion of the red brick facade, topped by a white cupola, is accented with white trim at the windows, roof line and between the three stories. It is flanked by two-story wings decorated in a similar vein with the addition of white Doric columns in front. *Open Mon.-Sat. except holidays.*

2. Old Economy Village *14th and Church Sts., Ambridge, Pa.* The town of Economy, established in 1824, was the third—and final—home of the Harmony Society, one of several 19th-century religious utopian experiments. The society, devoted to communal living, brotherhood, celibacy and pacifism, was founded in 1805 by the German-born "Father" George Rapp, and was disbanded 100 years later. The Harmonists' great industry and labor-saving equipment quickly made their new community very successful. The manufacture of textiles was the principal occupation, but a winery, distillery, lumber mill, brick-making plant and large flour mill also supplied products to Pennsylvania towns and cities. Preserved on this six-and-a-half-acre site (one-third the original acreage of the town) are 18 sturdy buildings, representing the economic and cultural center of Economy. In the midst of shrub- and flower-lined walks are the home of George Rapp, the communal dining hall and dwellings, craft shops and workrooms, all containing authentic furnishings, tools, household equipment and other memorabilia of these simple-living people. *Open daily except holidays. Small charge.*

BAKER HOUSE This is a typically austere Harmonist dwelling. Economy held about 100 such communal homes, of brick or wood, all built to the same dimensions and with the same floor plan. The three to 11 men and women living in each made up a family which was collectively responsible for work and schooling, and the distribution of goods given to it.

FEAST HALL On special ceremonial days all of the inhabitants of Economy, at one time as many as 1000, gathered together to eat in this building, men at one side, women at the other. The enormous quantities of food were prepared in the Feast Kitchen, which contains 12 massive kettles used in cooking. Several rooms were used as schoolrooms, while others served as a museum. Harmonist artifacts in the Feast Hall include their printing press, books, drawings and pamphlets, among others.

[**2.** *Great House*] *"Father" George Rapp's 25-room home remains in good condition. The Harmonists prospered from their manufacturing ventures; at one time the vault in the Great House held $500,000 in emergency funds.*

GREAT HOUSE The size and the many original furnishings of this 25-room house, home of George Rapp, show that the Harmonists' founder led a much less austere life than his followers. Behind the house is the community's large formal garden with a building, called the Grotto, where the Elders meditated, and a pavilion containing a statue of *Harmonie.*

3. Carnegie Institute *4400 Forbes Ave., Pittsburgh, Pa.* See feature display on page 173.

4. Frick Art Museum *7227 Reynolds St., Pittsburgh, Pa.* Helen Clay Frick, daughter of Pittsburgh industrialist Henry Clay Frick, erected the museum building for exhibiting a collection of fine arts. Like the Frick Collection in New York donated by her father, the objects—European paintings, sculpture, furniture, tapestries, Chinese porcelains—are shown in relation to one another in intimate settings. Emphasis in the collection is on the early Italian Renaissance and French Rococo periods, the latter beautifully illustrated in the French Period Room. The building itself, in proportion and scale, reflects early Italian Renaissance architecture. *Open Wed.-Sun. Sept.-July except holidays.*

5. Heinz Memorial Chapel *University of Pittsburgh, Pittsburgh, Pa.* This chapel, built in the 1930s, is a faithful example of French Gothic architecture. Of particular note are the stained-glass windows with both biblical and secular figures designed by Charles J. Connick, and the stone carvings on the interior and exterior. The parapet of the chapel is decorated with the seals of early colleges and universities. The building, a gift of the Heinz family, was designed by Charles Z. Klauder, who also designed the adjacent Cathedral of Learning. *Open Mon.-Sat. except holidays.*

6. Westmoreland County Museum of Art *221 N. Main St., Greensburg, Pa.* This privately endowed museum features period rooms. Four contain typically Victorian furnishings and memorabilia; two are 18th-century English in style, with carved pine paneling, furniture and silverware, and paintings by Reynolds, Gainsborough, Constable, Corot and Romney. The museum also has a permanent collection of American paintings among which are works by Whistler, Charles Willson Peale and Rembrandt Peale. *Open Tues.-Sun. except holidays.*

7. Fort Ligonier Memorial Foundation *S. Market St., Ligonier, Pa.* From 1758 to 1765 Fort Ligonier served as a staging area for British troops battling with the French for control of inland America and as a place of refuge for early settlers during Indian raids. Inner structures of the fort contain mannequins and furnishings of the period. All buildings have been rebuilt according to authentic military drawings and records of the original. On display in a museum on the site are a large collection of French and Indian War relics and

Water Lilies, *from the* Nymphéas *series by French Impressionist Claude Monet, hangs in the Museum of Art.*

3. Carnegie Institute

4400 Forbes Ave., Pittsburgh, Pa.

Millionaire philanthropist Andrew Carnegie bequeathed a legacy of cultural and educational institutions to the American people. In his book *The Gospel of Wealth* (1900) Carnegie expressed his belief that the rich should use their money for the betterment of mankind. At the age of 66, Carnegie sold his steel empire in order to practice his philosophy full time. Among other things, he endowed 2800 free public libraries and set up funds for educational, social and scientific research. The success of the Carnegie Institute, a four-and-one-half-acre cultural center which includes a natural history museum, art museum, library and concert hall, particularly pleased Carnegie. It was his gift to Pittsburgh, the city where he started on his way to a fortune. Of special note in the Natural History Museum are the dinosaur, Egyptian and marine exhibits. The Museum of Art has an excellent collection of 19th- and 20th-century French artists, a select number of Old Masters and contemporary works, and a wide sampling of decorative arts. The Music Hall and Library offer many free programs for children and adults. *Open Tues.–Sun. except holidays.*

This 13th-century reliquary chest of enamel and gilt copper from Limoges, France, is part of the museum's wide-ranging collection of decorative arts.

The skeletal remains of Diplodocus carnegiei, *on view in Dinosaur Hall in the Carnegie Museum of Natural History, were discovered in Wyoming in 1898. When Carnegie heard of the discovery, he sent funds and scientists out to the site to secure it for his new museum (opened in 1895). Replicas of* Diplodocus carnegiei *are exhibited in important museums in Europe and South America.*

artifacts from the fort found during excavation, dioramas of the troops' and settlers' frontier life and a Georgian room with period furnishings including a Reynolds portrait of the Lord Ligonier, for whom the fort was named. *Open daily Mar.-Nov. Adults $1.25, children small charge.*

8. Fallingwater *Mill Run, Pa.* The genius of architect Frank Lloyd Wright is demonstrated in this striking structure completed in 1939. Designed as a private residence, it is built over the waterfall of Bear Run, a stream that tumbles through huge slabs of sandstone. This same stone is used in the exterior walls, separated by cantilevered concrete decks, and the overall effect artfully suggests man's dependence on nature. Presented to the Western Pennsylvania Conservancy in 1963, the house is surrounded by acres of woodland plants. *Open Tues.-Sun. mid-Mar.-late Nov. $1.75 Sat., Sun., $1.50 Tues.-Fri.*

9. Woodrow Wilson Birthplace *24 N. Coalter St., Staunton, Va.* This brick Greek Revival dwelling was the birthplace of Wilson in 1856. The three floors open to visitors contain family possessions and furnishings. Many of Wilson's letters and books, some of the office equipment he used in the White House and an old Pierce-Arrow sedan, part of his White House fleet, are kept here. A short film consisting of old newsreels traces Wilson's career. The original Victorian garden with its century-old boxwood hedges has been restored. *Open Mon.-Sat. Jan.-Feb., daily Mar.-Nov., Mon.-Sat. Dec. Small charge.*

10. Swannanoa Palace *Rte. 250, Waynesboro, Va.* Eight years and the efforts of 300 master artisans were required to build this marble replica of an Italian Renaissance palace. The 52-room mansion high on a mountain top was completed in 1912 as the summer home of a Richmond industrialist. After serving as a country club, it was abandoned until 1948, when Walter and Lao Russell restored the house and its beautiful terraces and gardens for their "University of Science and Philosophy." The central baronial hall, gold-tapestried ballroom, library and oak-paneled dining room are filled with paintings and sculpture. The handsome Tiffany stained-glass window at the head of the marble double staircase, murals and the many wood carvings are of exceptional quality. *Open daily. Small charge.*

11. Cyrus McCormick Birthplace and Memorial Museum *Steeles Tavern, Va.* With the mechanical reaper that Cyrus McCormick invented in 1831, one man and a horse could reap as much grain in one day as previously required several men with scythes. A replica of the machine (as well as later models) that served to literally revolutionize the methods of agriculture is on display here in the blacksmith shop where it was designed and built. Also intact and open for inspection on the 634-acre McCormick homestead, known as Walnut Grove, are the large brick farmhouse where he was born and a restored late-18th-century gristmill. *Open daily May-mid-Oct.*

12. Lexington, Va.

The town, founded in 1777, was named for the Battle of Lexington, Mass. With the establishment of Washington College (now Washington and Lee University) and, later, of Virginia Military Institute, it became known as a cultural center. Perhaps the most famous of its residents were Robert E. Lee and "Stonewall" Jackson, both of whom were buried there.

George C. Marshall Research Library *Near V.M.I. Parade Grounds* Dedicated in 1964 to the memory of the famous U.S. Army Chief of Staff in World War II, U.S. Secretary of State (1947-49) and Nobel Peace Prize winner (1953), this excellent library holds a vast number of books, documents and microfilms on military and diplomatic history. Many photographs, awards and other memorabilia relating to Marshall's brilliant career make an interesting display. An electric map highlights episodes during World War II and a special room explains the significance of U.S. aid

[8] *Fallingwater, the weekend house Frank Lloyd Wright designed for Edgar Kaufmann in the mid-'30s, marked Wright's triumphant return as a consummate and daring architect. He was internationally known by 1914, but during the '20s he received few commissions. Fallingwater, with its smooth walls and slab roof, seems almost a part of the rock outcrop. The effect of unity given by the horizontal sweep of the concrete decks is carried out inside. All-glass walls open to terraces overlooking the falls, while stone walls close in the side of the house that faces upstream.*

to postwar Europe provided by the Marshall Plan. *Open daily. Small charge.*

Home of General Thomas J. "Stonewall" Jackson *8 E. Washington St.* The Confederate leader occupied this modest brick house, built in 1800, for two-and-a-half years while he was teaching at Virginia Military Institute. The only house he ever owned, it contains a large collection of Jackson memorabilia and many books about his career and the Civil War. *Open daily except Jan. 1 and Dec. 25. Small charge.*

Lee Chapel Museum *Washington and Lee University* Built in 1867-68, while Robert E. Lee was president of what was then known as Washington College, this lovely red-brick and limestone chapel with its rounded white-framed doors and windows is now a memorial to the Southern leader. It contains the white marble *Recumbent Statue of General Lee* by the Richmond sculptor Edward V. Valentine, a popular portrait of Lee by Theodore Pine and Charles Willson Peale's fine portraits of Washington and Lafayette. On the lower level are Lee's office—looking as it did when he was president—and a museum devoted to his life as a gentleman, general and educator. General Lee is buried here with other members of his family, including his father, "Light-Horse Harry" Lee. *Open daily.*

Virginia Military Institute *Off Rte. 11* Founded in 1839, this state-assisted military college was practically destroyed by Union shellfire in 1864. Of particular interest are periodic dress parades and bronze statues of Stonewall Jackson and *Virginia Mourning Her Dead,* a monument honoring the cadet corps which fought as a unit at the Battle of New Market, in 1864.

CADET BARRACKS Completed in 1850 and substantially enlarged in 1949, this castellated Gothic-style building of over 300 rooms serves all of the cadets as living quarters. A National Historic Landmark, its three main entrance arches are named for Washington, Jackson and George C. Marshall.

SUPERINTENDENT'S QUARTERS *412 V.M.I. Parade* Ten superintendents have occupied this Gothic-style residence since its completion in 1860. During the Union attack of 1864 the building was spared since two children inside it were too sick to be moved.

VIRGINIA MILITARY INSTITUTE MUSEUM *Jackson Memorial Hall* Located in a 1916 building, this interesting museum recounts the history of the institute through objects belonging to many of its distinguished graduates and faculty members. Cadet life today is also illustrated with a display of uniforms and a model barracks room. A huge painting in the assembly hall depicts the charge of the cadets at the Battle of New Market. *Open daily.*

13. Smithfield Plantation House *Rte. 314, Blacksburg, Va.* When this handsome frame mansion was built in 1772, it stood at the beginning of the frontier, surrounded by a protective stockade against marauding Indians and Tories. It served the 19,000-acre plantation of Colonel William Preston, one of the great land owners of the Allegheny region (he had claims to 120,000 acres). Today six of the rooms are furnished with Preston possessions and other 18th-century pieces. Several other rooms are set aside as a regional museum. On permanent display here are Indian artifacts, early tools and implements, and archaeological findings related to Smithfield and Draper's Meadow, the original frontier settlement on the site. *Open Wed., Sat., Sun. mid-Apr.-mid-Nov. Adults $1.25.*

[**16.** *McLean House*] *In 1893 the house was dismantled for re-creation as a museum. The project languished; weather and souvenir hunters took their toll of wood and bricks. What visitors see now is a faithful reconstruction.*

14. Roanoke Transportation Museum *Wasena Park, Roanoke, Va.* In several buildings and on the grounds of this park are early automobiles, trucks, horse-drawn vehicles and other forms of transportation ranging from a Canadian dogsled of about 1900 and a 1945 electric streetcar to an Air Force jet trainer and Navy jet fighter. The museum has one of the country's largest collections of railroad equipment—from steam engines to diesels. *Open daily May-Sept. Small charge.*

15. Booker T. Washington National Monument *Rte. 122 N., 16 mi. E. of Rocky Mount, Va.* For nine years, from his birth in 1856 until the end of the Civil War, the great educator and black leader lived in a slave cabin on what was then a small, hardworking plantation. The 207-acre site is now operating as a living historical farm. Several buildings, including a slave cabin and a tobacco barn, have been reconstructed. One of the monument's most popular demonstrations takes place on Sunday afternoons, when a girl in period costume, using antique utensils, cooks over an open fire in the same way that Washington's mother prepared meals for the main house long ago. Exhibits and a short movie on the life of *Up From Slavery*'s author can be seen at the Visitor Center. *Open daily except Dec. 25.*

16. Appomattox Court House National Historical Park *Rte. 24, 3 mi. N.E. of Appomattox, Va.* In this tiny village on Apr. 9, 1865, General Robert E. Lee surrendered the Army of Northern Virginia to General Ulysses S. Grant, bringing about the end of the Civil War. The village of 21 buildings and sites has been restored to closely reflect its 1865 appearance. The places mentioned here are of special historical interest. *Open daily. Small charge for automobile.*

COURT HOUSE Once a legal and political center for the county, the building has been reconstructed and now serves as a visitor center and museum. A 17-minute audio-visual program is presented at regular intervals.

MCLEAN HOUSE It was here that Lee and Grant met and defined the terms of surrender. The house has been reconstructed and refurnished; some of the furnishings are original McLean pieces.

17. Pennsylvania State University *University Park, Pa.* Penn State is one of the first (1855) land-grant universities in the country. In the lobby of the college's first building, Old Main, are a series of frescos, beautifully executed by Henry Varnum Poor from 1940 to 1949, which tell the story of the university's founding and goals. *Open Mon.-Fri.*

LION SHRINE The Nittany Lion is the symbol of the university's athletic prowess. Despite the intended symbolism of strength and power, this statue is of a touchingly curious creature who looks too concerned and interested to pounce. It was carved from a 13-ton block of Indiana limestone by Heinz Warneke.

MINERAL INDUSTRIES BUILDING MUSEUM This museum contains collections of fossils, minerals, rare gems and related items and has an art gallery.

18. St. Michael's Church *Loretto, Pa.* St. Michael's, a stone church with Roman and Byzantine motifs that was erected in 1899, is architecturally noteworthy because it is the earliest church building in the country with a steel framework. (Fittingly, Charles M. Schwab of Bethlehem Steel was the donor.) *Open daily.*

19. Swigart Museum *Rte. 22, E. of Huntingdon, Pa.* Stanley Steamers, a Marmon 16, Pierce Arrow, Duesenberg, Du Pont, Carroll and many other antique and classic steam-, gas- and electric-powered cars are displayed here, all in operating condition. There is a huge collection of automobile nameplates, and many U.S. and foreign license plates are mounted on large "turning pages." *Open Sat., Sun. May, daily June-early Sept., Sat., Sun. early Sept.-Oct. Adults $1.50, children small charge.*

20. Old Castle *Berkeley Springs, W. Va.* Its origin shrouded in romantic legend, this modern replica of a Norman castle was built in 1887 on a rise overlooking the town. It is furnished in 19th-century style. *Open Fri.-Sun. Jan.-May, daily June-Sept., Fri.-Sun. Nov.-Dec. Small charge.*

21. Belle Grove *Rte. 11, Middletown, Va.* This gray limestone house with white wood trim was completed about 1794 for James Madison's brother-in-law. Several of its features, including the graceful main entrance fanlight and Doric portico, were suggested by Thomas Jefferson. During the Civil War it was occupied by Union troops, and Generals Fremont and Sheridan made it their headquarters. The restored structure and 100 acres of land belong to the National Trust for Historic Preservation. Craft shows and other events are held regularly on the property, which encompasses a working farm. *Open daily Apr.-Oct. Adults and children over 6 small charge.*

22. Shenandoah County Court House *Woodstock, Va.* This building of native limestone was designed by Thomas Jefferson and further reveals his excellent sense of proportion. Erected in 1792, it is the oldest courthouse in use west of the Blue Ridge Mountains. *Open Mon.-Sat.*

[29] *Completed in 1878 by John Fiester of Manheim, Pa., this 12-foot-high carved and painted walnut clock has been delighting visitors for many years. All figures are hand-carved wood, operated by brass springs and weights. The elaborate clock has five windings, but is now operated by hand. When the skeleton strikes the skull it is the signal for the apostles to begin their march. The procession depicts the denial of Christ by Peter and the betrayal of Judas. Other figures are Satan, Justice and a crowing cock. In the lower section a music box plays when the two trumpeters appear. During the winter months the clock is operated at 11 A.M., 1, 3 and 4 P.M.; during summer, whenever anyone wants to see it.*

23. New Market Battlefield Park *Off Rte. 81, New Market, Va.* The focal point on this 160-acre tract is the Hall of Valor, a Civil War museum which traces the war's history from its beginning at Fort Sumter to the surrender at Appomattox, through photographs, maps, dioramas, weapon displays and films. The museum and park were established by a Virginia Military Institute alumnus as a memorial to the 247 V.M.I. cadets who in 1864 rushed from their barracks to join the fighting here, helping to stall a Union thrust into the Shenandoah Valley. Near the museum is the restored Bushong Farmhouse, around which much of the battle took place. *Open daily except Dec. 25. Small charge.*

24. Starkweather Art Museum *New Market, Va.* A collection of 57 oil and watercolor paintings by American artist William Starkweather is exhibited here in an attractive setting. Visitors find Starkweather's sensitive treatment of the light and shadow in his paintings particularly interesting. *Open daily. Small charge.*

25. Ash Lawn *Rte. 53, Charlottesville, Va.* This rambling hilltop house was designed and built in 1798 for James Monroe, fifth President of the U.S., by his close friend and neighbor, Thomas Jefferson. Jefferson's Monticello is within sight of Monroe's home, approximately two road miles distant. The stately boxwood gardens, featuring a marble statue of Monroe, are considered by many the finest in Virginia. The completely furnished house includes many pieces that belonged to the Monroes. *Open daily. Small charge.*

26. Monticello *Charlottesville, Va.* See feature display on pages 178–9.

27. University of Virginia *Charlottesville, Va.* The intellectual stimulus and the physical character of the university were both established by Thomas Jefferson: he—with Madison, Monroe and some other Virginians—was one of the founding fathers, and he was the designer of the "academical village" around which UVA centers to this day. Jefferson's ground plan set out the Rotunda, fashioned after the Pantheon of Rome (and now a National Historic Landmark), as the focal point of the Lawn. Flanking the Lawn, and connected by colonnades, are the pavilions that housed professors. The 68 students who were present for the opening in 1825 lived in dormitory rooms behind the pavilions and dined in the six "hotels." Each of the pavilions is unique, for Jefferson intended them to illustrate different aspects of architecture. Most of the buildings are backed by enclosed gardens, and some have the serpentine brick walls Jefferson also designed. Among the students at UVA in 1826 was Edgar Allan Poe, whose room is preserved by the Raven Society. *Open daily.*

28. Cornwall Furnace *Off Rte. 322, Cornwall, Pa.* Cornwall Furnace is an example of the kind of iron furnaces used in the U.S. in the 18th and 19th centuries. It was established by a Peter Grubb in 1742, and the iron it produced from then until 1883 when it closed was used for stoves, kitchenware, farm tools and munitions for the Revolution. The ore came from the nearby Cornwall Ore Banks. (These mines, now owned by Bethlehem Steel Company, are still in operation.) The furnace, which is 28 feet square at the base and built into the side of the hill to facilitate charging, is now a museum where the process of making iron is explained through a series of dioramas. Adjacent to the furnace is a 19th-century miners' village of stone houses now occupied by Bethlehem Steel workers. *Open daily except holidays. Small charge.*

29. Hershey Museum *W. Derry Rd. and Park Blvd., Hershey, Pa.* Founded in 1933 as a repository for an extensive collection of Indian artifacts from Alaska to South America, the museum now also includes early American china, glassware and Pennsylvania Dutch antique furniture. An 1878 Apostolic Clock is interesting because of its intricately carved wood case, music box and movements that register the days, months, zodiac signs and moon phases as well as hours of the day. There are also more than 500 military firearms dating from pre-Revolutionary days to World War II, several rooms furnished in turn-of-the-century style and antique automobiles. *Open daily except holidays. Adults and children over 5 small charge.*

30. Hershey Rose Gardens and Arboretum *Hershey, Pa.* In 1936 Milton S. Hershey, the founder of the Hershey Chocolate Plant, established a small public rose garden, which has been expanded since then into a 23-acre landscape of magnificent flowers and trees. During the summer, 42,000 rose bushes with 1200 varieties of blossoms, 30,000 tulips, 3000 daffodils, 14,000 annuals and 5000 chrysanthemums blossom among a wide variety of azaleas, rhododendrons, flowering shrubs and shade and evergreen trees. Visitors wander at their leisure through the grounds on a maze of grass-covered footpaths. *Open daily mid-Apr.-Nov.*

31. Automobilorama *Rte. 15 at Pennsylvania Tpke., near Harrisburg, Pa.* Here the history of the automobile may be traced from the first cars powered by steam and electricity to the present gas models. Over 250 antique, vintage and classic cars are on display—an 1898 Malden Steamer, 1905 Thomas Flyer, 1928 Auburn, 1929 Duesenberg J, 1901 Olds, 1910 Rauch & Lang Electric, to name a few. Several cars once owned by celebrities and a number of vehicles used in movies are in the collection, as well as a historic sampling of bicycles, motorcycles, early sleighs, carriages and music boxes. *Open daily. Adults $2.00, children small charge.*

32. Main Capitol Building *Third St., Harrisburg, Pa.* This is one of the largest capitols in the U.S. Its dome, modeled after St. Peter's Basilica in Rome, rises 272 feet from the ground to dominate the Harrisburg skyline. At the top is the golden female figure of "Miss Penn." Beneath the dome is the great rotunda, a grand stairway of Italian marble and paintings of the history of Pennsylvania by Edwin Austin Abbey. Other notable features are the bronze doors, statuary, murals and 14 circular stained-glass windows. *Open daily.*

33. William Penn Memorial Museum *Third and North Sts., Harrisburg, Pa.* Exhibits here relate to Pennsylvania's cultural, historical and natural heritage. Included are Indian artifacts, ethnological, geographical and topographical displays, dioramas of birds and mammals and period rooms illustrating Pennsylvania's economic, social and religious development. There is a Transportation Gallery with an Indian canoe, some early automobiles, fire engines and an airplane, and the Fine Arts Gallery. In Memorial Hall *The Young William Penn,* a modern 18-foot bronze statue, stands in front of a historical mural. Penn's original 1681 charter from Charles II is kept here. *Open daily except holidays.*

[31] *A 1928 Auburn leads this parade of aristocratic automobiles. Other treasures include Clark Gable's Packard, Doris Duke's Duesenberg, the chariot from the movie* Ben Hur *and the streetcar from* Meet Me in St. Louis.

The columned portico entrance to Monticello opens onto a hall which Jefferson used as his private museum.

26. Monticello

Charlottesville, Va.

Thomas Jefferson, honored in American history as a political theorist, statesman and politician, was a man of many talents and interests. The author of the Declaration of Independence, minister to France, first American Secretary of State and third President, he was also an accomplished natural scientist, inventor, philosopher, linguist, educator and architect. Jefferson devoted considerable time to architecture, and, like designers before and since, had definite ideas on the subject. In place of what he considered the excessive ornamentation of the then-popular Adam style, he advocated classic Roman architecture, the simple lines and noble associations of which he considered particularly appropriate to the new democratic republic. Jefferson designed the

The library contains some of Jefferson's favorite books, instruments and inventions. On the table at the window is a polygraph, a two-penned device for making simultaneous copies of a letter ("finest invention of the present age," said Jefferson). A camera obscura rests on the octagonal table. In the foreground are his architect's table and instruments. Jefferson used the red leather chair while presiding over Senate meetings as Vice President (1797–1801).

Virginia State Capitol and University of Virginia buildings in this style and helped to ensure its use in the new Federal Capitol. Of all his architectural projects, Monticello, Jefferson's home in Virginia's Albemarle County, was his most beloved. He built and remodeled it over a period of 40 years (from 1768 to 1809), incorporating many ideas that he had encountered in Europe while ambassador to France. The result is a classical structure unmistakably Jeffersonian. While most Southern estates of that period consisted of a large main house and outbuildings on property near a waterway, Jefferson contoured a mountain and leveled its top for his homesite, hiding the outbuildings (laundry, stable, servants' quarters, carriage house, kitchen, dairy and the like) beneath terraces on either side of the mansion. The use of low, second-story windows directly above the tall first-story windows and skylights in the third story gives the illusion of a one-story facade that, in fact, conceals 23 above-ground rooms on three floors. To save space Jefferson dispensed with the usual grand stairway, building instead two 21-inch-wide staircases tucked in unobtrusive niches. He exercised his flair for invention at Monticello to satisfy his love of comfort: Beds were set in alcoves away from drafts; a silent butler carried wine from the cellar to the dining room. Just for fun, he installed a mechanism for sliding glass doors as well as a clock whose weights as they dropped indicated the days of the week on the wall. The house is filled with the things Jefferson loved, many of them original: books, gadgets, paintings—no landscapes—and fine furniture. He was no less interested in the planting of trees, shrubs and flowers on his estate. The gardens near his home today reflect his original designs. *Open daily. Adults $2.00, children small charge.*

Jefferson designed his bedroom as a sitting room-study with alcove bed in between. He answered his mail at the swivel chair and table in the foreground.

Many items of Jeffersoniana are housed at Monticello. Shown here are personal cards he used as a private citizen and as U.S. minister to France.

Below the pendulum clock in the main hall are moose and elk antlers, mementos of the Lewis and Clark Expedition, which Jefferson commissioned for the exploration of the Louisiana Territory.

Among his other talents Jefferson was an amateur cellist who enjoyed quartets. He designed the four-sided music stand at rear.

[**35.** *Gates House and Golden Plough Tavern*] *The Gates House was built onto the tavern, as this rear view shows. The medieval, half-timbered tavern is the only known example of the Germanic type of architecture in the U.S.*

34. Old West *Dickinson College, Carlisle, Pa.* Old West was designed and built by an illustrious group of 18th-century Americans. In 1803 the noted architect Benjamin Latrobe donated working drawings for the functional yet stately college house, and Jefferson, Madison, John Marshall and Aaron Burr were among those who contributed to its cost. In line and proportion the structure is Greek in character yet it has a native quality too. It is constructed of Pennsylvania limestone with stucco arches framing the windows, and red sandstone quoins and keystones. The graceful exterior remains practically unchanged, but the interior has been substantially modified to maintain it as a functioning campus building. Old West, a National Historic Landmark, is currently used as the college's main administration building. *Open Mon.-Fri. except holidays.*

35. Historical Society of York County Museum and Library *250 E. Market St., York, Pa.* Eighteenth-century York is dramatically displayed in the Street of Shops authentically reproduced in the Society's museum. A diorama of York's Center Square in the 1830s can also be seen, as well as Indian artifacts, a Conestoga wagon, a canal diorama and an 1804 Tannenberg organ. The reference library includes genealogical records and local historical data. The society also maintains four restored buildings for which a combination ticket (adults, $1.50, children small charge) is available. *Open daily except holidays. Small charge.*

BONHAM HOUSE *152 E. Market St.* The house reflects the period, beginning in the 1870s, when the Bonham family lived here. The rooms are decorated in styles ranging from Victorian to Federal, and collections of Oriental porcelains, ivories, bronzes, silver and glass are displayed. *Open daily except holidays. Small charge.*

1812 LOG HOUSE *157 W. Market St.* The style of this reconstructed and relocated log building is typical of most dwellings in Colonial York. It is furnished in the austere manner of the early German settlers. *Open daily except holidays. Small charge.*

GENERAL GATES HOUSE *157 W. Market St.* The two-story brick house was the residence of General Horatio Gates in the early part of 1778 at the height of the conspiracy to overthrow General Washington, known as the Conway Cabal. The scheme is said to have been thwarted by General Lafayette in a meeting at Gates' home. *Open daily except holidays. Small charge.*

GOLDEN PLOUGH TAVERN *157 W. Market St.* The half-timber structure with large hewn logs and a steeply pitched roof is almost medieval in appearance. Built about 1740, it was a center of activity when York served as the seat of the Continental Congress (1777-78). *Open daily except holidays. Small charge.*

36. Gettysburg National Cemetery *Rte. 134, S. of Gettysburg, Pa.* Within this 17-acre cemetery stands the Soldiers' National Monument commemorating the 3706 Civil War dead who are buried here and marking the spot where President Lincoln delivered his immortal Gettysburg Address on Nov. 19, 1863. *Open daily.*

37. Gettysburg National Military Park *Gettysburg, Pa.* It was here that Lee's Army of Northern Virginia engaged General George Meade's Army of the Potomac during July 1-3, 1863, in the bloodiest battle ever fought on the North American continent. The defeat of Lee's forces was a turning point in the Civil War. The battlefield covers an area of 25 square miles, with about 3200 acres included in the park. Points of interest include the Eternal Light Peace Memorial, a bronze urn on a 40-foot shaft with a continually burning flame; Meade's headquarters; and the Pennsylvania, Virginia and North Carolina Memorials. The Visitor Center features films that explain the battle, various exhibits and the Gettysburg Cyclorama. *Open daily. Small charge for Cyclorama.*

38. Gettysburg National Museum *Rte. 134, Gettysburg, Pa.* A most helpful feature of the Gettysburg battlefield site is a 30-square-foot topographical map on which 500 electric lights flash to show troop movements and positions during the three-day Civil War battle in 1863. In the museum itself is a vast collection of Civil War memorabilia—such things as guns, sabers and the table on which General "Stonewall" Jackson's arm was amputated eight days before his death in 1863. A monument adjacent to the museum marks the spot where Lincoln delivered the Gettysburg Address. Visitors can rent taped accounts of the battle to take along with them while touring the nearby area where it was fought. *Open daily except holidays. Small charge except Dec. 25.*

39. Basilica of the Sacred Heart of Jesus *Edgegrove, Pa.* The area, known as Conewago, is the oldest Catholic community west of the Susquehanna River, and since Colonial times has been a center for missionary activity. The original cabin church was replaced by the present fieldstone and brownstone structure in 1787. Transepts and a semicircular apse were added in 1850 and the spire was erected 23 years later. The murals on the walls and ceiling are particularly striking in their bright coloration and expressive line. They were done in 1851 by Franz Stecher, a noted Austrian painter of portraits and religious subjects. *Open daily.*

40. Baldwin Steam Engine #202 *Hagerstown City Park, Hagerstown, Md.* The Baldwin Locomotive Works built this 48-foot, 110-ton steam engine in 1912,

[**36**] *Stevens Knoll in Gettysburg Cemetery is silent and peaceful now. Yet here are buried the men and boys who died in the bloody, three-day battle that marked the turning point of the Civil War. Union casualties were about 23,000, Confederate 28,000. Over a thousand bodies were never identified. The battle has been studied for generations by military historians and generals of later wars as an example of the movement of large numbers of men over an extensive area (the battlefield covers 25 square miles). In the distance the Soldiers' National Monument marks the spot where President Lincoln, in his extraordinarily brief, moving address, sought to bind up the nation's wounds.*

and for 40 years "old 202" served on the Western Maryland Railroad's run between Baltimore and Hagerstown. When the locomotive was retired from service, it was donated by the railroad to the children of Hagerstown, who are especially pleased that the bell and whistle still work. *Open Sat., Sun.*

41. Washington County Museum of Fine Arts *City Park, Hagerstown, Md.* Located beside a lake in Hagerstown's lovely City Park, the museum houses a collection of Old Masters, later European works of the 18th and 19th centuries and an American collection that includes Sully, Peale, Church, Durand and others. Sculpture, Oriental paintings and art objects, such as tomb jades, are also featured. The museum maintains an art library, and has regular lectures, concerts and educational programs. *Open Tues.-Sun. except holidays.*

42. Antietam National Battlefield Site *Rte. 65, N. of Sharpsburg, Md.* The Battle of Antietam, which raged throughout Sept. 17, 1862, was the first of Robert E. Lee's two efforts to carry the Civil War onto Northern soil. Outnumbered by more than two to one, his 41,000 Confederate troops were on the brink of defeat when A. P. Hill's division smashed a final Union attack. Total Union and Confederate casualties exceeded 23,000 killed and wounded with neither side gaining a significant tactical advantage. However, Lee's frustrated strategy cost the Confederacy diplomatic recognition by England and gave Lincoln sufficient justification for issuing his famous Emancipation Proclamation declaring all slaves in rebelling states free on the first day of 1863. The battlefield area includes more than 785 acres and there are many monuments, tablets and cannons. *Open daily.*

BLOODY LANE Confederate and Union forces fought for three hours for possession of this sunken road, and savage hand-to-hand encounters led to 4000 casualties. Photographs by Mathew Brady, the famous Civil War photographer, show that after the battle the road was literally covered with bodies.

BURNSIDE BRIDGE In Washington County there are still many limestone bridges similar to this small 1836 triple-arched structure spanning a narrow stream. It was here on this historic ground that a few hundred Georgia sharpshooters prevented an advance by General Ambrose Burnside's four divisions—a major factor in preventing a clear-cut victory for the Union.

CLARA BARTON MONUMENT This simple stone marker pays tribute to the Civil War's most famous nurse, who tended wounded troops during and after the battle. The American Red Cross was founded largely through her efforts and her name still stands as a symbol for enlightened humanitarian works.

MONUMENT TO CIVIL WAR DEAD This granite statue in the national cemetery here honors the memory of those who fought in the four-year conflict.

[**42.** *Burnside Bridge*] *Confederate troops used the bluffs above Antietam Creek to advantage in the bloody battle of September 17, 1862. The graceful, triple-arched limestone bridge was built in 1836.*

VISITOR CENTER MUSEUM Twenty-four colorful exhibits illustrate the many dramatic moments in the battle and its influence on the course of the Civil War. *Open daily except holidays.*

43. Barbara Fritchie Home and Museum *154 W. Patrick St., Frederick, Md.* Legend—aided by John Greenleaf Whittier—has it that in 1862 the 95-year-old Barbara Fritchie defiantly raised her U.S. flag in the face of Stonewall Jackson's Confederate march through Frederick. Whittier's famous poem depicts her fearlessly refusing to lower it: "Shoot if you must, this old gray head, but spare your country's flag." The museum contains many items belonging to Mrs. Fritchie. *Open daily except holidays. Small charge.*

44. Trinity Chapel *8 W. Church St., Frederick, Md.* Portions of this church were built at different times over a period of more than a century. The church building itself dates from 1880, the 60-foot tower comes from an earlier structure built in 1763 and received the addition of the spire in 1807. The time-span in construction is not apparent, however, and the tower, belfry, clock, lantern and spire are remarkably well integrated and proportioned. *Open daily.*

45. Harpers Ferry National Historical Park *Harpers Ferry, W. Va.* On the cold, wet night of Oct. 16, 1859, 18 men under the fiery abolitionist John Brown seized several buildings at the Federal Armory here and barricaded themselves inside with captured arms and several hostages. The next day Brown's hope of a slave uprising and black fortress in the Appalachians withered in the sharp reality of a bayonet charge led by Colonel Robert E. Lee and Lieutenant J.E.B. Stuart. Ten of Brown's men, including two of his sons, were killed; Brown himself was captured and subsequently hanged. His abortive raid made him a martyr to the abolitionist cause when the Civil War erupted 17 months later. The 1500-acre park site includes parts of the reconstructed town (damaged by the war and floods) and surrounding heights used as entrenchments by Confederate and Union forces during the war. Several of the restored buildings house interesting exhibits.

HARPER HOUSE Robert Harper died before this three-story house was completed for him in 1782, and it was converted into a tavern (where Washington and Jefferson stayed) and then back into a house. Today its rooms hold furniture used in this area during the Civil War era. *Open daily mid-June–early Sept., Sat., Sun. early Sept.-Oct.*

JOHN BROWN MUSEUM In this structure, built about 1838 by Gerard Bond Wager, a descendant of Robert Harper for whom the town is named, are exhibits on John Brown's life. The house is believed to be on the site of Harper's first home, a 1747 cabin. *Open daily.*

JOHN BROWN'S FORT This 1848 brick building was the engine and guard house of the Armory; Brown and his men occupied the east end, where the fire engines were kept. The building was dismantled for display at the 1893 World's Columbian Exposition in Chicago and was subsequently returned to West Virginia and rebuilt on the campus of Storer College. In 1968 it was moved to its present location on the old Arsenal Square, not far from its original site near the Armory.

MASTER ARMORER'S HOUSE U.S. Secretary of War Jefferson Davis approved plans for this handsome large brick building, completed in 1859. It was first occupied by the armory's paymaster clerk who was in residence at the time of Brown's ill-fated raid on the town. During the Civil War, Union officers used the house; today it is a museum with exhibits on the art of gunmaking. *Open daily mid-June–early Sept., Sat., Sun. early Sept.-Oct.*

[**45.** *Harper House*] *Attracted by the beauty of the area and the accessibility of two rivers, Robert Harper founded the town and started service on Harpers Ferry in 1747. His first two houses were located on the river flats, but for his third he chose a hilltop site. This house took seven years to build, and he was never to occupy it. In the 1830s an extensive addition, known as Wager House, was added. The oldest dwelling in Harpers Ferry, the house has been restored and furnished in the style of the mid-19th century. Visitors can climb up steps that were carved by hand out of natural sandstone at the end of the 19th century.*

STAGECOACH INN Completed in 1834, this restored building is now a Visitor Center with displays and an audio-visual presentation on the history of the park. *Open daily.*

46. Waterford Historic District *Waterford, Va.* Founded in 1740 by Quakers from Pennsylvania, Waterford still enjoys a rural setting in the Blue Ridge foothills. Many structures in the town, including several residences and the grain mill, date from pre-Revolutionary days. In the early 1800s, Waterford became known for its craft industries. The Waterford Foundation, an organization dedicated to restoring the town and to fostering the crafts practiced here in the 18th and 19th centuries, sponsors an annual homes tour and crafts exhibit in October.

47. Morven Park *Old Waterford Rd., Leesburg, Va.* Attractive boxwood gardens and nature trails surround the stately Greek Revival mansion on this 1200-acre estate. Once the home of Governor Westmoreland Davis of Virginia, the house contains the Davises' handsome furnishings. A nearby carriage house and museum building hold over 100 horse-drawn vehicles, including coaches, landaus and phaetons. Wildflowers and other native plants and birds draw visitors to the scenic trails. *Open Wed.-Sun. Apr.-Oct. Adults $1.75, children small charge.*

48. Oatlands *Rte. 15, S. of Leesburg, Va.* Oatlands, property of the National Trust for Historic Preservation, is a late-Georgian plantation home with Federal and Adamesque details. Built in 1800-03 by George Carter, it was constructed with lumber from his land and bricks fired on the estate. Most of the original structure has been preserved. The main feature of the facade is the portico supported by six Corinthian columns. Delicate cast-plaster trim highlights the interior in the entrance hall and the octagonal drawing room. The house is furnished throughout with superb examples of American, English and French antiques from the collection of Mr. and Mrs. William Corcoran Eustis, who later owned the house. In the formal garden are plantings of boxwood dating from the early 1800s. *Open daily Apr.-Oct. Small charge.*

49. Trinity Episcopal Church *Upperville, Va.* This impressive example of Norman architecture, modeled after 12th- and 13th-century French country churches, was designed by H. Page Cross. The third church on the site (the first was erected in 1842), it was begun in 1951 and opened for services nine years later. Most of the construction was done by local artisans, who also learned to forge their own tools in the tradition of medieval craftsmen. Particularly beautiful are Heinz Warneke's carvings—native plants, great Christian preachers and symbolic animals both real and mythological—on the pews, pulpit and columns. The stained-glass windows in the nave and choir were made in Amsterdam. *Open daily.*

50. Dulles International Airport *Off Rtes. 495 and 123, Chantilly, Va.* Dulles is one of architect Eero Saarinen's last and most impressive designs. The mammoth terminal seems to soar skyward, with its concave arched roof supported by angled pillars interspaced with glass walls. The airport makes use of the latest techniques to facilitate travel, such as mobile lounge units which "dock" passengers at their planes. The 193-foot traffic-control tower at the rear has a restaurant at its base. *Open daily.*

[50] *The late Eero Saarinen called Dulles Airport "the best thing I have done." Many visitors see an Oriental influence in the upcurved roof; its casual grace suggested to one critic a handkerchief dropped in the grass.*

51. Sully Plantation *Rte. 28, Chantilly, Va.* Built in 1794 by Richard Bland Lee, brother of General "Light-Horse Harry" Lee and uncle to General Robert E. Lee, this three-story white clapboard house has survived through the years much as it was originally, including the wood flooring and paneling. The house is completely furnished, some of the pieces having belonged to the Richard Lee family. In mid-May local artisans and craftsmen gather here to demonstrate their skills. There are six outbuildings typical of the era on the property. *Open daily except Dec. 25. Small charge.*

52. Clara Barton House *5801 Oxford Rd., Glen Echo, Md.* Clara Barton, founder and first president of the American National Red Cross, used her home as headquarters for the organization from 1897 to 1904. The interior design of the 38-room Victorian house—made of lumber used to build barracks for the victims of the Johnstown flood—resembles that of a Mississippi steamboat. Second- and third-floor octagonal galleries overlook a paneled hall on the ground floor where there were offices and reception rooms. There is a suspended captain's quarters with a lantern roof on the third floor. Throughout the house many of Miss Barton's personal possessions are on display. *Open Tues.-Sun. except holidays.*

53. Arlington National Cemetery *Arlington, Va.* Overlooking the Potomac and Washington, this is the national cemetery for American military men. Established in 1864, it contains the gravesites of many notable Americans, including William H. Taft, John F. Kennedy, Robert F. Kennedy, General John J. Pershing, William Jennings Bryan and General George C. Marshall. It is also the burial ground for thousands of servicemen who have died in action and for many other U.S. soldiers. *Open daily.*

ARLINGTON HOUSE (R. E. LEE MEMORIAL) This Greek Revival mansion, presently on the grounds of the Arlington National Cemetery, was built in the first years of the 19th century by George Washington Parke Custis, the grandson of Martha Washington. His daughter married Robert E. Lee in 1831. Lee lived here until 1861 when he resigned from the U.S. Army to join the cause of Virginia. A wide hall divides the central section of the mansion. On the south side is a large formal parlor and on the north is the family dining room and parlor. The house, built of bricks covered with stucco, is painted to resemble marble. Facing the Potomac, the grand portico with eight large Doric columns provides a superb view of Washington. The mansion is furnished with pieces of the period. *Open daily except Dec. 25. Small charge.*

MARINE CORPS WAR MEMORIAL This is a reproduction of the Joseph Rosenthal photograph of Marines raising the American flag on Iwo Jima during World War II. The 78-foot figures of the memorial are cast in bronze. Color ceremonies and carillon concerts are given regularly from April to September.

TOMB OF THE UNKNOWN SOLDIER Unidentified American soldiers from World War I, World War II and the Korean conflict are buried in this tomb. Guarded 24 hours a day, it commemorates all the military men who died in battle. The monument of Colorado-Yule marble is carved from one of the largest blocks ever quarried.

54. Theodore Roosevelt Memorial *Theodore Roosevelt Island, E. of Arlington, Va.* The 26th President of the U.S. was one of the great conservationists and is fittingly honored in this 88-acre wilderness preserve in the Potomac River. The island's swamps, marshes and forests support a variety of trees, flowers, birds and small animals, which can be seen along the trails. A 17-foot bronze statue of Roosevelt is backed by a 30-foot granite shaft. There are also four granite tablets inscribed with his philosophy of citizenship. The island, under the jurisdiction of the District of Columbia, is reached by a footbridge from the Virginia side off the George Washington Memorial Parkway. *Open daily.*

55. Washington, D.C.

In 1791 President George Washington chose the site and the man he wanted to plan a new U.S. Capital. By the following year Paris-born Pierre l'Enfant's sweeping design for the city, modeled in part on the splendid expanses of Versailles, was completed. Washington's growth was slow; it was not until 1800 that the government finally moved here from Philadelphia. Fourteen years later most of the public buildings were burned by the British. The Civil War saw an expanding city, however, and today Washington has a population of some 750,000 people, about two-thirds of whom work for the Federal Government. Although l'Enfant's elegant plan was in the end greatly modified, his broad avenues and sweeping vistas, combined with the monumental buildings and the riches they contain, have made the Capital unique among American cities.

Air and Space Building *Independence Ave., S.W.* See feature display on page 194.

[**53.** *Tomb of the Unknown Soldier*] *Two more unknowns have joined the World War I soldier: men who died in the Korean War and in World War II. The guard is changed every half hour during summer daylight hours.*

American National Red Cross *17th and D Sts., N.W.* Three handsome white marble buildings house the national headquarters of the American Red Cross. The main building, completed in 1917 as a memorial to the women who cared for the sick and wounded of both sides during the Civil War, contains statuary, paintings, stained-glass windows by Tiffany and special exhibits and displays that illustrate the society's past and present. *Open Mon.-Fri.*

Arts and Industries Building *900 Jefferson Dr., S.W.* See feature display on pages 194-5.

Christ Church *620 G St., S.E.* This "Folk Gothic" structure, built in 1807 for Washington's first Episcopal parish, is one of the District's oldest churches. Designed in brick by Benjamin Henry Latrobe, America's first professional architect, it is now stuccoed and has undergone other modifications. Additions of a chancel, entrance foyer and battlemented bell tower (which served as an observation post during the Civil War) have altered its shape. In 1955, however, the interior was restored to its original simplicity. James Madison and James Monroe worshiped here; John Philip Sousa is buried in the graveyard. *Open Mon.-Fri., Sun.*

Corcoran Gallery of Art *New York Ave. and 17th St., N.W.* Begun in 1859, the Corcoran was one of the first art museums in the U.S. Today it holds one of the nation's most impressive collections of American art, encompassing works dating from the 18th century to the present. Some of the finest paintings by Copley, Stuart, Rembrandt Peale (*Washington Before Yorktown*) and other early portraitists are on view as are scenes by important landscape artists. *A Light on the Sea* by Homer, *The Pathetic Song* by Eakins and Sargent's *Madame Pailleron,* hang in the galleries. Also of interest are *The Old House of Representatives* by Samuel F. B. Morse, better known for his achievements in telegraphy, and one of the first American still lifes, *The Poor Artist's Cupboard* by Charles Bird King. The Hudson River school is abundantly represented by Cole, Durand, Church and Kensett. Canvases by the Ashcan School, Hans Hofmann (*Golden Blaze*) and other leading artists of the 20th century also can be seen here. American sculpture includes figures by Powers, Remington, Saint-Gaudens and Daniel Chester French. There is an extensive group of bronzes by the French sculptor Antoine Barye. Paintings and prints ranging from the 17th-century Dutch to the 19th-century French Impres-

sionist schools comprise a large collection including Rembrandt's *A Musician,* Degas's *Ballet School,* a number of Corot's paintings and works by Rubens, Renoir, Pissarro and Monet, among many others. In the collection of 18th-century English portraits are works by Gainsborough, Lawrence and Reynolds. Fine furnishings, including a superb Louis XVI salon, are also on view. One wing of the building houses the Corcoran School of Art. *Open Tues.-Sun. except holidays. Small charge Thurs.-Sun.*

Daughters of the American Revolution, National Society Headquarters *1776 D St., N.W.* Three buildings of outstanding character not far from the White House comprise the headquarters of this nationwide organization.

CONSTITUTION HALL This auditorium, built in 1929 for the society's annual meetings, is one of the largest in the District and the scene of many concerts, recitals and lectures. John Russell Pope designed the handsome, classical-style hall. *Open Mon.-Fri. except holidays.*

D.A.R. MUSEUM Located in the Administration Building, this museum is devoted almost entirely to early U.S. history. The large collection includes crewelwork, China Trade porcelain, glassware, pewter, silver, clothing and other items predating 1830. *Open Mon.-Fri. except holidays.*

MEMORIAL CONTINENTAL HALL An outstanding genealogical library, where Rembrandt Peale's famous "porthole" portrait of George Washington hangs, is housed here. The third largest such library in the nation, it has served the public for many years. Twenty-eight rooms containing excellent period furnishings are maintained in the same building by the state organizations. *Open Mon.-Fri. except holidays.*

Decatur House *748 Jackson Pl., N.W.* This attractive three-story brick Federal dwelling on Lafayette Square was completed in 1819 for Commodore Stephen Decatur, famed for his defeat of the Barbary pirates several years earlier. Designed by Latrobe, it has many decorative details, handsome woodwork and a fine circular staircase. There are many antique furnishings, paintings and examples of silver, and the second floor features Victoriana. Henry Clay and Martin Van Buren also resided here. The interior was restored in 1944 according to Latrobe's drawings, and the house is now the headquarters of the National Trust for Historic Preservation. Adjoining Decatur House, in the former carriage house, is the Truxton-Decatur Naval Museum, administered by the Naval Historical Foundation. On display are objects relating to the U.S. Navy, Marine Corps, Coast Guard and Merchant Marine. *House open daily. Small charge. Museum open Tues.-Sun.*

[**55.** *Corcoran Gallery*] *George Bellows'* Forty-two Kids *shows the influence of Goya in the dynamic contrast between light and dark and in the vitality of the figures of boys playing along the New York waterfront.*

[**55.** *Folger Library*] *Posed against a typical Elizabethan theater is a treasure of Shakespearean artifacts, including Edwin Booth's costume as* Richard III, *a breastplate and dagger, and a Wedgwood bust of the Bard.*

Dumbarton Oaks *1703 32nd St., N.W.* The conference that led to the founding of the United Nations was held in this 1801 Georgian-style mansion. In 1940 the owners, Mr. and Mrs. Robert Woods Bliss, donated both the house and the grounds to Harvard University and provided funds for its operation. Today it is a center for research and publication in Byzantine and Pre-Columbian studies and in landscape architecture. Its treasures include magnificent collections of Byzantine and Pre-Columbian art, fine tapestries and furnishings, and paintings by American and European artists, including El Greco's *Visitation.* A new wing, with eight circular glass pavilions, was designed by Philip Johnson to house the Pre-Columbian collection. On the splendid grounds surrounding the house are covered walks, formal gardens, terraces, fountains and trees of many kinds. *Open Tues.-Sun. except holidays Sept.-June.*

Federal Trade Commission Building *Sixth St. and Pennsylvania Ave., N.W.* This massive 1937 structure, of modified Classic design, has a rounded, colonnaded portico on the north facade. Within are the offices of the government agency responsible for protecting consumers and keeping business competition free and fair. Two massive stone statues, both of a man (the FTC) struggling mightily to control a horse (Trade), flank the eastern facade, and four limestone relief panels over the main entrances depict Foreign Trade, Agriculture, Industry and Shipping. *Open Mon.-Fri.*

Folger Shakespeare Library *201 E. Capitol St., S.E.* Of interest to all who enjoy literature, the library includes many rare books and manuscripts of the Renaissance—as well as the Folios, Quartos, paintings, costumes and furnishings that make up the world's foremost collection of Shakespeareana. Many of the rare books and other treasures are displayed for visitors. The bequest of Mr. and Mrs. Henry Clay Folger, this center of research is administered by the Trustees of Amherst College. While the exterior of the 1932 building, decorated with bas-reliefs of scenes from Shakespeare's plays, is contemporary in style, the high-beamed, paneled interior reflects the Elizabethan age. It houses a scale model of Shakespeare's theater, the Globe, and a full-size replica of an Elizabethan theater. *Open Mon.-Sat. Jan.-mid-Apr., daily mid-Apr.-early Sept., Mon.-Sat. early Sept.-Dec.*

Franciscan Monastery *1400 Quincy St., N.E.* Founded and maintained by the Order of Friars Minor, Roman Catholic guardians of the shrines of the Holy Land, this unique complex re-creates many of these sites for American visitors. Replicas of the Holy Sepulcher, the Grotto of Bethlehem and the catacombs of Rome are among those that can be seen in the Byzantine-style church and on the surrounding grounds. A small museum of arts and crafts relating to the Bible and the Holy Land contains icons, artifacts from the Crusades and the finest collection of carved pearl pieces outside of Jerusalem. The grounds are beautifully landscaped with paths and gardens, including an outstanding rose garden. *Open daily.*

Freer Gallery of Art *12th St. and Jefferson Dr., S.W.* See feature display on page 190.

Georgetown Historic District It was here in 1791 that Washington met with French architect Pierre L'Enfant to discuss the capital to be built just up the Potomac and named in his honor. At the time when the city of Washington was still a plan, Georgetown was a thriving Potomac River tobacco port where merchants and shippers were building imposing brick homes. As railroads developed and the harbor proved too shallow for steam navigation, the port declined in importance. The location, however, so near the growing capital—with which it later merged in 1871—encouraged continued growth, and Georgetown evolved into a unique community of fine homes, tree-shaded streets, brick walks and smart shops. Citizens' committees were formed from time to time to prevent the destruction of buildings of architectural merit and historic houses. In 1950 the Georgetown Historic District was created by an act of Congress and in 1967 it was listed in the National Register.

The best way to see Georgetown is on foot. The streets are narrow for driving and the overhanging branches of the trees limit the view from a car. There are lovely houses on every street, but among the most rewarding strolls are along M Street between 30th and 31st Streets; N Street between 28th and 31st Streets; and west of Wisconsin Avenue between Potomac and 34th Streets. The streets are lined with private homes, and their fine proportions, workmanship and architectural details—doorways, dormers, columns, pilaster trim, hardware and ironwork—may be enjoyed from the street. An exceptional 1852 Victorian house is at the north end of the area at 3259 R Street, and there is another imposing facade at 3238 R Street. On Q Street between 30th and 31st Streets are the Cooke Row houses, exceptional examples of Victorian fancy. The mansions at each end of the row are in an ornate Mansard style, and the two middle villas show the Italian influence also in vogue at the time. Other outstanding buildings in the area include the following.

CONVENT OF MERCY *3525 N St., N.W.* The first Roman Catholic church in the area was built here in 1791-95 and named Trinity Church. It has been rebuilt except for the facade and belfry.

CONVENT OF THE VISITATION OF THE HOLY MARY *1500 35th St., N.W.* Founded in 1799 by the Poor Clare nuns, this girls' boarding and day school was the first of the Order of the Visitation in the country. The oldest building on the grounds is the chapel, erected in 1821. The main building was erected in 1874 and is an engaging example of the Victorian style that was popular at the time.

DUMBARTON HOUSE *2715 Q St., N.W.* This is the headquarters of the National Society of Colonial Dames of America. (It should not be confused with the Dumbarton Oaks estate on R Street, famed as the site of the conference that led to the founding of the United Nations.) Dumbarton House has been moved from its original site, refurbished and furnished by the Society. The house is a handsome combination of Georgian and Federal architectural details. It is not a faithful rendition of one particular style but reveals an evaluation of styles. The prominent families who have lived here through

[Georgetown] John Cox, mayor of the newly incorporated town of George Town, built a row of houses on N Street in 1790. Numbers 3327 to 3339 remain, and are still known as Cox's Row. Two of the houses are fine examples of the Federal style—well proportioned, with doors and windows flush with the outer walls, which are decorated with graceful plaques.

[Islamic Center] Glowing carpets provide seating for shoeless tourists who are learning about the Muslim religion and the architecture of this magnificent mosque. Verses from the Quran are worked in tile on the pillars.

the years made additions according to their current tastes. *Open Mon.-Sat. Sept.-June.*

GEORGETOWN PRESBYTERIAN CHURCH *3115 P St., N.W.* This building has been rebuilt to resemble the congregation's original church on Bridge Street.

GRACE EPISCOPAL CHURCH *South St. and Wisconsin Ave., N.W.* In 1866 this small neo-Gothic church was built to replace the original wooden mission for canal boatmen constructed 11 years earlier.

METHODIST EPISCOPAL CHURCH *3127 Dumbarton Ave., N.W.* The church was used as a hospital during the Civil War, from October 1862 to Jan. 8, 1863, and Walt Whitman worked here as a male nurse. The church was built in 1849, and the present facade was added in 1898.

OLD STONE HOUSE *3051 M St., N.W.* Built in 1765, this is the oldest pre-Revolutionary building in Washington. Demonstrations of Colonial household crafts are given here. *Open Wed.-Sun.*

ST. JOHN'S CHURCH *O and Potomac Sts.* William Thornton, the first architect of the Capitol, designed St. John's, the oldest Episcopal church in the area, and it was dedicated in 1809. The dome of the belfry rests on the single remaining tier of the three-tiered original.

Georgetown University *37th and O Sts., N.W.* In 1789 Archbishop John Carroll founded this, the nation's first Roman Catholic college and, later, the first university chartered by the Federal Government. Since its early days, when it was primarily a seminary, Jesuit-run Georgetown has grown to comprise 10 schools, including those of law, medicine, dentistry, nursing and foreign service.

ASTRONOMICAL OBSERVATORY A three-story brick building with rotating dome, this was among the first college observatories in the country, built in 1844 by Father James Curley. Among the astronomical instruments that have been developed here is one that led to the Baker-Nunn camera, used today for star photography. The university holds its astronomy classes here.

HEALY BUILDING This massive, gargoyled Victorian structure, with its tall clock tower, is the landmark of Georgetown's campus. The building is named for the remarkable man who commissioned it, Patrick F. Healy, S.J., the son of an Irish planter and a former slave. Father Healy, whose family includes other leaders in the Catholic Church (one brother was bishop of Portland, Maine, and one sister founded the Sisters of the Holy Family, an order of nuns devoted to teaching black children), was Georgetown's 29th president—and the first black president of a university. He was also the first black recipient of a Ph.D. During his administration (1873-82), Father Healy revitalized Georgetown, turning it into the fine university it is today. *Open daily.*

JOHN CARROLL STATUE Dedicated in 1912, this bronze statue by Jerome Connor depicts the seated figure of Georgetown's founder. Besides his role in the university's history, John Carroll, one of the illustrious Carrolls of Carrolltown, Maryland, was the first Catholic bishop in the U.S. and a Revolutionary patriot who was friend to Washington and Jefferson.

OLD NORTH BUILDING Georgetown's second building, a three-and-one-half-story Georgian structure, flanked by two octagonal towers, dates back to 1797. Many early historic personages, including George Washington, visited Old North. The building continues to serve the university and contains administrative offices, dormitories, a small chapel and the post office. *Open daily.*

Hirshhorn Museum and Sculpture Garden *Seventh St. and Independence Ave., S.W.* See feature display on page 191.

House of the Americas *17th St. and Constitution Ave., N.W.* Formerly known as the Pan American Union, this handsome white marble building, completed in 1910, is the headquarters of the Organization of American States (O.A.S.), which includes the U.S. and 23 other nations of the Caribbean, Middle and South America. The red-tile roof, statuary, iron balconies and grillwork heighten the Latin American flavor of the exterior, while the interior is graced by a typical Latin patio (glass-roofed, however), with tropical birds and a year-round display of exotic plants. The Hall of Heroes and Flags and the magnificent Hall of the Americas—site of inter-American meetings, concerts and glittering receptions—are of great interest to visitors from all nations. Changing exhibits of Latin American artists are featured in the gallery. *Open Mon.-Sat. except holidays. Small charge.*

Islamic Center *2551 Massachusetts Ave., N.W.* In the midst of the stolid mansions of Embassy Row, site of many embassies and chancelleries, the Islamic Center's architecture—complete with minaret—offers an exotic touch of the Near East. Maintained and administered by American Muslims and by the Muslim countries with diplomatic missions in Washington, the building houses a mosque, a library, a lecture hall, classrooms and offices of the Institute for Higher Study of Islamic Culture. Colorful abstract patterns decorate the walls and ceiling of the mosque, which is richly adorned with gifts from different Muslim countries—tiles from Turkey, rugs from Iran and a magnificent ivory and ebony inlaid pulpit. *Open daily.*

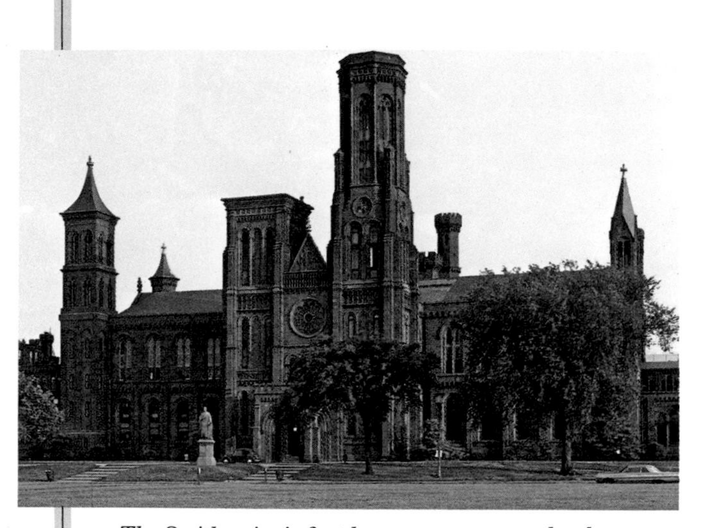

The Smithsonian's first home now serves as headquarters.

SMITHSONIAN INSTITUTION

Washington, D.C.

Fondly called "the nation's attic," the Smithsonian has spent nearly two lifetimes accumulating its vast stockpiles of treasure. It was founded in 1846 with half a million dollars bequeathed by James Smithson, a wealthy English scientist who had never crossed the Atlantic. Yet he wanted the capital of the United States to have "an establishment for the increase and diffusion of knowledge among men." Smithson's generous legacy fostered one of the world's largest enterprises devoted to the arts, the sciences and history. Its contribution to the "increase of knowledge" is unmeasurable. About a dozen separate museums hold around 69 million catalogued items, and of that vast number relatively few—under one percent—are on public display at any given time. The other aspect of Smithson's request—that his fortune should contribute to the "diffusion of knowl-

National Museum of History and Technology

14th St. and Constitution Ave., N.W.

The story of America and its inventive genius is given full display here. Farming machinery, automobiles and locomotives highlight transportation achievements; medical work ranges from George Washington's false teeth and early X-ray tubes to the world's first mechanical heart and iron lung. Whitney's cotton gin, Morse's telegraph equipment and Franklin's printing press are here, along with early cameras, typewriters and Gramophones. Military items include Washington's camp chest and tent and Clara Barton's Civil War ambulance cart. First Ladies are represented by a collection of their gowns worn by mannequins in period settings. Musical instruments, coins and stamps are among other fine exhibits. *Open daily except Dec. 25.*

Of the 12 million postal items, none is rarer than this 1918 airmail stamp: it is part of an original sheet of 100 on which the biplane was mistakenly printed upside down.

Even today's advertising would be hard put to match the showmanship of the late 19th-century cigar-store Indian. The tall and handsome figure is elaborately carved and painted—a brilliant lure for the tobacconist's shop.

edge"—has spurred the rise of the institution's reputation as the world's preeminent research center. Laboratories, observatories and institutes in this country and overseas conduct research programs in fields as varied as oceanography, biology, solar radiation and tropical studies. Scientific expeditions circle the globe. Many of the programs are shared with universities and other institutions; students at any level can draw on the Smithsonian's wealth of research material; and publications on new research are circulated here and abroad. In fulfilling its founder's wishes, the Smithsonian has extravagantly outdone itself. Each year about 15 million people enjoy as many of its astonishing exhibits as their time permits. For even if a visitor lingered just one minute over each object, it would take two and a half years to complete a tour. Headquarters for this multifold operation is a 12th-century Norman castle built in 1855. A sarcophagus on the main floor commemorates the Smithsonian's benefactor.

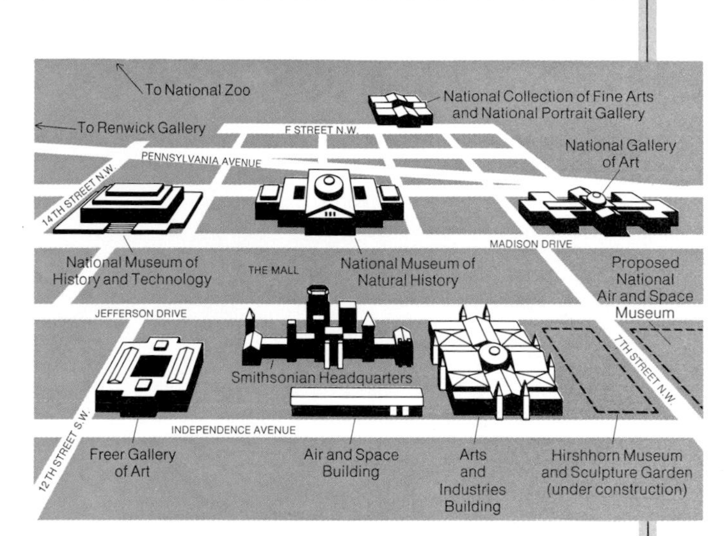

The Smithsonian Complex

The glittering scale model of the Huber steam tractor—which runs like the original—shows what was up-to-date in farm machinery at the turn of the century. It burned either wood or coal and built up steam to give it a mighty 30-horsepower thrust.

Among the many curious coins are this odd couple, the largest and smallest ever minted. The 1629 Bohemian 100-ducat piece upstages its tiny German companion, worth one thirty-second of a ducat.

America's most famous flag flew over Baltimore's Fort McHenry in the War of 1812. Still aloft after a night bombardment, it inspired Francis Scott Key to write his poem about the star-spangled banner.

Some of the National Gallery's proudest art flanks Rembrandt's noble Self-Portrait *and Verrocchio's bust of Lorenzo de' Medici. From top left: David's* Napoleon, *a Grünewald crucifixion beside El Greco's* Laocoön, *a Constable landscape, Raphael's* St. George and the Dragon, *da Settignano's bust of a little boy. From top right: a Gilbert Stuart portrait, Cézanne's still life, a van der Weyden portrait, de Heem's* Vase of Flowers, *Houdon's* Diana.

Freer Gallery of Art

12th St. and Jefferson Dr., S.W.

During his lifetime industrialist Charles L. Freer amassed one of the world's finest collections of Far Eastern and Near Eastern art. At his death in 1919 the extraordinary collection was given to the nation, along with a museum to house it and funds both for further purchases and continued study of Oriental art. Just as Freer found relief in his avocation from the commercial pressure of his times, today's visitors discover a certain tranquillity in viewing the graceful paintings, bronzes, sculptures and the delicate objects in jade, gold, stone and wood. Freer also bought paintings of 19th-century American artists such as Homer, Sargent and Hassam, and gathered together the world's largest assembly of works by Whistler, Freer's lifelong friend. *Open daily except Dec. 25.*

At 31, Freer bought a Japanese fan, his first piece of Oriental art. Now, grown to about 12,000 objects, the collection includes this serenely beautiful 13th-century Chinese bodhisattva, a Buddha-to-be.

National Gallery of Art

Sixth St. and Constitution Ave., N.W.

The lodestone of great works here was a gift made by financier Andrew Mellon in 1937: namely, more than 115 paintings and sculptures by such masters as Holbein, Titian, Rubens and Rembrandt, for which Mellon paid about $30 million. He added another fortune to construct and maintain the gleaming marble gallery. Mellon hoped his generosity would draw other prominent private art collections, and over the years more than 200 donors have given works. The gallery, which is administered independent of the rest of the Smithsonian, now boasts some 2200 paintings and 1740 sculptures. *Open daily except Jan. 1 and Dec. 25.*

Raphael's exquisite Alba Madonna *is in the gallery.*

Hirshhorn Museum and Sculpture Garden

Seventh St. and Independence Ave., S.W.

Like public-spirited Andrew Mellon and Charles Freer, Joseph H. Hirshhorn, a financier, in 1966 gave the country his magnificent collection of some 6000 paintings and sculptures. To display them, the Smithsonian is building a circular building with a sunken sculpture garden, an enormous reflecting pool and spacious, inviting walks. Paintings will highlight artistic achievements of the 20th century, featuring works by de Kooning, Rothko, Léger and Pollock. Approximately 2000 sculptures will reveal the development of this art from antiquity to modern times. Outstanding European and American sculptors of the 19th and 20th centuries will be eminently represented by men like Calder, Giacometti, Picasso and Matisse. *Open daily except Dec. 25.*

Moore's elongated King and Queen *grandly rest in the courtyard along with a hundred other works that include Rodin's* Burghers of Calais *and Matisse's bas-reliefs* The Backs.

National Zoological Park
3001 Connecticut Ave., N.W.

In 1890 the Smithsonian moved its small menagerie with about 200 animals to these woodland acres in Rock Creek Park. Today the National Zoo's eight buildings and special outdoor areas house 3000 mammals, birds and reptiles, representing more than 800 species and subspecies. The zoo was originally founded to preserve certain North American mammals, such as the bison and the elk. Its inhabitants now include some of the world's rarest animals, many endangered in their native habitats and breeding successfully here. The most celebrated newcomers are Ling-Ling and Hsing-Hsing, giant pandas from China. Other rarities are scimitar-horned Arabian oryxes, dragon-like Komodo monitor lizards from Indonesia and the catlike fossa and fanaloka from Madagascar. But visitors can also enjoy familiar zoo denizens like chimpanzees, bears, elephants, lions, rhinoceroses—and famous Smokey the black bear, his mate and Little Smokey. Among the most popular spots are the Bird House—birds fly freely in a lush rain forest—and the outdoor flight cage. *Open daily.*

Happiness for a giant panda is a game of throw-the-ball and splash-the-water. Zookeepers and visitors alike are delighted that the pandas feel at home in Washington.

The world's most famous single gem, the Hope Diamond (enlarged here to twice its size), glitters a rare and deep blue. The jewel weighs 44.5 carats.

National Museum of Natural History and Museum of Man
10th St. and Constitution Ave., N.W.

Of the 54 million objects amassed by the museum, only about one percent is ever on display at one time, but this is enough to dazzle even reluctant museum visitors. A horn-headed dinosaur that lived about 100 million years ago, a gigantic 12-ton Angolan elephant, an enormous Indian tiger, the last passenger pigeon, an Egyptian mummy, the Star of Asia sapphire—these are but a few of the exotic spectacles that fill various exhibit halls. Extensive displays reveal customs of Asian and African peoples, of Indians of the Americas, and of Pacific Islanders. A large number of the world's mammals are arranged in outstanding replicas of their natural environments, and separate space is devoted to sea creatures and bird life. The most renowned collection—and the world's largest—is a stunning array of minerals and gems. *Open daily except Dec. 25.*

This colorful grouping reveals many of the museum's areas of collection and research, such as paleontology, zoology and anthropology. The gorilla and the whale skeleton ferociously dominate their companions, an odd assortment of land, sea and air creatures.

The Hall of Life in the Sea holds one of the museum's most fantastic exhibits. A life-size fiberglass model of a blue whale, the largest mammal on earth, floats 30 feet above the floor. It took two years to construct the 92-foot behemoth.

Renwick's Grand Salon recalls a Victorian gallery.

Renwick Gallery
17th St. and Pennsylvania Ave., N.W.

In 1858 James Renwick, architect of the Smithsonian's original turreted building, designed a decorative French-style building of red brick and sandstone with a mansard roof to house the Corcoran collection of art, one of the first museums in the country. The building was used by the U.S. Court of Claims from 1899 until the 1960s when President Kennedy rescued it from planned demolition. Carefully restored and refurbished by the Smithsonian, it is now a showcase of late Victorian interiors (1860–75) and decorative arts and crafts. Exhibits include representations of Renwick's Washington buildings, America's design heritage and American wood furniture, and modern architecture and industrial design. *Open daily except Dec. 25.*

Indian Princess Pocahontas by an unknown Englishman is a prized painting in the Portrait Gallery.

In 1903 Orville Wright flew his flyer at Kitty Hawk for 12 seconds: history's first manned, powered flight.

Arts and Industries Building
900 Jefferson Dr., S.W.

The Arts and Industries Building and the nearby Air and Space Building are devoted to air and space displays. Here are the Wright brothers' original airplane; Charles A. Lindbergh's monoplane *The Spirit of St. Louis,* in which he flew the Atlantic; the first supersonic airplane; Mercury, Gemini and Apollo spacecraft; a moon rock and other lunar-exploration exhibits; and a real lunar module that served as a backup vehicle for those that took the astronauts to the moon's surface. Here too are prototypes of the thematic units around which exhibit halls will be organized in the new National Air and Space Museum that is being constructed nearby and is expected to open in 1976. The new museum will house most of the exhibits shown here. In the Hall of Aerospace Art are paintings and sculpture depicting man's adventures in the conquest of space. *Open daily except Dec. 25.*

In 1849 painter George Catlin, an impoverished expatriate living in London, offered his 600 oil paintings of American Indians to the Smithsonian for $65,000 but was refused. Thanks to a donation in 1879, some 590 of his works are now in the National Collection. While most American painters in the early 19th century concentrated on drawing-room portraits, Catlin painted scenes of Indian life. Here is Group of Dancers (probably eastern marginal Great Plains).

National Collection of Fine Arts National Portrait Gallery

9th St. between F and G Sts., N.W.

The National Fine Arts Collection of American painting, sculpture, prints and drawings from the nation's beginnings to the present is particularly strong in 19th-century, early-20th-century and contemporary works. The National Portrait Gallery maintains a painted record of U.S. Presidents and notable figures in all walks of American life, from Colonial days to the present. Both museums have temporary exhibits. Since 1968 these collections have been housed in one of the finest Neoclassic buildings in Washington and one with an interesting history. It served as a hospital during the Civil War and has been occupied by the Patent Office, Civil Service Commission and Department of Interior. *Museums open daily except Dec. 25.*

One room in the Arts and Industries Building is devoted to ballooning, the first technique that successfully lifted man off the planet Earth. It all started in 1783 when the Montgolfier brothers, two ingenious Frenchmen, rose above an amazed crowd in a hot-air-inflated sack. Europeans quickly succumbed to balloonomania, expressing their new enthusiasm in literature, art, music and many more high-flying escapades. The balloon exhibit is seen here through a fish-eye lens. The large sphere in the center is a Fu-go balloon. During World War II the Japanese floated them across the Pacific in an unsuccessful attempt to start fires in the U.S.

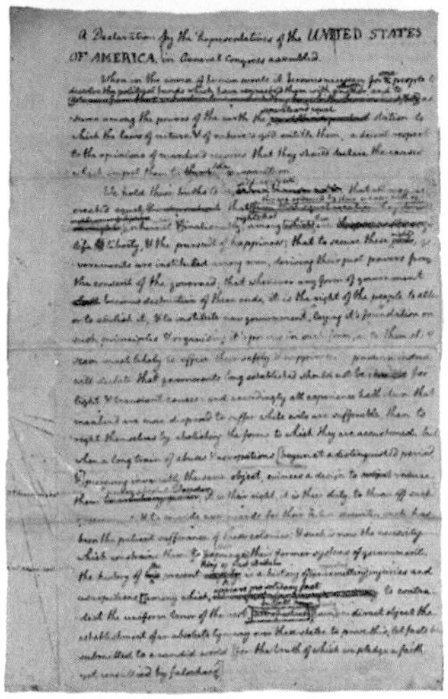

[Library of Congress] The Library's Great Hall was the focal point of controversy when the ornate Main Building was being built. Citizens protested that the government was throwing money away on marble furbelows and gold leaf. But most visitors today are impressed with the marble mosaic floor, great stairways, arches and ceiling murals. Thomas Jefferson's draft of the Declaration of Independence, with a few editorial changes by John Adams and Benjamin Franklin, is enshrined on the west side.

John F. Kennedy Center for the Performing Arts *2700 Virginia Ave., N.W.* This massive memorial to President Kennedy on the banks of the Potomac opened in 1971. Designed by Edward Durell Stone, its facilities include an opera house, a concert hall and two large theaters, one for drama, the other for films. Among the center's other attractions are the Hall of Nations, displaying flags of many countries; the Hall of States, where state flags are hung; and the upper-level terrace, which provides a fine view of the city. Many foreign governments contributed materials to the building, including the exterior marble (a gift from Italy) and most of the magnificent chandeliers. *Open daily.*

Library of Congress *10 First St., S.E.* Within these massive buildings are the possessions of the world's largest library—not only books (in 183 languages), but millions of manuscripts, maps new and old, prints, photographs, newspapers and microfilm. Although established in 1800 as a service to members of Congress, the library's facilities are currently available to all government agencies as well as to scholars, the general public and other libraries throughout the U.S. Here for scholars are one of the world's top collections of incunabula, or books printed before 1501, which includes a perfect copy on vellum of the Gutenberg Bible, and the largest collections of Slavic and Chinese books outside the U.S.S.R. and Asia. Students of American history can see Champlain's 1608 charting of sections of New England and Canada, what are believed to be maps drawn up by Lewis and Clark in 1804 and 1806, Colonial newspapers, a rough draft of the Declaration of Independence, Lincoln's first two drafts of the Gettysburg Address and Civil War photographs by Mathew Brady. In a lighter vein, they can listen to recordings of cowboy ballads, hillbilly songs and Creole and Indian folk songs or view George Gershwin's original handwritten score for *Porgy and Bess*—these are just a small part of the library's extensive musical collection that includes Stradivari instruments and manuscripts by Bach, Beethoven and other great composers. In the Motion Picture Section are almost 160,000 reels, including a three-second film, *The Sneeze,* copyrighted by Thomas Edison in 1894, and 3000 films that trace the development of the movie industry between 1894 and 1912. The earliest of the library's buildings—and the most elaborate by far—was completed in 1897 in Italian Renaissance style. Rich ornamentation and statuary—the Court of Neptune Fountain, marble columns, mosaic marble floors, allegorical and symbolic sculpture and busts of the world's most distinguished men of letters through the ages—decorate the building. *Exhibit halls open daily except Dec. 25; reading rooms open daily except holidays.*

Lincoln Memorial *Foot of 23rd St., N.W.* This classic white marble building, which resembles the Parthenon of Greece, is a fitting monument to the nation's 16th President. Designed by Henry Bacon, its exterior motif symbolizes the U.S. The 36 Doric columns of the portico represent the number of states in the Union at the time of Lincoln's death. The names of these states are carved on a frieze above the columns. The walls bear the names of the 48 states in existence in 1922, when the memorial was completed. Within is Daniel Chester French's famous 19-foot-high marble statue of the seated Lincoln and two Jules Guerin murals, *Emancipation* and *Reunion.* The Gettysburg Address and Lincoln's second inaugural address are carved in the walls. At night the interior and exterior are dramatically illuminated. *Open daily except Dec. 25.*

Martin Luther King Memorial Library *901 G St., N.W.* Mies van der Rohe's design for this four-story structure is an effective blending of black steel, brick and bronze-colored glass. The main building of the District of Columbia's public library system, it houses divisions devoted to black studies and Washingtoniana, the latter a rich source of materials dealing with the Capital's past and present. Visitors can study L'Enfant's plan for the city and Captain John Smith's map of explorations along the Potomac River, plus copies of early city directories and a complete microfilm file of Washington's first daily newspaper, *The National Intelligencer. Open Mon.-Sat.*

Medical Museum of the Armed Forces Institute of Pathology *6825 16th St., N.W.* This impressive new building designed by Edward Durell Stone, on the grounds of the Walter Reed Army Medical Center, houses exhibits dealing with human and animal diseases and with medical history from the Civil War to the present day. The museum holds the world's largest collection of microscopes, from a replica of the first crude model of about 1600 to the electron microscopes of today as well as displays of other medical instruments. Special displays relate to the Lincoln and Garfield assassinations. Exhibits on drug abuse, air pollution and other current problems affecting man and the environment are also featured. *Open daily.*

Memorial Evangelical Lutheran Church *Thomas Circle, Massachusetts and Vermont Aves., N.W.* Known also as Luther Place Church because of the bronze statue of Martin Luther that stands before it, this red sandstone edifice was dedicated in 1874 as a memorial to the return of peace after the Civil War. Depicted in its stained-glass windows are Luther and Reformation leaders of other sects, including Wesley, Calvin, Wyclif, Knox and Huss. *Open daily.*

Metropolitan Memorial United Methodist Church *Nebraska and New Mexico Aves., N.W.* Designed in the English Gothic style, the church was dedicated in 1932. It contains several stained-glass windows, memorials and a pulpit and lectern from an earlier church where Presidents Grant and McKinley worshipped. The window depicting the Transfiguration is especially beautiful. *Open Sun.-Fri.*

Museum of African Art *316-318 A St., N.E.* Appropriately, this museum, founded in 1964 to display Africa's rich contribution to art, was once the home of Frederick Douglass, the former slave who later gained prominence as an outspoken abolitionist and adviser to Lincoln. The Victorian building's 12 galleries hold wood, iron, brass, gold and ivory sculptures; musical instruments; crafts; textiles and clothing; as well as a display illustrating African influences on Western art. In addition to a room containing many of Douglass's documents, photographs and other memorabilia, there is a library, classroom and small auditorium where the museum carries out its educational program in African culture and Afro-American history. *Open daily.*

[National Archives] History comes alive for those who visit the Great Hall of the Archives Building and see with their own eyes the original documents of the Declaration of Independence, the Constitution and the Bill of Rights.

National Archives *Pennsylvania Ave., N.W.* Within this imposing classical-style building is the recorded history of the nation's past—documents directly associated with the U.S. Government from 1774 to the present. These include the original Declaration of Independence, Constitution and Bill of Rights, as well as a vast amount of maps, pictures, letters and other related material. Surprisingly, the early documents were only gathered together in 1934, when the National Archives was established. The building to hold them, designed by John Russell Pope, was opened the following year. Its colonnaded exterior, which includes one of the largest pediments in the U.S., is lavishly decorated with allegorical sculptures and massive 10-ton bronze entrance doors. The National Archives administers the Presidential Libraries and regional Federal Records Centers in other parts of the country. It produces extensive publications and audiovisual programs and, of course, has enormous research facilities. Our three most vital documents are on permanent display. *Open daily; research rooms open Mon.-Sat.*

National City Christian Church *Thomas Circle and 14th St., N.W.* Pope designed this handsome 1930 church, which is distinguished by a stately Ionic portico and a handsome 200-foot tower with a colonnaded lantern cupola and finial. Many lovely marble features adorn the interior. The pew, pulpit and Communion table often used by President James Garfield, an ordained minister, may be seen. President Lyndon B. Johnson also attended quite often, and the pew he used is marked. *Open daily.*

National Collection of Fine Arts and **National Portrait Gallery** *9th St. between F and G Sts., N.W.* See feature display on pages 194-5.

National Gallery of Art *Sixth St. and Constitution Ave., N.W.* See feature display on pages 190-1.

National Museum of History and Technology *14th St. and Constitution Ave., N.W.* See feature display on pages 188-9.

National Museum of Natural History *10th St. and Constitution Ave., N.W.* See feature display on pages 192-3.

National Presbyterian Church and Center *4101 Nebraska Ave., N.W.* This impressive Neo-Gothic complex of six buildings, dominated by the 173-foot Tower of Faith, stands on a site of more than 12 acres. Opened in 1969, the center serves many purposes, including the presentation of musical programs and religious dramas. The white marble interior of the church gleams with rich colors, the result of the magnificent jewel-like windows of faceted stained glass, which transmit light with shimmering variations. The Chapel of the Presidents, dedicated to Dwight D. Eisenhower, contains the pew he occupied at services and the prie-dieu on which he knelt at his baptism, as well as pews once used by Jackson, Grant and other U.S. Presidents. Eisenhower, Washington, Lincoln, Wilson and both Roosevelts are depicted in the chapel's stained-glass windows. *Open daily.*

National Shrine of the Immaculate Conception *Fourth St. and Michigan Ave., N.E.* This massive structure, the seventh largest church in the world and the largest Catholic church in the U.S., still awaits the completion of its final chapel, one for the Byzantine rite. The vast crypt was opened in 1926, but it was not until 1959 that the upper church was dedicated. Built solely of stone and masonry, the shrine combines Byzantine, Romanesque and contemporary architectural details. Brilliant blue and gold tiles cover the huge dome, and mosaics and sculptures decorate the exterior walls. Within are rich tapestries, stained-glass windows, various marbles, statuary and fine mosaics. Among the last are the huge *Christ in Majesty* in the north apse, and reproductions of Murillo's *Immaculate Conception* and Titian's *Assumption of the Virgin,* both gifts of the Vatican. The Knights Tower soars more than 320 feet in height and contains the shrine's superb carillon. *Open daily.*

National Zoölogical Park *3001 Connecticut Ave., N.W.* See feature display on page 192.

Notre Dame Chapel *Trinity College, Michigan Ave. and Franklin St., N.E.* This graceful domed structure, with its beautifully simple style combining classical and Byzantine elements, was completed in 1924. The following year it won for its architects the American Institute of Architects' gold medal for ecclesiastical design. Bancel La Farge's magnificent mosaic covering the ceiling above the main altar and the fine stained-glass windows are among its outstanding features. *Open Sun.-Fri.*

Octagon House *1799 New York Ave., N.W.* This unique eight-sided (but not octagonal) Federal-style brick dwelling was built in 1800 as the winter home of a wealthy Virginia family. Its architect was the eccentric Dr. William Thornton, who had designed the Capitol in 1792. When the nearby President's Mansion was destroyed during the War of 1812, the house served as the residence of President James Madison and his wife Dolley between 1814 and 1815. After years of ill-use, the house was taken over by the American Institute of Architects. Now owned by the A.I.A. Foundation, it has been carefully restored and decorated with outstanding Chippendale, Hepplewhite and Sheraton furniture. The superb woodwork and mantels, the wine cellar and brick-floored kitchen—as well as frequently changing exhibits on historic Washington, architects and architecture—are among its attractions. *Open Tues.-Sun. except holidays.*

[Octagon House] The round table in the Treaty Room is the original and is believed to be the one at which President James Madison ratified the Treaty of Ghent putting an end to the War of 1812. The table, which spins on its base, has wedge-shaped drawers that could be used for filing. Both the table and the specially woven rug help to emphasize the room's circular shape. The candle sconces decorated with eagles on the far wall were a gift from the Royal Institute of British Architects and date from 1790.

[Phillips Collection] Renoir painted The Luncheon of the Boating Party *(1881) after many visits to a restaurant on the banks of the Seine. The result was this enchanting scene of boatmen and their friends relaxing on the terrace.*

Phillips Collection *1600-1612 21st St., N.W.* An outstanding collection of 19th- and 20th-century American and European paintings is on display here in the former residence of the Phillips family. The museum is a delight, for the masterpieces it contains and for the warm, unrushed, homelike atmosphere that has been deliberately retained. The music room in itself is a museum piece. Among the works collected by Mr. and Mrs. Duncan Phillips are Renoir's *The Luncheon of the Boating Party,* paintings by van Gogh, Bonnard, Matisse, Cézanne, Monet and most of the other great Impressionists, plus a fine representation of Klee, Braque, Rothko and many other modern artists. Some displays are arranged to encourage comparisons between the work of different artists, and others feature many paintings by the same artist. There is, for example, the stunning effect of an entire room given to the work of the superb French colorist Pierre Bonnard. In 1971, with Mrs. Phillips as director, the museum celebrated its 50th anniversary. *Open Tues.-Sun.*

Renwick Gallery *17th St. and Pennsylvania Ave., N.W.* See feature display on page 194.

Robert A. Taft Memorial *Capitol Hill* This simple monument to the late senator from Ohio, son of a President and himself a three-time Republican candidate for presidential nomination, consists of a 10-foot-high statue of the senator, backed by a 100-foot-high bell tower. The superbly matched French bells of the carillon ring out frequently. *Open daily.*

St. John's Church *Lafayette Sq., N.W.* Benjamin Latrobe designed this Episcopal church in 1816 and served as its first organist and choirmaster. The Federal structure is often called the Church of the Presidents, because every Chief Executive since Madison has at-

tended services here. Renovations in the 1880s included the installation of fine stained-glass windows, many, including a copy of Leonardo da Vinci's *The Last Supper,* designed by the curator of the famed stained glass of Chartres Cathedral. *Open daily.*

St. Matthew's Roman Catholic Cathedral *1725 Rhode Island Ave., N.W.* The simple Renaissance-style exterior of red brick and sandstone, embellished by a handsome dome, belies the magnificence of the cathedral's interior, which gleams with superb mosaics and multicolored marbles. Of particular beauty are the white marble altar and baptismal font, made in India and decorated with insets of characteristic Indian floral designs. Murals, frescos and gold-leafed woods adorn many of the outstanding chapels in the church. An inscription on the floor before the main altar commemorates the funeral Mass of President John F. Kennedy, held here on Nov. 25, 1963. *Open daily.*

St. Paul's Episcopal Church *Rock Creek Church Rd. and Webster St., N.W.* Popularly known as Rock Creek Church, this is the only Colonial house of worship in the District of Columbia, serving a parish that dates from 1712. Completed in 1921, the present structure replaced the twice remodeled 1719 church, which was destroyed by fire. Rock Creek cemetery, a Washington landmark, contains the graves of many prominent early Americans and a number of fine sculptures. *Open daily.*

ADAMS MEMORIAL *Rock Creek Cemetery* This masterful seated bronze figure was completed in 1891 by Saint-Gaudens as a memorial to Marion Hooper Adams, wife of Henry Adams, the author, journalist and historian. It bears no inscription, and is known as both *The Peace of God* and *Grief. Open daily.*

Smithsonian Institution See feature display on pages 188-95.

Supreme Court of the U.S. *1 First St., N.E.* Facing the Capitol is the templelike home of the highest court in the U.S. Designed by Cass Gilbert and completed in 1935, the white marble structure has a monumental entrance, with a broad, imposing stairway, a portico surrounded by elaborate Corinthian columns and a sculptured pediment representing *Liberty Enthroned,* guarded by *Order* and *Authority.* The bronze doors are each divided into four sculptured panels depicting scenes in the development of law. The magnificent marble-finished courtroom where the nine justices sit is graced with columns and carved friezes. Limited seating for visitors is available on a first-come, first-served basis when the court is in session (from October through June). *Open Mon.-Fri.*

Textile Museum *2320 S St., N.W.* These two handsome brick buildings were designed by John Russell Pope as the residence of George Hewitt Myers, who founded the museum in 1925. The fine collection of non-European handwoven textiles includes some 600 Oriental rugs, many ancient Egyptian, Persian and Peruvian textiles, plus a number of Near and Far Eastern, Indonesian, Central and Southwestern American and other works ranging from 2000 B.C. to the present. *Open Tues.-Sat.*

Thomas Jefferson Memorial *South Bank of Tidal Basin* A picturesque location on the Tidal Basin heightens the beauty of this tribute to the third U.S. President. John Russell Pope's circular, colonnaded monument, dedicated in 1943, reflects Jefferson's own taste in architecture, and in its domed profile is strikingly similar to that of Monticello, Jefferson's Virginia home. The heroic statue of the President, by Rudulph Evans, is impressively located in the center of the interior and can be seen through any of the memorial's four openings. Engraved on the walls are quotations from Jefferson's most famous writings that illustrate some of his political and social principles. *Open daily.*

U.S. Botanic Garden *Maryland Ave. between First and Second Sts., S.W.* Fascinating varieties of plants from all over the world are on view in this colorful oasis near the Capitol. Founded in 1820, the garden's first greenhouse was built in 1842 to hold the botanical collection brought back from the South Seas by an official U.S. exploring expedition. Rare and tropical plants—palms, cactus, ferns, citrus, bromeliads and cycads—are featured. Special seasonal displays are held during the year. *Open daily.*

U.S. Capitol *Capitol Hill* It is perhaps appropriate that a young nation should declare an amateur designer, Dr. William Thornton, winner among the 17 contestants who submitted plans for a capitol in 1793. The building has been considerably enlarged and remodeled over the years but the essential character has not been altered. The cornerstone for Thornton's building, a Federal adaptation of classical Renaissance style, was laid by Washington in 1793; by 1800 the north wing of the Capitol was completed, permitting Congress to

[U.S. Capitol] The soaring dome and the seemingly infinite number of slender pillars that take the eye to the ends of this monumental building make it the dominant structure on Capitol Hill. The view that makes the greatest impression on visitors looks west out over the Mall toward the piercing shaft of the Washington Monument. Acres of carefully tended grounds, with noble old trees, fountains and statues, surround the building.

move to Washington from Philadelphia. During the War of 1812 part of the building was destroyed by a fire set by the British. By 1863, after several extensions and the addition of a dome higher than the original, the profile of the building which has dominated the center of the city for over 100 years was complete. Nearly 100 years later the east front was extended, but the original appearance of the Capitol was preserved.

The Capitol is a repository of art and decoration, most of it pertaining to the nation's political history. In the Great Rotunda with its 180-foot-high dome is a huge fresco by Constantino Brumidi. Statues of Presidents line its curved walls. Busts of the first 20 Vice Presidents can be seen in the Senate gallery; in the Senate Chamber below, Vice Presidents were inaugurated from 1861 to 1933. Another interesting room is Statuary Hall, originally the meeting place for the House of Representatives. Here are statues of persons from each state who were chosen as outstanding contributors to American life. The architectural development of the Capitol is traced in exhibit cases in the Crypt, featuring a 12-foot model of the Capitol and drawings of the additions and changes made by each of the Capitol's architects. The 68-acre park surrounding the Capitol was designed in the late 19th century by Frederick Law Olmsted. Guided tours are available (they include admission to the Senate and House galleries and a ride on the monorail subway connecting Senate and House with their office buildings). *Open daily except holidays.*

U.S. Department of State Diplomatic Reception Rooms *U.S. Department of State Building, 2201 C St., N.W.* High on the eighth floor of the State Department's severely modern building is this series of six gracious rooms, site of much of Washington's official entertaining. Thanks to gifts and loans from private individuals, foreign visitors and other official guests are received amid some of the finest early American furniture, paintings, silver, porcelain and other decorative arts. Each of the rooms is furnished in a style appropriate to a certain period in the life of the statesman for whom it was named. The Thomas Jefferson State Reception Room, for example, has several architectural features copied from Jefferson's home at Monticello in Virginia. The John Quincy Adams State Reception Room, with its Chippendale furniture, could be a Philadelphia drawing room of the late 18th century. The largest of the six rooms is the Benjamin Franklin State Dining Room, with a horseshoe-shaped table that can seat 124 people. Three smaller rooms, used for more informal entertaining, are also elegantly furnished. It is necessary to make reservations, by calling or writing the State Department, to see the masterpieces of Americana that fill these rooms.

[**55.** *Washington Cathedral*] *In addition to guided tours of the cathedral, visitors may see the Bishop's Garden with its Norman arch, and the Cottage Herb Garden, where cuttings from famous trees and shrubs are sold.*

U.S. Department of the Interior Museum *Interior Bldg., C St. between 18th and 19th Sts., N.W.* A broad range of displays is housed in the museum's galleries, which take up a first-floor wing of this massive building. Paintings, drawings, illustrated maps and dioramas depict episodes in early land distribution and development and the department's current role in maintaining the lands in its care, including the national parks. Several fine geological exhibits as well as excellent examples of Indian and Eskimo arts and crafts can also be seen. *Open Mon.-Fri. except holidays.*

Washington Cathedral *Mount St. Albans at Massachusetts and Wisconsin Aves., N.W.* Officially designated the Cathedral Church of St. Peter and St. Paul, this awesome edifice in 14th-century English Gothic style is a modern American counterpart of the great medieval cathedrals of Europe. Begun in 1907, it is not scheduled for completion until 1981, when it will rank as the sixth largest church in the world. Its position on Washington's highest elevation makes this Episcopal church even more imposing. The 301-foot-high Gloria in Excelsis Tower, which contains both a 53-bell carillon and a 10-bell peal for change ringing, dominates this section of the city. The vaulted interior contains beautiful stone carvings and ironwork reflecting a variety of architectural influences. The Chapel of the Holy Spirit has an outstanding wood reredos, painted and gilded by N. C. Wyeth. The Children's Chapel, scaled and decorated for the young, is one of two such cathedral chapels in the world. Among the many lovely features in the huge buttressed apse is the Jerusalem Altar, constructed with 12 stones from Solomon's quarry in Jerusalem, and exquisite stained-glass windows patterned after medieval French designs. *Open daily.*

Washington Monument *Constitution Ave. and 15th St., N.W.* Completed 85 years after his death in 1799, this memorial to the Father of His Country holds a unique, symbolic position in Washington. The unadorned 555-foot-high marble obelisk stands on the Mall, between the Lincoln Memorial and the Capitol. There is an elevator to the observation room, with spectacular views of the city and surrounding area. Walking down the 898-step iron stairway reveals the 190 inscribed memorial stones presented by nations, states, cities, societies and individuals. *Open daily except Dec. 25. Small charge for elevator.*

White House *1600 Pennsylvania Ave., N.W.* The official residence of the President of the U.S. since 1800—every President except Washington has lived here—this Georgian building was designed by Irish-born architect James Hoban. History, and each Presidential family, have left their mark on the whitewashed sandstone building. It was burned by the British in 1814 and subsequently rebuilt, received porticos in the 1820s,

[**55.** *White House*] *The oval Blue Room, above, is used for state receptions. Here ambassadors making their first formal visit to the White House are received. More informal gatherings take place in the Green Room, left, named for the green watered silk that covers the walls. Over the mantle is a portrait of Benjamin Franklin.*

and was renovated in 1902. The interior was completely gutted and rebuilt between 1948 and 1952. In 1961 Mrs. Jacqueline Kennedy began the project of bringing historical and authentic American furnishings and paintings to the President's home and restored many rooms to 19th-century decor. Ten years later, Mrs. Richard Nixon again refurbished the State Rooms, making them even more authentic to the period 1800–1825. Visitors to the White House pass through the Ground Floor Corridor and up the Grand Staircase to the East Room, the largest room in the mansion. Here hangs the Stuart portrait of Washington, which Dolley Madison saved from the British torches in 1814. The Green Room is an American Federal parlor (1800–1820) furnished in the Sheraton style with many pieces by master craftsman Duncan Phyfe. Hoban designed the oval Blue Room to be the most beautiful room in the house. Furnished with French Empire and Louis XVI pieces, it has beige French wallpaper with decorative blue borders which is based on an early-19th-century document. The Red Room is furnished in the American Empire style with important pieces by Charles Honoré Lannuier. The State Dining Room with its Georgian woodwork is just as McKim, Mead and White, the New York architects, designed it for Theodore Roosevelt. In addition to other paintings by Stuart, the White House collection includes works by the Peales, Sully, Cassatt, Whistler, Sargent, Eakins, Durrie, Inness and Homer as well as portraits of all of the Presidents and a number of First Ladies. Surrounding the mansion are 18 acres of lawns and gardens. *Open Tues.-Sat.*

Woodrow Wilson House *2340 S St., N.W.* Wilson, the 28th President of the U.S. and the only one to retire in Washington, lived in this handsome Georgian-style brick town house—now maintained by the National Trust for Historic Preservation—from the end of his second term in 1921 until his death three years later. The interior is virtually the same as it was during Wilson's occupancy, and contains original furnishings and gifts from foreign countries and dignitaries. The grounds include a terraced garden. *Open daily except Dec. 25. Small charge.*

56. Gunston Hall Plantation *Rte. 242, Lorton, Va.* George Mason, chief author of Virginia's Declaration of Rights—which later became a model for the U.S. Bill of Rights—and its first state constitution, commissioned this handsome Georgian brick mansion in 1755. It was completed three years later under the supervision of William Buckland, an indentured carpenter and joiner brought over from England by Mason. Buckland's designs for the interior were so outstanding that they set many styles of the period and he became known as a "taste maker" of his era. The interior of Gunston Hall, furnished with Queen Anne, Chippendale and Hepplewhite pieces, contains Buckland's fine carving in the Palladian drawing room and several lovely and unusual furnishings in the Chinese Chippendale dining room. The beautiful 18th-century gardens have boxwood hedges planted by Mason that are now 12 feet high. Also on the grounds, overlooking the Potomac River, are a reconstructed schoolhouse, a deer park and a nature trail. *Open daily. $1.50.*

57. Alexandria, Va.

Founded in 1732 by Scottish merchants, Alexandria quickly became a thriving port and a social, political and commercial center of Virginia. Washington helped to survey the town, in 1749, and maintained a home here, as did many other important Virginians of the period. Most of what was Colonial Alexandria is visible today in the section known as Old Town, along the Potomac, where the majority of the 18th-century buildings below are located.

Boyhood Home of Robert E. Lee *607 Oronoco St.* The spacious, well-preserved house and gardens where Lee spent part of his childhood occupy half a city block. The mansion, built in 1795, was owned for some years by the Fitzhugh family, and is still known as the Fitzhugh-Lee House. It is built of brick in the Federal style, with each room off the large central hall opening onto the garden. Other notable features include the Adamesque mantels in the master bedrooms, the decorative supports of the stair railings and the brick chimney oven in the kitchen. *Open daily. Small charge.*

Christ Church *118 N. Washington St.* Construction costs for this brick church were paid in tobacco upon its completion in 1773. Designed with white stone quoins and white keystones in the brick window arches, the structure has been slightly modified: a gallery was installed in 1787, chimneys were built in 1812 and a tower and steeple erected in 1818. Visitors can admire a fine Palladian window and a superb 18th-century brass and cut-glass chandelier from London. Washington was among those who regularly attended services here, and the church contains his original pew and family Bible. Lee was confirmed here in 1853, and in 1861 was offered command of the Army of Virginia following a meeting in the churchyard. *Open daily.*

Friendship Veterans Fire Engine Co. *107 S. Alfred St.* This distinguished fire-fighting company, now a historical society, was organized in 1774. The following year it was given its first fire engine by one of its most prominent members, George Washington. That small hand-drawn engine is on display in this reconstructed firehouse, as is other fire-fighting equipment of the 18th and 19th centuries. *Open Mon.-Sat.*

Gadsby's Tavern *128 N. Royal St.* This historic Georgian tavern and inn, opened in 1752, was a favorite meeting place in 18th-century Virginia. Washington had a long association with Gadsby's, and began—and ended—his military career here. In 1754 he was named a lieutenant colonel in the Virginia Militia and recruited troops at the tavern for his first command. He held his last military review here in 1798, a year before his death. It is now owned by the City of Alexandria, which is refurnishing many of the rooms with the trappings of a Colonial tavern and inn, helping to restore Gadsby's to the era when it was known as the finest public house in America. *Open daily Apr.-Nov. Small charge.*

[**57.** *Christ Church*] *James Wren, who is thought to be a descendant of the famous English architect Sir Christopher Wren, drew the plans for Christ Church. The steeple, with its strong yet graceful lines, was added later.*

Old Presbyterian Meeting House *321 S. Fairfax St.* This simple brick church was built in 1774 by the Scottish founders of Alexandria. Washington's funeral sermons were preached here on Dec. 29, 1799, when roads to his own church were impassable. The interior was completely renovated in 1837, after a disastrous fire, but is Colonial in appearance, with gated pews. In the churchyard are the Tomb of the Unknown Soldier of the American Revolution and the graves of several prominent Virginians. *Open daily.*

Ramsay House Visitors Center *221 King St.* Ramsay House is Alexandria's oldest dwelling, built in 1724 in a nearby town and moved to its present location 25 years later. The original owner, William Ramsay, was Alexandria's first (and only) Lord Mayor. The frame, gambreled structure serves as the information center for visitors to the city. A color film on Alexandria's history can be seen here, and hostesses provide information on its points of interest and directions for a walking tour. *Open Mon.-Sat. except holidays.*

58. Fort Washington *Fort Washington Rd. (off Rte. 210), Md.* Located 5½ miles south of Washington, D.C., this outstanding example of a 19th-century coastal fortification was completed in 1824 to replace an earlier structure destroyed in the War of 1812. The stone and brick complex, with a dry moat and drawbridge, includes officers' quarters, barracks, a magazine and guardroom, reconstructed batteries and a museum. In the 1840s it was modified according to recommendations made by Robert E. Lee, then an obscure U.S. Army lieutenant. Weekend cannon firings and monthly moonlight tours in summer are scheduled. *Open daily; museum open Sat., Sun., holidays Jan.-May, daily June-early Sept., Sat., Sun., holidays early Sept.-Dec.*

59. Mount Vernon *Mount Vernon, Va.* See feature display on pages 204-5.

60. Woodlawn Plantation *Mount Vernon, Va.* The plantation was originally a part of the Mount Vernon estate. George Washington set aside 2000 acres of his land for his nephew, Lawrence Lewis, when Lewis married Eleanore Parke Custis. The house, completed in 1805, was designed by Dr. William Thornton. It is in the Georgian style and is constructed of red brick trimmed with Aquia stone. The interior of the mansion is noted for finely detailed woodwork, carved marble mantels and molded plaster ornaments. The house, which belongs to the National Trust for Historic Preservation, contains many of the original furnishings, paintings of George and Martha Washington, and an early portrait of Nelly Custis. *Open daily except Jan. 1 and Dec. 25. Small charge.*

POPE-LEIGHEY HOUSE This simple but highly functional house designed by Frank Lloyd Wright was built in 1940 and reveals many of the architect's distinctive details. It is constructed of brick and glass with cypress paneling both inside and out, and the windows are designed to be an integral part of the walls. The interior has built-in furniture and a heated concrete floor. In 1964 the structure was dismantled and moved from its original site in nearby Falls Church through the efforts

[**60.** *Woodlawn Plantation*] *When Lafayette returned to America in 1824 for a triumphal tour of the country, he stayed in this bedroom at the Lewises' home. He had known Nelly Custis Lewis since she was a young girl.*

of Mrs. Robert Leighey and the National Trust for Historic Preservation. *Open Sat.-Sun. Mar.-Nov. Small charge.*

61. Aquia Church *Rte. 1, Stafford, Va.* Built in 1751 (to serve a parish then 90 years old), Aquia, although it is unusually large, is a fine example of the period's English church architecture. Constructed in the form of a Greek cross, it has three double-door entrances in each arm of the cross. The altar is at the east end of the church, and at the opposite end curved stairs lead to the former slave gallery. The church's Communion silver was brought from England in 1754, and its imposing three-tiered pulpit and Colonial box pews are among the last of their type still in existence. Set into the thick brick walls are two tiers of windows finished with distinctive stone quoins (the stone was quarried on nearby Aquia Creek). *Open daily.*

62. Fredericksburg, Va.

Founded in 1727, this historic town originally consisted of a trading post, a warehouse and 50 acres of land. By the latter half of the 18th century Fredericksburg had become an important center of Virginia commerce and culture, and played a vital role in the Revolutionary War. During the Civil War the town changed hands several times; the battles of Fredericksburg, Chancellorsville, the Wilderness and Spotsylvania Court House were fought for its control. The Information Center, at 2800 Princess Anne Street, provides directions for a self-guided tour that includes a number of well-preserved 18th-century buildings which were significant in the town's early history.

Court House *Princess Anne St. near George St.* A copy of a speech Washington gave in Fredericksburg in 1784 and the will of his mother, Mary Washington, are among the many historic documents displayed here. The Court House, built in 1852, has a domed tower with a bell made in the Paul Revere Foundry. The walnut ceiling with hand-carved walnut bridgework supports are original. *Open Mon.-Fri.*

Fredericksburg and Spotsylvania National Military Park *Sunken Rd. and Lafayette Blvd.* Scattered within a 17-mile radius of Fredericksburg are the 3600 acres that comprise this national military park. They take in portions of four major Civil War battlefields—Fredericksburg, Chancellorsville, the Wilderness and Spotsylvania Court House—scenes of disastrous fighting that accounted for some 100,000 casualties. Besides the battlefields themselves, studded with historic markers, the park's grounds take in the Fredericksburg National Cemetery and the buildings below. *Area open daily except Dec. 25.*

CHANCELLORSVILLE VISITOR CENTER *Rte. 3, 9 mi. W. of Fredericksburg* This battlefield museum features exhibits, artifacts and slide programs dealing with Fredericksburg's strategic battles. It is one of the two orientation centers for the park and—as at the Fredericksburg Visitor Center—uniformed guides provide aid, information and directions. *Open daily except Dec. 25.*

FREDERICKSBURG VISITOR CENTER *Sunken Rd. and Lafayette Blvd.* This is the headquarters of the Fredericksburg and Spotsylvania National Military Park and the starting point for tours of the battlefields. The building also serves as a museum. In addition to exhibits of small arms, photographs and war relics there are an electric map of the area and a diorama of wartime Fredericksburg. *Open daily except Dec. 25.*

JACKSON SHRINE *Guinea* During the battle of Chancellorsville, Confederate General Stonewall Jackson was mortally wounded by shots mistakenly fired by his own men. He died eight days later, on May 10, 1863, in this small house, then a plantation outbuilding. It is furnished with pieces of the period, including the bed on which Jackson died and part of the blanket that covered him. *Open Fri.-Mon. Jan-May, daily June-Aug., Fri.-Mon. Sept.-Dec.*

OLD SALEM CHURCH *Rte. 3, 4 mi. W. of Fredericksburg* General Robert E. Lee successfully resisted a Union attempt to turn the Confederate flank at Chancellorsville here. The action occurred May 3-4, 1863. *Open daily except Dec. 25.*

Fredericksburg Lodge No. 4, A.F. & A.M. *803 Princess Anne St.* One of the oldest Masonic lodges in the country, this brick building was the scene of Washington's initiation as a Mason in 1752. On display are the Bible used at that ceremony, the lodge's minute books of the period, a Gilbert Stuart portrait of Washington and many Masonic artifacts. The ceremonial furnishings of the 18th century are still in use. *Open daily except Jan. 1 and Dec. 25. Small charge.*

Fredericksburg Presbyterian Church *Princess Anne and George Sts.* This Greek Revival brick church, dedicated in 1833, still bears the scars of the 1862 bombardment of Fredericksburg. During the Civil War it was used as a hospital and Clara Barton is said to have worked here at that time. *Open daily.*

Historic Fredericksburg Foundation Museum *818 Sophia St.* Artifacts exhibited here recall the city's history, as does the museum itself. It was built about 1812 as the home of Captain Wells and his family. Legend has it that a Union spy boarding with them fell in love with one of the Wells daughters and then, unfortunately, was found out and exchanged for a Confederate soldier. A slide presentation of the city's history is shown. *Open daily. Small charge.*

Houdon made this plaster cast of Washington from life.

59. Mount Vernon

Mount Vernon, Va.

George Washington, although he came from a family of successful businessmen and landowners, had little formal education, and his first success in life came through a natural aptitude for surveying. At 21 the British governor of Virginia put him in charge of an expedition to the upper Ohio valley to secure it against the encroaching French. By the time he was 23 he was a colonel in charge of all Virginia troops. In 1759 Washington resigned his commission and settled at Mount Vernon, which he had inherited from his half brother. He married Martha Dandridge Custis and began the long, leisurely process of enlarging the Mansion House. The Mount Vernon estate was eventually expanded to more than 8000 acres divided into five farms, each with its own overseer, workers, livestock and buildings. The

While General Washington was Commander in Chief of the Continental Army, from 1775 to 1783, Lund Washington, a distant relative, supervised the building of Mount Vernon's north and south additions and the wing buildings connected by graceful colonnades. When Lund wrote that he had given provisions to a British man-of-war, Washington replied that he would rather "they had burnt my house, and laid the Plantation in ruins."

principal crop was tobacco, but Washington had to export all the tobacco he produced to Britain, sell through British merchants and buy what he considered poor quality British goods. So he cut back on the tobacco acreage and put his slaves to work making some of these trade goods, particularly cloth. He also planted more wheat, set up a mill and operated a Potomac fishery. The 500 acres around the Mansion House were developed less as a farm than as a gentleman's country seat. Vineyards, meadows and groves were laid out to please the eye. The house, set on a hill, already had a fine view of the Potomac and the low Maryland hills beyond. Mount Vernon is furnished with period pieces, many of them original, and on the grounds are the box-bordered flower garden and the dependent structures, such as the cook house and spinning house, where the work of the plantation was carried on. *Open daily. Adults $1.50, children small charge.*

The two-story, pillared veranda may have been a Washington invention. In summer, when cooling breezes blew off the Potomac, the Washingtons served tea to friends here.

George Washington was a very social man. According to one estimate, he entertained 2000 guests from 1768 to 1775. Some of these may have spent the night in the downstairs bedroom visible through the door. The mirrored "plateau" on the table holds a bisque ornament and crystal candelabras.

Washington died in this upstairs bedroom on December 14, 1799. Intending to build a gravel path and a fish pond, he was caught in a snowstorm while marking the trees that he wanted cut down. The resulting acute throat inflammation helped bring about his death the following day.

[**62.** *James Monroe Museum*] *James Monroe was Minister to France in 1794. One of the prizes he brought back with him is this handsome Louis XVI desk with its secret compartments and carved, gilded corner posts.*

James Monroe Museum and Memorial Library *908 Charles St.* The fifth President of the U.S. practiced law in this small brick building from 1786 to 1789. Built in 1758, it is now a National Historic Landmark and is furnished with the Monroes' belongings used in the White House, including the Louis XVI desk on which Monroe signed the message to Congress that put forth what was to become known as the Monroe Doctrine. The building also houses family jewelry, china, silver, sculptures, portraits and court costumes worn by the Monroes at Napoleon's court. The attached library holds books, documents, original manuscripts, letters and newspapers relating to Monroe and the Monroe Doctrine. Behind the house is a quaint walled garden. *Open daily except Dec. 25. Small charge.*

Kenmore *1201 Washington Ave.* The stately brick face of this mid-18th-century manor house contrasts sharply with the warmth and sumptuousness of its interior. The elaborate yet delicate plasterwork ceilings and overmantels are considered to be as fine as any of this period in America. Kenmore was the home of Colonel Fielding Lewis and his wife Betty Washington Lewis, sister of George Washington. Washington is said to have suggested the Aesop fable theme for the overmantel in the Great Room. The Washington family crest is portrayed on the dining room mantel. Carefully restored in the early 1900s, most of Kenmore's interior—ceilings, overmantels and other woodwork—is original. In its architecture, period furnishings in warm woods and colors and lovely gardens, Kenmore accurately reflects the pre-Revolutionary times when the Lewis family lived there. *Open daily except Jan. 1, 2, Dec. 25, 26. Adults $1.25, children over 6 small charge.*

Mary Washington House *1200 Charles St.* From 1772 until her death in 1789, Washington's mother lived in this brick-and-frame cottage purchased for her by her son so that she would be close to Kenmore, the home of her only daughter. Within are the original woodwork (doors, paneling, mantels) and authentic 18th-century furnishings, many of which belonged to Mary Washington. The English-style garden, re-created with shrubs and flowers typical of that time, contains Mrs. Washington's sundial and her boxwood plantings. *Open daily except Jan. 1, 2 and Dec. 25, 26. Small charge.*

Rising Sun Tavern *1306 Caroline St.* Washington, Patrick Henry, Jefferson, George Mason and Hugh Mercer were among the patriots that frequently met here to discuss strategy for ending British rule in America. Built in 1760 by Charles Washington, George's youngest brother, the tavern was a social center of Colonial Fredericksburg, and also served as a stage coach stop and post office. In recent years the clapboard building has been restored and refurnished with pieces from the period, including a desk owned by Jefferson and chairs that belonged to Monroe. A collection of American and English pewter is displayed, with gaming tables, boot racks and other tavern accessories. *Open daily except Jan. 1, 2 and Dec. 25, 26. Small charge.*

Stoner's Store Museum *1202 Prince Edward St.* In this replica of a 19th-century general store are over 13,000 items of Americana—including tools, guns, ladies' corsets, fly fans, buttons, coins, jewelry, clocks, churns, coffee mills, kitchen utensils and blacksmith equipment—all collected in the environs of Fredericksburg. The rambling white frame structure was built in 1796. *Open daily early Jan.-late Dec. Adults $1.25.*

63. George Washington Birthplace National Monument *Washington's Birthplace, Va.* Only the foundation remains of the house in which Washington was born. The house itself was destroyed by fire in 1779. The present memorial mansion, built in 1931, is not an attempt at restoration, but rather a replica of the typical 18th-century plantation house. It is furnished with Colonial pieces, some of which belonged to the Washington family. A reproduction of a Colonial kitchen is also on the grounds. The present farm recreates life on the Colonial plantation using early methods of cultivation, and raising the same crops and animals. Nearby, on the banks of Bridges Creek, is the Washington family burying ground with the graves of Washington's father, grandfather and great-grandfather. *Open daily except Jan. 1 and Dec. 25. Small charge June-early Sept.*

64. Stratford Hall *Off Rte. 214, Stratford, Va.* This large adapted-Jacobean Georgian mansion, completed about 1730 in what was then a wilderness area, was an ancestral home of the Lees of Virginia, a family that contributed much to the history of the U.S. The original owner, Thomas Lee, was Colonial Virginia's acting governor and the negotiator of the Treaty of Lancaster, which opened the Ohio Basin to white settlers. His sons Richard Henry and Francis Lightfoot Lee, both signers of the Declaration of Independence, were born here, as was Robert E. Lee, whose father, "Light Horse Harry," lived here from 1782 to 1810. Built of brick in Flemish bond, the 18-room house is in the shape of an "H," the crossbar of which is the Great Hall. Arches join the four chimneys on each side, forming pavilions above the hip roof. Stratford Hall is beautifully furnished, and contains many items that belonged to the Lees. The reconstructed stables, Thomas Lee's office, smokehouse and operating gristmill, as well as a small museum, are

[**62.** *Kenmore*] *The elaborate plasterwork in Kenmore's Great Room and throughout the house was executed by a French artisan "loaned" by George Washington and by Hessian soldiers captured in the Battle of Trenton.*

other points of interest on this 1500-acre plantation, once again in use as a working farm. *Open daily except Dec. 25. Adults $2.00, children small charge.*

65. Scotchtown *Rte. 685, 10 mi. N.W. of Ashland, Va.* Scotchtown, built around 1719, is one of Virginia's oldest plantation manor houses. From 1771 to 1777 it was the home of Patrick Henry (he was living here when he made his plea for liberty or death in 1775 at St. John's Church in Richmond), and was later the childhood home of Dolley Payne Madison, a cousin of Henry's. The one-and-a-half-story frame house and its garden were restored recently. *Open daily Apr.-Oct. Small charge.*

66. Richmond, Va.

Because of its central location, the city was made the site of the state capital in 1779. During the Civil War it was the capital of the Confederacy, and when it fell to Federal forces more than half the city was burned. Many buildings that predate the Civil War still stand, however, mingled with the skyscrapers and other structures of the modern industrial community.

Agecroft Hall *4305 Sulgrave Rd.* This half-timbered Tudor manor house was built in the 1470s, on what was then a bucolic site near Manchester, England. By the 1920s the house stood in an industrial, coal-mining area and was in great danger of deterioration. Today Agecroft Hall stands once again in a delightful setting, surrounded by lawns and gardens—thanks to Richmond resident T. C. Williams, who purchased it and had it dismantled and shipped to this city, where it was reconstructed on a site overlooking the James River. The house, which contains the original oak paneling, is furnished in the style of the Tudor period. Also typical of that era is the two-story Great Hall, which features a 10-by-25-foot mullioned bay window bearing its former owners' ancient arms in stained glass. *Open Tues.-Sun. except holidays. Small charge.*

Battle Abbey *428 North Blvd.* Famous Virginians and Confederates are memorialized in this 1912 Greek Revival building housing the museum and library of the Virginia Historical Society. Many excellent displays can be seen here, including portraits by Stuart, Charles Willson Peale and Sully, furniture and other possessions of Colonial notables and objects from the state's early years. A good collection of Confederate military items features uniforms worn by Robert E. Lee and Jeb Stuart, battle flags and weapons. Charles Hoffbauer's famous murals symbolizing the Confederacy's four seasons also are here. A fine historical library holds many valuable papers that belonged to Peyton Randolph, Washington, Jefferson, Lee and others, plus a large collection of maps, prints, photographs and early newspapers. *Open daily except holidays. Small charge.*

Edgar Allan Poe Museum *1914 E. Main St.* Memorabilia of the famous American poet and author of spine-chilling stories are displayed in four buildings, the most interesting of which is the Old Stone House, the city's oldest dwelling (built about 1686). On display, in addition to some of Poe's personal belongings, are an early-19th-century model of the city as Poe knew it and original illustrations for "The Raven" by John Carling. A reference library is open to students. *Open daily. Small charge.*

Executive Mansion *Capitol Sq.* Since 1813 Virginia governors have occupied this white brick Federal structure, a short distance from the capitol. It was saved from the great evacuation fire that razed parts of Richmond late in the Civil War, and the exterior survived a damaging fire in 1926. It has been considerably enlarged and refurbished over the years, always in keeping with its antebellum character. The high-ceilinged rooms, finished with finely detailed moldings, contain Chippendale, Hepplewhite and Sheraton furniture, portraits of Virginia notables and antique rugs. Dogwood, holly, English boxwood and magnolias frame the clipped lawns in the enclosed garden south of the house. The mansion's guests have included Lafayette, Edward VII when Prince of Wales, Marshall Foch and Churchill. *Open Tues.-Sun. Aug.*

[**64**] *From about 1730 to 1830, Stratford Hall, the solid brick center of a flourishing plantation, sent forth generations of Lees—leaders of men in times of war; scholars, statesmen and farmers in times of peace.*

John Marshall House *818 E. Marshall St.* The fourth Chief Justice of the U.S. lived in this handsome dwelling from the time of its completion in 1790 until his death in 1835. It is the only 18th-century brick house still standing in Richmond and retains the original woodwork, floors and paneling. Its rooms reveal the good taste of the period, with antique silver, china and furniture, much of which belonged to the Marshalls. Mrs. Marshall's 1783 wedding gown is on display. The house is maintained and operated by the Association for the Preservation of Virginia Antiquities. *Open daily. Small charge.*

Maymont Park *Hampton St. and Pennsylvania Ave.* The former 95-acre estate of Confederate officer Major James N. Dooley was donated to the city in 1925.

DOOLEY MUSEUM This is the Dooleys' former home, a lavish Victorian structure with furnishings of the era including several unusual "swan beds." Located near the mansion are the Italian gardens, featuring fountains, waterfall, statues, symmetrical flower beds and a pergola, and nearby are the Japanese gardens. *Open Tues.-Sun. in season.*

MAYMONT NATURE CENTER A unique "living museum" features predator birds and small mammals native to the state. A small barnyard and an extensive shell collection are also on display. *Open daily.*

MAYMONT-VIRGINIA WILDLIFE EXHIBIT On view here are animals native to Virginia, including deer, raccoons, foxes and many kinds of birds in a walk-through aviary. Farmyard animals and waterfowl are included in the exhibit. *Open daily.*

[**66.** *Monument Avenue*] *Some of the major figures of the Confederacy are memorialized along this Richmond street. In the foreground here is General "Jeb" Stuart, in the background is General Robert E. Lee.*

Monument Avenue Preservation Zone *Between Lombardy St. and Belmont Ave.* Monuments commemorating five famous Confederate heroes have been built along a 1.3-mile stretch of this gracious tree-lined boulevard, which is flanked by attractive townhouses and several churches, among them Grace Covenant Presbyterian Church and the First Baptist Church. Starting from east to west, the monuments are: General J.E.B. Stuart Monument (Lombardy St.), an equestrian statue by Fred Moynihan of the Virginia cavalry leader who was killed in 1864 at the age of 31; General Robert E. Lee Monument (Allen Ave.), showing the commander of the Army of Northern Virginia astride his famous horse Traveller, done in 1890 by J. A. Mercie; Jefferson Davis Monument (Davis Ave.), the president of the Confederacy carved by Edward Valentine in 1907; General Thomas J. "Stonewall" Jackson Monument (Boulevard), a fine statue of Jackson mounted on Sorrell, completed in 1919 by William Sievers; Commodore Matthew F. Maury Monument (Belmont Ave.), a statue of the marine writer, hydrographer and Confederate Navy officer, also by Sievers, completed in 1927.

Museum of the Confederacy *1201 E. Clay St.* The world's largest collection of Confederate memorabilia is housed in the White House of the Confederacy—the official residence of President Jefferson Davis between 1861 and 1865. The columned, Classic Revival building, completed in 1818, contains materials that illustrate the history of the South during the Civil War. On display are a pistol and other items belonging to Davis, the sword and uniform worn by Lee when he surrendered at Appomattox and the Great Seal of the Confederate States of America. Several rooms are furnished with Victorian pieces used when Davis was there. *Open daily except holidays. Small charge.*

Robert E. Lee House *707 E. Franklin St.* This modest three-story Greek Revival brick house, built in 1844, was the occasional home of General Lee during the Civil War. During the last year of the war Mrs. Lee and their daughters resided here, and it was to this house that Lee returned after the surrender at Appomattox. It is furnished with period pieces and some of Lee's personal belongings. *Open Mon.-Fri. Jan.-late May, Tues.-Sat. late May-early Sept., Mon.-Fri. early Sept.-Dec. Small charge.*

Valentine Museum *1015 E. Clay St.* The exhibitions in this museum complex revolve around three themes: Richmond life and history; a junior activities and museum center; and a textile resource and research center. Permanent exhibits augmented by rotating displays from the museum's large storage collections are housed in a building complex that includes the elegant neoclassic Wickham-Valentine House, built in 1812, which is maintained as a typical 19th-century Richmond residence with a lovely formal garden of the period; the 1840 Bransford-Cecil House; three Victorian row houses; and the sculpture studio of Edward V. Valentine. The buildings all interconnect on the first floor, and all are accessible to the public except the sculpture studio. Among the highlights of the various exhibits are examples from the costume collection, the third largest in America; artifacts of major North American Indian cultures from 10,000 B.C. to the present; the Half and Half Pipe Collection; a 19th-century toyroom; and a rare

[**66.** *Virginia Museum of Fine Arts*] *The tiny and intricate jeweled Easter eggs made by the celebrated Peter Carl Fabergé, court jeweler to Russia's last two Czars, are among the most popular exhibits at this large and lively museum. There is also a medieval hall, a good collection of contemporary painting, and outdoor sculpture.*

18th-century perfume distiller. The Richmond Research Library is also on the premises. *Open Tues.-Sun. except holidays. Small charge.*

Virginia House *4301 Sulgrave Rd.* An impressive Tudor mansion overlooking the James River, Virginia House was constructed in 1928 from the 400-year-old remains of an ancient building that had been recently demolished in Warwick, England. These materials were brought here and reassembled by two Richmond residents, who later gave the house to the Virginia Historical Society. The sandstone walls and the hand-hewn stones of the roof still bear the marks of the first masons, while the interior is graced by the original carved oaken stairway and balustrade, fine paneling and window glass. Tapestries and embroideries complement the Elizabethan and Queen Anne furnishings. *Open Tues.-Sun. Small charge.*

Virginia Museum of Fine Arts *Boulevard and Grove Ave.* The nation's first state-operated museum opened in 1936 in this large brick and stone Georgian-style building. Enlarged several times, it now comprises 14 main exhibition galleries, each with its own orientation theater. Paintings, prints, sculptures and decorative arts from many periods and countries are on display. Among the more notable holdings is one of the nation's leading collections of the art of India, Nepal and Tibet. An unusual collection of Imperial Russian jewels belonging to the Romanoff family includes an extensive grouping of the fabulous works of Fabergé. The gold and gem-studded Easter eggs, among other pieces, are fascinating in their ornateness and intricacy. One of the choice examples of 18th-century painting is Goya's *General Nicholas Guye.* Also on view here are works by Courbet, Monet, Renoir, Picasso, Hopper, Shahn and other European and American artists. In the garden court are a number of modern sculptures by Rodin, Lipschitz and Moore (*Reclining Figure*). *Open Tues.-Sun. Small charge Tues.-Fri.*

Virginia State Capitol *Capitol Sq.* A first-century Roman temple in Nîmes, France, provided the inspiration for the central section of this building, designed by Thomas Jefferson and Charles Louis Clérisseau and completed in 1800. Two wings were added in 1906 to hold the Senate and the House of Delegates. In the rotunda stands the Houdon statue of Washington, the only one made from life. Along the rotunda walls are marble busts of the other seven Virginia-born Presidents and of Lafayette, the latter also sculptured from life by Houdon. The lovely Old Hall of the House of Delegates contains busts and portraits of distinguished Virginians, as does the Old Senate Hall. Historical paintings hang here, including the *Battle of Yorktown* and the *Landing at Jamestown Island.* In the 12-acre park surrounding the Capitol is an equestrian statue of Washington and smaller statues of other noted Americans. *Open daily except Dec. 25.*

Wilton House Museum *S. Wilton Rd.* Wilton was built in 1753 for William Randolph III, a member of a prominent Virginia family. The exterior is classically Georgian in style; the rooms—every one of which is paneled from floor to ceiling—are Queen Anne appointed with beautiful 18th-century furniture. In 1934 the house was moved six miles up the James River from its original site and is now headquarters for the National Society of Colonial Dames in the Commonwealth of Virginia. The landscaping was a gift of the Garden Club of Virginia. *Open Tues.-Sun. Small charge.*

67. Haw Branch Plantation *Amelia, Va.* The large white mansion, surrounded by neat lawns and spreading magnolia, elm and tulip trees, dates from the 1740s and ranks with the most beautiful Georgian-Federal homes in Virginia. Unusual tobacco-leaf carvings grace the front and rear entrances, and a similar design is used on the interior woodwork. Many of the furnishings are antiques belonging to the Tabb family, the original owners, whose descendants live here today. An ancient outside kitchen with a seven-foot cooking fireplace and baking oven, a smokehouse and a one-room schoolhouse are also on the grounds. *Open daily except Thanksgiving Day and Dec. 25. $1.50.*

68. U.S. Army Quartermaster Museum *Fort Lee, Va.* Since 1775 U.S. Army soldiers have in general been fed, clothed, housed and equipped by the Quartermaster Corps. On display here are thousands of items—weapons, flags, uniforms, wagons, military saddles, among others—associated with the duties of the Quartermasters. Much of the collection is of historic interest, for example, the Civil War saddle of General Grant, Presidential flags and a roughly sewn banner, made by American prisoners of war in Japan, that was the first U.S. flag to fly over that country after its surrender in World War II. *Open daily except holidays.*

69. Berkeley Plantation *Off Rte. 5, W. of Charles City, Va.* Formal plantings of English and American boxwood, fresh green lawns and aged trees surround this 1726 Georgian mansion, thought to be the oldest three-story brick house in Virginia. The birthplace of Benjamin Harrison V, thrice governor of Virginia and a signer of the Declaration of Independence, the house is elegantly furnished, evoking the Golden Age of the James River plantations. On this land the first official Thanksgiving by American settlers took place in December 1619, and three years later the first bourbon whiskey in America was distilled. In 1862 General Daniel Butterfield composed "Taps" while quartered here. *Open daily. Adults $1.75, children small charge.*

70. Shirley Plantation *Rte. 5, Charles City, Va.* Ten generations of the Carter family have lived in this house. Built about 1723, it was the home of Elizabeth Hill Carter, the grandmother of Robert E. Lee. The plantation is the earliest in Virginia, having been founded in 1613, seven years before the Pilgrims landed at Plymouth. The house contains many of the original family furnishings, silver and portraits. One beautiful and renowned architectural element in the house is a graceful carved walnut staircase without visible supporting posts. *Open daily except Dec. 25. Adults $1.50, children small charge.*

71. Westover *Rte. 5, 7 mi. W. of Charles City, Va.* Wrought-iron gates, boxwood gardens and 100-year-old poplars grace the Westover property. The elegant brick house, considered one of the finest examples of Georgian architecture in the U.S., was built about 1730 by William Byrd II, a tobacco planter and the founder of Richmond. *Grounds open daily. Small charge.*

72. Chippokes Plantation State Park *Surry, Va.* This farm, once a part of Jamestown Colony, has been in continuous operation for more than 350 years. Captain William Powell, owner and a member of the colony, named the plantation for the Indian chief Choupouke, who had befriended the settlers. The buildings on the farm range in date from the 17th to the 20th century. Sites include the River House, slave quarters and the mansion, built in 1850. Many examples of early American memorabilia are on display. A formal six-acre garden may also be viewed. *Grounds open daily. Mansion and brick kitchen open Tues.-Sun. late May-Sept. Small charge for buildings, grounds free.*

[70] *Bright windows, a huge fireplace and authentic 18th-century kitchen implements suggest that the kitchen in this old house (the plantation itself even predates the Pilgrims) could return to life at any moment.*

[73. *Old Church Tower]* *This ancient tower, smothered in ivy, is all that stands today of the Jamestown settlement. Several earlier churches stood on this spot—in one of them the Indian princess Pocahontas was married.*

73. Jamestown National Historic Site *Jamestown, Va.* On May 13, 1607, with the arrival of three ships carrying male colonists, Jamestown Island, then a peninsula in the James River, became the site of the first permanent English settlement in America. The colony's early days were exceedingly difficult, and nine-tenths of the population perished from starvation or disease. But Jamestown survived, in great part because of John Rolfe's successful experiments in growing tobacco. In 1624 the royal colony of Virginia was founded, with Jamestown as its political, social and cultural center. Some 50 years later, however, political differences led to open rebellion and the burning of the town; the seat of government was subsequently shifted to Williamsburg, and Jamestown was soon abandoned. The Association for the Preservation of Virginia Antiquities and the National Park Service cooperate in administering the 20-acre site, a small portion of the original settlement. *Open daily except Dec. 25. Small charge.*

GLASSHOUSE One of America's first manufacturing industries began at Jamestown in 1608, upon the arrival of eight glassmakers from England. Today's glass factory was reconstructed near the site of the original one. The National Park Service holds daily demonstrations in the art here, using equipment similar to that used by the early colonists and producing similar items in the same green-colored glass.

NEW TOWNE This section of the original townsite was developed after 1620, and was the home of several prominent people, including Henry Hartwell, one of the founders of the College of William and Mary. Still visible are the foundations of some of the houses.

OLD CHURCH TOWER The only standing structure remaining from 17th-century Jamestown, this brick

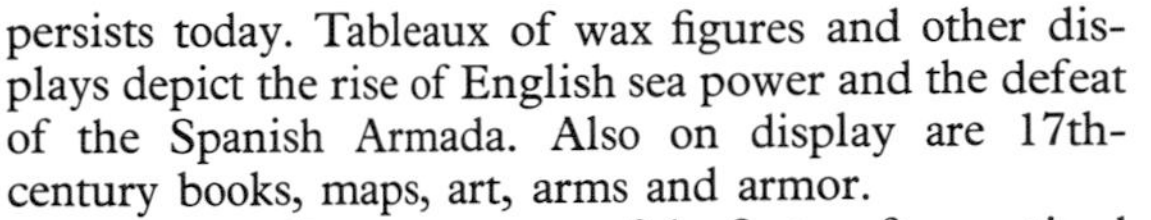

tower is believed to have been a part of the community's first brick church, which was built around 1639. (As was usual for the period, however, the tower was added later, sometime after 1647.) The site is now occupied by the Memorial Church built in 1907 by the Colonial Dames of America. Within are the foundations of the 1617 frame church, said to have been the scene of the first representative legislative assembly in America. The churchyard contains gravestones of early settlers.

STATUE OF JOHN SMITH Many historians believe that Jamestown would not have survived had it not been for the courage and strong leadership of Captain John Smith in the first two and a half years of the colony—he returned to England in 1609 after being injured by an explosion of gunpowder. The statue was designed by William Couper.

STATUE OF POCAHONTAS The marriage of Pocahontas, daughter of the Indian chief Powhatan, to John Rolfe helped bring about a period of peace between the Indians and the colonists. William Ordway Patridge designed this charming statue of the Indian princess.

VISITOR CENTER More than half a million Jamestown artifacts, most of them unearthed by the Park Service during archaeological excavations, are housed in this museum. The center also provides an orientation to Jamestown life by means of dioramas and a wide variety of film programs. *Open daily except Dec. 25. Small charge.*

74. Jamestown Festival Park *Glasshouse Pt., Jamestown, Va.* Adjacent to the Jamestown National Historic Site is this re-creation of the Jamestown settlement, constructed in 1957 to celebrate the 350th anniversary of the colonists' landing. *Open daily except Jan. 1 and Dec. 25. Small charge.*

JAMES FORT This full-sized reconstruction of the early triangular fort was built about one mile from the original site. The fort's buildings are wattle-and-daub structures of a type common in the 17th century, and include a church, a marketplace and several houses.

NEW WORLD PAVILION A variety of exhibits trace the history of the Indians and the white settlers in Virginia from the days of the first colony to 1776. The exhibits outline the contributions made by the early Virginians, that helped to create the new nation and to shape the national character.

OLD WORLD PAVILION Portrayed here are some of the European personalities and events that led to the establishment of the first permanent English settlement in North America and to the strong British heritage that persists today. Tableaux of wax figures and other displays depict the rise of English sea power and the defeat of the Spanish Armada. Also on display are 17th-century books, maps, art, arms and armor.

POTTERY Pottery was one of the first crafts practiced by the settlers. Here at this 17th-century-type pottery skilled potters work at the wheel creating earthenware bowls, cups, candlesticks and other pieces known to have been made at Jamestown. They are fired in a kiln adjoining the potter's shop.

POWHATAN'S LODGE Powhatan, father of Pocahontas, was chieftain of the Algonquin nation. This Indian long house, similar to ones he would have used, was reconstructed from a 1588 description of ceremonial lodges and from a depiction of one in a map of Virginia drawn by John Smith. The lodge consists of a sapling frame tied together with rawhide and covered with woven mats of cattails.

"SUSAN CONSTANT," "GODSPEED" AND "DISCOVERY" These are replicas of the ships of the Virginia Company of London that brought the first settlers (104 men and boys) to Jamestown in 1607. Like the originals, they are made of hand-hewn timbers and fitted with flaxen sails and are painted in the bright colors used at that time to scare away sea monsters and aid in identification and visibility. Full-size, they reveal the terribly cramped quarters of 17th-century sailing vessels. Visitors may board the ships at their moorings in the James River.

75. Carter's Grove Plantation *Rte. 60, 6 mi. S.E. of Williamsburg, Va.* This splendid red brick Georgian mansion on the James River is considered by some to be the most beautiful house in America. It was built in 1750–53 by Carter Burwell on the estate of his grandfather, Robert "King" Carter—one of the most influential and wealthiest men in Colonial Virginia. Its present 400-acre site takes in only a very small portion of the 300,000 acres Carter owned. A master woodworker spent six years on the interior which, if only for its magnificent paneled entrance hall and main stairway, is testimony to his artistic skills. Washington and Jefferson were among the distinguished guests entertained at the mansion when it was a center of Virginia's planter aristocracy. Legend has it that both proposed marriage to early loves in the mansion's southwest parlor—and both were rejected; the parlor is now called the Refusal Room. The mansion is owned and operated by the Colonial Williamsburg Foundation. *Open daily Mar.-Nov. and two weeks at Christmas. Adults $2.00, children small charge.*

[**74.** Susan Constant, Godspeed *and* Discovery] *The boats (shown here from left to right) brought the colonists to Jamestown across the stormy Atlantic in a space no bigger than a modern pleasure cruiser. The biggest,* Susan Constant, *displaced only 100 tons, the others were less than half that size. All were reconstructed in 1956 after careful study of British naval records.*

The tall cupola of the reconstructed Capitol looms through the trees. In the original building, Patrick Henry spoke stirringly against the Stamp Act that led to revolt.

The Peyton Randolph House was home to the statesman who became president of the First Continental Congress; Virginia's position on independence was debated here.

Sheep nibbling the grass on the Palace Green may have been a familiar sight to Williamsburg's original inhabitants, but strike a charmingly bucolic note for today's visitors. The Green runs between Duke of Gloucester Street, the main thoroughfare in the Historic Area, and the Governor's Palace, seen in the background here.

76. Colonial Williamsburg

Williamsburg, Va.

More than 40 years of work and many millions of dollars have been dedicated to the creation of this remarkable restoration. It is the most meticulously planned effort to bring a historic community back to life that can be seen anywhere in the country, and about a million people come to see it every year. Williamsburg was the capital of Virginia from 1699 to 1780, and many of the heroes of the American Revolution are intimately associated with it: Thomas Jefferson went to college here, Patrick Henry orated, and George Washington had his headquarters here before the Battle of Yorktown. But after the State Capitol moved to Richmond, the life drained from Williamsburg, and for nearly 150 years it drowsed as an increasingly dilapidated but still largely 18th-century country town. Then in 1926 a local rector got John D. Rockefeller Jr. interested in Williamsburg's lively past. Teams of scholars, historians, archaeologists, engineers and architects were set to work re-creating the Williamsburg of the 1770s. Working from an amazingly detailed plan of the town as it was in 1782, they have preserved and restored more than 80 surviving buildings, and have rebuilt some 50 other major structures on their former sites, with streets and gardens and authentically furnished interiors. In more than 20 craft shops artisans demonstrate the skills of 200 years ago; carriages and oxcarts travel the streets where cars are banned during the daytime; and costumed militia and fife-and-drum corps hold their drills on the Market Square Green several times a week from April through October. The entire Historic Area covers 172 acres, and is served by buses. *Adults $4.50, children 6–12, $3.00. Small additional charge for Governor's Palace.*

Formal English gardens surround the Governor's Palace, home of seven Colonial governors between 1720 and 1775. Britain's royal arms symbolizes their rule.

Horse-drawn carriages, driven by costumed coachmen, are one of the many period touches that bring a Colonial city to life. Visitors can ride them through the streets as an added enjoyment of the historic area.

Any 18th-century community had to have a mill to grind its flour—and at Williamsburg it was Robertson's, which has been reconstructed near the Peyton Randolph House. It works: visitors can buy newly ground flour.

Pieces of 18th-century ware are frequently dug up in excavations at Williamsburg, and in the Archaeological Laboratory skilled craftsmen mend and clean them. Many of them will ultimately be put on display.

Those Williamsburg buildings open to the public have been furnished with painstaking attention to period detail, as in this upstairs bedroom at the Governor's Palace. Note the rich hangings of the four-poster bed, and the tiled fireplace.

In a series of craft shops, Williamsburg visitors can watch early skills being practiced. Here a bookbinder is at work.

A silversmith can be seen busily engaged at his task in a shop entitled The Golden Ball on the main street.

Like all the craftsmen, the bakers work with authentic tools: a hearth with a real fire —no electric ovens for them.

77. Sir Christopher Wren Building *College of William and Mary, Williamsburg, Va.* Begun in 1695, this three-story brick building is the oldest academic structure in use in the U.S. After modifications by the college planners, only the chapel follows Sir Christopher Wren's original design. There is only one other house of worship in America designed by him. The Wren Building was the first major restoration to be carried out in Williamsburg by John D. Rockefeller, in the late 1920s. Among the rooms that once again appear as they did when Jefferson and Monroe (to name just two of the college's prominent students) studied here are the Grammar School Room, the Common Room used by the professors, the Great Hall, in which both the students and the faculty dined, and Wren's chapel. *Open daily except Dec. 25.*

78. Yorktown Visitor Center *Yorktown, Va.* The Battle of Yorktown was the last major battle fought in the Revolution. It was here that British General Cornwallis surrendered on Oct. 19, 1781. From the observation deck of the Visitor Center the entire field of action can be seen. The center features an orientation program on the battle and has many related displays including the tent used by Washington. *Open daily.*

79. Mariners Museum *Rtes. 60 and 312, Newport News, Va.* Housing one of the most complete maritime collections in existence, this museum brings together the history and romance of the sea and ships. Twelve well-arranged galleries contain dioramas of various historic nautical events, hand-carved figureheads, navigation instruments, relics and artifacts, ship fittings, armament and antique tools. The Whaling Room, with two fully equipped whaleboats, scrimshaw and Eskimo handiwork, and the Chesapeake Bay Room, devoted to the bay's historic past, are among the specific collections. A group of beautifully carved, extraordinarily detailed miniature ship models depicts vessels dating from the 15th century B.C. through the 19th century A.D. The museum also houses maritime paintings, prints, rare books, photographs, maps, charts, seamen's journals and log books. An outdoor display features a variety of small boats. *Open daily. Small charge.*

80. Fort Monroe *Fort Monroe, Va.* Sometimes called the Gibraltar of Chesapeake Bay, this is the largest masonry fort ever built by the U.S. Government. It was designed by Brigadier General Simon Bernard, a French military engineer who served as an aide to Napoleon, and took 15 years to build (from 1819 to 1834). During the Civil War it served as a Union military and naval base, and was one of the few forts in the South not captured by the Confederates. (Its impregnability was in part the result of the surrounding moat, eight feet deep.) The fort is now the headquarters for the U.S. Continental Army Command. *Open daily.*

CASEMATE MUSEUM A number of casemates, or chambers in the fort's walls, make up this museum, which contains many artifacts, maps, pictures and documents relating to Fort Monroe. Jefferson Davis was imprisoned in one of the casemates for several months after the Civil War. Models of the *Monitor* and *Merrimack,* the two great ironclad ships that battled in Hampton Roads, are on display, along with illustrations depicting the encounter (which was won by neither side). *Open daily.*

81. Norfolk, Va.

Because of its location on Chesapeake Bay, Hampton Roads and the Elizabeth River, Norfolk has been an important seaport and the most populous city of Virginia since 1683. It is the site of the largest naval base in the world (Norfolk Naval Station) and also has some restored 17th- and 18-century homes and outstanding museums.

Adam Thoroughgood House *Parish Rd., S. of Rte. 60* Time has obscured the true date and builder of this four-room Colonial house, but it is undoubtedly one of the oldest brick dwellings in the U.S. One brick bears the initials "A. T.," a clue that the house may have been constructed by Adam Thoroughgood, a tobacco planter and member of the House of Burgesses, who died in 1640. Its most notable exterior features are a steep A-gabled roof and a massive outside chimney. A charming 17th-century-style garden welcomes the visitor. *Open Tues.-Sun. Small charge.*

Chrysler Museum at Norfolk *Olney Rd. and Mowbray Arch* This modern building houses important

[77] *Although several fires have destroyed the interior over the past centuries, the original walls of this oldest American college building still stand. The great English architect Wren was said to have drawn up the original designs for it, and these were then "adapted to the Nature of the Country," as a contemporary account put it. Thomas Jefferson, a student at the College of William and Mary, and no mean architect himself, once proposed an extension, but it was never built.*

[79] *A room full of magnificent ships' figureheads is one of the features at the Mariners Museum: this striking figure was carved by John Haley Bellamy for the frigate* Lancaster *in 1880. A few years later the art was dead.*

works of art of every civilization, including 18th-Dynasty Egyptian, Oriental, European, Pre-Columbian and modern American. Highlights of the collection are Greek and Roman sculptures, Renaissance and Baroque paintings (Titian, Tintoretto, Rubens, Hals), fine representations of French Impressionism and contemporary European works of art exemplified by such outstanding painters as Picasso and Miró. Two centuries of U.S. art, ranging from paintings by Stuart, Sargent and Cassatt to Benton, Inness, Pollack and Warhol, are also exhibited. A distinguished collection of 7000 pieces of glassware can be seen in the Chrysler Institute of Glass collection. *Open daily except Jan. 1 and Dec. 25.*

General Douglas MacArthur Memorial *Bank St. and City Hall Ave.* Built to serve as a city hall, this large Classic Revival domed building was completed in 1850. It is now devoted entirely to a large collection of objects associated with one of the nation's most illustrious military leaders. Six murals trace MacArthur's career from his service at Vera Cruz in 1914 to his activities during World Wars I and II and the Korean War. Two reconstructed offices used by MacArthur, his 1950 staff car and a model of the U.S. Navy PT boat on which he escaped from the Philippines in 1942 can be seen, along with the familiar garrison cap with its resplendent gold braid, the corncob pipe and sunglasses, and other personal belongings. One of the murals depicts the Japanese surrender to the Allies on board the U.S.S. *Missouri* in 1945; the surrender documents and the pen used by MacArthur to sign them are also displayed. MacArthur's simple tomb is recessed in the floor of the rotunda whose marble walls are engraved with excerpts from his speeches and writings. *Open daily except Jan. 1 and Dec. 25.*

Hermitage Foundation Museum *7637 North Shore Rd.* A large Tudor-style mansion on graciously landscaped grounds overlooking the Lafayette River provides a domestic setting for the wide-ranging art and craft collection of William and Florence K. Sloane. Contemporary American and European paintings and sculpture, Oriental ivory carvings, bronzes and jade, Russian silver and icons, Italian and French lace, European furniture and ceramics are informally shown in 13 galleries. The Gothic drawing room has oak paneling, heavy beams, rood screen and wrought-iron hardware. *Open daily except Dec. 25. Adults and children over 6 small charge.*

Myers House *323 E. Freemason St.* Moses Myers, a wealthy importer and merchant, was the original owner of this sturdy 1792 brick Georgian house. His descendants lived here until 1931, and it is furnished principally with family possessions, including outstanding Chippendale, Sheraton, Duncan Phyfe and Hepplewhite pieces plus several family portraits by Sully, Stuart and John Bell. Among the guests entertained in the house were James Monroe, Daniel Webster, Lafayette and Stephen Decatur (a Myers son owned the pistols used in Decatur's fatal 1820 duel with Commodore Barron and these are on display here). The house also contains the family's extensive collection of early 19th-century music. *Open daily except Jan. 1 and Dec. 25. Small charge.*

Norfolk Chamber of Commerce Building *269 Charlotte St. and St. Pauls Blvd.* This stuccoed Greek Revival building was erected in 1841 to serve the Norfolk Academy. Its designer, Thomas U. Walter, modeled it after the Temple of Theseus at Athens. Of the simple Doric order, the 91-foot building is graced with two handsome, columned porticos, front and back. *Open Mon.-Fri.*

Willoughby-Baylor House *601 Freemason St.* In 1794 Captain William Willoughby, a prosperous merchant and contractor, built one of the first Georgian brick town houses in Norfolk (a Federal porch was added in 1824) on land where a Masonic hall stood before being burned to keep the British from occupying it during the Revolution. The house has been furnished with antiques in keeping with the way it was after Captain Willoughby's death in 1800. *Open daily except Jan. 1 and Dec. 25. Small charge.*

82. Carroll County Farm Museum *Center St., Westminster, Md.* Life on a 19th-century Maryland farm

[**81.** *Hermitage Museum*] *A carved limewood figure of the Chinese goddess of mercy, Kuan Yin, is one of the fine Oriental pieces to be found in informal display here.*

is re-created here. The 142-acre site is equipped with tools and farm implements of the period, and demonstrations of their uses are presented along with the crafts of spinning, weaving, quilting and blacksmithing. Buildings include a springhouse, smokehouse, barns, main farmhouse, and a log cabin schoolhouse. *Open Tues.-Sun. Apr.-Oct. Adults $1.50, children small charge.*

83. Union Mills Homestead *Rte. 140 and Deep Run Rd., 6 mi. N. of Westminster, Md.* Six generations of the Shriver family have occupied this 23-room clapboard house from 1797 to the present day. In 1863, before the Battle of Gettysburg, it was occupied on the same day by both Confederate cavalry and Union infantry. The house has served as an inn, a tavern, a post office, a country store, a magistrate's office and a schoolroom. It is now furnished with Shriver possessions accumulated over the years. The adjacent grist and flour mill operated by the first owners is now used as a museum of tools, farm equipment and artifacts of the 19th century. *Open May-Oct. Small charge.*

84. Hampton National Historic Site *535 Hampton Lane, Towson, Md.* For some, the early days of independence in the U.S. were a time of gracious and elegant living. Preserved here is a portion of one of the great estates of the time, which belonged for some 200 years to one prominent Maryland family, the Ridgelys. Only 45 of Hampton's original 7000 acres remain, but the handsome 1790 Georgian mansion (one of the largest houses of its period) and the gardens survive to tell the story of their past. The buff-colored stone and stucco house with its Great Hall is beautifully furnished, much of it with original family possessions, including European and American pieces, Aubusson rugs, fine china, paintings and most of the original chandeliers. These chandeliers figure in one of Hampton's many ghostly legends: the sound of their crystals falling to the floor and shattering signaled the imminent death of the lady of Hampton. A tour of the grounds reveals an herb garden, an early-19th-century formal garden, broad lawns and fine old trees. *Open Tues.-Sun. except holidays. Small charge.*

[85. *Baltimore & Ohio Museum*] *The form of transportation involved is, naturally, railroads, and the museum complex includes a very early railroad station and a roundhouse (shown here) full of historic trains.*

85. Baltimore, Md.

The city was founded in 1729 as a tobacco port, one of several along the eastern seaboard, and later became a shipping point for Maryland wheat and flour. During the American Revolution many privateers were outfitted here, and the city became an important shipbuilding center, the birthplace of the famous Baltimore clippers. When Philadelphia was threatened by British attack in 1776, the Continental Congress met in Baltimore. It was also the scene of the first casualties of the Civil War, as Federal troops were stoned by the citizens when they entered the city. Baltimore has retained its importance as a center for domestic and foreign trade.

Baltimore & Ohio Transportation Museum *900 W. Pratt St.* Perhaps the largest collection of locomotives, coaches and other railroad equipment from 1829 to the present is assembled in this three-building complex, which includes a roundhouse and the former Mount Clare Station. Built in 1830, the station is believed to be the oldest railroad depot in the world, and in 1844 Samuel Morse's first telegraph message from Washington, D.C. was relayed through it. Visitors can see a replica of the 1829 "Tom Thumb," the 1836 "John Hancock" and other fully operational locomotives, and observe displays on the development of rails, bridges and telegraphy. There are several dioramas, a model train layout and a collection of old toy trains. *Open Wed.-Sun. except holidays. Small charge.*

Baltimore City Hall *Fayette and Holliday Sts.* This is a massive but well-balanced public building constructed (1875) of bluestone and white marble. Its exterior presents a pleasing decorative mixture of round arch windows, mansard roofs and a cast-iron dome. *Open Mon.-Fri.*

Baltimore Museum of Art *Art Museum Dr.* The largest public collection in the U.S. of works by Matisse is part of the museum's notable assemblage of 19th- and 20th-century French art. Among the sculpture on display is an exceptionally fine casting of Rodin's *The Thinker.* There are also excellent collections of American paintings and decorative arts, Oriental art and Early Christian mosaics. Outstanding too are the extensive collections of African, Oceanic and Pre-Columbian works. The development of Maryland architecture and decorative arts is beautifully revealed in the eight period rooms shown in the American Wing. *Open Tues.-Sun.*

Basilica of the Assumption of the Blessed Virgin Mary *Cathedral and Mulberry Sts.* This, the mother church of Catholicism in the U.S., was designed by Benjamin Latrobe, one of the nation's foremost early architects. The cornerstone was blessed on July 7, 1806, by Bishop John Carroll and the church was dedicated for public worship on May 31, 1821, by Archbishop Ambrose J. Maréchal. Built of brick faced with granite, the Basilica is a cruciform church in the Romanesque style with a single dome over the crossing. The imposing portico, in Greek Revival style, is supported on 10 fluted columns of Nova Scotia stone, and is flanked, in effect, by the two basilica towers. The vaulted ceiling has coffered panels carved with rosettes of geometrical form. The main altar, still in use, was given by priests of Marseilles in 1821. *Open daily.*

Battle Monument *Calvert and Fayette Sts.* This 52-foot marble memorial commemorates the men who died defending Baltimore during the War of 1812, and

[**85.** *Fort McHenry*] *From the air, the famous fort whose sturdy defense against the British in the War of 1812 inspired the writing of "The Star-Spangled Banner" looks like a miniature early Pentagon. It still commands a fine view over Baltimore harbor, though nothing more warlike takes place here now than colorful military ceremonies by U.S. Marines on Thursday evenings in the summer. The fort the visitor sees dates from an expansion in 1830. At the time of the encounter, the buildings had only one story.*

it carries their names inscribed on the base. Begun in 1815, it is the oldest war memorial in the U.S. In 1827 it was adopted as the symbol of Baltimore, and now appears on the city's official flag and seal.

Carroll Mansion *Lombard and Front Sts.* Charles Carroll, a signer of the Declaration of Independence, lived here with his daughter and her husband. The house, built about 1812, is the best surviving example of the Baltimore merchant town house, with business offices and casual family rooms on the ground floor and formal rooms on the second floor. There is an elegant winding staircase, and nine rooms are furnished in period styles fashionable from 1800 to 1840. *Open Wed.-Sun. except Jan. 1 and Dec. 25.*

Cathedral of Mary Our Queen *5200 N. Charles St.* This modern version of the Gothic cathedral was completed in 1959. The Roman Catholic cathedral is faced with Indiana limestone and built in the traditional manner without the use of structural steel. Outstanding features include the many stone carvings and ornamented altars, large stained-glass windows, soaring arches over the sanctuary and the colorful interior walls. *Open daily.*

Conservatory of Bureau of Parks *Druid Hill Park* The Conservatory, a Victorian structure built in 1884, maintains several horticultural displays, including a wide variety of tropical plants. Brightening up the seasons are three special displays of chrysanthemums in November, poinsettias at Christmas, and an Easter exhibit of spring flowers. *Open daily.*

Fells Point Historic District *Aliceanna and Wolf Sts.* Named for William Fell, a Lancashire shipbuilder who purchased the land in 1730, this area is the original seaport of Baltimore. It was here that the U.S. Navy's first ship, the frigate *Constellation,* was built. Fells Point, which can best be seen on a walking tour, is almost unchanged from its earliest days. There are markets, churches, warehouses and many well-preserved examples of the typical 2½- and 3½-story buildings that were the homes of seamen, merchants, shipowners, shipbuilders and others involved in the activities of this historic port.

First Presbyterian Church *Park Ave. and Madison St.* Nathan G. Starkweather designed this spired Victorian Gothic church, which was completed in 1859. Baltimore's oldest Presbyterian church, the congregation was founded in 1761. *Open Sun.*

First Unitarian Church *Charles and Franklin Sts.* This neoclassical church was designed by Maximilian Godefroy and completed in 1818. The handsomely proportioned exterior of the building is Greco-Roman, with pillars and dome. Tiffany designed the chancel window and the mosaic depicting the Last Supper, which extends across the chancel above the altar. The pulpit, of bird's-eye maple, was also designed by Godefroy.

Fort McHenry National Monument *Fort Ave. at Locust Pt.* The fierce bombardment of Fort McHenry, and its successful defense against the British naval attack, flag flying continuously, inspired Francis Scott Key to write "The Star-Spangled Banner" in 1814. The earthworks, gun batteries and star-shaped fort commanded the entry to Baltimore harbor, and were essential to the defense of the city. The fort was completed about 1803, replacing old Fort Whetstone, and served the U.S. military through World War II. On display are historic flags and firearms. *Open daily. Small charge.*

Greek Orthodox Church of the Annunciation *22–24 Preston St.* The Greek Orthodox Church took over this Romanesque building in the 1930s, some 50 years after it was built as a Congregational church. Its present Byzantine character was acquired in 1963, when it was completely renovated and the interior richly redecorated with chandeliers and many icons, stained-glass windows and other ornamentation relevant to this faith. *Open daily.*

Homewood House *Charles and 34th Sts.* Completed in 1803 for Charles Carroll, Jr., son of a signer of the Declaration of Independence, this was one of the most elegant country houses of the Federal period. The local brick used in its construction was burned to achieve the desired warm color. The house consists of a one-and-one-half-story central section flanked by one-story pavilions and has marble steps leading to the main entrance and columned portico. Homewood House and its landscaped grounds are now the property of Johns Hopkins University.

Lovely Lane Church Museum *2200 St. Paul St.* This museum houses the historical collection of the

Baltimore Conference, Methodist Historical Society—books, manuscripts, artifacts and memorabilia relating to the history of Methodism in America. John Wesley's personal copy of Thomas à Kempis's *Imitation of Christ* is on display here, as is The Strawbridge Pulpit, the hand-hewn oak pulpit that was the first to be used by a Methodist preacher in America. Also on view here are the Charles Peale Polk portrait of Bishop Francis Asbury, the church's first bishop in this country, and his table and chair. *Open Mon.-Fri., Sun.*

LOVELY LANE UNITED METHODIST CHURCH This unusual Etruscan-style church, designed by Stanford White, was completed in 1887 at the direction of the pastor, Dr. John F. Goucher (after whom Goucher College was named). The fifth home of the Lovely Lane congregation, which was founded in 1772, it is on the order of early churches in Ravenna, Italy. An unusual feature of the building is a reproduction of a nighttime sky in the vault of the dome. *Open Mon.-Fri., Sun.*

Maryland Historical Society Headquarters *201 W. Monument St.* The Society occupies two handsome buildings, a stately house built in 1847 and a large modern addition of compatible design completed in 1967. A library of 80,000 volumes and nearly 2 million manuscripts deals with the history of Maryland and the U.S. Included are the original manuscript of Francis Scott Key's "Star-Spangled Banner," and papers of Charles Carroll of Carrolltown, Benjamin Latrobe and the Calvert family. There is also a museum with collections of furniture, silver, china and paintings; a maritime museum of the Chesapeake Bay area; period rooms and the Darnall Young People's Museum of Maryland History. *Open Tues.-Sat. except holidays. Small charge for library.*

Maryland Institute College of Art Mount Royal Station *1400 Cathedral St.* Founded in 1826, this is one of the country's oldest independent art schools. It is partially housed in the former Mount Royal Station of the B. & O. Railroad. The station, built in 1896 in the neo-Renaissance style, served as a passenger terminal until 1961. The institute acquired it three years later and completely renovated it to house a gallery, library, studios, auditorium, cafeteria and the Rinehart School of Sculpture. The structure, a national landmark, is made of Port Deposit granite with Indiana limestone trim. It has a glazed-tile roof and an imposing square clock tower 150 feet tall. The gallery features regularly held exhibits by students and faculty. *Open Mon.-Sat.*

Mother Seton House *600 N. Paca St.* Elizabeth Bayley Seton was the founder of the American Sisters of Charity. She lived in this handsomely proportioned little Federal house, built around 1800, for one year (1808-9), during which she opened a Roman Catholic school for girls here and saw the beginnings of her order. The house now contains period furnishings and features a stained-glass window of Mother Seton, who was beatified—the second step toward being canonized by the Roman Catholic Church—in 1963. *Open daily.*

OLD ST. MARY'S SEMINARY CHAPEL Designed by Maximilian Godefroy, and dedicated by Bishop John Carroll in 1808, this small brick chapel is one of the first Gothic Revival churches in the U.S. It was built to serve the first Catholic seminary in the U.S., opened in the One Mile Tavern in 1791 by French Sulpicians.

[Patterson Park Pagoda] Grim-looking cannons, dating from a time when Baltimore's Hampstead Hill was a strategic defense point, are lined up outside this gaily colored tower, built in 1891 and recently renovated.

The first U.S.-trained priest was ordained in St. Mary's original chapel in 1793. In the lower chapel Mother Seton took her first private vows in 1809, and it was there also that the first black community of nuns, the Oblate Sisters of Providence, was established in 1829. The Sister Servants of the Immaculate Heart of Mary trace their history back to the same chapel. In the 1960s the main chapel was renovated and restored. Four of the stained-glass windows, added in the 1880s, are from Chartres.

Mount Clare *Monroe St. and Washington Blvd.* Built in 1754, this elegant Georgian mansion was the home of Charles Carroll, Barrister (a designation used to distinguish him from the three other Charles Carrolls in his home town of Annapolis). It is the oldest country-style mansion now within the city limits and is built of pink brick laid (on the facade) in Flemish bond. The entrance is through a columned portico paved with gray and white marble, with a Palladian window above. The house is beautifully furnished with 18th-century pieces, many of which belonged to the Carroll family. Portraits of the Carrolls by Charles Willson Peale hang in the drawing room. *Open Tues.-Sun. Small charge.*

Mount Vernon Place Historic District *Charles and Monument Sts.* This cruciform-shaped park comprising Mount Vernon and Washington Places contains monuments to many distinguished Americans. In the late 19th century the area surrounding the park was one of Baltimore's best addresses. Among the points of interest are the University Club and the Peabody Institute. The following monuments are on display. Howard Monument: During the Revolutionary War General John Eager Howard led Maryland troops in a bayonet charge at the Battle of Cowpens; he is shown by sculptor Emmanuel Fremiet astride a powerful horse and the base of the monument bears the inscription from the medal awarded him by Congress for his bravery in that engagement. Lafayette Monument: This bronze equestrian sculpture by Andrew O'Connor honors General Lafayette for his assistance during the American Revolution; on the stone base of the 30-foot-high monument are inscriptions by Woodrow Wilson and by Raymond Poincaré, the president of France. Taney Statue: Roger Brooke Taney was appointed Chief Justice of the U.S. in 1836 and held that position at the time the court handed down its famous Dred Scott decision in 1857; Taney also served as U.S. Attorney General and as Secretary of the Treasury under President Andrew Jackson; the heroic bronze statue depicting the seated Chief Justice is by William Henry Rinehart and is a replica of one in front of the State House in Annapolis. Washington Monument: The focal point of Mount Vernon Place, the 178-foot-high tower was the first major monument erected (in 1829) in honor of George Washington; it includes a 16½-foot statue carved by Enrico Causici which represents Washington resigning his commission at Annapolis; exhibits at the base explain its history, and the Historical Information Center in the monument is operated by the Peale Museum. *Open daily except Jan. 1 and Dec. 25. Exhibit area free, small charge for tower.*

Mount Vernon Place United Methodist Church *N. Charles St. and Mt. Vernon Pl.* This cathedral church of the United Methodist denomination is an outstanding example of Victorian Gothic architecture. Built in 1870, it is located near the first public monument to George Washington. Next door is the Bishop Francis E. Asbury Memorial House, an interesting "upper-class" mid-19th-century town house. *Open Sun.*

Patterson Park Pagoda *Patterson Park and Eastern Ave.* The fanciful, bracketed four-story orange and yellow Chinese pagoda is an observation tower from which visitors can see the city. It commands a view of the harbor, Fort McHenry and landmarks in downtown Baltimore. The 60-foot pagoda is octagonal and has exterior and interior viewing decks. *Open daily.*

Peale Museum (Municipal Museum of the City of Baltimore) *225 Holliday St.* This is the oldest museum building in the U.S.; the original museum was established by Rembrandt Peale in 1814. When Peale's museum failed after 16 years, the building was used as the city hall, and later as a municipal office building. In 1931 it became the Municipal Museum and today paintings by the Peales—Rembrandt, Sarah and Charles Willson—and other important artists are exhibited. Also featured are examples of work by Baltimore silversmiths, including Samuel Kirk and Son and the Warner family. In the archives can be found many photographs, paintings, engravings, lithographs and maps relating to the early history of the city. *Open Tues.-Sun. except holidays.*

Star-Spangled Banner Flag House *844 E. Pratt St.* Built in 1793, this Federal period house was the home of Mary Pickersgill, who made the flag that flew over Fort McHenry during the British bombardment of September 1814. The sight of this flag inspired Francis Scott Key to write the poem which became the U.S. national anthem. Displays in the restored house include a handmade replica of the original 30-by-42-foot flag—which contained 15 stars and 15 stripes—as well as rare U.S. flags and Pickersgill possessions. Adjacent to the Flag House is an 1812 War Military Museum. *Open Tues.-Sun. except holidays. Small charge.*

U.S. Frigate "Constellation" *Pratt and Light Sts.* The *Constellation,* launched in Baltimore in 1797, was the first commissioned ship of the U.S. Navy, and is the world's oldest ship continuously afloat. Known as the Yankee Race Horse, the 36-gun warship was the first U.S. ship to defeat and capture an enemy vessel, and the first American man-of-war to enter the China Sea. She also carried American Marines to Tripoli to suppress the Barbary pirates. The *Constellation* last served as a flagship in the Atlantic Fleet during World War II. *Open daily. Small charge.*

[*Star-Spangled Banner Flag House*] *A replica of part of the famous banner that was "still there" by the "dawn's early light" drapes a table in the house of the woman who made it in 1813. The flag that inspired the national anthem was huge—30 by 42 feet—and a receipt displayed at the Flag House showed that the commander at Fort McHenry paid over $400 to have Mary Pickersgill sew it. The actual flag itself is now in the Smithsonian Institution in Washington, but a highly authentic reproduction can be seen here, as well as a copy of the anthem in Francis Scott Key's hand and a number of exhibits of the War of 1812.*

Walters Art Gallery *600 N. Charles St.* The gallery reveals the wide-ranging interests and careful selection of collectors William T. Walters and his son, Henry Walters. Visitors may see the world's largest display of bronze animal sculptures by Antoine-Louis Barye and one of the largest collections of Sèvres porcelain in America. Other collections include watercolors of the West by Alfred Jacob Miller, 19th-century French paintings, Islamic pottery, metalwork, sarcophagi from the tomb of Pompey's family, Byzantine treasures, and a large number of manuscripts. Individual works of significance include Manet's *At the Café* and the 4th-century Byzantine "Ruben's Vase," a beautifully carved vase of agate which at one time belonged to the Flemish master Rubens. *Open daily except holidays.*

86. Annapolis, Md.

The capital of Maryland is essentially a city of gracious homes situated two miles up the Severn River from Chesapeake Bay. Founded in 1649, it was made the state capital in 1695, and developed into an important seaport and a cultural and political center. Outstanding examples of Georgian, Federal and Victorian architecture as well as typical shops and waterfront buildings from earlier periods have contributed to its designation as a National Historic Landmark. Annapolis is well known as the home of the U.S. Naval Academy (see below) and St. John's College, chartered in 1784, on whose campus stands the Liberty Tree under which a peace treaty with the Indians was signed in 1652.

Brice House *42 East St.* See feature display on pages 224–6.

Chase Home *22 Maryland Ave.* See feature display on pages 224–6.

Hammond-Harwood House *19 Maryland Ave.* See feature display on pages 224–6.

Maryland State House *State Circle* Built in 1772, the state house is the oldest such building in the U.S. still used for its original purpose. It was here that the Treaty of Paris, formally ending the Revolutionary War, was ratified by the Continental Congress in 1784. The State House is a lovely Georgian brick-and-wood building whose main exterior feature is a striking 165-foot-high wooden dome added in 1779. The Old Senate Chamber, where General George Washington resigned his commission in 1783, is now a commemorative exhibit room. A statue of U.S. Chief Justice Roger Brooke Taney stands in front of the building on the spacious tree-shaded lawn. *Open daily except Dec. 25.*

St. Anne's Episcopal Church *Church Circle* Built in 1859, this church building is the third to serve St. Anne's on this site. The parish was founded in 1692 and in its early years was supported by a tax of 40 pounds of tobacco per taxpayer. Of particular interest is the Sands Memorial Window by Tiffany which won first prize for ecclesiastical art at the 1893 World's Fair. Still used, every Sunday, is the silver Communion service presented by King William III in 1695. Two of the signers of the Declaration of Independence, William Paca and Samuel Chase, were vestrymen of St. Anne's. *Open daily.*

U.S. Naval Academy The Naval Academy was founded in 1845 by George Bancroft, Secretary of the Navy under President Polk. It is located on 302 acres, the site of the former Fort Severn, at the mouth of the Severn River. Most of the buildings are in late-French Renaissance style and date from the early 20th century. The two oldest buildings on the grounds are the Waiting Room (1876) and the Guard House (1881). Bancroft Hall, probably the largest dormitory complex in the world, houses the entire 4200-man brigade of midshipmen and includes all the necessary support and recreation facilities. Throughout the Yard are many monuments and mementos commemorating American naval heroes. The tomb of John Paul Jones is in the crypt of the Academy's Chapel. Also of interest is the statue of Tecumseh, a bronze replica of a figurehead on the 1819 wooden ship U.S.S. *Delaware,* which has become an Academy celebrity. *Open daily.*

U.S. NAVAL ACADEMY MUSEUM The largest single collection of materials relating to the life of John Paul Jones is housed here. Also on display are collections of weapons, ship models, medals, rare books, paintings, artifacts and memorabilia of American naval history. *Open daily except holidays.*

William Paca House and Garden *186 Prince George St.* William Paca, a wealthy lawyer and planter who was interested in Colonial and Revolutionary

[**85.** *Walters Art Gallery*] *Rich colors glow from this miniature triptych (seven inches high and twice as wide) created in painted enamel by a master in Limoges, France, around 1510. The central panel is a Nativity, the side ones the Annunciation. The Walters Gallery has America's finest collection of such work—as well as an astonishingly wide range of European paintings, medieval and Byzantine art, Islamic manuscripts and many other precious things. A new wing is planned to provide more exhibition space for these treasures.*

political affairs and the third governor of Maryland, lived in this 35-room Georgian mansion situated on beautifully landscaped grounds. The extravagance of the garden, which has been restored to its original design, complements the handsome exterior of the house, which was built in 1765. Shrubs, trees and flowers are planted about the grounds, which also contain a small lake, a brook, garden structures, walks and elegant parterres. *Garden open Mon.-Fri.*

87. Sotterley Plantation *Rte. 245, E. of Hollywood, Md.* Sotterley has been a working plantation ever since the long, low clapboard main house was completed in the 1750s. The country-style exterior, with shuttered windows and a low veranda, belies a rich interior. Because it has been embellished through the centuries by the owners, its decor reflects individual tastes. There are a superb Chinese Chippendale staircase, antique chairs with Chinese lattice backs, two fine Queen Anne mirrors and early Sheffield candelabra. On the grounds are a barn, smokehouse, tobacco shed, tenant houses, English country garden and old warehouse in which there is a collection of early farm tools and artifacts that were excavated on the property. *Open daily June-Sept. Small charge.*

88. Reconstructed State House *Off Rte. 5, St. Mary's City, Md.* This two-story brick building is an accurate reproduction of the State House built in 1676 in Maryland's first settlement and provincial capital. It remained the seat of the Provincial Assembly until Annapolis became the capital in 1695, when it served as a courthouse and later as a chapel. It was dismantled in 1829 and its bricks were used in the construction of nearby Trinity Church. Special exhibits on the second floor of the present structure tell of the voyage of settlers from England in 1634 and their early life in the colony. *Open daily except Jan. 1 and Dec. 25.*

89. Everhart Museum *Nay Aug Park, Scranton, Pa.* Everhart is a composite of several kinds of museums within one building. In the natural history department are a planetarium, displays of birds of the world, American mammals and an exhibit of anthracite coal emphasizing its importance in the region. Among the permanent exhibits are European and American paintings and sculptures, American Indian arts and crafts, Oriental art objects, good examples of 19th-century American folk art and an extensive collection of Dorflinger glassware, a superior quality of blown and cut glass made locally between 1852 and 1921. Both the art and natural history departments present temporary exhibits. *Open Tues.-Sun. except holidays.*

90. Asa Packer Mansion *Packer Rd., Jim Thorpe, Pa.* The ornate elegance of the Victorian era has been retained in its original state in this elaborate home. Built in 1860 for the coal and railroad magnate and founder of Lehigh University, the mansion contains the Packers' furnishings, including the heavy wood and upholstery furniture of the period as well as marble furniture, paintings, silver, china and other Victorian bibelots. The dining room with upper walls covered in gold leaf and the lower graced with elaborate hand-carved paneling is typical of the lavish decoration. *Open Tues.-Sun. and Mon. holidays mid-May-Oct. Adults $1.25, children over 12 small charge.*

[**86.** *State House*] *The Maryland State Legislature still meets in this fine building, as they have ever since the War of Independence, making it the oldest state capitol in continuous use. In 1784 it served as the seat of Congress.*

91. Reading Public Museum and Art Gallery *500 Museum Rd., Reading, Pa.* Raphaelle Peale's 1847 *Lemons and Sugar,* Frederick Church's romantic *Cotopaxi,* and *The Balloon* by Julien Dupré are among the paintings exhibited here, together with collections of sculpture, graphics, Indian artifacts and minerals. The library in this classic-style structure, built in 1928, stresses art and natural history. On the museum's 25-acre site are a planetarium and an arboretum and botanical garden with lovely seasonal displays. *Open daily Sept.-May, Mon.-Fri., Sun. June-Aug. except holidays.*

92. Hopewell Village *5 mi. S. of Birdsboro, Pa.* Hopewell, founded in 1744, was one of the many small communities in the early industrial era in America whose economic base was the production of iron. As in any of the iron towns when they were prosperous, the central feature is the furnace and its attendant buildings—coaling shed and charcoal house, bridge house and casting house. Adjacent to these are the workers' homes, office store, ironmaster's mansion, barn, blacksmith shop and other village buildings. Hopewell is being restored to its 1820-40 condition by the National Park Service. *Open daily except Jan. 1 and Dec. 25.*

93. Ephrata Cloister *632 W. Main St., Ephrata, Pa.* Ephrata was one of the more successful experiments in communal living in Colonial America. Founded in 1732 by the German Pietist mystic Conrad Beissel, the community consisted of three orders—a celibate brotherhood and sisterhood and a married order of householders. They lived in austere surroundings and practiced a life of spiritual purification through self-denial. Entirely self-sufficient, members operated their own bakery, gristmill and farm. At its height in the mid-1700s, the cloister was the source of many fine printed books and hand-illuminated songbooks and religious music. The buildings were Germanic in character, made of wood and stone with small dormer windows. *Open daily except holidays. Small charge.*

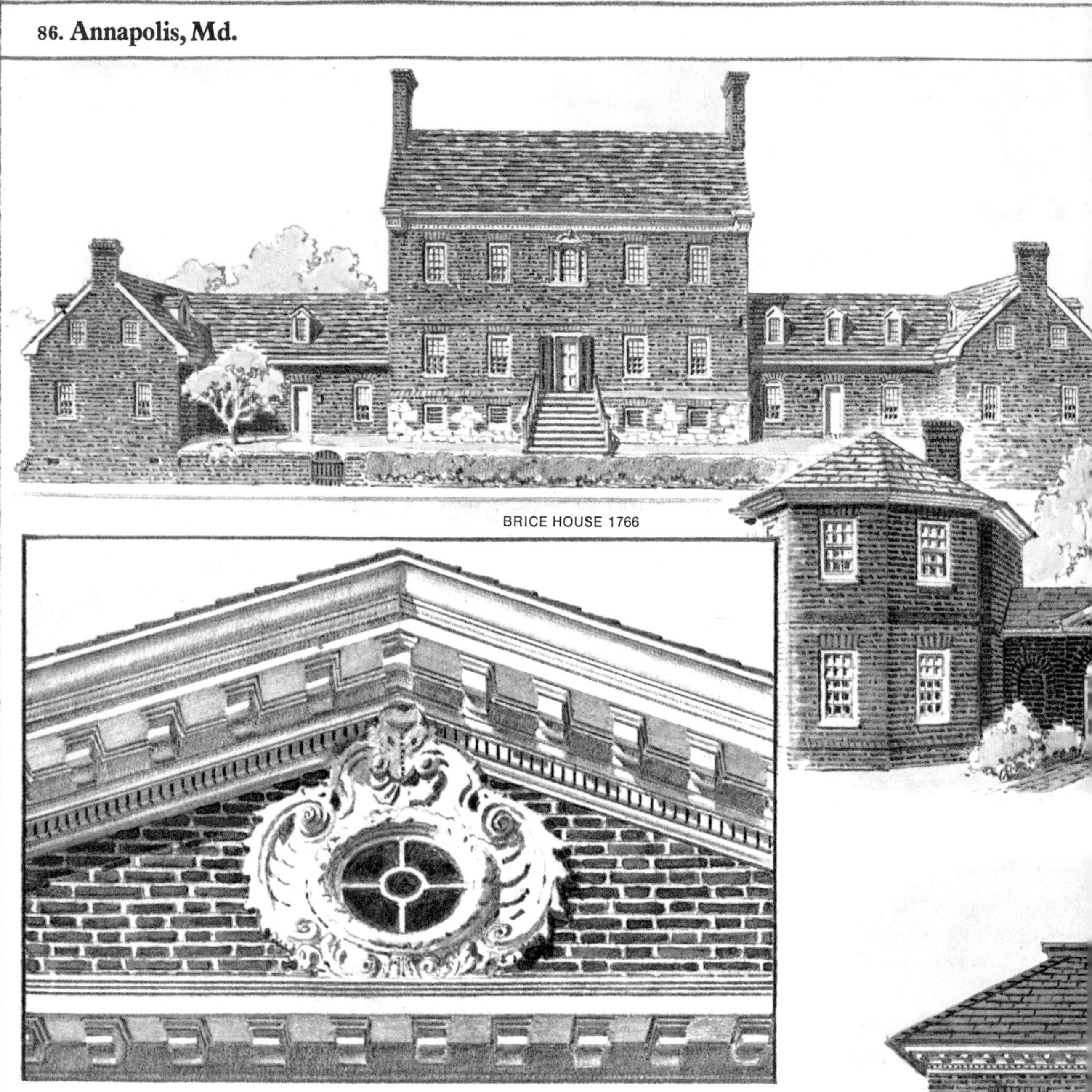

BRICE HOUSE 1766

PEDIMENT DETAIL
HAMMOND–HARWOOD HOUSE

The Elements of Georgian Brick Style

The Georgian brick architecture that flowered in 18th-century America was an offshoot of the English style named after the three Georges, Hanoverian kings who ruled England from 1714 to 1820. The style has survived because its elements—symmetry, pleasing proportion and attention to decorative detail—combine to produce houses that every age considers beautiful. Some of the best examples in this country are to be found in Annapolis. The three houses shown here, all designed wholly or in part by William Buckland, are typical. The Brice and Hammond-Harwood houses have characteristically large central sections with symmetrical connecting wings; the Chase Home has a projecting central bay. Exquisite details, such as the bull's-eye window in the triangular pediment (above), lighten the solidity of the Hammond-Harwood House; the doorway masterfully combines a variety of moldings and carvings with a fanlight. Buckland's skill as a woodcarver is seen in the door to the dining room in the Chase Home (far right). The broken pediment was a common Georgian device, but the tobacco-leaf motif is indigenous to Maryland.

HAMMOND—HARWOOD HOUSE
1774

CHASE HOME
1769-71

INTERIOR DETAIL
CHASE HOME

(*continued next page*)

86. Annapolis, Md.: Georgian Brick Style

(*See feature display on pages 224–5.*)

Settled in 1649 by 10 Puritan families fleeing Anglican persecution in Virginia, Annapolis was named for England's Princess (later Queen) Anne. Echoes of England persist today in street names like Duke of Gloucester and King George. Over the years Annapolis consolidated her position as one of the chief tobacco ports for the middle colonies. As her merchants and the nearby plantation owners prospered, they traveled to England for business and pleasure and sent their children to be educated abroad, bringing back English ideas, clothing and architectural styles to Colonial America. Annapolis was fortunate in having William Buckland (master builder of Virginia's Gunston Hall) as a resident. He and others, using the abundant local clay for bricks, were able to translate the latest English Georgian brick styles into the handsome mansions that grace the old city today. These solid, dignified houses, with their big, high-ceilinged rooms, suited their American owners perfectly and gave them an appropriate setting to continue the plantation tradition of lavish entertaining. Annapolis today has spread out onto three peninsulas; its town limits embrace four creeks. The first-known business was Thomas Todd's boatyard, and boat building and repair are important industries today, as are fishing and shellfishing in the rich Chesapeake Bay waters. Historic Annapolis (in 1965 the original area was designated a National Historic District) with its red brick sidewalks laid out in herringbone patterns and its 100 or so Georgian houses and public buildings is freighted with memories of its seagoing past.

Brice House *42 East St.* This privately owned house, built during the mid-18th century by James Brice and decorated by William Buckland, was restored during the 1950s. It is one of the largest Georgian brick homes in America. Two massive, 90-foot-high chimneys flank the central pavilion, which is connected by "hyphens" to the east and west wings.

Chase Home *22 Maryland Ave.* Samuel Chase, one of Maryland's four signers of the Declaration of Independence, all of whose Annapolis homes remain intact, began building this three-story house in 1769. Two years later Edward Lloyd bought the incompleted house and engaged William Buckland to finish it, both inside and out. The master builder's touch is evident in such features as the beautifully detailed Adamesque ceiling in the parlor and the Palladian window behind the remarkable cantilevered stairway in the entrance hall.

Hammond-Harwood House *19 Maryland Ave.* Built in 1774, this nobly proportioned house with its unusual semioctagonal wings is considered the most beautiful Georgian house in America and Buckland's masterpiece. It is the only house that can be completely attributed to him from conception to completion. It is authentically furnished with English and Maryland antiques. *Open Tues.–Sun. except Dec. 25. $1.50.*

94. Amish Farm and House *2395 Lincoln Hwy., E. of Lancaster, Pa.* This 165-year-old Amish homestead gives an idea of the totally self-sufficient way of life still practiced by the "plain people" of Pennsylvania Dutch country. The farm buildings and house are authentically equipped and furnished. Amish vehicles of transportation (Conestoga wagon, bobsled, sleigh, four-wheeled carriage) are on view. *Open daily. Adults $1.75, children small charge.*

95. Pennsylvania Farm Museum of Landis Valley *2451 Kissel Hill Rd., Lancaster, Pa.* In 1880 two Lancaster County brothers began a collection of everyday items illustrative of rural life in Pennsylvania. The farm and craft tools, furniture, household utensils, folk art and hunting equipment they acquired number over 150,000 pieces dating from "the age of homespun to the Gay Nineties." They are on display in representative buildings of the period: a tavern, village schoolhouse, country store, gunshop, wagon shed. Spinning and weaving demonstrations are given in the barn. *Open daily. Small charge.*

96. Rock Ford *881 Rock Ford Rd., Lancaster, Pa.* Rock Ford was the home of General Edward Hand, a medical doctor and the Adjutant General of the Continental Army. The large Georgian-style house, completed about 1793, remains architecturally unchanged and is in remarkably good condition; details such as stairs, doors, shutters, paneling and window glass (one window pane bears initials scratched on by Hand's son) are original. Washington was a guest here. *Open daily early Apr.–late Oct. Small charge.*

97. Wheatland *Marietta Ave. (Rte. 23), Lancaster, Pa.* This large 19th-century brick house was the home of James Buchanan before and after he served as the only unmarried President of the U.S. He purchased it in 1848 and owned it until his death in 1868. It has been fully restored; its 17 rooms contain many of his furnishings, china and silver. A carriage house contains a carriage which bears his name. *Open daily mid-Mar.–Nov. Adults small charge.*

98. Eagle Americana Shop & Gun Museum *Rte. 741, West Strasburg, Pa.* An outstanding collection of weapons, from the crossbow to World War II ordnance, is on display at this museum, including a number of Pennsylvania/Kentucky rifles used by early settlers for protection and by soldiers in the French and Indian Wars and the Revolution. Also on display are collections of early Americana—toys, coins, iron, glass, china, bottles and other artifacts. These are housed in an old stone mill built in 1740 which has at various times produced cornmeal, flour, grist and whiskey. *Open daily April–Oct., Sat., Sun. Nov. Small charge.*

99. Longwood Gardens *Rte. 1, Kennett Square, Pa.* Formal and informal gardens, sparkling fountains and magnificent conservatories—with four acres of plants under glass—make Longwood Gardens a delight at any season. The 1000-acre site, developed to its present condition by Pierre Samuel du Pont, was originally granted by William Penn to George Peirce in 1700. The mansion built by Peirce's son in 1730 still stands and

[99] *Plumes of water leap and flash in the Fountain Garden of one of America's most spectacular formal gardens. The view here is from the terrace in front of a group of conservatories housing azaleas, roses and palms.*

contains the gardens' administrative offices. Also surviving from the time when the site was known as Peirce's Park are some of the elegant trees planted by the family. Longwood Gardens' major features include the Fountain Garden, with spectacular illuminated displays in the evening; the Italian Water Garden, a replica of one in Florence, with fountains and pools; the Waterlily pools; All-America Rose Garden; Wildflower Garden; and extensive wooded areas and lakes. The conservatories include the Azalea-Camellia, Rose, Desert and Palm houses, and also display fine bonsai and tropical plant collections. An orchid display is changed weekly. Plays are presented in the open-air theater, which has a unique "water curtain." Organ concerts are held in the huge ballroom adjoining the conservatories. *Open daily. Small charge for gardens.*

100. Magic Age of Steam *Rte. 82, Yorklyn, Del.* Fifteen Stanley Steamers, a Toledo Jr. Steamer, a White Model H five-passenger touring car and one Doble Steamer (there were only about 25 made) are among the antique cars, most of them steam-powered, featured in this unique museum. In addition, exhibits of operating models of stationary engines and steam locomotives illustrate the history of America's Steam Age, dating from the end of the Civil War to the 1920s. The Auburn Valley, a miniature railroad, carries passengers on a short run over a 7½-inch-gauge track. *Open Sat., Sun. and holidays mid-Apr.-mid-Nov. Small charge.*

101. University of Delaware *Newark, Del.* The university originated as a small Presbyterian academy, founded in Pennsylvania in 1743. In 1833—long after the move to Delaware—it became New Ark College, in 1870 a land-grant college and the state university in 1921. Now occupying 1850 acres, the university has an enrollment of more than 10,000 and offers degrees in over 100 different fields.

MEMORIAL HALL Donations collected by school children helped to build this memorial to World War I servicemen. It has served the university as a library and as the home of the College of Arts and Sciences, and contains a beautiful carillon which plays both traditional and popular music on the hour. *Open daily.*

OLD COLLEGE Built in 1833, this handsome red brick home of the university's music department is the oldest structure on the campus. The entrance is graced by a wide stairway and white-painted portico supported by Doric columns. Inside, another monumental stairway leads to the second floor. *Open daily.*

STUDENT CENTER The center is the scene of many art exhibitions. These include traveling exhibits from prominent museums, regular shows of student and faculty works and the annual Delaware Valley Regional Art Exhibit. *Open Mon.-Fri.*

102. Hagley Museum *Rte. 141, Greenville, Del.* Here is the Brandywine River site of the first du Pont powder mills, built of local granite in 1802 and in continuous production until 1921. An 1814 textile mill houses the main exhibits, which trace American industrial development with working models and talking dioramas from the Colonial mills of Brandywine Valley to the modern corporation. In the Black Powder Exhibit Building a series of models demonstrates steps in manufacturing black powder. Jitneys travel through the 185-acre grounds of the indoor-outdoor museum. *Open Tues.-Sun. and Mon. holidays except Jan. 1 and Dec. 25.*

ELEUTHERIAN MILLS A 10-minute jitney ride along the Brandywine from the Hagley Museum, the family home of the du Ponts is a charming Georgian country house of buff-colored stucco over stone. The original dwelling was built by E. I. du Pont in 1803 and served as both residence and office until 1837, when a separate office was erected a few hundred feet away. Five generations of du Ponts have lived in the house, which was enlarged in 1805 and again in 1853. The last owner, Mrs. Francis B. Crowninshield, great-granddaughter of E. I. du Pont, bequeathed it at her death in 1958 to the Eleutherian Mills-Hagley Foundation. The comfortably-sized house contains early American, Federal and Empire pieces belonging to the family. Also on the site are a barn, built in 1803, containing a display of 19th-century vehicles; a coopers shop; farm tools and a collection of antique weathervanes; and Lammot du Pont's workshop. The Eleutherian Mills-Hagley Foundation also administers the Eleutherian Mills Historical Library nearby. Open to qualified researchers, the library has books and graphics devoted to American economic and technological history. It also holds the archives of E. I. du Pont de Nemours and Company and many of the du Pont family papers. *House open Tues.-Sun. and Mon. holidays mid-Apr.-early June, Oct.*

103. Wilmington, Del.

The largest city in Delaware, this has been an important shipping and industrial center since Colonial days. The first colony on this site, Fort Christina, was established by a Swedish expedition in 1638 and named for their queen. The area passed through Dutch and British hands before coming under the influence of William Penn and the Quakers. The town received its charter and the name of Wilmington in 1739.

Delaware Art Museum *2301 Kentmere Pkwy.* The emphasis here is on American art, but the several notable collections include a fine group of English Pre-Raphaelite paintings. Works by Eakins, Homer and

Ryder are featured as well as drawings and paintings by Howard Pyle, a native of Wilmington who influenced many American artists. One of his pupils was N. C. Wyeth, some of whose works appear here together with those of other members of the Wyeth family. There is also a major John Sloan collection. The museum library contains books and manuscripts relating to American art and late-19th-century English art. *Open daily except holidays.*

Fort Christina Historical Park *Seventh St.* Also known as The Rocks, this two-acre park on the site of the original Swedish settlement was dedicated in 1938 to celebrate the 300th anniversary of the founding of the colony. A log cabin stands on the grounds, a reminder that this form of construction was introduced in the New World by Delaware's Swedish settlers. The 25-foot-high black granite monument by the Swedish-American sculptor Carl Milles depicts scenes of Delaware's early colonization period. *Open daily.*

Greenbank Mill and Station *Adjacent to Wilmington & Western R.R. tracks, near intersection of Rtes. 2 and 41.* Greenbank Station is typical of a railroad station of the 19th century. From here the Wilmington & Western Railroad operates a run through historic Red Clay Valley, carrying passengers in gaily painted trains drawn by steam locomotives. Greenbank Mill, a 1790 water-powered mill that still grinds grain in the original manner, is across the stream from the station. *Mill and station open during scheduled train trips Sat., Sun. and holidays May-Nov. Small charge.*

Holy Trinity Episcopal Church *606 N. Church St.* Old Swedes Church, one of the oldest churches in the U.S., was consecrated in 1699 to serve a parish that was founded more than 60 years earlier. The stone building has hooded gable ends and a floor of rectangular brick tiles. Changes were made in the original structure after it was transferred from Swedish Lutheran to Episcopalian jurisdiction in 1791. These changes include the addition of the tower and elaboration of the severely plain interior. Oil portraits of several of the Swedish pastors are on display in the vestry. *Open Tues.-Sun. except holidays.*

HENDRICKSON HOUSE Also known as Old Swedes House, this 1690 building, now on the grounds of Holy Trinity Church, was built in Pennsylvania for a young Swedish farmer. It is made of stone, which was unusual for that period of frame construction. It has a gambrel roof and heavy log beams supporting the ceiling. The interior is attractively decorated with interesting wood paneling and period furnishings. *Open Tues.-Sun. except holidays.*

Old Town Hall *Sixth and Market Sts.* This Federal-style building, erected in 1798, is now the home of the Historical Society of Delaware, which has restored it to its original appearance, even to the dungeon jail cells. The society's museum here contains china, silver, furniture, portraits and other objects relating to the early history of the state, while its library holds genealogical materials and an outstanding collection of books and manuscripts on Delaware history. *Open Tues.-Fri. except holidays Jan.-July, Sept.-Dec.*

Public Building *1000-1020 King St.* Since 1916 this handsome neoclassical building with a columned facade has been the seat of the City of Wilmington and New Castle County governments. It also houses various courts, as well as the administrative offices of the Wilmington Police and Fire departments. An annual May exhibit, the Clothesline Fair, displays the works of local artists. *Open Mon.-Fri.*

[**103.** *Holy Trinity Church*] *Since its dedication in 1699, congregations have worshiped in Old Swedes, making it one of America's oldest churches in continuous use. The original 1699 pulpit is also the oldest in the land.*

104. Winterthur Museum and Gardens *Winterthur, Del.* See feature display on pages 230-1.

105. New Castle, Del.

Founded by the Dutch in 1651 (Peter Stuyvesant himself laid out the town's boundaries in 1655), New Castle went on to become an important shipping town, the colonial capital and, for one year (1776-7), the state capital. The central portion of the town is one of the best-preserved examples of a colonial settlement in the U.S. The narrow streets are lined with handsome brick houses maintained much as they were 200 years ago. On the third Saturday in May the annual A Day in Old New Castle takes visitors into many historic homes not otherwise open to the public.

Amstel House *Fourth and Delaware Sts.* This three-story Dutch house, built in 1730, was the home of Nicholas Van Dyke, seventh governor of Delaware. Now maintained as a museum by the New Castle Historical Society, its furnishings—even the kitchen utensils—are of the Colonial period. Period clothing, antique dolls and other mementos further enliven the house, scene of a 1784 wedding at which George Washington was a guest. *Open Tues.-Sat. Small charge.*

Buena Vista *Rte. 13* John M. Clayton, U.S. Senator and Secretary of State under Zachary Taylor (and a negotiator of the Clayton-Bulwer Treaty with Britain on a proposed canal in Central America), built this house in 1845. A two-story brick building in the Greek Revival style, it has a wide, columned veranda across the front. Senator Clayton was an early adherent of scientific farming and demonstrated its advantages here. The house and 52 acres of land were willed to the state in 1965 by Senator C. Douglass Buck, Sr., a

descendant of John Clayton. It is furnished with period pieces, many of them original. *Open Tues., Thurs., Sat.*

George Read House *The Strand* A splendid example of Georgian architecture, this 1801 mansion was the home of George Read II, son of a signer of the Declaration of Independence. He is thought to have designed the house himself, incorporating several Federal details into the exterior, including the arched, fanlighted entrance. Above the door is a Palladian window of the same width. A widow's walk at the peak of the roof commands a view of the Delaware River.

Immanuel Episcopal Church on the Green *Market and Harmony Sts.* Many additions have been made over the years to this historic church. It was built in 1703 to serve the first Episcopal parish in Delaware, established in 1689. The original simple rectangular building received an entrance porch and interior gallery in 1724, and in 1820 William Strickland added the spired tower and west transepts. The brick surface was stuccoed at a later date. The parish still owns the original baptismal font and the Communion silver given to it by Queen Anne in 1710. In the churchyard are the graves of many prominent Delaware citizens. *Open daily.*

Old Court House *Delaware St. on the Green* Built about 1732 on the site of the earlier 1688 courthouse, this fine brick building played an important role in Delaware's early history. As the Colonial capitol, it was the site of Delaware's approval of the Declaration of Independence and adoption of its first state constitution. Its octagonal cupola was the center of the "12-mile circle" that formed the Pennsylvania-Delaware boundary and part of the Mason-Dixon Line. The building has undergone many changes, such as the wings, which were added in 1765, and the replacement of the original gambrel roof which was destroyed by fire in 1777. The interior, including the courtroom, has been handsomely restored. *Open Tues.-Sun. except holidays.*

Old Dutch House *Third St. on the Green* Authentic Dutch Colonial furnishings and equipment can be seen in this small brick house. It is one of the state's oldest houses—probably the oldest brick house—built about 1690. *Open Tues.-Sun. Apr.-Oct. Small charge.*

106. Corbit-Sharp House *Main and Second Sts., Odessa, Del.* William Corbit, a prosperous tanner, completed this splendid Georgian dwelling in 1774, when Odessa was a thriving port. Now administered by the Winterthur Museum (as is the Wilson-Warner House, below), the house is noted for its fine woodwork and furnishings, its old kitchen and the beautiful grounds surrounding it. Included in the admission fee to this house (as well as in that to the Wilson-Warner House) is a visit to the nearby John Janvier Stable on Second Street. Built in 1791 for a master cabinetmaker, it is unusual because of its brick-and-wood construction. It contains a small carriage room and two box stalls. *Open Tues.-Sun. except holidays. Adults $1.25 (or combined admission to both houses and stable $2.00), children small charge.*

107. Wilson-Warner House *Main St., Odessa, Del.* Standing beside the Corbit-Sharp House is this equally fine dwelling, built about 1740 and expanded in 1769. Once the home of merchant David Wilson, it contains many fine paneled rooms, furnished primarily with 18th-century pieces. The old smokehouse, used for preserving meats, is still attached to the exterior of the kitchen fireplace. Corbit Library, the state's first public library, was located here until 1968. *Open Tues.-Sun. except holidays. Adults $1.25, children small charge.*

108. Dover, Del.

Dover, with a population of 25,000, is the capital of the second smallest state in the union (Rhode Island is the smallest). Within the city, located on the St. Jones River, are several Colonial buildings of historic and architectural note.

Delaware State Museum *316 S. Governors Ave.* Exhibits housed in four buildings touch on the social, cultural, industrial, agricultural and commercial elements in the growth of Delaware from early times. *Open Tues.-Sun. except holidays.*

CHAPEL Adjacent to the church, this building displays early firemen's equipment; plows and other agricultural tools of the pre-machine age; stone arrowheads, axes and pottery of the Delaware Indians; and a demonstration of early weaving on a handloom.

ELDRIDGE REEVES JOHNSON MEMORIAL BUILDING E. R. Johnson was an inventor and businessman who played an important role in the development of the U.S. recording industry. He founded the Victor Talking Machine Company in 1901, and on display here are the earliest models of talking machines as well as later ones. A reproduction of a 1920s Victrola dealer's store is featured in the exhibit, as well as the personal belongings of Mr. Johnson.

LOG CABIN BUILDING Within, there is a walk-in furnished cabin typical of those built by early Swedish settlers in Delaware. It dates from about 1704.

OLD PRESBYTERIAN CHURCH Built in 1790, the church has an impressive spiral staircase leading to the gallery. On display are the works of Delaware silversmiths, furniture and furnishings, costumes, and a Grand Harmonicon that is played daily.

[**108.** *E. R. Johnson Building*] *The dog Nipper listens to an early phonograph in this famous Francis Barraud painting that became the Victor trademark. It is at the museum, together with much phonographic memorabilia.*

Elliptical stairway built about 1820 gracefully dominates Montmorenci Stair Hall, whose furnishings also reflect the fine craftsmanship of the young Republic.

104. Winterthur Museum and Gardens
Winterthur, Del.

As soon as Henry Francis du Pont inherited Winterthur, his family's estate, in 1926 he began to develop it as a repository of 17th- to early-19th-century American interiors. He tripled the size of the house in order to display his ever-growing collection of furniture, silver, rugs, room paneling, facades, staircases, ceramics, glass, paintings and textiles. Twenty-five years later du Pont turned Winterthur into a public museum which today consists of more than 150 rooms—bedrooms, parlors, dining rooms and kitchens. Many are furnished in a style that could be found in a particular locality, for instance a parlor with furniture by New York cabinetmaker Dun-

Philadelphia highboy made in 1769 typifies the Rococo style popularized in England 10 or 15 years earlier by cabinetmaker Thomas Chippendale and developed to its highest form in the colonies.

Chinese Parlor contains American furniture in the "Chinese taste," a Chippendale style developed in response to the Anglo-American desire for Oriental design. Wallpaper was handpainted in China.

can Phyfe, and a bedroom with pieces made by Dutch settlers of the Hudson Valley. Other notable areas include the Hall of Statues with its carved wooden figures and the China Shop, devoted to the display of Chinese export porcelain. Over the years du Pont, a world-renowned horticulturist, landscaped the 910 acres surrounding Winterthur into flowered woods, parklands, a pinetum and gardens with masses of blooms. *Gardens open Tues.-Sun. mid-Apr.-Oct., Nov.-mid-Apr. by appointment. Small charge. Main museum: 16 rooms open Tues.-Sun. mid-Apr.-late May; adults $1.50, children small charge. Complete collection open late May-mid-Apr. by appointment; adults only, $4.00 a half day. South Wing (14 rooms) open Tues.-Sun. mid-Apr.-Oct., Tues.-Sat. Nov.-mid-Apr.; small charge.*

Autumn-blooming colchicum bulbs color a hillside in the gardens that are designed as a series of complementary natural settings of flowers, trees and shrubs.

Governor's House *King's Hwy.* This handsome 1790 brick building, also known as Woodburn, was restored in 1966 to serve as the residence of Delaware's governor. Hand-carved paneling highlights many of the rooms, which are furnished with period pieces. A spacious hall, opening onto terraces, takes up the west end of the structure. The house was an important station on the "Underground Railroad," and contains a secret shaft which runs from the basement to the attic with an opening in a first-floor cupboard. *Open Tues.*

Hall of Records *Legislative Ave.* Charles II's 1682 charter granting Delaware to James, Duke of York, and various documents signed by William Penn are among the many historic documents housed here. In addition, the Georgian Colonial style building, completed in 1938, holds other public records and many manuscripts and publications relating to the state's history. *Open Mon.-Fri. except holidays.*

John Dickinson Mansion *Kitts Hummock Rd.* John Dickinson, whose writings contributed much to the cause of Independence and earned for him the title "Penman of the Revolution," made his home in this brick Georgian dwelling. Built by his father in 1740, it is a splendid example of the plantation architecture once common in lower Delaware. Restoration of the house in the early 1950s brought in furnishings once owned by the Dickinson family or typical of the area in the 18th century. Although Dickinson refrained from signing the Declaration of Independence, thinking it too precipitate, he himself wrote most of the documents of the American Congress that preceded it and later drafted the Articles of Confederation. His letters and speeches supporting the Constitution were in part responsible for Delaware's being the first state to ratify it, on Dec. 7, 1787. *Open Tues.-Sun. except holidays.*

Legislative Hall *Legislative Ave.* The handmade bricks used in its construction help keep this 1933 Georgian-style building in harmony with the 18th-century Old State House, whose functions it has largely assumed. Within are the offices of Delaware's top executives, as well as the chambers of the Senate and House of Representatives. The second-floor gallery contains portraits of distinguished citizens of Delaware and other paintings from the state's collection. *Open Mon.-Fri. except holidays.*

Old State House *The Green* The east side of historic Dover Green is graced by this 1792 middle-Georgian building, the second oldest state house in the U.S. still in active administrative use. A well-proportioned Palladian window and the octagonal tower and cupola surmounting the roof are notable features.

109. Zwaanendael Museum *Savannah Rd. and King's Hwy., Lewes, Del.* This adaptation of the Old Town Hall in Hoorn, Holland, was built in 1931 to commemorate the 300th anniversary of Delaware's first Dutch settlement, Zwaanendael. The settlers, most of whom were from Hoorn, were massacred by Indians about 1632, but their colony holds great importance in the state's history. Surmounting the building's highly ornamented gabled facade is a statue of Captain David Pieterssen deVries, who dispatched the expedition. The museum contains mementos and artifacts relating to the Dutch settlers and to other aspects of the early history of southern Delaware. *Open Tues.-Sun. except holidays.*

110. Old Wye Church *Queenstown-Easton Rd., Wye Mills, Md.* Originally a chapel of ease, or an additional chapel, built to serve St. Paul's parish, this church was opened for worship in 1721. It is an excellent example of the early Colonial church, with high wooden pews numbered to reserve them for the members of the congregation. The brick church building and the adjacent one-room vestry house have been completely restored, the latter with pre-1767 furnishings. *Open Wed., Thurs., Sun. May-Nov.*

111. Chesapeake Bay Maritime Museum *St. Michaels, Md.* Exhibits relating to the history and traditions of the Chesapeake Bay area include a salt-water aquarium, a gaff-rigged oyster sloop and other work boats, a 129-foot lightship and marine paintings. A major feature is the Hooper's Strait Lighthouse, one of the last cottage-type screw pile lighthouses on Chesapeake Bay—the threaded iron pilings supporting the cottage and light were literally screwed into the bottom

[114] *Typical of the faithful restoration done in 1953-60 are the "three-decker" pulpit pew, the high-backed box pews made of southern pine salvaged from abandoned Maryland and Virginia 18th-century houses and the altar rail of native black walnut. The large red brick floor tiles and the altar table frame are original. One of the special pleasures of Old Trinity is its pastoral setting on the banks of Church Creek, screened from the highway by magnificent old trees.*

[118] *A vivid St. Christopher, painted in the late 15th century by the Flemish master Quentin Massys, is one of many notable works in the outstanding Kress Memorial Collection of Renaissance and Baroque work housed here.*

of the bay. It dates from 1879. *Open Tues.-Sun. Jan.-Apr., daily May-Oct., Tues.-Sun. Nov.-Dec. Adults $1.50, children small charge.*

112. St. Mary's Square Museum *St. Michaels, Md.* The history of the town of St. Michaels is honored in this small museum, which contains memorabilia of the town's shipbuilding days. There are two adjoining buildings, the older of which dates from the late 17th century. *Open Fri.-Sun. Apr.-Sept. Small charge.*

113. Historical Society of Talbot County Headquarters *29 S. Washington St., Easton, Md.* Furnishings of the Federal period, including pieces by Chippendale and Hepplewhite, are featured in the society's headquarters, a handsome brick town house. The four-story building, which has been restored, dates from the 1790s. There are regular exhibits of silver, china, toys, guns and other items of the period. The lovely garden contains plantings typical of the 18th century—boxwood, flowers such as lilies of the valley, and fruit trees. *Open Tues., Fri. Jan.-Mar., Tues., Fri.-Sun. Apr.-Dec. Small charge.*

114. Trinity Episcopal Church, Dorchester Parish *Off Rte. 16, Church Creek, Md.* Built about 1675, Old Trinity is the nation's oldest church standing in its original form and still regularly used by its congregation. A unique feature of this small brick church is the semicircular sanctuary with a six-foot radius. Buried in the cemetery are many soldiers of the Revolution. There are also many prominent Marylanders, including the daughter of a former Governor of Maryland, Anna Ella Carroll, "Maryland's Most Distinguished Lady," hailed as a member of the "unofficial cabinet of President Lincoln." Here too lies the last miller to run a nearby 18th-century gristmill—its two huge millstones marking his grave. *Open Wed.-Mon. Mar.-Dec., Sat.-Sun. Jan.-Feb.*

115. Eyre Hall *N. of Rtes. 13 and 680, Cheriton, Va.* Formal gardens and boxwood hedges surround a pleasant frame house that has been in the Eyre family since its construction in 1750. The well-appointed home is noted for its Dufour wallpaper and mantels carved with classic motifs. *Gardens open daily.*

116. Annie S. Kemerer Museum *427 N. New St., Bethlehem, Pa.* At her death in 1951 Annie Kemerer, a native of Bethlehem, bequeathed her valuable collection of Venetian, Bohemian and American glassware and furniture (mainly Queen Anne, Chippendale and Hepplewhite pieces) to that city. Among the other articles that she had acquired through a lifetime of collecting were locally made clocks and domestic objects once used by the 18th-century Moravian settlement of Bethlehem. One of the rooms of the museum holds changing displays from other collections. A 1698 English fire engine, early tools and fire-fighting equipment are exhibited in a separate building. *Open Mon.-Fri., 2 Sun. each mo. except holidays.*

117. Church Street *Bethlehem, Pa.* Moravians who had fled from religious persecution in Germany established Bethlehem in 1741 and lived here in a closed community for more than a century. At the community's center was the unique complex of buildings surrounding Church Street. Besides those discussed below, the area includes other interesting buildings, such as the Widow's House (built in 1768 and still a residence for widows and daughters of Moravian ministers) and the sandstone Bell House, whose peals set the community's schedule.

CENTRAL MORAVIAN CHURCH *Church and Main Sts.* This church, dedicated in 1806, was built with a truss construction of the roof and ceiling that eliminated the need for supporting columns. It has excellent acoustics for the great variety of music heard during services. Its belfry is a landmark of Bethlehem. *Open daily.*

MORAVIAN MUSEUM OF BETHLEHEM *66 W. Church St.* Furnishings, musical instruments, needlework and artwork are among the items here that give visitors a glimpse of what life was like in 18th-century Bethlehem. The museum is housed in the Gemein Haus, or community house, a five-story structure built in 1741 of logs, which are now covered with clapboard. The second building put up in Bethlehem, and the oldest still standing, it housed the entire community during the early years. *Open Tues.-Sat. except holidays. Small charge.*

OLD CHAPEL *Heckewelder Pl.* From 1751 until the early 1900s, the upper floor of this thick-walled stone building served as Bethlehem's place of worship—and it still is used for school services and special events. The ground floor was originally a dining hall for Moravian married couples.

118. Allentown Art Museum *Fifth and Court Sts., Allentown, Pa.* More than 30 paintings and sculptures from the Samuel H. Kress Memorial Collection of Renaissance and Baroque works can be seen in this redesigned church and adjoining annex. Two large galleries display the genius of many European masters,

[122] *The Washington Memorial Chapel, the lofty bell tower, and a museum containing George Washington's campaign tent and headquarters flag stand in a group at Valley Forge, facing the Grand Parade where Baron von Steuben drilled the demoralized troops in the spring of 1778; it was here, too, that the news arrived of the entrance of France into the war on America's side.*

including Tintoretto, Rembrandt, Hals, van Ruisdael and Jan Steen. Fine wood carvings by Yselin and Erhart can also be enjoyed. *Open daily except holidays.*

119. Mercer Museum of the Bucks County Historical Society *Pine and Ashland Sts., Doylestown, Pa.* Over a period of 33 years Dr. Henry C. Mercer put together a collection of more than 33,000 tools that were used by pre-Industrial Revolution American homemakers, artisans and craftsmen. Visitors gain an understanding of this country's early social life through these objects once commonly used by doctors, miners, bakers, tanners, glassblowers, potters, dressmakers, gunsmiths, carpenters, wagon builders, horologists, trappers, printers and many others in the trades, crafts and professions. Within the museum are an entire 19th-century country store, an early American kitchen, an 1800 bedroom and a mid-18th-century parlor. Hanging from four galleries circling a large center court are a whaleboat, fire engine, one-horse shay and dugout canoes. The museum building itself, the first all reinforced concrete structure in the country, is also of considerable interest. Dr. Mercer designed and built it in 1916. *Open Tues.-Sat. Mar., Tues.-Sun. Apr.-Oct., Tues.-Sat. Nov.-Dec. Small charge.*

[119] *A visitor walking through the tall center court of this remarkable building finds whaleboats, canoes, sleds—even an early fire engine—suspended above him in a rich display of early craftsmanship.*

120. National Shrine of Our Lady of Czestochowa *Ferry Rd., Doylestown, Pa.* This modern church was dedicated in 1966 in commemoration of 1000 years of Christianity in Poland and is a repository of religious art and culture. Of particular interest are windows of leaded stained glass, each measuring 2500 square feet. The history of Christianity in Poland is the subject of the west window wall in the Czestochowa Shrine; the east window wall depicts the contribution of Christians to American history. *Open daily.*

121. Valley Forge State Park *Valley Forge, Pa.* Washington's half-starved, half-clothed Continental army encamped here for the crucial winter of 1777–78. The 2255-acre park includes extensive remains of earthworks, trenches and the Grand Parade Ground where troops were drilled by Baron von Steuben. Among points of interest are Washington's Headquarters and stable, the Bake-House, Baron von Steuben's quarters and General Varnum's quarters. A slide show describing the park's history is offered at the Visitor Center. *Open daily.*

122. Washington Memorial Chapel *Rte. 23, Valley Forge, Pa.* This architecturally outstanding Gothic chapel adjacent to Valley Forge State Park was built as a monument to George Washington and the men of the Continental army who endured the bitter winter of 1777–8. Scenes from Washington's life are depicted in the stained-glass windows over the entry door in glowing colors. Other windows depict historical and religious subjects. The chapel is also noted for its ornate hand-carved woodwork. Flanking the chapel are the Cloister of the Colonies and the Bell Tower; the latter contains the Washington Memorial National Carillon. *Chapel open daily, tower open mid-June–early Sept.*

123. Barnes Foundation *North Latch's Lane and Lapsley Road, Merion, Pa.* Seldom have so many important paintings been so little seen as those at the

Barnes Foundation. Dr. Albert C. Barnes, who made a fortune from the patent medicine Argyrol, was a controversial and energetic art collector with definite ideas about the rules of color and composition. The Foundation was established in 1922 as a school to teach the principles in which he believed. The vast collection of paintings he assembled during his lifetime was intended to be seen by the students only, and it was not until after his death in 1951 that the public was allowed to view it on the limited basis explained below. The number of paintings is staggering. There are, for example, more than 200 Renoirs, some 60 Matisses, almost 100 Cézannes and 25 Picassos. Most of the works are by French artists, but many 20th-century American painters are also represented. The walls of the 30-room mansion are literally covered with paintings. Masterpieces are mixed with less successful works and with other art objects to illustrate principles of design and composition espoused by the school. This method seldom displays an individual work to its best advantage, but the total effect of so much genius compressed in one place is overwhelming. Most of the paintings have never been published in color or shown anywhere else. Because of its unique character the Barnes collection is included in the book, although it is not as readily accessible to the public as the other treasures here. *Open Fri.-Sun. Sept.-June except holidays (100 persons with reservations and 100 without admitted).*

124. Buten Museum of Wedgwood *246 N. Bowman Ave., Merion, Pa.* The impressive Buten collection of 10,000 examples of Wedgwood pottery, porcelain and stoneware dating from 1759 to the present is displayed in an interesting Tudor-style mansion. Daily gallery talks explain the significance of the many impressive displays. *Open Tues.-Thurs. Jan.-May, Oct.-Dec.*

125. Bryn Athyn Cathedral *Papermill Rd. and Huntingdon Pike, Bryn Athyn, Pa.* This beautifully proportioned Gothic cathedral is the center of the General Church of the New Jerusalem, founded on the writings of Emanuel Swedenborg. Dedicated for worship in 1919, its outstanding features include Romanesque and Gothic towers, stone carvings, fine wood and metal work and glowing stained-glass windows which fill the church with vibrant life and color. *Open Sat.-Thurs.*

126. Old St. Mary's Church and **New St. Mary's Church** *W. Broad St., Burlington, N.J.* Old St. Mary's, completed in 1703, was the first Episcopal church in New Jersey. In 1834 the original rectangular structure was enlarged in the form of a Latin cross but the early Colonial simplicity of the facade was maintained. A silver chalice, a paten and glass, gifts to the church from Queen Anne, are still in use. New St. Mary's, completed in 1854, was designed by Richard Upjohn, the architect who advocated the use of the Gothic Revival style in America. It is the first cruciform church built in the U.S. Also on the grounds is the Guild House, originally the rectory, built in 1799. *Open daily.*

127. Hope Lodge *Bethlehem Pike, Whitemarsh, Pa.* The original owner and builder of this Georgian manor house is believed to be a Mr. Samuel Morris, and the story goes that he built the stately home in 1750 for his bride-to-be but the marriage never took place. The interior details were handled in the classic Georgian manner with symmetrical wainscoting of wood, large fireplaces with Delft tiles, and classical pilasters and pediments. One unusual feature for a Georgian interior is the staircase located in the rear hall. The last private owners of the house restored and furnished it with fine period pieces. Hope Lodge (named by one of the early owners for his cousin Henry Hope, whose family later gave its name to the Hope Diamond) also played a part in Revolutionary War history. In 1777 Washington's troops briefly occupied the surrounding hills and it is believed that espionage directed at the British was carried out from the house. *Open Tues.-Sun. and holiday Mon. Small charge.*

128. Beth Sholom Congregation *Old York and Foxcroft Rds., Elkins Park, Pa.* This is the only synagogue designed by Frank Lloyd Wright, one of the best-known 20th-century American architects. It was dedicated in 1959. Wright used the triangle as the basic design unit in both the structure and decoration. One large triangular roof dominates a series of others on lower levels, the whole representing Mount Sinai and a symbol of the communion of God and Man. Inside, the triangle is reflected in the design of the ark, menorah, chandelier, pulpit, memorial tablets, lamps and door handles. *Open Sun.-Thurs.*

129. Philadelphia, Pa.

Philadelphia is one of the largest storehouses of American treasures, owing to its position during the Colonial and Revolutionary eras as a leading city in many respects: size, economy, culture, industry. The two-square-mile city laid out by William Penn in 1682 grew rapidly; by the mid-18th century it was the center of political activity against British rule and was the capital of the country until the Federal Government moved to Washington in 1800. The buildings, homes and churches where many of the most respected men in 17th- and 18th-century America worked, lived and prayed are still standing, the majority of them restored

[124] *Just a small corner of the Buten's astonishing collection of Wedgwood pottery, china and stoneware gives a good idea of the endless variety of shape and color within the 10 basic types by this famous maker.*

[City Hall] The ornate center of government in the City of Brotherly Love probably bears more elaborate sculptural decoration than any other building in America. Every one of the hundreds of statues and reliefs was designed by Alexander Calder, Scottish-born grandfather of the contemporary sculptor of the same name. Although carried out to an elaborate program, none of the sculptures bears any inscriptions; a leaflet detailing the principal ones is available at the hall itself. Everyone knows, however, that the 37-foot figure atop the tower is William Penn; it is said to be the largest sculpture on any building in the world. The view from the tower embraces the heart of the city.

and maintained as historic sites. Although Philadelphia's political influence declined in the 19th century, the city continued to grow economically and culturally. Several of its outstanding museums, parks and houses date from this period.

Academy of Natural Sciences of Philadelphia *19th St. and Benjamin Franklin Pkwy.* The Western Hemisphere's oldest natural science museum (founded in 1812) has some outstanding collections, notably its 20 million specimens of the world's plants and animals, displays of minerals, rare gems, dinosaur skeletons, and insects, including live bees. The Audubon Hall of Birds is a popular attraction, and children enjoy the live-animal shows presented daily. The academy's distinguished biology library of 150,000 volumes includes many important works. Lectures and films are scheduled regularly. *Open daily. Small charge.*

Betsy Ross House *239 Arch St.* The story goes that in 1776 a delegation from the Continental Congress called on Mrs. Elizabeth Ross in this quaint brick house and commissioned her to make the first American flag—13 red and white stripes and 13 white stars on a field of blue. It was officially adopted by Congress in 1777. The house, fully restored and furnished, is an interesting example of an 18th-century middle-class home. *Open daily except Dec. 25.*

Cathedral of SS. Peter and Paul *18th St. and Benjamin Franklin Pkwy.* One of the impressive sights on the Philadelphia skyline is the green copper dome and golden cross of the Ss. Peter and Paul Cathedral. (The model for the Roman Catholic cathedral, built between 1846 and 1864, is the Lombard Church of St. Charles in Rome.) The church is a prime example of Roman Corinthian architecture, with ornate columns supporting the pediment over the entry of the brownstone structure as well as the lofty vaulted ceilings of the interior. *Open daily.*

Church of St. James the Less *3227 W. Clearfield St.* St. James the Less, an Episcopal church built in 1846, is a replica of a 13th-century early Gothic parish church in Cambridgeshire, England. Its simplicity of proportion, line and decor influenced some prominent architects of the day, with the result that St. James became a model for many American mid-19th-century parish churches. The east window was designed by Henri Gerente, a renowned stained-glass artist who filled windows in Ely Cathedral, Cambridgeshire, and Ste.-Chapelle, Paris, two of the most famous churches in the world. *Open daily.*

Church of St. Vincent de Paul *109 E. Price St.* The facade of this Roman Catholic church, dedicated in 1851, is classically simple; window pediments and capitals on relief columns are the primary architectural ornaments. The considerably more ornate interior is restrained by subdued colors and the soft contours of carved marble worn with age. *Open daily.*

City Hall *Penn Sq., Broad and Market Sts.* Philadelphia's seat of government is a massive structure, the best example of 19th-century eclecticism in the country. The facade is an ebullient mixture of Renaissance windows, Grecian pediments and columns, Roman arches and relief panels, and scores of sculptures representing such things as the races of man, the continents, admonition and repentance, knowledge, sympathy, resolution. Atop the tower is a 37-foot-high statue of William Penn. Visitors can ride a special elevator to the top of the tower for a fine view of the city. The interior of the building is as rich in decorative detail—mosaics, friezes, frescos, bas-reliefs—as the exterior is in architectural extravagances. *Open Mon.-Fri.*

Cliveden *6401 Germantown Ave.* Benjamin Chew, a prominent lawyer and later chief justice of the province of Pennsylvania, built this elegant stone house between 1763 and 1767. Except for an 18-year interval, it was to remain in his family until 1972. A three-story structure with ornate chimneys, the mansion is noted for its main doorway, flanked by hand-carved pilasters and crowned by a dentiled pediment. It contains many of the original furnishings, including family portraits, Philadelphia Chippendale and Federal furniture and rare rococo mirrors. The mansion is now the property of the National Trust for Historic Preservation. *Open daily except Dec. 25. Adults $1.25, children small charge.*

Congregation Rodeph Shalom *615 N. Broad St.* Hand-appliquéd painted walls, a marble altar and bronze doors of the Ark that weigh 1000 pounds are outstanding features of this Byzantine-style structure, which was built in 1927 on the same site as an earlier synagogue completed in 1869. Extensive archives here relate to the Philadelphia Jewish community which dates from the 1790s. *Open Mon.-Fri.*

Deshler-Morris House *5442 Germantown Ave.* Sometimes referred to as the Germantown White House, this 1773 dwelling was the scene of Cabinet meetings and other official business during two short periods in 1793 and 1794 when President and Mrs. Washington lived here. General William Howe made his headquarters in this house when the British occupied Philadelphia in 1777. The house has been fully restored; the exterior is stucco and is noted for 24 large-paned windows. Many rooms are paneled and all have period furniture. *Open Tues.-Sun. Small charge.*

Drexel Museum Collection *Drexel University, 32nd and Chestnut Sts.* The highlight of this collection is an astronomical clock made in 1773 by David Rittenhouse. A famous astronomer and mathematician, Rittenhouse surveyed part of the Mason-Dixon Line and served as the first director of the U.S. Mint. The clock is his masterpiece and its works and superb case are virtually in their original condition. Also on view are Napoleon's chess table, Napoleonic china and 19th-century German and French paintings. *Open Mon.-Fri. during academic year.*

Edgar Allan Poe House *530 N. Seventh St.* Poe lived here from 1842 to 1844, the most peaceful years of his short, tormented life. First editions, portraits and other memorabilia are on view in the red brick house which is furnished as it might have been when Poe and his wife lived here. It was here Poe wrote "The Raven," "The Black Cat," "The Tell-Tale Heart" and "The Gold Bug" as well as many other of his most celebrated poems, tales and critiques. *Open daily except Easter Day and Dec. 25. Small charge.*

Elfreth's Alley *Between Second and Front Sts.* Elfreth's Alley is believed to be the nation's oldest continuously occupied street that is still in its original condition. Only six feet wide, it was laid out no later than 1704, and the earliest of its 33 two- and three-story houses were probably built in 1722. Although most of these unpretentious buildings are private homes, the Elfreth's Alley Association operates a museum at 126 Elfreth's Alley in the house where Jeremiah Elfreth, a blacksmith, once lived. It is completely furnished, a typical example of the 18th-century houses in the alley. The area has no particular historical significance, but it is known that Benjamin Franklin visited friends here, and its size and architectural qualities have qualified it as a National Historic Landmark. Several of the private homes are opened to the public during an annual fete on the first Saturday in June. *Museum open daily Apr.-Oct.*

[*Elfreth's Alley*] *Only a block from Philadelphia's bustling waterfront and a major highway bridge, and often threatened in the past with demolition, this little street is a perfectly preserved Colonial gem.*

Fairmount Park Colonial Houses *Fairmount Park* The 4000 acres of one of the world's largest city parks, situated in northwestern Philadelphia, stretch away from both banks of the Schuylkill River. They provide a fitting setting for these lovely homes, reminders of Philadelphia's early, calmer days.

CEDAR GROVE *Lansdowne Dr.* Its tranquil hillside setting, to which it was moved in 1927, is appropriate for this handsome gray fieldstone Quaker farmhouse, built about 1748 and greatly enlarged some 50 years later. The dwelling contains 18th-century furnishings, all accumulated by five generations of the Morris family, the former owners. Among the many fine pieces are outstanding examples of William and Mary, Queen Anne, Chippendale, Hepplewhite and Sheraton styles, some of which were made in Philadelphia. An herb garden is another notable feature of the house. *Open daily except holidays. Small charge.*

LEMON HILL *E. River Dr. at Boat House Row* This elegant stucco Federal mansion was completed in 1800 on the former estate of Robert Morris, the Philadelphia merchant who helped finance the Revolutionary armies and served as superintendent of finance after the war. The land is located high above the river and in Morris' time was known as The Hills. Henry Pratt purchased the property in 1799 and renamed the estate after the first lemon trees grown in America were developed in the greenhouse. The mansion's entranceway consists of twin curved stairways that rise to a fanlighted door topped by a fine Palladian window. The interior includes three unusual oval rooms, a curved floating staircase and many period furnishings. The Colonial Dames of America maintain the house. *Open every Thurs. and 2nd and 4th Sun. July-Aug. Small charge.*

MOUNT PLEASANT *Mount Pleasant Dr.* Completed in 1762 for a Scottish sea captain, this grand Georgian house demonstrates a remarkable symmetry of design; even the front and back facades are identical, both adorned with a handsome pedimented doorway with a fanlight and a fine carved Palladian window on the second story. This symmetry is carried through in the two flanking outbuildings and in the interior of the main house, where door balances door, window balances window. Boxwood gardens and fine Chippendale furniture are other notable features of this home, which John Adams in 1775 described as the "most elegant seat in Pennsylvania." The house has had many owners: one, Benedict Arnold, bought it as a wedding present for his bride but was convicted of treason before they could occupy it. Mount Pleasant is maintained by the Philadelphia Museum of Art. *Open daily except holidays. Small charge.*

STRAWBERRY MANSION *33rd and Dauphin Sts.* Three sections built in two architectural styles are harmoniously joined in this white stucco house. A Quaker judge constructed the central Federal-style portion in 1797; the two higher wings in the heavier Greek Revival style were added about 1820 by the second owner. (Strawberries grown from Chilean roots by this owner's son gave the structure its name.) Fine woodwork can be seen in the interior along with late-18th- and early-19th-century furniture, toys, artifacts and a collection of early American Tucker porcelain. The Committee of 1926 maintains the house. *Open Tues.-Sun. Feb.-Dec. Small charge.*

[*Independence Park*] *Independence Hall, home of the Liberty Bell, is the centerpiece of this collection of famous buildings in Philadelphia's heart—here flanked by Congress Hall and Old City Hall.*

SWEETBRIAR *Lansdowne Dr.* A combination of symmetry and delicate neoclassic ornamentation contributes to the simple elegance of this house, a fine example of Adamesque architecture. The mansion was built for Samuel Breck, a philanthropist who was a patron of John James Audubon as well as of several worthy Philadelphia institutions. It was restored in 1927 and furnished with period pieces of exceptional quality, many of which belonged to Breck himself, so that today Sweetbriar appears virtually as it did at the time of its completion in 1797. The Modern Club of Philadelphia maintains the house. *Open Mon.-Sat. Jan.-June, Aug.-Dec. Small charge.*

WOODFORD MANSION *33rd and Dauphin Sts.* This handsome brick dwelling, built in 1756 by Judge William Coleman, was restored in 1930 by the Naomi Wood Estate, which maintains it today. It is furnished with Miss Wood's collection—"an illustration of household gear during Colonial years"—which includes furniture, silver, unusual clocks, paintings and prints. An exceptional collection of polychrome English Delftware is shown in rooms with pegged floors, coved ceilings and walls painted in the original colors. Chippendale, William and Mary and Queen Anne furniture is displayed, as well as pieces by outstanding Philadelphia cabinetmakers. The second-floor living room is furnished completely in maple. Originally a one-story dwelling (where Benjamin Franklin was a frequent guest), the house was attractively enlarged by its third owner, David Franks, a Tory who entertained Lord Howe and his officers here during the British occupation of the city in 1777. *Open Tues.-Sun. Jan.-July, Sept.-Dec.*

Franklin Institute *20th St. and Benjamin Franklin Pkwy.* The original purpose of the Franklin Institute, founded in 1824, was to provide a center where scientists and craftsmen could gather together, with a technical library and research materials available to them. Exhibits of interest to the general public were also planned. The institute consists of a science library of books, periodicals and patents; the Fels Planetarium, whose 515-seat auditorium is used both for sky viewing and multimedia exhibits; Franklin Memorial Hall, dominated by a huge but sympathetic marble statue of Franklin by James Earle Fraser; and the Science Museum. The latter carries on the institute's tradition of excellence in their exhibitions (the Bell telephone was first exhibited here). Among the most popular exhibits are "Energy—What's It All About" and a pioneer airplane constructed with stainless steel. *Open daily except holidays. $1.50.*

Independence National Historical Park *313 Walnut St.* Many of the most important events in the nation's early history took place within a four-block area of old Philadelphia. Here the Continental Congress met, the Declaration of Independence was adopted, the Liberty Bell tolled and the Constitution was written. Here distinguished Colonial families lived and such important institutions as the First Bank of the U.S., Franklin's Philosophical Society and Christ Church were established. Some of the most interesting treasures within the park are listed below.

BISHOP WHITE HOUSE *Walnut St.* Bishop White, a founder of the Episcopal Church in America, was the first Episcopal bishop of Pennsylvania and served as rector of Christ Church and chaplain for both the Continental Congress and the U.S. Senate. He lived in an elegant row house which has been restored and furnished with many of its original pieces and others of the period. *Open Mon.-Fri.*

CARPENTERS' HALL *320 Chestnut St.* In Colonial days a carpenter was a supercraftsman who combined carpentry with architecture and building. The carpenters in Colonial Philadelphia formed a guild and between 1770-1774 built a guildhall. It is of brick in the shape of a squat cross with paned windows and a cupola. The building was used by many other groups besides carpenters. The First Continental Congress met here, and during the Revolution it was used as a hospital and as a storehouse for Continental army supplies. In 1790 it served as headquarters for the Secretary of War and later was occupied by the U.S. Customs and several societies and banks. *Open daily except holidays.*

CHRIST CHURCH IN PHILADELPHIA *Second St.* This church, completed in 1744, is a classic example of Georgian Colonial architecture. Its basically simple interior is embellished with a graceful English brass chandelier, beautifully proportioned Palladian window and a rare 18th-century Wineglass pulpit. The English foundry that cast the Liberty Bell also cast the eight (now 11) bells in Christ Church tower; they rang out with the Liberty Bell when the Declaration of Independence was announced, and they still ring daily. Because Christ Church was so closely associated with the Revolution—Washington, Franklin, Adams and many other patriots worshiped here—it is regarded by many as the most important Colonial church in America. *Open daily.*

CONGRESS HALL *Sixth St.* The hall was completed in 1787 to be used as the Philadelphia County Court House, but for ten years (1790-1800) it was occupied by the U.S. Congress. Here Washington was sworn in as President for his second term, and Adams took the oath as second President of the U.S. *Open daily.*

INDEPENDENCE HALL *Chestnut St.* This large brick Georgian building, built between 1732 and 1756, is associated with several dramatic events in the nation's early history. It served as Pennsylvania's State House and was used by the Second Continental Congress. Washington was chosen to command the Continental army in this building. On July 4, 1776, America's freedom from England was proclaimed here with the adoption of the Declaration of Independence, and in 1787 the U.S. Constitution was debated and written within its walls. From 1802 until 1828 the second floor was used as a museum by portraitist Charles Willson Peale; after 1830 state courts and city councils utilized the building. It deteriorated, however, until 1951 when restoration was finally begun. The building's most popular attraction is the renowned Liberty Bell. Cast in England in 1751, it cracked during testing and was recast. The present crack occurred during tolling for the funeral of Chief Justice Marshall in 1835. *Open daily.*

PEMBERTON HOUSE *Chestnut St.* This house was built in 1775 by Joseph Pemberton, a wealthy Quaker merchant; the exterior was reconstructed in the late 1960s. Inside is the Army-Navy Museum, with exhibits that show the activities of these services in the late 18th century. *Open daily.*

PENNSYLVANIA HORTICULTURAL SOCIETY GARDEN *325 Walnut St.* Next door to its headquarters the Society has maintained a garden typical of those in vogue among upper-class 18th-century families of the district. It is divided into three sections: a formal parterre with beds of flowers and shrubs surrounded by gravel walks and handsome edging plants and bounded at the back by a grape arbor; a small orchard; and a vegetable, herb and flower-cutting garden. *Open daily.*

[Independence Park-Christ Church] The harmoniously proportioned interior of "the nation's church" has seen many great Americans—such as Benjamin Franklin, whose simple tomb is in Christ Church Burial Ground nearby.

[Pennsylvania Academy of Arts] Charles Willson Peale's self-portrait, The Artist in His Museum, *showing the painter surrounded by his natural history collection, is among the stellar American works housed here.*

PHILADELPHIA EXCHANGE *313 Walnut St.* William Strickland, a noted 19th-century architect, built this Greek Revival structure between 1832 and 1834. For many years it housed the Philadelphia Stock Exchange. The exterior, completely restored, reveals Strickland's imaginative use of Greek design: atop the semicircular apse supported by Corinthian columns is a copy of a monument to Lysicrates which is used here as a tower. *Open daily.*

TODD HOUSE *Walnut St.* John Todd, a lawyer, bought this modest 1775 house in 1791 and came to live here with his wife Dolley. After his death in 1793 Dolley married James Madison and so became the First Lady of the White House when Madison took office in 1809. *Open daily.*

Museum of the Philadelphia Civic Center *Civic Center Blvd. and 34th St.* Assembled in a well-proportioned Greek Revival building are changing exhibits of international arts and crafts and permanent displays of ship models and unusual musical instruments. One exhibition of particular note is the "Philadelphia Panorama," which traces the planned development of the city. The museum offers a full program of concerts, films, operas, dance and lectures. *Open Tues.–Sun.*

Pennsylvania Academy of the Fine Arts *Broad and Cherry Sts.* Pennsylvania Academy, founded in 1805, is the oldest museum and art school in the country. While the collection contains European paintings and sculpture, emphasis has been on American art, with the result that today the academy owns an excellent historical and cultural survey of American art from the earliest days to the present. Among well-known works in the collection are West's *Penn's Treaty with the Indians,* Eakins' *Walt Whitman,* and a number of works by Cassatt, Andrew Wyeth, Charles Willson Peale (including *George Washington at Princeton* and *The Artist* *in His Museum*), Sargent, Whistler, Sully and Stuart. The Academy building, opened in 1876, was designed by Frank Furness and is a Victorian eclectic masterpiece of a pleasing mixture of pink granite, brownstone and brick. With these materials Furness created a facade composed of Gothic, Byzantine, Renaissance and Classic motifs and decorated with intricate floral designs. The interior is in a similar vein. *Open Tues.-Sun. Jan.-July, Sept.-Dec.*

Philadelphia Art Alliance *251 S. 18th St.* Many exhibits of works by contemporary artists are presented here in seven galleries. Displays include paintings, sculpture, prints, industrial designs and jewelry, as well as creations in glass, wood and metals. Gallery talks, recitals and programs of dance and drama are held regularly. *Open daily except holidays Jan.-June, Sept.-Dec.*

Philadelphia Maritime Museum *321 Chestnut St.* This selective collection traces man's history on the high seas from the late 18th century to the present, though emphasis is on the maritime history of the Eastern seaboard. On display are carved figureheads, ship models, whaling equipment, scrimshaw, maps, paintings, and exhibits on sunken treasure and underwater diving and photography. An important historical ship in the collection is an 1883 Portuguese square-rigged fishing vessel; visitors may board it at Pier 15 North on the Delaware River. *Open daily. Small charge.*

Philadelphia Museum of Art *Fairmount Park, Benjamin Franklin Pkwy. and 26th St.* A broad range of the world's finest art is housed in this magnificent classical-style building modeled after the Parthenon. In many of the 200 galleries, the works of art are displayed in settings appropriate to their period. For this reason the museum has acquired authentic architectural elements (Romanesque portals, French 18th-century paneled walls and the like), as well as entire rooms and houses—an 11th-century Spanish cloister and a 14th-century French Gothic chapel, for instance. Most intriguing are the Asian interiors, which include a Japanese tea house and garden, a 16th-century Indian hall and a Ming Dynasty palace reception room. European paintings from 1200 to 1800 are well represented, but the museum's strong point is American and early-20th-century European art. Some 40 canvases by Eakins and major works by Charles Willson Peale (*Staircase Group*), Andrew Wyeth, Kline, Hofmann and Stuart Davis hang in the American rooms. Among the museum's finest European paintings of the late 19th and early 20th centuries are *The Folkstone Boat* (Manet), *The Bathers* (Renoir), *Sunflowers* (van Gogh), *Three Musicians* (Picasso) and *Nude Descending a Staircase* (Duchamp), to name but a few. Fifteen galleries are devoted to early Philadelphia furniture, silver and Pennsylvania Dutch arts. In addition to the many sculptures reflecting major European trends (including Brancusi's famous *Bird in Space*), there are 13 superb tapestries from Rome's Palazzo Barberini. *Open daily except holidays. Small charge.*

Philadelphia Zoological Garden *Fairmount Park, 34th St. and Girard Ave.* America's first zoo, opened in 1874, now occupies 42 acres. Among its collection of over 1400 mammals, birds and reptiles are many rare species, including various apes, bears, tigers, rhinos, tortoises and European bison. Many of the animals live within moated enclosures instead of traditional cages. A major attraction is the imaginative Hummingbird Exhibit which houses several species of these colorful birds in a skillfully conceived natural surrounding of tropical plantings and rocks, with a 20-foot waterfall, and inhabited by lizards, turtles and fish. Visitors observe the birds at close range from a 60-foot-long bridge that spans the central exhibit area. Information on unusual characteristics of hummingbirds such as plumage iridescence, wing speed and migration habits is well presented. The Reptile House, alive with crocodiles, has a placid jungle stream occasionally disturbed by simulated thunderstorms. In the two-acre Children's Zoo small animals may be fed and petted. A panoramic view of the grounds may be had from the elevated Safari Monorail. *Open daily except holidays. Adults $1.75, children small charge. Hummingbird Exhibit, Children's Zoo and Safari Monorail small additional charge.*

[Philadelphia Museum of Art] The classical portico of the great museum looms above the Schuylkill River and the equally classical Fairmount Water Works in this striking vista. The latter may be reopened as an aquarium.

Rodin Museum *22nd St. and Benjamin Franklin Pkwy.* Only the Musée Rodin in Paris, which was given his works and control over their casting by Rodin himself, contains a larger collection of the brilliant sculptor's pieces. Gathered here and given to the city by movie-maker Jules E. Mastbaum are 80 bronze casts, plus original marble and plaster sculptures and a number of drawings and watercolors. Passing by a bronze of *The Thinker*, one enters the museum (commissioned by Mr. Mastbaum and completed in 1929) through a gateway modeled after the facade of Rodin's home in

France. Among the other outstanding works are *Age of Bronze, St. John the Baptist Preaching, The Burghers of Calais* and *The Gates of Hell.* At Rodin's death in 1917, only a plaster cast of the last work had been made. It was first cast in bronze for the Philadelphia museum, in 1924. *Open daily. Small charge.*

St. Mark's Church *1625 Locust St.* This Episcopal church designed by John Notman is considered one of the best examples of early Gothic Revival architecture. Completed in 1849, its interior reveals a quiet restraint that is most evident in the open timber roof and unplastered walls of hammer-dressed stone. *Open daily.*

Samuel S. Fleisher Art Memorial *715-721 Catharine St.* The Romanesque styling of this former Episcopal church makes it an appropriate setting for the Romanesque and medieval religious art collected by Mr. Fleisher, an ardent teacher of art as well as a collector. Between the 1890s and his death in 1944 he acquired a number of fine 13th- and 14th-century French limestone statuaries, 15th- and 16th-century primitive paintings and Russian icons, and an outstanding German triptych of 1480. Above the right aisle of the church is a stained-glass window with three panels designed and executed by the American artist John La Farge. Adjacent to the church is the memorial's art school, where graphics, sculpture and paintings by contemporary artists, notably Baskin, Calder, Shahn and Chagall, are shown. *Open Mon.-Sat.*

Society Hill The popular name for the oldest residential area in Philadelphia derives from the Free Society of Traders, William Penn's land company which was located here. Today the official name for the area is Washington Square East, which signifies a bold urban redevelopment program that has substantially restored 25 blocks of historic homes and buildings. Most of these are private residences, but the ones listed here are open to the public.

HILL-PHYSICK-KEITH HOUSE *321 S. Fourth St.* Henry Hill, a wealthy importer of Madeira wine and sympathizer of the American Revolution, built this handsome brick mansion in 1786 and resided here until his death four years later. It later became the home of Dr. Philip Physick, the most respected American surgeon of his day. (His patients included Andrew Jackson and Chief Justice John Marshall.) The house is filled with superb examples of Federal furniture, including several fine Philadelphia pieces. Adjoining the house is a replica of an early-19th-century walled garden with statuary and serpentine brick paths. *Open Tues.-Sun. except Jan. 1 and Dec. 25. Small charge.*

PERELMAN ANTIQUE TOY MUSEUM *270 S. Second St.* This handsome 1758 brick house holds an intriguing array of more than 2000 antique American toys and children's banks, collected by the museum's founder, Leon J. Perelman. There are extensive collections of ingenious cast-iron mechanical banks that perform all sorts of tricks at the drop of a penny, rare hand-painted tin toys produced in the mid-1800s, and varied antique cap pistols (one Punch and Judy model is set off by Punch knocking Judy on the back). An exhibit of cast-iron toys—boats, fire engines, wagons, circus carts, planes and trains—illustrates the amazing variety of U.S. transportation since 1860. *Open daily except holidays. Small charge.*

POWEL HOUSE *244 S. Third St.* Colonial notables including Washington, Lafayette and John Adams dined and danced in this elegant Georgian town house, the finest of its kind in Philadelphia. It was the home of Samuel Powel, the last mayor of Philadelphia under the British and the first after Independence. Among the original furnishings on view are a sewing table presented to Mrs. Powel by Martha Washington, some fine china, 18th-century drapery fabric and a magnificent 1790 Waterford crystal chandelier. A charming 18th-century walled garden stands next to the house. *Open Tues.-Sun. Small charge.*

Ukrainian Catholic Cathedral of the Immaculate Conception *830 N. Franklin St.* In the heart of downtown Philadelphia is the world's largest Ukrainian Byzantine Rite Catholic church, an impressive edifice recognizable from afar by its massive gold dome rimmed with 32 stained-glass windows. While the architectural shapes used in the building are traditionally Byzantine, the cathedral is built of reinforced concrete and limestone. The interior decor reflects this same combination of modern materials and Byzantine style: the aluminum windows and concrete walls are embellished with mosaics, icons and wall paintings. The first two Ukrainian Catholic bishops in the U.S. are buried in the crypt. *Open daily.*

U.S.S. "Olympia" *Pier 11 North, Delaware Ave. and Race St.* The *Olympia* was part of the "New Navy" that launched U.S. steel and ship-building industries and signaled America's arrival as a world power in the 1890s. In 1898, during the Spanish-American War, the 344-foot cruiser under Commodore George Dewey served as the flagship of the American fleet that destroyed the Spanish flotilla in the Battle of Manila Bay. It was on convoy duty in World War I, and in 1921 brought back the body of the Unknown Soldier from France. Decommissioned a year later, the ship has

[*U.S.S.* Olympia] *The oldest steel-built American warship still afloat, the* Olympia *was launched in 1891 and saw service in the Spanish-American War. Now restored as a naval museum, it has also starred in movies.*

been restored; on view are Dewey's quarters, the dispensary, machine shop and engine room and exhibits pertaining to the ship during wartime: photographs, uniforms, medals, weapons, charts, contemporary newspaper accounts and the like. *Open Tues.-Sat. Jan.-early Apr., daily early Apr.-late Nov., Tues.-Sat. late Nov.-Dec. Small charge.*

University Museum *University of Pennsylvania, 33rd and Spruce Sts.* One of the world's most comprehensive collections of ancient and primitive art is housed here, with emphasis on Near East, Amerindian, African and Oceanic cultures. The museum since it was founded in 1877 has been a leader of archaeological and anthropological fieldwork. Among the fine holdings, many of which were discovered on expeditions sponsored by the museum, are the lapis lazuli, gold and carnelian works from the royal cemetery at Ur, Pre-Columbian gold objects from the Americas, a granite sphinx of Rameses II and bas-relief war horses from the T'ang Dynasty. *Open Tues.-Sun.*

Woodmere Art Gallery *9201 Germantown Ave.* The permanent collection of American and European painting and sculpture, Oriental rugs, porcelain, textiles and furniture was donated to the public by Charles Knox Smith and is displayed in his former home, a spacious Victorian (1867) residence. In addition there are contemporary American paintings, sculpture and graphics. *Open daily except holidays.*

[**131**] *In this humble frame house on a Camden back street the author of* Leaves of Grass *lived the last eight years of his life, dying in 1892. His greatest fame was posthumous, and his closing years were marked by poverty.*

130. Camden County Historical Society Buildings *Park Blvd. and Euclid Ave., Camden, N.J.* The society maintains Pomona Hall, built in 1726 by Joseph Cooper, Jr. This Georgian-style, red brick house is furnished with English and American 18th- and 19th-century antiques. In an adjoining building is the society's museum with exhibits of lighting devices, fire-fighting equipment, toys, military objects and uniforms dating from the American Revolution. Early American crafts such as spinning, candle-making, coopering and blacksmithing are displayed in "shops." The library contains an extensive collection of materials on the history of New Jersey and the Camden area. *Open Sun., Tues.-Fri.*

[**129.** *University Museum*] *As a leading sponsor of archaeological expeditions around the world, the University of Pennsylvania has acquired a remarkable collection of ancient and primitive art. One of the star attractions in its museum is this* Ram-in-the-Thicket, *exquisitely fashioned of gold, lapis lazuli, shell, wood and silver. It was unearthed from a royal tomb in the ancient Mesopotamian city of Ur of the Chaldees.*

131. Walt Whitman House *330 Mickle St., Camden, N.J.* The last eight years of Whitman's life (1884-92) were spent in this Victorian row house, which is sparsely furnished as it was during that period. The setting accurately reveals the modest circumstance in which this famous American poet lived his declining years. Of particular interest are the clothing, books, manuscripts, letters and other Whitman memorabilia. The house is maintained as a State Historic Shrine. *Open Tues.-Sun. and Mon. holidays. Small charge.*

132. Burlington County Court House *High St., Mt. Holly, N.J.* This elegantly proportioned Georgian building, erected in 1796, replaced the original county courthouse built in 1683. The Court House bell, cast in England in 1755, has been used to announce the opening of court sessions ever since it was installed some 170 years ago. Over the front doorway is a bas relief of the New Jersey Coat of Arms.

133. Batsto Historic Site *Rte. 542, Hammonton, N.J.* Batsto is a rare example of an early Industrial Revolution village which through a series of economic misfortunes has remained in its original state. A Mr. Charles Reed established a bog-iron furnace here in 1766. Soon the village became one of the most important iron-making centers in the country, producing domestic items such as pots and stoves and munitions for the Government during the Revolution and the War of 1812, and remained so until the discovery of coal in

Pennsylvania in the 1830s. The furnace owners tried to establish a second industry by opening a glass factory, but when that enterprise was closed in 1867 the economy of Batsto failed and it became a ghost town. Before the village had much time to decay, Joseph Wharton (the man who founded the U.S. nickel industry and the University of Pennsylvania School of Business) bought the whole village and surrounding acreage with the idea of damming the rivers and streams in the vicinity in order to supply water to Philadelphia. His scheme was overruled by the state legislature, and so Batsto lay dormant but not destroyed from the 1870s until 1954, when the state acquired the land and began restoration of the town. Visitors may visit Batsto Mansion, a 36-room, mainly Victorian structure with furnishings of the period, a blacksmith and wheelwright shop, sawmill, gristmill, workers' cottages, pig barn. The general store contains a collection of Batsto glass. *Open daily. Small charge.*

134. Greenwich, N.J. John Fenwick, a Quaker refugee from religious persecution in England, founded Greenwich in 1675, seven years earlier than the founding of nearby Philadelphia. Built on the banks of the Cohansey River, Greenwich was once a thriving shipping town and the scene in 1774 of the Greenwich Tea Party, during which a cargo of British tea was burned. The main thoroughfare of the town is Ye Greate Street, along which original 18th- and 19th-century houses still stand. With more than 40 places of interest, for both historic and architectural reasons, the village is listed in the National Register of Historic Places.

GIBBON HOUSE *Main St.* The Cumberland County Historical Society has restored this 1730 brick house built by merchant Nicholas Gibbon. On the first floor is a fully equipped Colonial kitchen dominated by the typically large cooking fireplace then in use. Three windows in an upstairs bedroom were bricked up to avoid the glass tax the British imposed on the colonies. The house is furnished with Colonial and early Victorian antiques. *Open daily except holidays. Small charge.*

135. Historic Towne of Smithville *Rte. 9, Smithville, N.J.* Smithville is a reconstructed early-19th-century southern New Jersey village. Some 60 buildings typical of the era were found in various parts of New Jersey and have been brought here and reestablished along the streets and the mall. Among them are the original Smithville Inn (1781), a one-time stagecoach stop (which is once again operated as a restaurant), an 1800 gristmill, a smokehouse and a cobbler's shop. Many of the structures are used as stores (selling typical 19th-century wares), while in others examples of early American arts and crafts (pewters, brass, furniture) are on display. An 1889 Chesapeake Bay oyster boat is moored on the town lake. *Open daily.*

136. Victorian Village *Cape May, N.J.* In Victorian horse and buggy days when only natural air conditioning was available, the long, cooling beaches of Cape May were popular among East Coast city dwellers with enough money to escape the summer heat. Large resort hotels and private homes were built in the spacious Victorian manner of the day. Many of these have been restored by the city of Cape May with the aid of a $3,000,000 Urban Renewal grant. Among the most interesting are those described below.

CHALFONTE HOTEL *Sewell Ave. and Howard St.* Chalfonte is an L-shaped clapboard building with first- and second-floor verandas, and a large cupola on the roof. The hotel has survived since it opened in 1876 with most of the elaborate Victorian trim and many of the original furnishings and fixtures intact—including marble-top dressers and globe lamps lighted by gas. The original tub and bowl remain in the bridal suite, one of the few accommodations with bathroom facilities. *Open July-Sept. Rates vary with accommodations.*

CONGRESS HALL *Beach and Perry Sts.* Several 19th-century Presidents vacationed here. The present hotel, built in 1879, occupies the site of a hotel dating back to 1816. It is of brick and the main decorative feature of the facade is a three-story-high veranda supported by delicate columns. *Open in summer. Rates vary with accommodations.*

EMLEN PHYSICK ESTATE *1048 Washington St.* Dr. Emlen Physick of Philadelphia built this 15-room home in 1877. The exterior of the clapboard structure is a jumble of chimneys, dormer windows and porches piled under a fish-scale roof. The interior decoration is typically heavy and ornate. The entrance hall and stairs are embellished with carved Romanesque posts and a screen; tiled fireplaces, carved mantels with mirrors, pressed leather wall coverings and plaster ceiling fixtures are found throughout the house.

PINK HOUSE *Perry St.* Pink House is a delightful example of a small frame Victorian house with gingerbread trim.

VICTORIAN MANSION *635 Columbia Ave.* Originally Victorian Mansion was a private club for gentlemen, built by Southern planters. The elegant proportions and restrained decoration are reminiscent of plantation homes. Slender columns support a three-sided veranda above full-length windows on the ground floor. Much of the furniture and fixtures are original, including cast-iron chandeliers, pier glasses and a large copper and enamel bathtub. *Open June-Sept. Small charge.*

[**136.** *Chalfonte Hotel*] *Visitors to Cape May during July and August can still enjoy the experience of staying in a genuine Victorian hotel, with most of its fixtures and furnishings—including gas lamps—unchanged since 1876.*

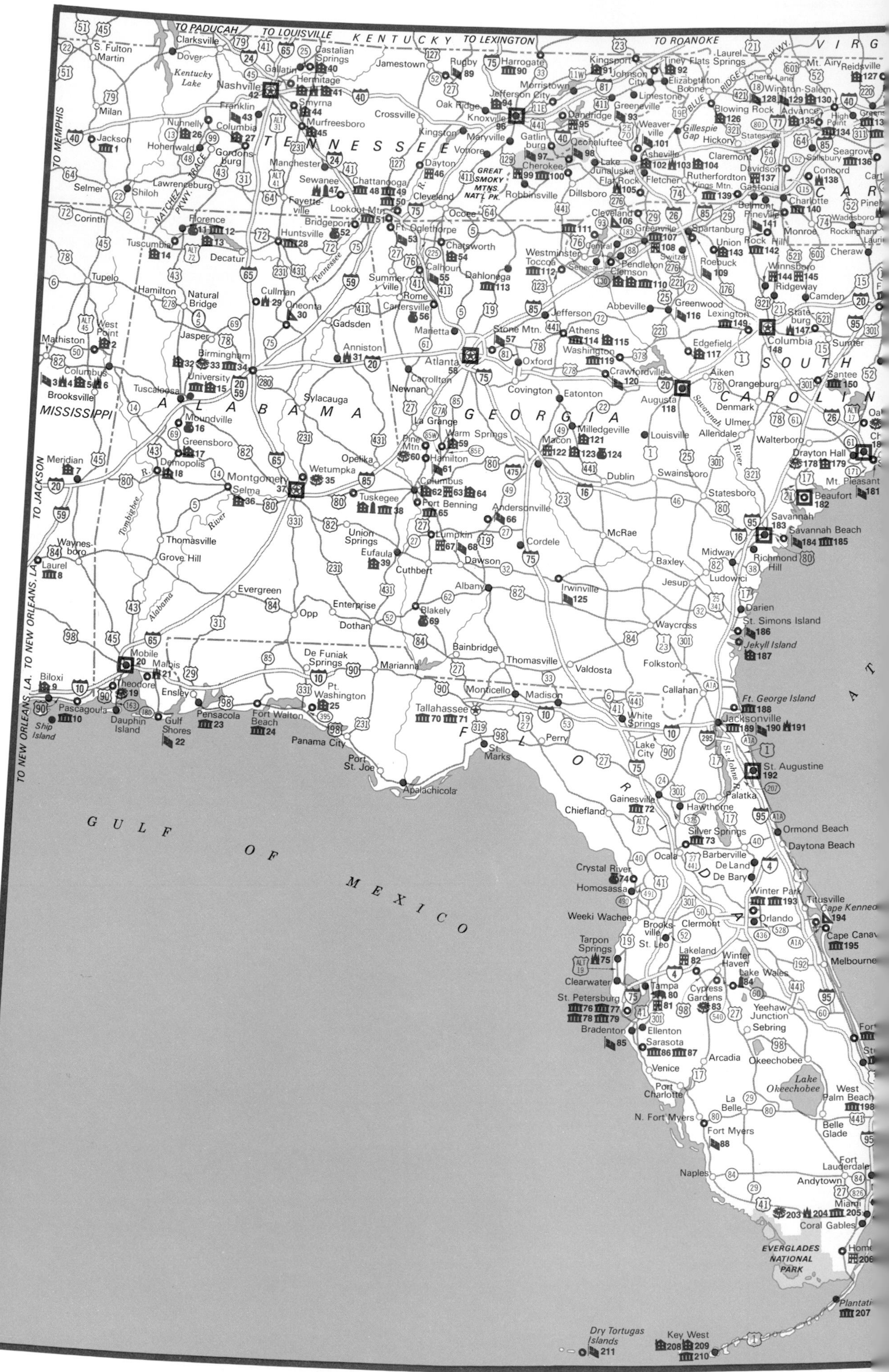
TO PADUCAH
TO LOUISVILLE
KENTUCKY
TO LEXINGTON
TO ROANOKE
TO MEMPHIS
TO JACKSON
TO NEW ORLEANS, LA.
TENNESSEE
ALABAMA
GEORGIA
MISSISSIPPI
FLORIDA
SOUTH CAROLINA
GULF OF MEXICO
GREAT SMOKY MTNS. NAT'L PK.
NATCHEZ TRACE PKWY.
BLUE RIDGE PKWY.
Kentucky Lake
Clarksville
Nashville
Gallatin
Castalian Springs
Hermitage
Franklin
Smyrna
Murfreesboro
Columbia
Jackson
Hohenwald
Gordonsburg
Manchester
Sewanee
Chattanooga
Jamestown
Rugby
Harrogate
Crossville
Oak Ridge
Knoxville
Kingston
Maryville
Vonore
Dayton
Cleveland
Lookout Mtn.
Kingsport
Johnson City
Elizabethton
Greeneville
Morristown
Jefferson City
Dandridge
Gatlinburg
Oconaluftee
Cherokee
Asheville
Lake Junaluska
Flat Rock
Robbinsville
Dillsboro
Boone
Blowing Rock
Winston-Salem
Charlotte
Gastonia
Shiloh
Corinth
Florence
Tuscumbia
Decatur
Huntsville
Tupelo
Hamilton
Natural Bridge
Cullman
Oneonta
Gadsden
Jasper
West Point
Birmingham
Anniston
Columbus
Tuscaloosa
Brooksville
Moundville
Greensboro
Demopolis
Meridian
Montgomery
Selma
Wetumpka
Tuskegee
Opelika
Sylacauga
Thomasville
Grove Hill
Evergreen
Waynesboro
Laurel
Mobile
Theodore
Biloxi
Pascagoula
Dauphin Island
Gulf Shores
Pensacola
Fort Walton Beach
Panama City
Atlanta
Marietta
Rome
Calhoun
Chatsworth
Dahlonega
Stone Mtn.
Athens
Washington
Crawfordville
Augusta
Macon
Milledgeville
Columbus
La Grange
Warm Springs
Pine Mtn
Lumpkin
Eufaula
Albany
Irwinville
Savannah
Savannah Beach
Jekyll Island
St. Simons Island
Columbia
Spartanburg
Greenville
Clemson
Charleston
Beaufort
Tallahassee
Marianna
Jacksonville
St. Augustine
Gainesville
Ocala
Silver Springs
Daytona Beach
Orlando
Winter Park
Cape Kennedy
Tampa
St. Petersburg
Clearwater
Bradenton
Sarasota
Fort Myers
Naples
Lake Okeechobee
West Palm Beach
Miami
Coral Gables
EVERGLADES NATIONAL PARK
Key West
Dry Tortugas Islands

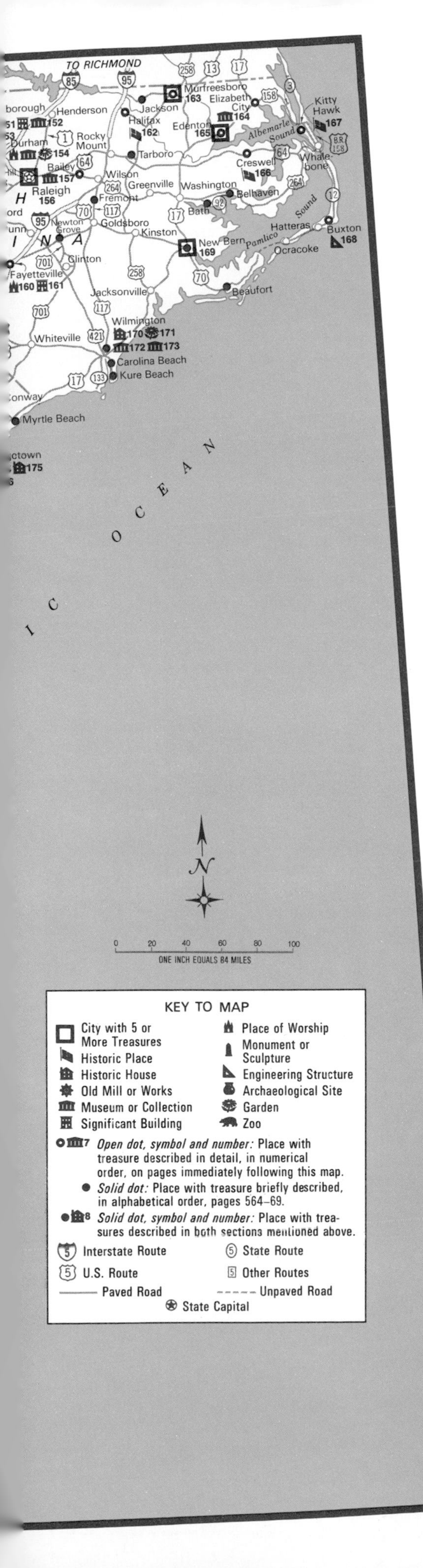

Prehistoric Indian mounds, Spanish forts, Georgian town houses, plantation homes, frontier mountain cabins, the Kennedy Space Center: the architecture is a reminder that this is a region whose treasures span hundreds of centuries and a fascinating diversity of peoples and cultures.

1. Casey Jones Home and Railroad Museum *211 W. Chester St., Jackson, Tenn.* Casey Jones, the railroad hero of song and story, was a real person. As the ballad says, he drove Engine No. 382—a 10-wheeled steam locomotive—to his death on April 30, 1900. A duplicate of the engine stands on the property of Jones's home, a simple cottage furnished as it was when he died. Although the house has been made a museum, it provides an accurate picture of the turn-of-the-century working man's home environment. An exact copy of Casey's "whip-poor-will" whistle (made by his son), telegraph instruments, lanterns, early dining-car menus and other memorabilia can be seen here. *Open daily. Small charge.*

2. Waverley Mansion *Off Rte. 50, West Point, Miss.* Colonel George Hampton Young, an admirer of Sir Walter Scott, named his lavish plantation house after the author's Waverley novels. Completed in 1852, the house took five years to build because of its size—8000 square feet—and Colonel Young's insistence on quality workmanship and the finest materials. Within are marble fireplaces and steps, intricate plaster and ironwork, hand-turned stair-rail spindles and red Venetian glass. The interior stairwell rises 65 feet from front entry to an octagonal cupola. The cupola served as a lookout over the plantation and, with windows open, drew off hot summer air—a kind of natural air conditioning. The house was restored by Mr. and Mrs. Robert Snow, Jr. in the 1960s. *Open daily. Small charge.*

3. Columbus, Miss. Originally having the unprepossessing name of Possum Town, this quiet river community was renamed Columbus in 1821. Its landed gentry thrived during the next century on the production and sale of cotton. In the early 19th century these families built large homes, often in the then popular Greek Revival style, and settled down to a gracious life in town. More than 100 of their residences remain standing, many owned by descendants of the original occupants. The impressive stately facades and gardens line broad streets in the historic center of town. Thirty or so may be seen on a walk from Second to Fifth Streets between Second Avenue and Eighth Avenue South and from Seventh Street North to Ninth Street North between Third and Seventh Avenues. Many of these homes are open to the public during Columbus's annual Pilgrimage Week, and by private appointment with the Chamber of Commerce at other times. Some of the pre-Civil War churches are also worth noting.

4. Annunciation Catholic Church *808 College St., Columbus, Miss.* This brick-and-stucco-faced Catholic church marked its 100th anniversary in 1963. Among its embellishments are lovely stained-glass windows and a 40-foot sky-blue ceiling with a medallionlike cluster of angels around a dove. *Open daily.*

5. Blewett-Harrison-Lee Home *316 Seventh St., N., Columbus, Miss.* Major Thomas G. Blewett built this two-story red brick house in the mid-1840s. It was later owned by his granddaughter, Regina Harrison, who married General Stephen D. Lee, the officer who gave the order for the first shot to be fired on Fort Sumter and thus began the Civil War. The architecture is an unusual blend of Georgian and Greek Revival. Of particular interest is the elaborate iron grillwork of the columns and railings on the front porch. Some of the handsome period furnishings and silver in the house had formerly belonged to the Blewett and Lee families. The home is used as the headquarters of the Pilgrimage tour each spring. *Open Tues., Thurs.*

6. First United Methodist Church *602 Main St., Columbus, Miss.* Built in 1860, this red brick, white steepled church is one of the oldest in Mississippi. The sanctuary is located on the second floor and has a balcony originally used for slaves. *Open Sun.-Fri.*

7. Merrehope *905 31st Ave., Meridian, Miss.* The core of this 26-room Greek Revival house was built in 1859 by Juriah McLemore Jackson and her husband, daughter and son-in-law of the first settler of what is now the city of Meridian. Subsequent owners added to and changed the initial structure, until the house reached its present size in 1904. Nine stately columns support the portico, and the interior features double parlors divided by columns. The house is furnished with Empire pieces, several of which are exceptional. Special events include "Trees of Christmas" decorated with hundreds of handmade ornaments and displayed for 10 days in December, and an antique show and sale in early May. *Open Tues.-Sun. Small charge.*

8. Lauren Rogers Library and Museum of Art *Fifth Ave. and Seventh St., Laurel, Miss.* More than 15,000 volumes are shelved in this library. There are books on art, genealogy, Mississippiana and nature, and a magnificent seven-volume set of the 1840 edition of John James Audubon's *Birds of America.* In the museum wings are exhibited over 600 baskets, including the handiwork of more than 45 American Indian tribes, as well as Indian clothes and jewelry. Fine paintings by American and European artists are also on display. *Open Tues.-Sun. except holidays.*

9. Beauvoir *Rte. 90, 5 mi. W. of Biloxi, Miss.* See feature display on page 247.

10. Spanish Fort Museum *4602 Fort St., Pascagoula, Miss.* Not a fort in the traditional mold, nor built by the Spanish, the museum is quite possibly the oldest standing building in the Mississippi Valley. Built in 1718 by French settlers as a carpentry shop, it was routinely fortified against Indian attack. Its 18-inch-thick walls are made of tabby brick. From 1780 to 1810 the building served as a Spanish military outpost and subsequently was known as the Old Spanish Fort. The museum contains 18th-century artifacts from the area. *Open daily. Small charge.*

11. Indian Mound and Museum *S. Court St., Florence, Ala.* Rising to 42 feet with a quadrilateral base, this Mississippi Culture mound is believed to have been built about 1200 A.D. and is the Tennessee Valley's largest domiciliary mound. On the grounds is a museum with displays of Indian artifacts, some of which date back 10,000 years. Audio-visual aids give the history of Indians in the region and in other areas of North America. *Open Tues.-Sun. Small charge.*

Tall windows look out on a veranda surrounding the front of Beauvoir, named for its fine view over the Gulf.

9. Beauvoir

Rte. 90, 5 mi. W. of Biloxi, Miss.

Twelve years after the Civil War ended, the former President of the Confederate States, Jefferson Davis, came to Beauvoir for a visit. A year later he bought the gracious one-and-a-half-story house overlooking the Gulf and moved in with his wife and one daughter. Davis was still a symbol of the old South and he held a special place in the hearts of Southerners. Until his death in 1889 the house was a social center for the Davises' many friends and admirers. In 1941 the house, the outbuildings and the 82 surrounding acres were restored. Much of the original furniture was found and put back in place, so that Beauvoir now looks as it did in the time of the Davis family. The Davis museum in the lower part of the house and the excellent small library are of value to anyone interested in the South in the mid-19th century. *Open daily except Dec. 25. Adults $2.00, children over 8 small charge.*

For three years Mr. Davis labored on writing his view of the Rise and Fall of the Confederate Government, *a copy of which is pictured above. At the left is the Library of East Cottage where he worked. A similar cottage on the other side of the house was furnished and kept for the Davises' married daughter, Margaret Davis Hayes.*

12. Pope's Tavern *Seminary St. and Hermitage Dr., Florence, Ala.* The tavern, built in the early 1800s, later served as a hospital during the Civil War. Still displaying the early glass in its windows, it now contains antique furniture and a museum collection. The grounds include flower, vegetable and herb gardens. *Open Tues.-Sat. Small charge.*

13. W. C. Handy Home and Museum *W. College St., Florence, Ala.* This humble log cabin was the birthplace of the "Father of the Blues" whose genius made the "St. Louis Blues," "Beale Street Blues" and other compositions part of America's musical heritage. In the adjoining museum are Handy's piano, trumpet, library and many of his awards. *Open Tues.-Sat. Small charge.*

14. Ivy Green (Birthplace of Helen Keller) *300 W. North Commons, Tuscumbia, Ala.* Within two years of her birth in 1880, Helen Keller was stricken with a disease that left her deaf and blind. The remarkable and moving story of how her dedicated teacher Anne Sullivan helped her surmount these severe handicaps is perpetuated here. The tiny cottage where Miss Keller lived and studied as a child is adjacent to the main house. Her braille library and typewriter plus many other mementos are displayed along with family furnishings. The grounds include the well where Miss Keller first learned the meaning of words when water was splashed on her hand as her teacher tapped out the letters for the word "water." *Open daily. Small charge.*

15. University of Alabama *University, Ala.* Founded in 1831, this university was practically destroyed by fire during a Union raid in 1865. Among the buildings that survived are a Norman-style round tower and the President's Mansion, built about 1840 in Greek Revival style.

ALABAMA MUSEUM OF NATURAL HISTORY *Smith Hall* The museum, established in 1848, holds a display of tools, weapons, pottery and other artifacts from a number of Central and South American and South Pacific cultures. Many fossils and minerals are also exhibited, and dioramas illustrate several geological periods. The Hodges meteorite, which fell on Sylacauga in 1954, can also be seen here. *Open daily during academic sessions.*

GORGAS HOUSE Two curved iron stairways rise to the veranda of this 1829 brick house, the first building on the campus. Originally used as a dining hall, it was redesigned as a residence around 1840. It is named for Confederate General Josiah Gorgas, who became president of the university in 1878. Period furnishings and an interesting collection of Spanish Colonial silver that belonged to Mrs. William C. Gorgas are displayed. *Open daily except holiday weekends.*

[19] *This may look like a photograph of a live wood thrush feeding its young among the azaleas, but the birds and the flowers are porcelain. A large collection of Edward Marshall Boehm's famous porcelain sculptures is on display in the Visitors' Lounge, enhancing the bird sanctuary aspect of the Bellingrath Gardens.*

16. Mound State Monument and Museum *Moundville, Ala.* Little imagination is needed to visualize the community of mound-building Indians that flourished here about 700 years ago. Forty mounds can be seen in the vicinity. The tallest of these earth platforms, a temple mound, rises 60 feet. Today visitors can climb to a reconstructed temple and see what religious rites were performed here. Daily Indian life is vividly revealed in the artifacts of the museum and in five huts containing life-size figures. *Open daily except Dec. 25. Small charge.*

17. Magnolia Grove *Rte. 14, Greensboro, Ala.* Admiral Richard P. Hobson, whose heroism during the Spanish-American War won him a belated Congressional Medal of Honor in 1934, was born in this handsome 1838 mansion. The house features bricks made by hand on the estate, cast-iron Corinthian columns along the back and an unsupported winding staircase. Many furnishings and much of the silver are family belongings, and a museum room holds Admiral Hobson's collection of souvenirs from foreign countries. *Open daily.*

18. Bluff Hall *Commissioners Ave., Demopolis, Ala.* Made of brick and stucco, this house was later modified by the addition of Greek Revival details. It was constructed in 1832 for Francis S. Lyon, a prominent lawyer who served in the U.S. and the Confederate congresses. The simple entrance facade has six large square portico columns and is embellished by a handsome door that includes a fanlight and glass side panels. Corinthian columns and pilasters in the drawing room and an ornamented dining room ceiling are among the interior attractions. *Open Sun. Small charge.*

19. Bellingrath Gardens and Home *Off Rte. 90, Theodore, Ala.* Out of a wilderness fishing camp 20 miles from Mobile, Mr. and Mrs. Walter D. Bellingrath created this magnificent estate, which now belongs to the Bellingrath-Morse Foundation. Constantly changing floral displays create a blaze of color throughout the year. The azaleas of early spring, over 200 varieties, some 20 feet high, are particularly spectacular, but are closely rivaled by the camellias, chrysanthemums and poinsettias that brighten other seasons. Special gardens dotting the 65-acre site include a rock garden planted with African violets, an Oriental garden and a fine rose garden. The Bellingrath mansion, of handmade brick with handsome iron grillwork accents, was completed in 1935. Its beautiful furnishings include fine antique pieces, silver, crystal and china. *Open daily. Gardens: adults $2.40, children over 6 $1.20; home: $3.00.*

20. Mobile, Ala.

Mobile's location at the head of Mobile Bay has been the chief factor in her development. Before becoming part of the U.S., the port was controlled by France, Great Britain and Spain, and the city reflects the cultures of these three nations. Today ships leave Mobile for worldwide ports, and shipbuilding is one of her main industries.

Battleship "Alabama" Memorial Park *Battleship Pkwy.* State residents saved the 680-foot U.S.S. *Alabama* from scrapping in 1962, and visitors can board this warship to see the captain's and crew's quarters, engine room, wheelhouse, bridge and other interesting aspects of the ship. The turrets of its 16- and 5-inch guns can also be entered. Launched in 1942 and assigned to North Atlantic convoy duty, this ship later supported landings at Tarawa, Saipan and Okinawa and led the U.S. fleet into Tokyo Bay. Also moored at the edge of this 75-acre park is the World War II submarine U.S.S. *Drum;* nearby are displays of Air Force, Coast Guard and Navy planes plus Army field equipment from World War II and Korea. *Open daily. Adults and children over 11 $2.00, children 6–11 small charge.*

Church Street East Historic District Some 70 19th-century buildings of historic and architectural interest can be seen in this area, including private homes, churches and structures adapted as offices, restaurants, hotels, shops and museums. Ornamental cast-iron verandas from the Gothic Revival era decorate many facades, but many of the buildings pre-date this period. Of particular interest along Government Street are the Presbyterian Church (1836) in the Greek Revival style; the Gaines-Quigley House (about 1860); and Barton Academy (1836), the state's first public school and hospital during the Civil War. Once used as a courthouse and jail, the Fort Conde-Charlotte House on Theatre Street has an interesting porch with Tuscan and Corinthian columns and a curious crowfoot railing design. Its rooms are furnished with 18th- and 19th-century pieces. The Church Street Graveyard, established in 1819, contains fascinating headstones and monuments, some inscribed in French and Spanish.

[**20.** *Battleship Memorial Park*] *Gangways provide visitors with access to the 35,000-ton U.S.S.* Alabama, *which won nine battle stars in the Pacific during World War II—and to its neighbor, the submarine U.S.S.* Drum.

[**20.** *Oakleigh*] *Set on a high point of land, the beautiful old house with its raised main floor is well adapted to a warm climate. The T-shape provides many rooms with exposure on three sides to any possible breeze.*

Mobile Art Gallery *Langan Park* The gallery building is characterized by a modern interpretation of the Moorish arch, a motif increasingly popular in Southern architecture. Founded in 1964, the gallery has built up impressive collections of 19th- and 20th-century American and European paintings and prints and of wood engravings. *Open daily except holidays.*

Oakleigh *350 Oakleigh Pl.* Sited serenely in a grove of the oaks for which it was named, the house, begun in 1833, has an unusual cantilevered outside staircase. It is furnished with Empire, Regency and early Victorian pieces. A Sully portrait is in the back parlor along with an interesting collection of silver and 19th-century jewelry. Oakleigh serves as headquarters for the Historic Mobile Preservation Society. *Open daily early Jan.–late Dec. Adults $1.25, children small charge.*

Phoenix Fire Station *203 S. Claiborne St.* Built in 1859 for the Phoenix Volunteer Fire Company, this handsome two-story brick structure with stone quoins was restored in 1964. Among its attractive features are a louvered cupola, a delicate iron balcony railing and a second-story ballroom. Old steam fire engines and fire fighting equipment dating from 1819 plus a collection of silver and china are on display. *Open Tues.–Sun.*

21. Malbis Memorial Church *Rte. 90, Malbis, Ala.* This brick and marble church commemorates the founding of the Greek Orthodox community at Malbis in the early 1900s. Modeled after a church in Athens, the 1965 edifice is strongly Byzantine in style. Among its most notable features are more than 100 hand-painted wall and ceiling murals, mosaics and hand-carved figures, imported Greek marble and 75-foot dome. The vivid colors of the interior are further enhanced by the unusual stained-glass windows. *Open daily.*

22. Fort Morgan *Rte. 180, Gulf Shores, Ala.* One of Napoleon's engineering officers designed this brick star-shaped fort which took 15 years to build (1819–1834). The third largest fort in the U.S., it is noted for its fine masonry and graceful arches. Over the entrance fly flags of Spain, France, England, Alabama (the Republic and the state), the Confederacy and the U.S., reflecting the political influences exerted over the area at various periods. Held by Confederate forces in 1861, the fort was captured by the Union three years later after the Battle of Mobile Bay. As late as World War II it was used as a military installation. The museum here has photographs of the fort showing the damage inflicted during the 18-day siege of 1864, later repaired. Excellent collections of guns, maps and military uniforms are among the museum's other displays. *Open daily except Dec. 25.*

23. Naval Aviation Museum *Naval Air Station, Pensacola, Fla.* Pensacola has been a navy base since President John Quincy Adams ordered this naval yard built in 1825. Since 1914 it has been the U.S. Naval Air Station. The museum here tells the story of American naval aviation from its beginning in 1911 to the present. On display are a variety of actual aircraft as well as engines, weapons, equipment, combat paintings and scale models of aircraft flown by naval aviators since 1911. Also here is the spacecraft Aurora 7, in which astronaut Scott Carpenter went into earth orbit in 1962. *Open Tues.–Sun. except holidays.*

24. Indian Temple Mound Museum *Rtes. 98 and 85, Fort Walton Beach, Fla.* The museum is next to Temple Mound, a National Historic Landmark and park, and contains Indian relics unearthed from the mound as well as other artifacts and exhibits that depict 10,000 years of Indian life in the Gulf Coast area. The earth mound was built about 1250 A.D. It was painstakingly erected with 500,000 basketloads of soil and has been restored to its original form. *Open Tues.–Sun. Adults and children over 9 small charge.*

[23] *Aviation progress in the course of 40 years is aptly summed up in this juxtaposition of the FF-1 Grumman fighter of the 1930s and an astronaut's space suit of the 1970s; both may be seen in the museum.*

25. Eden *1 mi. N. of Rte. 98, Point Washington, Fla.* William Henry Wesley, a lumber baron, built this plantation-style mansion in 1895. The two-story white frame house is surrounded on three sides by a veranda supported by large pillars. The interior reflects many styles, with European and American furnishings dating from the 1600s to the Victorian age. Among the period rooms are a Louis XVI drawing room, a library furnished in American Empire style, a Victorian bedroom and an Empire dining room. Handmade antique toys can be seen in a children's bedroom. Within Eden's parklike setting there are landscaped gardens, flowering trees and shrubs and gigantic old moss-covered oaks. *Open daily. Small charge.*

26. Pinewood Mansion *Rte. 48, Nunnelly, Tenn.* Samuel L. Graham built an Italian Renaissance mansion on his 6500-acre plantation just after the Civil War, decorating the interior walls and ceilings with elaborate plaster friezes. A sweeping staircase of Cuban mahogany is the focal point of this house, which has been fully restored and refurbished in a grand mid-19th century manner. *Open daily. Small charge.*

27. James Knox Polk Ancestral Home *301 W. Seventh St., Columbia, Tenn.* Our 11th President spent much of his boyhood in this elegant house, built by his father, Samuel Polk, in 1816. The house is a lesson in good craftmanship, with fine wide-board hand-pegged floors, carefully mortised window frames and hand-shaped bricks. Many of the furnishings were collected from other James Polk residences. Particularly interesting are such personal items as the National Fan, which Polk presented to his wife just before his inauguration. Its blue and gold surface is decorated with circular portraits of the first 11 U.S. Presidents. Also on exhibit are pieces of Presidential china displaying the American shield and seal, and a circular table, given to Polk when he retired as President, which has 30 white stars and the American Eagle inlaid on its Egyptian marble top. *Open daily except Dec. 25. Small charge.*

28. Burritt Museum *3131 Burritt Dr., Monte Sano Mountain, S.E., Huntsville, Ala.* This unusual 11-room house was built in the shape of a Maltese cross by Dr. William H. Burritt, who willed it to the city of Huntsville. The museum contains many items of regional historic interest, including ancient Indian artifacts, early medical and surveying equipment, toys, clothing and Civil War relics. A collection of color photographs shows wildflowers that grow in the vicinity. The Howard Weeden Room commemorates Maria Howard Weeden (1847–1905), Huntsville's most famous artist, whose poems and paintings portray the spirit of the Negroes who lived in the area before the Civil War. The scenic acres that surround the museum are sprinkled with wildflowers and more formal plantings, and there is a pioneer homestead on the grounds. *Open Tues.–Sun. Mar.–Nov.*

[27] *President James Polk gave this fan to his wife to complete the costume she wore at his Inauguration. Portraits of the first 11 Presidents are on one side, the signing of the Declaration of Independence on the other.*

29. Ave Maria Grotto *St. Bernard College, E. of Cullman, Ala.* More than 125 miniature buildings in stone and concrete are grouped on a landscaped hillside. They are replicas of churches, shrines and secular buildings from the Holy Land, Rome, the American Southwest and elsewhere. This creation represents many long years of effort by a Benedictine monk who also helped build the large stone Ave Maria Grotto that stands surrounded by these small structures and gives the entire site its name. *Open daily. Adults and children over 6 small charge.*

30. Horton Mill Covered Bridge *Rte. 75, N. of Oneonta, Ala.* This long wooden bridge was built in 1934. Restored and listed on the National Register, it is higher above the water—some 70 feet above a branch of the Warrior River—than any other covered bridge in the U.S. A picnic area and nature trails with many native plants form part of the attractive site. *Open daily.*

31. Church of St. Michael and All Angels *18th St. and Cobb Ave., Anniston, Ala.* Dedicated in 1890, this Norman Gothic Episcopal church, built of Alabama sandstone, contains several stained-glass windows depicting events in the life of Christ—the blank back wall symbolizes the 18-year-period of Christ's life about which little is known—a distinctive Italian marble altar and an alabaster reredos crowned by the figures of seven angels. Hand-carved ceiling braces and struts resemble the ribs of a ship, and their ends are decorated with angel heads. A 95-foot tower holds 12 bells. *Open daily.*

32. Arlington Antebellum Home and Gardens *331 Cotton Ave., S.W., Birmingham, Ala.* Late in the Civil War, a female Confederate spy is believed to have hidden in the attic of this eight-room mansion during its occupancy by Union General James H. Wilson. Constructed in its present form in the 1840s as an enlargement of a four-room dwelling built about 1820, its gracious Greek Revival styling includes six tapered square columns at the entrance portico. Pre-Civil War furniture can be seen inside, and the grounds feature more than six acres of period gardens, lawns and old magnolias. Annual events include an old-fashioned country fair held on the grounds in the fall and a festival in the mansion at Christmastime. *Open Tues.-Sun. except Jan. 1 and Dec. 25. Small charge.*

33. Birmingham Botanical Gardens *2612 Lane Park Rd., Birmingham, Ala.* Seven acres of Japanese gardens, complete with bridges, stone lanterns and a tea house donated by the Japanese government, can be enjoyed here. Other beautiful elements within the 67-acre area are the Wildflower Garden, one of the world's few floral clocks, a formal terrace walk and mass plantings of iris, daylilies and 125 varieties of roses. The Touch and See Trail for the blind is an outstanding feature, and a conservatory offers seasonal displays plus permanent exhibits of cacti and camellias. Facilities include a good library, a herbarium and a 500-seat auditorium. *Open daily.*

34. Birmingham Museum of Art *Eighth Ave. and 20th St., N., Birmingham. Ala.* Nearly 7000 objects, from ancient Egyptian artifacts to oils by contemporary artists, are housed in this functional modern (1959) building set off by formal plantings. Among the museum's notable collections are an impressive group of Italian Renaissance paintings, European paintings of the 17th through 19th centuries, craftwork by North American Indians, primitive art of the South Seas and a glittering collection of English and American silver. *Open daily except Jan. 1 and Dec. 25.*

35. Jasmine Hall Gardens *Off Rte. 231, S. of Wetumpka, Ala.* This privately-owned garden is best known for its copies of ancient Greek and Roman statuary. Included here are a replica *Winged Victory of Samothrace* and a good copy of the Temple of Hera in Greece. Visitors can also see original terra cotta lions, piping Pans and Venetian iron gates. *Open daily.*

36. Sturdivant Hall *713 Mabry St., Selma, Ala.* Fine Hepplewhite, Chippendale and Sheraton furniture can

[34] *An urn carved in the shape of the rain god by Zapotec Indians of Mexico in the 8th century is a feature of the Birmingham museum's collection of Pre-Columbian art. There are also fine Chimu gold objects from Peru.*

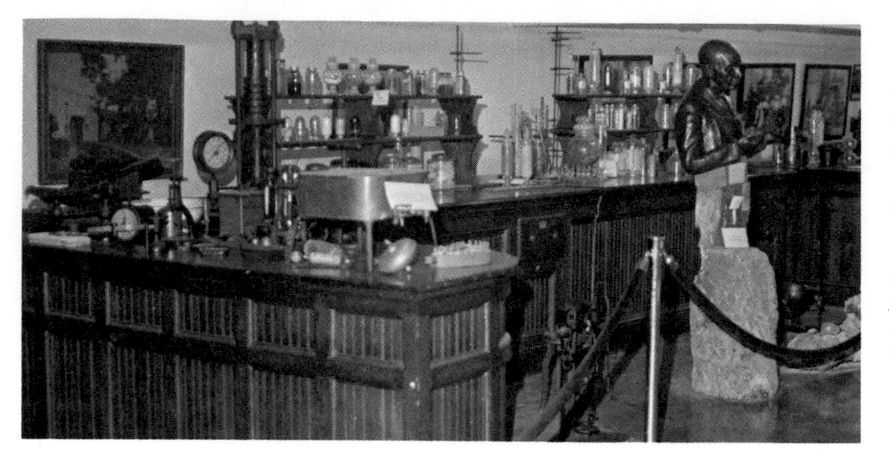

[**38.** *Carver Museum*] *Even in obtaining his laboratory equipment Dr. Carver demonstrated his ingenuity. His first laboratory, exhibited in the museum, was fashioned from discarded materials. With such crude apparatus he began the research that resulted in hundreds of new uses for the peanut, the sweet potato and even the clay from which they grew.*

be admired in this restored 1853 white-plastered brick house of neoclassic design. It also contains Indian relics and local genealogical material. The kitchen with its open hearth, the slave quarters, a smokehouse and a wine cellar can also be seen. *Open daily except Dec. 25. Adults and children over 12 small charge.*

37. Montgomery, Ala.

Alabama's capital was also the first capital of the Confederacy. Its many antebellum homes recall the days when it was a rich cotton market. Today Montgomery is one of the South's chief distribution points.

Alabama Chamber of Commerce Building *468 S. Perry St.* Also known as the Teague House, this 1848 Greek Revival brick mansion, with six Ionic columns supporting the entrance portico, retains much of its original charm, and has influenced the architecture of many other buildings in Montgomery. Early lighting fixtures and an attractive stairway can be seen on the ground floor, where the rooms are furnished with Empire and early Victorian pieces. *Open Mon.-Fri. except holidays.*

Alabama State Capitol *Bainbridge Ave. at E. end of Dexter Ave.* In this building the Confederate States of America came into being. Here, in 1861, the new government's first congress convened, adopted a constitution and chose a president—and Montgomery became the first capital of the Confederacy. Ten years earlier this National Historic Landmark had been erected on the foundations of the previous state capitol, which was destroyed by fire. The white building is T-shaped, three wings having been added to its square central portion. Six Corinthian columns support the three-story-high roof of the entrance portico—a bronze star marks the spot where Jefferson Davis stood as he was inaugurated President of the Confederacy—and an immense dome crowns this magnificent example of the Greek Revival style. In the interior, two free-standing, self-supporting spiral staircases twist to the third story; inside the dome 13-foot-high canvases showing key events of Alabama's history may be viewed from a balcony that circles the dome's interior. The hexagonal Senate Chamber remains almost unchanged from the days when it seated the first Confederate congress, as does the House of Representatives Chamber, the scene of Alabama's secession convention. On the grounds a nine-foot statue of Davis stands amid trees that were brought here from several Civil War battlefields. *Open daily except holidays.*

CONFEDERATE MONUMENT In 1886, on the north lawn, Jefferson Davis laid the cornerstone for this marble column flanked at four corners by life-size statues of Confederate soldiers and sailors. It is topped by a bronze figure of a woman laying down a sword and lifting a Confederate flag.

First White House of the Confederacy *Washington and Union Sts.* In 1861 Jefferson Davis and his family lived in this 1825 two-story clapboard dwelling for three months prior to the relocation of the Confederacy's capital to Richmond, Virginia. It was dedicated as a museum in 1921 after being moved to its present location. The house contains many personal belongings of the Davis family and features a shrine bearing a portrait of Davis. *Open daily except holidays.*

Murphy House *22 Bibb St.* This impressive Greek Revival structure was built in 1851 by a Virginian cotton merchant. The marble-floored portico has six massive fluted Corinthian columns, and a lovely cast-iron balcony overhangs the main entrance. The parlor is notable for its shell-patterned gilt cornices and Italian marble mantels carved with rose and grape designs. Among the Confederate leaders who visited the house was Jefferson Davis; Union forces occupied it immediately after the Confederacy's collapse. The building is now used for offices by a branch of the municipal government. *Open Mon.-Fri. except holidays.*

Ordeman-Shaw Complex *309 N. Hull St.* This complex comprises several houses restored to their original pre-Civil War condition. Visitors can admire authentic furniture from different periods and derive a sense of the life-style that prevailed here in the 1850s. *Open Tues.-Sun. except holidays. Adults $1.25, children small charge.*

DEWOLF-COOPER COTTAGE The Gothic-style building was completed in the 1850s by the publisher of the *Montgomery Advertiser* and presently serves as information center for the Montgomery Chamber of Commerce. Exhibits and a film on the history of the city may be seen, and tickets are available here for a tour of the complex.

ORDEMAN-SHAW HOUSE The Italian styling of this house gives it an attractive contemporary look that belies its age. Built between 1848 and 1853 by Charles Ordeman, a German architect and engineer, it contains several furniture styles of the period. The grounds include a number of interesting features such as the gardens, slave quarters, carriage house and other dependencies.

38. Tuskegee Institute *Tuskegee, Ala.* This coeducational professional and technical college was founded in 1881 by Booker T. Washington. From meager beginnings as a slave, he had risen to international prominence as an educator and spokesman for his people. Early students here were taught vocational subjects as well as liberal arts.

BOOKER T. WASHINGTON HOME Known as The Oaks, this rambling house of handmade bricks from the Institute's yard was completed in 1899. Washington's den holds several pieces of his furniture, including a hand-carved desk from the Orient. The building is now used as headquarters for the Institute's Office of Institutional Development. *Open Mon.-Fri.*

BOOKER T. WASHINGTON MONUMENT The heroic figure of the Institute's founder is shown removing the veil of ignorance from a crouching black man. The granite base of this eight-foot bronze monument, completed in 1922, is inscribed with quotations from the writings of the great educator.

GEORGE WASHINGTON CARVER MUSEUM In 1896 George Washington Carver became director of the Department of Agriculture at the Institute. Examples of his varied achievements are displayed in this brick building along with a number of awards he received. Samples of African art and dioramas showing contributions made to civilization by blacks can also be seen. A library holds many books and pamphlets on the cultures of Africa. *Open daily.*

39. Shorter Mansion *340 N. Eufaula Ave., Eufaula, Ala.* Good pieces of 18th- and early 19th-century furniture and a local historical museum can be seen inside this fine example of Greek Revival architecture. Built in 1906, its features include capitals on the portico columns and an elaborately carved design beneath the cornice and balustraded roof. *Open daily. Small charge.*

40. Cragfont *Castalian Springs, Tenn.* This large, austere house, built in 1798 for General James Winchester, is constructed of hand-chiseled stone, handmade brick and timbers hewn on the property. It is a good example of the transitional style between pioneer cabin and pillared mansion. General Winchester, a commander in the War of 1812, pioneer settler of Sumner County and one of the founders of Memphis, is said to have entertained Andrew Jackson and Lafayette here. Carefully restored, the house contains some lovely antiques, many from the Winchester family, and none later than 1825. *Open Tues.-Sun. mid-April-Oct. Small charge.*

41. Historic Hermitage Properties *Rachel's Lane, Hermitage, Tenn.* Andrew Jackson, seventh President of the U.S., made his home on this 625-acre estate for 40 years. On the grounds are Jackson's mansion, the church he attended and the house of his wife's nephew, who served as Jackson's secretary. The three buildings are within a mile of one another. *Open daily except Dec. 25. Adults $2.00, children small charge.*

HERMITAGE Andrew Jackson's home, though columned in the Greek Revival tradition of the day—it was built in 1819—is nevertheless a straightforward, relatively simple structure. Most of the furnishings within were owned by the Jacksons, including "Old Hickory"'s favorite armchair, his tobacco tin and even his hairbrushes. Also on view are the paintings of Jackson by Ralph E. W. Earl and the china used at the White House during Jackson's residency.

OLD HERMITAGE CHURCH Andrew Jackson's wife was a very religious woman, and to please her he contributed generously to the building fund for this

[**41.** *Hermitage*] *Jackson used the library as his office and spent much of his time here after he retired. Still a leader of the Democratic Party, he saw many political visitors in this room. Here also, sitting in the wood and leather chair, he read his letters and newspapers. Some of the furniture, gathered throughout Jackson's career, is older than the house. He used the marble topped table during the Battle of New Orleans. The flag by the window has 15 stars and stripes.*

simple red brick church. Bricks, all of which were handmade, were also used for flooring and for the two huge fireplaces that provided heat in winter.

TULIP GROVE Even the name of this lovely house evokes the charm and grace of the antebellum life in the South. It was the home of Andrew Jackson Donelson, Rachel Jackson's nephew. The white Doric columns and gabled roof stand out grandly against the mellowed red brick walls.

42. Nashville, Tenn.

Founded in 1779 by a hardy band of pioneers, Nashville has become a thriving industrial, educational and banking center of the southern U.S. The home of such distinguished Americans as Andrew Jackson, Sam Houston and Thomas H. Benton, this capital city is perhaps best known as the place where country music reigns supreme. The "Nashville Sound" was originated and first came to prominence here.

Belle Meade Mansion *110 Leake Ave.* Once the focal point of a world-famous thoroughbred nursery and stud farm, this graceful Greek Revival mansion is believed to have been designed by William Strickland, architect of Tennessee's State Capitol. The portico columns show nicks from fighting that occurred on the front lawn during the Battle of Nashville. Built for General William Giles Harding in 1853, it contains a winding staircase and many 19th-century furnishings. The large double parlor has a Victorian piano and two fireplaces with ornate mantels; in the library are several paintings of the famous racehorses once raised here. The double bedroom, with a pair of large beds covered with quilted canopies, was visited by President and Mrs. Grover Cleveland during their wedding tour. Outbuildings include an 1890s clapboard carriage house that contains a number of mid-19th-century carriages and a brick-and-stone dairy house of Tudor-Gothic style. One of the state's oldest houses is on the grounds. It is a 1793 log cabin which was purchased in 1807 by Harding's grandfather. *Open daily except Dec. 25. Adults and children over 6 small charge.*

Downtown Presbyterian Church *154 Fifth Ave., N.* Dedicated in 1851, this building designed by William Strickland is a rare example of the Egyptian Revival architecture that enjoyed considerable popularity in the mid-19th century. The exterior of the brick-and-stone structure remains almost unchanged, and only a few interior alterations have been made since 1882. An Egyptian temple motif is especially evident where multicolored pillars flank the altar. From 1862 to 1865 Union troops used the church as a hospital, and their horses were stabled in the basement. *Open Sun.-Fri.*

Holy Trinity Episcopal Church *615 Sixth Ave., S.* This outstanding example of Gothic-style architecture, built of blue limestone and cedar, was completed in 1853. It is much admired for its exterior design, original hand-carved furnishings and vaulted ceiling where the rafters are joined by carved emblems of the Trinity. During the Civil War, Union troops housed supplies and gunpowder here. Evidence of their occupation includes cleaver marks on the main altar, which the soldiers used as a butcher's block. *Open Sat., Sun.*

Nashville Parthenon *Centennial Park, West End* Opened in 1931, this structure is a remarkably accurate replica of the marble temple of Athena Parthenos which has dominated the hills above Athens since 438 B.C. Constructed of steel-reinforced conglomerate materials, it is the world's only exact-size copy of the famous building and shares with it the deliberate lack of uniformity that creates an illusion of strict balance. As a result, there are few straight lines anywhere in the design. All steps are of slightly different sizes, and the distances vary between each of the Doric columns in the peristyle. Accuracy of the reproduction extends to the 39 figures carved in the east and west pediments and to the griffins located at the corners of the roof, all of which substantially enhance the effect when the building is illuminated at night. Bronze doors, reputedly the largest in the world—they weigh 30 tons and stand 24 feet tall—are located off the east and west porticos and are the building's only entrances. Inside are reproductions of the famous Elgin marbles, once part of the original Parthenon and now in the British Museum. The basement rooms, which are a modern addition to the classic reproduction, house a permanent collection of 19th-century American paintings including works by Church and Homer. *Open daily except holidays.*

Peabody Arts Museum *George Peabody College for Teachers, Cohen Memorial Fine Arts Bldg., 21st Ave., S.* Doric columns decorate the entrance of this handsome brick building. Displayed here are Renaissance paintings from the Kress Collection, fine prints, contemporary painting and sculpture as well as a number of artifacts with regional historic significance. *Open daily during academic year.*

Tennessee Botanical Gardens and Fine Arts Center *Cheek Rd.* The permanent collection of the Fine Arts Center, housed in an impressive 60-room Georgian mansion known as Cheekwood, consists of American, European and Oriental sculptures, paintings and art objects dating from the 17th century to the present. The mansion is located on 55 landscaped acres containing formal gardens, statuary, fountains, flowing streams and pools. The new Botanic Hall, focal point for the study of regional environmental problems, is equipped with laboratory and library. *Open Tues.-Sun. except holidays. Small charge.*

Tennessee State Capitol *Sixth and Charlotte Aves.* On a rise in downtown Nashville stands Tennessee's imposing Greek Revival capitol, designed by the noted architect William Strickland. Construction of the building, which was modeled in part after the Erectheum on Athens' Acropolis, was begun in 1845. Strickland was supervisor of the project, and when he died in 1854, he was buried in a vault in the north portico wall. The building was completed in 1859, making it the nation's eighth oldest statehouse. The graceful exterior has Ionic facades, side porticos and a 79-foot tower and cupola. Considerable damage was inflicted on the structure in the Civil War when Union troops fortified it for use as a garrison, naming it Fort Johnson after Tennessee's military governor, Andrew Johnson. The marble balustrade on the beautiful first floor staircase is chipped from bullets fired by a guard at legislators who were leaving an 1866 session forced upon them by the state's Reconstruction governor. By the 1950s deterioration of the exterior limestone made restoration imperative, and a total restoration of the building was completed in 1960. Many attractions adorn the interior, including ceiling frescos, portraits of former

[**42.** *Nashville Parthenon*] *A million visitors a year come to gaze at this remarkable copy of the famous temple on the Acropolis in Athens—which, unlike the original, is in perfect condition. Originally built of temporary material for the Tennessee Centennial Exposition in 1897, it was rebuilt more durably in the 1920s and opened in 1931.*

governors and other state figures and murals depicting the discovery, settlement and development of the state. The legislative lounge, an exact replica of Sir Walter Scott's study, contains an ornate ironwork spiral staircase. Occupying the second floor are the chambers of the Senate and House of Representatives, the latter with fluted Ionic gallery columns and ornate chandeliers. On the grounds can be seen statues of Andrew Jackson and other well-known figures, as well as the tomb of President and Mrs. James K. Polk. *Open daily.*

Travellers' Rest Historic House *Farrell Pkwy.* John Overton, who built this house in 1799, was a law partner of Andrew Jackson and a founder of Memphis. Twelve rooms were added to the original four-room structure by succeeding generations of the Overton family. Since 1954 the house has been maintained as a historical museum. It contains Colonial- and Federal-style furniture and Tennessee historical records. The smokehouse on the grounds is now a museum of relics of the prehistoric mound-builder tribes who lived in the area around 1200 A.D. *Open daily except holidays. Small charge.*

Upper Room Chapel and Museum *1908 Grand Ave.* The Upper Room Chapel is located in a large and attractive building that also houses the headquarters of *The Upper Room,* a daily devotional guide. The chancel of the chapel is modeled on the room shown in Leonardo da Vinci's *The Last Supper.* On the wall behind the altar (a table like the one in the picture) is a limewood and walnut carving of Da Vinci's painting, 17 feet wide and 8 feet high, the work of Ernest Pellegrini. At the head of the stairs leading to the chapel is a lovely stained-glass window that tells the story of Pentecost. Paintings, books, porcelain and other items, all of a religious nature, are on display in the museum. The Agape ("Christian Love") Garden near the south wing has bronze statuary and trees, shrubs and seasonal flowers like those grown in the Holy Land. *Open daily.*

43. Franklin, Tenn. See feature display on pages 256-7.

44. Sam Davis Home *Off Rte. 24, Smyrna, Tenn.* The Davis family home, a frame house built in 1810, is now a state shrine commemorating Sam Davis, a member of the First Tennessee Volunteer Regiment in the Civil War. Captured behind Union lines with important military papers in his possession, he refused to reveal the identity of the friend who had given him the papers and was executed as a Confederate spy in Pulaski, Tennessee, on Nov. 27, 1863. The two-story house has a commanding view of the 168-acre farm, formal gardens and outbuildings: a kitchen, smokehouse, overseer's office and slave quarters. Davis is buried in the family cemetery on the grounds. A museum with items relating to Davis and the Civil War is also on the property. *Open daily. Small charge.*

45. Oaklands *N. Maney Ave., Murfreesboro, Tenn.* In 1862 Union troops quartered here were surprised by Confederate raiders who wounded their colonel and forced him to surrender the town of Murfreesboro. Consisting of four combined houses of different periods, the oldest dating from the early 1800s, the restored house today includes a handsome Romanesque Revival veranda with square chamfered columns and carved cornices over the windows. The floors are of ash with strips of cherry wood along the walls, and a winding staircase with hand-turned balusters graces the entrance hall. Some of the period furnishings are original to the house. A 19th-century-style garden is located on the grounds. *Open Tues.-Sun. Small charge.*

43. Franklin, Tenn.

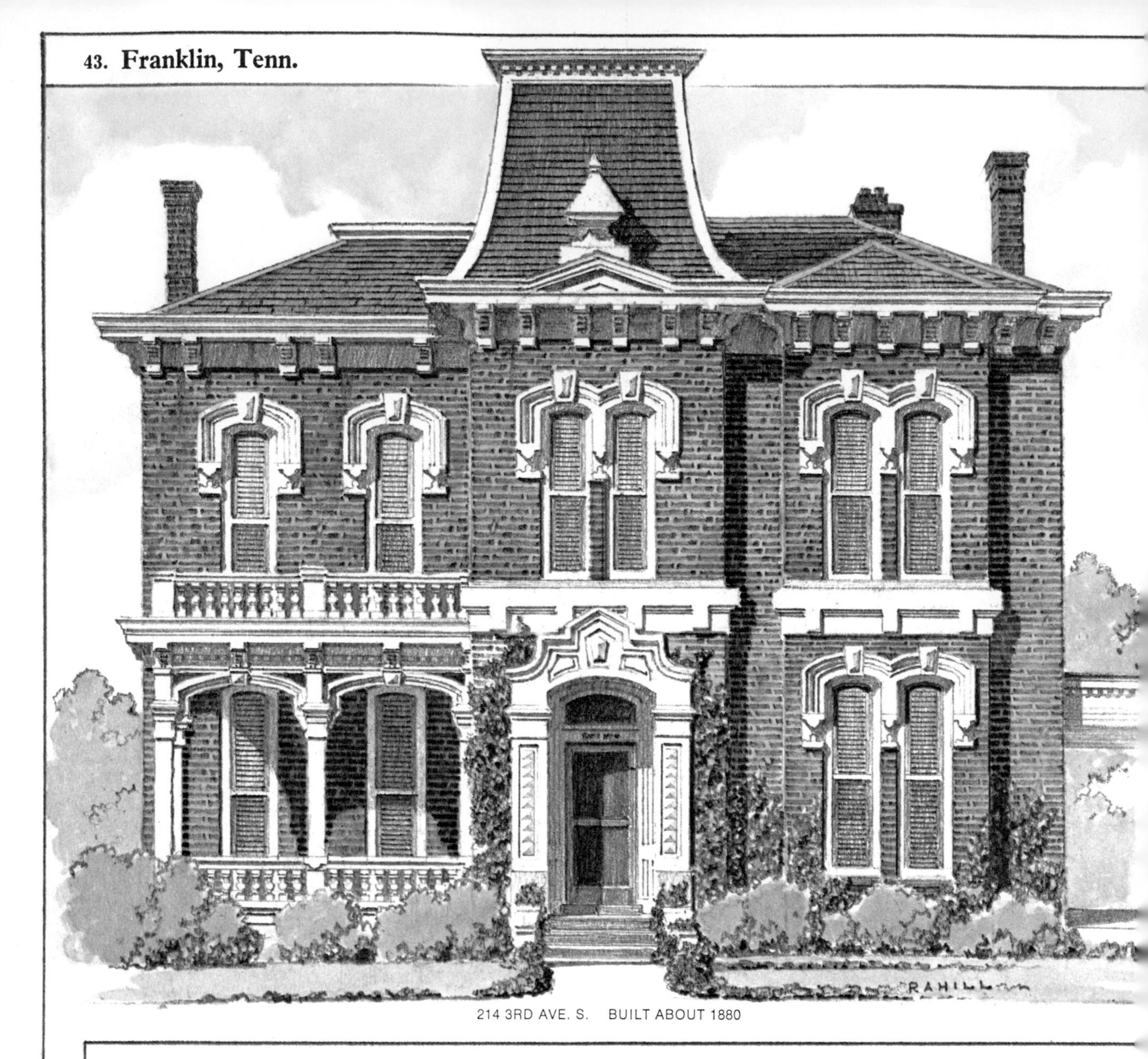

214 3RD AVE. S. BUILT ABOUT 1880

The Dynamic Expression of the New Machines

Wood was the most abundant building material in 19th-century America, and the newfound potential of the power-driven wood lathe and scroll saw extended the freedom of Victorian design. The front porch was also a peculiarly American addition to a house. It provided the family a protected vantage point from which to watch the rest of the small-town world pass by. To the designers and carpenters the necessary decorative posts, brackets, pendants, spindles and gable ends offered an irresistible challenge to the facility of the new machines.

BRACKET DETAIL, 134 4TH AVE. N.

PORCH GABLE WITH SPINDLES, 305 4TH AVE. S.

In the mid 1800s, with Queen Victoria on the throne, the tide of British Empire was at its height and English influence on manners, morals and the arts was manifest around the world. It was no wonder that a Victorian Era was established in America by a newly prosperous middle class that looked to England for guidance. In architecture the urge was to go beyond the Georgian style's prevalent austerity. A major influence was English architect Charles Lock Eastlake, whose *Hints on Household Taste* (published in Boston in 1872) went through seven printings here. Many of the architectural excesses of the time were attributable to enthusiastic extensions of Eastlake's ideas. The new direction was toward decorative embellishment. Designs were adapted from everywhere. In Victorian houses there are echoes of Greece, Italy, Egypt, France, Turkey, China, India and Siam. Most towns in America boast of a few good examples, but for its size Franklin is particularly rich. The houses are not open to the public, but the exteriors comprise a remarkable street-side museum of the style.

46. Rhea County Courthouse *N. Market St., Dayton, Tenn.* During the hot summer of 1925, Clarence Darrow and William Jennings Bryan battled over the origin of our species in this courthouse. The Scopes "monkey" trial held here received attention around the world. The solid red-brick building with traditional bell tower and the courtroom within appear the same today as at the time of the trial. *Open Mon.-Sat.*

47. University of the South *Sewanee, Tenn.* The campus of the University of the South, founded in 1857, spreads across 10,000 scenic acres atop Cumberland Plateau. Two notable buildings are described below.

ALL SAINTS CHAPEL In the tower of this Gothic structure is the 23-ton, 56-bell Leonidas Polk Memorial Carillon, which has a range of almost five octaves. The architect Ralph Adams Cram, who also designed the nave of the Cathedral of St. John the Divine in New York, used the Church of St. Mary the Virgin at Oxford University, England, as his model. Scenes in the stained-glass windows depict the first 100 years of the university's history. *Open daily.*

BRESLIN TOWER The tower, modeled after Magdalen College Tower at Oxford University, forms the entrance to the university's Convocation Hall. It rises to a height of 100 feet and measures 29 by 30 feet at the base. The cornerstone was laid in 1886, and the clock and Westminster chimes were added in 1900. Funds for construction of the tower were donated by Thomas and Elizabeth Breslin in memory of their daughter, Lucy. *Open Mon.-Sat.*

48. Houston Antiques Museum *201 High St., Chattanooga, Tenn.* A $9000 plated amberina glass pitcher is one of 15,000 pitchers in this museum collection, all gathered together by one person, Anna Safley Houston. So many items are displayed here that some literally hang from the ceilings. The collection includes some rare examples of blue Staffordshire and Liverpool pottery, Sandwich and Tiffany glass, and many items of copper and silver lusterware. Also on view are fine pieces of china, pewter and period furniture. *Open Sun.-Fri. except holidays. Small charge.*

[48] *A dazzling display of pressed glass glitters from every corner of the Pattern Glass Room in the Houston museum—as well as from the ceiling, where 200 pitchers hang from the rafters. Colored glassware is in the windows.*

[50] *Jacob's Dream, in which he saw a ladder ascending to heaven, has been exquisitely rendered in ivory by a Flemish artist of the mid-18th century; this is one of many treasures of religious art at the museum.*

49. Hunter Gallery of Art *10 Bluff View, Chattanooga, Tenn.* On a bluff 100 feet above the Tennessee River, this white columned former residence is a fitting environment for a representative collection of 18th- to 20th-century American art. Included are works of James Peale and Thomas Sully. The gallery also hosts exhibits of sculpture, photography, crafts and folk art. *Open daily Aug.-June except holidays and Christmas week.*

50. Siskin Memorial Foundation, Museum of Religious and Ceremonial Art *526 Vine St., Chattanooga, Tenn.* This collection of rare volumes and art objects of all religions was gathered by the late Dr. Harris Swift, chief rabbi of the British forces during World War II. Bibles—some in their original bindings and dating from the 16th century—printed in many different languages, an autographed edition of Dickens's complete works and 42 volumes of the writings of Voltaire are among the 3500 rare books in the library. A hand-chased ivory carving of Jacob's Dream is one of the many beautiful pieces of religious and ceremonial art on display. The museum is maintained by the Siskin Memorial Foundation, which also has a nondenominational chapel, rehabilitation center and facilities for social service, civic, religious and educational groups in a three-building complex. *Open Mon-Fri. except holidays.*

51. Lookout Mountain Museum *1110 E. Brow Rd., Lookout Mountain, Tenn.* Several life-size dioramas depict aspects of a Paleo-Indian culture known to have existed in this area 8000 years ago. A good collection of artifacts, mostly weapons and tools used by this primitive society, is also exhibited. During the Civil War the site of the museum was adjacent to the scene of the Battle Above the Clouds, in which control of an important vantage point was bitterly contested. A number of Civil War weapons are displayed to commemorate this event. *Open daily. Small charge.*

52. Russell Cave National Monument *Off Rte. 72, Bridgeport, Ala.* Archaeological work has established that early Indians inhabited this large cave continuously for almost 8000 years, until 1000 A.D. Pottery, tools and weapons recovered from the site are displayed at the Visitor Center and tell the story of several ancient cultures. An exhibit in the mouth of the cave explains digging techniques. The grounds also include a nature trail, and living history demonstrations are given in the summer. *Open daily.*

53. Chickamauga-Chattanooga National Military Park *Rte. 27, Fort Oglethorpe, Ga.* This military park, consisting of several areas in Georgia and Tennessee, marks the location of two fierce Civil War battles fought for control of Chattanooga, an important railroad center. Numerous monuments plus many plaques and cannon enable visitors to understand the various actions and the significance of the battles of Chickamauga and Chattanooga, which exposed the heart of the Confederacy to General Sherman's decisive "March to the Sea." The hilly, thickly wooded ground over which the fighting took place is little changed, although several hiking trails and picnic areas have been added. The Visitor Center at the Chickamauga Battlefield has many effective displays and houses the superb Fuller Collection of American military shoulder arms, the most complete grouping of its kind in the world. An audio-visual show on the battles is also given. *Open daily except Dec. 25.*

54. Vann House *Rtes. 76 and 225, Chatsworth, Ga.* James Vann, son of a Scotch trader and a Cherokee woman, was a chief of his tribe. He had helped Moravian missionaries become established at nearby Spring Place and they in turn helped him to build this two-story brick dwelling, the most elegant structure on what was then the land of the Cherokee Nation. The house, completed in 1805, is Federal in style with Georgian influences. At the front and back are narrow, two-story columned porticos, with a porch on each story. The interior of the restored house features the original bright blue, red, green and yellow colors and elaborate carving with many traditional Cherokee roses. The staircase is believed to be the oldest cantilevered design of its kind in the state. *Open daily.*

55. New Echota *Rte. 225, Calhoun, Ga.* In the early 1800s, the Cherokee Indians made a remarkable attempt to adopt a republican form of government. The capital of their nation was New Echota, founded in 1825. The experiment was short-lived, a victim of the U.S. government it emulated. Gold had been discovered on the Indian lands, and in the late 1830s most of the Cherokees were forced west into what is now Oklahoma. The Georgia Historical Commission maintains this 200-acre site, a portion of the original village. The one surviving building has been restored and several others reconstructed, and another building has been moved to this location. *Open daily.*

NEW ECHOTA PRINT SHOP The Cherokees were one of the first tribes to be literate in their own language. The first Indian newspaper in the U.S., the *Cherokee Phoenix,* was printed in English and Cherokee in this shop, now reconstructed, from 1828 to 1834. The publisher, Elias Boudinot, was three-quarters Cherokee and a graduate of Andover Theological Seminary. On display here are typecases, a printing press, a bookbinder similar to ones Boudinot used and a *Phoenix* of March 13, 1828.

SUPREME COURT OF THE CHEROKEE NATION For two weeks in the summer and two in the fall, the highest court of the Cherokee nation sat in this simple frame building—for the rest of the year, the structure served as a school and a mission. Here three men, acting as judge and jury, heard appeals of decisions made in the Cherokees' eight district courts. The building, erected in 1827, was reconstructed in 1961.

VANN TAVERN James Vann, the wealthy Cherokee chieftain who built the elegant Vann House near Chatsworth, also built this trading post and public stop, in 1805, in Buford, Georgia. Its durable construction is of hewn logs connected with wooden pegs. It was moved to its present location in 1957.

WORCESTER HOUSE Samuel A. Worcester, a Congregational missionary, was an important influence at New Echota, and a man who so loved his adopted people that he followed them westward. He built this two-story New England-style house, the only one of the village's buildings to survive, in 1827. The house is of frame construction, with double porches connected by a staircase, and is furnished with items from the period.

[52] *Excavations over the last 20 years have brought to light a wealth of early Indian artifacts here, showing that the cave was used in succession by several different Indian cultures. These range from the primitive Archaic man as far back as 6500* B.C. *to the Woodland Period man of 1000 years ago, who used pottery and more sophisticated weapons and developed a form of agriculture. A series of exhibits at the cave portray the lives of these ancient peoples and show some of the objects recovered from the site.*

[**57.** *Stone Mountain Confederate Memorial*] *The figures carved into the side of the mountain eclipse even Mount Rushmore's in extent, resting in a niche larger than a football field. Jet torches were used to complete the work.*

56. Etowah Indian Mounds *Rte. 61, Cartersville, Ga.* This is one of the more important prehistoric Indian settlements in the southeastern U.S. From about the 9th to the 16th centuries it was the site of a community of several thousand people. The area covers 40 acres and consists of three large ceremonial mounds and four smaller domiciliary ones surrounded by a deep moat. A museum presents the history of the mound dwellers through skeletons, pottery, weapons and other objects excavated from one of the mounds. *Open daily except holidays.*

57. Stone Mountain Park *Stone Mountain, Ga.* This 3200-acre "historical-recreational" park offers a variety of attractions. Its museums and restored buildings give visitors a glimpse of the Old South, while its facilities for hiking, camping, boating, fishing and swimming enable them to enjoy the present one. Besides those below, the park's attractions include a huge carillon, the Bells of Stone Mountain; a Game Ranch; demonstrations of the South's old industries; Confederate Hall, with a light-and-sound enactment of Sherman's march through Georgia; the Observation Tower, which holds the Georgia Forestry Information Center; the Indian Museum and the Plaza of Flags. *Open daily. Parking fee $2.00.*

ANTE-BELLUM PLANTATION What was life like on a pre-Civil War plantation? This complex of buildings offers a surprisingly realistic answer. The handsome porticoed main house and its dependencies are genuine—moved here from sites all over Georgia and carefully restored. Costumed hostesses, flower and vegetable gardens, barnyard livestock and open-hearth cooking in the Cook House enhance the realism. *Open daily. Adults $1.65, children over 6 small charge.*

ANTIQUE AUTO AND MUSIC MUSEUM Forty antique autos, including several one-of-a-kind, vie for a visitor's attention with music machines dating from 1900 and a collection of Tiffany-style lamps. *Open daily. Small charge.*

CIVIL WAR MUSEUM Union and Confederate Army uniforms, firearms and field and surgical equipment are attractively displayed here, along with artifacts relating to the naval history of the Civil War. The museum is in the Memorial Hall Information Center. *Open daily.*

STONE MOUNTAIN CONFEDERATE MEMORIAL CARVING Stone Mountain, the focus of the park, is the largest mass of exposed granite in the world. One face of this colossal monolith (which covers almost 600 acres) now holds the world's largest sculpture. Riding their mounts solemnly as if before a military review, the giant carved figures of Confederate President Jefferson Davis and Generals Robert E. Lee and "Stonewall" Jackson stand out in relief against the vastness of the mountain. Work on the sculpture, begun in the 1920s, was interrupted several times. It was finally completed in 1972.

58. Atlanta, Ga.

Atlanta began as a railroad terminal point in 1837 and was originally called Terminus. By 1864 it had grown in economic importance to such an extent that General Sherman had no choice but to attack it; 90 percent of the city was burned to the ground by his troops. Within four years, the favorable geography and climate of the city brought recovery and Atlanta became the state capital. Today, railways, highways and air lanes converge at this center of the "New South."

Atlanta Memorial Arts Center *1280 Peachtree St., N.E.* This $13,000,000 art center unites the per-

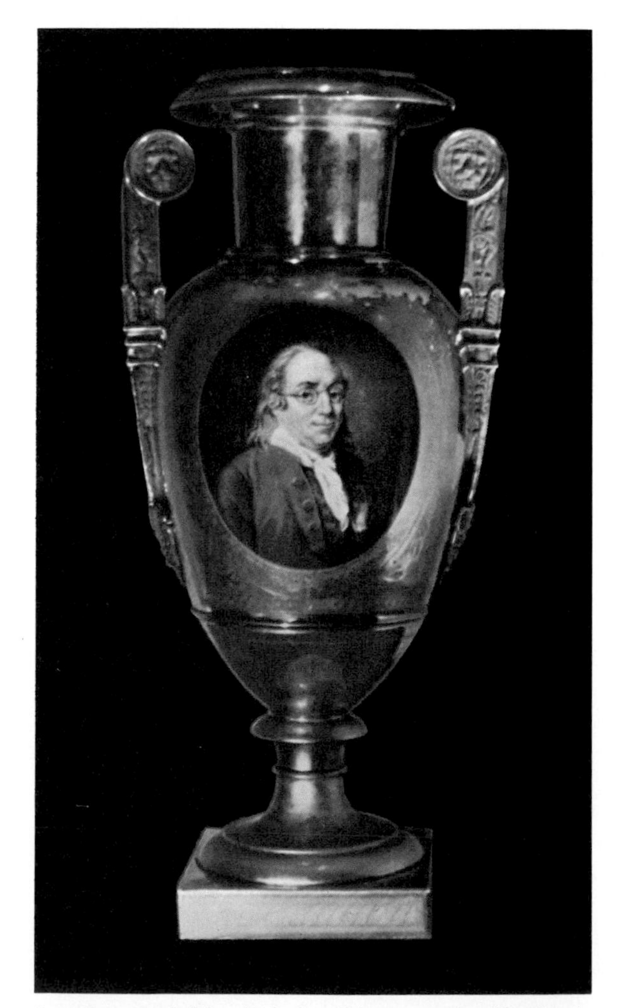

[**58.** *Governor's Mansion*] *A striking portrait of Benjamin Franklin decorates this 27-inch-high gilded porcelain vase. It is a copy of a portrait attributed to the French painter Charles Amédée Philippe Van Loo.*

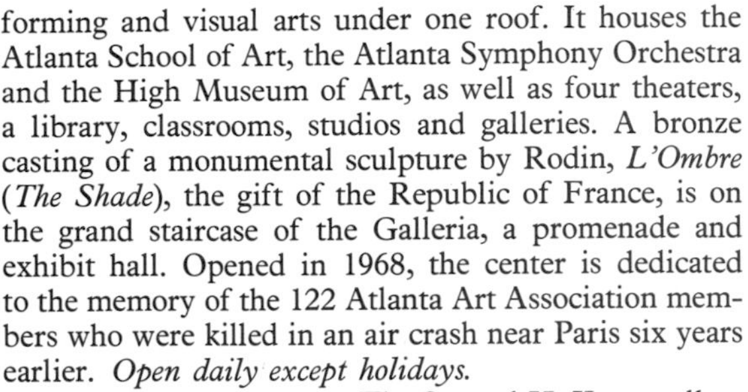

forming and visual arts under one roof. It houses the Atlanta School of Art, the Atlanta Symphony Orchestra and the High Museum of Art, as well as four theaters, a library, classrooms, studios and galleries. A bronze casting of a monumental sculpture by Rodin, *L'Ombre* (*The Shade*), the gift of the Republic of France, is on the grand staircase of the Galleria, a promenade and exhibit hall. Opened in 1968, the center is dedicated to the memory of the 122 Atlanta Art Association members who were killed in an air crash near Paris six years earlier. *Open daily except holidays.*

HIGH MUSEUM OF ART The Samuel H. Kress collection of Italian Renaissance painting and Northern European sculpture is an outstanding feature of this museum, which is located on three floors of the center. Also shown are works of 19th- and 20th-century American and European masters, including a selection of paintings by Monet and other Impressionists, prints by Toulouse-Lautrec, Gauguin and Picasso, and sculpture by Henry Moore. Regular lectures, films and numerous other programs are given in the Walter C. Hill Auditorium. The museum's Junior Activities Center serves the children of Atlanta with programs designed to make them visually aware. *Open daily except holidays.*

Cyclorama Building *Grant Park, Park Ave. and Boulevard, S.W.* The Battle of Atlanta, which took place on July 22, 1864, is re-created in this three-dimensional panorama consisting of an enormous circular painting and natural-looking figures and objects, combined with narration, music and sound effects. The painting, one of the largest of its type in the world (50 feet in height and 400 feet in circumference), was executed in 1885-6 and placed in its present location in 1921. The museum section of the imposing marble Cyclorama Building contains Civil War relics, including the "Texas," a railroad engine that was used by Confederate troops in the capture of James J. Andrews and his men after their daring 1862 raid through Southern lines. *Open daily except Jan. 1 and Dec. 25. Adults $1.25, children over 5 small charge.*

Georgia State Capitol *Washington St.* The gold-plated dome of this building is a conspicuous feature of the Atlanta skyline. The Renaissance-style capitol, completed in 1889, houses the state's executive offices and legislative chambers. The State Museum on the fourth floor has exhibits on Georgia's past and present, specimens of its wildlife and displays on its agriculture and industry. Paintings of prominent Georgians and commemorative plaques are displayed in the rotunda and in some rooms. On the five-acre grounds are many monuments and markers. *Open Mon.-Sat.*

Governor's Mansion *391 W. Paces Ferry Rd., N.W.* The handsome mansion of pink-toned molded brick is adorned with 30 white fluted Doric columns. The Greek Revival dwelling was built for Georgia's governors and dedicated in 1968. Included in the mansion's outstanding collection of early 19th-century American furnishings are pieces by Duncan Phyfe, Michael Allison, Charles Lannuier and John Needles; Chinese and English porcelain, Oriental rugs, antique silver and crystal chandeliers can also be seen. The cherry-paneled library contains books relating to Georgia's history as well as books by native authors. *Open Tues.-Thurs., Sun.*

Home of Joel Chandler Harris *1050 Gordon St., S.W.* Uncle Remus, Brer Fox, Brer Rabbit and the other "critters" lived in this gabled house, along with the most famous spinner of their tales. It was while living here at the "Wren's Nest" (from 1881 until his death in 1908) and working on the *Atlanta Constitution*, that Harris beautifully rewove the whimsical stories he had first heard as a child from slaves in the area. The house contains many of the original furnishings and many items associated with Harris and his work. *Open daily except holidays. Small charge.*

Shrine of the Immaculate Conception *48 Hunter St., S.W.* Although the original Catholic church on the site was spared during Sherman's burning of Atlanta, it was razed shortly thereafter to make way for this red brick Victorian Gothic building. Begun in 1869, it is the oldest surviving church in northern Georgia. The interior was extensively renovated in 1969. *Open daily.*

Swan House *3099 Andrews Dr., N.W.* This magnificent Palladian-type house, built in 1928, is one of the city's most elaborate homes. It is set on 18 acres of terraced lawns, wooded areas and formal gardens. Sweeping steps flanking a tiered fountain lead to the house. A feature of the striking interior, which contains much fine paneling and carved woodwork, is the main entrance hall with its free-standing circular staircase accented with wrought-iron balustrades. The Atlanta Historical Society, the present owner, has retained many of the 18th-century furnishings of the house's original owners. The main floor rooms are shown by guided tours. *Open daily except holidays. Small charge.*

[**58.** *Swan House*] *This splendid 18th-century-style mansion was built less than 50 years ago. Its design is authentic, however, and the collection of antiques with which it was furnished by its original owners can be enjoyed on guided tours. It now houses the Atlanta Historical Society, and the 18-acre grounds are tended by garden clubs.*

59. Roosevelt's Little White House and Museum *Rtes. 27A and 85W, Warm Springs, Ga.* Attracted to Warm Springs by the healing properties of its waters, the polio-afflicted Franklin D. Roosevelt built this unpretentious white clapboard cottage in 1932. Thirteen years later he died here, on April 12, 1945. Now the focal point of a state memorial, the small (six-room) but comfortable house has been kept essentially as it was on his last day. Inside are the same furnishings and books and the unfinished portrait by Mme. Elizabeth Shoumatoff for which Roosevelt was sitting when he was fatally stricken. The memorial also includes the Walk of the States, a pathway lined with stones and flags representing the 50 states and the District of Columbia; a warm springs fountain; and a museum which contains mementos of Roosevelt's life. A short movie on FDR in Georgia is shown at frequent intervals. *Open daily. Adults $1.25, children small charge.*

60. Callaway Gardens *Rte. 27, Pine Mountain, Ga.* Nature trails and some 18 miles of scenic drives through impressive stands of native pine and lushly landscaped areas are among the many pleasant diversions here. Visitors can enjoy four golf courses, 12 man-made lakes—many with swimming and boating—and other family recreation, including tennis and water skiing. Georgia industrialist Cason Callaway established the gardens as a memorial to his mother. Famous for the vivid array of flora, as varied and colorful as the seasons, they can be toured by bus, a one-hour trolley ride or on foot. The azaleas, in great drifts of color along the wooded trails and roads, are an especially popular highlight in the spring. A miniature train and tiny Mississippi River steamboat are especially popular with children. The 17th-century-style information center presents a short slide show on the history of the gardens. One can visit an authentic 19th-century Georgia log cabin or hear an organ concert at the Ida Cason Callaway Memorial Chapel which also has lovely stained-glass windows. There are added attractions in summer. *Open daily. Small charge. Additional charges for trolley, train and boat rides and for recreational facilities.*

61. Hamilton on the Square *Off Rte. 27 N., Hamilton, Ga.* The area surrounding the square of this once-flourishing town has been carefully restored and now includes a number of shops and museums that take the visitor back to the turn of the century. In addition to the attractions described below, there is an apothecary shop complete with old-fashioned ice cream parlor.

ANTIQUE AUTOMOBILE MUSEUM A good representation of automobiles from the early 1900s encompasses several pioneer gas, electric and steam models. One, a 1909 Sears Surrey, has a tiller in place of a steering wheel. Antique motorcycles and bicycles are also exhibited plus marble gear shift knobs, oil bottles and other early automotive equipment. *Open daily. Small charge.*

OLD STORE MUSEUM This imaginative re-creation of a general store, where chewing tobacco and high-button shoes compete for space with country hams and tin tea caddies, brings a vanished era back to life. All of the merchandise is authentic; many items unfamiliar to modern consumers are labeled. In a room behind the museum are located a smithy and carriage shop. This area also houses a collection of early carriages and saddlery, plus a number of interesting old baby carriages. *Open daily. Small charge.*

62. Illges House *1428 Second Ave., Columbus, Ga.* This stately house, built in the 1850s, is a magnificent example of antebellum Greek Revival architecture. Its brick exterior is plastered in front, and six intricately carved fluted Corinthian columns decorate a narrow portico. There is a cast-iron balcony over the pedimented main entrance and an unusual ironwork roof balustrade. The house is operated as an antique shop. *Open daily.*

63. Springer Opera House *103 Tenth St., Columbus, Ga.* From the 1870s to the 1920s, whenever actors, lecturers and singers toured the U.S., most of them stopped in Columbus to play this elegant theater. Today the pink brick structure, built in 1871, has been restored to its former Victorian splendor and is the permanent home of a community theater company. It has been designated the State Theater of Georgia. Edwin Booth, Maude Adams, Otis Skinner, Oscar Wilde, William Jennings Bryan, Geraldine Farrar and the Barrymores—among the many famous personalities who appeared on the Springer's stage—are remembered in the theater's museum in photographs, portraits, costumes and other memorabilia. The opera house is open to visitors twice weekly as part of the Heritage Tour of Columbus. *Open for performances and tours Wed., Sun. Tour: Adults $2.00, children small charge.*

64. Walker-Peters-Langdon House *716 Broadway, Columbus, Ga.* This Georgian cottage, built in 1828, is the oldest known structure in the city. It is constructed of clapboard and is furnished with American antiques of the 1830s. The building now serves as headquarters for the Historic Columbus Foundation. *Open Mon.-Fri.*

65. U.S. Army Infantry Museum *Fort Benning, Ga.* Displayed in four converted barracks on the world's largest infantry center are over 14,000 objects associated with the American infantryman, his allies and enemies from the French and Indian War to the present. In addition to uniforms, portraits and flags, several battlefield dioramas can be seen plus many weapons. A comprehensive collection of Japanese firearms from 1895 to 1945 is exhibited, along with U.S. firearms from 1813 models to the first M14 rifle and M60 machine gun ever produced. Weapons used by Communist forces in North Korea and Vietnam are also on view as are U.S. Army shoulder patches, unit distinctives and medals. A research library holds many books and 200,000 documents and photographs. Outside the museum are several pieces of artillery, tanks, trucks and other vehicles. *Open Tues.-Sun., closed holidays except July 4.*

66. Andersonville National Historic Site *Andersonville, Ga.* For a little more than a year (1864-5), this was the location of the infamous Andersonville Prison, where about 13,000 Union soldiers died. (The prison commandant, Captain Henry Wirz, was the only Confederate official to be executed for war crimes.) It was the largest of the Civil War prison camps, occupying 27 acres, and at one time as many as 32,000 men were

[**68.** *McDonald House*] *An impressive mansion typifying the style in which the wealthiest family in town would have lived in the 1840s, this was actually brought to Westville from nearby Cuthbert and has been extensively restored. Westville aims to show different period life-styles, and also includes middle-class and humble farm homes.*

contained behind the 15-foot-high stockade walls. In addition to the stockade area and its fortifications, the site includes the National Cemetery which contains the graves of the prisoners who died here, as well as those of 1000 veterans of later wars. Numerous monuments mark the area, which is gradually being developed. *Open daily except Thanksgiving Day and Dec. 25.*

67. Bedingfield Inn *Rte. 27, Lumpkin, Ga.* Stewart County's first physician built this frame residence and stagecoach stop in 1836. The house has been restored and furnished with many Empire pieces, its rooms are painted in bright shades that closely match the original colors. *Open daily June-Sept., Sat.-Sun. Oct.-May. Small charge.*

68. Westville Village *Rte. 27, Lumpkin, Ga.* At this reconstruction of an 1850 community, craftsmen demonstrate their skills in several authentic structures moved to the site. Weavers, basketmakers, potters, blacksmiths and other artisans work in settings complete with old furniture and equipment. Several annual events take place here, including a fair during the first week in November. *Open daily except Thanksgiving Day and Dec. 25. Adults $2.00, children small charge.*

FEAGIN HOUSE *Lamar St.* This 1840 Stewart County dwelling now serves as a house-museum that illustrates the life-style of a mid-19th-century middle-class family. Quilting demonstrations are given here regularly.

MCDONALD HOUSE *Troup St.* Edward McDonald began this house in nearby Cuthbert in 1843. It is restored and furnished with period pieces that typify an affluent owner's tastes. Its portico includes six squared columns.

MOYE HOUSE *Gilmer St.* This house was built in Cuthbert prior to 1840. The site includes a doctor's office furnished in the style of the times.

69. Kolomoki Mounds State Park *Off Rte. 27, N. of Blakely, Ga.* Ceremonial and burial mounds are remains of the Kolomoki culture which flourished in the 12th and 13th centuries. Archaeological excavations indicate that the earliest settlement here may have been made about 800 A.D., and that the site was abandoned about 1300 A.D. The largest mound in the group, known as the Great Mound, was the foundation for the village's temple. It measures 325 by 200 feet at its base and is 56½ feet high. There are also several smaller burial mounds. A museum at the site exhibits pottery and other artifacts found in excavations and features displays that illustrate the daily life of the Kolomoki people. *Open daily Apr.-Oct., Sat., Sun. Nov.-Mar. Small charge.*

70. Tallahassee Junior Museum *3945 Museum Dr., Tallahassee, Fla.* Even though the museum is intended for children, adults will be fascinated by the array of exhibits here. Man's interrelationship with animals is illustrated in the live animal exhibit, which boasts a bald eagle as well as native mammals and reptiles. The four main buildings have displays that include changing monthly exhibits in the arts and in the social and natural sciences. There are fresh and salt water aquariums and a large window for bird watching. Forty acres of nature trails are part of the museum complex, as is Big Bend Pioneer Farm. Eleven hand-hewn log buildings, some dating from 1880, have been assembled in a farm setting and equipped to recapture the life of early settlers in northwest Florida. *Open Tues.-Sun. early Jan.-mid-Dec. Small charge.*

[73] *The remarkable Rumpler car, shaped like a boat on wheels, is one of the most unusual of the large collection of carriages and cars shown at the Early American Museum near Silver Springs. Produced in 1921, the Rumpler failed to catch the public imagination; but like every other car in this fine collection, it is still in running condition. Many historic names are here, including Duesenberg, Pierce-Arrow and Stutz.*

71. University Art Gallery *Fine Arts Building, Florida State University, Tallahassee, Fla.* A good collection of American graphics and a number of Baroque paintings are the main attractions in this contoured brick building. Activities at the gallery include lectures, temporary exhibitions and intermuseum loans, and a Fine Arts Festival each February. *Open daily except holidays and college vacations.*

72. Florida State Museum *University of Florida, Museum Rd. and Newell Dr., Gainesville, Fla.* Following the theme Environment and Man, the museum's exhibits trace the anthropological and biological history of Florida and the Caribbean area. The artifacts displayed date from about 10,000 B.C., when man first arrived here; fossil remains and thousands of specimens of local animals and plants present a complete account of the region's life. Re-created environments include a cave that visitors can explore, a mangrove swamp and an archaeological site. Visitors may also use the unique "object library." The handsome building, which was completed in 1970, is modeled after the Indian ceremonial mounds of the region. *Open daily except Dec. 25.*

73. Early American Museum *Rte. 40E, Silver Springs, Fla.* Transportation is the main subject of this museum, and visitors can trace its development in America in the fine collection of over 100 carriages and early automobiles as well as in a souvenir of the space age—a full-size model of the Freedom 7 space capsule. Of particular interest among the antique cars (all of which are operational) are a 1909 Stanley Steamer and a 1921 Rumpler, a most unusual-looking car with a distinctive teardrop shape. Little-known vehicles like the Prescott and Gaylord automobiles can be seen along with some of the world's most famous models, such as a 1932 Stutz Super Bearcat and a 1935 Duesenberg S-J convertible. An elegant 1895 landau and a carriage used in *Gone With the Wind* highlight the exhibit of horse-drawn vehicles. The museum's reminiscences of bygone days also include a large toy collection; replica storefronts that recapture the aura of a typical 19th-century street; a bar known as Casey's Saloon in which there are a number of playable mechanical musical instruments; and a fashion shop containing over 300 antique dolls as well as a number of mannequins dressed in styles of the early 1900s. *Open daily. Adults $1.50, children over 5 small charge.*

74. Crystal River Historic Memorial *Off Rte. 19, N.W. of Crystal River, Fla.* The mound-building culture of the early North American Indians, which may have originated in Mexico and eventually made its way as far north as the Great Lakes, may have had its first location north of Mexico at this riverbank site. Ceremonies were held here from about the 2nd century B.C. until about the 15th century A.D. Visitors can walk along trails to view several interesting mounds, including a temple mound standing 40 feet high and a glass-covered crypt in the embankment of a burial mound displaying ancient remains. Over 450 burial sites have been discovered in the immediate vicinity. A museum exhibits pottery and other artifacts. *Open daily. Adults and children over 12 small charge.*

75. Universalist Church *Grand Blvd. and Read St., Tarpon Springs, Fla.* Eleven paintings by George Inness, Jr. (1854–1926), son of the noted landscape artist, can be seen in this 1909 stone-block church. Most of these paintings of landscapes and religious scenes were done specifically for the church by Inness, who wintered in Tarpon Springs and was a member of the congregation. *Open Tues.-Sun. Oct.-May except holidays. Small charge.*

76. Haas Museum *3511 Second Ave. S., St. Petersburg, Fla.* Natural history exhibits, including shell and mineral collections and a bald eagle's nest recovered intact, are among the main features here. There are also replicas of a cobbler's shop, blacksmith's shop, barber shop, dentist's office and an early fireplace kitchen. The museum, the Grace S. Turner House and the Lowe House are owned and maintained by the St. Petersburg Historical Society. *Open Tues.-Sun. Jan.-Aug., Oct.-Dec. Small charge includes all buildings.*

GRACE S. TURNER HOUSE *3501 Second Ave. S.* Early St. Petersburg is reflected in the furnishings and other objects in this bungalow. Most of them, including a serving table that belonged to the pirate Jean Lafitte, were donated by town residents. The children's room contains small-scale Victorian furnishings.

LOWE HOUSE *3527 Second Ave. S.* Cypress wood walls and pine floors characterize this 125-year-old house built in Anona, Fla. in the early 1850s. Complying with the wishes of its last resident, the St. Petersburg Historical Society moved the house with some of its original furnishings to its present site near the Haas

Museum. Next door, the society has preserved an old railroad station.

77. M.G.M.'s "Bounty" Exhibit *345 Second Ave. N.E., St. Petersburg, Fla.* In 1789 Fletcher Christian successfully led a mutiny against Captain William Bligh, of the *Bounty.* This exact working replica of the ship was made in Nova Scotia for the M.G.M. filming of the great classic sea adventure, *Mutiny on the Bounty,* during which the vessel traveled more than 50,000 miles. The ship, weighing 418 tons, is 118 feet long and carries 10,000 feet of sails and 10 miles of line. It is now permanently anchored in a historical exhibit in Vinoy Basin. The Polynesian setting reproduced there also features a replica of the longboat in which Captain Bligh and 18 crewmen were cast adrift and an outrigger sailing canoe from Tahiti. The cabins of the *Bounty* are furnished with 18th-century antiques. *Open daily. Adults $1.50, children small charge.*

78. Museum of Fine Arts *255 Beach Dr. N., St. Petersburg, Fla.* The museum's nine galleries house a broad collection of European and American art from the 17th to the 20th centuries. The museum is particularly proud of an oil-and-wood-panel painting, *Portrait of a Standing Woman,* by Pieter van den Bos, a contemporary of Rembrandt. Among the other exhibits are sculpture from India, Pre-Columbian pottery and gold and two authentic period rooms from England that were dismantled at their original sites and reassembled here. *Open Tues.-Sun. Adults small charge.*

79. St. Petersburg Historical Museum *335 Second Ave. N.E., St. Petersburg, Fla.* The museum, maintained by the St. Petersburg Historical Society, is one of Florida's largest, with more than 10,000 items in its collections. A 3000-year-old Egyptian mummy, a 400-year-old cypress canoe and a 1777 map of the Florida region can be seen. Collections include shells, china, Bibles, musical instruments, Indian artifacts and furniture. *Open daily except Dec. 25. Small charge.*

80. Busch Gardens *3000 Busch Blvd., Tampa, Fla.* This 285-acre tropical garden contains more than 2500 rare and colorful birds. Many of them are housed in a geodesic dome of gold-anodized aluminum and there are regular performances by trained macaws and cockatoos. One can take a monorail tour through the simulated African veld where hundreds of animals are allowed to run free, or get close-up views of them on the Trans Veld Railway. All the usual African animals may be seen, along with aardvark, gnu and scimitar-horned oryx. A zoo, called the Boma, features smaller African mammals and birds. Other popular attractions are the Tanzania Theater, the Old Swiss House, the boat ride and the Stairway to the Stars, an escalator that lifts the visitor 86 feet to a vantage point for viewing the surrounding countryside. *Open daily except Jan. 1 and Dec. 25. Small charge. Monorail rides small charge.*

81. University of Tampa *401 W. Kennedy Blvd., Tampa, Fla.* Plant Hall, the main building of the university, was formerly the Tampa Bay Hotel. The Moorish structure, completed in 1891, is a copy of the Alhambra in Spain. It is crowned with 13 silvered domes and minarets and contains approximately 500 rooms. Many of the classrooms, such as the Elizabethan Room, Florentine Room, Mediterranean Room, Rough Rider Room and 1776 Room, have been decorated using themes of various periods and cultures. Of particular interest are an early Otis elevator cage of hand-rubbed Honduran mahogany, Marie Antoinette's writing desk and a carpet ordered by Queen Victoria for Buckingham Palace. The Henry B. Plant Museum in the southern wing displays Tampa Bay Hotel furnishings from the 1890s as well as cabinets formerly owned by Isabella and Ferdinand of Spain and by Mary, Queen of Scots, and four chairs that belonged to Louis Phillippe. The De Soto Oak, where the explorer is believed to have bargained with the Indians, is on the campus. *Main building open daily, museum open Tues.-Sat. Sept.-July.*

82. Florida Southern College *West Campus, Lakeland, Fla.* On the 100-acre campus of this Methodist college are seven monumental buildings designed by Frank Lloyd Wright, constituting the world's largest complex of his architecture. Over a 20-year period, beginning in 1936, Wright created the interconnected structures, each of which bears the unmistakable stamp of his genius for blending a construction into its surroundings to make it appear almost an extension of nature. Among the most distinctive works is the Annie Pfeiffer Chapel with its steel trellislike tower instead of a traditional steeple. Inside this angular edifice, which contains an excellent collection of early American glass,

[81] *The main building of the University of Tampa, Plant Hall, is one of the most exotic-looking academic buildings in the country. During its hotel days, rickshaws were provided to carry guests down the long, wide corridors.*

[84] *The Singing Tower rises from the idyllic landscape of the Mountain Lake Sanctuary on peninsular Florida's highest mountain (295 feet). Frederick Law Olmsted, son of the famous 19th-century landscape architect of the same name, designed the sanctuary, which contains many rare and unusual plantings. The site is also home to a colony of wood ducks and 112 other wild bird species. At certain times of the year a naturalist is on hand to guide visitors through the reserve. The tower itself, of marble and coquina, houses a particularly fine 53-bell carillon, one of the largest in the U.S., on which a 45-minute recital is given daily. Visitors are advised to listen from a distance; the effect of the bells in this beautiful natural setting is quite haunting.*

interesting patterns of light shine through glass-wall inserts. Wright designed the circular Buckner Building as a library, but it now serves as an administrative center and contains a unique multi-terraced, semi-circular conference room where a bust of the architect is displayed. The only planetarium in central Florida is housed in the three-level Polk Science Building. Nearby is a Garden of Meditation where an authentic Hindu temple and two ancient stone elephants can be seen. Since Wright's death in 1959, his work at Florida Southern has been carried on by a protege, Nils Schweizer, who has designed or renovated many of the other structures on the campus. *Open Mon.-Fri.*

83. Florida Cypress Gardens *Rte. 540, Cypress Gardens, Fla.* This 106-acre garden is lavishly landscaped with more than 2200 varieties of plants. Many superb specimens of bougainvillea, camellias and gardenias vie for attention with magnolias, azaleas, poinsettias and other flora. Models in colorful antebellum costumes stroll along the paved pathways, posing for photographers in the many lovely settings available. Cypress trees rise from the water, their foliage festooned with Spanish moss. Visitors can admire a Japanese Garden, a Cactus Garden and a South Sea waterfall, or take a ride through the lagoons on an electric boat with a guide to identify the plants. Children enjoy Fantasy Valley where models of elves, dinosaurs, frogs and other creatures can be seen. Each day four Water Ski Reviews feature the famous Aquamaids demonstrating precision water skiing. A kite man on skis who often rises 300 feet in the air and the Aqua Ballerinas also form part of each program, which can be viewed from the marine stadium or from a special photo stadium built above the water. Among the annual events here are Festival Time in April and All-American Water Ski Championships in June. *Open daily. Adults $3.00, children over 11 $1.50. Electric boat ride small charge.*

84. Mountain Lake Sanctuary and Singing Tower *Lake Wales, Fla.* The tower, 205 feet high and built of Georgia marble and Florida coquina stone, stands atop Iron Mountain in a beautifully landscaped, 128-acre nature sanctuary. The carillon has 53 bells—the smallest 17 pounds, the largest nearly 12 tons. Recitals are given daily for 45 minutes at 3 P.M.; recorded selections are played every half hour. Edward Bok, a Dutch immigrant who became a successful publisher, established the place to show his gratitude to the American people. *Open daily. Small parking fee.*

85. De Soto National Memorial *W. of Bradenton, Fla.* The great Spanish explorer Hernando de Soto set out in 1539 from what is now western Florida, wandering with his men on a 4000-mile search for riches through much of the Deep South. This 25-acre park commemorates his journey, which lasted four years. It includes a marked nature trail and a visitor center that contains a mural of the expedition and objects relating to De Soto. A film is shown daily, and crossbow demonstrations are given on weekends. Each March a pageant dramatizes the story of the epic journey. *Open daily except Dec. 25.*

86. Bellm's Cars & Music of Yesterday *5500 N. Tamiami Trail, Sarasota, Fla.* An 1897 Duryea is the oldest automobile in this extensive collection of antique, classic and racing cars. In addition, over 1000 mechanical music machines, dating from as early as 1790, can be seen. Other items of interest include a bicycle collection, antique carriages, a blacksmith shop, a livery stable and many Early American articles and antiques. *Open daily. Adults $2.25, children over 5 small charge.*

87. Ringling Museums *Rte. 41, Sarasota, Fla.* See feature display on pages 268-9.

88. Thomas A. Edison Winter Home and Museum *2350 McGregor Blvd., Fort Myers, Fla.* Edison owned two of the earliest known prefabricated houses. They were built to his design in Maine in 1886 and transported in sections by schooner to Florida, where he wintered for more than 40 years, until his death in 1931. Maintained by the City of Fort Myers, his home has been kept just as he left it, and his laboratory is intact even to the chemicals still in the test tubes. Two large museums contain an outstanding collection of his experiments and inventions. Surrounding the buildings are 14 acres of botanical gardens from which Edison used to obtain plant materials for experiments. *Open daily except Dec. 25. Adults $1.50, children small charge.*

89. Rugby Restoration *Rugby, Tenn.* Rugby was established in 1880 as both a colony and a school for younger sons of the British gentry. The founder was Thomas Hughes, author of *Tom Brown's School Days,*

and a spokesman for the Cooperative and Christian Socialist movements. The school is no longer in use, but a number of the delightful "carpenter Gothic" buildings on the campus have been restored. Among them are Kingstone Lisle, the Hughes home, which contains the original furnishings; Hughes Public Library (formerly the schoolhouse), a repository of 7000 volumes of rare books and the furnishings used by the school; and Rugby's Christ Church. The church's rosewood reed organ, built in London in 1849, is still in use. *Open Tues.-Sun. June-Oct. Small charge.*

90. Department of Lincolniana, Lincoln Memorial University *Cumberland Gap, Harrogate, Tenn.* The Duke Hall of Citizenship on this campus houses one of the largest and most interesting collections of Lincolniana in the U.S. Papers, statuary, personal effects and many other records of the man and his role as 16th President of the U.S. are on display here. Of special interest are the famous Frederick Hill Meserve collection of Lincoln photographs and Gutzon Borglum's bust of the President. Also stored here is a huge collection of books, manuscripts, pamphlets and notes on Lincoln. Adjacent to the Lincoln Room is the Civil War Memorial Room, containing more than 6000 books and papers on the Civil War period. *Open daily.*

91. Allandale *Rte. 11-W, W. of Kingsport, Tenn.* The large main structure, an effective adaptation of a Colonial mansion, dates from the 1940s; a small five-room house built in 1861 is attached at the back. The big house incorporates a number of architectural elements salvaged from an 1847 Knoxville dwelling, including an imposing portico with four tall columns and a fine hand-carved staircase. Beautiful Jacobean, Queen Anne, Hepplewhite, Sheraton and Louis XIV furnishings are displayed, and the dining room contains a 17th-century Aubusson carpet. Peacocks, duck ponds and formal boxwood gardens can be seen on 25 surrounding acres. *Open Sun., Tues.-Fri. Apr.-Nov., Sun. Dec.-Mar. Small charge.*

92. Rocky Mount *Off Rte. 11E, Tiney Flats, Tenn.* For two years, from 1790 to 1792, this two-story log house served as the capitol of the newly created Southwest Territory, the area that in 1796 was admitted to the Union as the State of Tennessee. Built in 1770 by William Cobb, a prominent cotton planter, it has been fittingly restored and reflects the affluence and influence of its first owner (the furnishings even include several original Cobb pieces). The house was operated as a post office between 1838 and 1847, when the stagecoach route between Baltimore and Memphis ran past it. On the grounds are a reconstructed smokehouse and kitchen, built of white oak logs to match the house, as well as a museum with exhibits relating to eastern Tennessee's frontier years. Hostesses in period costumes guide visitors through the various buildings. *Open daily Apr.-Oct. Small charge.*

93. Andrew Johnson National Historic Site *Depot and College Sts., Greeneville, Tenn.* This memorial to the 17th President of the U.S. consists of three areas administered by the National Park Service. *Open daily except Dec. 25. Small charge June-mid-Sept.*

ANDREW JOHNSON HOMESTEAD This was Johnson's home from 1851 until his death in 1875. The two-story brick facade is set directly on the street; a double-deck veranda in the rear of the basic house extends along the side and end of an ell. The house and its furnishings, much of which were actually used by the Johnsons, reflect his taste for a simple life.

ANDREW JOHNSON TOMB Johnson is buried in the Monument Hill Cemetery. Over his grave is a marble shaft with a carving of the American eagle and the inscription "His faith in the people never wavered."

JOHNSON TAILOR SHOP Johnson rose to the Presidency from humble beginnings. He worked at his first trade, tailoring, in a small wooden clapboard structure now preserved within a brick building which also houses a Visitor Center and museum. The simple brick house in which he lived from sometime in the 1830s to 1851 is also part of the complex.

[**90**] *All of the famous Frederick Hill Meserve collection of photographs of President Lincoln line a wall in the Lincoln Room at Lincoln Memorial University, home of more than 16,000 pieces of Lincolniana. Items on display here include part of the Lincoln coin collection and one of the busts of the President by the celebrated sculptor Gutzon Borglum, who also created the design for the massive heads on Mount Rushmore. Space allows only a fraction of the huge collection to be shown. Visitors to the exhibits, in the college's Duke Hall of Citizenship, gain a better understanding of Lincoln and his role in history.*

87. **Ringling Museums**
Rte. 41, Sarasota, Fla.

The complex of buildings set in a spendidly landscaped park beside the blue waters of Sarasota Bay forms a perfect memorial to a master showman, John Ringling, the great circus magnate. The John and Mable Ringling Museum of Art, the centerpiece of the complex, has been described as the most beautiful art museum in the Western Hemisphere. It is a reproduction, on a colossal scale, of a typical 15th-century Italian villa. Colonnaded loggias surround a garden court replete with several fountains and a copy of Michelangelo's *David;* the loggias, as well as the gardens themselves, are full of sculptures Mr. Ringling bought on his European travels. Inside the galleries are the museum's real treasures: a collection of Baroque paintings widely regarded as the finest in the U.S. Mr. Ringling's taste ran largely to monumental and elaborate works, and the series of Rubens designs for tapestries (see facing page) are highly impressive examples of the Flemish master's grandest manner. The collection also contains notable pictures by El Greco, Tintoretto, Veronese, Murillo, Velázquez, Titian, Guardi, Hals, Rembrandt, Gainsborough and Reynolds. A fortunate aspect of viewing the collection in such a building is that there is space enough to give the paintings the elbow room they need for full appreciation. The Italianate feeling of the art gallery is continued in the Asolo Theater, a miniature jewel of an auditorium that was brought here from a hill town near Venice and reassembled inside an appropriate building on the grounds in 1957. It is the only original 18th-century Italian theater in the country, and its tiers of ornate boxes, built in an intricate horseshoe plan, preserve the feeling of the aristocratic playhouse it once was. The lobby is decorated with period art and furniture, and the theater houses a winter opera season and a spring and summer series of plays. The mansion that Mr. and Mrs. Ringling built for themselves at the water's edge is worth a visit all by itself. Called Ca' d'Zan, which means "house of John" in a dialect of Mr. Ringling's beloved Venice, it is a Venetian Gothic palace in pale pink stucco and glazed terra-cotta rising from Sarasota Bay much as the Doge's Palace rises from the Venetian lagoon. Inside, the Great Hall is perhaps the most impressive room, a towering Renaissance-style chamber hung with costly tapestries. Completing the complex is the Museum of the Circus, set up after Mr. Ringling's death. It is a treasure-house of circus memorabilia, from the spectacles of ancient Rome to the present day. *Open daily. Combination ticket adults and children over 12 $2.40.*

A bronze casting of Michelangelo's David *is impressively posed on a raised walkway at one end of the garden court of the Ringling Museum of Art. Replicas of classic and Renaissance sculptures and fountains adorn the terraces.*

The Flemish master Rubens and his assistants created many cartoons (designs to be carried out in tapestry), and perhaps the most magnificent of them is a set ordered by the Infanta Isabella for a convent. Two of them are in France, and four are here at the Ringling Museum. This vast canvas, Abraham Receiving Bread and Wine from Melchizedek, *is regarded as the most grandly conceived of the ones seen here. A large gallery was designed specially for the Rubens cartoons and gives their scale the maximum dramatic impact.*

The Museum of the Circus houses a unique collection of circus arts and artifacts covering five centuries. The celebrated bandwagon shown here, Five Graces, *used to head the Barnum and Bailey circus parades around the turn of the century and was drawn by a hitch of 40 matched horses.*

The Great Hall at the Ringling mansion has a lofty coffered ceiling surrounding a skylight of colored glass. Tapestries on the walls conceal the pipes of a huge organ, and much of the elaborately gilded furniture was purchased from the estates of two fellow millionaires, Vincent Astor and Jay Gould.

94. Glenmore Historic House Museum *Chucky Rd. and Old Hwy. 11E, Jefferson City, Tenn.* Dutch fireplace tiles, fine carved walnut and cherry woodwork and a graceful three-story winding staircase are among the handsome features of this restored mansion. Completed in 1869 for John Roger Branner, an executive of the state's first railroad, the brick, white-trimmed house is one of the finest Victorian dwellings in eastern Tennessee. Its 27 rooms include a ballroom on the second floor. Attached to the back of Glenmore is a small replica of the house, known as Doll Town. It served the early occupants as a winter home, since it was easier to heat than the high-ceilinged mansion. Also on the grounds are a two-story brick smokehouse, a frame barn and a carriage house. *Open Sat.-Sun. May-Sept. Small charge.*

95. Jefferson County Court House *Dandridge, Tenn.* This rambling white building with a columned facade was built in 1845 as a courthouse. It has continued to serve as the county center and courthouse, and it also houses a museum. On display are the marriage license issued to Davy Crockett in 1806, a copy of the town's first newspaper (printed in 1855), Civil War memorabilia and a variety of Cherokee Indian relics. The original map of Dandridge, drawn by Samuel Jack in 1793, can also be seen. The town was named for the nation's first First Lady, Martha Dandridge Custis Washington. *Open Mon.-Sat.*

96. Knoxville, Tenn.

Once a repair and supply stop for westbound wagon trains, Knoxville is now the trading center for the rich East Tennessee Valley and the headquarters of the Tennessee Valley Authority. Tennessee marble quarries are in the area, some within city limits, and one of the world's largest marble-finishing plants is in Knoxville.

Blount Mansion *200 W. Hill Ave.* The oldest (1792) frame house west of the Allegheny Mountains is a two-story clapboard dwelling with one-story wings, built in 1792 for William Blount, whom George Washington appointed governor of the Territory South of the Ohio River. Among the interesting 18th-century furnishings in the house are a tin and sweetgum chandelier, a fine Hepplewhite table and several English Chippendale chairs. A good collection of pewter is displayed in the kitchen, and in the parlor, added in 1794, is an Oriental rug with a design of Aesop's fable of the fox and the grapes. Just behind the house is Blount's office, with its exposed beams and horizontal paneling. It was the seat of government prior to Tennessee's admission to statehood in 1796. Blount, who was a signer of the Constitution, was named as one of the state's first U.S. Senators and remained active in politics until his death in 1800. *Open Tues.-Sun. Adults and children over 6 small charge.*

Craighead-Jackson House *1000 State St.* This brick house with stone lintels and dentil cornice was built in 1818. For its restoration, most of the interior woodwork, including a staircase with an unusual sunburst panel, was taken from two Knoxville houses of the same period. Its rooms are filled with outstanding 18th-century and early 19th-century furnishings from the collection of the philanthropist William Perry Toms. An exquisite Philadelphia Chippendale walnut clock case of about 1760 stands in the entrance hall, and the drawing room holds a 1770 London Chippendale piano. Many other valuable pieces representing the Hepplewhite, Sheraton and Chippendale styles can be admired along with examples of early 19th-century glass. There are changing displays of superb silver from 1623 to 1820, also from the Toms collection, and an arts festival is held in the garden in April. *Open Tues.-Sun. Small charge.*

Dulin Gallery of Art *3100 Kingston Pike* John Russell Pope, who in the 1930s designed several monumental structures in Washington, D.C., including the Jefferson Memorial, planned this large residence for the Dulin family in 1915. Visitors enter the handsome neoclassical-style house through an impressive elliptical hall with a marble fountain. While the exterior is primarily late 18th-century French in design, the interior

[**97**] *In 1818 John Oliver, a veteran of the War of 1812, made his way across the Great Smoky Mountains to the valley of Cades Cove and built a home there. He was the first permanent settler in what became a pioneer mountain community, and a reconstruction of his simple shack (left) is one of the highlights of a self-guiding automobile tour that visitors to the Great Smoky Mountains National Park can take through this remote valley. Some of the old farmhouses, mills and churches remain, others have been rebuilt, and the area is still farmed, under Park Service supervision, by descendants of the old settlers.*

shows the influence of Robert Adam's "antique style." The museum's permanent collection of prints, paintings and sculpture is augmented by frequently changing exhibits. Among the most interesting displays are the furnishings built to scale in the Thorne Miniature Rooms. *Open Tues.-Sun. Small charge.*

Frank H. McClung Museum *1327 Circle Park, University of Tennessee* Fine arts as well as history and natural history are represented here, but the emphasis is on anthropological materials. Displays illustrate how regional prehistoric Indian artifacts were made and used. An important exhibit is the Duck River Cache of chipped stone implements found in Humphreys County in 1894. *Open daily except holidays.*

James White's Fort *205 E. Hill Ave.* James White, the first settler of the area and founder of Knoxville, built the main house in 1786. The two-story structure has been restored, using its original exterior logs, joist rafters and floor, and moved to the corner opposite its initial site. A number of original furnishings can be seen inside. Later White added three log cabins for visitors and surrounded the complex with a stockade as protection against Indian attacks. *Open daily except Dec. 25. Small charge.*

Marble Springs Historic Farm *Neubert Springs Rd.* Tennessee's first governor, John Sevier, built this two-story log house prior to 1792 to serve as a trading post and rallying point for settlers in times of danger on the frontier. The restored dwelling is flanked by a rebuilt kitchen with a distinctive "stick" chimney. A springhouse and smokehouse can also be seen in the fenced-in clearing. *Open daily mid-Mar.-mid-Nov. Adults and children over 6 small charge.*

Ramsey House *Thorngrove Pike (6 mi. E. of Knoxville)* Constructed in 1797 of local marble and limestone, this simple but stately restored dwelling is thought to be Knox County's earliest stone house. Its builder was Francis A. Ramsey, a prominent citizen and public official, and it remained in the Ramsey family until 1866. Exhibits of old quilts, costumes, tools and implements are held from time to time, as are demonstrations of 18th-century home crafts. *Open Tues.-Sun. Apr.-Oct. Small charge.*

97. Cades Cove *Off Little River Rd., 27 mi. S.W. of Gatlinburg, Tenn.* Early in the 1800s a number of pioneer families settled in this isolated valley. Today the sturdy log cabins, churches, mills and farms that they built can still be seen in a lovely mountain setting. The Great Smoky Mountains National Park maintains this area as an open-air museum, while leasing some of the acreage for active farming. Visitors can take a self-guided automobile tour of the community and visually drift back in time to pioneer days. *Open daily.*

98. Pioneer Farmstead *Oconaluftee, N.C.* Pioneer history comes alive in this reconstructed farmstead. Log buildings and split-rail fences depict a way of life that has all but disappeared. During the summer weaving, blacksmithing, shake-making and other pioneer activities are demonstrated. *Open daily.*

99. Oconaluftee Indian Village *Rte. 441, Cherokee, N.C.* This fascinating replica of an 18th-century Indian community enables visitors to understand the Cherokee life-style. They lived in notched log cabins similar to those built by early white settlers. The religious and political center of this village is a seven-sided council house where animal pelts, ceremonial drums and gourd rattles can be seen. Various ritual devices are explained on the squareground by members of the tribe, who also demonstrate 10 Indian crafts including basketry, beadwork, pottery and dugout canoe making. Dances can be seen as part of *Unto These Hills*, a Cherokee drama presented nightly except Sundays in July and August. *Open daily mid-May-mid-Oct. Adults $2.50, children $1.25.*

[**100**] *The hand-carved Cherokee effigy masks to be seen here are among the finest authentic ones in existence. Up until about 100 years ago, the Indians used them in ceremonial dances and to help heal the sick.*

100. Museum of the Cherokee Indian *Rte. 441, Cherokee, N.C.* In 1838 the federal government forcibly removed most of the Cherokee from their lands in the southeastern U.S. to Indian Territory (present-day Oklahoma). Descendants of the few who escaped the roundup and the subsequent Trail of Tears live on the reservation where this museum is located. The museum houses the most extensive display of Cherokee artifacts ever assembled, including the rare effigy masks used by Cherokee medicine men and ceremonial dancers. Exhibits describe the making of many of the artifacts. Also kept here is the largest collection of original Cherokee documents and rare writings about the tribe. In these are found accounts of celebrated Cherokee such as Sequoyah, the inventor of the Cherokee alphabet and perhaps the only man ever to have devised an entire alphabet (the giant Sequoia redwoods of California were named for him), and Will Thomas, the only white man to become a Cherokee chief. *Open daily Apr.-Oct. Small charge.*

101. Vance Birthplace State Historic Site *Reems Creek Rd., Weaverville, N.C.* Zebulon Baird Vance was North Carolina's Civil War governor and later a U.S. senator. His house, built in 1795, has been reconstructed with materials from the original five-room pine log building and is furnished with 18th-century country-style pieces. Also on the site are a toolhouse, smokehouse, corncrib, loom house, springhouse and servants' quarters. Exhibits relating to the life of Governor Vance and a display of mountain handicrafts may be seen at the Visitor Center. *Open Tues.-Sun.*

[**102**] *The ceiling arches 75 feet above the table in the Banquet Hall of George Vanderbilt's Biltmore mansion. Over the elaborately carved triple fireplace are cast banners of 11 great powers when America was discovered.*

102. Biltmore House and Gardens *S. of Asheville, N.C.* George W. Vanderbilt's home was truly his castle, French Renaissance style. About 1000 men worked from 1890 to 1895 to build the 250-room mansion and landscape 35 acres of formal gardens amid many more acres of informal gardens and woodlands. Inside, the drawing room, banquet hall, library and other spacious rooms are graced with Persian rugs, tapestries, a Wedgwood mantel, ancient Chinese vases and an array of rare antiques, paintings, books and objets d'art, including an ivory chess set once owned by Napoleon. Outside, splendid gardens, walks and pools provide a fitting counterpart to the home. It is now a privately owned National Historic Site. *Open daily Feb.-mid-Dec. Adults $3.50, children over 5 $2.00.*

103. St. Lawrence Church *97 Haywood St., Asheville, N.C.* A Spanish architect, Rafael Guastavino, designed this Spanish Baroque-style Catholic church, completed in 1920. It is constructed of tiles and brick; copper covering the dome's tiles represents the only use of metal. Guastavino (who is buried in a crypt here) donated the large, self-supporting dome and brought the 17th-century walnut Crucifixion tableau above the main altar from Spain. His son, Rafael, Jr., who completed the church after his father's death in 1908, developed the luster glaze tiles used on the door of the crypt. Decorations in glazed polychrome terra cotta are another important feature, along with handsome, stained-glass windows and fine marble statues. *Open daily.*

104. Thomas Wolfe Memorial *48 Spruce St., Asheville, N.C.* In his autobiographical novel *Look Homeward, Angel,* Thomas Wolfe describes in powerful detail the boarding house, owned and operated by his mother, which was his childhood home. Furnished as it was in the early 1900s, the house retains the atmosphere and appearance that Wolfe so successfully memorialized in his novel. It became a literary shrine in 1949. *Open daily May-Oct. Small charge.*

105. Church of St. John in the Wilderness *Flat Rock, N.C.* This brick Episcopal church was originally built as a private chapel in 1836 and was enlarged in 1852 to assume its present appearance. Its simple interior of native wood has exposed beams and arches; the brass name plates of early pew owners can still be seen. Carl Sandburg's funeral service was held here in 1967. *Open daily.*

106. Poinsett Bridge *Rte. 25, N.E. of Cleveland, S.C.* The state's oldest span, this 1820 stone bridge with its keystone arch is still in use. It is named for Joel Poinsett, scientist and diplomat, who is also commemorated by the poinsettia plant which he introduced into this country from Mexico. *Open daily.*

107. Bob Jones University Art Museum *Bob Jones University, Rte. 29, 3 mi. N. of Greenville, S.C.* Devoted entirely to religious art, this important collection has major works by Titian, Tintoretto and Botticelli. Canvases by French, Italian and Flemish Baroque artists include works by Rubens, van Dyck and Rembrandt. Some of the 27 galleries are also decorated with handsome inlaid paneling. The paintings are complemented by period furniture, statuary and other art objects. A number of 15th- through 19th-century icons can be admired along with a collection of Near East religious antiquities. *Open Tues.-Sun. except holidays.*

108. Greenville City Hall *Main and Broad Sts., Greenville, S.C.* This elaborate brick Romanesque Revival structure bears a striking resemblance to the Smithsonian Building in Washington, D.C. Its castellated towers and precast terra cotta insets are among its exterior charms. Completed in 1892 as a post office, it has served its current function since 1938. The interior woodwork is outstanding and includes fine wainscoting and carved oak balustrades on the ornate staircase. Occupying a site once used as an Indian burial ground, the building is said to be haunted by ghosts whose bones were disturbed during construction. *Open Mon.-Fri. except holidays.*

109. Walnut Grove Plantation *Rte. 221, Roebuck, S.C.* Walnut Grove, an up-country plantation established on land included in a 1763 grant to its builder, Charles Moore, by King George III, has been completely restored. The main house is a plain two-story Georgian structure with worthy Queen Anne mantels, fine paneling, pre-1830 furniture and a colorful history. During the Revolution it was the scene of three murders committed by a notorious Tory, and some of Daniel Morgan's patriot riflemen stopped here before their victory at the Battle of Cowpens in 1781. On the plantation are a number of outbuildings: an authentically equipped kitchen built around 1764, a well house, smokehouse, blacksmith's forge and one of the area's first schools, Rocky Spring Academy. The restored garden

contains boxwood, flowers and herbs for cooking and medicine, and is shaded by venerable trees as old as the house itself. *Open Tues.-Sun. Mar.-Nov. Adults $2.00, children small charge.*

110. Clemson University *Clemson, S.C.* South Carolina founded Clemson Agricultural College in 1889 on land that Thomas G. Clemson had bequeathed the state. During Reconstruction this scientist and agriculturist had unsuccessfully tried to raise funds to give the South "an institution for the diffusion of scientific knowledge" that would aid in its return to prosperity. Today, Clemson's dreamed-of institution includes 52 main buildings on 600 acres and an adjacent forestry preserve that encompasses 23,000 acres.

FORT HILL About 1825, the year he was inaugurated Vice President of the U.S., John C. Calhoun acquired a plantation of 1100 acres. On it was a small house that he enlarged to 14 rooms, named Fort Hill and used as his country home until his death in 1850. The impressive frame structure, with three Doric-columned piazzas, contains a large number of Calhoun furnishings. In the parlor, where Thomas Clemson married Calhoun's eldest daughter, are a chair and sofa that belonged to George Washington. A dining room sideboard made of paneling from the frigate *Constitution* (Old Ironsides) was a gift of Henry Clay. *Open Tues.-Sun.*

HANOVER HOUSE A prominent French Huguenot completed this handsome clapboard dwelling in 1716, naming it after George I of England, the Hanoverian king who befriended these religious refugees. A magnificent example of a South Carolina low-country house, its Gallic gambrel roof contains pedimented dormer windows and external end chimneys. Shuttered gun slots in the basement wall indicate its builder's fear of Indian attack. Moved here in the early 1940s and restored, it has fine walnut paneling and 17th- and 18th-century furniture of great distinction, including a William and Mary armchair and a very early Queen Anne tea table. A rare 1694 Bible is also on display. *Open Tues.-Sun.*

RUDOLPH LEE GALLERY Located on the main floor of the College of Architecture building, this collection includes 17th- and 18th-century Flemish and Dutch paintings, most of which were brought from Europe by Thomas Clemson. Contemporary American graphics and paintings as well as architectural designs and models by students are also shown, and many temporary exhibits are held. *Open Mon.-Fri.*

111. Keowee-Toxaway Visitor Center *Intersection of Rtes. 130 and 183, 13 mi. N.W. of Clemson, S.C.* This modern building is located on the vast Duke Power Keowee-Toxaway electric power complex. Exhibits here are devoted to "The Story of Energy," a fascinating program that traces the nature of water, wind, fire and other elements. A number of "involvement exhibits," in which visitors take part, show how man has learned to control these forces. Highlights include a reconstructed coal mine, operational waterwheel and a simplified demonstration of how a nuclear reactor operates. Slide shows, closed circuit television productions and films are additional features of the center's educational program. A panoramic view of the complex, which includes a nuclear station, the Keowee Dam and man-made Lake Keowee behind it, can be seen from the lounge and from two exterior overlooks. *Open daily except Jan. 1, Dec. 24-25.*

112. Traveler's Rest *Rte. 123, 6 mi. E. of Toccoa, Ga.* The original section of this structure was built in 1784 as the residence of Major Jesse Walton, Revolutionary soldier and Indian fighter. Early in the 19th century the property was acquired by Devereaux Jarrett, who expanded it for use as an inn, trading post and post office. The building is of frame construction over a cobblestone basement; interior walls are paneled with chestnut

[107] *(above) Among the treasures in the Samuels Gallery of the Bob Jones University Art Museum are two Flemish stained-glass windows and* The Procession to Calvary *by the anonymous Master of St. Sang. (left) Two wings of a triptych by Colijn de Coter, a Flemish painter of the late 15th century, have been joined together to form this picture. Michael the Archangel is on the left, St. Agnes with lamb on the right.*

and walnut. The house is now operated as a museum and contains many of the original furnishings. Among these are a walnut swinging cradle and a tester bed dating from about 1820. Jarrett's account books, hotel registers and other memorabilia are on display. *Open Tues.-Sun. Nov.-Apr.*

113. Dahlonega Courthouse Gold Museum *Rte. 19, Dahlonega, Ga.* In 1828, with the reports of gold discoveries in what was then Cherokee Territory, prospectors swarmed into this section of northern Georgia. The story of that first major U.S. gold rush can be traced in the 1836 Greek Revival courthouse, the scene of many suits over mine claims. The museum in the handsomely restored building contains gold dust, nuggets, mining equipment and many old photographs. A number of these objects relate to the U.S. branch mint that once stood nearby and that receipted over $6,000,000 in gold between 1838 and 1861. In 1849 Matthew F. Stephenson, later assayer for the mint, stood on the porch of the courthouse and attempted to dissuade miners from leaving for the California gold fields. Pointing to a nearby peak, he exclaimed, "There's millions in it." Mark Twain is said to have paraphrased this remark when he wrote: "There's gold in them thar hills!" *Open Tues.-Sun. except Thanksgiving Day and Dec. 25.*

114. Georgia Museum of Art *University of Georgia, Jackson St., Athens, Ga.* American paintings from 1845 to 1945 form the core of the Eva Underhill Holbrook Memorial Collection of American Art which is housed here. A print collection of about 1500 works by European and American artists of the 17th, 18th and 19th centuries is also featured. Founded in 1945 with the donation of 100 paintings, the museum's collection has grown to include some 3000 objects. Among recent special exhibitions have been a retrospective show of the work of Lamar Dodd and the paintings and lithographs of Philip Pearlstein augmented by loans from other museums and private collections. *Open daily except holidays and college vacations.*

115. Taylor-Grady House *634 Prince Ave., Athens, Ga.* General Robert Taylor, a wealthy planter and cotton merchant, built this handsome Greek Revival house in 1839. It was later (1865-68) the home of Henry Woodfin Grady, a noted editor and speaker. The white two-story mansion has a portico on three sides supported by 13 large Doric columns linked by a graceful railing of iron grillwork. Now the home of the Athens Junior Assembly, it is attractively furnished with period pieces. *Open Sun., Mon., Wed., Fri. Small charge.*

116. Cokesbury Historic District *N. of Greenwood, S.C.* In the early 19th century, a village of three-story mansions and thriving cotton plantations was located here. It was a Methodist community named for Thomas Coke and Francis Asbury, the first two Methodist bishops in the U.S., and supported a Methodist boys school. After the Civil War when many families moved away, most of the homes decayed or burned. Only eight of the original 54 remain. Two have been restored, work continues on several others. *Open Tues., Wed., Sat. May-Oct.*

[114] *This poignant oil portrait,* Sissy, *by Robert Henri (1865-1929) is in the Holbrook collection of American painting. After 1905 Henri headed a group that spurned academicism and turned to themes of common life.*

COKESBURY COLLEGE This austere three-story Greek Revival building completed in 1854 served as the Masonic Female College until 1876. Later it was part of the Cokesbury Conference School and, from 1918 to 1954, a public school. Today it is fully restored in a landscaped setting of azaleas, shrubs and trees.

117. Oakley Park *Rte. 25, Edgefield, S.C.* This Greek Revival clapboard house, built in 1835, became the home of General Martin Witherspoon Gary, the "Bald Eagle of the Confederacy." General Gary was later a leader of a political group, known as the Red Shirts, which in 1876 wrested control of the state from the blacks, "scalawags" and "carpetbaggers" that made up the Republican Reconstruction government. The gracious dwelling has double-door entrances, topped by fanlights, that open onto front and rear piazzas and there are wide center halls on both floors. Plasterwork, handsome carved woodwork and period furnishings are among the outstanding interior features, and there is a museum room with books, manuscripts and Confederate battle flags. The house and the grounds, which include a garden, a well and several outbuildings, are maintained by the United Daughters of the Confederacy. *Open Tues., Fri. Small charge.*

118. Augusta, Ga.

Founded in 1735 and named after the mother of George III, Augusta was a battlefield of the Revolutionary War. At the end of the 18th century it was the state's chief tobacco market. In the 19th century cotton replaced

tobacco, and large-scale manufacture of the famous Georgia red brick began. The city is now a center of diversified manufacturing and a winter resort where golf is the chief recreation. The Masters Golf Tournament is held here each April.

Augusta Richmond County Museum *540 Telfair St.* This structure, built in 1802, was for 124 years the home of the Richmond Academy. During that period the original stark exterior was modified several times, the additions including cast-iron columns on the porch and Tudor-style crenellations on the roof. Now a museum, the building contains exhibits relating to local and military history, art, natural science and archaeology. *Open Tues.-Sun. early Jan.-late Dec.*

First Baptist Church *Eighth and Greene Sts.* This large domed structure, dating from 1902, is the third to be occupied by the church, which was founded in 1817. Within it are displayed the church's first Communion set and Bible; the original Communion table and pulpit chairs are still in use. The Southern Baptist Convention was organized on this site in 1845. *Open Sun.-Fri.*

First Presbyterian Church *642 Telfair St.* Robert Mills originally designed this 1812 church in the classical style, but today, after extensive remodeling in the 1840s and 1890s, it presents a mid-Victorian Gothic appearance. In 1861, after being refused seating by the Presbyterian General Assembly in Philadelphia, Presbyterian representatives from southern states met here and founded the Presbyterian Church in the Confederate States—today known as the Presbyterian Church in the U.S. Dr. Joseph Ruggles Wilson, father of Woodrow Wilson, was minister of this church for 12 years (1858-70). *Open Sun.-Fri.*

Gertrude Herbert Memorial Institute of Art *506 Telfair St.* Nicholas Ware, a mayor of Augusta and U.S. senator, built the institute's home, a three-story frame house, in 1818. Whether because of its lovely, lighthearted design or because of its high construction cost, the building came to be known as Ware's Folly. It has since been remodeled several times, but retains much of its original appearance and is noted for its exceptional staircase. Now the property of the art institute, it contains a collection of graphics and paintings and is the scene of frequent art exhibitions arranged by the institute or by the Augusta Art Association. The institute's art school offers classes for adults and children. *Open Mon.-Fri.*

Mackay House *1822 Broad St.* Built around 1760, this frame gambrel-roof structure is considered Augusta's oldest house and one of Georgia's most important Colonial buildings. Known for many years as Mackay's Trading House, it was a center for trade with the area's Indians. During the Revolutionary War it was the scene of a battle between American troops led by Colonel Elijah Clark on the one side and British, Tory and Indian forces on the other. Thirteen American survivors were hanged from the exterior staircase by the British commander. Mackay House has been beautifully restored to reflect its Colonial heritage: the first floor is furnished with 18th-century antiques; the second contains exhibits relating to the South's role in the Revolution; and the third features displays pertaining to Augusta's early Indian trade. *Open Tues.-Sun. except Thanksgiving Day and Dec. 25.*

St. John United Methodist Church *734 Greene St.* This brick edifice was built to replace an earlier structure which had been sold to a Baptist congregation. An eclectic mixture of Gothic and Victorian influences, its exterior features include rounded windows and entrances plus two towers of unequal heights. It remains one of the state's oldest Methodist churches. *Open daily.*

St. Paul's Episcopal Church *605 Reynolds St.* This brick structure, built in 1919, is the congregation's fourth church on the same site. The original St. Paul's was erected here in the shade of Fort Augusta in 1750—a large stone Celtic cross in the gardens marks the location of the fort. That church was destroyed by cannon fire during the Revolutionary War. A later building was the scene of the 1823 convention that created the Episcopal Diocese of Georgia. The present handsome red brick structure with a white-columned portico and cupola has an equally beautiful interior. It still has the original baptismal font, which was brought from England by St. Paul's first priest, the Reverend Jonathan Copp, in 1751. *Open Mon.-Fri.*

119. Washington-Wilkes Historical Museum *308 E. Robert Toombs Ave., Washington, Ga.* Civil War memorabilia, including Jefferson Davis's camp chest, and Indian relics fill the second floor of this 18-room white frame house. Furnishings in the first floor parlor, dining room and bedroom are as they might have been during the mid-19th century, while the high basement contains a restored antebellum kitchen and pantry. The comfortable front porch has lacy "carpenter Gothic" columns. Built around 1835, the house was owned by a succession of Washington families until 1955. *Open Tues.-Sun.*

120. Liberty Hall *Alexander H. Stephens Memorial State Park, Rte. 278, Crawfordville, Ga.* The two-story frame dwelling, standing in a state park named for its former owner, was the home of one of Georgia's most distinguished public servants. "Little Alex" Stephens was the diminutive lawyer and statesman who became a congressman, vice president of the Confederacy and later governor of Georgia (he died in that office in 1883). Stephens purchased the house in the 1840s and virtually rebuilt it in 1872. It was completely restored in the 1930s and is furnished with many of Stephens's own possessions; thus it truly reflects the graciousness of its owner and times. Hospitality was a key word here, and on the second floor is the Tramps' Room where many destitute transients spent the night. The slave quarters and several other outbuildings have also been restored. *Open Tues.-Sun. Small charge.*

CONFEDERATE MUSEUM Also located in the park is this white frame building in which the visitor can see Confederate uniforms, weapons and other items, as well as a number of Stephens's personal belongings. Letters, diaries and documents, including many written by Stephens during the Civil War, are also on view. *Open Tues.-Sun. Small charge.*

121. Old Governor's Mansion *Georgia College, 120 S. Clark St., Milledgeville, Ga.* From 1838 until 1868, when the state capital was moved from Milledgeville to Atlanta, Georgia's governors lived in this stately pale pink stucco mansion. It is an outstanding example of Greek Revival architecture and has an imposing portico with Ionic columns and a classical pediment. Its impressive interior, which includes rooms of many different shapes, features a 50-foot-high central rotunda topped by a coffered domed ceiling with gold-leaf decoration. The fine furnishings—primarily English Regency and American neoclassical—are typical of the era in which the house was built. During the Civil War the governor was captured here by Union troops, and General Sherman stopped here briefly during his march to the sea. Since 1890 it has served as the home of Georgia College presidents. *Open Tues.-Sun. except holidays. Small charge.*

122. Grand Opera House *651 Mulberry St., Macon, Ga.* This outstanding restoration contains one of the nation's largest stages. The stage is so large, in fact, that the chariot race for *Ben Hur* was once performed here with live horses. Sarah Bernhardt, Dorothy and Lillian Gish, Will Rogers and the Lunts are some of the personalities who have appeared in this historic theater. Built of brick in 1884, its exterior is notable for a unique five-story, cast-iron staircase. The interior is elegantly decorated with crystal chandeliers and velvet wall hangings. The original asbestos fire curtain is still in use, as are the hand-pulled riggings. Plays, symphony concerts, ballets and lectures are among the programs presented here. *Open Mon.-Fri. Small charge.*

123. Hay House *934 Georgia Ave., Macon, Ga.* In 1851, William Butler Johnston returned with his bride from Italy determined to reproduce an Italian villa in Macon. And so he did, with the guidance of architect James B. Ayers and the help of Italian artisans. The red brick 24-room house was seven years in construction and exhibits the elaborate craftsmanship typical of the Italian Renaissance. Today its superlative woodwork and plaster work are complemented by fine furnishings and art—collected primarily by the late Mr. and Mrs. Park Lee Hay, who bought the house in 1925. Hay House features several immense rooms with vaulted, ornamented ceilings. One of these, the ballroom, with a 50-foot-high, skylighted ceiling, was planned as the mansion's art gallery. *Open Tues.-Sun. except holidays. Adults $1.50, children small charge.*

[122] *A palatial theater in a comparatively small place—when it first opened in 1884 it could seat more than 15 percent of the town's 15,000 citizens—Macon's Grand Opera House has been handsomely restored to greatness.*

124. Ocmulgee National Monument *Rte. 80E, Macon, Ga.* Paleo-Indians began to arrive in the Ocmulgee area about 10,000 years ago. A major agricultural settlement of mound-building Indians developed here in the 900s. On this site you can see seven mounds and a reconstructed ceremonial lodge with its original clay floor. A Creek Indian Craft Shop is located at the Visitor Center, and modern Creek Indians of Oklahoma, Ocmulgee's descendents, work at the park. *Open daily except Dec. 25. Small charge.*

125. Jefferson Davis Memorial State Park Museum *Off Rte. 32, Irwinville, Ga.* Although this small building holds a number of interesting Civil War documents and other relics, an outdoor bronze bust of Davis is also a focus of attention for visitors. It marks the spot where he was taken prisoner by Michigan cavalrymen, thus foiling his attempt to continue the conflict even after Lee had surrendered at Appomattox. *Open Tues.-Sun. Small charge.*

126. Parkway Craft Center *Moses H. Cone Memorial Park, Blue Ridge Pkwy., N.E. of Blowing Rock, N.C.* Textile industrialist Moses H. Cone, the "Denim King," built this mansion around 1900 with materials hauled by oxen over 25 miles of rough mountain roads; he called it Flat Top Manor. It is located within a 3600-acre recreational area (formerly the Cone estate) that includes horse carriage and hiking trails and trout and bass lakes. The house is now used by the Southern Highland Handicraft Guild, which in summer presents demonstrations of old mountain crafts such as weaving, vegetable dyeing, wood carving and pottery making. *Open daily May-Oct.*

127. Chinqua-Penn Plantation House *Wentworth Rd., N.W. of Reidsville, N.C.* In 1925 Mr. and Mrs. Jefferson Penn's 27-room stone and log mansion was completed, and they began furnishing it with interesting and rare art objects that they gathered on world tours. European and Oriental antiques are found throughout the mansion, including two life-size Chinese statues of about 700 A.D., a number of Nepalese altar pieces, a 15th-century Byzantine mosaic, an African gilt bronze panther head, a Tibetan hitching post and a Peruvian mask. Today the house is maintained by the University of North Carolina at Greensboro. On the property are attractive gardens, greenhouses and an authentic Chinese pagoda. *Open Wed.-Sun. Mar.-mid-Dec. Adults $1.50, children small charge.*

128. Historic Bethabara Park *2147 Bethabara Rd., Winston-Salem, N.C.* This is the site of the first Moravian settlement in North Carolina, founded in 1753. Archaeological excavations have exposed the foundations of early buildings as well as numerous interesting artifacts. The palisade which encircled the original community has been reconstructed in the original trench. Restorations include the Bethabara Church and Gemein Haus, built in 1788; the 1803 home of a Betha-

And not one savage beast be seen to frown.
A little child shall lead them on in love.
When man is led and moved by sovereign grace.
His grim carnivrous nature then shall cease.

[130] Peaceable Kingdom of the Branch, *by Edward Hicks (1780–1849), is a touching example of primitive folk art in a collection of great American paintings of the last 200 years in Reynolda House. Hicks was a Quaker sign painter who did more than 50 pictures on the "Peaceable Kingdom" theme. His experience as a sign painter can be seen in the lettering of the quotations that surround this version. The lamb lying down with the lion is one obvious peace symbol in the picture; another, hardly discernible, is the group of Indians reading William Penn's treaty with them beneath Virginia's Natural Bridge.*

bara brewer; and a potter's house dating from 1782. A museum in the brewer's house contains unusual examples of Moravian pottery and exhibits showing the history of the settlement. The park has a nature trail with markers indicating rare herbs and wild flowers. *Open daily Easter Day–Nov.*

129. Old Salem *Off Rte. 52, Winston-Salem, N.C.* See feature display on pages 278–9.

130. Reynolda House *Reynolda Rd., Winston-Salem, N.C.* This was the former home of Richard J. Reynolds, founder of the tobacco company that later became R. J. Reynolds Industries. Completed in 1917, it was the center of a 1000-acre self-sustaining village and farm. The Reynolda House collection of American art—major works by Stuart, Andrew Wyeth, Copley, Church, Hassam, Johnson, Mount and many others—is on view here. There is also a large collection of fine antique furniture and a variety of art objects from the 18th and 19th centuries. *Open Tues.–Sun. Feb.–Dec. except Dec. 25. Small charge.*

131. Greensboro Historical Museum *130 Summit Ave., Greensboro, N.C.* In a former church that served as a hospital late in the Civil War are over 100 exhibits that re-create the history of Guilford County from its prehistoric Indian settlement to the present. Among the exhibits are period rooms, antique glassware and china, and military weapons and uniforms used in seven American wars. In the Dolley Madison Room are objects that relate to this vivacious First Lady, who was born in the county in 1768; several of her gowns, manuscripts, personal items and a portrait are exhibited. A replica of Greensborough Village as it was in the 19th century includes buildings associated with William Sydney Porter, the short-story writer who found fame and misfortune as O. Henry. Among these buildings are the schoolhouse where he studied, his uncle's drugstore where he worked as a pharmacist and a charming general store with round-top glass display cases and flour barrels. The museum also contains an extensive collection of O. Henry memorabilia and writings. *Open Tues.–Sun. except holidays.*

FRANCIS MCNAIRY HOUSE A settler from Pennsylvania, Francis McNairy, built this crude log structure in 1761. His son was a lifelong friend of Andrew Jackson, who lived in the house briefly while practicing law. The house was moved in 1967 to its present site beside the museum. Originally it stood near the Guilford Courthouse battlefield site and was used as a hospital after the 1781 battle.

132. Guilford Courthouse National Military Park *New Garden Rd., Off Rte. 220, 6 mi. N.W. of Greensboro, N.C.* Here, in March 1781, a British bayonet charge overwhelmed two lines of inexperienced American foot soldiers. In pressing their advantage, however, the outnumbered Redcoat ranks, thinned by earlier volleys, were shattered by the disciplined musketry of veteran Maryland infantry. Although royal artillery cannon fire broke up a counterattack and drove the Americans from the field, it was a Pyrrhic victory for Lord Cornwallis. Having sustained heavy casualties, he was forced to begin a long retreat that culminated in the momentous British surrender at Yorktown seven months later. Twenty-eight memorials stand on the battlefield, including a fine bronze statue of General Nathanael Greene, the American commander. By means of two self-guiding trails and a marked auto-tour, visitors may follow the movement of the battle. At the Visitor Center are a number of dioramas, uniforms and weapons of the period. *Open daily except Jan. 1 and Dec. 25.*

133. Weatherspoon Art Gallery *Walker Ave. and McIver St., University of North Carolina at Greensboro, N.C.* The emphasis here is on 20th-century American art, but there is also a small collection of Oriental and primitive art. Calder, de Kooning, Nadelman and Henri are among the leading artists represented. The gallery offers talks, lectures and many special exhibitions. *Open Sun.–Fri. during college year.*

This view looking north up Old Salem's Main Street shows several of the district's sturdy, gracious buildings. The Christoph Vogler House is in the foreground, with the John Vogler House and the Community Store beyond.

The living room of the John Vogler house is furnished with authentic details like a game table, bellows and music stand. Moravians have always been noted for their love of music; Vogler probably played in a brass choir.

129. Old Salem

Off Rte. 52, Winston-Salem, N.C.

What sets Old Salem apart from most other restored towns is the fact that it is inhabited. People live, work and go to school in the Old Salem Historic District and commute to jobs in surrounding Winston-Salem. Salem (from the Hebrew word for peace) was founded in 1766 by Moravians who moved down from their original settlement in Pennsylvania. The Moravians, devout Germanic people, valued education, craftsmanship and trade. They practiced communal living, dividing themselves into groups, called choirs, according to age, sex and marital status. Unmarried women lived in the Single Sisters' House, built in 1786. This house and the restored Girls Boarding School next door now serve as dormitories for Salem College. Six original buildings are open to the public: Boys School, Single Brothers' House, Miksch Tobacco Shop, Winkler Bakery, John Vogler House and Salem Tavern. The Tavern, reputed for its hospitality, was one of the first buildings erected by the Moravians, who from the beginning intended Salem to be a trading center. Old Salem today remains a fine example of town planning. The streets were carefully laid out on paper before a single tree was cut down—and the plans were followed. George Washington admired the gravity-flow water system, with its ingeniously bored log pipes. The Museum of Early Southern Decorative Arts, with 15 period rooms reflecting the styles and craftsmanship of the South between 1690 and 1820, rounds out a visit to this delightful window into the past. *Open daily except Dec. 25. Combination ticket adults $3.50, children $1.25.*

The original half-timbered Salem Tavern, built around 1772, burned down in 1784. Five days later a new brick building began to rise from the ashes. This is the kitchen of the 1784 tavern, which is now a museum. The more recent addition has a modern kitchen, from which food is served.

Modern day artisans, like this tinsmith making cookie cutters and candle sconces in the Single Brothers' House, keep up the tradition of craftsmanship that was a prominent feature of Moravian life. There were many skilled craftsmen among the Moravians who came to America from Europe in the 18th century. In another room a gunsmith may be putting the finishing touches to the wooden stock of a rifle.

134. High Point Historical Society Museum *1805 E. Lexington Ave., High Point, N.C.* High Point has for over a century been a center of the furniture industry in this country. In the museum's collection are 18th- and early-19th-century woodworking tools once in wide use throughout the area. Objects relating to the evolution of the hosiery industry are also exhibited here, as well as items depicting the history of High Point and its rural surroundings from Colonial times to the present. *Open Tues.-Sun. except holidays.*

135. Cooleemee Plantation House *Rte. 64, Advance, N.C.* Straight and curved lines are balanced delightfully in this beautiful interpretation of the Greek Revival style. The cruciform brick and white stucco building, with columned verandas, magnificent bay windows and tall octagonal belvedere, was completed in 1855. Descendants of the Hairstons who acquired the 4000-acre plantation in 1817 live here and have blended modern pieces with their family's original furnishings. Cotton and tobacco once grew at Cooleemee; now the land is devoted to forestry and recreation. About one and one-half miles from the house, on the shores of Forest Lake, is a camp resort operated by the Hairstons. *Open Wed., Sat., Sun. June-Aug. Small charge.*

136. Potters Museum *Rte. 220, N. of Seagrove, N.C.* A historical review of North Carolina folk pottery can be seen here. The craft was brought to the state by potters from Staffordshire, England. Jugs, jars, dishes, foot warmers, toys, grave markers, inkwells and many other examples of stoneware and earthenware—some dating from as early as 1750—are on display, and in addition there is a work area where present-day potters carry on their craft. *Open Mon.-Sat.*

137. Davidson College *N. Main St., Davidson, N.C.* Of the four pre-Civil War buildings on this campus, two, Eumenean Hall and Philanthropic Hall, continue to fulfill their original purpose of serving college literary societies. Both buildings have been renovated but still contain some of their original furnishings. *Open daily during college sessions.*

138. First Presbyterian Church *70 Union St. N., Concord, N.C.* The simple design of this 1927 brick church is an adaptation of 18th-century English ecclesiastical architecture. Its main exterior decorative element is a clock tower above which rises an elegant spire. Inside are traditional box pews, round-topped windows and a fine Palladian window at the rear of the chancel. A four-acre Memorial Garden contains attractive brick walks, huge trees, an old stone fountain and seasonal displays of bulbs as well as many shrubs and perennials. *Open daily.*

139. Kings Mountain National Military Park Visitor Center *Kings Mountain, N.C.* The third largest military park in the U.S. was the scene of a bloody battle in the autumn of 1780 when American troops encircled and killed or took prisoner every member of a British force led by Major Patrick Ferguson. Stone markers identify the graves of Ferguson and one of the American leaders, Major William Chronicle of the North Carolina militia. A one-mile self-guiding trail passes two large monuments within the 3900-acre expanse. The small museum contains a diorama and other exhibits that help explain the battle. In summer, firing demonstrations of American muskets and British "Brown Besses" are given. *Open daily except Dec. 25.*

140. Mint Museum of Art *501 Hempstead Pl., Charlotte, N.C.* This Federal-style building, designed by William Strickland, served as a branch of the U.S. Mint from 1837, when this area was one of the leading gold producers in the U.S., until the beginning of the Civil War. After the war it served as a federal assay office. Thomas Edison used the building between 1900 and 1903 to conduct several experiments in an attempt to extract gold from ore by means of electricity. Dismantled and reconstructed on its present site in 1935, the building today houses a fine collection of painting, sculpture and decorative arts. Emphasis is on Renaissance, Baroque, 18th-century English, 19th- and 20th-century European, American and Pre-Columbian art. In the Delhom Gallery is an unusually good collection of European and Oriental ceramics. Among the many temporary exhibits are several devoted to artists from southeastern states. *Open Tues.-Sun. except holidays.*

141. James K. Polk Birthplace State Historic Site *Pineville, N.C.* In 1795 James K. Polk, the 11th President of the U.S., was born on this site in a log cabin similar to the one that has been reconstructed here. Also on the site is a Visitor Center which offers a film on Polk's life and exhibits relating to his term in office and his achievements as President. *Open Tues.-Sun. except holidays.*

142. Nature Museum of York County *Mount Gallant Rd., Rock Hill, S.C.* Specimens of many species of mammals are displayed here in replicas of their natural habitats. Among the exhibits is a polar bear shot by Admiral Robert E. Peary at the North Pole in 1909. Also on display are films used by Thomas Edison in his Kinetoscope as well as records, photographs and other materials. The live-animal room and small outdoor zoo are popular with children. *Open Tues.-Sun. except holidays.*

143. Rose Hill *Rte. 16, S. of Union, S.C.* This former plantation house stands amid boxwoods and roses, overlooking a 41-acre grove of hickory and oak trees. The handsome Federal-style mansion, completed in 1832, was the country home of William H. Gist, an ardent advocate of secession during his term as governor (1858-60). Gist added two-story porches to the front and back and stuccoed the brick facade. There are delicate fanlights over the doors on both levels. A number of pre-Civil War furnishings and Gist family pieces are displayed inside, and there is a ballroom on the second floor. Operated as a state park, the adjacent acres include a picnic area. *Open Tues.-Sun.*

144. Fairfield County Court House *Congress St., Winnsboro, S.C.* Robert Mills, the noted architect from South Carolina, designed this imposing Greek Revival structure, built in 1822. The two rear wings were added in 1939 along with the graceful double stairway that rises to the second floor through the Doric columns of

[140] *Since the town of Charlotte was named in honor of the marriage of George III to Charlotte of Mecklinburg-Strelitz in 1761, it is appropriate to find their portraits in the city's Mint Museum. These two opaque glass medallions in the Delhom Gallery were made by James Tassie, a Scot. His art was popular and prominent people sat for portraits. Tassie's secret composition of opaque glass died with his nephew and successor, William.*

the building's portico. Records held here date back to the 1730s. *Open Mon.-Sat. except holidays.*

145. Town Clock-Market Building *Washington St., Winnsboro, S.C.* This clock, said to be the longest continuously running town clock in the U.S., has been telling time since 1834, the year the Market Building was completed. The clockworks and the bell in the tower above the clock were made in France, shipped to Charleston and hauled by wagons to Winnsboro. As in most early communities, the bell was used as a fire alarm, distress signal and proclaimer of great events and also announced the arrival of supplies. *Open Mon.-Sat.*

146. Florence Museum *558 Spruce St., Florence, S.C.* Primitive art—African pieces plus Pueblo pottery and other artifacts of southwestern Indians—and the highly sophisticated and detailed work of the Orient are featured here. Among the many fine Chinese pieces are ceramics, bronzes and frescos and a superb 19th-century silk costume embroidered with Imperial motifs. The museum, housed in a 26-room former residence designed in the International style, also contains 19th-century American furnishings. Changing exhibits display work by South Carolina artists. *Open Tues.-Sun. early Sept.-May.*

147. Church of the Holy Cross *Stateburg, S.C.* Consecrated in 1852, this Gothic Revival Episcopal chapel with its steep roofline is built of pisé de terre (rammed earth). In addition to several fine German stained-glass windows dating from 1852, the church still has its original organ and silver pieces. *Open Wed., Sun.*

148. Columbia, S.C.

This capital city was established by the South Carolina legislature in 1786 on the site of an early-18th-century trading post. At first it was a trading center, but industry, particularly textiles, gradually began to dominate the economy. In 1801 it became the home of South Carolina College (later to become the University of South Carolina). Much of the city was destroyed by Sherman's army in February 1865, but fortunately a number of important structures have survived.

Columbia Museum of Art and Science *1112 Bull St.* Most treasured of the museum's possessions are the magnificent Renaissance paintings from the Samuel H. Kress collection, including works by such masters as Tintoretto and Botticelli. There is also considerable emphasis on local art forms—paintings, silver, jewelry, ceramics and furniture—from all periods in the state's history. *Coast Scene on the Mediterranean,* an 1811 oil by South Carolina romanticist Washington Allston, is displayed here along with paintings, drawings, sculptures and graphics by contemporary artists and a collection of artifacts from the Spanish Colonial period. The art library is considered to be the most comprehensive in the state. The Gibbes Planetarium, part of the science center established in 1959, is a popular attraction, as are natural history displays of live snakes and game fish native to the state and of marine life found off its coast. Dioramas of native mammals and birds are also on view. Gathered together in a nature garden are excellent collections of native ferns, shrubs and wildflowers. *Open Tues.-Sun.*

First Baptist Church *1306 Hampton St.* This Classical-style edifice with huge brick columns dates from 1859. The building is rich in history. Its sanctuary was the scene of the first (1860) meeting of South Carolina's secession convention, and the first draft of the state's Ordinance of Secession was written at the Communion table, which is still in use. The church, seating 1500 persons, serves the largest congregation of Baptists in South Carolina. *Open daily.*

Governor's Mansion *800 Richland St.* Built in 1855 to house the officers of the Arsenal Military Academy, this white stucco dwelling has served as the official residence of the state's governors since 1879. Its well-balanced exterior design is embellished by attractive ironwork trim. The furnishings within include some that belonged to former governors. Stuart's portrait of the last chief justice of South Carolina to be appointed by King George III hangs here, as do a number of paintings by state artists. An interesting 66-piece silver service from the U.S.S. *South Carolina* and a set of china made for President James Monroe's wife are also exhibited. Magnolias, oaks, palmettos and a three-tiered fountain decorate the grounds.

LACE HOUSE *801 Richland St.* This 1853 dwelling undoubtedly derives its name from the abundance of iron grillwork used on its two-tiered porch, entrance steps and sidewalk railing. It is used chiefly for official entertaining by the governor and occasionally for meetings of local organizations.

[**148.** *University Museum*] *The Bernard Baruch Silver Collection includes (clockwise) a 1730 tray, 1728 sugar bowl, 1730 teapot, 1727 milk jug, 1760 sugar tongs and 1721 candlesticks. Baruch was a native of South Carolina.*

Hampton-Preston House *1615 Blanding St.* When General Sherman burned Columbia in 1865, this house was spared so that it could be used by the sisters of a Roman Catholic convent. It later served for many years as a school and college. Originally a plain brick dwelling with a slate roof, it was begun in 1820 and purchased three years later by General Wade Hampton, a veteran of the American Revolution and the War of 1812. He remodeled it about 1834, adding roof pediments with fan windows, an attic and a circular staircase. Modified further in the 1850s, the house is now stuccoed and carries a front piazza with eight columns plus cast-iron steps with delicately ornamented railings. Among those known to have been guests here are John James Audubon, Henry Clay and John C. Calhoun. Operated as a museum, the house contains a number of Hampton family furnishings that reflect their mode of gracious living prior to the Civil War. *Open Sun.-Fri. Small charge.*

Robert Mills Historic House and Park *1616 Blanding St.* The first American-born professional architect and the first Federal architect, Robert Mills (1781-1855), served under seven Presidents. Best known as the designer of the Washington Monument, the U.S. Treasury Building and other public buildings in Washington, D.C., he began plans in 1823 for this three-story brick residence. The handsome building with three-part Venetian windows, Ionic entrance portico and arcaded rear elevation never served as a home, however: the wealthy merchant who commissioned it died before it was completed, and it was soon purchased by a Presbyterian theological seminary which used it for more than 100 years. In 1962 the Historic Columbia Foundation rescued the house from demolition and established it as a memorial to Mills. The foundation added the elegant interior details and several outbuildings originally called for in Mills's plan but never incorporated, and furnished it with fine pieces from the Empire, Regency and Classic Revival periods. The four-acre site also includes a garden styled after those of the 1820s. *Open Tues.-Sun. except holidays. Small charge.*

South Carolina Confederate Relic Room and Museum *World War Memorial Building, Sumter and Pendleton Sts.* In addition to Confederate uniforms and equipment, this collection includes military items from all periods of South Carolina's history. Costumed mannequins in the likenesses of Francis Marion, Thomas Sumter and other state notables are displayed in glass cases as are some posts and spikes from Charles Fort dating from 1562, a torch used by Union troops during the burning of the city in 1865 and an authentic carpetbag from Reconstruction days. There is also a small collection of 19th-century dolls and children's wear. *Open Mon.-Fri. except holidays.*

South Carolina State House *Gervais St.* Begun in 1855 but not completed until 1907, this granite and marble Italian Rennaissance-style capitol is noted for its superb facade graced by wide stone steps and a handsome cupola. The building was shelled during General Sherman's attack on the city in 1865; large brass stars cover the damage made by cannonballs. A huge dome and cupola surmount the structure. Its interior features include a large second-story lobby with entrances to the Senate and House of Representative chambers and the Legislative Library. The lobby itself contains outstanding painted plaster ceiling cornices and a decorative wrought-iron and walnut balcony reached by two staircases of the same material and design. Mahogany doors with a carved broken pediment and pineapple design open into the governor's offices, where a 14-arm Georgian chandelier and a Copley portrait can be admired. The figurehead from the bow of the U.S.S. *South Carolina* is prominently displayed in the lower lobby. On the grounds are memorials to South Carolina's Civil War dead, the Confederate women and General Wade Hampton, among others. *Open Mon.-Sat. Grounds open daily.*

Trinity Episcopal Church *1100 Sumter St.* This English Gothic-style edifice with its ornate twin towers was built in 1846, modeled after the Cathedral of St. Peter in York, England. Its simple interior contains the original box pews, a marble baptismal font and altar designed by Hiram Powers, and 10 outstanding memorial stained-glass windows. A chapel added in 1958 is decorated with a fine Carrara marble altar and a number of English stained-glass windows depicting scenes from the life of Christ. The parish dates from 1812, and the adjacent churchyard contains several headstones from that period as well as the graves of later South Carolina dignitaries. *Open daily.*

University Museum *War Memorial Building, University of South Carolina, Sumter and Pendleton Sts.* The museum is noted for two unusual collections: gems and antique silver. More than 2000 stones cut by J. Harry Howard, nationally recognized lapidarist, are shown in the gem collection. Visitors can also admire some hundred varieties of beautifully worked gems, including rubies, sapphires and emeralds. The silver collection, donated by the estate of Bernard Baruch, includes a number of 18th-century tablespoons, platters, tea caddies and other superb examples of English silversmithing. A few fine Irish and Scottish pieces can be seen along with a Chinese filigree dish presented to Mr. Baruch by Mme. Chiang Kai-shek. A number of African artifacts and mementos from the South Pacific at the time of World War II are also on view. *Open Mon.-Fri. except holidays.*

Washington Street United Methodist Church *1401 Washington St.* This 1871 brick church is distinguished by its solid walnut woodwork, including pews, chancel, pulpit and balcony railing. The side pews are particularly interesting since they face toward the altar at angles that increase as they near the front of the building. A series of beautiful stained-glass windows installed in 1914 allegorically interpret the life of Christ through landscape scenes ranging from Bethlehem to Bethany. The grounds also contain Christ Chapel, a modern gray stone structure with handsome African mahogany woodwork and stained-glass windows that reflect the teachings and statements of Christ. The altar window is particularly lovely, containing gold laid over the sculptured lead tracery. *Open daily.*

Woodrow Wilson Boyhood Home *1705 Hampton St.* The Reverend and Mrs. Joseph Ruggles Wilson, parents of the 28th President of the U.S., lived in this clapboard house for three years (1872-75). It is a typical Victorian dwelling with bay windows and iron mantels painted to resemble marble. Some of the period furniture it contains belonged to Woodrow Wilson, including the bed in which he was born in 1856 and a desk he used while governor of New Jersey. Several trees planted by the Wilson family still grow on the grounds. *Open Tues.-Sun. except holidays. Small charge.*

149. Lexington County Homestead Museum *Rte. 378 and Fox St., Lexington, S.C.* The life-style of the region's early Swiss-German settlers is illustrated by this large frame house, built about 1832, and its farm outbuildings. The house has been completely restored and furnished with country antiques. A thresher house is filled with old farm tools and a log structure contains a loom and spinning wheels. The museum also has antique dolls and other toys and a large collection of Indian artifacts. *Open Tues.-Sun. Apr.-Dec. Small charge.*

150. Wings and Wheels *Rtes. 95 and 301, S. of Santee, S.C.* About 90 antique and classic cars as well as a number of aircraft that range from pre-1900 gliders to a Mercury space capsule are featured here. A 1911 Buick and a 1912 Hudson can be seen, but the main automotive attraction is a 1930 Duesenberg with a powerful 405-cubic-inch engine. A reproduction of the Wright brothers' plane that made the world's first powered flight in 1903 is here, as well as a World War I Spad from the famous Hat-in-the-Ring Squadron and a replica of Baron von Richthofen's Fokker triplane. Visitors can see a replica of the first U.S. passenger train, "The Best Friend of Charleston." *Open daily except Dec. 25. Adults $2.00, children over 6 small charge.*

151. Hillsborough, N.C. During North Carolina's Constitutional Convention, the proposal to include a Bill of Rights in the U.S. Constitution was made here in 1788. Bearing pre-Revolutionary names, Hillsborough's streets are noted for their fine 18th- and 19th-century architecture, ancient trees and sweeping lawns. The homes, all privately owned, may be found in the area bounded by Queen Street, Wake Street, Margaret Lane and Cameron Avenue. House tours, for which a fee is charged, are sponsored biennially by the Hillsborough Historical Society.

[150] *The hangar where the Wings and Wheels collection is housed is bigger than a football field. In the foreground is a 1912 Hudson touring car which has, like all the cars of those days, a collapsible top. Behind it is a replica of the first U.S. military aircraft, constructed by the Wright brothers for the U.S. Army in 1911.*

152. Orange County Courthouse *E. King and Churton Sts., Hillsborough, N.C.* This two-story Greek Revival building, completed in 1845, is constructed of red brick with white wood trim; the facade features a large Doric portico. Interior woodwork designs are styled after the Asher Benjamin pattern books. *Open Mon.-Fri.*

ORANGE COUNTY HISTORICAL MUSEUM The early history of Orange County is depicted in the old courtroom on the second floor of the courthouse. Among the objects to be seen are antique costumes and the work of early silversmiths. There is an 18th-century kitchen and a Homespun Room with a 150-year-old loom. Of special interest is a set of English weights and measures purchased by the county in 1760. *Open Tues.-Sun.*

153. St. Matthew's Episcopal Church *E. King St., Hillsborough, N.C.* This small, unadorned brick church was built here on a wooded knoll in 1824. By 1875 a tower and a slender spire had been added to the Gothic Revival structure. Two of the high-pointed windows contain early Tiffany glass. Among the graves in the tree-shaded, brick-enclosed graveyard is that of the renowned jurist Thomas Ruffin who donated the land on which the church was built. *Open Sun.*

154. Duke University *Durham, N.C.* This is one of the country's most generously endowed schools and one of the most beautiful. Its two campuses comprise almost 7000 acres.

DUKE UNIVERSITY CHAPEL *West Campus* This large English Gothic structure dominates the campus with a 210-foot tower that resembles the Bell Harry Tower of Canterbury Cathedral. The native-stone chapel was first used in 1932 and has since served for musical events as well as for interdenominational services. The nave, transepts and choir, seating more than 2000, exhibit fine workmanship in stone and wood. The limewood figures of Jesus and Sts. Peter and Paul in the Memorial Chapel reredos are particularly impressive. The many stained-glass windows contain scenes from the life of Jesus as well as Old and New Testament figures. The presentation of music in the chapel is enhanced by an organ with over 7000 pipes and a 50-bell carillon. *Open daily.*

DUKE UNIVERSITY MUSEUM OF ART *East Campus* The Brummer Collection of medieval sculpture and decorative art is the museum's most impressive holding. Important pieces in this collection are the fine 13th-century *Head of the Virgin* from the rood screen of Chartres Cathedral and four outstanding 12th-century French stone carvings of apostles. Also on view in the spacious galleries are some unusual wood carvings, marble and alabaster reliefs, bronzes and paintings. The building has a handsome paneled library. There are special exhibits of works by North Carolina artists. *Open Tues.-Sun.*

SARAH P. DUKE GARDENS *West Campus* At any season visitors enjoy the colorful plantings—from the late winter blooming of jasmine and honeysuckle to the spectacular displays offered by forsythias, azaleas and other flowering plants. The focal point is a formal circular terraced garden with Japanese cherry and crab-apple trees, walks and steps that descend to a pond. There is also a rock garden, and huge drifts of narcissus

[**154.** *Duke University Chapel*] *A soaring Gothic design and a wealth of stained glass are the features of the chapel, heart of the Duke campus. The glass, designed by G. Owen Bonawit of New York, fills 77 windows, and portrays more than 800 figures from the Bible. On the left are scenes from Jesus's life; above, He washes the disciples' feet.*

planted on the fringe of a pine forest bloom each spring. *Open daily.*

155. William Hayes Ackland Memorial Art Center *S. Columbia St., University of North Carolina, Chapel Hill, N.C.* The purpose of this museum, which opened in 1958, is to provide historical perspective of important styles of art. It has examples of painting, sculpture and drawing from antique through contemporary periods of both Western and Eastern cultures. Among major works owned by the museum are paintings by Rubens, Delacroix, Courbet, Pissarro and Max Weber. Also on display is Rodin's *Head of Balzac. Open Tues.-Sun. except holidays.*

156. Raleigh, N.C.

The capital of North Carolina was founded in 1741 and named in honor of Sir Walter Raleigh. Andrew Johnson, 17th President of the U.S., was born here. Besides being the seat of government in the state, it is an educational and cultural center and the retail outlet for the North Carolina tobacco-growing industry.

Andrew Johnson's Birthplace *Pullen Park* The 17th President of the U.S. was born in this small frame house on Dec. 29, 1808. The gambrel-roof structure has been moved from its original location in downtown Raleigh but has been preserved in its original form. The house contains furnishings of the period. *Open Sun.-Fri. Small charge.*

Christ Episcopal Church *120 E. Edenton St.* This neo-Gothic building, completed in 1849, was designed by Richard Upjohn along the lines of an English medieval parish church. The stone bell tower, connected to the church by an arched cloister, was added in 1861. Both the church and the tower are constructed of granite from a local quarry. The cruciform-shaped church has a shallow chancel with a white altar, stained-glass windows and galleries over the rear nave and wings of the transept. In the church's early days, the rear gallery was reserved for slaves. *Open daily.*

J. S. Dorton Arena *State Fair Grounds* The walls of this elliptical structure, which seats over 9000 people, are made entirely of glass. An outstanding feat of engineering, it has a saddle-shaped roof suspended on a network of cables from 90-foot parabolic arches, thus eliminating the need for structural steel supports.

North Carolina Museum of Art *107 E. Morgan St.* The only painting by Stefan Lochner (15th century) in America and the only bronze sculpture by Cellini in existence are among the many masterpieces arranged in 60 galleries here. Among the museum's other European works are a painting by Raphael and a sculpture by Riemenschneider, and it also has large collections of British and American painting and sculpture. The Mary Duke Biddle Gallery for the Blind is a unique part of the museum's program. *Open Tues.-Sun. except holidays.*

North Carolina Museum of History *109 E. Jones St.* Exhibits of over 300 years of Carolina history are on view here. These include archaeological displays; paintings, furnishings and decorative arts of the early settlers; and a communications display of major advances—first air flight, first voice carried over air waves—which originated in the state. The North Carolina State Archives in the same building contain millions

[**156.** *North Carolina Museum of History*] *The charter by which King Charles II established the colony of Carolina is on display here. The 1663 document states that the settlers were to enjoy the same rights as Englishmen.*

of documents relating to the state's history. *Open daily.*

North Carolina State Museum *101 Halifax St.* This natural history museum displays collections of native minerals, fossils, invertebrates and vertebrates. There is also an exhibit of materials relating to prehistoric Indians who lived in North Carolina and an exhibit of early whaling tools. *Open daily except holidays.*

State Capitol *Capitol Sq.* This Greek Revival structure, completed in 1840, stands on a six-acre square in the heart of Raleigh. The building has a large copper dome and deep porticos at the east and west facades. The columns of the porticos are Doric, copied from those of the Parthenon in Athens. The rotunda rises three stories; displayed in it are busts of prominent North Carolinians and historical tablets. The vestibules of the building are decorated with Ionic columns. Large stone stairways lead to the second-floor Senate Chamber and Hall of the House, which are no longer in use as the general assembly now meets in the State Legislative Building described below. Offices decorated in the Gothic style are on the third floor. Fifty varieties of native trees shade the landscaped grounds. *Open Mon.-Sat.*

State Legislative Building *W. Jones and Halifax Sts.* This five-domed marble contemporary structure by Edward Durell Stone, which has housed the North Carolina General Assembly since 1963, is the center of a complex of state buildings. It encloses over 200,000 square feet on four levels. From an open gallery on the third floor visitors can view the legislature in session. In front of the main entrance is a 28-foot terrazzo mosaic of the Great Seal of the State of North Carolina. At the four corners of the building are landscaped garden courts. The cruciform-shaped building also has a landscaped pool in the rotunda and roof gardens. *Open daily.*

157. Country Doctor Museum *Vance St., Bailey, N.C.* Two buildings once used by 19th-century doctors were moved to this site and restored with two typical country doctors' offices. They are equipped with an operating table-chair, surgeon's desk, pill-making machine, iron washstand, stock bottles, apothecary shelves, old instrument trays and blood-letting equipment. Medical displays at the museum include the evolution of the stethoscope, from the 1816 model used by its inventor to modern examples, and collections of early porcelain ointment jars and show globes. The Medicinal Garden of plants that are used for healing grows near the house. *Open Wed., Sun.*

158. Village Chapel *Pinehurst, N.C.* This nondenominational chapel is attractively located in a large grove of long-leaf pine trees. The building, with its tall graceful steeple, was designed by Hobart Upjohn about 1925. Serving a parish that contains a country club and five golf courses, the church offers an early service for golfers. *Open daily.*

159. 82nd Airborne Division War Memorial Museum *Ardennes St., Fort Bragg, N.C.* The eventful history of this famous U.S. Army unit is told here in photographs, documents and related objects. Examples of equipment used by the 82nd Airborne include C-46 and C-47 jump airplanes, a World War II glider and a 105mm howitzer. The world's largest collection of German daggers can also be seen, as well as impressive memorials to the division's recipients of the Medal of Honor and Distinguished Service Cross. A huge silver trophy bearing the names of officers who served in one of the division's regiments in World War II includes an 18-inch cup from which soldiers still drink after they have qualified as paratroopers and been officially assigned to the outfit. *Open Tues.-Sun.*

160. First Presbyterian Church *Bow and Ann Sts., Fayetteville, N.C.* Long, wide stone steps lead to this handsome Colonial-style edifice. It was built in 1832 to replace an earlier church destroyed by fire. Among its noteworthy interior features are several early-19th-century crystal chandeliers, handwrought hardware, carving on the galleries and an 1824 silver Communion service. *Open daily.*

161. Market House *Market Sq., Fayetteville, N.C.* Union General William T. Sherman described this pink brick structure in an 1865 letter as "an ancient market house of very tasteful architecture." An interesting example of Greek Revival styling modified by Spanish-Moorish arches, it was built in 1838 as a farmers' market where produce, meat and fish were sold. There are cleaver marks in its second-story pine pillars, one of which also contains a bullet fired during a skirmish late in the Civil War. A square tower houses an old Boston clock and a mid-19th-century bell and is surmounted by a cupola. Art shows are occasionally presented here, and the Fayetteville Museum of Art occupies the second floor. *First floor open daily, second floor open Wed., Sun.*

162. Halifax, N.C. The site was first settled in 1723 and developed rapidly into a thriving river port and commercial and political center. In the spring of 1776, the Halifax Resolves, the first official document in the 13 colonies to recommend independence from England, was adopted here by the Fourth Provincial Congress of North Carolina. (The Declaration of Independence signed by the Continental Congress almost three months later included some of its ideas.) During the Revolution British troops were quartered in Halifax prior to their retreat to Yorktown. In the town are a number of archaeological sites and four restored 18th- and 19th-century buildings which constitute a state historic site. One of them, the Colonial Clerk's Office on Main Street (built in 1832), is the Visitor Center. The others are described below.

CONSTITUTION HOUSE *Main St.* This small frame house, built about 1770, is believed to be the site of the drafting of the State Constitution in 1776. It is fully restored and consists of two rooms. A side hall contains furniture from the Revolutionary period. *Open Tues.-Sun. except Thanksgiving Day and Dec. 24-26.*

OLD JAIL *Main St.* Escaping prisoners burned two earlier jails that were on this site. The present brick building, completed in 1838, has gabled ends and an elaborate corbel cornice. *Open Tues.-Sun. except Thanksgiving Day and Dec. 24-26.*

OWENS HOUSE *Pennsylvania St.* This restored former home of a prominent merchant was built around 1760 and is now furnished with pieces that predate the Revolution. *Open Tues.-Sun. except Thanksgiving Day and Dec. 24-26.*

163. Murfreesboro, N.C.

Known in the 1740s as Murfree's Landing, the town took its name from William Murfree, its chief benefactor and one of the founders of Murfreesboro. During the 18th and 19th centuries it became an important river port and commercial center, trading naval stores and agricultural products for New England, West Indian and European commodities. Many of the homes and other buildings in the historic area centering on Broad, Williams and Main Streets are being preserved or restored through the efforts of groups of interested citizens.

John Wheeler House *403 E. Broad St.* This solid house was built by John Wheeler, a New Jersey merchant, early in the 19th century. Its brick walls are 18 inches thick; the fanlight and detailed cornice above the front entrance are outstanding. Remnants of the original wallpaper may be seen on the vertical pine boards of the entrance hall. The kitchen, once part of a complex of buildings separate from the main house, still stands. Also constructed of brick, it contains built-in cupboards, a hidden stairway and living quarters for servants on the second floor. Restored by the Murfreesboro Historical Association, the house has been listed in the National Register of Historic Sites and Buildings. *Open daily. Small charge.*

McDowell Columns Building *Chowan College, Jones Dr.* Massive white columns form the front of the double veranda of the impressive Greek Revival structure, one of the largest buildings in this style in North Carolina. Built in 1851 to house the Chowan Female Baptist Institute, it now serves as the administrative center of a coeducational junior college. *Open daily except Dec. 25.*

Roberts Village Center *Main St.* This late-18th-century house contains eight large rooms; it was enlarged to its present size in 1835. The original portion of the exterior has chimneys with Flemish bond brick-

work, and inside the original woodwork still remains. Four dependencies of the house—a dairy, kitchen, carriage house and office—have been restored. Today the building, operated by the town of Murfreesboro, contains a library, meeting rooms, civic offices and an information center. *Open daily.*

William Rea Store Museum *E. Williams St.* Considered to be the oldest commercial structure in North Carolina, this store was built in 1790 by William Rea, a Boston merchant and shipper. Constructed of brick, the building's walls are 20 inches thick. The first mechanical peanut pickers, developed in the 1880s, were produced here. The museum features exhibits on river trade, education, agriculture and the early development of Murfreesboro. *Open daily. Small charge.*

164. Museum of the Albemarle *Rte. 3, Elizabeth City, N.C.* Through exhibits of Indian artifacts and equipment used in early lumbering, hunting and farming, the museum tells about the history of this coastal part of the state, where colonization first began in 1583. Interesting exhibits include a display of hand-carved duck-hunting decoys and models of Coast Guard vessels from 1790. A collection of old toys is also on display each year from Thanksgiving to the end of December. *Open Tues.-Sun. except holidays. Small charge.*

165. Edenton, N.C.

Settled about 1660, Edenton was once a flourishing port and the home of such distinguished Colonial men as Joseph Hewes, a signer of the Declaration of Independence, and Dr. Hugh Williamson, who signed the Constitution. In 1774 the town was the scene of what came to be called the Edenton Tea Party, with 51 women meeting to protest a British tax on tea—an event believed to be the first organized political action by American women. The town is noted for many excellent examples of Colonial architecture. Notable among them are the buildings described below.

Barker House *S. Broad St.* The double galleries along the front of this handsome frame structure provide an excellent view of Albemarle Sound. The house was built about 1782 by Thomas Barker, a lawyer and London agent for the colony of North Carolina prior to the Revolution. (It was moved to its present site on the water and restored.) It is now the headquarters of Historic Edenton, Inc. and serves as a visitor's center-museum and orientation point for tours of the town. *Open Tues.-Sun. except holidays.*

Chowan County Courthouse *E. King St.* This is the oldest courthouse in the state and one of the most beautiful in the country. It was built of brick in 1767, in the Georgian style, with a simple symmetrical facade graced with a shining white clock tower and cupola rising above a pediment. *Open Mon.-Fri.*

Cupola House *S. Broad St.* This two-story frame house built about 1725 is a good example of Jacobean architecture, a transition between early 17th-century and 18th-century Georgian styles. It has a second-story overhang, central octagonal cupola and a heavy brick chimney at either end. The finial on the front gable is marked with the initials of one Francis Corbin and the year 1758 when he completed modifications that included the addition of a fine staircase. *Open Tues.-Sun. except holidays.*

James Iredell House *E. Church St.* Built in 1759, this large frame dwelling was purchased in 1778 by James Iredell, who served as attorney general of North Carolina and was appointed associate justice of the U.S. Supreme Court by George Washington in 1790. The double-tiered porches on the front were added around 1810. The grounds include a kitchen-museum, necessary house (privy), carriage house, schoolhouse and a formal garden. *Open Tues.-Sun. except holidays.*

St. Paul's Episcopal Church *W. Church St.* This Georgian edifice is the state's second oldest church building but it has been considerably rebuilt since its construction around 1736. During the Revolution it was closed because of its Tory congregation. Deterioration from disuse necessitated the repairs that were finally made between 1806 and 1809. After it was partially damaged by fire in 1949 the church was restored to its original appearance. Communion silver from 1725 is still used here. *Open daily.*

[**165.** *Barker House*] *Thomas Barker, who built this house about 1782, was a London agent for the Carolina colony before the Revolution. Moved to a new location at the edge of Albemarle Sound, the house is now a visitor center.*

[168] *Like a giant candy-striped barber's pole, America's tallest lighthouse rises from the windswept shore of Cape Hatteras. Visitors can climb a winding staircase to the balcony just beneath the light, some 180 feet above the long, curving beach—and with a clear view of the seas that break white over the treacherous Diamond Shoals the light is designed to warn against. Hundreds of ships have been lost on this coast, and there has been a lighthouse at Cape Hatteras since 1798; the present building dates from 1870 and has worked continuously since then except during the late 1930s and '40s when beach erosion forced its closing.*

166. Somerset Place State Historic Site *Pettigrew State Park, Creswell, N.C.* This Greek Revival great house, built around 1830, was once the center of a huge, totally self-sufficient rice and corn plantation. Before the Civil War some 20 outbuildings (a slave hospital, dormitory for sons and tutors and a slave chapel among them) stood on the property. Six of these outbuildings, including a storehouse, icehouse and kitchen-laundry, remain. The 14-room mansion has been restored and furnished with pieces from the 1850s. Lawns and gardens beside a nearby lake have been revived. *Open daily except Thanksgiving Day and Dec. 25.*

167. Wright Brothers National Memorial *Rte. 158, Kill Devil Hills, Kitty Hawk, N.C.* On Dec. 17, 1903, four years of experiments by Wilbur and Orville Wright culminated in man's first successful flight in a motor-driven, heavier-than-air machine. A large granite boulder marks the take-off spot where this historic 12-second event occurred, and numbered markers show the lengths of the four flights made that day. Visitors may drive around the 60-foot granite Wright Memorial Shaft on Kill Devil Hill or see it on foot. North of this hill is a reconstruction of the Wrights' camp, which includes a hangar-workshop and a storage building. At the Visitor Center full-scale replicas of a 1902 glider and the famous 1903 machine are displayed. *Open daily.*

168. Cape Hatteras Lighthouse *Cape Hatteras National Seashore, S.E. of Buxton, N.C.* This 208-foot brick tower was built in 1870 to replace one damaged during the Civil War. It is the tallest lighthouse in the U.S., and among the most distinctive with its spiraling black and white stripes that have been a daymark to mariners since 1873. Visitors who climb to the balcony beneath the light are rewarded by a fine view of Hatteras Island, Cape Hatteras and Diamond Shoals, an offshore area known as the "graveyard of the Atlantic" because of its treacherous shifting sandbars. Owned by the National Park Service, the lighthouse is operated by the U.S. Coast Guard. In good weather its beacon can be seen for at least 20 miles. *Open daily except Dec. 25.*

169. New Bern, N.C.

The town was founded by Swiss and German settlers in 1710. The first provincial congress to elect delegates to the Continental Congress met here in 1774 and 1775. New Bern was the provincial capital of North Carolina during the early years of the 18th century, and later it became an important mid-Atlantic seaport. Today the visitor can see a number of fine old buildings.

Attmore-Oliver House *511-3 Broad St.* This two-and-a-half-story residence was built in 1790 by Samuel Chapman and enlarged to its present size in 1834. The house has double porches which extend across the rear, quadruple chimneys and balconies with iron grillwork. It is furnished with antiques of the period. On the grounds are a brick smokehouse and a gambrel-roof cottage built in 1796. The house now serves as headquarters of the New Bern Historical Society and as an exhibition house. *Open Tues.-Sun. Apr.-Oct. Small charge.*

NEW BERN HISTORICAL SOCIETY MUSEUM This museum, which occupies one room of the Attmore-Oliver House, contains exhibits of Civil War memorabilia—books, maps, papers, flags, clothing and so on. Two interesting items are a silver bowl and ladle presented by the State of Massachusetts and a silver urn presented by the State of Rhode Island, both in memory of soldiers, natives of those states, who fell in battle here. *Open Tues.-Sun. Apr.-Oct. Small charge.*

Christ Episcopal Church *320 Pollock St.* The first church at this location was completed in 1750. Its foundation may be seen in the churchyard. The present church, dating from 1824, still has a silver Communion service, Book of Common Prayer and Bible presented by King George II in 1752. Each item is engraved with the royal coat of arms. *Open daily.*

First Presbyterian Church *412 New St.* Constructed of pine wood, the 1822 Greek Revival church was built by Uriah Sandy. The portico is supported by four large Ionic columns. The lower three sections of the bell tower are square, topped by an octagonal section. There are two tiers of windows, the upper ones arched. During the Civil War the church was used as a hospital by the Union army. *Open daily.*

New Bern Firemen's Museum *420 Broad St.* Early fire-fighting equipment is on display here. Included are two world-record horse-drawn steam fire engines, one dating from 1879 and one from 1884. Among the other displays are Civil War relics, a portrait of Baron de Graffenried, founder of New Bern, and artifacts from Berne, Switzerland. *Open Tues.-Sun. except holidays. Small charge.*

Tryon Palace Complex *613 Pollock St.* See feature display on pages 290-1.

U.S. Post Office and Court House *413-415 Middle St.* This elaborate Colonial-style structure, completed in 1935, houses the Federal offices of New Bern. Large murals in the courtroom, painted as a WPA project, depict the early history of the area. The handsome bronze lighting fixtures were specially designed and cast for this room. *Open Mon.-Sat.*

170. Burgwin-Wright House *224 Market St., Wilmington, N.C.* British general Lord Charles Cornwallis made his headquarters here in mid-April 1781, shortly after his army suffered severe losses at the battle of Guilford Courthouse in Greensboro. The house was built by John Burgwin, treasurer of the colony of North Carolina, in 1771. The foundations of the building were part of the stone walls of an abandoned jail which once occupied the site. The lower cellar of the house still has dungeons. There are remnants of a tunnel to the Cape Fear River which was constructed, it is supposed, as a means of escape for the family in case of attack from pirates. A large Palladian doorway and Ionic porch columns are the dominant exterior features. A three-story kitchen stands apart from the house, separated by an open courtyard. Furnishings are 18th-century antiques. The landscaped gardens about the house are still planted in an 18th-century manner. *Open Mon.-Fri. Small charge.*

[171] *Glowing azaleas frame the classical pillars of Orton House, heart of the rich plantation created early in the 18th century by Roger Moore. The house itself is not open, but the gardens are a springtime delight.*

171. Orton Plantation Gardens *Rte. 133, 18 mi. S. of Wilmington, N.C.* Roger Moore, one of the largest landowners in the Cape Fear area, established this plantation in 1725. The manor house (which is not open to the public) is a large two-story structure with massive front columns and is considered an outstanding example of the Greek Revival style of architecture. It is set in elaborately landscaped gardens that feature hundreds of Kurume and Indian azaleas, camellias, roses and dozens of other varieties of flowers. *Open daily. Adults $2.00 Mar.-Aug., $1.50 Sept.-Feb., children small charge.*

172. U.S.S. "North Carolina" Battleship Memorial *Eagle's Island, Wilmington, N.C.* This is the only battleship that participated in all the 12 major naval offensive campaigns in the Pacific Theater during World War II. The ship was brought here in 1961 as a memorial to North Carolinians who died in the war. The main deck, bridge, engine room, gun turrets, galley and living quarters of the officers and crew are open to visitors. A museum located in the main-deck wardroom features exhibits relating the history of the ship. Also on display is the Honor Roll with the names of 10,000 North Carolinians who died in World War II. *Open daily. Small charge.*

173. Wilmington-New Hanover Museum *814 Market St., Wilmington, N.C.* In addition to local history, this museum has a number of interesting exhibits. Among them are Victorian replica rooms, African tribal masks, Egyptian pottery, Chinese porcelain and a seashell collection. *Open Tues.-Sun. except holidays.*

174. Hopsewee *Rte. 17, S. of Georgetown, S.C.* Thomas Lynch built this low-country rice-plantation house around 1740 and it is still in practically its original condition. A clapboard building constructed of black cypress, it contains random-width pine floors, a handsome Georgian staircase and carved moldings varying in pattern from room to room. Its hip roof is pierced by two central chimneys serving eight fireplaces, and the waterfront face of the building includes a double-tiered piazza. A National Historic Landmark, the house has the distinction of being the home of the only father and son to serve together in the Continental Congress. The younger Lynch, who was born here in 1749, was one of the youngest signers of the Declaration of Independence. On 35 surrounding acres can be seen two cypress-shingled kitchen outbuildings with West Indies features plus many live oaks and magnolias. Tree-size camellias planted about 1840 can also be admired. *House open Tues.-Fri. Adults $1.50, students small charge. Grounds open daily. Small charge.*

Wrought-iron gates brought from a London house built in 1741 frame the long vista toward the main entrance.

The Council Chamber did double duty as a ballroom: George Washington was among those who danced here in 1791. Above the Sienna marble mantel is the royal coat of arms; on either side hang portraits of King George III and Queen Charlotte. The governor's writing desk rests on an Ispahan rug from a Portuguese palace.

This oblique overall view shows the grand design of Tryon Palace and its grounds overlooking the Trent River. The gigantic task of restoration involved purchasing houses already built on these six acres and demolishing them to prepare the site for the rather grand panorama of palace, outbuildings and gardens. With few exceptions, the trees, flowers and shrubs you see here are similar to those that were favorites in Colonial times. In this view the kitchen wing is at the left and the stable at the right. On the pediment over the main entrance is a re-creation of King George III's coat of arms. Sentry boxes flank the two gateposts.

169. Tryon Palace Complex

613 Pollock St., New Bern, N.C.

Tryon Palace, named for William Tryon, a royal governor of the colony of North Carolina, was completed in 1770 under the supervision of architect John Hawks. The Georgian-style palace served as the state capitol after the Revolution. By 1798, a few years after the capital moved to Raleigh, it had fallen into disrepair, and one cold winter night all but the two wings burned down. In 1952 the long process of restoration of the palace and surrounding buildings began, on the original foundations and from the original architectural drawings. Digging on the site turned up some helpful finds: bits of plaster molding with some of the original paint indicated the original color schemes, which have been faithfully followed. Chips of marble found here were used to re-create the marble fireplaces. The original varicolored brick can still be seen in the west (stable) wing. With an inventory which was originally made by Tryon as a guide, English and American 18th-century antiques were purchased to fill the rooms. Furnishings include portraits of royalty and furniture from English castles as well as native pieces such as a pair of tables from Newport, R.I. Today Tryon Palace has been completely restored and is surrounded by six acres of beautifully landscaped grounds. The complex includes the 1779 John Wright Stanly House and the 1805 Stevenson House. *Open Tues.-Sun. and Mon. holidays, closed other holidays. Palace and gardens, adults $2.00, children small charge; Stanly House, adults $1.50, children small charge; Stevenson House, small charge.*

Labyrinths dominate the Maude Moore Latham Memorial Garden, which honors the restoration's major donor.

The governor's bedroom features a Wilton carpet, a Chippendale mahogany bed, French bedspread and a Massachusetts Queen Anne highboy.

175. Pyatt-Doyle Town House *630 Highmarket St., Georgetown, S.C.* The age of this elegant clapboard house may be determined by the English bond brickwork pattern which was generally discontinued after 1800. Built with an unusual Bermuda coral stone foundation, the house is a typical low-country dwelling with double steps leading to a wide piazza. Original woodwork still exists with candlelight cornice moldings and pine floors; visitors may note that built-in closets are not a modern innovation. The staircase is especially interesting with its balusters set diagonally. The furnishings cover several periods from Queen Anne to early Victorian. *Open Mon.-Fri. except holidays. Small charge.*

176. Rice Museum *Front and Screven Sts., Georgetown, S.C.* Imaginative dioramas, maps, pictures and tools and other equipment trace the interesting history of the rice grown in this region. In the 1850s Georgetown was the world's largest exporter of this important crop. Chronological exhibits illustrate procedures for clearing swamps and constructing ditches, dikes and floodgates, and show how rice was planted, harvested, processed and marketed. The 1842 brick building is also noteworthy for the tower with its four-sided clock and 1866 bell. Formerly known as the Old Market Building, it has served as a police station and jail, and its second floor room was used as the town hall. Produce and fish were once sold on the ground floor. *Open daily. Adults small charge.*

177. Cypress Gardens *Off Rte. 52, Oakley, S.C.* Sunlight filters through Spanish moss clinging to ancient bald cypress trees which grow from the still black water of the lake that was once a reservoir for a huge rice plantation. The air is scented by thousands of blossoms in their season that adorn the banks of the lake and its islands. The visitor may glide through the gardens in a paddle boat, or wander along pathways and over small bridges connecting the islands. *Open daily mid-Feb.-Apr. Adults $2.50.*

[176] *The winnowing house in this diorama functioned like a sieve on stilts. Laborers would bring the hulled rice here on a windy day and pour it into the grate in the floor so that the chaff would blow away.*

178. Magnolia Gardens *Rte. 61, N.W. of Drayton Hall, S.C.* The gardens were begun prior to the Civil War by a clergyman who planted many superb camellias from the Orient. Magnolia Gardens consists of over 40 acres of flowers, trees (including fine magnolias) and lawns laid out beside the banks of the Ashley River. English novelist John Galsworthy called the setting "a miraculously enchanted wilderness." Backdrops of gnarled swamp cypresses loom over multi-hued azaleas, their reflections glimmering in adjacent waterways. A rustic bridge festooned with wisteria crosses a dark lagoon; in spring huge drifts of daffodils may be seen from brick-lined walks. Massive oaks flank the road to Magnolia Manor, which was built during Reconstruction to replace the home burned in the Civil War. The marble tomb of the gardens' designer survived this conflict but bears marks made by Union soldiers' bullets in 1865. *Open daily mid-Feb.-Apr. $2.50.*

179. Middleton Place *Rte. 61, N.W. of Drayton Hall, S.C.* Henry Middleton, president of the First Continental Congress, started the 65-acre garden on his vast plantation in 1741. It is the oldest landscaped garden in the U.S., and unquestionably one of the most beautiful. The basic format—that of an 18th-century green garden—remains the same despite two wars and a severe earthquake. Landscaped terraces, ornamental waterways and plantings arranged in complex geometric patterns delight the eyes in all seasons. Three plants from a large camellia garden begun in 1783 by French botanist André Michaux still survive. In the spring azaleas bloom throughout the garden. The main unplanned feature in this landscape of flowers, water and lawns is the Middleton Oak, estimated to be 1000 years old. In the garden also are several of the old plantation buildings, as well as the tomb of Arthur Middleton, signer of the Declaration of Independence. The original springhouse (1741) and pre-Revolutionary rice mill still stand. The Georgian mansion built by Henry Middleton was burned by Union troops in 1865. The south wing has been restored. Annual events held at Middleton Place, which is a National Historic Landmark, are the Greek Spring Festival (May), Arthur Middleton Birthday Celebration (June), Scottish Games (September) and a Lancing Tournament (October). *Open daily. Adults $2.50, children 12-18 $1.50, 6-11 small charge.*

180. Charleston, S.C.

Rich in history and culture, Charleston is a coastal city of lovely gardens and attractive homes, examples of the best in pre-Revolutionary and antebellum architecture. Originally called Charles Towne, it was settled by a group of hardy pioneers in 1670, and became a thriving seaport, with rice and indigo among its primary exports. In its many years of existence, it has endured war, earthquake and fire, as well as pirate attacks from the sea. Fortunately, many of the original structures have survived. There is a fascinating diversity of architecture as a result of the diverse origins of the people who settled here. Facades of some of the finest homes line the streets in the oldest section of the city near the water. The Thomas Rose house at 59 Church Street and the

[179] *In the mid-18th century 100 slaves worked for 10 years to carry out Henry Middleton's grand design for gardens that would rival some of the most famous of the formal European gardens. The sculptured terraces were carved out of a bluff above the Ashley River. The twin lakes, which resemble the spread wings of a butterfly, sparkle below. This was the view from the Georgian Middleton Mansion, of which now only the restored south wing remains.*

Ralph Izard house at 110 Broad Street are typical of early-18th-century Charleston architecture. The first floors of these houses are built level with the street. The Colonel William Rhett house at 54 Hasell Street is believed to be the oldest surviving home in Charleston—it dates from about 1712. As the city prospered, residences grew larger and more elaborate. The three-story Daniel Huger house at 34 Meeting Street, built about 1760, is a fine example of what is known as the Charleston "double house" (two rooms wide on the street side). Its interior is paneled throughout. The two-story Miles Brewton house at 27 King Street, dating from about 1769, is another double house; it has an especially grand two-story portico. A distinguished Federal structure built in 1800 is the William Blacklock house at 18 Bull Street. Large even for its time, the residence is elegantly detailed on the outside. At the height of the Georgian period in Charleston, around 1772, craftsmen erected the William Gibbes house at 64 S. Battery. The structure was renovated twice, and interestingly combines elements of several periods. The Josiah Smith house at 7 Meeting Street, constructed about 1783, is a sterling example of Georgian architecture. A large home, it features a sweeping double stair and lantern entrance. A walk through the residential district of old Charleston will reveal many charming residences and gardens in addition to the ones described above.

Charleston Museum *121-5 Rutledge Ave.* This museum organization is generally acknowledged to be the oldest in North America. Founded in 1773 by the Charles Town Library Society, its purpose was "promoting a natural history of the Province." On display are period rooms and collections of crafts and furniture that were typical of the area during Colonial days. In addition, there are exhibits of birds, animals and minerals. *Open daily. Small charge.*

City Hall Art Gallery and Council Chamber *80 Broad St.* Completed in 1801 as a bank, this graceful Adam-style stone building was purchased by the city in 1818. It is the nation's oldest active city hall. In the council chamber is an important collection of portraits, mostly of famous Southerners. The portraits, either through subject matter or artist or both, all have a historical connection with Charleston. Dominated by Trumbull's 1791 full-length portrait of George Washington and Samuel Morse's 1820 portrait of James Monroe, the room also contains a fine oil (from about 1795) of Christopher Gadsden by Rembrandt Peale, John Vanderlyn's portrait of Andrew Jackson, Charles Fraser's miniature watercolor of Lafayette and George P. Healy's portraits of John Calhoun and Confederate General Beauregard, as well as a number of busts of other notables. The black walnut furniture was made in Charleston specifically for this room. *Open Mon.-Fri.*

Dock Street Theatre *Church and Queen Sts.* This theater occupies the site of the first American building (opened in 1736) solely for theatrical productions. Reconstructed in the 1930s, its entrance facade is finished with an airy cast-iron balcony and six sandstone columns. The interior is made up of a number of rooms, including a drawing room, taproom and 19th-century hotel lobby, that were once part of the legendary Planter's Hotel. The theater's Georgian-style auditorium is paneled in black cypress and has bench-back seats. It is now used by a community-theater group active from September through May. Art exhibits are given at this time. *Open Mon.-Fri.*

Fort Moultrie *Sullivan's Island (off Rte. 703)* The first fort on this site was commanded by Major General William Moultrie, who led the successful battle against an attack by the British navy in 1776, the first decisive victory of the American Revolution. Rebuilt several times, the fort, now a National Monument, has served our troops in every major war through the close of World War II. Edgar Allan Poe was once stationed at Fort Moultrie, and the famous Indian chief, Osceola, is buried here. Cannons, muskets, shells and many other types of armament are on display. *Open daily except Jan. 1 and Dec. 25.*

Fort Sumter *Charleston Harbor* Begun in 1829 on a man-made island at the mouth of Charleston harbor and still unfinished in 1861, this fort was a remarkable engineering feat. About 70,000 tons of granite and other rock went into the foundation, and millions of handmade bricks were needed to form the five-foot-thick walls around the fort. Although the bastion took a terrible pounding during the Civil War, portions of the original walls are standing today. In the museum is the remainder of the flag that flew over the fort when the Civil War began. National Park Service historians conduct informative tours of Fort Sumter, now a National Monument. *Boats leave Municipal Yacht Basin at regular intervals. Adults $2.50, children small charge.*

[**180.** *Nathaniel Russell House*] *This music room is one of three oval rooms in the Russell House, which has been called "an exercise in ellipses." The theme of flowing curves is echoed in the harp and Empire sofa.*

French Huguenot Church *Church and Queen Sts.* A group of French Huguenot refugees who had settled in and around Charleston built their first church on this site in 1681. The Gothic-style church now standing here dates from 1845. It was badly damaged during the Civil War and practically demolished by the 1886 earthquake. The church was restored and now contains a number of marble tablets memorializing George Washington, Alexander Hamilton and other Colonial notables with Huguenot ancestry. The interior also includes a beautiful altar with a circular railing, box pews and an 1845 Henry Erben tracker organ with an interesting history. Dismantled by Union soldiers in 1865, it was about to be loaded onto a ship leaving for New York when it was saved by its organist. Restored in 1969, this rare instrument with two manuals and pedals plus 12 stops is used for recitals each spring. In the churchyard are many stones from the early 1700s that are inscribed in French. *Open daily.*

Gibbes Art Gallery *135 Meeting St.* The gallery is notable for its 18th- and 19th-century American portraits—especially those by West, Peale and Sully—and more than 250 miniatures of the same period portraying early Charleston residents. Among the miniatures are 60 works by Charles Fraser, a Charleston artist born in 1782. Henrietta Johnston, the first woman artist in British America, is represented by five pastel portraits completed between 1706 and 1720. The large Roman Revival-style marble bust of George Washington on display was created from life studies by Giuseppe Ceracchi. Among the 19th-century American landscape and genre painters, Henry Inman (*An Abby Window*) and Thomas Doughty (*Delaware Water Gap*) are represented. A collection of lithographs and engravings document many of the most important Revolutionary and Civil War battles. There are a number of Oriental carvings and ceramics and Japanese prints. *Open Tues.-Sun. except holidays.*

Heyward-Washington House *87 Church St.* George Washington, who rented this three-story hip-roof brick dwelling for one week during his tour of the South in 1791, remarked on its comfort, and considering the number of places Washington stayed his opinions are to be respected. It is a typical Charleston "double house" with centrally located halls built around 1770. Its first owner was Daniel Heyward, a rice planter and the father of Thomas Heyward, who was a signer of the Declaration of Independence. The main entrance with its fanlighted door, pediment and columns is reconstructed but the rest of the building is virtually original and its interior charms include a fine second-story paneled drawing room with interior paneled shutters and an outstanding Georgian mantel. The house is furnished throughout with superb period furniture made in Charleston. A separate kitchen and carriage house stand on the grounds, and a formal garden is planted with flowers known to have been cultivated in Colonial days. *Open daily. Small charge.*

Joseph Manigault House *350 Meeting St.* Charleston's early prosperity is evident in this elegant gray brick three-story dwelling completed in 1803. A fine example of the Adam style, it has bays on the north and east sides, a curved double veranda on the west and a broad double veranda at the main entrance. Rescued from ruin in 1933 and fully restored, the house is currently operated as a branch of the Charleston Museum. A fine unsupported staircase rises from the large front hall, and there is a secret stairway between the second and third stories. The plasterwork ceilings and cornices are outstanding. Collections of Louis XV, Louis XVI and early 19th-century Charleston furniture are displayed along with Waterford glass and English porcelain. The grounds include an attractive garden. *Open daily. Small charge.*

Kahal Kadosh Beth Elohim *86 Hasell St.* This handsome stone structure with a six-column portico and tall side windows, built in 1841, resembles a Greek Doric temple. It is the second oldest synagogue in the U.S. and serves the nation's oldest Reform Jewish congregation. In the Archives Room is an interesting collection of historical documents, including a letter of thanks from George Washington in answer to the congregation's congratulations on his election to the Presidency; the coat of arms and deed to the land of Francis Salvadore, the first Jew to hold public office in the nation and the first to be killed in the American Revolution; and the original prayerbook of Isaac Harby, the first Jew in the U.S. to develop a liberal Judaism, which later served as the basis for the Reform movement in this country. *Open Mon.-Sat.*

Nathaniel Russell House *51 Meeting St.* This beautiful example of the Adam style was built around 1809 by a Rhode Islander whose success as a merchant in Charleston earned him the title "King of the Yankees." The restrained lines of the exterior are enlivened by the use of red brick and marble trim about the windows, wrought-iron balconies and a superb fanlight above the entrance. A three-story bay overlooks the large garden. Rooms on each floor are reached by way of a graceful free-flying staircase. Their decor—English,

French and American period furniture, fine porcelains, silver, rugs and paintings—enhances the Adamesque architectural detail of the rooms. From mid-March to mid-April the house serves as headquarters for Historic Charleston Foundation's annual Festival of Houses, when over 60 private homes are opened to the public. *Open daily except Dec. 25. Small charge.*

Old Slave Mart Museum *6 Chalmers St.* This is the oldest museum in the U.S. dedicated to the Negro and it contains the only collection of handicrafts made exclusively by slaves. A comparison of this display with an exhibit of African arts and crafts reveals that the slaves employed techniques much the same as those used by free black men in Africa. In another display the history of slavery in the U.S. is told through a collection of letters, documents, pictures, including a list of slaves sold in this building. Art exhibits featuring the works of contemporary black artists throughout the state are held periodically. The building, constructed in 1820 as a fire house, was enlarged in 1856 and converted into a slave market. The front balcony was used by auctioneers; inside are several booths where buyers could examine slaves before bidding. *Open daily except holidays.*

Protestant Episcopal Church of St. Philip *142 Church St.* This is the third home of the oldest parish (organized in 1670) in South Carolina. The present Colonial-style church was built between 1835 and 1838. It has a stately spire which once contained a set of chimes that was melted down and recast as Confederate cannons during the Civil War. The interior of the church is noted for its plasterwork and a number of silver objects that survived the fire that destroyed one of the earlier buildings. Included in this collection are a 17th-century heart-shaped salver and a set of 1710 English Communion plate. In the church cemeteries are the graves of Edward Rutledge, a signer of the Declaration of Independence, Charles Pinckney, who signed the Constitution, John Calhoun, the famous statesman, and other South Carolina dignitaries. *Open daily.*

St. Michael's Episcopal Church *Meeting and Broad Sts.* The oldest church in Charleston, dedicated in 1762, is one of the finest examples of ecclesiastical architecture in Colonial America, and most of its original features have survived intact. Its design is in the tradition of James Gibbs, but owes much to the builder, Samuel Carty, from Ireland. It has a tall octagonal steeple rising above a two-story Doric-columned portico that graces a simple facade. The interior has galleries on three sides, a slightly recessed altar, a prominent pulpit and a few choice embellishments: a 1772 English wrought-iron chancel rail, an 1803 chandelier and several stained-glass windows. *Open daily.*

Unitarian Church in Charleston *8 Archdale St.* Henry VII's chapel in Westminster Abbey provided the inspiration for the rare Gothic fan tracery vaulting in the ceiling of this church. The building was begun in 1772 and was opened for worship in 1787. During the Revolution the unfinished building was occupied by British forces, who purportedly used it as a stable. It was completely remodeled in 1852 by architect Francis Lee, inventor of the spar torpedo used in the defense of Charleston during the Civil War. Originally part of the Independent Church, the congregation evolved to become the first Unitarian church in the South. *Open daily.*

U.S. Custom House *200 E. Bay St.* This neoclassic building was constructed between 1849 and 1879 at a cost of almost $3,000,000. Damaged by the Union bombardment in 1865 and by an earthquake in 1886, the building was restored in 1968 and again serves its original purpose. Inside, the stenciled etchings around the perimeter of the cortile ceiling have been restored, and there is an interesting display of an old ship register. *Open Mon.-Fri. except holidays.*

181. Boone Hall Plantation *Long Point Rd. (off Rte. 17), Mount Pleasant, S.C.* Major John Boone, a member of the "First Fleet" of original English settlers, established a cotton plantation on 17,000 acres of land granted to him in 1681. Surviving are 738 acres (still profitable—farm produce, cattle and pecans are raised today) and the original plantation buildings all of which were constructed of brick made on the plantation. These include nine cabins on "slave street" where house servants once lived, a circular smokehouse and the cotton gin house. The boat dock formerly used for loading bales onto ships bound for nearby Charleston has been renovated. A nave of oaks planted in 1743 arch over the avenue that leads to the mansion house, a reconstruction of the original antebellum home. It is set between two large formal gardens of azaleas and camellias. The ground floor of the house is open to visitors. Boone Hall plantation was used as a setting in the movie *Gone with the Wind* and other Hollywood productions. *Open daily except Thanksgiving Day and Dec. 25. Adults $1.75, children under 12 small charge.*

[181] *This three-quarter-mile-long avenue of moss-draped live oaks is ablaze with azaleas in spring. The mansion stands at the end of the avenue, surrounded by gardens. The nine brick cabins where the house servants lived are hidden behind the trees. The field slaves, who numbered about 1000, lived in smaller cottages on the 17,000-acre plantation. It was planted mostly in cotton in Colonial days.*

[**183.** *Factors' Walk*] *The old days when cotton was king come alive along Factors' Walk (far right). Here bales of cotton were unloaded for the merchants' inspection, and fortunes were made in the offices on the upper level. In the Cotton Exchange Building (near right), formerly the Savannah Cotton and Naval Stores Exchange, traders set the world price of turpentine, rosin and pine gum every day at noon. In the foreground is Menelas Park, named in honor of one of the directors of the exchange.*

182. Beaufort, S.C.

Three different flags—Spanish, French and Scottish—flew over this site before the British settlement was established in 1710. It was during its golden age as an agricultural center, from about 1820 to 1860, that many of the finest homes and buildings in Beaufort (pronounced *bewfort*) were constructed. These reflect various architectural styles: Georgian, Colonial, Greek Revival and the tropical architecture brought here by Barbadian planters. Beaufort was occupied by Union troops during the Civil War, and its buildings were spared the destruction that befell many other Southern cities. Particularly noteworthy private homes can be seen in the area centering on Bay Street and on the old historic Point.

Bank of Beaufort House Museum *1001 Bay St.* George Elliott, a wealthy Beaufort planter, built this handsome dwelling in about 1840. Today the facade, with its four massive pillars, is broken by a second-story veranda, added late in the 19th century. Notable interior features include the period furnishings, ceilings decorated with elaborate plasterwork, the original random-width flooring, gilded cornices and moldings and marble mantels. *Open Mon.-Sat. Small charge.*

Beaufort Baptist Church *600 Charles St.* This white stucco Greek Revival structure was erected in 1844. Its recessed front portico is topped by a pediment that extends the width of the building. The interior cove ceiling features particularly fine plaster ornamentation, done by slave artisans. Fluted Doric columns support the gallery that extends around three sides of the church. *Open daily.*

Beaufort Museum *713 Craven St.* A wide assortment of early Americana, including paintings, sculpture, stamps, cannon and Civil War relics and memorabilia, is on display in this castellated, fortresslike building, which is known as the Arsenal, and dates from the late 1700s. *Open daily.*

St. Helena's Episcopal Church *501 Church St.* This historic Colonial church dates from Beaufort's earliest days. The first church was built in 1724 for a parish founded 12 years earlier. It was enlarged in 1823 and again in 1840, making use of brick with cement stucco finishing. Doric pilasters and a fanlight frame the entrance of the church, and the interior has a cove ceiling with the chancel and altar in a semicircular apse. Still in use on special occasions is the Communion silver given to the church in 1734. In the churchyard, surrounded by a high brick wall, are the graves of many prominent citizens, including two generals of the Confederate Army. *Open daily.*

183. Savannah, Ga.

One of the first planned cities in the U.S. and, perhaps for that reason, one of the loveliest today, Savannah was laid out around squares and parks by its founder, James Oglethorpe, and William Bull in 1733. It served as the capital of the colony until 1786, when the seat of government was moved to Augusta, and was the chief cotton port in the U.S. when that product was king. More than 1100 of the city's stately 19th-century homes and commercial buildings are historically and architecturally important. (Devastating fires in 1796 and 1820 virtually obliterated 18th-century Savannah.) A great effort is currently being made to preserve and restore these reminders of the city's heritage.

Cathedral of St. John the Baptist *222 E. Harris St.* In 1898 a fire virtually destroyed the congregation's earlier cathedral on this site, but in less than two and a half years time they had replaced it with another French Gothic structure. The largest Catholic cathedral in the southeast, it has many lovely stained-glass windows, most of which were made in the Austrian Tyrol. The high altar, of Italian white marble, which survived the fire and hand-carved Stations of the Cross from Munich are among the treasures here. An Italian bronze bas-relief of St. John the Baptist stands in the garden. *Open daily.*

Christ Church *28 Bull St.* Built in 1838, this Greek Revival Episcopal edifice is the third church to occupy the site. Six Ionic columns are impressive features of the entrance porch. The interior is noted for a fine balcony and a superb ceiling cast from molds designed by Christopher Wren for St. Paul's Cathedral in London. The only Revere bell south of Washington, D.C., is still used regularly to announce services. Among the ministers who served early congregations was John Wesley (1736-37). *Open daily.*

Colonial Dames House *329 Abercorn St.* Andrew Low, an Anglo-American cotton merchant, built this handsome, stuccoed Victorian house in 1848. Later it was occupied by his son and the latter's wife, Juliette Gordon Low. The younger Lows spent much of their married life in England, where Mrs. Low became familiar with the Boy Scouts and Girl Guides, founded by Sir Robert Baden-Powell and his sister. It was in this house, after her return to the U.S., that Mrs. Low organized America's first Girl Scout troop in 1912. Besides its role in the history of scouting, the lovely house is of interest for its beautifully proportioned rooms, ornate ceilings, carved woodwork and crystal chandeliers. William Makepeace Thackeray, while in Savannah on lecture tours, and Robert E. Lee are known to have been guests here. Since 1928 the building has been the headquarters of the National Society of Colonial Dames of America in the State of Georgia. *Open Mon.-Sat. except holidays. Small charge.*

Congregation Mickve Israel *20 E. Gordon St.* This is the oldest Reform temple in North America. It was consecrated in 1878 to serve a congregation that dated from 1733, when a small number of Sephardic Jews landed in Savannah. The original Sefer Torah brought over with them and copies of letters sent by Levi Sheftal to George Washington along with his response are housed in a museum. *Open Mon.-Fri.*

Davenport House *324 E. State St.* In 1955 this superb example of late Georgian architecture, then more than 130 years old, was saved from destruction by the Historic Savannah Foundation. Used today as the organization's headquarters, the sturdy dwelling has been restored and refurnished with pieces from the period. The starkness of the building's brick facade is broken by the elliptical stairway, fine wrought ironwork, shutters and handsome entrance door. Of particular note in the interior is the drawing room, which has Ionic columns and an 18-branch crystal chandelier. *Open Mon.-Sat. Small charge.*

Evangelical Lutheran Church of the Ascension *Bull and State Sts.* This excellent combination of Norman and Gothic styles was built between 1876 and 1879; much of the work was done at night by the men of the congregation after their regular workday ended. In the uncolumned sanctuary are a splendid stained-glass window of the Ascension of Christ and an unusual baptismal font in the form of an angel holding a basin. Sixteen scenes in miniature from the congregation's history, beginning with its founding in 1741, are displayed in the downstairs auditorium. They are composed of tiny, parishioner-made buildings and furnishings and peopled with antique china dolls. *Open daily.*

Factors' Walk *Bay St. between E. and W. Broad Sts.* Early 19th-century cotton merchants known as factors gave their name to this area. Four- and five-story former warehouses extend for 10 blocks beside a sunken walk along the Savannah River. This is where the factors inspected bales of cotton for purchase and shipment. The buildings and streets in the area are made of stones once used as ballast on English merchant ships, and the bluff opposite the warehouses is faced with them. The newly restored Factors' Walk is once more a thriving part of downtown Savannah.

COTTON EXCHANGE BUILDING *100 E. Bay St.* Currently occupied by the Savannah Area Chamber of Commerce, this 1886 stone building has a number of intriguing decorative features: a leaded stained-glass window bearing the word "cotton," large fireplaces with hand-carved mantels, columns decorated with plasterwork designs and an ornate staircase. In front of the exchange is a small, round pool with a terra cotta griffin fountain. *Open daily except Dec. 25.*

FACTORS' WALK MILITARY MUSEUM *222 Factors' Walk* A 1775 cotton warehouse now holds a collection of Civil War flags, uniforms and objects recovered from numerous battlefields. Condeferate arms displayed include edged weapons, a Gatling gun, rifles and revolvers. The building itself is of interest, with its exposed beams and stone walls. A tape recording explains episodes in the Civil War that relate to Savannah. *Open daily. Small charge.*

OGLETHORPE BENCH *Corner of Bay and Whitaker Sts.* A bench marks the spot where James E. Oglethorpe and a group of colonists landed in 1733 to found the 13th colony of the New World.

Independent Presbyterian Church *Bull St. and Oglethorpe Ave.* Built as a replica of an earlier structure destroyed by fire, this 1890s church, with its soaring four-sectioned steeple, is reminiscent of 18th-century St. Martin-in-the-Fields in London, England. William Dean Howells wrote in 1919 of its Georgian interior, "It is of such exquisite loveliness that no church in London can compare with it." The congregation, organized in 1755, is the oldest Presbyterian denomination in Georgia. Lowell Mason was its organist for 10 years and this is where his now-famous hymn tunes were first heard. *Open Sun.-Fri.*

Juliette Gordon Low Birthplace *142 Bull St.* The spirited founder of the Girl Scouts of the U.S.A. was born in this elegant Regency-style town house in 1860 and lived here for 26 years, until her marriage to William Mackay Low. Now a national center of the Girl Scouts, the stuccoed brick house, designed by William Jay and completed in 1821, is maintained as a living memorial to "Daisy" Low. All phases of Mrs. Low's life are represented here and many of her creative achievements, including sculptures, paintings and poems, are on display. The building is superbly fur-

[**183.** *Juliette Gordon Low Birthplace*] *Above the mantel hangs a portrait of "Daisy" Low in the gown she wore when she was presented at Queen Victoria's Court in 1887, shortly after she was married to William Mackay Low.*

nished, much of it with pieces that belonged to the five generations of the Gordon family that occupied it. A lovely 1870s-style garden complements the house and its various outbuildings. *Open Mon.-Tues., Thurs.-Sun. except holidays. Small charge.*

Kiah Museum *505 W. 36th St.* American Indian artifacts, African art, silver, china and 18th- and 19th-century furniture form the basis of the personal collection of Mrs. Virginia Kiah, an artist and former art teacher. Animals and exotic plants can also be seen here, and there are antebellum and Civil War items that were excavated in Savannah and Washington, D.C. Temporary exhibits are held often. *Open Tues., Thurs. Sept.-May except holidays.*

Owens-Thomas House *124 Abercorn St.* William Jay, a British-born architect, designed this superb English Regency house at the age of 19. The dwelling, completed in 1819, has many attributes unusual for the period: indirect lighting in the dining room, curved doors and walls and a unique arched "drawbridge" on the second floor spanning the stairwell and linking the front and rear halls. There are outstanding Regency and Federal furnishings, many of which belonged to the Owens family who occupied the house for 120 years. One of its most distinguished chambers is the Lafayette Room where the French general stayed during his visit to Savannah in 1825. A walled garden behind the house contains plants that were typical of Southern gardens in the early 1800s. *Open daily Oct.-Aug. except holidays. Adults $1.25, children over 9 small charge.*

Telfair Academy of Arts and Sciences *121 Barnard St.* One of the southeast's oldest art museums, the Telfair was founded in 1875. Eleven years later it opened to the public in this stately structure designed by William Jay in 1818 as the home of the Telfair family. A collection of American graphic arts can be seen here along with one emphasizing early 20th-century works by Bellows, Hassam, Henri and Cassatt. A number of fine Colonial and Federal portraits are also featured. Textiles and antique furniture, including many Telfair pieces, are displayed; a small library contains rare books on such topics as architecture, botany and medicine. *Open Tues.-Sun. Feb.-Dec. except holidays.*

U.S. Customhouse *1-3-5 E. Bay St.* Built in 1852 of Massachusetts granite, this Greek Revival structure is the oldest federal building in the state. Each of its six huge columns (topped with tobacco-leaf capitals instead of the usual acanthus leaf) on the facade weigh over 15 tons. Halfway up, the central interior staircase divides in two, the sections spiraling to the top floor without any perpendicular support. Exhibit cases in the lobby contain Customs memorabilia and samples of imports that have entered Savannah. *Open Mon.-Fri. except holidays.*

Wesley Monumental United Methodist Church *429 Abercorn St.* John and Charles Wesley, the founders of Methodism, spent three years (1735-38) preaching and teaching in Georgia, much of the time in and around Savannah. This Gothic-style memorial to the two brothers, modeled after Queen's Kirk in Amsterdam, Holland, was begun in 1875 with contributions from Methodists throughout the world. The spacious sanctuary contains several magnificent Tiffany stained-glass windows dedicated to famous Methodists. *Open daily.*

184. Fort Pulaski National Monument *Rte. 80, Savannah Beach, Ga.* This remarkably well-preserved, five-sided fort stands on Cockspur Island in the Savannah River. Massive brick walls over seven feet thick surrounded by a moat demonstrate the skill and patience of early masons. Constructed between 1829 and 1847 with a dike and drainage system designed by Lieutenant Robert E. Lee, the fort includes a number of rooms furnished in the Civil War period and a parade ground. In 1862 the methods of construction used here were rendered obsolete by Union rifled cannon that pounded Pulaski's defenses during a 30-hour bombardment and brought about its surrender. Several shells are still imbedded in the walls. At the Visitor Center a number of displays illustrate the fort's design and history. North of the fort stands the Wesley Memorial commemorating the site where John Wesley knelt in thanks after safely crossing the Atlantic in 1736. *Open daily except Dec. 25. Small charge.*

185. Tybee Museum *Rte. 80, Savannah Beach, Ga.* Pictures, documents and dioramas illustrate 400 years in the history of this coastal area—from the days of early Spanish and French explorations, through the English settlement and pirate activities, to the present. Also displayed in this former fort are a large gun collection, old coins and uniforms. The Civil War Room contains objects associated with both the Union and the Confederacy. *Open daily May-Sept., Wed.-Mon. Oct.-Apr. Small charge.*

186. Fort Frederica National Monument *St. Simons Island, Ga.* These ruins of a fort and settlement stand as mute evidence of the conflict that once raged between England and Spain for possession of Georgia and the Carolinas. Built in 1736, the fort served as base for General James Oglethorpe and his regiment during the War of Jenkins' Ear (1739-48). The decisive Battle of Bloody Marsh, frustrating further Spanish colonial ambitions in North America, occurred nearby in 1742. Parts of the fort's walls and a barracks tower still guard the remains of the town of Frederica. Once a bustling town of 1500, Frederica now consists of a burial ground, the ruins of the fort and houses and a few grass-covered vestiges of the moat that once surrounded it. In the Visitor Center there are maps, excavated objects and a diorama that help to tell the story of this British outpost. Informal talks and the demonstration firing of 18th-century flintlock muskets form part of the summer program here. *Open daily.*

187. Jekyll Island Museum *329 Riverview Dr., Jekyll Island, Ga.* Thirteen years after its completion in 1892, William Rockefeller, the younger brother of John D. Rockefeller, Sr., purchased this gray-shingled, 25-room "cottage" with its wide verandas to use as a vacation residence. It has been restored and furnished to look just as it did when he lived there. The original Edwardian furnishings are notably unpretentious but tasteful and attractive. A handsome Tiffany glass window can be seen on a stair landing. Originally the house had no kitchen, since Rockefeller took all his meals at the exclusive Jekyll Island Club, whose members were reputed to control one-sixth of the world's wealth. *Open daily. Adults $1.50, children 6-12 small charge.*

[**183.** *Telfair Academy*] *The dining room at Telfair is a showcase for a number of portraits of Savannah citizens. All of the furniture here belonged to the Telfair family. The side chair, in a late classic design, was probably made in Philadelphia. The sideboard, with its serpentine front, Hepplewhite design and underwood of cypress and pine, was made for the Telfair family in Savannah or Charleston and found some years ago in Telfair's attic. John Frazee did the handsome marble mantel. Miss Mary Telfair, sister of the original owner, Alexander Telfair, left the mansion and its furnishings to the Georgia Historical Society in 1875.*

188. Kingsley Plantation *Fort George Island, Fla.* The two-story white Kingsley House, set in a 14-acre park, is believed to be the oldest plantation house in Florida. Besides displaying period pieces that belonged to the Kingsley family, the house has a museum of artifacts out of the island's past. Kingsley, who dealt extensively in slaves, married an African princess and gave her a small house nearby made of tabby brick (a mixture of oyster shells, lime, gravel and water). One of the old slave cabins has been restored. *Open daily. Small charge.*

189. Cummer Gallery of Art *829 Riverside Ave., Jacksonville, Fla.* The art collection of Mrs. Arthur Gerrish Cummer formed the nucleus of the fine works of art here, which have grown to number more than 1300 objects since the museum's opening in 1961. Medieval illuminated manuscripts, Renaissance portraits, rare tapestries and furniture share the gracious building with paintings by European masters such as Titian, Rubens and Goya and such famous American painters as Whistler, Homer and Eakins. The gallery also owns a superb collection of early-18th-century Meissen porcelain, which was the first hard-paste porcelain produced in Europe. Beautiful formal gardens surround the museum, which overlooks the St. Johns River. *Open Tues.-Sun. except holidays.*

190. Fort Caroline National Memorial *12713 Fort Caroline Rd., off Rte. 10, E. of Jacksonville, Fla.* In 1564 near this site on the St. Johns River, French colonists under the leadership of René de Laudonnière established the first European settlement north of Mexico. They were driven out the following year by the Spanish, who feared Fort Caroline might become a threat to their commerce. The National Park Service has reconstructed the French fort and its moat from a sketch by Jacques Le Moyne, a member of the original settlement, and has brought together in the Visitor Center many artifacts of the 16th century: European military, navigational and religious objects as well as relics of the area's Indians. *Open daily except Dec. 25.*

191. Riverside Baptist Church *2650 Park St., Jacksonville, Fla.* Addison Mizner combined features of Spanish and Byzantine architecture in this unusual limestone church, completed in 1925. Built in the shape of a cross, the center is octagonal. Blue glass in the windows and a blue-glass chandelier flood the interior with a calm blue light. *Open Mon.-Fri., Sun.*

192. St. Augustine, Fla.

The oldest city in the U.S. was founded as a military outpost by Captain-General Pedro Menéndez de Avilés of Spain in 1565, 55 years before the Pilgrims landed on the coast of New England, and remained a Spanish colony and military base until 1763. It became British property after the signing of the Treaty of Paris in that year. Twenty years later, in 1783, the city was returned to Spanish rule as the result of another treaty and remained under Spanish control until all of Florida was acquired by the U.S. in 1821. Thirty-one original buildings have survived and 29 additional buildings have been carefully reconstructed by various governmental agencies and private organizations. The restored area lies along Matanzas Bay waterfront and is bounded on the west by Cordova Street.

Arrivas House *46 St. George St.* One of the owners of this coquina (natural shell stone) structure, built about 1725, was Don Raimundo de Arrivas. A second-story addition of wood was added around 1788. On the first floor demonstrations of candle making, spinning and weaving are held. *Open daily.*

Benét House *65 St. George St.* One owner of this early 19th-century house was Pedro Benét, the great-grandfather of Stephen Vincent Benét and William Rose Benét, both Pulitzer Prize winners. The house, built around 1804, is made of coquina, and, typical of the St. Augustine style, has a high-pitched roof and entrance through a patio. *Open daily.*

[Castillo de San Marcos] Spanish and Indian workers labored almost 25 years building the castillo's 30-foot-high walls from coquina, a native rock formation of solidified seashells; the mortar holding the blocks was made of shell lime. The drawbridge spans a 40-foot-wide moat that extends around three sides of the 17th-century fort.

Castillo de San Marcos National Monument *1 Castillo Dr.* This Spanish fortress, constructed between 1672 and 1695, is the oldest masonry fort in the U.S. Assaulted by the English in 1702 and 1740, the castillo withstood both attacks. Inside the fort are guardrooms, powder magazines, prisons and living quarters. The walls of the fort are 13 feet thick at the base, tapering to nine feet at the top. *Open daily except Dec. 25. Small charge.*

Cathedral of St. Augustine *40 Cathedral Pl.* This church ministers to the oldest Catholic parish in the U.S., dating from 1565. The building, erected in the 1790s, was rebuilt after a fire in 1887. Only the nave of the cathedral is from the original structure. The church was refurbished in 1965 and contains a baroque gold tabernacle from Ireland, Spanish floor tiles and murals depicting the historic and religious life of St. Augustine. *Open daily.*

Fernández-Llambias House *31 St. Francis St.* Built before 1763, this is one of the few remaining houses in St. Augustine that can be traced to the first Spanish period. During the second Spanish period the building was occupied by Minorcan colonists. In 1854, the house became the property of the Catalina Llambias family, who owned it for some 65 years. The walls are made of coquina, the floor of oystershell, sand and lime. The house is handsomely furnished with a number of English, Spanish and American antiques. *Open 1st Sun. of each month.*

Flagler Memorial Church *36 Sevilla St.* Henry M. Flagler, who with his partner, John D. Rockefeller, founded Standard Oil Company, was one of the early developers of Florida. Flagler had this sumptuous Venetian Renaissance-style Presbyterian church built in 1890 as a memorial to his daughter. The interior of the 150-foot-high copper dome is inlaid with marble; 12 plaques of breccia violet marble, symbolic of the 12 apostles, are set in the marble tile floor. Santo Domingo mahogany woodwork in the church is all hand carved. The Aeolian-Skinner organ, a four-manual instrument, with 70 registers, 90 ranks of pipes, and seven divisions with festival trumpets, is considered one of the finest in the country. *Open daily.*

Government House *Cathedral and St. George Sts.* Government House, built as the residence and office of the governor, as well as the court and social center of Florida, later served as a post office, courthouse and customs office. The first structure on this site dates from 1598. The present building, erected in 1833–34, has several later additions. The building now houses historical displays, archaeological and curatorial laboratories and the research library of the Historic St. Augustine Preservation Board. *Open daily.*

Oldest House Museum Complex *St. Francis St.* The St. Augustine Historical Society has established a museum of the social, cultural and domestic history of St. Augustine. Exhibits are housed in three separate buildings on the same block. *Open daily. Adults and children over 10 small charge for all three houses.*

GONZÁLEZ-ÁLVAREZ HOUSE *14 St. Francis St.* A domestic interior in the typical Colonial St. Augustine style is re-created in this hip-roof dwelling which was built sometime between 1703 and 1727. Also known as the oldest house in St. Augustine, the first documented occupancy was by a Canary Islands' sailor and artilleryman. It has hand-hewn cedar beams and walls of coquina. The walled garden contains fruit trees and flowers listed on early records and known to have been grown in Colonial St. Augustine.

TOVAR HOUSE *22 St. Francis St.* Built in the first half of the 18th century, Tovar House was considerably modified in the early 1900s. Today it houses collections of tile, glass, ceramics and door locks. It is also called the House of the Cannonball: a British shot said to be from Oglethorpe's attack on the Spanish-held city is embedded in a wall.

WEBB MEMORIAL MUSEUM *20 St. Francis St.* This building is named for Dr. DeWitt Webb, a physician, naturalist and one of the founders of the St. Augustine Historical Society. Its displays include items of local significance.

Oldest Store Museum *4 Artillery Lane* During the last decades of the 19th century, C. F. Hamblen's general store supplied the St. Augustine community with many of its material needs. Items Hamblen stocked (hardware, farm machinery, automobiles, household

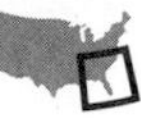

goods and dry goods) are displayed as they were then on wooden shelves, counters and in barrels. Also in the museum are replicas of a gun shop, blacksmith shop, ship chandlery and a collection of buggies and covered wagons. *Open daily. Small charge.*

Oldest Wooden School House *14 St. George St.* Constructed of cedar and cypress some time during the first Spanish occupation of Florida (1565-1763), this schoolhouse is said to be the oldest in the U.S. The schoolmaster lived on the second floor and taught his students in the one-room classroom below, which has been set up as it was in 1864. A few members of that class, the last one to be attended here, returned 67 years later for a nostalgic reunion. *Open daily except Dec. 25. Small charge.*

Old Spanish Inn *47 St. George St.* This 18th-century structure, built originally as a one-story coquina home, was later expanded to a good-sized two-story house. In 1957 it was remodeled to resemble a typical Spanish inn. Although it contains some 18th-century paintings and antiques, most of the furnishings are replicas of period pieces. Among the authentic items are rugs, candelabra, a copper bed warmer, an inlaid arcade chair, an Italian relief-carved drop-leaf table, a flax-spinning wheel and an 18th-century dish cupboard called a "confesionario." *Open daily. Small charge.*

Pan American Center *97 St. George St.* Latin American art is exhibited in this museum; paintings, sculpture, artifacts and antiques. The building is a reconstruction of the Colonial Hassett House and is typical of upper-class homes here in the late 18th century. It is constructed of coquina and has fireplaces on both floors. A part of the original foundation may be seen on the first floor. *Open daily. Small charge.*

Ribera House *20 St. George St.* Ribera House is a reconstruction on the original foundations of a home typical of those built in the 18th century by upper-class St. Augustine families. The two-story house was built with coquina and plastered inside and out to protect it from moisture. The house is furnished with 18th-century antiques and art objects. A two-room kitchen building, also reconstructed on the original foundation, stands behind the house. *Open daily. Small charge.*

Ximenez-Fatio House *20 Aviles St.* In the early 19th century, Andres Ximenez set up his furnishings store in this house which had been built between 1797 and 1802. It is constructed of coquina and native cedar, furnished with Spanish furniture of the period. The kitchen, a separate building, is believed to predate the house and is an excellent example of the architecture in early St. Augustine. Much of the original woodwork in both the house and the kitchen is still in good condition. It is now operated by the Florida Colonial Dames. *Open Thurs. Oct.-Apr.*

Zorayda Castle *83 King St.* Zorayda, built as a private residence in 1883, is a one-tenth scale replica of a section of the Alhambra Palace in Granada, Spain. Many of the interior walls are decorated with mosaic tiles and Moorish tracery. The castle includes harem quarters, the Egyptian Room which contains the Sacred Cat Rug said to be over 2300 years old (the rug was found in the casket of a mummy in the Valley of the Kings in Egypt), and the Court of Lions Hall whose walls are tiled with mosaics from a 12th-century Egyptian mosque. Throughout are exhibits of Oriental, Middle Eastern and European antiques collected by A. S. Mussallam, an antique rug merchant who lived here. *Open daily. Adults $1.25, children small charge.*

[Oldest School House] The weathered shingles and hand-hewn frames attest to the great age of the schoolhouse. In the fountain across the street, a boy and girl shelter from the spray under an umbrella.

[Flagler Memorial Church] Visible for miles, the shining copper dome of this magnificent church makes the great bronze Venetian cross above it seem small, although the cross is nearly 20 feet tall.

[**193.** *Morse Gallery*] *Louis Comfort Tiffany (1848–1933), son of the founder of the famed Tiffany and Company, was one of America's most influential designers, particularly of glass. He invented his own method of staining glass, and his window designs illuminate many homes, public buildings and churches around the country. Tiffany was also interested in home furnishings. All the furniture and glassware as well as the windows in this room were designed by him. The table, chairs and rug were made especially for Laurelton Hall, his house in Cold Spring Harbor, Long Island.*

193. Rollins College *Winter Park, Fla.* Rollins, founded in 1885, is a private, coeducational school with an enrollment of about 1200 in undergraduate and graduate studies. Noteworthy among the features of its lovely campus are the two collections described below.

BEAL-MALTBIE SHELL MUSEUM Almost every known species of shellfish (about 100,000) is represented in this unusual museum which is recognized as one of the finest of its kind anywhere. Dr. James H. Beal began the collection in 1888, gathering specimens from all over the world. Today over 250,000 shells, fascinating in their variety of shapes, sizes and colors, are attractively displayed in a Mediterranean-style building. Cameos carved from shells and other objects made out of shells are also on exhibit. *Open Tues.-Sun. Sept.-July except holidays. Small charge.*

MORSE GALLERY OF ART Founded in 1942 by Jeannette Genius McKean in memory of her grandfather, Charles H. Morse, this gallery houses the world's largest collection of windows by Louis Comfort Tiffany. Also on view are glass, furniture, enamels and lamps by this American master, as well as important works by many of his contemporaries, including Gallé, Majorelle and Lalique. *Open daily.*

194. John F. Kennedy Space Center *Cape Kennedy, S. of Titusville, Fla.* This immense installation, administered by the National Aeronautics and Space Administration, is the major U.S. launch base for all Mercury, Gemini and Apollo orbital and lunar landing missions. At the Visitor Center is a fascinating display of photographs, paintings and equipment relating to space exploration; films and a non-technical lecture on space projects are also offered. Main attractions at the center are Gemini 9 spacecraft, showing the effects of intensive heat caused by friction with the Earth's atmosphere during re-entry following a 72-hour manned space flight in 1966; models of the earlier Mercury capsule and Apollo Lunar Module landing craft; and a detailed scale model of a powerful Saturn V used to launch Apollo astronauts on moon missions. An escorted bus tour enables visitors to see the Moon Launch Pad and the towering Vehicle Assembly Building which, in itself, is a major accomplishment in engineering and construction. Also shown are the Apollo astronauts' training center, Mission Control and the Air Force Space Museum, where a comprehensive collection of objects traces the history and development of man's ventures into space. *Open daily except Dec. 25. Bus tour: adults $2.50, children 13–19 $1.25, 2–12 small charge.*

195. Real Eight Museum of Sunken Treasure *8625 Astronaut Blvd., Cape Canaveral, Fla.* For almost 300 years, the Spanish Empire regularly sent out fleets of ships to gather the treasures of its American colonies. In 1715 one such fleet failed to return. The galleons, carrying more than 1000 men and $14,000,000 worth of cargo sent from the Orient to Mexico by way of Manila, were wrecked in a hurricane off the coast of Florida. Nearly half of this fortune was recovered almost at once; the rest lay under the sea—some of it little more than 1000 feet from shore—for the next 245 years. At that time the Real Eight Company (the name is a combination of "piece of eight" and the Spanish equivalent, *ocho reales*) began to recover the remainder. Rare gold and silver pieces, gold jewelry and Chinese porcelains have been lifted from the sea. Visitors to the museum can view about one-fifth of this treasure, as well as dioramas and ship models. Audiotapes and a short film give the background of the fabulous discoveries. *Open daily except Jan. 1 and Dec. 25. Adults $2.25, children $1.25.*

196. St. Lucie State Museum *Pepper State Park, Fort Pierce, Fla.* This museum, designed like the spiraling shell of the chambered nautilus, houses exhibits and artifacts that recall the area's colorful past. Artwork tells the story of Indian, Spanish and American adventures, including the loss of ships and gold nearby. *Open daily. Small charge.*

197. Elliott Museum *Hutchinson Island, Stuart, Fla.* This museum honors Sterling Elliott, inventor of the addressing machine and the quadricycle, who pioneered the steering and transmission systems used in today's cars. Many of the 222 patented machines developed by Elliott and his son Harmon are on display. There is also a general store with a post office, antique carriages and automobiles, 12 Americana shops, an art gallery and a winter theater. *Open daily. Small charge.*

198. Norton Gallery *1451 S. Olive Ave., West Palm Beach, Fla.* Over 700 European and American paintings, including masterpieces of the early Italian Renaissance and works by Gauguin, Braque, Bellows, Hopper, Pollack and Motherwell, are on display in this handsome low building, completed in 1941. An outstanding sculpture collection features such works as Maillol's *Ile de France*, Brancusi's *Mademoiselle Pogany* and Moore's *Family Group II.* The Chinese Room contains many rare jades, bronzes and ceramics. The Norton School of Art offers classes in drawing and painting, sculpture, ceramics and ballet for students of all ages. *Open Tues.-Sun.*

199. Episcopal Church of Bethesda-by-the-Sea *S. County Rd. and Barton Ave., Palm Beach, Fla.* This handsome church, consecrated in 1931, re-creates the architectural features of some of Europe's great Gothic churches. Wood and stone carvings and a collection of ecclesiastical paintings, the finest of which is Murillo's *Madonna and Child*, are highlights of the interior. At one side of the church are the beautifully landscaped Cluett Memorial Gardens. *Open daily.*

200. Henry Morrison Flagler Museum *Whitehall Way, Palm Beach, Fla.* The collections at Whitehall, the former home of the pioneer developer of Florida, include paintings, dolls, fans, laces, silver and china. The mansion itself is well worth a visit. Built for the Flaglers in 1901, it provided a lavish background for the entertainment of their many guests and reveals the opulent taste of the very rich in that era. It served as a luxury hotel for many years, but has now been restored to its turn-of-the-century elegance. The entrance hall is lined with marble panels, benches and columns. The ballroom glitters with chandeliers, plate glass mirrors and damask drapes. Tapestries cover the wall of the music room and the chairs in the salon. *Open Tues.-Sun. Small charge.*

201. Ancient Spanish Monastery *16711 W. Dixie Hwy., N. Miami Beach, Fla.* A relic of the Middle Ages brought from the Old World to the New, this Cistercian monastery was built in the 12th century in the Spanish province of Segovia to celebrate a victory over the Moors. William Randolph Hearst bought it in the 1920s, had it dismantled and its 35,784 stones shipped to the U.S. in 10,751 crates. Today it is the home of an Episcopalian congregation and is known as the Episcopal Church of St. Bernard de Clairvaux, after the monastery's founder. The lovely building, surrounded by formal gardens, houses many ancient art treasures. *Open daily except holidays. Adults $1.50, children small charge.*

202. Bass Museum of Art *2100 Collins Ave., Miami Beach, Fla.* Paintings attributed to Botticelli, Rembrandt and El Greco can be seen in this museum's varied collections, as well as Impressionist and other modern works. Also on exhibit are sculptures, tapestries, altar vessels and vestments, gold coins and Tibetan bronzes. Autographs and first editions of famous composers can also be seen here. There are daily concerts of classical music. *Open Mon.-Sat.*

[195] *Some of the riches in the Museum of Sunken Treasure are shown here in an antique treasure chest with an old flintlock gun. The gold coins are doubloons, also called 8-escudo pieces, and they are now worth up to several thousands of dollars on the collectors' market. The silver coins are pieces of eight and they are worth hundreds of dollars apiece. The silver deteriorated somewhat after 250 years in the sea, but the gold resisted all corrosion.*

This aerial view shows Vizcaya's formal gardens, in the Italian style, which were carved out of a mangrove swamp.

205. Vizcaya

3251 S. Miami Ave., Miami, Fla.

The late James Deering, co-founder of the International Harvester Company, built Vizcaya on 30 acres of land overlooking Biscayne Bay. There are 10 acres of formal gardens in a rather grand version of the Italian style, with low hedges, parterres, canals, fountains and statuary. Guarding the private harbor is a stone breakwater in the shape of a great festive barge, decorated with obelisks and statues that symbolize the terrors and delights of the sea. The architects, F. Burrall Hoffman, Jr., Diego Suarez and Paul Chalfin, created the 16th-century-style Italian Renaissance palace to house Deering's magnificent collection of mostly Italian antique furniture, sculpture, textiles and ceramics, plus many exceptionally fine architectural details such as doorways, ceilings and wall panels from Italian palaces. The collection could never be duplicated or even approached today, since European countries have prohibited the removal of such national treasures as these. The building, now the Dade County Art Museum, is built of light-colored Florida limestone with a tile roof. Airy loggias and an interior court lighten the impact of the lavish rooms, which are furnished and decorated in a felicitous mixture of Renaissance, Baroque, rococo and Neoclassical styles. *Open daily except Dec. 25. Adults $2.00, children small charge.*

The wrought-iron gates from a Venetian palace are flanked by Neapolitan murals in the tea room.

The Neoclassical east loggia overlooks Biscayne Bay, and, like most of the rooms, opens on a patio.

203. Fairchild Tropical Garden *10901 Old Cutler Rd., Miami, Fla.* Over 4000 kinds of exotic plants from all parts of the tropical world flourish on the 83 acres of this botanical garden. Visitors see many rare, often bizarre, species in the collections of palms, orchids, bougainvillea, hibiscus and flowering trees, and walk through a lush tropical rain forest sustained by artificial rainfall. *Open daily except Dec. 25. Small charge.*

204. Plymouth Congregational Church (United Church of Christ) *3429 Devon Rd., Miami, Fla.* One man, a Spanish stonemason, built this simple mission-style church of native coral rock between 1915 and 1917, modeling it after a church in Mexico City. Its hand-carved walnut door, more than 350 years old, is from an ancient Spanish monastery. Plymouth Church is also known as the Church in the Garden because of its lovely cloister gardens with their fountains and covered walks. *Open daily.*

205. Vizcaya *3251 S. Miami Ave., Miami, Fla.* See feature display on page 304.

206. Coral Castle of Florida *28655 S. Federal Hwy., 2 mi. N. of Homestead, Fla.* Out of massive blocks of coral, some weighing as much as 35 tons, a frail Latvian immigrant carved this castle tower and the huge pieces of "furniture" in its courtyard. Singlehandedly—he claimed he had discovered how the Egyptians had built the Pyramids—Edward Leedskalnin quarried the blocks, put them behind an eight-foot wall of coral and transformed them into such objects as a one-ton rocking chair and a six-ton heart-shaped table. Other features include a nine-ton swinging gate that turns at the touch of a finger, a 25-foot obelisk and a 23-ton telescope. *Open daily. Adults $1.50, students small charge.*

207. McKee's Museum of Sunken Treasure *Treasure Harbor, Plantation Key, Fla.* In 1733 a fleet of Spanish treasure galleons was sunk in a hurricane in the Florida keys. Visitors to this museum, operated by diver Arthur McKee, can see coral-encrusted objects salvaged from these wrecks 222 years later. These include silver bars weighing from 60 to 75 pounds, gold doubloons, pieces of eight, jewelry and treasure from other shipwrecks in the Bullion Room. A 3000-pound cannon, cannonballs, swords, flintlock pistols, ivory tusks, silver plate and a 20-foot anchor are also on view. *Open daily. Adults $1.50, children small charge.*

208. Audubon House *Whitehead and Greene Sts., Key West, Fla.* John James Audubon lived in this elegant frame house in 1832 while painting the wildlife of the Florida Keys. On display is a rare complete set of "double elephant" folios of his *Birds of America.* The house, furnished with choice 18th- and 19th-century pieces, was built in 1830 by Captain John H. Geiger. *Open daily. Small charge.*

209. Ernest Hemingway Home and Museum *907 Whitehead St., Key West, Fla.* Hemingway lived in this Spanish Colonial-type house from 1931 to 1940. He built the first swimming pool in Key West, and in the study of the poolhouse he wrote some of his most famous works: *Death in the Afternoon, For Whom the Bell Tolls* and *The Snows of Kilimanjaro,* among others. Hemingway's furnishings and mementos can be seen in the house. Many of his plantings and numerous descendants of his original cats thrive in the garden today. *Open daily. Small charge.*

210. Martello Gallery and Museum *S. Roosevelt Blvd., Key West, Fla.* In 1846, when the U.S. was at war with Mexico, Congress authorized the building of six forts to defend the southeastern states from attack. Construction of the Martello Towers was begun in 1861, but they were never completed because rifled cannon (first used during the Civil War) made them obsolete. In 1954 the East Martello Tower was made into a museum. Within the rooms and dungeon of the fort are exhibits of Key West culture, a costume room, Hemingway Room, children's museum and galleries of art. There is an aviary and Lookout Tower as well. *Open daily except Dec. 25. Small charge.*

211. Fort Jefferson National Monument *Dry Tortugas Islands, 68 mi. W. of Key West (accessible only by boat)* Within the 90-square-mile area of the national monument, which includes the seven Dry Tortugas Islands and the surrounding shoals and waters noted for their coral reefs, natural sea gardens and seabird nesting grounds, is massive Fort Jefferson. The largest 19th-century coastal fort in the U.S., it was built to guard the Gulf of Mexico. The fort has walls eight feet thick and 50 feet high; it covers almost 16 acres. Construction started in 1846 and carried on for two decades until the new rifled cannon used in the Civil War made the fort obsolete. It continued to serve as a Federal prison, housing, among others, four men found guilty of conspiring to assassinate Lincoln: one was Dr. Samuel Mudd, who had innocently set the broken leg of John Wilkes Booth. *Open daily.*

[208] *Leaves of an original four-volume set of folios show a white pelican (top) and a pair of Key West doves (bottom). Audubon made paintings of the doves while he was staying at Captain Geiger's house in Key West.*

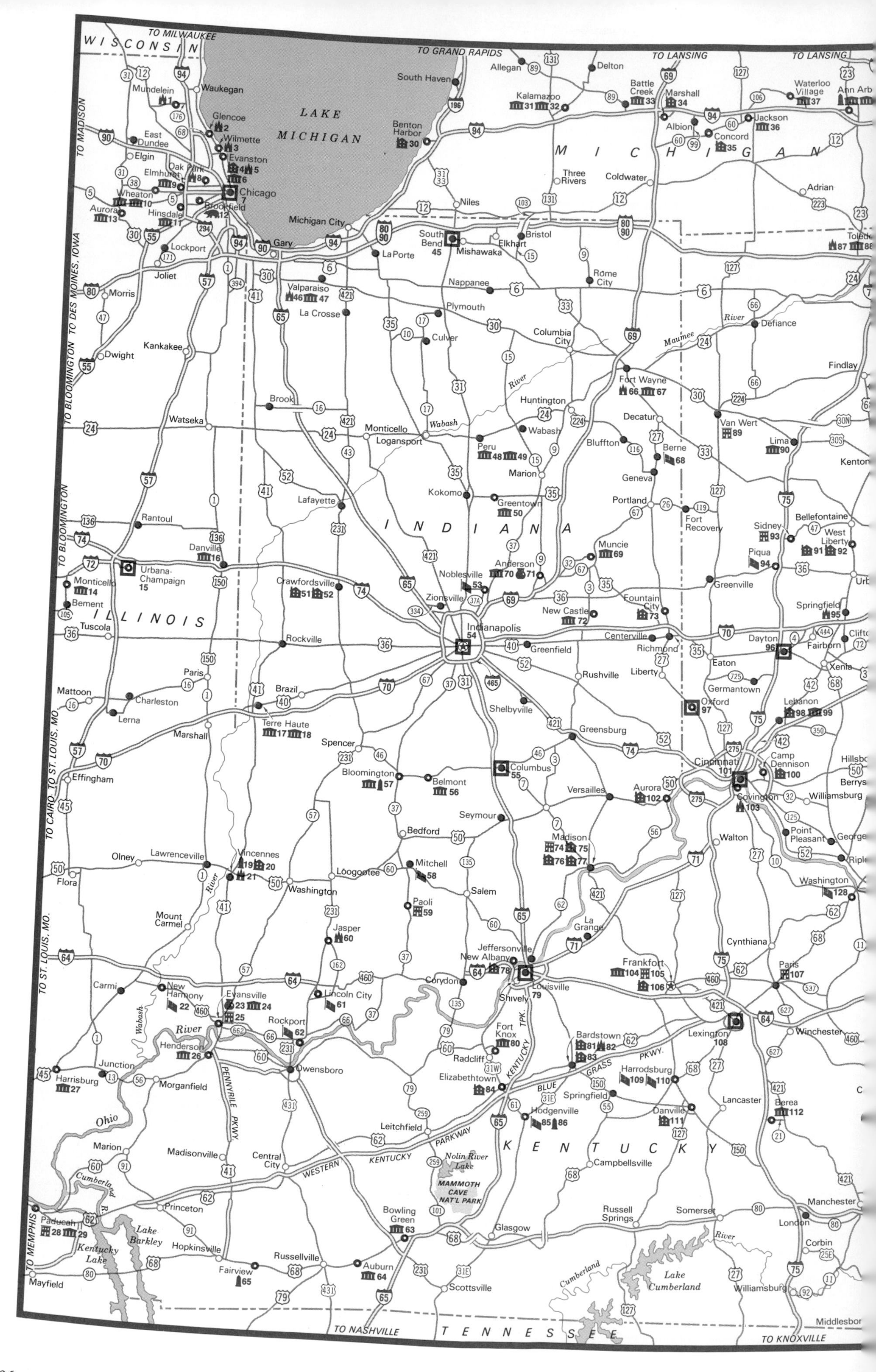

TO MILWAUKEE
WISCONSIN
TO MADISON
TO GRAND RAPIDS
TO LANSING
TO LANSING
LAKE MICHIGAN
MICHIGAN
INDIANA
ILLINOIS
KENTUCKY
TENNESSEE
TO BLOOMINGTON TO DES MOINES, IOWA
TO BLOOMINGTON
TO CAIRO TO ST. LOUIS, MO
TO ST. LOUIS, MO.
TO MEMPHIS
TO NASHVILLE
TO KNOXVILLE
Mundelein
Waukegan
Glencoe
Wilmette
Evanston
East Dundee
Elgin
Oak Park
Elmhurst
Wheaton
Aurora
Hinsdale
Brookfield
Chicago
Lockport
Joliet
Morris
Dwight
Kankakee
Gary
Michigan City
La Porte
Valparaiso
La Crosse
South Haven
Allegan
Delton
Kalamazoo
Battle Creek
Marshall
Albion
Concord
Jackson
Waterloo Village
Ann Arbor
Benton Harbor
Three Rivers
Coldwater
Adrian
Niles
South Bend
Mishawaka
Elkhart
Bristol
Rome City
Toledo
Nappanee
Plymouth
Culver
Columbia City
Fort Wayne
Defiance
Findlay
Maumee River
Huntington
Brook
Watseka
Monticello
Logansport
Wabash
Peru
Marion
Decatur
Bluffton
Berne
Geneva
Van Wert
Lima
Kenton
Kokomo
Greentown
Portland
Fort Recovery
Lafayette
Rantoul
Danville
Urbana-Champaign
Monticello
Bement
Tuscola
Crawfordsville
Noblesville
Anderson
Muncie
Sidney
Bellefontaine
West Liberty
Piqua
Greenville
Zionsville
Indianapolis
New Castle
Fountain City
Springfield
Centerville
Richmond
Dayton
Fairborn
Eaton
Xenia
Rockville
Greenfield
Rushville
Liberty
Germantown
Oxford
Lebanon
Mattoon
Charleston
Paris
Brazil
Terre Haute
Lerna
Marshall
Shelbyville
Greensburg
Effingham
Spencer
Bloomington
Belmont
Columbus
Versailles
Aurora
Cincinnati
Camp Dennison
Covington
Williamsburg
Seymour
Bedford
Madison
Walton
Point Pleasant
Olney
Lawrenceville
Vincennes
Flora
Loogootee
Mitchell
Washington
Salem
Paoli
Mount Carmel
Jasper
La Grange
Cynthiana
Jeffersonville
New Albany
Corydon
Louisville
Shively
Frankfort
Paris
Carmi
New Harmony
Evansville
Lincoln City
Rockport
Henderson
Owensboro
Fort Knox
Radcliff
Elizabethtown
Bardstown
Lexington
Winchester
Harrodsburg
Springfield
Danville
Lancaster
Berea
Junction
Harrisburg
Morganfield
Ohio
Wabash River
PENNYRILE PKWY
KENTUCKY TPK.
BLUE GRASS PKWY.
WESTERN KENTUCKY PARKWAY
Hodgenville
Marion
Madisonville
Central City
Leitchfield
Nolin River Lake
MAMMOTH CAVE NAT'L PARK
Campbellsville
Princeton
Paducah
Lake Barkley
Kentucky Lake
Hopkinsville
Fairview
Russellville
Auburn
Bowling Green
Glasgow
Scottsville
Russell Springs
Somerset
Lake Cumberland
Cumberland
Williamsburg
London
Corbin
Manchester
Middlesboro
Mayfield

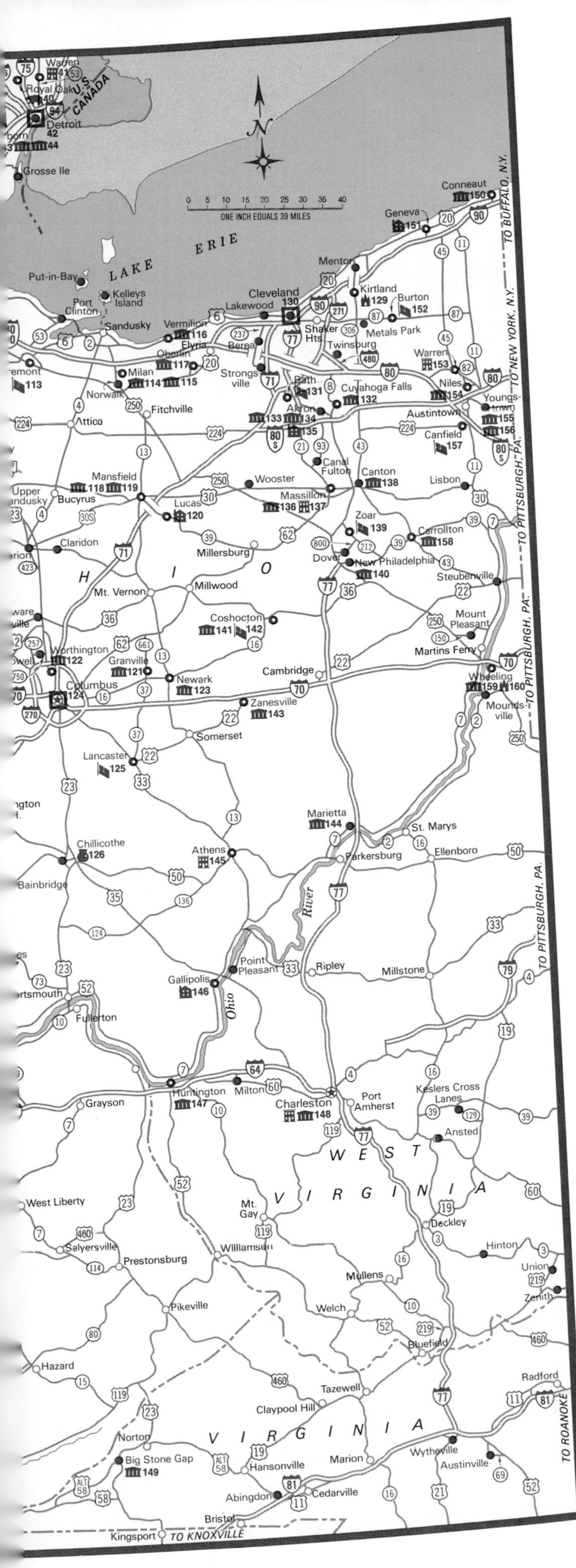

Pages 306–355

Though geographically east of center, this is where middle America begins. Long a prosperous agricultural and industrial area, much of its wealth is now manifest in its large, treasure-filled cities. The simpler riches of the Ohio and Indiana countryside—small-town churches, wood farmhouses, one-room schools—are reminders of the rural past. Some backwoods communities in Kentucky and the Virginias recall the time when this was the far west.

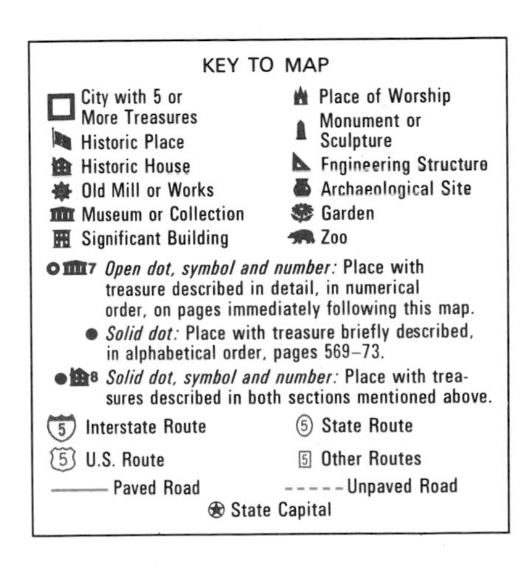

[7. *Art Institute*] *Grant Wood's* American Gothic, *a satirical portrait of his sister and a dentist, has become a symbol of the Puritan ethic of hard work. Equally famous is Georges Seurat's* Sunday Afternoon on the Island of La Grande Jatte. *Seurat's pointillism technique of color dots is an attempt to capture flickering light.*

1. Benedictine Sanctuary of Perpetual Adoration *Mundelein, Ill.* In the small but lavishly adorned church, the nave is flanked by marble colonnades with a procession of archways flowing to the ornate altar enclosure. Intricate artworks in bright enamel and mosaic depict Biblical scenes and personalities. Stained-glass windows shed a soft light while richly depicting some of the symbols and statements of religious faith. The edifice is a memorial to the International Eucharistic Congress held in Chicago in 1926. *Open daily.*

2. North Shore Congregation Israel *1185 Sheridan Rd., Glencoe, Ill.* Soaring skyward like a huge, exotically sculptured plant, the white concrete synagogue was designed by Minoru Yamasaki, the renowned architect. Fan vaults unfold like flower leaves to enclose the sanctuary, where daytime glare is softened by amber glass skylights and leaded-glass wall panels. Lighting effects are also designed for the raised marble platform that holds sacred objects associated with Jewish worship. The temple achieves, in both its graceful mass and simple detail, the architecture of light Yamasaki envisioned. *Open Mon.-Thurs.*

3. Bahá'í House of Worship *112 Linden Ave., Wilmette, Ill.* Sunken formal gardens divided by walkways lead to the nine entrances of the building, a stunning architectural symbol of Bahá'í faith in the oneness of God, religion and mankind. From the nine-sided base to the delicate tracery of the dome, the temple incorporates forms and symbols of the world's major religions: exterior pylons display the ancient hooked cross of Egypt, the star of David of Judaism, the cross of Christianity and the star and crescent of Islam. Interior design includes motifs of the nine-point Bahá'í star and the intricate design of the enormous dome. *Open daily.*

4. Evanston Historical Society Headquarters *225 Greenwood Ave., Evanston, Ill.* The society's headquarters is in the Charles Gates Dawes home, built in 1894. General Dawes, Vice President of the U.S. under Calvin Coolidge and a recipient of the Nobel Peace Prize, lived in the house until his death in 1951. The French Gothic mansion of 28 rooms with a theater, a ballroom and formal gardens bordering on Lake Michigan is maintained by the society as a museum. Possessions of the Dawes family are exhibited here as well as displays relating to the history of Evanston, Indian objects, furniture, glassware, coins, ceramics and costumes from the early 1800s. *Open Mon., Tues., Thurs.-Sat. Small charge.*

5. First Congregational Church of Evanston *Hinman and Grove Aves., Evanston, Ill.* A distinctive example of Colonial architecture in the Midwest, the brick church is handsomely proportioned and has a richly detailed exterior. Tall columns front the pedimented portico, and the ornate four-stage bell tower is topped by a slender spire. *Open Sun.*

6. Frances E. Willard House *1730 Chicago Ave., Evanston, Ill.* When Frances Willard died in 1898, Congress voted to put a statue of "the first woman of the 19th century, the most beloved character of her times" in the rotunda of the U.S. Capitol. Miss Willard, an educator and reformer best known as a founder and president of the WCTU, lived and worked in this Victorian wooden house with "Gingerbread Gothic" trim. It contains many of her furnishings and personal items, and three rooms serve as a temperance museum. *Open Mon.-Fri. except holidays.*

7. Chicago, Ill.

Although no longer "hog butcher for the world," the nation's second largest city is one of the world's leading ports and a center of manufacturing, trade and transport for much of the U.S. Few of Chicago's "treasures" are historically important: the Great Fire of 1871 destroyed almost every building in a three-and-a-third-square-mile area of the city. Rather, the majority of them are important for their architectural significance. Contrary to popular belief, New York City is not the home of the skyscraper. The first such steel, concrete and glass structure was built here in 1889 by William Le Baron Jenney. Under the direction of the leaders of the Chicago School of Architecture—men such as Dankmar

Adler, D. H. Burnham, John Wellborn Root and the great Louis H. Sullivan—and, later, Frank Lloyd Wright and Mies van der Rohe, Chicago's buildings continued to set new styles and to soar. Chicago also has beautiful parks, museums, art galleries and other cultural and educational facilities that make it one of the most sophisticated and vital cities in the country.

Art Institute of Chicago *Michigan Ave. and Adams St.* A superb El Greco, *Assumption of the Virgin,* a world-renowned Seurat, *Sunday Afternoon on the Island of La Grande Jatte,* and Grant Wood's famous *American Gothic* are three of numerous priceless paintings on view here, ranging from the 13th century to the present. The museum's collections of Impressionist and Post-Impressionist paintings are preeminent. Reaching out across the arts, the Institute exhibits include sculpture, drawings, prints, photographs and primitive arts. There are two great collections of Japanese prints in the U.S.: one of them belongs to the Art Institute, the other is in the Museum of Fine Arts in Boston. Nor is decorative art neglected. On display are 68 authentic reproductions in miniature (scaled one inch to one foot) of American and European period rooms, illustrating the development of interior styles over several centuries. A Junior Museum within the Institute offers art activities and education for young people. *Open daily except Dec. 25.*

Auditorium Theatre *50 E. Congress Pkwy.* Frank Lloyd Wright, who was once an apprentice for the building's architectural firm, Adler and Sullivan, called the auditorium "the greatest room for music and opera in the world, bar none." The theater was opened by President Benjamin Harrison in 1889, with Adelina Patti singing "Home Sweet Home." Closed in 1940, it was restored and reopened in 1967. The theater is efficiently designed to provide unimpeded sight lines from every seat, and its acoustics are considered among the finest in the world. The theater is located in a block-long granite building that originally also housed a hotel and offices. This space is now occupied by Roosevelt University. *Open Mon.-Fri. Tour: adults $2.00, children small charge.*

Basilica of Our Lady of Sorrows *3121 W. Jackson Blvd.* The majestic church, built in the classical style of the Italian Renaissance, has been a landmark of Chicago's West Side since its completion in 1902. The massive main altar dominates the interior, with many fine small altars and wood carvings from Fatima in the side chapels. Rich carving and coloring emphasize the beauty of the pilasters, arches and ornamented vaulted ceiling. The balconies holding the noted four-manual organ are modeled after the balcony of the Sistine Chapel. In the lower shrine is a replica of Michelangelo's *Pietà. Open Sat., Sun.*

Carson, Pirie, Scott Building *1 S. State St.* Louis H. Sullivan, who planned some of America's first skyscrapers, created the original design for this department store. Although only two sections of the store, built in 1899 and 1903-4, are actually his, two later additions are in keeping with his plan. The upper stories—the sections are 9 or 12 stories high—are covered in white terra cotta. The first and second stories, however, are lavishly decorated with cast-iron and terra cotta ornamentation, providing a striking frame for the show windows. *Open Mon.-Sat.*

Chicago Academy of Sciences *2001 N. Clark St.* The academy, devoted to the natural history of the region, has collections of birds, animals, reptiles, rocks and minerals. Exhibits depict such varying themes as the evolution of life on earth, the ecology of the Great Lakes and life of the Chicago coral reefs in the remote past. Especially impressive is a walk-in display showing "Chicago as a coal forest" in 300,000,000 B.C. *Open daily except Dec. 25.*

Chicago Historical Society Headquarters *North Ave. and Clark St.* The panorama of American history from Columbus to the 20th century is set out for the visitor in the society's interesting exhibits. Outstanding are the memorabilia of the Civil War and of Lincoln. Pioneer and 19th-century life—the furnishings, costumes and crafts—can be seen in the period rooms. Naturally, the Windy City is prominently featured here with Chicago's first locomotive, "The Pioneer," and exhibits on the Great Fire. Books, maps, pamphlets, magazines, newspapers and other materials are included in the society's 140,000-volume library of Americana. *Open daily except holidays. Small charge.*

Chicago Public Library *78 E. Washington St.* The classical exterior of the massive building, completed in 1897, belies the elaborate, almost Byzantine splendor within. Here, colored marbles, carved woods and hand-set mosaics are strikingly used. In the third-floor Humanities Department, for example, the ceiling is a large dome of stained glass which is supported by arches set with intricate mosaic scrolls and rosettes containing the symbols of famous printers. The mosaics, as well as the lamps throughout the building, were designed and executed by Tiffany and Company. One room, the Social Sciences and Business Department and Newspaper Division on the fourth floor, was designed to resemble a hall in the Doge's Palace in Venice. It has wainscoting of verd antique marble, paneled pilasters ornamented by masks and garlands, and a ceiling adorned with reliefs and moldings. *Open Mon.-Sat.*

[7. *Carson, Pirie, Scott Building*] *Architect Louis Sullivan had an unerring eye for elegant proportion and was a master of decorative design. The latter is well illustrated by the cast-iron foliage of the main entry.*

[*Chicago Water Tower and John Hancock Center*] *Chicago landmarks on Michigan Avenue: the Water Tower built when sedate mansions lined this street, and the 100-story John Hancock skyscraper built in 1969.*

Chicago Water Tower *800 N. Michigan Ave.* This Gothic structure, a minaretlike tower surrounded by saw-toothed battlements, is one of Chicago's most important landmarks. Completed in 1869 to house a standpipe for the city's water system, it was designed to be fireproof. Two years later it proved its worthiness when it escaped serious damage in the great Chicago fire, which destroyed almost every other building for miles around. Castellated Gothic was the style chosen by architect William W. Boyington. His elaborate design creates the effect of a medieval palace, today tucked away in the glass and steel of a modern city.

Civic Center *66 W. Washington St.* The sleek 31-story building, completed in 1966, is among the most outstanding civic structures in the U.S. Its wide expanses of glass, divided into three bays by the rust-colored structural steel frame, strongly reflect the influence of Mies van der Rohe. Skidmore, Owings and Merrill designed the center. *Open Mon.–Sat.*

PABLO PICASSO SCULPTURE The great Spanish artist designed this work for the Civic Center's sweeping plaza and donated it to the city. The abstract work is made of the same special steel as the building, weighs more than 160 tons and stands 50 feet high.

860–880 Lake Shore Drive Apartments These twin rectangular towers, designed by Mies van der Rohe and completed in 1951, were among the first buildings to take full advantage of glass and steel as a means of architectural expression. Narrow black steel mullions separate the windows into groups of four; the two inner windows are slightly wider than the outer two. The 26-story buildings are among the 35 landmarks of architectural distinction designated by the city of Chicago.

Field Museum of Natural History *Roosevelt Rd. and Lake Shore Dr.* This is one of the world's great museums of natural history and it can be visited and revisited with profit. Its collections are fascinating and seemingly endless. Here are exhibits on Stone Age man, later primitive peoples around the world, American Indians, Asian and African cultures—with examples of each group's artworks, weapons, ornaments and religious and utilitarian objects. Geological exhibits demonstrate the physical world, past and present, and the plants and animals that live in it are strikingly presented, many in their natural surroundings. *Open daily except Jan. 1 and Dec. 25. Small charge except Fri.*

Fountain of Time *Washington Park, W. of Cottage Grove Ave.* A heroic statuary group, made up of over 100 figures, represents humanity passing in review before Father Time, who watches solemnly from the opposite side of the fountain pool. The fountain is one of the finest works of Lorado Taft (1860–1936), an American sculptor, teacher and writer on art.

Garfield Park Conservatory *300 N. Central Park Blvd.* Covering four-and-a-half acres, the conservatory may well be the largest in the world. Its 5000 species and varieties of plants, gathered from tropical, semitropical and arid regions of the world, are arranged naturalistically. Each year the conservatory holds four major flower exhibitions—the azalea and camellia, Easter, chrysanthemum and Christmas shows—and a summer plant show. *Open daily.*

Glessner House *1800 S. Prairie Ave.* Henry Hobson Richardson, who greatly influenced the founders of the Chicago School of Architecture, designed this massive granite mansion in 1886. It is his last surviving work in Chicago. The Romanesque house, built around an open courtyard, presents a fortresslike facade to the street. There are few windows on this side, so that the city's noise and grime seldom penetrate. Now restored by the Chicago School of Architecture Foundation, the house contains many of the furnishings of John J. Glessner, a founder of International Harvester, who lived here with his family for 50 years. There is also a collection of Frank Lloyd Wright pieces. *Open Tues., Thurs., Sat., Sun. Small charge.*

Grant Park *Between E. 14th Blvd. and E. Randolph Dr.* This lakefront park in downtown Chicago has been called the city's front yard. There are many points of interest on its formally landscaped acres. The rose garden, one of the largest in the Midwest, has over 8000 plants arranged in a formal design reminiscent of Versailles. Another handsome formal garden is the Court of Presidents. Two important works of sculpture are Augustus Saint-Gaudens's seated statue of Lincoln and his equestrian statue of the Union General John A. Logan. Nearby is the Clarence Buckingham Fountain, resembling the Latona Fountain at Versailles but twice as large. *Open daily.*

Jane Addams' Hull-House *800 S. Halsted St.* In 1889 Jane Addams established here the most influential social settlement in the U.S. The activities carried on here influenced the settlement movement throughout the country and helped to improve the lot of slum dwellers. Hull-House and its adjacent Residents' Dining Hall are located on what is now the Chicago Circle

[Civic Center-Picasso Sculpture] Horse? Dog? Friendly prehistoric monster? Passersby on the Civic Center's grand plaza may decide for themselves. Picasso donated the design for the 50-foot-high sculpture with no label attached.

campus of the University of Illinois. The two restored buildings contain exhibits, pieces of the original Victorian furniture and other memorabilia of Jane Addams' work here, which she told about in her autobiography. *Open daily except holidays.*

John Hancock Center *875 N. Michigan Ave.* The 100-story glass and steel structure, a preview of the "vertical city" of the future, combines residential, commercial and recreational facilities. More than 800,000 square feet of office space, over 700 apartments, restaurants, shops, a department store and a swimming pool are among the features of the unique building. Visitors to the enclosed observatory at the 94th floor have an unobstructed view of four states. *Observatory open daily. Adults $1.25, children small charge.*

Lincoln Park *Lake Shore Dr. between North and Hollywood Aves.* This lakefront park of 1185 acres is Chicago's largest; it is also one of the city's loveliest and most interesting places. The Formal Garden contains over 8000 colorful plants arranged in formal patterns. Rock plants, annuals, shrubs and trees grace the Rock Garden, while the Grandmother's Garden is devoted mostly to old-fashioned plants—40,000 of them. Notable works of sculpture in the park include Saint-Gaudens's statue of Lincoln (standing) and Leonard Crunelle's of Richard J. Oglesby, U.S. senator and three times governor of Illinois. On a more elaborate scale is the Alexander Hamilton Memorial. This consists of a 13-foot bronze statue of Hamilton by John Angel, backed by a 78-foot pylon of black granite. Besides these attractions and the zoo and conservatory described below, the park has abundant facilities for indoor and outdoor recreation.

LINCOLN PARK CONSERVATORY *2400 N. Stockton Dr.* The conservatory, on three-and-a-half acres, is a living museum of plants from all over the world. Flower lovers enjoy its four seasonal shows: chrysanthemum, Christmas, azalea and camellia, spring and Easter. *Open daily.*

LINCOLN PARK ZOOLOGICAL GARDENS *100 W. Webster Ave.* More than 2300 mammals, birds and reptiles from almost every part of the world are found in the zoo's buildings and outdoor habitats. The zoo's special pride is its collection of great apes—orangutans, chimpanzees and gorillas—said to be the world's finest. Many of the animals roam in natural habitats surrounded by moats. In one, the Zoorookery, visitors can sit on flat stones and observe the waterfowl that live there. The sea lion pool offers underwater viewing. Youngsters can make the acquaintance of domestic animals on the five-acre Farm in the Zoo and can pet baby and small animals in the Children's Zoo. *Open daily.*

Monadnock Building *53 W. Jackson Blvd.* Four branches of a New England family built this 17-story structure which was completed in 1893; it was designed in four sections, each of which could be closed off if one or more units were sold. Two of Chicago's famous architectural firms—Burnham and Root and Holabird and Roche—designed the building, one taking the north half, the other the south. The designers reverted from the new steel-skeleton type of construction then becoming popular, and built the last masonry-supported skyscraper. They also opted for a solid, stark facade rather than the elaborately ornamented ones in vogue at the time. When erected the Monadnock was the world's largest office building and is still the largest masonry building. *Open Mon.-Fri.*

Museum of Contemporary Art *237 E. Ontario St.* Visitors to the museum, opened in 1967, can see what is presently happening in the world of art. There is no permanent collection; instead the museum mounts a new exhibit of contemporary art every six weeks, and is closed for one week between shows. Modern dance, multi-media and film programs are also presented. *Open daily except Jan. 1 and Dec. 25. Small charge.*

[Field Museum] Diorama in the Hall of the Stone Age shows Cro-Magnon man (30,000 B.C.) as sculptor. Exhibits here trace man's development from 1,000,000 years ago to the beginning of recorded history.

Museum of Science and Industry

57th St. and Lake Shore Dr., Chicago, Ill.

The world's largest and most popular science museum totally involves children and adults in an adventure of looking, listening and learning. Most exhibits are designed for visitor participation as well as viewing. Hundreds of displays are laid out on 14 acres of floor space, and some 3,200,000 people come to see them every year. One of the favorites is a reproduction of a working coal mine. Visitors descend into the main shaft by a hoist, then board an electric train that transports them to the working part of the mine, where demonstrations of old and modern mining methods and safety precautions are given. Farm buildings containing the latest agricultural machinery, prize animals and even fields are part of the museum's interesting exhibit on the operation of large Midwestern farms. In the physics section visitors operate displays which demonstrate laws of magnetism and electricity while listening to recorded explanations of their principles on telephone headsets. Here too are displays on the 16th- and 17th-century discoveries of Galileo and Newton, the inventions of Thomas Edison and Benjamin Franklin's kite experiments. Wherever possible exhibits present the developments of the scientific concepts involved, how these have been applied in inventions and manufacturing, and what their future use and social implications might be. The photography exhibit, for instance, traces photography from the development of the pinhole camera to space age sound-circuit photos and holography. It also explains how photographic techniques are applied in research and medicine and how they are used by millions of amateur photographers. Despite its name the museum does not restrict itself to scientific and industrial subjects. Colleen Moore's "Fairy Castle" which contains thousands of miniature treasures such as Cinderella's glass slippers, a diamond-studded fairy wand and King Arthur's round table set with a solid gold dinner service is displayed here, as is an international collection of old and new dolls. Visitors to "Yesterday's Main Street" (around 1910) may watch silent movies in the "Nickelodeon." At the spectacular miniature "Circus" visitors can see the Main Street parade, main-ring events, clowns and side shows. The history, technology and excitement of the big top are traced in the exhibit's dioramas, hand-carved pieces and eight-minute film. *Open daily except Dec. 25. Small charge for some exhibits.*

Animal City is a bubble-topped futuristic cage designed for a community of gerbils (small rodents) whose entire diet consists of water and a form of protein derived from petroleum. With the world population growing steadily every year and the supply of natural food projected to decline, scientists have been experimenting with man-made supplements like this one. These petroleum-fed gerbils, by the way, are at least as energetic as their naturally fed relatives. Animal City is one of many displays in the petroleum exhibit which show how and where crude oil is discovered and explain how petroleum and its products are made. A visitor-operated oil well-pinball machine dramatically illustrates the risks involved in searching for oil.

Museum exhibits are displayed in a vast classic structure originally built as the Palace of Fine Arts for Chicago's Columbian Exposition in 1893. Julius Rosenwald was the leader of a movement, in 1926, to reconstruct and adapt the building for use as a museum. For all the museum's acreage in floor space, the 75 separate halls and some 2000 exhibits, the floor plan is not difficult to comprehend.

In the museum's coal shaft a "miner" explains how coal is extracted from the mine by means of an undercutting machine (on the ground) and a drill (on the wall). A real hoist takes visitors into the shaft.

Outdoor exhibits include a World War II German submarine captured off North Africa in 1944 and the first (1934) streamlined passenger train, which was retired to the museum in 1960.

Movie star Colleen Moore's nine-foot-square Fairy Castle is an adult fulfillment of childhood fantasy, a home fit for none other than a fairy prince and princess who love antiques. It has its own electricity and plumbing: water pours into the princess' silver tub in her crystal and jade bath, and from garden fountains and a weeping willow tree. Jewel-adorned furniture sparkles under the miniature lights. Fairy fantasies, such as a gold goose and eggs and the Three Bears' chairs, each on a pinhead, abound in this dream castle come true.

Pullman Historic District *Bounded by 103rd and 115th Sts., Cottage Grove Ave. and Lake Calumet* George M. Pullman, whose design of the Pullman car made overnight train travel comfortable, established the area in 1880 to provide pleasant suburban living conditions for his employes and a home for his vast manufacturing enterprise. He hired an architect, Solon S. Beman, and a landscape designer, Nathan F. Barrett, to create the first planned industrial-residential community in the U.S. Most of the original brick buildings—row houses, apartments, single houses, a hotel and a church—remain and are being restored. The district, a National Historic Landmark, preserves much of its 19th-century atmosphere.

Queen of All Saints Basilica *6280 N. Sauganash Ave.* This Roman Catholic church in the Gothic tradition of Europe's great cathedrals was completed in 1960. Entrance is through a portal archway, above which is a Crucifixion group carved in limestone. In the interior, the walls of the nave are lined with narrow octagonal stone pillars. Above these, strikingly colored wooden trusses rise to form a series of arches along the similarly decorated vaulted ceiling. Other prominent features of the basilica include the handsome main altar and many stained-glass windows. *Open daily.*

Riverside Landscape Architectural District *Bounded by Harlem, Ogden and First Aves. and 26th St.* Riverside was the first planned model community in the U.S. The district remains almost exactly as it was laid out in 1869 by Frederick Law Olmsted, America's most eminent landscape architect, and his partner, Calvert Vaux. Olmsted planned "a village within a park," setting aside almost half of the original 1600 acres for parks, commons and other public uses. He forsook the conventional grid pattern of urban planning and let the roads curve gracefully, following the topography. Riverside includes many architecturally important buildings, among them the Coonley House (281 Bloomingbank Rd.), designed by Frank Lloyd Wright and called by him his best house; a Swiss cottage (100 Fairbank Rd.), designed by Olmstead and Vaux; a Gothic cottage (124 Scottswood Rd.), designed by W.L.B. Jenney; and two buildings designed by Louis H. Sullivan (277 and 281 Gatesby Rd.).

Rookery Building *209 S. LaSalle St.* Burnham and Root's design for this important office building is a combination of the solid, masonry styles that had been firmly established and the glass and skeletal structures that were slowly to come. Completed in 1888, the Rookery encompasses an interior court, an innovation that gave most of the offices natural lighting. Except for the first two floors, which are of rough-hewn granite, the 11-story structure is faced with brown brick with delicate terra cotta ornamentation. An elaborate archway graces the main entrance. In 1905 the lobby was remodeled by Louis Sullivan. Frank Lloyd Wright, who was a draftsman in the Sullivan firm, was reputedly responsible for the gold and ivory decorations of the lobby. The Rookery inherited its name from a previous building on the site, a favorite resting place of the city's pigeons. *Open Mon.-Fri.*

32 North State Building *32 N. State St.* The 15-story structure, completed in 1895 and formerly known as the Reliance Building, is built upon a structural cage of steel, with a white terra cotta sheathing. The building was put together in an unusual, piecemeal manner, beginning with a foundation and first story that were placed under an existing building on the site. Later

[**7.** *University of Chicago-Oriental Institute*] *Sculpture relief of a winged bull is one of a pair that once stood at the entry to the palace throne room of Assyrian King Sargon II (722-05* B.C.) *in Khorsabad, an ancient planned city that flourished in what is now northern Iraq. In many eastern religions the so-called winged bull (it actually combines the features of eagle, man and lion as well as bull) is similar in significance to the angel in Christianity. In Assyria the winged bull was considered a minor deity, a protector of doorways who drove the evil spirits away and let in the good. The bull's size was also meant to command human respect. This one carved from limestone is 16 feet high and 17 feet long and weighs 40 tons.*

the upper floors were removed and the present structure evolved. The building was designed by Charles Atwood of D. H. Burnham and Company. The large areas of glass made it a forerunner of the skyscrapers to come. *Open Mon.-Sat.*

University of Chicago *E. 58th St. and Ellis Ave.* This private, coeducational institution of higher learning and research was founded by John D. Rockefeller and incorporated in 1890. The campus of 165 acres lies on both sides of the Midway; most of the Neo-Gothic structures are to the north and the more modern buildings to the south. Saturday morning tours of the campus start at Ida Noyes Hall, 1212 E. 59th Street.

LAIRD BELL LAW QUADRANGLE *1111 E. 61st St.* Eero Saarinen designed this striking modern complex, with three low buildings grouped around the six-story library-office building, an open court and a reflecting pool. In the pool stands a soaring bronze sculpture by Antoine Pevsner, a Russian-born sculptor.

LORADO TAFT MIDWAY STUDIOS *6016 S. Ingleside Ave.* In these studios, much enlarged from their beginnings as a simple brick barn, the Midwestern sculptor worked with some of his associates from 1906 until his death 30 years later. Several of his plaster portrait busts and most of his maquettes are on view. The studios, which are used by the university's Department of Art, are a National Historic Landmark. *Open Mon.-Fri. Jan.-Aug., Oct.-Dec. during academic sessions.*

"NUCLEAR ENERGY" *Ellis Ave. between E. 56th and E. 57th Sts.* The 12-foot-high bronze sculpture by Henry Moore marks the site where Enrico Fermi and 41 other scientists achieved the first controlled self-sustaining nuclear chain reaction on Dec. 2, 1942. To commemorate the 25th anniversary of the birth of the atomic age, the sculptor created a work that resembles both a skull and a mushroom cloud, supported by what might be the archways of a great cathedral.

ORIENTAL INSTITUTE MUSEUM *1155 E. 58th St.* The museum of the Oriental Institute, which has carried out many expeditions in the Near East, houses one of the world's major collections of ancient art and archaeological findings from that area. Nearly every Near Eastern culture is represented—Assyrian, Babylonian, Iranian, Palestinian, Egyptian and others—from about 5000 B.C. to 1100 A.D. *Open Tues.-Sun. except holidays.*

ROBIE HOUSE *5757 S. Woodlawn Ave.* The handsome brick dwelling was designed by Frank Lloyd Wright in 1906 for the manufacturer Frederick C. Robie and was completed in 1909. It is one of Wright's "prairie houses," which, with their sweeping horizontal lines, revolutionized the architecture of American homes. The building contains some of the interesting original furnishings Wright designed for it. It is now occupied by the Adlai Stevenson Institute of International Affairs (which is not affiliated with the university) and is a National Historic Landmark.

ROCKEFELLER MEMORIAL CHAPEL *1156 E. 59th St.* The chapel, dedicated in 1928, is noted for its soaring, Gothic-style design by Bertram Grosvenor Goodhue. Built in the form of an irregular cross, it has a vaulted ceiling and handsome stone sculptures and wood carvings. The chapel was named for John D. Rockefeller, and its 72-bell carillon, one of the world's finest, was given to the university in memory of his wife, Laura Spelman Rockefeller. *Open daily.*

8. Unitarian Universalist Church (Unity Temple) *875 Lake St., Oak Park, Ill.* No spire or tower rises from the flat roof to proclaim a traditional church. Yet the unusual building, set in the center of town, is clearly a house of worship. Designed by Frank Lloyd Wright and completed in 1908, it was this great American architect's first public building and one of the earliest architectural uses of poured concrete. The feeling of simple but gracious dignity is carried logically to the interior, where the lighting comes from large skylights above glass ceilings and windows set high up in the walls beneath the roof. In 1961 colors chosen with the aid of the Wright Foundation were added to the interior walls. *Small charge for tours.*

9. Lizzadro Museum of Lapidary Art *220 Cottage Hill Ave., Elmhurst, Ill.* The display of gems, minerals, fossils and art objects made from gem materials dazzles visitors at every turn. Exhibits include graceful agate bowls, intricately shaped jade pagodas, prehistoric animals carved from jasper, a screen glistening with jade, lapis and ivory. *Open Tues.-Sun. except holidays. Small charge except Fri.*

10. Robert McCormick Museum and Flower Gardens *Off Roosevelt Rd., W. of Wheaton, Ill.* Extensive gardens surround the former residence of Colonel Robert R. McCormick, publisher of the Chicago *Tribune* for nearly 45 years, a member of the First Division in World War I and founder of the war memorial here. His Georgian residence-museum contains a wealth of books, paintings, statues, weapons, medals and manuscripts. *Open Wed.-Sun. except holidays.*

CANTIGNY WAR MEMORIAL MUSEUM OF THE FIRST DIVISION The sights and sounds of war are vivid in a World War I trench which visitors can enter and in a diorama that replays the 1918 battle of Cantigny. Weapons, maps, pictures and other memorabilia of the First Division's actions in both world wars provide striking exhibits. *Open Tues.-Sun. except holidays.*

11. Old Graue Mill and Museum *York Rd., Hinsdale, Ill.* An old trade comes alive as a white-aproned miller grinds corn in this waterwheel gristmill, the only one in the state still in operation. (The cornmeal, packed in old-fashioned cloth bags, is for sale.) Put into operation in 1852, the three-story brick and limestone mill served the surrounding farmlands for 60 years. At one time runaway slaves, headed for Chicago, were given refuge in the mill cellar. The old granary now contains furnishings, farm tools and implements of the middle and late 1800s. *Open daily May-Oct. Small charge.*

12. Brookfield Zoo (Chicago Zoological Park) *First Ave. and 31st St., Brookfield, Ill.* One of the most attractive zoological parks in the U.S., Brookfield has an outstanding collection of mammals, birds and reptiles, many in simulated natural habitats bordered by moats. Ibex, baboons and Dall sheep roam on rocky mountains, a pack of wolves in Wolf Woods; nearby, porpoises perform in the Seven Seas Panorama. A small fee entitles the visitor to a trip through the zoo on either a narrow gauge railroad or a trackless Safari train. *Open daily. Small charge except Tues. Children's Zoo small additional charge. Small parking fee.*

13. Aurora Historical Museum *304 Oak Ave., Aurora, Ill.* The main museum building, a museum piece itself, is a 20-room brick home built in 1856. The parlor has the original gas fixtures and carpet; some of the original furniture still remains. The unusual Blanford astronomical clock tells standard time plus time, date and day in 127 cities of the world, and shows the phases of the moon. The exhibits also include pioneer items, Indian artifacts, guns, mastodon bones and a collection of American flags. A carriage house on the grounds contains a collection of old cars and horse-drawn vehicles plus a blacksmith shop. *Carriage house open weather permitting. Small charge. Museum open Wed., Sun.*

14. Monticello and Sangamon Valley Railway Museum *Off Rte. 105, Monticello, Ill.* Railroad buffs find the answer to their enthusiasms at the museum. There are collections of railroad equipment and rolling stock to admire, and an actual train ride is available. On the hour, visitors can climb aboard a steam engine with an engineer, sit in a passenger car or ride a caboose over four miles of track. *Open Sat., Sun. late May-mid-June, daily mid-June-early Sept., Sat., Sun. early Sept.-Oct. Adults $1.25, children over 5 small charge.*

15. Urbana-Champaign, Ill.

Just one street separates the cities of Urbana and Champaign. Although administratively independent, the two form a commercial and social unit with a population of about 90,000.

University of Illinois The main campus of this great university, established in 1867, is divided between the twin cities of Urbana and Champaign, with some 32,000 students attending classes here. Free guided tours can be arranged at the Tour Office in the Illini Union building.

ASSEMBLY HALL *S. of Memorial Stadium* One of the world's most unusual multi-purpose buildings, the hall consists of two concrete bowls 400 feet across placed rim on rim; the inverted bowl forms the dome. The structure is held together not by pillars or beams but by 614 miles of fine steel wire wound around the rims. It can be comfortably converted from a 3600-seat theater to a 1700-seat arena. *Open daily.*

KRANNERT ART MUSEUM *500 Peabody Dr.* The museum's collections include ancient and medieval art, old-master paintings, American paintings of the 19th and 20th centuries, sculpture, prints, drawings, photographs, European and American decorative arts and Oriental and Pre-Columbian art. In the permanent collection are works by Hals, Ingres, Copley, Homer and Shahn. *Open daily except holidays.*

KRANNERT CENTER FOR THE PERFORMING ARTS *500 S. Goodwin Ave.* This unique complex is made up of five theaters; four are indoors and the fifth is an outdoor amphitheater. Architect Max Abramovitz has designed three distinctive-looking structures that rise from connecting lower levels; one level is a huge central lobby opening on each of the indoor theaters. Three ascending landscaped terraces provide a unifying motif for the exterior, as do the red brick and Indiana limestone materials from which the building was constructed. *Open daily except holidays.*

MUSEUM OF NATURAL HISTORY *Mathews Ave.* The museum has exhibits on early man in North America and on geology (including fossils), botany and animal life. The pride of the museum is a collection of objects that belonged to the geneticist Gregor Mendel. *Open Mon.-Sat.*

WORLD HERITAGE MUSEUM *Fourth floor, Lincoln Hall* The story of man from prehistoric cave-dwelling days to the 20th century is set forth here in an attractive and informative manner. Especially worth viewing are the Sumerian and Egyptian displays, medieval armor, ship models and the Black Africa exhibit. *Open daily during academic sessions.*

16. Vermilion County Museum *116 N. Gilbert St., Danville, Ill.* Lincoln often stayed in this two-story house when he visited his friend Dr. William Fithian, who had built it in 1855. Visitors can see the bed where Lincoln slept and other authentic period furnishings. The museum also features several more 19th-century rooms, Dr. Fithian's office, a dentist's office furnished in 1914 style, an art gallery and a small natural history museum. *Open Wed.-Sun. Small charge.*

17. Historical Museum of the Wabash Valley *1411 S. Sixth St., Terre Haute, Ind.* Housed in an attractive 1868 brick mansion are Indian artifacts, military items, grandfather clocks, documents, antique dolls and other memorabilia of the area's past. Rooms are furnished to show modern visitors a Victorian parlor, bedroom and nursery, a country store and a ladies' dress and hat shop. *Open Wed., Sun.*

18. Sheldon Swope Art Gallery *25 S. Seventh St., Terre Haute, Ind.* Wood, Benton, Marsh and Hopper are among the American artists whose works are exhibited here. The gallery's permanent collection also includes various examples of African, Oriental and Polynesian art. A fine print collection ranges from Renaissance to contemporary works. *Open Tues., Wed., Sat., Sun. Jan.-July, Sept.-Dec.*

19. George Rogers Clark National Historical Park *115 Dubois St., Vincennes, Ind.* A 22-acre landscaped park on the Wabash River memorializes the man who helped to win the Northwest Territory from the British

[**22.** *Labyrinth*] *As a symbol of the hard but rewarding righteous life, just one path leads to the small house at the center. There rough walls enclose a smooth interior, a reminder not to judge by external appearances only.*

[23] *Excavations atop this mound in the Indian village revealed the remains of a large building. From explorers' accounts of similar villages farther south, archaeologists reconstructed the kind of temple which once stood here. Windowless, it has three doors and smokeholes in the roof.*

during the Revolutionary War. An impressive rotunda containing a heroic statue of Clark dominates the park. Around its interior walls are seven large murals depicting scenes of his winter (1778–9) campaign. This successful drive culminated in the capture of the British Fort Sackville which stood here at the time. *Open daily except Jan. 1 and Dec. 25.*

20. Grouseland, William Henry Harrison Home *3 W. Scott St., Vincennes, Ind.* Harrison, ninth President of the U.S. (from March 1841 until his death one month later), built this handsome house while serving as governor of the Indiana Territory (1800–12). A Virginian, he incorporated the architecture and gracious style of his native state into his new home. The red brick dwelling, with a bow end and high white columns supporting the two-story portico, has been exactingly restored. It contains family portraits (two of Harrison are by Rembrandt Peale and John Jarvis), and many of the original furnishings; the beautiful silk-screened wallpapers were reproduced from ones common in the 18th century. The house is owned and maintained by the Francis Vigo chapter, Daughters of the American Revolution. *Open daily except holidays. Small charge.*

21. Old Cathedral *Second and Church Sts., Vincennes, Ind.* This historic church was founded by Jesuits in 1749 to serve the French who had settled the town of Vincennes in the early 1730s. The present white spired, red brick edifice, formally known as the Basilica of St. Francis Xavier, was begun in 1826 on the site of the original simple log chapel. A bell from the chapel, recast, hangs in the basilica's steeple. *Open daily.*

OLD CATHEDRAL LIBRARY Established in 1840, the library is now housed in a handsome modern (1968) building adjacent to the church. It contains various works of art, books and historic documents. Among the documents are letters by Sts. Isaac Jogues and Vincent de Paul, a 1619 copy of *The Voyages of Champlain,* and—the library's oldest manuscript—a letter of Pope John XXII written in 1619.

22. New Harmony Historic District *New Harmony, Ind.* Historically fascinating, the community was the home of two separate experiments to create utopias. In 1814 George Rapp and a group of German artisans established the town of Harmonie. Dissenters from the German Lutheran faith, the Harmonists practiced celibacy, held property in common, and preached the imminent second coming of Christ. In 1825 they moved to Pennsylvania, selling the place to a group led by Robert Owen, a Welsh-born reformer, who also wanted to build a perfect society. The colony, under his guidance, became prominent as a scientific and cultural center. However, in a few years the colony foundered. Some of the buildings that have been restored by the State of Indiana and other agencies are described below.

DORMITORY NO. 2 Unmarried men of Rapp's Harmonist Society originally occupied the building. Under Owen, it housed a printshop and was the center of much of the colony's cultural life. *Open Tues.-Sun. May-Nov. except holidays. Small charge.*

HARMONIST HOUSE The typical one-family frame dwelling has been restored by the National Society of Colonial Dames. It contains a small museum room. *Open daily May-Oct. Small charge.*

LABYRINTH A replica of a garden maze planted by the Harmonists, it represents the various paths offered in life and the reward given to the person who makes the correct choice. *Open daily except holidays.*

OLD FAUNTLEROY HOME The house was built by the Harmonists in 1815. Under Owen, it was the headquarters of the Minerva Society, the first women's club with a written constitution. *Open daily Apr.-Oct., Tues.-Sun. Nov.-Mar. except holidays. Small charge.*

OLD OPERA HOUSE This was the fourth dormitory erected by the Harmonists. During Harmonie's second period it was made into an opera house and, restored, is used to house summer theater performances.

ROOFLESS CHURCH The architect Philip Johnson designed the dome of this unusual contemporary (1960) church, which has the shape of an inverted rosebud and casts the shadow of a full-blown rose. Jacques Lipchitz created the bronze gate medallions and the statue, *Descent of the Holy Spirit,* inside. *Open daily.*

WORKINGMEN'S INSTITUTE Endowed in 1838 by Owen's associate, William Maclure, it existed to further educate those "who work with their hands." It houses an art gallery, museum and library. *Art gallery and museum open Tues.-Sun. May-Nov., Tues.-Sat. Dec.-May. Library open Tues.-Sun. Small charge.*

23. Angel Mounds State Memorial *8215 Pollack Ave., ¾ mi. S. of Rte. 662, Evansville, Ind.* How did Indians of the Middle-Mississippian culture live during the 16th century? Some of the answers are on view at this 421-acre archaeological site, unusual in that it has been little disturbed by industry. A good part of the site has been carefully reconstructed to look as it did when about 1000 Indians lived there, from around 1400 to 1500 A.D. Indian huts, earth mounds and a portion of the log and clay palisade that protected the village are reproduced. A new Interpretive Center contains models of the mounds and displays the findings of some 40 years of scientific excavation. *Open daily except holidays. Small charge.*

24. Evansville Museum of Arts and Science *411 S.E. Riverside Dr., Evansville, Ind.* The variety of exhibits here offers something to visitors of all ages. For example, one can step into a re-creation of a 19th-century doctor's office and apothecary shop, press a button and hear a description of the surgical equipment and medicines of the day, or view a restored steam engine, tender, club car and caboose on the grounds of the museum. The art collection includes works from Egypt, the Orient and the Indian cultures of the Americas, as well as paintings by old masters such as Titian, Zurbarán and Murillo. In the stairwell by the entrance hangs a group of Gobelin and Flemish tapestries. The museum was designed by Victor Gruen, and is a striking example of contemporary architecture. *Open Tues.-Sun. except Jan. 1 and Dec. 25*

25. Willard Library *21 First Ave., Evansville, Ind.* The library, which has been in continuous use since its construction in 1884, is a remarkable study in Victorian Gothic architecture: brick and limestone offer contrasting colors, large rosettes decorate arched windows, dormer windows interrupt the mansard roof and a tall tower is fancifully off-center. Inside features include fine woodwork, tiled floors, stained-glass windows and brass hardware. In the library is the country's biggest collection of old and rare books on the history of southern Indiana. *Open Tues.-Sun.*

26. John James Audubon Memorial Museum *Rte. 41, Henderson, Ky.* The print collection in this attractive, Romanesque-style building includes 126 pages from the original folio edition of *Birds of America,* the work of the great ornithologist John James Audubon, who spent nine years studying the birds and other wildlife of this wooded countryside. Audubon, Haitian-born, grew up in France and was sent to America at 18 to make his living. He supported himself by painting portraits and giving drawing lessons, but his great love and his life's work was to capture with his brush the marvellous variety of North American bird and animal life. Also displayed are oil paintings and numerous mementos of Audubon's career. The museum is in a state park, which contains a wildlife sanctuary. *Open daily Apr.-early Sept., Wed.-Sun. early Sept.-Oct. Small charge.*

27. Saline County Area Museum *1600 S. Feazel St., Harrisburg, Ill.* The three-acre complex portrays life in southern Illinois about 100 years ago. A one-room schoolhouse is complete with rows of desks, pot-bellied stove, recitation bench—and a sturdy hickory switch. A wagon, buggy and early farm tools fill a log barn. There is a general store and post office, and a log cabin containing a cord bed, bearskin rug and a land grant signed by President Andrew Jackson. The main building, once a farm home for the care of paupers, has among its many displays a portable dentist's chair and an imposing cure-all "quack box." Among the items in the re-creation of an early kitchen are a granite coffee pot and a pie safe (used to store food) of pine and pierced tin. *Open daily.*

28. City Hall *Fifth and Washington Sts., Paducah, Ky.* Edward Durell Stone, noted New York architect, has designed a simple, graceful building occupying a full city block in downtown Paducah. It bears a strong resemblance to his famous U.S. Embassy in New Delhi, India. The building has a flat, projecting roof supported by squared-off columns. The interesting triangular designs on the underside of the roof are echoed in the walk leading to the building and inside on the floor of the main hall. *Open Mon.-Fri.*

29. Market House *Second St., Paducah, Ky.* Once a market, in an area platted by General William Clark, the building now houses a museum, art gallery and theater. The museum has a wealth of local memorabilia, including the complete interior of a 100-year-old drugstore, a 1913 fire truck, old hand tools, home furnishings and Indian artifacts. The art gallery exhibits the work of important regional artists. *Open daily. Small charge for museum.*

[26] *Naturalist John James Audubon painted this admirable portrait of Daniel Boone from memory years after the two had met in the Kentucky wilderness. The watercolor of two ground squirrels is more typical of Audubon's work. He was the first naturalist-artist to depict life-size animals with their native habitat as background.*

[32] *A reconstructed tomb in the Kalamazoo Museum shows how Egyptian royalty had their bodies mummified and entombed in familiar richly decorated surroundings in anticipation of a comfortable afterlife.*

 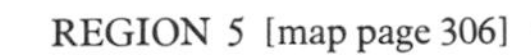 

30. Josephine Morton Memorial Home *501 Territorial Rd., Benton Harbor, Mich.* This 1849 frame house is the oldest residence in Benton Harbor. Four generations of the Morton family lived here before it became a memorial to early settlers of the area. The house is now a historic museum with six period rooms decorated in styles from 1850 to 1910, a display room of local historical exhibits and an area where carding and spinning demonstrations are given. The front porch was often called the Indian Hotel because the second Mr. Morton let it be used as a shelter by Indians who came to this community from their nearby village to sell their baskets. An 1840 barn on the grounds was moved three times before arriving at its present location. *Open Thurs., Sun. Apr.-Oct.*

31. Genevieve and Donald Gilmore Art Center *Kalamazoo Institute of Arts, 314 S. Park St., Kalamazoo, Mich.* The center's permanent collection features American paintings since 1900; also exhibited are sculptures and graphics from all over the world. The galleries, along with a library and art school, are housed in an elegantly modern structure—a work of art itself—designed by Skidmore, Owings and Merrill. *Open Tues.-Sat. July-mid-Aug., Tues.-Sun. mid-Aug.-June.*

32. Kalamazoo Public Museum *315 S. Rose St., Kalamazoo, Mich.* Among the most effective displays here is a reconstructed Egyptian tomb with accurate interior details, including a mummy, which can be observed through slots in the tomb's wall. Many original items from early Egyptian tombs can also be seen, and their significance is explained in occasional gallery talks. The replica Pioneer Room, made of hand-hewn logs, shows typical living quarters of this area's early homesteaders. An unusual geophysical globe with a diameter of over six feet is another attraction, painted to show the maximum summer vegetation of the earth as seen from space. *Open Mon.-Sat. except holidays.*

33. Kingman Museum of Natural History *175 Limit St., Battle Creek, Mich.* This "environmental observatory" is housed in the Leila Arboretum. Several displays—including "Life: An Ecological View," "A Window to the Universe" and "The Wide World: Man in His Environment"—trace the relationships in the universe. A planetarium and a small collection of live snakes, fish and turtles can also be visited. Wildlife, travel and adventure films and special programs are offered. *Open Tues.-Sun. except holidays. Small charge.*

34. Honolulu House *104 N. Kalamazoo Ave., Marshall, Mich.* Judge Abner Pratt built the unique dwelling in 1860 to duplicate the house he had occupied in Hawaii while serving as U.S. consul. The completely balanced design of its facade is dominated by a tower over the entrance, and the porch roof is supported by unusual triple pillars with carved scrollwork. The interior has ornate plaster ceilings. Redecorated in 1883, the house has been little changed since then and is currently used as headquarters for the Marshall Historical Society. *Open daily May-Sept. Small charge.*

35. Mann House *205 Hanover St., Concord, Mich.* The 11-room Victorian clapboard house is typical of the late-19th-century homes of prosperous small-town families. It was completed in 1884 by Daniel S. Mann, a farmer who took over the homestead in the 1830s. The house has been restored and is furnished as it was at the turn of the century with china, linens, handwoven fabrics and Victorian furniture. In the two-story carriage house are a buggy and cutter, farm implements and household items. *Open Tues.-Sun.*

36. Ella Sharp Museum *3225 Fourth St., Jackson, Mich.* The museum occupies several buildings, including the Merriman-Sharp House, a brick structure built in the 1850s. Located on land known as Hillside Farm, it is furnished according to the period between the mid-1800s and the first decade of the 20th century and vividly reveals life on a once-typical Michigan farm. In the second-floor Craft Room are displays and demonstrations of 19th-century American crafts. There is also a one-room schoolhouse, built about 1875, containing objects related to 19th-century education; a log cabin with tools and furnishings from the 1830s to 1850s; a gallery of changing exhibitions; and a well-stocked country store. Nearby is a small planetarium with shows on Sunday afternoons. *Open Sun. Jan., Tues.-Sun. Feb.-Dec. except holidays. Small charge for Merriman-Sharp House and planetarium.*

37. Waterloo Area Farm Museum *9998 Waterloo-Munith Rd., 3 mi. N.W. of Waterloo Village, Mich.* This restored brick farmhouse stands as a tribute to the hard-working Michigan farmers of the latter part of the 19th century. The 10 rooms have been furnished with authentic pieces; all labor and materials were donated by local residents. On the grounds are an icehouse, milk cellar, log bakehouse with a brick oven, toolhouse and windmill. *Open Tues.-Sun. late May-early Sept. Small charge.*

[40] *Detroit Zoo polar bears in one of their particularly social moods play and beg to an unseen human audience. Their spacious, moated living area is typical of the zoo's well-kept naturalistic animal quarters.*

38. University of Michigan *Ann Arbor, Mich.* The university was founded in 1817 and moved from Detroit to Ann Arbor 20 years later, but it did not enroll its first college class until 1841. Originally quite small, the university now comprises 18 colleges and schools and has additional campuses in Flint and Dearborn.

BURTON MEMORIAL TOWER The 10-story tower, named for a former president of the university, is 212 feet high. The top floor houses the 68-ton Charles Baird Carillon, made up of 53 bronze bells, the largest of which weighs 12 tons and the smallest, 12 pounds.

EXHIBIT MUSEUM *Alexander G. Ruthven Museums Bldg., 1109 Geddes Ave.* Dioramas are an outstanding feature of the museum. The exhibit of Indian clothing and implements is complemented by 14 small dioramas illustrating early Indian life in North America. To illustrate evolution there are dioramas of different environments with the animals that have adapted to each. On weekends the planetarium has demonstrations of astronomy. *Open daily. Planetarium small charge.*

KELSEY MUSEUM OF ANCIENT AND MEDIEVAL ARCHAEOLOGY *434 S. State St.* Among the fascinating exhibits to be seen here from time to time is Roman glass from the first through the fourth centuries that was excavated by the university's expeditions to Egypt between 1924 and 1935. Included are lamps, plates, goblets, bowls and pitchers, some of which were discovered stored in jars sunk into the dirt floors of dwellings. Their excellent condition enables visitors to study a variety of shapes and manufacturing techniques. *Open Mon.-Fri. Sept.-July except holidays.*

MUSEUM OF ART *Alumni Memorial Hall, State St. and S. University Ave.* Arts of the western world from the sixth century to the present plus those of Africa and Asia are amply represented here. Prints and drawings are included, with emphasis on those of the 20th century. Notable in the collection of American painting are Wimar's *Attack on an Emigrant Train* and Johnson's often-reproduced *Boyhood of Lincoln.* Works by Rodin, Arp, Lipchitz and David Smith are in a small but choice sculpture collection. *Open daily except holidays.*

39. St. John's Armenian Apostolic Church *22001 Northwestern Hwy., Southfield, Mich.* A saw-tooth conical gold dome crowned by a gold cross, distinctively Armenian in design, is the most arresting feature of this octagonal church. Although modern in feeling (it was consecrated in 1966), the church is characteristic of ancient Armenian ecclesiastical architecture. The Byzantine-style structure of Indiana limestone is faced with eight gabled bays adorned with arches and columns. Of particular note are the stained-glass windows, made in Chartres, France, which depict saints and include typical Armenian ornamental motifs. *Open daily.*

40. Detroit Zoological Park *Ridge and Ten Mile Rds., Royal Oak, Mich.* Barred cages are the exception in this 122-acre zoo. Instead, deep moats, many camouflaged with thick hedges, effectively isolate the animals. One of the most successful re-creations of a natural habitat is the African swamp site, where gazelles, flamingos, pelicans and cranes wander about in an area of pools connected by a stream. Simulated rock terraces studded with caves make a handsome setting for the world's largest display of polar bears. In the Penguinarium penguins zip through the chilly waters of their pool while visitors watch through large glass windows. The Holden Museum of Living Reptiles has many unusual features, including subterranean snakes in wall cases with removable lids for viewing. From mid-May to early October ponies, chimpanzees and other animals perform in the Holden Amphitheater animal shows. During summer months trains carry visitors through the zoo grounds and there are conducted tours on tractor trains. *Open daily mid-May-mid-Sept., Wed.-Sun. mid-Sept.-mid-May except holidays. Small charges for zoo, zoo railroad, animal shows and tractor train.*

41. General Motors Technical Center *Mound and Twelve Mile Rds., Warren, Mich.* The 38 steel and glass buildings occupying 330 acres were designed by Eero Saarinen. In place of traditional masonry walls, the architect specified laminated prefabricated panels only two-and-a-half inches thick. The tinted window glass and gray porcelain side paneling are in striking contrast to the vivid colors of the glazed brick end walls. Research laboratories, areas devoted to engineering, design and other General Motors operations and an auditorium with a 65-foot steel dome with aluminum shingles are shown on guided tours. The attractively landscaped grounds include a 22-acre lake with two fountains, one of which was designed by Alexander Calder. *Open Tues.-Sun. early June-early Sept.*

42. Detroit, Mich.

The city's location on waterways which connect two Great Lakes and two countries destined its importance from the start. Settled by the French as a trading post in 1701, strategic Detroit was held by British troops during both the Revolutionary War and the War of 1812. Since becoming an American city, its only conquest has been by commerce: the advent of the steamboat spurred trade and the arrival of Henry Ford's ingenious automobile created a manufacturing boomtown famous around the world.

Detroit Institute of Arts *5200 Woodward Ave.* The largest city-owned museum in the U.S. holds collections that combine broad range with unusual depth. Displayed in over 100 galleries are masterpieces of painting, sculpture and decorative art, including works from ancient Egypt, Greece, Rome, Africa and the Orient. European and American art of many periods is abundantly represented. Works by Botticelli, Giovanni Bellini, Titian, Rubens, Rembrandt, Bruegel and Gainsborough are here; among the Impressionist and Post-Impressionist paintings are works by van Gogh, Cézanne, Degas (*Dancers in the Green Room*), Renoir (*Seated Bather*), Monet and Matisse. American art includes oils by Whistler, Eastman Johnson, Eakins and Sloan. Among the reconstructions are a paneled room from a 16th-century English town house, a Gothic French chapel and several rooms from Whitby Hall, built outside Philadelphia in 1754, which contain William and Mary, Queen Anne and Chippendale furniture. The Rivera Court is noted for its remarkable frescos completed in 1933 by Diego Rivera. Symbolizing the development of man and his industrial society, the 27 panels include two particularly impressive murals that depict activities along an automobile assembly line. *Open Tues.-Sun. except holidays.*

Dossin Great Lakes Museum *Belle Isle* The colorful history of the Great Lakes and their ships is told in the museum, which contains a number of scale models and lithographs of the 19th-century steamers and later vessels. The first hydroplane to exceed a speed of 100 m.p.h. is also on display. The most ambitious exhibit is a restoration of the Gothic Room from a 1912 lake steamer; once a smoking lounge, its grand decor includes ornate, carved pillars and arches and a striking stained-glass window. *Open Wed.-Sun. Jan.-mid-Dec. except holidays.*

Jefferson Avenue Presbyterian Church *8625 E. Jefferson Ave.* The impressive Gothic-style stone edifice is considered one of the city's most beautiful churches. Dedicated in 1926, it serves a parish founded in the 1850s. The vaulted ceiling soars 90 feet above the sanctuary, which features many examples of fine hand-carved woods and stained-glass windows by Henry Lee Willet. *Open daily.*

[**42.** *Detroit Institute*] Women Admiring a Child *by American painter Mary Cassatt (1845-1926) is in the French Impressionist style. Cassatt exhibited with the Impressionists and lived in France after 1874.*

McGregor Memorial Conference Center *Wayne State University, 495 W. Ferry Ave.* Minoru Yamasaki designed the striking building, completed in 1958, using glass and marble-sheathed steel columns in geometric patterns. Endowed by the late philanthropists Mr. and Mrs. Tracy W. McGregor, the memorial contains 11 conference rooms and a 600-seat auditorium, all available for seminars, workshops, conferences and other programs of the university and the community. A definite but not overwhelming Japanese influence can be seen in the gardens and reflecting pool. The sculpture court is dominated by the bronze *The Nymph and the Faun,* created by the noted Italian sculptor Giacomo Manzu. *Open daily.*

Money Museum *National Bank of Detroit, 611 Woodward Ave.* More than 11,000 examples of ancient and modern coins, paper currency and tokens in this absorbing collection trace the development and history of money. Many curious objects used for barter during 40 centuries can be seen: cowrie shells, a Japanese money tree, salt bars and a 19th-century Mexican leather token. There is a wealth of early Roman, Chinese, Macedonian and Peruvian coins. Crude Lydian coins date from 640 B.C., and a Greek stater bearing a profile of Athena, the goddess of wisdom, was used about 330 B.C. A U.S. $10,000 bill and a rare four-dollar U.S. gold piece valued at $7000 are prize exhibits. *Open Mon.-Fri. except holidays.*

43. Dearborn Historical Museum *21950 Michigan Ave., Dearborn, Mich.* Between 1833 and 1837, 12 buildings were constructed here for use as a U.S. government arsenal to supply the Northwest Territory with arms. Today the Dearborn Museum is housed in two of these buildings and a 1950 annex. *Open Tues.-Sun. Mar.-Nov.*

COMMANDANT'S QUARTERS *Michigan Ave. and Monroe Blvd.* The commanding officer lived in this two-story house until 1875, when the arsenal was closed. The building, the oldest and most historic in the city, was considered a showplace when many pioneers were still living in log cabins. The brick house has been completely restored to its original elegance. It was used after 1875 as a residence, municipal offices and police station—and now contains displays of Indian artifacts, an arsenal-history room and several period rooms, one of which replicates an Army officer's bedroom from the 1840s.

MCFADDEN-ROSS HOUSE *915 Brady St.* Originally this 1839 building was the arsenal's powder magazine. It had two-and-a-half-foot-thick walls, a vaulted brick ceiling and copper-covered wooden doors, and some of these protective features may still be seen in the original section of the house. The abandoned structure was purchased in 1882 by Nathaniel Ross and converted into a farmhouse which was substantially enlarged in the 1920s. The museum has furnished the rooms in a Victorian manner. Local historical records and a library are on the second floor. In an exhibit annex are craft shops, wagons, a Model T Ford and agricultural items used from 1780 to 1945.

44. EDISON INSTITUTE

Dearborn, Mich.

From log cabins to sophisticated mechanical exhibitions, there is something to interest every member of the family at the Edison Institute, where Henry Ford assembled an amazing record of daily American life. The name honors Thomas Alva Edison, a personal friend, his inventive genius and his effect on life in the United States. The enormous complex includes Greenfield Village, an assemblage of American homes, shops, laboratories, mills and the like from different periods, the Henry Ford Museum of mechanical and decorative arts, a research library and the Ford Archives. *Open daily except holidays. Separate charge for museum and village: adults $2.25, children 6–14 small charge.*

Greenfield Village

The heart of the early American village was the green. Around it were the gathering places of the community: the church, the town hall, the shops and post office. Greenfield Village is reminiscent of this functional plan. To the east of the green, or common, and across a covered bridge, is the residential section, with houses whose dates range from the early 17th through the 19th century. Brought from Gloucestershire, England, a limestone cottage and its outbuildings represent the kind of house that many early settlers left. Nearby are two 17th-century American houses, one from New England, the other from Maryland. Included among the other houses brought to Greenfield Village from various sites around the country are the unpretentious homes in which some famous Americans lived, all furnished according to their period, location and inhabitants. On the west side of the common are early industries: craft shops, mills and factories. These are used to demonstrate how the villagers worked and how technology changed their living and working patterns from home industries to craft shops and then to factories.

Before grain can be ground in this 17th-century windmill from Cape Cod, its 54-foot sails must be spread with canvas. Nearby graze some English Cotswold sheep.

One of Thomas Alva Edison's most important innovations was the use of a team of researchers. Working in this and other laboratories he and his team turned out more than 1000 patentable devices, among them the incandescent light bulb and phonograph. Among the Edison labs preserved here is Menlo Park, his first and biggest.

Orville Wright was born in this typical late-19th-century house in Dayton, Ohio, and the family lived here for many years. Between aviation experiments and the bicycle business the two brothers found time to make several improvements to the interior and to add the elegant porch.

As a young circuit-riding attorney traveling around his home state of Illinois, Abraham Lincoln often practiced law in this small rural courthouse.

In the study of his new Federal-style house in New Haven, Noah Webster finished An American Dictionary of the English Language, *published in two volumes in 1828.*

Detroit has become famous for its fast-moving production lines, but in 1903, when the newly formed Ford Motor Company opened its first factory there, the plant was used only for the assembling of parts which had been manufactured elsewhere and hauled to this building by horses. Assembling 15 cars a day was the goal of the men, who worked on a few cars at once. It was not until 1913, after a new factory had been built for construction of the famous Model T, that the moving assembly line was introduced. Three of the early Fords once so laboriously assembled are pictured here by the first plant, now in Greenfield Village. From left to right they are the 1905 Model F Runabout, the 1903 Model A Runabout and a 1902 prototype Runabout.

At the end of a brick pathway lined with some of the flags once used in America is a reproduction of Independence Hall in Philadelphia. This is the entrance to the Henry Ford Museum. In the hall and in reproductions of Carpenter's Hall and Old City Hall are galleries devoted to American decorative arts. The Speaker's chair once actually used in Independence Hall is one of the cherished treasures in the collection of beautiful furniture made by America's greatest cabinetmakers and often associated with many noted personalities.

Henry Ford Museum

In the Henry Ford Museum the visitor may see many of the marvels that have been produced in America and the ever-changing tools that have been used. Dedicated in 1929, the vast museum is divided into three main parts. In the galleries of the American Decorative Arts are examples of furniture, clocks, silver, pewter, painting, sculpture, ceramics and glass from Pilgrim times through the 19th century. The largest section of the museum, the eight-acre Mechanical Arts Hall, contains the tools and machinery that were used and shows the evolution of agriculture, manufacturing, transportation and communications. The museum has the world's largest collection of objects that have served for transportation, from birchbark canoe and Conestoga wagon to Sikorsky's first practical helicopter, and various oddities such as the 10-man bicycle. Connecting the Decorative Arts Galleries and the Mechanical Arts Hall is the Folk Art Collection with the Street of Shops. Nearly every trade is represented along the old-fashioned street that shows the surroundings in which early American artisans worked or sold the things they made. There is a millinery shop and a collection of costumes, ranging from 18th-century handmade garments to early factory-produced clothing. Candlemaking, silversmithing, potterymaking, cabinetmaking and other skills are often demonstrated by costumed men and women, and the museum's Adult Education Division offers academic courses and instruction in such early crafts.

Made late in the 19th century, this colorful weather vane in the Folk Art Collection is complete in every detail. Even the steam pressure pump is modeled on one actually used in New Hampshire.

To demonstrate his skill in woodcarving, H. Card has put samples of his work outside his shop. Carved wooden signs such as a boot for a cobbler or a top hat for a hatter were formerly in common use.

During the latter 18th century, Sarah Furman Warner of Greenfield Hill, Conn., labored long on her needlework. There is no record of how much time she spent on her creation, but her meticulous stitching and intricate precise design have resulted in a masterpiece of the Folk Art Collection that will keep her name alive as long as her carefully chosen fabric lasts.

The Boston and Sandwich Glass Company is well represented at the Edison Institute, where elements of the original 1825 factory have been incorporated into a replica of the plant. Glassblowing techniques are demonstrated here. The Decorative Arts Galleries have a large collection of Sandwich glass of various types. The overlay Sandwich glass lamp at the right is in the lighting section of the Mechanical Arts Hall. It was made around 1875.

John Rogers sold thousands of plaster copies of his explicit sentimental bronze statuettes during the late 1800s.

More than 200 automobiles are here, the oldest a steam-powered horseless carriage made in 1863 by Sylvester Roper. Here is the slow electric car Mrs. Ford preferred and the 1902 racer Henry Ford drove at over 91 miles an hour. Also included here are early examples of fanciful decorations and accessories lavished on cars.

45. South Bend, Ind.

A French trading post was established on the south bend of the St. Joseph River soon after the site was visited by La Salle in 1679. Later it was taken over by John Jacob Astor's American Fur Company. Today the city is an important industrial and distribution center for northern Indiana.

University of Notre Dame *Rte. 31N* A Roman Catholic university for men, Notre Dame was established in 1842 by the Congregation of Holy Cross, a French religious order. In 1967 the university was turned over to lay control. Some 75 buildings of varying architectural styles stand on the 1250-acre campus.

ADMINISTRATION BUILDING With its golden dome surmounted by a statue of the Virgin Mary, the building is one of the nation's more celebrated campus landmarks. On the second floor are 10 murals of Columbus painted by Luigi Gregori. *Open daily.*

ART GALLERY *O'Shaughnessy Hall* The gallery houses an unusually good permanent collection of paintings and art objects of various periods and cultures. Included are such varied works as the portrait of Beatrice d'Este attributed to Veneto, a fine Ruisdael landscape and Picasso's *Le Miroir.* Special exhibitions of works gathered from other collections are held frequently. *Open daily.*

CHURCH OF THE SACRED HEART The handsome Gothic structure serves as the university church. In it can be seen Ivan Meštrović's sculpture *Pietà* and other art objects. *Open daily.*

GROTTO OF OUR LADY OF LOURDES This is a replica of the famed grotto at Lourdes in France. *Open daily.*

LOG CHAPEL The small simple building is a replica of the first structure on what was eventually Notre Dame's campus. The chapel was used by Father Stephen Badin, the first Catholic priest ordained in the U.S., and it contains his tomb. Mass is still said here.

NOTRE DAME MEMORIAL LIBRARY Thirteen stories high, this is the largest college library building in the world. An 11-story mural of Christ the Teacher adorns the modernistic facade.

[45. *Library*] *An impressive 132-foot-high mosaic mural of Christ as teacher with a host of saints and scholars rises above the library entrance. Artist Millard Sheets composed the monumental work of 7000 granite pieces.*

46. Seven Dolors Shrine *Off Rte. 6, 7 mi. N. of Valparaiso, Ind.* People of all faiths are welcomed to the rustic shrine that covers 160 partially wooded acres. A World War II memorial—a modern interpretation of the *Pietà*—stands near the entrance. The main grotto of the Seven Dolors has a life-size figure of Mary, her heart pierced by seven golden swords, standing high up in an arched block of tufa rock. The Lourdes Grotto features a Nativity scene; an altar to St. Francis of Assisi stands in the center of the grounds. In 1959 the Seven Dolors Chapel was added to the Friary, the residence of the Franciscan Fathers who maintain the shrine. *Open daily late May–Sept.*

47. Sloan Galleries of American Paintings *Henry F. Moellering Memorial Library, Valparaiso University, Valparaiso, Ind.* Changing exhibits of painting, sculpture and ceramics, illustrating major art trends, are presented here monthly. A permanent collection, displayed throughout the campus, focuses on American painting from about 1850 to 1950 and contains more than 400 works, many by Junius R. Sloan of the Hudson River school. *Open daily during academic sessions.*

48. Miami County Historical Museum *Miami County Court House, Rte. 24, Peru, Ind.* Colorful panels from old circus wagons and the stagecoach Tom Mix once used in a Wild West circus act are among the memorabilia exhibited on the fourth floor of the courthouse. Peru used to be winter quarters for seven renowned circuses and was known as the Circus Capital of the World. Also displayed are a fine collection of pioneer relics and paintings by George Winter and James Whitcomb Riley. Most intriguing are belongings of Frances Slocum, who in 1778 at the age of five was kidnaped by Indians and raised by an Indian family. Later she married a chief of thc Miami tribe. *Open Mon.-Sat. except holidays.*

49. Puterbaugh Museum *11 N. Huntington St., Peru, Ind.* The first-rate collection of American pioneer and Indian relics in the three-floor museum appeals to all visitors, while children are drawn to a steam automobile, circus collection and natural history displays. *Open Mon., Tues., Thurs., Sat. except holidays.*

50. Greentown Glass Museum *Greentown, Ind.* Between 1894 and 1903, a factory located in this community produced glassware in a variety of colors and interesting patterns. The 700 pieces here are effectively displayed in a room decorated in the style of the gaslight era of the early 1900s. Visitors can see several examples of chocolate glass and agate glass, both so rare they have become collectors' items. Some of the patterns used include teardrop and tassel, cord drapery and the rare holly amber. Indian head pitchers, miniature wheelbarrows and thistle trays are included in a collection of

[50] *These pitchers and glasses show some of the colors and patterns developed in the Greentown Glass Factory which closed in 1903 after a disastrous fire. Pieces produced there have become collectors' items.*

unusual receptacles. *Open Tues.-Sun. June-Sept., Sat., Sun. Oct.-May.*

51. General Lew Wallace Study *E. Pike St. and Wallace Ave., Crawfordsville, Ind.* Near the spot where the study stands, General Wallace wrote the phenomenally successful novel *Ben-Hur,* for which he is probably best remembered. Yet Wallace served with distinction in the Civil War and was also a fine painter, a statesman and, from 1881 to 1885, U.S. Minister to Turkey. That tour of duty explains the Byzantine aspect of the red brick study, designed by the general and built on the grounds of his estate in 1896. On display within are paintings by Wallace and portraits of him by others, many personal items, and, a favorite of the general's, the painting *Little Turkish Princess,* a gift from the Sultan of Turkey. *Open Wed.-Mon. mid-Apr.-Oct. except holidays. Small charge.*

52. Montgomery County Historical Society Headquarters *212 S. Water St., Crawfordsville, Ind.* Henry S. Lane, a close friend and political associate of Abraham Lincoln, lived for many years in this handsome Greek Revival house, presently occupied by the Historical Society. The house, which was begun in 1836, was purchased and enlarged by Lane in 1845. The Lanes' furniture, Mrs. Lane's banquet china, lovely cut glass and pressed glass, china dolls, cradles and some interesting mementos relating to Lincoln are on exhibit within. *Open Tues.-Sun. except holidays. Small charge.*

53. Conner Prairie Pioneer Settlement *Rte. 37A, 4 mi. S.W. of Noblesville, Ind.* The life of the early settler in Indiana is depicted here. The settlement was founded in the early 19th century by William Conner, one of the first traders in the newly formed Indiana Territory. Descriptions of some of the buildings follow. *Open Tues.-Sun. early Apr.-late Oct. Adults $1.50, children small charge.*

CONNER MANSION The two-story brick house was built by Conner in 1823, a splendid Colonial structure with a high-pitched roof and twin chimneys. Furnishings are antiques of the 1810-40 period.

FARMSTEAD Furnished as it would have been in the early 19th century, the log cabin reflects the home life of the settler. William Conner and his Indian princess wife, Mekinges, made their first home in a similar cabin. A log barn provided animal shelter, storage and a working area.

LOOM HOUSE Spinning, carding, weaving and other steps in the cloth-making process are demonstrated here just as they were performed during pioneer days. The restored building, of the 1825-30 period, is constructed of board and batten, with a broad plank floor.

MUSEUM A Conestoga wagon and a 150-year-old dugout canoe are among the exhibits. Other displays reflect various aspects of the early settler's life in central Indiana and the western frontier.

SCHOOLHOUSE A restoration of a typical country schoolhouse of the 1850s, the building is furnished with items of the period: a schoolmaster's desk, books, slates and other learning aids. A section of the wall is painted to provide a blackboard.

TRADING POST An essential feature of the fur trader's business, the log building was a destination for Indians and other trappers who brought furs to be traded for salt, blankets, cloth or hunting goods.

54. Indianapolis, Ind.

The city is not the outgrowth of a settlement but a planned state capital. The geographic center of the state was chosen for its site in 1821, and even though not on a navigable waterway, it is a focus for nationwide agricultural and industrial traffic. Woodruff Place Historic District, a residence park of private homes begun in 1872, is an enclave of Victorian architecture in the city's heart, graced with towering trees, fountains and cast-iron statuary.

Children's Museum of Indianapolis *3010 N. Meridian St.* For many years this was the only museum in the Indianapolis area, so the range of exhibits is unusually wide. American Indian artifacts, for example, are displayed in dioramas that show how they were made and used, and a 2500-year-old mummy dominates a handsome Egyptian room. Two of the most popular exhibits are the "Reuben Wells," an 1868 wood-burning locomotive hitched to a caboose, and the reconstructed interior of an 1829 log cabin. The focal point of a large toy collection is an elaborately landscaped electric train layout. *Open Tues.-Sun. except holidays.*

Indiana State Capitol *Ohio and Capitol Sts.* More than 12 acres of floor space are contained in this magnificent example of classic design. Ten years were required to build the limestone edifice, completed in 1888. Its 234-foot-high dome is supported by eight columns of Maine granite. On the third-floor level of the rotunda are imposing Carrara marble statues that represent justice, law, liberty, oratory, agriculture, commerce, history and art. Grand corridors, 68 feet wide, extend the entire length of each floor. The building is located on nine landscaped acres containing statues of prominent Indiana citizens. *Open Mon.-Fri.*

Indiana War Memorial *431 N. Meridian St.* In 1927 General John J. Pershing laid the cornerstone for

[**54.** *Museum of Indian Heritage*] *Treasures in the Eastern Woodland Indian exhibit include a ceremonial mask, beaded bandolier bag and vest and a mannequin that shows off a typically colorful costume.*

this large Indiana limestone structure, set in a five-block plaza. It is patterned after the Mausoleum at Halicarnassus in Asia Minor, one of the seven wonders of the world. Two marble staircases in the Grand Foyer lead to the imposing Shrine Room, where portraits of leading military figures from all the Allied nations in World War I are displayed. Light filters through stained-glass windows onto the enamel and marble Altar to the Flag. In the middle of the south stairway is the winged, 24-foot-high, seven-ton *Pro Patria,* one of the largest bronze statues ever cast. The extensive grounds include a large mall and plaza plus a black granite cenotaph honoring Indiana's World War I dead. At the base of a black granite obelisk are fountains that are illuminated at night with a rainbow of colored lights. *Open daily except holidays.*

Indianapolis Museum of Art *1200 W. 38th St.* The magnificent museum complex, consisting of a group of buildings in a beautifully landscaped park, houses collections that range over 4000 years. Every major period or school of fine arts is represented, with particular strength in the Oriental collection, 17th-century Flemish and Dutch paintings and 19th-century English and American portraits. A number of the museum's French Impressionist paintings rank with the finest to be seen in the U.S. The Krannert Pavilion, completed in 1970, is a striking structure of Indiana limestone and bronze glass. Here can be found the museum's main exhibits. Among the Impressionist works are *House in Provence* by Cézanne and *Landscape Near Arles* by Gauguin. Two major Edward Hopper paintings are among the treasures of the fine collection of American art. In an outdoor sculpture court are works by Indiana artists, including Robert Indiana, whose well-known *Love* appears in big steel letters outside and on canvas inside the galleries. The Clowes Pavilion houses the museum's old masters from the 12th century through the Renaissance, among which are two Titians, two Rembrandts and five El Grecos. The Lilly Pavilion of the Decorative Arts, built in the style of an 18th-century French chateau, is noted for its magnificent English, French and Italian furnishings and art objects. Among its 22 rooms is an exquisite Georgian library with a molded plaster ceiling and Sheraton and Hepplewhite furniture. *Open Tues.-Sun. Small charge.*

James Whitcomb Riley Home *528 Lockerbie St.* James Whitcomb Riley, the Hoosier poet, author of the familiar favorites "When the Frost is on the Punkin" and "The Old Swimmin' Hole," lived the last 23 years of his life in this brick house. Built in 1872, it is considered one of the finest examples of Victorian architecture in the country. The handsome furnishings are mostly in the Victorian style. Handpainted canvas decorates the walls and ceilings of some of the rooms. Many of Riley's personal possessions, including books, manuscripts, letters, his guitar and some articles of clothing, are on display. *Open Tues.-Sun. except holidays. Adults small charge.*

Museum of Indian Heritage *6040 DeLong Rd.* Dedicated to preserving and interpreting the rich Indian cultural heritage of North America, the museum has colorful displays depicting Eastern Woodland, Northwest Coast, Southwestern and Plains Indian cultures. Also featured are exhibits of rare archaeological artifacts of America's ancient past. All visitors receive a guided tour. *Open Tues.-Sun. Adults $1.25, children small charge.*

President Benjamin Harrison Memorial *1230 N. Delaware St.* Benjamin Harrison, the 23rd President of the U.S., lived in this house from 1874 until his death in 1901. Now a memorial museum, the house contains original furnishings and many personal effects of President Harrison. Visitors to the 16-room home (10 of which have been restored) can see Harrison's library, with his desk from the White House and mementos of his career; the front parlor, with crystal chandelier, handmade rug and gold Victorian furniture; Mrs. Harrison's sitting room, featuring her collection of gowns; a rosewood piano; and, in the master bedroom, both Harrison's massive, hand-carved bed and his baby crib. *Open daily. Small charge.*

Scottish Rite Cathedral *650 N. Meridian St.* A 212-foot-high Gothic carillon tower dominates this Masonic building, which is one of the largest of its kind in the country. The tower contains a 54-bell carillon with bells ranging from 19 pounds to over 11,000. The interior of the cathedral is resplendent with polished travertine marble walls decorated with Masonic emblems. A large bronze centerpiece in the floor depicts the signs of the zodiac and Scottish rite symbols. The auditorium, which seats 1100, is paneled in carved oak. *Open Mon.-Sat.*

Soldiers and Sailors Monument *Monument Circle* The nearly 285-foot monument in the heart of downtown Indianapolis commemorates Indiana's military men who served in wars prior to World War I. Just below the bronze statue of Victory at the top of the monument is a balcony, reached by an elevator, which provides a panoramic view of the city. At the monument's base is a circular plaza with statues and a fountain. *Open daily except holidays. Small charge.*

Tabernacle United Presbyterian Church *418 E. 34th St.* Stained-glass windows, which have been judged among the finest in the Midwest, are the outstanding feature of the handsome Gothic church. A total of 51 windows in the main sanctuary and four in the church tower depict the life and works of Christ and other Biblical scenes. *Open daily.*

55. Columbus, Ind.

Because of a few public-spirited citizens aware of how beautiful civic buildings can enhance the daily lives of a whole community, Columbus has become a showplace of modern American architecture. This midwestern town of 20,000 has some 35 buildings of outstanding architectural merit, including the Victorian Bartholomew County Court House described below and the post-World War II buildings shown in the feature display on pages 330-1.

Bartholomew County Court House *Third and Washington Sts.* The courthouse, completed in 1874, is a superb example of Victorian architecture. Its lofty central tower and fancy brickwork are reminiscent of the great French chateaus. Recently renovated, the courthouse continues to serve the county needs. One room—Court Room A, Room 24—is furnished much as it was nearly 100 years ago. *Open Mon.-Fri.*

56. T. C. Steele State Memorial *Off Rte. 46, S. of Belmont, Ind.* The studios of the Brown County Art Colony, which was once renowned in American art circles, are preserved on the wooded estate here. They house some 300 paintings by Theodore Clement Steele, one of Indiana's foremost artists at the turn of the century and a founder of the art colony. Steele began his career as a portrait painter, but his versatility is clearly apparent in the many landscapes and still lifes, as well as portraits, exhibited in his former studios. *Open daily May-Oct., Tues.-Sun. Nov.-Apr. except holidays. Small charge.*

57. Indiana University *Bloomington, Ind.* Bloomington is the main campus of this large university and architecturally it is an exciting amalgam of the old and the new. Among the visual highlights is the Calder stabile in front of the Musical Arts Building.

INDIANA UNIVERSITY ART MUSEUM *Fine Arts Bldg.* There is a surprising variety of paintings and art objects gathered here, ranging from the modern *Nude* sculpted by Aristide Maillol to an Egyptian jar more than 5000 years old. The collection of Greek and Roman art—one of the largest in the Middle West—and a strong, constantly growing collection of 20th-century works make this an important university museum. Featured among the sculptures is *Birth of Venus* by Robert Laurent, which stands in the center of Auditorium Plaza. *Open daily.*

THOMAS HART BENTON MURALS *Auditorium* The history of Indiana, its cultural and industrial progress, is depicted in a series of murals by Thomas Hart Benton. Painted for the Indiana exhibit at the 1933-4 Century of Progress International Exposition in Chicago, the murals are now on display in the Auditorium. A diversity of subjects is shown, starting with the *Mound Builders* and *Indians.* Cultural progress is portrayed along one side of the hall and industrial progress along the other. *Open Mon.-Fri.*

58. Spring Mill Village *Spring Mill State Park, Rte. 60, Mitchell, Ind.* The restored shops and mills of the village, once a frontier trading post, reflect the cultural and economic activities of the early and mid-1800s. An apothecary shop exhibits apothecary jars with their medicines, medical instruments, a dentist chair and illustrations of medical procedures. Tools and products of the leather-making craft along with a craftsman at work can be seen in the Munson House. A hat factory has hat molds, a dyeing machine and rack and other tools of the trade. A post office and general store dating from 1828 has items of the period on display and offers for sale typical products of the 1850s. Of particular interest is the three-story Hamer Grist Mill, built in 1817, the largest of its kind in southern Indiana, with a 500-foot flume and a 24-foot wheel. The power it can generate is used to grind corn, and the cornmeal is on sale to visitors. The power is also used occasionally to operate a nearby sawmill. Another operational structure is a distillery where the old-fashioned whiskey-making process is demonstrated. *Open Sat., Sun. Apr.-May, daily June-early Sept., Sat., Sun. early Sept.-Oct. Park admission $1.25 each car.*

[57. *Benton Murals*] Coal, Gas, Oil, Brick *is one of the murals Thomas Hart Benton did for the popular Chicago Exposition. It is the last of the series on the cultural and industrial progress of the state. The sculptural figures (co-workers on the project and friends were the models) and three-dimensional quality of the mural are typical of Benton's work. Unlike most other muralists of the day, the Missouri-born artist did not believe that walls should be decorated with flat patterns and effects only.*

What Do We Mean by Modern?

If a building is not obviously traditional—that is to say Federal, Georgian, Gothic, Romanesque or such—and if it is clean of line with the forms clearly defined, it can well be called modern. There are a number of schools of the style. They range from the precisely rectangular, beautifully proportioned forms of the Miesians (named for Ludwig Mies van der Rohe) to the arches, vaults and pierced walls of the neo-formalists to the massive masonry shapes and rich surface textures of the brutalist school. There are many permutations of these rather arbitrary categories, and there are good examples of the established styles as well as imaginative variations represented here in Columbus.

The architects include such well-known names as Harry Weese, John Carl Warnecke, TAC (The Architects Collaborative), Edward Larrabee Barnes, Gunnar Birkerts, Venturi and Rauch, I. M. Pei and Partners, Mitchell-Giugola, James Polshek, John M. Johansen, Eliot Noyes, Roche and Dinkeloo, Skidmore, Owings and Merrill, Victor Gruen Associates and Eero Saarinen, among others. In 1942 Saarinen's father, Eliel, designed the First Christian Church, a simple brick rectangle with a soaring rectangular bell tower standing adjacent. As the first of the modern buildings here, it was greeted with something less than total enthusiasm. Today, however, it is a landmark in the town and looks perfectly at home just across the street from the county library and the Henry Moore sculpture shown in the drawing at the right. Except for here in the downtown area, most of the buildings are rather widely distributed. This has the important advantage of bringing interesting architecture to many neighborhoods. But to really appreciate the full impact of what the work of a few great architects can do for a community, one must seek out the buildings.

W. D. RICHARDS ELEMENTARY SCHOOL, 1965

FIRST BAPTIST CHURCH, 1969

NORTH CHRISTIAN CHURCH, 1964

(*continued next page*)

55. Columbus, Ind.: Modern Style

(*See feature display on pages 330-1*)

In this small Indiana town there are more good examples of modern architecture than in any other place of its size in the world. The entire community has participated in this seeming miracle, but the movement was inspired and generously supported by one man, J. Irwin Miller, board chairman of Cummins Engine Corp. with headquarters in Columbus. The Cummins Engine Foundation was established in the 1950s and, as part of its program, pays design fees for public buildings done by firms on a list selected by two disinterested and "most distinguished architects." The first building under the program, the Lillian Schmitt Elementary School, was completed in 1957. The idea of good design has spread. Other companies now use outstanding designers and the Victorian buildings on Main Street have been refurbished and brightly painted. Most of the important buildings are open to the public. A brochure and tour map are available at the Visitors Center at 506 Fifth Street.

Cleo Rogers Memorial Library *536 Fifth St.* Designed by I. M. Pei, the brick building is understated and elegantly proportioned. The entry plaza and inner courtyard make a pleasant transition from the outside to the interior. Integral to the site is a monumental hollow bronze sculpture, *Large Arch,* by Henry Moore. *Open daily.*

First Baptist Church *3300 Fairlawn Dr.* Obviously modern in design, the church still observes the classic concepts. Architect Harry Weese used natural materials: slate for the roof; brick for the walls; and wood, naturally finished, for the interior. The steeply pitched rooflines and end walls soar upward toward the heavens in the revered tradition of the Gothic. *Open daily.*

Newlin House *2920 Franklin St.* Architectural fees for private buildings are not paid by the foundation, and there are only a few modern homes in Columbus. So that this important category could be represented, the Newlins graciously consented to have their house included here. Not open to the public, it can be seen from the street.

North Christian Church *Tipton Lane* Few architects have been more self-demanding than Eero Saarinen. This church was finished in 1964 just before he died. This is what he said about it: "I want to solve [this design] so that when I face St. Peter, I am able to say that of the buildings I did in my lifetime, one of the best was this little church . . . that speaks forth to all Christians as a witness to their faith." The church is a marvel of unity. The dramatic 192-foot spire, copper-sheathed ribs and slate roof look essentially the same from every angle of view. *Open daily.*

W. D. Richards Elementary School *Fairlawn Dr.* There are 10 schools of exceptional design in Columbus. Different in appearance, they are alike in dedication to the concept that a school should be adaptable to a variety of learning situations rather than forcing students to adapt to the building. Richards School, by architect Edward Larrabee Barnes, exemplifies the idea.

59. Orange County Court House *Town Square, Paoli, Ind.* Framed by trees, the courthouse has been unchanged in appearance and use since it was built. It is an exemplary representative of the Greek Revival architecture fashionable in public buildings in 1851 when it was completed. An aristocratic portico with huge Doric columns fronts the brick and stone structure, and a cast-iron stairway makes a suitably grand entryway. A three-stage cupola, which holds a clock, rises proudly over the building. *Open Mon.-Fri.*

60. St. Joseph Church *1215 N. Newton St., Jasper, Ind.* One of Indiana's largest churches, the Romanesque Catholic edifice was begun in 1867. It was designed and built entirely by the pastor and parishioners, who quarried, dressed and erected the native stone of its walls. A tall belfry and clock tower stands at the rear; the front is decorated by three small statues. The original simple interior, of plasterwork and wood, was renovated with sandstone and marble in the 1950s. There also are three superb mosaics which were installed in 1911. *Open daily.*

61. Lincoln Boyhood National Memorial *Rte. 162, Lincoln City, Ind.* When Abraham Lincoln was seven years old, his family moved to this site where they cleared and worked a frontier farm from 1816 to 1830. Here, in 1818, Lincoln's mother died and was buried. The memorial building of Indiana limestone consists of two halls connected by a visitor center with offices, an auditorium and a small museum of relics from the Lincoln era. The Abraham Lincoln Hall resembles an early chapel. The interior walls are of Indiana sandstone with a wainscot of cherry wood, hand-hewn hardwood beams and high-back benches of yellow poplar and cherry. The Nancy Hanks Lincoln Hall, a memorial to Lincoln's mother, contains a large stone-arched fireplace, wooden benches, a hand-braided rug, a large table and several chairs. The landscape over the fireplace shows the historic place on the Ohio River where the Lincolns crossed on their way into Indiana from Kentucky. *Open daily Apr.-Oct., Wed.-Sun. Nov.-Mar. except Jan. 1 and Dec. 25.*

LINCOLN LIVING HISTORICAL FARM This typical pioneer farm features, in addition to the original Lincoln homesite, a reconstructed log cabin, barn and barnyard, corncrib, chicken house and crafts shop. Farm animals and crops which are essentially the same as those raised by the Lincoln family are also exhibited along with farm implements and tools.

62. Lincoln Pioneer Village *City Park, Rockport, Ind.* The 1937 museum village is a memorial to Abraham Lincoln and the 14 years he lived here in Spencer County. *Open daily. Small charge.*

AZEL DORSEY HOME The home of one of Lincoln's teachers housed the first court of law held in Spencer County. The log structure, with floors of roughly hewed timber, still contains a desk and chairs from the first courthouse.

GENTRY MANSION James Gentry was a rich businessman and landowner who employed Lincoln to work on his farm and in his store for 25 cents a day. The house is furnished with items which belonged to the Gentry family during this period.

[61] *Lincoln's boyhood home, similar to this 18-by-20-foot hand-hewn notched log cabin, resembled those of many other midwestern pioneers. It had a dirt floor, sleeping loft of clapboard, daubed fireplace and stick chimney.*

JOHN PITCHER'S LAW OFFICE Lincoln often walked the 17 miles from his home to borrow or return law books from John Pitcher, the first lawyer who lived in the county, and it was through him that Lincoln gained an interest in legal affairs. Old law books and an office desk are still here.

LINCOLN HOMESTEAD The log cabin is a replica of the one occupied by the Lincoln family. Lincoln slept in a bed in the loft, reached by a stairway of pegs driven into the wall. Furnishings of the period include a bed of boughs and a spinning wheel.

MUSEUM OF EARLY TRANSPORTATION This replica of a tobacco warehouse contains early horse-drawn vehicles, including a hearse and several buggies. The building was constructed for use in the production of the movie *The Kentuckians.*

OLD PIGEON BAPTIST CHURCH Abraham Lincoln was the only member of his family who did not belong to the church, although he helped to build it. (The present building is a replica of the original.) A stairway leads to the loft where men who came from some distance to attend church could sleep overnight, while their wives and children stayed with neighbors.

63. Kentucky Building Library and Museum *Western Kentucky University, Bowling Green, Ky.* Among the exhibits here are prehistoric fossils, Indian artifacts and more than 1000 specimens of Kentucky birds, insects and mammals. Also featured are pioneer relics such as cooking utensils, spinning wheels and homemade shoes. The library contains more than 20,000 volumes relating to Kentucky life and history as well as rare prints, maps, newspapers and scrapbooks. Also here are important records, journals, account books and diaries of the nearby South Union Shaker community. *Museum open daily, library open Mon.-Sat.*

64. Shaker Museum *Rte. 68, 3 mi. N.E. of Auburn, Ky.* The museum has everything from a hogshair mattress to a trestle dining table—products of generations of hardworking Shakers, who established a cooperative colony here in 1807. In the collections are furniture, stoves, tools, textiles, baskets, clocks, drawings and books, all produced and used by the Shakers until the South Union Community was disbanded in 1922. The Auburn Shaker Festival is held each year during the first two weeks after Independence Day. *Open daily mid-May-mid-Oct. Small charge.*

65. Jefferson Davis Monument State Shrine *Rte. 68, Fairview, Ky.* A 351-foot-high concrete obelisk, the fourth highest monument in the U.S., memorializes the only president of the Confederate States of America, Jefferson Davis. An elevator takes visitors to the top where they can view the countryside. Twenty-two acres of parkland surround the monument, and a replica of Davis's log-house birthplace is nearby. *Open Tues.-Sun. Mar.-May, daily June-Aug., Tues.-Sun. Sept.-Nov., Sat., Sun. Dec.-Feb. Small charge.*

66. Concordia Senior College *6600 N. Clinton St., Fort Wayne, Ind.* Everything about this campus is new, from the lake (made by flooding nine acres of lowland) to the 31 buildings designed by the great architect Eero Saarinen in the pattern of a northern European village. Befitting the purpose of Concordia—the training of Lutheran ministers—the chapel, with its free-standing, tapered bell tower, is the campus centerpiece. Within, the main altar is simply a six-ton slab of Vermont granite, symbolizing the austere beauty of the entire college. Throughout the buildings there can be seen brilliantly conceived decorative motifs with the unified theme of rendering thanks to God, ranging from incised brick bas-reliefs to painted linen tapestries and cast-bronze shields. *Open Mon.-Fri.*

67. Lincoln Library and Museum *Lincoln National Life Insurance Building, 1301 S. Harrison St., Fort Wayne, Ind.* One of the nation's largest collections of printed material on Abraham Lincoln is enlivened by a variety of objects owned by the President and his family. Many portraits of Lincoln are on display, along with a large number of contemporary prints and photographs and more than 200 Lincoln busts, plaques and masks. The notable collection of original manuscripts includes 85 documents in Lincoln's handwriting. The library serves as a clearinghouse for Lincolniana and contains over 16,000 books, pamphlets, clippings, microfilms and periodicals. Among its famous visitors has been Carl Sandburg, one of Lincoln's most renowned biographers. Paul Manship's large bronze statue of Lincoln as a Hoosier stands outside the entrance to the building. *Open Mon.-Fri. except holidays.*

68. Amishville, U.S.A. *Amish Trnpke., 5 mi. S.E. of Berne, Ind.* This is an authentic Amish farm open to visitors. A tour includes the Grossdawdy Haus (granddaddy house), smokehouse, kettle house, washhouse and garden, all maintained in the old-fashioned style. Buggy and wagon rides are available. The farm is in Amish country—settled in the 1850s by Amish people who had left their homes in Europe to escape religious persecution. You can see them in the vicinity, leading much the same kind of simple life they did over 100 years ago—the men are mostly farmers, drive wagons, and wear beards and black coats; the women wear bonnets and shawls. One mile to the west, off the Amish Turnpike, is the only remaining covered bridge across the Wabash River. *Open daily except holidays. Small charge for tour and rides.*

[**79.** Belle of Louisville] *This old sternwheeler now offers only three-hour pleasure trips. In the 19th century such engine-driven flatboats were a most elegant way of traveling (for first-class passengers) and the chief means of shipping cargo on our inland waterways. Largely because of them such river cities as Louisville and St. Louis developed. For owners (often the captains), a steamboat was a profitable investment. They could recoup the purchase price within 20 weeks of use.*

69. Art Gallery of Ball State University *Muncie, Ind.* A superb collection of fine arts covers hundreds of years of creative work and styles. There is a splendid display of Roman glass of the first and second century. Fine Renaissance paintings include a DiCredi *Madonna and Child* on a wood panel. Landscapes of 19th-century American artists—among them, Thomas Doughty, Alexander Wyant, George Inness—are an impressive specialty, as are important works of contemporary art. *Open daily except holidays.*

70. Alford House, Anderson Fine Arts Center *226 W. Eighth St., Anderson, Ind.* Constructed in 1870, the white Greek Revival-style mansion on a tree-shaded knoll is typical of many stately 19th-century residences that line the streets of towns in mid-America. Today the headquarters of the Anderson Fine Arts Center, Alford House contains a collection of Midwestern art and each year hosts over a dozen special exhibits. *Open Tues.-Sun. Sept.-July except holidays.*

71. Mounds State Park *4306 Mounds Rd., Anderson, Ind.* Two thousand years ago Indians built nine mounds here which they used for cremation and burial. Most of them are circular, but two are fiddle-shaped and one resembles a figure eight. The largest is nine feet high and 384 feet across. Artifacts dug up by archaeologists from Indiana University are on the campus in Bloomington. *Open Sat., Sun. Apr.-May, daily June-Aug., Sat., Sun. Sept.-Oct. Small charge. Parking fee.*

72. Henry County Historical Society Museum *614 S. 14th St., New Castle, Ind.* The outstanding feature here is the building itself. Once the residence of a prominent Civil War general, William Grose, the 16-room mansion is restored and furnished in the Victorian style of the 1870s. Included among the exhibits are Indian relics, Civil War mementos, primitive paintings and wildlife displays. *Open Mon.-Sat.*

73. Levi Coffin House *Rte. 27 and Mill St., Fountain City, Ind.* The characters of Uncle Simeon and Aunt Rachel in Harriet Beecher Stowe's *Uncle Tom's Cabin* were drawn from Quaker merchant Levi Coffin and his wife Catharine. They built this substantial brick house in 1839. Over the years the Coffins aided more than 3000 escaped slaves. Their home sheltered many of them and became known as the Grand Central Station of the "Underground Railroad." In the crawl space beneath the roof and in other nooks and crannies as many as 17 slaves could be hidden at one time. The eight period rooms are staffed by costumed hostesses. *Open Tues.-Sun. June-mid-Sept., Sat., Sun. mid-Sept.-Oct. Small charge.*

74. Auditorium *West and Third Sts., Madison, Ind.* The Greek Revival structure, built in 1835, is the oldest public building in Madison and is said to be the finest example of this style in the whole region. It was originally designed by Edwin J. Peck for the Second Presbyterian Church. It now contains a public auditorium and several business offices, including those of the Greater Madison Chamber of Commerce.

75. J. F. D. Lanier State Memorial *Elm and W. First Sts., Madison, Ind.* The antebellum mansion, among the finest outside the South, was built in 1844 by J.F.D. Lanier, a prominent lawyer and banker. The building is Greek Revival in style, with imposing Corinthian columns supporting the two-story entrance portico. Inside, a lovely staircase spirals up gracefully for three stories. Many Lanier heirlooms are included in the furnishings. *Open daily May-Oct., Tues.-Sun. Nov.-Mar. except holidays. Small charge.*

76. Judge Jeremiah Sullivan House *304 W. Second St., Madison, Ind.* Madison's first lawyer, Jeremiah Sullivan, built this Federal-style home in 1818. The house contains most of the original woodwork: outstanding cornices, handmade doors, ash-board floors. The turned cherry handrail and square spindles of the staircase show particularly fine craftsmanship. Pots and pans of the period hang in the basement kitchen, and many items belonging to the Sullivan family are included in the room furnishings. Also featured are exhibits of glass, china and silver of the early 19th century. *Open daily May-Oct. Adults small charge.*

77. Shrewsbury House *301 W. First St., Madison, Ind.* As in the neighboring Lanier Mansion, a spiral staircase rises three floors in this Greek Revival house. Other notable features include unusually high ceilings, elaborate plaster cornices and Greek columns in some of the rooms. The double drawing room—still with the original paint—has furnishings of the mid-19th-century period when the mansion was built for Charles Lewis Shrewsbury, a river trader and internationally known pork packer. It stands on the bank of the Ohio River, where boatloads of Shrewsbury hams sailed for world markets. *Open daily Mar.-Dec. Adults and children over 12 small charge.*

78. Culbertson Mansion *914 E. Main St., New Albany, Ind.* The old glitter has been restored to this 26-room mansion built in Second Empire style, the largest residence on the Ohio River during the booming days of steamboat building in New Albany. It has been refurnished in the elegant fashion of the year 1868, when it was completed at a cost of nearly $125,000. Highlights include a grand ballroom with hand-painted ceiling, a cantilevered staircase and woodwork crafted throughout by skilled boatbuilders. The home was built for W. S. Culbertson, a financier and philanthropist. *Open Tues.-Sun. Apr.-Nov. Small charge.*

79. Louisville, Ky.

In 1778 George Rogers Clark brought soldiers down the Ohio to take the Illinois country from the British. With them came 20 families who maintained Clark's supply base here during the campaign. After his victory more settlers came and in 1780 the settlement at the "Falls of the Ohio" was named Louisville after Louis XVI of France, who had befriended the American cause. Today it is Kentucky's largest city and one of the South's chief industrial and educational centers.

"Belle of Louisville" *Riverfront Plaza and Fourth St.* An old-style riverboat with a sternwheel, the *Belle* makes three-hour afternoon cruises on the Ohio River, carrying her passengers back into the past. In the week preceding the Kentucky Derby (held on the first Saturday in May), they can watch the annual race she runs with another sternwheeler, the *Delta Queen* of Cincinnati. *Trips Tues.-Thurs., Sat., Sun. late May-early Sept. Adults $2.00, children small charge.*

[**79.** *J. B. Speed Museum*] *Regardless of whether scholars decide this equestrian statue is the only piece of sculpture done by Da Vinci, it will still be considered the finest 16th-century Italian bronze in America.*

Farmington *3033 Bardstown Rd.* Built from a design of Thomas Jefferson, this Federal-style house of 14 rooms was completed in 1810. Interesting Jeffersonian details include two magnificent octagonal rooms and a hidden stairway. The furnishings are American and English antiques made prior to 1820. Behind the house are an early 19th-century garden and a working blacksmith's shop. *Open Tues.-Sun. except holidays. Small charge.*

J. B. Speed Art Museum *2035 S. Third St.* The museum, named for a Louisville industrialist, James Breckinridge Speed, houses superb collections that range from 3000 B.C. to the present. Among its acquisitions are the bronze *Horse and Rider,* under international study as perhaps the only sculpture by Leonardo da Vinci. Works by Rubens, Gauguin and Monet are among its rare selections of paintings. Excellent examples of the decorative arts are also kept here, and an Elizabethan manor house room, considered the world's finest, forms part of a museum wing. *Open Tues.-Sun. except holidays.*

Jefferson County Courthouse *531 Jefferson St.* The Greek Revival structure, designed by Gideon Shryock, who pioneered that style in the Western states, was begun in 1837, but lack of funds prevented its being completed until 1860. A statue of Henry Clay stands in the great rotunda, which is surrounded by eight fluted Ionic columns. Outside the entrance there is also a statue of Thomas Jefferson. *Open Mon.-Sat.*

Kentucky Railway Museum *River Rd.* Steam locomotives, some the last survivors of their types, are found here along with diesel engines. A French boxcar, passenger coaches and streetcars are also displayed. Railroad artifacts and models round out the collection. *Open Sat., Sun., holidays late May-early Sept.*

Locust Grove House Museum *561 Blankenbaker Lane* In this attractive Georgian brick house, built about 1790, General George Rogers Clark spent his last years. The house, on 55 rolling acres, has been restored and furnished with period pieces and portraits. One example of the meticulous restoration is the handsome wallpaper in the ballroom, reproduced from fragments that remained of the original French paper. *Open Tues.-Sun. except holidays. Small charge.*

Louisville Zoological Garden *1100 Trevilian Way* The modern zoo, opened in 1969, features interesting groupings of animals by their geographical origins. The animals are confined by moats and roam in herds and family groups in effectively landscaped naturalistic habitat areas. Among the most interesting exhibits are those featuring aquatic animals and animals of the African plains and Australia. Signs explaining the exhibits are located throughout the zoo, and a miniature train runs around its perimeter. In the Children's Zoo animals can be petted and fed, and trained animal performances are given in the amphitheater. *Open Tues.-Sun. except Tues. following Mon. holidays. Adults and children over 5 small charge.*

80. Patton Museum of Cavalry and Armor *Fort Knox, Ky.* One of the larger collections of tanks and armor in existence, both American and foreign, may be seen here, including a rare 1918 U.S. Ford tank. Also on display is the staff car in which General George S. Patton, Jr., was fatally injured. *Open daily except Jan. 1 and Dec. 25.*

81. My Old Kentucky Home State Park *Rte. 150, Bardstown, Ky.* Stephen Foster is said to have composed "My Old Kentucky Home" while visiting his cousins the Rowans here in 1852. The plantation manor house was begun by Judge John Rowan in 1795, and it now stands amid 235 acres of parkland. The house retains many of the original furnishings, including the desk used by Foster. Paul Green's musical *The Stephen Foster Story* is presented in an outdoor amphitheater from mid-June through early September. *Open daily Mar.-Nov., Tues.-Sun. Dec.-Feb. Small charge.*

82. St. Joseph's Church *310 Stephen Foster, Bardstown, Ky.* When the handsome edifice was dedicated in 1819, it was one of only three Roman Catholic cathedrals in the U.S. Its limestone was quarried by pioneers who also fired the bricks, cut the lumber and made all the hardware used in the construction. The building is Neoclassical in design with Greek Revival exterior characteristics; its portico is adorned with Ionic columns made of poplar and crowned by a graceful steeple with a clock tower, lantern and tall spire. The basilicalike interior with its vaulted ceiling and Tuscan columns is dominated by several remarkable religious paintings generally believed to be by Rubens, Van Dyck and Murillo. *Open daily.*

[81] *The handsome brick mansion reflects the Georgian style of architecture that flourished in 18th-century America. A replica of the springhouse where Judge Rowan practiced law is on the grounds.*

83. Wickland *Rte. 62, Bardstown, Ky.* Superbly proportioned Georgian architecture and rooms graced with period furniture create a truly remarkable house. Interior highlights are hand-carved woodwork, extraordinary Adam mantels and a cantilever stairway. Built in 1813 by Charles Wickliffe, it was the family home of three governors: Wickliffe, his son and his grandson. *Open daily Mar.-Nov. Small charge.*

84. Brown-Pusey House *128 N. Main St., Elizabethtown, Ky.* Originally a stagecoach inn, the Georgian brick building was constructed around 1825. From 1871 to 1873 it served as headquarters for General George Custer while his regiment was stationed in the area, and he spoke well of the inn's hospitality: "I enjoy this old-fashioned hotel with its quaint landlady who is everything in one." Today's visitors find an equally warm atmosphere. It is a community house now, handsomely restored with many of its original furnishings, and retaining the charm of another era. *Open Mon.-Sat. except holidays.*

85. Abraham Lincoln Birthplace *Rte. 31E, Hodgenville, Ky.* The one-room log cabin believed to be the birthplace of Abraham Lincoln is now enshrined in a memorial building on the site of the Lincolns' Sinking Spring farm. The monument, completed in 1911, is a massive, Roman-templelike structure of granite and marble. Marked on the farm are the spring, a boundary oak and a rail fence typical of the period. There is a visitor center with exhibits depicting Lincoln's early life; one of these includes the Bible that belonged to his father. *Open daily except Dec. 25.*

86. Lincoln Statue *Public Sq., Hodgenville, Ky.* The seated figure of Abraham Lincoln was created by the sculptor A. A. Weinmann, a student of Saint-Gaudens. It was erected by the U.S. Congress and the State of Kentucky in 1909.

87. Rosary Cathedral *2561 Collingwood Blvd., Toledo, Ohio* This is the world's only cathedral to follow a 16th-century Spanish architectural form known as plateresque. The ornate structure, fashioned from limestone and granite, was dedicated in 1940. The exterior is distinguished by sturdy buttresses, bas-relief carvings and two bell towers that flank a rose window. Marble from Spain, Italy and France is used lavishly throughout the interior. On the ceiling 83 feet above the nave is a portrayal of the 28 kings and prophets from the Old Testament, while a view of Christ on the cross dominates the ceiling over the marble Communion rail. Elaborate frescos, paintings, carvings, statues and mosaics further embellish the vast nave and apse. *Open daily.*

88. Toledo Museum of Art *Monroe St. and Scottwood Ave., Toledo, Ohio* Paintings by the old masters and by 20th-century Americans, a medieval cloister, classical and Oriental art objects—all these and much more are housed in the museum's imposing Greek Revival building. Piero di Cosimo's superb *Adoration of the Child* is just one of the early Renaissance works. A mid-12th- to 14th-century cloister forms an appropriate setting for the museum's tapestries, stained-glass windows and

[88] *Maurice Prendergast, who lived in France and Italy during the 1890s, was one of the first American painters to work in the style of the French modernists. His delightful* Flying Horses *shows the influence of Bonnard.*

medieval decorative arts. Egyptian objects and sculpture and Greek, Roman and Near Eastern ceramics and statues comprise a rich and interesting chronology of ancient art in the Mediterranean area. The Oriental collection of bronzes, ceramics and lacquer is just as extensive. There is an impressive assemblage of 17th- to 19th-century French art. English and American artists of the 19th century are well represented. Paintings by Bonnard, Matisse and Modigliani contribute to an excellent 20th-century group. Rodin's 1881 statue of *Eve* and Moore's bronze *Reclining Figure* are among the many works in the sculpture collection. Appropriately for this glass-making city, the museum houses one of the world's most comprehensive collections of glass, ranging from sand-core specimens made in Egypt about 1350 B.C. to contemporary pieces. *Open daily.*

89. Brumback Library *215 W. Main St., Van Wert, Ohio* The nation's first county library is housed in a castlelike building given to Van Wert County by a former resident. Completed in 1901, the sandstone structure is a combination of Gothic and Romanesque styles, with turreted towers and a tile roof. The pleasing interior has marble floors and decorative vaulted ceilings. *Open Mon.-Sat.*

90. Allen County Museum *620 W. Market St., Lima, Ohio* Completely furnished period rooms, each reflecting a particular aspect of pioneer living, were installed by the Allen County Historical Society. There is an extensive collection of Indian baskets and a diorama of a prehistoric Indian burial. Other displays have such varied themes as fossils, minerals, guns and fire engines. The society has a library with a large collection of local and state histories and genealogies. *Open Tues.-Sun. except holidays.*

91. Castle Piatt Mac-A-Cheek *1 mi. E. of West Liberty, Ohio* Benjamin Piatt, a quartermaster general in the War of 1812 and later federal judge in Cincinnati, moved to the valley of the Mac-A-Cheek Indians in 1817. His sons built two imposing castles in the valley during the last half of the 19th century. Both are still owned by the family. Reminiscent of a fortified French chateau, the elaborate castle was built in 1864 by General Abram Saunders Piatt. Two-foot-thick walls were hand-chiseled from limestone quarried on the Piatt estate. The 35 rooms have walls lavishly paneled in walnut, ash or pine, floors inlaid with fine woods, and ceilings vividly frescoed. Furnishings are original, mostly Early American and French antiques. Relics of the many wars in which members of the Piatt family have participated are on display. *Open daily. Small charge.*

92. Mac-O-Chee Castle *2 mi. E. of West Liberty, Ohio* Colonel Donn Piatt, at one time chargé d'affaires to the court of Louis Napoleon, built this Flemish-style castle complete with towers and tall spires in 1879. The building is constructed of local limestone. Interior decor includes ornate woodwork, elegant frescos and rare tapestries, and the furnishings are mostly European and Asian antiques. *Open daily. Small charge.*

93. Peoples Federal Savings and Loan Association Building *Court St. and Ohio Ave., Sidney, Ohio* The innovative structure, completed in 1917, was the last major commission of the great architect Louis H. Sullivan. The building's stark lines are broken at one side by a series of high windows. An arch of blue mosaic tiles, bordered with multicolored terra cotta, above the entrance is the most elaborate ornamentation. (The tiles carry an appropriate message: "THRIFT.") The interior illustrates Sullivan's use of open space. His innovations here included a heated vestibule, cork floors in work areas, large double-paned windows, an early air-conditioning system and indirect lighting in the lobby. *Open Mon.-Fri.*

94. Piqua Historical Area *Piqua, Ohio* Indian villages, fur-trading posts and forts once occupied this region along the banks of the Great Miami River, and early trade routes and pioneer and military expeditions crossed here or passed nearby. Fort Piqua, built in 1794,

[91] *The Valley of the Mac-A-Cheek, named for the tribe of Shawnee Indians who lived here, is the unlikely setting for this fanciful Norman French chateau built of Ohio cream limestone by General Abram Saunders Piatt.*

became part of the land bought by John Johnston in 1804. Several of his farmstead buildings have been restored. *Open Tues.-Sun. Apr.-Oct. Small charge.*

BARN The large double-pen log structure, built around 1808, housed sheep and hogs and also served as a storage place for Indian trade goods during the War of 1812. Sheds and a threshing floor were added in 1826. Over a span of 100 years various changes were made, but now it is restored to its 1826 style.

CANAL BOAT The *General Harrison,* built long (68 feet) and narrow (12 feet) to negotiate locks, is typical of the cargo boats used for freight hauling on the Miami-Erie Canal from 1840 to 1850.

CIDER HOUSE Apple cider, an important product of the farm, was stored in this building, a reconstruction on the original site. To keep the area cool in the summer, there is a vent space between the roof and the ceiling.

INDIAN MUSEUM The museum depicts the Indians of the Ohio Valley as seen through the eyes of explorers, soldiers, traders and settlers. Indian artifacts and early trading merchandise are exhibited.

JOHNSTON HOUSE The first section of this Dutch Colonial house was completed in 1811, the second in 1815, after which the house took on a Georgian appearance. It was one of the first brick houses in the area and was John Johnston's home until about 1840.

95. Weaver Chapel-Thomas Library *Wittenberg University, Springfield, Ohio* A handsome modern building of brick and stone contains the chapel and library of this Lutheran university. The free-standing, 212-foot tower attests to the structure's combined facilities; on it are larger-than-life limestone statues of persons important in the spiritual and cultural heritage of Protestantism. The chapel's high, narrow stained-glass windows are unique. Reversing the usual technique of stained glass, Oliver Smith, the designer, used lead heavily, almost like a stencil, with the glass only filling in the design. In the three-story library is one of the nation's best collections of materials relating to Martin Luther. This includes a letter written by him and manuscripts and original editions of early Lutheran tracts, some with engravings by Lucas Cranach the Elder and Hans Cranach. *Open daily.*

96. Dayton, Ohio

The city's location at the confluence of four streams early set its course as a prominent commercial center. Hundreds of national products are manufactured here now, including tires and other automotive parts, cash registers, refrigerators and air conditioners. Despite all the city's emphasis on industry, Dayton remains an attractive and hospitable city with strong interests in its cultural heritage and development.

Carillon Park *Rte. 25S* Exhibits that depict the progress of transportation are featured in the 61-acre museum park. Displays include the Wright brothers' second airplane, a section of the Miami-Erie Canal with one of the original locks, a Concord coach, a Conestoga wagon, a steam fire engine and a 1912 Cadillac. A "grasshopper" locomotive is displayed in a replica of an early railroad station. Also exhibited is an early-day, water-powered gristmill. *Open Tues.-Sun. and Mon. holidays May-Oct.*

DEEDS CARILLON The 41-bell carillon, with its impressive tower, was a gift to the city by Mrs. E. A. Deeds. Carillon and celestron concerts are presented on Sunday evenings during summer months.

NEWCOM TAVERN Constructed of hewn logs, the two-story tavern, built in 1796, is the oldest building in Dayton. It has served as a post office, church and courthouse in the past; today it is used as a museum featuring early American relics and artifacts. *Open Tues.-Sun. and Mon. holidays May-Oct.*

Dayton Art Institute *Forest and Riverview Aves.* All the great art periods in history are represented in the thousands of items gathered together in this museum. Included are collections of European painting from the 16th to 19th centuries, 20th-century American painting, Pre-Columbian art and artifacts and Oriental

[**96.** *U.S. Air Force Museum*] *This 1911 Blériot is similar to the monoplane in which Louis Blériot, pioneer French aviator, made the first overseas flight in a heavier-than-air craft, crossing the English Channel in 1909. Blériot built France's first airplane factory; his planes were used as trainers by fledgling pilots of many nations.*

art. Among outstanding individual works are a Chinese burial urn dating from about 2200 B.C., a Mayan cylindrical vase from the ninth century, a Peruvian mummy mask, Rubens' *Study Head of an Old Man* and John Sloan's *Coburn Players.* The museum is housed in an Italian Renaissance-style palazzo on a hill overlooking the city of Dayton. *Open Tues.-Sun. except holidays.*

Dayton Museum of Natural History *2629 Ridge Ave.* Some museums are essentially storage houses, but this one, which has more than 80,000 specimens, stresses active participation. Children interested in nature become junior curators and staff members. They care for all the live animals in the Animal Fair, bring in specimens from field trips and catalogue them. There are exhibits on plant life, rocks, an Egyptian mummy, early Indian artifacts (many from a current dig nearby), an observatory and a planetarium. The functionally designed museum blends with its 17½ acres of land overlooking Stillwater River. *Open daily except holidays. Small charge Sun.*

U.S. Air Force Museum *Wright-Patterson Air Force Base, Springfield St. (N.E. of Dayton)* The museum is the oldest and largest in the world devoted to military aviation. About 130 aircraft, 10,000 artifacts, dioramas and models trace the development of flight from Da Vinci's early experiments to the latest rocket triumphs. World War II aircraft include a B-17 Flying Fortress, a Spitfire, a German V-1 buzz bomb and a Japanese suicide plane. More recent craft include the XB-70 "Valkyrie," an F-86 Sabre and a MIG-15. Atomic bomb cases similar to those dropped on Japan provide an awesome display. Rocket-age items include a Gemini III capsule, samples of space food, a moon rock and objects carried by astronaut Neil Armstrong. *Open daily except Dec. 25.*

Wright Brothers Memorial *Rte. 444 (N.E. of Dayton)* The pink granite monument commemorates the contributions made by Wilbur and Orville Wright to the development of aviation. A large bronze plaque tells of their achievements; a smaller plaque contains a list of 119 flyers trained by the Wright brothers. From here can be seen Huffman Field and Wright-Patterson Air Force Base. The Wrights made experimental flights at Huffman, the world's first airport and also the site of the first pilot training school. The first controlled turn was completed there in 1904.

97. Oxford, Ohio

In 1803 this area of southwestern Ohio was set aside as the future site of educational institutions. Miami University was established in 1809, and the village of Oxford was laid out the following year. Although in the midst of a farming region, it remains primarily a university town.

Miami University *High St.* Miami, a state institution, has an enrollment of more than 13,000 and branches in other cities in the state.

NUMISMATIC COLLECTION *King Library* Although this is not an especially large collection, it is of excellent quality. Displayed here is a good range of rare coins dating from about the sixth century B.C. to the third century A.D.

WILLIAM HOLMES MCGUFFEY MONUMENT *Campus Ave.* The noted author and educator compiled the first two of his six famous *Eclectic Readers* while a language

[**97.** *Miami University-McGuffey Museum*] *McGuffey wrote his first four readers in this house. The primers, spellers and readers were very popular—the major educational influence in the Middle West until the 1900s.*

teacher at Miami (1826-36). This monument, located in the courtyard of McGuffey Hall, includes a bronze bust of McGuffey and a charming group of young children reading a book.

WILLIAM HOLMES MCGUFFEY MUSEUM *Spring and Oak Sts.* This restored house, completed by McGuffey in 1833, contains many objects associated with him. These include a large collection of McGuffey readers, other early textbooks and the octagonal table desk he used while working on his readers. *Open Tues., Sat., Sun. Sept.-July except holidays.*

Pioneer Farm and Home *Brown Rd., Huseton Woods State Park* Artifacts of midwestern farm life in the early 19th century enliven this restored 1830s house and barn. Household furnishings, early farm tools, carriages, old bottles and stoneware are displayed. Annual features include a spring arts and crafts show and fall apple butter festival. *Open daily late May-Oct.*

Western College This small private college, now coeducational, was founded for women in 1853. Its art collection, displayed in several buildings, is worthy of note. The paintings include 19th-century American and French works by Inness, Blakelock and others; Japanese prints, Oriental artifacts and pottery pieces of the mound builders can also be seen. *Open daily.*

KUMLER MEMORIAL CHAPEL The college's lovely stone chapel is a reproduction of a 14th-century church in Normandy. Built in 1918, it has a semicircular apse, a tower with a dentil cornice beneath its steep roof and several fine stained-glass windows.

98. Glendower State Memorial *Rte. 42, Lebanon, Ohio* John Milton Williams, local lawyer and county prosecutor, built the Greek Revival mansion in the early 1840s. At that time the house was a single rectangular unit with front and rear porticos; later, wings were added. A captain's walk tops the large brick building. Interior features of the 13-room house include a central stairway, with cherry balustrade, that extends from the first floor to the attic. Furnishings are of the period. *Open Tues.-Sun. Apr.-Oct. Small charge.*

[**101.** *Cincinnati Art Museum*] *This display of European plucked lutes from the 15th through the 19th centuries shows the exquisite workmanship that went into the making of musical instruments. The lute at the far left, made in Italy around 1600, has Arabic letters in the ivory sound-hole rose. It was meant to be sold in Turkey.*

99. Warren County Historical Society Museum *105 S. Broadway, Lebanon, Ohio* Beautifully housed in Harmon Hall, the three-floor historical museum depicts life in southwestern Ohio from prehistoric days through the 19th century. Included in the museum are 14 charming shops surrounding an interior village green, five period rooms, a small chapel and a school, a log cabin, early farm equipment and vehicles, paleontology and archaeology exhibits and an unusually good Shaker display. Many fine examples of early American arts and crafts can be seen. There is an excellent genealogical research library. *Open Tues.-Sun. Small charge.*

100. Christian Waldschmidt House *7567 Rte. 50, Camp Dennison, Ohio* Christian Waldschmidt, who came here in 1794 from Lancaster County, Pennsylvania, completed this fieldstone "Pennsylvania Dutch"-style house in 1804. Near it he and his fellow settlers established a church, a store, a sawmill, distillery and—across the road from the house—Ohio's first paper mill. The house has now been restored and furnished to reflect those early pioneer days. Iron pots and kettles hang in the huge kitchen fireplace; the 18th- and early 19th-century furniture includes several Waldschmidt pieces. During the Civil War the house served as a Union Army induction and training center, and its ground-floor museum room holds a number of relics from this and earlier periods. *Open Sun. Apr.-May, Sat., Sun. June-Aug., Sun. Sept.-Oct.*

101. Cincinnati, Ohio

In 1788 settlers from New Jersey and other Mideastern states purchased a million acres of land along the Ohio River and established several settlements there. Two years later the main settlement was named for the Society of the Cincinnati, an organization of Revolutionary War officers that in turn had been named in honor of the Roman hero Lucius Quinctius Cincinnatus. The city grew quickly and became a manufacturing and trading center of the Midwest. It also became the gateway to the South as steamboats traveling the Ohio brought goods to and from the southern states. Today Cincinnati has a population of about half a million and continues as one of the region's important industrial and commercial cities.

Cincinnati Art Museum *Eden Park* On display in this handsome Greek Revival building is a superb collection of painting, sculpture, prints and decorative works spanning 5000 years in the history of world art. Works from ancient Egypt, Greece, Rome and the Near and Far East join Gothic and Renaissance masterworks and a wide representation of later European art. The impressive collection of American art includes several portraits by the Peales, Kellogg and Harding, and important works by Bingham, Inness (*Near the Village*), Hopper, Cassatt (*Mother and Child*) and Grant Wood (*Daughters of Revolution*). A number of magnificent period rooms are highlighted by the completely authentic Paris salon of the late 1700s. The 110 galleries here also hold one of the nation's finest collections of musical instruments plus many costumes. The museum's activities include temporary exhibits, lectures and art classes. *Open daily except Thanksgiving Day and Dec. 25.*

Cincinnati City Hall *801 Plum St.* A typical 1890s Romanesque castle of brownstone and granite with clock tower and cathedral steeple, the building is especially notable for its stained-glass windows. On each of three landings of the grand marble staircase are five huge windows portraying in brilliant colors the founding of Cincinnati, the building of the early log cabin city, Cincinnatus abandoning the plow for the sword and other themes of significance to the city. *Open Mon.-Fri. except holidays.*

Cincinnati Museum of Natural History *1720 Gilbert Ave.* Three walk-through exhibits make this an unusually interesting museum. Over 1300 stalactites and stalagmites decorate the dimly lit interior of a man-made, full-size cave. Rubber bats hang on the walls and live fish swim in a stream. "Talking telephones" help visitors understand the geological features and strange cave animals. The Ohio Wilderness Trail takes visitors through the woodland and marsh environment of the Ohio of 150 years ago, complete with native birds and animals and the changing seasons. Finally, the

Indian Path traces Ohio's Indian history from the Ice Age through modern times, with authentically detailed, full-scale dioramas. The museum's planetarium offers shows on weekends. *Open Tues.–Sun. except holidays. Small charge.*

Cincinnati Union Terminal *1301 Western Ave.* Completed in 1933 at a cost of more than $41,000,000, the station contains several impressive murals of inlaid Italian mosaic, the work of Winold Reiss. The largest of these, double panels in the front rotunda, depict individual figures ranging from Indians to modern-day workers, while in the background types of transportation and the development of Ohio River Valley shipping and industry are portrayed. *Open daily.*

Cincinnati Zoo *3400 Vine St.* Five Persian leopards are included in the cat collection of this zoo, the second oldest in the country and one of the nation's finest. The zoo has a remarkable record for breeding animals in captivity: more lowland gorillas were born here than in any other U.S. zoo. The Bird of Prey Flight Cage, 72 feet high, accommodates 16 large birds, among them some vultures and an American bald eagle. Another unusual feature is a large area in which elephants, a hippopotamus and pygmy hippos roam. *Open daily. Adults $1.75, children small charge.*

KEMPER LOG HOUSE James Kemper, who was a schoolteacher, farmer, surveyor and, later, a minister, moved his family into this dwelling in 1804, on the night his 15th child was born. The four-room log structure, which has been relocated to the zoo grounds, is the oldest surviving house in Cincinnati. It contains furniture, pewter and other household items of the period, most of which were Kemper family possessions. *Open daily May–Sept. Small charge.*

[**101.** *St. Peter in Chains and City Hall*] *The towers of church and state contend with each other in downtown Cincinnati, where the Greek Revival cathedral stands beside the late 19th-century Romanesque-style city hall.*

Irwin M. Krohn Conservatory *950 Eden Park Dr.* In large greenhouses surrounded by attractive trees and shrubbery is an excellent collection of desert and tropical plants. Many handsome varieties of ferns, palms, orchids and cacti are displayed. Five seasonal floral displays are presented every year. *Open daily.*

Plum Street (Isaac M. Wise) Temple *Eighth and Plum Sts.* Two tall, ornate minarcts contrast with the horizontal roof parapets above the entrance and give the synagogue a definite Moorish air. Gothic elements include several rose windows. The interior is lavishly decorated with rich gilding, Moorish-type arabesques and stained-glass windows framed by Hebrew inscriptions. Completed in 1866, the temple is named for the rabbi who pioneered Reform Judaism in the U.S. and founded Cincinnati's Hebrew Union College. *Open Fri. evenings and Jewish holidays.*

St. Gregory Seminary of the Athenaeum of Ohio *6616 Beechmont Ave.* The large granite and limestone building, housing the college seminary of the Archdiocese of Cincinnati, is an impressive example of Lombard Romanesque design. Part of its facade is decorated with an arcaded walk that extends on each side of a six-columned central portico. The chapel, modeled after a fifth-century church in Ravenna, Italy, has handsome stained-glass windows and graceful arches supported by Corinthian columns. In the marble-floored atrium is a huge painting, *Christ's Triumphal Entry into Jerusalem,* done in 1820 by Benjamin Haydon. Wordsworth, Hazlitt, Keats and other literary friends of the artist appear in the crowd around Christ. *Open daily.*

St. Monica Church *328 W. McMillan St.* St. Monica Church has been built and adorned with care. The facade is decorated with statues by Clement J. Barnhorn, an eminent ecclesiastical sculptor and native of Cincinnati. A massive bronze crucifix over the altar is also his work. The Shrine of the Sacred Heart and depictions of saints were painted by Carl Zimmerman in Byzantine style. Their brilliant colors, and those of the stained-glass windows imported from Munich, create a warm light that pervades the church. *Open daily.*

St. Peter in Chains Cathedral *Plum and Eighth Sts.* Amid the bustle of downtown Cincinnati, the cathedral is a calming sight. The gleaming white limestone edifice surrounded by green lawns merits the name of "White Angel" given it by its early parishioners. Built in 1845, it is the oldest cathedral west of the Allegheny Mountains and has been called "one of the most distinguished monuments of native American architecture." Today, after extensive renovations, it retains an extraordinary artistic unity. The architecture is Greek Revival at its best, and the interior decor reinforces the Greek motif. Fluted Corinthian columns, flanked by the Stations of the Cross in a style reminiscent of early Greek vases, guide the eye to the altar. Bronze statues, carved mahogany woodwork and cream and black marble give rich effect to classically pure lines. Among the cathedral's art treasures is a 16th-century crucifix by Benvenuto Cellini. *Open daily.*

[**101.** *Taft Museum*] *The classical restraint of early 19th-century Federal-style architecture and interiors provides dignified surroundings for the display of the Taft collections. Seen here is the ballroom.*

Taft Museum *316 Pike St.* The historic mansion, built in 1820, is an excellent example of the Federal style. The entrance portico, with four Doric columns and a wrought-iron railing, was the scene of the 1908 acceptance of the Republican Presidential nomination by William Howard Taft, half-brother of Charles Phelps Taft, owner of the house. Charles and Anna Sinton Taft's magnificent art collection is displayed in the gracefully proportioned rooms of their home, redecorated according to the taste of the 1820s with Duncan Phyfe furniture and English Regency and French Empire fabrics. On the walls hang portraits by such European masters as Rembrandt, Goya, Reynolds and Gainsborough, and such Americans as Sargent and Whistler. Landscapes are by Corot, Millet, Turner and Rousseau. The Tafts amassed one of the nation's best collections of French Renaissance painted enamel portraits and more than 200 Chinese porcelains from the 17th and 18th centuries. Concerts and exhibitions are presented during the year. Formal gardens adjoin the impressive house. *Open daily except Thanksgiving Day and Dec. 25.*

Tyler-Davidson Fountain *Fountain Sq., Fifth and Vine Sts.* In 1871 Henry Probasco donated this elaborate fountain, with carved figures representing the genius of water, to the city as a memorial for his brother-in-law. When the city's center was renovated recently the fountain was preserved, and now the sleek lines of modern buildings contrast with the rococo testimonial.

102. Hillforest *213 Fifth St., Aurora, Ind.* In 1852, when times were flourishing along the big rivers, Thomas Gaff began constructing this elegant house on a high bluff with a sweeping view of the Ohio River. Gaff, an industrialist who owned a fleet of cargo boats and palacelike steamboats that plied the rivers, built Hillforest in basic Italian Renaissance style. But the delicate columns that support one circular veranda on another, topped with a pilot house cupola, give the mansion a definite "Steamboat Gothic" appearance. Hillforest has been painstakingly restored inside and out, and furnished in mid-Victorian style. *Open Tues.-Sun. Apr.-Dec. Small charge.*

103. Cathedral Basilica of the Assumption *12th St. and Madison Ave., Covington, Ky.* Its superb stained-glass windows have given this 13th-century French Gothic-style Catholic edifice its popular name, the Cathedral of Glass. The church, modeled after Notre Dame, also contains four huge Frank Duveneck murals depicting episodes in the life of Christ and a number of sculptures by Clement Barnhorn. More than 60,000 pieces of Venetian mosaic tile appear in each of the fine Stations of the Cross. *Open daily.*

104. Liberty Hall Museum *218 Wilkinson St., Frankfort, Ky.* The imposing brick house was built around 1796 for John Brown, one of the first two senators to represent the young state of Kentucky. A distinguished statesman, Brown entertained famous guests such as James Monroe, Andrew Jackson and Zachary Taylor. Although the outside appearance of the house is Georgian, the interior reveals Federal influence. Splendidly furnished with antiques—many from the Brown family—it is a vivid glimpse of home styles 200 years ago. *Open Tues.-Sun. Small charge.*

105. Old State House *Broadway and St. Clair St., Frankfort, Ky.* Designed by Gideon Shryock, this is among the finest Greek Revival structures in the U.S. and Shryock's greatest achievement. Among its many distinctions is a self-supporting spiral staircase in the rotunda. The building was completed in 1830 and served as the capitol until 1910. It now houses the Kentucky Historical Society and a museum that contains Daniel Boone's "Ticklicker"—a flintlock rifle inscribed "Boons Best Fren"—Pontiac's tomahawk and the pistol with which Aaron Burr shot Alexander Hamilton in their 1804 duel in Weehawken, N.J. *Open daily.*

106. Orlando Brown House *Wapping and Wilkinson Sts., Frankfort, Ky.* This 1835 brick house is one of the few private residences designed by Shryock. It was a gift from U.S. Senator John Brown to his son Orlando. On display are the Browns' furniture, china and silver as well as family portraits by Matthew Jouett and John Neagle. *Open Tues.-Sun. Small charge.*

107. Duncan Tavern Historic Center *323 High St., Paris, Ky.* The imposing 20-room tavern of native limestone has existed longer than the state of Kentucky: it was built in 1788, four years before Kentucky was admitted to the Union. The tavern is furnished throughout with attractive period antiques and contains an excellent library of history and genealogy. The Anne Duncan House next door, a clapboarded log structure, also displays furnishings of the period, including fine examples of cabinetwork. *Open daily except holidays. Adults $1.25, children small charge.*

108. Lexington, Ky.

Lexington owes its name to a group of frontiersmen who were camping at its site in 1775 when news of the Battle of Lexington reached them. The city was founded four years later. Today it is the main center in the U.S. for the raising of thoroughbred horses.

[**101.** *Tyler-Davidson Fountain*] *Sumptuous curves of figures in the 100-year-old fountain are seen in relief against the sleek lines of a skyscraper.* Genius of Water *figure on top stands nine feet high, weighs two tons.*

American Saddle Horse Museum *Spindletop Farm, Ironworks Pike (7 mi. N. of Lexington)* The American saddle horse, a type that was developed chiefly in Kentucky, is bred for intelligence, stamina and show-horse brilliance. At this former saddle-horse nursery, the collections feature saddles, harnesses, carriages, equine oil paintings and trophies. *Open Tues.-Sun. Apr.-Oct. Small charge.*

Ashland *E. Main St. and Sycamore Rd.* Henry Clay, the "Great Pacificator" and architect of the Compromise of 1850, lived in the beautiful mansion for more than 40 years, until his death in 1852. The furnishings and other possessions of four generations of the Clay family can be seen. On 20 surrounding acres visitors can visit Clay's icehouses, smokehouses and caretaker's cottage, and a lovely garden. *Open daily except Dec. 25. Small charge.*

Headley Jewel Museum and Library *Old Frankfurt Pike (4 mi. W. of Lexington)* Jeweled bibelots in gold and platinum, most of them designed by George Headley and executed by leading jewelers around the world, are housed in an exquisitely proportioned building that is itself a masterpiece of design. The collection also includes specimen stones and minerals and snuff boxes of the 17th and 18th centuries. *Open Wed., Sat., Sun. Adults $2.00, students small charge.*

Hunt-Morgan House *201 N. Mill St.* Cavalry commander John Hunt Morgan, the "Thunderbolt of the Confederacy," lived in this town house built for his grandfather in 1812-4. It is a fine example of late Georgian architecture and the fanlight doorway, unsupported square staircase and courtyard are especially noteworthy. *Open Tues.-Sun. Feb.-Dec. except Thanksgiving Day and Dec. 25. Small charge.*

Memorial Hall *University of Kentucky, Limestone St. and Euclid Ave.* The hall's steeple, a landmark of the Bluegrass region, looks out over what was once part of the oldest buffalo trace in North America and is now one of Lexington's main arteries. The building is dedicated to the Kentuckians who died in World War I. *Open Mon.-Fri.*

Waveland State Shrine *Higbee Mill Rd., off Rte. 27* This Greek Revival mansion, completed in 1847, is the center of a restored plantation village that gives a picture of Kentucky life from pioneer days through the opulent antebellum period. On the 10-acre site are slave quarters, a blacksmith's and a harness and cobbler's shop, a country store, a printshop, an icehouse and a meat house. There is also a collection of Civil War weapons and pioneer household implements. *Open Tues.-Sun. except Jan. 1 and Dec. 25. Small charge.*

109. Old Fort Harrod State Park *Rtes. 68 and 127, Harrodsburg, Ky.* In Harrodsburg, in 1774, James Harrod and his companions made the first permanent settlement west of the Alleghenies, and this state park commemorates their achievement. It contains a reproduction of the fort they built, with blockhouses and cabins furnished with handmade utensils and furniture. In the old cemetery are graves of more than 500 early settlers. Inside the Lincoln Marriage Temple is the cabin in which Abraham Lincoln's parents were married in 1806. Other mementos of Kentucky history can be found in the 1830 Mansion Museum, which includes a Lincoln Room and a Confederate Room. An outdoor drama, *The Legend of Daniel Boone,* is performed nightly from late June through early September in the park's amphitheater. *Open daily Mar.-Oct., Tues.-Sun. Nov.-Feb. Small charge.*

110. Shakertown at Pleasant Hill *Rte. 68, N.E. of Harrodsburg, Ky.* The attractive village contains 27 19th-century buildings, 20 of which have been restored to reflect the life-style of the Shakers who lived here from 1805 to 1910. The handsome frame and brick structures, located in the midst of 2250 acres of original Shaker farmland, include the 1824 Center Family Dwelling House with exhibits and Shaker rooms, the 1809 Farm Deacon's Shop and the 1845 East Family Brethren's Shop with its display of early farm and carpentry tools. *Open daily except Dec. 25. Adults $2.50, children over 6 small charge.*

[**108.** *Headley Jewel Museum*] *An 18-karat-gold Benin king astride a rhinoceros carved from chloromelanite is one of designer Headley's bibelots on display. Rubies decorate the rhino's chain and the king's headdress.*

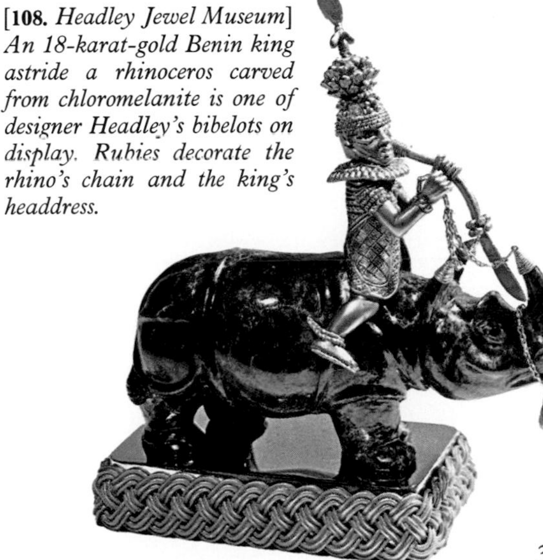

111. McDowell House and Apothecary Shop *125 S. Second St., Danville, Ky.* The first drugstore in the U.S. west of the Alleghenies, McDowell's Apothecary Shop, was opened in 1795 in the two-room brick building adjoining the large frame house that was the home of the proprietor, Dr. Ephraim McDowell. Both buildings have been restored and refurnished, and the shop is supplied with ointment jars, drawers full of old-fashioned drugs and other equipment of the period. In the home visitors can see the operating room where the pioneer surgeon performed a remarkable abdominal operation, a milestone in surgical history, on Christmas night, 1809. *Open daily except Dec. 25. Small charge.*

112. Wallace Nutting Museum *Berea College, Berea, Ky.* The collection comprises reproductions of early American furniture—a slant-top, carved-frame desk, a canopy bed, a four-drawer lowboy—all antiques in their own right. They were made by Wallace Nutting, who devoted much of his life to keeping alive the art of woodcraft. Berea College today carries on this craft, partly as a result of Nutting's efforts and support. *Open Mon.-Sat.*

113. Rutherford B. Hayes State Memorial *1337 Hayes Ave., Fremont, Ohio* Hayes was a prominent army general, a congressman and a governor of Ohio before he was elected the 19th President of the U.S. in 1876. It was in 1873 that he moved to his uncle's 25-acre estate, known as Spiegel Grove, a property he inherited within a year.

HAYES HOME The manor house at Spiegel Grove, where Hayes lived for 20 years, is a Victorian structure built between 1859 and 1863 by Sardis Birchard, his uncle; large wings were added in 1880 and 1889. The elaborate furnishings are those of the Hayes family, and include some items from the White House. *Open daily except holidays. Small charge.*

[112] *Twin bed with fluted posts and canopy frame is one of the Colonial designs copied by cabinetmaker Wallace Nutting. He is largely responsible for keeping alive the tradition of handcrafted American furniture.*

HAYES LIBRARY AND MUSEUM More than 10,000 volumes from Hayes's personal library, along with his personal papers, correspondence, diaries and other materials are housed here. A research library contains more than a million manuscripts and 100,000 books relating to 19th-century America. The museum features items that belonged to the Hayes family, including a doll house, a sideboard from the White House, a Presidential carriage, White House china, Civil War and Indian relics. *Library open Mon.-Sat. except holidays, museum open daily except holidays. Small charge for museum.*

RUTHERFORD B. HAYES TOMB A granite burial monument, located on a knoll within the estate, marks the graves of the President and his wife, Lucy Webb Hayes. The monument was designed by President Hayes, and the stone was quarried on his father's Vermont farm. Hayes died on Jan. 17, 1893.

114. Milan Historical Museum *10 Edison Dr., Milan, Ohio* A fine collection of art glass, dolls, period furniture and antique toys and guns are among the attractions of this museum of early Americana. They are housed in an 1840s brick dwelling, once the home of the doctor who assisted at the birth of Thomas Edison. Behind the house are a reconstructed blacksmith shop and a country store with authentic wares and post office corner. Next to it is the Edna Roe Newton Memorial Art Building, containing paintings and decorative objects from all parts of the world. *Open Tues.-Sun. Apr.-Oct.*

115. Thomas A. Edison Birthplace Museum *9 Edison Dr., Milan, Ohio* The great inventor of the microphone, electric incandescent light, phonograph and dozens of other devices (he held 1097 U.S. patents) was born in this brick cottage in 1847. Edison bought the dwelling in 1906. It was not until a visit in 1923 that he found his old home—ironically—was without electricity and he promptly had it wired. Today the house contains family objects, original furnishings, and letters, pictures and sketches that belonged to Edison. *Open Fri.-Sun. mid-Feb.-Mar., Tues.-Sun. Apr.-Nov. Adults and children over 6 small charge.*

116. Great Lakes Historical Society Museum *480 Main St., Vermilion, Ohio* Preservation of Great Lakes history is the objective of this museum. Situated on the south shore of Lake Erie, it houses special collections of paintings, ship models, engines, marine artifacts and the Clarence S. Metcalf reference library. *Open Tues.-Sun. and Mon. holidays Mar.-mid-Dec., Sat., Sun. and holidays mid-Dec.-Feb. Small charge.*

117. Allen Memorial Art Museum *Oberlin College, Lorain and Main Sts., Oberlin, Ohio* The first college museum west of the Allegheny Mountains, this handsome Italian Renaissance-style building houses one of the finest collections of art on any U.S. campus. In addition to an extensive art library, there are a spacious sculpture court and picture galleries where art from ancient Egypt to the present is effectively displayed. European masterpieces include a canvas by Rubens and prints by Dürer and Rembrandt. Oriental rugs, Japanese woodcuts, a fine costume collection and 1400 American pressed glass goblets are also exhibited. *Open daily.*

[118] *Kingwood Hall, the French Provincial-style home built by the industrialist Charles Kelley King in 1926, is now used as an educational, cultural and recreational center. Collections of coins, stamps and minerals as well as wildlife are exhibited. Nature trails have been laid out on the grounds, and each summer 12 separate gardens blossom with beautiful displays of flowers.*

118. Kingwood Center *900 Park Ave. W., Mansfield, Ohio* Formerly the private estate of an affluent industrialist, Charles Kelley King, the 47-acre tract is landscaped with impressive displays of flowers, trees and shrubs. Bird fanciers can see geese, ducks, pheasants and peafowl in the gardens. Kingwood Hall, the estate's 27-room mansion, has many original furnishings as well as a lending library of books on botany, gardening and nature study. Flower and art shows, lectures and demonstrations are regularly scheduled. *Grounds open daily, mansion open Tues.-Sat. except holidays.*

119. Oak Hill Cottage *2310 Springmill St., Mansfield, Ohio* Novelist Louis Bromfield referred to this Gothic-style brick house as Shane's Castle in *The Green Bay Tree* (1924). Built in 1847, with carved woodwork around the edges of its gable roof, it is reputed to have been a stop on the "Underground Railroad" for escaped slaves. The house contains decorative Victorian furniture, and there are gas chandeliers and marble fireplaces in every room. *Open daily. Small charge.*

120. Louis Bromfield Malabar Farm *Rte. 1, Lucas, Ohio* The famous American author and conservationist purchased almost 600 acres here in 1939 and transformed them into a model farm employing the latest agricultural methods. Today the farm is an important center of agricultural and ecological research. The large frame house consists of 31 rooms furnished exactly as they were at the time of the novelist's death in 1956. The author's study contains his semicircular desk, a typewriter and the card table he used for writing, as well as his collection of books and many personal belongings. Bromfield is buried on the grounds, which include nature trails, picnic areas and a rose garden where Hollywood stars Humphrey Bogart and Lauren Bacall were married. Wagons drawn by tractors carry visitors around the farm on Sundays between May and the end of September. *Open daily. Small charge; wagon tour small additional charge.*

121. Museum of Burmese Arts and Crafts *Denison University, Granville, Ohio* More than 900 items of Burmese art are on display here. The collection is the principal U.S. reference source for study of this specialized and absorbing art interest. Included is a rare 11th-century standing Buddha, the only one of its type to be seen in a Western museum. *Open Mon.-Fri. mid-Sept.-mid-May.*

122. Ohio Railway Museum *990 Proprietors Rd., Worthington, Ohio* Restored trolleys, electric interurban and railway cars form the bulk of this unusual collection, all of which is in operating condition. Visitors can take scheduled trips on an electric or steam train with a post office car, a coach-baggage car, two Pullman cars and an observation car fitted with a kitchen, berths and wicker furniture, or on several streetcars. A full-size reproduction of a typical small town depot of the 1880s serves as a museum which displays photographs and many objects once associated with Ohio railroading. *Open Sun. Apr.-May, Sat., Sun. June-Aug., Sun. Sept.-Nov. Small charge.*

123. Licking County Historical Society Museum *Sixth St. Park, Newark, Ohio* A fine old Federal-style house, built about 1820 and known as the Sherwood-Davidson House, serves as the society's museum. It is furnished as a distinguished mid-19th-century home and contains many impressive antique furnishings and decorative pieces. Among these are an 18th-century Dutch grandfather clock that plays four tunes and a silver collection dating from the period of King George III. The pedimented fan doorway and two-story recessed porch topped by a low elliptical arch are striking features of the exterior. Behind the museum is the handsome 1835 Buckingham House, scene of the society's meetings and temporary exhibits. *Open Wed., Fri.-Mon. Adults small charge.*

124. Columbus, Ohio

Columbus, located in the center of Ohio, was established in 1812 as the state capital. It has since become one of Ohio's important centers of industry and commerce, with a population of about half a million. As the home of Ohio State University and other colleges, it is noted for its educational facilities. The city is named for Christopher Columbus.

Columbus Gallery of Fine Arts *480 E. Broad St.* The gallery's home, a handsome Italian Renaissance-style building, was constructed in 1931. The one painting no one should miss is Rubens' *Christ Triumphant Over Sin and Death.* The Howald Collection contains an impressive number of works by modern masters: five each by Picasso and Matisse, seven by Derain, 28 by John Marin. The Bellows Room honors Columbus-born George Bellows—13 of his paintings hang here. *Open daily.*

German Village *1 mi. S. of city center* Red brick houses with wrought-iron fences and brick sidewalks along cobblestone streets make this a distinctive section of the city. In the mid-19th century German settlers built these solid houses with their thick walls and cut-stone lintels. About 450 of the original homes, stores and other buildings have been restored in the 233-acre historical district. Bazaars and shops offer handcrafted items; sausage houses provide regional food.

Ohio Historical Center *Rte. 71 and 17th Ave.* Two buildings in one, the center houses at ground level the museum services of the Ohio Historical Society, with three main display areas: natural history, archaeology and history. In the three-story, cantilevered block that seems to float above the museum base are the society's library, archives and offices. In the mall areas of the museum, artifacts made by Ohio's prehistoric mound builders are displayed in pits that make glass partitions unnecessary. *Open daily.*

Ohio Statehouse *Broad and High Sts.* Abraham Lincoln and Stephen A. Douglas made speeches from the fourth (and present) Ohio state capitol, which was completed in 1861. Eight huge Doric columns set off the entrance. The floor of the rotunda contains 4892 blocks of marble, including varicolored pieces symbolizing the 13 original states. The great dome, which rises about 120 feet, is decorated with plaques commemorating the eight U.S. Presidents who came from Ohio. *Open daily.*

MY JEWELS MONUMENT Seven Ohio citizens who gained fame in the Civil War are commemorated by this monument on the statehouse grounds. It consists of a statue of Cornelia, the Roman matron who said that her sons were her greatest jewels, extending her arms toward the figures of Grant, Sheridan, Sherman, Garfield, Chase, Stanton and Hayes grouped below.

125. Square 13 Historical District *Bounded by Main, Broad, Wheeling and High Sts., Lancaster, Ohio* More than a dozen architecturally handsome homes of the early 19th century ring Square 13, the first land plot laid out by Lancaster's town planner, Ebeneezer Zane, in 1800. Pillared doorways, curved windows and hand-carved cornices are among the many graceful notes of these houses, which feature Greek Revival, Italianate and Federal architecture.

SHERMAN HOUSE STATE MEMORIAL *137 E. Main St.* Judge Charles Sherman built a small frame house here in 1811 and expanded it within a few years for his family of 11 children. Two famous sons—General William Tecumseh Sherman and Senator John Sherman—were born in the home, which the family occupied for 33 years. The original dining room, master bedroom and

[**124.** *Gallery of Fine Arts*] Polo at Lakewood *painted in 1910 by George Bellows is one of many of his works in the museum. Bellows was born in Columbus and lived there until he left to study in New York City.*

children's room are restored; later additions include a reception room that held the judge's office and an area given over to a re-creation of General Sherman's field tent and its equipment. Sherman family memorabilia and other Civil War items are also at hand. *Open Tues.-Sun. June-Oct. Small charge.*

126. Mound City Group National Monument *4 mi. N. of Chillicothe, Ohio* Early American Indians of the prehistoric Hopewell culture used the site as a burial ground: 23 mounds are enclosed within low earthwork walls. The Visitor Center contains exquisitely crafted tools, ornaments and ceremonial objects. *Site open daily except Jan. 1 and Dec. 25. Visitor Center open daily June-early Sept.*

127. Serpent Mound State Memorial *Rte. 73, Peebles, Ohio* The mysterious and fascinating effigy of a giant snake curves along a hilltop for almost a quarter of a mile. The prehistoric Adena Indians probably constructed the serpent some time between 1000 B.C. and 700 A.D. Excavations have established that the religious or mystical design (its significance is still unknown) was first laid out with stones and lumps of clay and covered with soil. Several nearby conical mounds have yielded remains of the Adena Indians and their implements, and the memorial's museum holds artifacts, diagrams, a diorama and the reconstructed cross-section of an actual grave. *Open daily.*

128. Washington Historic District *Washington, Ky.* Laid out in 1785 on land purchased from Simon Kenton, the great Indian fighter, Washington was a stopping place for westward-bound pioneers and grew rapidly into a trading center. Thirty-three of the early buildings still stand, flanked by the original flagstone sidewalks. In 1969 the town was placed on the National Register of Historic Places. The buildings described below are located on Main Street, once a part of the buffalo trace—the trail followed by annual migrations of buffalo. *Buildings below open daily May-early Sept., Fri.-Sun. early Sept.-Dec. $2.00 or small charge each house.*

ALBERT SIDNEY JOHNSTON HOME General Johnston, one of the South's ablest officers, spent his childhood

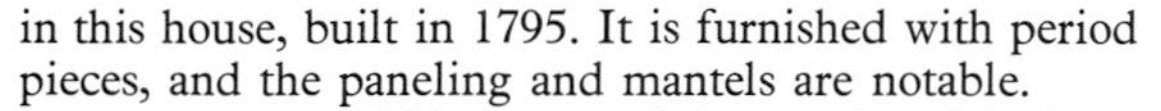

in this house, built in 1795. It is furnished with period pieces, and the paneling and mantels are notable.

CANE BRAKE This is one of the town's original log houses and is typical of its earliest structures. It is now a state shrine to Simon Kenton.

MEFFORD'S STATION George Mefford's little log cabin is a "flatboat" house—he used wood from his boat to build some of the interior walls and flooring. The house dates back to 1787 and was the first in the area to be built outside a protected fort.

OLD CHURCH MUSEUM The 1848 structure, once a Methodist church, houses church memorabilia.

PAXTON INN Built about 1810, the inn has been restored and furnished with period pieces. Its features include a museum and a genealogical library.

129. Kirtland Temple *9020 Chillicothe Rd., Kirtland, Ohio* The temple of the Reorganized Church of Jesus Christ of Latter Day Saints was completed in 1836. The two-foot-thick walls of the three-story building are constructed of native stone on a framework of oak beams and are plastered white. The interior of the temple still contains the original hand-molded and carved pulpits and pews. Pulpits are located in both the front and back of the sanctuaries, and pews are designed so the congregation can face either way. The architectural effect, both inside and out, is one of simple elegance. *Open daily.*

130. Cleveland, Ohio

Founded in 1796 by General Moses Cleaveland, the pioneer surveyor of northern Ohio, the great city on Lake Erie grew slowly at first. Only when water routes opened south to the Ohio River and along the Great Lakes did Cleveland mushroom commercially. Today it is Ohio's largest city and home of prominent steel, iron, shipping and tool industries. Cleveland is also distinguished for one of the country's first professional resident theaters and an internationally renowned symphony orchestra.

Arcade *401 Euclid Ave.* One of the largest structures of its kind in the U.S., the enclosed area, completed in 1890, extends between two 10-story office buildings. Covered by a vast skylight is a 300-foot-long promenade, with five levels of shops along the sides. The decorative iron grillwork on the balcony balustrades and the newel posts at the head of the grand staircase are especially worth seeing. *Open daily.*

Cleveland Cultural Gardens *East and Liberty Blvds., Rockefeller Park* The cultures, philosophies and histories of a number of countries are reflected in the unique 35-acre landscaped area on a wooded hillside. Paved paths connecting the different ethnic gardens take visitors past outstanding plantings, plaques, busts, inscriptions and monuments devoted to particular cultures. There are Irish, Hebrew, American, German and Italian gardens as well as 15 other displays. *Open daily.*

Cleveland Museum of Art *11150 East Blvd.* See feature display on pages 348–9.

Cleveland Museum of Natural History *Wade Oval, University Circle* These interesting and diverse collections stress the natural history of Ohio and the Cleveland area, with fine exhibits of vertebrate paleontology, ecology and anthropology. Displays include an Ohio dinosaur, the Johnstown Mastodon and the skull of a 350,000,000-year-old armored fish. Fluorescent minerals are featured in a display of precious stones. Other facilities include a research library, observatory and planetarium. *Open daily except holidays. Adults and children over 6 small charge except Tues.*

Cleveland Public Library *325 Superior Ave.* The country's second largest public library is housed in two neoclassic buildings linked by attractive gardens. Choice items from its collections of rare books, Orientalia and chess books are displayed in changing exhibits. In the magazine room, a mural by William Sommer re-creates early 19th-century Cleveland. *Open Mon.-Sat.*

Cleveland Zoological Park *Brookside Park* Many of the 1100 animals here at the nation's fifth oldest zoo live in conditions resembling their native habitats: five different species of bears shelter in simulated rock grottos, hoofed animals roam across a plain, and lions and tigers stalk a veld (all, of course, separated from visitors by moats). A yak herd and the beautiful Bird Building with its exotic species and the adjacent Waterfowl Lake are among the special attractions. The Children's Farm includes a red barn and friendly animals. Key-operated "Talking Story Books" throughout the attractively landscaped grounds describe exhibits for children. *Open daily except Jan. 1 and Dec. 25. Adults and children over 6 small charge.*

[127] *This quarter-mile-long serpent mound was probably built by the Adena Indians. Numerous mounds exist in the eastern half of the U.S., and the prehistoric Indians who built them as burial, religious, temple and home sites had highly developed cultures as evidenced by artifacts found in their graves. It is unfortunate that the builders did not have the spectacular aerial view of their work that the airplane affords. They did, however, have a perspective.*

This French 16th-century tapestry is a woven allegory on the changing conditions of life from youth to old age.

Cleveland Museum of Art
11150 East Blvd., Cleveland, Ohio

The Cleveland Museum is not only among the country's finest in terms of the quality and range of its collections, it is also one of the most beautifully situated and pleasant to visit. The main building, Greek Revival in design, encloses a spacious garden court and, in turn, is seen within a graciously landscaped park of wooded terraces, flowering gardens, fountains and a lagoon. The thoughtful design of the building enables visitors to see all the collections and gain an overview of the major art periods and cultures of the world. This can be done here without developing a case of museum fatigue. In the relatively short span of about 60 years, there have been gathered together works by the greatest artists in Western painting from the Renaissance to the 20th century, such as Rembrandt, Rubens, Velázquez, Holbein, El Greco, Goya, Reynolds, Turner, Copley, van Gogh, Matisse, Picasso and de Kooning. In the medieval collection are three late Gothic tapestries and part of the Guelph Treasure of 11th-century ritual articles from the German cathedral of Brunswick. On view in the Treasure Room are textiles, ivories, jewelry and enameled pieces from the Coptic, early Christian and Byzantine civilizations. The museum is world renowned for its superb collection of Japanese art. The highly stylized paintings and decorative motifs of objects on view are outstanding not for originality but for the fine and subtle execution of ancient art formulas. First-rate examples of Chinese and Indian art may be seen, too, as well as Oceanic, African and Pre-Columbian works. Noteworthy in the last two collections are a 17th-century African bronze altar portrait of a Benin king and a Mayan head from Honduras sculpted from volcanic stone. Frequently special exhibits are mounted, and the lectures, films and concerts that make up the museum's educational and musical arts programs take place in a wing designed by architect Marcel Breuer and completed in 1971. Guides to the special exhibits and to the permanent collections are available. *Open Tues.–Sun. except holidays.*

In his 1883 painting Frieze of Dancers, *Degas's favorite subjects secure their ribbons before performing.*

George Wesley Bellows (1882–1925), the noted American painter from Columbus, Ohio, was especially interested in depicting the life of the common man. Like other early 20th-century American realists, his main concern was to capture movement and emotion on canvas. In Stag at Sharkey's *he emphasizes the attraction of a boxing-match crowd to the violence and grace of the sport but, in the realistic tradition, does not make a moral comment on their reactions. The picture is charged with animal energy.*

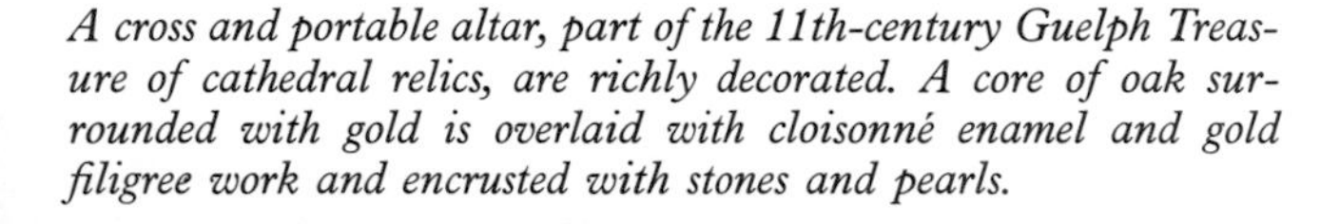

A cross and portable altar, part of the 11th-century Guelph Treasure of cathedral relics, are richly decorated. A core of oak surrounded with gold is overlaid with cloisonné enamel and gold filigree work and encrusted with stones and pearls.

Cuyahoga County Court House *1 Lakeside Ave.* The mural at the south end of the second floor, *Signing of the Magna Carta,* was completed by English artist Sir Frank Brangwyn. The mural at the opposite end, *Constitutional Convention of 1787,* was executed by Violet Oakley of Philadelphia. The building was erected in 1912 at a cost of approximately $5,000,000. *Open Mon.-Fri. except holidays.*

Garfield Monument *Lake View Cemetery between Euclid and Mayfield Aves.* In July 1881, James A. Garfield, the 20th President of the U.S., was shot by an assassin only four months after taking office and died two months later. He is buried in this Gothic-Romanesque memorial, a circular tower 50 feet in diameter and 180 feet high. At the base is a square stone porch with life-size bas-relief panels depicting episodes from Garfield's life. Inside the memorial hall, light filtering through 14 stained-glass windows (representing the 13 original states and Ohio) illuminates a handsome marble statue of Garfield. Deep red granite columns support the dome, decorated in gold and stone mosaics. *Open daily Apr.-Oct.*

Park Synagogue *3300 Mayfield Rd.* The wedge-shaped complex of interconnected brick buildings serves the world's largest Conservative Jewish congregation. It was designed by Eric Mendelsohn and completed in 1950. The most striking feature is a copper-covered dome over the sanctuary that rises 65 feet above floor level. The dome rests on a band of clear glass windows with a view of 33 acres of wooded grounds. In the synagogue's Gallery of Contemporary Art is a unique 75-foot wall created by Yaakov Agam. Thirty-six colored plastic panels move on tracks at the touch of a visitor's finger, offering innumerable chances to make an "original" abstract design. *Open daily.*

St. Michael the Archangel Church *3114 Scranton Rd.* The stone Catholic church, dedicated in 1892, is an excellent example of Gothic Revival architecture. It is distinguished by two spires of similar design but unequal height. The Historic American Building Survey of the National Park Service has cited St. Michael's for "outstanding beauty in architecture." The interior, with vaulted arches and high-ceilinged center nave, also has statues and decorations made of hand-carved oak imported from Germany. *Open daily.*

Shaker Historical Society Museum *16740 S. Park Blvd.* From 1821 to 1889 much of what is now Shaker Heights was owned by the North Union community of Shakers. Relics and historical materials of those early settlers are exhibited in this Tudor-style building. Visitors can see the Shakers' simple but beautifully crafted furniture and clothing and their labor-saving tools and inventions—all of which help toward understanding this unique group of people. *Open Tues.-Fri., Sun. except holidays.*

Soldiers' and Sailors' Monument *3 Euclid Ave.* William McKinley, then governor of Ohio, dedicated the monument on July 4, 1896, to the memory of Cuyahoga County citizens who served in the Civil War. The monument, designed by Levi T. Scofield, is an ornamental column rising 125 feet from a 100-foot square base. Around the base are bronze statues of servicemen in fighting scenes. Inside the monument are a number of bronze historical panels, one of which, with Abraham Lincoln as the central figure, represents the emancipation of the slaves. *Open Mon.-Sat. except holidays.*

Temple *University Circle and Silver Park* Tiled domes and graceful arches lighten the bulk of the Byzantine-style temple. The center of the limestone edifice is the seven-sided hall of worship, where the dome is 88 feet above floor level. Within the building is the Temple Museum of Religious and Ceremonial Art and Music. Exhibited here are Biblical antiquities, tapestries and ritual silver—more than 500 items related to Jewish religious ceremonies and everyday life. *Open Sun.-Fri. Jan.-May, Mon.-Fri. June-Aug., Sun.-Fri. Sept.-Dec. except Jewish holidays.*

War Memorial Fountain *The Mall* Man's spirit rising above the flames of war is depicted by the striking 35-foot bronze figure surrounded by four polished granite carvings. Names of World War II and Korean War dead are engraved on the base. Designed by Ohioan Marshall Fredericks, the impressive memorial was dedicated in 1964.

[**130.** *Western Reserve Museum*] *In 1970 the Western Reserve Historical Society opened an American Empire parlor in the Hay Wing of the museum. The wallpaper and the hangings are reproductions, but the mahogany furniture appeared in Cleveland's finest homes between 1815 and 1845. The room provides a glimpse of the lifestyle of the period and a study in furniture change. The earlier pieces follow ancient classical designs. Later cabinetmakers made heavier furniture and used less gilding. Furniture produced by machine in the 1840s became even less detailed.*

Western Reserve Historical Society Museum and Library *10825 East Blvd.* The collections are housed in a complex of adjoining buildings, two of which were originally constructed as private residences in Italian Renaissance style. Although the emphasis is on Ohio's history, there is a wide range of objects and printed materials relating to all areas and periods of American life and of other countries as well. A collection of American decorative arts is arranged in a number of period rooms, including a handsome American Empire parlor illustrating early 19th-century life in Cleveland. The costume collection is one of the largest in the Midwest and ranges from 1790 to the present. Children enjoy the 1890 Bingham doll house. A comprehensive collection of Indian artifacts and the 13½-foot sloop *Tinkerbelle* in which Robert Manry sailed across the Atlantic in 78 days are also on display. The Education Department includes several craft shops in which live demonstrations are given of mid-19th-century crafts and domestic industries. A rotating exhibition gallery presents new exhibits every two or three months devoted to various aspects of American life. Among the most impressive holdings from other nations is the Napoleon collection, one of the most outstanding of its kind in the western hemisphere. The large library exhibits letters signed by every signer of the Declaration of Independence and prominent Revolutionary War figures and by every U.S. President. The history archives collections trace the achievements of Cleveland's most prominent leaders through letters, speeches, diaries and other manuscripts and many clippings from periodicals. *Open Tues.-Sun. except holidays.*

FREDERICK C. CRAWFORD AUTO-AVIATION MUSEUM More than 150 automobiles, eight airplanes and several horse-drawn carriages and fire engines are displayed in this building. Among the cars, many of which are fully restored, are a 1913 Austro Daimler (the Prince Henry model), two early Wintons and a 1932 aluminum-bodied Peerless—the only one of its kind in existence. Restoration work can be observed in a mechanics' shop, and visitors can wander along a replica turn-of-the-century cobblestone street and enter shops that include a music store, blacksmith shop, general store, pharmacy and saloon. The "Bumblebee," a 1911 Curtiss pusher plane that once served Cleveland's waterfront, is among the aircraft shown. *Open Tues.-Sun. except holidays. Small charge.*

131. Hale Farm and Western Reserve Village *2686 Oak Hill Rd., Bath, Ohio* In the first half of the 19th century, settlers from New England streamed into this area, which Connecticut had claimed until 1800 and named its Western Reserve. Visitors to the museum village can glimpse the life of those hardy pioneers, who brought with them so much of their native East. The nucleus of the complex is the attractive Federal brick house built here in 1826 by Jonathan Hale, a farmer from Connecticut. Many of the furnishings belonged to the Hale family. Other buildings of Connecticut's Western Reserve in Ohio have been moved here and rebuilt around a village green. These include a Greek Revival-type clapboard dwelling, a saltbox house typical of the style still common in New England, a log schoolhouse dating from around 1816 and a small country law office. All these are appropriately furnished with

[131] *A skilled woodworker arrived in Bath about 1820, 10 years after the Hale group. Woodcarving demonstrations are given daily in the village cabinet shop whose walls are covered with tools used in the early 1800s.*

period pieces. Spinning and weaving are demonstrated in a barn behind the farmhouse, and cabinet- and candle-making as well as blacksmithing can be observed in craft shops. Farm animals graze in pastures on the grounds, which include a picnic area and a nature trail. *Open Tues.-Sun. May-Oct., Dec. Small charge.*

132. Railways of America *3656 Akron-Cleveland Rd., Cuyahoga Falls, Ohio* A red brick railroad station flanked by locomotives and Pullman cars shelters what is probably the world's largest collection of operating model trains. The collection, including replicas of historic American trains, contains about 2000 freight, locomotive and passenger cars, which run on nearly two miles of track. Relics of early railroading are also on display. *Open daily except holidays. Small charge.*

133. Akron Art Institute *69 E. Market St., Akron, Ohio* Art of the 20th century is the attraction here, and works by Stella, Margritte, Picasso, Warhol and Robert Indiana are featured. A library has a good collection of slides, video-tape films and art periodicals, and there is a handsome sculpture court surrounded by a hand-forged wrought-iron fence. Tempory exhibits of photographs, ceramic sculpture, prints, etchings and such are presented regularly. *Open daily except Dec. 25.*

134. Perkins Mansion *550 Copley Rd., Akron, Ohio* Colonel Simon Perkins, son of Akron's founder and business partner of abolitionist John Brown, built the Greek Revival mansion of local sandstone in 1835-7. The stately house has an imposing two-story portico supported by four graceful columns. The mansion, which is maintained by the Summit County Historical Society, contains many original furnishings as well as historical exhibits. Ten acres of landscaped grounds hold a carriage house, well and laundry. *Open Tues.-Sun. except holidays. Small charge.*

135. Stan Hywet Hall *714 N. Portage Path, Akron, Ohio* The magnificent 65-room Tudor-style mansion is one of the great houses in the U.S. Stan Hywet (from the Anglo-Saxon for "stone quarry"—the house is on the site of an old quarry) was completed in 1915 for Frank A. Seiberling, founder of the Goodyear Tire and Rubber Company and the Seiberling Rubber Company. The Seiberlings incorporated many features from Elizabethan English manors into their home and imported craftsmen to work on the house, which is filled with fine antique furnishings from the 14th through 18th centuries. Fascinating pieces, exquisite carvings and stained-glass windows all contribute to this re-creation of Renaissance England. The estate's 65 acres (one-fifth the original grounds) are beautifully landscaped—a rose garden, a long birch allée and an English walled garden, for example—making them a delight at any season. *Open Tues.-Sun. except holidays. Adults $2.00, children over 5 small charge.*

136. Massillon Museum *212 Lincoln Way E., Massillon, Ohio* The brick house of James Duncan, founder of Massillon, was built about 1835 and has served as a museum since 1933. The exhibits, including paintings, prints, furniture, textiles, china, pottery and sculpture, relate to the arts and crafts of Ohio and to the history of the area. *Open daily.*

137. Massillon Woman's Club *210 Fourth St. N.E., Massillon, Ohio* Five Oaks, which now houses the club, was built in 1892 as the home of J. Walter McClymonds. The predominantly Romanesque structure is made of stone from a local quarry and is noted for its many intricate and elaborate stone carvings. The house has three stories, a turret and a large front porch with clustered columns that give an arcaded effect. The double entry door is made of heavy oak with large iron strap hinges. The house contains numerous Tiffany stained-glass windows, including the skylight over the billiard room. Many of the lighting fixtures are also Tiffany. Fine carved woodwork may be seen throughout the house, which also contains statues, paintings, decorative art objects and many of the original furnishings. *Open Mon.-Wed., Fri., Sat. Sept.-June.*

138. Cultural Center for the Arts *1001 Market Ave. N., Canton, Ohio* The attractive brick and stone structure houses eight galleries featuring the Canton Art Institute's collection of American and European painting and sculpture and a number of items associated with President William McKinley. There are also two theaters used by the Players Guild, a community theater group, and a recital hall that is the scene of lectures, ballets, operas and other events. In the Great Court is the impressive bronze Pegasus Fountain by Henry Mitchell, and several abstract works can be seen in a central courtyard. *Open Tues.-Sun.*

139. Zoar Village State Memorial *Rte. 212, Zoar, Ohio* In 1817 300 Zoarites, religious separatists from Wurttemberg, Germany, bought 5500 acres here. Early communal experiments brought economic success, and their village became virtually self-sustaining. Although farming was the major activity, small industries also prospered; the Zoarites became well known for the manufacture of stoves, woolens and pottery. But failure to adopt modern agricultural and industrial methods caused the settlement to dissolve in 1898, and its dwindling assets were divided among 222 residents. Close to a dozen original buildings still stand. Among them are a bakery, built before 1840, which produced around 80 loaves of bread daily; a tinshop where villagers' utensils were manufactured; a garden and greenhouse where plants and bulbs were so expertly tended they were sought throughout the Midwest; and the house of Joseph Bäumeler, the community's first leader, which is now a museum whose exhibits include objects manufactured by Zoarites. *Open Tues.-Sun. and Mon. holidays Apr.-Oct. Small charge.*

140. Rena's Miniature Rooms *1315 E. High Ave., New Philadelphia, Ohio* The work of one woman, Mrs. Rena Poteet, the collection of 24 tiny period rooms encompasses fully furnished bedrooms, parlors and kitchens in Early American, French Provincial and Victorian styles. The intricate details—minute painted designs on dishes and furniture, one-inch candles, a spinning wheel that turns, quilts the size of handkerchiefs, even minuscule newspapers—lend authenticity to the rooms. *Open daily June-Aug. Small charge.*

141. Johnson-Humrickhouse Memorial Museum *Sycamore and Third Sts., Coshocton, Ohio* Pioneer furnishings, implements, utensils and guns are highlights

[135] *Comfortable overstuffed sofas and chairs do not detract from the Great Hall's impressive Tudor design. From the stone floor to the exposed rafters three stories above, the room has beautiful antique pieces.*

of the museum. Prehistoric Indian artifacts and relics, including hundreds of baskets and arrowheads, fill the Indian Room. An extensive Oriental collection contains Chinese and Japanese porcelain, jade, ivory figurines, lacquerware, weapons and carved screens. European artwork is represented in pottery, pewter, glass and laces. The impressive collections are housed in an 1853 brick school building. *Open Tues.-Sun. except holidays.*

142. Roscoe Village *Rte. 16, Coshocton, Ohio* Once a thriving wheat-shipping port on the Ohio-Erie Canal, this community sank into oblivion in the early 1900s with the coming of the railroad. An extensive restoration program begun in 1968 has brought many of the original handsome buildings back to life. Among these are a blacksmith's shop, with the smith on hand, and a craft house, where demonstrations of old-time handicrafts are given. Guides in period costumes conduct tours through the 1830s Williams House, which is furnished with many fine antiques. Several structures now house attractive shops, including an elegant restaurant, reflecting the period of Roscoe's heyday. Rides on horse-drawn wagons and on a reconstructed canal boat are available nearby. *Open daily. Small charge for Williams House.*

143. Zanesville Art Center *1145 Maple Ave., Zanesville, Ohio* Paintings by Rembrandt, Goya, Gainsborough and Marin are in the permanent collection of this fine art museum. Among the other exhibits are primitive and Oriental art objects and a collection of early glass made in Ohio. An English paneled room from about 1700 can also be seen. The library contains reference materials on the fine and applied arts. *Open Sat.-Thurs. except holidays.*

144. Campus Martius Museum *Washington and Second Sts., Marietta, Ohio* During Marietta's early years the settlers, sent by the Ohio Company of Associates, lived in a stockaded village known as Campus Martius ("Field of Mars"). The site is now occupied by this museum, which contains objects associated with Ohio's pioneers. Besides china, furniture, glassware and paintings and temporary exhibits of guns, archaeological items and period clothing, the brick building shelters one of Campus Martius's houses—the restored 1788 frame home of Rufus Putnam, superintendent of the Ohio Company. Ship models, equipment and photographs are displayed in a wing that houses the River Museum, a collection devoted to the early history of the Ohio River. On the grounds is the company's Land Office (also built in 1788), a one-room structure of logs and clapboard siding. It was the first office building in the Northwest Territory. *Open daily except holidays.*

145. Manasseh Cutler Hall *Ohio University, Athens, Ohio* In 1816 work began on this handsome brick Federal structure for the first institution of higher learning in what was then the wilderness of the Northwest Territory. Completed in 1818, it was the university's only building for almost 20 years. It is named for the minister, doctor and lawyer who was responsible for provisions regarding public education in the Northwest Ordinance of 1787 and who later wrote a model charter for Ohio University. Cutler Hall with its central cupola and clock was restored to its original exterior appearance

[139] *This fanciful birdcage is one of many Zoarite-made articles on display at Number One House. The largest house in the community was built in 1835 and soon became the home of the leader, Joseph Bäumeler.*

in 1947. It is the university's main administrative building. *Open Mon.-Fri. except holidays.*

146. Our House State Memorial *434 First Ave., Gallipolis, Ohio* Henry Cushing, a leading citizen of Gallipolis, built this tavern in 1819. The Federal-style brick structure contains public and private dining rooms, a ballroom, a taproom, a ladies' parlor and three bedrooms. The kitchen is located in a small detached brick building behind the tavern. The completely restored structure has been refurnished to give the appearance of an early 19th-century tavern. *Open Tues.-Sat. Apr.-Oct. Adults small charge.*

147. Huntington Galleries *2033 McCoy Rd., Park Hills, Huntington, W. Va.* A concrete and brick addition designed by Walter Gropius, his last work, and opened in 1970 has greatly enhanced the facilities here which now include a library, two additional exhibition galleries, a print gallery and a 300-seat auditorium. A sculpture court and studio workshops devoted to weaving, photography, ceramics, painting and other media also form part of the complex. Rembrandt, Utrillo and Braque are among European artists represented, and the extensive American collection offers works by Whistler, Homer, Cassatt and Hopper. Among the modern American artists' work are sculptures by Seymour Lipton and Leonard Baskin and paintings by Robert Motherwell,

Paul Jenkins and Andrew Wyeth. Several examples of European furniture and decorative arts are displayed along with Georgian silver. *Open Tues.-Sun.*

148. West Virginia State Capitol *E. Kanawha Blvd., Charleston, W. Va.* The limestone building, completed in 1932, bears an obvious resemblance to the U.S. Capitol. It is further enhanced by a handsome portico with eight Roman-style columns and huge bronze entrance doors. A decorative 300-foot-high gilt dome situated over the central section supports a two-ton rock crystal chandelier. The attractive marble interior is notable for its ground floor Doric vestibule and mosaic foyer columns. The wings of the building house the state supreme court, law library and the archives. *Open daily except holidays.*

STATE MUSEUM West Virginia's history is traced in the museum beneath the main rotunda of the Capitol. Highlights include a 1791 property survey signed by Daniel Boone, whose powder horn and beaver traps are displayed, and several land grants bearing the signatures of George Washington, Patrick Henry and other Colonial dignitaries. The mahogany table that was used for the signing of the Declaration of Independence is here along with the 35-star U.S. flag flown at Gettysburg in 1863 during Lincoln's immortal address. A replica pioneer kitchen is furnished with 18th- to mid-19th-century items. Other displays feature native coal and miners' equipment, coins and antique dolls. *Open daily except holidays.*

149. Southwest Virginia Museum *W. First St. and Wood Ave., Big Stone Gap, Va.* A fine collection of flintlocks and other firearms, early medical instruments and a set of Minton china presented to Benjamin Disraeli by Queen Victoria are among the varied attractions here. Also displayed in the 1890s stone structure are Indian artifacts, many relics of the American Revolution and the Civil War and several dioramas of the area's early industries. Handmade quilts and other examples of early folk crafts, period furniture and paintings can also be seen. In the small library there are historical documents and papers of regional significance. *Open Tues.-Sun. except holidays.*

150. Conneaut Historical Railroad Museum *Depot and Mill Sts., Conneaut, Ohio* The steam era of railroading is relived in the exhibits centering around this old New York Central station. A steam locomotive, railroad cars, lanterns, timetables, stock certificates, scale model trains and other railroad memorabilia can be seen in indoor and outdoor displays. *Open daily late May-early Sept.*

151. Shandy Hall *6333 S. Ridge W., Geneva, Ohio* The Federal-style frame dwelling, built in 1815 by Colonel Robert Harper, is one of the oldest houses in the Western Reserve. It was occupied for 120 years by members of the Harper family. Now owned by the Western Reserve Historical Society, the house still contains much of the original furniture and china. The most interesting of its 17 rooms is the large, elaborate banquet hall and its early 19th-century French wallpaper with a panoramic Italian scene. The house was named after the 18th-century novel *Tristram Shandy* by Laurence Sterne. *Open Tues.-Sun. May-Oct. Adults and children over 5 small charge.*

[156] *William M. Harnett painted* After the Hunt *in 1884. It clearly shows the sense of design and purity that made Harnett a leading painter of the deceptively dimensional, precisely detailed trompe l'oeil still lifes.*

152. Geauga County Historical Society Museum and Pioneer Village *14653 E. Park, Burton, Ohio* A rural community of the mid-19th century, complete with homes, shops, a church and schoolhouse, even a depot of the Baltimore and Ohio Railroad, has been painstakingly reconstructed here around a typical village green. The buildings, all of which are at least 100 years old, were moved to their present location and restored by the Geauga County Historical Society. Many of them bear strong traces of New England styling, a remembrance of the time when the northeastern region of Ohio was the Western Reserve of Connecticut. The typical 19th-century shops include a general store, ladies' dress and hat shop, cabinetmaker's shop and smithy. One of the houses, a rambling brick dwelling, has been outfitted as a museum and now displays mementos of the county's early days. *Open Tues.-Sun. Adults $1.50, children over 12 small charge.*

153. City Hall *391 Mahoning Ave. N.W., Warren, Ohio* Henry Bishop Perkins, a prominent politician of the area, built the 20-room mansion now used as a city hall. The building, constructed in 1871 and set on seven landscaped acres, was designed to resemble a Tuscan villa. The house is noted for its carvings in both stone and wood. Many of the present furnishings were there during the visits of five U.S. Presidents: Grant, Hayes, Garfield, Benjamin Harrison and McKinley. *Open Mon.-Fri. except holidays.*

154. National McKinley Birthplace Memorial *40 N. Main St., Niles, Ohio* Almost the exact spot where the 25th U.S. President was born in 1843 is marked by this impressive Greek Revival marble memorial designed with Doric columns. In addition to a large statue of McKinley, the structure contains an auditorium and a museum that displays a number of his belongings. *Open daily.*

155. Arms Museum *648 Wick Ave., Youngstown, Ohio* Headquarters of the Mahoning Valley Historical Society, this was formerly the home of Mr. and Mrs. Wilford Paddock Arms. Designed by Mrs. Arms and built in 1905, the mansion is now a museum exhibiting possessions of the Arms family, including furniture, silver, glassware, Oriental rugs and family portraits. Other displays feature early farm and household tools, Indian relics, armor and guns. Mannequins display period clothing in several rooms. *Open Wed.-Sun. except holidays. Small charge.*

156. Butler Institute of American Art *524 Wick Ave., Youngstown, Ohio* In 1917 a fire destroyed almost the entire art collection in the residence of industrialist Joseph G. Butler, Jr. Mr. Butler resolved to build a fireproof structure where new acquisitions could be seen by the public. The resulting marble building in a Roman architectural style was opened in 1919, and its spacious galleries now hold more than 3500 works by American artists. One of the strongest collections of American art in the U.S., the works encompass watercolors, oils, prints and drawings, as well as many outstanding contemporary Ohio ceramics. A Winslow Homer oil was the first important purchase, followed by many other 19th-century canvases by artists such as Audubon, Samuel F. B. Morse and George Inness. Among the 20th-century works are paintings by Edward Hopper, Ben Shahn and John Marin. Here, too, is a unique collection of miniatures of every U.S. President from Washington to Nixon. There are more than 40 paintings and prints of clipper ships, over 100 early glass bells and an outstanding collection of paintings of the American Indian. *Open Tues.-Sun.*

157. Pioneer Village *Canfield Fair Ground, Canfield, Ohio* Eight authentic frame buildings have been moved here and restored to re-create the flavor of an early Western Reserve community. Visitors can enter a furnished law office and a doctor's office, a country store, log cabin, library and blacksmith shop as well as an old schoolhouse. The railroad depot features a watchman's tower and early caboose. *Open daily June-Aug.*

158. McCook House *Public Sq., Carrollton, Ohio* The handsome Federal-style house was home to the prominent McCook family from about 1837 to 1853. Daniel McCook and eight of his sons along with five nephews valiantly fought for the Union cause in the Civil War. The two-story brick house is now a museum and memorial to this historic Ohio family. It contains period rooms, family memorabilia and exhibits of Civil War objects. *Open Wed.-Sun. and holidays June-Sept. Small charge.*

159. Mansion Museum *Oglebay Park, Wheeling, W. Va.* Home styles from frontier days to Victorian times are reflected in the eight period rooms of this 1835 plantation house, which has undergone several alterations since it was first built. A spinning wheel, pewter plates and wrought-iron cooking utensils share a pioneer kitchen; Hepplewhite and Sheraton furniture grace an 18th-century dining room; Queen Anne and Chippendale decor fill a Federal bedroom. An addition built in 1967 has an auditorium, a gallery of local historical exhibits and an outstanding glass collection that includes what is said to be the largest existing cut-glass piece, the Sweeney Punch Bowl. *Open daily except Jan. 1 and Dec. 25. Adults $1.25.*

160. St. Joseph's Cathedral *13th and Eoff Sts., Wheeling, W. Va.* Lombard Romanesque in design, the Roman Catholic cathedral immediately impresses with its solid front: two octagonal turrets handsomely flank the recessed fluted entrance archway topped by a rose window. Interior features include the nave's sturdy columns and soaring arches, five marble altars, 12-foot-high marble wainscoting in the sanctuary and stained-glass windows depicting the life of St. Joseph. Consecrated in 1926, the building was mostly constructed from Indiana limestone, expertly smoothed and carved. *Open daily.*

[159] *Although the house was not built until 1835, the rooms represent periods from 1720 to 1850. In contrast to the Victorian parlor, crowded with bric-a-brac, this 18th-century dining room is spacious and uncluttered. During the late 18th and early 19th centuries the taste was for elegantly simple classic lines. Rare Hepplewhite and Sheraton furniture rests on a rug from China. The scenic French wallpaper was made in 1815.*

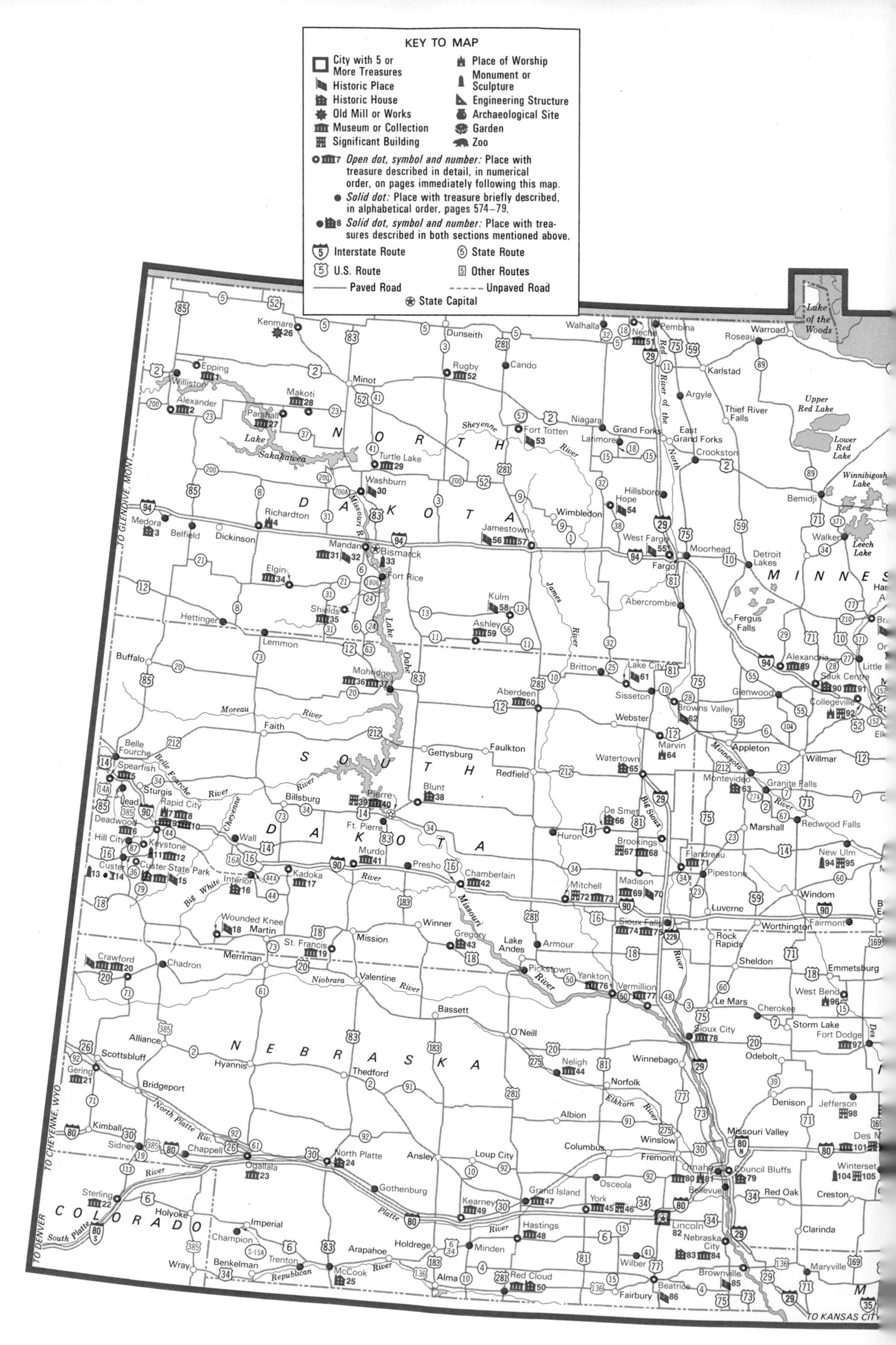
KEY TO MAP
City with 5 or More Treasures
Historic Place
Historic House
Old Mill or Works
Museum or Collection
Significant Building
Place of Worship
Monument or Sculpture
Engineering Structure
Archaeological Site
Garden
Zoo
7 Open dot, symbol and number: Place with treasure described in detail, in numerical order, on pages immediately following this map.
Solid dot: Place with treasure briefly described, in alphabetical order, pages 574–79.
8 Solid dot, symbol and number: Place with treasures described in both sections mentioned above.
5 Interstate Route
5 U.S. Route
5 State Route
5 Other Routes
Paved Road
Unpaved Road
State Capital
NORTH DAKOTA
SOUTH DAKOTA
NEBRASKA
COLORADO
MINNES
TO GLENDIVE, MONT.
TO CHEYENNE, WYO.
TO DENVER
TO KANSAS CITY
Lake of the Woods
Kenmare 26
Dunseith
Walhalla
Neche 51
Pembina
Warroad
Roseau
Karlstad
Epping 1
Williston
Cando
Rugby 52
Minot
Makoti 28
Alexander 2
Parshall 27
Lake Sakakawea
Argyle
Thief River Falls
Upper Red Lake
Lower Red Lake
Niagara
Fort Totten 53
Sheyenne River
Grand Forks
East Grand Forks
Larimore
Crookston
Turtle Lake 29
Washburn 30
Missouri R.
Red River of the North
Hillsboro
Hope 54
Wimbledon
Bemidji
Winnibigosh Lake
Medora 3
Belfield
Dickinson
Richardton 4
Jamestown 56 57
West Fargo 55
Fargo
Moorhead
Detroit Lakes
Walker
Leech Lake
Mandan 31 32
Bismarck 33
Fort Rice
Elgin 34
Kulm 58
Shields 35
Ashley 59
Hettinger
Lemmon
Lake Oahe
James River
Abercrombie
Fergus Falls
Buffalo
Mobridge 36 37
Britton
Lake City 61
Sisseton
Alexandria 89
Sauk Centre 90 91
Collegeville 92
Little
Glenwood
Aberdeen 60
Browns Valley 62
Moreau River
Faith
Webster
Marvin 64
Belle Fourche
Belle Fourche River
Spearfish 5
Gettysburg
Faulkton
Redfield
Watertown 65
Appleton
Willmar
Minnesota River
Montevideo 63
Granite Falls
Sturgis
Lead
Deadwood 6
Rapid City 7 8 9 10
Cheyenne
Billsburg
Blunt 38
Pierre 39 40
Ft. Pierre
Big Sioux
De Smet 66
Marshall
Redwood Falls
Hill City
Keystone 11 12
Wall
Huron
Brookings 67 68
Flandreau 71
New Ulm 94 95
Custer 13 14
Custer State Park 15
Murdo 41
Presho
Chamberlain 42
Madison 69 70
Pipestone
Interior 16
Big White River
Kadoka 17
Mitchell 72 73
Windom
Luverne
Missouri
Winner
Sioux Falls 74 75
Worthington
Fairmont
Wounded Knee 18
Martin
Mission
St. Francis 19
Gregory 43
Armour
Lake Andes
Rock Rapids
Sheldon
Emmetsburg
Crawford 20
Chadron
Merriman
Niobrara
Valentine
Pickstown
Yankton 76
Vermillion 77
West Bend 96
Le Mars
Cherokee
Storm Lake
Bassett
Sioux City 78
Fort Dodge 97
Alliance
Scottsbluff
Gering 21
Hyannis
O'Neill
Neligh 44
Winnebago
Odebolt
Thedford
Norfolk
Elkhorn River
Bridgeport
North Platte Riv.
Albion
Denison
Jefferson 98
Kimball
Sidney
Chappell
Ogallala 23
North Platte 24
Ansley
Loup City
Columbus
Winslow
Missouri Valley
Fremont
Omaha 80 81
Council Bluffs 79
Des M
101
Winterset 104 105
Sterling 22
Gothenburg
Grand Island 47
Osceola
Bellevue
Red Oak
Creston
Holyoke
Imperial
Champion
Kearney 49
York 45 46
Lincoln 82
Nebraska City 83 84
Platte River
Clarinda
Hastings 48
South Platte
Trenton
Arapahoe
Holdrege
Minden
Wilber
Wray
Benkelman
Republican
McCook 25
Alma
Red Cloud 50
Fairbury 86
Beatrice
Brownville 85
Maryville

First fur, then gold, free land and a chance to begin anew lured settlers into this region, forcing the Indians out. Many treasures here—sod houses, forts, abandoned mines, ghost cities—recall the short-lived, action-packed and legendary epic of the Old West.

REGION 6

Pages 356–399

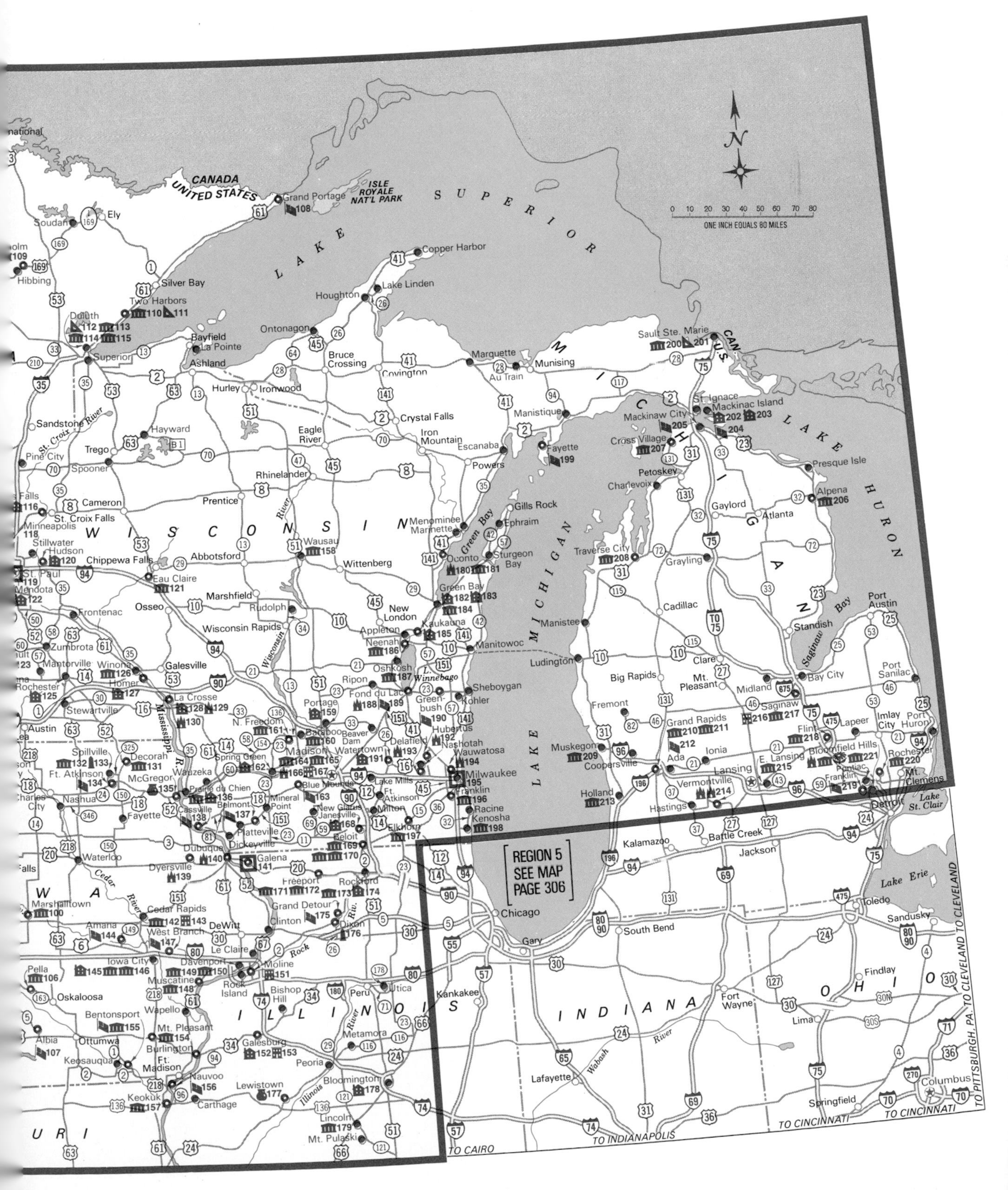

1. Buffalo Trails Museum *Main St., Epping, N.D.* The three-building complex is made up of restored frontier structures: a hardware store, a machinery display and harness shop and a grocery store. Effective exhibits include a diorama of an Assiniboin Indian village and oil paintings by local artist Elmer Halvorson. Costumed figures set in frontier home situations tell the early story of the upper Missouri River area. Also here are exhibits of Indian artifacts, local geology and archaeology. A prime attraction is the recorded interviews with early pioneers of the area. The museum received a Certificate of Commendation from the American Association for State and Local History in 1968. *Open daily June-Aug. Small charge.*

2. Lewis and Clark Trail Museum *Rte. 85, Alexander, N.D.* Although there is a replica of an early-day millinery shop, an old country store and a Pioneer Room with early settlers' artifacts, the main attraction here is the Lewis and Clark Room. A highlight of the exhibits here is a letter from President Thomas Jefferson to Congress requesting an appropriation of funds for the momentous search for an overland route to the Pacific. There are also brief biographies of Jefferson, Lewis and Clark. A roster of the men who accompanied the two famed explorers is also exhibited, as are paintings of Indians by Russell and Catlin. A diorama built of willows depicts Fort Mandan, where Lewis and Clark spent the winter of 1804-5. *Open daily June-early Sept. Adults small charge.*

3. Chateau de Mores *Rtes. 10 and 94, Medora, N.D.* In 1883 Antoine de Vallombrosa, a French marquis and adventurer, founded Medora as the center of a vast cattle and meat-packing enterprise and named it for his wife. That same year his chateau was built, a 26-room frame house that blends outwardly with its Badlands setting. Inside, however, its furnishings are in a style familiar to the titled European guests who once were lavishly entertained here. Much of the furniture that belonged to the Marquis de Mores and his family remains, as well as paintings, handcrafted armor, a gun collection and some personal clothing. *Open daily. Small charge.*

4. Assumption Abbey *Richardton, N.D.* The most impressive building of this Benedictine monastery complex is the Gothic-Romanesque church, known as the "Cathedral of the Prairies." Its hooded twin steeples are topped with gray slate roofs surmounted by burnished crosses. The early structures (1899-1909), which form a quadrangle enclosing a spacious garden, were largely built by the monks themselves, using red bricks made from local clay baked in a kiln on the grounds. In recent years a gymnasium, high school and junior college have been added to the expanding institution. The library, housed in a 1942 building, is an official depository for government publications. *Open daily.*

5. Lyndle Dunn Wildlife Art Collection *Library-Learning Center, Black Hills State College, Spearfish, S.D.* Almost 70 works in several media by nature artist Lyndle Dunn are featured in the upper lounge of this building. In addition to the accurate paintings of fish, birds and mammals, the collection includes several hunting and fishing scenes and a number of outstanding landscapes. A replica of the artist's studio is also of interest to visitors. *Open daily.*

6. Adams Memorial Museum *Deadwood, S.D.* The valuables here tell the picturesque story of frontier settlement in the Black Hills. Cases display minerals and extraordinary Indian artifacts. There are pictures of Calamity Jane and "Wild Bill" Hickock and a General Custer picture collection. Other displays are school and church bells, spinning wheels, a gun collection and a Pioneer Room. One of the most popular features is the first steam locomotive Homestake engine drawn to the Black Hills in 1879 by a bull team. *Open daily.*

7. Chapel in the Hills *Rte. 40, Rapid City, S.D.* Stavkirke Church is a charming replica of a stave church built around 1150 A.D. in Borgund, Norway. The chapel is constructed entirely of wood inside and out and elaborately carved. Like the Norwegian original, decoration of the structure reflects both Christian and pagan themes. Simulated prows of Viking longboats employing dragon heads extend from the roof, and serpents and animals in violent combat are prominent among the interior carvings. The St. Andrew's crosses in the interior are part of the chapel's structural trussing. *Open daily May-Oct.*

8. Horseless Carriage Museum *Rte. 16, 10 mi. S.W. of Rapid City, S.D.* The development of the horseless carriage is the main exhibit here. Unusual early cars and outstanding ones such as the Stutz, Stanley Steamer and Fords from 1915 to 1947 are featured, joined by other mechanical devices, from the first German jet aircraft engine to a large collection of antique music boxes and one of early firearms. Mannequins model clothes of earlier days, and there are many other reminders of pioneer life. *Open daily May-Oct. Adults and children over 12 $1.50, children over 5 small charge.*

9. Museum of Geology *O'Harra Memorial Bldg., South Dakota School of Mines and Technology, E. St. Joseph St., Rapid City, S.D.* A well-preserved fossil of a female oredont creates much interest here: enclosed in the skeleton are two unborn young, an unusual circumstance among such excavated remains. Estimated to be 30 million years old, this relative of sheep, pigs and camels is displayed along with many other animal fossils recovered from the Badlands. A large collection of min-seen, as well as meteorites and samples of gold. *Open* erals, ores and rocks from the Black Hills can also be *daily June-Aug., Mon.-Fri. Sept.-May except holidays.*

10. Sioux Indian Museum and Crafts Center *1002 St. Joseph St., Rapid City, S.D.* The past and present arts of the Sioux are shown here in exhibits of their costumes, adornments and other objects that relate to religion, warfare and the hunt. All of the decorative pieces on display here are richly worked with beads, porcupine quills and feathers. Special exhibits feature work by contemporary Sioux artists and craftsmen. There is also a nonprofit museum-shop that sells the work of various Indian craftsmen and artists as well as literature on Indian topics. *Open Mon.-Sat. late May-Sept., Tues.-Sun. Oct.-late May except holidays.*

Designed to be seen from below, the monument is lofty and dignified. Rock in foreground is debris from sculpting.

11. Mount Rushmore National Monument

Keystone, S.D.

The massive granite heads of Presidents Washington, Jefferson, Theodore Roosevelt and Lincoln atop Mount Rushmore commemorate the monumental importance of their contribution to American democracy, as was the aim of the sculptor, Gutzon Borglum. Between 1927 and 1941 whenever weather permitted and funds were available, Borglum-trained miners worked, standing on scaffolds or suspended in seats on the face of the 6000-foot-high mountain. They first measured, then drilled, blasted, chipped and smoothed away 450,000 tons of granite in accordance with Borglum's scale models. It took the miners six-and-a-half years to engineer-sculpt the four 60-foot-high faces. (A full figure at the same scale would be 465 feet tall.) The visitor's viewpoint is an observation center below. While sunlight strikes the monument most of the day, the faces are best seen in morning light, or, from June to September, at night when they are floodlighted and a special program is offered in the amphitheater. *Open daily.*

During construction scaffolding was used for close-up work. Here men chip and smooth an 11-foot-wide eye. Much of the work on the sheer face of the mountain was done from swinging seats, three of which are seen here.

[16] *In the early 1900s a few crops and cattle barely supported thousands of families who acquired homestead sites like this one free of charge from the government on condition that they cultivate the land.*

12. Shrine to Democracy Wax Museum *Rte. 16A, Keystone, S.D.* Highly realistic wax effigies of every U.S. President from Washington to Nixon can be seen here in settings that recapture momentous events in their careers. Katherine Stubergh Keller and her husband Tom Keller created these figures, which also include several foreign leaders, such as Churchill and Stalin, and notable people and scenes in the nation's history. Particularly popular are the depictions of Lee's surrender at Appomattox, General Custer and Chief Sitting Bull's Council. *Open daily May–Oct. Adults and children over 12 $2.00.*

13. Crazy Horse Memorial *Off Rtes. 16 and 385, 5 mi. N. of Custer, S.D.* The monumental project, a singlehanded creation of sculptor Korczak Ziolkowski, will be finished around 1978 when an estimated 6 million tons of granite will have been blasted from Thunderhead Mountain. The gigantic figure, carved in the round and mounted on a galloping buffalo pony, is Chief Crazy Horse, the master strategist who briefly united the Sioux nations in 1876 to strike a crushing blow to Custer and his command at the Little Big Horn. Ziolkowski's life work will forever honor the brave Indian. The admission fee includes a tour through the artist's studio-home where visitors can see Ziolkowski's antique collection and some of his past works. *Open daily. $2.00 each car.*

14. Wiehe's Frontier Museum *25 N. Fifth St., Custer, S.D.* The 1899 groceries and general merchandise store holds what looks like a storehouse of props for a Wild West movie. There are gold dust and nuggets from nearby French Creek, along with mining tools and gold scales. Firearms by Colt and Winchester, photographs of outlaws, sheriffs and cavalry officers, Indian objects, relics from saloons and ghost towns and music boxes are among the other authentic mementos of an adventurous Western history. *Open daily mid-June–Aug. Small charge.*

15. Custer State Park *E. of Custer, S.D.* Besides fishing, camping, swimming and boating, this state park in the Black Hills offers several historical attractions for visitors. *Open daily. Park admission $2.00.*

BADGER CLARK MEMORIAL The poet laureate of South Dakota, Charles Badger Clark (1883–1957), lived alone in this stone and lumber cabin for nearly 30 years. He built a home in this rustic spot with his own hands, then wrote poems about the lovely Black Hills, cowboy lyrics and other works. A memorial plaque honors "this friendly and understanding man," and visitors can see his personal effects and furnishings in the home just as he left them upon his death. *Open daily June–Aug.*

CUSTER STATE PARK MUSEUM The museum building, constructed of native stones, seems rooted in the hillside, a fitting tribute to its natural setting. Inside, suitably, are natural history exhibits, including geological specimens native to the Black Hills. Indian artifacts and pioneer memorabilia form other displays. *Open daily June–Aug.*

GORDON STOCKADE This is a replica of the stockade built during the winter of 1874–5 by the adventurous Gordon party. The group of 26 men, one woman and a boy arrived here after a 78-day trek, lured by news of gold to be found in the Black Hills. Trespassers on Indian land, they fenced in their rude cabins on the bank of French Creek with a strong, high stockade. With homes built and defenses prepared, they panned for gold in the creek bed and began to see their hardships rewarded. But within a few months a cavalry expedition arrived to escort the illegal squatters out of the territory. *Open daily.*

16. Prairie Homestead Historic Site *Interior, S.D.* The dug-out, sod-wall, dirt-roof house on its original site vividly shows what it was like to homestead on the Great Plains in the early 1900s. Cottonwood logs face the lower walls, while buffalo-grass sod was used for the upper portions; part of the house—a food storage cave and a chicken coop—extends into the excavated bankside. Hitched onto the hut for a living room is a former claim shack. All the furnishings would be familiar to pioneer homesteaders: they either belonged to this home or are typical of those in the hundreds of thousands of sod houses that once dotted the prairies. *Open daily June–Sept. Small charge.*

17. Red Cloud Indian Museum *Off Rte. 90, Kadoka, S.D.* A fine collection of feather bonnets, beaded moccasins and other clothing and ceremonial apparel, along with weapons and utensils, illustrates the superb workmanship that distinguishes these handcrafted Indian objects. Various displays, many with mannequins, depict the life-style of Indian tribes in the region. *Open daily mid-May–mid-Sept. Small charge.*

18. Wounded Knee Massacre Site *Wounded Knee, S.D.* On Dec. 28, 1890, more than 400 Sioux, many of whom were exhausted and sick, were apprehended with their leader Chief Big Foot by the U.S. 7th Cavalry about five miles northwest of this site. Although they surrendered at once, they were escorted to Wounded Knee Creek and detained overnight in a canyon. The next morning, during a search for weapons by the Army, a shot rang out. What followed was a storm of gunfire that killed about 250 defenseless Indian men, women and children. Situated on the Pine Ridge Indian Reservation, the mass grave of Big Foot and 129 of his followers continues to serve as a bleak reminder of the massacre. This tragic event was the last full-scale encounter between the northern Plains Indians and the Army. *Open daily.*

19. Buechel Memorial Sioux Indian Museum *St. Francis Mission and School, St. Francis, S.D.* In 1902 the Reverend Eugene Buechel, a Jesuit priest, began this outstanding collection of artifacts, presented to him by the Sioux whom he served for almost 50 years. Ghost Dance shirts, pipes, colorful headdresses and rawhide objects are displayed, as well as articles that once belonged to Crazy Horse, Red Cloud and other famous Sioux chiefs. *Open daily late May-early Sept.*

20. Fort Robinson *Rte. 20, 4 mi. W. of Crawford, Nebr.* The fort was erected in 1874 to provide military protection for the nearby Red Cloud Agency. In the heart of Sioux country, it was the base camp for several important Indian campaigns. Several buildings representative of various construction periods still stand: a wheelwright's shop, blacksmith shop, officers' quarters, harness repair shop and a reconstruction of the guardhouse where Crazy Horse, the Sioux war leader who defeated Custer, was killed in a struggle after surrendering. *Open daily Apr.-mid-Nov.*

FORT ROBINSON MUSEUM Housed in a 1905 building which served as post headquarters, the Nebraska State Historical Society Museum contains Indian artifacts, military items and other relics of the fort's early history. Various exhibits depict the early life of the Indian and the white man. *Open daily Apr.-mid-Nov.*

TRAILSIDE MUSEUM OF NATURAL HISTORY Operated by the University of Nebraska, this museum is known for its interpretive exhibits illustrating the geologic history and wildlife of the area, which is noted for its fossils. *Open daily late May-early Sept.*

21. Scotts Bluff National Monument *Rte. 92, Gering, Nebr.* Scotts Bluff is a 700-foot rock promontory overlooking the North Platte Valley through which passed the famed Oregon Trail. In the 19th century the massive bluff was a landmark for the fur traders, explorers, gold seekers and settlers who traveled this route to the western wilderness. The Pony Express and the first overland telegraph also followed the Oregon Trail. Exhibits in the Oregon Trail Museum here depict the story of the westward migration: tools and vehicles of

[21] *For emigrants heading west on the Oregon Trail, Scotts Bluff, seen in the picture at the right, was a welcome sight, for the pioneers believed this was the midpoint of their journey. Here they rested awhile before tackling the difficult and dangerous terrain that lay beyond. Transportation along the trail, which originated in Independence, Missouri, forked near Salt Lake and ended in Portland and Sacramento, was by wagon trains made up of prairie schooners like the one shown here. These prairie schooners, drawn by two or four horses (the heavier Conestoga wagons required six), were perfectly suited to 19th century pioneer travel. They were used for carrying possessions and provided protection during Indian raids. Made as durable as possible, the schooners forded rivers and streams en route and, the long journey over, were used as farm wagons.*

the period are displayed, as is a collection of paintings by pioneer artist William Henry Jackson. *Open daily except Dec. 25. Small charge each car.*

22. Overland Trail Museum *Off Rte. 80S, Sterling, Colo.* The world's largest branding iron collection is displayed here, along with many other objects associated with early settlers in the area. A diorama depicts part of the Battle of Summit Springs in which the U.S. 5th Cavalry defeated Cheyennes in the last important fight with the Plains Indians in Colorado. "Buffalo Bill" Cody, chief scout for the 5th Cavalry, gained some of his reputation as an Indian fighter in this 1869 engagement. *Open daily Apr.-Oct.*

23. Mansion on the Hill *1004 Spruce St., Ogallala, Nebr.* Cut stone and ornately carved wood trim decorate the Victorian brick house that was built for a banker in 1887. Maintained as the Keith County Historical Society Museum, it contains its original woodwork as well as a variety of objects with regional significance, including furniture and clothing, and in the library, local photographs and documents. *Open daily June-Aug.*

24. Buffalo Bill's Ranch *Rte. 1, N. Platte, Nebr.* Famed Indian scout and hunter William F. ("Buffalo Bill") Cody built the 19-room frame dwelling in 1886 when fortunes from his renowned "Wild West Show" were running high. It holds Victorian furniture, a number of Indian relics, many Cody belongings and family photographs. Some wallpaper depicts scenes from Cody's colorful life. Called "Scout's Rest" by its owner, the house was visited by such other Western notables as Annie Oakley. Located on the grounds are an icehouse, a wine cellar and an original log cabin that was moved here from one of Cody's other ranches. A barn contains original 1880s posters from Cody's show and serves as a theater for film showings. *Open daily late May-early Sept.*

25. George W. Norris Home *706 Norris Ave., McCook, Nebr.* During 40 years in Congress, George Norris earned the title "Gentle Knight of Progressive Ideals" for his support of projects, such as the TVA, which empowered the federal government to undertake programs for the national good. He purchased this simple but comfortable house in 1899 when he was a district judge, and it remained his home until he died in 1944. It contains many original furnishings, including Norris's prized Persian rugs, and an exhibit that traces the highlights of the senator's career. *Open Sat., Sun. Apr.-late May, Tues.-Sun. late May-early Sept., Sat., Sun. early Sept.-Oct.*

26. Danish Mill *Kenmare, N.D.* Handmade gears cut from the hard wood of a maple tree in the restored windmill transfer power generated by the winglike vanes to the two 1800-pound millstones which once ground as much as 200 sacks of grain each day. Built in 1902 by a Danish farmer, the handsome red-shingled structure tapers to a top section that revolves so the vanes could always be faced into the wind. This is one of just seven similar mills in the U.S.—and the only one with its original millstones. *Open daily.*

27. Paul Broste Rock Museum *Parshall, N.D.* Paul Broste, a farmer, spent his spare time executing the oil paintings and collecting the unusual items displayed here. Among them are agates, quartz crystals, corals, petrified stumps and rocks that Broste cut and polished into multicolored spheres. He designed the building, which is made of native granite boulders with translucent agate slabs in the windows, and planned the interior decoration that features two spherical trees made of rocks. *Open daily. Small charge.*

28. Makoti Threshing Association Museum *Makoti, N.D.* The stars of the museum's extraordinary collection are gigantic tractors of the early 1900s. The 1909 gas-driven Hart Parr weighs 10 tons, including an 1125-pound flywheel; the drive wheels of the 1914 Big Four are more than eight feet high; fully loaded, the 1914 30 h.p. Minneapolis double-cylinder steam engine weighs 22 tons. Second billing goes to antique cars such as the Staude-MAK-A-Tractor, the 1913 Model T Ford touring car and the 1928 Essex Super Six. Altogether more than 100 operational antique farm machines, including cars, threshers, tractors and trucks, fill the three steel-enclosed buildings.

29. Schlafmann Museum *Rte. 200, 5 mi. S.E. of Turtle Lake, N.D.* Visitors may listen to some all-but-forgotten sounds of the 19th century in this museum of mechanical musical instruments. Besides nickelodeons and player pianos there are an 1850 German barrel organ, a uno-fon used by a circus in the late 1800s, a merry-go-round band organ, a coin-operated military band organ and many more instruments, most of which are in working condition. *Open daily late May-Aug. Small charge.*

30. Fort Mandan *4 mi. W. of Washburn, N.D.* This replica of the Lewis and Clark winter camp of 1804 is built of 14-foot palisaded cottonwood logs. It stands in the Missouri River bottom near the site of the original fort from which the famous party set out for further exploration. During the winter they obtained much valuable information on local Indian tribes, topography and other subjects. *Open daily.*

31. Beck's Great Plains Museum *Rte. 1806, 2½ mi. S. of Mandan, N.D.* Assembled here is an absorbing conglomeration of articles that depict life-styles in the area from pioneer times to the 1920s. There are old-fashioned clothes, phonographs, automobiles, firearms, washing machines—and 170 types of barbed wire. Displays include furnishings of a barbershop, a dentist's office, a general store and a two-story 1877 log house, one of the oldest homes from nearby Bismarck. *Open Sat., Sun. mid-May-late May, daily June-Aug., Sat., Sun. Sept.-Oct. Small charge.*

32. Fort Lincoln State Park Museum *Rte. 1806, 4½ mi. S. of Mandan, N.D.* Various aspects of local military history and Indian lore are presented in the museum, where visitors can learn of the park's historical significance. It contains a reconstructed Indian village and a rebuilt blockhouse of Fort McKeen, which was established in 1872. The following year the fort was renamed for Abraham Lincoln, enlarged and soon ac-

[33] *The Shoshone Indian woman Sakakawea, who acted as an interpreter for the Lewis and Clark expedition through the Louisiana Purchase, is credited with maintaining peaceful relations with Indians all along the way.*

commodated the 7th Cavalry led by Lieutenant Colonel George A. Custer. It was the base of Custer and his troops until their fatal encounter at the Little Big Horn. *Open daily May-Oct. Small charge.*

SLANT INDIAN VILLAGE Five earth mound dwellings have been reconstructed to show how the Mandan Indians lived here from about 1738 to 1764. The village received its unusual name because the houses are built on the side of a hill.

33. Sakakawea Statue *Capitol Grounds, Bismarck, N.D.* On the journey from the Dakotas to the Pacific Ocean, one of the invaluable members of the Lewis and Clark expedition was the Shoshone Indian woman Sakakawea. Known as the Bird Woman, she guided the explorers, helped them get food and horses from her tribesmen, and at one time saved the expedition's records from an overturned canoe. The fine bronze statue depicts Sakakawea walking with her baby son on her back, as she did throughout the march across the continent. *Open daily.*

34. Grant County Museum *Railroad Ave. and Main St., Elgin, N.D.* Relics of pioneer life in the Dakotas are on view in Elgin's one-building museum complex. In the original railroad depot, built in 1910, are a restored ticket office and waiting room, plus a replica sod house with furnishings from the days of the early settlers. A restored one-room schoolhouse in the depot freight room comprises the second half of the museum, and antique farm machinery stands on the grounds. *Open daily June-early Sept.*

35. Weinhandl Museum *Shields, N.D.* Here you can see a Sioux Indian dictionary copyrighted in 1851, prehistoric arrowheads, old bottles and jars, cut glass and antique toys. The collections are housed in Shields' old railroad depot. *Open Mon.-Sat. June-Aug.*

36. Land of the Sioux Museum *511 N. Main St., Mobridge, S.D.* This small museum holds a fine collection of items relating to Sioux Indians in general and Sitting Bull in particular. Paintings and photographs of the famous chief, who lived near here, and historical records dealing with him are displayed. Indian history and culture are depicted in 10 outstanding murals by Sioux artist Oscar Howe. One shows a little-known episode which occurred in 1862 when a small band of Cheyennes rescued several white captives from the Santee Sioux. A sumptuous feather blanket, intricate beadwork, an eagle-feather headdress and many other artifacts are on display. *Open daily mid-May-mid-Sept.*

37. Mobridge Municipal Auditorium *Off Rte. 12, Mobridge, S.D.* Ten colorful murals with Indian themes, the work of Oscar Howe, cover the walls of the modern auditorium. The murals are divided into two groups: *The Ceremonies of the Sioux* are depicted on the south wall and *History Along the Missouri* is shown on the north wall. *Open Mon.-Fri.*

38. Mentor Graham House *Commercial St., Blunt, S.D.* The man who taught Abraham Lincoln the rudiments of grammar, diction and surveying moved into this small frame house at the age of 84 and lived here until his death a year later in 1885. He had met Lincoln in Illinois in 1829 when the latter was a flatboatman and fell in love with one of Graham's students, the beautiful and ill-fated Ann Rutledge. The modest dwelling holds 1880s furniture, including a huge walnut bed, a dresser and a commode. Several old photographs and engravings still hang on the walls. *Open daily Apr.-Oct.*

39. South Dakota State Capitol *Pierre, S.D.* The capitol, dominated by a copper-sheathed dome, is set in wooded grounds by a 10-acre lake. An artesian well that feeds the lake contains so much natural gas that it flames up in a perpetual burning fountain, especially spectacular at night. Inside the building, light filters through stained-glass panels in the dome down to the simulated marble pillars and the mosaic floor of the rotunda, 96 feet below. The magnificent Ionic-style marble staircase rises two stories. *Open daily.*

40. South Dakota State Historical Society Museum *Soldiers and Sailors World War Memorial Bldg., Pierre, S.D.* Star of the museum is the Vérendrye Plate, a small lead tablet inscribed in Latin and French. In 1743 it was placed on a hill overlooking the Missouri River by the French-Canadian explorer Pierre Gaultier de Varennes, Sieur de la Vérendrye, who was searching for a route to the Pacific. Long sought by historians, since Vérendrye had referred to the plate in his diary, it was accidentally discovered by schoolchildren in 1913. Indian artifacts ranging from the Paleo period through the time of contact with Europeans are also displayed. *Open daily except holidays.*

This 1886 steam engine still works, as do most of the 150 pieces of equipment in the Thieszen Farm Machinery Collection. Twenty-four antique automobiles are also displayed. Steam engines for plows, tractors, mills and threshers helped transform the prairie, which pioneers called the Great American Desert, into the thriving agricultural region it is today.

47. Stuhr Museum of the Prairie Pioneer

Rte. 34, S. of Grand Island, Nebr.

Architect Edward Durell Stone's shining white, flat-roofed museum building seems to float on its island in a crescent-shaped lake. The ultramodern structure, filled with relics of Nebraska's early days from 1870 to 1915, makes an intriguing contrast with the larger outdoor displays. Some 55 buildings have been brought here from surrounding towns, meticulously restored and arranged as a typical prairie town. Railroad tracks, complete with rolling stock, form the town's eastern boundary and an old depot stands ready to receive people and goods. Facing the tracks is a wide Main Street of typical western-style buildings, some false-fronted: a bank, barbershop and general store, hotel and houses, post office, blacksmith shop and barns. The Stuhr Museum was named for Leo B. Stuhr, the son of pioneer parents, who gave the land and money for it. He and his fellow townsmen have made possible a trip back to a simpler, smaller world, to the days when Nebraska was young. *Main building open daily except holidays. Outdoor museum open daily June-early Sept. Small charge.*

41. Pioneer Auto Museum *Rtes. 90 and 83, Murdo, S.D.* More than 140 antique and classic cars are scattered over a three-acre site, given a still more ancient air by the 25 authentic buildings from pioneer days. Automobile enthusiasts will enjoy inspecting a 1902 Oldsmobile, 1909 Sears-Roebuck, 1925 Stanley Steamer and a 1931 Packard touring car. An interesting collection of sleighs, buggies and other horse-drawn vehicles is housed in a livery barn. Also displayed are music boxes, antique furnishings, early bicycles and motorcycles, 45 old tractors and other farm equipment. Buildings include a 1906 jail, a homesteader's claim cabin and an early schoolhouse. *Open daily Apr.-Oct. Adults $1.25, children small charge.*

42. Old West Museum *Rtes. 90 and 16, 3 mi. W. of Chamberlain, S.D.* Two covered wagons and an 1898 Army ambulance wagon are among the outstanding attractions here. Visitors can also see a variety of Indian artifacts and an excellent collection of the types of guns once used in the area. A small stagecoach, a one-room schoolhouse and an authentic territorial jail are exhibited along with powder horns, early china, dolls and a unique picture of a buffalo made from hundreds of buffalo teeth found in the prairies. The grounds shelter live buffalo and longhorn steers. *Open daily May-mid-Oct. Adults and children over 5 small charge.*

43. Soper's Sod Museum *Rte. 18, E. of Gregory, S.D.* At the turn of the century when settlers came to the treeless prairies, it was considered a mark of security and distinction to have a sod house like this one, the replica of a family home built in 1905. A plow turned 108 tons of earth to build strong walls two feet thick, which make the "soddie" warm in winter, cool in summer. An authentic interior luxury is plasterwork, but the cement floor is a modern comfort, as are the electric lights, added to provide better viewing of old household utensils and furniture. *Open daily Mar.-Oct.*

44. Pioneers Antelope County Historical Society Museum *Neligh, Nebr.* Cells and barred windows attest to this brick building's service as the county jail from 1901 to 1964, but it was originally built as a college gymnasium in 1892. The Indian Room contains a good collection of artifacts, and many early household items can be seen in a reconstructed pioneer log cabin. Period clothing, a handmade rug loom and a 13-star American flag are also prize exhibits. *Open Sun., Fri. Mar.-Nov.*

45. Anna Palmer Museum *211 E. Seventh St., York, Nebr.* Civil War relics are of particular interest here, an understandable feature since York was settled by veterans of the conflict. Visitors can appreciate the lifestyle of the time when they see the period bedroom and living room, which are arranged with mannequins dressed in the apparel of the time. A replica sod house contains china, glassware and furniture, all made before 1870 when York became a town. *Open Mon.-Sat.*

The Milisen House, built in Grand Island about 1879, has been restored and authentically furnished, down to the dinnerware and 1890s wallpaper.

The Danish Lutheran Church (1888) stands somewhat apart from the re-created town, near the Wood River. The striped steeple is visible for miles.

46. York County Courthouse *York, Nebr.* Artful details distinguish the exterior of this massive stone structure, which was built in 1886. A high entrance portico includes a dentil pediment, and a large central tower is crowned by a sleek dome. Beneath the dome are representations of a plow, a rake, a hoe, a sheaf and a cogwheel, symbolic of the area's rich agricultural heritage. *Open Mon.-Fri. except holidays.*

47. Stuhr Museum of the Prairie Pioneer *Rte. 34, S. of Grand Island, Nebr.* See display above.

48. Hastings Museum *Rte. 281 and 14th St., Hastings, Nebr.* Birds, mammals, fish, reptiles and insects form part of the impressive natural history exhibits here. Known as the "House of Yesterday," the museum also contains many displays that dramatize the history of the Great Plains and the American Indian: an 1880s country store and post office, complete with candy and chewing tobacco; a Sioux eagle-feather headdress and beaded vest; pioneer corn-husk and rag dolls; a covered wagon and a stagecoach. The museum's J. M. McDonald Planetarium features daily shows and frequently changing programs dealing with various aspects of the universe. *Open daily. Small charge.*

49. Fort Kearney Museum *315 S. Central, Kearney, Nebr.* Odd and colorful items are the rule here. There are bleeders, a favorite tool of early physicians; instruments of torture; a dinosaur egg; prehistoric elephant teeth; the first music box manufactured in the U.S. and a rare vase from the Pitcairn Islands. These are just some of the curiosities in the museum's collections of armor, guns, masks, Indian artifacts and Oriental and archaeological finds. A popular attraction is a glass-bottomed boat ride on the museum's private lake. *Open daily May-Aug. Small charge.*

50. Willa Cather Pioneer Memorial Museum *N. Webster St., Red Cloud, Nebr.* Letters, first editions and other items relating to the life of Willa Cather are exhibited in the library of a 19th-century bank building. In addition to the Cather archives and memorabilia, the museum contains pioneer artifacts and works by several Nebraska artists. *Open daily May-Sept.*

WILLA CATHER CHILDHOOD HOME *Third and Cedar Aves.* Willa Cather described this one-and-a-half-story frame house in *The Song of the Lark.* It was her family's home from 1884-1904. The original wallpaper, with small red and brown roses, may be seen in Miss Cather's upstairs bedroom. The furnishings are late 19th century. *Small charge.*

51. Paton's Isle of Memories *Neche, N.D.* Four buildings make up this museum dedicated to preserving the memory of rural life in 19th-century America. A 90-year-old one-and-a-half-story wooden frame house is completely furnished with period pieces. A one-room 1882 schoolhouse is still filled with initial-carved desks, blackboards and even some old report cards. The other attractions here are a wooden village church with arched windows, and a Quonset hut housing a large collection of Americana, including a 70-year-old bicycle, an 1890 piano-harp, many phonographs and replicas of an old-time kitchen, post office, sitting room and blacksmith shop. *Open daily June-late Oct.*

52. Pioneer Village Museum *Off Rtes. 2 and 3, Rugby, N.D.* The geographical center of the North American continent is marked by a white stone near this museum. The reconstructed pioneer village includes a 19th-century railroad depot, a bank, a one-room schoolhouse, a log cabin with appropriate furnishings, a church and a blacksmith shop. Two buildings are used to house 600 dolls dating back to 1885 and collections of antique guns, cars, farm implements and musical instruments. *Open daily mid-June-Oct. Small charge.*

53. Fort Totten Historic Site *Off Rte. 57, Fort Totten, N.D.* Built in the 1860s, Fort Totten remains the best-preserved fort from the days of the Plains Indian wars. Now located in a Sioux and Chippewa reservation, the fort consists of a parade ground surrounded by several original brick buildings. These include a row of officers' houses, enlisted men's barracks, quartermaster's storehouse and quarters for the commanding officer, surgeon and chaplain. The former hospital now houses the Lake Region Pioneer Daughters' Museum, containing many items that typify life in the old territory. There is also a National Game Preserve nearby. *Open daily.*

54. Steele County Historical Society Buildings *Hope, N.D.* Housed in the society's four-building complex are furniture, clothes, pictures, machinery and other artifacts that tell the story of the early prairie days. A restored 19th-century frame schoolhouse contains a pioneer kitchen, musical instruments, and school and church items used by the settlers. Nearby is a two-story brick house furnished in pieces typical of the late 1800s. An old general store and a building housing a collection of early machinery complete this view of the past. *Open Sun. late May-early Sept.*

55. Bonanzaville, U.S.A. *West Fargo, N.D.* In the 1870s land in North Dakota was bought in huge blocks of 7000 to 75,000 acres, and as many as 1000 men might work one farm. Now, in Bonanzaville, more than 25 structures with appropriate furnishings re-create a village typical of the Red River Valley in the days of bonanza farming. There is the Town Hall with its two-cell jail; the bandstand; a livery stable full of simple buggies and elegant carriages; the U. R. Next Barbershop, built in 1900; a two-story farmhouse with the original furnishings; and the railroad depot, with a caboose and passenger coach on the siding. The museum presents literally thousands of objects and furnishings—and an atmosphere that brings back the region's "good old days." *Open daily June-mid-Oct., Tues.-Fri. mid-Oct.-May. Small charge.*

56. Frontier Village *Off Business Loop W., Jamestown, N.D.* The pioneer life of the prairies is re-created in authentic buildings, which were moved here to establish the settlement. An 1883 frame church and a log cabin can be seen, as well as a drugstore, a printshop and a 1911 schoolhouse. Beside the town's first railroad depot stands a restored caboose. Nearby is a mammoth 60-ton concrete buffalo, symbol of the great herds that once roamed the open grasslands here. *Open daily late May-early Sept.*

57. Stutsman County Memorial Museum *321 Third Ave. S.E., Jamestown, N.D.* Constructed in 1907 for a lumber magnate, the brick building contains local memorabilia: Indian artifacts, military relics and medical instruments are the highlights. Temporary exhibits are often presented, and a regional history library is available. *Open Sun., Wed. June-Sept.*

58. Whitestone Hill Battlefield State Historic Site *Off Rte. 56, S. of Kulm, N.D.* The last significant battle between whites and Indians east of the Missouri River was fought here in 1863 when the U.S. Cavalry fell on a Sioux camp. Displays and items related to the battle are housed in a small museum. The grounds include a monument commemorating the military dead in the hilltop cemetery, along with hiking trails, campsites and picnic areas. *Open daily June-Aug.*

59. Christopher Rott Museum *Ashley, N.D.* Old pendulum clocks, antique chairs and china, guns, Edison phonographs and seven spinning wheels are just a few of the objects that line the walls and hang from the ceiling of this small but extensive folk museum. The private collection also encompasses pioneer utensils, clothing and farm machinery. Several vintage cars can be seen as well, including a 1923 Model T touring car, 1927 Model T sedan, 1928 Model A roadster, 1939 Lincoln Zephyr and even a 1935 Oldsmobile hearse. *Open daily May-Aug. Small charge.*

60. Dacotah Prairie Museum *21 S. Main St., Aberdeen, S.D.* Several displays here center on the Plains Indians and early settlers, the trophy room contains mounted animals from India, Africa and the Arctic, and the museum's art gallery features changing monthly exhibits. Several fine period rooms include an 1870s scene, with an ornate organ, a corner stove, a painted gas lamp and costumed mannequins. The collection is housed in a three-story structure that was built as a bank in 1888, the original vaults still serving as storage rooms. *Open daily.*

61. Fort Sisseton State Park *Lake City, S.D.* Fort Sisseton, built in 1864 (and known as Fort Wadsworth), is the oldest fort in South Dakota. It consists of a large parade ground surrounded by breastworks and a number of restored brick and stone buildings, including a hospital, officers' quarters, 1870s library-schoolhouse, blacksmith shop and guardhouse. Although these structures are not open to the public, a visit here offers an excellent idea of conditions during the days of early settlement. *Open daily. Park admission $2.00 May-Sept.*

62. Sam Brown Memorial State Park *Browns Valley, Minn.* Army scout Sam Brown, often called the frontier Paul Revere, made an incredible 150-mile round-trip horseback ride in 1866 to warn a scout outpost in the Dakota Territory of an impending Indian

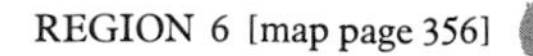

[**60**] *A Victorian parlor of the 1870s is overfilled by today's standards with such status symbols as an organ, Victrola, painted gas lamp and a plethora of patterns. The room and the dress are typical of solid middle-class Victorian style. The newly completed (1869) cross-country railroad speeded the current fashions in the East to those in the West who could afford them. The hundreds of thousands of homesteaders, of course, could not.*

uprising. (It turned out to be a false alarm.) On his return leg, he lost the trail in a spring snowstorm and nearly died of exhaustion and exposure before making his way back. The park contains the log cabin built by his father, Major Joseph Renshaw Brown, in 1863—the first house in Traverse County—in which many of Sam Brown's possessions can be seen. Also on the property are a perfect "little red schoolhouse" with period desks, maps and schoolbooks on display, and the Sacred Rock, a large rock faintly engraved with Indian hieroglyphics (a copy of the figures is kept on view). *Open daily late May-early Sept.*

63. Swensson House *Rte. 6, Montevideo, Minn.* In 1901, at the age of 58, Olof Swensson, a Swedish immigrant who worked as a lay preacher and farmer, gathered and cut local stones for the foundation of a new family home. In two years Swensson, with help from his daughter, completed a 22-room wood and brick structure with 59 windows and 38 doors, all framed with hand-carved woodwork. A chapel, which occupies most of the second floor, and several other rooms were paneled by Swensson with tin sheeting. The house remained in the family until 1967 and it still contains original furnishings, many of which are handmade. On the grounds are a large barn, a gristmill with granite millstones, and the family burial ground. *Open Sun. May-Sept. Small charge.*

64. Blue Cloud Abbey *Marvin, S.D.* Named for a prominent Christian Sioux, this modernistic Benedictine abbey was dedicated in 1967. The exterior of the sandstone building is decorated with a granite mural of the Virgin, and the visitors' lounge contains an interesting abstract mural depicting the arrival of the Benedictines to work with the Indians of the Dakotas some 100 years ago. To further the education of today's Indians—and of whites seeking information on Indian philosophy and culture—the monks recently founded the American Indian Culture Research Center here. Among other facilities, it offers an extensive advisory service and library, and a small display of beadwork, ceremonial pipes and scale models that explain Indian customs. *Open daily.*

65. Mellette House *421 Fifth Ave. N.W., Watertown, S.D.* In 1889 Arthur C. Mellette was elected the first governor of the new state of South Dakota, having served as the last chief executive of the Dakota Territory. His restored 1883 brick house is a typical Victorian structure, with two floors and a three-story corner tower. Inside are original furnishings, including family portraits and two pianos with massive carved legs. A spiral staircase and fireplace frames are examples of the interesting woodwork. *Open Tues.-Sun. May-Sept.*

66. Surveyor's House *De Smet, S.D.* The one-time railroad house, removed from the countryside to the town of De Smet, has been restored as a memorial to Laura Ingalls Wilder, well-known author of children's books. When she was 12 years old, her father, a timekeeper and paymaster for the railroad construction camps, moved his family into the little wooden surveyor's house where they lived in the winter of 1879-80. Six of Mrs. Wilder's books have their locale in De Smet. *Open daily June-Aug. Small charge.*

[**68**] *The charming* After School *by South Dakota artist Harvey Dunn (1884-1952) is one of the many scenes he painted of pioneer life in his state. Dunn himself grew up in a claim shanty on his family's homestead.*

67. Charles Coughlin Campanile *South Dakota State University, Brookings, S.D.* This 1929 gift from an alumnus soars 170 feet and offers from its top a fine view of the surroundings, including the Minnesota border 20 miles away. A set of chimes sounds the hours, plays college songs and announces special university observances. *Open daily June-Aug.*

68. South Dakota Memorial Art Center *Medary Ave. and Harvey Dunn St., Brookings, S.D.* Highlighted in the modern building are 57 oils by South Dakotan Harvey Dunn (1884-1952), who gained fame as a combat artist in World War I and later portrayed the pioneer history of his state. *Something for Supper* and *Bringing Home the Bride* are among his major canvases that faithfully record early prairie scenes. *Street Fight* and *The Doughboy* tell of the American soldier in World War I. Here too are paintings by Rockwell Kent, Thomas Hart Benton and Reginald Marsh. Prominent Sioux artists Oscar Howe and Andrew Standing Soldier are represented in the growing Indian collection. More than 1500 superb examples of the world-famous embroidered linens of South Dakotan Vera Way Marghab are visitor favorites. *Open daily.*

69. Lake County Historical Museum *Dakota State College, Madison, S.D.* The modern brick and stone building houses material that helps the viewer to understand the early years of the state and county. Indian relics, old household and farm items, coins, silver and a collection of animals and birds can be seen. *Open Sun., Tues.-Thurs.*

70. Prairie Village *Rte. 34, W. of Madison, S.D.* Most of the 40 or so buildings in the 140-acre site on the shores of Lake Herman were moved here from towns throughout the state, but the flavor of an authentic pioneer community has been preserved. In addition to an 1877 claim shanty, a sod house and a two-story, hand-hewn log dwelling built in 1872, visitors can enter an 1884 one-room schoolhouse and a late 19th-century depot. All of these structures are furnished, and the 1912 opera house offers theater productions during the summer. Much farm equipment is on display here, including more than 100 antique gas-operated tractors. Among the working steam-powered machines are a German locomotive, an 1893 carousel with hand-carved horses and a popcorn wagon. In late August steam fans gather from all over the country for the annual Steam Threshing Jamboree. *Open daily May-Sept. Adults $1.50, children over 12 small charge.*

71. Moody County Museum *E. Pipestone Ave., Flandreau, S.D.* A dentist's office in any setting is not notably popular, but the old one reproduced here at least consoles modern viewers that they are much better off today. Another exhibit shows a pioneer bedroom with a wardrobe trunk at the foot of the ample double bed. Antique automobiles and carriages, old-fashioned dolls and clothes, Indian artifacts and moccasins, old books and newspapers—all make absorbing displays. Nearby —a separate part of the museum—stands a rural schoolhouse, completely outfitted and ready for class. *Open Sun. late May-early Sept.*

72. Corn Palace *604 N. Main St., Mitchell, S.D.* The unique corn-covered structure is of Moorish design, with minarets, turrets and domes. Each year the exterior decorations, made entirely of corn and other local grains and grasses, are changed—sometimes requiring up to 3000 bushels of corn. For more than 20 years the noted artist Oscar Howe has created the designs for the 11 panels that circle the palace. The building, used as a municipal auditorium, is the scene of the Corn Palace Festival during the last week in September. *Open daily late May-early Sept.*

73. Friends of the Middle Border *1311 S. Duff St., Mitchell, S.D.* The way people—Indians, pioneers and soldiers—lived in the Dakota Territory comes alive again in displays of costumes, tools and weapons. There is also a good collection of horse-drawn vehicles, antique cars, furniture and farm equipment. Visitors especially enjoy the 1882 schoolroom and the early country store and railroad depot. Harvey Dunn's *Dakota Woman,* James Earl Fraser's *Lewis and Clark,* as well as works by Childe Hassam and Oscar Howe are among the fine art displayed. In the large history library are relics of Hamlin Garland, O. E. Rolvaag and others who wrote of homestead days. *Open daily June-early Sept. Small charge.*

74. Memorial to the Battleship U.S.S. "South Dakota" *Rte. 16, Sioux Falls, S.D.* Cables stretched around the circular brick building mark the length and beam of the famous battleship that won 14 battle stars for service in the Pacific during World War II. One of the *South Dakota*'s bells may be rung by visitors coming to see the many mementos and photographs of the ship on which Admirals Chester Nimitz and William "Bull" Halsey both served. Especially interesting are the official Navy scale model of the vessel, and another model showing part of her engine room. The museum's teak walls and ceiling paneling were taken from the ship's deck. *Open daily May-early Sept.*

75. Pettigrew Museum of Natural Arts and History *131 N. Duluth Ave., Sioux Falls, S.D.* This was the home of R. F. Pettigrew, the state's first U.S. senator. An excellent exhibit of Indian objects encompasses an authentic Blackfoot tepee and many Sioux artifacts such as wampum, warbonnets and a rare Ghost Dance shirt. Rocks, minerals, wildlife specimens and fossils provide a good insight into the state's natural history. Among the many other displays are a superb gun collection and photographs of famous Plains Indian chiefs. Senator Pettigrew's papers are available for study in the library. *Open daily except holidays.*

76. Yankton County Territorial Museum *Westside Park, Yankton, S.D.* The reconstructed 1860s office of the Dakota Territory's first governor contains a buffalo rug and a buffalo overcoat, a desk, a stove and a wall clock that help evoke an image of the time. Other period rooms here at the museum are a bedroom, a schoolroom, a kitchen and a parlor with a square grand piano especially designed to save space. A sod-buster plow, an old wooden sleigh and an Indian tepee are also displayed, as are materials relating to Yankton, the territory's first capital. *Open Tues.-Sun. late May-Dec.*

77. W. H. Over Dakota Museum *University of South Dakota, Rte. 50, Vermillion, S.D.* Full-size and miniature dioramas provide a cross section of the natural history and ecology of South Dakota. Visitors can see an extinct breed of Badlands sheep, a prairie dog town, and the habitats of beaver, bison and antelope. There are a replica of a Sioux Indian encampment and an exhibit of objects used in the Sioux Ghost Dance. The museum houses the studio and gallery of Oscar Howe, the well-known Sioux artist whose colorful abstract paintings are based on the Sioux culture. *Open daily except holidays.*

78. Sioux City Public Museum *2901 Jackson St., Sioux City, Iowa* Fine paneling, an elaborately carved staircase and many fireplaces are of particular interest in this large 1890 quartzite mansion where local history is preserved. The Rumsey Historical Room contains documents, photographs and letters related to Sioux City's pioneer years; tools from early trades are shown elsewhere. Nature exhibits include bird dioramas, while plant and animal fossils record vanished wildlife. The Indian collection has clothing and decorative artistry worked with quills and beads. *Open Tues.-Sun. except holidays.*

79. Historic General Dodge House *605 Third St., Council Bluffs, Iowa* Grenville Mellen Dodge, Civil War general, U.S. congressman and railroad magnate, built this 14-room house in 1869, the year he finished, as chief engineer, construction of the Union Pacific Railroad. One of the finest examples of Victorian architecture in the Midwest, the mansion reflects postbellum opulence. It has been restored and contains many possessions of the Dodge family and other excellent examples of Victorian furniture and decorative accessories. *Open Tues.-Sun. Feb.-Dec. except Thanksgiving Day and Dec. 25. Small charge.*

80. Joslyn Art Museum *2200 Dodge St., Omaha, Nebr.* See feature display on pages 370-1.

81. St. Cecilia's Cathedral *701 N. 40th St., Omaha, Nebr.* Massive buttresses in a scroll design surround the nave of the impressive Catholic cathedral, which was begun in 1907 but not completed until 1959. The Spanish Renaissance styling is evident in the church's tall twin towers, plain shafts rising to highly decorative cupolas. Triple bronze doors open into the vaulted nave, where the eye is drawn at once to the white Carrara marble altar and the large bronze crucifix over it. Exquisite paintings and carvings of saints, the Stations of the Cross in circular bronze medallions, stained-glass windows and mosaic work in side chapels adorn the sanctuary. *Open daily.*

[72] *Since long before the dawn of recorded history man has celebrated the harvesting of his crops. The way they do it in Mitchell, South Dakota, is to decorate the minareted, brick Corn Palace convention hall with thousands of bushels of locally grown corn and grasses. For the past 25 years South Dakota Indian artist Oscar Howe has designed the varicolored corn murals using a different theme each year. Then, for a week in September, Mitchell holds a festival of agricultural displays, a carnival, parades and big band shows at the Palace. The idea originated in 1892 with two local businessmen who wanted a new way to celebrate an ancient tradition.*

Man With a Falcon *by Titian (1477–1576). This wealthy 16th-century Italian is one of many public figures who had their portraits painted by Titian in the 1520s after the master's fame had spread far beyond his hometown of Venice. The subject looks as dignified as a prince of the church or state, a quality with which Titian imbued most of his portraits regardless of the sitter's social position. Titian painted prolifically—religious and mythological figures, portraits and landscapes—for 70 years, exceeding the production of other masters, such as Rembrandt and Rubens.*

Fort Laramie *is one of 113 watercolors in the museum sketched by A. J. Miller, who accompanied Scottish Captain W. D. Stewart on a hunting trip along the Oregon Trail in 1837. Fort Laramie was built in 1834 as a fur-trading post. Indians camped outside while they bartered beaver pelts for dry goods, beads and whiskey. When the fur trade declined in the 1840s the fort became an important supply center and an army post charged with protecting wagon trains from hostile Indians. Today it is a National Historic Site* *(see page 541).* *After this trip Miller expanded some of his sketches into oils for Stewart's castle in Scotland, then became a portrait painter in Baltimore. He also sold copies of his Western sketches.*

80. Joslyn Art Museum

2200 Dodge St., Omaha, Nebr.

Joslyn is one of the particularly noteworthy small museums in the country. It has a substantial collection of European and American paintings which includes works by Rembrandt, Veronese, El Greco, Corot, Renoir, Inness, Homer, Wood and Benton, and objects representative of 5000 years of art from around the world. The cultural and historic context of the collection is emphasized by displaying the fine and decorative arts of a particular period together with material which shows how and where they were employed. For example, a painting by Titian, the most renowned painter of the Venetian school, is seen beside Venetian sculpture and carved furniture of the period. The museum's regional collection is presented in an exhibit of "Life on the Prairie" which begins with a display of Stone Age artifacts—pottery, flints, bows and arrows—of the people who first inhabited the area. European exploration, exploitation and settlement of the plains is documented with maps, paintings, prints, photographs, period rooms, crafts and tools. Most interesting and informative are the paintings and prints. Impressions by artists who were on the scene are the only true visual record we have of the now vanished Old West. Represented are George Catlin (1796-1872), who painted the daily and ceremonial life of Plains Indians in wonderful, sympathetic detail; Karl Bodmer (1809-93), a Swiss artist who made illustrations for the German naturalist Prince Maximilian of Wied on a scientific study in North America; A. J. Miller (1810-74), commissioned to sketch on a Scot's Western hunting trip; and American army officers, stationed at prairie outposts, who recorded the life around them. Many of these vital works by Bodmer and Miller are owned by the Northern Natural Gas Company, which has loaned them to the museum. *Open Tues.-Sun. Small charge except Sat.*

Sixth- and fifth-century B.C. *Greeks decorated their utilitarian objects with extraordinarily fine drawings. Here are a krater (top) used for mixing wine and water, and two amphorae in which wine and oil were stored.*

Before railroads were laid, Conestoga wagons such as this carried freight westward; they were the prototype of the lighter-weight prairie schooner.

Wahktageli (*"Big Soldier"*) *by Karl Bodmer. Bodmer's sketches of Indians, plants and animals are beautifully executed and accurate in detail.*

 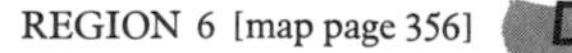

[83] *J. Sterling Morton, founder of Arbor Day, built his 52-room mansion on homestead property that was originally virgin prairie. His example inspired Nebraska farmers to beautify their land by planting trees.*

82. Lincoln, Nebr.

Lincoln, the state capital, prospered in the 19th century because it is located in a salt basin. In 1867 its name was changed from Lancaster to Lincoln to honor the assassinated President. It is a transportation, cultural and trading center of Nebraska.

Fairview *4900 Sumner St.* The famous orator and politician William Jennings Bryan lived in this then tranquil rural retreat from 1902 to 1917. Mementos of his career remain in the house. The carved wood furniture is typical of the period, while the Oriental objects are splendid souvenirs of a family trip around the world. *Open Thurs.-Sun. June-Aug. Small charge.*

Lincoln Children's Zoo *2800 A St.* The opportunity for personal contact with llamas, goats, Sicilian donkeys, sheep, deer, tortoises and other animals is provided at the zoo's animal compound. Other features of this children's zoo, one of the largest in the world, are the Stegosaurus fountain; the crooked house; and Zooville Square, a miniature version of an 1880s' Nebraska town. *Open daily May-Sept. Small charge.*

Nebraska State Capitol *1545 J St.* See feature display on page 373.

Nebraska Statehood Memorial *1627 H St.* The Italianate mansion was once the residence of Thomas Perkins Kennard, one of three men chosen by legislators in 1867 to pick a capital site for the new state of Nebraska. They all chose Lincoln, and each had substantial masonry houses built to show confidence in the city's future. Only the Kennard home remains, now restored to its 1870 appearance. Furnishings reflect a well-to-do household of the era and many items—a desk, a bookcase, a fireplace—belonged to Nebraska's early governors. The hitching post outside is from the first governor's mansion. *Open Tues.-Sun.*

Sheldon Memorial Art Gallery *University of Nebraska, 12th and R Sts.* Philip Johnson designed the elegant columned building of Italian marble in the early 1960s. Prominent among the 19th- and 20th-century American artists featured here is Robert Henri (1865-1929), with a group of canvases that spans his career. Paintings by Maurer, Sloan, Eakins and Blakelock, and such contemporary artists as Hartley, de Kooning and Rothko can also be admired. There is a sculpture garden, and films, lectures and temporary exhibits are additional attractions. *Open Tues.-Sun. except holidays.*

83. Arbor Lodge State Historical Park *W. of Nebraska City, Nebr.* After newspaperman J. Sterling Morton built his house here in 1855, he landscaped the surrounding barren prairie and advocated home beautification for his readers. His deep interest in the land persisted. In 1872 he founded Arbor Day, still celebrated annually by the planting of trees, and later became the nation's second Secretary of Agriculture. Splendid trees and shrubs—more than 170 varieties—may be seen around the 65-acre estate, and flowers crowd a terraced garden designed by Frederick Law Olmsted in 1903. The stately Greek Revival mansion holds much of the Morton family furniture as well as china, glassware and Tiffany light fixtures. Farm implements, fire engines and early carriages are other estate exhibits. *Open daily mid-Apr.-Oct. Small charge.*

84. Wildwood Center *Wildwood Park, Steinhardt Park Rd., Nebraska City, Nebr.* The completely furnished Wildwood Period House, built in 1869, is the main attraction in the complex. Its 10 rooms have authentic decor from 1860 to 1880, including an 85-key Steinway piano, an 1878 reed organ and English and French wallpaper. An iron stove is the centerpiece of the serviceable kitchen, and the pantry is properly equipped with bins for flour, coffee and sugar. Puppet shows are presented in a remodeled chicken coop on the grounds, and arts and crafts classes are given in a barn. *Open Tues.-Sun. mid-Apr.-mid-Oct. Small charge.*

85. Brownville Historic District *Brownville, Nebr.* The frontier town, founded in 1854, was once an important trading center on the Missouri River, for here steamboats from the East met freight wagons headed for Denver and Santa Fe. The historic district encompasses many houses, business offices, churches and other buildings of the steamboat era. Descriptions of four buildings open to the public are given below. *Open Sun. May, Tues.-Sun. June-early Sept., Sun. early Sept.-mid-Oct.*

BROWNVILLE MUSEUM *Main St.* Furniture, clothing, household items, toys and musical instruments from the town's early history are on view here in the Victorian home of a riverboat captain. Old quilts and comforters colorfully decorate one bedroom. *Small charge.*

CARSON HOUSE *Main St.* Richard Brown, the town's founder, built a two-story brick dwelling in 1860. John Carson, a local financier, acquired the residence in 1864 and added frame wings and a brick carriage house. The furnishings of the home are the originals used by the Carson family. The carriage house is now an art gallery. *Small charge.*

LONE TREE SALOON *Main St.* At one time Brownville could boast 13 saloons, but this is the one reputedly favored by Jesse James. It formerly was the Opera House and is now a mill producing stone-ground flour.

MUIR HOUSE *Second and Atlanta Sts.* The Italianate mansion was built between 1868 and 1872 by Robert Muir. Now a museum, the two-story brick house contains Victorian furniture, clothing and household items. Embroidery, paintings and watercolors are displayed along with sculpture and decorative arts. *Small charge.*

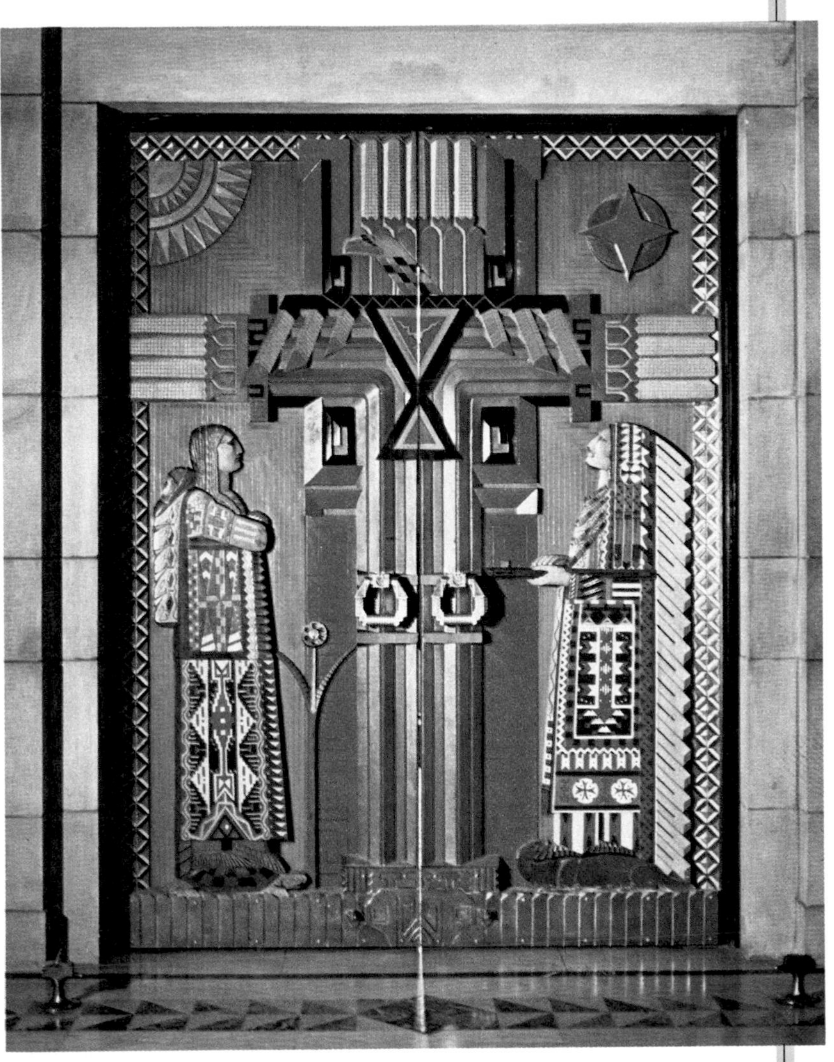

A massive but clean-lined 400-foot tower dominates Nebraska's capitol. Over the gold mosaic dome a giant figure of the Sower *strides. The "Indian" doors (right) feature the Tree of Life—the green cross with ears of corn at the ends—and the Thunderbird, ruler of the heavens.*

The rich detail in the north hall—bricks, mosaics, lamps—is not overwhelming because of the vast scale. The mural honors Nebraska's sodbusters.

82. Nebraska State Capitol

1545 J St., Lincoln, Nebr.

Up to 1922, when ground was broken for the Nebraska State Capitol, most state capitols were variations on the classical theme of the U.S. Capitol in Washington. But the 1920s marked the coming of age of the skyscraper. Elevators could zoom up 20 or 30 stories; concrete poured on a steel frame and reinforced with steel bars meant that floor could rise on floor almost, it seemed, to infinity. Architect Bertram Grosvenor Goodhue, in this modernist structure, made the mass and height of the tower, its details smoothed and simplified, work against the horizontals—the shallow flight of steps leading to the entrance and the quadrangle of low buildings around it. Inside, the floors and walls of the enormous public rooms, illuminated by massive, elaborate chandeliers, glow with finely worked mosaics. Many different kinds of marble and wood, often richly carved, provide color and textural contrast. Symbols and stories in murals and mosaics range from the signs of the zodiac to the coming of the pioneers. The state capitol, which so successfully blends art and architecture, was justly famous in its time. *Open daily except Dec. 25.*

86. Homestead National Monument *Rte. 4, Beatrice, Nebr.* Daniel Freeman filed his claim for this site on Jan. 1, 1863, one of the first to act under the newly passed Homestead Act, which permitted any citizen to claim 160 acres of unused government land. Displays at the Visitor Center show household items, tools and other simple relics of the period. An 1867 timbered cabin, moved here from a neighboring farm, illustrates a homestead dwelling with its typical furnishings, all authentic. *Open daily except holidays.*

87. Lumbertown U.S.A. *Rte. 77 off 371, N. of Brainerd, Minn.* Walk through the swinging doors of an old-time saloon, or visit an old-fashioned ice cream parlor (where ice cream is sold) in this re-creation of an 1870s lumber town, complete down to a cobbler's shop, livery stable, printshop and undertaker's parlor. These restored and reconstructed buildings are furnished as if it were still 1870. Also entertaining: a ride around the area on a replica of an old Northern Pacific train, or a cruise aboard the riverboat *Blue Berry Belle. Open daily late May-mid-Sept. Small charge.*

88. Mille Lacs Indian Museum *Off Rte. 169, 10 mi. N. of Onamia, Minn.* From prehistoric times until fur traders came in the 18th century, Chippewa and Sioux Indians lived peacefully in this area. Territorial fighting began after the Chippewa obtained guns from the traders, and in 1745, after a long battle here, the Chippewa won, forcing out the Sioux. In this museum the political, social and cultural history of these tribes is recalled by means of dioramas and displays of weapons and tools—some of which are prehistoric—and clothing. *Open daily May-Sept. Small charge.*

89. Kensington Runestone Museum *206 N. Broadway, Alexandria, Minn.* Did a band of Vikings explore Minnesota 130 years before Columbus reached America? The inscription on a 200-pound stone says they did. In the runic writing of ancient northern Europe, the Kensington Runestone tells of Viking experiences in the area and is dated 1362. When it was discovered by a pioneer Kensington farmer in 1898, some scholars declared it a hoax. Sincc then, evidence points to its authenticity. The original stone is displayed in this museum with ancient weapons and tools found on the Vikings' route along Minnesota waterways. Also here are Indian artifacts, a pioneer cabin and exhibits of the state's wildlife. *Open daily May-Sept., Mon.-Fri. Oct.-Apr. Adults and children over 6 small charge.*

90. Sinclair Lewis Boyhood Home *812 Sinclair Lewis Ave., Sauk Centre, Minn.* In his famous novel *Main Street* (1920), Sinclair Lewis tarnished the myth of idyllic smalltown American life by describing its indigenous provincialism. The setting of the book, Gopher Prairie, is actually Sauk Centre, where Lewis lived until 1903 when, at the age of 18, he left for Yale University. Neither the town nor the house in which Lewis grew up, a two-story clapboard structure with gingerbread trim, have changed much over the years. The home contains furniture and other items that belonged to the Lewis family, and a visit here evokes the turn-of-the-century era. Lewis, who went on to write a number of insightful novels on American life, won the 1930 Nobel Prize for literature, the first American so honored. *Open daily late May-early Sept. Small charge includes admission to Sinclair Lewis Museum.*

[86] *A homesteading family of 12 lived in this 14-by-16-foot, two-story cabin; a cramped home but easier to heat than a bigger place. The owner built it of logs and clay bricks, using materials from his land.*

91. Sinclair Lewis Museum *Library Bldg., Original Main St., Sauk Centre, Minn.* Part of Bryant Library, which Sinclair Lewis remembered fondly because its books provided him with so many vicarious boyhood adventures, has been turned into a Lewis museum. It contains autographed copies of Lewis's novels, his writing desk and personal effects. Highlights of the author's life are presented in a sound-and-slide show. *Open daily late May-early Sept. Small charge, or included in admission to Sinclair Lewis Boyhood Home.*

92. St. John's Abbey and University *Rte. 32, Collegeville, Minn.* This Benedictine monastery, the world's largest, was founded in 1856. The monks conduct the university, as well as a seminary and a college preparatory school, all of which fit easily on the 2400-acre campus. Worldwide attention has been focused on St. John's since renowned architect Marcel Breuer began designing a series of buildings for the campus, including the two noted below. *Open daily.*

ABBEY AND UNIVERSITY CHURCH OF ST. JOHN THE BAPTIST Reinforced concrete and honeycomb glass are the materials used for this outstanding contemporary structure, dramatic without and approaching the awe-inspiring within. Before the church stands a 112-foot-tall concrete bell banner that commands attention even from great distances.

ALCUIN LIBRARY In deference to the church, architects Breuer and Hamilton Smith gave the rectangular library building a low profile, saving its drama for the interior. There, huge concrete "trees" rise through the main floor to support the roof, eliminating the need for columns and freely opening the space within.

93. Oliver H. Kelley Farm *Off Rte. 10, near Elk River, Minn.* The founder of the Grange movement, Oliver Hudson Kelley, homesteaded this 200-acre farm around the middle of the 19th century. Unlike most farmers of his time, he experimented with crops, built a large irrigation system and wrote about agriculture. Kelley conceived the idea of forming a national farmers' organization with social and educational programs, and the first meeting of the National Grange of the Patrons of Husbandry took place in his 11-room farmhouse on

Dec. 4, 1867. The house is furnished to reflect a typical farm home of the 1860s and '70s. *Open daily May-Sept., Sat., Sun. Oct. Adults small charge.*

94. Hermann's Monument *Center St., New Ulm, Minn.* German-Americans erected this monument to freedom, unity and self-government in 1897 in New Ulm, a small town settled by German immigrants 43 years earlier. Hermann, the Cheruscan, a Germanic warrior, united all the German tribes in 9 A.D. and led them to victory against occupying Roman legions. The bronze statue of him is 32 feet high; an observation platform in the monument provides a panoramic view of the countryside. *Open daily May-mid-Oct.*

95. New Ulm Post Office *Center St. and Broadway, New Ulm, Minn.* The New Ulm Post Office, built in 1910, is a delightful Victorian structure of red brick horizontally striped from rooftop to basement with white stone. Its crenelated gables topped with white finials, and flower boxes set in each window, reinforce the building's Dutch feeling. *Open daily.*

96. Grotto of the Redemption *West Bend, Iowa* The life of Christ unfolds here in a unique construction. Begun in 1912 by a priest, Father Paul Dobberstein, who worked on it until his death 42 years later, the shrine is still being added to. Nine separate grottoes depict the Stable of Bethlehem, the Trinity, the Ten Commandments, Gethsemane and other Biblical scenes. Gems, semiprecious stones, seashells, fossils and petrified wood from the U.S. and many foreign countries appear in the intricate designs, and the 14 Stations of the Cross are rendered in mosaics. Life-size statues from Italy grace the landmark, which is flanked by a small lake. *Open daily.*

97. Blanden Art Gallery *920 Third Ave. S., Fort Dodge, Iowa* A former Fort Dodge resident donated the gallery to the city in 1931. Contemporary paintings by European and American artists, such as Chagall, Miró, Motherwell and Klee, are featured in the permanent collection, which also includes drawings, Japanese prints and Pre-Columbian and African art objects. Contemporary sculpture is represented in the works of Moore, Marin and Lipchitz. *Open Tues.-Sun. except holidays.*

98. Mahanay Memorial Carillon Tower *Courthouse Sq., Jefferson, Iowa* The 162-foot glass and concrete shaft holds a carillon of 32 bells and, atop its roof, 14 chime bells. They make an unusual orchestra that can be heard in concerts daily all across the town. An elevator rises to an observation deck where visitors can watch the bells gong quarter hours and hours. *Open daily mid-May-mid-Oct. Small charge.*

99. Iowa State Center *Iowa State University, Ames, Iowa* The New York Philharmonic performed at the 1969 opening of the Stephens Auditorium, the first building in this lively cultural center. Serving not only the university but the surrounding community as well, the complex comprises the structures described below, a Little Theater and a proposed Continuing Education Building. *Open daily.*

C. Y. STEPHENS AUDITORIUM Cultural events have a magnificent setting in this modern hall. Cantilevered loges flank three balconies beneath a flowing hemlock ceiling. Stage center, a brilliant seamless curtain, handwoven in Japan on a gigantic loom, symbolizes the university's excellence in science.

JAMES H. HILTON COLISEUM An audience of 14,000 can enjoy events in this impressively designed indoor amphitheater, one of the largest in the state.

100. Fisher Foundation Collection *Fisher Community Center, Marshalltown, Iowa* Paintings and sculptures of 19th- and early 20th-century French artists are featured here. Matisse's *Portrait of Madame Matisse dans la Grace* and Degas's *Dancers on Stage* share the company of fine works by such Impressionists as Monet, Pissarro and Sisley. *Open daily.*

101. Des Moines Art Center *Greenwood Park, Des Moines, Iowa* The striking building, opened in 1948, is itself one of the center's greatest treasures—Eliel Saarinen was the architect, and 20 years later a sculpture wing designed by I. M. Pei was added. Inside there are equal delights. In only a quarter century the center has built up impressive strength in 19th- and 20th-century European and American art, with work by such sculptors as Rodin, Moore, Calder and Arp and such painters as Monet (*Cliffs at Etretat*), Bellows, Hopper, Klee and Kuniyoshi (*Amazing Juggler*). There is also a choice collection of primitives and graphics. *Open Tues.-Sun.*

[**92.** *Abbey and University Church*] *A dominant campanile astride the church entrance is the chief exterior indication of the building's function. Architect Marcel Breuer designed the bell banner to serve a number of purposes. It provides a dramatic entry into the church; open spaces in the upper portion hold a cross and bells; and the slab itself reflects sunlight into the church.*

[**103**] *The 16th-century trestle table in the Common Room came from a monastery near Salisbury, England. Here Mrs. Weeks entertained at tea parties. The Van Dyck portrait of Cardinal Domenico Rivarola (right) is the most valuable of several paintings in the room.*

102. Iowa State Capitol *Grand Ave. and E. Ninth St., Des Moines, Iowa* The magnificent edifice was completed in 1886 after 15 years of construction. It is sometimes called the Golden Dome after its central dome (275 feet high and 80 feet in diameter), which is thought to be the largest gold dome in the U.S. Beneath it the rotunda boasts Edwin Howland Blashfield's monumental painting *Westward,* six mosaics by Frederick Dielman and eight murals by Kenyon Cox. One of the most superb rooms in the building is the law library, with circular staircases and balconies, all of beautiful iron grillwork. The statehouse is situated on 165 acres offering 150 varieties of flowers and several monuments. *Open Mon.-Fri. except holidays.*

IOWA STATE MUSEUM Adjacent to the capitol is a museum dealing with various aspects of Iowa's history. A billion years of geologic time is recorded here by rocks and fossils from every type of natural formation in Iowa. Animals common during pioneer days—some are no longer found in the state—are displayed. The wide range of exhibits includes Indian artifacts and pioneer relics, one Conestoga wagon and early American glassware. *Open daily.*

103. Salisbury House *4025 Tonawanda Dr., Des Moines, Iowa* Cosmetics tycoon Carl Weeks built this sumptuous manor house, a replica of one called King's House in Salisbury, England. Among the features duplicated are a 13th-century Gothic porch with a Tudor flint and stone section. The 42 rooms are filled with antiques, paintings—including a portrait by the master Van Dyck—and authentic Renaissance appointments. The Iowa State Education Association now owns the building. *Open Mon.-Sat. Adults and children over 11 small charge.*

104. Clark Tower *City Park, Winterset, Iowa* The 25-foot-high crenelated tower was dedicated in 1927 to the memory of Caleb and Ruth Clark, who were among the first families to settle here in 1846. Built of limestone quarried in the immediate vicinity, the tower contains a number of windows with keystone arches. The view from the top is of the Middle River Valley and the beautifully landscaped Winterset City Park. *Open daily.*

105. Madison County Court House *Winterset, Iowa* A local judge carved the huge black walnut newel-posts on the staircases in the handsome Greek Revival structure, built in 1876 of native limestone. Objects associated with early settlers are displayed in the Madison County Historical Rooms. The large dome is topped by a cupola decorated with four clock dials facing north, south, east and west. *Open Mon.-Fri. except holidays.*

106. Pella Historisch Museum and Park *507 Franklin St., Pella, Iowa* The restored 1849 brick Van Spanckeren House serves two purposes: to preserve the boyhood home of Western lawman Wyatt Earp, whose family lived in the building's east half from 1850 to 1864, and to house mementos of the Dutch community that was settled here in 1847. Early furniture, a collection of Delftware and a quaint Dutch fireplace are among its many attractions. The grounds also include an operating gristmill—appropriately surrounded by tulip gardens—and a craft shop where wooden shoes and pottery are still being made. *Open Mon.-Fri. Mar.-Nov. Small charge.*

107. Main St. Restoration *Albia, Iowa* It is not actually Main Street but the Town Square of this southern Iowa town of 4500. With an eye to the aesthetic values of authentic Americana, the citizens of Albia have cleaned and sandblasted the square's handsome old two- and three-story buildings—in a range of Victorian and later styles—scraped and painted the wooden cornices and windows, repainted walls and made other improvements in an unusual and eye-catching restoration. The result is an attractive and functional reminder of the past, an excellent example that could be followed by many other towns and cities today.

108. Grand Portage National Monument *Grand Portage, Minn.* The white man's first business venture in the Northwest was fur trading, and the trading post here was the center of activity. It was the "great depot" of Montreal's North West Company, where voyageurs brought goods from the East and furs from the Northwest. The Grand Portage (or "great carrying place") was a nine-mile trail from the Lake Superior trading post around the unnavigable falls of the Pigeon River. The stockade, built of hewn timbers, the blockhouses and the Great Hall have been reconstructed and appear much as they did in the 18th century. The 709-acre site encompasses the original portage and a stretch of Lake Superior shoreline. *Open daily.*

109. Minnesota Museum of Mining *W. Lake St., Chisholm, Minn.* Chisholm, known as the "Iron Bowl City" because of its location in the center of the Great Mesabi Range, is a most logical location for the museum. At one time there were more than 100 operating mines in the area. Exhibits in the museum—a castlelike structure—bring mining, past and present, to life. Visitors can take a guided underground tour of a mine drift and see precisely what a working mine is like. Aboveground, they can view a huge 1910 steam shovel, a 1907 steam locomotive, trucks, ore wagons and even a jet plane, all either made of Mesabi Range iron or once used in range mining. *Open daily late May-early Sept. Small charge.*

110. Lake County Historical Society and Railroad Museum *Foot of Sixth St., Two Harbors, Minn.* An old railroad depot houses paintings, photographs and artifacts that tell the industrial story of this port area. The discovery of iron ore about 100 years ago spurred lumbering and railroading, and aspects of these colorful activities are featured in the displays. Two early steam locomotives stand outside: the small wood-burning one was used to lay track, and the mammoth coal-burning Mallet—the most powerful steam locomotive ever built—hauled ore. *Open daily late May-early Oct.*

111. Split Rock Lighthouse *Rte. 61, 20 mi. N.E. of Two Harbors, Minn.* Early ore-carrying ships of Lake Superior depended upon the lighthouse to keep them away from treacherous reefs and shallows. The lighthouse was built in 1909 at the edge of a 124-foot-high cliff which was accessible only by water; all construction materials were brought by boat and hoisted up the bluff. Although the octagonal brick tower no longer serves navigational needs, it sends its light across the waters in summer, and tourists can inspect its original two-paneled lens. The lighthouse is now part of a 100-acre state park named for it. *Open daily May-early Sept.*

112. Aerial Lift Bridge *Foot of Lake Ave., Duluth, Minn.* This unusual symbol of Duluth spans the ship canal at the entrance to the harbor. Built in 1905 as an aerial bridge, it was reconstructed in 1930 into a lift bridge that can be elevated 138 feet in less than 55 seconds. And this happens often as international ships ply the port harbor. Both ship and bridge watchers wait for the moment when the 900-ton span reaches its full height: it is counterbalanced then by two equally heavy concrete blocks.

113. A. M. Chisholm Museum *1832 E. Second St., Duluth, Minn.* Poised for flight, an impressive bronze eagle from Japan stands before the two-story building. Formerly the Duluth Children's Museum, the museum today is of general interest, with natural history exhibits and historic displays from many countries. In the collection, for example, are a worn and tattered 20-star American flag, sewn in 1818; a number of American Indian relics; and a 16th-century English suit of armor. *Open Mon.-Sat. and 1st Sun. of month.*

114. St. Louis County Historical Society Headquarters *2228 E. Superior St., Duluth, Minn.* Twelve oil paintings and 20 charcoal drawings of the Chippewa Indians hang in the society's museum. All were superbly done in 1857 by Eastman Johnson, a highly regarded artist of the period. Also on display here are room settings, clothing, jewelry and tools dating from the early days in the area. The society also has an extensive library and manuscript file on the history of the region. *Open daily June-Aug., Mon.-Fri. and 1st Sun. of month Sept.-May except holidays.*

115. Tweed Museum of Art *University of Minnesota, 2400 Oakland Ave., Duluth, Minn.* An unusually fine collection of art for a university museum began with the collection of Mr. and Mrs. George P. Tweed which was donated in 1950. Paintings range from the 16th century to the present and are housed in a light and airy building of crisp and well-defined architecture. *Open daily except holidays.*

116. W.H.C. Folsom House *Government Rd., Taylors Falls, Minn.* Both the Federal and Greek Revival styles are evident in the two-story, 10-room home. Built in

[114] *Eastman Johnson, a highly successful genre painter who died in 1906, became interested in painting the Chippewa Indians during a visit to his sister in Superior, Wisconsin, in 1857. This oil,* Canoe of Indians, *shows one type of canoe the Chippewas used on lakes and rivers.*

[**118.** *Minneapolis Institute of Arts*] *Patriot-silversmith Paul Revere made this tea service in 1792 in the neoclassic style (note the elliptic curves, fluted sides and delicate tracery), then the highest fashion in silver and furniture. It was only after the Revolutionary War that matched tea services such as this one became popular.*

1855 for an enterprising Yankee lumberman who later became a state senator, the house is constructed of pine, with pegged and mortised timbers. Woodwork a foot wide frames interior windows and doorways. Original furnishings include a square piano and family pictures. A special exhibit shows the development of the St. Croix River Valley, which the dwelling overlooks. In the back of the house is a charming garden of wild flowers. *Open Tues.-Sun. June-Sept. Small charge.*

117. Church of St. John the Evangelist *6 Interlachen Rd., Interlachen Park, Hopkins, Minn.* One of the fine contemporary churches in America—and honored by architectural awards—St. John's is an extraordinary combination of natural materials, space and light. Sweeping brick walls, soaring paneled ceilings, benches of oak—all give a powerful simplicity to the main sanctuary. Completed in 1969, the Roman Catholic church also has an adjoining community center. *Open daily.*

118. Minneapolis, Minn.

Minnesota's largest city is situated at the Falls of St. Anthony on the Mississippi River. Within its boundaries are 22 lakes and lagoons. Begun as a fort built to protect the fur trade, the city today, with its twin city St. Paul, is a center for wheat-flour milling and the manufacture of precision instruments.

American Swedish Institute *2600 Park Ave.* The 33-room castle was the symbol of success to Swan J. Turnblad, who made his fortune as publisher of the nation's largest Swedish-American newspaper. The chateaulike building is made of Indiana limestone, with exterior sculptures by Herman Schlink. The interior plaster ceilings, also by Schlink, are notable for the many elaborate designs. Ulrich Steiner's impressive wood carvings include the griffins of the stairway and the cherubs that surround the music room. The home contains 11 tile ovens imported from Europe and a unique art-glass window. It now houses the American Swedish Institute and has exhibits of pioneer historical items, Swedish glass, textiles and 17th- and 18th-century antiques. *Open Tues.-Sun. except holidays. Small charge.*

Hennepin County Historical Society Museum *2303 Third Ave. S.* How did the main street of a typical rural town appear in the early 1900s? An exhibit called "Main Street U.S.A." in one wing of the society's museum provides a revealing look backward. On the "street" are 11 buildings, none higher than six feet, furnished with more than 1500 miniature items collected from the four corners of the globe. Many are handmade. More than 50,000 relics from Minnesota's pioneer days are on view in the main areas of the museum. *Open Tues.-Sun.*

Minneapolis Institute of Arts *201 E. 24th St.* A considerable portion of this fine museum is devoted to American art—landscapes by Thomas Moran, Gilbert Stuart portraits and a Thomas Sully copy of a Stuart painting of Washington, among others. Also here are furnished Early American rooms and the Templeman tea service, the most complete silver service by Paul Revere in existence. The institute is equally strong in European art and decorative works, with selections from Rembrandt, Van Dyck, Titian and van Gogh, and elaborate furnishings and period rooms. In addition, the collections include an exceptional group of Chinese bronzes, Greek and Roman sculpture and more than 40,000 prints and drawings dating from the 15th century to the present. Additions designed by Kenzo Tange, renowned Japanese architect, are being added to the institute. *Open Tues.-Sun. except Dec. 25.*

Northwestern National Life Insurance Building *20 Washington Ave. S.* Seattle-born architect Minoru Yamasaki, creator of New York City's mammoth World Trade Center, designed the six-story building in Gateway Center as the insurance company's home office. The elegant modern structure, completed in 1964, is supported by 63 slender columns with flaring capitals, which are accentuated by panels of dark green marble veined in a book-leaf pattern. Floor-to-ceiling windows flank the panels. Entrance to the building is through a 56-by-114-foot portico that is topped by an 85-foot-high ceiling. The white marble lobby is dominated by the Harry Bertoia sculpture *Sunlit Straw,* a 14-by-46-foot work composed of thousands of brass-coated steel rods. *Open Mon.-Fri. except holidays.*

University Gallery *316 Northrop Memorial Auditorium, University of Minnesota* Works of 20th-century American artists are featured in the gallery's permanent collection. These include paintings, drawings and prints by Feininger, O'Keeffe, Marin, Weber and Dove. Prints, drawings, sculpture and the decorative arts also form the collection. *Open Sun.-Fri. except holidays.*

Walker Art Center *Vineland Pl.* Lipchitz's *Prometheus Strangling the Vulture II,* Segal's *The Diner* and Oldenburg's *Falling Shoestring Potatoes* are among the many outstanding examples of 20th-century sculpture emphasized at this cultural center. Also featured are contemporary paintings by European and American artists; one of the holdings is Hopper's *Office at Night.* Selected jades and porcelains from the T. B. Walker collection are exhibited, along with prints and a group of late 19th-century American landscapes, including Church's *Scene in the Catskill Mountains.* New design concepts are a feature of the museum. *Open Tues.-Sun.*

119. St. Paul, Minn.

St. Paul, Minnesota's capital, overlooks the Mississippi River, and with its twin city, Minneapolis, forms a commercial, industrial and transportation center. The majority of early settlers were of German and Irish origin, and their influence affects the character of the city today.

Alexander Ramsey House *265 S. Exchange St.* The first governor of Minnesota Territory lived in this 1872 French Renaissance mansion with a mansard roof. The 16-room house is constructed of native limestone. Among its notable features are a hand-carved staircase, walnut and butternut woodwork, 15-foot ceilings and arched doorways. Many of the original Victorian furnishings were preserved by the governor's descendants who occupied the home until 1964, when it was turned over to the Minnesota Historical Society. In the adjacent carriage house, reconstructed from the original plans, are period carriages and an interpretive exhibit. *Open Tues.-Sun. Small charge.*

Burbank-Livingston-Griggs House *432 Summit Ave.* Appearances are indeed deceiving at this elegant mansion. Built in the early 1860s by a wealthy businessman, the three-story stone house looks typically Victorian outside. Little Victoriana, however, is found within. In the 1930s most of the interior was stripped and 10 rooms were installed from splendid French and Italian villas of the 17th and 18th centuries. To complement the intricate paneling and mirrored walls, authentic period furniture, paintings and decorative objects were acquired abroad. This wealth survives, giving visitors a glimpse of several periods and cultures. *Open Tues.-Sun. Small charge.*

Cathedral of St. Paul *225 Summit Ave.* Atop a hill overlooking downtown St. Paul is the cathedral of the Roman Catholic Archdiocese of St. Paul and Minneapolis, a Renaissance structure which is an adaptation of Michelangelo's design for St. Peter's Basilica in Rome. The great green dome rises 306 feet from the ground and is 96 feet in diameter. The interior is decorated in an ornate, neo-Baroque style with an abundance of bronze work, colored marble, elaborate stone carvings, paintings and stained-glass windows. *Open daily.*

City Hall-Court House *Fourth and Wabasha Sts.* A 55-ton white onyx statue of the Indian God of Peace stands three stories tall in the concourse of this striking 1930s building. The figure, the work of Swedish-American sculptor Carl Milles, is set on a turntable that moves slowly to the right and then to the left during a two-and-a-half-hour interval. Above the marble concourse, each of the 18 floors is finished with a different variety of wood. In the council chamber are murals showing scenes of pioneer days in Minnesota Territory. *Open daily.*

Fort Snelling *Rtes. 5 and 55* The original fort, the first permanent outpost of white settlers in Minnesota, was established in 1820 to help eliminate British influence in the Northwest. Constructed by troops of the U.S. 5th Infantry, it consisted of 13 stone buildings and two wooden ones enclosed by a 1500-foot stone wall. The buildings—towers, guardhouse, school-chapel, magazine, shops and barracks—are being restored or reconstructed to show how the fort looked in the 1820s, when 200 to 350 regimental troops and dependents lived there. Visitors may watch military drills and ceremonies and such day-to-day frontier activities as blacksmithing, carpentry, baking and candle-dipping. *Open daily Apr.-late Oct. Adults small charge.*

Gibbs Farm Museum *2097 W. Larpenteur Ave.* In the heart of the city is a farm museum operated by the Ramsey County Historical Society. The farmhouse, now part of a four-building complex, began as a one-room cabin built in 1854 by the pioneering Gibbs family. It was expanded into its present two-story frame structure in the 1870s. Demonstrations of pioneer arts and crafts—spinning, weaving, candle-dipping and butter-churning—are held here. In the white barn is a collection of carriages and sleighs that belonged to railroad tycoon James J. Hill. In the red barn early agricultural tools and implements are displayed. During summer, children attend the one-room schoolhouse, where they are taught by methods used 100 years ago. *Open Tues.-Fri., Sun. May-Oct., mid-Dec.-mid-Mar.*

Minnesota Museum of Art *305 St. Peter St.* The largest permanent collections in this public museum are those of Oriental graphics, ceramics and textiles; 20th-century drawings, sculptures and paintings; and African, Northwest Coast Indian and contemporary American crafts. In addition, the museum organizes national competitions every other year in drawing and in fiber, clay and metal, exhibiting the winning works both here and on extensive tours. *Open Tues.-Sat. Small charge.*

Minnesota State Capitol *Aurora and Cedar Sts.* In planning the capitol, architect Cass Gilbert sought to achieve an integration of Italian Renaissance architecture and art. Completed in 1905, it is made of marble, granite, limestone and sandstone. The huge Baroque dome is one of the largest self-supporting marble domes in the country. At its base, above the main entrance, is a sculpture group called the *Gold Horses,* the work of Daniel Chester French and Edward Potter. From here there is a fine view of St. Paul and Minneapolis. The elaborate interior contains many sculptures, paintings and murals. *Open daily except holidays.*

[124] *Louis Sullivan was a master at integrating decorative motifs. This chandelier, its twisting, organic forms reminiscent of Art Nouveau, both blends and contrasts with the curve and sinuous designs of the arch.*

120. Octagon House *1004 Third St., Hudson, Wis.* The house, built in 1855, is in the octagonal style that became popular during the mid-19th century. It is furnished with authentic pieces of the period, many of them handmade. Of particular interest is the collection of rare dolls in the children's playroom. The carriage house and garden house contain museums. *Open Tues.-Sun. May-Oct. Small charge.*

121. Paul Bunyan Camp Museum *Carson Park, Eau Claire, Wis.* The museum is a memorial to the day when the pine tree was king in northern Wisconsin, when logging was a major industry in the area and when lumberjacks were legendary men. It re-creates a logging camp of the 1890s, complete with bunkhouse, dining hall, cooking shanty, blacksmithy, stable and sheds. Every building contains authentic furnishings and equipment—vivid reminders of a bygone way of life. *Open daily early May-Aug., Thurs.-Mon. Sept.*

122. Sibley House *Mendota, Minn.* Thought to be the oldest residence in Minnesota, this large three-story limestone dwelling was built in 1835 by Henry H. Sibley, fur trader and later the state's first governor. The house has been restored and carefully furnished with period pieces—some belonging to the Sibley family. *Open daily mid-Apr.-Oct. Small charge.*

123. Episcopal Cathedral of Our Merciful Saviour *515 N.W. Second Ave., Faribault, Minn.* After seven years and expenditures of more than $100,000, the cathedral was completed under the direction of Minnesota's first bishop, the Right Reverend Henry B. Whipple, in 1869. It was the first Episcopal edifice built in the U.S. to serve as a cathedral. The handsome, stately English Gothic structure's magnificent stained-glass windows include two donated by Christian Indians in gratitude for the aid provided by Bishop Whipple whom the Indians called "Straight Tongue." The cathedral tower by Ralph Adams Cram and the carillon were dedicated in 1902 in memory of the bishop, who died the previous year. *Open daily.*

124. Security Bank and Trust Company *Cedar and Broadway, Owatonna, Minn.* Louis Sullivan, designer of the stately building, believed that the design of any structure should complement its function. Stone, baked clay and bronze were used in the construction of the spacious, square building completed in 1908. It features four large arches richly ornamented with terra cotta, an elaborate bronze pediment over the front entrance, four large, ornate chandeliers that illuminate the main banking hall and an intricately embellished central clock. *Open Mon.-Fri. except holidays.*

125. Mayowood *Rte. 125, Rochester, Minn.* Dr. Charles H. Mayo, one of the founders of the famed Mayo Clinic, had this 38-room mansion built in 1911 according to his own design. It incorporates various architectural ideas that he acquired on worldwide travels and, considering its vast size, it is quite homelike and comfortable. The house is constructed of poured concrete; the outside walls are over a foot thick. The layout of the ground floor—a 48-foot-long living room, an equally long gallery, dining rooms, library and service areas—provides for natural ventilation and lighting, ease of access and lovely views of the surrounding countryside. The house is furnished with antiques and art objects of many periods and styles, all collected by the Mayo family. These include a number of French pieces and mementos of Napoleon, whom Charles Mayo greatly admired. Arrangements to see the home must be made at the Olmstead County Historical Society headquarters in Rochester. *Open Sat., Sun. Apr., Wed., Fri., Sat., Sun. May, Tues.-Sun. June-Aug., Wed., Fri., Sat., Sun. Sept.-Oct., Sat., Sun. Nov. Adults $1.75, children small charge.*

126. "Julius C. Wilkie" Steamboat Museum *Levee Park, Foot of Main St., Winona, Minn.* The museum is housed in its principal exhibit, the 96-foot wood-hull stern-wheeler *Julius C. Wilkie,* built in 1898 and the last of its kind on the upper Mississippi. The proud steamboat still contains all its original equipment and machinery. Displays of navigation instruments, ships' bells, pilots' whistles and a working air calliope are among the reminders of this colorful era in shipping. Here too are an array of steamboat models and the country's largest collection of documents relating to inventor Robert Fulton. *Open daily May-Sept. Small charge.*

127. Bunnell House *Rtes. 61 and 14, Homer, Minn.* Tudor styling, vertical siding and scalloped trim make this an unusually elaborate pioneer home. Built in the early 1850s for Willard Bunnell, a fur trader and one of the area's first white settlers, the three-story house is now owned by the Winona County Historical Society. The interior, furnished in the mid-19th-century manner, is as fashionable as the exterior. *Open daily June-early Sept.*

128. Hixon House and County Historical Museum *427 N. Seventh St., La Crosse, Wis.* Gideon C. Hixon, one of the city's early residents, completed this 15-room

frame home in 1857. A banker and industrialist, he outfitted it with all the conveniences of the day, and it still contains many of his family's furnishings and art treasures. The house has five fireplaces. The hallway walls are covered with embossed velvet and the dining-room walls are decorated with hand-painted canvas. *Open daily June-early Sept. Small charge.*

129. Maria Angelorum Chapel *St. Rose Convent, 912 Market St., La Crosse, Wis.* The red brick Romanesque structure with windows of Bavarian stained glass was completed in 1906 by the Franciscan Sisters of Perpetual Adoration. The elaborately decorated chapel contains handcrafted altars of Italian marble with onyx pillars, gold bronze ornamentation and inlaid mosaics of mother of pearl and Venetian glass. Scenes from the history of the three Orders founded by St. Francis—the Friars Minor, Poor Clares and Third Order Secular—are all portrayed in a series of paintings displayed in the sanctuary. *Open daily.*

130. St. Joseph the Workman Cathedral *530 Main St., La Crosse, Wis.* In this Roman Catholic cathedral, dedicated in 1962, the old blends with the new. The design is contemporary but of Gothic inspiration, with a tower that rises more than 216 feet from the ground. The stained-glass windows are especially striking. In the Blessed Sacrament Chapel the walls are black marble and the altar is of gold-colored mosaic glass. *Open daily.*

131. Vesterheim, Norwegian-American Museum *502 W. Water St., Decorah, Iowa* Vesterheim—"western home," as the Norwegian immigrants called their new home in America—has one of the most comprehensive collections of a single immigrant group in the U.S. Among the featured exhibits are a replica of a 19th-century three-room house from Norway and a one-room pioneer cabin from northeast Iowa, both completely furnished. Colorful Norwegian and Norwegian-American arts and crafts, household furnishings and costumes are displayed. The story of Norwegian-American pioneer industries is told in a separate building, the Stone Mill. It includes a restored and operating blacksmith shop. On the last weekend in July the Nordic Fest, a festival of arts, crafts, music and dance, is held. *Open daily May-Oct. Small charge.*

132. Bily Clock Exhibit *Spillville, Iowa* Frank and Joseph Bily's carvings of clock cases make an extraordinary display of masterful woodworking. An eight-foot cherry and walnut clock—four years in the making—has detailed bas-reliefs of pioneer history, with chimes that play "America." A Gothic cathedral crowns one clock, and every hour figures of the 12 Apostles appear. Panels depicting the history of travel—by land, sea and air—front another clock, symbolically topped by a mighty eagle. A timepiece shaped like a violin commemorates Antonín Dvořak, who lived in this building during the summer of 1893. *Open Sat., Sun. Mar., daily Apr.-Nov. Adults and children over 7 small charge.*

133. Dvořak Memorial *Riverside Park, Spillville, Iowa* The simple stone monument honors the famous Czech composer Antonín Dvořak, who spent the summer of 1893 in Spillville. Although he went there primarily to rest after a strenuous year as director of the New York Conservatory of Music, he made final corrections on his ninth symphony (*New World*) and composed the *Quartet in F Major* during his stay.

134. Fort Atkinson State Monument *Rte. 24, ½ mi. N. of Fort Atkinson, Iowa* The fort's distinction is that it was built in 1840 to protect quarreling Indian tribes from one another. After it was abandoned in 1849, many of the buildings deteriorated or were vandalized. The present fort, reconstructed around a blockhouse, powder magazine and part of a stone barracks that remained, is now complete with cannon house, stockade and parade grounds. The barracks houses a museum displaying a large map of the Indian buffer zone, an Indian canoe, pictures of the old fort and various artifacts connected with its military history. *Open Tues.-Sun. mid-May-mid-Oct.*

135. Effigy Mounds National Monument *McGregor, Iowa* Close to 1500 years ago, Indians who lived in the region buried their dead in curious mounds, some shaped like bears, some like birds; others are conical or linear shaped. Almost 200 of them, mostly in clustered groups, are scattered around the park, evidence of the once-active communities that farmed and hunted here. In the Visitor Center are related pictures and a special audio-visual presentation explaining what is known about these Indians and their customs. *Open daily except Dec. 25.*

136. Villa Louis *Villa Louis Rd., Prairie du Chien, Wis.* A prominent fur trader built this large dwelling in the Georgian style in 1843. It was substantially modified 29 years later by his widow, who gave it its current Victorian appearance. The house stands on the remains of a 2000-year-old Indian burial mound, near the confluence of the Mississippi and Wisconsin Rivers. Many

[131] *This beautifully worked cupboard was built by Lars Christianson of Benson, Minnesota, around 1880. Christianson here transcended the usual limits of folk art and produced a genuinely artistic piece of furniture. His skill is apparent in the handling of decorative details like the moldings, drawer pulls and the spindles on the lower chest. Other furniture in Vesterheim is decorated in colorful folk style in the Norwegian technique of painting on wood called rosemaling. Also on display is Christianson's elaborate altar, carved largely with a jackknife. It is in the folk art tradition—virtually covered with stylized figures from the New Testament.*

original late 19th-century furnishings—rugs, lace curtains, china and glassware, Waterford crystal chandeliers and paintings—grace the rooms. In the library are more than 3000 volumes printed prior to 1890, including a Bible printed in Holland in 1565 and an original Audubon series. *Open daily May-Oct. Adults $1.20, children small charge.*

MUSEUM OF PRAIRIE DU CHIEN Located in the coach house of Villa Louis, this museum stands on the site of Fort Crawford (1816), where Zachary Taylor and Jefferson Davis served as young officers. Dioramas trace the development of the region and include scenes of the Hopewell mound builders, early fur traders and events during the War of 1812.

137. First Capitol State Park *Belmont, Wis.* Belmont was frontier land when the capital of the Wisconsin Territory was established here in 1836. Today, visitors can see the restored original wooden buildings that housed the territorial legislature and the supreme court. The capitol structure is furnished much as it was originally, while the supreme court building has been made into a museum which depicts old Wisconsin life. Prefabricated in Pittsburgh, the buildings' parts were transported into the wilderness by boat and ox-drawn wagon and subsequently assembled. After Madison became Wisconsin's capital, the structures at Belmont were used as barns. *Open Mon.-Fri. Apr.-May, daily June-Aug., Mon.-Fri. Sept.-Oct.*

138. Stonefield *Nelson Dewey State Park, Cassville, Wis.* Once part of the estate of Nelson Dewey, Wisconsin's first governor, the village is a replica of a typical 19th-century frontier community. The large house near the village—Dewey's restored home—suggests modern comforts with its Oriental rugs and other splendid furnishings, but once visitors cross the covered bridge into the village itself, time stops in the 1890s. Around the green stand a one-room schoolhouse equipped with slates and sturdy two-seater desks, a pharmacy complete with cure-all ointments and powders, a general store lined with household supplies, a firehouse, a blacksmith shop, a bank and a railroad station. Altogether 25 buildings recall everyday life of 80 years ago, and at the farm museum—Dewey's old cattle barn—an array of tools vividly tells of the farmers' hard-working days. *Open daily May-Oct. Adults $1.50, children over 7 small charge.*

139. Basilica of St. Francis Xavier *Dyersville, Iowa* Completed in 1889, the church was proclaimed a basilica (one of a small number in the U.S.) by Pope Pius XII in 1956. Noble twin spires rise 212 feet on either side of the main entrance, each crowned by gold-leaf crosses. The main altar, crafted from Italian marble and Mexican onyx, stands beneath a remarkable ceiling fresco: a dazzling Lamb of God is surrounded by saints of the Old and New Testaments. *Open daily.*

140. Church of the Nativity *1225 Alta Vista, Dubuque, Iowa* Outstanding features of the contemporary church are its bold simplicity of form and the 42 stained-glass windows, designed and made in the cathedral city of Chartres by French artist Gabriel Loire. The polished limestone floor of the sanctuary leads to a striking altar. The imposing background wall of the sanctuary, fashioned from bricks, depicts nine angels in low relief. *Open daily.*

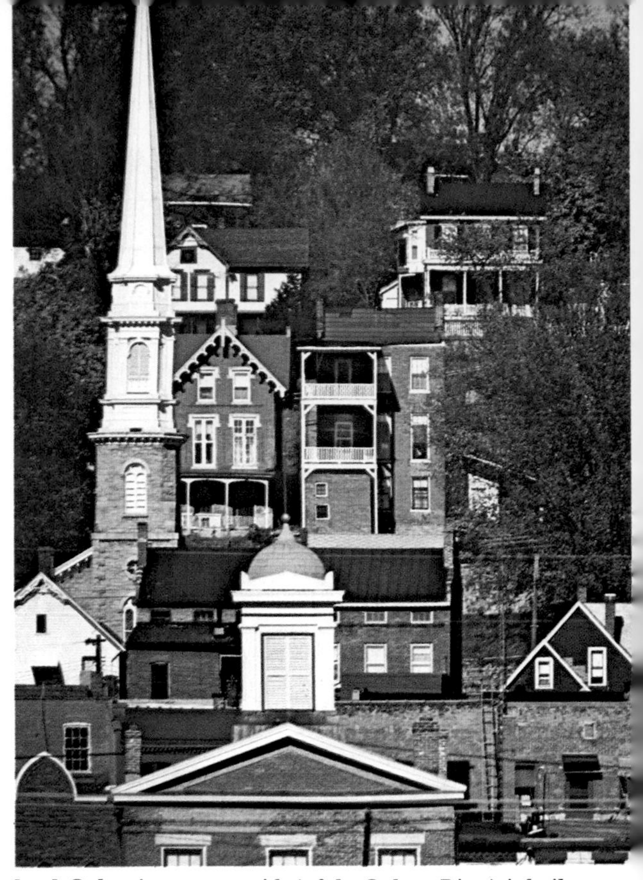

[141] *Galena's steep west side (of the Galena River) is built on five levels. The Greek Revival Market House, its copper dome oxidized to green, is in the foreground; behind it is the spire of the First Presbyterian Church.*

141. Galena, Ill.

The town of Galena achieved fame and fortune in the mid-19th century from nearby lead mines and because of its accessibility to Mississippi River boat traffic. Its citizens celebrated their prosperity by building imposing Federal-, Southern-, Victorian- and Greek Revival-style homes on Quality Hill and in other parts of town. The older areas have been proclaimed a historic district, and biennial tours are made to the most interesting houses. Other attractions include 11 museums and such survivals from the past as the old firehouse and the custom house, now a post office.

Dowling House *Main and Diagonal Sts.* John Dowling, pioneer merchant, built the two-story stone structure in 1826. It is the oldest surviving building in Galena. The restored house is now furnished in the original manner, as a frontier residence and trading post. *Open daily May-Oct. Small charge.*

Galena Historical Museum *211 S. Bench St.* Aspects of the region's earlier days are reflected in the various documents and collections, which include clothing, books and dolls as well as Civil War memorabilia. A proud possession of the museum is Thomas Nast's *Peace in Union,* a life-size painting depicting Lee's surrender to General U.S. Grant, once a Galena resident. *Open daily May-Oct. Small charge.*

Grace Episcopal Church *Prospect St.* This small, early English-style stone church nestles against a wooded hillside, its vine-covered tower dominating the entrance and framing the gracefully arched doorway and window. Inside are the original pews and a hand-carved walnut altar. The lovely stained-glass windows were imported from Belgium. *Open daily.*

Market House *411 Meeker St.* Once the place where farmers brought their produce and housewives shopped for groceries, the 1845 building is the last of its kind in the Midwest. Today it is a state memorial and houses exhibits of Illinois and Midwestern architecture. *Open daily except holidays.*

Stockade *208 Perry St.* A refuge for settlers during the Black Hawk War of 1832, the stockade had a formidable wall of tall pointed timbers. A log house and underground rooms remain intact and displayed here is a choice collection of Indian relics. *Open daily May-Oct. Small charge.*

Ulysses S. Grant Home State Memorial *511 Bouthillier St.* The handsome, two-story brick residence, with wide overhanging eaves, white wooden trim and green shutters, was a gift of Galena's grateful citizens to Grant when the hero came back after the Civil War. He lived in it for brief periods from 1865 to 1880. Many of the Grants' possessions are in the house: the dining-room table is set with china they used in the White House, and every room has souvenirs they brought back from their trip around the world in 1877-9. (Grant's pre-Civil War home, at 121 High Street, can be visited from May through October.) *Open daily except holidays.*

142. Grant Wood Memorial Window *Veterans Memorial Coliseum, Mays Island, Cedar Rapids, Iowa* The creator of *American Gothic* designed this striking stained-glass window as a memorial to America's fighting men. Completed in Germany in 1929, the 24-by-20-foot window is dominated by a heroic female figure wearing a mourning veil and holding a victor's laurel wreath and the palm branch of peace. Below her stand six U.S. soldiers dressed in the military uniforms of the U.S. from the Revolutionary War through World War I. *Open Mon.-Fri.*

143. Iowa Masonic Library *813 First Ave. S.E., Cedar Rapids, Iowa* This is one of the oldest (1845) and largest Masonic libraries in the U.S. Its 100,000 volumes deal with subjects Masonic and non-Masonic; among the latter are the Iowa history, Robert Burns and Abraham Lincoln collections. Two museum rooms display Masonic relics and such diverse items as a Washington medal by Saint-Gaudens and incised Babylonian clay bricks. There are also stained-glass windows with Masonic symbols as motifs. *Open Mon.-Fri.*

144. Amana Colonies *Amana, Iowa* Seven small villages—Amana plus East, Middle, High, West and South Amana and Homestead—all in a 20-mile area were settled in 1855 by the Ebenezer Society, a sect of religious refugees from Germany. Amana became one of the most successful communities of its type in America. Its enterprises included woolen mills, meat-smoking plants, bakeries and craft industries that are still locally famous for their products. Now they also make major appliances, such as food freezers, and Amana farms and vineyards produce ham, bacon and sausage and wines.

[**146.** *Museum of Natural History*] *The last passenger pigeon, once one of our most common species, died in 1914. The museum has several specimens such as these in Bird Hall where the North American collection is outstanding.*

Factories make clocks, woolen goods and furniture. The villages still retain much of their character of over 100 years ago. The Amana Heim in Homestead (3 miles south of Amana, on Rte. 6) is an old home preserved as a museum. *Open daily.*

145. Plum Grove *Carroll Ave., Iowa City, Iowa* This simple but sturdy brick house honors the early history of Iowa and its first territorial governor, Robert Lucas. Lucas built the seven-room home in 1844 after an eventful career in the army and in local and national politics. A State Historic Monument, it has been carefully restored, even to the replanting of plum trees, which years ago surrounded the residence and suggested its name. Every room boasts a fireplace, and each is furnished in the authentic style of the times. Many pieces once belonged to Governor Lucas and his family. *Open Tues.-Sun. mid-Apr.-mid-Nov.*

146. University of Iowa *Iowa City, Iowa* Founded in 1847, the coeducational university offers graduate and undergraduate courses in diverse areas of study, from dentistry to fine arts.

MUSEUM OF ART *Riverside Dr.* Grant Wood was but one noted artist who taught at the University of Iowa during the 1930s when most U.S. colleges ignored creative arts. As a result of the university's early involvement in the arts, it has one of the finest art collections in academic America today. Included are works by Picasso, Pollock, Beckmann, Miró and Rouault. In addition, the museum has an impressive collection of 17th- and 18th-century English silver, Tibetan sculpture and primitive art. *Open daily.*

MUSEUM OF NATURAL HISTORY *Macbride Hall* Archaeological, zoological, geological and botanical treasures are featured here. Exhibits range from single-celled protozoans to the most highly evolved animals, the vertebrates, which include man himself. There are particularly fine displays of North American birds. Ethnological materials representative of Eskimo and tribal societies can also be seen. *Open daily except holidays.*

[151] *Architect-designer Alexander Girard's 180-foot-long collage is a nostalgic collection of 2000 objects—memorabilia reflecting rural America in the 19th and early 20th centuries, a way of life that has all but vanished.*

147. Herbert Hoover National Historic Site *N. of Rte. 80, West Branch, Iowa* In addition to the buildings described below, this attractive park holds a statue of Isis presented by Belgian schoolchildren in gratitude for Hoover's extraordinary efforts to get food to their country during World War I. The graves of President and Mrs. Hoover are also here. *Open daily except holidays.*

BLACKSMITH SHOP The frame structure is similar to the shop operated by the President's father, Jesse Clark Hoover. A large bellows, a brick forge and the blacksmith's tools are the main features.

HERBERT HOOVER BIRTHPLACE COTTAGE Hoover's first five years, from his birth in 1874 until 1879, were spent in this board cottage, now restored. Built by his father, it contains three rooms with family photographs and period furniture, including some original pieces.

HERBERT HOOVER PRESIDENTIAL LIBRARY Objects associated with Hoover's career as a mining engineer, Secretary of Commerce, President, humanitarian and elder statesman are exhibited in the limestone building. Among the displays are a reconstruction of Hoover's White House office and the Walnut Library, which contains rare books plus several exquisite K'ang Hsi and Ming porcelains collected by Mrs. Hoover during their years in China. *Small charge.*

QUAKER MEETINGHOUSE Hoover's mother frequently addressed the congregation in this austere frame building, with its plank benches and iron stoves. Hoover himself was a lifelong Quaker.

148. Laura Musser Art Gallery and Museum *1314 Mulberry Ave., Muscatine, Iowa* Peter Musser, pioneer Muscatine lumberman, built the 22-room Edwardian mansion in 1908. A music room was specially added later to hold an enormous 731-pipe player organ. The building is now used as an art gallery and museum, featuring paintings and other works, mostly by Midwest artists. Civil War mementos include weapons, diaries and pictures. There are many other artifacts related to Iowa and Mississippi River Valley history. The museum also holds the excellent Albert Bliven Memorial Collection of African Art. *Open Tues.-Sun. except holidays.*

149. Davenport Municipal Art Gallery *1737 W. 12th St., Davenport, Iowa* A wide variety of artworks is displayed in this attractive contemporary gallery. Among the European acquisitions is Lawrence's *Portrait of Sarah K. Siddons;* the American works include many paintings by Grant Wood, one of Remington's *Bronco Buster* sculptures and caricatures by Hirschfeld. The collection of Mexican Colonial paintings is said to be one of the best outside of Mexico. Haitian painting and sculpture are amply represented, as are Oriental prints and various aspects of the decorative arts. *Open Tues.-Sun. except holidays.*

150. Davenport Museum *1717 W. 12th St., Davenport, Iowa* The entire globe is represented and nearly 35 centuries are spanned in the museum's many-sided art, history and natural science exhibits. Its holdings range from ancient Egyptian miniature burial boats to scale models of post-Civil War steamboats, from the primitive sculpture of Pacific-island and Middle American cultures to exquisite Chinese porcelains and cloisonné. *Open daily except holidays. Small charge.*

151. Deere & Company Administrative Center *John Deere Rd., Moline, Ill.* Architect Eero Saarinen designed this dramatic building complex, which was honored with an award by the American Institute of Architects in 1965. A unique three-dimensional mural by Alexander Girard depicts long-ago life in rural America and the attendant growth of this farm-equipment company by means of documents, photographs, posters, tools and other objects of farm life. The company's products, both old and new, are also on display here. *Open daily.*

152. Carl Sandburg Birthplace *331 E. Third St., Galesburg, Ill.* The modest three-room cottage is a fitting shrine for earthy Carl Sandburg, eminent American poet and Lincoln biographer. Sandburg, son of an immigrant railroad worker, was born here in 1878. The Lincoln Room, attached to the house, displays Sandburg and Lincoln memorabilia. In the rear is Sandburg Park, where the poet's ashes rest beneath "Remembrance Rock," a boulder of red granite. *Open Tues.-Sun. except holidays.*

153. Old Main *Knox College, Galesburg, Ill.* Early on Oct. 7, 1858, the roads around the small college town of Galesburg were thronged. Nearly 20,000 people gathered to hear the fifth of the famous Lincoln-Douglas debates, which took place east of Old Main, a fine example of American Gothic, on the campus of Knox College. In his speech Lincoln for the first time condemned slavery as a moral evil. Bronze plaques mark the door before which the debate was held. The window through which Lincoln stepped to the debating platform is also marked. A selection of furnishings from the mid-19th century can be seen in the Alumni Room of Old Main. *Open Mon.-Sat. except holidays.*

154. Heritage Museum *McMillan Park, Mount Pleasant, Iowa* Early tractors and other antique agricultural machinery are displayed here in a museum area covering more than an acre. A reconstructed country kitchen, Corliss engines and some transportation vehicles can also be seen. For five days through Labor Day this is the scene of the Midwest Old Settlers and Threshers Reunion, when all the machines are demonstrated by enthusiastic volunteers. At this time, also, visitors can see the last of the "folk theaters" that once traveled across the country, presenting shows in tents. *Open daily late May-early Sept. Adults small charge.*

155. Bentonsport National Historic District *Bentonsport, Iowa* Once a thriving river town—the largest west of the Mississippi in the 1850s—Bentonsport is now a museum of 19th-century homes, stores, churches and other buildings. The whole of it is being preserved by county interests and by local citizens. Fully restored are the post office, built in 1852 of solid walnut, and a general store, its porch loaded with merchandise of 100 years ago. Inside the store are an old cracker barrel, a gigantic coffee grinder and an 1893 chewing gum machine. *Buildings open daily Apr.-Oct.*

MASON HOUSE MUSEUM Built in 1846, this was Bentonsport's luxury hotel, its average rate $2.50 a week for room and board. Most of the original furnishings are still here, including the high maple and walnut bar where steamboat captains swapped river tales, and the bridal suite with its marble-topped dressers and sit-up bath. *Small charge.*

156. Nauvoo Historic District *Nauvoo, Ill.* More than 30 historic sites have been restored in old Nauvoo to give visitors an idea of what it was like here during the seven tumultous years, beginning in 1839, when the village suddenly became the largest community in Illinois and the national center of the Church of Jesus Christ of Latter-day Saints (Mormon). Just as suddenly, in 1846, the Mormon settlers abandoned their fine homes and businesses by the thousands and departed on the arduous trek across the plains and mountains to the Great Salt Lake, under the leadership of Brigham Young. Four of the most interesting buildings are listed below. *Open daily.*

BRIGHAM YOUNG HOUSE Brigham Young built the solid two-story brick house in 1844. Authentic "country style" furnishings give it a warm, homey air.

JOSEPH SMITH CENTER *Main and Water Sts.* The Joseph Smith Homestead, a two-story log house, was partially built in 1803; Joseph Smith purchased it in 1839. The restored homestead is furnished with pioneer pieces—a musket above the fireplace, candles on the walls and shelves of pewterware and warming pans. The Joseph Smith Mansion House, a handsome frame residence with gray shutters, was built in 1842 as a permanent home for the prophet and is more elaborately furnished than the homestead.

VISITOR CENTER *Main and Young Sts.* The large windows in the foyer of the handsome modern building provide an overall view of the restored area. On display are a model of the Nauvoo Temple (which was burned by vandals in 1848), a statue of Prophet Joseph Smith and paintings relating to Nauvoo Mormons and their westward trek.

157. "George M. Verity" Keokuk River Museum *Victory Park, Keokuk, Iowa* This steamboat is one of the nation's few remaining Mississippi River sternwheelers that is unaltered from its heydey in the 1920s and 1930s. Then the 162-foot towboat constantly worked the river, moving barges between St. Louis and Minneapolis. Visitors can explore the 15-cabin boiler deck, the spacious pilot house, the ample lounge and the staterooms. Pictures and other mementos of riverboating days add to the authentic atmosphere. *Open daily mid-Apr.-Oct. Small charge.*

158. Venne Art Center *521 Grant St., Wausau, Wis.* Six fireplaces, several Oriental rugs and many original furnishings can be seen in the 19-room mansion, which was built by an early Wisconsin lumberman and more recently served as the home of artist Claude E. Venne. A large collection of Wisconsin Indian artifacts is on view, and changing exhibits of paintings and crafts by central Wisconsin artists are presented. Other attractions include a 19th-century French tapestry and an intricate petit point tapestry completed by Queen Victoria when she was 19. *Open Mon.-Sat. May-Oct.*

159. Old Indian Agency House *Portage, Wis.* The U.S. government built this two-story clapboard house in 1832 for John Harris Kinzie, agent to the Winnebago Indians. (Kinzie's father was the first white settler at Fort Dearborn, now Chicago.) One of the oldest surviving dwellings in the state, it contains handsome furniture, most of which is American Empire style. None of the furniture was made later than 1833, when Kinzie moved to Chicago. Interesting objects include a cherry clock (1810) in the front hall and a piano (1830) in the parlor. The dining room contains a mahogany sideboard, a banjo clock with a stenciled case and four Hitchcock chairs. In the kitchen are old kettles, flintlocks and a rocking bench with a "fence" to protect a baby. *Open daily except Dec. 25. Small charge.*

160. Circus World Museum *426 Water St., Baraboo, Wis.* Pleasant memories from the days of traveling circuses are awakened at this museum, located in the original winter quarters buildings of Ringling Brothers Circus. More than 100 ornately carved and painted circus wagons have been restored and are displayed in the huge Circus Parade Pavillion. Six- and eight-horse teams of Percherons pull some of the wagons and help unload the circus trains. Visitors can see a re-creation of P. T. Barnum's fabulous 19th-century sideshow and a one-ring presentation of trained animal and aerial acts. Steam and air calliope concerts are given regularly. Youngsters enjoy an antique merry-go-round, the goat- and pony-cart rides and the animated miniature circus. *Open daily mid-May-mid-Sept. Adults $2.50, children under 12 small charge.*

[160] *This gilded and mirrored circus wagon, every square inch embellished with griffins, cupids, Greek heads and wreaths, must have been a sensation as it rolled down small-town Main Streets behind dappled Percherons.*

161. Mid-Continent Railway Historical Society Museum *Off Rte. 136, North Freedom, Wis.* The lively sensations of railroading in the early 1900s can be experienced along a four-and-a-half-mile stretch of track that once served as a branch line on the Chicago & North Western Railway. Visitors board trains at a restored depot from which a variety of steam locomotives, coaches and cabooses make the trip. A caboose used to be called a conductor's castle; there are seven of them here among nearly 100 pieces of equipment on display and in use. Volunteers, train buffs all, keep the old trains running and in good repair. *Open daily late May-early Sept., Sun. early Sept.-mid-Oct. Adults $2.00, children small charge.*

162. House on the Rock *Rte. 23, Spring Green, Wis.* When Madison sculptor Alex Jordan first saw the jagged chimney rock, which rises 59 feet out of a hill 450 feet above a valley, he felt it would be the perfect place for a house. In 1945 Mr. Jordan began what was to become a 20-year project, quarrying more than 5000 tons of sandstone from nearby bluffs and welding them to the rock with mortar and steel cable. The house is built on several different levels around and through the rock itself. Rooms are built around trees, rock has been incorporated into ledges for seating. Waterfalls splash into pools, enormous stone fireplaces burn whole tree trunks. The architecture is strongly Oriental; windows are canted out over the valley. House on the Rock is part of a larger complex: visitors pass from it to the Mill House, with its 16-foot mill wheel and the world's largest fireplace, into the "Streets of Yesterday." Here shops such as a drugstore, barbershop and clock shop recall the gaslit era of the 1880s. *Open daily Apr.-Nov. Adults $2.00 Mon.-Sat., $2.25 Sun. and holidays, children small charge.*

163. Little Norway *Blue Mounds, Wis.* The 1856 homestead of a Norwegian settler, nestled by a secluded stream in the Valley of the Elves, comprises a dozen or so log buildings constructed in the Norwegian style. The largest, modeled after a 12th-century Norwegian stave church, was built in Norway to be exhibited at several world expositions of the late 1800s. Within the buildings are handsome Norwegian antiques, such as chests, rocking chairs and cupboards, as well as handcrafted pencil boxes, fur boots, butter molds, embroidered wall hangings and other useful objects of decorative character. Altogether the settlement provides a memorable glimpse of how pioneer immigrants lived and worked. *Open daily May-late Oct. Adults $1.25, children over 5 small charge.*

164. Elvehjem Art Center *University of Wisconsin, 800 University Ave., Madison, Wis.* Almost 2000 art objects are included in the collections of this fine arts museum, making it one of the three largest university art museums in the U.S. The painting collection, which features works by such diverse artists as Gainsborough, Giovanni di Paolo, Giorgio Vasari, Helen Frankenthaler and Salvator Rosa, is especially strong in Dutch and Italian works of the 16th and 17th centuries. A complete set of Goya's *Caprichos* is found in the print and drawing collection. Sculpture is represented by works of Rodin, Maillol, Frank Gallo and others. Other collections include Greek vases, African and medieval sculpture, Indian miniatures and Tibetan art. There is also a large art library. *Open daily except holidays.*

165. State Historical Society of Wisconsin Library and Museum *816 State St., Madison, Wis.* The emphasis here at the society's headquarters, a large Renaissance-style building completed in 1900, is on the history of Wisconsin and the Midwest. The Draper Manuscripts, relating to the early West (1750–1815), form one of the library's prize collections. Dioramas depict the history of Wisconsin from prehistoric days to early European exploration, fur trading and pioneer settlement. Period rooms display typical settings of the 19th and 20th centuries. The society also has an outstanding collection of more than 3000 United Artists feature films, short subjects and cartoons, and shows them frequently for educational purposes. *Open Mon.-Sat.*

166. Unitarian Meeting House *900 University Bay Dr., Madison, Wis.* One of Madison's most memorable sights, the meetinghouse, completed in 1951, stands on a knoll overlooking Lake Mendota. It was designed by Frank Lloyd Wright, a lifelong member of the congregation; Wright's father was secretary of the congregation when it was organized in 1879. The basic plan of the meetinghouse is a triangle much like a prow—a dramatic, thrusting roof that forms a chapel, spire and parish hall in one. The roofing is green copper laid in strips that emphasize the design's boldness. *Open Tues.-Sat.*

167. Wisconsin State Capitol *Rtes. 90 and 94, Madison, Wis.* The capitol, a splendid example of Roman Renaissance architecture, is located in a landscaped park in the heart of Madison. The granite dome is only a few inches shorter than that of the U.S. Capitol. Lavish use of varicolored marble and granite in the interior plus a number of handsome murals make the building one of more than ordinary interest. The dome and the cruciform plan of the structure are especially striking at night because of indirect lighting. *Open daily.*

168. Tallman Restorations *440 N. Jackson St., Janesville, Wis.* A villa in the Italian style, the 26-room house was completed in 1857 by W. M. Tallman, a land speculator. Reputedly the largest dwelling in Wisconsin before the Civil War, it cost $33,000 (about $500,000 by today's values), and is furnished much as it was then. A notable exhibit is the arms collection, which includes firearms and other weapons, some dating from the Middle Ages and from many different countries. Also on the property are an 1842 stone house and a carriage house that has been converted into a local history museum. *Open Sat., Sun. early May-late May, daily late May-early Sept., Sat., Sun. early Sept.-Oct. Adults $1.50, children small charge.*

169. Bartlett Museum *2149 St. Lawrence Ave., Beloit, Wis.* Norwegian pioneer objects, farm tools, Indian items and early glassware displayed in this limestone former residence reflect life in Beloit during the past 100 years. Relics from four wars, period clothing and a sizable doll collection are also on view, and the museum's reference library includes many old manuscripts, newspapers and almanacs. *Open daily except holidays. Small charge.*

170. Beloit College *Beloit, Wis.* Beloit, founded in 1846, is a coeducational liberal arts institution with an enrollment of some 1700. The college maintains two museums of some importance.

[163] *The Norway Building, more fantasy than building, is an 1885 model of a 12th-century Norwegian church. Made of hewn oak, it is beautifully hand-carved throughout. Fire-breathing dragon heads on the gable ends were meant to ward off evil spirits. The shingles resemble the scales of a fish. Inside, the faces of pagan kings and queens peer down from beam ends. The house, a museum of Norwegian culture, has exhibits that include hand-carved skis, chests and household objects, an Edvard Grieg manuscript and a collection of silver and jewelry.*

LOGAN MUSEUM OF ANTHROPOLOGY The museum, one of the oldest in the U.S., houses a fine collection of Old Stone Age artifacts from Europe and North America. Among the other well-displayed exhibits are tools and clothing of North and South American Indians, a full-scale reproduction of a Pueblo Indian house and carvings and ornaments from New Guinea and Africa. *Open daily early Jan.-mid-Apr., early May-mid-Aug., early Sept.-mid-Dec.*

T. L. WRIGHT ART CENTER Graphics, especially of the Post-Impressionist and German Expressionist schools, are the main attractions here. There are a number of Oriental decorative objects, including a collection of Korean pottery from about 1000 A.D. The center's most important painting is by the 16th-century German artist Lucas Cranach. Sculptures by Barlach and Moore are also featured. *Open daily except holidays.*

171. Rawleigh Museum *223 E. Main St., Freeport, Ill.* The museum's displays include sculpture, paintings, mosaics, tapestries, Dresden china figures and coats of armor, as well as some Oriental pieces. Two of its most impressive exhibits are a life-size copy of Da Vinci's *Last Supper* and a Ching dynasty lacquered screen 18 by 9 feet. *Open Mon.-Fri.*

172. Stephenson County Historical Society Museums *1440 S. Carroll Ave., Freeport, Ill.* At this location are not only two museums but also a delightful arboretum containing a wide variety of old large trees. The Historical Museum, housed in an attractive 1857 stone house, contains memorabilia of Jane Addams, who was born in nearby Cedarville, cast-iron toys, Indian beadwork and other local historical items. At the Farm Museum visitors can see how rural Illinoisans lived and worked long ago. *Historical Museum open Fri.-Sun. except holidays, Farm Museum open Fri.-Sun. June-Sept. except holidays.*

173. Erlander Home Museum *404 S. Third St., Rockford, Ill.* John Erlander, one of the city's early settlers and a leading furniture manufacturer, built the house for his family in 1871. Today it is a museum of local and Swedish history, with about 1500 items, among them Swedish furniture, dolls and other objects associated with immigrants from Sweden, who played a large role in Rockford's development. *Open Sun.*

174. Tinker Swiss Cottage *411 Kent St., Rockford, Ill.* The charming 20-room house is based on sketches made of Swiss chalets by R. H. Tinker, a wealthy Rockford businessman, who built it in 1865. Many of the rooms are wood-paneled; others are interestingly decorated with sketches and murals. The chalet contains the original furnishings, which include many fine antiques, paintings and exquisite glass and china. The octagonal library was modeled on that of Sir Walter Scott at Abbotsford, Scotland. *Open Wed., Thurs., Sat., Sun. Small charge.*

175. John Deere Historic Site *Off Rte. 2, Grand Detour, Ill.* John Deere built the "plow that broke the prairies." Pioneer farmers in Illinois found that the area's heavy soil stuck to their wood and iron plows, requiring constant scraping. In 1837, blacksmith Deere made their lot easier by developing a steel plow which scoured itself clean. From his small enterprise developed Deere & Company, a major manufacturer of farm equipment, now headquartered in Moline. The remains of his blacksmith shop can be viewed in an exhibition building. The historical complex also includes Deere's house, furnished in the style of the 1830s, and a reconstructed 19th-century blacksmith shop with a working forge. *Open daily.*

176. Lincoln Monument State Memorial *Lincoln Statue Dr., Dixon, Ill.* The monument stands in a small park that overlooks the Rock River on the site of the Dixon Blockhouse. The statue shows the youthful Lincoln in 1832, at the time of the Black Hawk War. When that Indian disturbance broke out, Lincoln enlisted immediately and was unanimously chosen captain of his volunteer company.

177. Dickson Mounds Museum *Lewistown, Ill.* About 1000 years ago Indians, who had an advanced culture here, buried their dead in a large mound. Today visitors can examine it in the modern museum building, suggestive of such a mound, along with more than 200 skeletons buried in it and the artifacts that were placed with them as grave offerings. A few hundred yards from the museum is the Eveland Village site, the remains of a village that dates from 950-1200 A.D. *Open daily except holidays.*

178. Clover Lawn *1000 E. Monroe Dr., Bloomington, Ill.* David Davis, an intimate of Lincoln, was instrumental in obtaining for him the Republican nomination in 1860 and was later appointed to the U.S. Supreme Court by the President. Davis's 20-room brick mansion, a variation of the Italian villa style, was completed in 1872, and exemplifies luxurious living in that day. The house contains most of its original Renaissance-style furnishings. The Italian marble fireplaces and the stencil-painted wall decorations are noteworthy. The photographic plates in the bay window of the sitting room were made by John Wesley Powell on the Colorado River. *Open Tues.-Sun. except holidays.*

179. Lincoln College Museums *Lincoln College, 300 Keokuk St., Lincoln, Ill.* Two interesting historical collections are housed in the college's McKinstry Memorial Library. In the Lincoln Collection are more than 2000 books, artworks and other Lincolniana, including a table at which the 16th President studied. The Museum of the Presidents honors every chief executive, with documents written or signed by the Presidents, and their pictures and commemorative medals. *Open daily.*

180. First Church of Christ, Scientist *Main and Chicago Sts., Oconto, Wis.* This was the first structure in the world built as a Christian Science church. An interesting Gothic-style frame building, it was completed in 1886. The original Kimball reed organ is still in use. Pictures and objects associated with the church's early days can be seen in the reading room. *Open Mon., Wed., Fri. June-Aug.*

181. Oconto County Historical Museum *917 Park Ave., Oconto, Wis.* The museum's collections are

[186] *Most of these pieces were made in France in the mid-19th century. The first and third vases from the left, top row, have traditional millefiori ("thousand flowers" in Italian) bases. Thin rods or tubes of different colored glass were heated and fused together, then stretched out like taffy. The bunches of rods were then cut crosswise and "slices" were set in the base. In the overlay paperweight, bottom left, is an upright bouquet of colorful flowers surrounded by green foliage. The overlay was cut on sides and top and then encased in clear glass. The egg-shaped "lady's hand-cooler," second left, is ribbed, the one next to it is multi-faceted, both giving a pleasing tactile effect. Note the devil silhouette in the center of the weight at bottom right.*

housed in the Beyer Home—a mansion of the Civil War period and the first brick house built in Oconto County —and in a modern annex on the grounds. Wisconsin was the center of the prehistoric Copper Culture people, so called because they were the first-known people in America to use copper for tools. A settlement at the present site of Oconto was flourishing about 5556 B.C. Archaeological finds are displayed, as well as materials relating to the time when Oconto was a fur-trading post. *Open daily late May-mid-Sept. Small charge.*

182. Cotton House *2632 S. Webster Ave., Green Bay, Wis.* The large, gracious house ranks as one of the outstanding examples of Greek Revival architecture in the Midwest. Captain John W. Cotton, one of the first graduates of West Point, built it in the early 1840s. Many of his family's possessions are here, including a canopied four-poster. Other furnishings are authentic to the period of the Cottons' residency. *Open Tues.-Sun. May-Oct. except holidays. Small charge.*

183. Hazelwood *1008 S. Monroe Ave., Green Bay, Wis.* Morgan L. Martin, a Wisconsin pioneer, lawyer and distinguished legislator, built this frame house about 1837. Its dormer windows and broad front porch add to its homey, modest appearance. But it is generously furnished with period antiques, including the table at which Martin and other politicians drafted the state's constitution. *Open daily Apr.-Nov. Small charge.*

184. National Railroad Museum *2285 S. Broadway, Green Bay, Wis.* The era of steam railroading still lives at the museum: it displays an outstanding collection of historic locomotives and cars. Of special interest are President Eisenhower's locomotive, command car and staff car from World War II and a Pullman parlor car used by Sir Winston Churchill. The collection also includes 15 steam engines, among them the largest ever built. An old-fashioned depot houses hundreds of railroad relics. Visitors may take a ride on an 1890 train with a steam locomotive. There is also a narrow-gauge steam train for children. *Open Sat., Sun. May, daily June-mid-Sept., Sat., Sun. mid-Sept.-Oct. Adults $1.50, children small charge.*

185. Grignon Home *Augustine St., Kaukauna, Wis.* Charles A. Grignon, grandson of Charles De Langlade, the "Father of Wisconsin," erected the large three-story frame house with classical details in 1836. All of the artifacts are also displayed. *Open Tues.-Sun. late* furnishings are Grignon family pieces. Some Indian *May-early Sept. Small charge.*

186. John Nelson Bergstrom Art Center and Museum *165 N. Park Ave., Neenah, Wis.* Works by Wisconsin artists are included in a permanent display of regional painting in the large, Tudor-style building, the former Bergstrom residence. Evangeline Bergstrom's collection of more than 700 antique and modern glass paperweights is considered one of the world's best. Glass decanters and goblets from Austria, Bavaria and Germany, as well as decorative Victorian glass baskets, are also featured. *Open Tues.-Thurs., Sat., Sun. June-Aug., Wed., Thurs., Sat., Sun. Sept.-May.*

Off the Coast of Cornwall by George Inness (1825–94) is an example of his later work, which moved away from a meticulous rendition of grand natural scenes to an emphasis on the intimate moods of nature. He sought to project their effect on the human spirit by means of bold brushstrokes, color and light. Born in New York, Inness traveled and painted a good deal in this country and in Europe. Though not generally recognized by the public until the latter part of his life, Inness' work had a tremendous influence on other American landscape painters of his time.

187. Paine Art Center and Arboretum

1410 Algoma Blvd., Oshkosh, Wis.

Three centuries of English domestic interiors are represented within this rambling Tudor mansion. It was built over a period of 20 years and furnished with Gothic, Tudor, Jacobean, Georgian and Victorian interiors—exposing visitors to centuries of architecture and the decorative and fine arts—by Mr. Nathan Paine, an Oshkosh lumber baron. After his death in 1947 it was opened to the public as a cultural center. Part of Mr. Paine's collection of outstanding antique Persian rugs, paintings and sculpture has been carefully integrated into the period rooms; the rest is displayed in special galleries. Well represented in the painting collection are 19th-century French artists of the Barbizon school of landscapists (Corot, Millet) and American landscapists of the Hudson River school (Inness, Moran, Blakelock). Throughout the year the center mounts special exhibits of its own and traveling art shows. On acreage surrounding the center marked trails lead through an arboretum and gardens arranged with appropriate seasonal plantings. *Open Tues.–Sun. late May–early Sept., Tues., Thurs., Sat., Sun. early Sept.–late May.*

This Chinese porcelain vase from the Cheng Hua period (1406–87) of the Ming dynasty is on view in the museum's new Chinese Gallery of decorative arts.

Lumber-rich millionaire Nathan Paine began to build his Tudor manor house in the 1920s toward the end of the era when it was popular among American tycoons and the architects who served them to use period European architectural styles for their homes. The view here is of the rear of the house as seen from the carefully planned garden.

188. Cathedral Church of St. Paul the Apostle *51 W. Division St., Fond du Lac, Wis.* This impressive Episcopal church is built in the Gothic style and laid out like the cathedrals of England. The life-size wood carvings of the Apostles were made in Oberammergau. Noteworthy also are the carvings of the choir stalls and sanctuary. The graceful arches of the cloister look out on the Close, a broad expanse of lawn and gardens. *Open daily.*

189. Historic Galloway House and Village *336 E. Pioneer Rd., Fond du Lac, Wis.* The center of this interesting complex is a 30-room Victorian farmhouse with a square tower, the Galloway House. Featured in the interior are stenciled ceilings, fine carved woodwork and many of the original furnishings. A number of restored buildings have been gathered around it by the Fond du Lac County Historical Society, creating a village of the late 1800s with country store, log house, carpenter shop, blacksmith shop, printshop, gristmill, schoolhouse and other pioneer buildings. Exhibits include farm equipment and vehicles, tools, household items, dolls and dollhouse furniture, clothing and many more 19th-century items collected mostly in the region. *Open Tues.-Sun. and Mon. holidays June-Sept. Adults $1.50, children small charge.*

190. Old Wade House State Park *Rte. 23, Greenbush, Wis.* The Wade House, a white-pillared stagecoach inn, was built in the mid-19th century to serve travelers on the plank road between Sheboygan and Fond du Lac. The inn, which has been carefully restored, contains the furnishings of its early days, rare butternut woodwork and mannequins in period costumes. Within the 300-acre park are other early structures, including a gracious home known as Butternut House, a sugaring cabin, a smokehouse and a blacksmith shop. A carriage museum on the grounds features 75 antique horse-drawn vehicles, the collection of Wesley W. Jung. *Open daily May-Oct. Adults $1.50, children small charge.*

191. Octagon House *919 Charles St., Watertown, Wis.* John Richards, a teacher, lawyer and mill operator, built the eight-sided house about 1854. It consists of eight rooms on each of three floors—there is also a kitchen floor and a roof lantern—radiating from a cantilevered spiral staircase running through the center of the house from first floor to lantern. The staircase, a work of art as well as an engineering marvel, features basswood treads and a hand-turned cherry rail and spindles. Along the stairwell are two faucets which drained the rainwater trapped on the roof. This is but one part of the ingenious water system in the house. The parlor contains original family photographs and Victorian furniture, including Watertown's first piano. *Open daily May-Oct. Adults and children over 6 small charge.*

FIRST KINDERGARTEN IN U.S. Mrs. Carl Schurz, wife of the German-born American politician, founded the nation's first kindergarten in Watertown in 1856. The small building that she used for her German-speaking classes has been moved to the grounds of the Octagon House. Costumed dolls and period furniture create the illusion of a class in session.

[191] *Phrenologist Orson Fowler's book on the merits of octagon houses,* A Home for All *(1848), influenced John Richards who built this one. A central circular staircase extends to the tower, giving access to all the rooms.*

192. Shrine of Mary-Help of Christians *Holy Hill, Hubertus, Wis.* The shrine, a handsome Romanesque church, stands at the top of a lofty hill, making it the highest church in the state and affording a spectacular view of the countryside. Maintained by Carmelite friars, the sanctuary casts a peaceful spell as the stained-glass windows shed their many-colored light. The richly carved white marble altar, crowned by a mosaic depicting the Trinity, Mary, Joseph and the 12 Apostles, is a highlight of the interior. *Open daily.*

193. Church of St. John Chrysostom *Genesee and Church Sts., Delafield, Wis.* Built in the early 1850s of solid oak inside and out, St. John's is an unusually fine example of a frontier parish church. The stone altar was fixed into the ground first and the neo-Gothic building constructed around it. All the hinges, latches and nails were carefully handwrought by local craftsmen. Even after more than 100 years of use, the Episcopalian church still impresses visitors with its unspoiled simplicity and its strangely contemporary design. *Open daily.*

194. Greek Orthodox Church of the Annunciation *9400 W. Congress St., Wauwatosa, Wis.* Frank Lloyd Wright was 86 when he drew the plans for this striking church; it was his last major building. Few will fault the great architect for calling it "my little jewel—a miniature Sancta Sophia." It is a unique contemporary synthesis of the Greek cross, circle and dome, the three elements of Byzantine church architecture. The blue-tiled dome, which gives the edifice a flying-saucer look, rests on more than 700,000 ball-bearing-like structural devices. *Open daily. Small charge.*

[**195.** *Marquette Art Collection*] *This brilliantly glazed terra cotta* Madonna and Child, *with its fruited wreath and hovering angels, is typical of the work of Luca della Robbia, 15th-century Florentine sculptor.*

195. Milwaukee, Wis.

Milwaukee, Wisconsin's largest city, has an attractive setting on a crescent-shaped bay of Lake Michigan. It is a center of industry and a major Great Lakes port. German immigrants settled here in droves in the mid-19th century, and the city still has a strong German flavor.

Marquette University Art Collection *Memorial Library, Marquette University* Flemish and Italian masterpieces of the Renaissance highlight this collection of mostly religious works. It is also distinguished by 17th- to 19th-century French tapestries; French, Italian and American bronzes; and ivory carvings from Germany, Spain and Italy. Among the artists whose work is exhibited here are Dürer, Reynolds, Matisse and Dali. The latter's *The Madonna of Port Lligat* is especially popular. In the Marquette Room are antique furniture, crystal and silver objects and Oriental rugs. *Open daily.*

Milwaukee Art Center *750 N. Lincoln Memorial Dr.* The attractive modern building contains an excellent collection of 20th-century art in all media and is especially strong in contemporary works. All periods of American art are well represented. Among the works by European old masters is Zurbarán's superb *St. Francis.* A mile north of the Art Center on Lake Michigan is its branch museum for the decorative arts. This is housed in the Villa Terrace, an elegant Mediterranean-style mansion. *Open daily except holidays.*

Milwaukee County Historical Center *910 N. Third St.* Built of gray marble, the French Renaissance-style structure reveals its banking origins in one exhibit: a mannequin in period clothing is standing in a teller's cage. In addition to exhibits relating to early settlers, fashions and transportation, visitors can see military relics and old fire-fighting equipment. The Children's World offers fascinating insights into how youngsters lived, played and worked a century ago. There is also a gallery devoted to Victoriana which features a fully furnished section of a local brewer's house. Pushbuttons in a turn-of-the-century drugstore illuminate the common cures of yesteryear. *Open daily except holidays.*

Milwaukee County Zoological Park *10001 W. Bluemound Rd.* A great deal of planning has gone into this zoo, which displays one of the country's largest collections of animals—both in number and variety. The result is a park that for the most part shows animals as they occur in the wild: in continental groupings, with predator and prey seemingly together. Bars are few, and buildings make extensive use of glass, so animals can be easily seen. Grass, trees, shrubs and flowers enhance the natural appearance. In the African wildlife exhibit grazing animals such as elands and impalas are separated from lions by concealed moats. Also using the moat arrangement, elephants, rhinos, black bears and tigers coexist in the Asian exhibit. The Reptile House and Aquarium complex features a 40-foot replica of the Amazon River, complete with two waterfalls. Baby animals, an egg hatchery and a farm-in-the-zoo are among the features of the Children's Zoo. A miniature train and zoomobiles help visitors get around. *Open daily. Small charge. Small additional charge for Children's Zoo, miniature train and zoomobile.*

Milwaukee Public Museum *800 W. Wells St.* This is the nation's fourth largest natural history museum, and its life-size dioramas illustrate a number of the world's cultures. The display on Eskimo life, for example, is complete with a walk-in igloo. The Central American exhibit features a Guatemalan market with taped marimba band music, while visitors can stroll through a simulated Melanesian ceremonial house and Ikoma village. There are numerous displays of plant and animal life, and an ecological tour of the world that includes prairie and woodland settings where bird sounds and pine scents add to a feeling of authenticity. The "Streets of Old Milwaukee" enables visitors to walk along gaslit plank sidewalks and brick streets with a dry goods store, optometrist's office, apothecary shop and other buildings, and view silent films in a nickelodeon. *Open daily except holidays. Small charge.*

St. John Cathedral *802 N. Jackson St.* In 1935 a fire almost entirely destroyed this Spanish Renaissance-style church, leaving only its exterior walls and magnificent three-stage tower. The tower has been a landmark since 1853, when the Roman Catholic cathedral was first dedicated; its elaborate scrolls, pilasters and columns have long made it a favorite subject of artists. The spacious interior, restored in the early 1940s, seats 1400 and is noted for the beautiful Italian marble in a wide range of colors. Pews and other furnishings are of white oak. Twin rows of Corinthian columns adorn the nave, and 12 hand-carved wooden lanterns hang from the high ceiling. *Open daily.*

[**195.** *Milwaukee Public Museum*] *The museum's lifelike dioramas provide a geographic and ecological tour of the world. "The Bison Hunt," a glassless diorama 40 feet in diameter with a painted, curved background, is so realistic visitors almost feel themselves a part of the turbulent scene. Perhaps 15 million buffalo grazed on the Great Plains in the early 19th century. The Plains Indians literally lived on the great animals, using their flesh, hide and bone for food, clothing, tepees, cooking pots and tools.*

196. EAA Air Museum *11311 W. Forest Home Ave., Franklin, Wis.* A 1911 Curtiss A-1 (the oldest licensed flying plane in the U.S.), a World War I German Pfalz fighter, an R.A.F. S.E. 5A, a German Stuka and a Japanese Nakajima from World War II are among the 84 historic airplanes on exhibition here in the second largest collection of its kind in the country. The museum also displays a wide variety of airplane models, propellers and engines. *Open daily except holidays. Small charge.*

197. Webster House Museum *9 E. Rockwell St., Elkhorn, Wis.* A local land office in the 1830s, the old frame building later served as the home of Joseph P. Webster, composer of the famous hymn "In the Sweet By and By" and the Civil War camp song "Lorena." On view in the house are many furnishings and household treasures of the Webster family and other pioneers of Walworth County. *Open Tues.-Sun. May-Sept., Sat., Sun. Oct. Small charge.*

198. Kenosha Public Museum *5608 10th Ave., Kenosha, Wis.* The two most interesting displays here are 25 early Chinese ivory carvings and nine dioramas made between 1927 and 1936 by students of American sculptor Lorado Taft under his supervision. The dioramas include the interior of a fifth dynasty Egyptian temple, the "Gates of Florence in 1400," "Michelangelo and His David" and detailed interpretations of the studios of Phidias, Praxiteles, Donatello and Niccola Pisano. *Open daily.*

199. Fayette State Park *Fayette, Mich.* In the late 19th century Fayette prospered as an iron-smelting center. Today the village is a ghost town but, thanks to exacting restoration, it still gives visitors an excellent understanding of its exciting days a century ago. Now maintained by the state, the town's buildings include residences with period furnishings, a doctor's office, an opera house and a hotel. Rebuilt charcoal and lime kilns and partially restored blast ovens help explain the principles of early iron smelting. The Visitor Center overlooking the townsite contains an exhibit wing in which the story of Fayette is told in further detail. *Open daily mid-May-mid-Oct. Small charge each car.*

200. Museum Ship "Valley Camp" *1113 Kimball St., Sault Ste. Marie, Mich.* The 1917 Great Lakes freighter, still operational, is now a historical monument. The *Valley Camp,* which measures 550 feet long and 58 feet wide, has steamed a total of 3 million miles and carried 16½ million tons of cargo. A guided tour reveals the ship's three gigantic holds, ballast tanks, pilot house, captain's quarters, engine room, galley and seamen's quarters. One entire hold is given over to a display of marine artifacts. *Open daily May-mid-Oct. Adults $1.50, family $3.00.*

[**198**] *This carved ivory Chinese Emperor, one of a royal pair, is seated on a chair decorated with six dragon heads. The unknown artist's skill is particularly apparent in the designs on the robe and hat and in the beads.*

[**204**] *The East Blockhouse, built in 1798, is one of three that guarded the perimeters of Fort Mackinac. Inside, visitors can see a panorama of the Straits from the gunports. Exhibits tell the story of how the old fort buildings were restored. Artifacts unearthed in the area include a 1760 Irish coin and a 1796 uniform button.*

201. St. Marys Falls Canal *Off Portage Ave., Sault Ste. Marie, Mich.* Also known as the Soo Locks, this is the only water link for ships between Lake Superior and Lake Huron: a long set of falls with a drop of about 21 feet. The newest of the five locks (one is on the Canadian side of the falls) accommodates freighters up to 1000 feet long and 105 feet wide. The U.S. Army Corps of Engineers operates the locks and a park from where ships passing through can be watched. At the information center is an operating model of a lock. *Open daily early Apr.-early Dec.*

202. Beaumont Memorial *Market St., Mackinac Island, Mich.* The charming shingled house is a replica of the Old American Fur Company store that stood here from 1818 to 1834. It became a historic spot in 1822 when an 18-year-old voyageur, Alexis St. Martin, was accidentally shot in the stomach. Dr. William Beaumont, Fort Mackinac's post surgeon, was summoned to attend the wounded man. Although the doctor saved the young man's life, the wound never completely healed, and an opening about the size of a quarter was left in St. Martin's stomach. Through this aperture, the doctor discovered how the human digestive system works. After years of study he published the report on his findings in 1833. Dioramas in the building dramatically depict the extraordinary events. *Open daily late June-early Sept.*

203. Biddle House *Market St., Mackinac Island, Mich.* Considered the oldest home still standing on Mackinac Island, the neat clapboard dwelling probably dates, in part at least, from the early 1780s. Fur trader Edward Biddle lived here in the 1820s, and his descendants occupied the house for the next century. It has been carefully restored, and the furnishings reflect the styles of the 1820s. *Open daily late June-early Sept.*

204. Fort Mackinac *Huron Rd., Mackinac Island, Mich.* High on a bluff overlooking the city of Mackinac Island and its harbor are the gleaming white buildings of Fort Mackinac. Blockhouses, barracks and officers' quarters contain exhibits and period settings with costumed figures that illuminate the fort's colorful history. Begun by the British in 1780 and still unfinished when it was occupied by the Americans 16 years later, Fort Mackinac was the most important military installation on the Great Lakes. The island figured prominently in the fur trade from 1780 to 1840. Thick stone walls surround the 14 original buildings. "Soldiers" in period uniforms fire off cannon and muskets in the summer, to the delight of visitors. *Open daily mid-May-Sept. Adults and children over 12 $2.00.*

205. Fort Michilimackinac *Straits Ave., Mackinaw City, Mich.* In 1715 French troops built palisaded Fort Michilimackinac overlooking the Straits of Mackinac that separate Lake Huron and Lake Michigan. For the next 65 years—the last 20 under the British—the fort guarded the vital straits. The eight buildings surrounded by a log palisade are reconstructions based on extensive research. Visitors are particularly intrigued with the barracks that contains 30 displays and four murals. Dioramas dramatize the 1763 massacre of British troops at the fort by Chippewas during Pontiac's Rebellion. Other points of interest include the king's storehouse, the commanding officer's house and the French Church of St. Anne. French and British traders' homes contain period furnishings. Among the more illustrious soldiers to command the post was Major Robert Rogers of Rogers' Rangers, who in 1766 sent out an ill-fated expedition to find the Northwest Passage. *Open daily mid-May-mid-Oct. Adults and children over 12 $2.00.*

206. Jesse Besser Museum *491 Johnson St., Alpena, Mich.* The museum has one of America's most significant collections of materials from the early Indian cultures around the Great Lakes. Exhibits, arranged chronologically, show the craftsmanship of these North American peoples over a period of 20,000 years. A

"copper cache," the work of copper-mining Indians, features three completed and 31 partially completed pieces. Other museum facilities include a planetarium and re-creations of late 19th-century Alpena shops. *Open Tues.-Sun. Small charge for planetarium.*

207. Great Lakes Indian Museum *Cross Village, Mich.* The art and industry of the Ottawa, Chippewa, Potawatomi and other tribes of the woodlands and plains are celebrated in the interesting collection of Indian clothing, weapons, tools and beadwork. Several exhibits demonstrate the uses of various raw materials and how barter items acquired by Indians in the fur trade affected their culture. *Open daily mid-June-early Sept. Small charge.*

208. Con Foster Museum *Clinch Park, Grandview Pkwy., Traverse City, Mich.* In this small museum are thousands of items from the days when Michigan belonged to Indians and pioneers. There are also mementos of all the wars fought by the U.S. The museum was named for a retired showman who helped in the development of Clinch Park. On the park grounds are a zoo housing native wildlife and an aquarium with native game fish. *Museum open daily late May-mid-Sept. Small charge. Park open daily.*

209. Hackley Art Gallery *296 W. Webster Ave., Muskegon, Mich.* *Tornado Over Kansas,* a forceful oil by John Steuart Curry, is one of the museum's proudest possessions, which also include a Dürer engraving, a drawing by Degas and etchings and dry points by Rembrandt, Picasso and other artists. *St. Jerome* by the Flemish master Joos van Cleve; *The Home Signal,* Winslow Homer's fine 1876 work; the vibrant *Ecstasy* by Romanticist Ralph Blakelock and *Magic of the Sea* by Albert Ryder are some of the museum's other fine paintings. Persian miniatures, Japanese prints and sculpture are also in the collection, which is frequently augmented by changing exhibitions. One of Muskegon's lumber barons, Charles H. Hackley, established the museum, with its Greek Revival building, in the early 1900s. It is often the scene of lectures, study groups and art classes. *Open Mon.-Fri. July-Sept., daily Oct.-June except holidays.*

210. Grand Rapids Art Museum *230 Fulton St., Grand Rapids, Mich.* The impressive Pike House (see also pages 396 and 398), now serves as a museum. Seven galleries are devoted to the fine arts, with a particular focus on German Expressionism. There are also Renaissance paintings, 18th- and 19th-century French oils and contemporary American works. Comprehensive displays of graphics, decorative arts and textiles are also featured. *Open daily Sept.-May, Tues.-Sun. June-Aug. except holidays.*

211. Grand Rapids Public Museum *54 Jefferson Ave. S.E., Grand Rapids, Mich.* This large museum is notable for the wide variety of its exhibits. Indian artifacts, a planetarium and displays of animals in their native habitats are among the historical and scientific exhibits. Gaslight Village, with its paved street of cedar blocks, brings back the "good old days" of the 1870s to 1890s with a number of fully re-created shops, such as a gunsmith's, harness maker's and apothecary's, as well as a doctor's office, fire station and other buildings. Some of the furniture Grand Rapids has produced for more than a century is on display here in period rooms, and miniature examples of houses throughout the world are displayed in terrains typical of each country. Other attractions include several early 20th-century shops, located in reconstructed Old Town; a garden center where demonstrations in horticulture are given; and the 100-acre Blandford Nature Center (off W. Leonard Street), where fields and woodland, a pond, stream and small farm provide a setting for nature studies. *Open daily except Dec. 25. Small charge for planetarium.*

[209] *John Steuart Curry, born on a Kansas farm, may have seen twisters like the one he painted in* Tornado Over Kansas. *Here the farm family, hastening toward the storm cellar, seem more worried about the escaping cat than the approaching whirlwind. Curry studied art in Kansas City and Chicago and became a successful free-lance illustrator. After he returned from a year in Europe he began to paint scenes of the circus, farm life, sports events and other American subjects. Curry, along with Thomas Hart Benton and Grant Wood, became a leader of the Regionalist movement of the 1930s. He died in 1946.*

Inspiration From Everywhere

In the 19th century Americans looked to the architectural past for inspiration. Greek Revival was the first style to take a firm hold: Americans considered the architecture of the oldest democracy in the world symbolically fitting for their own aspirations. Across the country thousands of homes were built on the ancient principles of symmetry and solid proportion, their exteriors characterized by massive white pillars. As people tired of the formality but desired cultural associations older than anything their American past could offer, an interest in more picturesque styles developed. By the 1850s homes were built in such diverse traditions as Egyptian, Moorish, Dutch, Flemish, French Baroque, Tudor and Mediterranean, to name only a few. Architects also combined elements from various styles in one design, creating peculiarly American versions of the originals. In the Heritage Hill district of Grand Rapids, Michigan, are some 1500 houses, examples of 70 different architectural styles. Four especially popular motifs are depicted here.

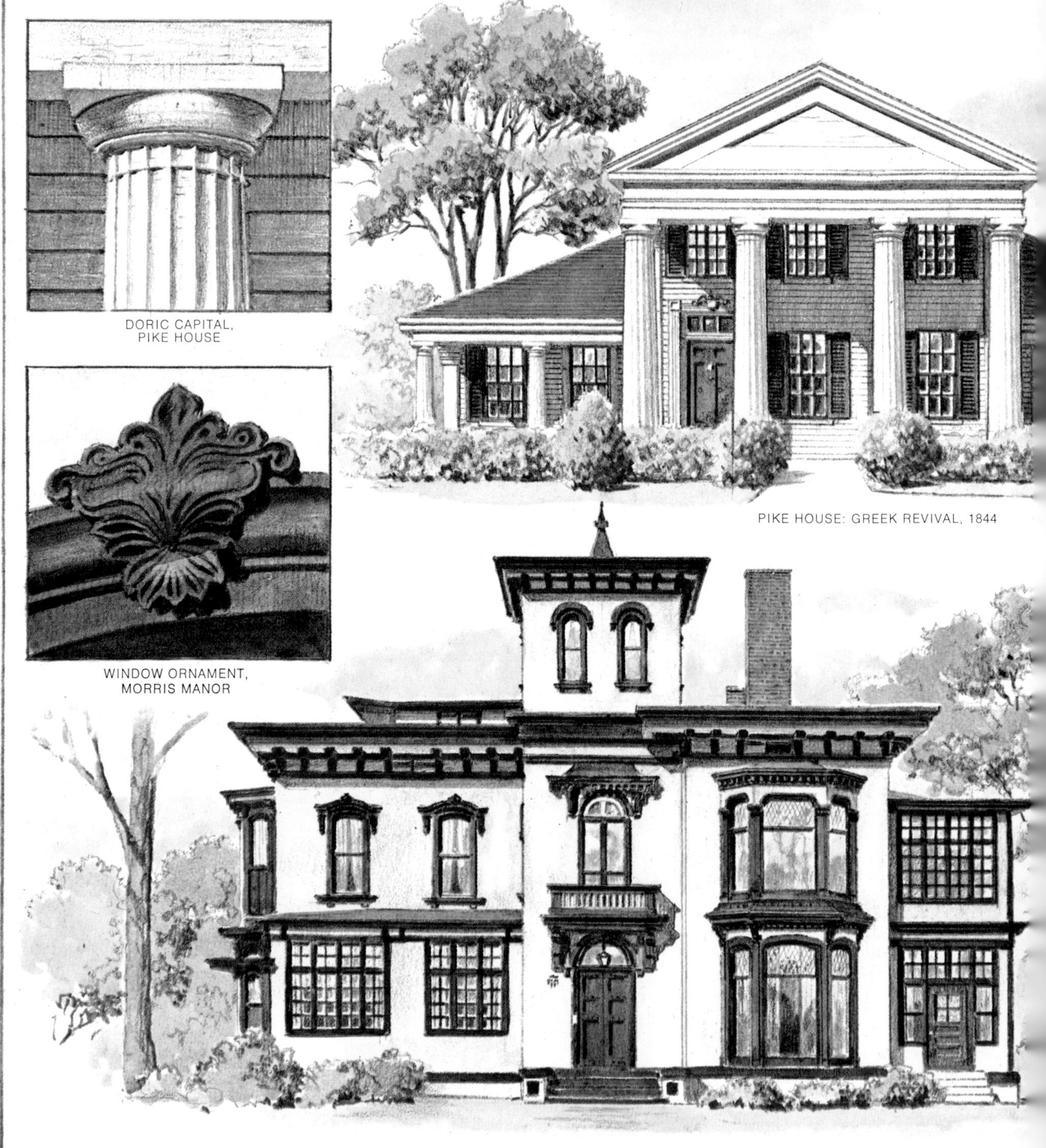

DORIC CAPITAL, PIKE HOUSE

WINDOW ORNAMENT, MORRIS MANOR

PIKE HOUSE: GREEK REVIVAL, 1844

MORRIS MANOR: ITALIAN VILLA REVIVAL, 1865

GABLE WITH DECORATIVE TRIM, THOMPSON HOUSE

THOMPSON HOUSE: GOTHIC REVIVAL, 1866

LION'S HEAD DOWNSPOUT, FRIANT HOUSE

FRIANT HOUSE: QUEEN ANNE (MEDIEVAL REVIVAL), 1892

(*continued next page*)

212. Grand Rapids, Mich.: The Great Revivals

(*See feature display on pages 396–7.*)

Despite the Civil War and periods of economic instability, America doubled in size, wealth and population in the 1800s. Grand Rapids was one of many American cities to develop then, growing from a fur-trading post in 1826 to a manufacturing city of about 100,000 in 1900. A number of families made small fortunes from the manufacture of lumber and furniture, the city's main industries, while many others grew rich in the retail trades. Because income taxes were moderate (they were nonexistent from 1872 to 1913), their wealth accumulated. One of the ways they used their money was for building houses on a grand scale and in a grand manner. The Voigt House, 115 College Avenue, S.E., for instance, is an 1895 romanticized version of King Henry II's chateau in Chenonceaux, France. Thanks to the efforts of the Heritage Hill Association, the charm of this fashionable 19th-century neighborhood is preserved. A drive through these streets reveals worldwide architectural echoes.

Friant House *601 Cherry St., S.E.* Lumber baron Thomas Friant built his house in the Queen Anne style which originated in England as a revival of 16th- and 17th-century architectural ideas. As can be seen from the facade, the American version is characterized by the use of many different materials for textural effect, asymmetry, rectangular and rounded windows, bays, turrets, leaded glass and fanciful exterior detailing. Note the delightful lion's head on the downspout.

Morris Manor *434 Cherry St., S.E.* This house is in the Italian villa style, one of the most popular of the 19th-century revivals because it combined picturesqueness with practicality. Sensible floor plans did not have to be sacrificed for the sake of overall effect, and later additions only increased its pleasant, rambling character. A smooth facade, asymmetry, square tower, large rounded windows, bracketed eaves and gently pitched roof line are hallmarks of the style. Built in 1865 by lumberman Robert Morris, the house was originally surrounded by 20 acres of land beautifully landscaped by Morris's wife.

Pike House *230 Fulton St., E.* The tremendous popularity of the Greek Revival style during its heyday from 1820 to 1845 is in large part responsible for its decline thereafter. While it was beautifully simple and uplifting, the great number of Greek Revival homes, offices, churches and public buildings built during this period tended to deaden its effect. The bilateral symmetry, Doric pillars, simple pediment across the portico of this house (now an art museum; see entry 210, page 395) are typical elements of the style, but the low flanking wings are rather unusual.

Thompson House *32 Union Ave., S.E.* The gingerbread ornamentation at the eaves, the rooftop spires and broad, spindled arches forming a loggia or gallery are typical early Gothic Revival details. They do much to lighten the aspect of this sturdy home built for a local physician-business-man.

213. Baker Furniture Museum *E. Sixth St., Holland, Mich.* A detailed history of furniture design—from early European to modern American—is set forth for visitors to this unique museum. More than 1500 examples of antique furniture include pieces fashioned from a variety of woods. Operated by a furniture company, the museum is organized into several galleries devoted to specific influences such as French Directoire, English Regency, Italian Classic and Romantic, and Provincial (from the "provinces" of America, England, Italy and France). A paneled Georgian room, which once graced a London mansion, contains many beautiful mahogany period pieces. Ornamental wood and stone carvings, old woodworking tools, some Far Eastern items and a series of prints dealing with antiques complete the collection. *Open daily May-mid-Oct. Adults and children over 12 small charge.*

214. First Congregational Church *On the Square, Vermontville, Mich.* The white rectangular frame building with a tall steeple is a classic example of traditional New England church architecture. It was built in 1862 by Congregationalists who came here from Vermont in 1836. One goal, among others, was to "remove the moral darkness" from the West. The original pews remain, as do the lovely stained-glass windows of cathedral glass (the colors are ground into the glass). *Open Sun.*

CHAPEL *On the Square* This is Vermontville's oldest building. It was built in 1843 and through the years served as a church, school, meetinghouse and general store. Today it is a museum dedicated to the preservation of the town's history. *Open Sat. late Apr., July-Aug.*

215. Kresge Art Center Gallery *Michigan State University, East Lansing, Mich.* The history of art from the prehistoric period to the present can be traced here, but the gallery's collection is strongest in small Pre-Columbian and African sculptures and 20th-century paintings and prints. Two early Spanish works to admire here are a 15th-century Gothic wood carving, *Seated Bishop,* and a 17th-century painting by Zurbarán, *The Vision of St. Anthony of Padua.* Exhibitions by students and staff members are regularly featured, and the gallery is also often used for lectures, films and musical events. *Open daily.*

216. Federal Building (Old Post Office) *Federal and Jefferson Sts., Saginaw, Mich.* Conical towers, copper ornaments, stone dragons and allegorical figures enliven the massive building—a fanciful blend of Roman and French Gothic architectural elements. Modeled after the ancestral chateau of the famous de Tocqueville family, the building was opened in 1898 as a post office and remains one of the nation's most beautiful structures ever used for this purpose. Interior attractions include fine Colorado marble and two blind spiral staircases with peepholes once used by postal inspectors. *Open Mon.-Fri. except holidays.*

217. Saginaw Art Museum *1126 N. Michigan Ave., Saginaw, Mich.* A few old masters are included among the paintings on view in the museum's six galleries, along with prints and a collection of Indian pottery,

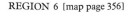

[**221.** *Art Galleries*] Orpheus Fountain *contains eight such youthful bronzes, all listening to music, according to their sculptor, Carl Milles. He did not include Orpheus, a mythological Greek musician, among the figures.*

beads and other artifacts. Monthly exhibits on varying subjects are presented, and activities encompass art classes, lectures, films and gallery talks. *Open Tues.-Sun. Sept.-July except holidays.*

218. Flint Institute of Arts *DeWaters Art Center, 1120 E. Kearsley St., Flint, Mich.* In addition to a fine collection of tapestries, sculpture, furniture and other decorative arts of the Italian Renaissance, the Flint Institute of Arts is known for its outstanding examples of French and American art of the 19th and 20th centuries. These include canvases by Sisley, Vuillard (*Woman Lighting a Stove in a Studio*) and Utrillo, as well as works by Mary Cassatt, John Singer Sargent, Heade (*Sunrise on the Marshes*), Cropsey and Andrew Wyeth (*The Sweep*). Other exhibits encompass prints; antique French paperweights; Oriental objects in bronze, jade and ivory; and European glass drinking vessels of the 18th and 19th centuries. Special exhibitions, art classes, concerts and lectures form part of the institute's program. *Open daily.*

219. Historic District of Franklin Village *Franklin, Mich.* Now a suburb of Detroit, Franklin was a rural community at the time of its founding in the 1820s. Many of the buildings dating from the town's early days still stand in this historic district. Among the private homes are the Christopher Kline House, which was built about 1840 and shows the influence of New England architecture, and the William Clemens House, also built during the 1840s, which was once occupied by a cousin of Mark Twain. The commercial structures still in use include a former gristmill, a tavern and hotels.

220. Meadow Brook Art Gallery *Oakland University, Rochester, Mich.* The gallery's interesting permanent collection of African art consists of 300 objects that include elaborate masks and carved figures from a number of tribes. Temporary exhibitions of contemporary art, Western and Oriental paintings, sculptures and graphic arts are featured throughout the year. *Open Tues.-Sun. during academic year.*

221. Cranbrook *Bloomfield Hills, Mich.* An unusual and striking complex of gardens, buildings and works of art covers the 300 acres of this educational and cultural center. Cranbrook was founded by the late Mr. and Mrs. George G. Booth, who named it after the Booth family's ancestral village in England.

CHRIST CHURCH CRANBROOK *470 Church Rd.* An impressive example of English Gothic architecture, the church was designed in the 1920s by Goodhue Associates, the architects for the Washington Cathedral in the nation's capital. Notable among the many works of art within are the silver and enamel altar cross by Arthur Nevill Kirk, the sanctuary fresco by Katherine McEwen and the tapestries and stained-glass windows, several dating from the 12th and 13th centuries. *Open daily.*

CRANBROOK ACADEMY OF ART GALLERIES *500 Lone Pine Rd.* Swedish-born sculptor Carl Milles was associated with Cranbrook for 21 years and left behind 71 of his works. His *Orpheus Fountain,* a circle of slender bronze figures around a mist of water, stands at the north side of the galleries building. The building was designed by architect Eliel Saarinen, the first president of the academy, and contains more than 1000 art objects—paintings, prints, ceramics and sculpture. Best known are collections of work by Saarinen and Milles. *Open Tues.-Sun. except holidays. Small charge.*

CRANBROOK HOUSE GARDENS *380 Lone Pine Rd.* Around the former home of Mr. and Mrs. Booth are 40 acres of impressive formal and informal gardens, statuary, water cascades, quiet pine-tree-lined walks and a 400-seat Greek-style theater. *Open daily May-Oct. Small charge, which may be applied to admission to Galleries or Institute of Science.*

CRANBROOK INSTITUTE OF SCIENCE *500 Lone Pine Rd.* Natural phenomena are presented here in lively and, in many cases, functioning exhibits. Included are some of the nation's finest specimens of rocks and minerals, and exhibits in physics, math, biology and anthropology in which models, graphics and do-it-yourself projects bring the subjects alive. Also here are a planetarium, observatory and a nature center with programs tailored to age levels and interests of special groups. *Open daily except holidays. Adults $1.25, children small charge. Small additional charge for planetarium.*

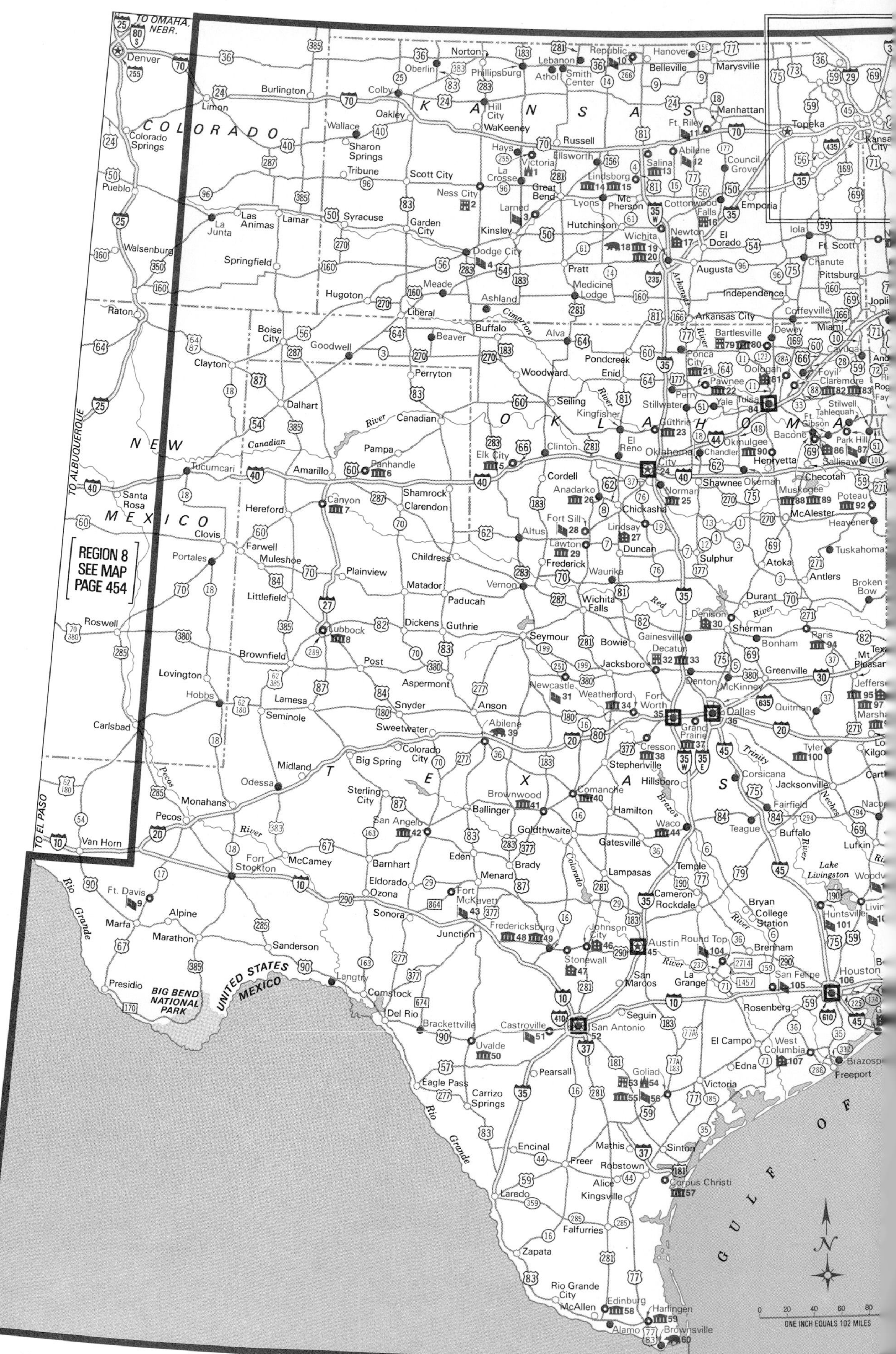
TO OMAHA, NEBR.
Denver
Limon
COLORADO
Colorado Springs
Pueblo
La Junta
Las Animas
Lamar
Walsenburg
Springfield
Raton
Burlington
Syracuse
Hugoton
Garden City
Dodge City
Scott City
Tribune
Sharon Springs
Wallace
Oakley
Colby
Oberlin
Norton
Phillipsburg
Hill City
WaKeeney
Hays
Victoria
La Crosse
Ness City
Larned
Great Bend
Russell
Ellsworth
Lindsborg
Salina
Abilene
Ft. Riley
Manhattan
Topeka
Kansas City
Council Grove
Emporia
Mc Pherson
Lyons
Hutchinson
Newton
Wichita
El Dorado
Cottonwood Falls
Kinsley
Pratt
Medicine Lodge
Meade
Ashland
Liberal
Augusta
Independence
Arkansas City
Iola
Ft. Scott
Chanute
Pittsburg
Coffeyville
Lebanon
Athol
Smith Center
Republic
Belleville
Hanover
Marysville
KANSAS
Boise City
Goodwell
Beaver
Buffalo
Alva
Woodward
Perryton
Clayton
Dalhart
Canadian
Pampa
Panhandle
Amarillo
Canyon
Hereford
Tucumcari
Santa Rosa
Clovis
Portales
Farwell
Muleshoe
Plainview
Littlefield
Lubbock
Childress
Shamrock
Clarendon
Matador
Paducah
Dickens
Guthrie
Seymour
Vernon
Altus
Elk City
Clinton
Cordell
Anadarko
Fort Sill
Lawton
Frederick
Chickasha
Norman
Oklahoma City
El Reno
Kingfisher
Guthrie
Stillwater
Perry
Pawnee
Ponca City
Pondcreek
Enid
Seiling
Bartlesville
Dewey
Tulsa
Okmulgee
Henryetta
Shawnee
Okemah
Chandler
Muskogee
Tahlequah
Stilwell
McAlester
Atoka
Antlers
Durant
Ardmore
Sulphur
Duncan
Lindsay
Waurika
Wichita Falls
OKLAHOMA
NEW MEXICO
REGION 8 SEE MAP PAGE 454
Roswell
Lovington
Hobbs
Carlsbad
TO ALBUQUERQUE
TO EL PASO
Van Horn
Pecos
Monahans
Odessa
Midland
Big Spring
Lamesa
Seminole
Brownfield
Post
Snyder
Sweetwater
Abilene
Anson
Aspermont
Colorado City
Sterling City
San Angelo
Ballinger
Brownwood
Comanche
Stephenville
Weatherford
Fort Worth
Dallas
Grand Prairie
Cresson
Denton
McKinney
Sherman
Denison
Gainesville
Decatur
Jacksboro
Bowie
Newcastle
Paris
Bonham
Greenville
Tyler
Corsicana
Jacksonville
Hillsboro
Waco
Temple
Cameron
Rockdale
Bryan
College Station
Huntsville
Lufkin
Fairfield
Teague
Buffalo
Austin
San Marcos
Seguin
San Antonio
Castroville
Uvalde
Del Rio
Brackettville
Eagle Pass
Carrizo Springs
Laredo
Encinal
Zapata
Rio Grande City
McAllen
Edinburg
Harlingen
Brownsville
Alamo
Kingsville
Alice
Corpus Christi
Robstown
Mathis
Sinton
Victoria
Goliad
Edna
El Campo
Rosenberg
Houston
Freeport
West Columbia
San Felipe
Brenham
La Grange
Round Top
Fredericksburg
Johnson City
Stonewall
Junction
Sonora
Ozona
Eldorado
Fort McKavett
Menard
Brady
Eden
Goldthwaite
Lampasas
Gatesville
Hamilton
Fort Stockton
McCamey
Barnhart
Sanderson
Langtry
Comstock
Alpine
Marathon
Marfa
Ft. Davis
Presidio
BIG BEND NATIONAL PARK
UNITED STATES
MEXICO
TEXAS
Rio Grande
Pecos River
Colorado
Brazos
Red River
Canadian River
Cimarron River
Arkansas River
Trinity
Neches
Lake Livingston
GULF OF
ONE INCH EQUALS 102 MILES
0 20 40 60 80
N

REGION 7

Pages 400–453

The treasures of this region are convincing evidence that America is more a coexistence of many cultures than a melting pot. Here, proudly preserved, is the heritage of Indians in Oklahoma, Spanish and French colonizers in Texas and Louisiana, slaves in Mississippi and German, Swedish, Russian and English settlers in the Midwest.

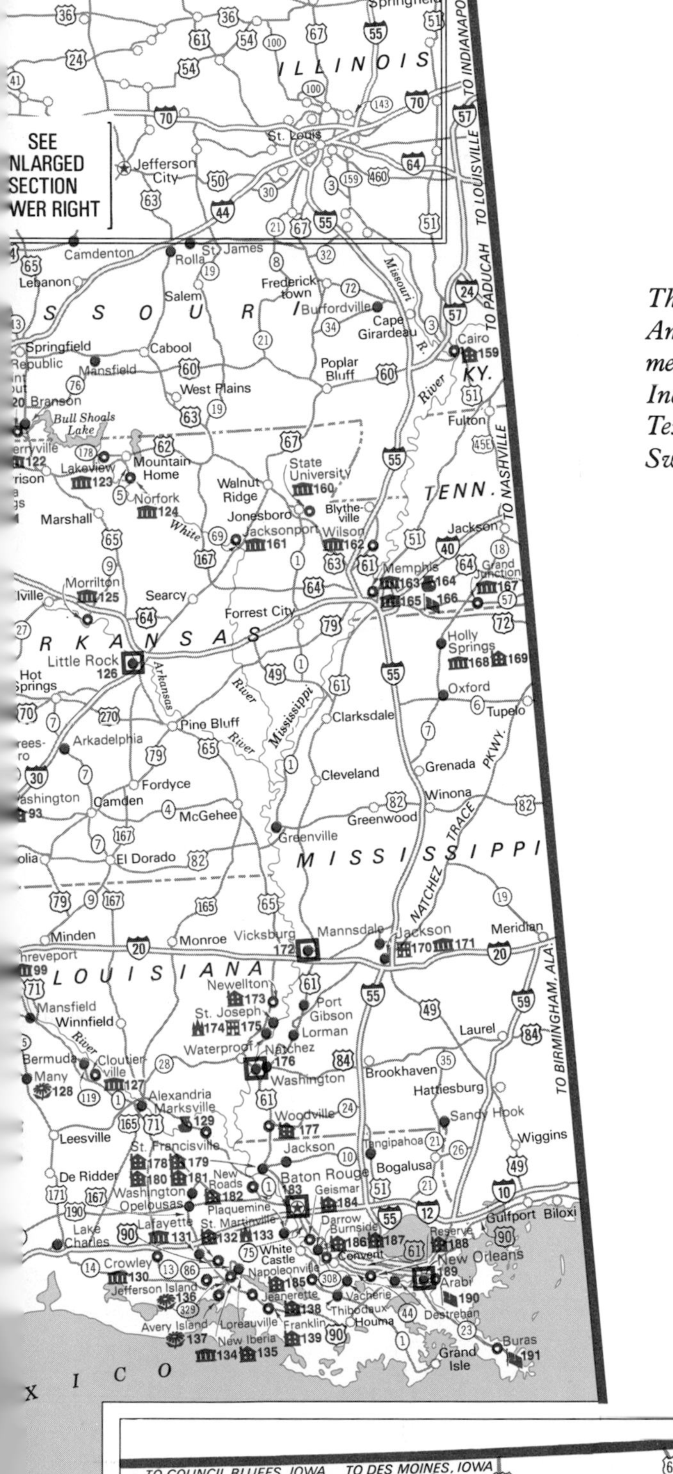

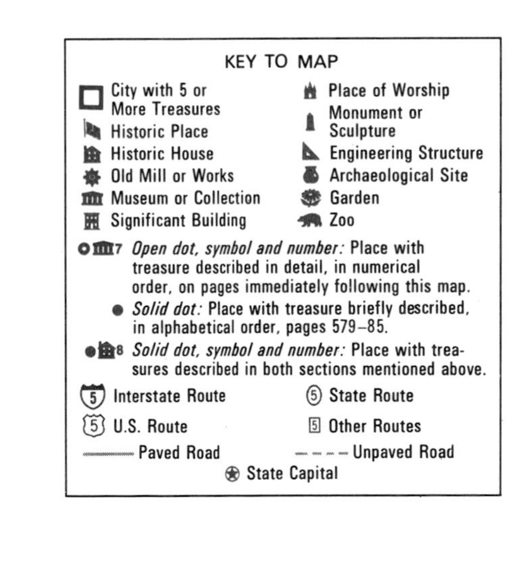

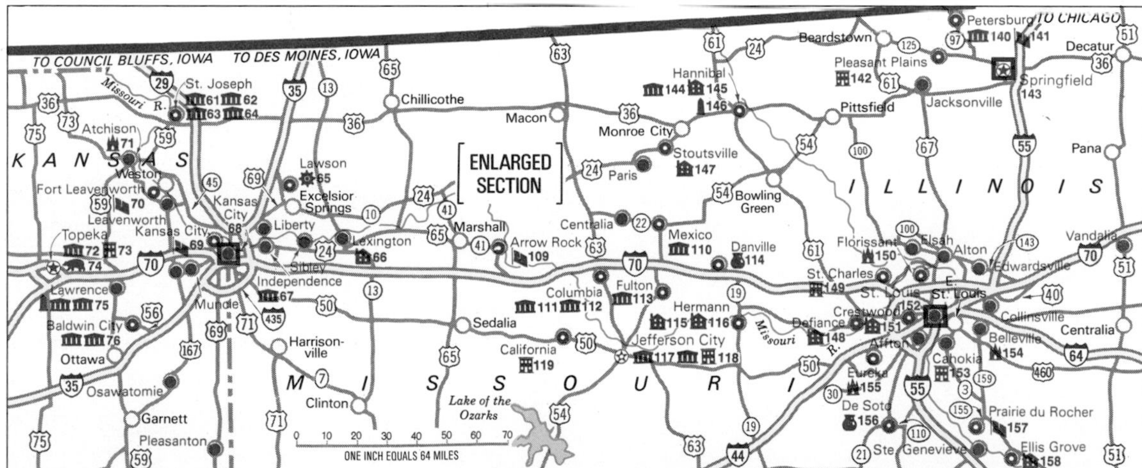

1. St. Fidelis Church *Victoria, Kans.* Twin towers rise 141 feet above the native limestone church, dominating the adjacent flatlands. Begun in 1908 the "Cathedral of the Plains" took two years to build. Its early parishioners not only raised money for the Romanesque edifice, they also contributed hours of hard labor cutting and hauling stone to the site. Inside, massive hand-polished Vermont granite pillars support the vaulted ceiling and lead the eye to the ornately decorated high altar. About 40 stained-glass windows, imported from Bavaria, are masterpieces of delicate design and color. *Open daily.*

2. Ness County Bank Building *106 S. Pennsylvania Ave., Ness City, Kans.* Surrounded by low buildings and flat country that stretches to the horizon, the imposing three-story stone edifice has aptly been dubbed the "skyscraper of the Plains." Finished in 1890, the castlelike structure has lavishly hand-carved entry arches, second-story arched windows and much intricate detailing, all cut from native limestone by skilled local craftsmen. *Open daily except holidays.*

3. Fort Larned National Historic Site *Rte. 156, 6 mi. W. of Larned, Kans.* For almost 20 years Fort Larned was an important military post on the Santa Fe Trail. It was abandoned in 1878, after being used during several Plains Indian campaigns. Nine of the fort's original stone buildings are still in good condition; these include officers' quarters, two barracks, a quartermaster warehouse, a commissary storehouse and workshops. The buildings house displays of 19th-century military equipment, horse-drawn vehicles, Indian artifacts, tools, costumes and other pioneer relics. *Open daily.*

4. Boot Hill and Old Front Street *Dodge City, Kans.* A gunman who was killed and buried with his boots on gave the famous burial ground its name; more than 50 bodies were interred here between 1872 and 1879, when this cattle town was known as "the wickedest little city in America." Hangman's Tree draws a crowd, since three horse thieves are known to have swung from it. At the foot of the cemetery is a reconstruction of Dodge City's main street in the 1870s. Visitors can enter cigar and liquor stores, a barbershop, a dry goods store and other old-time establishments. *Open daily.*

BEESON MUSEUM The 10,000 items displayed here include the 1872 town charter, a letter written by lawman Bat Masterson to the Colt Firearms Company, many frontier medical instruments and a newspaper clipping advertising Doc Holiday's services as a dentist. A shotgun used by Marshal Wyatt Earp is part of the valuable gun collection.

BOOT HILL MUSEUM The wide range of rifles and revolvers here includes Sharps and Winchester models and a rare Colt revolving rifle. Other attractions encompass stuffed animals and reptiles common to the area in the 1870s, old music machines that still play period songs, Indian artifacts and old cowboy equipment.

HARDESTY HOUSE Original furnishings in the restored home of an early cattle baron include Victorian pieces, old books, carpets, drapes and ornate kerosene lamps.

LONG BRANCH SALOON Visitors can sidle up to the bar here to order a drink of sarsaparilla and admire the portraits of Wyatt Earp, Doc Holiday, Bat Masterson and other famous figures from the community's past. A separate room holds early gambling devices which still work. A variety show with can-can girls is presented nightly between the first Saturday in June and the last Saturday in August, and gunfights are staged each evening on the street outside. *Small charge for variety show.*

OLD FORT DODGE JAIL A small office and two cells can be seen in the simple clapboard structure that dates from 1864. It served as the town's first jail.

5. Old Town Museum *W. Rte. 66 and Pioneer Rd., Elk City, Okla.* The gingerbread house, a replica of a turn-of-the-century home, is appropriately outfitted with vintage clothing, furniture and other possessions of early Oklahoma settlers. One of the 11 rooms shows a schoolroom with desks smartly lined up before a chalkboard and pot-bellied stove. Others depict a pioneer parlor, bedroom, a child's nursery and a doctor's office. There are also rodeo relics and, on the grounds,

[8] *Sunbonnets, rifles, old maps and photographs evoke the Texas of 1875–1900. The area is called* Llano Estacado (*staked plain*), *perhaps because the early Spanish explorers had to stake their route to find their way back.*

[9] *A partially restored officers' quarters and nearby ruins recall the days when Fort Davis played a key role on the southwestern frontier. This part of West Texas was the domain of Apache and Comanche Indians, who had long plundered isolated villages and haciendas in northern Mexico. Their raiding trails intersected the San Antonio-El Paso Road. By 1854 Indian attacks on white men using this road had increased so alarmingly that the Texas military authorities ordered Fort Davis built.*

a gazebo where concerts and melodramas are staged during the summer. *Open Tues.-Sun. Small charge.*

6. Carson County Square House Museum *Elsie and Fifth Sts., Panhandle, Tex.* The central building of the museum is the Square House, a ranch dwelling built in the 1880s. The museum features items that vividly tell the story of the area from the time of the prehistoric Indians to the oil boom. A silver medallion is a relic of Coronado's trek across the plains. A diorama illustrates pioneer ways, and buffalo hunters once fired the Sharps rifles. An early chuck wagon, a Santa Fe Railroad caboose and ranch paraphernalia all figured in bygone enterprises. A reconstructed and furnished dugout—half underground—shows what home was like for most early settlers. *Open daily.*

7. Panhandle-Plains Historical Museum *West Texas State University, 2401 Fourth Ave., Canyon, Tex.* Early cattle brands around the entrance door set the mood for the collection, which highlights the area's colorful past with Indian and pioneer objects. The Comanche and Kiowa exhibits are compelling, as are the prehistoric Indian artifacts. The museum's outstanding paintings include 500 works from the collection of early Western artist Frank Reaugh. Visitors also enjoy examining a chuck wagon, a miniature hand-carved ranch and an array of 800 guns. The library and archives are devoted to regional history. *Open daily except Dec. 24-5.*

8. Museum of Texas Tech University *Fourth St. and Indiana Ave., Lubbock, Tex.* Geology, paleontology and the natural history of this region are among the major collections housed in the modern museum building. Art is displayed and the history of the area is caught in exhibits here and, in the old museum building, in Peter Hurd's rotunda mural. On the grounds are a planetarium and ranch buildings that illustrate the development of ranching from the 1830s to the early 1900s. *Open Tues.-Sun. except holidays.*

9. Fort Davis National Historic Site *Fort Davis, Tex.* Between 1854 and 1891 troops stationed at Fort Davis, then a key post in West Texas, protected travelers on the Overland Trail against robbers and Indian raids. The route was used by migrants and fortune hunters lured West by available land and tales of gold. At its most active period the fort consisted of some 50 adobe and stone buildings. The officers' quarters and cavalry barracks have been partially restored. In the latter are military and Indian exhibits and a model of the fort. *Open daily. Small charge.*

10. Pawnee Indian Village Museum *Rte. 266, Republic, Kans.* The round museum encloses the carefully excavated floor of a circular Pawnee earth lodge dating from the early 1800s. Once part of a village of more than 30 lodges, the dome-shaped home, 50 feet in diameter, had a timber framework covered with saplings, thatch grass and about a foot of sod. Two families lived in large lodges like this one; their common living area centered around the fire pit. Scattered about the floor, exactly as they were found, are whetstones, knives, scrapers and other implements. Recessed cases in the museum's wall hold more artifacts from the village, which once supported 1000 Pawnees. Visitors may tour the remains of the village, where markers explain the various sites. *Open Tues.-Sun. except holidays.*

11. Fort Riley *Fort Riley, Kans.* The famed 7th Cavalry protected traffic on the Santa Fe Trail from this post, which was established in 1853. Many of the original buildings may be seen in a tour of the historic military reservation. *Open daily.*

CUSTER'S HOME George A. Custer and his wife lived here in 1866-7. He was a lieutenant colonel at the time, nine years before the Little Big Horn massacre. The two-story house, which features a screened front porch, was built in 1855 and is one of the oldest surviving structures at Fort Riley.

FIRST STATE CAPITOL The stone building, formerly a warehouse, was the site of the first meeting of the Kansas Territorial Legislature in 1855. The lower floor was used as the house chamber; the senate occupied the second floor. A museum now, the restored building is furnished with period pieces.

ST. MARY'S CHAPEL Built in 1855 as an Episcopal chapel, the native limestone structure later served as a school and as an all-faith chapel. St. Mary's was renovated and enlarged in 1938 and is now a Catholic chapel.

U.S. CAVALRY MUSEUM The building, first the post hospital and later post headquarters, now houses the Cavalry Museum with exhibits relating to military history, especially of the cavalry, and local history. Swords, guns and uniforms are part of the display. A Sherman tank and a half-track stand guard outside.

12. Dwight D. Eisenhower Center *S.E. Fourth and Buckeye Sts., Abilene, Kans.* The complex, set on 13 acres, honors the World War II commander of Allied forces in Europe and the nation's 34th President. *Open daily except holidays. Adults small charge.*

DWIGHT D. EISENHOWER LIBRARY The research collection in the modern stone building interprets Eisenhower's life as a soldier, President and former President through more than 16 million manuscript pages, 22,000 volumes, films, audio tapes and photographs. The wartime papers of General Walter Bedell Smith and other high-ranking U.S. officers are held here, along with the personal and staff files of several former Cabinet members, including those of John Foster Dulles.

DWIGHT D. EISENHOWER MUSEUM Dedicated on Veterans Day, 1954, the museum was established to house materials and objects related to Dwight D. Eisenhower's life. It contains over 30,000 square feet of galleries, with exhibits that not only show the fine art objects collected by and given to Eisenhower, but also tell the story of his careers as a military leader and as President.

EISENHOWER HOME The two-story clapboard dwelling with original furnishings was occupied by members of Eisenhower's family from 1898 to 1945, when his mother died. "Ike" spent his boyhood in the house, leaving here for West Point in 1911.

PLACE OF MEDITATION The small limestone chapel for all faiths contains the graves of Eisenhower and his three-year-old son Doud. A fountain plays on the terrace in front of the structure.

13. Smoky Hill Historical Museum *Oakdale Dr., Salina, Kans.* Amid the trappings of an old country store, relics of bygone days are exhibited. Among them are a fine collection of Indian artifacts, cowboy gear, and the garb and tools of early pioneers. Also on view are some crude belongings of Stone Age man. *Open Tues.-Sun. except holidays.*

14. Birger Sandzen Memorial Gallery *Bethany College, Lindsborg, Kans.* The museum is a restful, low-lying brick building on the campus of the college where the Swedish-born painter Birger Sandzen (1871-1954) taught for 52 years. Sandzen, an eloquent advocate of art galleries for small towns as well as cities, is fittingly honored: of the nine exhibit areas, four hang his works. A garden courtyard shows off a lovely fountain, *The Little Triton,* given by its creator, the sculptor Carl Milles. Also here are paintings by Poor, Raymer, Bashor, Hartley, Nordfeldt and Curry. *Open Tues.-Sun. except holidays. Small charge.*

15. McPherson County Old Mill Museum and Park *120 Mill St., Lindsborg, Kans.* Grouped here are buildings that tell the early history of Kansas and Lindsborg's Scandinavian heritage. In the museum pioneer life is simulated by the re-creation of a fully equipped general store, a turn-of-the-century parlor and an old-fashioned kitchen. Maps and historical documents trace the growth of both town and county, and native animal exhibits fill a natural history room. Next door is the tall Smoky Valley Roller Mill, the state's only water-driven flour mill still standing. A restored schoolhouse, topped by a bell tower, boasts period desks and blackboards. *Open Tues.-Sun. except holidays.*

16. Chase County Courthouse *Pearl St., Cottonwood Falls, Kans.* Perfect balance is evident in the facade of the three-story native limestone building that was completed in 1873 and is the state's oldest courthouse still in use. Its French Renaissance style reveals a strong Victorian influence, particularly noticeable in the ornate wrought-iron balustrade around the mansard roof and over the central clock tower. A decorative cornice can be seen above the pedimented double windows on the second floor. The interior contains a handsome walnut circular staircase. *Open Mon.-Fri.*

17. Warkentin House *211 E. First St., Newton, Kans.* Bernhard Warkentin was a pioneer miller and Mennonite leader who brought hardy Turkey Red wheat

[17] *Bernhard Warkentin, a Russian-born Mennonite, built this sprawling, comfortable house in 1886. Warkentin came to America in 1872 as a tourist. When he saw the fertile lands of south central Kansas, he decided to stay. He set up mills and spread the word to his fellow Mennonites back in Russia, encouraging them to come to Kansas and bring Turkey Red winter wheat with them—an agricultural innovation that greatly increased the production of wheat in this country.*

[20] *Winslow Homer, noted for his skillful handling of light, would wait patiently for hours to see a certain effect—sun shining on water, or, as here in* In the Mowing, *on wheatfields ripe for the harvest.*

from his Russian homeland to this country—a significant contribution to America's grain agriculture. Built in 1886, his house is an elaborate Victorian period piece with large porches and dormer windows. Inside are many of the original furnishings, lovely wood paneling and leatherette wainscoting—along with Italian marble fireplaces and glittering crystal chandeliers. *Open daily June-Aug., Sat., Sun. Sept.-May. Small charge.*

18. Sedgwick County Zoo *5555 Zoo Blvd., Wichita, Kans.* Hundreds of animals are exhibited in settings that underscore the interrelationship of animals and their habitats. Exhibits include two children's farms, one American and the other Asian; a herpetarium; an African veld; and a jungle building. Visitors can take a boat ride through landscaped gardens and past many of the exhibits. *Open daily.*

19. Wichita Art Association *9112 E. Central, Wichita, Kans.* Visitors approach the contemporary brick and concrete structure over a footbridge that spans a small watercourse, setting a quiet mood for contemplation of the arts. But inside they find more than a repository of treasures: in lively studios and classrooms young and old learn silversmithing, ceramics, weaving, lithography, sketching and painting. In the Children's Theatre students take part in drama and ballet. The gallery collection contains fine painting, sculpture, Oriental artifacts and antique glass. *Open Tues.-Sun. Sept.-mid-July except Thanksgiving Day and Dec. 25.*

20. Wichita Art Museum *619 Stackman Dr., Wichita, Kans.* Homer's *In the Mowing,* Hopper's *Sunlight on Brownstones,* a Cassatt *Mother and Child* and Shahn's *The Blind Botanist* are but a few of the exceptional works of American artists on exhibit. This is the only museum west of the Mississippi devoted exclusively to American art: altogether its paintings, drawings and sculptures comprise one of the finest collections in the country. Also on display is a large assemblage of exquisite porcelain birds. *Open Tues.-Sun.*

21. Ponca City Indian Museum *1000 E. Grand Ave., Ponca City, Okla.* Peyote ritual objects, an Osage bridal costume, Kaw ceremonial dress, baskets and kachina dolls—these are some of the extraordinary Indian artifacts that belong to the permanent collection. The museum often holds special exhibits of contemporary Indian arts and crafts. An additional attraction here is the building itself, a former governor's home grandly furnished and featuring an indoor pool and a hanging stairway. *Open Wed.-Mon.*

22. Pawnee Bill Museum *Rte. 64, W. of Pawnee, Okla.* "Major" Gordon William Lillie (1860-1942), known as Pawnee Bill, was an interpreter, teacher, adopted white chief of the Pawnee Indians and a Wild West showman. His 14-room ranch house stands here with its original furnishings, including tapestries, rare books and art objects. The ranch buildings include a log cabin Lillie built by hand and a new museum building housing Wild West memorabilia and Indian curios. On surrounding parkland buffalo and longhorn cattle graze. *Open daily except Dec. 25.*

23. Oklahoma Territorial Museum *402 E. Oklahoma Ave., Guthrie, Okla.* Historical materials and memorabilia relating to the Oklahoma Territory are exhibited in the modern museum, opened in 1973. The collections displayed here depict territorial life from 1889 to 1907. Adjoining the museum is the Guthrie Carnegie Library, a two-story domed structure that was the first Carnegie library built in Oklahoma. The last territorial governor and the first state governor both took their oaths of office on the building's front steps. The library features reference materials on early Oklahoma history. *Open daily.*

24. Oklahoma City, Okla.

The site of Oklahoma City was begun as "Oklahoma Station" on the Santa Fe Railway in 1887. Its location here in the "Oklahoma Country" of Indian Territory was opened for settlement in the run on Apr. 22, 1889. By the evening of that day, more than 10,000 settlers had made the run and camped on the site of the town. The city today is Oklahoma's largest commercial and financial center.

National Cowboy Hall of Fame and Western Heritage Center *1700 N.E. 63rd St.* Storybook tales of pioneers, cowboys and Indians come to life in the museum's colorful detailed exhibits. The focal point is a gigantic statue of a defeated Indian warrior slumped in his saddle and holding a downturned spear, the famous *End of the Trail* by James Earle Fraser, who also designed the buffalo-Indian head nickel. Western settlement is recorded in paintings, life-size dioramas, a stagecoach, a sod house, a gun shop, an Indian village and a cowboy chuck wagon. The Rodeo Hall of Fame, crammed with saddles, buckles, boots, spurs and trophies, honors champion riders. A room-size relief map, using light and sound, tracks the historic trails pioneers followed westward. *Open daily except holidays. Small charge.*

Oklahoma Art Center *3113 Pershing Blvd.* In the striking circular building is a large collection of modern art—paintings, drawings, prints and sculptures that include works by such contemporary artists as Robert Indiana and Ellsworth Kelly. The old masters are represented by Rembrandt's superb etching *The*

[**24.** *Oklahoma State Capitol*] *Towering oil derricks, like this one at the capitol's main entrance, dot the 100 acres surrounding the impressive capitol complex. Flanking the capitol's plaza are replicas of the 14 different flags that have flown over Oklahoma since 1541. Coronado first claimed the area for Spain; England and France challenged Spain; Mexico owned the Oklahoma Panhandle for 15 years; Texas flew two different flags over the Panhandle; and Choctaw Indians had their own nation in southeastern Oklahoma.*

Raising of Lazarus. Americana is featured in commemorative designs of the extensive glass collection. The American Birds of Dorothy Doughty are also on display. A sculpture court admirably counterpoints the center's interior galleries. *Open Tues.-Sun.*

Oklahoma City Zoo *Eastern Ave. and N.E. 50th St.* Natural habitats are one of the hallmarks of fine zoos, and several are featured here. In one area wild dogs such as dingoes, coyotes and maned wolves roam; in another, rare antelopes and deer. The newest grouping features South American animals: Andean condors, giant rheas, Paraguayan monkeys, llamas and pampas cats. Of the zoo's more than 500 species, the most admired is the trio of rare mountain gorillas (one of a number of species here that are in danger of extinction in the wild), though several hundred peacocks draw their share of attention as they stroll the walks with visitors. *Open daily. Small charge.*

Oklahoma Historical Society Museum *N.E. 19th St. and Lincoln Blvd.* The museum features one of America's largest collections of items pertaining to Indians: murals and paintings, an old Sioux tepee, scalps, Creek bows and arrows, a Cherokee hunting coat, clothing and tools of the Plains tribes. Another outstanding collection reveals artifacts excavated from Oklahoma's ancient Spiro Mounds. The travel conveyances on display range from a pioneer wagon and stagecoach to a 1915 Ford. *Open daily except holidays.*

Oklahoma Science and Arts Foundation Museum and Planetarium *3000 Pershing Blvd., Fair Park* Rare objects from ancient civilizations highlight the museum's collections. From Mesopotamia are 4000-year-old tablets recording everyday affairs such as a temple offering and a wagon rental. In the Egyptian displays is a mummified cat that died in 2500 B.C. Of the two human mummies, Princess Menne, who died in 331 B.C., gets more attention; small hieroglyphics adorn each side of her breastplate, and her face mask is fashioned of hammered gold. Artifacts of the Pre-Columbian Indians include Mayan figures and heads. The museum's ivory collection features more than 200 Oriental, European and African pieces. At hand for stargazers is the Kirkpatrick Planetarium, the only planetarium in the state, which puts on frequent programs. *Open daily. Small charge for planetarium.*

Oklahoma State Capitol *23rd St. and Lincoln Blvd.* Like many state capitols in the country, Oklahoma's is a grand, classic structure with a pillared portico, pediments and marble hallways, but it is unique in one respect. On the grounds are several oil wells which have provided millions of dollars in revenue for the state since the first one was drilled in 1941. Within the building a great staircase rises to the fourth floor, where three large Gilbert White murals adorn the walls, along with portraits of famous Oklahomans such as Will Rogers, Jim Thorpe and Sequoyah. Two large, modern office buildings flank the capitol's attractive landscaped gardens. *Open Sun.-Fri. except holidays.*

25. University of Oklahoma Museum of Art *410 W. Boyd St., Norman, Okla.* Among the specialties are ancient Oriental paintings, statues and porcelains, and North African jewelry, pottery and textiles. The modern galleries, with movable, carpeted walls, highlight graphics by Dürer and Rembrandt, and prints by Goya and Picasso. The museum also contains an impressive collection of 200 American Indian paintings and contemporary art in all media. *Open Tues.-Fri. Aug., Tues.-Sun. Sept.-July except holidays.*

26. National Hall of Fame for Famous American Indians *Rte. 62, Anadarko, Okla.* A 10-acre park serves as a fitting outdoor shrine to distinguished Indians. Bronze portrait busts stand on the grounds and include historic scouts, warriors, educators, statesmen and tribal leaders. Among the 18 figures commemorated are Osceola, the Seminole leader; Sacajawea, the Shoshoni woman who aided the first Lewis and Clark expedition; Sequoyah, the Cherokee silversmith who created an alphabet for his people; and Pontiac, the Ottawa chief. *Open daily.*

27. Erin Springs Mansion *Rte. 76, 2 mi. S. of Lindsay, Okla.* In 1871 Frank Murray, an adventurous Irish immigrant, married a young widow of Indian ancestry and settled at the stage stop of Erin Springs. The land was part of the Chickasaw Nation, and Murray, through his marriage, could acquire it. Within a short time he had 20,000 acres supporting corn and cattle—the largest farm in the Indian Territory. Murray soon built a home to match his holdings, the first permanent house within 25 miles. The impressive building has rock walls two feet thick, and columns rising to a gallery and fan window. It was completed in 1883 (remodeled in 1902) and furnished in the lavish style reproduced in it today. *Open Tues.-Sun. except holidays.*

28. Fort Sill *Fort Sill, Okla.* Established in 1869 as a cavalry fort, the enormous compound served soldiers, settlers, missionaries and homesteaders in Indian territory. Comanches, Arapahoes, Cheyennes, Kiowas and Apaches are among the famous Indian tribes that figured in the fort's history, and the post cemetery is regarded as the Indian "Arlington" because of the many chiefs buried here. Nearly all the original stone buildings still stand, and they are actively used as facilities for the U.S. Army Field Artillery Center and as Fort Sill Museum exhibit halls that tell dramatic stories of the past. Among the outstanding features is the old guardhouse in which Geronimo was imprisoned. (The great Apache chief died at the fort and is buried here.) The exhibits in it honor soldiers and Indians alike, and one display shows how the fort looked in 1875. The 1870 stone corral contains army and pioneer horse-drawn vehicles, blacksmith tools, harnesses and Indian tepees. The oldest Oklahoma house of worship in continuous use is the 1875 Post Chapel. In Hamilton Hall, field artillery equipment displayed includes battle flags, muskets and gunners' tools. Other buildings feature weapons, military banners and uniforms. *Open daily except Jan. 1-2 and Dec. 25-6.*

29. Museum of the Great Plains *601 Ferris Ave., Lawton, Okla.* The history, culture and settlement of the central plains region are the focus of displays here. Dioramas portray prehistoric Indian hunters trapping a mammoth, Indian women building a grass hut, and a farm during the dust-bowl days. Fur traders, cowboys, hunters and settlers are all spotlighted in various aspects of the exhibits. Outside the museum, beside a vintage wood depot, stands a gigantic 1926 Frisco locomotive that traveled the rails—for almost two million miles—until 1952. *Open daily except holidays.*

30. Eisenhower Birthplace State Park *208 E. Day St., Denison, Tex.* The 34th President of the U.S. was born on Oct. 14, 1890, in the modest two-story clapboard house, which was restored after World War II. It contains period furnishings and an early telephone that conveys greetings from "Ike" when cranked. A handsome quilt that he helped his mother make in his childhood can be seen here, as well as an original Eisenhower painting of an American Indian. *Open Tues.-Sat. Small charge.*

31. Fort Belknap *Rte. 251, New Castle, Tex.* A key site in the early defense of the Texas frontier, the fort's first log buildings were erected in 1851. Important cavalry and infantry units occupied it during its prime years, and it was a major stop on the route of the Butterfield Overland Mail Company. The restored buildings include the commissary, powder magazine, corn house, kitchen and two infantry quarters. A museum contains relics of frontier days and a collection of ladies' apparel featuring gowns worn by Mrs. Douglas MacArthur, Mrs. Dwight Eisenhower and Mrs. Lyndon Johnson. *Open Sat.-Thurs.*

32. Wise County Courthouse *Town Sq., Decatur, Tex.* Each block of Texas pink granite used in the 1895 structure was cut to size at a quarry in Burnet, shipped here by train and hauled to the site by mules. A staircase rises to the top of a clock tower decorated with many narrow window arches and columns. County and state offices and courts still operate here. *Open Mon.-Fri. except holidays.*

33. Wise County Heritage Museum *1602 S. Trinity St., Decatur, Tex.* Operated as a junior college until 1965, the restored 1891 limestone building now houses a museum and auditorium where theatrical productions are occasionally staged. Displays relating to prehistoric life as well as pioneer artifacts and Indian costumes can be seen in the museum. *Open daily June-mid-Oct., Sat., Sun. mid-Oct.-May. Small charge.*

34. Texas Railroad Museum *301 Fort Worth St., Weatherford, Tex.* A former Santa Fe railroad station provides an appropriate setting for the museum. On display are Engine No. 208, a locomotive built in 1912 and since owned by five different lines; Business Car No. 4, a luxuriously appointed car built in 1899 and used by railroad executives; a caboose dating from the early 20th century; and an old New Orleans streetcar. Other exhibits include vintage timetables, dining car menus and an old-time scale model railroad. *Open daily June-Aug., Sat., Sun. Sept.-May. Small charge.*

35. Fort Worth, Tex.

At the end of the Mexican War a military camp was established here in 1849 and named after General William Jenkins Worth. This became the site of Fort Worth, one of Texas's fastest growing urban areas.

[28] *The story of American field artillery, from 1638 to 1900, is told in Hamilton Hall's displays of cannon, flags, muskets and paintings. The "Siege of Yorktown" diorama and the Civil War exhibits are outstanding.*

Charles M. Russell painted Wild Meat for Wild Men *in 1890, the same year his* Studies of Western Life *was published. Russell knew his subject from the saddle up—he worked in Montana as a sheep rancher, trapper and cowboy for more than 10 years. By 1893, well established as an artist, he abandoned the life of a working cowboy. In 1903 he had his first New York show, and the same year cast the first of his many small bronzes. Today Russell, along with Remington, is regarded as one of the finest artists to record the American West.*

Architect Philip Johnson used a wide-angle portico design for this museum, making the most of the site on a hill overlooking Fort Worth. Henry Moore's bronze Upright Motives *in the plaza provides vertical contrast.*

Amon Carter Museum of Western Art

3501 Camp Bowie Blvd., Fort Worth, Tex.

The late Amon G. Carter, founder and publisher of the Fort Worth *Star-Telegram,* was prominent in the development of West Texas and Fort Worth. Carter, born and raised in a frontier community, never lost his admiration for the hardworking men of the frontier. During his life he was able to buy many works of art that caught the spirit of the Old West. His collection of the pictures, drawings and bronzes of Frederic Remington and Charles M. Russell was outstanding, and it formed the nucleus of the Amon Carter Museum of Western Art. Designed by Philip Johnson and opened in 1961, the museum's handsome building is considered an architectural landmark in the Southwest. Behind the portico is the facade of 15 sections of optical glass set in bronze. The bronze front doors open into a gallery two stories high extending the width of the building. It is dominated by Remington bronzes, including *Bronco Buster* and *Coming Through the Rye.* The scope of the collections has been broadened to include paintings, prints and photographs from the early 19th century to the present. The focus is on tracing the American cultural momentum from East to West, carrying with it the diverse heritage of earlier traditions, toward the ever-receding frontier. Georgia O'Keeffe's *Dark Mesa and Pink Sky* is here, and so is Grant Wood's *Parson Weems' Fable,* showing a pint-sized George Washington, with the mature face of the Gilbert Stuart portrait, confronting his father by the cherry tree. Contemporary art includes Leonard Baskin's massive walnut sculpture *Augur* and, in keeping with the Western emphasis, his ink drawing of Sitting Bull. The dreamlike landscape of Albert Bierstadt's *Sunrise, Yosemite Valley* seems to sum up the promise of a young America. *Open daily June-Aug., Tues.-Sun. Sept.-May.*

The wide-eyed horses drumming up a cloud of dust, the wounded man falling out of his saddle into the arms of a companion, lend an almost palpable urgency to Frederic Remington's A Dash for Timber.

Fort Worth Art Center Museum *1309 Montgomery St.* European and U.S. art of the 20th century is exhibited here through paintings, sculptures, prints and drawings. Among the most impressive holdings are Eakins's 1883 oil, *The Swimming Hole,* and *Allegory,* a 1948 tempera work by Shahn. Picasso is represented by his bronze *Head of a Woman* and an oil entitled *Femme Couchée Lisant.* Several changing exhibitions are given each year, and works by emerging Southwestern artists are often displayed. A small library is especially strong in books on modern art. *Open Tues.-Sun.*

Fort Worth Museum of Science and History *1501 Montgomery St.* An extensive collection of medical artifacts is featured in the Hall of Medical Science, which includes history of medicine and physiology sections, as well as period rooms representing a drug dispensary and a doctor's and dentist's offices. The past of Texas comes alive in the Hall of Texas History in a log cabin, blacksmith shop and general store. A new addition to the Hall of Man is the Aldenhoven Collection of Pre-Columbian art, featuring among other things a Jalisco shaft-tomb burial. Natural history is represented by live and mounted animals. The museum also contains a planetarium with regular shows. *Open daily. Small charge for planetarium.*

Kimbell Art Museum *Will Rogers Rd. W.* Art from prehistoric times through such 20th-century masters as Matisse and Picasso is displayed in a remarkably innovative building designed by Louis I. Kahn. The nucleus of the works here is the former private collection of the late Fort Worth industrialist Kay Kimbell, which focused on 18th-century English portrait painters such as Gainsborough, Reynolds and Romney. An extensive collection of Pre-Columbian and Asian art and works by Tintoretto, Bellini, Rubens, Boucher and Goya have also been assembled for the museum. A series of 12th-century French frescos transferred to canvas from the walls of a chapel near Avignon are impressive, as is a rare 13th-century English altarpiece. *Open Tues.-Sun. except holidays.*

Log Cabin Village *2121 Colonial Pkwy.* Life on the frontier leaps out of the pages of history books here. Seven authentic log and mud structures, beautifully handmade with simple tools, hold period furnishings and household equipment. In the Pickard Cabin (about 1856) is some original furniture; the Parker Cabin (1848) holds an early loom, a telling reminder of pioneer resourcefulness. Details on each owner are fully documented. A gristmill stands on the grounds, and common frontier crafts are demonstrated by volunteers in 19th-century costumes. *Open daily. Small charge.*

36. Dallas, Tex.

The first Anglo-American settled here in 1841. Since then, Swiss, German, French and many other immigrant groups intermingled to transform Dallas into the cosmopolitan city it is today. A center for the arts, banking and insurance, Dallas is also one of the nation's top fashion markets.

Age of Steam Railroad Museum *Washington Ave., State Fair Park* The world's largest steam engine is among the immense engines displayed in the exhibit that focuses on railroading's golden age. A long passenger train, completely restored, brings back the days when the best way to travel was by rail. The earliest station in Dallas, built in 1872, is preserved here as are a switcher, a four-wheel caboose and a New Orleans trolley car. *Open daily June-Aug., Sat., Sun. Sept.-May. Adults small charge.*

Dallas Garden Center *Forest and First Aves., State Fair Park* A lush tropical garden with orchids, bromeliads and other exotic plants gathered from all over the world flourishes in the center's Tropical Room—a modern 40-foot-high conservatory with some 6800 square feet under glass. The room even includes a cascading waterfall and a lofty catwalk which gives visitors a treetop view. The center contains more than seven acres of formal and informal gardens laced with lagoons. One feature is the Herb and Scent Garden, designed for the blind. *Open daily except Dec. 25.*

[**35.** *Art Center Museum*] *An artist of the Southwest, Georgia O'Keeffe is noted for voluptuous forms, soft coloring and large-scale objects as evident in this oil,* Yellow Cactus Flower, *painted in 1929. She is one of the early American modernists (Max Weber and John Marin were others) who were interested in learning from 20th-century European trends. They were greatly influenced in this respect by Miss O'Keeffe's husband, Alfred Stieglitz, the famed photographer. He was instrumental in introducing abstract art to this country and, through his New York galleries, in presenting European and American modernists to the public.*

[**35.** *Museum of Science and History*] *These five-inch-high clay warriors, an aggressive one with raised club threatening a frightened, seemingly defenseless opponent crouching behind his shield, form part of the museum's excellent collection of Pre-Columbian art from Mexico. These fellows, far more endearing than imposing, are from the west coast of Mexico. They were made by Indians of the Colima area, probably sometime between 100* B.C. *and 250* A.D., *and were intended as tomb companions for the dead; the holes on the top of their heads indicate they were also used as ceremonial whistles.*

Dallas Health & Science Museum *First and Forest Aves., State Fair Park* Technically complicated aspects of health and science are presented in winning fashion here. Features of the anatomy, reproduction and diseases are all shown in absorbing exhibits, many automated. The most popular are a transparent man and woman that describe functions of their bodies in electronic voices. Models show how babies are born, and other displays tell how to maintain good health. There is also a planetarium at the museum. *Open daily except Dec. 25.*

Dallas Museum of Fine Arts *Second Ave., State Fair Park* The museum's strong collection of 20th-century paintings by American artists stars Hopper's *Light-House Hill,* Bellows' *Emma in Blue* and Pollock's *Cathedral.* The extensive group of Congolese sculpture is probably the finest anywhere in the world. Other splendid possessions cover Pre-Columbian items, Oriental screens, sculpture from ancient Greece, Impressionist works and regional art. *Open Tues.-Sun.*

Dallas Theater Center *3636 Turtle Creek Blvd.* The only public theater designed by Frank Lloyd Wright, the smoothly sculptured building seems rooted in its landscape, fulfilling the architect's credo that a good structure should be "at home on its site like a swan on a lake." The sweeping auditorium, which holds 416 seats, flows around a revolving stage that thrusts into the hall, creating an intimate connection between audience and performers. *Open daily. Small charge.*

Dallas Zoo *621 E. Clarendon Dr., Marsalis Park* Klipspringer, dik-dik, saiga antelope, Gambian oribi and red duiker—these are among the rare hoofed animals that live here in moated enclosures. A three-level tropical rain forest is home to colorful free-flying birds, and a beautifully landscaped pool belongs to stilt-legged flamingos. There are primates such as orangutans, gorillas, gibbons and chimpanzees; large mammals include giraffes, elephants and lions. Among the many rare or vanishing species are the okapi, the Siberian tiger and the clouded and snow leopards. *Open daily. Small charge except Sat.*

Texas Hall of State *State Fair Park* Lavish use of different types of marble and wood lend a luxurious air to the handsome building which was erected in 1936 to commemorate the Centennial of Texas Independence. In the Hall of Six Flags a huge gold wall medallion symbolizes the different powers that have controlled Texas. The Hall of the Heroes contains bronze statues of Stephen F. Austin, William B. Travis, Sam Houston and other notable Texans. The museum features dioramas depicting Indian life, Coronado marching through Texas, the defense of the Alamo and other events. The Dallas Historical Society operates the building as a museum of Texas history with changing exhibits drawn from its rich collections of Texana. *Open daily except 2 wks. preceding annual State Fair.*

37. Southwestern Historical Wax Museum *Off Dallas-Fort Worth Trnpke., Grand Prairie, Tex.* The almost legendary history of Texas and the Southwest comes to life vividly through the museum's remarkable full-size wax figures. A total of 48 scenes, including Wild Bill Hickok deep in a card game and the Earp brothers' bloody gunfight at O.K. Corral, feature figures of history-book renown: Sam Houston, Pancho Villa, Davy Crockett, Billy the Kid, Bat Masterson, Geronimo, and Bonnie and Clyde are among the most famous. Exhibited too are Indian artifacts, antique weapons and other Americana. *Open daily except Dec. 25. Adults $2.00, children under 12 small charge.*

38. Pate Museum of Transportation *Rte. 377S, Cresson, Tex.* Antique, classic and special interest automobiles, stagecoaches, wagons, an early railcar, aircraft and space-flight materials make up the exhibits here. The 35 automobiles particularly delight visitors: youngsters admire the styling of old-fashioned vehicles, and their parents can reminisce about them. *Open daily.*

[*45. Capitol Complex-Governor's Mansion*] *Like many antebellum Southern homes, this is Greek Revival in style. Sam Houston's bedroom while governor (1859-61)—the bed was his—is now a guestroom.*

39. Abilene Zoological Gardens *Rte. 36 and Loop 322, Abilene, Tex.* Asian and African elephants, llamas, elands, tigers, sloth bears, polar bears, giant turtles and giraffes are among the animals here. Habitats, separated by open moats, include Australian, South American, African veld and Texan plains. The zoo also features a large waterfowl exhibit and a children's area where small animals may be fed and petted. *Open daily. Small charge.*

40. Burks Museum *Rte. 16, N. of Comanche, Tex.* Part of the museum is housed in a log structure which was once the Cora Courthouse. Built in 1856, it is the oldest existing courthouse in the state. The two-room building and surrounding acreage contain exhibits of early farm implements. A 1921 Model T Ford and Nichols-Shepard woodburning steam engine are among the 12,600 items to be seen here; there is also a complete blacksmith shop and pioneer store. *Open Sun. May-Aug. Small charge.*

41. General Douglas MacArthur Academy of Freedom *Howard Payne College, Brownwood, Tex.* An astonishing replica of a medieval castle chamber featuring a huge mural depicting the signing of the Magna Carta in 1215 and an exact copy of the historic Assembly Room in Philadelphia's Independence Hall are the highlights here. The building, home of the college's social studies honors program, is dedicated to landmarks in Western democracy. It also includes a Mediterranean Room with exhibits on ancient Greek, Egyptian and Israelite civilizations. Mementos of General MacArthur are also on display, including one of his familiar gold-braided Army caps, sunglasses, medals and swords. *Open daily except holidays.*

42. Fort Concho Preservation and Museum *716 Burges St., San Angelo, Tex.* Between 1867 and 1889 the post protected the Texas frontier. During eight of those years it was the headquarters of the famed 10th Cavalry, a crack regiment of blacks known as the "Buffalo Soldiers." Today the best-preserved fort of the Indian war period in Texas, it has twenty of the original buildings, including the 1875 administration building and four rebuilt barracks, all of which now serve as a museum. Displays feature a diorama of the fort, natural history exhibits, pioneer relics and guns. *Open daily except holidays. Adults and children over 5 small charge.*

43. Fort McKavett State Historic Park Site *Off Rte. 29, Fort McKavett, Tex.* Once a large frontier post, the fort was garrisoned from 1852 to 1883 with the exception of the years 1859-68. Restoration continues on several buildings, which include the officers' quarters, barracks and mess halls. Visited by Generals Robert E. Lee and William T. Sherman, the key fort was commanded by several famous soldiers including Colonel William R. Shafter, who later led U.S. Army forces in Cuba during the Spanish-American War, and Colonel Abner Doubleday, originator of baseball. *Open daily.*

44. Armstrong Browning Library *Baylor University, Waco, Tex.* More than 1000 letters and other manuscripts written by and to Elizabeth Barrett Browning and Robert Browning help to make up what is probably the world's largest collection of Browning material. Here also are books, paintings, furniture, periodicals and personal items that belonged to the two poets. The collection was established by Dr. A. J. Armstrong, chairman of the university's English Department from 1912 to 1954. It is housed in an imposing three-story building decorated with 46 stained-glass windows illustrating poems and themes of the Brownings. Similar themes are depicted in panels in the building's bronze entrance doors. *Open daily.*

45. Austin, Tex.

Named after Stephen F. Austin, the "Father of Texas," this is the capital of the Lone Star State. No matter what the weather, the moon shines here each night. The townspeople are proud of their towerlights: 26 mercury vapor lamps which bathe the city in artificial moonlight.

French Legation *802 San Marcos St.* The handsome restored house is a mixture of Greek Revival and Louisiana bayou styles, with slender square pillars supporting a veranda along the entrance facade. It was built

 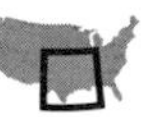

in 1840 to serve as the official residence of the French chargé d'affaires to what was then the Republic of Texas. In addition to the few pieces brought from France by its first occupant, the house holds remarkable period furnishings. Copper, brass and iron decorate the authentic early French Creole kitchen, which has been restored. *Open Tues.-Sun. Adults and children over 12 small charge.*

Lyndon B. Johnson Library *University of Texas, 2313 Red River St.* This is the first U.S. Presidential library to be established at a university. The large stone building contains eight floors, three of which are open to the public. It holds an overwhelming 31 million documents relating to the 36th President's career from 1935 to 1969. Displays include letters received by Johnson from international figures, a replica of the Oval Room office in the White House and an exhibit that traces the colorful story of Presidential campaigns since that of George Washington. Many items are associated with Johnson's years as chief executive, including gifts he received while President. An audio-visual presentation highlights life in the White House. *Open daily.*

Texas State Capitol Complex A dozen major buildings, old and new, are spread out over the 26 acres in the heart of Austin that form the state's center of government. Those of particular interest are described below.

GOVERNOR'S MANSION *1010 Colorado St.* Every Texas chief executive has lived in the elegant structure since its completion in 1856. It has the broad verandas and white pillars that characterize antebellum Southern mansions. Several rooms are open to the public, including the Sam Houston Room, which contains the huge mahogany four-poster that Governor Houston used here, as well as Stephen Austin's desk. Other interior attractions range from portraits by Reynolds and Gainsborough to an elaborate long-case clock once owned by Napoleon. *Open Mon.-Fri.*

MEMORIAL STATUES A variety of statues stand about the Capitol grounds, including a bronze of a typical Texas cowboy, another representing the Texas Rangers and a memorial to the Civil War's Confederate dead.

OLD LAND OFFICE BUILDING *112 E. 11th St.* The famous writer O. Henry spent four years as a draftsman in the German Romanesque-style building and featured it in two of his short stories. Completed in 1857 and used as the state's Land Office until 1918, it now houses two museums. On the first floor the Daughters of the Confederacy Museum displays Confederate relics; on the second, the Daughters of the Republic of Texas Museum contains objects from the Texas Revolution, mementos of Sam Houston and documents and costumes from pioneer days. *Open Tues.-Sat. except holidays.*

TEXAS STATE CAPITOL *Congress Ave.* As might be expected, the huge edifice is one of the biggest of all state capitols. It covers three acres, is more than 300 feet high from basement to the top of the Goddess of Liberty statue on the dome and has about 18 acres of floor space. Built mostly of granite, it was constructed (1882-8) in the Classical style. A number of mosaics and murals in the building depict scenes from Texas history, and there are heroic statues of Stephen Austin and Sam Houston. *Open daily except Dec. 25.*

46. Lyndon Baines Johnson Boyhood Home *Johnson City, Tex.* Lyndon Johnson lived with his family in the one-story Victorian house from 1913 until his marriage in 1934. The white frame house was the scene of an early political speech when Johnson first ran for Congress. Today it has been restored and again looks comfortably lived in, with family furniture and mementos of LBJ's career. *Open daily except Dec. 25.*

47. Lyndon Baines Johnson Birthplace *Stonewall, Tex.* Here in the Texas hill country the 36th President was born in 1908 in a one-story, two-bedroom farmhouse. The modest home has been reconstructed on the same site with some of the materials from the original house. It is furnished with many of the belongings of Johnson's parents and grandparents. When LBJ was five, his family moved to another home in Johnson City. *Open daily except Dec. 25.*

48. American Heritage Museum *Rte. 290 E., Fredericksburg, Tex.* Among the many items of Americana exhibited at the family-owned museum are an early cotton gin, a 19th-century loom and spinning wheel, and

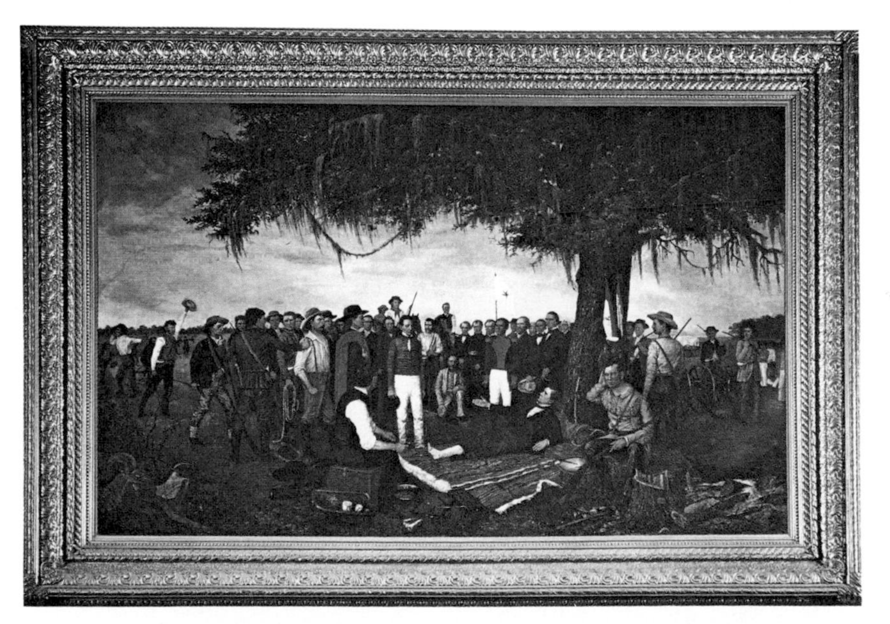

[**45.** *Capitol Complex-State Capitol*] The Surrender of Santa Anna *by William Henry Huddle (1847-92). In February 1836, after Texas had seceded from his country, Mexican President Antonio Santa Anna led 5000 troops against the Alamo, wiping out the Texans inside. In April a Texan army led by General Sam Houston defeated the Mexicans at San Jacinto. The painting shows General Houston (later President of Texas and a U.S. Governor and Senator), his leg wounded in battle, accepting Santa Anna's surrender.*

[52. *Alamo*] *Like the other missions established in the Southwest by Spanish Franciscans, the sturdy Alamo had a dual purpose: to convert the Indians and to underscore Spanish military authority, as symbolized in the nearby Presidio. Mission-building was important in maintaining Spain's Colonial power.*

[52. *Mission San José*] *Called the "Queen of the Missions of New Spain," Mission San José's church is noted for its graceful, Renaissance-style limestone carvings such as those seen here on the facade.*

collections of old dolls, costumes, china, tools and guns. Kitchen utensils, furniture and other household items are displayed, along with a replica of an early general store and pioneer artifacts. *Open daily. Small charge.*

49. Vereins Kirche *112 W. Main St., Fredericksburg, Tex.* The octagonal structure, known as the Coffee Mill, is a replica of a building erected by German settlers in 1847. The original served as a church, school and town hall, and was also used as a refuge from Indian attacks. Today it houses the Chamber of Commerce offices, where historical displays pertaining to early Fredericksburg can be seen. *Open Mon.-Sat.*

50. Ettie R. Garner Memorial Building and Museum *333 N. Park St., Uvalde, Tex.* The two-story brick mansion was the home of John Nance Garner, Vice President of the U.S. under Franklin D. Roosevelt. Garner, who died in 1967 at the age of 99, donated the house to the city as a memorial to his wife Ettie. It contains materials collected by Garner during his political career, which encompassed nearly 65 years. Included are oil portraits of Garner and his wife, a collection of gavels, posters, formal clothes worn on official occasions in Washington, antique furniture and guns. *Open daily.*

51. Castroville Historic District *Castroville, Tex.* Nearly all the buildings in this historic village in Texas contribute to its European character. It was settled by peasants brought here by Henri Castro from Alsace in the 1840s. Many of the original small dwellings with their thick whitewashed limestone walls, overhanging roofs and porches have been inhabited by the same family for generations, and the town is restoring some buildings that have decayed for lack of use. Castroville is beginning to grow, but its distinct qualities remain in contrast with modern Texas. Guests can still stay at the Landmark Inn, once a stagecoach stop, and use its separate lead-lined bathhouse.

52. San Antonio, Tex.

San Antonio was a primary Spanish, then Mexican outpost until the Texas Revolution in 1835-6. Dating from 1718, when the Spanish first established Mission San Antonio de Valero, the bilingual town (both Spanish and English are spoken) has a varied cultural flavor. Fiesta San Antonio, a joyous Mexican celebration, takes place during the last two weeks in April.

Alamo *Alamo Plaza* Mission San Antonio de Valero, destined to become the "Cradle of Texas Liberty," was founded in 1718, the first of a mission chain established to Christianize the Indians. Work on the existing structure began about the middle of the 18th century but was uncompleted when the mission was abandoned in 1793. Later the building served as a military depot and fortress. On Feb. 23, 1836, the Mexican army, led by General Santa Anna, attacked the Alamo and demanded its surrender. The 188 defending Texas soldiers, who included Jim Bowie, Davy Crockett and William Travis, unanimously elected to stand their ground. After a 13-day siege the last of the defenders were killed during the final onslaught of 5000 Mexican soldiers. "Remember the Alamo!" became the battle cry that carried the Texans on to victory at the Battle of San Jacinto. Materials associated with the mission and Texas history are on display in the Alamo Museum. The Long Barrack Museum contains artifacts of the Spanish, Indians and early Texas settlers. The final hours of the siege are depicted by a diorama. A library contains books and documents relating to the state's history and paintings that depict early San Antonio and Texas subjects. *Open daily except Dec. 24-5.*

King William Street Historic District King William (named in honor of Wilhelm I of Prussia) is a broad street lined with fine old Victorian homes, most of them built in the 1870s and '80s. It was laid out by Ernst Altgelt, the founder of Comfort, Texas, for the wealthy German population of San Antonio. At that time Germans were the largest ethnic group in the city. Most of these homes are still privately owned, but one of the grandest—the Steves House, No. 509—is open to the public. It is a rambling stone house with a mansard roof and is furnished with antique pieces, the kind in fashion among early well-to-do San Antonio German families. *Open daily except Dec. 25. Small charge.*

Marion Koogler McNay Art Institute *6000 N. New Braunfels Ave.* A Spanish mansion, with a tropical patio and 23 landscaped acres, provides a congenial setting for the art here. In the entrance hall are El Greco's *Head of Christ* and Rivera's *Delfina Flores.* Impressionists represented include Gauguin, Cézanne and Pissarro. The large print collection features works by Toulouse-Lautrec, Manet, Johns and Oldenburg. The sculptures, housed in two new pavilions added to the museum in 1970 and 1973, are dominated by Rodin's mighty *Burghers of Calais.* Medieval and Gothic art, pottery and textiles, and New Mexican arts and crafts are also prominently displayed. *Open Tues.-Sun. except holidays.*

Mission Nuestra Senora de la Purisima Concepcion de Acuna *807 Mission Rd.* Twin towers and a domed ceiling surmount the massive, rather Moorish church, which was completed in 1755 and is the oldest unrestored stone church in the U.S. The design of the mission is a cruciform, and a triangular pediment representing the Trinity stands above the entry. The building has walls almost four feet thick and is noted for its outstanding acoustics. Original frescos still adorn the chapel. *Open daily late May-early Sept., Sat., Sun. and holidays early Sept.-late May. Small charge.*

Mission San Francisco de la Espada *9800 Espada Rd.* In the 18th century Franciscan friars established five missions in San Antonio, of which this is one. The mission church, built in 1731, has been completely restored and the Franciscan fathers who live here hold services in it. Foundations of the old surrounding walls, a granary and a fortified tower are clearly visible. Part of the mission's original irrigation system, built in the 1740s, may be seen at the nearby San Antonio River; some of the ditches are still in use. *Open daily. Small charge.*

Mission San José *6539 San José Dr.* In 1720 a Franciscan priest, Father Antonio Margil de Jesús, founded the mission, and throughout the 18th century buildings were added. The complex ranks as a superior example of early Spanish mission architecture. Several structures are preserved. The church, built in 1768–82, features exceptional stone carvings. These can be seen on the lavishly detailed facade and on one particularly fine curved window. A winding hewn-oak stairway leads to the sturdy belfry. *Open daily. Small charge.*

CONVENT Sixty-four picturesque arches and broken cloisters of both Roman and Gothic design are all that remain of the missionaries' 1749 living quarters. The two-story dwelling which had spacious galleries also accommodated guests and contained offices and storage space for weapons and other needs of the mission.

GRANARY The stone structure, one of the oldest in San Antonio, was in continuous use for more than 200 years. Built in the early mission years, it has served as a granary, chapel, fort—and a home. The flying buttresses and vaulted roof were added around 1768. It houses a model of the original mission.

INDIAN QUARTERS Living quarters for Indians were constructed along the walls, and at one time 350 Indians lived and worked here. The stone apartments—one for each family—usually contained a small kitchen.

OLD MILL The flour mill was built in 1790 and was the first in Texas. The lower story is the original; the second floor is a restoration. Original mill machinery can be seen.

Mission San Juan Capistrano *Off Rte. 181* Named for a Franciscan friar from Capistrano, Italy, the mission has the simplest architecture of those built in San Antonio. The main feature is the three-arched bell tower. The church and the missionaries' residence, both erected in 1731, have been restored. *Open daily. Small charge.*

National Shrine of the Little Flower *906 Kentucky Ave.* Our Lady of Mount Carmel and St. Thérèse, completed in 1931, is a Romanesque mission-style church with two massive towers flanking its triple arched entry doors. The shrine's most notable feature is an exquisite replica of the Shrine of the Little Flower in Lisieux, France. Other interior appointments include elaborately hand-carved statues and altarpieces and a series of exceptional stained-glass windows. *Open daily.*

Paseo del Rio *Downtown San Antonio* Winding stone stairways lead to the rustic but sophisticated Paseo del Rio (River Walk) along the San Antonio River, that represents a model of superb urban renewal. Terraced and landscaped with an elegant variety of trees and shrubs—including wild olive, cypress, palm and jasmine—the walk offers a tranquil promenade only a stone's throw from downtown San Antonio's bustle. Lined with small shops, sidewalk cafés, restaurants, nightclubs and a unique outdoor theater, the Paseo del Rio is the scene of frequent festivals and art shows. River taxis and paddleboats are available.

San Antonio Convention Center *HemisFair Plaza* The modern three-building complex contains an exhibition hall; banquet or assembly hall; a 10,000-seat arena; and a 2800-seat theater for the performing arts. The theater overlooks Paseo del Rio, the picturesque winding river walk, and can be reached by water taxi. Above its front entrance, running across the entire width, is a mural executed in 11 types of unpolished stone, by Mexico's brilliant Juan O'Gorman, that symbolizes the confluence of civilizations—pre-Hispanic to Anglo-American.

San Antonio Zoological Gardens and Aquarium *3903 N. St. Marys St.* An old quarry, with roughhewn granite grottoes, provides a perfect setting for the zoo. Thirty-four different species of antelope, including several rare and endangered ones, are among the prize collection of hoofed animals. Many varieties of birds are represented, including the unusual shoebill stork. The zoo is one of the first to breed and raise whooping cranes and has the first flamingo colony to reproduce in a zoo, plus the first white rhinoceros birth in captivity outside South Africa. The waterfowl collection is considered among the finest in the world. The aquarium presents exotic fish from all parts of the world. *Open daily. Small charge.*

San Fernando Cathedral *114 Military Plaza* The first San Fernando church was completed in 1749 by settlers who had come from the Canary Islands. It was built in what was then the center of town, and Santa Anna made use of its tower as an observation lookout during the siege of the Alamo. The present building, completed in 1875 (fire destroyed the earlier one), makes use of some undamaged parts of the original structure and retains the feeling of the early Spanish-style church. Some Alamo heroes are buried here. *Open daily.*

Spanish Governor's Palace *105 Military Plaza* Governors of the Spanish Province of Texas lived in the aristocratic 10-room house for almost 100 years. Although the exact construction date is uncertain, the Hapsburg coat of arms and the date 1749 are prominently carved over the entrance arch. The building has beautifully hand-carved doors, walls almost three feet thick, beamed ceilings and a pebbled mosaic patio—a typical Spanish sanctuary lush with bright flowers, vines and trees around a fountain. An intimate chapel holds religious artifacts; copper and brass cooking pots hang in the simple kitchen. Handcrafted furniture—a combination of lovely Spanish antiques and plain Colonial items—decorates the ballroom, living room and bedrooms. *Open daily except Dec. 24-5. Adults and children over 6 small charge.*

Temple Beth-El *211 Belknap Pl.* The richly decorative scrollwork on the facade of the imposing 1927 synagogue reflects local Spanish influence. High above the three entrance doorways stand the tablets of the Commandments, and the motif of the ironwork designs is the Star of David. In the interior is a lovely marble Ark, its bronze doors enclosing the scrolls of the Torah; on either side of the Ark stand the traditional seven-branched candelabra. Stained-glass windows eloquently portray ancient Jewish symbols. *Open daily.*

University of Texas Institute of Texan Cultures *HemisFair Plaza* Multimedia techniques are employed in this historical research center to dramatize the contributions of various ethnic groups to the history and culture of Texas. The Irish, Negroes, Indians, Norwegians, Germans and Mexicans are among the 26 different groups who helped to build Texas. Exhibits make use of films and slides, color, architectural form, sound and movement in the treatment of history as a mosaic of biography. Displays include artifacts, paintings and sculpture associated with each ethnic group. The institute contains a large domed theater where 360-degree multiscreen shows are presented. *Open Tues.-Sun. except holidays.*

Witte Confluence Museum *HemisFair Plaza* Spacious galleries encircling an open-air sculpture garden provide a gracious setting for temporary exhibitions. On permanent display in Transportation Hall are antique automobiles, a mule-drawn streetcar, a World War I airplane and other interesting examples of transportation. *Open daily. Small charge.*

Witte Memorial Museum *3801 Broadway* Founded in 1926, the museum is dedicated to science, history and art. The wide scope of displays includes many related to Texas—its wildlife and ecology, early furniture and decorative arts—as well as circulating art exhibits. On the lovely landscaped grounds behind the museum are four restored historic houses dating from 1840-60: the John Twohig House, the Francisco Ruiz House, the Celso Navarro House and a frontier log cabin. *Open daily. Small charge.*

53. Goliad County Courthouse *Court House Sq., Goliad, Tex.* The formidable-looking courthouse is a three-story limestone structure erected in 1894. Although the building has been considerably remodeled, its original carved staircase and splendid wainscoting have happily survived. On the lawn of the courthouse is the Cart War hanging tree, a great oak where guilty parties in the 1857 border skirmish were executed. *Open Mon.-Fri.*

54. Mission Espiritu Santo *Goliad State Park, Rtes. 77A and 183, Goliad, Tex.* The mission was established by the Franciscan order near Matagorda Bay in 1722, but in 1749 it was relocated at its present site. The buildings, once used for the purpose of converting Indians, have been carefully preserved. A small museum has materials relating to the early mission period in Texas. *Open daily. Small charge for park admission.*

[63] *Among the exhibits is a blacksmith shop like the ones that kept Pony Express horses fit to travel the 1966 hard, fast miles between St. Joseph and Sacramento, California. In the year and a half the Pony Express was in operation, about 100 riders took part in the 10-day journey, which required about 160 manned relay stations. It was tough, dangerous work and the company knew it. Its advertisement read: "Wanted: Young, Skinny, Wiry Fellows . . . Must be expert riders willing to risk death daily. Orphans preferred . . ."*

55. Old Market House Museum *S. Market and Franklin Sts., Goliad, Tex.* The 1870s building was originally a marketing place with stalls that were rented to farmers and cattlemen for the sale of produce and meat. It later became the home of the Goliad fire department. Now preserved as a museum, the old structure houses historical documents, photographs, farm equipment and household items from the mid-19th century to the early 1900s. *Open daily June–Aug.*

56. Presidio La Bahia *Rte. 77A, 1 mi. S. of Goliad, Tex.* Spanish troops were garrisoned here in 1749 to protect the Mission Espiritu Santo on the opposite bank of the San Antonio River. The post was captured by a group of Texans in 1835; after announcing the Goliad Declaration of Independence on December 20, they flew the Goliad flag. Several buildings and stone walls of the fort have been restored, and the chapel is still in use. *Open daily.*

LA BAHIA MUSEUM In the officers' quarters are an exceptional collection of artifacts from various groups that formerly occupied the site, including Indians, Spaniards and American colonials. *Open daily. Small charge.*

57. Corpus Christi Museum *1919 N. Water St., Corpus Christi, Tex.* Natural history is the specialty here: Gulf Coast shells and other marine specimens, land animals and minerals. Recessed into walls is a fascinating array of aquariums, and terrariums are also on display. Other exhibits depict aspects of local history, including archaeological finds. *Open Tues.–Sun.*

58. Hidalgo County Historical Museum *County Sq., Edinburg, Tex.* The windows are still barred on the brick and white stucco building with a red tile roof. Completed in 1910 and serving for the next 12 years as the first county jail, the structure includes a hanging tower complete with trap door. Among many objects of local historical interest here are Pancho Villa's rifle and saddlebag. *Open Wed., Sat., Sun. Small charge.*

59. Confederate Air Force Flying Museum *Rebel Field, Harlingen, Tex.* World War II combat aircraft are the museum's main feature, and aviation fans can view 36 restored and operational models. In addition to a P-38 Lightning, B-17 Flying Fortress and other U.S. fighters and bombers, the collection includes four German Messerschmitts and a British Spitfire. Uniforms, weapons, engines and other objects in the museum trace military flying and warfare from 1939 to the present. *Open daily. Small charge.*

60. Gladys Porter Zoo *500 Ringgold St., Brownsville, Tex.* This unique specialized zoo houses one of the largest collections of rare and endangered species in the world. Built on an old channel of the Rio Grande, it is divided by moats and rock-cliff barriers into four continental "worlds" that eliminate the need for traditional cages. The majority of the animal inhabitants in the 26½-acre zoo are young paired breeding stock; some are the last-known specimens of breeding age in captivity. White rhinos, tapirs, Siberian tigers, orangutans and lowland gorillas are among the rarest. *Open daily. Adults $1.50, students and children small charge.*

[64] *A Crow pictograph on elk hide of a buffalo hunt is one of the North American Indian artifacts in the St. Joseph Museum. Its quality of line and uninhibited use of space are surprisingly sophisticated.*

61. Albrecht Gallery *2818 Frederick Blvd., St. Joseph, Mo.* The gallery is mainly devoted to contemporary American art, although changing exhibits feature the works of well-known European artists of all periods. The Georgian-style building, formerly a residence, with its carved woodwork, marble trim and ornate moldings, provides an attractive setting for the sculpture and paintings including works by Henri, Rivers, Bell and Thiebaud. On the surrounding four acres are an attractive rose garden, several sculptures and a children's creative playground. *Open Tues.–Sun. Small charge.*

62. Patee House Museum *12th and Penn Sts., St. Joseph, Mo.* The four-story building, opened in 1858 as the "finest and largest hotel west of the Mississippi," features the headquarters office of the Pony Express, located here in 1860. It also houses a woodburning 1860 vintage Hannibal & St. Joseph engine, tender and mail car and thousands of items of pioneer Western Americana. Special exhibits include an early-day altar and stained-glass windows, a country store, barbershop, Victorian house facade, antique cars and vehicles. Relics and photographs of the Civil War, World Wars I and II, General Custer and Jesse James are displayed. *Open daily late May–late Sept.*

63. Pony Express Stables Museum *914 Penn St., St. Joseph, Mo.* Before the completion of telegraph lines in 1861, almost 100 young men served as riders for the Pony Express from St. Joseph to Sacramento, California. They braved extreme climates and encounters with hostile Indians on the 1966-mile trip, which was once made in less than eight days. This brick building was the starting point and formerly housed the horses. It now contains a collection of photographs, drawings, saddles, weapons and other objects associated with the historic service. Maps trace the express routes, and models show stagecoaches and riverboats. *Open daily May–mid-Sept.*

64. St. Joseph Museum *11th and Charles Sts., St. Joseph, Mo.* Housed in this 1879 Gothic-style gray sandstone mansion overlooking the Missouri River are extensive and excellent collections on the North American Indian, local and Western history, and natural history of the Midwest. Ethnological exhibits illustrate a

[67] *Missouri artist Thomas Hart Benton and President Truman chose* Independence and the Opening of the West *for the theme of the mural surrounding a door in the museum lobby of the library. Independence was a starting point for wagon trains heading west on the Oregon and Santa Fe Trails. Mr. Benton depicts the town's life in those days: Indians threatening and offering the peace pipe; trading; blacksmithing; trappers passing through; wagon trains being outfitted while mothers and children wait for the long journey to begin.*

cross section of Indian cultures and life-styles. Historical exhibits include those on early St. Joseph, overland trails, the Pony Express, western expansion and the Civil War. Natural history exhibits include archaeology, geology and vertebrate animals. *Open daily May-mid-Sept., Tues.-Sun. mid-Sept.-Apr.*

65. Watkins Mill *Off Rte. 69, S.W. of Lawson, Mo.* When Waltus Watkins opened the three-story brick textile mill in 1861, it was western Missouri's first factory. A large number of machines used for producing woolen goods can still be seen, and some are operated for visitors. The original power plant with a steam engine and boiler and a trading store are included. Nearby are Watkins's 1850 brick dwelling, a smokehouse, a schoolhouse and a church—all of which were the center of a prosperous plantation. *Open Tues.-Sun. Adults and children over 6 small charge.*

66. Anderson House *Battle of Lexington State Park, Lexington, Mo.* Blood-stained floors on the second story of the antebellum dwelling attest to its role as a field hospital for both Union and Confederate troops during and after a Civil War battle here in 1861. The spacious three-story house still contains rafters broken by cannonballs that fell through its roof. Built in 1853 by Colonel Oliver Anderson, a hemp manufacturer, the house stands in a lovely 75-acre park. Its attractions include a U-shaped winding staircase and other woodwork made of local walnut, and room furnishings from the 1850s. *Open daily except Jan. 1 and Dec. 25. Adults and children over 6 small charge.*

67. Harry S. Truman Library and Museum *Rte. 24 and Delaware St., Independence, Mo.* A replica of the 33rd President's White House office here includes many personal belongings. Truman's rough draft of his famous "Fair Deal" message to Congress and papers from the Potsdam Conference are on display. There are exhibits of the 1948 election campaign. Original Presidential documents on loan from the National Archives feature Wilson's 1917 declaration of war against Germany, Roosevelt's memorable 1941 "Day of Infamy" address, Truman's V-E Day message and Kennedy's order establishing the Peace Corps. Other highlights are gifts presented to Truman, the 1945 Japanese surrender document and the table on which the U.N. Charter was signed in 1945. The library holds books, films and 10 million papers associated with the Truman Administration. The Truman grave site in the courtyard may be visited. *Open daily. Adults small charge.*

68. Kansas City, Mo.

A fur-trading post established in 1821 attracted the first permanent settlers to Kansas City, which was named for the Kansas Indians and Kansas River. The second largest city in Missouri, it is known as a great industrial center as well as for its beauty. Complementing the extensive park and renowned boulevard system are the more than 50 fountains located throughout the city. Many of these fountains are colorfully lighted, and some operate year-round.

Country Club Plaza *47th and Main Sts.* Begun in the 1920s, this was the nation's first suburban shopping center. Visitors admire the Spanish-style architecture, red tile roofs and tile mosaics. Giralda Tower, a plaza landmark, is modeled after the famous Moorish structure in Seville, Spain. Near it stands the Seville Light, a graceful fountain incorporating a 38-foot marble shaft topped by an ornate bronze chandelier. As is true of the rest of Kansas City, the plaza features numerous other fountains as well as statuary and other artwork. During the Christmas season the entire complex is beautifully outlined in lights. *Open daily.*

ALEMAN COURT Kansas City artist John Podrebarac's *Panorama of Americas,* a mural painted on porcelain, is displayed in the charming court, with its fountain and 17th-century Spanish cast-iron gates.

J. C. NICHOLS MEMORIAL FOUNTAIN The huge memorial to the plaza's originator and developer features a central water jet that falls on four equestrian figures surrounded by dolphins and cherubs.

Liberty Memorial *100 W. 26th St.* The impressive World War I memorial, dedicated in 1926, is dominated by a limestone shaft that soars 217 feet to an eternal flame. Concerts are played daily on a 305-bell carillon housed in the shaft. A museum here contains one of the nation's finest collections of World War I

posters and many relics associated with the U.S. Army's famous Rainbow Division. In Memory Hall heroic murals and illustrated maps recall aspects of the war. *Open Tues.-Sun. except holidays. Small charge for elevator to top of memorial.*

Nelson Gallery of Art and Atkins Museum *45th St. and Rockhill Rd.* The scope and depth of about 20,000 works of art displayed in this magnificent building assure it a place in the front rank of American museums. The collection ranges from Sumerian vases from 3000 B.C. to contemporary works, with one of the finest groupings of Chinese art in the U.S. Located throughout the galleries are outstanding re-creations of a medieval French cloister, Indian and Chinese temples and a Jacobean room. Among the European masters are Bruegel and Rubens (Flemish); Rembrandt (Dutch); Bellini, Caravaggio and Titian (Italian); El Greco, Goya and Murillo (Spanish); Cézanne, Gauguin and Renoir (French); and Constable, Gainsborough and Turner (English). American portraiture is represented by works of Sully, West, Waldo, Rembrandt Peale and Copley. Other attractions include ancient sculpture, miniatures, Chinese furniture and medieval armor. *Open Tues.-Sun. except holidays. Small charge Tues.-Fri.*

Wornall House *Wornall Rd. and 61st Terr.* Westward pioneer trails once crossed here; a Civil War battle was fought nearby, and the house became both headquarters and hospital. Built in 1858 by John B. Wornall, a local farmer and banker, the Greek Revival brick mansion saw gracious living, supported by slaves, and an eventful era. A two-story L-shaped structure, its front door stands beneath a grand pillared portico. The house has been restored—partly with the help of documents preserved by the Wornall family—and refurnished with period pieces. *Open Tues.-Sun. Adults $1.50, children small charge.*

69. Shawnee Methodist Mission *53rd St. and Mission Rd., Kansas City, Kans.* The group of two-story brick buildings, built between 1839 and 1845, housed a mission and school for Indian children established in 1830. Both original furnishings and reproductions of the originals may be seen in the three remaining buildings. Also exhibited are historical items relating to the mission's early history. Rooms have been restored to their 1840s appearance, when the mission was under the supervision of its founder, the Reverend Thomas Johnson. *Open daily except holidays.*

70. Fort Leavenworth *Fort Leavenworth, Kans.* Established in 1827 on bluffs above the Missouri River, the military post offered protection to wagon trains moving west on branches of the Oregon and Santa Fe Trails, which crossed the river at this point. It served as headquarters for the Army of the West in the Mexican War, and soldiers stationed here have left to fight in seven other wars. Historic houses on the 7000-acre post include the 1841 home of post sutler Hiram Rich; the Rookery, built in 1832 and the oldest house in Kansas; and Otis Hall, where Major and Mrs. Dwight D. Eisenhower lived while he was studying at the Command and General Staff College. Also to be seen here are the Memorial Chapel, built in 1878 of stone quarried nearby; a bronze statue of Ulysses S. Grant by sculptor Lorado Taft; and a national cemetery with graves of veterans from the War of 1812 through the Vietnam conflict. The Fort Leavenworth Museum has an excellent collection of military and civilian horse-drawn vehicles, including a 1790 Conestoga wagon and a sleigh that belonged to General George Custer. There are fascinating exhibits here of U.S. Army uniforms and 4500 miniatures of the world's regiments between 1880 and 1914. *Open daily.*

71. St. Benedict's Abbey Church *Atchison, Kans.* A 30-foot cross surmounts the tower of the limestone edifice, which was completed in 1957. Its modernistic brick and Indiana limestone interior includes oak pews and choir stalls and three dramatic frescos painted by Jean Charlot. The central high altar of Italian marble is a dominant feature, and the Blessed Sacrament Chapel altar is made of Alabama marble. There are several smaller chapels in the crypt, one of which includes altars dedicated to a number of Benedictine saints. *Open daily.*

72. Kansas Historical Society Headquarters *10th and Jackson Sts., Topeka, Kans.* Kansas newspaper editors and publishers established the society in 1875, so it should not be surprising that the collection of newspapers here is one of the largest in the U.S. The museum has colorful displays dealing with Kansas's past

[**68.** *Country Club Plaza*] *The first suburban shopping center in the country was developed in 1922 by J. C. Nichols who was rightly convinced that the U.S. would soon become a nation on wheels making his plan a success. The center, whose architectural style is basically Spanish, has grown into a carefully landscaped multi-block complex of shops, theaters, apartments and offices. Seen here is the magnificent Nichols Memorial Fountain with the Giralda Tower in the background.*

and period rooms, including a Victorian parlor and a sod house interior. *Open Mon.-Sat., museum open daily except holidays.*

73. Kansas State Capitol *Capitol Sq. (bet. Jackson and Harrison Sts.), Topeka, Kans.* Built of gleaming white limestone in a French Renaissance design with Corinthian detailing, the majestic capitol, begun in 1866, was completed in 1903. Many of the building's corridors, walls and panels are faced with exquisite marbles from many parts of the world. Elaborate allegorical frescos adorn the interior of the great dome. Among the murals is Kansas-born John Steuart Curry's gigantic *Tragic Prelude*—a dramatic image of John Brown in a pre-Civil War scene—and a series of eight great moments in Kansas history by David H. Overmyer. *Open daily.*

74. Topeka Zoological Park *635 Gage Blvd., Topeka, Kans.* Hand-raised twin polar bears, each a little over one pound at birth, and the first American golden eagle ever hatched and raised in a zoo are among the animals here. The new Tropical Rain Forest is a balanced community of plants and animals featuring a waterfall and tropical birds in free flight. In the mammal building are baby gorillas, Asian elephants featured in a training session, an animal incubator room and a nursery. *Open daily. Small charge.*

75. University of Kansas *Lawrence, Kans.* One of two large universities in Kansas, this highly respected center of learning spreads over and around Mount Oread in Lawrence. Its campus includes several buildings of interest to visitors.

CAMPANILE The slender bell tower on the brow of Mount Oread honors students and alumni who died in World War II. The campanile houses a 53-bell carillon—the largest bell weighs seven tons, the smallest, 10 pounds. A recital is held every Wednesday and Sunday. *Open daily.*

MUSEUM OF ART A fine selection of medieval and Italian Renaissance art, 17th- and 18th-century European paintings and 19th- and 20th-century American art hangs in the halls of the Romanesque-style building. Two of the most admired works are *West India Divers* by Homer and a sculpture *Madonna and Child* (about 1500) by Riemenschneider. *Open daily except Thanksgiving Day and Dec. 25.*

MUSEUM OF NATURAL HISTORY Through artful panoramas and dioramas, the museum brings to life the immediate and the very distant past. The panorama of North American mammals is not only spectacular in its size and attention to detail, but includes fascinating audio effects for the viewer. Two consistently popular exhibits are the bald eagle in its natural habitat and the taxidermic remains of the horse Comanche, a survivor of the Battle of the Little Big Horn. One floor of the building is devoted to anthropological relics from the Great Plains. *Open daily except holidays.*

76. Baker University *Baldwin City, Kans.* In 1858, even before Kansas became a state, Baker University was established. One of its earliest benefactors was Abraham Lincoln, who in 1864 donated $100 to start a science department.

OLD CASTLE MUSEUM *Fifth and Elm Sts.* The university's first home, the formidable stone building now displays Indian artifacts and pioneer utensils, tools and school books. The collection of old newspapers includes the Ulster County (N.Y.) *Gazette* that reported the death of George Washington in 1799 and the New York *Herald*'s account of Lincoln's assassination. *Open Tues.-Sun. Feb.-mid-Dec.*

QUAYLE RARE BIBLE COLLECTION *Library Bldg.* An authentic 17th-century Jacobean drawing room is an apt setting for exquisite Bibles illuminated by monks, two copies of the first edition of the King James Bible and incunabula (books printed before 1501). Gathered by Bishop William A. Quayle, once Baker's president, the collection also features a Nuremberg Chronicle, a medieval synagogue roll and pre-Christian cuneiform tablets. *Open Tues.-Sun. Feb.-mid-Dec.*

77. Bushwhacker Museum *231 N. Main St., Nevada, Mo.* The stone Federal-style building was originally the sheriff's quarters, the first structure to be

[80] *The Indian heritage of the Southwest—Pueblo, Apache and Navaho—fills Woolaroc's Second Room, left. The museum has outstanding Western art, baskets, pottery and blankets. Above are two Zuni clay pots. Today only a few Zuni women practice this ancient craft.*

erected after the town was destroyed by Union troops during the Civil War. Attached to it is the jail, containing cells that still show prisoners' signatures and drawings on the walls. Several displays reflect this aspect of the building's past, including metal food troughs, old tools and medical equipment. In the main section are Civil War relics, artifacts of Osage Indians and early settlers and a collection of old guns. *Open daily May-Nov. Small charge.*

78. George Washington Carver National Monument *S.W. of Diamond, Mo.* The farm was the Civil War birthplace of the distinguished teacher, botanist and agronomist. The monument encompasses Carver's birthplace cabin site, a statue of the former slave as a boy, the Moses Carver house and the family cemetery, all found along a wooded trail. At the Visitor Center exhibits tell of Carver's life and work, while a demonstration garden grows some of the same crops that he used as a source for developing hundreds of useful by-products. *Open daily except Dec. 25.*

79. Price Tower *S.E. Sixth St. and Dewey Ave., Bartlesville, Okla.* According to Frank Lloyd Wright, the skyscraper is a "technical, spirited American natural." The master architect designed this one to stand on its own, a single monument in a small, uncongested city. An office building, it is structurally cantilevered in four sections, each side protected by copper louvers that shield occupants from the glare of the sun. The 19-story building was completed in 1956. *Open Mon.-Fri.*

80. Woolaroc Museum *Rte. 123, 14 mi. S.W. of Bartlesville, Okla.* Buffalo, deer and elk are among the animals that graze in the enormous game refuge adjoining the museum. They are a fitting backdrop to the impressive exhibits in seven large rooms that trace the history of man in the New World. Excavated materials reveal the story of prehistoric farmers and hunters; baskets and blankets show off the skills of Pueblos, Apaches and Navahos; a stagecoach dramatizes the pioneer's westward push; and paintings by artists such as Remington and Russell depict a whole range of Western life-styles. *Open daily.*

81. Birthplace of Will Rogers *Will Rogers State Park, Oologah, Okla.* Will Rogers was born in this house in 1879 and lived in it until he was about 18. Though weatherboarded, the house was built of hand-hewn logs, a circumstance enabling Will later in life to compare himself to Abraham Lincoln: "I got the log house end of it O.K.," he said, "All I need now is the other qualifications." The seven rooms of the two-story home are furnished with period pieces. *Open daily.*

82. J. M. Davis Gun Museum *Rte. 66, Claremore, Okla.* The world's largest privately-owned gun collection—once sought by the Smithsonian Institution for $5,000,000—is housed in a modern building complete with a library and research facilities. Some 20,000 firearms of every era, size and design include such curiosities as Jesse James's .45 Smith and Wesson, Wild Bill Hickok's derringer, Napoleon's handgun and a 500-year-old Chinese hand cannon. Among the other collector's items in the museum are sabers, swords, knives, Indian spears and axes, beer steins and handcuffs. *Open daily except Dec. 25.*

83. Will Rogers Memorial *Rte. 88, 1 mi. W. of Claremore, Okla.* Will Rogers bought this land to build a permanent home—and such it turned out to be, for he is now buried here. The personality of the cowboy, actor and humorist is immediately evident in the genial bronze statue of him sculpted by Jo Davidson. Visitors to the memorial, which consists of four principal galleries and a research library, can enjoy Rogers's droll humor by listening to taped excerpts of his radio broadcasts and can see the costume he wore as Sir Boss in the movie *The Connecticut Yankee.* Saddles and exquisite horse blankets are among his many personal possessions, and the Saddle Room mural portrays notable episodes in his eventful life. *Open daily.*

84. Tulsa, Okla.

In 1901, when the area's first important oil well was brought in, the Creek Indian village of Tulsey Town started on the road to becoming the "oil capital of the world." Besides the hundreds of oil companies that are located here today, Oklahoma's second largest city is the home of manufacturing plants, meat processors and publishing firms, as well as numerous educational and cultural institutions.

Boston Avenue Methodist Church *1301 S. Boston Ave.* Designed in 1925 by Adah Robinson, the massive stone edifice was one of the nation's first contemporary high-rise buildings. Wide steps rise to the entrance doors, over which soars a skyscraper tower. Interior attractions include terrazzo floors and a splendid circular sanctuary. A mosaic of 700,000 pieces of glass tile symbolizes the strength and faith of Oklahoma's Indians and early settlers. *Open daily.*

First United Methodist Church *1115 S. Boulder Ave.* Considered the finest Gothic-style cathedral in the Southwest, the church is noted for its two graceful towers and huge stained-glass window on the entrance facade. A sandstone structure with limestone trim, it was dedicated in 1928. Interior attractions include a vaulted ceiling with huge oak trusses, several superb stained-glass windows and a magnificent Aeolian organ with more than 7500 pipes. The garden is landscaped with Biblical plants. *Open daily.*

Oral Roberts University Prayer Tower *7777 S. Lewis Ave.* A modern interpretation of the traditional cross, the 200-foot tower is covered with gold and blue mirrors. Its wide observation deck bears a metal "Crown of Thorns." The deck offers a fine view of the surrounding gardens, and visitors can hear taped descriptions of each vista. A 99-bell carillon plays hymns three times each day. *Open daily.*

Philbrook Art Center *2727 S. Rockford Rd.* An ornate Italian villa, the former home of oil magnate Waite Phillips, stands on 23 acres of landscaped grounds and gardens, providing an apt setting for the art museum. On exhibit are Italian Renaissance painting and sculpture, a collection of Chinese jade and decorative art, and American Indian baskets and pottery. Other notable possessions include African sculpture, landscapes of 19th-century European and American artists and paintings by American Indians. *Open Tues.-Sun. except holidays. Adults small charge.*

This stone raven pipe found buried in the Gilcrease excavations at Bedford Mounds in Illinois was used as a votive offering by Hopewell Indians. It dates from between 200 B.C. *and 200* A.D., *during the golden age of Woodland Indian craft. The Hopewells probably used some kind of abrasive rock as a carving instrument and sand-filled reeds as a drill for making holes.*

Thomas Gilcrease Institute of American History and Art

2500 West Newton, Tulsa, Okla.

The oil boom in Oklahoma early in the 20th century made Thomas Gilcrease a millionaire before the age of 21. His good fortune enabled him to devote the rest of his life to his main interest, the study and collecting of artistic and historic objects related to the Americas. The items he amassed included some 5000 examples of American painting and sculpture from Colonial times to the present; aboriginal artifacts; historic documents and letters pertaining to Spanish and English colonization and early U.S. history; and rare books (an original Aztec codex, a 1664 edition of Roger William's *Bloody Tenant,* for example). These are all housed in the institute which he founded in 1942. To learn more about the indigenous peoples of America, Gilcrease, whose ancestry was part Creek Indian, sponsored archaeological excavations that uncovered Indian mounds near St. Louis and a nine-acre Indian village in Arkansas. Artifacts from these diggings are shown together with prehistoric American Indian art from other sections of the U.S. and Central America. Before World War I, when most Americans were unappreciative of American art, Gilcrease recognized both its artistic and historic merit. He collected the work of artists who chronicled the life of cowboys, Indians and settlers in the Old West, preeminent among whom were Remington, Russell and Catlin. Well represented too were 18th-century artists such as West, Sully and Charles Willson Peale and 19th-century romantic landscapists such as Moran, Bierstadt and Miller, whose idyllic scenes of virgin land were greatly admired by urban Americans. Nor did he neglect to acquire the works of contemporary American Indian artists and Southwestern painters. The wealth of Americana he accumulated is today one of the largest collections of its kind in the world. *Open daily.*

Attack on the Wagon Train *by Charles M. Russell. While not as common as cowboy movies suggest, Indian attacks were one of the dangers that wagon trains encountered. Fire, storms and buffalo stampedes were others.*

Interior View of Fort William *by Alfred J. Miller. Miller sketched these Indians waiting to trade pelts for white men's goods in 1837. It was the only on-the-scene likeness of the fort made during the fur-trade years.*

Indian Troupe *by George Catlin. Catlin painted these nine Ojibway Indians in London in 1844. Their trip had been sponsored by a promoter who convinced Catlin that they should participate in his London painting exhibit and series of lectures on American Indians. (It was not uncommon for groups of Indians to be taken on exhibition tours of Europe.) While Catlin's work was praised by the press, by Queen Victoria and by the public, it was no more a financial success in England than it had been in the U.S. On the verge of destitution, Catlin was forced to sell over 120 paintings, most of them for $3.00 apiece, to an English friend, Sir Thomas Phillipps. They are now in the Gilcrease collection.*

85. Prairie Grove Battlefield State Park *Prairie Grove, Ark.* A 55-foot smokestack is the monument on this battlefield. The stack was moved here from Rhea's Mill and re-erected stone by stone to commemorate the indecisive battle fought here between Confederate and Union forces on Dec. 7, 1862. Nearby is Vineyard Village, a re-creation of an Ozark Mountain community of the mid-1800s. Buildings include a two-story log house, a barn, a well house and slave quarters. Also on the grounds are a one-room log schoolhouse, a church and the Hindman Museum containing relics of the battle. *Open daily.*

86. George M. Murrell Home *Park Hill, Okla.* Murrell, who built the two-story frame mansion in 1845, was a white man who married into the Cherokee tribe and accompanied it on the "Trail of Tears." Many of the original furnishings remain, including a Cherokee rosewood double bed with matching armoire and a rosewood sofa. China, silver, books, historical documents and Indian relics are on display. *Open daily Mar.-Nov.*

87. Tsa-La-Gi (Cherokee Cultural Center) *Park Hill, Okla.* Three large brick columns at the site are the remains of the Cherokee Female Seminary that opened in 1851. The ruins are regarded by the Cherokees as a symbol of their efforts to achieve equality through education. This is now the setting of a re-created 18th-century Cherokee village, the Cherokee National Museum and a large outdoor amphitheater where Professor Kermit Hunter's Cherokee drama, *Trail of Tears,* is presented from late June to late August. *Open Tues.-Sun. May-early Sept.*

88. Five Civilized Tribes Museum *Agency Hill, Honor Heights Dr., Muskogee, Okla.* The museum is devoted to preserving the traditions and records of the Cherokee, Chickasaw, Choctaw, Creek and Seminole Indians, tribes driven from their southeastern homes in the early 19th century and resettled in Oklahoma. The museum is housed in the original 1875 Union Indian Agency building, which was restored in 1966. An art gallery holds remarkable paintings and sculptures, and tribal exhibits highlight an extraordinary array of artifacts—jewelry, costumes, utensils, instruments, music and photographs. History and culture are further revealed through newspapers, treaties and other documents. *Open daily except Dec. 25. Small charge.*

89. Horseless Carriages Unlimited *2215 W. Shawnee, Muskogee, Okla.* This may be the most luxurious used-car lot in the world: some 60 antique and classic cars, each in fine running order, plus a variety of other vehicles are on display here. The more famous automobiles were specially crafted for celebrities: a 1909 Daimler and a 1911 Rolls-Royce for maharajas, a 1930 Cadillac for a Rothschild, Alfried Krupp's 1938 Mercedes and Churchill's 1954 Humber. The array of cars changes, as some are sold and new purchases are made, but the collection always boasts vintage beauties. *Open daily except holidays. Adults $1.50, children small charge.*

90. Creek Indian Nation Council House *Town Sq., Okmulgee, Okla.* Forced out of their Georgia homeland in 1836, Creek Indians settled around Okmulgee. Some 40 years later they drew up a constitution, proposed their own government within the federal system and constructed this capitol. The handsome 1878 sandstone building holds chambers for two governmental bodies—the House of Kings and the House of Warriors—where Creek Council meetings are still held. The Creek flag hangs here, and chairs represent each tribal town in the Creek nation. On display are items the tribes brought to Oklahoma, along with Indian paintings, a large mural, map, crafts, clothes and weapons. *Open daily.*

91. Fort Smith National Historic Site *Rodgers Ave. and Second St., Fort Smith, Ark.* Fort Smith was built in 1817 to keep peace among Indian tribes, white hunters and squatters in the frontier wilderness. Only the foundations of the first fort stand, along with two buildings of the second fort which was begun in 1838. The stone commissary serves as a museum of Indian and pioneer artifacts. The handsome brick barracks serves as a visitor center and contains the partially restored court of Isaac C. Parker, who presided here from 1875 to 1896. *Open daily.*

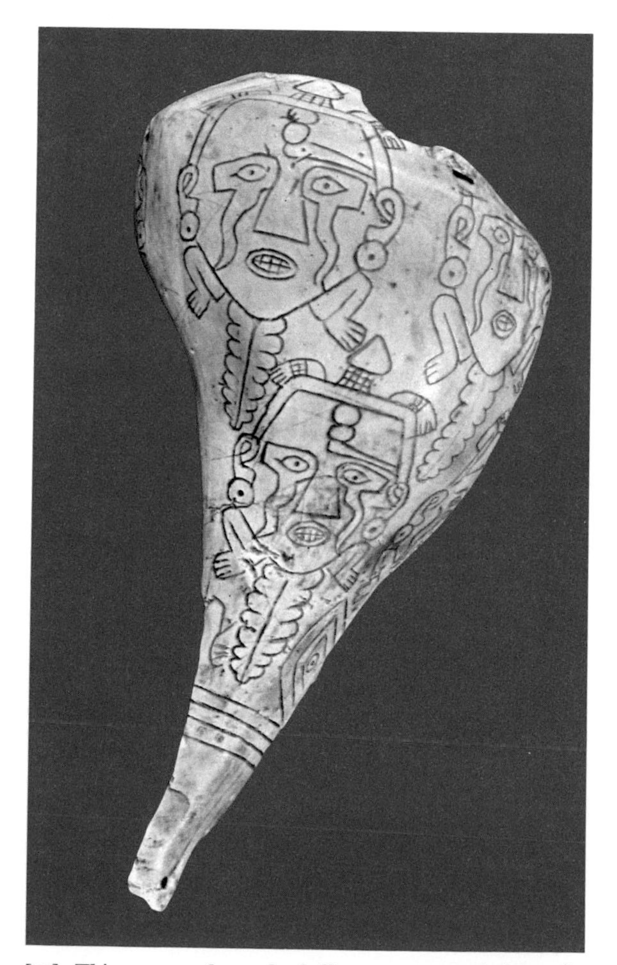

[92] *This engraved conch shell was excavated from the nearby Spiro Mound Complex, where Indians buried their dead from about 900 to 1450* A.D. *The biggest mound was 370 feet long and 39 feet tall at its highest point.*

92. Kerr Museum *Poteau, Okla.* The Eastern Oklahoma Historical Society maintains the museum in part of the striking native stone residence of the late Senator Robert Kerr. Many artifacts excavated from the nearby Spiro Indian Mounds are displayed, along with an 11th-century rune stone thought to be of Norse origin. Pioneer tools and weapons and a collection of fossils, rocks and minerals are on exhibit. Here too is an exact reproduction of Senator Kerr's Washington office. Regional art shows and temporary displays of china, silver and glassware are regularly presented. *Open daily except holidays. Adults and children over 6 small charge.*

93. Block-Catts House *Washington, Ark.* The slaves of Abraham Block started building this house in 1828, cutting virgin timber and dressing it by hand. Now restored, the New England saltbox-style home still has its original siding, floor, millwork, hand-carved balustrade on the upper veranda and chimney of handmade sun-dried brick. The interior doors are called Christian doors, because of their cross and open-Bible design. The dwelling is elegantly furnished with period pieces. *Open daily. Adults $2.00, children 6-15 small charge (fee includes 4 other buildings).*

94. Flying Tigers Air Museum *Rte. 82 W., Paris, Tex.* A large collection of aircraft—all operable and licensed—from primary trainers to early jet fighters, is featured here. Included are examples of famous World War II planes—North American's F-51 Mustang, Lockheed's P-38 Lightning, Boeing's B-17 Flying Fortress and Grumman's F4F Wildcat. Some of the craft have been flown in such films as *Twelve O'Clock High* and *Catch-22. Open daily.*

95. "Atalanta" *Austin St., Jefferson, Tex.* Financier Jay Gould's opulent 88-foot private railroad car dates from the 1890s and is richly paneled in mahogany and maple. Once known as a "palace on wheels," it has been restored and now rests across the street from the Excelsior Hotel. The car contains a lounge, four staterooms, dining room, kitchen, pantry and bath. *Open daily. Small charge.*

96. Excelsior House *211 W. Austin St., Jefferson, Tex.* Presidents Grant, Hayes and Lyndon Johnson were among the hotel's distinguished visitors; the register also boasts the signatures of Oscar Wilde, Jay Gould and the Barrymores. Built in the early 1850s, its 15 rooms hold sleigh beds, button and spool beds, marble-topped dressers and other handsome period furnishings. The two-story building is still operated as a hotel by volunteer help recruited from a local garden club. A decorative wrought-iron railing runs along the front gallery and a charming fountain is found in the hotel's intimate courtyard. *Open daily. Small charge.*

97. Jefferson Historical Society and Museum *223 W. Austin St., Jefferson, Tex.* This red brick structure, built in 1890, was formerly a U.S. post office and courthouse. More than 6000 items in the society's collection are exhibited here. There are Caddo Indian artifacts, antique furniture, weapons, dolls, rare china, pioneer tools, Civil War relics and even a boot that belonged to Annie Oakley. Documents relating to Texas history, including papers of Sam Houston, are also on view. *Open daily. Small charge.*

[**99**] *George Catlin, the noted genre and portrait painter, did this watercolor of General Sam Houston on ivory. Catlin was one of the first artists to depict the American Indian; he produced over 1000 Indian paintings.*

98. Harrison County Historical Museum *Old Courthouse, Peter Whetstone Sq., Marshall, Tex.* The distinguished 1901 county courthouse contains a remarkably varied collection. There is pottery, dating from 400 B.C., that was found in Harrison County. Indian, pioneer and Civil War artifacts form significant exhibits. Paintings, porcelains, silverware, ceramics, clocks, early phonographs and musical instruments all present vivid insights into local history. *Open Sun.-Fri. except holidays and Dec. 18-25. Small charge.*

99. R. W. Norton Art Gallery *4700 Creswell Ave., Shreveport, La.* American art of the 18th and 19th centuries on view here provides a visual documentary of much of the country's history. Frederic Remington is admirably represented by about 40 paintings and sculptures, including the oil *Coming to the Rodeo* and a bronze *Bronco Buster.* Paintings and more than 150 bronze sculptures by Charles M. Russell tell of Indian life and cowboy activities. The landscape collection features Bierstadt's romantic *Yosemite Valley* and a nostalgic work by Inness entitled *Going out of the Woods.* Highlights of the gallery's European possessions are a series of late 16th-century Flemish tapestries and a large collection of Wedgwood pottery. *Open Tues.-Sun. except holidays.*

100. Goodman Museum *624 N. Broadway, Tyler, Tex.* The building housing the museum is an antebellum mansion dating from the 1850s. The house contains a circular staircase, crystal chandeliers and six fireplaces. The Empire and Victorian furnishings and accessories, including a unique set of Rose Medallion china, belonged to the Goodman family. Among the contents of the museum are the medical instruments of Dr. William J. Goodman, pioneer Tyler physician; a 100-year-old square grand piano; and a collection of antebellum and Civil War documents. *Open daily except Dec. 25.*

101. Sam Houston Memorial *Rte. 75, Huntsville, Tex.* On the 15-acre site are several buildings important in the life of the great Texan leader, hero of San Jacinto, twice president of the Texas Republic, U.S. senator from Texas and governor of the state. The home, built in 1847, was his family residence until 1858. It is a typical story-and-a-half Texas house with a dog run. Also here are his law office (1847); another home, resembling a steamboat, where he died in 1863; and the Sam Houston Museum, with exhibits on his life and the history of Texas. *Open daily except Thanksgiving Day and Dec. 25.*

102. Alabama-Coushatta Indian Reservation *Rte. 190, Livingston, Tex.* More than 400 members of the Alabama and Coushatta tribes live on these 4600 acres, the only Indian reservation in the state. The making of traditional goods such as jewelry and baskets can be seen in the Living Indian Village, as well as demonstrations of dancing, costume-making and cooking. Tribal artifacts fill the museum. Visitors can tour a woodland area on a miniature train. *Open daily Mar.-May, Sat., Sun. June-early Sept., daily early Sept.-Nov. Adults $3.75, children $2.50.*

103. Heritage Garden Village and Museum *Woodville, Tex.* Here is a complete pioneer village with 30 authentic buildings: an 1866 log cabin, post office, smithy, apothecary shop and other typical business establishments, all containing appropriate furnishings and equipment. Visitors can crank up the old-time wall telephone, operate an early sewing machine, churn butter and sit in an 1890s barber chair. *Open daily except Thanksgiving Day and Dec. 25. Small charge.*

104. Winedale Stagecoach Inn *Rte. 2714, 5 mi. E. of Round Top, Tex.* Built around 1834 of native cedar and enlarged 14 years later, the two-story structure was restored and later presented to the University of Texas in 1967. Inside is a collection of early Texas furniture, and a room with designs painted on the ceiling around 1856. The 130 acres surrounding the house include a theater barn, smokehouse and restored log cabin kitchen. *Open Thurs.-Sun. except holidays. Small charge.*

105. Stephen F. Austin State Park *San Felipe, Tex.* The 664-acre park is a memorial to the "Father of Texas." It contains a replica of Austin's simple log cabin, a well dug by the colonists and a monument with a statue of the pioneer leader. A plaque describes the historic events that unfolded here before 1836, when San Felipe ceased to be Texas's political center. The site of the ferry crossing on the Brazos River marks a 200-year-old route between Texas and Mexico. *Open daily. Small charge each car.*

106. Houston, Tex.

The headquarters of NASA Manned Spacecraft Center began as a riverboat landing in 1836. The city derives its name from the general of the Texas army who won independence from Mexico, Sam Houston. Industrial, financial and shipping activities for much of the state are centered here in Texas's largest city.

Alley Theatre *615 Texas Ave.* One of the nation's finest resident professional companies is headquartered in a structure that matches its distinguished tenants. The bold, powerfully sculpted building broken by massive towers suggests a citadel of drama. Inside are an intimate arena stage, the seats banked on four sides, and

[**106.** *Bayou Bend Collection*] *The Belter Room is named after German immigrant cabinetmaker John H. Belter, who made the rococo-revival-style furniture such as the pieces seen here as popular in the Victorian era as Scandinavian-style furniture is in our own. The magnificent pieces made in Belter's large New York factory were known for their excellence of design and craftsmanship. The rosewood étagère on the end wall, made solely for the display of bric-a-brac, is typically Victorian in function as well as style. The* Self Portrait With Wife and Daughter *by Charles Willson Peale, at far right, a painting of the Federal era, hangs in the Drawing Room at Bayou Bend.*

 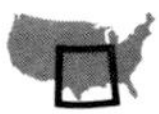

a curving main theater where the stage reaches into the audience and side runways stretch to the back of the auditorium—flexible design features that offer close contact between players and their audience. *Open Mon.-Fri. Small charge.*

Astrodome *Kirby and Fannin Sts.* This is the first fully air-conditioned, enclosed domed sports arena in the world; it accommodates baseball, football, basketball and many other sports events. The building, with an outside diameter of 710 feet and a clear span of 642 feet, is an engineering marvel. The dome has more than 4500 skylights. At the top, over the playing field, a retractable gondola carries auxiliary sound equipment. The building also contains the largest scoreboard in the world, with a half acre of information surface. As many as 66,000 spectator seats are available for some events. This was the first sports arena to make use of a synthetic playing surface known as Astroturf. *Open daily. Small charge.*

Bayou Bend Collection *1 Westcott St.* The collection of the Museum of Fine Arts of Houston, the largest in the Southwest devoted to American decorative arts, is housed in a "Latin Colonial" mansion, formerly owned by Ima Hogg, daughter of Texas Governor James Stephen Hogg. The collection, which can be seen only by reservation, made either by mail or by telephone, comprises 24 American period rooms with furniture and accessories dating from 1640 to 1870. Included are works of such noted cabinetmakers as Duncan Phyfe, John Townsend, Samuel McIntire and John Seymour. Exhibits include American glass, porcelain and silver, and paintings by American masters such as Peale, Copley and Stuart. *Open Tues.-Sat. Sept.-July.*

Harris County Heritage Society Buildings *Sam Houston Park* The society's restored 19th-century buildings, all but one moved to the park from other locations, represent the architecture of early Houston and Harris County and contain notable period furnishings. Among the interesting structures are those described below.

KELLUM-NOBLE HOUSE Sam Houston was a guest in the two-story house, which contains a few relics of the Texas leader. Built on this site in 1847 by Nathaniel Kellum, the owner of a brickmaking establishment, it is believed to be the city's oldest brick house. During the 1850s it was operated as a private school.

LONG ROW Here is a reconstruction of Houston's first shopping center—including a barbershop and a general store, originally built in 1837 but later burned. *Open daily except holidays. Small charge.*

NICHOLS-RICE-CHERRY HOUSE Moved to the park in 1960, the Greek Revival house dates from around 1850. It was built by General Ebenezer Nichols and contains a number of pre-Civil War items.

PILLOT HOUSE Eugene Pillot completed the typical mid-Victorian dwelling in 1868, and it remained in his family for 96 years. It included what is thought to be the city's first inside kitchen.

Institute for the Arts *Rice University, Stockton St. and University Blvd.* Ancient Egyptian, African and American Indian artworks are displayed in the innovative wooden building sheathed with corrugated sheet-iron. For purposes of display flexibility, the museum's inner walls are movable. A number of Surrealist paintings can also be seen, such as Magritte's 1963 *The Telescope* and works by Ernst. The several James Love sculptures include his playful *Big Jack,* which stands outdoors near the entrance. *Open Tues.-Sun.*

Museum of Fine Arts *1001 Bissonnet St.* Several distinguished collections range from ancient Egyptian objects to works by contemporary artists such as Pollock and Motherwell. Among the old masters represented are Fra Angelico, Bellini and Canaletto. Paintings by Cézanne, Renoir, Monet and Matisse show the importance of French contributions to modern art. The museum also holds outstanding sculptures by Rodin, Picasso and Calder. One of the nation's largest private collections of Remington paintings of the Old West is here, as well as a fine display of Southwest Indian artifacts, Pre-Columbian art and primitive works from Africa, Australia and the South Pacific. *Open Tues.-Sun.*

Rothko Chapel *Texas Medical Center, Branard and Yupon Sts.* The simple octagonal edifice is a sanctuary which owes allegiance to no one religion—a spiritual environment created by paintings without images by artist Mark Rothko, whose 14 panels are considered among the world's most distinguished 20th-century religious art. Outside the chapel, which was dedicated in 1971, Barnett Newman's 26-foot-high steel memorial to Dr. Martin Luther King, the *Broken Obelisk,* rises nobly from a reflecting pool. *Open daily.*

San Jacinto Battleground *Off Rte. 134* (*E. of Houston*) In the spring of 1836, 910 Americans defeated a larger Mexican force here in a mere 18 minutes. The 460-acre state park, located on the Houston Ship Channel, pays tribute to the event, which led to the annexation of Texas by the U.S. and the subsequent acquisition of almost one million square miles of additional territory following the Mexican War. *Open daily.*

BATTLESHIP "TEXAS" In 1948 Texas citizens saved the vessel—veteran of two world wars—from being scrapped, and visitors can now explore the last-surviving

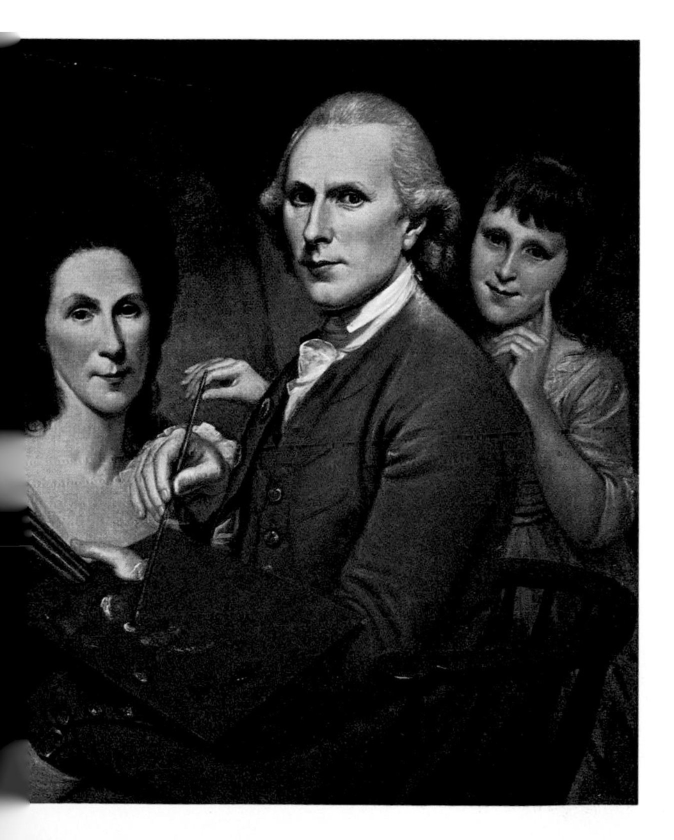

dreadnought, which was the flagship off Normandy on D-Day and later served in the Pacific. Of special interest are the Admiral Nimitz and Trophy Rooms and the Cruiser Houston Room, which memorializes the U.S.S. *Houston,* sunk by the Japanese in 1942. *Open daily June-Aug., Tues.-Sun. Sept.-May. Adults and children over 12 small charge.*

SAN JACINTO MONUMENT Completed in 1939, the 570-foot buff limestone shaft sheathes the tallest masonry monument in the world. It is topped by a 35-foot star and has an observation platform that offers a fine view of the surrounding area. Four bronze doors in the base bear reliefs of flags of the six powers that have controlled Texas, and eight huge panels relate the story of Texas at the time of the struggle against Mexico. Situated in the base of the monument is the San Jacinto Museum of History, where regional history—from the days of early Mexican Indian cultures through the Civil War—can be traced through relics, documents, maps, paintings and photographs. *Open daily June-early Sept., Tues.-Sun. early Sept.-May. Small charge for elevator.*

107. Varner-Hogg Plantation *West Columbia, Tex.* The first owner of the land on which this Greek Revival house stands was Martin Varner, who in 1824 received a grant of some 4500 acres from Mexico. Prior to the Civil War the two-story, columned manor house was the center of a large sugarcane plantation; later it became the home of James Stephen Hogg, governor of Texas from 1891 to 1895. The house, situated on 65 acres that are now a state historic park, was restored in 1920 and is furnished with antiques of the 1835-50 period. *Open Tues., Thurs.-Sun. Small charge.*

108. Bishop's Palace *1402 Broadway, Galveston, Tex.* The outstanding 1886 mansion was first the home of Colonel Walter Gresham, a prominent businessman and politician, and later purchased by the Galveston-Houston Catholic diocese for its bishop. Superb woodwork and jeweled-glass windows distinguish the Victorian stone structure. Exterior decor features wrought-iron railings and several fanciful chimneys. The winding interior staircase is a masterpiece of carved English oak. Visitors marvel at English damask wall coverings, silver hardware and Venetian crystal chandeliers. *Open Wed.-Mon. except holidays. Adults $1.50, children under 12 small charge.*

[**109.** *Tavern*] *In the 1830s travelers on the Santa Fe Trail could dine at this Federal-style tavern on the bank of the Missouri River just above the ferry crossing. Visitors to historic Arrow Rock can still do so today.*

109. Arrow Rock State Historic Site *Rte. 41, Arrow Rock, Mo.* The first building at Arrow Rock was a blockhouse and trading post built in 1813. The first ferry crossing the Missouri River at this point was established in 1817, and the site became a town (originally called New Philadelphia) in 1829. This was a starting point for traders traveling westward along the Santa Fe Trail. Historic buildings within the site include the Old Court House, Dr. Matthew Walton Hall House, George Caleb Bingham House and several others, two of which are described below. The 19th-century character of the town is little changed and Arrow Rock was the setting for the latest film version of Mark Twain's *Tom Sawyer.*

ARROW ROCK TAVERN Judge Joseph Huston built the first section of this Federal-style building in 1834; the taproom and ballroom were added in the 1840s. The two-story brick structure is furnished with early 19th-century pieces, mostly those common to Missouri pioneers. The taproom is now a museum with exhibits on the Santa Fe Trail and the state's early history. *Open daily except Jan. 1 and Dec. 25. Small charge.*

CALABOOSE The Arrow Rock jail is a small, single-room stone structure built in 1871. According to legend it was used only once—the prisoner created such a disturbance that he was released. *Open daily.*

110. Audrain County Historical Society *501 S. Muldrow St., Mexico, Mo.* The 1857 restored weatherboard house is decorated with carvings on the two-story entrance portico and on a roof enclosure that resembles a New England captain's walk. Its rooms contain much 19th-century furniture, including a rare 1847 rosewood and mahogany piano, and some 400 dolls. Other collections include antique three-face glass, period clothing and some 100 original Currier and Ives prints. On the grounds is the American Saddle Horse Museum, in which mementos of riders and equipment for horses are displayed. *Open Tues.-Sun. Mar.-Nov., Tues.-Sat. Dec.-Feb. except holidays. Small charge.*

111. Museum of Art and Archaeology *University of Missouri, Columbia, Mo.* See feature display on facing page.

112. State Historical Society of Missouri Art Gallery *Hitt and Lowry Sts., Columbia, Mo.* The society's collection includes 16 paintings by George Caleb Bingham, distinguished Missouri artist of the 19th century. Among these is one of Bingham's most famous paintings, *Order No. 11* (also called *Martial Law*), which shows the tragic effects on a Missouri family of a military order issued by a Union general during the Civil War. Seven of Thomas Hart Benton's World War II paintings are here, and 80 colored engravings by Karl Bodmer that depict the life of Western Plains Indians. Bill Mauldin is represented in the collection of original editorial cartoons. *Open daily except holidays.*

The wood polychrome statue of St. Constantine from Bohemia is early 18th century.

This glazed pottery head-vase of a young girl is a Roman piece about 2000 years old.

111. Museum of Art and Archaeology

Library 4D11, University of Missouri, Columbia, Mo.

Like hundreds of university museums across the country, the Museum of Art and Archaeology has grown rapidly in size and importance as Americans have become increasingly more interested in art. What began as a small campus-study collection in 1957 became a bona fide museum collection in 1961 with the gift of 14 paintings of the 15th to 18th centuries from the Samuel H. Kress Foundation. This foundation, organized by the man who made a fortune with a five-and-ten-cent-store chain, has donated works of art to scores of American museums, including some 20 university museums. The museum now has over 5000 objects; these include gifts, purchases and material from the university's archaeological excavations. There are sculptures, paintings, drawings and prints dating from the 15th century to the present; Middle and Far Eastern art; primitive art from Africa, Oceania and South America; and the state's largest collection of Egyptian, Near Eastern, Greek and Roman art. In a relatively short time the museum has become a valuable research institution and an enriching cultural asset. *Open daily.*

This Mayan chieftain with detachable headdress was fashioned around 800 A.D.

The bronze walking lion is probably from Alexandria, 3rd or 2nd century B.C.

River Scene With Castle *by Jan van Goyen, 1637. Van Goyen's specialty was the lyrical representation of waterways such as this. Art flourished in 17th-century Holland; portraits, interiors and landscapes became legitimate subjects for paintings in themselves, and were no longer necessarily subordinated to religious themes.*

[113] *The Great Fire of 1666, which destroyed two-thirds of London, gave Sir Christopher Wren the opportunity of a lifetime. St. Mary the Virgin, Aldermanbury, was one of scores of London churches he rebuilt. It is now in its third incarnation in Missouri as the Winston Churchill Memorial and Library. The exterior stones were scrubbed clean of three centuries of London grime and set again in Wren's simple yet elegant design. The elaborately carved lyres gracing the Palladian window are original; the corner pine cones are typical Wren touches.*

113. Winston Churchill Memorial and Library in the U.S. *Westminster College, Fulton, Mo.* In 1946 Winston Churchill came here and delivered his historic "Iron Curtain" speech. Centerpiece of the memorial to that occasion and to the great statesman is the Church of St. Mary, Aldermanbury—a London landmark from the 12th century to 1965. Gutted by the Great Fire in 1666, restored by Christopher Wren and gutted again by an incendiary bomb during the London blitz in 1940, the church was dismantled stone by stone and reassembled here, and the interior was reconstructed on the basis of 17th-, 18th- and 19th-century plans and engravings. The church's lower level holds official documents and memorabilia, including the carbon typescript of the "Iron Curtain" speech and letters Churchill wrote to one of his daughters. Outside is an eloquent bronze statue of the indomitable world leader simply labeled "Churchill." *Open daily except holidays. Small charge.*

114. Graham Cave State Park *Danville, Mo.* The natural rock-shelter, which is 20 feet high and 120 feet wide, has served as a campsite and shelter for man since the Ice Age. Excavations indicate that the cave was used by Indians perhaps as early as 7850 B.C. Archaeologists are still at work here in the summer, uncovering priceless fragments to add to the accumulation of ancient pottery, bone needles, grinding stones and flint scrapers. The cave is the first archaeological site to be designated a National Historic Landmark. *Open daily.*

115. Pommer-Gentner House *108 Market St., Hermann, Mo.* Built before 1848 by Ferdinand and Caroline Pommer, the attractive masonry house was purchased in 1882 by G. Henry Gentner, a German cabinetmaker and carpenter. Its Greek Revival features have been carefully restored, and its rooms hold early furniture that reflects the German heritage of the town of Hermann. *Open Thurs.-Tues. Apr.-Oct. Adults and children over 12 small charge.*

116. Strehly House *131 W. Second St., Hermann, Mo.* The masonry structure was completed about 1842 by two German immigrants who published abolitionist newspapers in the basement. A limestone block once used in lithography serves as the front doorstep, and a number of blocks for printing cloth can be seen inside. Although it was originally a one-story building, a three-story wing was added in 1860 for use in a wine enterprise. The vaulted cellar was once used to store wine, and a fermenting room contains a rare hand-carved cask. *Open Thurs.-Tues. May-Oct. Adults and children over 12 small charge.*

117. Cole County Historical Museum *109 Madison St., Jefferson City, Mo.* A former governor built the four-story brick building in 1871, and it once served as an official residence. Several rooms are stylishly decorated with Victorian furnishings. A collection of gowns worn by the state's first ladies at inaugural balls can be admired, along with 400 American, English, German and Venetian wine and cordial glasses, old silver, photographs and maps. *Open Tues.-Sat. early Jan.-mid-Dec. except Memorial Day and July 4. Small charge.*

118. Missouri State Capitol *High St., Jefferson City, Mo.* The four-story Greek Revival structure spreads over almost three acres, its great pillared dome rising 260 feet to a bronze figure of Ceres, goddess of grain. The building has 134 columns, comprising one-fourth of all the stone used in the structure. The interior features several outstanding murals executed by Frank Brangwyn and Missouri artist Thomas Hart Benton. In the senate chamber, which is surrounded by 16 marble columns, are murals by Richard E. Miller. Throughout the building murals depict Missouri's history and legends, as do statues and other decorations. *Open daily.*

MISSOURI STATE MUSEUM Historical items, Indian artifacts, early firearms, military flags and a variety of pioneer relics are exhibited here. Included is a stagecoach built in Palmyra, Missouri, in 1840. Also featured is a collection of historical photographs and archaeological finds of the area.

119. Moniteau County Courthouse *California, Mo.* Noted for its domed octagonal cupola, the 1868 brick Greek Revival structure also features a unique portico dome supported by massive curved Corinthian brick columns. Handsome cornices and a fanlight over

the front entrance have an elegant effect. The main hall contains objects of local historic significance. *Open Mon.-Fri. except holidays.*

120. Ralph Foster Museum *School of the Ozarks, Point Lookout, Mo.* The rich and varied history of the Ozarks unfolds on 11 floors here. Of particular note are displays describing prehistoric Indian cultures, such as that of the Bluff Dwellers, with artists' conceptions of the Indians' life-styles complemented by rare artifacts. The Ozarks Hall of Fame honors natives such as artist Thomas Hart Benton and Rose O'Neill, originator of the Kewpie doll which at one time was a national fad. Coins of many nations, apothecary antiques and cameos are exhibited, and one floor is devoted to a large collection of rifles and pistols. The museum also maintains a working replica of an Ozarks gristmill. *Open daily except Jan. 1 and Dec. 25.*

121. Miles Mountain Musical Museum *Rte. 62, Eureka Springs, Ark.* In 1895 a music lover could have purchased a Regina music box for about $300; the valuable record changer—precursor of today's hi-fi—is still automatically changing 15-inch discs here. It competes in volume with a fascinating array of "nickel-grabbers": one-man bands, a hurdy-gurdy, early Edisons and Gramophones and the Violano Virtuoso—popular in the early 1900s in saloons and ice cream parlors. Altogether there are dozens of exotic musical pieces on view in the museum along with button pictures and old clocks. *Open daily May-Oct. Adults $1.50, children over 6 small charge.*

122. Saunders Memorial Museum *113-15 E. Madison Ave., Berryville, Ark.* In the enormous collection of small arms here are guns that once belonged to Jesse James, Wild Bill Hickok, Billy the Kid and many other frontier swashbucklers. Pancho Villa's single action Colt .45 is on display, along with a brace of double-barrel pistols of 1735 and a 12th-century hand cannon. Also here are antique rugs, tapestries, silverware and Indian artifacts. *Open daily Mar.-mid-Nov. Small charge.*

123. Penrod's Museum *Bull Shoals Dam, Lakeview, Ark.* Fifty years of collecting by Mr. and Mrs. J. L. Penrod have resulted in a museum overflowing with fascinating Americana trivia—ranging from North American Indian artifacts to 41 pieces of American coin-glass made in 1892 and soon after outlawed by the U.S. Treasury, and a bicycle built-for-two with the seats side by side. Collections include mechanical penny banks, penny-in-the-slot music boxes, original Audubons, two George Washington inauguration buttons and rare antique dolls. *Open daily Apr.-Oct. Small charge.*

124. Wolf House *Norfork, Ark.* This first courthouse in Arkansas was built by Indian labor shortly after the Louisiana Purchase. The structure, preserved in its rough, frontier setting, is said to be the oldest two-story log house in the state. It was also used as an inn, serving such notables as Sam Houston and his brother. On display are more than 400 items of Americana ranging from an antique pole peeler to ironstone egg cups. *Open daily June-Oct. Small charge.*

125. Museum of Automobiles *Petit Jean Mountain, Morrilton, Ark.* The Winthrop Rockefeller collection of antique, vintage and classic automobiles is on display here. More than 40 cars, all in mint condition, are exhibited. Included are an 1899 Winton, a 1901 Panhard & Levassor, a 1903 Cadillac and a 1907 Rolls-Royce. The collection is housed in an enormous modern building, its roof suspended by cables to eliminate interior pillars. *Open daily except Jan. 1 and Dec. 25. Adults $1.50, children small charge.*

126. Little Rock, Ark.

Situated on the south bank of the Arkansas River, the city derived its name from the rocky formation of the riverbank. The largest city and capital of the "Land of Opportunity," Little Rock is Arkansas' principal commercial, manufacturing and cultural center.

Arkansas Arts Center *MacArthur Park* Among the most exciting works here are the portrait of *General James Miller,* painted by Samuel F. B. Morse, inventor of the telegraph; *George Washington,* an oil painting by James Peale; Bassano's *Adoration of the Shepherds; The Scout,* by America's great artist of the West, Frederic Remington; and *Andromeda* (1912) by Redon. The arts center is a beautiful modern cloister constructed of glass, brick and copper. *Open daily except Dec. 25.*

Arkansas First State Capitol *300 W. Markham St.* The fine example of Greek Revival architecture, designed by a noted user of that style, Gideon Shryock, was completed in 1836. The building houses outstanding displays including portraits of noted Arkansans; the gowns of Arkansas' first ladies; memorabilia from the U.S.S. *Arkansas;* a flag gallery; the Senate and House Chambers and the Governor's office; and period rooms furnished by historical organizations. The History Commission and archives are located in the west wing. *Open daily.*

Arkansas State Capitol *W. Capitol Ave.* A circle of Ionic columns supports a massive dome and cupola over the center of the imposing Greek Revival structure, built of Arkansas marble and granite. Columns of the same design also appear along the facade, where broad stone steps grandly rise to the entrance portico. Ornate balustrades extend along the roof and around the base

[125] *This 1936 Mercedes 500K was made by the German firm of Daimler-Benz, the world's oldest automobile manufacturers. The Mercedes was named for the daughter of Daimler's French agent, who thought a non-German name would increase sales.*

of the dome. Interior attractions include a display of state manufactures and an admirable mineral collection. *Open daily except Dec. 25.*

Arkansas Territorial Restoration *Third and Cumberland Sts.* Still grouped on their original sites are 13 buildings recalling Arkansas' earliest beginnings. The two-story log Hinderliter House, the oldest structure in Little Rock, is here, as well as the home honoring the man who delivered Arkansas' first Constitution to Washington; the home of the state's fifth governor Elias N. Conway; and the residence and printshop of the founder of the *Arkansas Gazette,* the oldest newspaper published west of the Mississippi River. *Open daily. Small charge.*

Museum of Science and History *MacArthur Park* The museum is in the Tower Building of the old arsenal built 1838–40 to protect settlers in the new state of Arkansas from hostile Indians. It was here that General Douglas MacArthur was born, Jan. 26, 1880. On display are curios, including stuffed birds, fluorescent rocks, minerals and Indian artifacts. Other exhibits include a history of glass and objects from the ancient cultures of Mexico, Central America, the Amazon, Egypt and Mesopotamia. *Open Tues.-Sun.*

127. Bayou Folk Museum *Off Rte. 1, Cloutierville, La.* Named for *Bayou Folk* (1894), a collection of Creole short stories by Kate O'Flaherty Chopin, the museum (once Mrs. Chopin's house) is dedicated to preserving the history of this Cane River country. The early 1800s building—a Louisiana classic constructed with handmade bricks, pegged cypress and pine beams and square nails—has period furniture among its displays. Next door is an early doctor's office, appropriately furnished and equipped; and out back is a timber blacksmith shop, now full of farm paraphernalia. *Open Sat., Sun. Mar.-Nov. Small charge.*

128. Hodges Gardens *Rte. 171, Many, La.* Spectacular landscaping around an abandoned stone quarry is one of the focal points in the 4700-acre garden. Seasonal accents are provided by mass groupings of many varieties of camellias, azaleas, day lilies and chrysanthemums along the shores of an enormous lake. An island in the lake is devoted to a memorial to the 1803 Louisiana Purchase, including the nation's largest terrazzo map. Visitors can walk along paths, climb stone stairways and cross bridges among the gardens, or drive through them on 12 miles of roads where signs mark attractions. One of the state's biggest wildlife refuges is here, and grazing elk and deer can be seen. *Open daily. Adults and children over 12 $2.50.*

129. Marksville Prehistoric Indian State Park *Rte. 1, E. of Marksville, La.* Extensive burial, temple and refuse mounds surrounded by the vestiges of an earth barricade prove the existence of a village here as long ago as 400 B.C. A Spanish mission-style museum building holds examples of pottery and other relics retrieved from the 40-acre site. Here too pictures illustrate life in the Mississippi Valley from the time of earliest man to the present. The grounds include a picnic area and a small zoo with native wildlife. *Open daily. Small charge.*

130. Blue Rose Museum *Off Rte. 13, S.W. of Crowley, La.* Named after a variety of rice developed in the area in 1912, the Acadian-style house dates from 1848 and was moved to its present location in 1964. Its square nails, mud and moss walls and pegged construction are especially evident in the second-story front section, where dances were once held for plantation workers. Original cypress paneling can be seen on the front porch and also on the ground floor walls on which a simulated wood grain design was created with paint in the 1880s. The house contains a fine collection of cut glass, china, silver and antiques, including a rosewood bed and dresser that once belonged to a cousin of Lincoln and is similar to the Lincoln bed in the White House. *Open Mon.-Fri. Mar.-Dec. Small charge.*

[135] *In New Iberia, in the heart of the Mississippi bayou country, the hauntingly beautiful Shadows-on-the-Teche, facing the city's Main Street, is surrounded by live oaks, rare camellias and landscaped grounds. Behind are the quiet waters of the Bayou Teche. Sugar and cotton built the mansion and made the good life possible for its owners in pre-Civil War days. Last of the Weeks family to live here was Weeks Hall, who restored the Shadows and spent 36 years developing the gardens. During the 1920s and '30s the house and its imaginative inhabitant drew visiting celebrities such as Henry Miller, Mae West, H. L. Mencken and Cecil B. De Mille.*

131. Lafayette Museum *1122 Lafayette St., Lafayette, La.* An unusual open cupola stands on the roof of the clapboard dwelling that was the boyhood home of Alexander Mouton, governor of Louisiana from 1843 to 1846. Built around 1800 the house has a two-story front veranda supported by square pillars. Furnishings include original pieces used by various occupants, and room exhibits feature Confederate artifacts and costumes worn by past royalty of the city's carnival balls. The original Acadian kitchen is connected to the main house by porches, and an old smokehouse stands on the attractively landscaped grounds. *Open Tues.-Sun. except holidays.*

132. Acadian House Museum *Longfellow-Evangeline State Park, N. of St. Martinville, La.* Like a friend's home, the entrance to the 200-year-old house is through a garden and a back door. The museum is devoted to the ways of the Acadians, the French settlers who were driven from Nova Scotia. This is demonstrated not only by displays of crude tools and handmade furnishings but by the congenial home itself. Its basement and fireplaces were made of clay bricks that the Acadians hand-shaped and sun-dried. They built the upper-story walls from a mixture of mud and moss, boarding them on the outside and plastering them inside. *Open daily except Jan. 1 and Dec. 25. Small charge.*

133. St. Martin de Tours Catholic Church *St. Martinville, La.* After the French-speaking Acadians were expelled from their Canadian settlement by the British, most of them arrived here in 1765 and established their church. St. Martin of Tours is the patron saint of the church, the town and the parish. The present structure of stone and plaster was completed in 1838. Its baptismal font, sculptured from marble, and the sanctuary lamp were gifts from King Louis XVI and Marie Antoinette. *Open daily.*

EVANGELINE'S MONUMENT Near the church the graceful statue of Evangeline sits above the grave of Emmeline Labiche. The story of Emmeline's search for her fiancé after they were exiled from Nova Scotia on different ships inspired Longfellow's famous poem.

MUSÉE DE PETIT PARIS DE L'AMERIQUE Its name and many of its possessions come from the late 18th century when aristocrats, fleeing from the French Revolution, brought their jewels, gowns and festivals to this backwoods parish, giving it—for a while—the name Le Petit Paris. On display are Mardi Gras costumes and antique furniture. *Open daily except Easter Day and Dec. 25. Small charge.*

134. Justine *Rte. 86, E. of New Iberia, La.* Moved here by barge in 1965, the clapboard dwelling was completed in 1822 with native cypress paneling and a fine Gothic-style stairway. Enlarged later, the house is noted for a huge second-story dormer window crowned by a split pediment. Much early Victorian furniture and an 18th-century Louis XV desk can be seen here along with period glassware and china, some of which date from the 1700s. The kitchen has examples of primitive pottery, iron and tin utensils and graniteware objects. *Open Wed.-Sun. Small charge.*

JUSTINE BOTTLE MUSEUM Demijohns, sarsaparilla bottles, flasks and medical jars are among the curious containers displayed in this former country store built in 1898. An 11th- or 12th-century Persian saddle bottle and glass containers carried by Civil War soldiers are star attractions in the display of more than 2000 bottles. *Small charge.*

135. Shadows-on-the-Teche *117 E. Main St., New Iberia, La.* Eight columns and twin galleries connected by two outside stairways distinguish the facade of this elegant town house, made of rose-colored bricks. Built in the 1830s in the midst of sugar plantations, it was allowed to deteriorate after the Civil War. In 1922 Weeks Hall, great-grandson of the builder, restored the house; the family possessions were recovered and returned. Now the 16 rooms of the mansion, which is a property of the National Trust for Historic Preservation, are resplendent with original silver, furniture and family portraits. In the handsome dining room are a Waterford crystal chandelier and a marble floor. *Open daily except Dec. 25. Small charge.*

136. Rip Van Winkle Gardens *Rte. 675, Jefferson Island, La.* Marked paths and carefully tended lawns invite visitors to walk through the 20-acre expanse and admire an outstanding English-style garden. The camellia collection includes imported specimens, and hundreds of roses, orchids, azaleas, gardenias and yellow jasmines have their corners. An Oriental Garden blooms with native iris and camellias, and the Alhambra Garden copies its namesake in Granada, Spain. The 1870 house here—closed to the public—was built of cypress by Joseph Jefferson, the 19th-century actor whose portrayal of Rip Van Winkle made him world famous. Earlier, the land was owned by pirate Jean Lafitte's brother-in-law, and pots of gold and silver coins unearthed in 1923 suggest this was once a hideout of Lafitte. *Open daily. Adults $2.25, children small charge.*

137. Jungle Gardens and Bird City Sanctuary *Avery Island, La.* In the late afternoon each day, tens of thousands of snowy egrets glide smoothly back to their nesting spots here, providing an astonishing sight viewable from the spectators' platform. But any time of day visitors on foot or by car can pass among the garden's 200 acres lushly cultivated with rare plants from all over the world. There are groves of live oaks hung with Spanish moss, clumps of bamboo and a dazzling array of flowers, including more than 100 varieties of azaleas and camellias that bloom all winter. A Chinese garden surrounds a small temple of Buddha. *Open daily. Adults $1.75, children under 12 small charge.*

138. Albania Mansion *Old Rte. 90, E. of Jeanerette, La.* The plantation that once surrounded the large clapboard dwelling furnished the materials to build it. Hand-hewn laths hold the original plaster strengthened with animal hair. Completed in 1842, the house occupies part of an early French land grant. A beautiful spiral staircase rises three stories, and the high-ceilinged rooms are decorated by cornices over doors and windows. Although the furniture is mostly early Victorian, there are a number of fine French pieces, including a seven-piece set of 1793 Directoire furniture and bedroom objects from the Louis XV and XVI eras. *Open daily Feb.-Dec. Adults $2.00, children under 12 small charge.*

139. Oaklawn Manor *Bayou Teche, Franklin, La.* The white pillared mansion was the splendid centerpiece of one of Louisiana's largest antebellum sugar plantations. It was built in 1837 by Alexander Porter, a U.S. senator, and is set among oak trees nearly 500 years old. The three-story mansion contains sumptuous hand-carved marble fireplaces, crystal chandeliers, rare tapestries and a fine collection of antique furniture, some of which dates from the 17th century. *Open daily. Adults $2.00, children small charge.*

140. New Salem Carriage Museum *Rte. 97, 3 mi. S. of Petersburg, Ill.* Among the 133 horse-drawn vehicles on display is an 1860s handmade wagon that was said to have been ordered by Lincoln when he was President; he was shot before taking possession. General Grant's carriage is on view along with coaches, sleighs, carts and wagons. There is also a full collection of accessories—harnesses, sleigh bells, lap robes, dusters and foot warmers. An 1858 covered bridge stands by the museum. *Open daily May-early Nov. Small charge.*

141. New Salem Village *New Salem State Park, Petersburg, Ill.* New Salem is a fascinating re-creation of the village where Abraham Lincoln lived (from 1831 to 1837) and worked as store clerk, postmaster, surveyor, soldier and legislator. Here he educated himself in law and the classics. Today ox-drawn wagons ply the winding dirt street among the 26 cabins, timber houses and shops, all but one reconstructed. There are split-rail fences, crops, gardens, livestock and a staff demonstrating some of the crafts once practiced here—all against a background of trees, flowers and vegetable gardens. *Open daily except holidays.*

BERRY-LINCOLN STORE Lincoln and William Berry moved their grocery store into this "fancy" building—the only one in town with siding and one of the few having a front porch. The large room was the store; the lean-to was a storeroom and, for a time, Lincoln's bedroom.

HILL-MCNAMAR STORE On its shelves are groceries and general merchandise packaged and displayed as they were long ago. It was the first store built in New Salem. Lincoln clerked here and probably served a portion of his postmastership in it.

MILLER AND KELSO CABIN Joshua Miller was the village blacksmith and wagonmaker. Jack Kelso was a fisherman, trapper and philosopher. When they married sisters, they built this log "duplex," which is authentically furnished. Lincoln became acquainted with the works of Blackstone, Shakespeare and other classic writers that Kelso loaned him.

ONSTOT COOPER SHOP At night Lincoln studied here by the firelight, using the barrelmaker's wood shavings as fuel. It is the only original building in New Salem.

RUTLEDGE TAVERN Pioneer cooking on the hearth is done here in the large room believed to have been the combined kitchen, dining room and guest sitting room. When Lincoln boarded here, he slept in the loft—the quarters for male guests.

142. Clayville Stagecoach Stop *Rte. 125, Pleasant Plains, Ill.* Built around 1824 this was one of the region's first brick structures, serving as a popular inn in pre-railroad days. The Federal building reflects the era between 1830 and 1850 when it was often used for Whig meetings, some of which Lincoln, the proprietor's lawyer, attended. The hardware, walnut mantels and most of the flooring are original; much of the period furniture was made locally. Two early log cabins stand nearby, including one that dates from 1817, and an old barn serves as a museum of early farm tools. A folk arts guild demonstrates pioneer arts and crafts and operates a crafts shop on the premises. *Open daily May-Oct. Small charge.*

[**143.** *Illinois State Capitol*] *The capitol, on a nine-acre plot, is built in the form of a Latin cross. Far below the foundation that supports the great Baroque dome is one of the richest coal veins in Illinois.*

143. Springfield, Ill.

Located on Sangamon River in central Illinois, Springfield was selected as the state capital through the efforts of Abraham Lincoln and eight other members of the Illinois legislature. Rich with Lincoln memorabilia, the city is an important industrial and agricultural center. Its many parks and recreational facilities encompass 1000 acres.

Abraham Lincoln Museum *421 S. Eighth St.* Lincoln once owned the land occupied by the museum. Built prior to 1850 the building was purchased soon after his assassination by his one-time law partner, John Todd Stuart. A remarkable life-size wax figure of Lincoln leaving Springfield to assume his duties as President is known to be an exact likeness: molds were taken of his face and hands by sculptor Leonard Volk when Lincoln lived in the house across the street. Much material associated with the 16th President is here, including a desk from his law office and original documents. Dioramas, uniforms, frontier tools, weapons, Mathew Brady photographs of the Civil War and ex-

hibits relating to slavery are also displayed. *Open daily except holidays. Small charge.*

Illinois State Capitol *Second St. and Capitol Ave.* The massive building, begun in 1868 and completed 20 years later, has been in use since 1876. It is one of the state's most elaborate structures: tiers of columns, arches and curved windows cover its Indiana limestone facing. The central rotunda rises to the huge dome, which is decorated with murals and bas-reliefs. The Reference Library is pine-paneled, and the Public Catalog Room is noted for its ornate ivory-coated ceiling. Outside are bronze statues of Lincoln and his political rival, Stephen Douglas. A granite slab carries Lincoln's farewell speech, delivered when he left Springfield for Washington for his first term as President. *Open daily.*

Illinois State Museum *Spring and Edwards Sts.* Dioramas depict man's 10,000 years in eastern North America and his development from food collector to food producer. Life-size habitat groups include animals once common in the state, as well as present wildlife. Early crafts range from pioneer utensils to a superb set of 19th-century hand-carved furniture and a fine collection of clocks spanning 200 years. Modern arts and crafts are also on display, and impressive ethnographic collections—baskets, blankets, ceramics, jewelry and the like—provide new exhibits periodically. *Open daily except holidays.*

Lincoln and Mary Museum *Eighth St.* The building is an accurate replica of the 1836 brick house owned by Ninian Edwards, brother-in-law of Mary Todd, who married Abraham Lincoln there in 1842. Mrs. Lincoln often revisited the original house following her husband's assassination, and she died in it in 1882. Twenty-eight dioramas depict episodes from Lincoln's life, including his service as a storekeeper and lawyer, scenes of his marriage and his acceptance of the Presidential nomination. *Open daily Apr.-Oct. Small charge.*

Lincoln-Herndon Building *Sixth and Adams Sts.* The restored three-story brick structure was built in 1840 and soon became closely connected with Abraham Lincoln's career as a lawyer. Its ceilings, walls and floors are original, and much period furniture is on display. A 19th-century store is re-created on the first floor and an early post office on the second. *Open daily. Small charge.*

ABRAHAM LINCOLN'S OFFICES Stephen Logan and later William Herndon maintained a law practice with Lincoln on the third floor. Visitors can enjoy an authentic 1840s atmosphere here, in a setting that includes original documents, journals and newspapers, many of which were discovered under the attic floor.

FEDERAL COURT Lincoln practiced law for 15 years in this long room. Furnishings include the raised judge's bench, clerk's table, wooden spectator benches and three quaint candle chandeliers.

Lincoln Home *424 S. Eighth St.* The 1839 clapboard dwelling was purchased by Lincoln in 1844 from the minister who had married him and Mary Todd two years earlier; it was the only house he ever owned. Originally a one-story structure, a second floor was added by the Lincolns in 1856. They lived here—where three of their sons were born—until leaving for Washington in 1861. The interior is typically Victorian. Lincoln's shaving mirror, his wife's sewing box and their sons' toys are among the objects displayed. Lincoln was notified of his nomination for the Presidency in the north parlor. *Open daily except holidays.*

CORNEAU HOUSE *422 S. Eighth St.* Moved next to the Lincoln Home in 1962, the frame building takes its name from its fourth owner, Charles Corneau, a druggist. Built about 1850, the remodeled interior holds period furniture. The house now serves as a reception center for visitors to the Lincoln Home. *Open daily except holidays.*

Lincoln Tomb State Memorial *Oak Ridge Cemetery* The 16th President's widow asked that Lincoln be buried here; this impressive monument was dedicated in 1874. Constructed of nine kinds of marble, it includes a tall obelisk surrounded by four sculptures representing the Army and Navy during the Civil War. A 10-foot bronze statue of Lincoln stands at the base of the shaft, directly over the tomb entrance. A bronze version of Daniel Chester French's famous marble seated figure of Lincoln dominates the foyer, and statuettes leading to the burial chamber trace episodes in the Great Emancipator's life. Texts from the Gettysburg Address and three other Lincoln speeches appear on tablets. Mary Todd Lincoln and three of their sons are also buried here. *Open daily except holidays.*

Old Illinois State Capitol *Downtown Sq.* Completed in 1839, the large Greek Revival building served as the state's fifth capitol until 1876. Between 1966 and 1968 it was totally dismantled and rebuilt with the original limestone blocks, and its interior was painstakingly restored. The capitol is closely associated with Abraham Lincoln's career: he served in the 12th General

[**143.** *Illinois State Museum*] *Pottery-making was a major industry of 19th-century Illinois. Here both stoneware and redware clays abounded, attracting potters from Pennsylvania, Ohio and New Jersey, from England and Germany. By 1900 Illinois' pottery production was second in the U.S. Shown are typical examples, along with other Illinois products, including quilts and woven coverlets.*

Assembly in its last session (1840-1), researched cases in its law library and delivered his memorable "House Divided" speech here. He also used the governor's quarters to receive visitors after his acceptance of the nomination for the Presidency. Following his assassination in 1865 his body lay in state here the night before the burial in Oak Ridge Cemetery. The building now holds more than 500 period pieces, including original furnishings, banners used in Lincoln's campaigns and furniture from his funeral train. *Open daily except holidays.*

Springfield Art Association *700 N. Fourth St.* The original section of this house was 10 years old when it was purchased in 1843 by Benjamin Edwards, a prominent Springfield lawyer and friend of the Abraham Lincolns. There were frequent political and social gatherings here, and Lincoln is known to have spoken from an upper window to a crowd in the adjacent grove. The house was remodeled and enlarged in the 1850s, and the present attached gallery was completed in 1969. Visitors can see much fine 19th-century furniture, including a marble-topped walnut table from Lincoln's home. *Open Tues.-Sun.*

Thomas Rees Memorial Carillon *W. Fayette Ave. and Chatham Rd., Washington Park* Decks on three levels of the 132-foot tower let visitors examine the carillon's playing mechanism and its 66 Dutch bells. Dedicated in 1962 to the memory of a prominent Illinois newspaper publisher, the concrete, brick and steel structure is the world's third largest carillon—its bells weigh more than 37 tons. It is surrounded by colorful gardens. The International Carillon Festival is held here in June. *Open daily June-Aug.; concerts Wed., Sun. July-Aug., Sat., Sun. Sept.-June.*

Vachel Lindsay Home *603 S. Fifth St.* The celebrated Illinois poet (1879-1931) spent most of his life in this modest clapboard house. It was built in 1824 and was at one time the home of Lincoln's sister-in-law. Many of Lindsay's letters and manuscripts as well as several poems and drawings are exhibited. *Open daily June-Aug. Small charge.*

144. Mark Twain Boyhood Home and Museum *208 Hill St., Hannibal, Mo.* Mark Twain, less well known as Samuel Clemens, spent several years of his early life in the two-story clapboard house. The fence made famous in *The Adventures of Tom Sawyer* still stands beside it. Built in 1844 by Twain's father, the restored house holds period furnishings. Displayed in the adjoining museum are manuscripts, furniture, photographs and other objects relating to Twain and his characters, as well as a number of original Norman Rockwell paintings. *Open daily except Dec. 25.*

145. Rockcliffe Mansion *900 Bird St., Hannibal, Mo.* The three-story brick mansion, once the home of lumber tycoon John J. Cruikshank, has been completely restored to its former elegance. The furnishings are mostly the antiques acquired by the Cruikshank family. Of particular interest are the drawing room, which features a mantel of pure white Italian onyx; the reception hall, furnished like one in an English country home; and the Moorish room, graced with four Corinthian columns and elaborate arches supporting a blue dome. *Open daily. Adults $1.25, children small charge.*

[146] *At the end of Main Street, Hannibal, Missouri, is a statue by Frederick C. Hibbard of Tom Sawyer and Huckleberry Finn, a memorial to the town's most famous residents apart from their creator, Mark Twain.*

146. Tom and Huck Monument *Main St., Hannibal, Mo.* The monument to adventurous youth consists of life-size statues of Mark Twain's immortal heroes, Tom Sawyer and Huckleberry Finn. Believed to be the first statuary in the U.S. honoring fictional characters, the monument stands at the foot of Cardiff Hill—Twain's "Holliday's Hill."

147. Mark Twain Birthplace Memorial Shrine *Mark Twain State Park, Stoutsville, Mo.* The great humorist was born in the simple two-room cabin here. It is furnished as it might have been when the writer's family lived in it. A modern building encloses the cabin and provides display room for many Twain mementos, including furniture and articles from his homes, books from his personal library and the manuscript used to set *Tom Sawyer* into type for the first time. *Open daily except holidays.*

148. Daniel Boone Home *Rte. F, 5 mi. W. of Defiance, Mo.* America's famous frontiersman supervised and helped to build (1803-10) the blue limestone Georgian home in which he died in 1820. Its walls are 30 inches thick. Gunports served for defense against Indian attack. Boone carved much of the woodwork himself, including five walnut fireplaces. The house has been restored and furnished with many items that belonged to Boone or his family. A long rifle and powder horn, such as those he used, hang over the dining room fireplace. On the grounds is the "Judgment Tree," a huge old elm under which Boone, acting for the Spanish government, arbitrated disputes between the white men and the Indians. *Open daily. Small charge.*

149. First Missouri State Capitol *208-14 S. Main St., St. Charles, Mo.* Following Missouri's admission to the Union in 1821, this series of three connected brick buildings functioned as the seat of state government for five years. Its second floor areas served several courts

and provided chambers for the senate, house and governor. The ground floors were used as the residence and dry goods and hardware store of the two brothers who constructed the center building. The structures have been restored, and each room holds period furnishings. Several Sheraton and early Empire pieces can be seen in the governor's office, and the store is stocked with early 19th-century goods. *Open daily. Adults and children over 6 small charge.*

150. Old St. Ferdinand's Shrine *1 Rue St. Francois, Florissant, Mo.* This is one of the oldest Roman Catholic churches in the Louisiana Purchase Territory. It was built in 1821, replacing the original 1789 log structure. The shrine, no longer used as a church, assumed its present Gothic appearance in 1880. The famous Jesuit missionary and peacemaker, Pierre Jean De Smet, known to the Indians as "Black Robe," was ordained here in 1827. Early altars and altar furniture, an 18th-century French tabernacle, pressed-glass chandeliers and two early 19th-century paintings are displayed. *Open daily except holidays.*

151. Sappington House *1015 S. Sappington Rd., Crestwood, Mo.* This Federal-style house was built by Thomas Jefferson Sappington, a farmer, in 1808. The two-story brick structure was built with slave labor; the bricks, of varied design, were handmade at the site. Wooden pegs rather than nails were used throughout the house. Furnishings are American antiques of the period. An Adam fireplace with double columns is the focal point of the living room. *Open Tues.-Sun. except holidays. Small charge.*

152. St. Louis, Mo.

"Gateway to the West" is another name for St. Louis. Here the Missouri and Mississippi Rivers come together, and here was the last chance for pioneer families to get supplies before pushing west in the great trek to the Pacific. Founded as a trading post in 1764, St. Louis was part of the Louisiana Purchase. It grew rapidly in size and importance during the 19th century. Steamboats plied their way back and forth from New Orleans. Two universities were founded. The first Dred Scott trial was held in the city, and the ubiquitous hot dog and the ice cream cone were first introduced to America at the St. Louis Exposition in 1904. The diversity of St. Louis still exists. It continues to be a major transportation center. Mementos of the past, which include many fine old mansions, mingle with new skyscrapers. Several old steamboats lined up on the riverfront are now used as restaurants. A modern landmark of steel, the Gateway Arch, towers over the West's first cathedral and the city's historic mid-19th-century courthouse.

Campbell House Museum *1508 Locust St.* The history of the city's early days and fur trade are preserved in this typical three-story Victorian town house. Once owned by fur trader Robert Campbell, its first two floors contain their original furnishings and Mrs. Campbell's gowns from 1840 to 1870 can be admired in a costume room. General William Tecumseh Sherman is among those known to have been entertained here, and President Ulysses S. Grant once addressed a crowd from the balcony off the double parlor. *Open Tues.-Sun. Small charge.*

[**152.** *Campbell House*] *The parlor of fur trader Robert Campbell's home in St. Louis is furnished in the elegant yet comfortable French manner which was at the height of fashion in mid-19th-century America.*

Chatillon-DeMenil House *3352 DeMenil Pl.* Henri Chatillon, a fur trader and hero of the book *The Oregon Trail,* built a simple four-room farmhouse here in 1848. He later sold the home to Dr. Nicholas DeMenil, who had it transformed from a summer retreat into a three-story Greek Revival mansion. Four massive Ionic columns and iron railings dominate the facade of the brick structure. The house contains elegant 19th-century French furnishings. A large natural cavern, known as Cherokee Cave, is located under the property. *Open Tues.-Sun. except holidays and 2nd wk. in Jan. Small charge.*

Christ Church Cathedral *1210 Locust St.* The imposing Gothic Revival edifice, built in the 1860s, serves one of the oldest Episcopal parishes (1819) west of the Mississippi. It is built largely of buff-colored sandstone, though gray limestone was used for additions such as the ornate 1912 bell tower. Its interior beauties include a superbly hand-carved stone altar and reredos from England, Tiffany windows and an Italian marble baptismal font. A mosaic in the narthex depicts episodes from the 15th Psalm, and there is a fine organ with more than 3600 pipes. *Open daily.*

Eads Bridge *Washington Ave. and the Wharf* The National Historic Civil Engineering Landmark was the first significant railroad span over the Mississippi River. Opened in 1874, it bears the name of its designer. Recognizable by three cantilevered steel arches, it was the first bridge to make considerable use of steel and includes parts that can be removed for repair. Its lower deck holds two railroad tracks. *Small toll.*

Eugene Field House *634 S. Broadway* The author of "Little Boy Blue" and other well-known children's poems was born in the three-story brick town house in 1850. Completed in 1845, the Federal structure is the sole survivor of a dozen row houses that were demolished in 1936. Its ground-floor furnishings reflect

the years when Field was a child; many of his books, manuscripts and other personal items are displayed on the top floor. Almost 700 antique toys are also on view. *Open Tues.-Sun. except holidays. Small charge.*

General Daniel Bissell House *10225 Bellefontaine Rd.* General Bissell (1768–1833), who built this brick house between 1812 and 1816, enlisted as a fifer in the Revolutionary War at the age of 12 and served in this area from 1804 until the outbreak of the War of 1812. The house was occupied by his descendants until 1962 and has since been restored. Its Federal architecture is unusual for this part of the country, and its furnishings reflect styles between 1812 and 1850. *Open Wed.-Sun. except Jan. 1 and Dec. 25. Small charge.*

"Goldenrod" Showboat *400 N. Wharf St.* Old-fashioned melodramas are still staged on the 1909 Mississippi River craft, now a National Historic Landmark. The largest showboat of its kind ever built, it served as the model for Edna Ferber's *Showboat.* Moored here since 1937 and restored, it is decorated with ornate woodwork, stained glass and brass. Ragtime concerts are given, and smorgasbord dinners are served. A gallery holds pictures of personalities associated with the boat and newspaper articles about its history. *Open Fri., Sat. Performances: Fri. $2.75, Sat. $3.00.*

Jefferson Barracks Historical Park *10000 S. Broadway* Several buildings standing in a 452-acre park are the remains of an important military post established in 1826 to serve the frontier lands. Included are a house in which civilian laborers lived and a stable, both built in 1851. The stone powder magazine is now a museum housing photographs, prints, maps and dioramas that portray notable events at the fort where such soldiers as Grant, Lee, Sherman and Jefferson Davis served. *Open Wed.-Sun. except Jan. 1 and Dec. 25.*

Jefferson National Expansion Memorial *Wharf St. between Washington Ave. and Poplar St.* A monument to Thomas Jefferson and the other leaders responsible for America's westward expansion, this park was created in the 1940s on the original site of St. Louis. The warehouses that marked the more-than-80-acre riverside area were torn down. Only the historic Old Cathedral and Old Courthouse were left standing, eventually to be framed by the gleaming Gateway Arch.

BASILICA OF ST. LOUIS, KING OF FRANCE *209 Walnut St.* Popularly known as the Old Cathedral, this Roman Catholic edifice was the first cathedral west of the Mississippi. It was dedicated in 1834 to serve a parish founded in 1770; in 1961 it was designated a minor basilica by Pope John XXIII. The interior of the Greek Revival stone structure has been handsomely restored and includes a museum relating to the cathedral's early history. *Open daily.*

GATEWAY ARCH *Third and Chestnut Sts.* Soaring 630 feet, the remarkable steel arch is the nation's tallest national monument. Designed by the late Eero Saarinen and dedicated in 1968, it pays tribute to the Louisiana Purchase and the early pioneers who passed through St. Louis, the "Gateway to the West," on their journey to conquer the wilderness. Passenger gondolas carry visitors to an observation deck. Underground, movies document westward expansion and the arch's construction, and a museum features paintings, pioneer items and exhibits. *Open daily except Jan. 1 and Dec. 25. Small charge for gondola.*

OLD COURTHOUSE *11 N. Fourth St.* The stately Greek Revival building, which is topped with a massive Renaissance dome, was built between 1836 and 1865. It has been the scene of many historic events, including the suits brought by the slave Dred Scott to win freedom for himself and his wife. The courthouse has recordings, dioramas and other exhibits relating to the settlement of the West and the growth of St. Louis. *Open daily except Jan. 1 and Dec. 25.*

Missouri Botanical Garden *2315 Tower Grove Ave.* This is one of the largest public gardens in the world. Visitors walk among labeled trees and gardens, including a rose garden containing 2000 plants in more

[Jefferson Memorial-Gateway Arch] The arch, one of the nation's tallest and most dramatic monuments, is visible for miles, a soaring ribbon of steel whose color and shape are changed by sunlight and shadow.

[Missouri Botanical Garden] The oldest botanical garden in the western part of the country has on its grounds the newest kind of greenhouse: an aluminum and plexiglass geodesic dome called the Climatron. In it are exotic tropical plants in settings similar to their native habitats.

than 100 varieties. The Camellia House, one of the first greenhouses west of the Mississippi, holds remarkable winter-blooming specimens. The darkened glass walls of the Lehmann Building mirror the surrounding area of the garden. Inside are more than two-and-a-half million dried herbs, an extensive library and research laboratories. The Climatron was the first climate-controlled geodesic dome devoted to the raising of plants. Also on the grounds is the restored Tower Grove House, once the country home of Henry Shaw, the garden's founder, which contains Victorian furnishings. Henry Moore's *Reclining Figure,* composed of two massive rocklike parts, is located in the garden. *Open daily except Dec. 25. Adults and children over 5 small charge.*

Missouri Historical Society Museum *Jefferson Memorial Bldg., Lindell Blvd. and De Baliviere Ave.* The history of Missouri, with a focus on St. Louis, is displayed in considerable detail here. There are exhibits devoted to costumes and the decorative arts, rare toys, the founders of St. Louis, Indian tribes, the Lewis and Clark expedition, Charles A. Lindbergh, transportation on the Mississippi, old fire-fighting equipment, firearms and dozens of other noteworthy subjects. *Open daily except holidays.*

Museum of Science and Natural History *Clayton Rd. and Big Bend Blvd.* The museum, housed in two old mansions, has a wide range of exhibits, reflecting the institution's history of more than a century. One extensive display shows the evolution of animals and man, featuring a full-size transparent model of a woman that "talks" about herself. The story of lighting includes a bicycle, the pedals of which are used to generate electricity and to illuminate bulbs. The dinosaur collection vies for popularity with Egyptian treasures and lunar-flight materials. Here, too, is one of the finest Midwest collections of Pre-Columbian Indian artifacts —about 70,000 catalogued pieces. *Open Tues.-Sun.*

National Museum of Transport *3015 Barrett Station Rd.* The museum came into existence in 1944 when a group of history-minded St. Louisans decided to save a mule-drawn streetcar destined for scrapping. That simple start fostered an ever-burgeoning collection: today's museum vehicles include old automobiles, buses, trucks, horse-drawn carriages, locomotives, railway cars and aircraft. *Open daily. Adults $1.50, children over 5 small charge.*

Oakland *7802 Genesta St.* The home was built about 1854 for Louis A. Benoist, one of the leading bankers and financiers of the Midwest. Architect George I. Barnett designed the white limestone house in various styles: the gabled roof has Greek features, windows suggest Romanesque arches, and porches are in the American tradition. The lofty four-story Italianate tower afforded Benoist a view of his large estate, which now belongs to Lakewood Park Cemetery. *Open daily.*

Priory of St. Mary and St. Louis Church *500 S. Mason Rd.* Winner of numerous architectural awards, this stunning building looks more like a gigantic sculpture than a church—except for its crowning cross. The circular structure, constructed of white, thin-shelled concrete arches, rises like a triple-tiered fountain. Fiberglas windows fill the walls of the 40 lower-level arches and softly shed light on the spacious interior room. The top tier of slender arches forms a bell tower and creates a skylight above the central altar. *Open daily.*

St. Louis Art Museum *Forest Park* The museum's unusually comprehensive collection includes works from nearly every major art period and style. Whether one is interested in Pre-Columbian pottery, the European great masters or the decorative arts of Africa, China, Japan or ancient Egypt, it is likely that there will be a number of choice objects here to engage the attention. The building itself is the only permanent structure retained from the St. Louis World's Fair of 1904. *Open Tues.-Sun. except Jan. 1 and Dec. 25.*

St. Louis Cathedral *4431 Lindell Blvd.* See feature display on page 440.

St. Louis Medical Museum and National Museum of Medical Quackery *3839 Lindell Blvd.* The medical museum depicts the development of medical practice in St. Louis since 1800 in 33 dioramas, both miniature and life-size. Actual instruments, furniture and wearing apparel of famous physicians lend authenticity to the displays. The fascinating quackery exhibits show 165 items of bogus apparatus, unapproved drugs and faddish foods confiscated by the U.S. Food and Drug Administration. *Open daily early Apr.-early Sept., Mon.-Sat. early Sept.-early Apr. except holidays.*

St. Louis Zoological Park *Forest Park, Off Rte. 40* Not far from downtown St. Louis is the magnificent 83-acre zoo. Visitors can observe the ways of more than 3000 animals from all over the world, often in family groups and in simulated natural habitats—such as the veld, rain forest or pampas. From May to September the zoo puts on free animal shows: elephants, seals and chimpanzees demonstrate their extraordinary intelligence. At the Children's Zoo youngsters can pet harmless animals. *Open daily.*

Wainwright Building *705 Chestnut St.* This 10-story building, designed by the firm of Adler and Sullivan in 1890, is the first high-rise, steel-frame struc-

St. Louis Cathedral

4431 Lindell Blvd., St. Louis, Mo.

The glory of St. Louis Cathedral lies in its mosaics. It has the world's largest collection, and the quality is superb—these are quite possibly the finest mosaics in the western hemisphere. The cathedral, begun in 1907 and built in modified Byzantine style with a Romanesque facade, is in the form of a Greek cross. Three successive domes form the nave, two half-domes the side transepts. Byzantine churches are noted for an air of mystery and awe; the domes, graduating from smaller to larger spaces, help create this effect. The interior of the central dome, 80 feet in diameter, is the largest spherical surface ever covered by mosaics. Linking the domes and the straight angles of the base are large curving triangles called pendentives. In typical Byzantine church style—sixth-century Sancta Sophia in Istanbul is the classic example—these are covered with mosaic figures and symbols on a background of gold. The hierarchy of images created from millions of tiny pieces of glass, marble, precious and semi-precious stones and gold leaf ranges from God, the saints and archangels to historic Missourians. The strong, simple forms and the two-dimensional effect that occurs as light scintillates over the rough-textured surface make the mosaics clearly visible even from a distance. In this cathedral, sparkling with gold and rainbow colors, religion has been well served by art. *Open daily.*

This view looks away from the main altar toward the entrance. The rose window by Tiffany and Company carries out the circular theme of arches and domes. The angel kneels among some of the 14 monolithic marble columns in contrasting colors that support the altar canopy.

The cathedral, magnificent in conception yet delicate in detail, makes a tremendous impact as one faces the main altar. As in all Byzantine-style churches, the mosaics are both highly decorative and an integral part of the architecture they embellish. One of the most interesting effects is the dynamic tension between curved and straight lines: domes, arches and rose window oppose the massive columns and the bands of contrasting marble on the walls. The altar itself stands on a circle in a square enclosed in concentric circles that flow outward like ripples on a lake.

ture which visually and functionally represents the purpose for which it was built. The large windows on the ground floor providing display space for stores give way to smaller, uniform windows on succeeding floors. The 10th or attic story, used for storage and mechanical equipment, has round windows decorated with leaf scrolls and is topped by an overhanging roof. The plain brown sandstone facing of the first two stories is replaced in the upper stories by red brick piers and terra cotta panels with foliage reliefs. *Open Mon.-Fri.*

Washington University Gallery of Art *Steinberg Hall, Forsyth St. and Skinker Blvd.* Housed in a spacious modern building, the collection ranks with the best in any U.S. university. Painting, sculpture, drawings and prints span the 16th to the 20th centuries and include prominent works by European masters such as El Greco, Reynolds, Rodin, Miró and Picasso. The gallery also features important collections of ancient coins and Greek vases. *Open daily except holidays.*

153. Cahokia Court House *214 W. First St., Cahokia, Ill.* The oldest house in Illinois, built about 1737, is typical of the Colonial homes of French settlers who came there from Canada. Its steeply cantilevered roof comes down over the tops of the windows, and its walls are constructed of vertical timbers and rubblestone. From 1793 until 1814 the building served as a U.S. courthouse and the center of government of the Illinois Territory. Moved from its original site in 1904, it was brought back and faithfully reconstructed in the late 1930s. Today it is a museum, and visitors can inspect artifacts recovered from the site as well as other material connected with the building's history. *Open daily except holidays.*

154. St. Peter's Roman Catholic Cathedral *Third and Harrison Sts., Belleville, Ill.* Its great tower and slender spire dominate the flat farmlands and small-city skyline—as they should. For the remarkable 1866 cathedral is an English Gothic stone poem, modeled on England's Exeter Cathedral. The influence of that famous building is particularly clear in the detail and variety of the delicate window tracery. The cavernous interior, recently renovated, is divided by fluted columns, intricate capitals and vaulted arches. *Open daily.*

155. Black Madonna Shrine *Rte. FF, 8 mi. S. of Eureka, Mo.* Brother Bronislaus Luscze, a Franciscan monk, built the multicolored rock grottoes with his own hands over a period of 22 years. They are constructed of local rock, costume jewelry and fragments of glass. The shrine, with a great variety of religious monuments, features a mosaic portrait of Our Lady of Czestochowa, known as the Black Madonna. This is a duplicate of the famous Miraculous Picture in Czestochowa, Poland, allegedly painted by St. Luke. *Open daily. Small parking fee.*

156. Washington State Park *Rte. 21, De Soto, Mo.* This 1101-acre park, which is believed to have been the site of prehistoric Indian ceremonial grounds, contains a large number of symbolic Indian rock carvings, called petroglyphs. Several hundred of these, probably made between 1000 and 1600 A.D., are exhibited at two locations within the park. The petroglyphs are designs of birds, footprints, arrows, human figures, claws and geometric shapes. Archaeological evidence indicates that these figures were memory devices to guide the Indians in various stages of ceremonial activities. Also here are nature trails and a museum with archaeological exhibits relating to early Indian culture. *Open daily.*

157. Fort de Chartres State Park *Rte. 155, N. of Prairie du Rocher, Ill.* The French constructed the fort between 1753 and 1756, but ceded it to the British who occupied it two years later. Renamed Fort Cavendish, it was the center of British authority in Illinois until its abandonment in 1772. The only stone fort in the Mississippi Valley, its 18-foot walls are still being reconstructed along with several buildings that stand in the four-acre interior: on view are a barracks, a powder magazine and a combined chapel-guardhouse. A museum containing period objects stands on the base of the original storehouse. The restored gateway suggests the invulnerability of the post, which the British described as the largest and best-built fort in North America. *Open daily except holidays.*

158. Pierre Menard Home *Ellis Grove, Ill.* The home is understandably called the finest example of southern French Colonial architecture in the central states. Construction was begun in 1802 by Pierre Menard, who became (1818) the first lieutenant governor of Illinois. Sandstone and limestone excavated from the vicinity were used for the foundation, walls and walks. Oak, walnut and hickory—all native woods—were employed for the frame and finishing. The fine exterior is matched by interior furnishings, some original, but all representative of the Menard era—from the fourposters to the delicate china dinner service on a polished antique table. *Open daily except holidays.*

159. Magnolia Manor *2714 Washington Ave., Cairo, Ill.* Former President and Mrs. Grant were given a reception here in 1880. The 14-room red brick residence was built in 1869 by a wealthy local merchant as a showplace. And that it still is, despite its being sheltered from the street by a sparkling fountain and magnolia trees. In the stately entrance hall is a curving staircase with balustrades carved from solid cherry; from its base visitors can see the skylight at the top of the fourth floor. The walnut bedstead in the southeast bedchamber is the one in which Grant slept. *Open daily. Small charge.*

160. Arkansas State University Museum *State University, Ark.* Students built the museum that presents some of the natural history of Arkansas; and students are its archivists, artists, laborers and guides. In it is an elaborate cutaway display depicting life in an Arkansas temple mound dating from 700 to 800 A.D. Also shown are a colorful tableau of stuffed Mississippi Flyway waterfowl and exhibits of East African wildlife. The Lutterloh china and glass collection is outstanding. *Open Sun.-Fri.*

161. Jacksonport Courthouse Museum *Jacksonport State Park, Jacksonport, Ark.* On many occasions when Jacksonport was a bustling river town, the tiered benches in the courtroom here were pushed back for one of "Society's" fancy balls. The red brick courthouse,

built from 1869–72, is notable for its high ceilings and tall arched windows. On the second floor is the restored court-ballroom; the ground floor has a Pioneer Room with handmade furniture, a Victorian parlor, a Gay Nineties Room and a War Memorial Room displaying Confederate relics and uniforms from the Civil War contests fought for control of the town. Harbored near the museum is the triple-decked stern-wheel steamboat, the *Mary Woods No. 2. Museum open Tues.–Sun. except Jan. 1 and Dec. 25. Small charge.*

162. Henry Clay Hampson II Memorial Museum of Archaeology *Rte. 61, N. of Wilson, Ark.* Over the course of 70 years, Dr. J. K. Hampson, a local physician and archaeologist, amassed a vast collection of prehistoric Indian artifacts from Nodena Mound and nearby areas in the mid-Mississippi Valley. More than 40,000 of his finds are displayed in the tidy modern museum. Besides dozens of human skulls, the visitor can see spear points, household implements, beads, toys, earplugs and handsome pottery effigy pots in the form of human heads, birds, turtles and frogs. *Open Tues.–Sun. except holidays.*

163. Brooks Memorial Art Gallery *Overton Park, Memphis, Tenn.* Thirteen galleries house a superb painting collection that includes Renaissance masterpieces, English landscapes and American works of the 18th and 19th centuries. Other highlights are notable prints and exceptionally crafted porcelains and glass objects. Generous gallery space is reserved for regional and traveling national exhibits. *Open Tues.–Sun. except holidays.*

164. Chucalissa Indian Town *1987 Indian Village Dr., S. of Memphis, Tenn.* Nine reconstructed grass-roofed mud houses and a large temple mound give visitors an idea of what life was like in the Middle Mississippian period of Indian culture that flourished here between 1000 and 1600 A.D. Two excavated areas have been roofed over as exhibits; in one—the Burial Exhibit—skeletons are arranged as found in the excavation. Choctaw Indians demonstrate early crafts and act as guides. The site is now operated by Memphis State University, which sponsors continuing excavations. *Open Tues.–Sun. mid-Jan.–mid-Dec. except Thanksgiving Day. Small charge.*

CHUCALISSA MUSEUM Weapons, tools and other artifacts of several southeastern Indian cultures are displayed here, along with interesting exhibits that help explain archaeological techniques. A short slide lecture presents the history of early American Indians.

165. Memphis Pink Palace Museum *232 Tilton Rd., Memphis, Tenn.* Originally designed as the palatial home of financier Clarence Saunders, the structure has been known as the Pink Palace almost from the day its pink Georgia marble walls began to rise. The museum deals largely with the history and natural history of the mid-South. Exhibits on archaeology, natural history and exploration and settlement of the area reflect the increasing regional emphasis. A hand-carved, animated scale model three-ring circus and a display of African big game animals are among the other exhibits which deal with a variety of subjects. *Open Tues.–Sun.*

166. Victorian Village *Adams and Jefferson Aves., Memphis, Tenn.* Nine of the city's oldest residences plus four carriage houses, a dollhouse and a playhouse stand on this Historic District. Five are under the protection of the Association for the Preservation of Tennessee Antiquities and a few have been restored. The structures described below are generally considered among the nation's most beautiful examples of mid-19th-century architecture.

FONTAINE HOUSE OF JAMES LEE MEMORIAL *680 Adams Ave.* Named for its second owner, this restored French Victorian dwelling was first occupied in 1871 by industrialist Amos Woodruff. Built of brick, with a tower, the building has furniture that ranges from Colonial through late Victorian; one tower room holds Woodruff family possessions. The grounds include a children's dollhouse, a brick carriage house that is now used for meetings and special events, and the charming 1890 Gingerbread Playhouse with its peaked tin roof and stained-glass decorations. *Open daily except holidays. Small charge.*

MALLORY-NEELY HOUSE *652 Adams Ave.* Built around 1852 at approximately the same time as the Pillow-McIntyre House, the Mallory-Neely House is turreted and towered in true Victorian style. James Neely acquired the house in 1883 and renovated it, adding, among other things, the stained-glass windows and doors. His daughter, Mrs. Barton Lee Mallory, lived here most of her long life, and the furniture and objets d'art all belonged to her family. *Open daily except holidays. Small charge.*

PILLOW-MCINTYRE HOUSE *707 Adams Ave.* A classic Greek Revival mansion of mellow brick glowing softly pink and two-story Corinthian columns, the Pillow-McIntyre House stands out from the more Victorian architecture of the area. The present owners, Lary-Vanlandingham Inc., an interior decorating firm, have restored the house with knowledge and care, furnishing it with choice antiques, some of which are older than the house. *Open Mon.–Fri.*

167. Ames Plantation *Off Rte. 18, N. of Grand Junction, Tenn.* The 18,600-acre tract, once privately

[**166.** *Fontaine and Mallory-Neely Houses*] *Although towered and turreted like a house in a Charles Addams cartoon, the Fontaine House (far left) was actually a happy home and saw many parties, including one at which John Philip Sousa's band played. Except for a muting of the original bright colors, the 25 rooms of the Mallory-Neely House have remained almost unchanged since the 1890s. The west drawing room (left) is a typical parlor of a prosperous family of the time. The four-panel Chinese silk screen was bought for the house at the St. Louis Exposition in 1904.*

owned, is now operated by the University of Tennessee for agricultural research. Cotton and corn, cattle and hogs are raised on the demonstration farm. Forestry and quail management are part of valuable wildlife studies pursued here. The grounds also contain an 1847 manor house with period furnishings. *Open daily.*

168. Kate Freeman Clark Art Gallery *Holly Springs, Miss.* When she died in 1957, Kate Freeman Clark left funds to build this gallery to hold her paintings. Talented as a teenager, Miss Clark left her home early to study art in New York. There she lived for about 30 years, executing more than 1000 canvases but refusing to sell even one work despite numerous offers. In 1923, at 47, she stored her works, returned to Holly Springs and never painted again. This extraordinary collection of her portraits, landscapes and still lifes reveals a rare artistic depth.

169. Montrose *Holly Springs, Miss.* A wide brick walk bordered with ancient boxwood leads to the pillared portico of the Greek Revival brick mansion. The house is noted for its circular stairway, Czechoslovakian crystal light fixtures, parquet floors and period antiques. Montrose was built in 1858 by Alfred Brooks as a wedding present for his daughter; it is now the home of the Holly Springs Garden Club.

170. Mississippi State Capitol *Mississippi and High Sts., Jackson, Miss.* The dignified classic Renaissance limestone structure, complete with a golden eagle-capped dome and beautifully proportioned wings, was built in 1901-3. Dominating the interior decor is a lavish variety of marble: the main rotunda is faced with a resplendent white Italian marble. The two legislative halls, with domed ceilings of copper and Bohemian stained glass, and the governor's offices are worth a visit for their splendor. *Open daily.*

171. Old Capitol Restoration *N. State and Capitol Sts., Jackson, Miss.* The proud old building was the state capitol from 1839 to 1903. Its halls once resounded to speeches by Andrew Jackson, Henry Clay and Jefferson Davis, and here secession became law in 1861. The slender columns in the front, the handmade exterior bricks and the cast-iron balcony railings are original. Interior chambers have been restored and the old state offices now house the State Historical Museum for Mississippi. Here dioramas depict De Soto's discovery of the Mississippi in 1541, the landing of the first steamboat at Natchez in 1811 and other historic events. *Open daily June-Aug., Tues.-Sun. Sept.-May.*

172. Vicksburg, Miss.

Vicksburg, rich in history, was the site of one of the Civil War's most decisive campaigns which ended in victory for the Union forces. Today the city is a major Mississippi port and hardwood market.

Cedar Grove *2200 Oak St.* John A. Klein, a local financier, built the grand pillared antebellum mansion between 1840 and 1858. Its 17 rooms include double parlors, a formal dining room and a ballroom—fine settings for lavish dances, recitals and other family entertainings. Cedar Grove was damaged during the Civil War bombardment of Vicksburg: its most dramatic battle scar is a cannonball lodged in the parlor wall. Much of the original elegant decor remains, such as French and English furniture, French mirrors and Bohemian glass. Old imported clocks line the downstairs mantelpieces. *Open daily Feb.-Nov. Adults $1.50, children under 12 small charge.*

McRaven *1445 Harrison St.* Known as the "Home of Three Periods," the original house was a frontier cottage built in 1797. It was modified with Louisiana Creole features and enlarged in 1836 and remodified 13 years later with Greek Revival elements. The architecture of each section remains unchanged. Interior details, which also reveal various design influences, include a flying-wing staircase, hand-carved window facings, plaster medallions and elaborate wall moldings. Many of the original furnishings remain. Featured are a rosewood John Belter parlor set and Chickering piano, a French ormolu chandelier and splendid Empire pieces. Century-old trees and a garden surround the dwelling. *Open daily mid-Feb.-mid-Nov. Adults $1.50, children under 12 small charge.*

Old Court House Museum *Court Sq.* The entrance porticos of the proud 1858 landmark are splendidly supported by tall fluted Ionic columns. The cupola and tower contain one of the oldest original clocks still in use in the U.S. which went unscathed even during the long siege of the city in 1863. The second-floor courtroom is the building's showplace: a gigantic chandelier hangs from the 23-foot ceiling; the iron grillwork is original and still divides visitors from the judge's bench. Museum exhibits include Confederate guns, antebellum costumes and riverboat memorabilia. *Open daily except holidays. Small charge.*

Steamer "Sprague" Museum *China St. and Waterfront* "Big Mama," as the *Sprague* was known on the river, is the world's largest stern-wheel towboat. It carried a crew of 55 and moved more tonnage up and down the Mississippi than any other steamboat. Now a riverboat museum, the mighty craft houses the River Hall of Fame; exhibits re-create the history of riverboating with models and mementos of famous boats and portraits of the steamboat era's notables. *Open daily. Adults $1.50, children small charge.*

Vicksburg National Military Park and Cemetery This is the battlefield of the 47-day siege of Vicksburg which ended when Confederate forces surrendered on July 4, 1863. Grant's victory here is considered one of the turning points of the Civil War. The battlefield contains the remains of nine Confederate forts, 12 Union approach trenches, earthen parapets and gun emplacements. Historical markers designate major points of interest. The 1581 Union soldiers who died in the Battle of Vicksburg are among those buried here. *Open daily except Dec. 25.*

SHIRLEY HOUSE "The white house," as it was known to Union soldiers, is the only surviving wartime structure within the park. During the siege it was headquarters for the 45th Illinois Infantry. The two-story frame house, then the home of James and Adeline Quincy Shirley, has been restored to its 1863 appearance.

STATUE OF GENERAL GRANT A bronze equestrian statue of General Ulysses S. Grant commemorates his victory at Vicksburg and marks the site of his headquarters during the siege.

VISITOR CENTER Artifacts of the Civil War and historical materials related to the siege of Vicksburg are exhibited in the center's museum. A motion picture vividly portrays the campaign and the siege.

173. Winter Quarters *Off Rte. 65, 3 mi. S.E. of Newellton, La.* The only plantation house in the area that General Grant did not burn on his 1863 march to Vicksburg began as a rustic three-room winter hunting retreat. Rooms were gradually added and now it is a rambling, unpretentious but comfortable home fronted by a broad shady veranda overlooking Lake St. Joseph. Painstakingly restored and furnished, it provides a comprehensive picture of life in the home of a well-to-do planter, and also houses mementos of the Civil War. *Open daily June–Sept. Small charge.*

174. Christ Episcopal Church *Courthouse Sq., St. Joseph, La.* The unusual Gothic design of the little wooden church harmonizes with the picturesque village and countryside in which it is set. The proportionately tall square tower capped by a pyramidal spire and wooden cross give it a simple spiritual quality. It was built in 1872 and retains its neat and trim character. *Open daily.*

175. Tensas Parish Court House *St. Joseph, La.* This handsome brick courthouse was built in 1906 in the popular octagonal style. It was thoroughly modernized in 1964 but the beauty of the original Greek Revival architecture remains intact. The building, which contains a library and plantation museum, is topped by a cupola, and Ionic columns support a gable at each of its four entrances. *Open daily Mar.–May, Mon.–Fri. June–Feb.*

176. Natchez, Miss.

The oldest city along the Mississippi River, Natchez was once the chief center of wealth and culture in Mississippi. Today much of the Old South atmosphere still prevails amidst the many stately antebellum homes.

Auburn *Duncan Park* The elegant brick mansion, built in 1812, was among the first in the Mississippi Territory to display classic Greek architectural details. A noble entrance doorway is matched by another on the second-story gallery; each has graceful side windows and transom fanlights. Outstanding features inside are splendid hand-carved woodwork in most rooms and a balanced spiral staircase that completes a perfect circle between first and second stories. A billiard hall and a carriage house are also popular attractions. *Open daily. Small charge.*

Briars *31 Irving Lane* Historically, the Briars is remembered as the home in which Jefferson Davis married Varina Howell in 1845. Architecturally, it is a typical planter's home, built in 1812. High on a bluff overlooking the Mississippi River, the comfortable one-and-a-half-story frame house has a wide gallery extending across the front. Slender pillars support the sloping roof, the line of which is broken by four large dormer windows. The house, which typifies antebellum days, is being preserved as part of Confederate Memorial Park. *Open daily except holidays. Small charge.*

[**172.** *Steamer* Sprague *Museum*] *Piloting the* Sprague *along the Mississippi while pushing 46 coal barges was a tricky business. A tug helped "Big Mama" maneuver the tow, but barges often got out of control and were wrecked.*

Cherokee *N. Wall and High Sts.* This mansion has a split personality: its rear section was built in 1794 on a Spanish land grant in the Spanish style; later, in 1810, five rooms and a classical Greek Revival facade were added, with twin columns and a pedimented portico. Prominent interior features are two drawing rooms with crystal chandeliers and a winding staircase. The 19th-century furnishings include a Sheraton desk, a Moorish octagonal taboret inlaid with ivory and Meissen vases. *Open daily except holidays. Small charge.*

D'Evereux *Rte. 61* Four years of skillful labor—around 1840—created the classic simplicity of this Greek Revival home. Six fluted columns rise two stories both in front and in back of the house. A hip roof, a captain's walk and a cupola harmonize perfectly with the architectural design. Many original American furnishings are still in place, all reflecting an atmosphere of gracious hospitality that has long been a heritage of this proud home. *Open Mon.-Sat. Small charge.*

Elms *S. Pine St.* Surrounded by inviting gardens and stately trees, this gracious home beckons the visitor back through time to the romantic days when Spain ruled the area. The three-story house with broad galleries around two sides was built in 1782, possibly by Spanish governor Don Pedro Piernas. Among the house's many intriguing features are an especially beautiful wrought-iron stairway, a unique multikey system of bells used to summon servants to various rooms and a charming octagonal summerhouse. *Open daily except Thanksgiving Day and Dec. 25. Small charge.*

Longwood *Lower Woodville Rd.* The largest octagonal house in the country—and probably the most eccentric—was begun in 1858 in an uninhibited attempt to develop a fresh native architectural expression. But construction was interrupted by the Civil War, during which four of Longwood's five floors and its onion-domed glass-enclosed tower were boarded up. Plans to face the entire structure with Italian marble were abandoned. Dr. Haller Nutt, the original owner, and his family personally finished nine rooms on the ground floor for a home, and they and their descendants lived here for more than a century. Their furnishings remain in place. *Open daily except Dec. 24-5. Small charge.*

Rosalie *100 Orleans St.* Great crises of American history were reflected in small events that occurred in this stately mansion. There is the room in which General Grant slept; and there is the table at which Jefferson Davis dined, only a room away from the library where the white marble fireplace mantel is smoke-stained from the roaring fires built by Union soldiers. The original furnishings are still here. The double parlor has two complete sets of Belter rosewood furniture and rich draperies of apricot brocade, while not far away, above the back doorway, hang the slave bells that summoned the house servants from their quarters. *Open daily except holidays. Small charge.*

Stanton Hall *401 High St.* Built in 1851 by Frederick Stanton as a replica of his Irish ancestral home, this is said to be the most palatial mansion in Natchez. It occupies a full city block, and its parlor and music room combined measure 70 feet in length. The brick is of burned Natchez clay, but the other materials were brought from Europe: hand-carved woodwork, marble mantels and bronze chandeliers. *Open daily except Dec. 24-5. Small charge.*

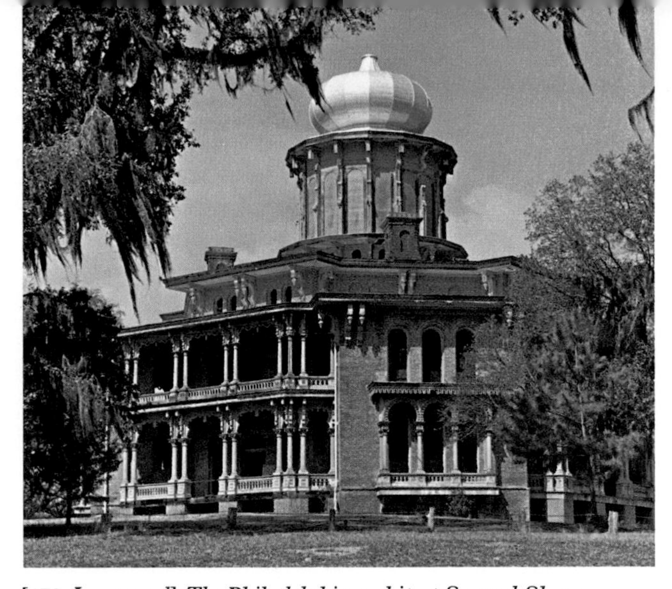

[**176.** *Longwood*] *The Philadelphia architect Samuel Sloan designed this unique octagonal house which was destined never to be completed. It contains 32 huge rooms, each of which opens on a veranda or a balcony.*

177. Rosemont Plantation *Rte. 24, E. of Woodville, Miss.* The family home of Jefferson Davis, U.S. senator and president of the Confederacy, is an unpretentious clapboard dwelling, but its rustic setting and generous verandas still suggest the comfort and peace Davis often returned to find. Little altered through the years, the cottage and plantation are being carefully restored to their early 19th-century style. On the grounds is the cemetery where five generations of the Davis family are buried. *Open daily. Adults $1.50, children small charge.*

178. Cottage Plantation *Rte. 61, 6 mi. N. of St. Francisville, La.* The cottage, built in 1795, was gradually extended, the last section being added in 1850. A long front porch a few steps aboveground has 12 slender pillars supporting the eaves of a sloping roof from which dormer windows project. Most of the original furnishings that were here when Andrew Jackson visited after the Battle of New Orleans can still be seen. One of the features of the plantation are the outbuildings: two slave cabins, a milkhouse, school, outside kitchen and carriage house. *Open daily except Dec. 25. Adults $1.50, children small charge.*

179. Myrtles Plantation Mansion *Rte. 61N, St. Francisville, La.* Ghosts reputedly prowl about the grounds and stairways of this 26-room French-type manor, built about 1830. Eerie shadows are cast by the beautiful iron-lace railings and pillars of the 160-foot gallery that extends around much of the old manor. In contrast, the interior sparkles with French and Irish crystal chandeliers. Most of the rooms contain mirror doorknobs, intricate moldings and Italian marble fireplaces. The music room shines with small golden harps, a Steinway and 36 violins dating back as early as 1560. *Open daily. Adults and children over 10 small charge.*

180. Oakley House *Audubon Memorial State Park, St. Francisville, La.* "The rich magnolias . . . the holly, the beech, the tall yellow poplar . . . surrounded once more by numberless warblers and thrushes, I enjoyed the scene," wrote naturalist-artist John James Audubon of his first impression of Oakley in 1821. For four

A double row of live oaks was the traditional approach to the great house of a Southern plantation. Few oak alleys today can match the one that leads to Rosedown.

181. Rosedown Plantation and Gardens

St. Francisville, La.

The Golden Age of the plantations reached its peak in the decades before the Civil War in the Louisiana parishes of East and West Feliciana. Here, immensely profitable crops of cotton, sugarcane, indigo and tobacco made millionaires of planters like Daniel Turnbull, who built Rosedown in 1835. The Turnbulls had traveled in Europe, visiting Versailles and the gardens of England and Italy. European furnishings followed them home to the U.S. and up the Mississippi to Rosedown; camellias and azaleas were imported from the Orient to blend with native plants in the gardens. Rosedown today is a complete and faithful restoration, although now the entire house is air-conditioned to protect it from the punishing Delta climate. Most of the furnishings are original, reflecting the excellent taste of the Turnbulls and the styles of the Victorian, Empire and Federal periods. Cuttings from the original plants flourish in the gardens, and ancient trees and shrubs—cryptomeria, true cypress, crape myrtle and cedar—have grown enormously. *Open daily except Dec. 24-5. Adults and children over 12: house and gardens $4.00. Children under 12: house $2.00, gardens free with adult.*

Daniel Turnbull bought the massive mahogany bedroom suite made for Henry Clay, defeated candidate for President, and built a wing to put it in.

The graceful mahogany staircase is the focal point of Rosedown's entrance hall. The wallpaper was created in France by Joseph Dufour in the early 1830s.

months he lived here, tutoring the owner's daughter and painting some (reportedly 32) of his famous illustrations for *Birds of America.* Built in 1799, Oakley has long jaloused galleries reminiscent of West Indies houses. Many first-edition prints from *Birds of America* hang in the rooms, which contain Sheraton and other fine furniture. One wing of the plantation barn serves as a museum. *Open daily except holidays. Small charge.*

181. Rosedown Plantation and Gardens *St. Francisville, La.* See feature display on facing page.

182. Parlange on False River *Rte. 1, 6 mi. S. of New Roads, La.* This 1750 dwelling is a rare relic of the type of construction known as *bousillage.* The two-story structure has galleries on all sides; its lower floors are built of brick and its upper ones of cypress. The house is still occupied by descendants of its builder, Marquis de Ternant, and is still a working plantation. Most of the furnishings—Oriental rugs, hand-carved desks and cabinets and portraits by the court painter of Napoleon III—are family heirlooms. *Open daily. Small charge.*

183. Baton Rouge, La.

An important industrial center and the state capital, Baton Rouge is a picturesque city of lakes and bayous, parks, winding drives and beautiful antebellum homes.

Louisiana Arts and Science Center *502 North Blvd.* Once the Governor's Mansion, the pillared 1930 building now houses exhibits that range from a simple explanation of electricity to a 2000-year-old Egyptian mummy. Also on view are an early country store, an Acadian house, a rare collection of miniature furniture, Eskimo and Tibetan art objects and sculptures by Croatian artist Ivan Meštrović. A planetarium adjoins the center. *Open Tues.-Sun. except holidays. Small charge for planetarium.*

Louisiana State Capitol *N. Third St. and Boyd Ave.* The soaring 34-story tower, completed in 1932, is the nation's tallest state capitol. Its lavish interior is embellished with fine marble from every major marble-producing country in the world. Statues, murals, friezes and other artwork in and on the building commemorate Louisianians' history and aspirations. From the observation tower visitors can view the surrounding gardens, the city and the Mississippi. *Open daily.*

Louisiana State University *Highland Rd.* Founded in 1860 just before the Civil War, the school saw precarious beginnings. When war broke out, its early president, William Tecumseh Sherman, resigned and later assumed a command in the Union Army. The school closed soon after, and its students joined the Confederate ranks. General Sherman was again of service to the school when he requested that it be saved from destruction by Union forces.

ANGLO-AMERICAN ART MUSEUM *Memorial Tower* The cultural influence of England on America is the theme in the museum, housed in Memorial Tower. Here is an impressive collection of paintings, prints and drawings—including works by Hogarth, Reynolds and Rembrandt Peale—most of them superbly displayed in six English and American period rooms. Magnificent wall paneling, a huge fireplace and brick floor tiles decorate the Jacobean Room of the early 17th century; 18th-century Georgian decor fills two other rooms. American styles can be seen in a Colonial Pennsylvania sitting room, a Federal-style Mississippi plantation drawing room and a Victorian hall from a New Orleans town house. *Open daily during academic sessions.*

MEMORIAL TOWER *Tower Dr.* Known also as the Campanile, the 175-foot clock tower was erected in 1924 to honor Louisianians who died during World War I. An electronic carillon chimes the quarter hours, and music from the university radio station is broadcast twice a day. *Open daily except Jan. 1 and Dec. 25.*

MUSEUM OF NATURAL SCIENCE *Dalrymple Dr.* Large dioramas of wild parrots, ivory-billed woodpeckers and whooping cranes introduce the major specialty here—birdlife of Louisiana. These rare, magnificent birds are matched by most of the species common in the state today, many presented in carefully reconstructed outdoor scenes. The museum also contains exhibits of native animals and vast research collections. *Open Sun.-Fri. June-Aug., daily Sept.-May.*

Old State Capitol *North Blvd. and St. Philip St.* Standing on the high bluffs above the Mississippi, this castlelike building was completed in 1849. Its unusual Gothic Revival design, incorporating crenellated battlements, prompted Mark Twain to call it the "monstrosity of the Mississippi." The capitol, however, has survived his criticism, along with fire, war, alterations and restorations. The spiral staircase, stained-glass windows and striking stained-glass dome are among the interesting features. *Open daily except holidays.*

St. Joseph Cathedral *Main and Fourth Sts.* Catholics have been served for over a century by St. Joseph's, although three extensive restorations have taken place since the cornerstone was laid in 1853. The church is now a romantic blend of old and new, of aesthetic pleasure and practicality. The most notable details are the delicate stained-glass windows, the mosaic Stations of the Cross and the magnificent mahogany crucifix by sculptor Ivan Meštrović. *Open daily.*

184. Belle Helene Plantation *Rte. 75, 2½ mi. S. of Geismar, La.* Sugarcane planter Duncan Kenner built this monumental house for his lovely Creole wife in 1841. Originally called Ashland, it is a classic-style temple surrounded by a gallery of 28 solid brick columns, each four feet square and 30 feet high. A grand interior hallway divides antique-filled rooms, ending at a spiral staircase that winds to the attic. The antebellum mansion stands among ancient live oaks festooned with moss. *Open daily. Small charge.*

185. Madewood Plantation House *Rte. 308, Napoleonville, La.* The noble Greek Revival mansion, built between 1840 and 1848 for Thomas Pugh of North Carolina, is fronted with six fluted Ionic columns that rise beyond a bedroom gallery to a pediment decorated with a fan window. A handsome entrance hall with Corinthian columns extends through the house; at the back, an unsupported winding staircase climbs to twin doorways flanked by similar columns. Among the rare furnishings are original Hogarth etchings, a 17th-century Italian altarpiece and a Mathew Brady photograph of Robert E. Lee. A huge fireplace dominates the kitchen; a family cemetery is on the grounds. The outbuildings include a brick and cypress carriage house. *Open daily. Adults $2.00, children small charge.*

186. Houmas House *River Rd., Burnside, La.* John Smith Preston built the Greek Revival mansion in 1840 on part of an early Spanish land grant. Flanking it are hexagonal brick *garconnières,* charming sleeping quarters for boys. The showplace mansion is surrounded on three sides by 14 impressively tall Doric columns and broad verandas. Inside features include a lovely three-story spiral staircase and antique furnishings, such as decorative armoires, that show off early Louisiana craftsmanship. Gleaming copper and brass utensils hang from the fireplace in the Colonial kitchen. *Open daily except Dec. 25. $2.50.*

187. Tezcuco Plantation Home *Rte. 44, Burnside, La.* The elegant house, which is set high on its foundation and features three outside staircases, was built in 1855. A Greek Revival structure with French Creole embellishments, it boasts delicate ironwork along its side and front galleries. Interior attractions include ornate plaster cornices and rosettes on the 15-foot-high ceilings, doors painted to look like grained wood, and a wealth of New Orleans antiques. On the spacious grounds huge live oaks and magnolias are laced with Spanish moss, wisteria and honeysuckle vines. *Open Mon.-Sat. $2.00.*

188. San Francisco Plantation House *Rte. 44, 2 mi. N. of Reserve, La.* Spacious galleries, Gothic arches and iron railings all lend a fanciful air to the extraordinary "Steamboat Gothic" mansion. Built in 1849-52, it took 100 slaves to burn, shape, set and plaster the brick of the walls and the square columns. The rooms are filled with ornate fireplaces, massive mirrors, carved grillwork, ceiling scrolls and French and English 17th- and 18th-century furniture. *Open daily. Small charge.*

[189] *The best way to see the French Quarter (Vieux Carré, or Old Square) of New Orleans is on foot. The decorative details of historic houses catch the eye and the antique shops and art galleries invite investigation.*

189. New Orleans, La.

This major port of entry is a city of contrast, encompassing tradition, new industry, jazz, the Mardi Gras, internationally famous cuisine and football's Sugar Bowl. But New Orleans had a different start. The sandy soil was so damp that houses were built without basements, many raised above the ground. Even the tombs of the cemeteries rise in tiers along the walls rather than being sunk into the ground. Founded in 1718 by Jean Baptiste Le Moyne, Sieur de Bienville, the city was carefully planned. To the dismay of its French inhabitants, it was ceded to Spain 44 years later. It became French again in 1800, but by the time the citizens had learned of the change, New Orleans had become part of the U.S. under the Louisiana Purchase. In the meantime the French and Spanish citizens had merged into a single group, the Creoles, who banded together against newcomers. The Americans were forced to build their houses away from the French Quarter (Vieux Carré) and as a result the finest old American homes are in the Garden District. As the name implies, these mansions are surrounded by large grounds, whereas the houses lining the narrow streets of the French Quarter give mere glimpses of their gracious, flowered patios. The balconies of the Creole houses are noted for the lacy ironwork. There are many other famous landmarks in the city, including the 33-story International Trade Mart and the Mississippi River Bridge, one of the longest cantilevered spans in the U.S.

Andrew Jackson Monument *Jackson Sq.* "Old Hickory" is depicted sitting erect upon his horse in the center of the French Quarter, doffing his hat in salute to the city that honored him for its defense in 1815. His horse's forelegs rise high, contrary to sculptural tradition, which holds that the horse of a hero who has died a natural death must have all four feet on the ground. Sculptor Clark Mills (1815-83) achieved a unique balance in the 10-ton statue, which is supported only by the horse's rear legs.

Banque de la Louisiane *417 Royal St.* See feature display on pages 450-2.

Casa Hové *723 Toulouse St.* When a Spanish grandee purchased the house in 1797, it was already about 80 years old—one of the earliest homes in the Mississippi Valley. Its Spanish styling complements a lovely brick patio and arched carriageway where a replica of a Christopher Wren stairway rises to the upper floors. Inside, the exposed ceiling beams and original wrought-iron hardware are striking, as are the living room fireplaces with hand-carved fronts. Among the early furnishings are a Duncan Phyfe gaming table, Baccarat wall sconces and a gold Directoire sofa that was presented to a New Orleans family by Louis Philippe of France. English pewter and brass chandeliers decorate the lower hall. *Open Mon.-Sat. except holidays. Adults and children over 11 small charge.*

Cathedral of St. Louis, King of France *721 Chartres St.* Since 1727 a parish church has stood on this site, serving first French, Spanish, Swiss and German colonists and finally Americans. The present edifice—dating from 1794 and substantially rebuilt in 1851—admirably honors St. Louis' long history. The Baroque entrance facade of this minor basilica, flanked by steeples, rises to an imposing spire. Inside, the nave and its pillared balcony flow to an enormous mural over

[**189.** *Andrew Jackson Monument*] *Behind the statue of Jackson is the Cathedral (now a basilica) of St. Louis where the city gathered in thanksgiving after the Battle of New Orleans. Jackson Square was then a parade ground called the Place d'Armes, the heart of the French Quarter. In the 1850s it was landscaped through the efforts of the Baroness de Pontalba, daughter of the wealthy Spaniard whose money had rebuilt the cathedral in the late 18th century. Many notable and historic old buildings surround Jackson Square today.*

the main altar that portrays St. Louis announcing the Seventh Crusade. Magnificent stained-glass windows depict other episodes in the saint's life, and rare statues and paintings add decorative grace notes. *Open daily.*

Elmwood Plantation *5400 River Rd.* The Mississippi Valley's oldest plantation was a 1719 grant from Louis XIV of France. The house, built in 1762, consisted originally of two floors, but the top story was destroyed by fire in 1938. The restored ground floor has barred windows and gun slots in the east wall. Louisiana's first American governor is believed to have lived here in the mid-19th century. The house is surrounded by groves of massive oaks. *Open daily.*

French Market *Decatur St.* A series of buildings, begun here in 1813, are connected by columned arcades and landscaped pedestrian malls. The roofs are framed by huge pegged cypress beams and decorated with several charming cupolas. This famous landmark is a hive of shops busy selling vegetables and fruits, fine china and crystal. Visitors make a habit of stopping at stalls to enjoy coffee and French pastry, a traditional market snack. *Open daily.*

Gallier Hall *545 St. Charles Ave.* It's worth a stroll around Lafayette Square to see the facade of this Greek Revival building. It was designed by James Gallier, Sr., as a city hall (erected in 1850) and may be the most beautiful example of its style in the U.S.

Gallier Residence *1132 Royal St.* See feature display on pages 450–2.

Gardette-Le Prêtre House *716 Dauphine St.* See feature display on pages 450–2.

Girod House *500 Chartres St.* See feature display on pages 450–2.

Historic New Orleans Collection *Merieult House, 533 Royal St.* In 1792 a French shipping merchant built the elegant house as a place of business as well as a residence. Remodeled in the 1830s, it boasts graceful cornices and mantels and serves as an appropriate setting for this remarkable collection. In 11 galleries rotating exhibits feature the story of Andrew Jackson and the Battle of New Orleans in 1815, the Mississippi River from the time of De Soto's discovery, plantation life and the Civil War occupation. A reference library includes early documents about pirate Jean Lafitte, many of Andrew Jackson's letters, royal edicts and more than 100 military letters written during the War of 1812. Every known print of the Battle of New Orleans can be seen here. *Open Thurs.-Sat. Small charge.*

Lafitte's Blacksmith Shop *941 Bourbon St.* Legend says that Jean and Pierre Lafitte, notorious smugglers, had a smithy in the one-story house as a front for their illegal dealings. But the house, now a little public bar, is famous in its own right as a French Colonial dwelling constructed more than 200 years ago of soft bricks reinforced with timbers. *Open daily.*

Longue Vue Gardens *7 Bamboo Rd.* Japanese plum trees line the entrance lane to the five tranquil gardens surrounding a large mansion situated on eight acres. In the Spanish Court, neat boxwood hedges and handsome tree roses accent a colonnaded loggia. Camellias and roses bloom in another area, and plants such as petunias and coleus—in artful containers—flank a miniature canal. The Yellow Garden features flowers and shrubs that bloom in shades of gold. Pebbled paths link the gardens, each highlighted by graceful fountains and sculptures. *Open Tues.-Sun. except holidays mid-Sept.-mid-July. Adults $2.00, children small charge.*

[**189.** *Lafitte's Blacksmith Shop*] *Early French colonists in Louisiana found that* briquette entre poteaux, *a combination of cypress posts and bricks, made a more durable house than did either of the two materials alone.*

URSULINE CONVENT

GARDETTE-LE PRÊTRE HOUSE

GALLIER RESIDENCE

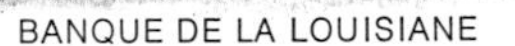

BANQUE DE LA LOUISIANE

From Wrought Iron to Cast Iron

The blacksmiths of Spain were famous for their artistry, and the Spanish colonists imported fine examples of wrought-iron work for their houses here. In the mid-1800s, when the process of casting iron into decorative shapes became popular, there was a ready market in New Orleans. The influence of traditional Spanish wrought iron (above left) is seen in the latter-day casting (above right)—both details from balcony rails in the French Quarter.

GIROD HOUSE

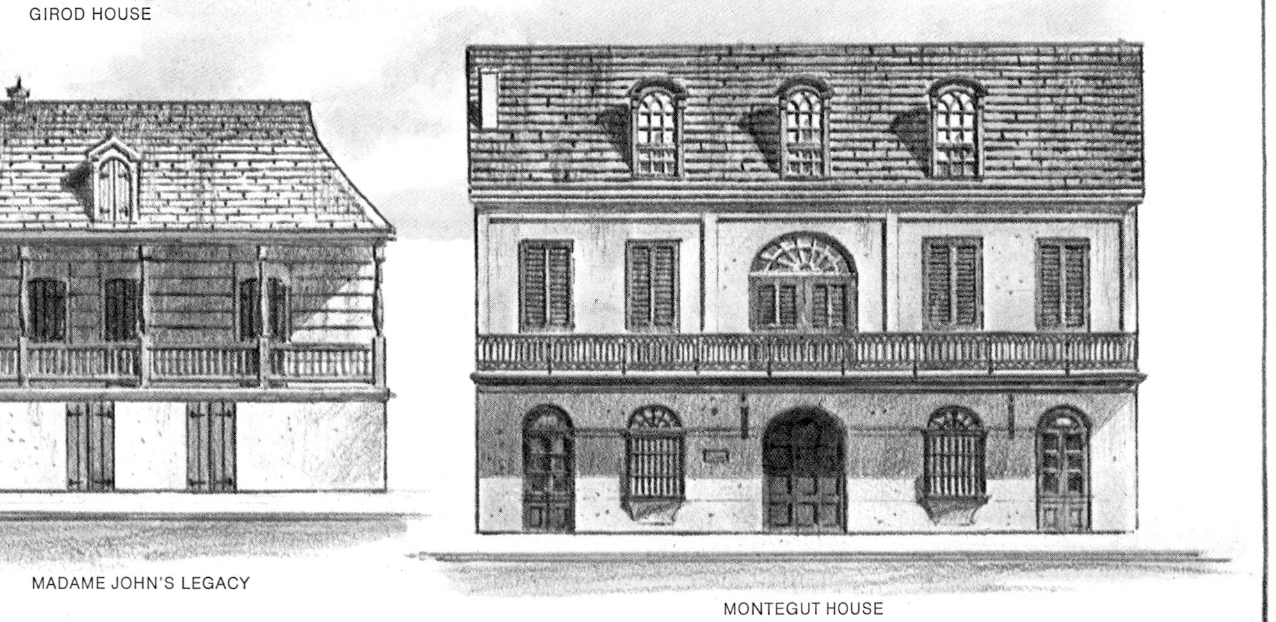

MADAME JOHN'S LEGACY

MONTEGUT HOUSE

(*continued next page*)

189. New Orleans, La.: French and Spanish Colonial Styles

(*See feature display on pages 450–1*)

The French Quarter, the oldest section of New Orleans, was planned and laid out as a walled town by the colonizing French in 1718. The 18th-century Gallic preference for formality and rationality of design is still much in evidence in the architecture here, but there are few purely French buildings left. After Spain took possession of the city in 1762 many houses were embellished with galleries of Spanish wrought iron in fanciful designs, lush courtyards and other features from Spain. A few decades later planters arrived from the West Indies and brought island methods for coping with heat and humidity: second-story wide-roofed verandas, ground floors of stone without below-ground foundations. The unique architectural heritage of New Orleans was charmingly blended and maintained by the Creole descendants of the early Spanish and French colonists. Their influence is also evident in the local cuisine, a blend of Mediterranean flavors with West Indian accents, and in the leisurely life-style for which the city remains justly renowned.

Banque de la Louisiane *417 Royal St.* Built about 1800 as a residence, then used as a bank, the building is now the home of Brennan's, a famed French restaurant. The cantilever balconies, dark shutters and inner court are typically Spanish. *Open daily.*

Gallier Residence *1132 Royal St.* James Gallier, Jr., a noted city architect, built this French- and Spanish-style home in 1857. Films on the art of ornamental iron- and plasterwork are shown in the three-window-wide right wing, formerly a warehouse. *Open Tues.–Sun. Adults $1.50, children small charge.*

Gardette-Le Prêtre House *716 Dauphine St.* The filigree galleries, added several decades after the house was built in 1836, show the Creoles' love of decorative ironwork.

Girod House *500 Chartres St.* The three-story main wing was built in 1814 for Nicholas Girod, mayor of New Orleans. It adjoins his brother's two-story section, dating from 1800, which faces St. Louis Street. Like the city itself, the two parts are a mélange of French and Spanish details.

Madame John's Legacy *632 Dumaine St.* Built in 1788 in the French Colonial tradition, the house has no basement and its sturdy ground floor supports a wooden second story.

Montegut House *731 Royal St.* The house was built in 1795, but it lost some of its early ornamental details—such as garlands of flowers draping the capitals of the second-floor pilasters—when it was remodeled about 1830. The central carriage door leads to a rear courtyard.

Ursuline Convent *1114 Chartres St.* The oldest building in New Orleans, completed in 1750, is pure French in character. It has been used as a convent, school, orphanage, bishop's residence and rectory. *Open Tues., Thurs.–Sat. Small charge.*

Louisiana State Museum The various cultural and artistic influences exerted on Louisiana through the years are depicted in several interesting displays in eight buildings in the French Quarter. Five buildings are described below. Another, Madame John's Legacy, appears in the feature display at left and on pages 450–1.

ARSENAL *600 Block St. Peter St.* Also known as Battle Abbey, the 1839 Greek Revival structure was built to serve as the state arsenal. It was an important depot for arms and ammunition during the Mexican and Civil Wars and the "White Rebellion" of 1873–4.

CABILDO *Chartres and St. Peter Sts.* The Spanish erected the stuccoed brick building in 1795 as a civic administration center, and the Louisiana Purchase was signed here in 1803. It then became city hall, later housed the state supreme court, and is now devoted to displays on the French, Spanish and American periods in Louisiana history. Other exhibits relate to Mississippi River steamboats and plantations. *Open Tues.–Sun. Adults and children over 12 small charge.*

1850 HISTORIC HOUSE *Lower Pontalba Bldg., 523 St. Ann St.* The restored row house is part of what is believed to be one of the nation's first two apartment buildings. Furnished in the 1850s style, it contains exhibits on the history of the Pontalba Buildings. Visitors can also see a courtyard and servants' rooms. *Open Tues.–Sun. Adults and children over 12 small charge.*

PRESBYTERE *751 Chartres St.* Begun in 1791 as a priests' house, the second floor was added in 1813 by the U.S. government for use as a courthouse; the third floor and mansard roof were added in 1847. On view are numerous portraits, paintings, early fashions and exhibits associated with Mardi Gras. The administrative offices and workrooms for the entire museum complex are on the third floor. *Open Tues.–Sun. Adults and children over 12 small charge.*

U.S. BRANCH MINT *400 Esplanade Ave.* In 1835 William Strickland designed the Greek Revival structure, which minted money until 1909. During the Civil War, the Confederacy unsuccessfully attempted to continue the production of coins here.

Montegut House *731 Royal St.* See feature display on pages 450–2.

New Orleans Jazz Museum *Royal Sonesta Hotel, 340 Bourbon St.* America's original art form is honored in the collection of memorabilia that traces the history of jazz from African rhythms to contemporary styles. An exhibit area features objects related to jazz and those who made it famous: cornets belonging to Louis Armstrong, Bix Beiderbecke and Emmanuel Perez; a mandolin played by Freddie Keppard when he was a child; and the bugle that was the first instrument Louis Armstrong ever played. Visitors can examine many documents and photographs, as well as dial telephones to hear vintage and modern jazz selections. *Open Mon.–Sat. Small charge.*

New Orleans Museum of Art *Lelong Ave., City Park* In 1911 Isaac Delgado gave the city of New Orleans funds to erect the museum's original building, a neoclassic structure. The museum collections, which include works from Pre-Columbian times to the modern era, have grown tremendously since then and recently three new wings were added. Among the permanent exhibitions here are contemporary light sculpture, African and Oriental art, the Kress Collection of Italian

[**189.** *Louisiana State Museum-Cabildo*] *The three major periods in the history of Louisiana—French, Spanish Colonial and American—live on in the stones and exhibits of the Cabildo. The oldest part (1750s) was the French Corps de Garde (police station). The Spanish Colonial government incorporated this section when they built the Cabildo in 1795. The third floor, added in 1847, reflects a new American spirit. The Cathedral of St. Louis is at the right.*

masters, Spanish Colonial painting and 19th-century Louisiana works. *Open Tues.-Sun. except holidays.*

St. John the Baptist Catholic Church *1139 Dryades St.* The intricately detailed brickwork on this Romanesque-style church, completed in 1871, is considered by some to be the finest masonry in the city. (Since the building was erected on land that had originally been a marsh, more bricks were used in the massive foundations than in the visible portion of the church.) Noteworthy features include a fine series of stained-glass windows, an elegantly simple interior and a gold leaf dome at the top of the steeple. *Open daily.*

St. Mary's Assumption Church *Constance and Josephine Sts.* Severely damaged by a 1965 hurricane, this Roman Catholic church is being restored as funds become available. Completed in 1860 and originally serving mostly German-immigrant parishioners, St. Mary's is a masterpiece of German Baroque architecture. There are Bavarian stained-glass windows, and the vaulted ceiling boasts ornamental plasterwork. Fluted columns are richly embellished with hand-painted statues and Corinthian capitals. The magnificent high altar from Munich has more than 30 carved wood statues of saints and angels beneath a moving statue of the Virgin Mary. *Open Sun.*

St. Patrick's Church *724 Camp St.* Noted architect James Gallier designed the Gothic-style edifice, modeling it after Yorkminster in England. Built of rough brick resembling uncut stone, it was the city's tallest building when it was completed about 1840. The sweeping interior reveals gracefully vaulted ceilings and a sanctuary considered among the most beautiful of any Southern church. Three huge 1841 frescos—*The Transfiguration, Christ Walking on the Sea* and *St. Patrick Baptizing Irish Princesses*—stand behind a magnificent altar carved by Gallier. Among other impressive decorations are superb wall paintings and a gold and diamond studded monstrance modeled after the Celtic Cross of Cong. *Open daily.*

Tulane University *6823 St. Charles Ave.* Founded in 1834, the university occupies land once part of a sugar plantation. Its main campus consists of 100 landscaped acres encompassing 65 buildings, including those administered by Newcomb College, the first (1886) separate women's college founded within a university in the U.S. A walking tour of the campus takes visitors past gracious old buildings and sleek modern ones. One of the latter is the Howard-Tilton Memorial Library, completed in 1968. Besides numerous books, documents, tape recordings and microfilms, the library houses the Archive of New Orleans Jazz. At Dinwiddie Hall visitors can enjoy the small but choice collection of ethnological and archaeological objects belonging to the Middle American Research Institute. Among the displays are carved alabaster vases from Honduras, Mexican carved shell ornaments and modern Guatemalan textiles, as well as a number of Pre-Columbian items. *Campus open daily, Institute open Mon., Tues., Thurs., Fri. during academic sessions except holidays.*

Ursuline Convent *1114 Chartres St.* See feature display on pages 450–2.

190. Chalmette National Historical Park *Arabi, La.* Relics remain on these grounds from the fierce battle for New Orleans on Jan. 8, 1815. Over this soil General Andrew Jackson led courageous, virtually untrained troops from four states to a resounding victory over the better-trained British forces. Markers and cannons indicate the line of defense. A lovely antebellum, white-columned house, once the residence of René Beauregard, son of Confederate General Beauregard, now serves as Visitor Center for the park. Nearby stands a 100-foot-high white monument—a timeless memorial to Jackson and his men. *Open daily except Shrove Tues. and Dec. 25.*

191. Fort Jackson *Off Rte. 23, Buras, La.* The walls of the fort—solid red brick and 17 feet thick—tower above the Mississippi River; the gun emplacements are reinforced with granite. It is not surprising that construction of the stronghold, named after General Andrew Jackson, took 26 years (1822–48). In April 1862, it was besieged by Union naval forces under Admiral Farragut for nine days and nights. The restored, star-shaped fort was reopened in 1962. Markers on the property tell of its history, and a museum within the fort contains relics found during the painstaking restoration. *Open daily.*

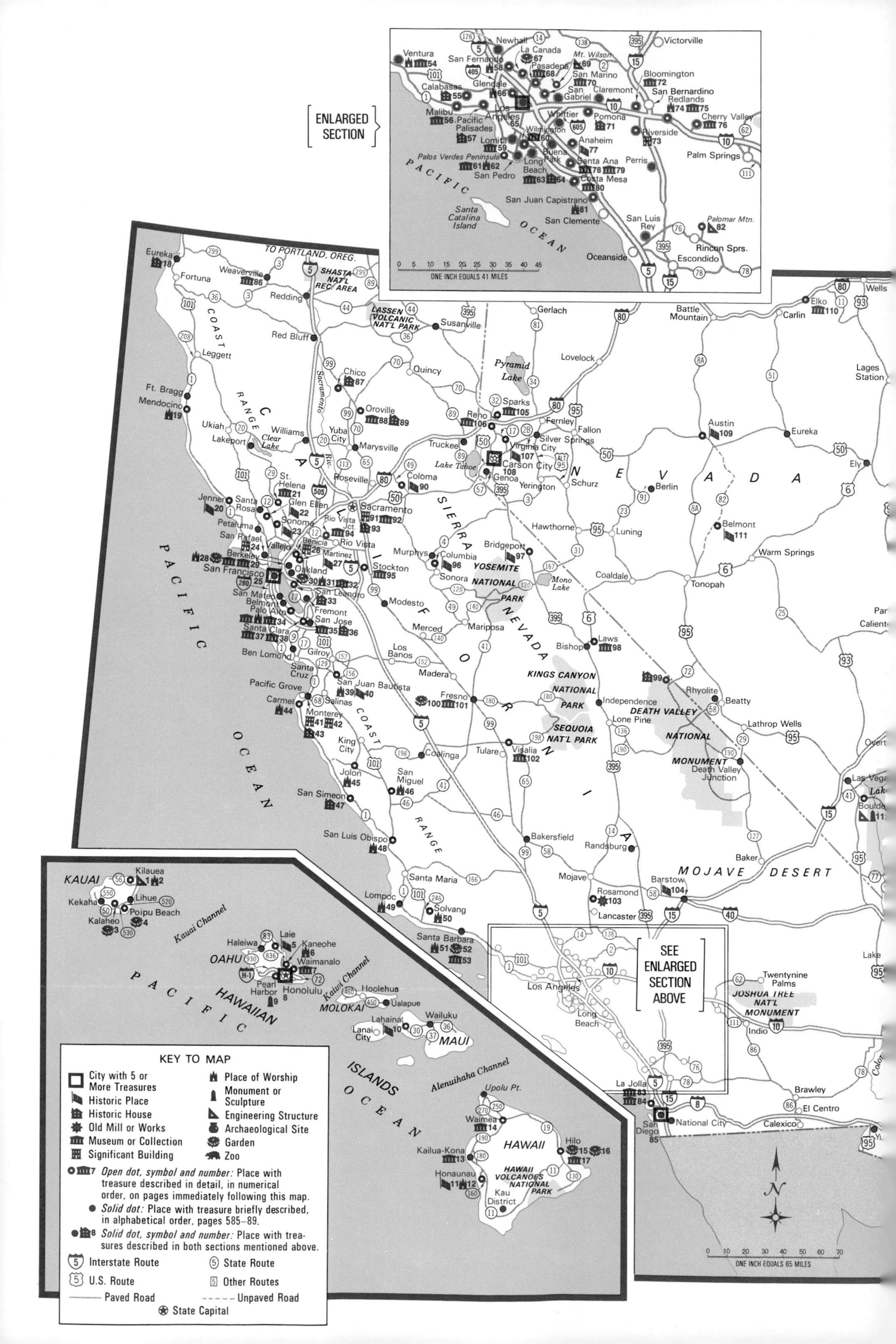
ENLARGED SECTION
Ventura 54
Newhall
La Canada 67
Mt. Wilson 69
Victorville
San Fernando 58
Pasadena 68
San Marino 70
Bloomington 72
Calabasas 55
Glendale 66
San Gabriel
Claremont
San Bernardino
Redlands 74 75
Malibu 56
Los Angeles 65
Whittier
Pomona 71
Cherry Valley 76
Pacific Palisades 57
Wilmington 60
Riverside 73
Lomita 59
Anaheim 77
Palm Springs
Palos Verdes Peninsula 61 62
Buena Park
Santa Ana 78 79
Perris
San Pedro
Long Beach 63 64
Costa Mesa 80
PACIFIC OCEAN
San Juan Capistrano 81
Santa Catalina Island
San Clemente
San Luis Rey
Palomar Mtn. 82
Rincon Sprs.
Oceanside
Escondido
ONE INCH EQUALS 41 MILES
Eureka 18
Fortuna
Weaverville 86
TO PORTLAND, OREG.
SHASTA NAT'L REC. AREA
Redding
LASSEN VOLCANIC NAT'L PARK
Susanville
Gerlach
Battle Mountain
Elko 110
Carlin
Wells
Red Bluff
COAST RANGE
Leggett
Pyramid Lake
Lovelock
Lages Station
Chico 87
Quincy
Ft. Bragg
Mendocino 19
Oroville 88 89
Sparks 105
Reno 106
Ukiah
Williams
Yuba City
Marysville
Fernley
Fallon
Austin 109
Eureka
Lakeport
Clear Lake
Truckee
Silver Springs
Virginia City 107
Carson City 108
Lake Tahoe
Genoa
Yerington
Schurz
Ely
NEVADA
Berlin
Sacramento Riv.
Roseville
Coloma 90
St. Helena 21
Jenner 20
Santa Rosa
Glen Ellen 22
Sacramento 91 92 93
Sonoma 23
Rio Vista Jct. 94
Petaluma
San Rafael 24
Vallejo
Benicia 26
Rio Vista
Berkeley 28 29
Martinez 27
San Francisco 25
Oakland 30 31 32
Hawthorne
Luning
Belmont 111
SIERRA NEVADA
Bridgeport 97
Murphys
Columbia 96
YOSEMITE NATIONAL PARK
Stockton 95
Sonora
Mono Lake
Warm Springs
Coaldale
Tonopah
San Mateo
San Leandro 33
Belmont
Palo Alto 34
Fremont
San Jose 35 36
Santa Clara 37 38
Modesto
Merced
Mariposa
Bishop
Laws 98
Caliente
Ben Lomond
Gilroy
Los Banos
CALIFORNIA
Santa Cruz
Madera
KINGS CANYON NATIONAL PARK
Pacific Grove
San Juan Bautista 39 40
Rhyolite 99
Beatty
Carmel 44
Salinas
Fresno 100 101
Independence
DEATH VALLEY NATIONAL MONUMENT
Monterey 41 42 43
Lone Pine
SEQUOIA NAT'L PARK
Lathrop Wells
King City
Coalinga
Tulare
Visalia 102
Jolon 45
San Miguel 46
Death Valley Junction
Las Vegas
PACIFIC OCEAN
San Simeon 47
Boulder
San Luis Obispo 48
Bakersfield
Randsburg
Baker
Santa Maria
Mojave
MOJAVE DESERT
Barstow 104
Rosamond 103
Lompoc 49
Solvang 50
Lancaster
Santa Barbara 51 52 53
SEE ENLARGED SECTION ABOVE
Los Angeles
Long Beach
Twentynine Palms
JOSHUA TREE NAT'L MONUMENT
Indio
Brawley
El Centro
Calexico
La Jolla 83 84
San Diego 85
National City
KAUAI
Kilauea 1 2
Lihue
Kekaha
Poipu Beach
Kalaheo 3
Kauai Channel
Laie 5
Haleiwa
Kaneohe 6
OAHU
Waimanalo 7
Pearl Harbor 9
Honolulu 8
Kaiwi Channel
Hoolehua
Ualapue
MOLOKAI
Lahaina 10
Lanai City
Wailuku
MAUI
PACIFIC
HAWAIIAN ISLANDS OCEAN
Alenuihaha Channel
Upolu Pt.
Waimea 14
HAWAII
Hilo 15 16 17
Kailua-Kona 13
Honaunau 11 12
HAWAII VOLCANOES NATIONAL PARK
Kau District
ONE INCH EQUALS 85 MILES
KEY TO MAP
City with 5 or More Treasures
Historic Place
Historic House
Old Mill or Works
Museum or Collection
Significant Building
Place of Worship
Monument or Sculpture
Engineering Structure
Archaeological Site
Garden
Zoo
7 Open dot, symbol and number: Place with treasure described in detail, in numerical order, on pages immediately following this map.
Solid dot: Place with treasure briefly described, in alphabetical order, pages 585–89.
8 Solid dot, symbol and number: Place with treasures described in both sections mentioned above.
Interstate Route
State Route
U.S. Route
Other Routes
Paved Road
Unpaved Road
State Capital

Like the scenery, many treasures here are large in scale and spectacular: the Golden Gate Bridge and Disneyland in California; Hoover Dam in Nevada; the ancient, multistoried apartments of cliff-dwelling Indians in Colorado; the Mormon Temple in Utah.

REGION 8

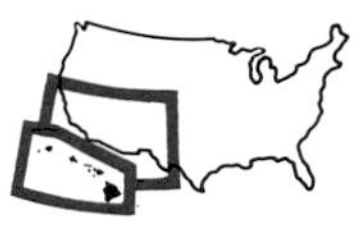

Pages 454–505

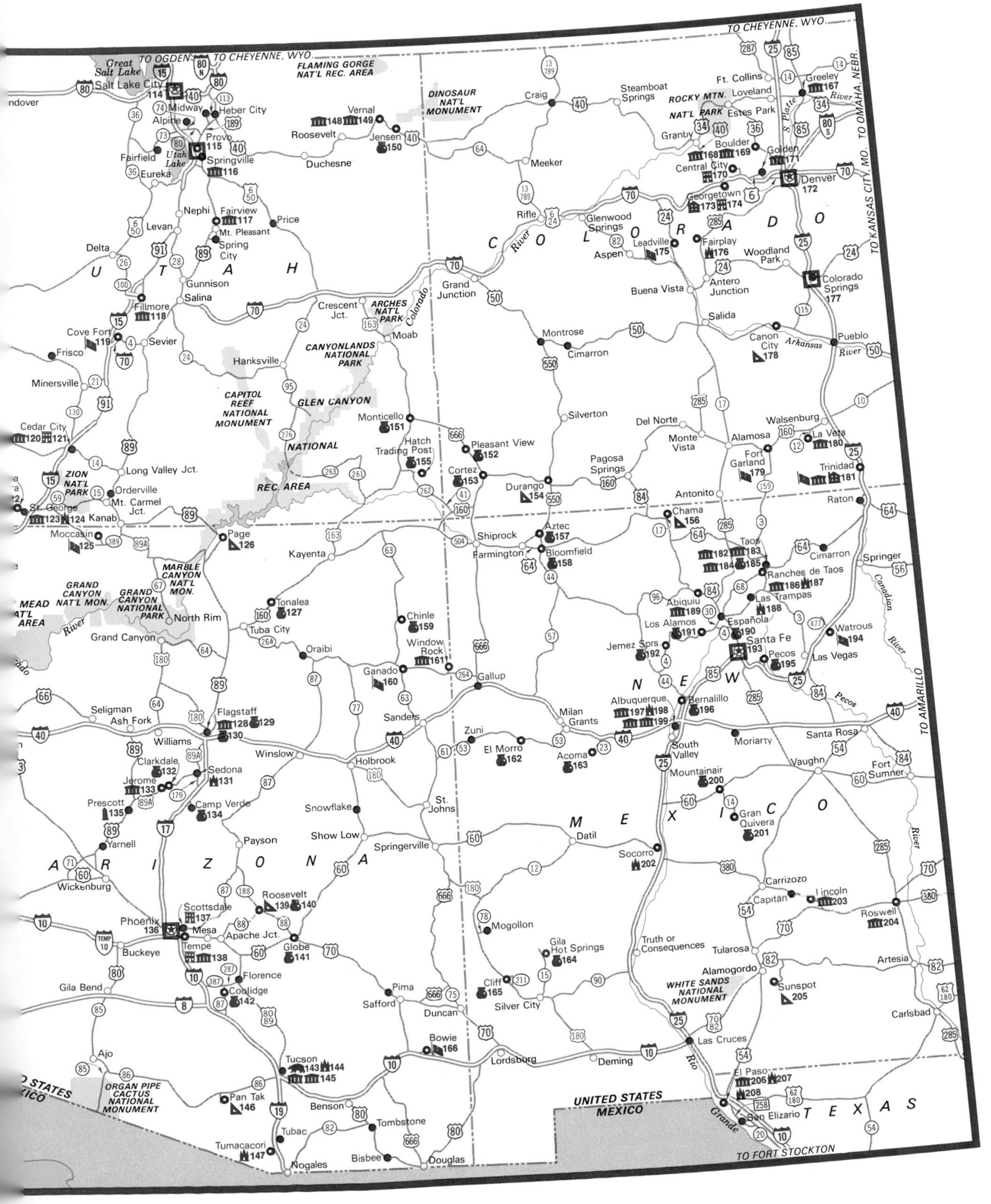

1. Kilauea Point Lighthouse *Off Rte. 56, Kilauea, Kauai, Hawaii* Located on a high bluff at the northernmost tip of the Hawaiian Islands, the lighthouse contains a "clamshell" lens, a two-sided optical instrument about 12 feet high and four tons in weight that floats in a bath of mercury. It is believed to be the largest of its kind in the world. Its powerful beacon is a guide to ships up to 23 miles at sea and to planes for 90 miles. *Open daily.*

2. St. Sylvester's Church *Kilauea, Kauai, Hawaii* At first appearing round, the striking Roman Catholic church is in fact an octagonal structure built of local lava rock and wood. The interior design features an altar centrally located, benches nearly surrounding it like a theater in the round. Exposed rough beams slant to the paneled ceiling, and the walls are decorated with remarkable frescos by prominent Hawaiian artist Jean Charlot. *Open daily.*

3. Olu Pua Botanic Garden *Rte. 50, Kalaheo, Kauai, Hawaii* Chinese fan palms, blue jade vines, white violet shrubs, dogbone trees and leopard plants are among the thousands of exotic plants displayed in the gardens. In addition to plants native to Kauai, the "Garden Isle," many of which grow nowhere else in the world, there are international botanic displays. Located on a former plantation manager's estate, the grounds take in a jungle setting, an Oriental scene, a sunken garden and a flowering terrace. *Open daily except Jan. 1. Adults $1.50, children under 12 small charge.*

4. Plantation Gardens *Poipu Beach, Kauai, Hawaii* Cacti from all over the world, some reaching an astounding height of 30 feet and weighing three tons, flourish in the lush tropical garden. More than 3500 varieties of plants, including succulents, aquatic plants, orchids and plumeria, overrun the seven acres. *Open daily. Adults and children over 11 small charge.*

5. Polynesian Cultural Center *55-402 Iosepa St., Laie, Oahu, Hawaii* Visitors can travel through the South Seas without leaving the 16-acre compound of the center, which is sponsored by the Church of Jesus Christ of Latter-day Saints. Villages of Fiji, Samoa, Tahiti, Tonga, old Hawaii and the Maori of New Zealand are impressively re-created. Arts, crafts, clothing, customs, cooking and sports from these far-flung islands are presented to make the buildings more meaningful. An evening musical revue called "Invitation to Paradise" features folk songs and dances of the islands. The "Pageant of the Long Canoes," another daily revue, is performed in a procession of Polynesian outrigger canoes. *Open Mon.-Sat. except Thanksgiving Day and Dec. 25. Villages: adults $3.00, children under 12 $1.50; show: adults $5.00, children under 12 $2.50.*

6. Byodo-in Temple *Valley of the Temples Memorial Park, 47-200 Kahekili Hwy., Kaneohe, Oahu, Hawaii* An 18-foot carved gold statue of Buddha is housed in the temple, a replica of an ancient Japanese one. Above the Buddha stands a carved screen depicting his 52 followers. The main hall is shaped like a bird poised for flight, and gold phoenixes perch on the steeply pitched roof. Other structures include a bell house, with a three-ton brass bell cast in Japan, and a ceremonial teahouse. The buildings have a magnificent setting: rugged mountains in the background, a large lake in front and classical Japanese gardens all around. *Open daily. Small charge.*

7. Sea Life Park *Makapuu Point, Waimanalo, Oahu, Hawaii* An offshore coral reef is re-created in an enormous 300,000-gallon tank here. More than 1000 tropical fish, representing about 100 species, and marine plants and animals can be seen through glass windows at different levels. Other exhibits include the Ocean Science Theater, a glass-walled tank in which whales and porpoises perform. A replica of the square-rigged whaling ship *Essex,* which inspired Melville to write *Moby Dick,* lies in a lagoon aptly called Whaler's Cove. *Open daily. Adults $3.50, children over 6 $1.75.*

8. Honolulu, Oahu, Hawaii

Stretched out between the fluted green slopes of the Koolau Range and the blue-green Pacific, Hawaii's capital city defies the saying that East and West never meet. In Honolulu Buddhist temples share a place with Christian churches, Chinese markets thrive along with ultramodern shopping centers, galleries display Polynesian crafts and Renaissance art. For most visitors, the East-West meeting place offers superb hotels, shops, restaurants and water sports—especially in the famous Waikiki area—which create a unique vacation place.

Aliiolani Hale *King and Mililani Sts.* Originally intended as a royal palace, the imposing structure, completed in 1874, became the home of government offices and the legislature. Here the Hawaiian monarchy was overthrown in 1893 and a provisional government founded. Today it is Hawaii's Judiciary Building. In front of it stands a statue of Kamehameha I, who united the warring islands into one kingdom. Panels on the base of the statue commemorate Captain Cook's discovery of the islands in 1778. *Open Mon.-Fri.*

[6] *Byodo-in, a replica of a 900-year-old Buddhist temple near Kyoto, Japan, was dedicated in 1968 to the memory of Hawaii's first Japanese immigrants. The original temple is considered the most beautiful building in the Kyoto area. The wings, raised on stilts, give the building a delightfully airy feeling.*

Bernice P. Bishop Museum

1355 Kalihi St., Honolulu, Hawaii

Princess Bernice Pauahi Bishop was the last direct descendant (a great-granddaughter) of Kamehameha the Great, the Hawaiian chief who unified the islands at the end of the 18th century. The treasures she inherited formed the nucleus of the memorial museum founded in 1889 by her husband, Charles Reed Bishop. The museum has grown from a single lava rock building into one of the world's great natural history museums with more than 10 million specimens. The collections of Pacific tropical flora, insects and land shells are outstanding. Among the most popular of the ethnographic and historical displays are the carved images of Hawaiian gods and the elaborate Hawaiian featherwork. *Open daily except Dec. 25. Adults $2.00.*

In the Monarchy Room feather-topped scepters stand guard by the throne of King Kalakaua, an elected monarch who ruled Hawaii from 1874 to 1891.

A real 55-foot sperm whale hangs in Hawaiian Hall, recalling the early 19th century when whaling made Hawaii prosperous. Exhibits on three levels trace Hawaiian history.

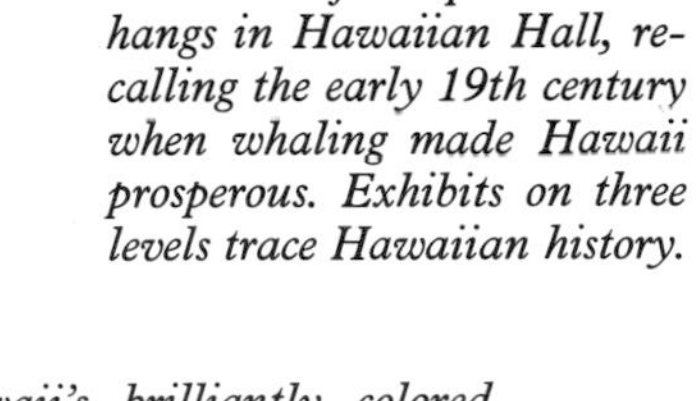

Hawaii's brilliantly colored birds supplied the feathers for these symbols of high office—a feather cloak and a feather helmet. Kukailimoku, the war god, appears as a feather-covered image.

First Church of Christ, Scientist *1508 Punahou St.* Set beneath tall monkeypod trees on stately lawns is an outstanding example of uniquely Hawaiian church architecture. Built in 1923 the church is a masterful blend of native volcanic rock and local wood fashioned into traditional church design. The spacious natural wood interior, topped by an open beam ceiling, is noted for its atmosphere of perfect serenity. *Open Sun., Wed.*

Honolulu Academy of Arts *900 S. Beretania St.* The layout of 25 galleries around a series of lovely courtyards studded with trees, walks and sculpture is almost as inviting as the art displayed inside. Outstanding among these works are paintings, sculpture, ceramics and decorative arts from Japan, China and Korea. But Western art is also featured in small but select collections that range from Mediterranean antiquities to American and European works of the past three centuries. *Open Tues.-Sun.*

Honpa Hongwanji Mission of Hawaii *1727 Pali Hwy.* The star attraction of the Buddhist temple is a superb statue of Buddha, an image of utmost grace and serenity. The lacquered and gold-leafed wooden statue enshrined in the temple's altar was carved in Japan around 800 years ago. It is believed to be the work of Hokyo Koun, a famed 12th-century sculptor of Buddha figures. *Open daily.*

Iolani Palace *King and Richards Sts.* The only royal palace in the U.S. was occupied by Hawaii's last monarchs, King Kalakaua and his successor Queen Liliuokalani. The large European-style building, completed in 1882, has two-story lanais on all four sides. After the monarchy was overthrown in 1893 the palace served for many years as the seat of government. Much of it was converted to offices and legislative chambers, but now the elegantly furnished throne room has been restored to its former grandeur. Most imposing are replicas of the two original gilded throne chairs flanked by towering feather *kahilis,* which stood as symbols of royalty. Also on the palace grounds are the Iolani Barracks, a picturesque coral block building that once housed the royal guard. *Palace open Mon.-Sat.*

Makiki Christian Church *829 Pensacola St.* A typical reflection of Hawaii's multinational heritage, the United Church of Christ offers services in both Japanese and English. The original portion of the church, built in 1932, is in the form of a Japanese castle. The lobby and nave are decorated with 164 painted panels: some depict flowers, fruits and vegetables; others illustrate Japanese proverbs. *Open daily.*

Queen Emma's Summer Palace *2913 Pali Hwy.* In summer, Queen Emma and King Kamehameha IV used to retire to this mountain retreat to enjoy a favorite pastime: gardening. The building is now a museum displaying furniture, clothing, jewelry and other royal family effects. Also on exhibit are Hawaiian artifacts such as weapons, stone implements, feather capes and leis and the feathered *kahilis* of royalty. *Open Mon.-Sat. Small charge.*

St. Andrew's Cathedral *Queen Emma Sq.* Ninety-one years elapsed between the laying of the cornerstone by King Kamehameha V and the completion in 1958 of this edifice, one of the oldest Episcopal cathedrals in the U.S. Basically French Gothic in style, the building's most impressive feature is its west window: about 50 feet high and 20 feet wide, the resplendent expanse of stained glass forms the church's entire facade and is one of the largest such windows ever built in this country. In front of the cathedral is a magnificent fountain with a heroic statue of St. Andrew preaching. *Open daily.*

Soto Mission of Hawaii *1708 Nuuanu Ave.* Gold flowers, an 800-year-old statue of Buddha and many rich accessories enhance the interior of the Soto Zen Buddhist temple. In this stunning setting, priests explain the beliefs and ceremonies of Buddhism. Erected in 1952, the building is modeled after a temple in India and is landscaped with a replica of Japan's Kyoto Gardens. *Open Mon.-Sat. except Jan. 1.*

University of Hawaii *E. of University Ave.* The only university within a 2000-mile radius, the Manoa campus spreads over about 300 acres of grounds, beautifully landscaped with hundreds of tropical plants. Some 24,000 students are enrolled annually.

EAST-WEST CENTER *1777 East-West Rd.* The center, in a complex of contemporary buildings, was established in 1960 to promote better understanding among the peoples of Asia, the Pacific area and the U.S. About 2000 students, mid-career professionals and senior scholars from some 40 countries and territories come here each year for study, research and career development. Symbolic of the center's goals are its scenic Japanese garden and the Thai pavilion, a gift from the King of Thailand. *Open daily.*

HAWAII HALL *2500 Campus Rd.* Completed in 1912 this first building on the campus reveals Hawaiian adaptations of neo-Georgian design. *Open Mon.-Fri.*

9. U.S.S. "Arizona" National Memorial *Pearl Harbor, Oahu, Hawaii* The U.S.S. *Arizona* was sunk during the Japanese attack on Pearl Harbor in 1941: the battleship took five direct hits with armor-piercing bombs. The bodies of most of the 1177 casualties are still trapped in the sunken hull. Spanning the broken

[8. *Honolulu Academy of Arts*] *The peaceful, rotund* Buddhist Altar Attendant, *the work of a 19th-century Korean sculptor, is an engaging example of the Oriental collection of the academy. The only general art museum in the central Pacific area, it is the cultural center of Hawaii. The founder, Mrs. Charles Montague Cooke, was a descendant of New England missionaries to Hawaii and an ardent art collector. The handsome building, designed by Bertram G. Goodhue Associates, has a high peaked roof, broad lanais or verandas and galleries that open onto interior garden courts.*

[8. *Iolani Palace*] *This brick building is the most interesting, both architecturally and historically, in Honolulu's Civic Center. King Kalakaua (1882-91) was a 33rd-degree Mason; the cornerstone was laid in 1879 with Masonic rites, and the first big social event was a banquet for 120 Masons. Queen Liliuokalani (1891-3) was held prisoner here in 1895 after her overthrow and her unsuccessful attempt to restore the monarchy.*

vessel is the memorial, a white concrete bridgelike structure, the names of the dead inscribed on the end wall. A museum displays the ship's 2000-pound bell, photos of the attack and commemorative plaques. The Navy provides boat service to the memorial. *Open Tues.-Sun. and Mon. holidays, closed other holidays.*

10. Lahaina Historic District *Rte. 30, Lahaina, Maui, Hawaii* During the 19th-century heyday of American whaling Lahaina was a thriving seaport. The city also served for a while as the capital of the kingdom of Hawaii. Several structures from this period and other historic properties have survived: the two-story white stucco home of Protestant medical missionary Dwight Baldwin, dating from the 1830s; Hale Pa'i, the missionaries' printing house at Lahainaluna; the seamen's cemetery and the U.S. Marine Hospital. *Open daily. Small charge for Baldwin Home.*

11. City of Refuge National Historical Park *Rte. 160, Honaunau, Hawaii* In the early 1800s Hawaiians maintained sacred places where vanquished warriors, refugees of island wars and people who broke taboos could find sanctuary. This site, on a six-acre lava shelf fronting the Pacific and bounded by a tremendous stone wall, is the only such refuge that has survived almost intact. Besides a reconstructed temple-mausoleum and other important relics of the refuge's past, visitors can see aspects of early Hawaiian life and ride an outrigger canoe on a coral lagoon. *Open daily.*

12. Painted Church *Off Rte. 160, Honaunau, Hawaii* Although its official name is St. Benedict's Catholic Church, the small white Gothic-style structure is best known for the paintings that adorn its interior and create an illusion of great space. Murals on the walls depict Biblical scenes, while columns are topped with palm fronds painted against a pale starry sky on the ceiling. Behind the altar, a trompe l'oeil painting suggests the apse of a cathedral with arches and columns receding in space. *Open daily.*

13. Hulihee Palace *Alii Dr., Kailua-Kona, Hawaii* Governor John Adams Kuakini built the two-story balconied structure in 1838 on the site of the first residence of King Kamehameha I. Now a museum, the palace contains collections of impressive Hawaiian artifacts: Hawaiian royal furniture, including a fourposter and a state dining table, personal effects of the kings, queens and chiefs, and a royal portrait gallery. *Open Mon.-Sat. Small charge.*

14. Kamuela Museum *Rtes. 250 and 270, Waimea, Hawaii* The history of the islands is reflected in the museum's wide-ranging exhibits of art objects and ancient artifacts. Furniture and other items from the homes of Hawaiian royalty tell of a vanished life-style. The years of conflict become apparent with the displays of military flags, guns and swords. Most telling is the collection of items brought to the islands by settlers from many different countries who arrived in the 19th century. *Open daily. Small charge.*

15. Kong's Floraleigh Gardens *1477 Kalanianaole Ave., Hilo, Hawaii* An ancient lava flow here spreads over two acres that were once thick with jungle growth. Now they are magnificently landscaped with orchids and other tropical plants. Throughout the gardens are small craters and caves, picturesque waterfalls, bridges and graceful pools covered with lilies. *Open daily. Small charge.*

16. Liliuokalani Gardens Park *25 Aupuni St., Hilo, Hawaii* The 25-acre oasis of artful nature is believed to be among the largest and most authentic Japanese gardens outside the Orient. The landscaped grounds are dotted with languid pools and laced with graceful paths and arched bridges. Scattered about are many *toros,* traditional Japanese stone lanterns, and small pagodas where strollers can rest and contemplate the scenery. In one corner of the garden is an authentic Japanese tea ceremony house. *Open daily.*

17. Lyman House Memorial Museum *276 Haili St., Hilo, Hawaii* The oldest home on the island was built in 1839 by Reverend and Mrs. David Belden Lyman, who came to Hawaii as missionaries seven years earlier. The comfortable frame home with its two-story lanai (veranda) is furnished as it was when the Lymans lived here. A large modern annex holds choice collections of island artifacts: a rare prehistoric Hawaiian stick god, fragile Polynesian feather leis, outstanding samples of kapa wood cloth and other interesting mementos of the past. *Open daily except holidays. Small charge.*

18. Carson Mansion *143 M St., Eureka, Calif.* The epitome of gaudy Victorian architecture, this 18-room house was completed in 1886 for lumber baron William Carson. Built of fir and redwood, the exterior is richly decorated with carved pillars, railings and gable cornices. A fancifully ornate tower rises over the front entrance, and several of the windows contain stained glass. The landmark building, now a private club, is set in attractively landscaped grounds.

19. Mendocino Presbyterian Church *44867 Main St., Mendocino, Calif.* A 90-foot bell tower dominates the English Gothic-style structure set high on a bluff above the Pacific. The handsome native redwood church was dedicated in 1868. The pealing of its first bell was overwhelmed by the noisy surf, so in 1870 a formidable successor was installed. It weighs 1000 pounds and is manually tolled from the front entry. Inside the church are the original kerosene lamps, the chandelier and a square grand piano built in 1850. *Open daily.*

20. Fort Ross State Historic Park *Rte. 1, 12 mi. N. of Jenner, Calif.* The restored structures were originally built in 1812 by Russian fur traders from Alaska on what was then Spanish land. Seal and sea otter pelts from the coast of California were sent to markets in China, Manchuria, Siberia and Europe until 1841, when Captain John Sutter purchased the fort. Surrounded by more than 350 acres, the complex includes a redwood stockade, blockhouses and the commander's house. *Open daily except Thanksgiving Day and Dec. 25.*

21. Silverado Museum *1347 Railroad Ave., St. Helena, Calif.* The largest collection of Robert Louis Stevenson memorabilia on public display is here in this handsome 1884 stone building. More than 3000 items are included, ranging from original manuscripts and rare first editions to portraits, Stevenson's writing desk and even locks of his hair. The site was chosen because Stevenson spent his honeymoon in an abandoned bunkhouse at nearby Silverado Mine, where he completed the first draft of *Silverado Squatters. Open Tues.-Sun. except holidays.*

22. Jack London State Historic Park *London Ranch Rd., W. of Glen Ellen, Calif.* The 40-acre park in the Valley of the Moon contains London's grave and the ruins of Wolf House, which burned in 1913, just a few weeks before the writer and his wife planned to move in. Objects associated with the author of *Call of the Wild* and *The Sea Wolf* are displayed in a large fieldstone house (now a museum), built by London's widow in 1919 as a memorial to her husband. Known as the House of the Happy Walls, it holds London's brass bed, his collection of South Seas artifacts and some of his work. *Open daily except holidays. Adults small charge.*

23. Sonoma State Historic Park *Sonoma, Calif.* In 1835 Mexican General Mariano Guadalupe Vallejo established what is today the town of Sonoma, then consisting of a few houses and a soldiers' barracks facing an eight-acre plaza. American revolt against Mexican rule began in 1846 when the Mexican flag flying over the plaza was pulled down and the California emblem, with a star and a grizzly bear, replaced it. Today the Bear Flag Monument there commemorates the event. Most of the original buildings are still intact, as is the mission church nearby.

MISSION SAN FRANCISCO SOLANO *Spain and E. First Sts.* Paintings of California's missions are on display here. Founded in 1823 this was the last of the Franciscan missions of upper California. The adobe structure has been restored and relics of its early history are now exhibited here. *Open daily except holidays. Adults small charge.*

SONOMA BARRACKS The balconied building was put up about 1837 to house the soldiers assigned to General Vallejo and the Sonoma garrison. After Mexican dominance ended, U.S. troops were quartered here. *Open daily except holidays.*

VALLEJO HOME *Spain and S. Third Sts.* General Vallejo moved here from his plaza residence. The redwood frame structure with dormer windows, a steep pitched roof and carved eaves, stands at the end of a long lane flanked by splendid trees. On the grounds is the Swiss Chalet, originally a storehouse, constructed of prefabricated timbers imported from Europe and bricks once used as ballast on sailing ships. It contains memorabilia of the Vallejo family and items from early Sonoma history. *Open daily except holidays. Adults small charge.*

[25] *This No. 61-California cable car is poised at the top of California Street on Nob Hill. The pagoda is in Chinatown. Such cars offer the easiest and most exciting way to see San Francisco's breathtaking views.*

24. Marin County Civic Center *San Rafael, Calif.* The impressive complex, rising from the ground like a Roman aqueduct, was planned by Frank Lloyd Wright and completed by his associates after his death in 1959. The first part of the complex, the Administration Building (completed in 1962), contains a central mall covered by a plastic skylight, which extends the entire length of the building and provides a setting for an indoor garden. Its interior features include continuous balconies with circular openings, reminiscent of the exterior's repetitive circular shapes. The Hall of Justice building follows through with the circular architectural theme with its round courtrooms. This design is reinforced by curved tables and curved rows of spectator seats. *Open Mon.-Fri. except holidays.*

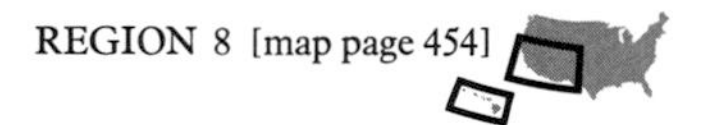

25. San Francisco, Calif.

Many people consider this cosmopolitan metropolis the most beautiful city in the U.S. Situated on a peninsula separating San Francisco Bay from the Pacific, it is blessed with a perpetually springlike climate. The city sprawls over nearly 50 square miles of rumpled hills bearing such evocative names as Nob, Russian and Telegraph. Since its founding in 1776 the city has undergone many changes, including those caused by disasters such as the earthquake and three-day fire of 1906 when some 28,000 buildings were destroyed. Today the city is a major cultural, financial and shipping center where glistening modern office buildings tower over Victorian structures and contrast with the distinctive architecture of the largest Chinatown in the western world.

Cable Car Barn *1200 Mason St.* Nearly every visitor rides at least once on one of San Francisco's 39 cable cars, which have been designated National Historic Landmarks. At the red brick car barn, built about 1886, tourists can find out how these delightful anachronisms operate: the system's 10½ miles of inch-and-a-quarter-thick steel cable endlessly reel in and out at a steady nine miles per hour. Here too is a small museum of cable car relics and the repair shop. The barn is gradually being restored to its original gaslight-era appearance. *Open daily.*

California Palace of the Legion of Honor *Lincoln Park* Although visitors might expect it to be some sort of hall of fame, this is really an art museum. The curious name arises from the fact that the grandiose French Neoclassic-style building is a replica of the Palace of the Legion of Honor in Paris. More than 40 bronze, plaster and marble sculptures by Rodin, including his famous *Thinker,* make up one of the finest Rodin collections in the U.S. Other displays include paintings from the 16th to the 20th centuries and an outstanding selection of graphics, along with porcelains, furniture, tapestries and other decorative arts. *Open daily.*

Cannery *2801 Leavenworth St.* In a remarkable architectural adaptation, the original brick Del Monte Fruit Cannery, which survived the 1906 earthquake and fire, has been transformed into an engaging complex of colorful shops, art galleries and restaurants. Visitors can stroll through a central walkway, cross bridges between two three-story buildings and enjoy fine views of the Bay area from several balconies. *Open daily.*

Chinatown *N.E. section of city* Broadway, Bush, Kearny and Stockton Streets form the borders of the 16 square blocks that hold the largest Chinese community outside Asia. Its main street is Grant Avenue, a colorful procession of intriguing tearooms, shops, temples, schools, theaters, nightclubs and groceries filled with exotic fare.

BUDDHA'S UNIVERSAL CHURCH *720 Washington St.* For 11 years volunteers of all races and faiths worked in their spare time to build the striking church. Finished in 1963, the results reward the astonishing labor of love. The altar in the gold-hued main chapel takes the form of a ship, the Buddhist vessel of truth; the altarpiece is a six-foot-high mosaic of Buddha. Two small chapels and a roof garden are other sanctuaries for quiet meditation. *Open 2nd and 4th Sun. of month.*

CHINESE HISTORICAL SOCIETY OF AMERICA MUSEUM *17 Adler Pl. off 1140 Grant Ave.* The museum of the only organization in the U.S. devoted to the history of the Chinese in America contains artifacts, documents and photographs that record the vital role played by the Chinese in California's pioneer days, including their contribution to the building of the first transcontinental railroad. Among the items here are clothing of early frontier workers, scales for weighing gold, an opium pipe, a fighting spear and a redwood sampan once used for fishing. *Open Tues.-Sun. except holidays.*

OLD ST. MARY'S CATHOLIC CHURCH *660 California St.* Constructed of New England bricks, Chinese granite and native redwood, the handsome Gothic-style church was dedicated in 1854. At the time it was the largest building in San Francisco and the largest church in California. Although it was gutted by the fire that followed the earthquake of 1906, it was soon restored to its former splendor and continues to serve as a treasured link with the city's turbulent past. *Open daily.*

PORTSMOUTH SQUARE *Kearny, Clay and Washington Sts.* In the mid-1830s, when San Francisco was a tiny settlement known as Yerba Buena, it centered around this historic square. Here were the marketplace, the custom house that also served as a fledgling municipal building, and the first rude house—a tent made of a ship's sail and supported by redwood pillars.

Civic Center This complex of government buildings occupies an area of seven square blocks near downtown San Francisco. The center is landscaped with small flower gardens and scattered plantings.

[**25.** *California Palace of the Legion of Honor*] *The decorative arts of 18th-century France are well represented in this Louis XVI salon. These were cabinetry's golden days: the more ornate a piece, the better the Court liked it.*

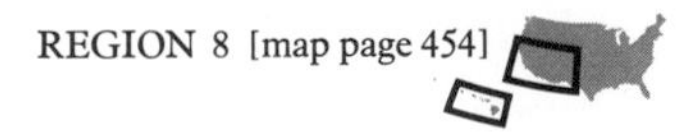

CITY HALL City Hall was the first building erected in the Civic Center. Completed in 1915, it is a grand French Renaissance-style structure faced in California granite, and topped by a 300-foot-high copper dome. Interior walls are finished in Manchurian oak and Indiana sandstone, and the floors are covered with three acres of inlaid marble. Reproductions from the city archives are sold on the main floor. *Open Mon.-Fri. except holidays.*

HEALTH CENTER *1490 Mason St.* Located above the east end of the Broadway Tunnel, the center serves the Chinatown community. Its chief decorative feature on the exterior is a huge sculptured Chinese dragon. The center was designed by architect Clarence Mayhew. The sculpture is the work of Pattie Bowler. *Open daily.*

OPERA HOUSE One of the two War Memorial Buildings, the Opera House is a French Renaissance-style structure completed in 1932. It is constructed of California granite and terra cotta, with a main facade 231 feet wide. The theater has a seating capacity of 3285. The main lighting fixture, suspended over the center of the orchestra section, is 27 feet in diameter and is composed of a series of metallic rays which give the effect of an illuminated star. *Open during performances.*

PUBLIC LIBRARY The library is known for its outstanding Special Collections Department. Included are collections of historical materials relating to San Francisco and California; the Richard Harrison collection of calligraphy and lettering; the Schmulowitz collection of wit and humor, comprising 16,000 items in 35 languages; and the development of the book, containing about 1600 items. *Open Mon.-Sat. except holidays.*

Coit Memorial Tower *Telegraph Hill* A superb panorama of the city and bay can be seen from the top of this tower on the crest of the hill. The glass-enclosed observation gallery, reached by elevator, is 540 feet above the waters of the bay. Built with funds left to the city in 1929 by Lillie H. Coit, the tower honors San Francisco's volunteer firemen of the 1850s and 1860s. As a young girl, Lillie Coit was made an honorary member of one of the volunteer companies. *Open daily.*

Embarcadero Center *Market, Sacramento and Clay Sts.* A prototype of expert urban planning, the five-block complex replaces an old waterfront area with a mix of commercial and cultural buildings. When the project is complete four office towers will counterpoint an array of shops, galleries and restaurants. Broad pedestrian malls, landscaped and raised above the streets, link the various buildings with the Golden Gateway Center, a neighboring development of office buildings and residential town houses, and invite leisurely strolling in the area.

Ghirardelli Square *900 N. Point St.* From its original quarters in an old woolen mill where uniforms were manufactured during the Civil War, Domingo Ghirardelli's chocolate manufacturing business eventually grew to a two-and-a-half-acre complex of handsome crenellated brick buildings. In the 1960s the business was sold and the chocolate factory closed down. Fearing the buildings would be razed, a group of citizens purchased the property and refurbished it in a remarkably successful team effort of urban preservation. Now it is a delightful, multilevel complex of landscaped plazas, restaurants, art galleries and shops. *Open daily.*

Golden Gate Bridge *Doyle Dr. and Golden Gate Strait* The city's most famous landmark, connecting it with Marin County, is one of the longest single-span suspension bridges ever built. With sidewalks for pedestrians and bicycles, its total length is 8981 feet, while the main span between the two 746-foot-high towers is 4200 feet long. The supremely graceful structure was completed in 1937 and has been a major source of civic pride ever since. *Small toll for southbound cars.*

Golden Gate Park *N.W. section of city* More than 1000 city acres are generously set aside here for recreation. There are outdoor attractions—wooded trails to walk, an arboretum, botanical gardens and lakes to

[*Golden Gate Bridge*] *On May 27, 1937, when the bridge was completed, some 200,000 people celebrated the event by walking the mile-long distance between San Francisco and Marin County. The next day the bridge was opened to vehicles. With its sweeping lines and superb natural setting, it tops most bridge buffs' list.*

[Ghirardelli Square] The big Ghirardelli sign welcomed ships into San Francisco Bay for decades, until World War II doused its lights. Now it glows again over Ghirardelli Square, yet another jewel in San Francisco's crown. This view is over the waters of the Bay past the steps of Aquatic Park. The towers of Russian Hill rise behind the lights of the shops and restaurants.

admire, fields for archery and ball playing—as well as galleries and museums to explore.

CALIFORNIA ACADEMY OF SCIENCES Anyone interested in natural history will find rich rewards in the many features of the complex. Rare minerals and fossils, exotic birds and mammals can be studied. An aquarium stars sea creatures from every corner of the world, and a planetarium features daily astronomical shows. *Open daily. Small charge.*

CONSERVATORY About 100 years ago the domed glass house with its choice plants welcomed its first visitors. The conservatory's earliest bulbs and plants came from London and were shipped cross-country by the Wells Fargo Express: when an exotic royal water lily bloomed, it was a much-heralded civic event. Following that early tradition, sightseers still come to gaze at the lush tropical plants and the ever-changing floral displays. *Open daily.*

JAPANESE TEA GARDEN Begun in 1894, the authentic Oriental landscape is a Shangri-la of serene walks, pools, bridges and pagodas artfully arranged among ornamental shrubs and lovely trees. Outstanding sights are the cherry blossom trees—especially in springtime bloom—the venerable Monterey pines and the dwarf bonsai-type trees. *Open daily.*

M. H. DE YOUNG MEMORIAL MUSEUM The largest and oldest municipal museum in the West was founded in 1895. It displays a full range of fine arts from around the world, including a good sampling of works by old masters. A prime attraction is the Center of Asian Art and Culture in the Avery Brundage Wing. Featured here are nearly 6000 works of Oriental art, collected by the former president of the International Olympic Committee, including one of the world's largest and best assemblages of jade carvings. *Open daily.*

Grace Cathedral *1051 Taylor St.* The third largest Episcopal cathedral in the U.S. was finally completed in 1964, 36 years after construction began. Although it is traditional French Gothic in style, the building, made of reinforced concrete to withstand possible earthquake damage, successfully combines many modern furnishings with ancient works of art. The most notable features are more than 60 brilliant stained-glass windows. The oldest are traditional in design, while two newer series are contemporary—and truly spectacular in concept and execution. *Open daily.*

Jackson Square *Jackson and Montgomery Sts.* The daring undertaking of a few home-furnishings wholesalers in 1951 spurred the preservation of the historic city enclave. They bought several rundown buildings here, restored their Federal-style brick facades and elegantly refurbished the interiors. Encouraged by this imaginative move, other design and decorative professionals remodeled other houses; retail dealers followed to open stores selling fine furnishings. It is fitting that once again the area is a business hub: it used to be the commercial center of the gold-rush boom, offices frenetically serving struck-rich miners and Wells Fargo coaches. For visitors, the streets offer sightseeing bounties: splendid window shopping, proud buildings of the 1850s and 1860s, and alleyways like Hotaling Place—still outfitted with hitching posts—that retain the charm of a bygone era.

Palace of Fine Arts *Marina Blvd. and Lyon St.* The original Palace of Fine Arts was built in 1915 as a temporary structure for the San Francisco International Exposition, which celebrated the opening of the Panama Canal. The architect, Bernard Maybeck, wished to convey "the sad, minor note of old Roman ruins covered with bushes and trees." His "palace," of plaster and chicken wire, was a huge success, and with its romantic lagoon setting and elegant design it inspired generations of San Franciscans. Finally, when total ruin threatened the building, the city passed a bond issue to finance a complete reconstruction. The new Palace, finished in 1967, is a remarkable facsimile; built of concrete, unlike the old, it will last. The rotunda has been transformed into a science Exploratorium, where visitors can explore the gyroscope, lasers, optical illusions and other wonders. *Grounds open daily; Exploratorium open Wed.-Sun.*

St. Mary's Cathedral *Geary and Gough Sts.* St. Mary's is a modern (1970) poured concrete building which expresses the wonder and majesty of Renaissance cathedrals. The ceiling is divided by stained-glass windows, each six feet wide, which form a multicolored cross that extends 139 feet down the walls. In the center of the column-free interior which seats 2400 is a baldachino made of thousands of aluminum rods held together by gold-plated wires. The exterior of the church is faced with Italian travertine marble. *Open daily.*

San Francisco Maritime Museum *Foot of Polk St.* Standing right on the waterfront is a more or less ship-shaped building with rounded ends, porthole windows and recessed upper stories, the "decks" of which are bound by ship rails. Inside, the city's maritime heritage is vividly portrayed with scale models of ships, old figureheads, anchors, historic photographs and other maritime relics. But the museum's choicest displays of living history are moored at nearby Fisherman's Wharf:

the *Balclutha,* a square-rigged merchant ship dating from 1886, and the paddle-wheel tug *Eppleton Hall,* built in 1914. *Open daily. Ships: adults $1.50, children small charge.*

San Francisco Maritime State Historic Park *2905 Hyde St.* The floating museum consists of four refurbished historic ships moored to a pier near famed Fisherman's Wharf. All are distinctive craft developed for special types of West Coast shipping: a double-end, paddle-wheel ferry steamer that once carried passengers across the bay; a flat-bottomed sailing-scow schooner used for carrying hay and other bulky cargoes; a sleek, three-masted lumber schooner; and a wooden steam-powered schooner used for transporting both lumber and passengers. *Open daily. Small charge.*

San Francisco Zoological Gardens *Zoo Rd. and Skyline Blvd.* More than 1200 mammals and birds are housed in this 95-acre zoo, which was the first one to display an entire gorilla family and the first in the U.S. in which musk-oxen have been raised. The collections include many rare specimens such as black rhinoceroses, white rhinoceroses, pygmy hippopotamuses, snow leopards and trumpeter swans. Areas of special interest are the great ape grottoes, bear grottoes, monkey island and a tropical walk-through aviary. Storyland and Zoocus are of special interest to children, who may feed and pet small animals at the Children's Zoo. *Open daily. Small charge.*

Temple Emanu-El *Arguello Blvd. and Lake St.* A towering archway announces the entrance to this temple of Levantine design and gives way to a courtyard surrounded by colonnaded porches. Bronze and glass doors open into the temple vestibule where marble columns and bronze lamps stand beneath a vaulted ceiling. Highlights of the spacious main sanctuary are a lower pulpit for preaching, an elaborate canopied upper pulpit for reading from the sacred scrolls and the venerable Ark, a bronze container encrusted with richly decorative enamel work. *Open daily.*

26. Benicia Capitol State Historic Park *First and G Sts., Benicia, Calif.* In 1853 the availability of marriageable young ladies in Benicia is said to have lured the state legislature into accepting the two-story brick Greek Revival building as the seat of California government. Modeled after Virginia's statehouse, it features six interior columns made from ship masts of New England cedar. After serving its intended purpose for one year, it was later used for church services and as a city hall. It has been restored and furnished in mid-19th-century style. *Open daily except holidays. Adults small charge.*

27. John Muir National Historic Site *4203 Alhambra Ave., Martinez, Calif.* John Muir—explorer, naturalist, conservationist and "The Father of the National Parks"—lived here from 1890 to 1914. The 17-room frame house, built in 1882, holds Victorian furnishings, Muir memorabilia and copies of his historic works. The second-floor library contains the flat-topped desk on which he wrote most of his books and articles. At the Visitor Center audio-visual shows recount Muir's life and philosophy. Also on the grounds is an 1849 adobe ranch house surrounded by vineyards and orchards. *Open daily except holidays. Small charge.*

28. First Church of Christ, Scientist *2619 Dwight Way, Berkeley, Calif.* Architect Bernard Maybeck, a pioneer in designing buildings crafted of natural materials, created the 1910 church with an entryway of imaginative colonnades and trellises. Gothic motifs are apparent, but the use of exposed concrete, rough glass and sculptured pine and redwood beams reflect the innovative artistry of an American design master. The splendid interior is illuminated by handmade fixtures which shed a mellow light on the carved panels, trusswork arches and pews. *Open Sun., Wed.*

29. University of California *Berkeley, Calif.* The campus spreads over 720 acres, between Hearst Street and Bancroft Way. Many of the buildings are made of white granite with red tile roofs. This style of architecture, plus Berkeley's luxuriant vegetation and hilly setting on San Francisco Bay, gives the university the air, in places, of a Mediterranean village. This is one of the world's largest and most prestigious universities, unu-

[28] *The plants around the windows were carefully chosen so that the outline of the foliage would enhance the interior. Such concern with plants seems especially suitable for the masterpiece of the man who is said to have suggested that all the sidewalks be painted green to make the town look more rural. Leaving the rough natural materials exposed, Maybeck managed to give the interior a rich medieval effect intensified by the mellow lighting.*

sual in that it is both intellectually stimulating and visually beautiful. The atmosphere of excitement and ferment comes through even to the casual visitor.

BOTANICAL GARDEN More than 15,000 different plant species are grown on the 25-acre site in Strawberry Canyon. Among the attractions is the world's most complete array (5000 species) of cacti and succulents. Eight acres are used for plants native to the state, and several of California's unique plant communities—such as the northern Pygmy Forest—are duplicated. Rhododendrons, irises and magnolias share the scene with exotic African shrubs and South American flowers. The Indian Nature Trail, lined with plants once used for food, is especially popular. *Open daily except Dec. 25.*

LOWIE MUSEUM OF ANTHROPOLOGY The museum, located in Kroebler Hall, specializes in archaeology, human biology and ethnology, with particular emphasis on ancient Egyptian, African and American Indian objects. *Open daily. Small charge.*

UNIVERSITY ART MUSEUM The world's largest university art museum features nine angular galleries connected by balconies and ramps extending from a central gallery. In addition to superb collections that range from Oriental art objects and old masters through European and American works of the 20th century, there are 45 paintings by abstractionist Hans Hofmann—the nation's largest collection of this artist's work. *Open daily.*

30. Lakeside Park Garden Center *666 Bellevue Ave., Oakland, Calif.* Traditional Buddhist and Shintoist symbolism is employed in the arrangement of the authentic Japanese garden. It features elaborate displays of stone lanterns, pebble-fringed pools glittering with fish and quiet corners studded with sculpturelike rocks. Among the many varieties of flowers and shrubs are a full acre of dahlias and a garden spangled with 200 kinds of chrysanthemums. *Open daily except holidays.*

31. Oakland Mormon Temple *4770 Lincoln Ave., Oakland, Calif.* Commandingly set on a hill overlooking San Francisco Bay, the massive temple appears as a Shangri-la vision with its shining white walls and golden spires. The building, dedicated in 1964, is illuminated at night and visible for many miles. Its extravagantly landscaped grounds feature rows of palm trees, flower gardens and ornamental fountains and pools. Guides at the Visitor Center tell the story of the church and its activities. The temple itself is open only to Mormons in good standing. *Visitor Center open daily.*

32. Oakland Museum *1000 Oak St., Oakland, Calif.* The history, culture and natural sciences of California are depicted in the exhibits here. The museum contains a large collection of paintings, sculpture, photography and crafts by California artists and reflecting on California themes. Permanent exhibition features include California life-styles, the state's distinctive ecological regions and a multimedia center. *Open Tues.-Sun. except holidays.*

33. Casa Peralta *384 W. Estudillo Ave., San Leandro, Calif.* The Peralta ancestral villa in Spain served as a model for the luxurious home built at the turn of the century. An imposing white wall with Spanish motifs surrounds the grounds; inside it is faced with tiled

[**34.** *Stanford Memorial Church*] *Architect Clinton Day designed a heavy-walled Romanesque church with rounded arches. The Venetian mosaic, in 15th-century Byzantine style, portrays The Sermon on the Mount.*

scenes from *Don Quixote.* Spanish artisans fashioned the many beautiful architectural features which include columns, mosaics, tilework and ironwork. It is furnished with lovely period pieces and displays many historical items relating to San Leandro. *Open Sat., Sun.*

34. Stanford University *Palo Alto, Calif.* In 1885 Senator and Mrs. Leland Stanford set aside an estate of 8800 acres and established this institution as a memorial to their son—its formal name is Leland Stanford Junior University. The main buildings, in the style of the Spanish missions, are made of warm-toned sandstone with red tile roofs. This liberal arts university has long had an excellent academic reputation.

HOOVER INSTITUTION ON WAR, REVOLUTION AND PEACE This is one of the world's largest repositories of books, papers and other documents relating to world conflicts and to the political, social and economic changes of the 20th century. It also contains one of the country's best Oriental research libraries. The institution was founded by Herbert Hoover in 1919, and memorabilia of the 31st President fill special rooms. The Hoover Tower affords sky-high views of the Stanford campus. *Open daily except holidays.*

STANFORD MEMORIAL CHURCH Superb Venetian mosaics are the church's most striking feature. A splendid portrayal of *The Sermon on the Mount* covers the entire facade of the Romanesque structure. Other mosaics on the interior include reproductions of Michelangelo's *Prophets* and Cosimo Rosselli's *Last Supper.* New Testament themes are brilliantly highlighted in the more than 50 stained-glass windows. *Open daily.*

STANFORD MUSEUM Founded by Senator and Mrs. Leland Stanford in 1891 as a memorial to their son, the museum has been growing ever since. Its collections now range from Pre-Columbian American art and ancient Roman coins to contemporary prints and drawings. Besides European painting and sculpture from the Renaissance to the present, there are an outstanding Oriental

[35] *The Rosicrucian Administration Building is patterned after an Egyptian mortuary temple on the banks of the Nile. The huge, pylon-faced structure is flanked by statues of Horus, the hawk-headed god of the sun.*

collection (including many jade carvings), a famous collection of Cypriot antiquities and examples of Melanesian art. *Open Tues.-Sun.*

35. Rosicrucian Egyptian Museum *Park Ave., San Jose, Calif.* An authentic reproduction of a 12th dynasty tomb (about 2000 B.C.) is on display in this copy of an Egyptian temple. The only one of its kind in the U.S., the museum exhibits mummies, sarcophagi and other interesting objects. There are displays of Egyptian, Assyrian and Babylonian antiquities: jewelry, textiles, ancient scrolls, clay tablets, metal utensils, and statuary and figurines of gods and pharaohs. Dioramas depict the life-style of ancient Egyptians. *Open daily.*

36. Winchester Mystery House *525 S. Winchester Blvd., San Jose, Calif.* A crew of carpenters worked night and day, seven days a week, for 38 years to build the bizarre house. Sarah Winchester, heiress to the Winchester Arms fortune, lived in fear of haunting spirits and when a spiritualist told her that the sound of workmen's hammers would keep antagonistic ghosts away, she set about building a home whose construction would virtually go on forever. The house had nine rooms when she bought it, 160 when she died in 1922. It contains 2000 doors, about 10,000 windows, 47 fireplaces, 50 staircases—one leading nowhere—and one intriguing secret passage. *Open daily except Dec. 25. Adults $2.50, children small charge.*

37. De Saisset Art Gallery and Museum *University of Santa Clara, Santa Clara, Calif.* The permanent collection is comprised of paintings, sculpture, graphics, photography, videotapes, porcelains, crystals, ivories, tapestries and antique furnishings. One gallery displays rare artwork, manuscripts and artifacts from the California mission period. Monthly exhibitions are also featured. *Open Tues.-Sun. Sept.-July.*

38. Triton Museum of Art *1505 Warburton Ave., Santa Clara, Calif.* The paintings of Theodore Wores, including many Santa Clara Valley scenes, are featured here. Other collections include 19th-century marble sculpture, and 19th-century English and American paintings. The four octagon-shaped museum buildings, a blend of Spanish and Oriental architecture, are set in a sculpture garden. *Open Tues.-Sun.*

39. Old Mission *Old Plaza, San Juan Bautista, Calif.* Mission San Juan Bautista, dating from 1797, is the largest of California's 21 mission churches and the only one with three aisles. Its baptismal font is of hand-carved native sandstone. Original decorations still color the thick adobe walls, and there is a vividly painted carved wood statue of St. John the Baptist. The museum exhibits church vestments and other relics of early California missions. On the grounds are a flower-lined patio and a cemetery with graves of more than 4300 Indians. *Open daily.*

40. San Juan Bautista State Historic Park *Old Plaza, San Juan Bautista, Calif.* In the 1830s, under Spanish rule, San Juan Bautista became the judicial and administrative headquarters of Alta California, the Spanish name for the southern and central sections of the present state of California. The buildings facing the plaza erected during that period include a hotel, residences, stables, a blacksmith shop and a granary. *Open daily except holidays. Small charge.*

CASTRO HOUSE Jose Maria Castro, prefect of the district and later commanding general of Spanish military forces in California, built this adobe house in 1840-1 to serve as his headquarters. It is furnished in the style of the 1870s. In a back garden are a lovely pepper tree older than the house and huge cast-iron cauldrons used in the hide-and-tallow industry.

PLAZA HOTEL In 1858 Angelo Zanetta purchased a one-story adobe structure facing the plaza and added a wooden second story, a balcony and several bedrooms. It has been restored to the way it looked in the 1870s when it was a popular stage stop.

ZANETTA HOUSE The house was named for Angelo Zanetta, its owner, who built it about 1868, using the adobe bricks from an old dormitory for unmarried Indian women. The first floor served as the Zanetta family residence; the second, which rests on solid redwood beams, was used for dances, shows and public meetings. Furnishings reflect the fashions of 100 years ago.

41. California's First Theatre *Scott and Pacific Sts., Monterey, Calif.* The former lodging house and barroom became the state's first theater in 1848 when a show was presented by minstrels Tips, Tops and Taps and four Army volunteers. To accommodate this entertainment, rough benches, candles and lamps and a stage were installed. The building retains many of its original features, along with theatrical memorabilia. Weekly shows are presented by the Troupers of the Gold Coast. *Open Tues.-Sun. Small charge.*

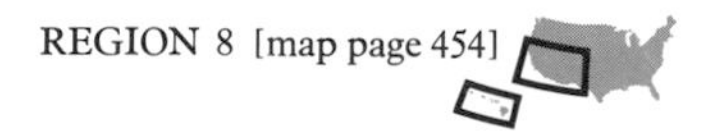

42. Old Custom House *1 Custom House Plaza, Monterey, Calif.* The flags of three countries—Spain, Mexico and the U.S.—have flown over this building, the oldest government building west of the Rockies. The two-story adobe structure was begun by the Spanish in 1814. It stands at the point on the coast where Commodore John Drake Sloat landed in 1846 and first raised the American flag in California. The Old Custom House has now been restored to its 1840s appearance, complete with bales, boxes and other freight as if ready for inspection. Tools, furniture, china, wine and cigars are among the items displayed. *Open daily.*

43. Robert Louis Stevenson House *530 Houston St., Monterey, Calif.* Stevenson was a tenant here in the fall of 1879 while visiting his soon-to-be-wife, Mrs. Fanny Van de Grift Osbourne. Now a memorial to the great author the two-story adobe house, built in the 1830s, contains many of his personal effects, diaries, scrapbooks, manuscripts and first editions. The Stevenson family also donated some of his furniture, including a 14-foot mahogany dining table over 150 years old. *Open daily except holidays. Adults small charge.*

44. Mission San Carlos Borromeo del Rio Carmelo *3080 Rio Rd., Carmel, Calif.* Dedicated in 1797, the beautiful restored sandstone church was established as a mission in 1770 by Father Junipero Serra, the famous Franciscan missionary, whose tomb lies under the stone sanctuary floor. Indian converts cut and hauled the stones for the walls, which curve toward a graceful arched ceiling. Inside are original Indian wall decorations, a statue of Our Lady of Bethlehem brought from Mexico in 1769 and original paintings and candlesticks. Declared a minor basilica in 1960 by Pope John XXIII, the church has a Moorish-type bell tower and a simple arched entry crowned by a star window. In the monastery is a memorial to Serra and other early Franciscans. *Open daily except Thanksgiving Day and Dec. 25.*

45. Mission San Antonio *Off Rte. 101, Jolon, Calif.* The large adobe compound, with its long arcaded cloisters and red tile roofs, has stood here since 1773 and is still operated by Franciscan friars. In addition to the rebuilt convent and workshops, there are replicas of an old gristmill and a wine press. A restored 1813 chapel is graced with three arched doorways surmounted by bell towers. Missals, vestments and other mission possessions are on view, along with Indian baskets, silver jewelry, sculptures and paintings. *Open daily.*

46. Mission San Miguel Archangel *801 Mission St., San Miguel, Calif.* This mission is noted for the well-preserved condition of its original decorations, including the interior frescos by Esteban Munras and his Indian helpers. The equally well-preserved wall pulpit is brightly painted in several colors, and three statues are set in panels behind the altar. Of interest is the mission's corridor—composed of arches in a variety of shapes and sizes. Paintings, Indian tools and mission artifacts are on display. *Open daily.*

47. Hearst San Simeon State Historical Monument *Rte. 1, San Simeon, Calif.* See feature display on pages 468–71.

48. Mission San Luis Obispo de Tolosa *Chorro and Monterey Sts., San Luis Obispo, Calif.* The fifth in the chain of missions founded by Father Junipero Serra, it dates from 1772. The mission church contains remarkable original statues and old paintings depicting the Stations of the Cross. The mission museum exhibits relics of the period, including early handmade vestments and a collection of Chumash Indian artifacts. In the garden are trees from California's first olive grove. *Open daily except holidays.*

49. La Purisima Mission State Historic Park *N.E. of Lompoc, Calif.* Years of painstaking work have gone into the restoration of the large 1812 mission. Buildings include the church, the padre's residence and the guardhouse in the Shops and Quarters Building. Ten structures are carefully furnished in period style and a museum holds a collection of valuable mission objects. The enormous park features a five-acre garden and a corral complete with burros and sheep. Trails are available for hiking and horseback riding. *Open daily except holidays. Adults small charge for museum.*

50. Old Mission Santa Ines *1760 Mission Dr., Solvang, Calif.* An 18th-century Mexican polychrome wood carving of St. Agnes ("Ines" in Spanish) stands in a niche above the altar in the 1804 mission church, which is elaborately decorated with other carvings, paintings and religious objects of the period. These include paintings of the Stations of the Cross—crude copies of 18th-century Italian woodcuts—a painting of St. Francis and a hand-carved confessional. A museum holds vestments and other interesting mission relics. *Open daily except Thanksgiving Day and Dec. 25. Small charge.*

[44] *A visitor who spends an hour or so wandering on the grounds of the Mission San Carlos at Carmel cannot help but feel a sense of tranquillity. Olive and pepper trees spice the air, water splashes in the patio fountain, doves coo in the bell tower. The simple days of the past, when Franciscan friars and Indian converts labored together to build the mission, are again recalled.*

47. Hearst San Simeon State Historical Monument

Rte. 1, San Simeon, Calif.

Rising above a 1600-foot hill overlooking the Pacific Ocean are the white twin towers of an extravagant monument to a prodigal man. William Randolph Hearst was "The Chief" of a publishing empire founded in 1887 at the age of 23 when his father gave him the San Francisco *Examiner.* He was the only son of George Hearst, who had made a fortune in mining, and Phoebe Apperson Hearst, whose interest in art became in her son a mania for collecting. His taste ran to the ornate, Baroque and medieval. Spending between $1,000,000 and $4,000,000 a year, Hearst filled warehouses with paintings, sculpture, tapestries, ceilings, fireplaces, choir stalls. He acquired whole rooms from European castles and even had the stones of an entire Spanish monastery packed away. He developed a great desire to build a palace to display his treasures. San Simeon, begun in 1919, was his favorite project because it was unending. In fact it was never finished, though he lived there for nearly 30 years. The architect, Julia Morgan, a friend of Hearst's mother, had a formidable task: to design the buildings around the collection. Each of the 100 rooms in the main house, La Casa Grande, had to be separately drafted without an overall floor plan. In some cases the walls were erected after massive pieces of furniture had been installed in a planned room. The resultant grandiose hodgepodge was a luxuriously livable museum, especially strong in tapestries and madonnas. Hearst also collected animals and had the country's largest private zoo on his hill. *Open daily except Thanksgiving Day and Dec. 25. Tours: adults $3.00 and $4.00, children 6–12 $1.50 and $2.00.*

Each of La Casa Grande's Hispano-Moresque towers has a belfry with 18 carillon bells and a bedroom. The two bedrooms are known as the Celestial Suite.

George and Phoebe Hearst called this part of their enormous ranch (it stretched along 50 miles of coastline) Camp Hill and brought their son to it for picnics. He called it La Cuesta Encantada, "The Enchanted Hill," and his money created a spell. The barren soil of the rocky hilltop bloomed with gardens as well as buildings. Rich topsoil was laid and water piped in. Keeping the few native oak trees, Hearst had other trees transported to the hill. Special soil was mixed for special plants, solid rock blasted, retaining walls built, until 123 acres were terraced and set with exotic plants and statuary. The gardens are noted for the variety of beautiful roses.

Mountain vistas provide a backdrop to the classic Greco-Roman temple facade and Etruscan-style colonnades that frame the sparkling waters of the Neptune Pool where several of the statues of Carrara marble seem to float. Ten feet deep and 104 feet long, the pool was a favorite gathering place for guests and was illuminated at night.

Julia Morgan must be given full credit for the splendid medieval effect of the refectory, whose fittings range from the 15th to the 19th centuries. Much of the room, such as the ceiling, the choir stalls and the tables, came from monasteries and churches. Forty guests could dine at the long tables where, standing incongruously among the baronial magnificence and heavy silver, were bottles of catsup and other condiments. Hearst liked these sentimental reminders of the days when he picnicked on the site of San Simeon with his parents and later with his wife and children. Guests were given a menu which included the name of the film to be shown later in the theater.

47. **Hearst San Simeon State Historical Monument** *(continued)*

Ornate gilded Renaissance columns flank the main entrance to the Assembly Room, largest in La Casa Grande. Its size was dictated by the 84-foot-long ceiling carved in the 1500s for an Italian palazzo. The walls are lined with choir stalls and hung with Flemish tapestries, one attributed to Rubens. The teak floors are covered with valuable Persian rugs. Overstuffed sofas and chairs in which Hearst's guests relaxed with their predinner cocktails provide the only contemporary note in the room.

Hearst kept in touch with his enterprises by telephones all over the grounds, but he really worked in the Gothic Study where even the lampshades, made from the pages of Gregorian chant books, maintain the medieval theme. Only a favored few ever saw this study or the unique barrel-vaulted ceiling of the Gothic Suite's sitting room.

The three guest houses, with a total of 47 rooms, were finished before La Casa Grande was begun. The guest rooms of Casa del Mar overlook the Pacific, and Casa del Sol has a fine view of the setting sun. The view of the Santa Lucia Mountains gave the second and smallest guest house its name, Casa del Monte. One of its four bedrooms contains the Cardinal Richelieu bed. Carved of heavy black walnut from Lombardy, the imposing 17th-century bed has signs of high church rank and royal connection on the headboard.

Craftsmen brought from Italy installed the mosaic tiles, glittering with real gold, of the indoor Roman Pool. The statues are copies of classical Greek and Roman works.

Like many of the furnishings of the opulent Doge's Suite, The Portrait of a Gentleman *in the sitting room is Venetian, painted during the 16th century.*

Lining the walls above the bookcases in the main library (pictured at left) is one of the world's finest collections of Greek and Etruscan vases.

51. Mission Santa Barbara *E. Los Olivos and Upper Laguna Sts., Santa Barbara, Calif.* Founded in 1786 by the successor to Junipero Serra, the Santa Barbara Mission is one of the most beautiful of all California missions. The present twin-towered, tile-roofed church was finished in 1820. Parts of the monastery were built earlier. On display are religious vestments, living quarters furnished in period style and an altar built by the Indians soon after the mission was founded. Indian artifacts and crafts, tools, historic relics and interesting examples of Mexican art of the 18th and 19th centuries can also be seen. On the grounds are a Moorish fountain built in 1808 and the Indian cemetery. *Open daily. Adults small charge.*

52. Santa Barbara Botanic Gardens *1212 Mission Canyon Rd., Santa Barbara, Calif.* The grounds here invite visitors to quiet strolls in a splendid mountain-backed canyon setting. Seventy acres and five miles of meandering trails cover a variety of California's habitats, each with its distinctive trees, shrubs and flowers. Areas are devoted to desert plants and meadow flowers, arroyo ferns and chaparral plants. A woodland section features oaks and pines; redwoods flourish along the garden's Mission Creek. The Old Mission Dam, built in 1806, is also located on the grounds. *Open daily.*

53. Santa Barbara Museum of Natural History *2559 Puesta del Sol Rd., Santa Barbara, Calif.* The extensive egg collection of William Leon Dawson, author of the four-volume *Birds of California,* was the nucleus of this museum. It has since branched out to include collections of much of the flora and fauna of southern California. Displays feature marine life, geology and paleontology, minerals, insects and California Indian artifacts. An arcaded central patio filled with trees and shrubs adds to the visitor's enjoyment. *Open daily except Dec. 25.*

54. San Buenaventure Mission *211 E. Main St., Ventura, Calif.* Dating from 1782, this was the last of the nine missions founded by Father Junipero Serra. The present church building was completed in 1809. The walls, almost seven feet thick, are constructed of adobe, stone and tile. The rafters and baptismal font are original, but the carved wooden doors are replicas. Original Indian paintings are at the entrance to the baptistry. Over the main altar is a statue of St. Bonaventure, patron saint of the mission. The center crucifix is of Spanish design and is believed to be about 400 years old. *Open daily.*

MISSION MUSEUM Wooden bells, the only ones used in the California missions, are on display in the museum. Other exhibits include the original church doors, baptism and death records written and signed by Father Serra and an exquisitely hand-carved confessional made by anonymous Indian artisans. *Open daily.*

55. Leonis Adobe *23537 Calabasas Rd., Calabasas, Calif.* A Basque sheep rancher, known as "The King of Calabasas" because of his enormous land holdings, once lived in the dwelling with his Indian wife. Begun in the 1840s and later modified, it boasts twin galleries on its entrance facade, the upper one decorated with an ornate fretwork railing. Its furnishings reflect the comfortable style of the 1870s. Outside are a replica of a Mexican beehive oven along with a windmill and several old farm implements. *Open Wed., Sat., Sun. except holidays.*

56. J. Paul Getty Museum *17985 Pacific Coast Hwy., Malibu, Calif.* The distinguished works collected by Mr. Getty and shown here feature Greek and Roman statuary, 18th-century French furniture and decorative arts, and English, Italian and Dutch paintings of the 15th to the 18th centuries. Sample highlights are a Greek torso from the Elgin collection, Rembrandt's *St. Bartholomew* and three works by Tintoretto. Bonnard's *Nude* and Rubens' *Hunt of Diana* are also stellar attractions. *Open Tues.-Sun.*

57. Will Rogers State Historic Park *14253 Sunset Blvd., Pacific Palisades, Calif.* This 186-acre ranch was the humorist's home from 1928 until his death in 1935. The estate and its 18-room ranch house are maintained as they were during the Rogers family's occupancy. Within the house are original furnishings as well as Rogers' collection of Western and Indian art and his cowboy mementos. On the grounds are a stable, corrals, a roping arena and several riding trails. A statue shows Rogers astride Soapsuds, his favorite roping pony. *Open daily except holidays. Small charge.*

58. Mission San Fernando Rey de Espana *15151 San Fernando Mission Blvd., San Fernando, Calif.* With the Russians advancing south from Alaska in the late 18th century the Spanish government decided to secure their unguarded colonial territory in California. They did so with a small military force and several Franciscan Fathers. Within 65 years the friars established 21 self-sufficient missions and converted thousands of Indians to Christianity. Together the fathers and Indians established California's first farms, orchards and industries. San Fernando Rey de Espana was one of the most flourishing missions. After 1846 it was dissolved but several of the adobe buildings—the school, convento, church, workshops—have been restored. They provide insight to early California colonial existence. *Open daily except Dec. 25. Small charge.*

59. Kuska Museum *24201 Walnut St., Lomita, Calif.* Nellie and Joseph Kuska have perfected the American habit of collecting. Over many years they have amassed more than 20,000 items: china, glassware, gems, buttons, books, bottles, costumes and dolls. Among the most outstanding items are a Sèvres dish made for Russia's Catherine the Great; two steins that belonged to Hitler; an 1840 whiskey bottle made by Philadelphia's E. C. Booz Company, famous for its contribution to the drinking vocabulary; and a rare French doll whose jeweled necklace contains miniature reproductions of famous Louvre paintings. *Open daily.*

60. Banning Museum *401 East M St., Wilmington, Calif.* Shipwrights and carpenters from the clipper ships built the Colonial-style mansion for General Phineas Banning (of the California State Militia) in 1864. Banning, a native of Wilmington, Delaware, moved to southern California in 1851. He founded the California town of Wilmington as well as local railroads,

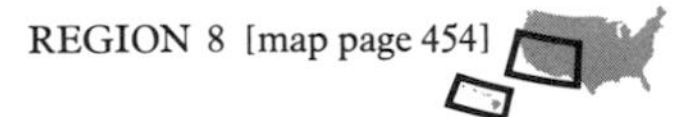

[**65.** *Bradbury Building*] *This landmark office building has come the full business cycle. Filled with prestige tenants early in the 20th century, it declined after the Depression. Now it is restored and prosperous again.*

shipping companies and stagecoach lines. Banning designed his own home, a simple but elegant three-story frame house with a two-story portico, square cupola and 30 rooms, many of which are furnished with Victorian antiques. To the rear of the house are the stables and coach house which contain a collection of horse-drawn vehicles. *Open Sun. Small charge.*

61. Marineland of the Pacific *Palos Verdes Dr. S., Palos Verdes Peninsula, Calif.* Orky, the largest killer whale in captivity, and Bubbles, the famous pilot whale, are among the disarming denizens at the world's largest showplace of marine life. Whales, dolphins, sea elephants, freshwater otters, walruses and more than 100 other kinds of sea animals live here. The Flamingo Garden, Turtle Pool, Octopus Grotto and Piranha Tank are among the displays. The world's biggest fishbowl, a four-story tank with 540,000 gallons of water, contains more than 3000 fish. Regular shows—starring whales, sea lions, dolphins and sea elephants—are presented at two stadiums. *Open daily. Adults $3.50; children 12 to 17 $2.00, 5 to 11 small charge.*

MARINELAND SKY TOWER A panoramic view of the Pacific, Marineland and the Palos Verdes coastline unfolds from the tower, which soars 344 feet above the ocean. During the four-minute ride to the top, the glass-enclosed elevator car slowly revolves around the tower, offering a procession of spectacular views.

62. Wayfarers' Chapel *5755 Palos Verdes Dr. S., Palos Verdes Peninsula, Calif.* This unique structure, known as the "Glass Church," is a memorial to Emanuel Swedenborg, the 18th-century Swedish mystic whose writings became, after his death, the basis of the Swedenborgian Church. Swedenborg's vision of a sanctuary made of living trees has been interpreted by architect Frank Lloyd Wright into a church that lets in as much of nature as possible. Its walls and ceiling are mostly glass, and the evergreens around the chapel seem to be almost a part of it. The chapel, set on a high bluff overlooking the Pacific, is situated on three-and-a-half acres of gardens landscaped with Biblical and other plants. A lofty triangular stone tower, topped by a cross, stands in front, visible for miles out to sea. *Open daily.*

63. Rancho Los Alamitos *6400 Bixby Hill Rd., Long Beach, Calif.* The adobe house was begun in 1806 on a 300,000-acre Spanish land grant. Situated on the site of an ancient Indian village, it was enlarged and modified by several owners. The house is filled with late 1800s furniture and boasts an outstanding pressed glass collection. Only seven-and-a-half acres of the original land grant remain, but this remnant is used to good advantage. Five gardens, graced with statuary, are planted with roses, herbs, cacti and native plants. *Open Wed.-Sun. except holidays.*

64. Long Beach Museum of Art *2300 E. Ocean Blvd., Long Beach, Calif.* The fine permanent collection of painting and sculpture here includes a dramatic single work of sculptor George Rickey, especially commissioned for the museum's hilltop site. Called *Two Lines Up-Spread,* the sculpture resembles an ultramodern weather vane: a thin stainless steel rod 30 feet high supports two sleek blades that move with the offshore breezes and create ever-changing designs. *Open Tues.-Sun. except holidays.*

65. Los Angeles, Calif.

The City of the Angels is a sprawling giant which rambles over 450 square miles. Founded by the Spanish in 1781, Los Angeles remained a small town until the 1880s, when a rate war between railroads—one dollar would bring you here from Kansas City—lured thousands to the city. Another boom occurred between 1920 and 1930, when the population more than doubled—to about 1,200,000—and an even greater population wave followed World War II. Some came for the climate, some to take jobs in the new factories, others to become famous on the Silver Screen. Today, Los Angeles is the third largest city in the U.S., with almost 3,000,000 Angelenos, and has attractions that range far beyond Hollywood and Vine. Museums, parks, colorful markets and churches are only a few of its enticements.

Art Galleries of the University of California at Los Angeles *405 Hilgard Ave.* Although European and English paintings as well as changing temporary exhibitions can be admired here, the prize attraction is a spacious sculpture garden. The landscaped park, with graceful winding walks, holds 37 major works by eminent 20th-century artists. Included are masterpieces by Rodin, Lipchitz, Arp, Calder and Moore. David Smith, Barbara Hepworth and Maillol are also represented, and Matisse's talent is revealed in four bronze reliefs. *Open Tues.-Sun.*

Bradbury Building *304 S. Broadway* Old and failing in health, mining and real estate mogul Lewis

[*Los Angeles County Museum of Art*] *Cézanne's* Still Life With Cherries and Apricots, *left, is one of the museum's most popular post-Impressionist works.* The Duchess of Alba *by Reuben Nakian lolls in the sculpture plaza.*

Bradbury decided in 1892 to erect a lasting monument to cap his career. He turned down the building plans of a prominent architect and accepted instead the remarkably original design of a young, untested draftsman, George Wyman. The fortunate decision created an extraordinary five-story office building of glazed brick walls, fine wood paneling, tiled floors and marble staircases. But the showpiece is the spacious central court: balconies circle it, staircases rise at either end and cage elevators climb openly to the top—all decorated with exquisite wrought-iron grillwork and bathed by daylight that pours through the glass-paneled roof. *Open Mon.-Fri.*

California Museum of Science and Industry *700 State Dr., Exposition Park* Displays on mathematics, aviation traffic control, mechanical sciences, communications and energy are among the 20 permanent exhibits here. The sight-and-sound "touch" subjects are especially popular with children. In the Hall of Health are models of a human fetus and man's nervous system, plus a translucent woman which shows the placement of organs. There are also displays on bone structure, the glandular system and the effects of narcotics on the body. Exhibits in the Hall of Dentistry and the Space Museum are equally interesting. On the grounds is a rose garden with gazebos where visitors can relax. *Open daily except Thanksgiving Day and Dec. 25.*

El Pueblo de Los Angeles *N. Main St. between Arcadia St. and Sunset Blvd., Alameda and Spring Sts.* Originally occupied by one of only two pueblos established in California by Spaniards, the 42-acre area encompasses several restored buildings. These reflect the architectural development of the city since 1815 and include the two-story brick Pelanconi House (1860) and the brick and cut stone Garnier Building (1890). It was an established market in the 1890s, but the site later deteriorated until its restoration as a State Historic Park was begun in 1953.

AVILA ADOBE Kit Carson knew the house well, and General Fremont used it as the seat of U.S. Government in the late 1840s. The oldest (1818) dwelling in Los Angeles, it has thick walls and 15-foot ceilings. Its French doors were brought around Cape Horn by ship.

OLD MISSION CHURCH The original section of the adobe edifice was begun in 1814, making it the city's oldest church in continuous use. It is noted for its earth floor and bell tower.

OLD PLAZA FIREHOUSE The 1884 brick building served its initial purpose until the late 1890s and was subsequently converted into a restaurant and saloon. It now holds late 19th-century fire-fighting equipment.

OLD SPANISH PLAZA In the 1890s produce wagons were backed up to the plaza's circular perimeter and business was conducted in the center. The bronze statue of Filipe de Neve, founder of the pueblo, was installed in 1931. All landscaping here is historically authentic.

OLVERA STREET Almost 70 stalls, shops and several restaurants attract visitors to the brick-paved arcade with its strong Mexican influence. Named for Judge Agustin Olvera who once lived at the end of the street, it is one of the city's oldest thoroughfares.

PICO HOUSE Completed in 1870 as a hotel, it was the city's first three-story courtyarded structure. Its builder, a Mexican named Pio Pico, was twice governor of California; he sold half of the San Fernando Valley to raise enough cash to erect the hotel.

Griffith Observatory *Griffith Park* The facility includes the Halls of Science museum, an observatory and a planetarium. The museum houses an operating weather-tracking station, a seismograph and a large cloud chamber for detecting cosmic rays. Two research-quality telescopes in the observatory can be used by the public; a triple-beam solar telescope and a spectrascope for the solar system are also located here. Space sciences and astronomy programs are presented in the planetarium, which has a 75-foot dome: projectors produce sunsets, eclipses and the Northern Lights. *Open daily mid-June–mid-Sept., Tues.-Sun. mid-Sept.–mid-June. Small charge for planetarium.*

Los Angeles County Museum of Art *5905 Wilshire Blvd.* These three modern buildings, flanked by pools with fountains and a sculpture plaza, hold a broad range of art. There are ancient Egyptian, Indian and Oriental works; medieval, Renaissance and Baroque paintings and sculpture, textiles and tapestries and outstanding examples of glass-making art. Visitors can admire several periods of English and French art as well as a fine collection of American paintings from the 18th century to the present. Among the impressive holdings are portraits by Rembrandt, Copley, Stuart and Sargent, several Matisse bronzes, *The Israelites Gathering Manna in the Desert* by Rubens and Cézanne's *Still Life With Cherries and Apricots. Open Tues.-Sun. except holidays.*

Los Angeles Zoo *Golden State and Ventura Freeways* Arranged by continents the outdoor displays offer landscaped settings that closely resemble the animals' natural habitats. More than 3000 animals, including some 50 endangered species, are on view throughout the 113-acre park. Apart from impressive apes and large cats, there are sea lions, elephant seals, bears, alligators and 500 kinds of snakes and amphibians. Many exotic mammals such as wombats, Tasmanian devils and tree kangaroos are at home here. A walk-through flight cage is a haven for bird watchers, and youngsters crowd the Children's Zoo with its farm animals and baby animal nursery. *Open daily except Dec. 25. Adults $1.25, children over 11 small charge.*

Museum of Natural History of Los Angeles County *900 Exposition Blvd.* More than 30 halls and galleries contain striking displays of wildlife set against backgrounds of North American and African scenery. Other exhibits relate to California and the history of the West. Skeletons of mastodons, saber-tooth cats and other prehistoric animals recovered from La Brea tar pits are notably popular features. There is also a fine collection of arms and armor. *Open Tues.-Sun.*

Music Center of Los Angeles County *135 N. Grand Ave.* Three bold modern buildings offer Los Angeles a full range of programs in the performing arts. The 2100-seat Ahmanson Theatre schedules musicals, ballets and dramas, while the Mark Taper Forum provides 750 seats for intimate drama, lectures, recitals and civic presentations around a thrust stage. In the huge Dorothy Chandler Pavilion symphony orchestra concerts, musical comedies, operas and recitals are held. In front of the Pavilion Lipchitz's bronze *Peace on Earth* is set in a large reflecting pool. *Open daily.*

St. John's Episcopal Church *514 W. Adams Blvd.* Looking like a misplaced Italian church, the stately building is, in fact, a re-creation of a church in Toscanella, Italy. The huge bronze entrance doors are framed by a series of receding arches and surmounted by an intricately laced rose window. Inside, a Florentine ceiling copied from an 11th-century Italian church flows to the altar enclosure, sumptuously decorated with mosaic and marble work, and a triptych carved in oak. *Open daily.*

St. Sophia Cathedral *1324 S. Normandie Ave.* Dedicated in 1952 the Byzantine-style edifice is widely considered the western hemisphere's most beautiful Greek Orthodox church. It was modeled after the Hagia Sophia in Istanbul. The exquisite interior is brilliantly decorated with paintings large and small, goldleafed carvings and 21 massive crystal chandeliers from Czechoslovakia. A huge icon of the Virgin and Child dominates the sanctuary, and the lavishly embellished dome ceiling depicts Christ. *Open daily.*

Southwest Museum *234 Museum Dr., Highland Park* The history, archaeology, ethnology and the arts and crafts of North, Central and South American Indians are shown here with displays of clothing, weapons, stonework, basketry and pottery. Children enjoy the buffalo skin tepee, and Chief Kicking Bear's painting on muslin of the Battle of the Little Big Horn is of particular interest. One entrance features a 260-foot tunnel with dioramas of Western Indian cultures. *Open Tues.-Sun. mid-Sept.-mid-Aug. except holidays.*

University Galleries *University of Southern California, University Park* Flemish, Dutch and Italian masterworks of the 17th century displayed here include canvases by Breugel, the Elder and Younger; Hobbema; Rembrandt; van Ruisdael and Jan Steen. Also exhibited is Rubens' oil *The Nativity.* The collection features eminent 18th-century British and 19th-century French works. Romantic paintings of the Hudson River school highlight the 19th-century American collection. *Open Mon.-Fri. Sept.-July.*

Watts Towers *1765 E. 107th St.* Logger, miner, construction worker and tile setter Simon Rodia, an Italian immigrant, proved himself a masterful jack-of-all-trades when he went to work on the towers. From 1921 to 1954 he built the eccentric constructions of steel pipes, broken bottles, seashells, bed frames, tiles and whatever odds and ends suited his creative fancy. The three main pop-art spires rise 100 feet, a monument to Rodia's engineering skill as well as his determined desire "to do something big." *Open daily. Small charge.*

[Watts Towers] Simon Rodia's fantastic spires, glittering with the myriad bits and pieces he collected in a lifetime of turning junk into art, twine their way skyward. The tallest of the towers are 100 feet high.

Wilshire Boulevard Temple *3663 Wilshire Blvd.* A massive dome with inlaid mosaics crowns the monumental building. Its interior beauties include marble and wood mosaics, stained-glass windows, bronze chandeliers and Belgian marble columns. Lunettes bear scenes of the Creation, prophets, priests and rabbis, and murals depict the story of the Jewish people from the time of Abraham to Columbus. Other rare possessions are gold and silver embroidered Ark curtains from several 19th-century European synagogues and a collection of letters and documents of U.S. Presidents and other notables. *Open Fri., Sat.*

66. Forest Lawn Memorial-Parks *1712 S. Glendale Ave., Glendale, Calif.* The Hall of the Crucifixion-Resurrection contains the world's largest religious painting, *The Crucifixion,* by Jan Styka, while *The Last Supper* in stained glass highlights the Great Mausoleum's Memorial Court of Honor. Also included on 300 acres are three well-known churches, such as the Church of the Recessional, patterned after the original in England where Rudyard Kipling worshiped as a youth. A collection of Kipling's manuscripts and mementos are exhibited in several rooms here. *Open daily.*

67. Descanso Gardens *1418 Descanso Dr., La Canada, Calif.* California oaks, giant redwoods, pines and other splendid trees shade an astonishing collection of 100,000 camellias, 10,000 varieties of rhododendrons and masses of azaleas, lilacs and chrysanthemums. One rose garden traces the development of this ornamental favorite from its earliest days; another includes every All-America rose winner since 1940. Other areas are devoted to orchids, begonias, fuchsias, irises and a handsome Japanese garden. *Open daily except Dec. 25.*

68. Pasadena Museum of Modern Art *Orange Grove and Colorado Blvds., Pasadena, Calif.* The collection of 20th-century art here is one of the finest in the nation. The nucleus is German Expressionist, featuring the works of the Blue Four—Paul Klee, Alexei Jawlensky, Lyonel Feininger and Wassili Kandinsky. The museum also sponsors several major exhibitions each year of the works of outstanding contemporary artists and photographers. The splendidly modern H-shaped complex is a fitting counterpoint to its distinguished holdings. *Open Tues.-Sun. except holidays. Small charge.*

69. Mount Wilson Observatory *Mount Wilson, Calif.* Astronomers here study the universe through the 100-inch Hooker telescope—the second largest reflecting telescope in the world—and also a 60-inch instrument. The larger one can be seen from a visitors' gallery. The altitude here in the San Gabriel Mountains is 5713 feet. *Open daily. Parking $2.00.*

70. Huntington Library, Art Gallery and Botanical Gardens *1151 Oxford Rd., San Marino, Calif.* See feature display on pages 478-9.

71. Adobe de Palomares *491 E. Arrow Hwy., Pomona, Calif.* Don Ygnacio Palomares built this 13-room ranch house in 1854. A typical Spanish home of the period, it is constructed with adobe bricks, a shake roof and cloth ceilings. It is furnished with authentic pieces, including some that belonged to the don. On the grounds are a blacksmith shop and some original ranch equipment. *Open Tues.-Sun. except holidays.*

[73] *Even a picture can't convey the spirit and size of this unique hotel. Moorish arches, fountains and statuary grace the many courtyards and patios; lacy wrought-iron balconies and tile roofs cast the spell of Old Spain.*

72. San Bernadino County Museum *18860 Orange Ave., Bloomington, Calif.* This museum specializes in the history of early man and the natural sciences as they relate to the county and region. The museum, which has sponsored important archaeological work, features exhibits that explain the on-going research. Objects excavated from the Calico dig in the Mojave Desert indicate that man may have inhabited North America more than 50,000 years ago. The Hall of North American Mammals and the collection of birds' eggs—one of the nation's largest—are popular with visitors. *Open daily.*

73. Mission Inn *3649 Seventh Ave., Riverside, Calif.* Described by Will Rogers as "the most unique hotel in America," the vast mission-style inn is a rambling maze of courtyards, patios, terraces, roof gardens, sun porches and towers. The inn is furnished with a notable collection of Spanish antiques, paintings and other works of art that its founder, Frank A. Miller, and his family gathered over the years. Many famous people have visited the inn. *Tours daily. Small charge.*

74. Asistencia Mission *26930 Barton Rd., Redlands, Calif.* The Franciscan Fathers of Mission San Gabriel began building this outpost in 1830, but mission secularization forced them to abandon it four years later. It was subsequently used as a home by several families and later sold to the Mormons. The 14-room building, which now contains two museum rooms and a wedding chapel, has been restored by the county with adobe bricks and tile roofs. Items relating to the mission, ranch life and pioneer history are displayed. *Open Tues.-Sun.*

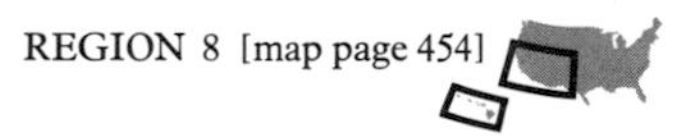

75. Sand Artist Bible Land *Rte. 10, 7 mi. E. of Redlands, Calif.* Sand sculptor Ted Conibear, using common sand and water, has created a series of scenes from the life of Christ. The realistic life-size figures in warm reddish tones have been placed in appropriate settings. Scenes include "The Last Supper," "Jesus and the Woman of Samaria," "The Babe in the Manger" and "Jesus Blessing the Children." *Open daily.*

76. Riverside County Art and Culture Center, Edward-Dean Museum of Decorative Arts *9401 Oak Glen Rd., Cherry Valley, Calif.* An exquisite collection of priceless antique European and Oriental furniture, paintings, tapestries, porcelains and other decorative objects is displayed in a series of rooms that capture the atmosphere of an elegant 18th-century home. Most impressive is the Pine Room, with handcarved paneling that was originally made in the 17th century for the state bedroom at the country home of the Earl of Essex. *Open Tues.-Sun. except holidays.*

77. Disneyland *1313 Harbor Blvd., Anaheim, Calif.* A fabulous world of fact and fantasy springs to life on these 74 acres, where 54 imaginative attractions appeal to young and old alike. The classic Disney characters—Mickey Mouse, Donald Duck and all the rest—are here, as well as a tantalizing variety of ingenious rides, displays and happenings, many of them devoted to the American past. Adventureland, Fantasyland and Tomorrowland add new dimensions to the basic theme. Disneyland can be considered a historic place because, when it opened in 1955, it was the first to bring together all these disparate elements and present them in a thoroughly organized and totally engaging way. Encouraged by its phenomenal success, other multithemed parks have sprung up in various parts of the country and seem destined to become a permanent part of the American scene. *Open Wed.-Sun. Jan.-early June, daily early June-early Sept., Wed.-Sun. early Sept.-Dec. Adults $3.50, children over 11 $2.50, under 12 small charge.*

78. Charles W. Bowers Memorial Museum *2002 N. Main St., Santa Ana, Calif.* Near the front entrance of the Mediterranean-style former home is a statue of Cabrillo, the Spanish explorer who discovered San Diego Bay. It is one of many items relating to the Spanish pioneer period in California exhibited here. The permanent collections include arts and crafts of the American Indian, antique dolls, rare seashells, paintings and anthropology and natural history displays. *Open Tues.-Sun. except holidays.*

79. Movieland of the Air *Orange County Airport, Santa Ana, Calif.* More than 50 planes, many of them currently featured in movies and TV shows, are included in this collection of antique aircraft. The indoor and outdoor displays include Fokkers, Jennies, a Curtiss Pusher Blériot and a J2F6 Grumman Duck. Aviation memorabilia in wide variety and a collection of model aircraft are also exhibited, along with weapons and arms, balloons and photographic materials. Barnstorming flights and other aerial demonstrations are frequently presented. *Open Tues.-Sun. Adults $1.75, children small charge.*

80. Briggs Cunningham Automotive Museum *250 E. Baker St., Costa Mesa, Calif.* Although not the world's largest collection of automobiles, this is considered one of the finest: almost 100 operational antique, classic and sports cars from 1898 to the present are displayed. Some prize vehicles are a 1927 Bugatti eight-cylinder Royale, a 1913 Isotta-Fraschini and a 1914 Rolls-Royce Colonial. Four handsome Hispano-Suizas, six Bentleys and a Stutz DV-32 Super Bearcat can also be studied. A display of automotive art includes many original paintings and drawings. *Open Wed.-Sun. Men $2.00, women, students, military and children over 12 $1.50.*

81. San Juan Capistrano Mission *Ortega Hwy., San Juan Capistrano, Calif.* Almost overrun with bright flowers, cascading vines and gnarled trees, the mission—famous for the regular appearance of its migrating swallows—is a place of utmost tranquillity. The great stone church of 1806 was destroyed by an earthquake, but the ruins of its walls, pillars, archways and cloister form impressive counterpoints to the lush garden setting. The 1778 adobe chapel, built by Father Junipero Serra, with its gilded altar has been completely restored. *Open daily. Small charge.*

[76] *The Grinling Gibbons Pine Room was named for the English carver (1648-1720) who founded a school of ornamental woodcarving. Gibbons' skill is evident in the overmantel border and the mantel itself. The portrait above the mantel is by Sir Peter Lely. Prominent in this view is the 18th-century Waterford crystal chandelier and the 19th-century Ispahan carpet of Sarouk design. A Louis XIII reclining chair is at right; behind it is a case of Chinese and Tibetan gilt bronzes of the 17th and 18th centuries.*

Scholars come from all over the world to use the Huntington Library facilities. Among its 5½ million precious manuscripts and books are a 1410 manuscript of Chaucer's Canterbury Tales, *a Gutenberg Bible, the earliest editions of Shakespeare, and Benjamin Franklin's autobiography written in his own hand.*

70. Huntington Library, Art Gallery and Botanical Gardens

1151 Oxford Rd., San Marino, Calif.

Railway executive Henry Edwards Huntington's instinct as a collector was for in-depth specialization. For the now-famous gardens at San Marino, he was interested in experimenting with tropical plants. Today the Botanical Gardens contains shrubs, trees and other plants from every part of the world. In art he narrowed his field to English paintings, particularly portraits of the late 18th and early 19th centuries, with a secondary emphasis on the French decorative arts. His mansion of white marble, a fitting place to live with such paintings and furniture, is now the Art Gallery. Within a few years of his retirement in 1910, the financier had built his burgeoning library into one of the finest rare book collections in the country, requiring an expanding staff and, eventually, a special building. Huntington accumulated historical documents and reference books as well as the classics. The result is a research library renowned for original sources in British and American history and literature. Once, stretched out on a hospital bed, Huntington compared his visiting art and book dealers to the two thieves who were beside Christ on the cross. Still, he continued to buy, and set up a trust fund to maintain and increase his collections after his death. *Open Tues.-Sun. Nov.-Sept. except holidays.*

In the Botanical Gardens visitors may wander across broad lawns through acres of camellias to the Japanese Garden. They can sit in the Shakespeare Garden (right) with its colorful flower beds or can enjoy the bizarre shapes of cacti in the Desert Garden, which contains one of the world's great collections of succulents.

The Blue Boy *had turned green by 1922, but the azure that flowed from Thomas Gainsborough's brush in 1779 shone again when the discolored varnish had been removed.*

Pinkie, *Sir Thomas Lawrence's portrait of Elizabeth Barrett Browning's aunt, is another of the well known paintings hanging in the main gallery.*

[82] *The huge Hale telescope dwarfs the men standing below. Just above them is the famous 200-inch mirror. At the top of the skeleton tube is a capsule in which the astronomer rides while photographing objects in space.*

82. Palomar Observatory *Palomar Mountain, 15 mi. N. of Rincon Springs, Calif.* Man's largest collection of giant telescopes is found at this complex of domed buildings on a 2040-acre plateau more than a mile high. In operation here is the largest optical instrument in the world—the Hale telescope. It weighs 530 tons but moves with the precision of a finely crafted watch. Along with other Palomar instruments, the telescope is used to probe the universe by means of photographs, spectra and photoelectric measurements. *Open daily.*

83. La Jolla Museum of Contemporary Art *700 Prospect St., La Jolla, Calif.* The building, set in beautifully landscaped grounds overlooking the Pacific Ocean, holds a fine collection of 3000 paintings, sculptures, prints, drawings and other objects, with the emphasis on modern American and European art. Of particular note are works by Kirschner, Morisot, de Kooning, De Rivera and Irwin. *Open Tues.-Sun.*

84. T. Wayland Vaughan Aquarium-Museum *University of California, San Diego, 8602 La Jolla Shores Dr., La Jolla, Calif.* Operated by the Scripps Institution of Oceanography the living museum includes 20 tanks swarming with fish and invertebrates from the waters off southern California and the west coast of Mexico. The Hall of Oceanography features 30 exhibits relating to research currently being conducted in the world's oceans. *Open daily.*

85. San Diego, Calif.

Renowned for its idyllic climate this city has long been popular as a resort. But thanks to its location on one of the world's great natural harbors, it is also a major industrial, shipping and naval center. Founded by Spaniards and ruled for many years by Mexico, it still has a distinctively Spanish Colonial appearance, especially in the historic Old Town.

Balboa Park This 1400-acre park is the city's cultural and recreational center. The California-Pacific International Exposition was held on the site in 1935-6; many exposition buildings have been preserved.

AEROSPACE MUSEUM Pioneer and modern aircraft, space capsules and aviation memorabilia are displayed. *Open daily.*

BOTANICAL BUILDING An old Santa Fe Railroad station is the setting for displays of tropical and subtropical plants from all over the world. *Open daily.*

FINE ARTS GALLERY Works by Rembrandt, Titian and Canaletto are included in the gallery's outstanding collection. All major schools since the Renaissance are represented. *Elizabeth With a Dog* by Thomas Eakins and Georgia O'Keeffe's *The White Trumpet Flower* are in the American collection. Henry Moore's monumental bronze, *Reclining Figure: Arch Leg,* is one of the most popular works of sculpture. *Open Tues.-Sun.*

HALL OF CHAMPIONS San Diego athletes are commemorated in this sports museum, which features photographs, portraits and memorabilia. *Open daily.*

HOUSE OF PACIFIC RELATIONS This complex of 15 cottages serves as a cultural headquarters for 20 different national groups. Outdoor entertainment is presented on the central lawn during the warm months. *Open Sun.*

MUSEUM OF MAN Exhibits depict the history of the Indians and the progress of man in the Americas. *Open daily. Small charge.*

NATURAL HISTORY MUSEUM Mammals, birds, marine life, insects and geological materials are exhibited. Selected works from the Ellen Browning Scripps collection of 1200 exquisite watercolors of California wildflowers by Valentien are displayed. *Open daily except Jan. 1 and Dec. 25. Adults small charge.*

OLD GLOBE THEATRE Two theatrical groups perform here regularly: the San Diego Community Theatre and, during the summer months, the San Diego National Shakespeare Festival.

SAN DIEGO ZOOLOGICAL GARDEN This is the world's largest collection of mammals, birds and reptiles. More than 5500 animals representing about 1600 species and subspecies are exhibited, including such rare ones as the pygmy chimpanzee, lion-tailed macaque and green tree python. The zoo features three walk-through bird cages, free seal acts, moving sidewalks which transport visitors easily from simulated canyons to mesas and an aerial tramway. In the children's zoo are a glass-enclosed nursery for baby primates, a rodent tunnel, walk-through bird displays, a seal pool and a tortoise ride. *Open daily. Adults $1.50.*

SPANISH VILLAGE ART CENTER Painters, sculptors, silversmiths and other artists and craftsmen can be seen working in the studios in which they display and sell their work. *Open Sat., Sun.*

TIMKEN ART GALLERY Spanish Baroque paintings from El Greco to Goya form the nucleus of this outstanding collection of old masters. The gallery also features an excellent collection of early Russian icons. *Open Tues.-Sun. Oct.-Aug.*

Bark "Star of India" *1306 N. Harbor Dr.* When all of its 19 sails are billowing in the wind, this 205-foot-long iron sailing vessel—the oldest merchant ship still afloat—is a spectacular sight. It was originally

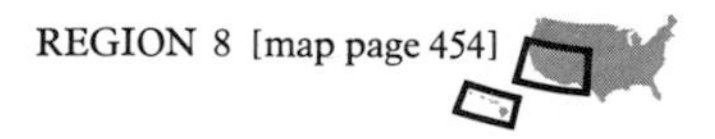

launched in 1863 and circled the globe 21 times before being abandoned in 1923. Now permanently anchored on the San Diego waterfront, the *Star of India* has been completely restored and refurbished as a maritime museum, providing an authentic picture of the way merchant sailors lived a century or so ago. *Open daily. Small charge.*

Old Town San Diego State Historic Park *4016 Wallace St.* A number of old houses and shops surrounding a plaza have been restored to the way they looked when California was under Mexican rule. One of the most interesting homes is the Casa de Estudillo, a large adobe built by a well-to-do Mexican family in the 1820s. Among the other buildings restored to their original appearances is the small frame structure where the first edition of the San Diego *Union* was published in 1868 and the Machado/Stewart Adobe. *Open daily. Small charge.*

Serra Museum, Library and Tower Gallery *2727 Presidio Dr., Presidio Park* Serra Museum, commemorating San Diego's 400-year history, is perched atop Presidio Hill, known as the "Plymouth Rock of the West." It was here that Father Junipero Serra established the first mission in California on July 16, 1769. The museum was built in 1929 in the classic mission style. The tower affords a splendid vista of modern San Diego. *Open Tues.-Sun.*

Whaley House Museum *2482 San Diego Ave.* Thomas Whaley, a New Yorker, sailed to San Francisco via Cape Horn in 1849 during the gold rush but soon journeyed on to San Diego, where he became a successful businessman. His Greek Revival-style home, completed in 1857, is said to be the oldest brick home in southern California. It has been restored and furnished with a good collection of period pieces. *Open Wed.-Sun. Small charge.*

86. Joss House *Weaverville, Calif.* One of the last few remnants of Weaverville's once-flourishing Chinese community is this Taoist temple built by Chinese who were lured to the town in the 1850s by gold rush fever. To preserve the building as a reminder of the Chinese cultural influence on the development of California, it was given to the state's park system. Entry to the temple, which is painted bright blue and white to resemble tiles, is through a carved wooden gate, past a statue of an ancient Chinese official who guards the structure from evil spirits. The interior is painted red, the Chinese symbol of happiness. It features three elaborately carved wooden canopies behind the altar. Exhibits include Chinese art objects, mining tools and weapons used in an 1854 tong (Chinese secret society) war. *Open daily except holidays. Adults small charge.*

87. Bidwell Mansion State Historic Park *525 Esplanade, Chico, Calif.* President Rutherford B. Hayes, Susan B. Anthony and General William T. Sherman were among the many notables to visit the 26-room Victorian dwelling, which was completed in 1868. The two-story stucco structure with an imposing tower over the front entrance was the home of General John Bidwell, a politician and pioneer agriculturist. The house, with its hooded windows and ornate balustrades, is an architectural museum in itself. *Open daily except holidays. Adults small charge.*

88. Chinese Temple *1500 Broderick St., Oroville, Calif.* During California's gold rush days Oroville was the home of the largest Chinese settlement in the state. Funds for the temple complex, begun in 1863, as well as many of its furnishings were given to the community by the emperor of China. The temple, now a museum of Oriental treasures of the past, survives as one of the most authentic of its kind in the U.S. A recent addition, connected by way of a garden courtyard graced with a copper pagoda, contains a rare tapestry collection, banners, parasols and rugs. Other rooms hold additional art objects, jewelry, intricately woven costumes and other Chinese artifacts. *Open daily. Small charge.*

89. Judge Charles F. Lott House *1067 Montgomery St., Oroville, Calif.* The Victorian frame house was built in 1856 for Judge Lott and his family. It is still furnished with the Lotts' splendid antique pieces. A fireplace, added in the 1930s by Jesse Sank, features rocks of many kinds and colors, and polished stones that romantically spell out the word LOVE—a tribute to Sank's 20-year courtship of and 30-year marriage to the Lotts' daughter, Cornelia. The house is set on an entire block of landscaped grounds, now a park with rustic picnic facilities for public use. *Open daily mid-Jan.-Nov. Small charge.*

[**85.** *Bark* Star of India] *The sturdy, iron-hulled merchant ship carried trade goods to India, emigrants from England to New Zealand and Australia, timber out of Puget Sound and salmon from Alaskan fishing grounds to California.*

90. Marshall Gold Discovery State Historic Park *Rte. 49, Coloma, Calif.* In 1848 James Marshall's chance discovery of gold at John Sutter's sawmill here led to the famous California gold rush a year later. Visitors to this 230-acre park can view the reconstructed mill as well as a blacksmith shop, an old stone jail and other early buildings. Marshall's cabin has been preserved, and his grave is marked by a statue of him pointing to the exact spot where his great discovery was made. A museum contains maps, Indian and pioneer objects and displays relating to the influence of gold on the nation. On the grounds are picnic areas, hiking trails and fishing sites. *Open daily except holidays. Adults small charge.*

91. California State Capitol *10th St. between L and N Sts., Sacramento, Calif.* Surrounded by a landscaped park that features thousands of trees and plants from around the world, the monumental building is capped by an impressive dome. On the main floor are commemorative statues and murals, while in the rotunda are exhibits of fine arts and historical materials. *Open daily.*

92. E. B. Crocker Art Gallery *216 O St., Sacramento, Calif.* The oldest museum west of the Mississippi was established in 1873 by Judge Edwin Bryant Crocker, a prominent Californian who played a key role in founding America's first transcontinental railroad. Judge Crocker built the imposing Italian Baroque-style structure especially to house his collection of more than 700 paintings, 1600 drawings and 400 prints. Sculpture, ceramics, American glass, furniture and a variety of Oriental art have been added to the museum's collection since it was given to the city in 1885. *Open Tues.-Sun. Small charge.*

93. Governor's Mansion *16th and H Sts., Sacramento, Calif.* California had no official executive residence until 1903, when the state purchased this Victorian Gothic-style mansion, built in 1877-8 for a successful hardware merchant. Outstanding features of its highly ornamental facade are the tall cupola and broad bay windows. Spacious rooms, elaborate fireplaces, intricate millwork and many fine period furnishings contribute to the charm of the mansion's interior. *Open daily except holidays. Adults small charge.*

[97] *In the 1880s Bodie's hectic streets were lined with shops, hotels, homes, bars and more bars. Those still standing along the silent streets are, like this one, permanently suspended in a state of decay.*

94. California Railway Museum *Rte. 12, Rio Vista Junction, Calif.* Two cars from the New York elevated railway that were built in 1888 and a century-old cable car are among the many historic pieces of rolling stock displayed at the restored railroad station, which was once a stop on the Sacramento Northern Railroad. Artifacts relating to railroad history, telegraphic equipment and the world's oldest operating gasoline mechanical passenger car are also on view. Visitors can ride some of the old cars on a one-and-a-quarter-mile stretch of track. *Open Sat., Sun. and holidays except Dec. 25. Small charge for rides.*

95. Pioneer Museum and Haggin Galleries *1201 N. Pershing Ave., Stockton, Calif.* This handsome three-story building houses an extensive local and state history collection displayed in exhibits such as the Storefronts Gallery, Vehicle Gallery, California, Pioneer and Indian Rooms and rooms from an 1860s ranch house. The Haggin Galleries' art collection is mainly composed of 19th-century American and European paintings, including several works by Gerome, Bonheur, Bierstadt and Inness; European and American graphics; and Victorian and Oriental decorative arts. *Open Tues.-Sun. except holidays.*

96. Columbia State Historic Park *Off Rte. 49, Columbia, Calif.* Once known as the "Gem of the Southern Mines," the mining town flourished between 1850 and 1860. During one frantic decade $87,000,000 in gold was removed from these hills. Restored buildings, scattered over an eight-block area, include the Wells Fargo office, a brick schoolhouse, a bank and an array of saloons and hotels. An early firehouse holds colorful period equipment, and plays are presented in the old theater during July and August. Visitors can take a ride in a real stagecoach or tour a goldmine. *Open daily except Thanksgiving Day and Dec. 25. Small charge for stagecoach ride.*

97. Bodie State Historic Park *Bodie Rd., S. of Bridgeport, Calif.* Gold discovered here in 1859 prompted the establishment of a town that by thc 1880s had burgeoned to 10,000 residents. Bodie was notorious for its 65 saloons, street fights, robberies and frequent killings. Now a ghost town, Bodie's remaining frame and brick buildings are maintained in a state of "arrested decay." Visitors can see several former residences, a sawmill, blacksmith shop, jail, schoolhouse and a church. *Open daily.*

98. Laws Railroad Museum and Historical Site *Rte. 6, Laws, Calif.* Situated on almost 12 acres are the vestiges of the last narrow-gauge railroad operated west of the Rocky Mountains. In use from the early 1880s to 1960 the line was once known as "The Slim Princess." Along with an operational 1909 10-wheel locomotive and several cars, the site contains six buildings, including the depot and agent's office that date from 1883. The agent's home displays period furniture, several old sewing machines and costumes. Railroad

[99] *Walter Scott was a prospector of the type known as desert rat—that is, unsuccessful. Yet he persuaded his friend Albert Johnson, a Chicago millionaire, to build this Moorish-style mansion as a home for the two of them in the burning hills of California's Death Valley. Many of the furnishings were imported from Europe. The fireplace in the baronial room above is one of 18 in Scotty's Castle.*

memorabilia and branding irons are exhibited in the depot. *Open daily except holidays.*

99. Scotty's Castle *Death Valley, Calif.* Castles in the desert are apt to be more legendary than real, but this handsome tile-roofed extravaganza is hardly a mirage. Built in the 1920s, it is a result of the friendship between prospector Walter Scott ("Death Valley Scotty") and millionaire Albert Johnson. The castle, complete with towers and archways, contains superb Spanish and Italian furniture, Mallorcan rugs and art. *Open daily. Adults and children over 11 small charge.*

100. Forestiere Underground Gardens *5021 W. Shaw Ave., Fresno, Calif.* With such simple tools as a pick, a shovel and a wheelbarrow and an incredible amount of hard labor, Baldasare Forestiere, a Sicilian who came to the U.S. at the turn of the century, created a lush Mediterranean setting around his house. When he died in 1946, he had devoted 40 years of his spare time to removing unfertile surface soil and planting sunken gardens 10 to 25 feet below grade. Among the five acres of patios, grottoes, courts and stone archways, all linked by paths, the self-taught horticulturist expertly cultivated shrubs, vines, flowers and trees such as figs, date palms, pears, loquats and citruses. *Open late Dec.-Nov. Adults $1.50, children small charge.*

101. Fresno Arts Center *3033 E. Yale Ave., Fresno, Calif.* American contemporary prints and paintings are the specialty here. There are also some small choice collections of Oriental painting, sculpture and pottery; some Mexican paintings; and a group of African figures from Kenya. One of the most valuable—and charming—works is an 18th-century panel by Sweden's Johannes Nilsson, a traditional folk painting crowded with vivid scenes. *Open Tues.-Sun. Sept.-July except holidays.*

102. Tulare County Museum *27000 Mooney Blvd., Visalia, Calif.* Tulare County Museum is set in a 150-acre park beside Cameron Creek. The museum itself contains local pioneer artifacts such as old pumps, saddles, a homemade tractor, buggies, Yokut Indian baskets and domestic tools. A pioneer village consisting of a jail, blacksmith shop, schoolhouse, harness shop and log cabin has been reconstructed on the grounds. A bronze of James Earle Fraser's equestrian statue *End of the Trail* is displayed here, as is Solon Borglum's *The Pioneer. Open daily Apr.-mid-Oct., Mon.-Fri. mid-Oct.-Mar. Small charge.*

103. Burton's Tropico Gold Mine, Mill and Museum *Off Rosamond Blvd., 5 mi. W. of Rosamond, Calif.* Millions of dollars in gold were removed from the Tropico mine between 1894, when gold was discovered here, and the mine's closing in 1956. Now visitors may tour underground passageways to see how the gold was mined. In the adjoining mill guides explain how the ore was processed in ingots. A mining camp typical of those that surrounded successful sites has been reconstructed. The miner's cabin, assay office, general store, schoolhouse, miners' hall and other buildings assembled here show how the sourdoughs lived. *Mine and mill open Thurs.-Mon.; camp open Sat., Sun. Oct.-May. Adults $2.25, children $1.50.*

104. Calico Ghost Town Regional Park *Off Rte. 15, E. of Barstow, Calif.* Wyatt Earp often visited the town, which was the scene of a rich silver strike in 1881. During the next five years, $86,000,000 worth of ore was removed from its mines. One mine is open to visitors today. The restored town also features an assay shop, firehouse, general store and a museum. Paintings of Old West gunfighters hang in Lil's Saloon. *Open daily except Dec. 25. Small charge.*

Harrah's has a full line of Fords, also many Chevrolets and Chryslers; and there are names out of the past such as Pierce Arrow, Pope-Hartford, Reo and Hupmobile.

105. Harrah's Automobile Collection

Second St., 3 mi. E. of Reno, Nev.

Harrah's Automobile Collection is the world's largest collection of antique, vintage and classic cars. (Antique cars are those built prior to 1915, vintage cars date from 1916 to 1942 and classic cars are usually luxury models from the 1920s and '30s that have been singled out by the Classic Car Club of America.) More than 1100 of Harrah's 1500-odd total are on display. The collection is an attraction of Harrah's Hotels and Casinos of Reno and Lake Tahoe, the Nevada gaming resorts. On the 10-acre grounds are showrooms, a large shop area for restoration and separate buildings for body work, upholstering, brass repair and such. Visitors can see cars and car parts being restored and cars put in top running condition by some of the 70 craftsmen who work here. Other features of the collection include antique motorcycles, boats and airplanes, and there is also an excellent automotive research library. *Open daily. Adults $2.50, children over 6 small charge.*

Packard once ranked among the top cars; this 1930 Speedster Runabout shows why.

This 1913 Cadillac roadster has a self-starter and wood-spoke wheels.

This 1907 Thomas Flyer, an American-made four-cylinder runabout, won an incredible New York-to-Paris automobile race. Six open cars—three French, one Italian, one German and the Thomas—with their crews left Times Square for the West Coast on Feb. 12, 1908. No one had yet driven across the U.S. in winter; roads were sometimes nonexistent. But four cars reached Seattle and were shipped to Japan and Vladivostok. In Siberia they followed centuries-old caravan routes and the roadbed of the trans-Siberian railroad. After 169 days the Thomas was declared the winner.

The 1912 Stutz Bearcat cost about $2000. Its pistons packed 60 horsepower.

In 1933 the 13-horsepower Austin American coupe was a forerunner of the compact.

Tyrone Power owned this 1930 Duesenberg Berline.

[107] *Mount Davidson rears up to the left in this view of Virginia City's main street. The white-painted spire of St. Mary's in the Mountains can be seen at the right. Many of the Victorian homes above and below the street have been restored by private owners.*

106. Fleischmann Atmospherium-Planetarium *University of Nevada, N. Virginia St., Reno, Nev.* The special domed theater here is the scene of a striking series of motion pictures relating to planets, galaxies, ocean depths, thunderstorms, sunrises—and just about any other natural phenomenon, past or present. Spectators, ensconced in reclining seats, are completely surrounded by the images on the screen. The astounding effect is obtained by means of a "fish eye" projector called the atmospherium and the dome's curved screen. Solar system models, weather dioramas, meteorites, antique scientific instruments and astronomical transparencies are among the educational exhibits. *Open daily June-Aug., Tues.-Sun. Sept.-May. Adults $1.50, children small charge.*

107. Virginia City, Nev. During the 1860s and 1870s, the glory years of the Comstock Lode, this was the queen city of Nevada. As riches poured from its silver mines, the city attracted businessmen, adventurers and rogues from all over the world. It was the home of bonanza kings who built extravagant palaces, indulged their most absurd whims, helped finance the Civil War and contributed much to the building of San Francisco. The incomparable glitter of the period is still reflected in the architecture of the remaining buildings.

CASTLE *70 South B St.* No expense was spared when Robert Graves, a superintendent of the Empire Mine, built his mansion in 1868. Modeled after a Norman castle, it was known as the "House of Silver Doorknobs." The front doors and the hanging staircase are made of black walnut imported from Germany. The chandeliers are handcut Bohemian rock crystal. Fireplaces throughout the house feature Italian marble, with ornate gold-leaf mirrors above the mantels. Other imported furnishings include French mirrors and clocks, Dutch vases and a 14-foot dining-room table of English walnut. *Open daily late May-Oct. Small charge.*

MACKAY MANSION *D St.* This was the home of John MacKay, richest of the Comstock millionaires, who was noted for his philanthropy and public works. The three-story brick dwelling, its walls nearly two feet thick, was built in 1860, and is filled with authentic Victorian furniture. A colonnaded second-floor porch encircles the house. *Open daily May-Oct. Small charge.*

PIPER'S OPERA HOUSE *B and Union Sts.* The theater, one of the most famous in the old West, starred some of the greatest performers of the day: Sarah Bernhardt, Edwin Booth and Joseph Jefferson all appeared here. *Open daily May-Oct. Small charge.*

ST. MARY'S IN THE MOUNTAINS *D St.* Gothic in design, with a large bell tower and high steeples, the 1868 church replaced an earlier frame structure. Two of the original stained-glass windows are intact. The works of more than 70 artists are displayed in its art gallery. *Open daily.*

108. Carson City, Nev.

In a broad valley more than 4000 feet above sea level by the Sierra Nevadas a trading post was established in 1858 and named for Kit Carson, the famous frontiersman. In 1864, over the claims of the more populous Virginia City, Carson City remained the capital of Nevada when it became a state. The discovery of the fabled Comstock Lode and other silver mines boosted the economy, and the booming town became the social center of the area. Several new millionaires built mansions here. A mint, now the Nevada State Museum, coined almost $50,000,000 between 1870 and 1893.

Bliss Mansion *710 W. Robinson St.* Lumber magnate D. L. Bliss built the three-story house in 1879 in a style worthy of his fortune. A solid frame structure set on sandstone, it has 21 spacious rooms. There are seven fireplaces made of marble imported from Vermont, Georgia and Italy. The staircase is made of hand-turned black walnut, with gold-leaf molding. Window catches, keyholes and other metal fixtures are fashioned from Comstock silver, and doorknobs feature quicksilver under glass. Furnishings are equally lavish: highlights are a Victorian banquet table, a carved bedroom suite and a collection of Oriental art.

Bowers Mansion *4005 Rte. 395 N. (10 mi. N. of Carson City)* Sandy Bowers, one of the first of the Comstock Lode millionaires, spent $400,000 to build his granite residence in 1864. The 16-room mansion, a mix of Georgian and Italian styles, is a solid two-story structure with three handsome levels of porches and balustrades that rise to a charming cupola. The house contains ornate chandeliers, marble statues and elaborate antique furnishings, including some pieces that belonged to the Bowers family. *Open daily mid-May-Oct. Adults and children over 5 small charge.*

Governor's Mansion *606 N. Mountain St.* Clustered columns supporting a large portico, plus a balustraded porch, highlight the exterior of the white mansion, completed in 1909 and constructed of sandstone bricks. The main entrance doors are replicas of those at the Governor's Palace at Williamsburg, Virginia. Inside, a grand stairway rises elegantly beneath a crystal chandelier, one of many gracing the house. The antique

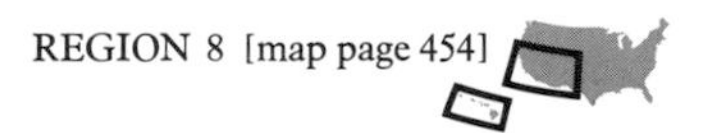

furnishings are from several periods and include a splendid 1782 Duncan Phyfe dining-room set.

Nevada State Capitol *N. Carson St.* Appropriately for the "Silver State," a silver dome, supported by hand-hewn logs, dominates this 1871 stone building shaped like a Greek cross. Solid granite steps lead to an entrance door paned with sparkling French crystal. Nevada's industries and resources are depicted in a decorative frieze that runs around the first floor corridor, the arches, wainscoting and floors of which are richly faced with Alaskan marble. In the governor's chambers are furnishings of the late 19th century. *Open daily.*

Nevada State Museum *N. Carson St.* The old U.S. Branch Mint in Carson City now houses a museum that features an array of items relating to Nevada and its history. Here are some of the coins produced during the mint's 23 years of service, including silver dollars, stamped CC—now rare collectors' pieces. A weapon display focuses on guns of the West; regional wildlife is carefully showcased; and Indian lore comes alive in a life-size diorama of a camp scene. There are also mineral displays and an extraordinary replica of a typical Nevada mine tunnel. *Open daily except holidays.*

109. Austin, Nev. During the 1860s Austin was a silver boomtown. It was noted for its camel pack trains, local pony express and for the Gridley Sack of Flour Auctions in which one R. C. Gridley, by auctioning a single sack of flour again and again, raised $275,000 to help Civil War wounded. Much of the flavor of the period is retained in the historic district in the center of the town. Several original buildings, including a brick courthouse and three brick churches, are still standing. On the edge of Austin is an abandoned stone structure known as Stokes Castle.

110. Northeastern Nevada Museum *1515 Idaho St., Elko, Nev.* The small but choice museum features items that tell of local history—including prehistoric finds—and regional wildlife. Among the most popular exhibits is a full-size bar from a saloon in the ghost town of Halleck, complete with fancy backbar and an early cash register. Next door stands the Ruby Valley Pony Express Station, one of the more picturesque vestiges of pioneer transport. *Open daily.*

111. Belmont, Nev. The ghost town, once the flourishing municipal seat of Nye County, now boasts a population of three and a few lonely surviving buildings from its heyday. During the mid-19th century the town held a large immigrant population—notably Irish, English and German settlers—and was the scene of violent English-Irish feuds that often lasted several years. Among the early structures still intact are a sturdy two-story brick courthouse, topped by a smart cupola, and the Cosmopolitan Saloon, a weathered and picturesque relic of bonanza days.

112. Hoover Dam *Boulder City, Nev.* Rising a mighty 726.4 feet from bedrock, this is one of the tallest dams in the western hemisphere. The monumental bulwark stretches 1244 feet across Black Canyon, its wall 660 feet thick at the base, a mere 45 feet at the top. Behind it the Colorado River backs up for 110 miles to form Lake Mead—one of the world's largest manmade lakes—a gargantuan water reservoir. The dam's hydroelectric plant hums with 17 generating units. In the Visitor Bureau a color film dramatizes the dam's development; in the Exhibits Building a topographic model shows the Colorado River basins. *Open daily. Tour: adults small charge.*

HOOVER DAM SCULPTURES At the west end of the dam is a pair of imposing sculptures called *Winged Figures of the Republic,* the work of Oskar J. W. Hansen. The heroic figures—30 feet high and made of more than four tons of bronze—flank a huge flagpole. The sculptures are set on a terrazzo floor that features a celestial map of Sept. 30, 1935, the day President Franklin Roosevelt dedicated the dam.

113. London Bridge *Lake Havasu City, Ariz.* When British authorities decided to tear down historic London Bridge, the McCulloch Oil Corporation, founder of the planned community of Lake Havasu City, purchased the structure and laboriously moved its 11,000 tons of granite blocks from the Thames to Arizona. It now spans

[112] *The view above looks downstream from above the dam. The four intake towers are in the foreground. The view at left looks up the Colorado River toward the dam and Lake Mead. The U-shaped powerhouse straddles two states, Nevada and Arizona.*

[**114.** *Temple Square-Temple*] *The multi-towered temple, one of eleven in active use in this country, is the scene of the most sacred Mormon ceremonies. The temple dominates the square, a 10-acre oasis surrounded by a high wall in the heart of Salt Lake City. The site for the square was chosen by Brigham Young in 1847; six years later, work on the temple began. Huge blocks of granite were hauled by oxen from a quarry 20 miles away, and slowly the majestic building rose. The golden figure of the angel Moroni that tops the tallest tower is the work of Cyrus E. Dallin, the noted Utah-born sculptor.*

a section of Lake Havasu on the lower Colorado River. As rebuilt here the massive stone landmark is reinforced with modern engineering wizardry, proudly defying the nursery-rhyme warning that "London Bridge is falling down." Near the bridge is an English village complex.

114. Salt Lake City, Utah

The city was first settled by Mormon emigrants from Illinois in 1847 and remains the world headquarters of the Church of Jesus Christ of Latter-day Saints. Perched in an arid mountain valley at an altitude of over 4300 feet, the 62-square-mile city is the major metropolis of the Great Basin. Its economy is based largely on farming and mining for gold, silver, copper, lead and zinc. The Great Salt Lake, 15 miles west of the city, the water of which is about 25 percent salt, is the area's best-known natural attraction.

Beehive House *67 E. S. Temple St.* A carved wooden beehive, symbol of Utah and of the Mormon belief in the dignity of honest work, rests atop the cupola on the home of Mormon leader Brigham Young. Completed in 1854, the gracious mansion has been restored and furnished with many of the original belongings of Young and his several families when he lived here as president of the church and governor of the Utah Territory. Young's own room, his offices, the sitting room, ceremonial Long Hall, kitchen, family store and all the rest of the house reflect the spirit and beliefs of this influential man. *Open Mon.-Sat.*

Brigham Young Forest Farm Home *732 Ashton Ave.* A pioneer showplace today as well as in 1863 when it was built, the comfortable house served as a home for Brigham Young and his family, a center for community entertainments and headquarters of Young's farm, where he experimented with growing fruits, vegetables and livestock that would prosper in Utah uplands. The formal parlor suggests its use for special occasions, and the casual family room still recalls such old-fashioned activities as sewing, quilting and spinning. *Open Mon.-Sat. Mar.-Oct.*

Cathedral of the Madeleine *331 E. S. Temple St.* From the carvings of Christ and the 12 Apostles over the main entrance to the murals of the Holy Trinity and saints of the Old and New Testaments behind the altar, the grand Catholic cathedral is filled with interesting works of art. Many paintings and fine wood carvings lend an air of warmth and intimacy to the spacious interior, where light filters through German-made stained-glass windows noted for their unusually realistic portraits. The cornerstone was laid in 1900 and the building completed in 1909. *Open daily.*

City and County Building *451 Washington Sq.* Topped by a 303-foot-high bell tower, the exterior of the immense Romanesque-style structure is an intriguing medley of turrets, towers, arches, balconies, carved friezes and medallions. The interior is also highly ornamented in the style of the 1890s, when the building was completed. It served for a time as the state capitol (1896–1915), and today is used for its original purpose of housing both city and county offices. Visitors who climb to the bell tower are rewarded with a superb vista of the city. *Open Mon.-Sat.*

Council Hall *Capitol Hill* The site of historic events such as the passage of a female suffrage act in 1870, the building was for 28 years the seat of government of Salt Lake City and the meeting place of the territorial legislature. Its elegant offices and meeting rooms are furnished much as they were in the years following its completion in 1866. Today Council Hall serves as the home of the Utah Travel Council and is a visitor information center. *Open daily late May-early Sept., Mon.-Fri. early Sept.-late May.*

Hogle Zoological Garden *2600 Sunnyside Ave.* More than 1000 animals—from penguins to polar bears—live in the 52-acre zoo. Its canyon setting, well-landscaped grounds and new exhibits make this one of the truly fine zoos. In one building small mammals, birds and reptiles live in climatically controlled areas where visitors can experience the typical temperature and humidity conditions of the animals' native habitats, whether desertlike or tropical. *Open daily except Jan. 1 and Dec. 25. Small charge.*

Keith/Brown Mansion *529 E. S. Temple St.* After walking under a portico supported by four massive stone columns, visitors pass through ornate glass and wrought-iron doors and enter a two-story octagonal room paneled in solid cherry and topped by a domed stained-glass window. The elegant Renaissance-style mansion, one of the most beautiful in the city, was completed in 1900 by Utah mining mogul David Keith. The building and adjoining carriage house were recently restored for use as corporate offices, but great care was taken to retain their historic and aesthetic qualities. *Open Mon.-Fri. except holidays.*

McCune Mansion *Brigham Young University, Salt Lake Center, 200 N. Main St.* When mining and railroad magnate Alfred McCune was building his brick and stone mansion at the turn of the century, it is said that he stopped counting the costs when they reached $500,000. The results are truly splendid: exquisitely carved oak and mahogany paneling, staircases and ceilings; lavish fireplaces, including one of Nubian marble that reaches from floor to ceiling in the main hall; and even silver fittings in the bathrooms. Today classes are held in these sumptuous surroundings. *Open Mon.-Fri. except holidays.*

Temple Square *Main and S. Temple Sts.* Just as Salt Lake City is the world headquarters of the Church of Jesus Christ of Latter-day Saints, Temple Square is the focal point of the church's history within the city. On the landscaped grounds of the walled, 10-acre city block are many of the most famous structures associated with the church.

ASSEMBLY HALL The granite Gothic-style building fringed with delicate spires is a place of public worship. It was completed in 1882. *Open daily.*

CHURCH MUSEUM *Bureau of Information Bldg.* The plow used to turn over the first acre of land in the Salt Lake valley, pianos hauled across the plains by teams of oxen and the press on which the area's first newspaper was printed are only a few of the fascinating relics of Utah's history to be found in the museum. *Open daily.*

OLD HOUSE The oldest house standing in Salt Lake City was built in 1847, shortly after the arrival of the first Mormons. The simple log cabin, now protected from the elements by a massive pergola, is an enduring symbol of the faith of those rugged pioneers.

SALT LAKE TABERNACLE The home of the famed 375-member Mormon Tabernacle Choir is noted for acoustics so perfect that a pin dropped near the pulpit can be heard distinctly at the opposite end of the vast hall. The organ, with nearly 11,000 pipes, is considered one of the world's finest, and recitals are presented daily. (Visitors can also hear the choir itself—at Thursday evening rehearsals and Sunday morning broadcast sessions.) The building, constructed after a plan suggested by Brigham Young, represents a remarkable architectural feat: the roof is an immense oval dome 250 feet long and 150 feet wide, supported only by interlocking wooden arches. *Open daily.*

SALT LAKE TEMPLE OF THE CHURCH OF JESUS CHRIST OF LATTER-DAY SAINTS The most imposing building on the square is the monumental granite structure with three richly ornamented towers on each end. The tallest tower is 210 feet high and is surmounted by a soaring gold-leafed statue of the angel Moroni with a trumpet. Brigham Young selected the site for the temple four days after his arrival in the valley and actual construction began in 1853, but the building was not completed until 40 years later. As is the rule for all Mormon temples it can be entered only by members in good standing with the church.

SEA GULL MONUMENT In the spring of 1848, as hordes of crickets threatened to destroy the Mormon's first crop of 5000 acres of grain, flocks of sea gulls arrived and devoured the insects, thereby saving enough grain to sustain the settlers through the winter. The event is commemorated in this unusual monument consisting of two bronze gulls in flight atop a granite shaft.

STATUES OF JOSEPH AND HYRUM SMITH Joseph Smith, the first prophet and first president of the Church of Jesus Christ of Latter-day Saints, and his older brother Hyrum were murdered by an anti-Mormon mob in Carthage, Illinois, in 1844. It was this bloody event that caused the Mormons to abandon Illinois and seek a new home in the West.

VISITOR CENTER Murals and paintings depict the life of Christ and the history of the Mormon faith. Films and other displays explain the beliefs and ceremonies of the members. *Open daily.*

"This Is the Place" Monument *Pioneer Trail State Park, 2701 Sunnyside Ave.* At the end of the heroic Mormon trek from Illinois to the West, Brigham Young rose from a sickbed on his wagon, viewed the valley of the Great Salt Lake and said, "This is the Place, drive on." Exactly 100 years later, on July 24, 1947, this colossal 60-foot-high monument to Utah's pioneer history was dedicated on the spot where Young uttered his prophetic words. The sculptor was Mahonri M. Young, a grandson of the Mormon leader. In the adjacent Visitor Center a stirring mural depicts the hardships and final triumph of the Mormons' epic journey. *Open daily except holidays.*

Thomas Kearns Mansion and Carriage House *603 E. S. Temple St.* A poor farm boy from Nebraska, Thomas Kearns made a fortune at Utah's famed Silver King Mines. His palatial, turn-of-the-century French Renaissance-style mansion is noted for its elaborately carved woodwork, tile and parquet floors, rare tapestries, marble, silver, paintings and statuary. For 20 years the official residence of Utah's governors, the house is now the headquarters of the Utah State Historical Society. Works by contemporary Utah artists are displayed in galleries in the mansion and the adjacent carriage house. *Open Mon.-Fri. except holidays.*

University of Utah After a shaky beginning—it opened in 1850, then closed after one session and remained closed until 1867—this state university today has an enrollment of almost 20,000 in a wide variety of schools. There are several attractions for visitors on its 653-acre campus.

UTAH MUSEUM OF FINE ARTS *Arts and Architecture Center* Major emphasis at the only sizable art museum in the area is on 19th-century French and American landscape painting. The varied holdings in the modern facility also include tapestries, French and English antique furnishings, Egyptian and Oriental objects and contemporary graphics. *Open Sun.-Fri. except holidays.*

UTAH MUSEUM OF NATURAL HISTORY With exhibits as diverse as the reconstructed skeletons of three dinosaurs and a collection of Indian artifacts ranging from 10,000 years ago to recent times, the museum explores the full spectrum of natural history in Utah and the Great Basin. There are dioramas of life-size mule deer

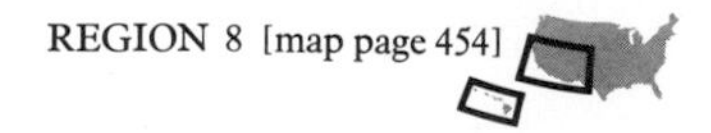

and marsh birds in their natural habitats, miniature replicas of prehistoric Indian ruins, the world's only known set of pterodactyl tracks and a variety of other exhibits portraying the interlocking worlds of man and nature. *Open daily except holidays. Small charge.*

Utah State Capitol *Capitol Hill* The magnificent domed structure of granite and marble sits amid landscaped gardens on a hill overlooking the city. In many of its more than 200 rooms are outstanding murals, paintings and statues of prominent Utahans. The Gold Room, used for state receptions, contains table, chairs and chandeliers covered with gold leaf made from ore from Utah mines. There is also an exhibition area with displays of the state's industrial, mineral and scenic resources. On the grounds is an impressive monument honoring the Mormon Battalion's 2000-mile march from Iowa to California during the Mexican War of 1846. *Open daily May-Sept., Mon.-Sat. Oct.-Apr.*

115. Provo, Utah

The Mormons reached the fertile valley of the Provo River and established themselves there in 1849. The city is an agricultural and manufacturing center surrounded by some remarkable scenery, such as Provo Canyon and 12,000-foot Mount Timpanogos.

Brigham Young University Founded in 1875 by the Mormon church, the university draws at least half its students from outside the state. Its beautifully landscaped campus attracts visitors, as do its fine museum collections.

EARTH SCIENCE MUSEUM *Eyring Science Center* Minerals from around the world make dazzling displays, but most compelling are the remains of dinosaurs and other extinct prehistoric animals. *Open Mon.-Fri.*

FINE ARTS COLLECTION *Harris Fine Arts Center* A choice selection of 15,000 drawings, paintings and sculptures prominently features the works of Utah artists. *Open Mon.-Fri.*

LIFE SCIENCE MUSEUM *Heber J. Grant Bldg.* Highlights of the displays are mounted animals and insects. There are several dioramas of birds, including their eggs, in natural habitats. *Open Mon.-Sat.*

MUSEUM OF ARCHAEOLOGY AND ETHOLOGY *Maeser Bldg.* A copy of a Mexican stela stands at the entrance to the Mesoamerican Room, where glyph panels and other ancient relics are on view. Artifacts from Navaho, Hopi, Apache and other Southwestern Indian cultures are featured, as well as displays depicting the life-style of Iroquois Indians. *Open Mon.-Fri.*

Provo Stakes Tabernacle *90 S. University Ave.* The handsome red brick building with two tall octagonal towers flanking its facade is one of the largest of all Mormon churches. It was completed in 1898. The spacious interior, which is noted for its fine acoustics, has been the site of concerts by composer and pianist Sergei Rachmaninoff, violinist Fritz Kreisler and other famous artists. *Open daily June-Sept.*

116. Springville Museum of Art *126 E. 400 S., Springville, Utah* Although a Gainsborough landscape and an impressive oil by Turner (*Ship Burning at Sea*) form part of the permanent collection, the main strengths of this museum lie in its American works. Rockwell Kent and Childe Hassam are among those represented, and a fine bronze, *Lady Godiva,* by Anna Hyatt Huntington can be seen, along with several sculptures by Utah artist Cyrus E. Dallin. *Open Tues.-Sun. Apr.-late Mar. except holidays.*

117. Fairview Museum of History and Art *Fairview, Utah Love and Devotion,* a larger-than-life study of a couple who were married for 82 years, is one of several sculptures here by prominent Utah artist Avard T. Fairbanks. On a much smaller scale are miniature carvings by a local artist whose subjects range from a Wells Fargo coach to a replica of the Taj Mahal. The museum's varied offerings also include local Indian artifacts, a broad range of pioneer memorabilia and a collection of antique wagons, engines and old-time earthmoving equipment. *Open daily Apr.-Sept.*

118. Territorial Statehouse *50 W. Capitol St., Fillmore, Utah* Utah's first capitol was originally planned as a grandiose cross-shaped structure with a dome. By 1855, however, only this south wing was completed; after a few sessions in Fillmore the legislators removed the seat of government to Salt Lake City, and the stately red sandstone building is now a museum. The legislative hall contains antiques and an art collection, some of the offices are furnished as replicas of rooms in pioneer homes and some contain paintings, Indian artifacts, tools, weapons and other relics. *Open daily June-Aug., Mon.-Fri. Sept.-May.*

AMERICAN ROSE SOCIETY TRIAL ROSE GARDEN The statehouse grounds feature extensive beds planted with dozens of varieties of All-American prize-winning roses, which bloom from June to late autumn. *Open daily.*

119. Old Cove Fort *Off Rte. 15, Cove Fort, Utah* Mormons under the direction of Brigham Young completed the stone fort in 1867 during the Black Hawk War as a protection against Indian raids. Its sturdy portholed walls and 12 rooms are in practically their original condition, and wooden pegs and square nails are visible in door and window frames. In addition to a fine collection of period furniture, visitors can study numerous Indian and pioneer relics. *Open daily Apr.-Oct. Small charge.*

120. Dr. and Mrs. William R. Palmer Memorial Museum *75 N. 300 W., Cedar City, Utah* Piute Indian basketry, leatherwork, an especially fine collection of beadwork and other artifacts plus many early pioneer tools are displayed in this museum maintained by the Iron County School District. Many of the objects were given to Dr. Palmer, a Mormon missionary and businessman, by the Piute Indians, who eventually made him a member of their tribe. *Open Mon.-Fri. except holidays.*

121. Southern Utah State College *Cedar City, Utah* This four-year liberal arts college traces its origin to the establishment of a normal school here in 1898. The auditorium in the college's 1904 Old Administration Building was Cedar City's first community center. The oldest building on the campus, Old Main, was completed in just six months in 1898. It was built by hand of local material by dedicated citizens who contributed all the time, labor and money that went into its construction. *Open Mon.-Fri. Sept.-July.*

[127] *As the Anasazi drew together and began to build their apartment-house villages, several cultural centers developed. One of these is preserved in Navajo National Monument, which has three great cliff dwellings. Regularly scheduled tours are led to Betatakin, but because of its fragility Inscription House (shown here) cannot be visited by tourists. The smallest of the three dwellings and the farthest from the Visitor Center, Inscription House was named for nearly illegible marks thought to have been made by a Spaniard in 1661. "Anasazi" is a Navaho word, and the ruins of this center of Anasazi culture are named for the Navaho and preserved on Navaho tribal land. The Navaho preserve several other ancient Anasazi settlements, yet the Anasazi were ancestors of the modern Pueblo Indians, not of the Navaho.*

122. Jacob Hamblin Home State Historic Site *Rte. 91, Santa Clara, Utah* The two-story 1862 sandstone dwelling also served as a fortress for Jacob Hamblin, the Mormon scout and missionary known as the Buckskin Apostle. Situated in Dixie State Park, the building has been restored and contains authentic pioneer furnishings. *Open daily.*

123. McQuarrie Memorial Hall *Off Rte. 91, St. George, Utah* Utah's Dixie region—so-called because cotton and other semitropical crops can be grown here—was settled in 1861. It was then an arid wasteland, and many of the earliest pioneer homes were small adobe huts or simple dugouts in the ground. Old photographs, tools, spinning wheels, looms, furniture and other possessions of the pioneers in the museum memorialize the harsh realities of their existence as they gradually established themselves here. *Open Mon.-Sat. June-Sept.*

124. St. George Temple of the Church of Jesus Christ of Latter-day Saints *401 S. 200 E., St. George, Utah* The white plastered walls of the lofty building rise above the town like a beautiful mirage. The oldest Mormon temple west of the Mississippi, it was completed in 1877 by the hardy, self-sacrificing pioneers who settled St. George. Like all Mormon temples, it is open only to members of the church in good standing, but at the adjacent Visitor Center guides outline its purpose and uses, and a color motion picture provides views of the interior and explains the rites performed in the temple. *Open Mon.-Sat.*

125. Pipe Spring National Monument *Moccasin, Ariz.* Built in 1870 by Mormons as a defense against Indian raids, the stone fort became part of a cattle ranch and served as an important stopping place for early travelers. The main section and several outbuildings contain displays of pioneer furnishings and artifacts. Demonstrations of ranch chores such as cattle branding and quilting are given. *Open daily.*

126. Glen Canyon Bridge *Page, Ariz.* Spanning Glen Canyon an impressive 700 feet above the Colorado River, the steel arch bridge is the highest in the world. The structure, which is 1271 feet long and constructed from more than 4000 tons of steel and 2550 cubic yards of concrete, was built in 1957-9. It accommodates a 30-foot-wide roadway flanked by pedestrian walks. Just upstream from the bridge is the massive sweep of Glen Canyon Dam, which holds back Lake Powell.

127. Navajo National Monument *30 mi. N.E. of Tonalea, Ariz.* These cliff dwellings—the largest complex in Arizona—were the homes of Anasazi Indians (a Navaho name meaning "the ancient ones"), who abandoned them about seven centuries ago. Betatakin ("Ledge House" in Navaho), the most accessible ruin, is located in a natural alcove protected by sheer canyon walls. The ruin contains 135 rooms, including living quarters, granaries and one kiva (a round, well-like ceremonial chamber). A primitive eight-mile trail leads to Keet Seel ("Broken Pottery"), the largest cliff dwelling in the state, with 160 rooms. The trails and many of the back roads in this part of the country are often rough and rugged. Travel is not advisable without proper directions and equipment. Pottery, jewelry and implements found at the ruins are among the exhibits at the Visitor Center. *Open daily.*

128. Museum of Northern Arizona *Fort Valley Rd., Flagstaff, Ariz.* Indian culture, both prehistoric and modern, and the natural history of the Colorado Plateau are the museum's featured subjects. Archaeological exhibits include items more than 2000 years old, tools, pottery and jewelry among them. Dioramas show how ancient Indians lived, and the customs and crafts of contemporary Indians are also displayed. Pictorial exhibits of geologic formations and fossils are a part of the natural history displays. Of particular interest are a replica of a Hopi kiva, Hopi kachina dolls and a room hung with Navaho rugs. *Open daily Mar.-mid-Dec.*

129. Walnut Canyon National Monument *Rte. 40, 8 mi. E. of Flagstaff, Ariz.* Within the 1879-acre national monument are the remains of the cliff dwellings of the prehistoric Sinagua Indians, dating from the early 1100s. The Sinagua built their one-room stone homes in the cavelike recesses of the 400-foot-deep canyon walls, and at one time there were more than 300 houses. A paved trail leads directly to 25 of the rooms. The canyon itself and many other rooms may be seen at a distance from another trail. A museum at the Visitor Center contains displays of the life and culture of the Sinagua who lived here in peace, farming at the rim of the canyon for 150 years. *Open daily. Small charge.*

130. Wupatki National Monument *Off Rte. 89, 35 mi. N. of Flagstaff, Ariz.* Within the monument's 56 square miles are about 800 Indian ruins dating from the 12th century. The largest dwelling, the Wupatki ruin, is a four-story sandstone structure with about 110 rooms (Wupatki means "tall house" in Hopi). Some original support timbers still stand, easily viewed in rooms reached today, as long ago, by ladder. Nearby are a masonry-lined ball court and a circular amphitheater. The small Nalakihu ruin was the dwelling of three prehistoric cultures (Nalakihu is a Hopi word for "house standing alone"). An unexcavated fortresslike structure called the Citadel tops a lava mesa and had about 40 rooms; some of its features are explained by interpretive panels at the site. Exhibits at the Visitor Center explain the life-style of the Indians who flourished on these richly historic mesas. *Open daily.*

131. Chapel of the Holy Cross *Rte. 179, Sedona, Ariz.* The architectural form of the front of this impressive modern shrine rooted between two spurs of red sandstone, with an enormous cross soaring 90 feet toward the sky, was dictated by the site. The rose-hued chapel, built in 1956, seems a natural outcrop of its spectacular setting in Oak Creek Canyon. Visitors enter through two lofty anodized-aluminum doors that extend from the threshold to the ceiling. *Open daily.*

132. Tuzigoot National Monument *Off Rte. 89A, E. of Clarkdale, Ariz.* The fortresslike pueblo, once an active village with 110 large rooms, some two stories high, was built on a ridge. It was constructed by Sinagua Indians in the early 12th century and occupied by them

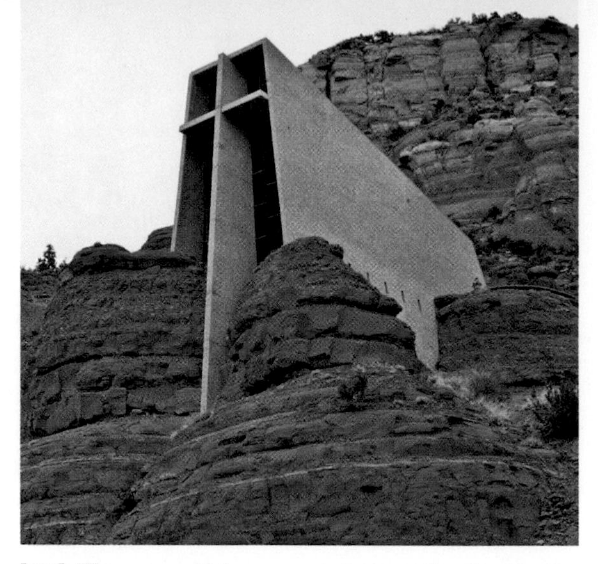

[131] *The cross, which appears to support the church, also, on the inside, supports the altar and a tormented figure of Christ. The enormous windows flanking the cross frame a vivid and violently sculptured landscape.*

for about 300 years. Few doorways are evident, as the Indians entered their rooms through roof hatches, using ladders. A museum contains bone and stone implements, mosaic pendants, pottery, basketry, jewelry and other artifacts excavated here. *Open daily except Dec. 25.*

133. Jerome Mine Museum and Gallery *Main St., Jerome, Ariz.* Perched high on the side of Cleopatra Hill, Jerome today remains proud of its rich mining heritage. Here a complex of copper mines once made men's fortunes, including that of James S. Douglas, who owned Little Daisy Mine. The Douglas mansion, built in 1917, now houses a museum of mining relics and exhibits of Jerome's bonanza days. Dioramas depict life in the mining town during the late 19th and early 20th centuries, a model shows the location of about 85 miles of tunnels and a photo gallery features Jerome's early buildings. The mineral display features a darkroom for viewing fluorescent rocks. *Open daily except Dec. 25. Small charge.*

134. Montezuma Castle National Monument *Rte. 17, 5 mi. N. of Camp Verde, Ariz.* About 800 years ago Sinagua Indians built the Castle, a five-story apartment house in a cavity 70 feet up the face of a cliff. Constructed of limestone chunks, boulders and adobe, the 19 rooms were reached by a series of ladders; when the lowest one was hauled in, the sanctuary became an inaccessible fortress. The Visitor Center holds pottery, turquoise and shell jewelry, bone awls, stone axes and other hand-crafted artifacts of the ancient culture. To the left of the Castle are the ruins of another five-story pueblo, and seven miles to the northeast, still part of the national monument, is Montezuma Well, a lake that provided irrigation for the nearby Indian farmlands. *Open daily. Small charge.*

135. Bucky O'Neill Monument *Courthouse Sq., Prescott, Ariz.* The bronze equestrian statue, designed by Solon H. Borglum, commemorates the Arizonans who died in the Spanish-American War. The statue is of Captain Bucky O'Neill, the war's first cavalry volunteer, who organized the famous Rough Riders.

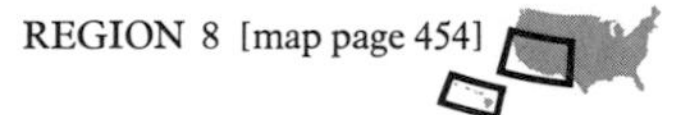

136. Phoenix, Ariz.

Arizona's capital is the Southwest's prototype boom town. In only 100 years it has grown from a cotton-growing community of 30 to a cosmopolitan city of 600,000. The arrival of the railroad in 1887 spurred its early development, but it was not until 1911, when the Roosevelt Dam was finished, that Phoenix had an adequate water supply. As the desert became an oasis, settlers moved in, industries soon followed and many tourists inevitably became fulltime residents, because nature generously endowed the Phoenix valley with mountains ringing the horizon, picturesque desert and a climate in which most days are brilliantly cloudless.

Arizona State Capitol *1700 W. Washington St.* Set in a park beautifully landscaped with cacti as well as trees and flowers, the dignified building was the territorial capitol before it became the statehouse in 1912. It is built of soft-hued native tufa stone and topped by a broad copper dome. Inside, a museum holds a choice collection of artifacts related to the history of Arizona. *Open Mon.-Fri.*

Heard Museum *22 E. Monte Vista Rd.* Indian artworks, both ancient and modern, are the prize possessions here. Primitive Indian artifacts represent works of the Pueblo, Pima, Papago, Hohokam and Apache tribes. Southwestern archaeological and ethnological materials are handsomely displayed as are the bold, imaginative arts and crafts of today's Southwest Indians. Senator Barry Goldwater's colorful collection of more than 400 kachina dolls fills a separate room. More than 5000 volumes in the library relate to American Indians. *Open daily except holidays.*

Phoenix Art Museum *1625 N. Central Ave.* Chinese tomb figures from the T'ang dynasty and Sir Victor Sassoon's collection of Chinese ivories are among the leading exhibits. The museum also contains works representing Renaissance, Baroque and Far Eastern art as well as American contemporary. Outstanding paintings include Picasso's *Woman at the Beach,* Jean Baptiste Greuze's *Self Portrait,* Andrew Wyeth's *Farmhouse* and George Inness' *Perugia.* Costumes, decorative arts and sculpture from various periods are also shown here, along with 16 fascinating miniature copies of famous rooms. *Open Tues.-Sun. except holidays.*

Phoenix Zoo *5810 E. Van Buren St.* Rare Arabian oryx, white rhinos, DeBrazza's monkeys, Asiatic leopards and giant anteaters are among the more than 1100 different animals "at home" here. The animals mostly live in moated natural settings, part of 123 landscaped acres of tawny desert terrain, rolling hills and sky-blue lakes in Papago Park. Trained animal shows, a safari train and a children's zoo are popular attractions. *Open daily. Small charge.*

Pioneer Arizona *Rte. 17, Pioneer Rd. exit* Pioneer life of the late 19th-century Southwest is re-created in this living-history museum. Arizona's first Bicentennial (1976) project now has 21 buildings ranging from an 1860 ranch, complete with livestock and crops, to a miner's camp, bank, stage station, saloon, wagonmaker's shop, craft shops and homes. All are furnished with original artifacts. Animals in common use on ranches at that time are also part of the village setting. *Open daily except Dec. 25. Adults $1.50, children small charge.*

Pueblo Grande Museum *4619 E. Washington St.* The Hohokam Indians, prehistoric desert farmers, occupied this site from 300 B.C. to 1400 A.D. The museum features exhibits related to the late Hohokam culture, including its arts and crafts and rare archaeological finds. The building, which includes three research laboratories, is designed after the stepped, truncated pyramids of Mexico which influenced the Hohokam. The site contains a large Hohokam platform structure and the remains of four prehistoric irrigation canals. A completely excavated ball court is near the mound. *Open Sun.-Fri. except holidays.*

137. Taliesin West *Shea Blvd. and 108th St., Scottsdale, Ariz.* Now the architectural office and school of the Frank Lloyd Wright Foundation, the stunning complex was designed by Wright and built by his students as his winter headquarters. Set beneath magnificent mountains and overlooking miles of desert floor, the buildings clearly evidence Wright's hallmark: they seem to belong to the desert itself. Long, low walls are formed of native boulders set in concrete, and all design motifs reflect the sharply outlined landscape. *Open daily mid-Oct.-mid-May. $2.50.*

138. Arizona State University *Tempe, Ariz.* Founded nearly 100 years ago the school was for many years devoted to the education of future teachers. After World War II demands for a broader curriculum resulted in startling growth and academic diversity. Today the university comprises 10 colleges and schools; its campus of strikingly modern buildings is dispersed over 320 gracefully landscaped acres.

GRADY GAMMAGE MEMORIAL AUDITORIUM Frank Lloyd Wright's building, which was dedicated in 1964

[137] *Taliesin was a legendary Welsh poet. The translation of his name, Shining Brow, seems appropriate at Taliesin West, where the intense desert sun is softly filtered through the white canvas roof into the drafting room in which architects work in the environment designed by Mr. Wright.*

and named for a former university president, is one of the Southwest's foremost centers for the performing arts. The auditorium looks like a fanciful pink carousel from the outside, but its interior is a paragon of functional beauty. The proscenium stage contains a steel acoustical shell that telescopes into place for symphonic and other non-theatrical performances. The sweeping grand tier, supported by a gigantic 145-foot girder, and the second balcony stand free from the back walls, so that sound reflects to each of the auditorium's 3000 seats. *Open daily.*

UNIVERSITY ART COLLECTIONS *Matthews Center* Audubon's *Osprey and the Otter and the Salmon,* Homer's *Corn Husking* and Eakins's *Portrait of Woman* are among the outstanding paintings here. Other artists represented in one of the largest and most distinguished collections of American art west of the Mississippi include Stuart, Bellows, Remington, Inness and Andrew Wyeth. Exhibits also include works of American and European sculptors, a large international print collection and American ceramics of the 19th and 20th centuries. *Open Sun.-Fri. except holidays.*

139. Theodore Roosevelt Dam *Rte. 88, Roosevelt, Ariz.* Mule-drawn wagons hauled supplies for the building of this gargantuan dam on the Salt River, an astonishing job that took eight years' work before its dedication in 1911. The government's first major reclamation project, the structure is the world's highest masonry dam (280 feet). It stores water that irrigates some 250,000 acres in the broad Phoenix valley. The lake created by the massively thick arched dam is now a favorite recreation spot.

140. Tonto National Monument *Rte. 88, Roosevelt, Ariz.* The farming Salado Indians, who flourished in this rugged landscape more than 600 years ago, constructed homes in two natural caves in steep cliffs and on a terraced ledge. The dwellings formed perfect strongholds against possible invasion. The three cliff dwellings were built of rough quartzite blocks set in adobe mortar; today the ruins are easily accessible by way of a self-guiding trail. One ruin contains 40 rooms, another 19 and the third 12. Various Salado artifacts such as stone and shell pendants, polychrome pottery, axes and bone awls are handsomely displayed at the Visitor Center. *Open daily. Small charge.*

141. Besh-Ba-Gowah Indian Ruin *Ice House Canyon Rd., Globe, Ariz.* The adobe ruins are the remains of a settlement of Salado Indians that flourished here between 1225 and 1400. Besh-ba-gowah is an Apache term meaning "metal camp," the current Indian name for Globe, a center for copper refining. The pueblo village once held about 200 rooms and surviving or restored portions include living and storage rooms, doorways and passageways, patios and fire pits. Pottery, basketry, ornaments, weapons and tools found in the burial grounds can be seen at the Museum of Gila County in Globe. *Open daily.*

142. Casa Grande Ruins National Monument *Rte. 87, N. of Coolidge, Ariz.* When the Hohokam Indians farmed in the Gila River Valley more than 600 years ago, the remarkable four-story earthen structure here—the Casa Grande, or "Big House"—may have been a ceremonial building, but its exact function is unknown. Surrounding it are the remains of a walled village containing several individual rooms. Other prehistoric villages are also evident within the monument's boundaries. A museum exhibits artifacts of the Hohokam and illustrates the fascinating life-styles of the period. *Open daily. Small charge.*

143. Arizona-Sonora Desert Museum *Tucson Mountain Park, Tucson, Ariz.* Hundreds of desert creatures displayed in surroundings closely simulating their natural habitats are the specialty of the justly famous museum. The animals, which are all indigenous to the Southwest, particularly to the Sonora Desert, include bighorn sheep, coyotes, bobcats, otters, beavers and mountain lions. In addition there are reptiles, birds and vampire and fruit-eating bats. Easy-to-follow exhibits in the Orientation Room explain the ecology of the desert, in particular the kangaroo rats and fringe-toed lizards, which exemplify adaptation to harsh desert living. A tunnel exhibit is devoted to the intricacies of underground life. There are also plant and mineral displays and a regional garden. *Open daily. Adults $2.00.*

144. Mission San Xavier del Bac *9 mi. S. on San Xavier Rd., Tucson, Ariz.* Franciscans completed the elaborately domed and arched church in 1797, a fine example of Spanish Colonial architecture. Brickwork

[**145.** *Arizona State Museum*] *These carved stone palettes that once held paints for decorating the body are from Snaketown, once the site of a flourishing desert community (300* B.C.*-1100* A.D.*). The Hohokam inhabitants worked out an elaborate canal system to irrigate their crops and still had time to develop sophisticated art forms. They invented shell etching before the Europeans did. The horned lizard on the center palette was a favorite motif.*

[150] *Most of the dinosaurs embedded in the quarry wall were plant-eaters like this* Camerasaurus supremus *whose leg bone is being carefully reliefed. Modern animals abound among the monument's beautiful canyons.*

and a dazzling white plaster are fashioned into graceful balconies and parapets, and the entrance facade is a masterpiece of decorative art. The baroque interior features expert brick and plaster craftsmanship, original paintings and a richly ornamented altar. *Open daily except holidays.*

145. University of Arizona *Tucson, Ariz.* The Arizona territorial legislature established the university in 1885—27 years before Arizona was admitted to the Union as the 48th state. On the 100-acre campus are two museums of interest to visitors.

ARIZONA STATE MUSEUM The museum contains an extensive group of archaeological materials relating to the prehistoric Indians of the area, who lived here from about the 8th century B.C. The remains of a mammoth, about 10,000 years old, are displayed along with the spear points that were used to kill it. Arts and crafts of modern Southwest Indians are also exhibited. *Open daily except holidays.*

MUSEUM OF ART A wide-ranging collection covers many centuries and art styles, but it features outstanding works in three areas. The Kress Collection is a fine array of Renaissance art. Prominent French artists are represented by Matisse, Léger, Dubuffet and Utrillo. The excellent American collection covers the 19th century to the present, including Hopper's painting *The City,* Calder's mobile *Blue Moon Over the Steeple* and works by Pollock, de Kooning and Rothko. *Open daily.*

146. Kitt Peak National Observatory *Off Rte. 386, S. of Pan Tak, Ariz.* Located atop Kitt Peak on the Papago Indian Reservation, the observatory is a self-contained community devoted to solar, stellar and planetary research. The McMath Solar Telescope, the largest of its kind in the world, is in operation here. In addition to an array of instruments worthy of the best science fiction, the complex contains an 84-inch and four smaller reflecting telescopes used to detect characteristics such as the motion, composition and brightness of stellar objects. A new 158-inch telescope, the second largest in the U.S., is used for stellar and galactic study. *Open daily except Dec. 25.*

147. Tumacacori National Monument *Tumacacori, Ariz.* The Mission of San José de Tumacacori, started by Jesuits in the late 18th century, was used until 1848, when it was abandoned before being completed. Parts of the elegant baroque church still remain: the dome, plastered walls, painted decorations and ceiling of the sacristy. Behind the church lies a walled cemetery with an unfinished circular mortuary chapel. A patio garden at the Visitor Center displays plants of the area. A museum contains maps, drawings, artifacts and dioramas detailing early Indian and Spanish history. *Open daily. Small charge.*

148. Uintah County Daughters of Utah Pioneers Museum *Fifth W. and Second S. Sts., Vernal, Utah* The focal point of this collection of pioneer objects is the medicine cabinet built and used by Vernal's first physician, Dr. Harvey Coe Hullinger, who delivered his last baby at the age of 96. Two early kitchen stoves are among the many pioneer relics displayed. *Open daily late May–mid-Sept.*

149. Utah Field House of Natural History *235 E. Main St., Vernal, Utah* Outside this compact museum are dramatically posed, life-size models of some of the many kinds of dinosaurs that once roamed the area, as well as a replica of the 76-foot-long skeleton of *Diplodocus,* a vegetarian dinosaur that lived in this region 140 million years ago. Inside are displays of the geology, paleontology, wildlife and other natural phenomena of the Uinta Mountain and Basin area. The archaeological exhibits include a diorama showing Indians of the Basketmaker culture. *Open daily.*

150. Dinosaur National Monument *Off Rte. 40, 7 mi. N. of Jensen, Utah* Some 140 million years ago this now-arid landscape was alive with dinosaurs, many of which apparently became mired on a sandbar in a now-extinct river or were washed into the area during floods. Their remains have been revealed in the most concentrated deposit of dinosaur bones ever discovered. Early in this century about 350 tons of fossils of 14 different kinds of dinosaurs were removed from the site and sent to museums across the country. Today visitors can enter a structure whose north wall is the actual face of the quarry and watch technicians chipping away to expose the astonishing array of fossil bones embedded in the rock. *Open daily.*

151. Newspaper Rock State Historic Monument *Off Rte. 163, 14 mi. N. of Monticello, Utah* Mysterious symbols drawn by Indians at several periods cover a large section of rock on a canyon wall. Some of these picturesque rock drawings (petroglyphs) are thought to be 1000 years old. None have been deciphered. Other petroglyphs are found in the canyon. *Open daily.*

152. Lowry Pueblo Ruins *9 mi. W. of Pleasant View, Colo.* At one time a three-story building of about 40 rooms, the pueblo housed a community of 50 to 100 Anasazi Indians. Built about 1075 A.D., it was occupied intermittently for 100 to 150 years, then abandoned. Now the crumbling masonry walls have been partially reconstructed and visitors can walk where a peaceful community of Indians eked a living from the land nearly 1000 years ago. The Great Kiva, or circular underground ceremonial chamber, is one of the largest ever found. *Open daily.*

153. Mesa Verde National Park *Off Rte. 160, 10 mi. E. of Cortez, Colo.* This tableland, cut by steep canyons and covering about 300 square miles, was inhabited for some 1300 years by Anasazi Indians. Visitors can see excavated ruins of the pit houses and pueblos they built on mesa tops and in natural caves halfway up the cliffs. Chapin Mesa Museum has many examples of pottery, baskets, weapons and other artifacts, and dioramas showing the stages of Anasazi culture. *Open daily. $2.00 each car or small charge each person.*

BALCONY HOUSE Like a stronghold, the ruin stands at a strategic spot in the wall of Soda Canyon. Its 40 rooms are reached by a 32-foot ladder.

CLIFF PALACE The largest of the cliff dwellings is reached by descending a long, steep stairway. Two hundred rooms, some in four-story apartments, and 23 kivas make this an important and impressive example of the villages that were built in this region by the prehistoric Indians.

FAR VIEW HOUSE The ruins of this large mesa-top pueblo suggest that a community existed here between 900 and 1200 A.D.

FEWKES CANYON RUINS Four separate dwelling areas nestle in this short branch of Cliff Canyon. Symmetrical Fire Temple was probably used for ceremonies; it is visible from the drive above but may not be entered. New Fire House holds two caves with living rooms and three kivas, while Oak Tree House encompasses 30 living areas and seven kivas. A virtual ruin, Mummy House derives its name from the preserved body of a child found there.

PICTOGRAPH POINT TRAIL The three-mile path starts at the museum and runs along the side of Spruce Tree and Navajo Canyons to Pictograph Point, where Indian rock petroglyphs may be seen.

SPRUCE TREE HOUSE Situated in a cave in Spruce Tree Canyon, the complex of 114 living and storage rooms and eight kivas was built over the course of about 100 years. The best preserved and third largest cliff dwelling in the park, it can be seen on a self-guided tour during summer months.

SUN TEMPLE Mystery surrounds the 131-foot-long structure, believed to have been intended for ceremonial functions. Never completed and found to hold only a few stone-working tools, it has a D-shaped main section with walls three feet thick.

154. Narrow Gauge Durango Train *Rio Grande Depot, 479 Main Ave., Durango, Colo.* The last of the regularly scheduled narrow-gauge railroad trains has been in operation since 1882. Leaving Durango in the morning, the chugging steam engine draws a string of vintage Victorian passenger cars for the all-day round trip to Silverton, a colorful mining town 45 miles to the north. The route, in many places on high, narrow cliffs, passes through spectacular Rocky Mountain scenery. *Open daily late May-early Oct. Adults $8.00, children under 12 $5.00.*

155. Hovenweep National Monument *Off Rte. 666, E. of Hatch Trading Post, Utah* Named for the Ute Indian word meaning "deserted valley," Hovenweep was not always lonely mesa country. Between 400 and 1300 A.D., Pueblo Indians peacefully lived here: they farmed corn, beans and squash; hunted animals; crafted tools, jewelry, clothing and religious objects. Their legacy today is a collection of scattered ruins—pueblos, cliff dwellings and stone towers. Square Tower, impressively preserved, reveals expert stone masonry, mute testimony to communities of accomplished artisans. *Open daily.*

156. Cumbres & Toltec Scenic Railroad *Chama, N.M.* This 64-mile narrow-gauge railroad was built in the 1880s to serve the mountainous area between Chama and Antonito, Colorado. The scenic route passes over breathtaking Toltec Gorge and through Cumbres Pass at 10,015 feet—one of the world's highest railway crossings. The original coal-fired locomotives pull open-air coaches made from boxcars built in 1904. *Trips Fri.-Mon. May-June, daily July-Aug., Fri.-Mon. Sept.-mid-Oct. Adults $14.00, children $5.00.*

157. Aztec Ruins National Monument *1 mi. N. of Aztec, N.M.* This is one of the largest Pre-Columbian pueblo communities in the Southwest. Early settlers erroneously labeled the Indian inhabitants Aztec, although they were unrelated to the Aztecs of Mexico. The largest of the pueblos, dating from the early 12th century, is a three-story, U-shaped structure, covering two acres and containing about 500 rooms. This was built around a great kiva, which has been completely restored. Pottery, weapons, bones, tools and other ar-

[**153.** *Cliff Palace*] *At the height of the Anasazi culture, some 400 people lived in Cliff Palace. The name was given to the multistoried community by Richard Wetherill and Charles Mason, who came upon it unexpectedly in 1888. The walls of several kivas can be seen near the cliff's edge. They were roofed over and entered by ladders. The roofs, like the roofs of other rooms, were used for daily activities.*

[163] *The Indians of Acoma Pueblo, also called Sky City, were able to resist the Spaniards until 1629, when the Acoma mission was established, because their fortress-like mesa provided tactical advantage. Only a few Indians still live on the mesa, but many return for the impressive ceremonies.*

chaeological finds are displayed in the museum. *Open daily. Small charge.*

158. Chaco Canyon National Monument *Rte. 57, Bloomfield, N.M.* Within the 21,500-acre monument are the ruins of 12 prehistoric pueblos and more than 300 smaller sites. The largest of the pueblos was Pueblo Bonito, a five-story masonry structure covering three acres. Built about 900 years ago, it contains 800 rooms and 32 kivas. Pueblo Bonito could accommodate 1200 persons. Pottery, jewelry, tools and other artifacts of the ancient Anasazi people who lived here until the 13th century are displayed at the Visitor Center. Dioramas help re-create their daily life. *Open daily.*

159. Canyon de Chelly National Monument *Chinle, Ariz.* Four different Indian cultures—the Basketmakers, the Pueblo, the Hopi and the contemporary Navahos—have made their homes in spectacular de Chelly (pronounced d'shay) Canyon and the others that make up the national monument. The cave dwellings along the canyon walls, built between 1100 and 1300 A.D., are the remains of the Pueblo civilization. White House, named for its white-plastered front, is the most famous ruin; it stands at the opening of a cave beneath a towering sheet of rock. Mummy Cave Ruin features a three-story tower, and Antelope House still has 150-year-old pictures of antelopes painted by a Navaho artist. Relics of the four Indian cultures are on display. *Open daily.*

160. Hubbell Trading Post National Historic Site *Rte. 264, W. of Ganado, Ariz.* John Lorenzo Hubbell (1853–1930), known on the frontier as Don Lorenzo, became the owner of the trading post shortly after its founding in 1876. It is the oldest on the Navaho reservation and is still in operation. The 150-acre site includes the Hubbell home and office and the trading post. The home contains its original furniture, Navaho rugs and blankets, brass beds, paintings, artifacts and a 1500-volume library of Western lore. Navaho blankets, rugs, silver jewelry and paintings are on sale in the old trading post. *Open daily. Small charge.*

161. Navajo Tribal Museum *Window Rock, Ariz.* The natural history of the area and the cultures of prehistoric Pueblo cliff dwellers and early Navahos form the basis of the many exhibits here. Artifacts of Southwestern Indians are displayed, with an emphasis on Navaho objects. Facilities include a research library, photographic files, a herbarium and a zoo housing native mammals and birds. *Open daily.*

162. El Morro National Monument *Off Rte. 53, El Morro, N.M.* Over the centuries El Morro, a massive sandstone promontory, has gained the name Inscription Rock. More than 1200 markings made here tell the story of various peoples. There are prehistoric Zuni symbols, and Spanish inscriptions, the first dating from 1605. American adventurers and settlers heading West added their own fascinating graffiti. Footholds rise to the ruins of two Zuni pueblo villages at the top of the bluff, one partially excavated. Exhibits in the Visitor Center tell the history. *Open daily except Dec. 25. Small charge.*

163. Acoma Pueblo *Rte. 23, Acoma, N.M.* High on a mesa above a windswept plain live a few families of Acoma Indians in the oldest continuously inhabited homesite in the U.S. Though its origins are undetermined, the pueblo has been occupied since 1075 and was flourishing when a Coronado expedition came upon it in 1540. The fortress village was built with extraordinary toil and dedication; stone, mud, timber and all other building materials were hauled up to the 350-foot mesa on backs or hoisted with grass ropes. In 1629 the adobe San Estevan Mission church was completed, a handsome twin-towered structure with nine-foot-thick walls and 40-foot-long roof logs. It has an altar hand-carved with crude tools, old statues and paintings. *Open daily. Adults $1.50, children small charge.*

164. Gila Cliff Dwellings National Monument *Rte. 15, Gila Hot Springs, N.M.* A pit house dating from between 100 and 400 A.D. is the oldest ruin in the monument. The common dwellings of the Mogollon culture prior to about 1000 A.D., pit houses were circular, built in the open, with the floor below ground level. They were replaced by square houses, built of masonry or adobe, and cliff dwellings. There are five cliff dwellings here, with a total of about 35 rooms. The Mogollons were skilled potters and some of their artifacts excavated at the site are exhibited at the Visitor Center, along with interpretive displays of Mogollon and Pueblo life-styles. *Open daily except Jan. 1 and Dec. 25.*

165. Kwilleylekia Ruins *Rte. 211, Cliff, N.M.* This is considered the last great pueblo erected by the Salado Indians. It dates from the early 15th century and consisted of about 300 rooms in three blocks of houses. The tallest was four stories high. The settlement was ruined by a flood in the late 16th century. Pottery, tools and other artifacts excavated at the site are splendidly arranged in the Visitor Center. Also at the site is a cactus garden of rare species. *Open daily Apr.–Nov. Adults and children over 12 small charge.*

[**172.** *Civic Center-Art Museum*] *The Hindu god Shiva dances the destruction of the universe in a ring of flame. This three-part South Indian bronze sculpture from the mid-13th century is one of the finest in the world.*

166. Fort Bowie National Historic Site *13 mi. S. of Bowie, Ariz.* The 5th California Volunteer Infantry established Fort Bowie in 1862 to protect the vital water source at Apache Pass. It was a key post in bloody campaigns against Cochise, Geronimo and other great Apache leaders. Now all that remains are the ruins of the two forts built here. They can be reached by way of a fairly rugged mile-and-a-half foot trail. A trail guide leaflet relates vivid stories of the fort, its men and the treacherous pass. Nearby are the stone foundations of a stage station once operated by the Butterfield Overland Mail Company. Historic photographs and artifacts are shown at the site. *Open daily.*

167. Meeker Memorial Museum *1324 Ninth Ave., Greeley, Colo.* Inspired by Horace Greeley's advice to "Go West, young man," Nathan Meeker left New York to become one of the founders of Greeley in 1870. His home is furnished with fine antiques from the period, as well as family items. *Open Mon.-Sat.*

168. Pioneer Museum *1655 Broadway, Boulder, Colo.* The area's history is revealed through life-size dioramas with period furniture and costumed mannequins. Among the scenes displayed are an 1870 bedroom, an 1866 kitchen, an apothecary shop and a general store. Collections of old typewriters, clocks and fans can be seen, as well as many early photographs and paintings with regional significance. *Open daily June-Sept., Sat., Sun. Oct.-May. Adults and children over 11 small charge.*

169. University of Colorado Museum *Henderson Bldg., Boulder, Colo.* Numerous scientific displays and an art gallery attract visitors to the museum. It is especially rich in Indian material and holds the earliest known feather headdress. Of special interest are the Halls of Earth and Life. The Hall of Man stresses North American prehistory with emphasis on the Southwest and Plains area. *Open Mon.-Fri. except holidays.*

170. Opera House *Central City, Colo.* The sturdy stone building was erected in 1878 by pioneers who were determined to bring culture to their growing community. It has remained the local center for dramatic presentations ever since. Nowadays visitors file through the arched doorways during the summer months of July and August to witness not only classic operas but also popular Broadway plays presented by professionals and aspiring young performers. *Open daily mid-May-early Aug. for tours, July-Aug. for performances.*

171. Colorado Railroad Museum *17155 W. 44th Ave., Golden, Colo.* In the late 1800s railroads were the lifelines linking remote mining camps and towns throughout the West. Most of the lines have now been abandoned, but part of the rich heritage is preserved at this outdoor museum. Scattered over 12 acres is a large collection of narrow-gauge and standard-gauge locomotives and rail cars dating from the 1870s to the present. Old documents and photographs are exhibited in a replica of an 1880-style rail depot. *Open daily. Small charge.*

172. Denver, Colo.

Denver, at the western edge of the Great Plains, calls itself the Mile High City—in this case not just a boast but the exact truth. Colorado's capital has one of the most dramatic settings in the country, with a 150-mile stretch of the Front Range of the Rocky Mountains looming to the west like a great wall. Denver blossomed during the gold rush of 1859, and after 1870, when the silver bonanzas began and rail service was established, its growth was assured. It is now the cultural and industrial center of the Rocky Mountain region.

Colorado State Capitol *1475 Sherman St.* The stately granite building, finished in 1902, is dominated by a 272-foot-high dome, which was covered with gold leaf in 1910 in tribute to Colorado miners and their rich ore finds. A series of steps lead to the arched entrance; on one is a plaque indicating the location is exactly one mile above sea level. The capitol's outstanding interior feature is the lovely rose onyx wainscoting lavished throughout the building. *Open daily June-Aug., Mon.-Fri. Sept.-May except holidays.*

[**172.** *Forney Transportation Museum*] *D. W. Griffith, the famous motion picture director, bought this Spanish-made 1923 Hispano-Suiza for $35,000. An oversize, high-powered six-wheeled machine—one of the true classics—it has often appeared in movies as an officer's staff car.*

Colorado State Museum *200 14th Ave.* The white marble building holds a fascinating trove relating to Colorado history. Exhibits highlight prehistoric and more recent Indian cultures, the development of mining and railroads, the cattle and sheep industries and the growth of pioneer Denver. Weapons, a few of Kit Carson's possessions, objects associated with early fur trappers and examples of pioneer crafts are also on display. The library holds rare books, documents and photographs. *Open daily except Dec. 25.*

Denver Botanic Gardens *909 York St.* The sweeping concrete and Plexiglas Boettcher Memorial Conservatory is the main feature on the 20-acre tract. Containing a fine collection of tropical and subtropical plants, the large structure is also noted for its naturalistic waterfalls, streams, pools and paths. Among the many outdoor attractions here are the seasonal displays of annuals and perennials. There are Japanese and herb gardens, and an experimental area for woody and herbaceous ornamentals. *Open daily except Dec. 25.*

Denver Civic Center *14th Ave. and Broadway* In this three-block area are a number of handsome public buildings and monuments. Trees, shrubs and wide lawns lend a parklike air.

"BRONCHO BUSTER" Sculptor Alexander Phimister Proctor appears to defy the laws of gravity with this exciting bronze. The broncho is poised on his forelegs, the rest of his body rearing into the air, and the cowboy on top pitches forward in imminent danger of falling.

CITY AND COUNTY BUILDING The massive civic structure, occupying an entire city block, is built in modified Roman style. The curved front is colonnaded with Doric columns that rival the largest ever erected in Greece and Rome. At Christmas, the building drops its sober air when it is bathed in a fantasy of colored lights. *Open Mon.-Fri.*

DENVER ART MUSEUM Exhibits on seven floors of the modern building encompass 20,000 objects that represent the art of all major historical periods and cultures. Works from Europe, the Orient and the Americas are on view along with examples of North American Indian, African and Pacific Island native arts. Particular strengths of the museum are evident in its collections of Renaissance painting and sculpture, East Indian art objects and 20th-century art. Late 15th-century French Gothic, Tudor English and 17th-century Spanish Baroque are the periods dramatized by three reconstructed rooms. *Open Tues.-Sun. except holidays.*

GREEK AMPHITHEATER Built in the classic style, the outdoor theater is often used by Denverites for square and folk dancing, as well as civic functions.

"ON THE WAR TRAIL" Proctor also did this bronze statue of an Indian with his spear at the ready.

"PIONEER MONUMENT" The monument, designed by Frederick MacMonnies, comes in three parts. On top is a bronze equestrian figure of Kit Carson. Below him cornucopias overflow with fruit and vegetables, and below these stand allegorical bronze figures of The Hunter, The Prospector and the Pioneer Mother and Child.

PUBLIC LIBRARY The library, founded in 1889, originated the open shelf system and sponsored the first children's library and the first circulating picture collection. It is noted for its outstanding Western History collection and its assemblage of Western paintings.

[**172.** *Governor's Mansion*] *Most of the furniture in the library was imported from Italy and France. Magnificent pieces of jade and quartz from the 16th and 17th centuries are displayed in the lighted case.*

Open Mon.-Sat. June-Aug., daily Sept.-May except holidays.

VOORHIES MEMORIAL The memorial, honoring a pioneer mining man, is a colonnade of large stone pillars that form a pleasant passageway in the Civic Center.

Denver Zoological Gardens *City Park* A wide assortment of animals live here in carefully re-created natural settings. The range area with moated pens enables visitors to observe herds of horned and hoofed mammals; a walk-through aviary and the children's zoo are other popular favorites. Seals, bears, elephants, lions, monkeys and waterfowl—all have their places. *Open daily. Adults small charge.*

Forney Transportation Museum *1416 Platte St.* About 250 automobiles, carriages, sleighs, railroad engines and coaches, airplanes, bicycles and fire-fighting equipment are shown. Among the antique and classic cars are Amelia Earhart's 1922 "Gold Bug" Kissel Kar, Ali Khan's Rolls-Royce, a 1904 Franklin, a 1917 Cole and a 1936 Packard. The 1941 "Big Boy" is one of the world's largest steam locomotives. *Open daily except Dec. 25. Adults $1.50, children small charge.*

Governor's Mansion *400 E. Eighth Ave.* Completed in 1908 and presented to the state in 1960, the brick Colonial-style mansion reveals a number of Greek Revival features. In addition to its high-ceilinged rooms—some containing fine paneling, fluted Ionic columns and stained-glass windows—the house is noted for its furnishings. These include a Louis XVI satinwood desk, a 1740 French tapestry and a 16th-century Italian sideboard. A fine collection of antique quartz and jade can also be admired. *Open Tues. May-Oct.*

Molly Brown House *1340 Pennsylvania St.* Guides in costumes of the early 1900s conduct tours through the 1890s house, home of the famous "Unsinkable Molly Brown" who survived the *Titanic* disaster in 1912. A stone structure with tall chimneys and tile roofs, it has been restored to reflect styles at the turn of the century. Many of Mrs. Brown's possessions are here. *Open Tues.-Sun. Small charge.*

U.S. Mint *320 W. Colfax Ave.* Some $2,500,000,000 in gold bullion is thought to be stored in the five-story stone building. One of the two largest-capacity mints in the world, it has 59 coin presses, 39 of which can each form 700,000 pennies a day; nickels, dimes, quarters, half dollars and dollars are also minted here. Visitors are especially fascinated by the display of $1,000,000 in gold bars. A nick made by a bullet in the main hallway's marble paneling serves as a reminder of the 1922 holdup of a Federal Reserve Bank truck outside the building. The mint has never lost a cent. *Open Mon.-Fri. July-mid-June except holidays.*

173. Hamill House *Third and Argentine Sts., Georgetown, Colo.* From the discovery of the Belmont Lode in 1864 until the silver panic of 1893, Georgetown lived up to its reputation as "Silver Queen of the Rockies." Hamill House, the gracious Victorian home of a wealthy mine owner, was once reputed to be the most luxurious dwelling in the territory. Although restoration is still going on, many of the mansion's rooms are completely furnished, with the original ceiling and wall coverings, walnut woodwork and fireplaces intact. *Open daily May-Sept., Tues.-Sun. Oct.-Apr. Small charge.*

174. Hotel de Paris *Sixth St., Georgetown, Colo.* A touch of France in the Old West, the famous hostelry sheltered famous people such as railroad tycoon Jay Gould and financier Russell Sage as well as local miners and their families. The handsome establishment was opened in 1875 by Louis Dupuy, an eccentric Frenchman with epicurean tastes. Luxurious furnishings, imported china, statuary and other works of art all contributed to the graciousness of the setting in which Dupuy served gourmet meals. The entire hotel remains as it was during the town's heyday as a silver-mining center. *Open daily mid-June-mid-Sept. Small charge.*

175. Leadville, Colo. The town began as a mining camp when gold was discovered at nearby California Gulch in 1860, but its real prosperity came with the discovery of vast silver deposits. Buildings surviving from Leadville's heyday are reminders of the luxurious life-styles enjoyed by the fortunate ones who struck it rich in fabled bonanzas.

HEALY HOUSE–DEXTER CABIN *912 Harrison Ave.* Though its straight-lined exterior seems rather stark, the interior of Healy House, built in 1878, is a trove of relics epitomizing Victorian elegance. Red velvet, gilt, hand-carved furniture, stained-glass windows and mirrors backed with diamond dust abound. Dexter Cabin, on the same property, also has a rough exterior that belies its interior elegance. Built in 1879 as a hunting lodge and retreat by mining tycoon James V. Dexter, it contains a fully furnished period kitchen and a gem of a parlor with a crystal chandelier, a Persian rug, lavish wall coverings and fine furniture. *Open daily mid-May-Sept.*

HERITAGE MUSEUM AND GALLERY *Ninth St. and Harrison Ave.* Dioramas here depict Leadville's history. Mining memorabilia range from an old ore cart on original tracks to a full range of mining lamps, while antique candle holders contrast with the types in use today. There is also a gallery of contemporary art. *Open daily late May-Sept. Small charge.*

HISTORIC HOME OF H.A.W. TABOR *116 E. Fifth St.* In this simple Victorian cottage a legend began, for it was built by the fabulous "Silver King," Horace Tabor, and his first wife, Augusta. Tabor went bankrupt in the silver panic of 1893 and died penniless. The old Tabor House, where Horace and Augusta once entertained former President U. S. Grant, has been authentically restored. *Open daily. Small charge.*

HOUSE WITH THE EYE MUSEUM AND CARRIAGE HOUSE *127 W. Fourth St.* A stained-glass window shaped remarkably like a human eye in the roof of the house accounts for its name. Exhibits, designed to show how working miners lived, include furniture, old player pianos, paintings by miners' wives and old mining implements. The carriage house in the rear contains a number of historic vehicles such as a buggy owned by "Baby Doe" Tabor, the "Silver King"'s second wife, and an ornate horse-drawn hearse. *Open daily late May-early Sept. Small charge.*

TABOR OPERA HOUSE *306-10 Harrison Ave.* When Tabor opened his opera house in 1879, many claimed it was the biggest and best west of the Mississippi. The New York Metropolitan Opera Company performed here, as did Houdini, Anna Held and many others whose pictures line the entrance hall. The stage today remains set as though for a performance. Visitors can also view 10 sets of original hand-painted scenery and the cramped below-stage dressing rooms. *Open Sun.-Fri. late May-early Oct. Small charge.*

[**177.** *Air Force Academy*] *Walter A. Netsch, Jr., of Skidmore, Owings and Merrill designed the striking Cadet Chapel. Its 17 aluminum spires are 150 feet high, although they seem smaller in the awesome setting of the Rampart Range of the Rocky Mountains. Thin strips of stained glass cut the spires. In the Catholic chapel are magnificent Venetian glass mosaics; the Jewish synagogue boasts a Torah more than 500 years old. Between the chapel and the symbolic eagle and eaglets are the Air Gardens.*

176. Sheldon Jackson Memorial Chapel *Sixth and Hathaway Sts., Fairplay, Colo.* Though built without the aid of architects, the small frame Gothic-style chapel remains a delight to see. It was erected in 1874 by Dr. Sheldon Jackson, a missionary who had arrived in this historic gold-mining area two years earlier. A favorite subject for artists and photographers, the church is still used for weekly services. *Open daily.*

177. Colorado Springs, Colo.

Few cities in the country have been so favored by nature as Colorado Springs. It was established as a resort in 1871 by the president of the Denver and Rio Grande Railroad, and tourism has been one of its main businesses ever since. Strange red rock formations cover much of the city's western edge, and Pike National Forest, dominated by Pikes Peak, lies just to the west. The mountain views are spectacular.

Colorado Springs Fine Arts Center *30 W. Dale St.* American art displayed here ranges from works by prehistoric Indians to drawings, paintings and sculpture by contemporary artists. A survey collection of European, Oriental, African, Pacific and South American works is also on view. Art classes, lectures, special exhibits and plays form part of the center's varied program. *Open daily except Jan. 1 and Dec. 25.*

May Natural History Museum of the Tropics *8 mi. S.W. on Rte. 115* One of the world's best collections of mounted tropical insects, including many large and colorful specimens, is displayed here. Star billings go to a 17-inch insect from New Guinea that resembles a stick, Indian moths with 10-inch wingspans, tarantulas and a nine-inch Congo scorpion. *Open daily May–Sept. Adults and children over 6 small charge.*

Pioneers' Museum *25 W. Kiowa St.* Early American pressed glass, carriages, portraits and photographs tell the colorful story of the Pikes Peak region since its first exploration in 1806. Over 500 rare smoking pipes, many minerals, a number of New England antiques and a quantity of Plains and Pueblo Indian relics are also displayed here. Particularly fascinating is the rebuilt section of an 1874 dwelling, the home of Helen Hunt Jackson, author of the novel *Ramona*, with original furnishings. *Open Tues.–Sun. except holidays.*

U.S. Air Force Academy *10 mi. N. on Rte. 25* As modern as the space age, the striking complex of glass, aluminum and marble buildings stands on a plateau backed by towering mountains. Besides seeing buildings such as the Field House, a multipurpose sports arena, visitors can watch the cadets on parade and see a show in the planetarium. On summer Sundays there are band concerts and organ recitals. *Open daily.*

CADET CHAPEL The remarkably handsome modern building topped by 17 gleaming aluminum spires contains four chapels serving different faiths.

178. Suspension Bridge *Canon City, Colo.* Located in a municipal park, the quarter-mile bridge spans the Royal Gorge, a staggering 1053 feet above the Arkansas River. The highest suspension bridge in the world, it stands above the site of a violent 1870s skirmish between two railroad lines, both determined to reach rich ore fields. Fine views unfold from hiking trails on both sides of the canyon. *Open daily. Adults $1.25, children over 7 small charge.*

179. Old Fort Garland *Fort Garland, Colo.* Commanded in 1866-7 by Kit Carson, the frontier fort was built to protect settlers from Indian raids, but also served to secure the Colorado goldfields from Confederates during the Civil War. The old adobe buildings have now been restored and some of the quarters feature life-size mannequins dressed in authentic uniforms. *Open daily mid-Apr.–mid-Oct.*

180. Francisco Plaza Museum *La Veta, Colo.* In 1862 Colonel John Francisco, one of the original settlers in the area, built the rambling, L-shaped structure that bears his name. Intended both as a home and as a fort for defense against Indian raids, this structure and others moved to the site are now a museum depicting the realities of day-to-day life in the early Colorado Territory. Exhibits include a pioneer parlor, bedroom, kitchen, one-room log schoolhouse, blacksmith shop and saloon, all equipped with furniture, tools and utensils of the types that were used by the first settlers. *Open daily May–Oct.*

181. Trinidad, Colo. In the late 1800s this frontier town on the mountain branch of the Santa Fe Trail was headquarters for many of the largest cattle companies in the West. Its colorful history is reflected in the buildings on Main Street described below.

BACA HOUSE AND PIONEER MUSEUM The two-story adobe residence was erected in 1869 by a rancher and freighter, Don Felipe Baca. Across a courtyard is a one-story structure once used as a guesthouse and servants' quarters by the Baca family. It now holds exhibits relating to the area's settlement and its ranching past. *Open daily mid-May–mid-Oct.*

BLOOM HOUSE The ornate brick and sandstone home was built in 1882 by Frank G. Bloom, a well-to-do banker and cattleman. Behind the house is a delightful Victorian garden. *Open daily mid-May–mid-Oct.*

182. Harwood Foundation of the University of New Mexico Center *Ledoux St., Taos, N.M.* Besides many paintings by regional artists, the restored adobe complex holds collections of wood sculpture, Persian miniatures, Spanish and colonial furniture and local glass- and tinware. Primitive Spanish and Indian art objects are also displayed. Facilities include an auditorium and a library richly stocked with books on the Southwest. *Open Mon.–Sat.*

183. Kit Carson Home and Museum *E. Kit Carson Ave., Taos, N.M.* The famed Indian scout purchased the 1825 adobe house in 1843 and lived here with his wife and children for 25 years. Part of the dwelling is furnished in the period of Carson's occupancy, and several other rooms contain displays relating to the Spanish Colonial and fur-trading days and to early Indians of the region. The museum also sponsors lectures and has a good research library. *Open daily except holidays. Adults and children over 6 small charge.*

184. Stables Gallery *Rte. 3, Taos, N.M.* Remodeled from an old dwelling, this 12-room adobe-style building is a showcase for Taos artists. On the three surrounding acres are lilac gardens, an auditorium and the old stables, which now house an art school. *Open daily.*

185. Taos Pueblo *Rte. 3, N. of Taos, N.M.* New Mexico's highest mountains make a dramatic backdrop for Taos Pueblo, where more than 500 Indian families live. The two well-preserved multilevel pueblos are estimated to be 800 years old. A National Historic Landmark, Taos Pueblo has frequent ceremonial dances and fiestas. *Open daily. Small charge each car.*

MISSION OF SAN GERONIMO DE TAOS Used by members of the pueblo, the church stands near the ruins of the ancient mission, completed in 1612, which was all but destroyed by the U.S. Army in 1847.

186. Fort Burgwin Research Center *Rte. 3, E. of Ranchos de Taos, N.M.* At the site of a reconstructed U.S. Cavalry outpost established in 1852, Southern Methodist University conducts summer field courses in archaeology and ethnology. Displayed at the fort's museum are pottery, tools, arrowheads, spear points and many other artifacts recovered from nearby prehistoric Indian sites. There are also fascinating exhibits explaining the methods and techniques archaeologists use to piece together information about vanished cultures. *Open daily June–Aug.*

187. St. Francis of Assisi Church *Rte. 64, Ranchos de Taos, N.M.* Twin bell towers and large buttresses are among the distinguishing features of this church, completed in 1755 by Spanish settlers. It is a fine example of Spanish Colonial church architecture and contains the original wood altar backdrop and beams. On display are a silver cross that predates 1700 and silver ceremonial chimes from the early 1600s. Henry Ault's oil painting, *The Shadow of the Cross,* is called a mystery painting because in some lights Christ seems to be carrying a cross. *Open daily.*

188. Church of San José de Gracia de Las Trampas *Las Trampas, N.M.* The adobe walls of this 18th-century structure are six feet thick and are covered on the outside by mud plaster. Built more than 200 years ago by the dozen town founders, the church is an excellent example of Spanish Colonial architecture and contains wood carvings, early paintings, drawings and numerous artifacts of the period. *Open daily.*

189. Ghost Ranch Museum *Rte. 84, 17 mi. N.W. of Abiquiu, N.M.* Display techniques of a museum, zoo and botanical garden are all employed here to emphasize the importance of conserving natural resources. Live exhibits feature native wildlife and plants of the Southwest. In the half-acre Beaver National Forest a bilingual mechanical beaver explains the use being made of timber, water, wildlife and recreation resources in the national forests. Other exhibits include a forest fire display, fossils, a conservation diorama and geological materials. *Open daily.*

190. Puye Cliff Ruins *Rte. 5, 14 mi. W. of Espanola, N.M.* The ancient Pajaritan culture inhabited this plateau as late as the 17th century. The ruins consist of nearly two miles of cliff dwellings and a large pueblo, Top House Ruins, at the top of Puye Mesa. The pueblo is believed to have contained as many as 2000 rooms and three kivas. The site also preserves the remains of an irrigation canal, a large reservoir and the Pajaritan

[**193.** *Cristo Rey Church*] *This hand-carved stone altar screen, or reredos, is very old-world Spanish in feeling. A figure representing God and the Trinity is at the top; the Virgin Mary occupies a place of honor below.*

burial grounds. Santa Clara Indians, descendants of the Pajaritans, provide guide services. *Open daily. Adults and children over 13 small charge.*

191. Bandelier National Monument *Rte. 4, 12 mi. S. of Los Alamos, N.M.* From about 1200 to 1550 Indian farmers lived in this region of deep-cut canyons and creek waters, built homes and planted gardens of corn, beans and squash. Trails lead from the end of a paved road to the ruins of dwellings, man-made caves and storage rooms, many clustered in Frijoles Canyon. At the Visitor Center a slide program describes daily living in ancient times and display cases show crude stone and bone implements, glazed pottery and other items hand fashioned by the people who once lived here. *Open daily. Small charge.*

192. Jemez State Monument Museum *Rte. 4, Jemez Springs, N.M.* This is the dual site of the prehistoric Giusewa peublo, dating from about 1300, and the 17th-century mission of San José de los Jemez. The pueblo ruins comprise three kivas and a few dwellings. The mission church, founded in 1621–2, was constructed of sandstone. Its walls were up to eight feet thick, and a large octagonal tower lent it a fortresslike appearance. On two walls of the nave were some extraordinary murals, probably executed by Indians in the mission's early years. A reproduction of the murals and materials relating to both the pueblo and the mission fill the museum. *Open Wed., Thurs.*

193. Santa Fe, N.M.

About 60 miles northeast of bustling Albuquerque lies a unique city that has managed to thrive, and still preserve its heritage and atmosphere. Santa Fe, the oldest government seat in the U.S. (founded in 1610), is still a cultural and political center. The inhabitants, of Spanish and Anglo background, seem to like what they are doing and where they are. Many artists have chosen to make their homes along the narrow streets where the houses, even those not built of the traditional cool adobe, still follow the Spanish-Pueblo style. The town probably looked much the same when the Santa Fe Trail ended in the Plaza.

Cristo Rey Church *Cristo Rey St.* Considered to be the largest adobe structure in the U.S., the church is built like a fortress, with walls two to seven feet thick. Its prize possession is an exquisitely hand-carved stone reredos dating from 1761, a massive screen with three tiers of statuesque figures and decorative scrollwork. *Open daily.*

Fine Arts Museum *W. Palace Ave.* Works by George Bellows, Robert Henri and other American artists identified with the early days of the Santa Fe and Taos art colonies are displayed here along with an excellent collection of modern and traditional works by Southwestern Indian artists and other contemporary art of the Southwest. The St. Francis Auditorium resembles the interior of a Spanish mission chapel. Changing exhibits stress the theme of man in the Southwest. The Fine Arts Museum is a part of the Museum of New Mexico as are the Laboratory of Anthropology and two museums on Santa Fe's picturesque Plaza, the Museum of International Folk Art and the Palace of the Governors. *Open daily mid-May-mid-Sept., Tues.-Sun. mid-Sept.-mid-May.*

Institute of American Indian Arts Museum *Cerrillos Rd.* The works of Indian artists from more than 400 different tribes form the museum's outstanding permanent collection. About 6000 paintings are exhibited, along with sculpture, jewelry, printed textiles, beadwork, costumes, prints and drawings. Other featured attractions include fascinating displays of prehistoric, traditional and contemporary Indian artifacts. *Open Mon.-Fri. except holidays.*

Laboratory of Anthropology *Camino Lejo* While most of the building is devoted to research on the origin, development and history of the region's peoples, there is one hall with interesting exhibits for the public. Contemporary Pueblo Indian pottery is also displayed. *Open daily.*

Museum of International Folk Art *Camino Lejo* Work from more than 50 countries can be admired in the modern building. Of particular interest are world folk costumes and an outstanding collection of Spanish Colonial folk art. *Open daily mid-May-mid-Sept., Tues.-Sun. mid-Sept.-mid-May.*

Museum of Navaho Ceremonial Art *704 Camino Lejo* The octagonal building represents a large Navaho hogan (house), and the collection reflects all aspects of Navaho culture, with emphasis on Navaho religion. Most unusual are the 600 sand painting reproductions. There are also numerous rugs and other hand-crafted objects plus a large collection of ceremonial items. More than 2000 recorded legends and chants are preserved here, and the reference library is devoted to Navaho culture. *Open Tues.-Sun.*

Oldest House in the U.S.A. *215 E. DeVargas St.* The lower walls of the ancient structure, made of primitive puddled adobe, are the last remains of the Analco Pueblo, dating from about 1200 A.D. The rest of the

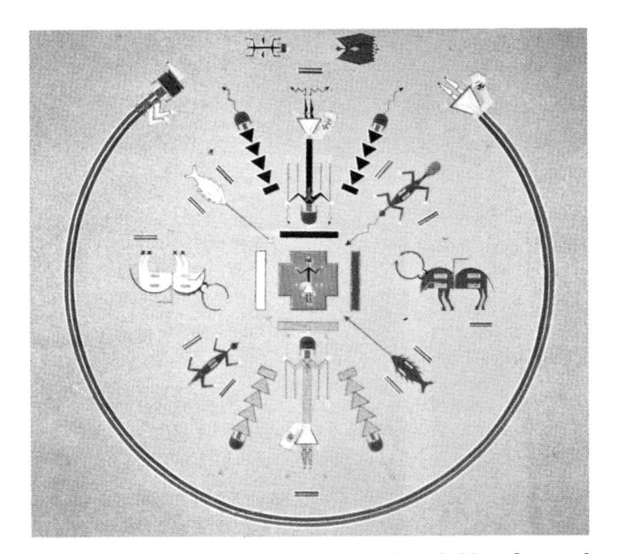

[**193.** *Museum of Navaho Ceremonial Art*] *Navaho sand paintings like these are used in rituals to cure the sick. After the medicine man has performed his ceremony, he destroys the painting he made for it.*

venerable house is believed to be the age of the nearby 17th-century San Miguel Mission. Spaniard slaves probably lived here, and it was once quarters for a Spanish officer. Other occupants have been Franciscan fathers, converted Indians, early traders and feared sisters whose weird collection of owl feathers, dried toads and cats' eyes caused them to be called witches by the local inhabitants. *Open daily Mar.-Oct., Wed.-Sun. Nov.-Feb.*

Our Lady of Light Chapel *219 Old Santa Fe Trail* In 1873 the Sisters of Loretto built a beautiful new stone chapel. It had a fine rose window, high arched ceilings, a lovely choir loft at the back and a problem. There was no way to reach the loft and no one could figure out how to fit in a staircase. One day an itinerant carpenter appeared and offered his help to the nuns. With his simple tools he built a superb circular wooden staircase. Vanishing before he could be paid, he left a masterpiece of construction in which no nails or supports are evident. *Open daily. Adults and children over 12 small charge.*

Palace of the Governors *Palace Ave.* Completed eight years before the Pilgrims reached Plymouth, this thick-walled adobe structure is the oldest public building in the U.S. The Indians held it for 12 years after the Pueblo Revolt in 1680. The Confederate Army held it for a month in 1862. As territorial governor Lew Wallace wrote part of *Ben-Hur* here. It remained the capitol of the Territory until 1900 and now holds displays on its own history plus artifacts and dioramas of pre-Spanish history. In the Hall of the Modern Indian, which was originally the old Santa Fe Armory, are collections that depict contemporary Indian life-styles. Farming practices, arts and crafts such as weaving and pottery and jewelry making plus family and religious life are shown in interesting displays. An outstanding library is open to the public. *Open daily mid-May-mid-Sept., Tues.-Sun. mid-Sept.-mid-May.*

St. Francis Cathedral *Cathedral Pl.* European architects and stonemasons built this French Romanesque-style structure between 1870 and 1889. The brown sandstone edifice exhibits both Moorish and

Gothic features and is the sixth church on the site. The vaulted interior ceiling is covered with volcanic rock. Archbishop Lamy, under whose auspices the cathedral was erected, is buried beneath the main altar. He was the subject of Willa Cather's novel *Death Comes for the Archbishop. Open daily.*

LA CONQUISTADORA CHAPEL The chapel contains America's oldest Madonna—Our Lady of the Conquest—brought here in 1625 by Fray Alonso Benavides, Franciscan supervisor of the New Mexico missions. The small wooden statue is decorated with arabesques over gold leaf. It occupies a place of honor in the beautiful gilded altar. *Open daily.*

San Miguel Mission *401 Old Santa Fe Trail* The thick-walled church—the nation's oldest—was built in 1610 by Tlaxcalan Indians from Mexico under the supervision of Franciscan missionaries. Among the interesting objects on view are 14th-century Indian artifacts excavated from beneath the church, a handsome 1798 altar backdrop with portraits and hand-carved wooden statues and two picture-charts dating back to 1630 drawn by Franciscans on animal hides. Tourists may ring San Miguel's 780-pound bell made of gold, silver, copper and iron, which was cast in Spain in 1356. *Open daily.*

194. Fort Union National Monument *Rte. 25, 8 mi. N. of Watrous, N.M.* Situated on the famous Santa Fe Trail, the military post was active between 1851 and 1891. The ruins of Fort Union visible today date from the 1860s, and a museum holds relics from the Civil and Indian Wars period. Troops from the fort fought both Confederate soldiers and Indian tribes—Apaches, Utes, Kiowas, Navahos and Comanches. Wagon wheel ruts from early trading days still clearly show in the valley surrounding the fort. *Open daily. Small charge.*

195. Pecos National Monument *Rte. 84-85A, Pecos, N.M.* The site is believed to have been one of the largest Anasazi Indian settlements in the Southwest. Between the 12th and 15th centuries the multistoried pueblo grew to 660 rooms and at least 22 kivas. When the Spanish arrived in 1540 they found a community of some 2000 people. Pecos became an important base of operations for Spanish explorers, and Spanish friars established the first mission sometime in the early 17th century. The ruins of a later church, built in the late 1700s, are here, along with the remains of pueblo structures and a restored kiva. *Open daily except Dec. 25.*

196. Coronado State Monument *Off Rte. 44, 2 mi. W. of Bernalillo, N.M.* The pueblo of Kuaua is the ancient home of Indians of the Tiwa culture. Coronado came into contact with these people, whose settlement dates from about 1300 A.D., when he visited the area in 1540. The pueblo comprises about 1200 ground-level rooms and six kivas preserved in outline form. One of the kivas contains a nearly complete set of multicolored murals (reproductions) of ceremonial figures and activities. Artifacts from the site and some original murals are exhibited at the Visitor Center. *Open Fri.-Wed. except holidays. Small charge.*

197. Museum of Albuquerque *Yale Blvd., S.E., Albuquerque, N.M.* This museum features displays relating to the history of the Southwest from 20,000 B.C. to the present. Among the permanent collections are pueblo paintings, archaeological finds, costumes, decorative arts, crafts and wildlife displays. New Mexico's role in the space program formed the basis for a recent special exhibition, one of many presented by the museum. *Open Tues.-Sun. except holidays. Small charge except Sun.*

198. San Felipe de Neri Church *Old Town Plaza, Albuquerque, N.M.* Franciscan fathers built the original church, the first in the city, on this site in 1706. It was rebuilt in the 1790s, and later remodeling added two large bell towers—each with Gothic windows and pointed spires—and a gable roof. An unusual feature is the stairway to the choir loft, which winds around the trunk of a large spruce tree. *Open daily.*

199. University of New Mexico *Albuquerque, N.M.* The largest university in the state was founded in 1889 and features many picturesque pueblo-style buildings on its spacious campus. Its library and museums specialize in the rich heritage of the Southwest.

MAXWELL MUSEUM OF ANTHROPOLOGY The collection of American Indian art ranks as one of the most complete and distinguished in the U.S. Displays concentrate on tribal artistry in rugs, jewelry, pottery, baskets and kachina dolls. There is also an impressive assortment of textiles and jewelry from Iran and Pakistan. *Open Mon.-Sat. except holidays.*

UNIVERSITY ART MUSEUM *Fine Arts Center* Indian and Western paintings are included in the permanent collection, which focuses on 19th- and 20th-century paintings, prints, sculpture and photographs. A special

[196] *Visitors to Coronado State Monument can climb down a ladder into this kiva, painted with authentic reproductions of the murals found here. Eighteen times over the decades the walls of the kiva were painted with ceremonial murals and then plastered over. Archaeologists have found a way to peel off one layer of plaster at a time to reveal the design of the various murals underneath.*

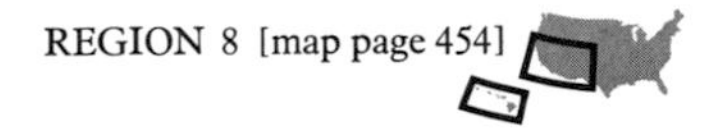

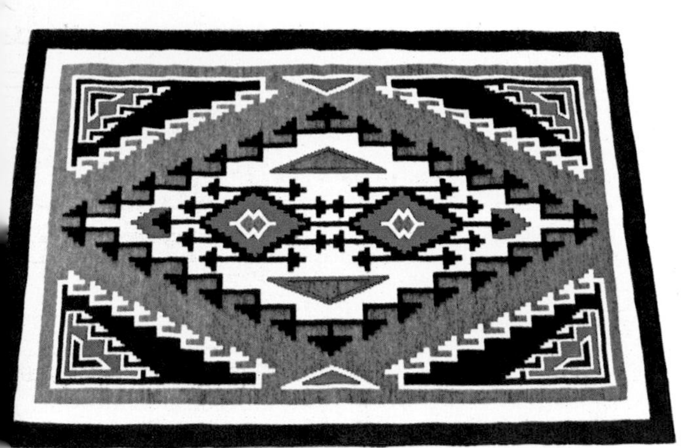

[**199.** *Maxwell Museum of Anthropology*] *The angular geometric patterns used in this rug are typical of Navaho Indian design. Such rugs were traditionally made on simple vertical looms suitable to a nomadic way of life.*

attraction is the display of Spanish Colonial silver. *Open Sun.-Fri. Sept.-July.*

200. Abo State Monument *Off Rte. 60, 10 mi. W. of Mountainair, N.M.* The Tompiros Indians occupied the site around the beginning of the 14th century. Visitors today can see the unexcavated pueblo ruin and the remains of a 17th-century Franciscan mission church and friar house, San Gregorio de Abo. The red sandstone church, believed to have been erected in the 1630s, was fully equipped for Catholic worship—it even contained an organ. Abo was abandoned about 1672 after Apache Indian attacks. *Open daily.*

201. Gran Quivira National Monument *Rte. 14, 1 mi. E. of Gran Quivira, N.M.* Preserved within the monument are the remains of two 17th-century Franciscan churches, San Buenaventura and San Isidro, as well as the ruins of a Mogollon community, Pueblo de las Humanas. The Mogollons, who began the pueblo about 1350, inhabited the area from the ninth century until 1675. Archaeological and historical materials are on display in the Visitors Center, along with exhibits which depict the life-style of the Mogollon culture. *Open daily. Small charge.*

202. Old San Miguel Mission *403 El Camino Real, Socorro, N.M.* Thick walls, one of which dates from 1598, and large carved rafters are among the venerable features of the church, completed in 1626. The last governor of New Mexico under Mexican administration is buried under one of the four sub-floors. *Open daily.*

203. Old Lincoln County Courthouse *Lincoln, N.M.* The two-story building houses the jail from which young William Bonney, the storied Billy the Kid, made a notorious escape in 1881. It was erected in 1874 as a general store and converted into a courthouse in 1880. Constructed of thick adobe bricks, the building boasts fine woodwork of native pine, fixed in place by handwrought square nails. The landmark is now a museum exhibiting materials relating to the history of this section of the frontier, with mementos of Lincoln County and Billy the Kid. An annual Billy the Kid pageant the first weekend of August features a folk play, old-time fiddlers contest, parade of the 1880s and White Oaks to Lincoln Pony Express race. *Open daily except Dec. 25. Small charge.*

204. Roswell Museum and Art Center *100 W. 11th St., Roswell, N.M.* The art of the Southwest, including a dazzling collection of works by Peter Hurd and his wife, Henriette Wyeth, is the notable feature here. Visitors can also see the rocket gadgetry and replica workshops of the great space pioneer Dr. Robert H. Goddard, whose experimental work near Roswell (1926–41), was the beginning of modern rocketry. Other important collections feature Chinese scrolls, 20th-century American paintings and sculptures, and Southwestern Indian arts and crafts. This remarkably varied and interesting museum also contains natural history exhibits, an aquarium and a planetarium. *Open daily except Jan. 1 and Dec. 25.*

205. Sacramento Peak Observatory *Sunspot, N.M.* The world's largest assembly of specialists and equipment for the study of the sun is located here. In addition to the various telescopes, spectrographs and other instruments, visitors can see the 16-inch coronagraph (for observation of the sun's outer atmosphere), the biggest in the world outside the Soviet Union. The 350-foot Tower Telescope is the only such instrument in the world and is used to study small features on the sun's luminous surface and its lower atmosphere. A magnificent far-reaching view stretches out from the site on the 9200-foot mountain. *Open Mon.-Sat.*

206. El Paso Museum of Art *1211 Montana Ave., El Paso. Tex.* Originally a private residence built in 1910, the museum now includes two modern wings and exhibits impressive possessions. Almost 60 paintings and sculptures by European masters from the 13th to 19th centuries comprise the Kress Collection, with works ranging from Botticelli (*Madonna and Child*) and Tintoretto to Van Dyck. Many fine examples of Mexican Colonial art and 19th- and 20th-century American and European graphics are also displayed as are a number of 19th- and 20th-century American paintings. *Open Tues.-Sun.*

207. Temple Mount Sinai *4408 N. Stanton St., El Paso, Tex.* At first sight, the wildly irregular shape of the building seems unruly and undisciplined: thin shelled concrete leaps and bends without apparent purpose. But once inside, visitors can appreciate architect Sidney Eisenshtat's grand design, for the arches and windows in the prayer hall put worshipers in close touch with the sky, the desert and the lovely hills that lie beyond. *Open daily.*

208. Ysleta Mission *Our Lady of Mount Carmel, 131 S. Zaragosa Rd., El Paso, Tex.* Founded in 1682 by Spanish padres and Tigua Indians, the mission is said to be the oldest in Texas. A Moorish bell tower and the Spanish-looking roofline are indications that the church has been rebuilt and altered a number of times. The walls, constructed of adobe brick, are as much as four feet thick. Indian crafts are demonstrated on the grounds and dances are performed at a museum run by Tigua Indians. The surrounding land has been farmed since the mission's inception. *Open daily.*

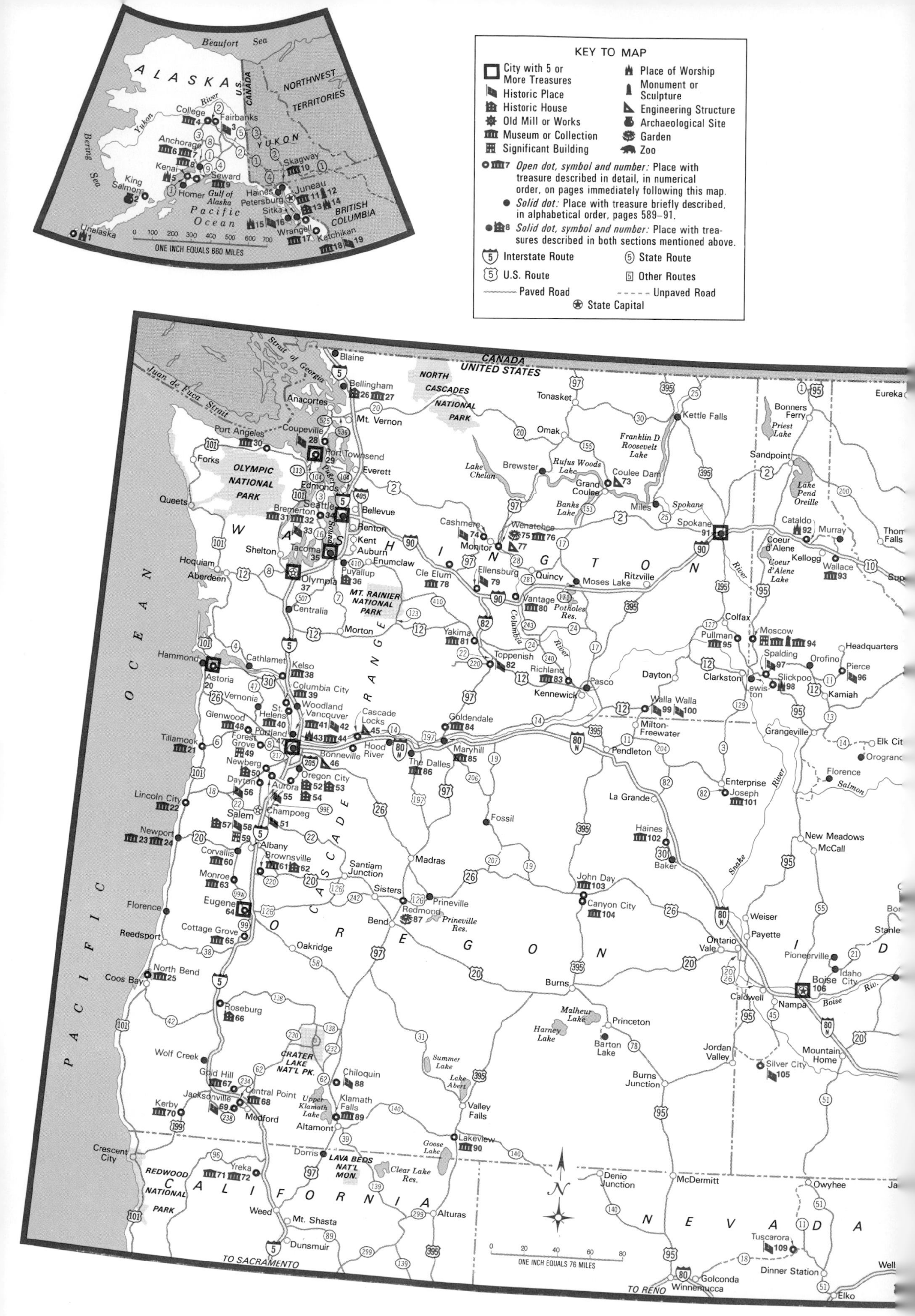
KEY TO MAP
City with 5 or More Treasures
Historic Place
Historic House
Old Mill or Works
Museum or Collection
Significant Building
Place of Worship
Monument or Sculpture
Engineering Structure
Archaeological Site
Garden
Zoo
Open dot, symbol and number: Place with treasure described in detail, in numerical order, on pages immediately following this map.
Solid dot: Place with treasure briefly described, in alphabetical order, pages 589–91.
Solid dot, symbol and number: Place with treasures described in both sections mentioned above.
Interstate Route
State Route
U.S. Route
Other Routes
Paved Road
Unpaved Road
State Capital
ALASKA
Beaufort Sea
NORTHWEST TERRITORIES
YUKON
U.S. CANADA
Bering Sea
Yukon River
College
Fairbanks
Anchorage
Kenai
Seward
King Salmon
Homer
Gulf of Alaska
Pacific Ocean
Haines
Skagway
Juneau
Petersburg
Sitka
Wrangell
Ketchikan
BRITISH COLUMBIA
Unalaska
ONE INCH EQUALS 660 MILES
CANADA
UNITED STATES
Strait of Georgia
Juan de Fuca Strait
NORTH CASCADES NATIONAL PARK
OLYMPIC NATIONAL PARK
MT. RAINIER NATIONAL PARK
WASHINGTON
OREGON
IDAHO
CALIFORNIA
NEVADA
PACIFIC OCEAN
CASCADE RANGE
Blaine
Bellingham
Anacortes
Mt. Vernon
Coupeville
Port Angeles
Port Townsend
Forks
Everett
Edmonds
Seattle
Bremerton
Bellevue
Renton
Kent
Auburn
Tacoma
Queets
Shelton
Puyallup
Enumclaw
Hoquiam
Aberdeen
Olympia
Centralia
Morton
Tonasket
Omak
Brewster
Lake Chelan
Cashmere
Wenatchee
Monitor
Ellensburg
Cle Elum
Quincy
Vantage
Moses Lake
Ritzville
Yakima
Toppenish
Richland
Kennewick
Pasco
Columbia River
Potholes Res.
Franklin D. Roosevelt Lake
Rufus Woods Lake
Coulee Dam
Grand Coulee
Banks Lake
Miles
Spokane
Kettle Falls
Colfax
Pullman
Clarkston
Dayton
Walla Walla
Milton-Freewater
Goldendale
Maryhill
Hammond
Astoria
Cathlamet
Kelso
Vernonia
Columbia City
St. Helens
Woodland
Vancouver
Cascade Locks
Glenwood
Forest Grove
Portland
Bonneville
Hood River
The Dalles
Tillamook
Newberg
Dayton
Oregon City
Aurora
Champoeg
Lincoln City
Salem
Newport
Albany
Corvallis
Brownsville
Monroe
Santiam Junction
Sisters
Madras
Prineville
Redmond
Prineville Res.
Bend
Eugene
Florence
Reedsport
Cottage Grove
Oakridge
North Bend
Coos Bay
Roseburg
Wolf Creek
Gold Hill
Central Point
Jacksonville
Kerby
Medford
Crater Lake Nat'l Pk.
Chiloquin
Upper Klamath Lake
Klamath Falls
Altamont
Summer Lake
Lake Abert
Valley Falls
Lakeview
Goose Lake
Fossil
John Day
Canyon City
Burns
Malheur Lake
Harney Lake
Princeton
Barton Lake
Burns Junction
Pendleton
La Grande
Haines
Baker
Enterprise
Joseph
Ontario
Vale
Jordan Valley
Crescent City
Redwood National Park
Yreka
Dorris
Lava Beds Nat'l Mon.
Clear Lake Res.
Weed
Mt. Shasta
Dunsmuir
Alturas
To Sacramento
Denio Junction
McDermitt
To Reno
Winnemucca
Golconda
Tuscarora
Dinner Station
Elko
Owyhee
Eureka
Bonners Ferry
Priest Lake
Sandpoint
Lake Pend Oreille
Cataldo
Murray
Coeur d'Alene
Kellogg
Wallace
Coeur d'Alene Lake
Moscow
Spalding
Lewiston
Slickpoo
Orofino
Pierce
Kamiah
Headquarters
Grangeville
Florence
Salmon River
Snake River
Weiser
Payette
New Meadows
McCall
Pioneerville
Idaho City
Boise
Boise River
Caldwell
Nampa
Mountain Home
Silver City
ONE INCH EQUALS 76 MILES

Just over a century ago settlers came to the Northwest determined to farm, mine and raise cattle despite hostile Indians, a difficult climate and the lawless and greedy among themselves. Proud of this heritage, Northwesterners of today have not forgotten the hard lives of their ancestors. Scores of large and small museums serve to document their colorful, recent past.

REGION 9

Pages 506–544

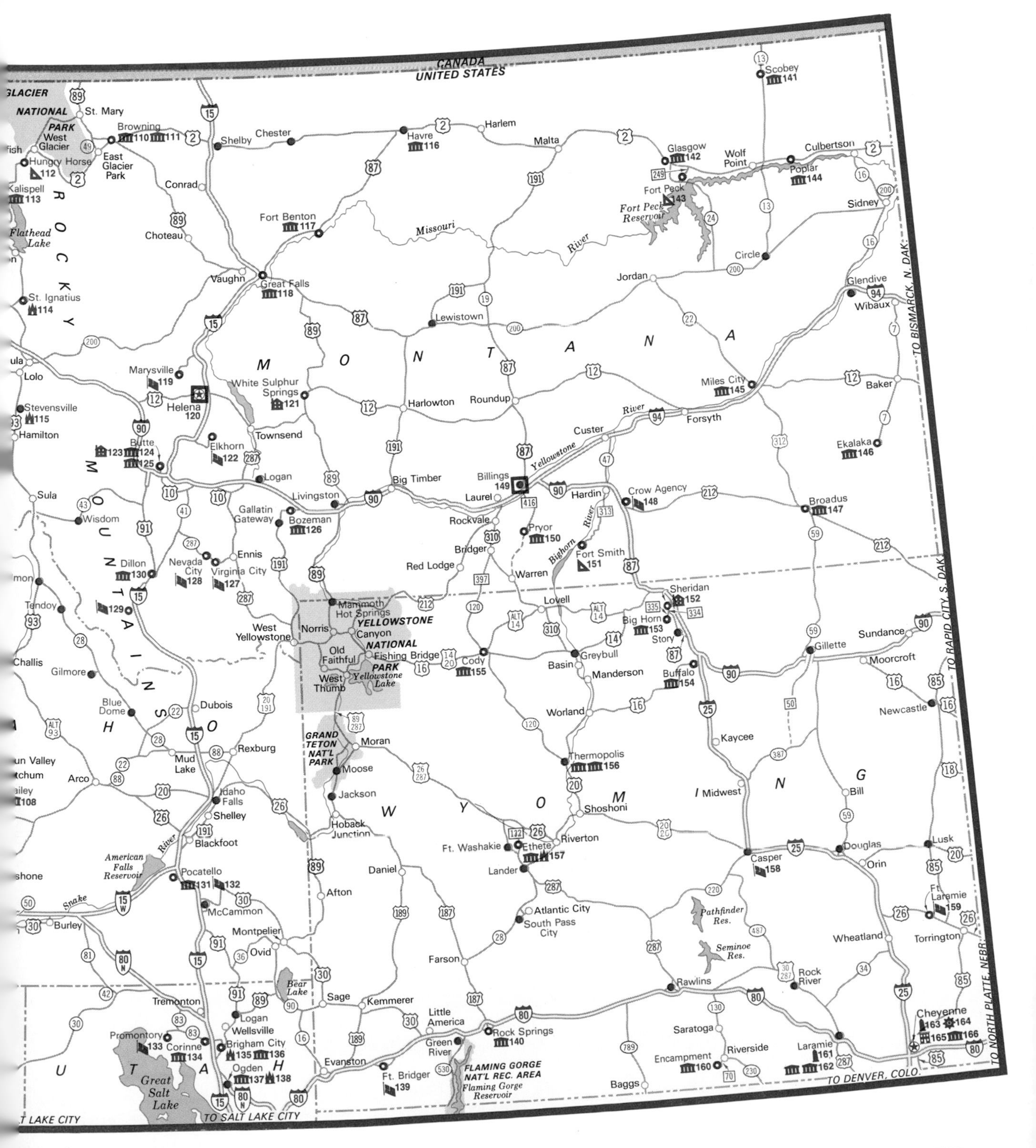

1. Holy Ascension of Christ Orthodox Cathedral *Unalaska, Alaska* John Veniaminov, later Bishop Innocent, the Russian Orthodox priest who introduced that religion to America, completed this frame church in 1826. Now a National Historic Landmark, it is noted for its traditional "onion" domes and hand-carved icon screen with icons brought here from Russia. The two smaller side chapels are later additions to the main structure. *Open daily.*

2. Katmai National Monument *King Salmon, Alaska* The 4200 square miles protected here include magnificently rugged landscapes pocketed with huge lakes, active volcanoes and wildlife. Although it looks far from hospitable, the land has been inhabited by man since around 2400 B.C. The most vivid evidence of Eskimo life stands at the site of a prehistoric village: a pit house, built hundreds of years ago with stone and bone tools, is sheltered now by a log cabin. Its dugout basement is covered with a framework of spruce logs, once expediently roofed with moss and clay. *Open daily June–early Sept.*

3. Alaskaland-Pioneer Park *Moore St. and Ave. of Flags, Fairbanks, Alaska* The compact 40-acre park compresses much of the variety of America's biggest state into a small area. In one corner is Gold Rush Town, a re-creation of a turn-of-the-century mining camp. In Mining Valley visitors can see how the sourdoughs panned for gold, and in the Wildlife Park native animals are on view. One can also ride the replica of an 1885 train to the Native Village and watch Eskimos, Indians and Aleuts demonstrating their crafts in reproductions of native dwellings. *Park open daily, buildings and exhibits open daily late May–early Sept.*

4. University of Alaska Museum *University of Alaska, College, Alaska* Mammoth tusks, a desk piece carved from walrus ivory, an eider skin parka and baskets woven from spruce roots—these are among the extraordinary archaeological and cultural objects exhibited here. Native Alaskan displays feature household goods, clothing and hunting gear, while historical items focus particularly on the days of Russian colonization and the Klondike gold rush. Around 7000 mammal specimens, 3500 birds and 40,000 plants in a herbarium reveal the diversity of Alaskan wildlife. *Open daily.*

5. Russian Orthodox Church *Mission St., Kenai, Alaska* This spruce-log church, built in 1896, was declared a National Historic Landmark in 1971. It is filled with mementos of Alaska's early days, when Russian fur traders settled at the Kenai River. Original Russian icons, paintings, wedding crowns and old Slavonic language books are displayed. *Open Sun.*

6. Alaska Transportation Museum *3833 International Airport Rd., Anchorage, Alaska* Various kinds of vehicles used in Alaska are on display: cars, kayaks, motorcycles and airplanes flown by bush pilots. Much as the railroads opened up the West in the continental U.S., the planes flown by courageous bush pilots opened up Alaska for settlement and development. *Open daily except Thanksgiving Day and Dec. 25.*

7. Anchorage Historical and Fine Arts Museum *121 W. Seventh Ave., Anchorage, Alaska* The modern museum offers a dramatic introduction to Alaskan and Arctic life from prehistoric times to the present. Exhibits cover aspects of early Russian colonization; of English, Spanish and French explorers; and of the ex-

[12] *The four-story totem, a gift to Juneau from the city's Rotary Club, stands at the head of Seward Street. The close-up shows the third story, "Tcaawunk and the Land Otter Men." Outcast as a child for pretending to be a medicine man, Tcaawunk gained real powers after repairing a heron's broken bill. He became such a famous shaman that when a white land otter was wounded by a villager, the otter men carried Tcaawunk off to their underground village to heal their prince. Before doing so, Tcaawunk demanded a great deal of wealth. The morning after his return, Tcaawunk went to look at his booty and found to his dismay that it had turned into seaweed and kelp.*

ploits of whalers and gold miners. Exceptional Eskimo, Aleut and Indian artistry is amply highlighted in displays of woven baskets, stone lamps, masks, sculpture and artifacts, ancient and new. Also featured are temporary art exhibitions from Alaskan and international sources. *Open Tues.-Sun. late May-early Sept., Tues.-Sat. early Sept.-late May except holidays.*

8. Fort Richardson Fish and Wildlife Museum *Fort Richardson, Anchorage, Alaska* One of the easiest ways to encounter polar bears face to face is here, where they are displayed among their fellow Arctic mammals, all full mounts. Brown and black bears also rear up threateningly, upstaging companion specimens such as moose, caribou, Roosevelt elk, Dall sheep, fox and beaver. Trophy fish are among the other displays at Alaska's largest wildlife museum. *Open daily.*

9. Resurrection Bay Historical Society Museum *State Bldg., Seward, Alaska* In a large basement room are displayed a fine collection of Attu Indian baskets, objects carved from baleen (whalebone), an Eskimo dogsled and historic photographs and newspaper clippings from early pioneering days around Resurrection Bay. *Open Mon.-Sat. June-Aug.*

10. Soapy Smith Museum *Second St., Skagway, Alaska* In the 1890s confidence man and outlaw Soapy Smith operated this saloon in the boomtown of Skagway. It is now a museum of those exciting days in Alaska's history, with photographs, newspapers and other relics. An early Skagway streetcar is also displayed, and a wildlife exhibit takes up one section of the museum. *Open daily June-Aug. Small charge.*

11. Alaska State Museum *Wittier St., Juneau, Alaska* The full sweep of Alaskan history comes to life in the museum. Exhibits range from arts and artifacts of aboriginal tribes that lived 2000 years ago to relics of the sourdoughs who arrived during the gold rush. A dazzling collection of objects made by artisans of all the native Alaskan cultures is the outstanding feature: there are totem poles, masks, birchbark canoes, caribou-skin garments ornamented with dyed porcupine quills and hundreds of other superbly crafted objects. *Open daily except holidays.*

12. Four-Story Totem *Upper Seward St., Juneau, Alaska* For more than 150 years the Haida Indians of the Queen Charlotte Islands have been carving "story masters," decorative objects that look like totem poles but instead of tracing lineages illustrate characters in Indian myths. This giant example, cut from red cedar wood about 1940, is in a sense a whole story book. Instead of the usual single story, it portrays (from top to bottom) the casts of characters in four separate myths: one about a monster frog, another about a fisherman who was captured by bears and two about the strange experiences of two medicine men.

13. Governor's Mansion *716 Calhoun Ave., Juneau, Alaska* The two-and-a-half-story frame structure completed in 1912 for the territorial governors is a stately New England Colonial-style building commanding a magnificent view of Juneau, the Gastineau Channel and spectacular snowcapped mountains on Douglas Island. At the side entrance is a large yellow cedar totem pole carved for the governor by the Tlingit Indians and illustrating some of their legends.

[14] *The labor of Tlingit Indians built this tiny church dedicated to the patron saint of fishermen. The Russian Orthodox church was supported by missionary funds from Moscow until 1917, and most of its members are Eskimo.*

14. St. Nicholas Russian Orthodox Church *326 Fifth St., Juneau, Alaska* Built in 1894, the octagonal clapboard structure with the traditional onion-shaped dome is the oldest Russian church standing in southeastern Alaska. Inside the tiny building is a collection of ancient icons brought from Russia in the 19th century, as well as an interesting assortment of old vestments, liturgical books and other church furnishings. *Open mid-June-mid-Sept. Small charge for adults.*

15. St. Michael's Cathedral *Lincoln and Maksoutoff Sts., Sitka, Alaska* This building is a reconstruction erected after a fire in 1966 totally destroyed the original 1848 Russian Orthodox church. Fortunately, most of the contents of that historic church, such as 19th-century vestments, chalices and wedding crowns, were saved from the fire, and are on display here. Among the elaborate icons is the *Kazan Mother of God*, which was painted in 1800. The Russians' missionary activity among the Indians is evidenced by the first editions of Indian church services and translations of the Bible. *Open daily June-Aug.*

16. Sitka National Historical Park *Lincoln St., Sitka, Alaska* The 107-acre park is the site of the 1804 Battle of Alaska, where Russian forces attacked and forced out the area's Tlingit Indians. New Archangel, the settlement the Russians then established, became the town of Sitka. Part of the Indian heritage is preserved in a splendid collection of ancient totem poles scattered along a trail through lush evergreen forest. The Visitor Center also serves in part as a cultural center where native crafts are demonstrated and taught to new generations of Indians of southeastern Alaska. *Open daily.*

[19] *The tallest totem poles were for potlatches, ceremonial feasts whose purpose was to enhance the prestige of the host. Although the poles were a source of pride, they were seldom repaired and were abandoned when the Indians left their homes. In front of the community house here is another type—a heraldic pole. Usually attached to the front of a house, often with a small entrance, it bore the family crest. Crests painted on the house front were less expensive. Expert totem carvers, who served a long apprenticeship, received high fees.*

17. Tribal House of the Bear *Wrangell, Alaska* This Alaskan Indian community house was once a trading post and the scene of such tribal ceremonies as the potlatch. Indian wood carvings, costumes and other historic objects have been gathered together here and may be seen by tourist groups. A number of fine totem poles, some said to be 200 years old, stand inside. *Open daily.*

18. Tongass Historical Society Museum *629 Dock St., Ketchikan, Alaska* Set on the wooded banks of Ketchikan Creek, the salmon-rich waterway that first attracted Indians and pioneers to this area, the museum holds beautiful articles made by local Indians. These include paintings, photographs, prints and other objects of regional significance. There are also skillfully painted Indian bentwood boxes; a 19th-century Tlingit shirt decorated with mother-of-pearl buttons; a Chilkat blanket made from mountain goat wool and cedar bark. A Chinese tea chest is a legacy of fur-trading days, while a Colt rifle and a muzzle loader recall pioneering exploits. *Open daily June-Aug., Tues.-Sun. Sept.-May.*

19. Totem Bight State Park *Off Tongass Hwy., N. of Ketchikan, Alaska* The Ketchikan area is noted for the totem poles by local Indians. There are many colorful totems salvaged from deserted villages and now restored. They depict legends of the Tlingits and other native tribes. An intricately carved and painted ceremonial house is interesting and informative. *Open daily.*

20. Astoria, Ore.

Astoria was founded in 1811, when John Jacob Astor established a fur-trading post in this far northwest corner of Oregon, near the mouth of the Columbia River. It is the oldest white settlement in the Northwest. Plants along the waterfront process salmon, tuna and other fish, and ocean liners start the long voyage across the Pacific from the docks.

Astoria Column *Coxcomb Hill* The picturesque 125-foot tower in a parklike hilltop setting is decorated from top to bottom with a spiral frieze depicting events in the discovery, exploration and settlement of the Pacific Northwest. Those who climb the 166 steps to the observation platform are rewarded with a splendid panorama of the city, the surrounding mountains, the Columbia River and the Pacific Ocean. *Open daily.*

Clatsop County Historical Museum *441 Eighth St.* Captain George Flavel, one of the early bar pilots on the Columbia River, was also a shrewd businessman who amassed a fortune by controlling piloting and towing operations at the river's mouth. As a symbol of his success, he built a delightfully ornate three-story Victorian mansion and filled it with lavish furnishings. His home is now a museum of regional history exhibiting Indian artifacts, antiques dating from the mid-19th century, when this area was settled by whites, and a collection of relics recovered from ships wrecked on the Oregon coast. *Open daily June-Sept., Tues.-Sun. except holidays Oct.-May.*

Columbia River Maritime Museum *1618 Exchange St.* From intricate scrimshaw carved by lonely whalers to massive beacon lights, all the objects in the museum commemorate the rich maritime heritage of the oldest American seaport on the West Coast. Ship models, figureheads, paintings and hundreds of other nautical mementos tell the story of fishing, whaling and other maritime industries of the Northwest. Moored outside is the lightship *Columbia*, which for 52 years guided ships at the mouth of the Columbia River. *Open daily May-Sept., Tues.-Sun. except Dec. 25 Oct.-Apr. Small charge.*

Fort Clatsop National Memorial *Off Rte. 101, 4½ mi. S.W. of Astoria* After a grueling 18-month overland journey from the Mississippi River, Captains Meriwether Lewis and William Clark finally reached their objective, the Pacific Ocean, in November 1805. Deciding to spend the winter near the mouth of the Columbia River, members of the expedition built Fort Clatsop. The original log structure has long since disappeared, but this full-size reproduction is based on Clark's own sketch of the floor plan. Exhibits and a slide program trace the route of the expedition and explain its historical significance. *Open daily except Dec. 25.*

Pioneer Finnish Home *Cullaby Lake* Superb workmanship is evident in this cedar-log dwelling, skillfully hewed by hand by a Finnish immigrant, Erik Lindgren. Built in the early 1900s in the depths of the Oregon forest, its dovetailed walls are finished on the inside with a smooth shave. Dismantled and moved to this site—along with a sauna-smokehouse—it has been partially reconstructed by master craftsmen. *Open daily.*

21. Tillamook County Pioneer Museum *2106 Second St., Tillamook, Ore.* The former county courthouse has been effectively converted into a showcase of regional history and wildlife. About 500 specimens of animals and birds are found in the natural-habitat dioramas: there are marsh birds, seabirds and shorebirds; scenes with deer, bobcats, coyotes. Chunks of beeswax, part of the cargo of a Spanish galleon wrecked in the early 1700s, are among the historical curiosities. Indian artifacts, antique automobiles, musical instruments, guns, clocks, furniture and photographs—all tell the story of the area's early settlers. *Open daily May-Sept., Tues.-Sun. Oct.-Apr.*

22. Laceys' Antique Museum and Doll House *3400 N. Hwy. 101, Lincoln City, Ore.* From the four-foot-tall antique china doll dressed in the style of the 1860s to the life-size wax figure of Queen Elizabeth II, this is an amazing collection. With more than 4000 dolls from around the world, many authentically costumed, it is one of the largest private doll collections in the West. The museum also features antique china, furniture, guns, buttons, music boxes and a Gay '90s hurdy-gurdy. *Open daily. Small charge.*

23. Old Yaquina Bay Lighthouse *Yaquina Bay State Park, Newport, Ore.* The 1871 lighthouse is one of the oldest on the northern Pacific Coast of the U.S. It is now operated as a museum with exhibits of marine artifacts, historical materials and a large collection of seashells. A marker commemorates Captain James Cook's first sighting of the coast in 1778. *Open Tues.-Sun. June-Sept., Fri.-Sun. Oct.-May.*

24. Oregon State University Marine Science Center *Marine Science Dr., Newport, Ore.* Instead of "Do Not Touch" warnings here, there are some exhibit signs that encourage contact: at the Handling Pool, children delight in picking up and studying snails, crabs, urchins,

[**20.** *Columbia River Museum*] *One of the crew of the* Columbia Rediviva *painted this watercolor and three others in the museum. The Boston ship was the first to enter the great river that bears her name, in 1792.*

anemones and chitons. Just as popular is the sinuous octopus that tolerates petting. Behind aquarium walls are hundreds of species of fish and invertebrates, while mounted displays feature coastal birds. Other exhibits describe ocean phenomena and commercial fishing gear. *Open daily except Dec. 25.*

25. Coos-Curry Museum *Simpson Park, North Bend, Ore.* Local history is traced here through a wide variety of objects. Indians, the earliest settlers, are represented by a fine collection of artifacts: arrowheads, baskets, implements and articles of clothing, including an exquisitely beaded robe. Pioneers are seen through their household possessions: an antique typewriter and sewing machine, a Chickering piano, a simple spinning wheel, a washing machine and an extraordinary little baby buggy. *Open Tues.-Sun.*

26. Gamwell House *1001 16th St., Bellingham, Wash.* Gingerbread, turrets, several ornate balconies and elaborate brick chimneys make the clapboard structure an outstanding example of late Victorian architecture. Built in 1890, its exterior features also include hand-carved pillars and railings.

[**20.** *Fort Clatsop*] *Sitka spruces tower over the small fort reproduced from the plan Clark sketched on the inside of the elk-skin cover of his field book. The Clatsops were a friendly local tribe. Here Lewis and Clark carefully detailed the Indian customs, flora, fauna, difficulties with food and the climate—rain. Only 12 days of their four-month stay were rainless.*

[27] *The arts of a vanished Northwest era are represented in a choice exhibition. Many masks had feathers and animal teeth. This pre-1900 Eskimo one of painted wood is a classic example from the Lower Yukon River.*

27. Whatcom Museum of History and Art *121 Prospect St., Bellingham, Wash.* Artworks by living Northwest artists and the history of this region are stressed in the museum, which was built in 1892 as the city hall. A fire in 1962 destroyed part of the impressive Victorian structure, including its large central clock tower, but it has since been restored. Changing exhibits with items of local historic and artistic significance are offered, and lectures, concerts and other events are frequent. Sculptor George Rickey's stainless steel *Two Lines Oblique* is on display outside the museum. *Open Tues.-Sun.*

28. Central Whidbey Historic District *Coupeville, Wash.* Settled in the early 1850s, Whidbey Island is noted for its well-made log blockhouses, built for protection against Indians. These—and a number of other interesting buildings—are centered around Coupeville, one of the state's oldest towns, and include the Alexander Blockhouse, Davis Blockhouse and Old Courthouse, all of which date from 1855. In front of the Alexander Blockhouse are several canoes, including a Skagit Indian war canoe made around 1850.

FORT CASEY LIGHTHOUSE Fort Casey, built in the 1890s as part of the Puget Sound Defense System, is now a state park. Some of the old artillery and fortifications can still be seen. The Interpretive Center contains exhibits on the history of the defense system, from 1900 to World War II. *Open daily May-early Sept.*

29. Port Townsend, Wash.

Victorian structures still proudly stand in this former port of entry, which was settled in 1851. Situated on a peninsula where Puget Sound joins the Strait of Juan de Fuca and still served by an 1879 lighthouse, the area has architecture largely reflecting styles from the late 1800s: St. Paul's Episcopal Church dates from 1865; the Old German Consulate, with fanciful spires, from 1890. The Old Bell Tower, originally used for summoning firemen, has been restored. Altogether 200 buildings are marked with dates of construction and names of original owners.

Fort Worden *1 mi. N.* Coast artillery installations were garrisoned here during World Wars I and II. A number of original concrete buildings and gun emplacements can still be seen. The fort is flanked by a park which offers picnic spots and fine views of the shoreline. *Open daily.*

Jefferson County Courthouse *Jefferson and Cass Sts.* A 100-foot clock tower rises above the Romanesque structure, which was built of brick and carved stone in 1891. It is the second oldest courthouse in the state and is still in use. *Open Mon.-Fri.*

Jefferson County Historical Museum *City Hall, Water and Madison Sts.* Displayed in a former courtroom, the exhibits here tell the story of Port Townsend, and a collection of books and family records is held in a library. It is said author Jack London was once locked up in the basement jail of the 1892 building, still used as a city hall. *Open daily May-Nov.*

Rothschild House *Franklin and Taylor Sts.* A strong New England flavor is evident in the modest eight-room frame house. Built in 1868 by a merchant, it has been restored and holds period furnishings. The grounds include an old-fashioned flower and herb garden. *Open Tues.-Sun. June-Sept.*

30. Pioneer Memorial Museum *Olympic National Park, 2800 Hurricane Ridge Rd., Port Angeles, Wash.* A huge relief map of the Olympic Mountains serves as an orientation to the nation's only remaining rain forest region. Exhibits highlight the distinctive animals and plants that flourish here and, through rare and ancient artifacts, tell the story of various coastal Indian tribes. *Open daily except Dec. 25.*

31. Kitsap County Historical Museum *837 Fourth St., Bremerton, Wash.* The focal point of the collection of regional objects is several pieces of ornately carved

[33] *Visitors may go straight to the U.S.S.* Missouri *at the westernmost pier, or see the famous ship as part of the tour of the shipyard. The "Mighty Mo," commissioned in June 1944, had shot down 11 Japanese planes and was the flagship of Admiral William F. Halsey when the formal Japanese surrender was signed on her forward deck.*

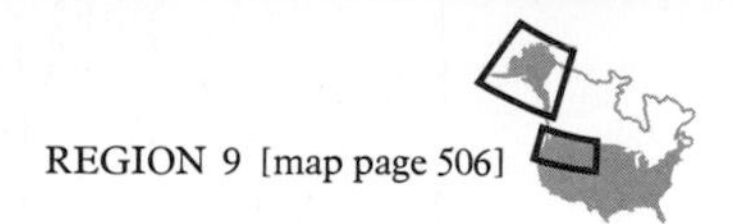

furniture made by a woman who lived in the county for decades. Her work includes a desk, china cabinet and a handsome fire screen. *Open Tues.-Sat. except holidays.*

32. Naval Shipyard Museum *Washington State Ferry Terminal Bldg., Bremerton, Wash.* Early steam engines, weapons and large models of naval vessels are exhibited here along with photographs of ships, the Puget Sound Naval Shipyard and other installations. *Military Courage,* a statue presented to the U.S.S. *Seattle* by France after World War I is also displayed. *Open Wed.-Sun. except holidays.*

33. U.S.S. "Missouri" *Puget Sound Naval Shipyard, Bremerton, Wash.* In 1945, representatives of Japan boarded the huge battleship in Tokyo Bay to sign the surrender document ending hostilities in World War II. A plaque in the forward, or "surrender," deck marks the spot where this historic event occurred. The large guns and other equipment on the vessel can also be seen by visitors, and a museum has been set up in the wardroom. *Open daily.*

34. Seattle, Wash.

The lumber camp named for a friendly Indian had become a prosperous town by the time most of it burned to the ground in 1889 and determined citizens rebuilt it. Then in 1897 Seattle suddenly became a boomtown. When gold was discovered in Alaska, Seattle was the departure point. But many people stayed, and the population grew. Dramatically situated on the hills of an isthmus between Puget Sound and Lake Washington, the city has four lakes within its limits, an unusual number of beautiful parks and mountain views in every direction. The protection of Elliot Bay has made Seattle a great seaport, and a few old ships have been preserved as museums.

Charles and Emma Frye Art Museum *704 Terry Ave.* This modern structure houses a collection of paintings that is especially strong in works from the Munich school during the last half of the 19th century. An impressive group of 19th- and 20th-century American art can also be admired, including *Landscape* by Childe Hassam, an oil by William Harnett and a watercolor by Andrew Wyeth. *Open daily except Thanksgiving Day and Dec. 25.*

Henry Art Gallery *University of Washington* The outstanding Horace C. Henry Collection of 19th- and early 20th-century American and European art includes works by Homer (*An Adirondack Lake*), Blakelock (*Moonlight* and *Landscape*), Hassam (*Old House and Garden, Long Island*) and Corot. This is complemented by the museum's good coverage of ethnic and contemporary art—including that of the Northwest—and handicrafts. There are also an extensive collection of Japanese folk pottery and frequent traveling exhibits. *Open Tues.-Sun. except holidays.*

King Street Station *303 S. Jackson St.* The 1906 railroad station is dominated by a massive tower, a noble copy of the famous campanile in the Piazza de San Marco in Venice, Italy. Constructed of red brick masonry, the imposing shaft features terra cotta and cast stone ornamentation, a four-face clock and a tile roof. *Open daily.*

Museum of History and Industry *2161 E. Hamlin St.* Historical dioramas, ship figureheads and fashions are among the many displays here relating to the story of the Pacific Northwest and Seattle's first 100 years. Children particularly enjoy the 1888 cable car and the miniature 14-room Southern Colonial mansion complete with tiny exquisite furnishings. The Aviation and Natural History Wings, the latter dominated by a huge Kodiak Island brown bear, are also popular. There are many photographs, and the facilities include a good research library. *Open Tues.-Sun. except holidays.*

Pike Place Public Markets *1431 First Ave.* More than 300 vegetable, fruit, fish and flower stalls, piled with temptingly fresh and attractively displayed goods, draw shoppers to this public market, where farmers and fishermen sell direct to consumers. Several arts and crafts shops are also located here. Opened in 1907 and now occupying three blocks, the market is listed on the National Register of Historic Places. *Open Mon.-Sat. except holidays.*

"Relief" *Northwest Seaport, Washington St. and Alaskan Way* The Pacific Coast's oldest steam-driven lightship was built in 1904 and served for 56 consecutive years. Visitors can see her original engine as well as a variety of navigational aids, lights and interesting exhibits on lifesaving, the lighthouse service and the Coast Guard. *Open Tues.-Sun. Small charge.*

Seattle Art Museum *Volunteer Park* See feature display on pages 514-5.

Seattle Center The site of the 1962 Seattle World's Fair, this 74-acre expanse offers a wide range of attractions in a setting originally designed to anticipate architectural tastes of the 21st century. There is an opera house, a large coliseum for sports events, an amusement park and the 600-foot Space Needle with observation deck and revolving restaurant. The illuminated International Fountain continues to draw crowds to its changing water patterns accompanied by music. *Open daily.*

[**34.** *Seattle Center*] *Since 1962 the Space Needle, symbol of the World's Fair, has become a favorite Seattle landmark. A small charge entitles visitors to an impressive 43-second ride up 600 feet to the observation deck, which is open daily until midnight, or to the restaurant. The view of the bay and the mountains is spectacular. The monorail at the base of the Needle is an easy means of transportation to the Center from downtown Seattle. This mile-long skyride provides visitors with another perspective of the city.*

Lush Still Life *by the Dutch artist A. van Beyeren (1620-90) is a gift to the museum from the Kress Collection.*

Seattle Art Museum

Volunteer Park, Seattle, Wash.

The emphasis at this museum, built atop one of the city's seven hills, is on the art of the Far East. On the grounds are marble camels, rams, lion-dogs and tigers which once lined avenues leading to the tombs of Chinese emperors and honored commoners. Within are galleries of Oriental sculpture, painting, screens, lacquer, ceramics and jade carvings representative of Asiatic civilization from 4000 B.C. to the present. Like the building itself, most of these objects are gifts of Dr. Richard E. Fuller, a geologist and director of the museum since it opened in 1933, and his mother. They began collecting exquisite examples of Oriental art in 1919. The jade carvings especially are spellbinding for their gentle array of color and intricate detail. Outstanding among the museum's Western art, which includes Renaissance, Baroque, primitive and American works, are paintings by two local, world-renowned painters: Mark Tobey and Morris Graves. (The museum houses the largest public collection of Tobey's works.) Their mystic images reflect the influence that their deep involvement with Oriental calligraphy and philosophy has had on their work. Other contemporary works as well as traveling exhibits are housed in the museum's Pavilion at the Seattle Center. *Open Tues.-Sun. except holidays.*

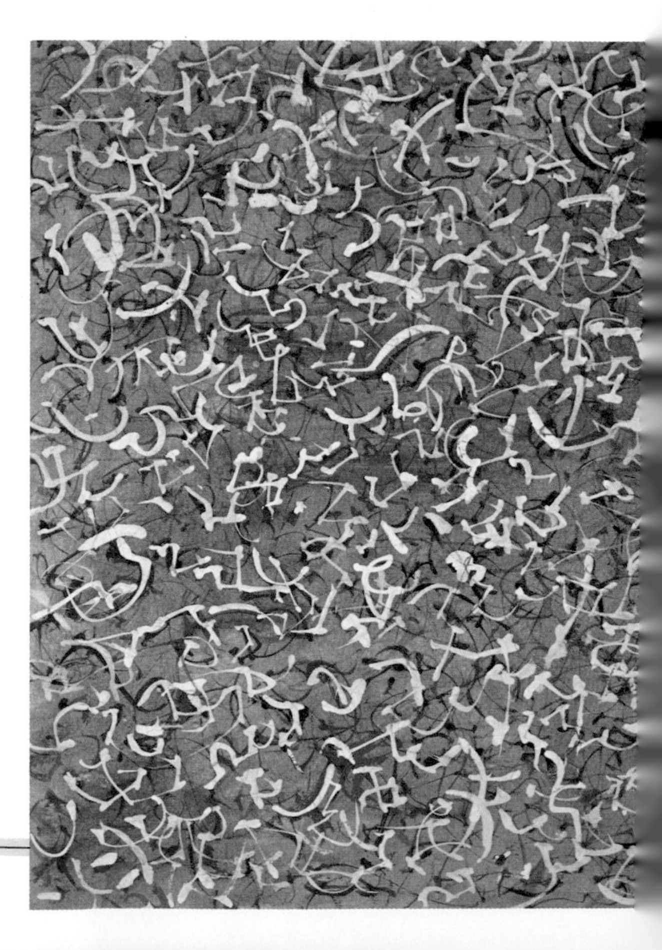

An involved intertwining of lotus flowers and stems covers the lid of this magnificent jade box which is a little over four inches in diameter. Flying around the central wheel are five bats, Chinese symbols of happiness. To achieve depth in the design, the motifs were carved on both sides.

With the aid of his ancient woodworking tools, the unknown Chinese sculptor who created this Monk at the Moment of Enlightenment *was able to preserve an awesome instant of religious experience. This nearly-life-size figure of polychromed wood was made during the Yuan dynasty (founded in 1279 by Kublai Khan), when for 89 years the Mongols ruled China.*

Vritten on the Plains #2 *is y Seattle artist Mark Tobey. 'ightly controlled lines, Orintal in feeling, are characeristic of Tobey's work. Less iterested in shapes, Tobey ses lines to express the ressed, rhythmic pulse of life.*

PACIFIC SCIENCE CENTER The former U.S. exhibit at the fair, this cluster of buildings is reached through several modernistic Gothic arches. Among its interesting features are the Boeing Spacearium with a huge overhead dome, the Astronomy-Aerospace Building and the Life Science Building, which includes a Northwest Indian ceremonial house. *Open daily. Adults $1.50, children small charge.*

WASHINGTON STATE FIRE SERVICE HISTORICAL MUSEUM Also known as the Hall of Fire Engines, the building houses almost 20 hand-drawn fire apparatus, three horse-drawn units and 17 motorized pumpers, ladder trucks and aerial rigs. Photographs, paintings, documents and pieces of equipment depict the history of fire fighting throughout the state. A facsimile of a famous 1914 waterfront fire scene has real flames and fire boats shooting water. *Open Wed.-Sun. May, daily June-Aug., Sat., Sun. Sept.-Oct.*

University of Washington Arboretum *Lake Washington Blvd. E. and Arboretum Dr. E.* Two hundred acres of bucolic landscaping stand as a fine counterpoint to the surrounding city scenery. Trails run past waterways and hundreds of trees, shrubs and flowers, a blaze of hues in spring when Japanese cherries, camellias and rhododendrons bloom and in autumn when leaves change color. In one corner of the park lies the tranquil Japanese Garden, complete with ponds, bridges, stone lanterns and a teahouse. *Arboretum open daily. Japanese Garden open daily Mar.-early Nov., Sat., Sun. mid-Nov.-Feb. Small charge for Japanese Garden.*

"Wawona" *Northwest Seaport, Washington St. and Alaskan Way* This three-masted wooden sailing vessel was built in 1897 and is now one of the last survivors of hundreds of similar ships once seen off the Pacific Coast. Used for transporting lumber and later as a cod fisher, she is currently undergoing restoration. Exhibits on board include paintings, photographs, tools and fishing gear. *Open Tues.-Sun. Small charge.*

Woodland Park Zoological Gardens *5500 Phinney Ave. N.* Rare snow leopards, four young gorillas and seven species of bear are among the 1500 mammals, birds and reptiles exhibited here. Especially impressive is the Tropical House with its collection of reptiles in natural settings. The children's zoo includes a waterfall and man-made brook that flows into a pond for water fowl, and the Poncho Theater shows natural history films and plays. *Open daily.*

35. Tacoma, Wash.

A sawmill built in 1852 on the shores of Commencement Bay marked the beginnings of Tacoma—today's "Forest Products Capital of America" and one of the country's leading ports. The city is framed by mountains—the Olympic Mountains to the west and the Cascade Range to the east—and was given the Indian name for its most spectacular backdrop: snowcapped, 14,410-foot-high Mount Rainier.

Camp Six Logging Exhibit *Point Defiance Park* Camp Six, designed by a veteran logging engineer, is a 20-acre re-creation of the days of steam logging in western Washington, from 1880 to 1940. Some of the equipment is the last of its kind. Included here are donkey engines, tracks and trestles, a logging locomotive, railroad car camps and bunkhouses. *Open daily.*

[**35.** *Tacoma Art Museum*] Natalie With a Blue Skirt *by William Glackens is one of several recent gifts of paintings to the museum. Founded in 1895 as the Tacoma Art League, the museum is now in a handsome new building.*

Fort Nisqually *Point Defiance Park* This is a replica of a pioneer fur-trading fort built by the Hudson's Bay Company of London in 1833, reconstructed with early-day materials and tools where possible. Only two of the original buildings remain and the fort's granary, built in 1843, is the oldest standing structure in Washington. The two bastions for defense have been rebuilt. A museum features pioneer relics, Indian artifacts and other memorabilia. *Open daily mid-June-early Sept., Tues.-Sun. early Sept.-mid-June.*

Narrows Bridge With a center span of 2800 feet and a total length of more than a mile, this is one of the longest suspension bridges in the U.S. Support towers rise to a height of 507 feet above the water. The bridge, which connects Tacoma and the Olympic Peninsula, was completed in 1950 at a cost of $18,000,000.

Northern Pacific Passenger Station *1713 Pacific Ave.* Once an important and crowded terminal for transcontinental trains, the palatial 1911 building now largely stands in proud memory of its former days of railroading glory. But the interior still elegantly reflects its old-fashioned high style: there are lavish Italian marble walls and terrazzo floors, and the waiting room roof is richly faced with copper. *Open daily.*

Old Tacoma City Hall *Seventh St. and Pacific Ave.* When the city government moved to modern quarters in 1959, some citizens wanted to demolish the old 1893 city hall. Others thought the handsome brick building, dominated by a 195-foot bell tower, should be saved. Eventually the preservationists won out. Although the interior has been completely reconstructed into a five-story complex of restaurants and smart shops, the ornate Italianate exterior still looks much as it did at the turn of the century. *Open daily.*

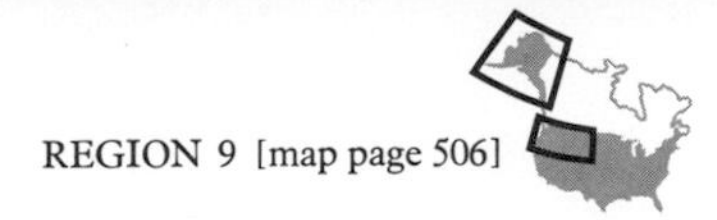

Tacoma Art Museum *12th and Pacific Aves.* Frequently changing exhibitions augment the small permanent collection housed in the museum's neoclassic building. This collection includes an Andrew Wyeth (*Braddock's Coat*), one of the *Moon Shot Series* by Rauschenberg and works by Dubuffet, Stella, Matta and Glackens. There is a small reference library and a Children's Gallery. *Open daily.*

Tacoma Totem Pole *Ninth and A Sts.* Alaskan Indians were hired to carve and paint this totem pole in 1903. Crafted from a single cedar tree and 105 feet high, it is believed to be the tallest in the nation. Various symbols, including representations of a killer whale, a wolf, a grizzly bear, human figures and Tads-doh, the great raven woman—all capped by a large eagle—depict the story of an Indian tribe.

Washington State Historical Society Museum *315 N. Stadium Way* A profusion of artifacts from prehistoric times to pioneer days, manuscripts such as the original journal kept by Narcissa Whitman on her trip from New York to Fort Vancouver in 1836, rare maps and pictures make the society's museum and library a major center of Pacific Northwest history. The museum is noted for its illuminated photo murals and for its unique exhibits on Indian and pioneer life in the Pacific Northwest and Alaska. Dioramas, models and artifacts illustrate the changing life of the region, and exchanges with other museums relate its history to that of other parts of the world. *Open Tues.-Sun. except holidays.*

36. Ezra Meeker Mansion *321 E. Pioneer Ave., Puyallup, Wash.* This 17-room Victorian mansion was the home of the "Hop King of the World," who gained national prominence in the early 1900s with his campaign to honor the pioneers of the Oregon Trail by erecting monuments along the route West. To promote his campaign he traveled the Trail—at the age of 76—by ox-drawn wagon; later by automobile; and—at 94—by airplane. The house he built in 1890 is noted for its six ornate fireplaces decorated with European tiles, and for its stained-glass windows, carved woodwork and widow's walk. *Open Sun. Feb.-May, Sat., Sun. June-early Sept., Sun. early Sept.-mid-Dec. Small charge.*

37. Olympia, Wash.

The capital city of Washington, while not as large as most of the other cities on Puget Sound, is among the oldest communities in the Pacific Northwest. Its first settlers came in the 1840s, and it was named the capital of the territory in 1853. Located at the southern end of Puget Sound, Olympia is the gateway to the beautiful Olympic Peninsula.

Capitol Group *Jefferson St. and Capitol Lake* Sixteen buildings completed between 1920 and 1971 make up this complex on eight acres of landscaped grounds. In addition to the legislative and judicial buildings described below, there are several administrative office buildings; a 71-foot totem pole beautifully carved by Chief William Shelton of the Snohomish tribe; an imposing memorial to the fighting men of World War I; and an illuminated fountain.

GOVERNOR'S MANSION Dwarfed by the other buildings yet unique in its own right is this 1907 house. It was designed as the governor's private residence while keeping in mind that hospitality is part of a governor's official role. The 35-foot ballroom, the formal dining and drawing rooms and the reception hall are all generously and graciously proportioned.

LEGISLATIVE BUILDING Dominated by a 287-foot dome surrounded by Corinthian columns, the imposing sandstone building is a superb example of modified Roman-Doric style. Eight massive Corinthian columns top the steps leading to the main entrance, where bronze doors bear bas-reliefs portraying the state's major industries. Dominating the rotunda is a huge bronze chandelier designed by the Tiffany Studios and supported by a chain more than 100 feet long. *Open daily June-Aug., Mon.-Fri. except holidays Sept.-May.*

TEMPLE OF JUSTICE Flanking the Legislative Building is this sandstone structure with Doric columns along its facade that blend with the Roman-Doric style of its neighbor. It houses the State Supreme Court, where the hearings are open to the public, and the State Law Library. *Open Mon.-Fri. except holidays.*

WASHINGTON STATE LIBRARY In contrast to the other buildings yet harmonious with them is this contemporary edifice that holds more than one million books, documents and special materials. A stunning marble mosaic wall designed and executed by James Fitzgerald stands free in the entrance lobby. The Washington Room, devoted to history of the Northwest, has four semi-abstract murals by Kenneth Callahan depicting the people of Washington's history and the state's rugged landscape. *Open Mon.-Fri. except holidays.*

State Capitol Museum *211 W. 21st Ave.* A fine collection of art as well as displays on the history and natural resources of the region can be admired in the 25 exhibit rooms of this former private residence. Eskimo, Northwest Coast and Plateau Indian artifacts range from examples of basketry and beadwork to weaving and implements. There is also a large exhibit of shells and a number of fossils, fish, mushrooms, minerals and petrified woods. Furniture, clothing, china, glassware, guns and early musical instruments reflect the area's history. *Open Tues.-Sun. except holidays.*

[**37.** *Capitol Group*] *The buildings overlook Puget Sound, with the Olympic Mountains and Mount Rainier as a backdrop. The Legislative Building's 287-foot masonry dome has survived two major earthquakes.*

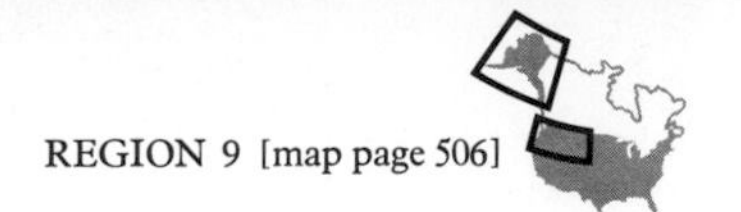

[45] *The "Oregon Pony" was considered a junior iron horse, hence its name. Transported by ship from San Francisco to Portland and hauled inland on a barge, it replaced mules on a four-and-one-half-mile portage road in 1862.*

38. Cowlitz County Museum *Court House Annex, Kelso, Wash.* Prominently displayed are a split-log cabin, a parlor, a kitchen, a country store, a barbershop and a livery stable—all reconstructions that evoke lifestyles on the frontier 100 years ago. Other legacies of pioneer days are dolls, clothing, quilts, tools and guns. There is also a choice collection of Indian artifacts. *Open Tues.-Sun.*

39. Caples House Museum *Columbia City, Ore.* Continuously inhabited by members of the pioneering Caples family for almost 100 years, the 1870 saltbox house still contains the furnishings used by the family. The rosewood grand piano came around Cape Horn by ship, but most of the furniture was made locally. The grounds include an old carriage house, which now holds period costumes; a country store; and a tool shed. *Open Tues.-Sun. Feb.-Dec. Small charge.*

40. Columbia County Museum *Strand St., St. Helens, Ore.* Historical materials relating to early Oregon pioneers are exhibited here, including antique furniture and logging pictures and equipment. The museum is housed on the second floor of a 1906 courthouse; one courtroom retains its former appearance and another houses books, county records and other regional memorabilia. *Open Thurs., Fri.*

41. Clark County Historical Museum *1511 Main St., Vancouver, Wash.* One of the first printing presses used in the Washington Territory is among the historical items on display here. Other exhibits include dioramas depicting the history of Fort Vancouver and Hudson's Bay Company, an 1890 country store, a pioneer doctor's office, a collection of old dolls and many Indian and pioneer artifacts. *Open Tues.-Sun.*

42. Fort Vancouver National Historic Site *E. Evergreen Blvd., Vancouver, Wash.* From 1825 to 1849 the British Hudson's Bay Company made its headquarters for the Pacific Northwest here, creating an important fur-trading center—and the future city of Vancouver. Later the fort site became a part of the first U.S. military post in the area. Over 100 years ago fire destroyed the fort, but its original building sites are marked, and parts of the stockade and a gate were restored in 1966. The Visitor Center contains items relating to fur-trading enterprises, military artifacts, maps and paintings. *Open daily except holidays.*

43. St. James Church *12th and Washington Sts., Vancouver, Wash.* The brick Gothic-style structure, built by Bishop Aegidius Junger in 1884, served as the cathedral for the Roman Catholic Archdiocese of Seattle until 1907. Now a parish church, it contains a hand-carved oak altar and reredos, shipped from Belgium by way of Cape Horn, and an ornate pulpit. Early furnishings and statues grace the sanctuary. *Open daily.*

44. Ulysses S. Grant Museum *1106 E. Evergreen Blvd., Vancouver, Wash.* The first building erected in Vancouver was the two-story log house (now sheathed with a protective siding), built in 1849. Three years later young Captain U. S. Grant served as quartermaster at this first military post in the territory. The main floor was the company headquarters and the officers' mess; upstairs were living quarters. The house now contains furniture owned by Grant, a rosewood piano, books, petroglyphs, antique china and glassware and Indian artifacts. *Open Fri.-Wed. Small charge.*

45. Cascade Locks Park *Cascade Locks, Ore.* The riverside site is steeped in history: Lewis and Clark camped nearby in 1805, early wagon roads passed close by, the railroad came in 1883 and locks to bypass rapids were built in 1896. Through old photographs of these sites and artifacts of pioneering settlers, the past is recalled in a museum, which is housed in one of the still-standing lock tenders' quarters. Also at hand is the quaint "Oregon Pony," the first steam locomotive built on the Pacific Coast and the first used in Oregon. *Museum open Tues.-Sun. May-Oct.*

46. Bonneville Dam *Bonneville, Ore.* Built in two sections connected by an island, the gigantic dam created a lake 48 miles long in the Columbia River Gorge. It is no real obstacle to salmon, shad and other fish that migrate upstream to spawn; the dam is bypassed by three fish ladders—steplike series of pools through which the fish swim on their way up and over the dam. Visitors watch at underwater viewing windows where the traveling fish are counted as they pass the ladders during the main March-November migration season. In the powerhouse, 10 generators convert the rushing-water energy into electric power; next to the powerhouse, the navigation lock moves large ships and pleasure craft past the dam. *Open daily.*

47. Portland, Ore.

Settled in 1844, Portland has grown to be Oregon's largest city. It stands astride the Willamette River at the western end of the Columbia River Gorge. In this

[**47.** *American Rhododendron Society*] *In spite of the wide range of color, these blooms are all rhododendron—including the subgenus azalea. The gardens also feature flowering trees set among the tall native Douglas firs.*

city of contrasts, snow-covered mountains rise to the north and east—with Mount Hood as the magnificent focal point—but the effects of the Japanese Current produce a mild climate. Roses and rhododendrons are grown here in profusion and this is also an educational, cultural and outdoor recreation center.

American Rhododendron Society Gardens *S.E. 28th Ave. and Woodstock Blvd.* One of the world's largest collections of rhododendrons and azaleas, from the least-known species to the most popular hybrids, comes into vivid springtime bloom here along the quiet winding trails in a natural wooded area. The gardens are located on a peninsula in Crystal Springs Lake and feature companion plants and a lovely rock garden. *Open daily.*

Auditorium Forecourt *S.W. Third Ave. and Clay St.* A man-made waterfall 80 feet wide is the magnificent focal point of this sculptured bi-level terrace-garden. About 13,000 gallons of water cascade over the thick concrete tiers every minute, running through a maze of huge concrete slabs. Facing the Civic Auditorium, the forecourt of pools and waterfalls was designed by landscape architect Lawrence Halprin.

Bybee-Howell House *Howell Park Rd., Sauvie Island* The two-story frame structure is Sauvie Island's oldest surviving residence. It was begun in 1856 by James F. Bybee, one of the island's early settlers, and was owned for more than a century by the family of Benjamin and Elizabeth Howell, who in time came to own more than 1000 acres on the island. The house has been carefully restored to its original appearance and contains period furnishings. It is now part of 120-acre Howell Territorial Park. *Open daily.*

FARM MUSEUM The reconstructed old farm outbuildings contain implements, weapons, stone carvings and other Indian artifacts discovered on the island, as well as relics of early settlers. *Open daily May–Oct.*

Central Lutheran Church *21st Ave. and N.E. Hancock St.* Native cedar and bricks are fashioned here into a sleek modern church, built in 1951. Sunlight falls on the imposing marble altar and the chancel area, creating a spacious, open atmosphere, while stained-glass windows add rainbow colors to the striking interior. *Open daily.*

Contemporary Crafts Gallery *3934 S.W. Corbett Ave.* Crafts of the Pacific Northwest, including ceramics, jewelry, sculpture and weaving, are handsomely exhibited here. The gallery also contains a permanent collection of prize-winning crafts from previous exhibitions. A small library features craft books and periodicals, and a sales gallery offers the works of more than 300 area artist-craftsmen. *Open daily except holidays.*

Lloyd Center *2 blocks E. of Broadway and Union Ave.* An exemplary city complex within the heart of a city, the center encompasses a hotel, offices, an ice-skating rink, free parking facilities and about 100 stores, all designed to make shopping more a welcome happening than a strenuous outing. Wide pedestrian malls, landscaped with trees and flowers, invite leisurely walks past pools, fountains and sculpture. There are frequent entertainments such as band concerts, sidewalk sales and special exhibits. *Open daily.*

[**47.** *Auditorium Forecourt*] *Few people can resist dipping their toes in the pools of this monumental urban renewal project. However, no one is expected to do so. The pools and streams were deliberately made wading depth, and the various levels of the platforms enable children and adults to reach them easily. The tallest waterfall is 18 feet high. The more adventurous can stand perfectly dry in a specially designed niche behind one waterfall and peer through the cascading waters.*

National Sanctuary of Our Sorrowful Mother *8840 N.E. Skidmore St.* The sanctuary was established in 1924 by the Order of the Servants of Mary, which maintains it. A replica of Michelangelo's *Pietà* is a focal point above the altar in the impressive Our Lady's Grotto—a cavelike opening carved in a 150-foot-high granite wall and the central attraction of the 58-acre sanctuary. Among the shrine's tranquil gardens and groves stand imposing statues of Christ and saints, while a series of wood carvings strikingly depict the Seven Sorrows of Mary. *Open daily.*

Old Church *1422 S.W. 11th Ave.* The wooden structure with its tall steeple is considered an outstanding example of Victorian "carpenter Gothic" architecture. Finished in 1883 as the Calvary Presbyterian Church, it still contains the original fine Hook & Hastings pipe organ. Much of the building has been restored to its 19th-century appearance, including the Lannie Hurst Parlour, which has been furnished with authentic Victorian pieces. The handsome Old Church is now used as a community center. *Open Tues.-Sat. except holidays.*

Oregon Historical Society Headquarters *1230 S.W. Park Ave.* A rich assortment of items here highlight aspects of the state's history. Pioneer tradesmen like the weaver, harness maker, cooper and tanner are represented by artifacts they once used. A full-size 1845 wagon shares space with a remarkable collection of model horse-drawn vehicles of the 19th century. Exhibits reveal everyday life-styles of the state's Indian tribes: their housing, clothing, salmon drying racks, trading and crafts. There is an extensive reference library. *Open Mon.-Sat.*

Oregon Museum of Science and Industry *4015 S.W. Canyon Rd.* Visitors here quickly learn that science is more fun than baffling. There is a ship's bridge with equipment to handle, an illuminated transparent woman who speaks of her body's functions and a huge walk-in heart that describes its vital role. Forty exhibits tell how electricity works, and 20 more relate the story of fluid mechanics. Among the other outstanding specialties are NASA exhibits, agricultural displays featuring a mechanical cow and a live beehive, and a planetarium which offers daily shows. *Open daily except Dec. 25. Small charge.*

Oregon Pioneer Savings and Loan Association Building *401 S.W. Fifth Ave.* Built in 1915, the massive but graceful Greek Revival landmark was spared demolition when the Savings and Loan Association bought it from the First National Bank of Oregon in 1972. The cornice, friezes and soaring columns of the front facade closely resemble those of the Lincoln Memorial in Washington, D.C. The building's noble scale is matched by its interior: one huge three-story space capped by a glass roof. *Open Mon.-Fri.*

Pittock Mansion *3229 N.W. Pittock Dr., off W. Burnside St.* Completed in 1914, the French Renaissance mansion was built for newspaper publisher Henry L. Pittock, founder of Portland's *Daily Oregonian.* Each room features opulent design details such as polished hardwood and marble floors, expertly crafted wood- and plasterwork, carved oak doors and bronze staircase railings. The original Tiffany glaze still decorates the Turkish smoking room's walls. Among the mansion's original lavish features are an elevator to all floors, an inter-room telephone system and a central vacuum cleaner. From the handsome oval drawing room, high above the city, the visitor can see hills and mountains in two states and five peaks of the Cascade range. The mansion's 46-acre site is now part of Portland's park system. *Open Wed.-Sun. Small charge.*

Portland Art Museum *1219 S.W. Park Ave.* The museum's specialty is the art of Northwest Indians and Eskimos: carvings, masks and rattles attest to their artistry and exceptional skill. Other collections include Japanese prints, sculpture and pottery; Renaissance masterpieces; 19th- and 20th-century French and American paintings; and Cameroon art. There are also notable works by artists of the Northwest. *Open Tues.-Sun. Small charge.*

Portland Children's Museum *3037 S.W. Second Ave.* Natural history is the dominant theme here, and the main attraction is a small zoo with about 40 animals that can be handled. The evolution of animal life is traced in a winding 60-foot Time Tunnel, and in a simulated environment of early man (including a cave) children can try their hand at basket weaving, grinding maize and other ancient crafts. There are dolls and stuffed animals, an Arctic display and a room filled with games and puzzles. *Open Mon.-Sat.*

[**47.** *Portland Art Museum*] *These two works of art show the diversity of the museum known primarily for its regional holdings. The portrait of Madame de Pompadour, mistress of Louis XV, is one of seven by François Boucher. Usually lavish with color, the rococo painter dressed her in blue for each portrait. Sculptor Constantin Brancuşi (1876–1957) found beauty in increasingly abstract forms. Yet no matter how streamlined, his forms are, like the* Muse *at the far left, imbued with a feeling of life.*

[47. *Washington Park-Japanese Garden*] *Largest of the garden's Oriental arrangements is the Strolling Pond Garden, whose waterfalls, ponds and irregular terrain symbolize the world in miniature.*

Portland City Hall *1220 S.W. Fifth Ave.* In 1963 a replica of the famous Liberty Bell in Philadelphia was presented to the city of Portland by a group of citizens. A reproduction of the bell hangs in the city hall, in itself an historic landmark. Built in 1895, the building is a combination of Renaissance and Greek Revival styles. *Open Mon.-Fri. except holidays.*

INDIAN PETROGLYPH ROCK At the Fourth Avenue entrance to the city hall is a large basalt rock with human associations far older than those of the Liberty Bell. On it an unknown people carved mysterious petroglyphs which have never been deciphered.

Portland Zoological Gardens *4001 S.W. Canyon Rd.* Among the hundreds of animals here are several species of bear, macaques, camels, yaks and Siberian tigers. Other features are the rare breeding elephant "herd," the seal and sea lion complex, an animal nursery, the walk-through aviary scaled for children, and pleasant gardens. The Children's Zoo provides the opportunity for personal contact with animals as well as a boat ride. The zoo's noted Zooliner, an 1870s-design steam train, takes passengers over two-and-one-half miles of narrow-gauge track. The railroad connects the zoo with the International Rose Test Gardens and the Japanese Gardens in Washington Park and offers a panoramic view of the city and of Mount Hood. *Open daily except Dec. 25. Small charge.*

St. Johns Bridge *Foot of N. Philadelphia St.* Completed in 1931 at a cost of almost $4,000,000, the suspension bridge spans 1207 feet of water, and the structure's overall span is more than 2000 feet. There is a 40-foot-wide roadway for vehicular traffic and a walkway for pedestrians.

Washington City Park *Arlington Heights* The large wooded park encompasses several attractions and provides a superb panoramic view of the city and distant Mount Hood. *Open daily.*

INTERNATIONAL ROSE TEST GARDEN Some 10,000 rose bushes, representing more than 500 varieties, are on colorful display here in season in the "City of Roses." This outstanding garden, established in 1917, serves as a testing center for new varieties. The main display area of five acres contains thousands of hybrid teas, floribunda, grandiflora and miniatures, banked by terraces of rhododendrons growing against a background of fir trees. There is also another garden featuring flowers popular during Shakespeare's lifetime. *Open daily.*

JAPANESE GARDEN Five traditional Oriental nature arrangements are featured here: the Strolling Pond Garden, the Moss Garden, the Sand and Stone Garden, the Flat Garden and the Tea Garden. The grounds also contain placid reflecting pools, pagodalike stone lanterns, a Haiku poetry stone and a graceful moon bridge. *Open Tues.-Sun. Apr.-Oct. Small charge.*

Zion Lutheran Church *S.W. 18th Ave. and Salmon St.* Architect Pietro Belluschi designed the elegant modern building, constructed in 1950 of brick and wood, to give the appearance of a village church. Its bronze entrance doors feature a graceful ascending angel design. Interior arches of laminated wood soar upward with Gothic-style majesty, a chancel window sheds light through violet and amber stained glass and a copper-sheathed altar stands beneath a shimmering wall-mounted cross. *Open Sun.-Fri.*

48. Trolley Park *Off Rte. 6, W. of Glenwood, Ore.* Whether it's on the double-decker from Blackpool, England, the open "breezer" from Sydney, Australia, or the closed city car from Portland, Oregon, visitors will be riding on an authentic operating trolley system in this unusual 42-acre park. And at the end of the mile-long line riders can lunch in a streamside picnic area accessible only by the trolley. In the car barn and repair shop are several other vintage trolley cars in the process of restoration. *Open daily July-early Sept., Sat., Sun. early-late Sept. Small charge.*

49. Old College Hall *Pacific University, Forest Grove, Ore.* The oldest structure in continuous educational use west of the Mississippi River had its beginnings in 1850 at a community building bee. Settlers from miles around camped on the grounds for two weeks while the men framed in the hall, the women cooked and the children played. Today the neat clapboard structure houses a chapel and meeting room and a museum devoted to Oriental artifacts, Indian relics and mementos of the area's pioneers. *Open Mon.*

50. Minthorn House *Second and River Sts., Newberg, Ore.* Herbert Hoover's boyhood bedroom, complete with the original furnishings, is the most impressive of many Hoover relics and souvenirs at this memorial to the former President. Following the death of his parents, 10-year-old Hoover came here to live with his uncle Dr. Henry Minthorn. The comfortable white clapboard dwelling surrounded by a tidy picket fence was built in 1881 and is the oldest house in Newberg. *Open Tues.-Sun. Small charge.*

51. Champoeg Memorial State Park *Champoeg, Ore.* By a vote of 52 to 50, Willamette Valley settlers determined to establish the provisional government of Oregon here in 1843. The event is commemorated with a monument in the gently rolling riverside park, which includes the Pioneer Mother's Cabin (open Tues.-Sun. Feb.-Nov.) and several other historical attractions as well as picnic facilities. *Open daily.*

CHAMPOEG PIONEER MUSEUM With the establishment of the first farms in the valley, the fur-trading period came to an end and more permanent settlement began. Relics of that early pioneer life are displayed here. *Open daily May–Sept., Fri.–Sun. Oct.–Apr.*

ROBERT NEWELL HOUSE, DAR MUSEUM The home of the man who surveyed and laid out the settlement of Champoeg was the only building in town that survived a disastrous flood of the Willamette River in 1861. The house is now a museum whose diverse collections range from Indian artifacts to the gowns worn by the wives of Oregon governors at their inaugural balls. On the grounds stands a two-room frame schoolhouse that was built about 1850 and is typical of its kind. *Open Tues.–Sun. Feb.–Nov. Small charge.*

52. Ainsworth House *19195 S. Leland Rd., Oregon City, Ore.* Four large columns dominate the facade of the Greek Revival mansion, built in 1850 as the home of Captain John C. Ainsworth, a Mississippi River pilot who emigrated to Oregon and made a fortune in steamboating, banking and railroading. Now a museum, the house contains two sea chests from the U.S.S. *Constitution,* "Old Ironsides," and one from the flagship of the War of 1812, the *Independence.* The antique furnishings are of the period. *Open Sat., Sun. Small charge.*

53. Barclay House *719 Center St., Oregon City, Ore.* This was the home of a Hudson's Bay Company doctor, Forbes Barclay, a founder of Oregon City, one of its first mayors and its first school superintendent. The pioneering doctor had the house built in 1850, in a New England style, of wood shipped from the East Coast around Cape Horn. A comfortable veranda spans the front. The house contains fine antiques and a collection of historical artifacts. *Open daily.*

54. Dr. John McLoughlin House *713 Center St., Oregon City, Ore.* In the days of the fur-trading empire of the Hudson's Bay Company, Chief Factor Dr. John McLoughlin ruled the western territory for 22 years. His friendliness toward the U.S. resulted in strained relations with Hudson's Bay, and in 1845 McLoughlin resigned and built a large frame house in Oregon City, which he had helped to found. One of the few houses of the period still standing, the McLoughlin home is Colonial style adapted to pioneer conditions. Now a National Historic Site, the dwelling has been restored to its original condition, furnished with McLoughlin family pieces and other period furniture, and moved from its original site to a park donated to the city by Dr. McLoughlin in 1850. *Open Tues.–Sun. except Dec. 25. Small charge.*

55. Aurora Colony Historical Society Buildings *Second and Liberty Sts., Aurora, Ore.* Determined to live each day according to the golden rule, to own property communally and to produce for their common good, a band of German religious idealists settled in Oregon in the 1850s. The Aurora Colony, which eventually numbered several hundred members, flourished for more than 30 years and came to own communal farms radiating for many miles from the town. With the death in 1877 of its leader and founder, Dr. William Keil, the group disbanded and its assets were equitably divided among the remaining members. Three buildings, now on a single property, present the lives and beliefs of these devout pioneers. *Open Wed.–Sun. except holidays. Small charge includes all buildings.*

KRAUS HOUSE The prim white frame house, built in 1864, is a typical family home of the kind the colonists built after becoming established in the Aurora area. Basic furnishings, from the delicately spooled trundle bed to the colony cupboards and chairs, are authentic and hand-made, typifying the colonists' craftsmanship.

OX BARN MUSEUM Evidence of the industry and culture of the Aurora colonists is preserved and displayed in the attractive museum. The handsome two-story structure, originally an ox barn, is filled with handcrafted furniture, tools, utensils, garments and other articles made and used by the colonists.

STEINBACH CABIN The crude log cabin with plank floors and roughly finished walls was the first home of one of the colony's farming families. The simple furnishings convincingly reflect the austerity of Aurora Colony farm life.

56. Fort Yamhill Blockhouse *City Park, Dayton, Ore.* Built of sturdy logs pierced by gun slots, the unusually shaped two-story blockhouse is a remnant of Fort Yamhill, a pioneer outpost that was established near Grand Ronde, Oregon, in 1856. *Open daily.*

57. Bush House *600 Mission St., S.E., Salem, Ore.* Asahel Bush, Salem banker and newspaper publisher, built the Victorian mansion in 1877–8 in a lovely setting among oak woods. Splendidly old-fashioned in appearance now, the house originally incorporated such modern conveniences as central heating and indoor plumbing. It still contains original gaslight fixtures, 10 marble fireplaces and much of the original wallpaper. Period furnishings include many articles that belonged to the Bush family. Next door in the Bush Barn Art Center are exhibits of works by Northwest artists. *Open Tues.–Sun. Small charge.*

58. Mission Mill Museum *Mill St., S.E. 12th–14th Sts., Salem, Ore.* Buildings here tell the story of Oregon's cultural and spiritual pioneers and fledgling industries. Among the most influential settlers in 1834 was Methodist missionary Jason Lee. Lee's house and the Parsonage, both built in 1841, are here. While the frame home has yet to be restored, the Parsonage is again furnished in 19th-century style. Added to these historic mission buildings is the John D. Boon House, a five-room slab dwelling built in 1847 by another Methodist minister. On the grounds are the Thomas Kay Woolen Mill buildings, erected in 1889–96 by a pioneering industrialist. The mill produced woolen goods like mackinaws, flannels and blankets for Klondike gold rushers and other customers throughout the Northwest. Plans are underway for exhibits featuring textile industries, fire vehicles, pioneer farm equipment and domestic crafts. *Open late May–early Sept. Small charge.*

59. Oregon State Capitol *Court St., Salem, Ore.* Oregon's impressively simple capitol, dedicated in 1938, is a low marble building with a large central rotunda. Massive sculpture groups, depicting *The Covered Wagon* and *Lewis and Clark Led by Sacajawea,* flank the en-

[64. *University of Oregon-Museum of Art*] *The courtyard is a pleasant place to rest after admiring treasures like this ivory figure of Ho-Hsien-Ku, the only female Taoist immortal. It was carved by an artist of the Ch'ing dynasty between 1736 and 1796.*

trance, and a heroic-size figure of *The Pioneer* tops the rotunda tower. *Open daily early June-early Sept., Mon.-Sat. early Sept.-early June.*

60. Horner Museum *Gill Coliseum, Oregon State University, Corvallis, Ore.* A large and diverse collection here features items of natural history and Indian and pioneer life. Ancient fossils include fragments of prehistoric animals, including elephants and mastodons. There are mounted animals and birds and displays of butterflies and insects. Arrowheads, necklaces, war bonnets and tomahawks highlight Indian cultures. Pioneer days come to life through a wide range of household items, woodworking tools, clothing, quilts and bicycles. *Open Tues.-Sun.*

61. Linn County Historical Museum *Brownsville, Ore.* The pioneer era of Linn County, which was formed in 1847, is re-created here in rooms decorated with furnishings collected in the area. Also on exhibit are equipment from an early doctor's office, a cobbler's shop, a blacksmith shop, a country store, a post office and a bank. *Open Tues.-Sun. mid-June-mid-Sept., Sat., Sun. mid-Sept.-mid-June.*

62. Moyer House *Brownsville, Ore.* With its stark straight lines softened by elaborate cornices and cutout designs, the large white house stands out in sharp contrast to the fir-covered hill in the background. A Brownsville pioneer and businessman, John M. Moyer, built the Italian villa-style home in 1881 with wood sawed in his own mill. Several rooms have unusual board ceilings decorated with painted designs. The house is furnished with period pieces, including some items that belonged to the Moyer family. *Open Tues.-Sun. mid-June-mid-Sept., Sat., Sun. mid-Sept.-mid-June.*

63. Oregon's House of Guns and Museum of Vanishing Americana *Fifth and Orchard Sts., Monroe, Ore.* Because of the nation's early history of pioneering settlers equipped with little more than courage and firearms to subdue the land, Americans tend to be more fascinated with than fearful of guns. The collection here astounds even the least avid fancier: there are 275 Winchester pieces and 350 other types of history-making arms. *Open Mon.-Fri.*

64. Eugene, Ore.

Eugene was named for its first settler, Eugene F. Skinner, who arrived here in 1846. It is a lumbering and manufacturing center, the seat of the University of Oregon and reveals remarkable advances in architecture and city planning.

Lane County Pioneer Museum *740 W. 13th Ave.* Farm equipment, old vehicles, logging gear, toys, clothing and household furnishings depict the daily activities of Lane County's early settlers. The museum's library houses the Lane County archives, old photographs, manuscripts and other paper material relating to the county's development. *Open Sat.-Thurs.*

University of Oregon The state university, located near the heart of the city, first opened its doors in 1876, and its first class of five members was graduated in 1879.

DEADY HALL The first building on campus was built in 1876 and named for Judge Matthew P. Deady, who was then president of the Board of Regents. It is a remarkably attractive structure in the Victorian style, with a mansard roof.

MUSEUM OF ART Behind the tapestrylike facade of the handsome brick structure are three floors of galleries filled with treasures. The extensive Oriental collections include Japanese folding screens, delicate Chinese ivory carvings, ancient stone Buddha heads and thousands of other works from China, India, Japan, Korea and Cambodia. The vast collection of works by contemporary artists of the Pacific Northwest is highlighted by 502 works by artist Morris Graves, noted for his mystical impressions of birds. *Open Tues.-Sun. except holidays.*

MUSEUM OF NATURAL HISTORY Masks and other artifacts portray the heritage of the Indians of the Northwest. In addition to displays of local plants and animals, there are exhibits of fluorescent minerals and explanations of volcanism, which played an important role in the area's geological history. *Open Mon.-Fri. except holidays.*

VILLARD HALL The second oldest building on the university's campus was named for a local railroad tycoon, Henry Villard. The handsome structure, adjacent to Deady Hall, was completed in 1885 and is also in the Victorian style.

65. Railroad Town U.S.A. *525 Row River Rd., Cottage Grove, Ore.* Old locomotives and passenger coaches provide fitting museum space for displays of colorful railroad memorabilia. And in addition an actual train ride is available. The vintage 1914 and 1925 engines of the Oregon Pacific and Eastern Railway haul passenger cars over a 35-mile, two-and-a-quarter-hour round trip through some of the state's ruggedly beautiful country which is steeped in the history of lumbering and mining. *Museum open daily. Small charge. Weekend train excursions mid-May-Sept. Adults $3.90, children 12-17 $2.75, 5-11 $1.50.*

66. Lane House *544 S.E. Douglas Ave., Roseburg, Ore.* The white frame house, built in the 1850s, was once the home of General Joseph Lane, first territorial governor of Oregon and first U.S. senator from the state, whose family occupied it for more than 100 years. Now a museum, it contains antiques contributed by descendants of pioneer families—pieces mostly brought across the Plains on wagons, shipped around Cape Horn or handmade in Oregon. Other interesting period furnishings include kitchen utensils, a Franklin stove, handwoven spreads and feather beds. There are also memorabilia of General Lane, who was a hero of the Mexican War, ancient weapons and Indian relics on display. *Open Sat., Sun.*

67. Old Oregon Historical Museum *2335 Sardine Creek Rd., Gold Hill, Ore.* Some 2500 items are displayed in the pioneer-style wood building, many focusing on the area's stagecoach and gold-mining era of the 1850s and 1860s. Old newspapers and other documents record the bygone times, wagons recall the hardships of early transportation, a gun collection tells of lawless days and penny arcade machines highlight past entertainment. In addition the museum features a collection of rare Indian artifacts. *Open daily Mar.-Oct. Small charge.*

68. Crater Rock Museum *2002 Scenic Ave., Central Point, Ore.* The large collection of agate, jasper, jade and other choice rock and mineral specimens is dominated by native Oregon material: many of the specimens were collected at famous mines that operated in southern Oregon in the 1800s and early 1900s. There are also fossils, multicolored sections of petrified wood and a fine display of local Indian arrowheads, spear points, fish hooks and other implements crafted from jasper and agate. *Open daily.*

69. Jacksonville Historic District

Jacksonville, Ore.

In 1851 gold was found in Rich Gulch and soon a town grew up nearby. You can still pan for gold around Jacksonville, or take a stagecoach ride and see it much as it was at its peak in the 1880s: white frame churches, carefully kept old homes, picket fences, even part of the old wooden sidewalk on California Street, the same neat brick buildings such as Odd Fellows Hall, constructed in 1855 with two feet of earth between roof and ceiling to prevent fire arrows from destroying it during Indian raids. From 1853 to 1900 the town photographer did a thriving business, so the main building of the Jacksonville Museum, in the old Jackson County Court House, has a pictorial record of the place and its people—Indians, farmers, Chinese, miners, judges, children. Bypassed by the railroad, the once lively trade center lost its position as county seat. Shops were boarded up; population declined. In 1963 a proposal for a four-lane highway to cut through Jacksonville aroused its citizens. After a successful fight to have the plan revoked, they turned to restoring the neglected old buildings. Now art galleries and antique shops are opening in this picturesque and historic setting.

This road leads to the cemetery overlooking the revitalized town. From the tombstones at the right, one can imagine the hardships of early inhabitants.

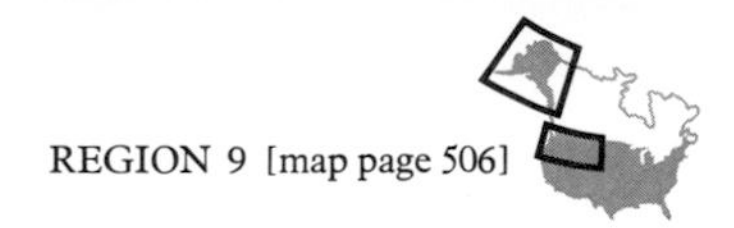

70. Josephine County Historical Kerbyville Museum *Rte. 199, S. of Kerby, Ore.* Local history comes to life in the environs of this 1878 home of a local merchant. The house itself is furnished with possessions of county pioneers. In the large modern annex are an old-fashioned country store, a genuine turn-of-the-century post office, a large gun collection and two moonshining stills that once were active in the valley. On the landscaped grounds are a log schoolhouse dating from 1898 and an assortment of mining, logging and farming equipment. *Open daily May–Oct.*

71. Siskiyou County Gold Display *311 Fourth St., Yreka, Calif.* A large collection of gold nuggets and other ores from this county can be seen in the foyer of the Siskiyou County Courthouse. Gold was first discovered here in 1851. Minerals and gems are still to be found in the area and maps showing some of the possible locations are available here. *Open Mon.–Fri. except holidays.*

72. Siskiyou County Museum *910 S. Main St., Yreka, Calif.* County history from prehistoric times to the early 1900s is recorded here in displays of fossils, Indian artifacts, costumes, firearms and dolls and other antique toys. There is a replica miner's cabin, and several other reconstructions highlight such early enterprises as a country store, a blacksmith shop and millinery and music shops. The museum building itself is modeled after an 1854 hotel, one of the county's stage stops on the Oregon Trail, which is still standing. *Open Tues.–Sun. except holidays.*

73. Grand Coulee Dam *Coulee Dam, Wash.* Completed in 1942, this massive engineering marvel is the largest concrete dam ever built. It contains over 10 million cubic yards of concrete and rises 550 feet above bedrock. The spillway, illuminated in summer, is half as wide and twice as high as Niagara Falls. Constructed as part of the Columbia Basin Project, it will provide water for more than one million acres of once-arid land. There is a visitor center and numerous view points; frequently revised tapes orient visitors on current activity. *Open daily.*

74. Old Mission Pioneer Village *E. Sunset Hwy., Cashmere, Wash.* The Chelan County Historical Society has moved a number of buildings to this site, recreating a typical late-19th-century Western community. The log Old Mission is a replica of the mission founded here by Oblate Fathers. Miners once brought ore samples to the 1879 assay office for evaluation, and farmers brought their horses to be shod at the blacksmith shop, built in 1889. A barbershop, general store, one-room schoolhouse and two homesteaders' cabins are some of the village's other attractions. *Open daily Apr.–Oct.*

WILLIS CAREY HISTORICAL MUSEUM The museum features displays on the history of the Columbia River, including archaeological remains from the Stone Age as well as artifacts of more recent periods.

Among the many visitors to the U.S. Hotel (above) was a U.S. president, Rutherford B. Hayes. Restored and refurnished, part of the 1880 hotel now serves as a bank. The museum headquarters are in the former courthouse (right), whose cupola has been a town landmark since 1883.

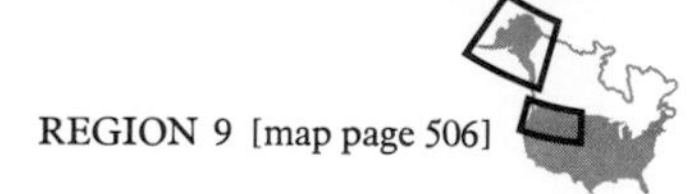

75. Ohme Gardens *Off Rte. 2, 3 mi. N. of Wenatchee, Wash.* For more than 40 years the Ohme family have worked to transform wilderness acres into splendidly tranquil gardens. Stone pathways now wander among bright alpine flowers set in stone outcroppings, past quiet pools, through shrubs and trees native to the Northwest. The nine-acre grounds lie high above the Wenatchee valley, offering far-flung views of the Cascade Range and the Columbia River. *Open daily Apr.-Oct. Adults $1.25, children over 11 small charge.*

76. North Central Washington Museum *Chelan and Douglas Sts., Wenatchee, Wash.* A colorful totem pole marks the entrance to the museum, which specializes in displays focusing on local history and artwork. Petroglyphs, rock carvings, beadwork and basketry highlight a legacy of Indian artistry, while clothing, needlework and home equipment recall pioneer days. Natural history is represented by fossils and by stuffed specimens of native mammals and birds. *Open Mon.-Sat. except holidays.*

77. Rocky Reach Dam *Rte. 97, 7 mi. N. of Wenatchee, Wash.* The L-dam spans the broad Columbia River, and observation windows overlook the turbulent spillway. In the powerhouse the Gallery of Electricity presents the historical development of electric energy. Also displayed are archaeological finds, Indian artifacts and industrial exhibits. In the Information Center there is a windowed area providing an underwater look at the fish ladder where salmon can be seen. *Open daily.*

78. Cle Elum Historical Museum *S. First St., Cle Elum, Wash.* The collection consists mainly of displays relating to the development of the telephone. Early manual switchboards and telephones can be seen along with a reconstruction of Cle Elum's first telephone office. Temporary exhibits of dolls, sleigh bells, old buttons, bottles and other items are often presented. *Open Tues.-Sun. late May-early Sept.*

79. Olmstead Place State Park *Off Kittitas Hwy., E. of Ellensburg, Wash.* On this site in 1875 Civil War veteran Samuel Olmstead established his homestead. Several of the sturdy structures he built can still be seen in this 218-acre park. The main house, built in 1875 of cottonwood logs, is still furnished with original pieces. Other attractions here include an 1892 barn, an 1894 wagon shed and a collection of early farm and ranch machinery and equipment. A National Historic Site, Olmstead Place serves to depict the development of agriculture in the state. *Open daily Apr.-Nov.*

80. Wanapum Dam Tour Center *Rte. 243, Vantage, Wash.* Bone and stone tools and weapons of the Wanapum Indians are among the large collection of archaeological finds exhibited here. Other displays include relics pertaining to the fur trade, Indian wars, mining and steamboating. Early life along the Columbia River is depicted in several paintings and dioramas: the largest is a 30-foot mural of life and historical events along the river. Chief Moses of the Columbia Indians, cattle drives and homesteading are the subjects of displays. A diorama of steamboating days is built around a replica of a pilothouse. The center also provides an impressive overview of Wanapum Dam. *Open daily Apr.-Nov.*

81. Yakima Valley Museum *2105 Tieton Dr., Yakima, Wash.* The area's original inhabitants were Yakima Indians and many relics of their culture are on display in this museum of local history. Then came white settlers from the East: to remind the present generation of their ancestors' way of life, an early-day post office, blacksmith shop, and a pioneer living room and kitchen have been re-created. Also on display are period costumes, household effects, mineral specimens and a choice collection of glassware. *Open Wed.-Fri., Sun. Jan.-late Dec.*

82. Fort Simcoe State Park *Rte. 220, 29 mi. W. of Toppenish, Wash.* This was the advance post of the 9th

[85] *This gracefully proportioned mansion-museum has an unusually dramatic setting overlooking the Columbia River and the Eastern Oregon plateau. One of the most popular exhibits is an ivory chess set carved in India during the early 1800s. The set contains the largest-known pieces in this traditional Madras style.*

[**86**] *While most army forts consisted of crude wooden buildings within a stockade fence, Fort Dalles was not enclosed and all of its buildings were in the same Gothic cottage style as the surgeon's quarters seen here. Captain Thomas Jordan, in charge of building Fort Dalles, and Louis Scholl, the supervising architect, were probably influenced by* Architecture of Country Houses *by A. J. Downing, a popular architectural tastemaker in mid-19th-century America.*

Regiment of the U.S. Infantry from 1856 to 1859. Located on the site of an ancient tribal gathering place known as Mool-Mool (bubbling water), it later served as an Indian agency and as a school. Around the parade ground, five of the original structures have been restored: the commandant's house, a square-log blockhouse and three captains' quarters. Two blockhouses and one barracks have been reconstructed. *Open daily mid-Apr.-mid-Sept.*

FORT SIMCOE MUSEUM Exhibits in the brick museum depict the history of Fort Simcoe and the surrounding area. On display are archaeological finds, Indian artifacts and crafts and military items relating to the Indian wars. *Open daily mid-Apr.-mid-Sept.*

83. Hanford Science Center *Federal Bldg., 825 Jadwin Ave., Richland, Wash.* Established by the Atomic Energy Commission, the center contains exhibits that dramatically reveal the work being done here on the peaceful uses of atomic energy. Among the equipment visitors can operate are a geiger counter and remote-control arms. Photographs, models, tape recordings, motion pictures and animated displays are designed to make atomic science both understandable and entertaining. *Open Tues.-Sun.*

84. Museum of Klickitat County Historical Society *127 W. Broadway, Goldendale, Wash.* Pioneer furniture, two organs, sleigh bells and harnesses are among the collections housed in the 1902 20-room frame house. McEwen's Brand Room contains leather patches bearing over 300 early cattle brands. An old steam traction engine can be seen outside on the lawn. *Open daily May-late Oct. Adults and children over 12 small charge.*

85. Maryhill Museum of Fine Arts *Off Rte. 14, W. of Maryhill, Wash.* Art from Europe and America is exhibited in 22 galleries in this palatial building. In addition to sculpture and drawings by Rodin, there are some personal belongings of Rumania's Queen Marie, including the throne and throne room furnishings from her summer palace near Bucharest. Visitors can also see many Northwest Indian artifacts, ship models and a large collection of chessmen. *Open daily mid-Mar.-Nov. Small charge.*

86. Fort Dalles Surgeon's Quarters *15th and Garrison Sts., The Dalles, Ore.* The only surviving building of 19th-century Fort Dalles is the surgeon's quarters, erected in 1856 and now housing a museum of historical relics. Featured here is the restored parlor, a collection of military guns and an 1800s pendulum clock. Nearby sheds contain fine collections of pioneer wagons and antique automobiles. *Open Tues.-Sun. May-Sept., Wed.-Sun. Oct.-Apr.*

87. Petersen Rock Gardens *Off Rte. 97, 7 mi. S.W. of Redmond, Ore.* Obsidian castles, agate mansions, bridges, towers, terraces and ponds—all constructed of thousands of different kinds of rocks—are fabulously displayed here. The garden is the 17-year work of Rasmus Petersen, a Danish farmer who immigrated to Oregon in 1906. Throughout the garden are many trees and flowers, free-roaming peacocks and a lagoon filled with water lilies. Rare rock specimens are exhibited in a museum. *Open daily.*

88. Collier Memorial State Park *Chiloquin, Ore.* In addition to fishing, hiking and picnicking, visitors to the park can explore a variety of historical attractions. *Open daily.*

LOGGING MUSEUM The early days of Oregon's major industry are recalled in an intriguing collection of old logging equipment, ranging from iron ox yokes to steam-driven tractors, log haulers with wheels twice as high as a man's head, and a massive boom for loading logs on railroad cars. There are also sections of logs from giant Oregon trees.

PIONEER VILLAGE Moved to a site on the banks of Spring Creek near the logging museum are several rugged cabins built long ago by trappers, miners, loggers and homesteaders.

PIT HOUSES In the park are a number of semisubterranean pit houses that were occupied by Indians before Mount Mazama exploded and formed nearby Crater Lake some 7500 years ago. One of the dwellings has been excavated and partially restored.

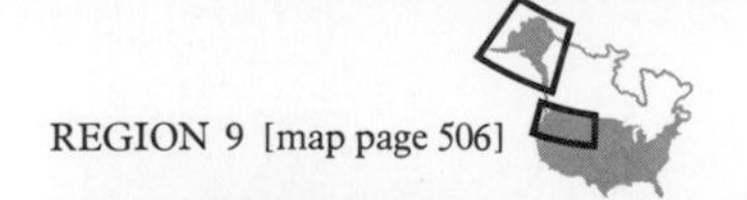

[90] *Mr. and Mrs. Schminck each came from pioneer families. Mrs. Schminck's parents had made the long wagon trek to Oregon before gold was discovered in California. Inherited family treasures were the nucleus of the museum. Through donations and painstaking repair work by Mrs. Schminck, the collection of china-head and bisque dolls displayed in the children's room now numbers 177. Many of the dolls are dressed in handmade clothes in the style of the period in which they were made. Some are more than 100 years old.*

89. Klamath County Museum *1451 Main St., Klamath Falls, Ore.* Because Klamath and Modoc Indians once lived in the area, the museum has developed an extensive Indian collection. The early pioneer display includes a sheepherder's wagon and other exhibits trace the area's history through the world wars. Another section is devoted to regional wildlife. *Open Tues.-Sun. except holidays.*

90. Schminck Memorial Museum *128 S. "E" St., Lakeview, Ore.* Convinced that ordinary everyday things are as worthy of preservation as the unusual and decorative, Lula and Dalpheus Schminck spent their lives collecting everything from old flatirons to china dolls. Their vast collection remains in their modest stucco home, which now seems ready to burst at the seams with Indian artifacts, glassware, handmade quilts, shaving mugs, candle molds, vintage telephones, sidesaddles and almost every other imaginable object of domestic Americana. *Open daily. Small charge.*

91. Spokane, Wash.

About 100 years ago a man on a horse came to the 70-foot falls of the Spokane River. Seized with enthusiasm, James Glover took out a claim. The falls are now in the central business district of Spokane, the second largest city in the state. It lies in a fertile agricultural area, but its original growth came from its proximity to the rich mines of Coeur d'Alene and British Columbia. Like many frontier towns, Spokane was razed by fire (1889), but unlike most it had a resident architect, Kirtland Cutter. He designed several public buildings for the city, but the majority of his work was done on the elaborate mansions that mining millionaires proceeded to build. These handsome homes still stand, reminders of an effort at formal elegance amid gambling halls, mud and dust.

Cathedral of St. John the Evangelist *127 E. 12th Ave.* A magnificent carillon and organ are among the many riches of the impressive Episcopal church, and recitals are given on both instruments. The former was designed in England and consists of 49 bells that weigh more than 40 tons, while the latter includes over 5000 pipes. The stone cathedral was begun in 1925 and reflects English Gothic taste with a strong French influence. It features outstanding wood carving, needlepoint cushions and a carved marble baptismal font. A superb trefoil design over the Italian limestone reredos is typical of the several beautiful stained-glass windows in the church. *Open daily.*

Duncan Gardens *Manito Park, W. 4th-21st Aves.* A 90-acre park provides the setting for hundreds of bright-blooming annual and perennial flowers and plants. Among the many attractions are dazzling rose and lilac gardens, greenhouses full of luxuriant plants and a conservatory for special year-round exhibitions. Throughout the grounds are restful fountains, lagoons and ponds. *Open daily.*

Eastern Washington State Historical Society Headquarters *W. 2316 First Ave.* Arts and crafts practiced by the Northwest Indians are featured here, along with exhibits relating to the history of the area. Dioramas depict Fort Spokane in 1818 and the Cataldo Mission in the 1850s; a natural history section has specimens of birds of eastern Washington. There is also a library of western Americana. *Open Tues.-Sun. except holidays.*

CHENEY COWLES MEMORIAL MUSEUM The Spokane Art Exhibition is held here each year from June through August. The museum contains a large permanent collection of the fine arts. *Open Tues.-Sun. except holidays.*

GRACE CAMPBELL MEMORIAL HOUSE The English-style mansion is symbolic of Spokane's "Age of Elegance" when fortunes were made in gold mining. Built in 1898, the house is constructed of brick and stucco with a half-timber trim. It is noted for its outstanding woodwork and for its fine reception room dominated by a fireplace lavishly decorated with gold. Furnishings are of the period and include some of the original antiques. *Open Tues.-Sun. except holidays.*

Pacific Northwest Indian Center *Gonzaga University* A furnished longhouse plus displays of regional Indian clothing, weapons and implements are included in the outstanding Indian collection housed in this modern five-story circular building. In the main lobby is a wall made of rocks bearing original prehistoric petroglyphs and a large decorative map that shows the areas inhabited by the various Pacific Northwest tribes. The research division incorporates thousands of volumes on Indian history and culture, photographs, maps and important manuscripts, including those of early Jesuit missionaries in the Northwest. *Open Mon.-Fri. Small charge.*

St. Charles Parish Church *N. 4514 Alberta St.* Daring design is the hallmark of this modern Roman Catholic church (finished in 1961) with a floating shell roof. The bell tower—a 92-foot shaft with strips of pierced copper scrollwork—stands apart from the concrete and masonry structure. A metal sculpture of St. Charles Borromeo dominates the entrance, flanked by enameled copper door panels that tell the story of Christ. Other features include vivid stained glass, a marble slab altar, a metal sculptured altar screen depicting saints, a rough mahogany reredos and a powerful, crafted-iron crucifix. *Open daily.*

92. Coeur d'Alene Mission of the Sacred Heart *Off Rte. 10, Cataldo, Idaho* Using no tools more complex than an auger, a broad axe, a pulley, a penknife and a few ropes, Jesuit missionaries and a band of Indians built the state's oldest building between 1848 and 1853. Large hand-pegged timbers still visible in the sanctuary attest to the builders' strength and perseverance, while the paintings and hand-carved altar, statues and decorative ceiling panels are monuments to their faith, craftsmanship and sense of beauty. *Open daily mid-Apr.-mid-Oct. Small charge.*

93. Coeur d'Alene District Mining Museum *509 Bank St., Wallace, Idaho* The biggest silver dollar in the world is on display at the well-organized museum in the heart of one of the country's major mining districts. Old hand-made equipment, an antique scale for weighing gold dust, mineral specimens and drawings and models all tell the story of mining past and present. *Open Mon.-Sat. June-Aug., Mon.-Fri. Sept.-May.*

[**92**] *The walls of this church were originally plastered with mud from the Coeur d'Alene River. The columns are a reminder of the Greek Revival style of architecture that was sweeping the country.*

94. University of Idaho *Moscow, Idaho* The coeducational university was founded in 1889, a year before Idaho became a state. The oldest arboretum in the West is located on its pleasantly landscaped campus.

ADMINISTRATION BUILDING The turreted clock tower dominating the handsome brick building is the university's symbol and its most famous landmark. *Open daily during academic sessions.*

COLLEGE OF MINES The hallways of the starkly modern building are lined with exhibits of mineral specimens. *Open daily during academic sessions.*

STUDENT UNION BUILDING In the main lounge is a large iron sculpture of warrior *Joe Vandal,* the university's mascot. *Open daily during academic sessions.*

UNIVERSITY MUSEUM Located along the central mall, the museum contains many artifacts of state and local history; it includes an exhibit on the spotted Appaloosa horse, which was developed in the area by the Nez Perce Indians. *Open Mon.-Fri.*

[**91.** *Historical Society-Campbell House*] *Within the Tudor exterior, architect Kirtland Cutter created a rococo reception room in rose and gold with this magnificent fireplace, one of 10 in the house.*

[105] *The men who once attended services in the church fought a full-scale war underground in 1868 when two adjacent operations broke into the shafts of the Golden Chariot Mine. Using steam hoses and guns, miners battled the claim jumpers inside War Eagle Mountain and outside. Called the Owyhee War, it was the biggest of such hostilities. Occasional claim jumping wars did not hinder the productivity of the 250 mines in the hills around Silver City, however. At one time the town was the center of the second largest silver-producing area in the country.*

95. Museum of Anthropology *Washington State University, Pullman, Wash.* The prehistory of man in this region is documented through archaeological finds, including material from Marmes Rockshelter, one of the Northwest's oldest sites. Here too is an outstanding collection of Indian basketwork—some 300 samples from tribes in the U.S. and Canada. Other exhibits feature Ashanti gold weights, Taoist god figurines and New Guinea artifacts. *Open Mon.-Fri. during academic sessions.*

96. Pierce, Idaho On Sept. 30, 1860, near what is now the town of Pierce but was then the forbidden lands of the Nez Perce Indians, Captain Elias D. Pierce and a party of prospectors panned less than five cents worth of gold—thereby setting off the first Idaho gold rush and bringing about the formation of the Idaho Territory two-and-a-half years later. Pierce was founded that winter and soon became the seat of Shoshone County. The first courthouse-jail, a two-story hand-hewn log structure erected in 1862, is still intact, the oldest building in town. Near the courthouse is an early stamp mill used to crush gold ore, one of the few remaining in Idaho. Other buildings in the city date from the late 19th and early 20th centuries.

97. Nez Perce National Historical Park *Spalding, Idaho* This unique national park—the first of its kind—comprises 23 separate historic and scenic sites scattered over 12,000 square miles of the hills and prairies of northern Idaho. The park is a venture involving the Nez Perce Indians, the National Park Service, other government agencies, private organizations and individuals. It was established in 1965 to commemorate the Nez Perce and the explorers, fur traders, missionaries, miners, loggers and homesteaders who opened up the area for whites. Most of the sites are along U.S. Routes 12 and 95. The two below are within easy driving distance of each other.

FORT LAPWAI *Lapwai* Two original buildings remain of this Army post founded in 1862 to protect both the miners and the Nez Perce during the Clearwater gold rush. *Open daily.*

PARK HEADQUARTERS *Spalding* The park headquarters, with excellent interpretive facilities for the entire area, is located at the site of the second mission founded by the Presbyterian missionary Reverend Henry H. Spalding. Traces of his 1840 saw and flour mills are visible, and other buildings of that busy era can be seen. *Open daily.*

98. St. Joseph's Mission Church *Slickpoo, Idaho* Nestled among tall trees in a pleasant valley is this neat white church with a gleaming cross atop its bell tower. St. Joseph's was built in 1874 by a Jesuit priest, Father Joseph M. Cataldo, who worked to convert the Nez Perce Indians to Catholicism. Although the church is no longer active, Nez Perce descendants gather here for a reunion at a Mass held on the last Sunday of each May. *Open daily mid-Mar.-mid-Oct.*

99. Fort Walla Walla Park *Walla Walla, Wash.* The 96-acre park and museum complex occupies part of the land of the original Fort Walla Walla, established in 1856. Some original and several restored buildings may be visited. The park also features nature trails, a bridle path and other recreational facilities. *Open daily May-Sept.*

OLD FORT WALLA WALLA CEMETERY The cemetery contains the graves of soldiers of the 1st Oregon Volunteer Cavalry, 1st Washington Infantry and others who died in the early Indian wars. *Open daily May-Sept.*

PIONEER VILLAGE An early schoolhouse, a pioneer cabin, a country store, a blacksmith shop, a replica of a log fort and several other structures are found here. These are furnished in the manner of the mid-19th century and contain memorabilia and historical items. The Babcock railway depot holds artifacts pertaining to early Western railroading. Adjacent to it is an exhibit of 19th-century farm equipment, pioneer tools and a covered wagon. *Open Sat., Sun. June-Aug. Small charge.*

100. Whitman Mission National Historic Site *Rte. 12, W. of Walla Walla, Wash.* Marcus and Narcissa Whitman established a mission here among the Cayuse

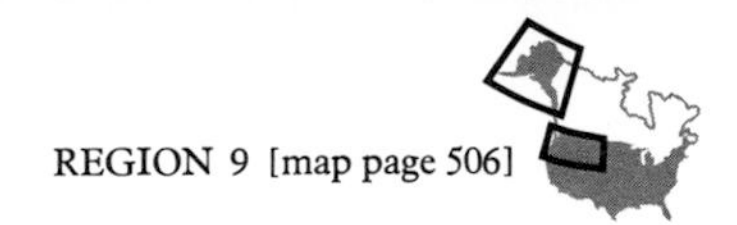

Indians in 1836. Mrs. Whitman was one of the first two women to make the overland trip across the continent. Eleven years later the missionary couple and at least 11 other whites were massacred by the Cayuse. The historic site includes a monument to the Whitmans, the graves of the massacre victims, a millpond and the early mission grounds. Historical materials relating to the Pacific Northwest's missionary period are exhibited in the Visitor Center. *Open daily except holidays.*

101. Kooch's Museum *Main St., Joseph, Ore.* For 30 years Mr. and Mrs. Raymond Kooch have been inveterate collectors of items relating to the history and settlement of Wallowa County. Some of the 2500 objects in their collection are now displayed in reconstructions of a pioneer kitchen, bedroom, parlor and other rooms. Also on exhibit are horse-drawn wagons and sleds, a 1914 Franklin automobile, farm implements, tools, lanterns, garments, dolls, glassware, historic photographs and a dizzying array of other memorabilia. *Open daily late May-early Sept. Small charge.*

102. Eastern Oregon Museum *Haines, Ore.* Items shipped around Cape Horn, carried across the plains by ox-drawn wagons or handmade locally comprise the large collection of pioneer possessions on display here. What was up-to-date equipment at the turn of the century looks quaintly picturesque now: cast iron stoves and heaters, hand-pumped washing tubs, old-time hay and grain implements, buggies and hacks. A completely outfitted blacksmith shop and a saloon bar highlight the frontier-day atmosphere of hard work and easygoing entertainment. *Open daily Apr.-Oct.*

103. Kam Wah Chung Co. Building *Gleason Park, John Day, Ore.* Following the discovery of gold nearby in 1862, the building was the trade center for the many Chinese who came to work in the local gold fields. Here they gathered to consult with the herb doctor, buy provisions, do their banking, worship at the shrine or simply gossip with friends. The main part of the picturesque stone and plank building was completed in 1867, and much of the interior remains exactly as it was 50 years ago. Plans are underway to refurbish the building as a museum.

104. Herman and Eliza Oliver Historical Museum *101 S. Canyon City Blvd., Canyon City, Ore.* Within 10 years of the discovery of gold at nearby Whiskey Flat in 1862, $26,000,000 worth of the precious ore had been mined in this area. Gold collections, mineral specimens and mining relics recall the local gold rush, while pioneer relics memorialize the farmers and lumbermen who later settled in Grant County. Indian and Chinese artifacts are also on display and the Greenhorn City Jail is located on the museum grounds. *Open Tues.-Sun. Apr.-Oct. Adults and children over 7 small charge.*

JOAQUIN MILLER CABIN The Oregon poet who was later to be known as the Poet of the Sierras wrote his first verses while living in this cabin in Canyon City, where he ran a newspaper. The rustic home, next to the museum, is furnished much as it was when Miller and his family lived here.

105. Silver City, Idaho Now deserted except for a small summer population, this is Idaho's largest ghost town. During the gold rush of the 1860s, Silver City became a prosperous mining center and the seat of Owyhee County, which it remained until 1934. About 40 of the city's early structures survive. Points of interest include the Golden Chariot Mine on War Eagle Mountain overlooking the town; the Stoddard House, a two-story Victorian home built about 1884 and noted for its ornate gingerbread trim; and the Idaho Hotel, built in 1866, which contains some early furnishings. *Open daily.*

106. Boise, Idaho

The capital of Idaho and its largest city (population 85,000) is set beside the Boise River. Boise is an anglicized derivation of *Les Bois,* which was the name used by early French-Canadian trappers. It is a modern industrial center today, but reminders of the city's gold rush beginnings are evident in the abandoned mines and ghost towns in the 2,958,356-acre Boise National Forest nearby.

Boise Gallery of Art *Julia Davis Park* The only public art museum in the state, the sleek contemporary building houses a well-rounded permanent collection that includes American, European and Oriental paintings and sculpture, with special emphasis on the work

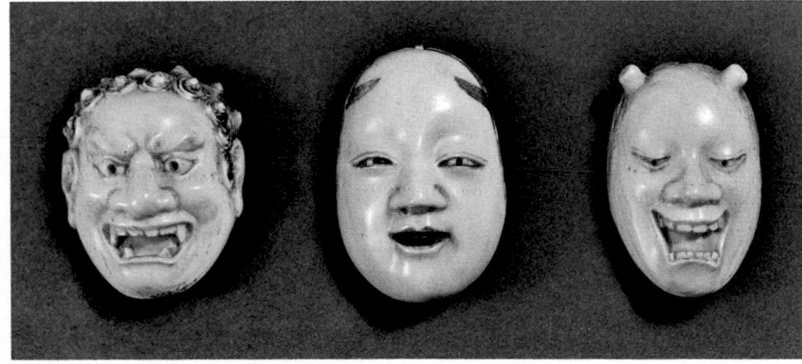

[**106.** *Gallery of Art*] *Near the end of the 17th century, it became fashionable in Japan to wear a small medicine case at the kimono sash, and the art of carving toggles (netsuke) for them developed. Most netsuke, like these 18th- and 19th-century ones, were made of ivory.*

of Idaho artists. There are also temporary exhibits of photography, graphics, architecture, crafts and other art forms and movements of both the past and the present. *Open Tues.-Sun. early Jan.-late Dec. except Thanksgiving Day.*

First United Methodist Cathedral *1110 Franklin St.* This striking church, completed in 1960, is known as the Cathedral of the Rockies. With its soaring tower and arched entrance, the church combines Gothic features with a simplified modern style. Most impressive is the rose window of stained glass over the entrance. *Open daily.*

Idaho State Capitol *Capitol Blvd.* Idaho's state capitol is a traditionally classic structure of stone and marble with a 190-foot-high central dome and Corinthian columns supporting a front portico. Of interest to visitors are exhibits of rare ores on the first floor. *Open daily.*

Idaho State Historical Museum *610 N. Julia Davis Dr.* The Idaho State Historical Society maintains this attractive museum. Featured here are exhibits on early pioneer and Indian life in the state, an operating miniature railway and historical interiors such as a saloon, blacksmith shop and Chinese temple. *Open daily.*

PIONEER VILLAGE Just east of the main museum is a collection of examples of early Idaho domestic architecture: a variety of log cabins, an old adobe house, barns and sheds. In some of the latter are old vehicles such as sleighs, stagecoaches, carriages, wagons and fire engines. *Open daily.*

Idanha Hotel *10th and Main Sts.* When the Idanha opened its doors in 1901 it was the grandest hotel in all Idaho, and even today its fanciful round-corner turrets give it a fairy-tale-castle air. Guests such as Theodore Roosevelt and Buffalo Bill strolled through the ornate Victorian lobby, which looks much as it did when the century was young. *Open daily.*

St. Michael's Cathedral *518 N. Eighth St.* Today's capital city was just a mining boomtown when the sturdy sandstone cathedral was dedicated in 1902. Designed in English Gothic style, the building saw the addition of a tower in later years—a memorial to soldiers killed in World War II. The most prominent feature of the cathedral's vaulted interior is a lovely Tiffany window. *Open Sun.*

[**111**] *At far left are horn spoons and other household implements; in the center is a painted rawhide tepee door. The eagle-feather headdress indicated success in war and was worn as a badge of honor.*

[**106.** *Union Pacific Depot*] *The depot is on the rim of a high ledge that skirts the city. Facing it, at the other end of a broad boulevard, is the capitol. The tower and surrounding gardens are illuminated at night.*

Union Pacific Railroad Depot *1701 Eastover Terr.* Although the last passenger train passed through Boise in 1971, the lovely depot—built less than 50 years earlier—remains one of the city's most picturesque landmarks. The massive Spanish-style stucco and red tile building, surrounded by the parklike Platte Gardens, is dominated by an 80-foot clocked bell tower. The waiting room is silent nowadays, but the tower's Westminster chimes continue to toll each quarter hour, as if to beckon tourists to come and admire the depot's pleasing architecture and setting.

U.S. Assay Office Building *210 Main St.* Soon after Idaho's gold rush began in the 1860s, an assay office was needed where gold and silver could be evaluated and purchased by the U.S. Mint. This dignified sandstone building, measuring just 48 by 46 feet, was erected in 1871 to house the assayer's office, laboratories and vaults. The second floor contained living quarters. The office is now the property of the Idaho Historical Society, which maintains it as a museum of the state's mining history, with displays of minerals, mining machinery and other artifacts. *Open Mon.-Fri.*

107. Custer, Idaho *Off Rte. 93, 10 mi. N. of Sunbeam, Idaho* Now a ghost town, this was once a thriving mining camp. The old seven-story mill has long since collapsed, but the nearby gold dredge is still standing. The schoolhouse, saloon and a number of ramshackle miners' cabins also survive from the late 1800s and early 1900s, when the fabulous General Custer and Lucky Boy mines were yielding millions of dollars worth of gold and silver.

U.S. FOREST SERVICE MUSEUM In what was once the Custer schoolhouse is a museum containing old mining

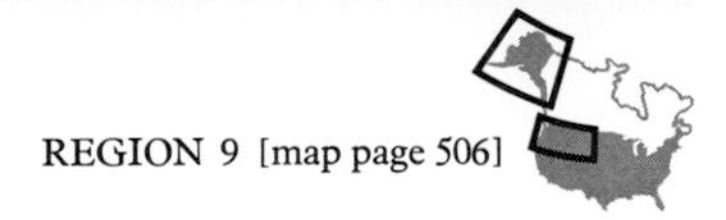

relics that evoke a living image of the town's booming past. *Open daily mid-May–Sept.*

108. Blaine County Historical Museum *Hailey, Idaho* An unusual attraction at the small museum is a collection of 5000 buttons, pennants and other political campaign memorabilia dating back to 1868. Also on display are a fine collection of arrowheads fashioned by local tribes and many articles associated with the area's past, including mementos of poet Ezra Pound, who was born in Hailey. *Open Wed.-Mon. mid-June–mid-Sept. Small charge.*

109. Tuscarora, Nev. When the Central Pacific Railroad was completed in 1869 and thousands of Chinese laborers were laid off, Tuscarora was one of the few towns in the West that would take them in. At one time 3000 to 4000 Chinese were living here, forming the second largest Chinatown west of the Rockies. Some found good pickings in the placer claims abandoned by white miners. The remains of an old mine and the smelter can still be seen. Around 30 old wooden buildings remain, some of which are still inhabited. A small museum contains displays of minerals, old photographs, artifacts and historical documents. *Open daily. Small charge for museum.*

110. Museum of Montana Wildlife *Browning, Mont.* Beyond a naturalistic waterfall at the museum's entrance, pools of light bathe mounted specimens of Montana animals depicted in lifelike stances. A grizzly bear seven feet tall, a 2000-pound bull buffalo and many others seem ready to spring to life. A second room contains 13 dioramas with miniature native wild animals portrayed in simulated natural habitats. The art gallery displays a selection of sculptures by Bob Scriver, the well-known Western artist-taxidermist and the museum's founder, who created the exhibits. *Open daily May–Oct. Small charge.*

111. Museum of the Plains Indian and Crafts Center *Browning, Mont.* The skill and artistry of the Plains Indians are shown in displays of costumes and accessories decorated with beads and porcupine quills, featherwork, carvings and designs painted on leather. Indian artists and craftsmen are featured in special exhibitions. Of particular interest is an audio-visual color slide production, *Wings of Change. Open daily June–Sept., Mon.-Fri. Oct.–May.*

112. Hungry Horse Dam *Hungry Horse, Mont.* Among the world's four largest and highest dams when completed in 1953, the colossal arched wall—close to half a mile long—checks the South Fork of the Flathead River and creates a reservoir 34 miles long. Like other great dams, it stores water, controls floods and—via four generators—turns out needed electric power. The Hungry Horse Reservoir, surrounded by Flathead National Forest, has also become a vast recreational center for camping, hunting and fishing and boating. *Open daily late May–early Sept.*

113. Hockaday Center for the Arts *Kalispell, Mont.* At this regional culture center programs are presented that include art classes, music recitals, plays and films. About 30 traveling exhibits are featured annually. *Open Mon.-Sat. except holidays.*

114. St. Ignatius Mission *Rte. 93, St. Ignatius, Mont.* The sizable brick church of this Catholic mission, which was founded by Jesuits in 1854 to serve the Flathead and Salish Indian tribes, was built in 1890. The upper walls and ceiling are adorned with 56 remarkable frescos, painted by a Jesuit brother who was an untrained artist. The church also contains many artifacts from the mission's early history, including a grinding stone from the original flour mill. Standing beside the sturdy building is the original church, a small log structure erected in 1854. *Open daily.*

[114] *Although the third church to be built at the St. Ignatius Mission was unusually large for its time and place, its interior might have remained rather austere had it not been for lay brother Joseph Carignano. He painted the many frescos illustrating man's relationship with God. It took him just 14 months, although he worked on embellishing the church only during time he could spare from his regular chores as cook, handyman and dishwasher. The triptych over the main alter is of St. Ignatius of Loyola.*

115. St. Mary's Mission *Charles St., Stevensville, Mont.* The log church, built in 1841 by Father Pierre de Smet, a Jesuit from St. Louis, was the first Christian mission established in the Northwest. The original church was later enlarged. Items related to the history of St. Mary's are exhibited inside and in a small museum. Next door is the compact mission log cabin that housed the first pharmacy and rude hospital in Montana; it now contains pioneer artifacts. The Bitteroot Mountains make a spectacular backdrop for the buildings. *Open daily.*

116. H. Earl Clack Memorial Museum *Fairgrounds, Havre, Mont.* The significance of the buffalo in Indian life is graphically highlighted in exhibits that explain the methods of killing, butchering, preserving and cooking meat, and treating and using the animals' hides. Other displays relate to the history of the Chippewa-Cree Indians and describe their use of native plants. There are dioramas depicting a cattle drive, a ranch scene, a rodeo and the surrender of Chief Joseph, as well as other interpretive exhibits of life on the northern frontier. *Open daily late May-early Sept.*

117. Fort Benton Museum *Front St. in City Park, Fort Benton, Mont.* A major fur-trading center, a crossroads of half a dozen overland trails, a vital supply center of the early West and a terminus for steamboats on the upper Missouri River, Fort Benton figures so prominently in Montana history it has reason to call itself the state's birthplace. Artifacts in the museum relate the town's colorful history, and dioramas tell the story of important events in its growth during the 19th century. *Open Sat., Sun. May, daily June-Aug., Sat., Sun. Sept.*

118. C. M. Russell Museum *1201 Fourth Ave. N., Great Falls, Mont.* The two-story frame house here was the home of the renowned cowboy artist Charles M. Russell from 1900 until his death in 1926. Next door is the comfortable studio where Russell did most of his work—a log cabin made from telephone poles. Original furnishings are still in place, along with his easel, other painting gear and his favorite Indian and cowboy artifacts. In the Russell Museum is a stunning collection of his paintings and bronzes—around 300 altogether—that vividly recapture the reality of the cowboy and Indian West. *Open daily June-Aug., Tues.-Sun. Sept.-May. Small charge.*

119. Marysville, Mont. A maverick Irishman named Thomas Cruse discovered gold here in 1876, and his Drum Lummon mine yielded a fortune of $50,000,000 before he sold it. Other prospectors found lucrative veins in the neighborhood, creating at the same time a thriving town that was the terminus of two railroad lines. Only a handful of families live here now, surrounded by ramshackle proof of past wealth and activity: part of Cruse's mine and the remains of other abandoned mines, two churches, the old school, deserted homes and stores. *Open daily.*

[122] *Though deserted now and tumbling down, old buildings like the Grand Hotel in Elkhorn once were filled with life. In the town's heyday as a silver-mining center, the notorious Calamity Jane ran a restaurant here.*

120. Helena, Mont.

Helena developed in 1864 as a gold prospector's outpost named Last Chance Gulch. The first four settlers struck gold in a vein lining the edges of what is now the main street, and by 1870 Last Chance Gulch, by now called Helena, was the most important settlement in the Montana Territory. It remains important today as the capital of Montana, a center of industry, agriculture and government in Prickly Pear Valley beneath the foothills of the Big Belt Mountains.

Archie Bray Foundation Museum *2915 Country Club Ave.* The workshops and craftsmen at the foundation, nationally known as an institution that fosters talent in the ceramic arts, produce outstanding artifacts. Glassblowing and weaving are part of the expanding creative program too, and other crafts such as leatherwork and metal sculpture are likely to be introduced. Funds for the institution come from the sales of works by resident craftsmen. A permanent collection of ceramic pieces as well as frequently changing craft exhibits amply attest to the superb work being done here. *Open Mon.-Sat.*

Cathedral of St. Helena *Lawrence and Warren Sts.* Rich in graceful Gothic detail, the twin-spired limestone edifice, begun in 1908, is a replica of Vienna's Votive Church. More than two dozen statues stand in niches outside the building, and 56 Bavarian-made windows—each protected by half-inch plate glass—form a gallery of stained-glass paintings. In the magnificent nave, massive pillars and decorated archways flow to the altar, while hand-forged bronze light fixtures hang from the ceiling like jeweled pendants. *Open daily.*

Governor's Old Mansion *304 N. Ewing St.* The state's executive mansion from 1913 to 1959, this sturdy brick and terra cotta building was completed in 1885 at a cost of $85,000. It was designed by noted architect Cass Gilbert and today still reflects the architecture and furnishings of the 1800s. Many of the 20 rooms have details of fine woodwork. *Open Mon.-Sat. Adults and children over 11 $1.50, under 12 small charge.*

Montana Historical Society Museum and Galleries *225 N. Roberts St.* Montana's history, from prehistoric times to its industrial development, is carefully spotlighted here. Dioramas portray aspects of Indian cultures, fur trading, gold mining, open-range cattle drives, homesteading days and early industry. Territory Junction, an 1880s street scene, depicts a post office, blacksmith and saddle shops, a drugstore and nine other frontier enterprises. The galleries feature the work of Charles M. Russell (1864-1926) as well as that of a number of contemporary artists. Among other displays are 40 antique Ford cars, including the first production model of 1903. *Open daily except holidays.*

Montana State Capitol A dome of Montana copper caps the imposing neoclassical limestone structure, completed in 1912. Interior finishings feature multihued Tennessee marbles, and imbedded in the terrazzo floor of the rotunda is Montana's state seal. White marble faces the main stairway; its balustrade and newel posts are fashioned from copper. Paintings of historic events and persons as well as commemorative statues decorate various halls and chambers, but the outstanding single work is Charles M. Russell's enormous painting *Lewis and Clark Meeting the Flatheads,* in the House of Representatives chamber. *Open daily early June-late Aug., Mon.-Fri. early Sept.-late May.*

Reeder's Alley The row of picturesque brick buildings was constructed in the 1860s by Louis Reeder, a Pittsburgh stonemason, to house miners; later residents included mule skinners and Chinese laundrymen. Contemporary craftsmen have refurbished the alley dwellings, turning most of them into attractive studio workshops. *Open daily.*

PIONEER CABIN Clamps rather than nails were used to build this hand-hewn log cabin, constructed (1864-9) by two gold-mining brothers. It must have been the talk of the town, for it was the first in Helena to have glass windows and a sewing machine. Gaslights and handmade chairs are among the period furnishings, which also include the original bathtub. *Open daily mid-Apr.-Sept.*

121. Castle *White Sulphur Springs, Mont.* When rancher-miner-businessman B. R. Sherman built his castlelike stone mansion in 1892, he is said to have chosen a hilltop site so that he could look down on the homes of his banker and his doctor on the flats below. Now refurbished with antiques and other furnishings of the 1890s, the house presents a convincing picture of the way Montana's well-to-do lived at the turn of the century. *Open daily mid-May-mid-Oct. Adults and children over 6 small charge.*

122. Elkhorn, Mont. The setting now for an artist or an on-location movie company, the deserted, weatherbeaten buildings—shingles askew, clapboards loose, porches broken—are all that remain of the once-thriving silver-mining town. Though ramshackle and faded, the many buildings still conjure up ghosts of the time when quick money was a possible dream. *Open daily June-Aug.*

123. Copper King Mansion *219 W. Granite St., Butte, Mont.* From the intimate billiard room to the 62-foot-long ballroom, this 30-room red brick mansion connotes Victorian elegance. William Andrew Clark, one of the wealthiest copper magnates, built the house in the 1880s, and its present owners have restored and furnished it with period antiques. Many rooms have frescoed walls and ceilings, paneled and trimmed mostly with mahogany, oak, cherry, sycamore and other fine woods. Hand-carved mantels, stained-glass windows, inlaid floors and Oriental rugs—all add to the opulence that suited wealthy Victorians. *Open daily. $1.50.*

[123] *It took four years to build this mansion, and when it was finished the Butte newspaper printed a long article describing the house and its appointments down to the heating system and the size of the water tank. The article noted that the glass for the window on the landing of the main staircase, which is shown here, had not yet been stained, but little else was lacking. In 1888 Butte was proud of the evidence the mansion gave of fashionable modern style in a mining town. Now it is proud of this reminder from the days of its lavish past.*

124. Mineral Museum *Library-Museum Bldg., Montana College of Mineral Science and Technology, Butte, Mont.* In this building with interior walls of polished Montana travertine, rock hounds can examine a collection of about 1300 specimens representing more than 670 varieties of minerals. These include large Brazilian amethyst geodes, fine pieces of green malachite and blue azurite and many other minerals from all parts of the world. A special room houses a display of fluorescent minerals that glow with unexpected colors when illuminated by ultraviolet light. *Open daily mid-June-early Sept., Mon.-Fri. except holidays early Sept.-mid-June.*

125. World Museum of Mining *Butte, Mont.* A wooden ore cart with wheels hewn from a solid log is typical of the ingenuity of the mining pioneers whose lives and labors are memorialized at this 35-acre indoor-outdoor museum. Antique underground fire-fighting equipment, handmade tools, a 100-year-old Chilean grinding mill with a granite wheel for crushing gold ore, and hundreds of other items show how men have labored to extract the earth's riches. The saloon, assay office, general store and other buildings in Hell Roarin' Gulch, a reconstructed mining camp, show how the miners spent their time aboveground. Dominating the scene is a 100-foot-high headframe straddling the vertical 3200-foot-deep shaft of Orphan Girl Mine, a now defunct zinc and silver mine. *Open daily early June-mid-Sept., Tues.-Sun. mid-Sept.-early June.*

126. Museum of the Rockies *Montana State University, Bozeman, Mont.* In this museum, dedicated to interpreting the physical and social heritages unique to the northern Rockies region, emphasis is placed on permitting visitors to be part of the exhibits by providing the opportunity to touch and use appropriate artifacts. Besides exploring the tools and trades of our pioneers and settlers, the visitor encounters the hard facts of earth science, paleontology, natural history, anthropology and technology. Frequently special programs are featured at the museum, such as demonstrations on the fashioning of tools from stone. *Open daily except holidays.*

127. Virginia City, Mont. When Bill Fairweather and five companions found gold in Alder Creek in 1863, they did not know their discovery would prove to be one of the richest gold strikes in the West. But word spread rapidly and within a year an estimated 35,000 people were living in 18-mile-long Alder Gulch. Virginia City, the mining camp that sprang up beside the creek, prospered and soon became Montana's second territorial capital. Road agents prospered also—secretly led by the town sheriff, Henry Plummer—and vigilante committees grew up to combat them. Eventually the strike played out and Virginia City went into a decline, but today many of the old false-front buildings along its wooden sidewalks have been restored and refurbished as a living museum of Western history. A brewery, livery stable, drugstore, saloon and opera house are among the old-time establishments modern-day visitors can enjoy, while two museums shed more light on this fascinating bit of Americana. *Most buildings open daily late June-early Sept.*

MADISON COUNTY-VIRGINIA CITY MUSEUM The relics of the vigilantes and road agents here recall Virginia City's lawless beginnings. The more peaceful days that followed are evoked by old furniture, musical instruments, cowboy outfits, a chuck wagon, mining equipment and other regional artifacts. There are also rock specimens and mounted animals from the area. *Open daily June-mid-Sept.*

[129] *Bannack looks like many a former Western boomtown. Most of it was built between October and December 1862, when the miners, who had been in the area since July, realized they had better prepare for a cold winter.*

THOMPSON-HICKMAN MUSEUM AND LIBRARY The elegant stone mansion was built by a family that struck it rich in the mines. Now it is a historical museum with a large collection of relics from the old gold camps. One room houses the very comfortable local library. *Open daily June-Sept.*

VIRGINIA CITY OPERA HOUSE Just as the miners used to flock to the shows of old-time touring companies, visitors today can come to this converted livery stable to watch nightly presentations of authentic 19th-century melodramas put on by a professional troupe. *Open daily late June-early Sept. Adults $2.25, children under 12 small charge.*

128. Nevada City, Mont. Once a "suburb" of Virginia City, this mining camp has been reconstructed on its original site one-and-a-half miles west down Alder Gulch. Several buildings of the gold-rush period were moved here from nearby locations; others were rebuilt. The jail, firehouse, saddle shop, barbershop, museum and other buildings are crammed with relics of mining history. A nostalgic collection of nickelodeons is displayed in the music hall. *Open daily mid-June-early Sept. Small charge for museum.*

129. Bannack, Mont. Montana's first territorial capital had its beginnings with the discovery of gold in the territory in 1862. Bannack boomed into a brawling, lusty mining town—the site of frontier violence and vigilante justice, territorial politics, gold mining in all its phases and everyday frontier life. It is essentially a ghost town now, but the weathered remains of pioneer homes, businesses and the jail are reminders of the times when hard-working miners and notorious outlaws walked and fought on these same streets.

130. Beaverhead County Museum *15 S. Montana St., Dillon, Mont.* Settlers came early to Dillon and this corner of Montana because the Lewis and Clark trail passed through here, blazing the way for adventurous trappers and gold hunters. The museum's various exhibits record the historic settlement. There are forged iron implements, including an array of branding irons, firearms and household articles such as glassware and china. Relics of mining enterprises include samples of ore as well as antique photographs of equipment. *Open daily June-Aug., Sun.-Fri. Sept.-May.*

131. Bannock County Historical Museum *Center St. and Garfield Ave., Pocatello, Idaho* The mounted head of the only moose known to have been killed by a locomotive, an old-time conductor's uniform and old-fashioned tools are but a few of many mementos of railroading history exhibited here. The displays of Indian culture include baskets, intricate beadwork and exhibits of Indian foods and their preparation. There is also an exhibit on the Northwest's earliest industry —the fur trade. *Open Tues.-Sun.*

132. Old Fort Hall Replica *Ross Park, Pocatello, Idaho* In 1834 an adventurous New Englander established a fur-trading post beside the Snake River, which two years later was sold to Hudson's Bay Company. The post was finally abandoned about 1855 but, in the meantime, had become an important stopping point for

[135] *In keeping with Mormon beliefs, this tabernacle was paid for with contributions of money, material and labor from the Mormon community. Many of the craftsmen who built the church were recent converts to the faith.*

wagon trains heading west on the Oregon Trail. Within the stout stockade walls of this exact reproduction are several log dwellings, a blacksmith shop and a museum with exhibits explaining the role of Fort Hall in opening the Northwest—first to trappers and then to settlers. *Open daily Apr.-mid-Sept.*

133. Golden Spike National Historic Site *Promontory, Utah* On May 10, 1869, a crowd gathered at this site for a momentous event: about 1800 miles of railway between Omaha, Nebraska, and Sacramento, California, had been laid and at 12:47 P.M. a golden spike was driven into the last tie. The news was instantly telegraphed across the nation that the East and West coasts were at last linked by rail. Today an obelisk marks the significant spot, two old engines stand symbolically facing each other on unused rails and a Visitor Center exhibits mementos of the historic railroad. *Open daily.*

134. Railroad Museum *Corinne, Utah* This grand collection of trains and railroading memorabilia appropriately stands near the Golden Spike National Historic Site. Railroad buffs can explore passenger cars, a mail-car, a caboose and engines of the Southern Pacific and Union Pacific lines. There is also a fine display of train photographs and steam-era artifacts. *Open daily May-Sept. Small charge.*

135. Box Elder Tabernacle *Second and Main Sts., Brigham City, Utah* Mormon leader Brigham Young selected the site for this tabernacle; after the first church burned, the present one was finished in 1890. A blend of Gothic and neoclassical styles, it features steep, peaked buttresses supporting stone walls that are broken

by arched windows. Ornamental plasterwork decorates the ceiling, but the most prominent adornment is the 1000-pipe organ, the music source vital to Mormon worship. Unlike Mormon temples, which can be entered only by church members, visitors are permitted in tabernacles. *Open daily June–Aug.*

136. Brigham City Museum-Gallery *24 N. Third W., Brigham City, Utah* A prominent feature of the museum-gallery is its Golden Spike Railroad display which commemorates the linking of the railroads of the West with those of the East at nearby Promontory in 1869. Other exhibits include panoramic views of the area, beautiful bird exhibits, paintings and a photography collection. There are also displays of materials relating to early Utah pioneers and the growth of Brigham City. An Indian collection features a diorama of Navaho family life and some Indian beadwork. Regular shows feature the work of local artists and a number of works by Utah sculptor Avard Fairbanks are on display. *Open Mon.–Sat.*

137. Bertha Eccles Community Art Center *2580 Jefferson Ave., Ogden, Utah* A small permanent art collection, monthly exhibits and art classes are among the attractions in this interesting Victorian frame structure. Built in 1884 as a private residence, it later served as a college dormitory. *Open Sun.–Fri.*

138. St. Joseph's Church *514 24th St., Ogden, Utah* For 40 years after its dedication in 1903, this stone Gothic-style building was the only Catholic church in northern Utah. St. Joseph's, built of native gold and red sandstone, has lovely stained-glass windows and a hand-carved altar. *Open daily.*

139. Fort Bridger State Historic Site *Fort Bridger, Wyo.* Jim Bridger, fur trapper and mountain man, established a trading post here in 1843. It grew into an important supply center for westward travelers. After being taken over by Mormon settlers, the fort became an army post in 1858 and later served also as an overland stage depot and Pony Express station. Surviving structures include the old guardhouse, commissary, barracks, trader's store and Pony Express stables. Buildings are furnished in their original manner. Weapons and other military items, Indian artifacts, pioneer relics and memorabilia of Wyoming's fur-trapping days are exhibited in the fort's museum. *Open daily May–Sept., Sat., Sun. Oct.–Apr.*

140. Fine Arts Center *301 Blair Ave., Rock Springs, Wyo.* This extraordinary museum contains a large collection of contemporary American paintings, many of them acquired through the fund-raising efforts of students at Rock Springs High School. The first painting, purchased with donations in 1939, was Henrietta Wood's *Shack Alley.* At present the center contains about 165 oils, watercolors, lithographs and etchings. Included are works by Grandma Moses, Aaron Bohrod and Frederic Taubes. *Open Mon.–Sat.*

141. Daniels County Museum and Pioneer Town *Scobey, Mont.* Daniels County residents donated most of the labor and the buildings to preserve relics of the region's early days. Some 30 structures have been brought to the 20-acre site and reconstructed and furnished in the style of the early 20th century, when Scobey was settled. Buildings include a one-room schoolhouse, a tar-paper homestead shack and a two-story farm home. Old cars, tractors and other farm machinery are exhibited in the museum. An annual threshing bee, held around the first of July, features a parade of antique cars, old steam engines and tractors. *Open daily May–Sept. Small charge.*

142. Pioneer Museum *Rte. 2, W. of Glasgow, Mont.* The Valley County Historical Society supports this new museum, the theme of which is "From buffalo bones to sonic boom." In chronological order around the room, dioramas and artifacts portray stages in the region's history. Real tepees are rarely held intact, but prominent in the outstanding Indian collection is a tepee made of 23 decorated elk hides which belonged to the late chief First-To-Fly of the Assiniboine tribe. An old chuck wagon and a locomotive are among the many

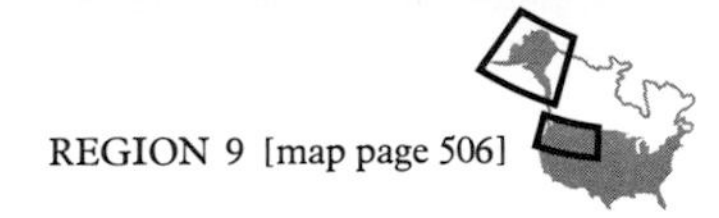

[**149.** *Gallery '85*] *Montana-born sculptor Earl Heikka's realistic portrayals of the Old West are highly prized now, more than 30 years after his death. This bronze, 41 inches long, is one of 12 cast of his* Trophy Hunters.

relics illustrating pioneer days. An aviation display represents a nearby Air Force base, now closed. *Open daily late May-early Sept.*

143. Fort Peck Dam *Fort Peck, Mont.* The mammoth earthen dam, constructed with hydraulic dredges, is the largest of its sort in the world. It was authorized in 1933 by President Franklin D. Roosevelt as a work-relief project, offering several years of employment to thousands of men under the supervision of the U.S. Army Corps of Engineers. It controls flooding of the Missouri River, and the enormous lake it creates is a popular recreational ground. A museum features exhibits of area wildlife as well as some spectacular dinosaur bones and other fossils. *Museum and power plant open daily late May-early Sept.*

144. Poplar Museum *Rte. 2, Poplar, Mont.* An old jail, which served its original purpose until 1966, houses the museum. Sioux and Assiniboine Indian art and artifacts are exhibited. A chieftain's buckskin suit, with buffalo robe and warbonnet, is prominently displayed, along with a large bell that came from the local Indian boarding school. Works by local artists depict the life of the Plains Indians. In the museum yard is the *Pride of Poplar,* one of the last ferry boats on the Missouri River. *Open daily June-Aug.*

145. Range Riders Museum *Miles City, Mont.* The museum is a large wooden structure filled to the rafters with memorabilia from the era of the white man's westward expansion into Indian territory. On view here are buffalo heads, army caissons, soldiers' uniforms, range wagons, old photos of the first Montana ranches and much more. *Open daily Apr.-Oct. Adults small charge.*

146. Carter County Museum *Ekalaka, Mont.* No one will ever see a live 35-foot-long duck-billed dinosaur, *Anatosaurus,* but here visitors can see the completely reconstructed skeleton of one of these strange creatures that lived about 100 million years ago. Vying for attention with this are other paleontological specimens, including a unique skull of *Pachycephalosaurus,* the "bone-head" dinosaur. Also on view are artifacts of early men in America and relics of Montana pioneers. *Open Tues.-Sun. except holidays.*

147. Mac's Museum of Natural History *Broadus, Mont.* For more than 70 years, R. D. "Mac" McCurdy has been collecting everything from Indian beadwork to buffalo skulls. His neatly arranged collections are now exhibited in the local high school for study by students and visitors. More than 4000 Indian artifacts, including arrowheads from 49 states, are displayed with mineral specimens, seashells, insect specimens, birds' eggs and hundreds of other striking items. *Open Mon.-Fri.*

148. Custer Battlefield National Monument *Off Rte. 212, Crow Agency, Mont.* Among the marble markers scattered over the rolling grassland is one pinpointing the spot where Lieutenant Colonel George A. Custer of the 7th Cavalry was killed during his famous "last stand" at the Battle of the Little Big Horn in June 1876. Faced by a force of Sioux and Cheyenne warriors, Custer and about 225 men under his command were killed in the last great Indian victory against the white man's westward march. Exhibits at the Visitor Center provide a description of the battle. For the past several years, early in July, local residents have staged a reenactment near the battle site. Four miles from the main battlefield is the site where the rest of the 7th Cavalry, under Captain Frederick W. Benteen and Major Marcus A. Reno, in a similar conflict, suffered few casualties. A memorial marks the spot. *Open daily.*

149. Billings, Mont.

Fred Billings, president of the Northern Pacific Railroad, gave the town its name. Food processing and oil refining are the main industries. Billings is located in the Midland Empire, a vast agricultural and oil-producing area that spreads out over 36,000 square miles. Summer rodeos and fairs draw thousands of visitors.

Gallery '85 *Emerald Dr.* Successfully combining the old and the new, the striking contemporary building on the site of a "buffalo jump" is paneled on the inside with weathered boards salvaged from old homesteads. In addition to memorabilia and paintings of the artists of the Old West, there are works of contemporary Western artists and craftsmen. *Open Mon.-Sat. Apr.-Dec.*

"Range Rider of the Yellowstone" *On the Rimrocks near Logan International Airport* This bronze statue of a range rider standing beside his grazing horse was posed for by famous silent-screen star William S. Hart. The memorial to the city's early settlers, the work of Charles Cristadoro, is perched on a 400-foot escarpment that affords a fine view of the Yellowstone Valley.

St. Patrick's Church *217 N. 31st St.* Principal church of a parish founded in 1880 to serve a small community of railroad workers, the edifice features characteristically Gothic styling. Pointed arches outline doors and windows, and a graceful tower rises to slender peaked turrets and a tall spire. Highlight of the interior is an array of stained-glass windows, particularly the lovely rose window of the Apostles. *Open daily.*

Yellowstone Art Center *401 N. 27th St.* In this ingeniously renovated county jail, the former solitary confinement block is now a ceramic lab and the one-time "drunk tank" a jewelry lab. The center presents traveling exhibits, as well as many loan exhibitions ranging from Western Americana through the graphics of Picasso, Braque and Matisse. There is also an outstanding collection of African sculpture. *Open Tues.-Sun.*

Yellowstone County Museum *Logan International Airport* At Billings' modern airport, jets whiz over a rustic log cabin that is filled with mementos of the area's frontier days. The building—the city's turn-of-the-century social center—was moved log by log and stone by stone to its present location in the 1950s. A huge stone fireplace dominates a typically furnished living room of the 1890s. Other rooms in the expanded facility contain old ranch wagons, saddles, cattle brands, guns, old-time clothing and many other relics of years past. On the grounds is the last steam switch engine operated in Billings by the Northern Pacific Railway. *Open Tues.-Sun.*

Yellowstone County Western Heritage Center *N. 29th St. and Montana Ave.* Memorabilia of Calamity Jane, Buffalo Bill and the Custer massacre highlight the famous "Treasures of the West" collection in this young but growing regional history museum. There are also interpretive exhibits of the works of cowboy author-artist Will James, who lived in Billings, and a unique display of Stetsons—the classic cowboy hats—worn by famous Westerners. *Open daily June-Aug., Tues.-Sun. Sept.-May. Small charge.*

150. Chief Plenty Coups State Monument *Pryor, Mont.* Chief Plenty Coups, a distinguished leader of the Crow Indians, lived here in a two-story house until his death in 1932. (The chief's name is a rough English translation of his Indian name—more formally he would be called Many Achievements.) Four years before he died he donated his land and home to the public as a park. The Visitor Center exhibits many of his personal things, including the medicine bundles he considered a source of power, his medicine pipes, his rifle and correspondence. Indian artifacts and regalia are displayed along with several Indian and Western paintings. On the 195-acre grounds are the graves of the chief and his two wives. *Open daily May-Oct.*

[153] *The attitude of the bemused cowboy in Charles M. Russell's* The Cowboy and the Lady Artist *hints at a future romance, in the tradition of the Eastern schoolmarm brought into conflict with the rough life of the West.*

151. Yellowtail Dam *Fort Smith, Mont.* The arch-type dam rises 525 feet between the walls of Bighorn Canyon—the highest dam in the Missouri River Basin. Bighorn Lake, a meandering waterway, stretches behind it for 70 miles. At the Visitor Center, travelers can enjoy an audio-visual program about the dam's construction and historical displays. Yellowtail stands within the vast sportsground, the Bighorn Canyon National Recreation Area. *Open daily.*

152. Trail End Historic Center *400 Clarendon Ave., Sheridan, Wyo.* Cattle baron John B. Kendrick, who served as U.S. senator and state governor, built the three-story brick mansion between 1908 and 1913. The elaborate interior with much carved woodwork has Kendrick family furnishings on the first floor, including mahogany dining-room furniture, crimson and gold carpets and draperies and custom-made chandeliers. Wyoming historical materials, a gun collection and two refurnished bedrooms can be seen on the second floor. On the third floor is a large ballroom complete with a balcony for an orchestra. On display are works of Wyoming artists. *Open daily. Small charge.*

153. Bradford Brinton Memorial Ranch *Rte. 335, Big Horn, Wyo.* The ranch-museum is a memorial to American history and art, dedicated to Bradford Brinton, art and book collector, nature enthusiast and businessman, who bought the ranch in 1923. In the gracious 20-room white clapboard house, in a style more typical of a Vermont village than a Wyoming ranch, are the original handsome furnishings and a vast collection of art, including works by Charles M. Russell, Audubon, Bellows and Remington. The rare book and document collection contains a letter written by Lincoln, a William Penn paper, books from the 17th and 18th centuries, a George Washington document, and Robert Louis Stevenson and Samuel Johnson materials. Indian artifacts, hunting trophies, antique wagons, buggies and saddles are displayed in various outbuildings. *Open daily mid-May-early Sept.*

154. Johnson County-Jim Gatchell Memorial Museum *Main and Fort Sts., Buffalo, Wyo.* Prehistoric artifacts and other archaeological finds are on display along with pictures, dioramas of the old West, Indian artifacts and other historical materials that tell the stories of Buffalo and of Johnson County. An early chuck wagon, a bedroll wagon and a sheep wagon are prize articles. *Open daily June-early Sept.*

155. Buffalo Bill Historical Center *720 Sheridan Ave., Cody, Wyo.* See feature display on pages 542-3.

[159] *The stuffed birds, barometer, medical books and instruments in the post surgeon's study reflect his varied roles. The surgeon kept the post weather records; he also sent information on request to the Army Medical Museum. Officers' Row, right, faces the parade ground. The low building on the right is the post trader's store.*

156. Memorial Museums *Fifth and Arapahoe Sts., Thermopolis, Wyo.* This Wyoming organization, dedicated to preserving Western pioneer materials and fostering art in the state, maintains two galleries here. *Open Tues.-Sun. June-mid-Sept.*

CONRAD GALLERY AND MUSEUM The works of artist-in-residence Rupert Conrad are presented here. Painting, sculpture and calligraphic studies are represented. Included is a larger-than-life bas-relief of a Nativity scene and several smaller sculptures in bronze, wood and terra cotta. Many of Conrad's paintings and drawings are inspired by calligraphy.

FIFTH AVENUE GALLERY The cupola on the building was the trademark of Clyde C. Ellis, who designed and built it in 1911 as Tom Skinner's saloon. It contains exhibits of pioneer memorabilia and paintings by Wyoming artists such as Dean States and James Boyle.

157. St. Michael's Mission *Ethete, Wyo.* The Episcopal mission was established in 1913 as a church and school for the people of the northern Arapahoe tribe. The buildings of the mission are located around the perimeter of a large circular driveway. Among them are a general purpose hall, a foster home for teenagers and residential cottages. *Open daily.*

ARAPAHOE CULTURAL MUSEUM An unusually complete collection of art and artifacts of the Arapahoe Indians—all assembled by members of the tribe as representative of their culture—is exhibited here. Included are quill- and beadwork, tools, clothing, jewelry, warrior regalia and paintings. A large mural is located at the museum entrance. *Open daily June-early Sept.*

CHURCH OF OUR FATHER'S HOUSE This log church, decorated with Indian motifs, is the oldest structure within the mission complex. A large picture window, located behind the altar, provides a stirring view of the nearby Wind River Mountains. *Open daily.*

158. Old Fort Caspar *13th St., Casper, Wyo.* From 1858 to 1867 the fort served as a relay station for the Pony Express and as headquarters for soldiers charged with protecting the wagon trains westward-bound on the Oregon Trail. It was originally known as Platte Bridge Station, but in 1865 its name was changed to honor the memory of Lieutenant Caspar Collins. The young officer was killed while trying to rescue a fallen comrade during a battle with 3000 Sioux and Cheyenne who had attacked a wagon train. (Lieutenant Collins also gave his name to the city, but a clerical error changed the name to Casper.) Pioneer and Indian relics, dioramas and military equipment are on display at the restored fort. *Open daily mid-May-mid-Sept.*

159. Fort Laramie National Historic Site *Rte. 26, 3 mi. S.W. of Fort Laramie, Wyo.* Famous names of the old West such as Jim Bridger and Calamity Jane are linked with the fort. First established as a private fur-trading center in 1834, it was bought by the Army in 1849. For the next 41 years it served as a vital military base, its soldiers safeguarding the passage of wagon trains moving westward along the Oregon Trail. There are remains of 21 buildings, many of them restored: the sutler's store, magazine, guardhouses and old bakery. "Old Bedlam," a two-story building, contained post headquarters and officers' quarters, now restored and furnished in the style of the 1850s and '60s. In the commissary storehouse are relics of the fort's illustrious past. *Open daily except Jan. 1 and Dec. 25.*

OLD ARMY BRIDGE The arched bridge, built in 1875, is believed to be the oldest surviving military iron bridge west of the Mississippi. Replacing a ferry, it provided a quicker link between Cheyenne and the region north of Fort Laramie.

160. Grand Encampment Museum *Encampment, Wyo.* The town's current population of some 350 started the museum complex to preserve the history of the copper-mining boom, which lasted from 1897 to 1908 and brought some 3000 people hurrying to the area. The museum features several historic buildings that have been moved here to form part of a pioneer town: a log cabin, a stage coach station, a bakery and ice cream parlor and a ranch house are among them. These and other structures house a general store, a saloon and pioneer living quarters. Early horse-drawn vehicles used in the area are also on display. The Doc Culleton Building contains stock certificates of the overpromoted copper mines, mining equipment, wearing apparel and other old-fashioned items. *Open daily late May-early Sept., Sat., Sun. early Sept.-Oct.*

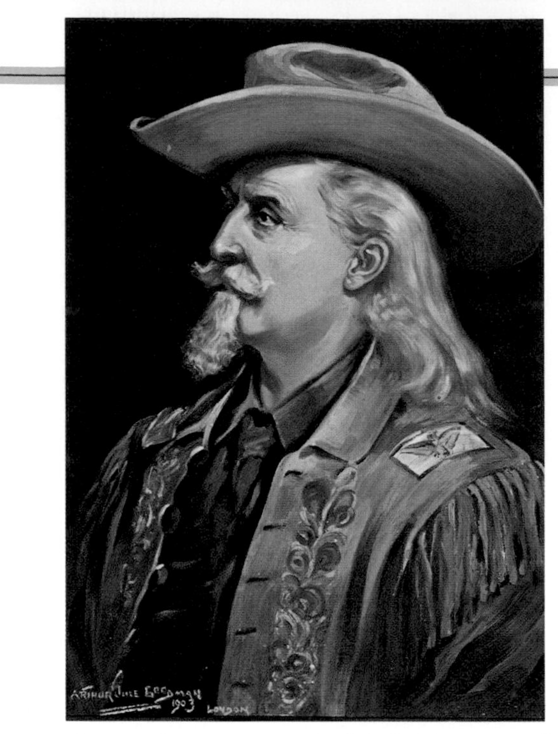

A man of many careers, Buffalo Bill is portrayed here in his role as Chief Scout for the Army.

155. Buffalo Bill Historical Center

720 Sheridan Ave., Cody, Wyo.

Actually three museums in one, this rambling modern building commemorates a West that is no more. It grew out of Buffalo Bill's wish to present the Old West realistically. The Buffalo Bill Museum memorializes the life and accomplishments of the famous frontiersman, scout, buffalo hunter and showman, Colonel William F. "Buffalo Bill" Cody. Mementos ranging from his clothing, guns and saddles to posters advertising his fabulous Wild West Show trace the career of this colorful character who played a unique role in taming the West. In the Whitney Gallery of Western Art an unparalleled collection of painting and sculpture documents the life and times of the cowboys, Indians and pioneers of a bygone era, with works by the most famous artists who knew the Old West at first hand. The Sioux, Blackfoot, Crow and other Indian tribes are represented. In the Plains Indian Museum elaborately beaded costumes, feathered headdresses, weapons and other paraphernalia tell the story of the first human inhabitants of the northern plains. *Open daily May–Sept. Small charge.*

A treasure trove of painting and sculpture that realistically portrays life in the Old West, the spacious Whitney Gallery of Western Art includes many of the finest works of Frederic Remington, Charles M. Russell, George Catlin and other artists who recorded the Western scene.

Annie Oakley, nicknamed Little Sure Shot for her unerring marksmanship, was one of the stars of Buffalo Bill's Wild West Show, an extravaganza of cowboys, Indians and buffalo that toured the U.S. and Europe for 15 years.

Authentic costumes worn by chiefs and other members of many Western tribes are featured in the Plains Indian Museum.

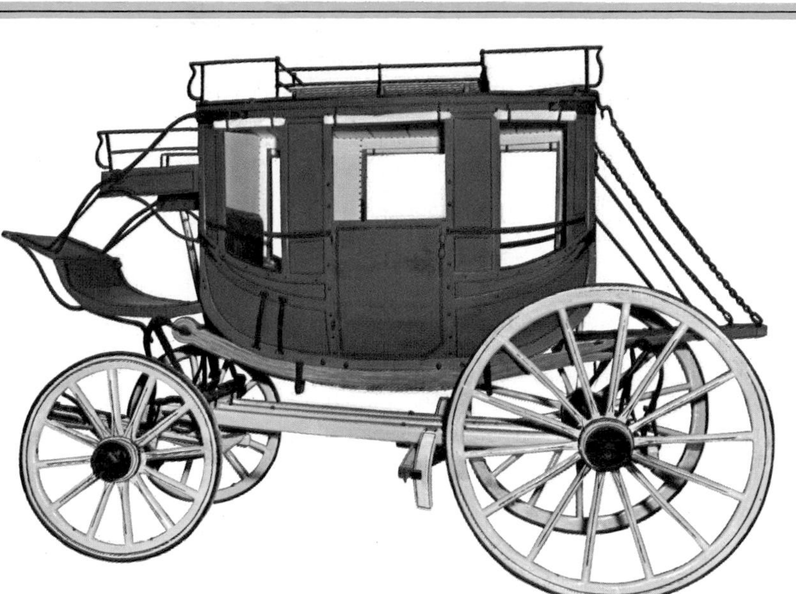

This old-time stagecoach, once the target of masked bandits and marauding Indians, carried five crowned heads of Europe after Buffalo Bill acquired it for use in opening parades for his Wild West Show.

Albert Bierstadt's Indian Encampment in the Rockies *reveals his love for the grandeur of the Western mountains. The collection of Bierstadt paintings in the Whitney Gallery of Western Art is one of the largest anywhere.*

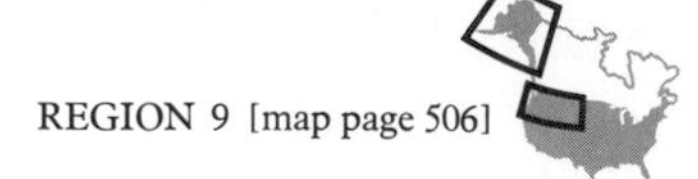

161. Abraham Lincoln Memorial Monument *Rte. 80, 9 mi. E. of Laramie, Wyo.* Sculptor Robert I. Russin created the striking memorial to President Lincoln in 1959 for Wyoming's commemoration of the 150th anniversary of the great leader's birth. The 12-foot-tall bronze bust rests on a 30-foot-high granite base. It is appropriately located at the summit of the Laramie Range, the highest point on the old transcontinental Lincoln Highway.

162. University of Wyoming *Laramie, Wyo.* The coeducational state university, now with an enrollment of about 8000, was established in 1886. Its 400-acre campus is situated near the center of Laramie.

ART MUSEUM *Fine Arts Center* American art of the 19th and 20th centuries, Oriental art and examples of 18th- and 19th-century European art form the museum's permanent collection. It is housed in the modern, recently completed Fine Arts Center, which also contains the university's art, music and theater departments. *Open Sun.-Fri. during academic year.*

GEOLOGY MUSEUM *Geology Bldg.* The star exhibit here is the 75-foot fossil of *Brontosaurus,* a dinosaur that lived in Wyoming about 150 million years ago. Other exhibits include the skull of a giant mammoth, a full-scale copper model of *Tyrannosaurus rex* and a skeleton of a *Mosasaur,* a large lizard from the Wyoming seas of about 80 million years ago. Fossils of extinct crocodiles, turtles, rhinoceroses, camels and giant pigs are other fascinating remains of prehistoric life. *Open daily except holidays during academic sessions.*

163. Ames Monument *Rte. 80, 30 mi. W. of Cheyenne, Wyo.* Ames Monument, a 60-foot-high red granite pyramid, is visible from miles around. It is dedicated to the memory of Oakes and Oliver Ames, Jr., two brothers who were instrumental in financing and managing construction of the transcontinental Union Pacific Railroad. When completed in 1883, the pyramid stood near a busy town long since gone. Henry Hobson Richardson, architect par excellence of American Romanesque architecture, designed the monument and Augustus Saint-Gaudens, the popular and influential turn-of-the-century sculptor, created the medallions of Quincy granite that adorn it.

164. "Big Boy" *Holiday Park on E. Lincoln Way, Cheyenne, Wyo.* The largest steam locomotive ever built—it weighs 1,208,750 pounds, is nearly 133 feet long, holds 28 tons of coal and 25,000 gallons of water—"Big Boy" and its fellow engines used to roll along the rails between Cheyenne and Ogden, Utah, for the Union Pacific Railroad. Retired in 1956, the gleaming workhorse now rests proudly in the city park, a monument to be admired after its strenuous 15-year hauling career. *Open daily.*

165. Wyoming State Capitol *Capitol Ave., Cheyenne, Wyo.* A 145-foot-high gold-leaf dome caps the impressive seat of Wyoming government. The Corinthian structure, similar to the U.S. Capitol, is constructed of Wyoming limestone. A statue of Esther Hobart Morris, prominent in the women's suffrage movement, stands in front of the building and other commemorative statues are located elsewhere on the grounds. On display in the rotunda are specimens of two of the state's more important wildlife species, the elk and the buffalo. Also decorating the rotunda are oil paintings of famous Wyoming frontiersmen. *Open daily.*

166. Wyoming State Museum *State Office Bldg., Central Ave. and 23rd St., Cheyenne, Wyo.* The area's native Indian cultures, both prehistoric and historic, are revealed in exhibits of archaeological findings. Among the other exhibits to be seen are interpretive displays of Wyoming's cultural heritage, including the eras of the soldier, the pioneer and the cowboy. *Open daily June-Aug., Mon.-Sat. Sept.-May.*

[**162.** *Geology Museum*] *Most visitors are awed by the size of this fossilized skeleton of* Brontosaurus, *a dinosaur that prowled the Wyoming wilderness at a time when parts of the state were covered by lush, tropical swamplands. When scientists discovered the deposit of bones, they had to fit them together one by one until they were able to reconstruct the entire skeleton. Fossils of many other extinct creatures on exhibit in the museum help scientists unravel the state's fascinating geological history.*

More Treasures to Enjoy

Starting below, and grouped by regions, are descriptions of nearly 2000 other treasures to see. There is a page reference to each of the large regional maps, on which all the towns listed here are indicated by a solid brown dot. The states and towns are arranged alphabetically within each region. Each place has a symbol (the same as on the large maps) to indicate the kind of treasures you will find, and a key is included at the bottom of every page.

REGION 1 [map page 52]

Maine

Ashland

ASHLAND LOGGING MUSEUM *Garfield Rd.* Lumbering memorabilia shown here include Lombard log haulers and a "king's arrow" pine once marked for a ship's mast. *Open Mon.-Sat. June-Aug.*

Bangor

BANGOR HOUSE *Main and Union Sts.* Opened about 1834, the hotel is one of the first in the Greek Revival style in America. *Open daily.*

PENOBSCOT HERITAGE MUSEUM OF LIVING HISTORY *City Hall, Harlow St.* Visitors may touch the educational exhibits relating to regional history. *Open Mon.-Fri.*

Bath

WINTER STREET CHURCH *Washington St.* One of the best examples of the American Gothic Revival in New England, this huge church has a towering spire and an elaborately carved exterior.

Blue Hill

JONATHAN FISHER MEMORIAL *Main St.* This hip-roof house, designed by the first minister of Blue Hill, contains many of his handicrafts. *Open Tues., Fri., Sat. July-mid-Sept. Small charge.*

Brunswick

PEARY-MacMILLAN ARCTIC MUSEUM *Hubbard Hall, Bowdoin College* Eskimo artifacts and memorabilia from the expeditions of Admirals Robert Peary and Donald Macmillan are displayed here. *Open daily mid-June-Sept.*

PEJEPSCOT HISTORICAL SOCIETY MUSEUM *12 School St.* Exhibits of area history are on view in this 1827 meetinghouse. *Open Mon.-Fri. mid-June-Sept.*

ST. PAUL'S CHURCH *27 Pleasant St.* This small wooden chapel, designed by Richard Upjohn, has not been altered since its completion in 1845. *Open Sun.*

Calais

ST. CROIX HISTORICAL SOCIETY HOUSE *Main St.* The town's oldest house, built in the 1700s, contains early furniture and artifacts. *Open daily July-Aug.*

Camden

CONWAY HOUSE *Rte. 1 and Conway Rd.* An 18th-century house, barn and blacksmith shop are adjacent to a museum of area history. *Open Tues.-Sun. July-early Sept. Small charge.*

Caribou

NYLANDER MUSEUM *393 Main St.* Geological specimens, art, shells, insects and pioneer implements are exhibited. *Open daily Apr.-Dec.*

Castine

WILSON MUSEUM *Perkins St.* Included are a museum, with local historic and worldwide prehistoric artifacts, and the 18th-century John Perkins House. *Open Tues.-Sun. late May-mid-Sept.*

East Corinth

ROBYVILLE BRIDGE *Robyville Village* The state's only fully shingled bridge was built in 1876.

Dover-Foxcroft

DOVER-FOXCROFT BLACKSMITH SHOP MUSEUM *Chandler Rd.* A Civil War smith's tools are displayed here. *Open daily May-Oct.*

East Machias

FIRST CONGREGATIONAL CHURCH *High St.* Thc 1836 church has a tracker-type two-rank pipe organ dating from 1872. *Open daily June-Sept.*

Ellsworth

STANWOOD HOMESTEAD MUSEUM *Rte. 3 and Bar Harbor Rd.* The birthplace of pioneer ornithologist Cordelia J. Stanwood is set in Birdsacre, a wildlife preserve. *Grounds open daily, museum open daily mid-June-mid-Oct.*

Farmington

NORDICA HOMESTEAD MUSEUM *N. off Rte. 4* The birthplace of Lillian Nordica contains the singer's memorabilia. *Open Tues.-Sun. June-early Sept. Small charge.*

Fort Kent

FORT KENT MEMORIAL *Rte. 1* Lumbering and Indian relics are collected in this 1839 blockhouse. *Open daily late May-early Sept.*

Fryeburg

FRYEBURG ACADEMY *Main St.* The second oldest academy in Maine, where Daniel Webster once taught, has been in continuous operation since it was chartered in 1792.

HEMLOCK BRIDGE *3 mi. E. off Rte. 302* The oldest covered bridge in Maine (1857) is of Paddleford truss construction.

Gardiner

CHRIST CHURCH *On the Green* An early example of the Gothic Revival in New England, the granite church has a groin-vaulted ceiling and stained-glass windows. *Open daily.*

GARDINER LIBRARY-LIBRARY HALL MUSEUM *152 Water St.* The museum has pottery, Indian artifacts and a model steamboat collection.

Hallowell

ST. MATTHEW'S CHURCH *Union St.* The board-and-batten exterior of this Episcopal church, built in 1860, makes it rare among 19th-century Gothic Revival structures in New England. *Open daily.*

Harpswell Center

HARPSWELL MEETINGHOUSE *Rte. 123* This clapboard, two-story frame building, erected in 1757, is now a town hall.

Islesboro

SAILORS' MEMORIAL MUSEUM *Grindle Point* Nautical items are displayed in an old lighthouse. *Open daily mid-June-Sept.*

Kennebunk

FIRST PARISH CHURCH *Main St.* The 1773 church has a steeple bell cast by Paul Revere. *Open Sun.*

Kennebunkport

OLDE GRIST MILL *Mill Lane* This rare tidewater gristmill was in operation from 1749 to 1937. *Open daily late May-early Sept.*

Key: Historic Place · Historic House · Old Mill or Works · Museum or Collection · Significant Building · Place of Worship · Monument or Sculpture · Engineering Structure · Archaeological Site · Garden · Zoo

Kittery

FORT MCCLARY MEMORIAL *2 mi. S. on Kittery Point Rd.* The site of this hexagonal blockhouse was fortified as early as 1715. *Open daily late May-mid-Oct. Small charge.*

Lewiston

STANTON MUSEUM *Carnegie Hall, Bates College* The museum contains excellent collections of native birds and a rare Audubon folio. *Open Mon.-Thurs.*

Machias

CENTRE STREET CONGREGATIONAL CHURCH *Centre St.* The clock tower of this 1836 wood Gothic church holds a bell signed by Paul Revere. *Open daily.*

Monhegan Island

MONHEGAN MUSEUM *Lighthouse Hill* Displays deal with the island and its history. *Open Tues.-Sun. early July-early Sept.*

Ogunquit

MUSEUM OF ART OF OGUNQUIT *Shore Rd., Narrow Cove* The permanent collection has works by modern North American artists. *Open daily early July-early Sept.*

Old Town

PENOBSCOT INDIAN RESERVATION *Indian Island* An early missionary church, old fire-fighting equipment and the Godfrey collection of local artifacts at the Library can be seen here. *Open daily.*

Orono

UNIVERSITY OF MAINE ANTHROPOLOGY MUSEUM *Stevens Hall* The museum has prehistoric American cultural relics and habitat groups. *Open Mon.-Fri.*

Paris

HAMLIN MEMORIAL HALL *Paris Hill* An unusual granite structure, a jail until 1899, is now a library. *Open Tues.-Sat. mid-June-Aug., Tues., Sat. Sept.-mid-June.*

Pemaquid

HARRINGTON MEETING HOUSE *Old Harrington Rd.* The balcony of this 1772 building has a museum of the old town of Bristol. *Open Mon., Wed., Sat. July-Aug. Small charge.*

Popham Beach

FORT POPHAM MEMORIAL *Rte. 209* Circular staircases lead to the towers of this semicircular granite fort. *Open daily late May-early Sept. Small charge.*

Porter

PORTER BRIDGE *S. off Rte. 25* The handsome two-span covered bridge was built in 1858.

Portland

MAINE HISTORICAL SOCIETY LIBRARY *485 Congress St.* The largest collection of Maine resource material and memorabilia is here. *Open Mon.-Fri. except holidays.*

NEAL DOW MEMORIAL *714 Congress St.* The Federal-style mansion, originally the home of temperance leader Neal Dow, is now a museum, library and headquarters of the Maine W.C.T.U. *Open Mon.-Sat.*

PORTLAND CITY HALL *389 Congress St.* The design of this turn-of-the-century building is based on New York City Hall. *Open Mon.-Fri. except holidays.*

TATE HOUSE *1279 Westbrook St.* The weathered clapboards, gambrel roof and massive chimney are notable. *Open Tues.-Sun. July-mid-Sept. except July 4 and Labor Day. Small charge.*

Skowhegan

SKOWHEGAN HISTORY HOUSE *Elm St.* The house, built in 1839, is now a museum of area history. *Open Tues.-Sat. mid-June-Sept.*

SKOWHEGAN INDIAN *High St. and Madison Ave.* Bernard Langlais carved the 62-foot-high wooden Indian, dedicated to the memory of Maine's Indians.

Solon

FEDERATED CHURCH *Rte. 201* The oldest pipe organ in Maine is still used in church services. *Open Sun.*

South Bristol

OLD WALPOLE MEETING HOUSE *Rte. 129* The pulpit of this 1772 meetinghouse is elaborately hand-carved. *Open Sun. July-Aug.*

South Solon

SOUTH SOLON MEETING HOUSE *E. Madison Rd.* Students have recently covered the walls of this 1842 meetinghouse with frescoes. *Open daily mid-May-mid-Oct.*

South Windham

PARSON SMITH HOMESTEAD *89 River Rd.* The original pegged windows still remain in this 1764 house.

Sunset

DEER ISLE-STONINGTON HISTORICAL SOCIETY MUSEUM Memorabilia from all over the island are collected in the Salome Sellers house. *Open Wed., Sat., Sun. July-mid-Sept.*

Union

EDWARD A. MATTHEWS FARM MUSEUM *Fairgrounds* Farm tools, wagons, sleighs, a country kitchen and cooper, cobbler and blacksmith shops are on display. *Open Tues.-Sun. July-Aug.*

Waldoboro

OLD GERMAN CHURCH *Rte. 32* The 1772 church is now painted yellow, and its plain interior has box pews and a high "wineglass" pulpit. *Open daily May-Oct.*

Waterville

REDINGTON MUSEUM *64 Silver St.* In an 1814 frame house the Waterville Historical Society has collected period furnishings, artifacts and documents of the area. *Open Tues.-Sat. mid-May-Sept.*

Winslow

FORT HALIFAX MEMORIAL *Rte. 201* A log blockhouse—the oldest in the country (1754)—is all that remains. *Open daily late May-early Sept.*

Wiscasset

OLD LINCOLN COUNTY JAIL AND MUSEUM *Federal St.* The granite jail now houses a collection of early tools and Americana. *Open daily mid-June-Sept. Small charge.*

Yarmouth

YARMOUTH HISTORICAL SOCIETY MUSEUM *Merrill Memorial Library, Main St.* Objects and documents of early Yarmouth are displayed. *Open Wed., Sat. mid-Apr.-mid-Dec.*

York

CAPE NEDDICK LIGHT Commonly known as Nubble Light, this pretty lighthouse attracts photographers and artists.

JOHN HANCOCK WAREHOUSE *Lindsay Rd. and York River.* York's only Colonial commercial building houses early tools and ship models. *Open daily late June-mid-Sept. Small charge.*

Massachusetts

Haverhill

BUTTONWOODS *240 Water St.* The Haverhill Historical Society has headquarters in this 1814 mansion. Nearby are the John Ward House (1641) and Tenny Hall. *Open Tues.-Sat. June-mid-Sept., Tues., Thurs., Sat. mid-Sept.-June. Small charge.*

WHITTIER'S BIRTHPLACE *305 Whittier Rd.* The childhood home of John Greenleaf Whittier was the setting for his poem *Snow-Bound. Open Tues.-Sun. Small charge.*

Newburyport

PETTINGILL-FOWLER HOUSE *180 High St.* The 1792 Georgian-style house, now a private club, has two large interior chimneys.

New Hampshire

Canaan

OLD NORTH CHURCH *Canaan St.* The 1828 church has many-paned Gothic-style windows, said to have been added during the 1850s.

Center Sandwich

SANDWICH HISTORICAL SOCIETY MUSEUM *Rtes. 109 and 113* Here are 19th-century furnishings, antique shoemaker tools and a collection of gowns and laces. *Open Mon.-Sat. July-Aug., Sat. June, Sept.*

Charlestown

FOUNDATION FOR BIBLICAL RESEARCH AND PRESERVATION OF PRIMITIVE CHRISTIANITY *Main and Paris Sts.* Early Bibles and historical material on Christian Science are in an 18th-century setting. *Open Tues.-Sat. except holidays.*

Chesterfield

CARRIAGE AND SLEIGH MUSEUM *Coach House, Rte. 9* Horse-drawn vehicles dating from the late 18th century are on display. *Open daily May-Oct. Small charge.*

Durham

THOMPSON HALL *University of New Hampshire* The university's first building is a fine example of the Romanesque-Revival style. *Open Mon.-Fri. except holidays.*

Groveton

NORTHUMBERLAND - GROVETON BRIDGE *E. off Rte. 3* The 1852 covered bridge is of Paddleford truss construction.

Hanover

WEBSTER COTTAGE *Dartmouth College* Daniel Webster (Class of 1801) lived in this quaint 1780 cottage while a student at Dartmouth. *Open Tues.-Thurs., Sat., Sun. June-Sept., Sat. Oct.-May.*

Harrisville

HARRISVILLE This is an early 19th-century mill town with fine buildings and millers' homes.

Haverhill

ALUMNI HALL *Court St.* Built in 1848 in the late Classic-Revival style, the building was originally a courthouse.

Jaffrey

OLD MEETING HOUSE *On the Common* Begun during the Battle of Bunker Hill, this white frame clapboard building was restored in 1922. Nearby is an early schoolhouse. *Open Fri., schoolhouse open Sat., Sun. June-Sept.*

Lyme

LYME CONGREGATIONAL CHURCH *Main St.* Completed by 1812, the church still has doors on the pews and the original 27 contiguous horse sheds. *Open Sun.*

Manchester

MANCHESTER HISTORIC ASSOCIATION *129 Amherst St.* The association has collected local antique furniture and other historic items relating to Manchester. *Open Tues.-Sat. except holidays.*

Nashua

HUNT MEMORIAL BUILDING *Main St.* Built in 1903, the library is a good example of the early work of New Hampshire-born Ralph Adams Cram.

Newbury

CENTER MEETING HOUSE *Rtes. 103 and 103A* The pews in this 1832 community church face the vestibule. *Open Sun. July-Aug.*

New Hampton

DANA MEETING HOUSE *Dana Hill Rd.* The unrestored meetinghouse was built in 1800 by Free Baptists. *Open daily.*

Newport

NEWPORT CLOCK MUSEUM *The Common* More than 400 clocks and watches from all over the world dating over five centuries are displayed. *Open daily. Small charge.*

North Groton

MARY BAKER EDDY HISTORIC HOUSE This is a home of the founder of Christian Science.

Peterborough

ST. PETER'S CHURCH *Vine St.* This meetinghouse-church has been active since 1873. *Open daily.*

Portsmouth

PORTSMOUTH PUBLIC LIBRARY *Islington St.* The library, in the style of Charles Bulfinch, was built in 1809 as a boys' school. *Open Mon.-Sat. except holidays.*

SOUTH UNITARIAN UNIVERSALIST CHURCH *292 State St.* The otherwise austere granite church is dominated by a massive Tuscan portico. *Open daily.*

Rindge

CATHEDRAL OF THE PINES *Cathedral Rd.* Two national war memorials are part of this outdoor international shrine. *Open daily May-Oct.*

Rumney

MARY BAKER EDDY HISTORIC HOUSE *Stinson Lake Rd.* This was the home (1860-2) of the founder of Christian Science. *Open Tues.-Sun. late May-Oct. Small charge.*

Salem

SALEM TOWN HALL *Main St.* The original roof trusses, hand-hewn in 1738, are visible in the loft of this meetinghouse. *Open Mon.-Fri.*

Sandown

OLD MEETING HOUSE *Fremont Rd.* This 1774 meetinghouse has a high wine-goblet pulpit and square box pews. *Open daily.*

Warren

MORSE MUSEUM *Main St.* Collections of African big-game hunting, curios and native shoes are displayed. *Open daily June-Sept.*

Wentworth

WENTWORTH CONGREGATIONAL CHURCH *On the Common* Originally built as a meetinghouse in 1828, the church has an attractive square-staged steeple. *Open daily.*

West Franklin

DANIEL WEBSTER BIRTHPLACE *Rte. 127* The restored frame house where Webster was born and spent his boyhood years contains period antiques and family mementos. *Open daily June-mid-Oct. Small charge.*

New York

Albion

PULLMAN MEMORIAL UNIVERSALIST CHURCH *E. Park and S. Main Sts.* Tiffany windows adorn the sanctuary of the Gothic-style church.

Alexandria Bay

1000 ISLANDS BRIDGE *Collins Landing* The five-span, seven-mile-long bridge crosses the St. Lawrence River. *Small toll.*

Arcade

ARCADE AND ATTICA RAILROAD *278 Main St.* Rides on a steam-engined passenger train are offered. *Sat., Sun., holidays June, Oct., Wed., Sat., Sun. July-Aug. Adults $2.00, children small charge.*

Auburn

CAYUGA MUSEUM OF HISTORY AND ART *203 Genesee St.* Art, historical and scientific exhibits are featured here. *Open daily except holidays.*

OWASCO STOCKADED INDIAN VILLAGE *Emerson Park* This is an authentic on-site reconstruction of a prehistoric Owasco Indian village. *Open July-Aug. Small charge.*

Auriesville

NATIONAL SHRINE OF THE NORTH AMERICAN MARTYRS *Rtes. 5-S and 288* The first North American saints were martyred here. *Open daily May-Oct.*

Ausable Chasm

AUSABLE CHASM ANTIQUE AUTO MUSEUM *Off Rte. 9* The Walter H. Church collection of early automobiles is on display. *Open Sat., Sun. May-mid-June, daily mid-June-Oct. Small charge.*

Batavia

HOLLAND LAND OFFICE MUSEUM *131 W. Main St.* The 1815 building was used for Holland Purchase Land Company sales. *Open daily except holidays.*

Bolton Landing

MARCELLA SEMBRICH MEMORIAL STUDIO *Rte. 9N* The opera singer's summer studio has mementos of her career. *Open daily July-mid-Sept.*

Brewerton

FORT BREWERTON MUSEUM *5439 Library St.* Relics of the 1759 fort are on display. *Open Mon.-Sat. June-Aug., Sat., Sun. Sept.-May.*

Bridgewater

UPSTATE AUTO MUSEUM *Rte. 20* More than 100 old autos are shown. *Open Sun., holidays May, Oct., daily June-Sept. Small charge.*

Brownville

BROWN MANSION *216 Brown Blvd.* The Georgian-style mansion was completed in 1815 by General Jacob Brown. *Open Wed., Sat.*

Buffalo

ST. MARY'S SHRINE CHURCH *Broadway and Pine Sts.* The oldest (1850) Catholic church in Buffalo is constructed of native limestone in the Neoclassic style. *Open daily.*

ST. PAUL'S CATHEDRAL *Main and Church Sts.* The Victorian Gothic church was designed by Richard Upjohn, Sr., in 1850. *Open daily.*

TEMPLE BETH ZION *805 Delaware Ave.* Ben Shahn created the stained-glass windows in this 1966 temple. *Open daily.*

Caledonia

BIG SPRINGS HISTORICAL SOCIETY MUSEUM *Main St.* Items from Scottish settlers' homes are included here. *Open Fri. May-Nov., Sun. Dec.-Apr.*

Castile

MUSEUM OF INDIAN AND PIONEER HISTORY *Letchworth State Park* Behind the museum is a log cabin built by Mary Jamison, the legendary "White Woman of the Genesee." *Open Tues.-Sun. May-Nov.*

Chazy

ALICE T. MINER COLONIAL COLLECTION *Rte. 9* Period furnishings and utensils are collected in a house dating from 1824. *Open Tues.-Sat.*

Childs

COBBLESTONE CHURCH *Rte. 104* In this 1834 Federal-style church is a museum of 19th-century cobblestone masonry. *Open daily mid-June-mid-Sept.*

COBBLESTONE SCHOOLHOUSE *Rte. 104* Greek Revival in style, the 1849 building is authentically restored. *Open daily mid-June-mid-Sept.*

Clayton

1000 ISLANDS MUSEUM *Riverside Dr.* Area history exhibits include fine handmade duck decoys. *Open daily June-Oct. Small charge.*

1000 ISLANDS SHIPYARD MUSEUM *750 Mary St.* A collection of antique boats is on display. *Open daily. Small charge.*

Crown Point

PENFIELD HOMESTEAD MUSEUM *Ironville Rd.* The 1828 Federal mansion is a museum of local history. *Open daily mid-May-mid-Oct. Small charge.*

Elmira

PARK CHURCH *Main and Church Sts.* This elaborate Romanesque-style Congregational church was completed in 1876. *Open daily.*

Fayette

PETER WHITMER FARM *S. off Rte. 96* The Church of Jesus Christ of Latter-day Saints was organized here. *Open daily.*

Fishers

GHOST CITY OF VALENTOWN MUSEUM *Off Rte. 96* The restored 1879 shopping and community center features a Lightning Man's show. *Open daily Apr.-Oct. Small charge.*

Fonda

MOHAWK-CAUGHNAWAGA MUSEUM *Rte. 5* An Indian museum is at the site of the excavated village of Caughnawaga. *Open daily June-Sept.*

Fort Edward

OLD FORT HOUSE *29 Lower Broadway* Items of early America are displayed in this pre-Revolutionary tavern. *Open daily July-Aug.*

Fort Plain

FORT PLAIN MUSEUM *Upper Canal St.* Indian artifacts and historical items from the nearby fort are displayed. *Open daily July-Aug. Small charge.*

Geneseo

LIVINGSTON COUNTY HISTORICAL MUSEUM *30 Center St.* The cobblestone schoolhouse, built in 1838, is now a museum of local history. *Open Tues.-Thurs. May-Oct.*

Herkimer

FORT HERKIMER CHURCH *Rte. 5 S.* This 1740 church served as part of a stockade during the French and Indian War. *Open daily Apr.-Nov.*

HERKIMER COUNTY HISTORICAL SOCIETY MUSEUM *400 N. Main St.* Local Colonial items are displayed here. *Open Mon.-Sat. July-Aug.*

Jamestown

JAMES PRENDERGAST LIBRARY ART GALLERY *509 Cherry St.* Among exhibits here are late 19th-century French, German and American paintings. *Open Mon.-Sat. June-Aug., daily Nov.-Apr.*

Johnstown

FULTON COUNTY COURT HOUSE *N. William St.* This is the only Colonial courthouse still in use.

Le Roy

LE ROY HOUSE *23 E. Main St.* The early 19th-century stone house was built as a residence and land office for the owners of the Triangle Tract. *Open Sun. July-Aug.*

Lewiston

POWER VISTA *5777 Lewiston Rd.* The Visitor Center of the Niagara Power Project features dioramas, a terrain map and a mural by Thomas Hart Benton. *Open daily.*

Liverpool

FORT STE. MARIE DE GANNENTAHA *Onondaga Lake Pkwy.* Here is the replica of a log fort built by the French in 1656. *Open daily.*

SALT MUSEUM *Onondaga Lake Pkwy.* Articles used in salt-making are shown. *Open daily.*

Lyons

WAYNE COUNTY MUSEUM *21 Butternut St.* An 1854 jail houses exhibits of county history. *Open daily.*

Montour Falls

MEMORIAL LIBRARY *Main St.* A collection of Seneca Indian relics is featured. *Open Mon.-Sat.*

Norwich

CHENANGO COUNTY MUSEUM *Rexford St.* Early-settler, railroad, Chenango Canal and Indian memorabilia are shown. *Open Wed., Sat., Sun. June-Aug.*

Ogdensburg

ST. MARY'S CATHEDRAL *415 Hamilton St.* This is a modern version of Gothic architecture. *Open daily.*

Oneida

COTTAGE LAWN *435 Main St.* The Madison County Historical Society has organized a regional center for traditional crafts here. *Open Tues.-Sun. May-Oct.*

Owego

TIOGA COUNTY HISTORICAL SOCIETY MUSEUM *110 Front St.* Indian, pioneer and military relics are displayed. *Open Tues.-Sun.*

Painted Post

TOWN OF ERWIN MUSEUM *Town Hall, Monument Sq.* Colonial, Civil War and Indian relics are on view. *Open Mon.-Sat. July-Aug., Tues.-Thurs. Sept.-June.*

Palatine Bridge

REFORMED DUTCH CHURCH OF STONE ARABIA *Rte. 5* The church, built of local pale gray sandstone in 1788, is still active. *Open Sun. Apr.-Dec.*

Palmyra

MARTIN HARRIS HOME *Maple Rd.* The first printings of *The Book of Mormon* were paid for by mortgaging this farm. *Open daily May-Oct.*

Penn Yan

OLIVER HOUSE MUSEUM *200 Main St.* Here are artifacts of Algonquin and Seneca Indians and early settlers. *Open Thurs. except holidays.*

Remsen

OLD STONE CHURCH *Prospect St.* Still in use, the 1831 church was solidly built by Welsh immigrants.

Rochester

TEMPLE B'RITH KODESH *2131 Elmwood Ave.* A monumental bronze-cast ark stands under a 12-sided wooden and glass dome in the synagogue's prayer hall.

Rome

FORT STANWIX MUSEUM *112 Spring St.* Displays, dioramas, maps and artifacts depict the cultural and historical development of the area. *Open Tues.-Sun. except holidays.*

Sackets Harbor

PICKERING-BEACH MUSEUM *503 W. Main St.* The museum has Early American furnishings and artifacts from the War of 1812. *Open daily June-Aug. Small charge.*

SACKETS HARBOR BATTLEFIELD STATE PARK The park includes the War of 1812 battlefield, ruins of fortifications and an interpretation center. *Open daily July-Aug.*

St. Johnsville

FORT KLOCK *1 mi. E. on Rte. 5* The fortified 18th-century farmhouse and trading post is furnished with antiques. *Open Tues.-Sun. June-Aug. Small charge.*

MARGARET REANEY MEMORIAL LIBRARY *19 Kingsbury Ave.* Documents and objects of local history are exhibited here. *Open Mon.-Sat.*

Sandy Creek

RAIL CITY MUSEUM *Rte. 3* Steam locomotives can be ridden here. *Open daily June-Sept. Adults $1.50, children small charge.*

Saranac Lake

ROBERT LOUIS STEVENSON COTTAGE *Stevenson Lane* Staying here in the winter of 1887-8 to treat his illness, the author wrote some essays. *Open daily July-Aug. Small charge.*

Schaghticoke

KNICKERBOCKER MANSION *2 mi. S.W.* This 1770 brick mansion is near the spot where a 1676 peace treaty was signed with the Mohawk Indians. *Open late May-Sept.*

Schenectady

SCHENECTADY MUSEUM *Nott Terrace Hts.* Changing art, science and planetarium shows are given. *Open Tues.-Sun. except holidays. Small charge for planetarium.*

Springfield Center

DENNYS TOY MUSEUM *Rte. 80* Oldtime toys and miniature trains are displayed. *Open daily Easter Day-mid-Oct. Small charge.*

Stillwater

SARATOGA NATIONAL HISTORICAL PARK *Rte. 4* The park commemorates a decisive battle of the Revolutionary War. *Open daily except holidays.*

Stone Arabia

TRINITY LUTHERAN CHURCH *Rte. 5* This church was built by Palatine settlers in 1792. *Open daily.*

Ticonderoga

FORT MOUNT HOPE *½ mi. E.* Relics of the fort are on display in the restored blockhouse. *Open late May-late Oct.*

Tupper Lake

JACKMAN GALLERY OF ART *3 mi. S. on Rte. 30* Here are works of early Adirondack painters. *Open daily.*

Utica

JUNIOR MUSEUM OF ONEIDA COUNTY *1703 Oneida St.* History, natural history and science exhibits are geared to children. *Open Tues.-Sun.*

Wellsville

DAVID A. HOWE PUBLIC LIBRARY *155 N. Main St.* Lincoln portraits and old prints are housed here. *Open Mon.-Fri. June-Aug., Mon., Tues., Thurs.-Sat. Sept.-May.*

Whitehall

SKENESBOROUGH MUSEUM *The Boulevard* Models of a 1776 shipyard and the flagship *Saratoga* are among the displays. *Open daily mid-June-early Sept. Small charge.*

WILLIAM MILLER MEMORIAL CHAPEL The small white chapel is a memorial to the founder of the Advent Christian Church.

Wilton

GRANT COTTAGE *Mount McGregor* President Ulysses S. Grant stayed here in 1885 to improve his health and finish his memoirs.

Pennsylvania

Erie

ANTHONY WAYNE BLOCKHOUSE *560 E. Third St.* Over the grave of General Wayne is a replica of the blockhouse in which he died. *Open daily.*

CATHEDRAL OF ST. PAUL *131-3 W. Sixth St.* This late 19th-century Episcopal cathedral is basically Gothic in style. *Open daily.*

CHURCH OF THE COVENANT *247 W. Sixth St.* The huge Gothic edifice was built in 1929. *Open daily.*

PRESQUE ISLE LIGHTHOUSE *Presque Isle State Park* The lighthouse has been an aid to lake navigation since 1872.

Vermont

Albany

HAYDEN HOUSE *Rte. 14* A winding staircase and a third-floor ballroom are among the features of this elegant 1850s house.

Arlington

ST. JAMES EPISCOPAL CHURCH *Rte. 7* The stone Gothic structure is said to be the oldest (1827) Episcopal parish in Vermont. *Open daily.*

Bellows Falls

INDIAN CARVINGS *S. of Vilas Bridge* Mysterious faces with dots for eyes and mouth were carved here in two large groups before the first settlers arrived.

Brattleboro

BROOKS MEMORIAL LIBRARY *224 Main St.* The modern library displays works by artists William Morris Hunt and Larkin Mead. *Open Mon.-Sat.*

Brookfield

MARVIN NEWTON HOUSE *Brookfield Center* The 1835 clapboard house contains period furniture, clothing and tools. *Open Sun. July-Aug.*

Burlington

BILLINGS CENTER *University of Vermont* This student center was designed by Henry Hobson Richardson in the late 19th century. *Open daily.*

ST. JOSEPH'S CHURCH *85 Elmwood Ave.* The oldest French-Canadian parish in New England is Vermont's largest church. *Open daily.*

Calais

KENT MUSEUM *Kent's Corner* Nineteenth-century furniture and a country store are displayed. *Open Tues.-Sun. July-Aug. Small charge.*

East Poultney

EAGLE TAVERN *On the Green* This 18th-century tavern was a favorite meeting place for Ethan Allen and his Green Mountain Boys.

Fairlee

WALKER MUSEUM *1 mi. S. on Rte. 5* Ethnological collections here include a Persian bazaar and a Japanese room. *Open daily July-Aug.*

Ferrisburg

ROBINSON FAMILY MEMORIAL MUSEUM ("ROKEBY") *Rte. 7* Heirlooms are shown in this 1789 house. *Open daily mid-May-mid-Oct. Small charge.*

Hartford

SECOND CONGREGATIONAL CHURCH *Main St.* This 1828 church is unusual for its single row of windows and two-door entrance bay. *Open Sun.-Fri.*

Isle La Motte

ST. ANNE'S SHRINE The state's first Mass was said here at the site of Fort St. Anne, erected in 1666. *Open mid-May-mid-Oct.*

Manchester

MUSEUM OF AMERICAN FLY FISHING *Rte.. 7* The museum tells the history of the sport. *Open daily.*

Middlebury

EMMA WILLARD HOUSE *131 S. Main St.* The founder of the first school for women lived here in 1814. *Open Mon.-Fri.*

HALPIN BRIDGE Forty-one feet above the water, this is the second highest covered bridge in Vermont.

Montpelier

SUPREME COURT BUILDING *111 State St.* This structure of light Barre granite houses the Vermont Department of Libraries. *Open Mon.-Fri. except holidays.*

THOMAS WATERMAN WOOD ART GALLERY *135 Main St.* Paintings by the 19th-century Montpelier artist are displayed. *Open Mon.-Fri.*

North Fairfield

PRESIDENT CHESTER A. ARTHUR BIRTHPLACE *Off Rte. 36* This is a replica of the house in which the President was born in 1830. *Open Tues.-Sun. July-Aug. Small charge.*

Northfield

NORWICH UNIVERSITY MUSEUM *On the Campus* Here are mementos of Norwich alumni. *Open daily during academic sessions, Tues.-Sat. during vacations.*

Norwich

NORWICH CONGREGATIONAL CHURCH-UNITED CHURCH OF CHRIST *Church St.* This 1817 meetinghouse has a Paul Revere bell. *Open daily.*

Old Bennington

BENNINGTON BATTLE MONUMENT *Monument Circle* The 306-foot stone monolith commemorates the 1777 Revolutionary battle here. *Open daily Apr.-Oct. Small charge.*

Proctor

MARBLE EXHIBIT *Main St.* Varieties of marble from many countries are on display. *Open daily late May-mid-Oct. Small charge.*

Putney

WINDHAM COLLEGE The modern campus was designed by Edward Durell Stone in 1954. *Open daily.*

Rockingham

OLD ROCKINGHAM MEETING HOUSE *Rte. 103* The oldest (1787) meetinghouse in Vermont is a fine example of Colonial architecture. *Open daily mid-June-Aug. Small charge.*

St. Johnsbury

"AMERICA" *Courthouse Sq.* The Italian marble statue by Larkin Mead honors the Civil War dead.

West Brattleboro

CREAMERY BRIDGE *Off Rte. 9* The 1879 covered bridge is 80 feet long and has a sidewalk on its western flank.

REGION 2 [map page 102]

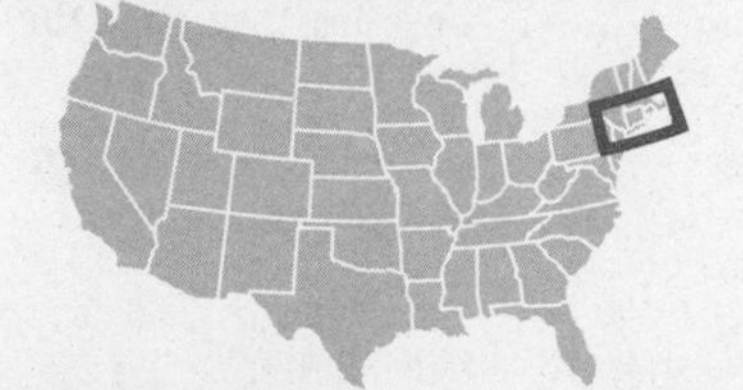

Connecticut

Bridgeport

BARNUM MUSEUM *820 Main St.* The 50,000-piece Brinley Model Circus is exhibited here, as well as memorabilia of P. T. Barnum and Tom Thumb. *Open Tues.-Sun. except holidays.*

MUSEUM OF ART, SCIENCE AND INDUSTRY *4450 Park Ave.* Changing exhibits of regional interest can be seen in nine galleries. *Open Tues.-Sun. except holidays.*

Brooklyn

MEETING HOUSE ON THE GREEN The octagonal domed belfry is typical of many Colonial New England churches. *Open Sun.*

OLD TRINITY CHURCH *Church St.* The nearly square Colonial church has a four-sided hip roof. *Open Sun. June-Aug.*

Clinton

ADAM STANTON HOUSE *63 E. Main St.* Collections of antique furniture, china and glass are displayed. *Open Tues.-Sun. May-Oct.*

Coventry

NATHAN HALE HOMESTEAD *South St.* The 1776 home contains memorabilia of the great patriot. *Open daily mid-May-mid-Oct. Small charge.*

East Granby

OLD NEW-GATE PRISON AND COPPER MINE *Newgate Rd.* The copper mine was a prison from the Revolution until 1827. *Open Tues.-Sun. late May-Oct. Small charge.*

East Haven

BRANFORD TROLLEY MUSEUM *17 River St.* Riding on an old trolley car, visitors view more than 50 other antique electric cars. *Open daily July-Aug., Sat., Sun., holidays June, Sept., Sun., holidays Apr.-May, Oct.-Nov. Small charge.*

East Windsor

WAREHOUSE POINT TROLLEY MUSEUM *Rte. 140* About 45 electric trolleys and locomotives from 1892 to 1947 are on display. *Open Sat., Sun., holidays May-Nov., Sun., holidays Dec.-Apr. Small charge for rides.*

Farmington

FIRST CHURCH OF CHRIST, CONGREGATIONAL *75 Main St.* This 1771 meetinghouse has a slender graceful spire and is beautifully preserved. *Open Mon.-Fri. except holidays and Thanksgiving weekend.*

Greenwich

PUTNAM COTTAGE *243 E. Putnam Ave.* The oldest house in Greenwich has an unusual scalloped shingle exterior. *Open Mon., Thurs.-Sat. Small charge.*

Guilford

FIRST CONGREGATIONAL CHURCH *On the Green* The 1829 Greek Revival-style meetinghouse has a conical spire. *Open daily.*

THOMAS GRISWOLD HOUSE MUSEUM *171 Boston St.* Period rooms from 1735 through to the present day, plus late 19th- and early 20th-century costumes are featured. *Open Wed.-Sun. Apr.-Nov. Small charge.*

Hartford

FIRST CHURCH OF CHRIST IN HARTFORD *675 Main St.* The 1807 brick building has an elaborate tower and a columned portico. *Open daily.*

Lebanon

GOVERNOR JONATHAN TRUMBULL HOUSE *On the Common* The well-furnished home of the state's first governor is near his store, which served as his Revolutionary War headquarters. *Open Tues.-Sat. May-Nov. Small charge.*

Manchester

ANTIQUE AUTO MUSEUM OF MANCHESTER *Rte. 86 and Slater St.* The beautifully restored cars date from 1909 to 1939. *Open daily mid-June-early Sept., Sat., Sun. early Sept.-mid-June. Small charge.*

Meriden

ST. ROSE OF LIMA CHURCH *35 Center St.* The fine Gothic church has a marble altar and jewel-like stained-glass windows. *Open daily.*

Moodus

AMASA DAY HOUSE *On the Green* There are interesting original stenciled designs on the stairs and upstairs hallway. *Open daily mid-May-mid-Oct. Small charge.*

Mystic

WHITEHALL MANSION *Rte. 27* The gambrel-roof mansion has handsome paneling and antiques. *Open Sun.-Fri. Small charge.*

New Haven

MORRIS HOUSE *325 Lighthouse Rd.* Decorative arts of the 17th, 18th and 19th centuries are displayed in an 18th-century plantation house. *Open Sun.-Fri. May-Oct.*

NEW HAVEN COLONY HISTORICAL SOCIETY MUSEUM *114 Whitney Ave.* Exhibits tracing the growth of the New Haven Colony are shown. *Open Tues.-Sun.*

New London

HEMPSTED HOUSE *11 Hempstead St.* This restored 1678 house is the oldest in New London. *Open daily mid-May-mid-Oct. Small charge.*

SHAW MANSION *11 Blinman St.* The 1756 stone mansion differs from others here since it was built by Acadian settlers from Nova Scotia. *Open Tues.-Sat. Small charge.*

New Preston

NEW PRESTON CONGREGATIONAL CHURCH The 1824 stone church is noted for its masonry and unchanged interior. *Open Sun. July-Aug.*

Niantic

THOMAS LEE HOUSE *Rte. 156* The 1660 saltbox is the oldest frame house in Connecticut. *Open Wed.-Mon. late May-mid-Oct. Small charge.*

Norwich

CATHEDRAL OF ST. PATRICK *213 Broadway* The 1879 church is a splendid example of English Gothic style. *Open daily.*

Ridgefield

ALDRICH MUSEUM OF CONTEMPORARY ART *258 Main St.* An outstanding art collection is shown in this 1783 mansion. *Museum open Sat., Sun.; sculpture garden open daily. Small charge for museum.*

KEELER TAVERN *132 Main St.* A British cannonball fired in the Battle of Ridgefield is buried in the cornerpost. *Open Wed., Sat., Sun. Small charge.*

Sharon

GAY-HOYT HOUSE *Main St.* This 1775 brick home has an interesting smokehouse on the grounds. *Open Tues., Sat. May-Oct.*

South Glastonbury

WELLES-SHIPMAN-WARD HOUSE *972 Main St.* This elegant house is an outstanding example of mid-18th-century Connecticut Valley architecture. *Open Sun. May-Sept. Small charge.*

Stonington

OLD LIGHTHOUSE MUSEUM *Stonington Point.* The maritime museum has a stone tower which gives a view of three states. *Open Tues.-Sun. July-early Sept. Small charge.*

Stratford

CAPTAIN DAVID JUDSON HOUSE AND MUSEUM *967 Academy Hill* The restored 1723 home contains period furnishings. Local antiques are displayed at the adjacent museum. *Open Wed., Sat., Sun. Apr.-Oct. Small charge.*

Uncasville

TANTAQUIDGEON INDIAN MUSEUM *1819 Norwich-New London Tpke.* Mohegans built and run this Indian folk museum. *Open daily May-Oct.*

Warren

WARREN CONGREGATIONAL CHURCH *Rtes. 341 and 45* This 1820 church has an unusual pulpit and many historic antiques. *Open daily.*

Washington

GUNN MEMORIAL LIBRARY HISTORICAL MUSEUM *Washington Green* An outstanding collection of American Indian artifacts and Connecticut historical objects are displayed. *Open Tues., Thurs., Sat.*

Waterbury

OUR LADY OF LOURDES CHURCH *309 S. Main St.* Underneath the sanctuary is a reproduction of the famous Grotto of Our Lady of Lourdes in France. *Open daily.*

West Hartford

NOAH WEBSTER HOUSE *227 S. Main St.* Birthplace of the famous lexicographer, this farmhouse contains 18th-century furnishings. *Open Sun., Thurs. Small charge.*

Westport

UNITARIAN CHURCH IN WESTPORT *10 Lyons Plain Rd.* This fine 1965 church has a dramatic, steeply soaring roof. *Open Sun.-Fri.*

Wethersfield

ISAAC STEVENS HOUSE *211 Main St.* The 18th-century frame house contains family heirlooms and an early toy collection. *Open Tues.-Sun. May-Oct., Tues.-Sat. Nov.-Apr. Small charge.*

SILAS DEANE HOUSE *203 Main St.* This 1766 mansion has an elaborately carved mahogany staircase. *Open Tues.-Sun. May-Oct., Tues.-Sat. Nov.-Apr. Small charge.*

Wilton

WILTON HERITAGE MUSEUM *249 Danbury Rd.* The 18th-century farmhouse contains period furniture, costumes and tools. *Open Sat., Sun. Sept.-July.*

Windsor

OLIVER ELLSWORTH HOMESTEAD *778 Palisado Ave.* The birthplace of the third Chief Justice of the U.S. is filled with choice antiques. *Open Tues.-Sat. May-Oct. Small charge.*

Windsor Locks

BRADLEY AIR MUSEUM *Bradley International Airport* Many types of aircraft are on display; some of them can be boarded by visitors. *Open daily June-Sept., Sat., Sun., holidays Oct.-May. Small charge.*

Winsted

WINCHESTER HISTORICAL SOCIETY *225 Prospect St.* The Federal mansion houses a fine gun collection. *Open Mon., Tues., Thurs.-Sat. mid-June-mid-Sept. Small charge.*

Woodbury

FIRST CONGREGATIONAL CHURCH *Main St. and Judson Ave.* The lovely white frame Colonial church was built in 1819. *Open Sun., Mon., Wed., Fri.*

GLEBE HOUSE *Hollow Rd.* Built in 1690, the house was the site of the 1783 election of the first Episcopal bishop in America. *Open Wed.-Sun.*

Massachusetts

Amherst

EMILY DICKINSON HOUSE *280 Main St.* The Federal mansion was the home of the famous poetess for most of her life.

MEAD ART BUILDING *Amherst College* The museum houses a major collection of American art of all periods. *Open daily Sept.-July.*

Andover

AMOS BLANCHARD HOUSE *97 Main St.* The original interior woodwork is intact in this three-story Federal house. *Open Mon., Wed., Fri.*

Arlington

JASON RUSSELL HOUSE *7 Jason St.* This house was the scene of the massacre of 11 minutemen by the British in 1775. *Open Tues.-Sat. Apr.-Oct.*

Ashley Falls

COLONEL ASHLEY HOUSE *Cooper Hill Rd.* The oldest house in Berkshire County has fine original pine paneling. *Open Wed.-Sun. July-early Sept., Sat., Sun. June, early Sept.-Oct. Small charge.*

Belchertown

STONE HOUSE *Maple St.* Built of local stone in 1827, the home contains period furnishings. *Open Wed., Sat. mid-May-mid-Oct. Small charge.*

Beverly

BALCH HOUSE *448 Cabot St.* Built in 1636, this is considered to be the oldest wooden frame house in the U.S. *Open Mon.-Fri. mid-June-mid-Sept. Small charge.*

Boston

BUNKER HILL MONUMENT *Monument Sq.* In 1775 the outnumbered Americans repulsed the British twice at the site of the 220-foot monument. *Open daily except Thanksgiving Day and Dec. 25. Small charge.*

DORCHESTER HEIGHTS NATIONAL HISTORIC SITE *G St. and Thomas Park* The Americans won their first victory over the British here in 1776. *Open daily.*

FIRST CHURCH IN ROXBURY *John Eliot Sq.* The oldest frame church in Boston has a Paul Revere bell and two Willard clocks. *Open Sun. Sept.-June.*

GIBSON HOUSE MUSEUM *137 Beacon St.* The Victorian museum is in a mid-19th-century town house. *Open Tues.-Sun. except holidays. Small charge.*

NATIONAL SOCIETY OF THE COLONIAL DAMES OF AMERICA IN MASSACHUSETTS *55 Beacon St.* Asher Benjamin designed this fine Federal house, which was later occupied by historian William H. Prescott.

OLD WEST CHURCH *131 Cambridge St.* The 1806 church, designed by Asher Benjamin, contains a C. B. Fisk organ. *Open daily.*

ROBERT GOULD SHAW MEMORIAL *Beacon and Park Sts.* The outstanding bronze bas-relief by Augustus Saint-Gaudens was unveiled in 1897.

SYMPHONY HALL *Huntington and Massachusetts Aves.* The acoustics of this hall, designed by McKim, Mead and White, are superb. *Open during scheduled performances.*

U.S. CUSTOM HOUSE *1-8 McKinley Sq.* The observation tower of the historic 1847 building offers a magnificent harbor view. *Open Mon.-Fri. except holidays.*

Braintree

GENERAL SYLVANUS THAYER BIRTHPLACE *786 Washington St.* The "Father of West Point" was born in this 1720 saltbox. *Open Tues., Sun. mid-Apr.-mid-Oct., Tues., Sat. mid-Oct.-mid-Apr. Small charge.*

Brewster

OLD GRIST MILL *Satucket Rd.* Corn is still ground in this Colonial mill. Above it is a museum of early industry. *Open Wed., Fri., Sat. July-Aug.*

Brookline

JOHN FITZGERALD KENNEDY NATIONAL HISTORIC SITE *83 Beals St.* In each room Mrs. Joseph P. Kennedy's voice on tape tells about her memories of this house where JFK was born. *Open daily. Small charge.*

Cambridge

COOPER-FROST-AUSTIN HOUSE *21 Linnaean St.* Cambridge's oldest house has a steeply pitched roof and pilastered chimney. *Open Mon., Tues., Thurs., Sat. June-Oct., Mon., Thurs. Nov-May. Small charge.*

Chatham

CHATHAM RAILROAD MUSEUM *Depot Rd.* Housed in an 1887 railroad station, the museum contains railroad memorabilia. *Open Mon.-Fri. late June-early Sept.*

Chestnut Hill

HOME OF MARY BAKER EDDY AT CHESTNUT HILL *400 Beacon St.* Mrs. Eddy founded *The Christian Science Monitor* while living in this gray stone mansion in 1908. *Open daily mid-May-mid-Oct., Mon.-Sat. mid-Oct.-mid-May except holidays.*

Concord

CONCORD ART ASSOCIATION *15 Lexington Rd.* During the summer American art from the Revolutionary War period and the early 19th century is displayed. Exhibits change at other times. *Open Tues.-Sun. Feb.-mid-Dec. Small charge.*

Cummington

WILLIAM CULLEN BRYANT HOMESTEAD *Luther Shaw Rd.* Bryant's childhood home is furnished with souvenirs of his travels. *Open Tues.-*

Sun. mid-June–early Sept., Sat., Sun. early Sept.–mid-Oct. Small charge.

Danvers

DANVERS HISTORICAL SOCIETY MEMORIAL HALL MUSEUM AND ARCHIVAL CENTER *Page St.* The museum contains witchcraft memorabilia, and the archival center has the largest collection of material on the subject in the U.S. *Open Mon., Wed., Fri.*

PAGE HOUSE *11 Page St.* Jeremiah Page, a colonel in the Revolution, built this home in 1754. *Open Wed. mid-June–mid-Aug.*

REBECCA NURSE HOUSE *149 Pine St.* According to tradition, Rebecca Nurse, one of the witchcraft martyrs, lived in this 17th-century saltbox. *Open Tues., Wed., Fri. July–Aug. Small charge.*

SAMUEL HOLTEN HOUSE *171 Holten St.* This architecturally important house was originally built in 1670 as a two-room structure. *Open Wed. July–Aug.*

Duxbury

JOHN ALDEN HOUSE *105 Alden St.* This dwelling, built in 1653, was the home of a son of John and Priscilla Alden. *Open daily late June–early Sept. Small charge.*

MYLES STANDISH MONUMENT RESERVATION *Captains Hill* The tall stone monument offers an excellent view from its top. *Open daily June–Aug. Parking fee.*

East Weymouth

ABIGAIL ADAMS BIRTHPLACE *North and Norton Sts.* The restored 17th-century Cape Cod house contains period furnishings. *Open Tues.–Fri., June–early Sept. Small charge.*

Fall River

BATTLESHIP "MASSACHUSETTS" *Battleship Cove* Particularly impressive are the gun mounts of this huge World War II ship. Nearby is the submarine *Lionfish. Open daily except Thanksgiving Day and Dec. 25. Adults $2.50 June–Sept., $2.00 Oct.–May. Children small charge.*

CATHEDRAL OF ST. MARY OF THE ASSUMPTION *Spring St.* Fall River granite was used for this impressive Gothic-style church, completed in 1856. *Open daily.*

Framingham Centre

FIRST BAPTIST CHURCH IN FRAMINGHAM *1200 Worcester Rd.* A fine Christopher Wren-style steeple tops the 1825 church. *Open Sun.*

FIRST PARISH IN FRAMINGHAM *Vernon St. and Edgell Rd.* An excellent replica of a Georgian Colonial-style meetinghouse, this brick church was built in 1927. *Open Sun.*

Gloucester

CAPE ANN HISTORICAL ASSOCIATION HOUSE AND MUSEUM *27 Pleasant St.* The 1804 Captain Elias Davis House contains period furnishings and toys. The adjoining museum has a large collection of Fitz Hugh Lane paintings. *Open Tues.–Sat. except holidays. Small charge.*

FISHERMEN'S MEMORIAL *Stacy Blvd. and Western Ave.* This bronze statue commemorates the local fishermen lost at sea.

Groton

GOVERNOR BOUTWELL HOUSE *Main St.* Mementos from the Lincoln and Grant administrations can be seen in this Victorian house. *Open Sat. late May–late Sept.*

Hadley

FIRST CONGREGATIONAL CHURCH, UNITED CHURCH OF CHRIST *Middle St.* The spire of the 1808 church is crowned by a gilded weathercock. *Open Tues.–Sun.*

FORTY ACRES *130 River Dr.* Six generations of family furnishings make this 1752 frame house unusually interesting. *Open mid-May–mid-Oct. Small charge.*

HADLEY FARM MUSEUM *147 Russell St.* Farm and home implements from Colonial times through the Civil War are displayed. *Open Tues.–Sun. May–mid-Oct.*

Hingham

OLD ORDINARY *21 Lincoln St.* This 1680 house-museum was once a stagecoach stop. *Open Tues.–Sat. June–Aug. Adults $1.50, children small charge.*

Ipswich

JOHN HEARD HOUSE *40 S. Main St.* There is a handsome Palladian-style window over the doorway of this 1795 Federal home. *Open Tues.–Sun. May–Oct. Small charge.*

Lincoln

DECORDOVA AND DANA MUSEUM *Sandy Pond Rd.* A landscaped 30-acre park surrounds this arts center. *Open Tues.–Sun. except holidays.*

Lowell

WHISTLER HOUSE AND PARKER GALLERY *243 Worthen St.* Etchings of James Abbot McNeill Whistler are on display at his birthplace. *Open Tues.–Sun. Sept.–June.*

Lynn

LYNN HISTORICAL SOCIETY MUSEUM *125 Green St.* Furnished period rooms can be seen in the Hyde-Mills House. An early shoe shop and museum are adjacent. *Open Mon.–Fri. except holidays.*

Marblehead

ST. MICHAEL'S CHURCH *Pleasant St.* A graceful, 12-branched brass chandelier embellishes one of the country's oldest (1714) Episcopal churches. *Open daily.*

Nantucket

MARIA MITCHELL BIRTHPLACE *1 Vestal St.* The home of the first American woman astronomer is the only house on the island with a widow's walk which is open to the public. *Open Mon.–Sat. mid-June–mid-Sept. Small charge.*

North Oxford

BIRTHPLACE OF CLARA BARTON *Clara Barton Rd.* Mementos of Miss Barton's years in the American Red Cross and other activities can be seen. *Open Tues.–Sun.*

North Swansea

MARTIN HOUSE *G.A.R. Hwy.* Early pewter and furniture are displayed in this 18th-century farmhouse. *Open daily May–Nov. Small charge.*

North Woburn

COUNT RUMFORD HOUSE *90 Elm St.* The birthplace of scientist Benjamin Thompson contains models of his experiments. *Open Tues.–Sun.*

Norwell

JACOBS FARM *Main St. and Jacobs Lane* This mid-18th-century farmhouse with later additions contains period furnishings. *Open Tues., Thurs., Sat. June–Sept. Small charge.*

Osterville

OSTERVILLE HISTORICAL SOCIETY AND MUSEUM *Parker and West Bay Rds.* The well-furnished house was built in 1795 by a sea captain. *Open Sun., Thurs. July–Sept.*

Pittsfield

HEADQUARTERS HOUSE *113 E. Housatonic St.* The Berkshire County Historical Society has exhibits in this villa. *Open Mon.–Fri. except holidays. Small charge.*

MAJOR BUTLER GOODRICH HOUSE *823 North St.* This restored Federal house contains many fine Hepplewhite and Chippendale pieces. *Open Tues.–Sun. July–mid-Oct. Small charge.*

Plymouth

HARLOW OLD FORT HOUSE *119 Sandwich St.* Demonstrations of 17th-century crafts are held at this 1677 Pilgrim home. *Open daily mid-June–mid-Sept. Small charge.*

PLIMOTH PLANTATION *Rte. 3A* This is a complete re-creation of the 1627 Pilgrim settlement. Moored at State Pier is a replica of the *Mayflower. Open daily Apr.–Nov. Adults $1.50, children small charge; small additional charge for* Mayflower.

Provincetown

CAPE COD PILGRIM MEMORIAL ASSOCIATION MONUMENT AND MUSEUM The monument commemorates the 1620 landing of the Pilgrims and the museum houses exhibits of early Cape Cod. *Open daily. Small charge.*

CHURCH OF ST. MARY OF THE HARBOR *519 Commercial St.* The works of local artists enhance the interior of this lovely waterfront chapel. *Open Sun.*

CHURCH OF ST. PETER THE APOSTLE *Prince St.* Stained-glass windows depict the arrival of Columbus, the landing of the *Mayflower* and the blessing of Provincetown's fishing fleet. *Open daily.*

OLDEST HOUSE IN PROVINCETOWN *72 Commercial St.* The 1746 house was built of timbers from wrecked ships. *Open daily June-Sept. Small charge.*

Quincy

JOHN ADAMS BIRTHPLACE *133 Franklin St.* The 1681 saltbox house had a lean-to added at a later date. *Open Tues.-Sun. mid-Apr.-Sept. Small charge.*

JOHN QUINCY ADAMS BIRTHPLACE *141 Franklin St.* Like its neighbor, the 1716 Colonial house has period furnishings. *Open Tues.-Sun. mid.-Apr.-Sept. Small charge.*

Rockport

PAPER HOUSE *Pigeon Hill St.* Approximately 100,000 newspapers were used to construct this house and its furniture. *Open daily late May-Sept. Small charge.*

Royalston

ROYALSTON COMMON Of the more than 20 untouched 19th-century buildings on the common, the Greek Revival-style church and the Rufus Bullock Mansion are particularly noteworthy.

Salem

PIONEER VILLAGE *Forest River Park* Reproductions of the first shelters built in 1630 by Salem settlers may be seen. *Open daily June-Oct. Small charge.*

Sandwich

YESTERYEARS MUSEUM *Main and River Sts.* Originally a church, the building now has exhibits of old dolls, dollhouses and toys. *Open Sat., Sun. May, daily late May-mid-Oct. Small charge.*

Saugus

BOARDMAN HOUSE *17 Howard St.* This 17th-century home is of interest architecturally because of its original framework and interior details.

Scituate

CUDWORTH HOUSE *First Parish Rd.* Now the Scituate Historical Society, the 1797 house has period furnishings. *Open Wed.-Sat. mid-June-mid-Sept. Small charge.*

Sharon

KENDALL WHALING MUSEUM *27 Everett St.* A whaleboat, scrimshaw, paintings and whaling gear are shown. *Open Tues., Wed. Small charge.*

Shrewsbury

FIRST CONGREGATIONAL CHURCH OF SHREWSBURY *Church Rd.* This classic New England meetinghouse was built in 1766. *Open daily.*

Springfield

ALEXANDER HOUSE *284 State St.* Attributed to Asher Benjamin, this lovely Federal-style home has an impressive reception hall with a fine vaulted ceiling.

FIRST CHURCH OF CHRIST, CONGREGATIONAL *Court Sq.* The 1819 church has a richly decorated tower topped with a four-foot weathercock. *Open daily.*

GEORGE WALTER VINCENT SMITH ART MUSEUM *222 State St.* Exhibits include decorative arts of the 20th century and 19th-century American paintings. *Open Tues.-Sun.*

MUNICIPAL GROUP *36 Court St.* There is a panoramic view from the 300-foot observation tower, one of three impressive structures here. *Open Mon.-Fri. Apr.-Nov.*

NAISMITH MEMORIAL BASKETBALL HALL OF FAME *460 Alden St.* The museum is dedicated to America's only major native sport. *Open daily except holidays.*

Stoughton

MARY BAKER EDDY HISTORIC HOUSE *133 Central St.* The founder of Christian Science lived in this frame house in 1868-70. *Open Tues.-Sun. May-Oct. Small charge.*

Swampscott

MARY BAKER EDDY HISTORIC HOUSE *23 Paradise Rd.* Mrs. Eddy had her first healing here in 1866. *Open daily mid-May-mid-Oct., Mon.-Sat. mid-Oct.-mid-May except holidays. Small charge.*

Taunton

OLD COLONY HISTORICAL SOCIETY *66 Church Green* Of particular interest is the Taunton Silver Room. *Open Tues.-Sun. July-Sept., Mon.-Sat. Oct.-June except holidays. Small charge.*

Templeton

FIRST CHURCH OF TEMPLETON *Wellington Rd.* Elias Carter, a master builder and carver, built this graceful church in 1811. *Open Sun.*

Waltham

ROSE ART MUSEUM *415 South St., Brandeis University* A fine display of early ceramics is a feature. *Open Tues.-Sun. except holidays.*

Watertown

BROWNE HOUSE *562 Main St.* An authentically furnished 17th-century parlor with crewel hangings is the chief attraction here. *Open Mon., Wed., Fri. June-Oct. Small charge.*

Wayland

FIRST UNITARIAN PARISH IN WAYLAND *Old Boston Post Rd.* The tower and belfry of this 1815 church are among the best in New England.

Wellesley

BABSON WORLD GLOBE *Babson College* The 28-foot diameter sphere has a scale of 24 miles to the inch and rotates on its axis. *Open daily except Thanksgiving Day and Dec. 25.*

COLEMAN MAP BUILDING *Babson College* From the balcony is seen a giant relief model of the U.S., just as it would look from the upper stratosphere. *Open daily except Thanksgiving Day and Dec. 25.*

JEWETT ARTS CENTER *Wellesley College* The noteworthy architect Paul Rudolph designed this building, which houses a museum. *Open daily Sept.-May except holidays.*

Wenham

WENHAM HISTORICAL ASSOCIATION AND MUSEUM *132 Main St.* An old house, doll collection and two early shoe shops are of interest. *House and museum open Mon.-Fri. Mar.-Jan. except holidays; shops open Mon.-Fri. May-Oct. Small charge.*

West Barnstable

WEST PARISH MEETINGHOUSE Paul Revere's foundry cast the bell in this 1717 church, oldest Congregational edifice in America. *Open daily.*

West Falmouth

SACONESSET HOMESTEAD *Rte. 28A* Known as the Ship's Bottom Roof House, this is now a museum of early Americana. *Open daily June-Oct. Small charge.*

Westfield

WESTFIELD ATHENAEUM *6 Elm St.* A pre-1700, authentically furnished house is a popular attraction. *Open Mon.-Fri. July-Aug., Mon.-Sat. Sept.-June.*

Westford

FIRST PARISH CHURCH UNITED A cupola belfry and graceful spire top this pitched-roof church.

Weston

CARDINAL SPELLMAN PHILATELIC MUSEUM *235 Wellesley St.* Postage stamps of the world are displayed by country and by topic. *Open Sun., Tues., Thurs.*

West Springfield

OLD DAY HOUSE *70 Park St.* Period furnishings are found in this 1754 brick saltbox house. *Open Wed.-Sun. Small charge.*

Worcester

AMERICAN ANTIQUARIAN SOCIETY *185 Salisbury St.* The largest single collection of printed source material about this country's first 250 years (1620-1876) is housed here. *Open Mon.-Fri. except holidays.*

ROGERS KENNEDY MEMORIAL *Elm Park* A stone pedestal with 16 bas-reliefs depicting pioneer life is topped by appropriate bronze figures.

TEMPLE EMANUEL *280 May St.* A collection of handwritten scrolls of all the books of the Hebrew Bible is on display. *Open daily.*

New Jersey

Caldwell

GROVER CLEVELAND BIRTHPLACE *207 Bloomfield Ave.* Cleveland's personal belongings fill this two-and-one-half-story frame house. *Open Tues.-Sun. and Mon. holidays. Small charge.*

Clinton

CLINTON HISTORICAL MUSEUM A working mill since 1763, the museum features 18th- and 19th-century Americana. *Open daily Apr.-Oct. Small charge.*

Elizabeth

BOXWOOD HALL *1073 E. Jersey St.* The 1749 shingle house has classic Georgian details. *Open Tues.-Sun. Small charge.*

Farmingdale

DESERTED VILLAGE *Allaire State Park, 4 mi. S. on Rte. 524* The 19th-century village includes an ironworks, a general store and workers' dwellings. *Open Sat., Sun. Mar., daily Apr.-Oct. Small charge.*

Flemington

RAGGEDY ANN ANTIQUE DOLL AND TOY MUSEUM *171 Main St.* Here are hundreds of antique dolls, dollhouse furnishings and toys. *Open Tues.-Sun. Feb.-Dec. Small charge.*

Franklin

FRANKLIN MINERAL MUSEUM *Evans St.* A full-sized mine replica and a display of fluorescent minerals are here. *Open Tues.-Sun. mid-Mar.-mid-Dec. Small charge.*

Freehold

MONMOUTH COUNTY HISTORICAL BUILDING *70 Court St.* Exhibits include Emanuel Leutze's painting, *Washington at Monmouth. Open Tues.-Sun. Jan.-mid-July, Aug.-mid-Dec.*

Highlands

TWIN LIGHTS *On the Bluff* From the North Tower is a view of the ocean and New York Bay. There is also a nautical museum. *Open Tues.-Sun. late May-early Sept.*

Holmdel

HENDRICKSON HOUSE *Longstreet Rd.* This fine Dutch Colonial house is painted in its original colors. *Open Thurs.-Sun. May-Oct.*

Middletown

MARLPIT HALL *137 Kings Hwy.* The Dutch Colonial home has period furnishings and an herb garden. *Open Tues., Thurs., Sat., Sun. Feb.-Dec. except Thanksgiving Day and Dec. 25.*

Millburn

ST. STEPHEN'S CHURCH *119 Main St.* The building is one of the finest surviving examples of a Gothic wood church. *Open daily.*

Montclair

ISRAEL "KING" CRANE HOUSE *110 Orange Rd.* A working 18th-century kitchen is attached to this Federal mansion. *Open Sun. Sept.-June.*

Morristown

MORRIS MUSEUM OF ARTS AND SCIENCES *Normandy Heights and Columbia Rds.* An outstanding feature is a diorama of an early Indian village. *Open Tues.-Sat. July-Aug., daily Sept.-June.*

Newark

NEW JERSEY HISTORICAL SOCIETY MUSEUM AND LIBRARY *230 Broadway* The building contains a library on New Jersey history and a museum with fine antiques. *Open Tues.-Sat. except holidays.*

OLD FIRST CHURCH *820 Broad St.* The original congregation of this 1791 church building was founded in Newark in 1666. *Open Sun.-Fri.*

New Brunswick

BUCCLEUCH MANSION *Buccleuch Park* The three-story Georgian mansion has an interesting fanlight on the top floor. *Open Sat., Sun. late May-Oct.*

JOHNSTON HISTORICAL MUSEUM *Rtes. 1 and 130* Displays trace the history of the Boy Scouts of America. *Open daily except holidays.*

Paterson

PATERSON MUSEUM *268 Summer St.* There are a fine indigenous mineral collection and an excellent display of New Jersey Indian artifacts here. *Open Mon.-Sat.*

Plainfield

DRAKE HOUSE MUSEUM *602 W. Front St.* Colonial and Empire furnishings are displayed in the 1777 headquarters of George Washington. *Open Mon., Wed., Sat.*

Princeton

HISTORICAL SOCIETY OF PRINCETON *158 Nassau St.* The restored Georgian-style Bainbridge House features period furnishings, historical exhibits and a library. *Open daily.*

River Edge

VON STEUBEN HOUSE *Main St.* Built in 1739, this Dutch Colonial house has displays of antique furniture, Indian crafts and toys. *Open Tues.-Sun. Small charge.*

Rutherford

KINGSLAND-OUTWATER HOUSES *245 Union Ave.* The Colonial Kingsland House and the early 19th-century Outwater House were restored by Fairleigh Dickinson University. *Open Mon.-Fri.*

Short Hills

TEMPLE B'NAI JESHURUN *1025 S. Orange Ave.* The elegant contemporary building was designed by Pietro Belluschi, former dean of the M.I.T. School of Architecture. *Open Mon.-Sat.*

Shrewsbury

CHRIST CHURCH *Rte. 35 and Sycamore Ave.* The pre-Revolutionary church contains a Queen Anne Communion set and a rare 1717 Oxford Bible. *Open Sat., Sun.*

Somerville

OLD DUTCH PARSONAGE *63 Washington Pl.* This Dutch Colonial building was built in 1751 with bricks from Holland. *Open Tues.-Sun. Small charge.*

WALLACE HOUSE *38 Washington Pl.* George Washington used this home as his headquarters in 1779; his campaign trunk is on display. *Open Tues.-Sun. Small charge.*

Spotswood

ST. PETER'S EPISCOPAL CHURCH *505 Main St.* The carvings on the exterior of this mid-18th-century wooden Gothic church are noteworthy. *Open daily.*

Trenton

OLD MASONIC LODGE BUILDING *Lafayette and S. Willow Sts.* One of the oldest Masonic Temples in the U.S., the 1793 fieldstone building has exhibits of Masonry memorabilia. *Open Mon.-Fri.*

West Orange

TURTLE BACK ZOO *560 Northfield Ave.* Among the 850 animals is the largest turtle collection on the East Coast. *Open daily. Small charge.*

New York

Albany

CATHEDRAL OF THE IMMACULATE CONCEPTION *125 Eagle St.* Built in 1852, the fine Gothic cathedral has stained-glass windows from Munich. *Open daily.*

FIRST CHURCH IN ALBANY *N. Pearl St. and Clinton Sq.* The wooden pulpit, Communion silver, hourglass and Bible are among the oldest in the U.S. *Open Sun.-Fri.*

HISTORIC CHERRY HILL *S. Pearl St.* The Dutch-Georgian house was completed for Philip van Rensselaer in 1768 and was occupied by his descendants until 1963. *Open Tues.-Sun. Small charge.*

JOSEPH HENRY MEMORIAL BUILDING *Washington and Elk Sts.* This beautifully proportioned building is one of the finest remaining works of Albany architect Philip Hooker. *Open Mon.-Fri.*

TEN BROECK MANSION *9 Ten Broeck Pl.* The Federal mansion has columned porticos at front and rear and a balustraded roof. *Open Tues.-Sun. except holidays.*

Amagansett

TOWN MARINE MUSEUM *Bluff Rd.* Displays include a whaling boat, harpoons and model ships. *Open daily July-early Sept. Small charge.*

Beacon

MADAM BRETT HOMESTEAD *50 Van Nydeck Ave.* Built in 1709, this home contains seven generations of family possessions. The old kitchen is intact. *Open Wed.-Sat. mid-Apr.-mid-Nov. Small charge.*

Cold Spring

FOUNDRY SCHOOL MUSEUM OF THE PUTNAM COUNTY HISTORICAL SOCIETY *63 Chestnut St.* The 140-year-old schoolhouse has exhibits of the former West Point gun foundry and the Hudson River. *Open Sun., Wed.*

Key: Historic Place · Historic House · Old Mill or Works · Museum or Collection · Significant Buildir

Cooperstown

BUSCH WOODLANDS AND MUSEUM *Rte. 80* Nature trails, museums, railroad cars and wild animals offer a glimpse into America's early days. *Open daily May-mid-Sept. Adults $1.95, children small charge.*

COOPERSTOWN AND CHARLOTTE VALLEY RAILROAD *1 Railroad Ave.* Visitors may ride in a turn-of-the-century train pulled by a steam engine. *Open Sat., Sun., holidays late May-early July, early Sept.-Oct., daily early July-early Sept. Adults $2.50, children $1.50.*

COOPERSTOWN ART ASSOCIATION *22 Main St.* The former library is the scene of an annual exhibition of contemporary arts and crafts. *Open daily July-Aug. Small charge.*

COOPERSTOWN INDIAN MUSEUM *1 Pioneer St.* On display are New York State Indian artifacts ranging back 10,000 years. *Open daily mid-May-mid-Oct. Small charge.*

Coxsackie

BRONCK HOUSE MUSEUM *Rte. 9W* This complex of buildings reflects three centuries of upper Hudson Valley history. *Open Tues.-Sun. mid-June-Sept. Small charge.*

Delhi

DELAWARE COUNTY HISTORICAL ASSOCIATION FRISBEE HOUSE MUSEUM *Rte. 10* The elegant Federal house is fully furnished. *Open Sat., Sun. and holidays late May-Sept.*

East Hampton

CLINTON ACADEMY *Main St.* The first chartered academy in New York State now houses Montauk Indian relics, whaling gear, shipwreck mementos and tools. *Open daily July-early Sept. Small charge.*

"HOME SWEET HOME" *14 James Lane* Composer John Howard Payne was born in this 1660 saltbox house. *Open Wed.-Mon. Small charge.*

MULFORD FARM *James Lane* The early saltbox house has primitive 18th-century furniture. *Open daily July-early Sept. Small charge.*

East Setauket

SHERWOOD-JAYNE HOUSE *Old Post Rd.* This saltbox house is furnished with an outstanding collection of antiques. *Open Wed.-Sun. May-mid-Oct. Small charge.*

Fishkill

TRINITY EPISCOPAL CHURCH *Main St. and Hopewell Ave.* The interior has been restored to a Colonial appearance. *Open daily.*

Goshen

HALL OF FAME OF THE TROTTER *240 Main St.* Collections of lithographs and dioramas tell the story of the trotter. *Open daily.*

Huntington

CONKLIN HOUSE *New York Ave. and High St.* This 18th-century farmhouse is maintained by the Huntington Historical Society as a museum of American decorative arts. *Open Sun., Tues.-Fri. Small charge.*

THOMAS POWELL HOUSE *434 Park Ave.* The 17th-century house contains a fine collection of early Huntington pottery and antique costumes. *Open Sun. Small charge.*

WALT WHITMAN HOUSE *246 Walt Whitman Rd.* Birthplace of the famous poet in 1819, this simple shingled farmhouse contains Whitman memorabilia. *Open daily except Jan. 1 and Dec. 25.*

Hurley

TOWN OF HURLEY NATIONAL HISTORIC SITE The preserved houses on the main street are all more than 200 years old.

Kinderhook

VAN ALEN HOUSE *Rte. 9H* Washington Irving chose this Dutch homestead as the setting for his *Legend of Sleepy Hollow. Open Tues.-Sun. late May-mid-Sept. Small charge.*

Monroe

MUSEUM VILLAGE OF SMITH'S CLOVE *Rte. 17* Nearly 30 restored buildings house displays of 19th-century American tools and crafts. *Open daily mid-Apr.-Oct. Adults $2.00, children over 7 small charge.*

Mount Vernon

ST. PAUL'S CHURCH *897 S. Columbus Ave.* This 1763 church holds the oldest existing organ built by Henry Erben and a 1758 bell.

Newburgh

CRAWFORD HOUSE *189 Montgomery St.* The Georgian home has exquisite carvings and ornamentation.

WASHINGTON'S HEADQUARTERS *Washington and Liberty Sts.* Washington announced the end of the Revolution from this Dutch stone house in 1783. *Open Wed.-Sun. except holidays.*

New Rochelle

THOMAS PAINE COTTAGE *20 Sicard Ave.* Mementos of the patriot may be seen here and in the Thomas Paine Memorial Building nearby. *Open Tues.-Sun.*

NEW YORK CITY

Bronx

HALL OF FAME FOR GREAT AMERICANS *181st St. and University Ave.* The semicircular granite colonnade contains nearly 100 bronze busts of notable Americans. *Open daily.*

VALENTINE-VARIAN HOUSE *Bainbridge Ave. and 208th St.* This fieldstone farmhouse, now the Museum of Bronx History, displays artifacts, photographs and paintings. *Open Sun. Small charge.*

Brooklyn

BROOKLYN HEIGHTS HISTORIC DISTRICT *Atlantic Ave., Court and Fulton Sts., East River.* Half the 1300 buildings were built before the Civil War; many have been restored.

LEFFERTS HOMESTEAD *Prospect Park and Flatbush Ave.* The pre-Revolutionary farmhouse burned down and was rebuilt in 1777 with salvaged lumber. *Open Wed., Fri.-Sun. Nov.-May except holidays.*

LONG ISLAND HISTORICAL SOCIETY LIBRARY *128 Pierrepont St.* The 19th-century building boasts an impressive arched entrance set between decorated columns. *Open Tues.-Sat. Sept.-July except holidays.*

Manhattan

ABIGAIL ADAMS SMITH MUSEUM *421 E. 61st St.* This restored 18th-century stone building was originally a carriage house. *Open Mon.-Fri. Sept.-July. Small charge.*

AMERICAN GEOGRAPHICAL SOCIETY *Broadway and 156th St.* The collection includes maps and globes dating from the 17th century. *Open Mon.-Fri. except holidays.*

AMERICAN NUMISMATIC SOCIETY *Broadway and 155th St.* The history and use of coinage and collections of medals and decorations are displayed. *Open Tues.-Sun.*

ASIA HOUSE GALLERY *112 E. 64th St.* Historic arts of Asia are shown in a beautiful modern building designed by Philip Johnson. *Open daily Oct.-early June.*

CARNEGIE HALL *154 W. 57th St.* The acoustics of the 1891 Italian Renaissance-style structure are world famous. *Open during scheduled performances.*

CASTLE CLINTON NATIONAL MONUMENT *Battery Park* The fortification, with its eight-foot-thick walls, was built to protect New York Harbor in the years preceding the War of 1812. *Open daily.*

CHASE MANHATTAN PLAZA *William and Pine Sts.* Featured is the Sculptural Water Garden, designed by Isamu Noguchi, with huge black basalt rocks and fountains. *Open daily.*

CHINESE MUSEUM *7 Mott St.* There are displays of Chinese musical instruments and foods as well as audio-visual exhibits of Chinese customs and culture. *Open daily except Dec. 25. Small charge.*

DYCKMAN HOUSE *Broadway and W. 204th St.* The 1783 Dutch farmhouse is furnished with Colonial antiques. *Open Tues.-Sun.*

EAST COAST MEMORIAL *Battery Park* This impressive monument commemorates the World War II servicemen who died in the Atlantic.

ELMER HOLMES BOBST LIBRARY AND STUDY CENTER AT NEW YORK UNIVERSITY *70 Washington Sq. S.* This architecturally outstanding building was designed by Philip Johnson.

New York City (*continued*)
FRAUNCES TAVERN MUSEUM *Pearl and Broad Sts.* The second and third floors of this historic 1719 building contain mementos of Washington and the Revolution. *Open Mon.-Fri.*
HAMILTON GRANGE NATIONAL MEMORIAL *Convent Ave. and 141st St.* Alexander Hamilton lived in this Federal house for the last three years of his life. *Open Mon.-Fri.*
MILTON STEINBERG HOUSE OF THE PARK AVENUE SYNAGOGUE *50 E. 87th St.* The entire facade is a huge stained-glass window 35 feet wide and four stories high, with 91 separate panels. *Open daily.*
MUSEUM OF AMERICAN FOLK ART *49 W. 53rd St.* This museum is devoted to the craftsman-artist. *Open Tues.-Sun. Sept.-July. Small charge.*
MUSEUM OF CONTEMPORARY CRAFTS *29 W. 53rd St.* There are exhibits of ceramics, ceramic sculptures, textiles, tapestries, rugs and woodwork. *Open Tues.-Sun. Small charge.*
MUSEUM OF PRIMITIVE ART *15 W. 54th St.* This is the only museum devoted solely to the arts of the indigenous cultures of the Americas, Africa and Oceania. *Open Wed.-Sun.*
NEW YORK CITY FIRE DEPARTMENT MUSEUM *100 Duane St.* The museum displays antique fire-fighting apparatus. *Open Mon.-Sat.*
NEW YORK CULTURAL CENTER *2 Columbus Circle* Built for Huntington Hartford, the elegant museum was designed by Edward Durell Stone. It is now operated in association with Fairleigh Dickinson University. *Open Tues.-Sun. Small charge.*
NEW YORK STOCK EXCHANGE *20 Broad St.* Guides escort visitors through this financial marketplace housed in a 1903 Beaux Arts Eclectic landmark building. *Open Mon.-Fri.*
OLD CUSTOM HOUSE *1 Bowling Green* The most outstanding feature of the ornate building is the rotunda with murals by Reginald Marsh. *Open Mon.-Fri.*
OLD MERCHANT'S HOUSE *29 E. Fourth St.* Original furnishings are featured in this 1832 Greek Revival town house.
PLAZA HOTEL *Fifth Ave. at 59th St.* Built in the style of a French Renaissance chateau, this is one of New York's most elegant buildings. *Open daily.*
ST. MARK'S CHURCH IN-THE-BOWERY *10th St. and Second Ave.* The fieldstone church, built in 1799, sits peacefully surrounded by its cemetery. *Open Sun., Tues.-Fri.*
VILLARD HOUSES *Madison Ave. and 50th St.* The impressive complex of Italian Renaissance-style brownstone mansions was designed by McKim, Mead and White.
WASHINGTON ARCH *Washington Sq. and Fifth Ave.* The white marble arch ornamented with bas-reliefs was designed by Stanford White.

Richmond (Staten Island)
FORT WADSWORTH MILITARY MUSEUM *School Rd. and Bay St., Fort Wadsworth* America's oldest continuously manned fort contains objects from the Revolutionary War through Vietnam. *Open Sat., Sun., holidays.*
GARIBALDI AND MEUCCI MEMORIAL MUSEUM *420 Tompkins Ave., Rosebank* On view are Meucci's models for the telephone he invented and memorabilia concerning the Italian patriot Garibaldi. *Open Tues.-Sun. except holidays.*
JACQUES MARCHAIS CENTER OF TIBETAN ART *338 Lighthouse Ave., Richmondtown* The museum, a Tibetan temple, contains Tibetan art and literature. Gardens are filled with stone sculptures. *Open Sat., Sun. Apr.-Nov. Small charge.*

North Blenheim
OLD BLENHEIM BRIDGE *Schoharie Creek* The 232-foot-long bridge, built in 1855, is said to be the world's longest single-span covered wooden bridge.

North Salem
HAMMOND MUSEUM AND ORIENTAL STROLL GARDENS *Deveau Rd.* The museum of humanities is surrounded by serene pools and Oriental gardens. *Museum open Wed.-Sun., Mon. holidays late May-Dec., garden open late May-Oct. Small charge.*

Old Bethpage
OLD BETHPAGE VILLAGE RESTORATION *Round Swamp Rd.* An agricultural village of the early 1800s has been brought to life. *Open daily. Adults $1.50, children small charge.*

Orient
ORANGE WEBB HOUSE *Village Lane* The two-story wooden house has pillars in front and a delightful summer kitchen. *Open Tues., Thurs., Sat., Sun. July-mid-Oct.*

Ossining
OSSINING HISTORICAL SOCIETY MUSEUM *196 Croton Ave.* Historical artifacts of the Ossining area include some famous Hudson River paintings. *Open Mon., Wed., Sat.*

Oyster Bay
PLANTING FIELDS ARBORETUM AND COE MANSION *Planting Fields Rd.* The mansion, a superb example of Elizabethan architecture, is closed, but visitors can enjoy the 400 acres of landscaped grounds around it. *Open daily. Adults $1.50.*
RAYNHAM HALL *20 W. Main St.* A Victorian wing was added to the 1738 saltbox in 1851. The furnishings reflect both eras. *Open Wed.-Sun. Small charge.*

Purchase
PEPSICO WORLD HEADQUARTERS *Anderson Hill Rd.* Outstanding modern sculptures surround the multitiered building designed by Edward Durell Stone. *Sculpture garden open daily.*

Rensselaer
FORT CRAILO *9½ Riverside Ave.* The fine old Dutch manor house was built in the early 18th century. Rooms are furnished in period style. *Open Tues.-Sun.*

Rhinebeck
OLD RHINEBECK AERODROME *Rte. 199* Visitors can see many old airplanes (1900-20), most of them originals. *Open daily mid-May-Oct. Small charge. Sun. air shows: adults $2.00, children small charge.*

Riverhead
SUFFOLK COUNTY HISTORICAL SOCIETY MUSEUM *300 W. Main St.* Fine china and memorabilia of Colonial textile production are here. *Open Mon.-Sat. except holidays.*

Roxbury
WOODCHUCK LODGE *Memorial Field* The summer home of naturalist John Burroughs has been restored. *Open daily mid-May-mid-Sept.*

Rye
SQUARE HOUSE *1 Purchase St.* The early 18th-century house has hand-hewn framing, huge fireplaces and original paneling. *Open Sun., Tues.-Fri. except holidays.*

Schoharie
OLD STONE FORT MUSEUM *N. Main St.* Indian artifacts, antique firearms and household furnishings are displayed. *Open daily June-Aug., Tues.-Sun. May, Sept.-Oct. Small charge.*

Setauket
THOMPSON HOUSE *N. Country Rd.* The 17th-century house has high chimneys and massive fireplaces. *Open Wed.-Mon. May-mid-Oct. Small charge.*

Southampton
ELIAS PELLETREAU SILVERSMITH SHOP *Main St.* On display in the hip-roofed wooden building is a collection of silver that Pelletreau made here more than 200 years ago. *Open Fri., Sat. Small charge.*
HALSEY HOUSE *S. Main St.* Built in 1648, this is the oldest English frame house in New York State. *Open daily mid-June-mid-Sept. Small charge.*
LONG ISLAND AUTOMOTIVE MUSEUM *Rte. 27* More than 100 restored antique cars, trucks and fire engines from 1906 on are displayed. *Open daily late May-Sept. Adults $1.50, children small charge.*
SOUTHAMPTON HISTORICAL MUSEUM *Meeting House Lane* The museum features whaling exhibits, a

one-room schoolhouse and a pre-Revolutionary barn. *Open daily mid-June-mid-Sept. Small charge.*

Troy

RENSSELAER COUNTY HISTORICAL SOCIETY MUSEUM *59 Second St.* Also known as the Hart-Cluett Mansion, this handsome Federal house is filled with 19th-century antiques. *Open Tues.-Sat. except holidays.*

Vails Gate

KNOX HEADQUARTERS *Rte. 94* General Henry Knox used this 1754 fieldstone house during the Revolution. *Open Wed.-Sun.*

NEW WINDSOR CANTONMENT *Temple Hill Rd.* This restored Revolutionary War winter camp includes an original officers' hut. *Open Wed.-Sun. mid-Apr.-Oct.*

Water Mill

OLD WATER MILL MUSEUM *Old Mill Rd.* Visitors enjoy using the Colonial looms, spinning wheels and tools on display here. *Open Wed.-Mon. mid-June-Sept.*

West Bay Shore

SAGTIKOS MANOR HISTORICAL SOCIETY HOUSE *Montauk Hwy.* The 1692 Colonial home served as headquarters for General Sir Henry Clinton during the Revolution. *Open Sun., Wed., Thurs. May-mid-Sept. Small charge.*

Woodstock

WOODSTOCK ARTISTS ASSOCIATION *28 Tinker St.* Located in one of America's most famous art colonies, the building features changing exhibits of local artists. *Open Fri.-Mon.*

Yonkers

HUDSON RIVER MUSEUM *511 Warburton Ave.* The museum, housed in a Victorian mansion and a contemporary building, sponsors continuous exhibits of art, science and industry. *Open Tues.-Sun. except holidays. Small charge.*

Rhode Island

Bristol

BRISTOL ART MUSEUM *Wardwell St.* Once a ballroom, the museum has changing exhibits of paintings and sculpture. *Open daily June-mid-Sept.*

BRISTOL HISTORICAL AND PRESERVATION SOCIETY MUSEUM *48 Court St.* Exhibits tracing Bristol's history are housed in the original county jail. *Open daily Apr.-Dec.*

HAFFENREFFER MUSEUM OF ANTHROPOLOGY *Mount Hope Grant* Outstanding collections of American Indian, Eskimo and aboriginal artifacts are on display. *Open Tues.-Sun. June-Aug., Sat., Sun. Sept.-Jan., Mar.-May.*

Coventry

GENERAL NATHANAEL GREENE HOMESTEAD *Taft St.* Washington's adjutant during the Revolution built this handsome frame house. *Open Wed.-Sun. Mar.-Nov.*

East Greenwich

GENERAL JAMES MITCHELL VARNUM HOUSE *57 Pierce St.* Carved paneling graces the interior of the 1773 home. *Open Sun. June-Aug. Small charge.*

VARNUM MILITARY AND NAVAL MUSEUM *Main and Division Sts.* There are relics of the French and Indian Wars and other Colonial wars as well as a collection of uniforms and equipment.

Jamestown

JAMESTOWN WINDMILL *N. Main Rd.* The 18th-century gristmill has been restored to operating condition. *Open Sat., Sun. July-Aug.*

Kingston

FAYERWEATHER HOUSE *Mooresfield Rd.* The simple 1820 wooden house with its central chimney belonged to the village blacksmith. *Open Tues.-Sat. Apr.-mid-Dec.*

PETTAQUAMSCUTT HISTORICAL SOCIETY MUSEUM *Kingstown Rd.* The 18th-century granite jail now contains period furniture, Indian artifacts, tools and a 19th-century schoolroom. *Open Tues., Thurs., Sat. Small charge.*

SOUTH COUNTY ART ASSOCIATION *1319 Kingstown Rd.* Changing art and ceramics exhibits are scheduled six or more times a year for three weeks at a time in the 1802 Helme House. *Open Tues.-Sun. during exhibitions.*

Lincoln

ARNOLD HOUSE *449 Great Rd.* The house was built in 1687 and enlarged during the 1700s. The big end chimneys make it a typical Rhode Island "stone-ender." *Small charge.*

Little Compton

UNITED CONGREGATIONAL CHURCH *Commons* The simple white frame church is a fine example of a New England Colonial meeting-house.

WILBOR HOUSE *W. Main Rd.* Built during the 17th, 18th and 19th centuries, the two-story frame house contains period furnishings. *Open Tues.-Sun. mid-June-early Sept. Small charge.*

Narragansett

TOWERS *Ocean Rd.* This 50-foot-high stone arch spanning the highway was designed by Stanford White in 1883 as part of a casino.

Newport

ARTILLERY COMPANY OF NEWPORT RHODE ISLAND MILITIA *23 Clarke St.* The nation's oldest military organization has a comprehensive collection of American and foreign uniforms. *Open Tues.-Sun. May-Sept., Sat. Oct.-Apr.*

BAPTIST HOME OF RHODE ISLAND *2 Shepard Ave.* This mansion is considered the finest specimen of Queen Anne architecture in the U.S. *Open Mon.-Fri.*

BREAKERS STABLE *Coggeshall Ave.* The building houses a large collection of carriages and coaches—all in working order—owned by the Vanderbilts. *Open daily July-early Sept. Small charge.*

BRICK MARKET *127 Thames St.* The building with its classic arches and columns was designed in 1762 by Peter Harrison to serve as Newport's first shopping center. *Open Mon.-Sat.*

H.M.S. "ROSE" *Newport Harbor* The 20-gun, largely reconstructed frigate is the last remaining example of a full-sized ship of the Revolutionary War. *Open daily Apr.-Nov. Small charge.*

NATIONAL LAWN TENNIS HALL OF FAME AND TENNIS MUSEUM *194 Bellevue Ave.* Housed in the historic Newport Casino, the museum is devoted to the history of tennis. *Open Mon.-Fri. mid-May-late May, daily June-Oct. Small charge.*

NAVAL AND UNDERSEAS MUSEUM *Spring and Church Sts.* Displays include artifacts from undersea explorations and famous shipwrecks. *Open daily May-Sept. Small charge.*

NEWPORT HISTORICAL SOCIETY *82 Touro St.* Attached to the museum of Newport memorabilia is the 1729 Sabbatarian Meeting House. *Open Tues.-Sat. except holidays.*

OLD STONE MILL *Touro Park* Some historians believe that this squat round structure was built by Norsemen in the 11th century.

REDWOOD LIBRARY AND ATHENAEUM *50 Bellevue Ave.* Designed to resemble a Roman temple, this is the oldest library building in continuous use in the U.S. *Open Mon.-Sat. except holidays.*

ST. GEORGE'S SCHOOL CHAPEL *Purgatory Rd.* This lovely English Gothic-style chapel contains statues of saints and disciples by sculptor Joseph Coletti. *Open daily.*

ST. MARY'S CHURCH *Spring St. and Memorial Blvd.* John F. Kennedy and Jacqueline Lee Bouvier were married in this church, the oldest Roman Catholic parish in the state. *Open daily.*

SANFORD-COVELL HOUSE *72 Washington St.* The house, with its fine period furnishings, is an excellent example of Victorian architecture. *Open Tues., Thurs., Sat. June-Sept. Small charge.*

WANTON-LYMAN HAZARD HOUSE *Stone St. and Broadway* The 1675 Jacobean house is the oldest still standing in Newport. *Open daily July-early Sept. Small charge.*

Newport (*continued*)

WHITE HORSE TAVERN *Farewell and Marlborough Sts.* The gambrel-roof Jacobean building is America's oldest (1673) tavern still dispensing libations. *Open daily.*

North Kingstown

SOUTH COUNTY MUSEUM *Scrabbletown Rd.* The exhibits depict daily life in Rhode Island more than a century ago. *Open Tues.-Sun. late May-Sept. Small charge.*

Portsmouth

CHURCH OF ST. GREGORY THE GREAT *Portsmouth Abbey and School* There is an outstanding wire sculpture by Richard Lippold over the main altar. *Open daily.*

Providence

BAJNOTTI MEMORIAL FOUNTAIN *Kennedy Plaza* Presented to the city in 1900, the bronze figures depict the flight of the soul.

BENEFICENT CONGREGATIONAL CHURCH *300 Weybosset St.* Built in 1810, this unusual building is often referred to as "The Round Top Church." *Open daily.*

BETSY WILLIAMS COTTAGE *Roger Williams Park* The furnished 1773 cottage is surrounded by more than 400 acres of beautiful parkland. *Open Fri.-Wed.*

CATHEDRAL OF ST. JOHN *271 N. Main St.* The present building of the Mother Church of the Episcopal Diocese of Rhode Island was erected in 1810. *Open daily.*

FLEUR-DE-LYS BUILDING *7 Thomas St.* Providence artist Sidney Burleigh built this half-timbered studio in 1886.

GRACE CHURCH IN PROVIDENCE *Westminster Mall* This brownstone Victorian Gothic edifice was consecrated in 1846 and recently renovated. *Open daily.*

MARKET HOUSE *N. Main and College Sts.* The handsome brick Georgian building has a tablet showing where the floodwaters reached during the "great gale of 1815." *Open Mon.-Sat.*

PROVIDENCE ART CLUB *11 Thomas St.* Changing exhibitions of local art are on display in these two 18th-century buildings. *Open Mon.-Fri. June-mid-Aug., daily Sept.-May.*

PROVIDENCE ATHENAEUM *251 Benefit St.* This Greek Revival library building contains outstanding paintings and rare books. *Open Mon.-Sat.*

PROVIDENCE COUNTY COURTHOUSE *250 Benefit St.* This building is an adaptation of early Federal architecture. It was built in 1933. *Open Mon.-Fri.*

PROVIDENCE PUBLIC LIBRARY *150 Empire St.* The library has notable collections of Rhode Island history. *Open Mon.-Fri. July-Aug., Mon.-Sat. Sept.-June.*

ST. JOSEPH'S CHURCH *86 Hope St.* The oldest Catholic church in Providence, built of varicolored fieldstone, has a fine view of the harbor.

WAR MEMORIAL GROTTO *Providence College, River Ave. and Eaton St.* The grotto, with its amphitheater, altar and statues, was built to honor alumni killed in World War I. *Open daily.*

Saunderstown

GILBERT STUART MEMORIAL *Gilbert Stuart Rd.* The birthplace of the famous portrait painter (b. 1755) has a working gristmill and snuffmill. *Open Sat.-Thurs. except Dec. 25. Small charge.*

Watch Hill

FLYING HORSE CAROUSEL *Bay St.* Six generations of children have ridden the hand-carved wooden ponies. *Open Sat., Sun. late May-early June, daily mid-June-mid-Sept. Small charge.*

Wickford

OLD NARRAGANSETT CHURCH *Church Lane* The silver Communion service still in use at the 1707 church was presented by Queen Anne. *Open Fri.-Sun. July-Aug.*

REGION 3 [map page 170]

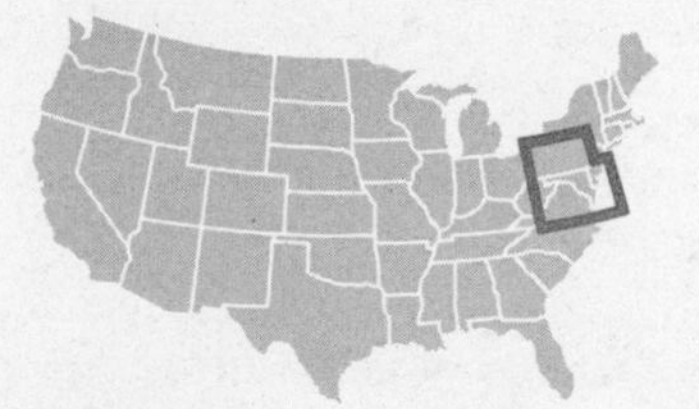

Delaware

Camden

CAMDEN FRIENDS MEETING HOUSE *122 E. Camden-Wyoming Ave.* The 1805 building has a gambrel roof and dormer windows. *Open Sun.*

Cowgill's Corner

OCTAGONAL SCHOOLHOUSE *Rte. 9* The one-story, one-room 1836 structure is a perfect octagon. *Open Sat., Sun. except holidays.*

Dagsboro

PRINCE GEORGE'S CHAPEL *Rte. 26* The barrel ceiling of this 1757 chapel forms a cross.

Delaware City

FORT DELAWARE STATE PARK *Pea Patch Island* The pentagonal bastion was a Union prison. *Open Sat., Sun., holidays late May-Oct.*

Dover

CHRIST EPISCOPAL CHURCH *S. State and Water Sts.* The original 1734 brick church forms the nave of the present structure. *Open daily.*

OLD POST OFFICE *43 The Green* The 1718 hand-split clapboard dwelling was a post office from 1818 to 1825. *Open 1st wk. May.*

Frederica

BARRATT'S CHAPEL AND MUSEUM *Rte. 113* The Methodist Episcopal Church in the U.S. was planned here in 1784. *Open Tues.-Sun.*

Greenville

DELAWARE MUSEUM OF NATURAL HISTORY *Rte. 52* Exhibits of mollusks, mammals, birds and eggs can be seen. *Open Wed.-Sun. Adults $1.25, children small charge.*

Laurel

OLD CHRIST CHURCH *3 mi. E. on Rte. 24* The native pine interior of this 1771 frame church is original. *Open Sun. June-Aug.*

Lewes

ST. GEORGE'S CHAPEL, INDIAN RIVER HUNDRED *8 mi. W. on Rd. 285* The 1794 chapel has a Palladian window and fine paneling. *Open Sun.*

Middletown

OLD ST. ANNE'S EPISCOPAL CHURCH *1 mi. S. on Rte. 896* The original box pews remain in this 1768 brick church. *Open Sun. June-mid-Sept.*

New Castle

ACADEMY BUILDING *Third and Harmony Sts.* Built in 1798, this was the first school in New Castle.

NEW CASTLE PRESBYTERIAN CHURCH *Second St.* The 1707 Colonial church was restored in 1950. *Open daily.*

Odessa

DRAWYERS CHURCH *½ mi. N. on Rte. 13* The Presbyterian church was built in 1773 of locally made brick. *Open 1st Sun. June.*

Smyrna

ALLEE HOUSE *Dutch Neck Rd.* The restored Queen Anne period house is furnished with antiques. *Open Sat., Sun. except holidays.*

South Bowers

ISLAND FIELD ARCHAEOLOGICAL MUSEUM AND RESEARCH CENTER *Milford Neck* Skeletons lying in open graves can be seen in the ninth-century Indian burial ground.

Wilmington

FIRST PRESBYTERIAN CHURCH *Park Dr. and West St.* Built in 1740, the brick church has a gambrel roof.

District of Columbia

Washington

ALL SOULS CHURCH, UNITARIAN *16th and Harvard Sts., N.W.* A Revere bell hangs in the tower of this magnificent church. *Open daily.*

ALVA BELMONT HOUSE *144 Constitution Ave., N.E.* One of the oldest houses on Capitol Hill is now National Women's Party headquarters.

AMERICAN SECURITY AND TRUST CO. *15th St. and Pennsylvania Ave., N.W.* The bank was designed to complement the classical architecture of its neighbor, the U.S. Treasury. *Open Mon.-Fri. except holidays.*

ANDERSON HOUSE *2118 Massachusetts Ave., N.W.* The Society of the Cincinnati occupies the neo-Palladian mansion. *Open Tues.-Sun.*

ARTS CLUB OF WASHINGTON *2017 I St., N.W.* When the White House burned in 1814, this Federal town house was the Executive Mansion. *Open daily except holidays.*

CHAPEL HALL *Gallaudet College* The central building of the institution for the deaf is Gothic Revival in style. *Open Mon.-Fri.*

CHRISTIAN HEURICH MEMORIAL MANSION *1307 New Hampshire Ave., N.W.* The late 19th-century house is Norman Revival in style. *Open Mon., Wed., Sat. except holidays.*

DISTRICT BUILDING *14th and E. Sts., N.W.* The mid-Victorian-style white marble "City Hall" was completed in 1908. *Open Mon.-Fri.*

DOLLEY MADISON HOUSE *1520 H St., N.W.* Mrs. Madison lived in this stucco house from 1837 to 1849.

EXPLORERS HALL, NATIONAL GEOGRAPHIC SOCIETY *17th and M Sts., N.W.* Famous National Geographic expeditions are depicted in life-size displays. *Open daily except Dec. 25.*

FIRST BAPTIST CHURCH *16th and O Sts., N.W.* Stained-glass windows depict the history and spirit of Baptist churches. *Open Sun.*

FORD'S THEATRE *511 10th St., N.W.* Performances are held nightly in the theater where Lincoln was shot. In the basement is a museum of Lincolniana. *Open daily.*

FREDERICK DOUGLASS HOME *14th and W Sts., S.E.* The Colonial-style brick and stucco house was the home of the former slave who became a prominent abolitionist. *Open daily.*

GALLERY OF ART *Howard University, Sixth and Fairmont Sts., N.W.* The Alain Locke Collection of African Art is notable. *Open Mon.-Sat.*

HOUSE OF THE TEMPLE *1733 16th St., N.W.* The Masonic headquarters resembles the Temple of Halicarnassus in Asia Minor *Open Mon.-Sat.*

KLUTZNICK EXHIBIT HALL *1640 Rhode Island Ave., N.W.* Here is the second largest U.S. collection of Judaica. *Open Sun.-Fri. except holidays.*

MOUNT VERNON PLACE UNITED METHODIST CHURCH *900 Massachusetts Ave., N.W.* Broad steps lead to the high colonnaded portico of the 1917 stone church. *Open daily.*

NATIONAL RIFLE ASSOCIATION MUSEUM *1600 Rhode Island Ave., N.W.* Over 1000 arms are displayed. *Open daily except holidays.*

NAVY MEMORIAL MUSEUM *Bldg. 76, Washington Navy Yard* Among the Navy memorabilia is an excellent collection of naval guns. *Open daily except holidays.*

NEW YORK AVENUE PRESBYTERIAN CHURCH *1313 New York Ave., N.W.* Many U.S. Presidents have been associated with this historic church. *Open Tues.-Sun.*

OLD CITY HALL *451 Indiana Ave., N.W.* The city's fourth oldest government building is an outstanding example of Greek Revival architecture. *Open Mon.-Fri. except holidays.*

PENSION BUILDING *Fourth, Fifth, F and G Sts., N.W.* Seven inaugural balls were held in this massive building, now a courthouse. *Open Mon.-Fri. except holidays.*

ST. ALOYSIUS CHURCH *19 I St., N.W.* A large painting by Brumidi hangs in this Baroque-style Catholic church. *Open daily.*

U.S. DEPARTMENT OF AGRICULTURE BUILDING *14th St. and Independence Ave., S.W.* This is one of the last Neoclassical government buildings completed in the city. *Open Mon.-Fri.*

U.S. DEPARTMENT OF COMMERCE BUILDING *14th St. and Constitution Ave., N.W.* The monumental building is in the Italian Renaissance Palazzo style. *Open Mon.-Fri.*

WASHINGTON WARD CHAPEL *2810 16th St., N.W.* The Mormon chapel is built of Utah bird's-eye marble.

WATKINS GALLERY *American University* Works by American artists of the mid-20th century are displayed. *Open Mon.-Fri.*

Maryland

Annapolis

OLD TREASURY BUILDING *State Circle* Colonial currency was issued here in this 1735 building. *Open Mon.-Fri.*

Baltimore

BABE RUTH SHRINE AND MUSEUM *216 Emory St.* The rebuilt birthplace of the famous baseball player is flanked by a three-building museum. *Open daily. Small charge.*

BALTIMORE COURT HOUSE *St. Paul and Lexington Sts.* Historical murals decorate the interior of this white marble building. *Open Mon.-Fri.*

EDGAR ALLAN POE HOUSE *203 Amity St.* The home of the renowned poet from 1832 to 1835 is furnished with period antiques. *Open Sat. Small charge.*

EUTAW PLACE BAPTIST CHURCH *Eutaw Pl. and Dolphin St.* Thomas Ustick Walter, architect of the dome and wings of the U.S. Capitol, designed this 1869 church.

FIRE ENGINE HOUSE NO. 6 *416 N. Gay St.* This 19th-century building, recently renovated, has a Venetian Gothic clock tower. *Open daily.*

FIRST AND FRANKLIN STREET PRESBYTERIAN CHURCH *500 Cathedral St.* In 1844 Robert Long designed this red brick Tudor-style church. *Open Sun.*

FRANCIS SCOTT KEY MONUMENT *Eutaw Pl. and Lanvale St.* The 30-foot-high monument was sculpted by Jean Mercié and erected in 1911.

ST. VINCENT DE PAUL CHURCH *Fayette St. and the Fallsway* This 1840 Roman Catholic church is in the Neoclassical style. *Open daily.*

Big Pool

FORT FREDERICK STATE PARK *Off Rte. 70* The only extant Colonial-period British fort in the U.S. is here. *Open daily May-mid-Oct.*

Burkittsville

WAR CORRESPONDENTS MEMORIAL *Gathland State Park, off Rte. 17* Civil War correspondent George Alfred Townsend erected this unique monument.

Chestertown

OLD ST. PAUL'S CHURCH *8 mi. S. on Rte. 20* The oldest continuously used church in the state was built between 1711 and 1713. *Open daily.*

Cumberland

EMMANUEL CHURCH *16 Washington St.* This 1851 church is on the site of an old fort. *Open daily.*

HISTORY HOUSE *218 Washington St.* The 1866 Victorian-style house is a museum of local history and period furniture. *Open Sun. May-Oct.*

Emmitsburg

ST. JOSEPH'S PROVINCIAL HOUSE *Off Rte. 15* Mother Elizabeth Seton is entombed here. *Open daily.*

Frederick

ROGER BROOKE TANEY HOME-FRANCIS SCOTT KEY MUSEUM *121 S. Bentz St.* The home of Chief Justice Taney dates from 1799. *Open daily May-Oct. Small charge.*

Hagerstown

JONATHAN HAGER HOUSE AND MUSEUM *19 Key St.* The fortified home of the town founder was built in 1740 over two springs. *Open Tues.-Sun. May-Oct. Small charge.*

ZION EVANGELICAL AND REFORMED CHURCH *201 N. Potomac St.* Several beautiful stained-glass windows brighten the stone walls of this 1774 church. *Open daily.*

La Plata

CHRIST CHURCH *Off Rte. 301* The Gothic-style church was constructed just after the Civil War. *Open daily.*

Leonardtown

ST. ANDREW'S EPISCOPAL CHURCH *St. Andrew's Church Rd.* A large, hand-painted reredos is a notable feature of this 1767 church.

Port Tobacco

ST. IGNATIUS CHURCH *Chapel Point* Built in 1798, this is one of the oldest Roman Catholic churches in the U.S. The adjacent St. Thomas Manor (1741) is said to be the oldest Jesuit residence in continuous use in the world. *Church open daily.*

St. Mary's City

TRINITY EPISCOPAL CHURCH *Off Rte. 5* The church was constructed in 1829 of brick from the dismantled State House. *Open daily.*

Warwick

ST. FRANCIS XAVIER OR OLD BOHEMIA SHRINE *Off Rte. 282* The mission church was founded in 1704. *Open Sun. June-Sept.*

Westminster

HISTORICAL SOCIETY OF CARROLL COUNTY *210 E. Main St.* A doll collection and a pictorial history of the first Rural Free Delivery service are displayed. *Open Tues.-Sun.*

New Jersey

Atlantic City

ABSECON LIGHTHOUSE *Rhode Island and Pacific Aves.* The restored tower guarded the inlet from 1857 to 1933. *Open Tues.-Sun. June-Sept. Adults small charge.*

Barnegat Light

BARNEGAT LIGHTHOUSE *Long Beach Island* The brick tower was built by General George G. Meade. *Open Sat., Sun. early-late May, early Sept.-Oct., daily late May-early Sept. Small charge.*

Cape May Court House

HISTORICAL MUSEUM *Main St.* Local history is told through displays in the basement of the Cape May County Court House. *Open Mon.-Sat. except holidays.*

Deerfield Street

DEERFIELD PRESBYTERIAN CHURCH *Deerfield St.* This stone church, built in 1771, houses a fine Aeolian-Skinner organ. *Open Sun.*

Haddonfield

INDIAN KING TAVERN *233 King's Hwy. E.* The New Jersey legislature met here in 1777. *Open Tues.-Sun. Adults small charge.*

Mount Holly

HISTORIC BURLINGTON COUNTY PRISON MUSEUM *128 High St.* Robert Mills designed this 1810 prison. *Open Tues.-Sat. except holidays.*

Somers Point

SOMERS MANSION *Shore Rd. and the Circle* A shipwright built this early 18th-century house with a roof resembling an upturned hull.

Swedesboro

TRINITY EPISCOPAL (OLD SWEDES) CHURCH *King's Hwy. and Church St.* The Georgian-style church was erected in 1784. *Open daily.*

Woodbury

HUNTER-LAWRENCE HOUSE *58 N. Broad St.* Colonial memorabilia gathered by the Gloucester County Historical Society can be seen in this 1765 house. *Open Wed.*

New York

Narrowsburg

FORT DELAWARE *¾ mi. N. on Rte. 97* Patterned after a 1750s settlement, the fort is a museum of pioneer life. *Open Sat., Sun. June, early-late Sept., daily July-early Sept. Adults $1.25, children small charge.*

Pennsylvania

Airville

INDIAN STEPS MUSEUM *E. of intersection of Rtes. 74 and 425* Seven rooms are devoted to Indian relics and plaster casts of ancient petroglyphs. *Open daily Apr.-Oct. except Mon. holidays.*

Allentown

LIBERTY BELL SHRINE *622 Hamilton St.* A replica of Philadelphia's Liberty Bell is displayed in Zion Reformed Church where the original bell was hidden (1777-8) from the British. *Open daily mid-Apr.-mid-Oct., Wed.-Mon. mid-Oct.-mid-Apr.*

TROUT HALL *414 Walnut St.* Period furnishings and local artifacts of the Lehigh County Historical Society are on view in this 1770 house. *Open Tues.-Sun.*

Altoona

BAKER MANSION *Baker Blvd.* This 1846 Greek Revival house is the museum of the Blair County Historical Society. *Open Thurs.-Sat. mid-May-mid-Oct. Small charge.*

Athens

TIOGA POINT MUSEUM *724 S. Main St.* Here are exhibits of Indian lore and Stephen Foster memorabilia. *Open Mon., Wed., Sat.*

Avella

MEADOWCROFT VILLAGE *Penowa Rd.* The 18th- and 19th-century structures moved here re-create a rural community. *Open daily May-Nov. Adults $2.00, children small charge.*

Birdsboro

DANIEL BOONE HOMESTEAD *Boone Rd.* Among the buildings on this 600-acre complex is an 18th-century farmhouse. *Open daily. Small charge.*

Boalsburg

BOAL ESTATE *Rte. 322* The Boal Mansion (1789), the Columbus Family Chapel from 16th-century Spain and the Boalsburg Museum may be visited. *Open daily May-Oct. Adults $1.25, children small charge.*

PENNSYLVANIA MILITARY MUSEUM *28th Division Shrine, Rte. 322* A reconstructed World War I battlefield is among the military exhibits. *Open Tues.-Sun. Small charge.*

Brookville

E. M. PARKER INDIAN MUSEUM *247 E. Main St.* Local Indian relics are on display. *Open Mon.-Fri. May-Aug.*

Carlisle

CARLISLE BARRACKS On the grounds are the Hessian Guardhouse and Omar N. Bradley Museums. *Open Tues.-Sun. May-Sept.*

Chadds Ford

BRANDYWINE BATTLEFIELD PARK *Rte. 1* The headquarters of Generals Washington and Lafayette are here. *Open daily late May-early Sept., Sat., Sun. early Sept.-late May.*

BRANDYWINE RIVER MUSEUM *Rte. 1* A converted gristmill serves as a museum focusing on the work of illustrator Howard Pyle and the Wyeth family. *Open daily. Small charge.*

Columbia

FIRST NATIONAL BANK MUSEUM *S. Second and Locust Sts.* Here an early 19th-century bank is preserved in its original setting.

NATIONAL ASSOCIATION OF WATCH AND CLOCK COLLECTORS MUSEUM *514 Poplar St.* Here are exhibits of clocks, watches and books relating to horology. *Open Mon.-Fri.*

Dawson

PHILIP G. COCHRAN MEMORIAL UNITED METHODIST CHURCH *Howell and Griscom Sts.* This fine church is a 20th-century version of the English Gothic style. *Open Sun.*

Devon

OLD ST. DAVID'S CHURCH *Valley Forge Rd.* The stone church, still in use, was built in 1715. *Open daily.*

Doylestown

MORAVIAN POTTERY AND TILE WORKS *E. Court St. and Swamp Rd.* Tours are conducted to explain the ceramic process. *Open Wed.-Sun.*

Easton

FIRST UNITED CHURCH OF CHRIST *27 N. Third St.* Treaties between the Delaware Indians and the Continental Congress were signed in the 1776 sanctuary, now restored.

Farmington

FORT NECESSITY NATIONAL BATTLEFIELD *Rte. 40* The reconstructed fort and the 1818 Mount Washington Tavern are on this site. *Visitor center open daily Apr.-mid-Nov., tavern open daily.*

Fort Washington

CLIFTON HOUSE *473 Bethlehem Pike* A mid-19th-century inn is furnished with period antiques. *Open Sun., Wed. Sept.-June.*

Gettysburg

GETTYSBURG BATTLE THEATRE *571 Steinwehr Ave.* Flags and equipment are displayed and "Battlerama" is enacted. *Open daily. Adults $1.25, children small charge.*

HALL OF PRESIDENTS AND FIRST LADIES *789 Baltimore St.* Here are life-size, speaking wax models. *Open daily Apr.-Oct. Adults $1.25, children small charge.*

LINCOLN ROOM MUSEUM *Wills*

Key: Historic Place   Historic House   Old Mill or Works   Museum or Collection   Significant Buildin

House, Lincoln Sq. Lincoln prepared the Gettysburg Address here. *Open daily Apr.-Sept. Small charge.*

NATIONAL CIVIL WAR WAX MUSEUM *Steinwehr Ave. and Culp St.* An audio-visual presentation with more than 200 life-size figures shows the causes, leaders and battles of the Civil War. *Open daily. Adults $1.50, children small charge.*

Harmony

HARMONY MUSEUM *Rte. 68* A one-hand German tower clock, dated about 1650, is on display. *Open Tues.-Sun. June-Sept. Small charge.*

Harrisburg

FORT HUNTER MUSEUM *5300 N. River Rd.* Period furnishings enhance an 1814 house on the site of Fort Hunter. *Open Tues.-Sun. May-mid-Oct. Small charge.*

JOHN HARRIS MANSION *219 S. Front St.* The collections of the Historical Society of Dauphin County are displayed in the 1766 home of the city founder. *Open Mon.-Fri. July and last 2 wks. Aug., Mon.-Sat. Sept.-June.*

Horsham

GRAEME PARK *County Line Rd.* This 1721 house was built as a distillery. *Open Sat., Sun. May-Oct.*

Hunterstown

GREAT CONEWAGO PRESBYTERIAN CHURCH This 1787 stone church served as a field hospital during the Battle of Gettysburg. *Open Sun.*

Lancaster

AMISH HOMESTEAD *3 mi. E. on Rte. 462* Tours are conducted around this old-order Amish farm. *Open daily mid-Mar.-Nov., Sat. Dec.-mid-Mar. Small charge.*

LANCASTER COUNTY HISTORICAL SOCIETY HEADQUARTERS *230 N. President Ave.* Here are items of local and national historical interest. *Open Tues.-Sat.*

PENN DUTCH SHO-PLACE *6 mi E. on Rte. 30* Relics of the Pennsylvania Dutch and other Americana are displayed. *Open daily. Adults $1.50, children small charge.*

TRINITY LUTHERAN CHURCH *31 S. Duke St.* This fine Colonial church serves the oldest congregation in the city (1729). *Open daily.*

Lititz

MORAVIAN CHURCH *Church Sq.* Several other Moravian buildings surround this historic 1787 church.

Meadville

BALDWIN-REYNOLDS HOUSE MUSEUM *Terrace St.* Items of local historical interest can be seen in this 1843 mansion. *Open Wed., Sat., Sun. late May-early Sept. Small charge.*

Mercer

JOHNSTON TAVERN *5 mi. S. on Rte. 19* This 1831 stone structure was a stopping place for stagecoach passengers. *Open Tues.-Sun.*

Middletown

SANT PETER'S LUTHERAN KIERCH *Union and High Sts.* This brownstone church was built in 1767.

Philadelphia

AMERICAN PHILOSOPHICAL SOCIETY LIBRARY *105 S. Fifth St.* Part of this 1959 building was copied from the 1789 library that stood on this site. *Open Mon.-Fri.*

CONYINGHAM-HACKER HOUSE *5214 Germantown Ave.* Relics of Germantown are in this 1772 house. *Open Tues., Thurs., Sat.*

GLORIA DEI (OLD SWEDES') CHURCH *Delaware Ave. and Christian St.* The old church was built in 1700 by Swedish colonists. *Open daily.*

HISTORICAL SOCIETY OF PENNSYLVANIA *1300 Locust St.* Here are American historical manuscripts and paintings. *Open Tues.-Fri. Sept.-July.*

"MAN FULL OF TROUBLE" TAVERN *125-7 Spruce St.* The restored 18th-century tavern is now a museum of decorative arts. *Open Tues.-Sun. Apr.-Nov., Sat., Sun. Dec.-Mar. Small charge.*

OLD ST. JOSEPH'S CHURCH *321 Willing's Alley* The first Roman Catholic church in the city was founded in 1733. *Open daily.*

PHILIP H. & A. S. W. ROSENBACH FOUNDATION MUSEUM *2010 Delancey Pl.* Rare books and manuscripts are displayed in a 19th-century townhouse. *Open Mon.-Fri. June-July, Tues.-Sun. Sept.-May. Adults small charge.*

TRINITY CHURCH, OXFORD *Oxford Ave. and Disston St.* This 1711 church is still used. *Open Sun.*

Pittsburgh

FORT PITT MUSEUM *Point State Park* Exhibits in a reconstructed bastion tell the history of the city and state. *Open daily. Small charge.*

STEPHEN COLLINS FOSTER MEMORIAL HALL *University of Pittsburgh, Forbes Ave.* Here is the world's largest collection of the Pittsburgh composer's memorabilia. *Open Mon.-Fri.*

Pottstown

POTTSGROVE MANSION *W. King St.* The 1750s mansion, built by John Potts, founder of Pottstown, has period furnishings and flower and herb gardens. *Open Tues.-Sun.*

Reading

HISTORICAL SOCIETY OF BERKS COUNTY *940 Centre Ave.* Here are a library and exhibits of local history. *Open Tues.-Sat. except holidays.*

Slippery Rock

OLD STONE HOUSE *Rte. 8* The restored inn was built in 1822. *Open Tues.-Sun. Small charge.*

Soudersburg

MILL BRIDGE CRAFT VILLAGE *S. of Rte. 30 on Ronks Rd.* Along with a gristmill, cider press and blacksmith shop, there are demonstrations of local arts and crafts. *Open Mon.-Sat. Apr.-Oct., Sat. Nov. Adults $1.50, children 6-12 small charge.*

Stroudsburg

QUIET VALLEY FARM MUSEUM *Off Rte. 209* Costumed guides do the chores of 18th- and 19th-century farm life. *Open daily mid-June-early Sept. Adults $2.00, children small charge.*

Towanda

FRENCH AZILUM *S.E. on Rte. 6* An 1835 house and reconstructed log cabins stand on a site occupied (1793-1803) by refugees from the French Revolution. *Open Thurs.-Tues. late May-late Oct. Small charge.*

Trappe

AUGUSTUS LUTHERAN CHURCH *E. Seventh Ave. and Main St.* A fine example of Colonial German architecture, the 1743 church is little altered. *Open Sun. May-Sept.*

Washington

DAVID BRADFORD HOUSE *175 S. Main St.* The home of the Whiskey Rebellion leader was built in 1788. *Open Tues.-Sun. Small charge.*

Watsontown

WARRIOR RUN CHURCH *Rte. 147* This 1835 red brick church is basically Greek Revival in style.

West Chester

DAVID TOWNSEND HOUSE *225 N. Matlack St.* The 1790 house is furnished with antiques and period pieces. *Open Tues.-Thurs., Sat. May-Oct.*

Wyoming

SWETLAND HOMESTEAD *885 Wyoming Ave.* This 19th-century house is furnished in the period. *Open Tues.-Sun. June-Sept. Small charge.*

York

LITTLE RED SCHOOL HOUSE MUSEUM *12 mi. W. on Rte. 30* The century-old one-room school is complete with pot-bellied stove and children's books and lunchboxes. *Open Sat., Sun. Apr.-May, early Sept.-Oct., daily June-early Sept. Small charge.*

Virginia

Accomac

ST. JAMES EPISCOPAL CHURCH *Daugherty Rd.* On one wall of this 1838 church is a unique trompe-l'oeil decoration. *Open daily.*

Aldie

OAK HILL FARMS *Rte. 15* The home of James Monroe was built in the Palladian style in 1821 from plans drawn by Thomas Jefferson.

Alexandria

GEORGE WASHINGTON MASONIC NATIONAL MEMORIAL Extensive

Alexandria (*continued*)
Washington memorabilia are displayed in the elaborate 333-foot-high shrine. *Open daily except holidays.*
STABLER-LEADBEATER APOTHECARY MUSEUM *107 S. Fairfax St.* Hand-blown bottles can be seen in this 1792 shop. *Open Mon.-Sat.*

Arlington
NETHERLANDS CARILLON TOWER *Arlington Ridge Rd. and Arlington Blvd.* The 49-bell carillon was a gift from the Netherlands to the U.S.

Brookneal
RED HILL SHRINE *5 mi. S.E. on Rte. 600* Here is Patrick Henry's last home, law office and burial place. *Open daily except Dec. 25. Small charge.*

Burrowsville
BRANDON EPISCOPAL CHURCH *Rte. 10* This church has two Tiffany windows and Communion silver from the mid-1600s. *Open daily.*

Charlottesville
ALBEMARLE COUNTY COURTHOUSE *Court Sq.* The historic building was a center for county citizens including Thomas Jefferson, James Monroe and James Madison. *Open daily.*
HISTORIC MICHIE TAVERN MUSEUM *2½ mi. S.E. on Rte. 53* A striking portrayal of Revolutionary life can be seen in Patrick Henry's boyhood home. *Open daily except Jan. 1 and Dec. 25. Small charge.*

Clarksville
PRESTWOULD HOUSE *2 mi. N.* Scenic wallpaper covers many walls of the 1795 plantation house. *Open Sun., Wed. June-Aug. Small charge.*

Colonial Heights
VIOLET BANK MUSEUM *Virginia Ave.* General Lee's 1864 summer headquarters is now a Civil War museum. *Open daily May-Sept.*

Covington
HUMPBACK BRIDGE *3 mi. W. off Rte. 60* This 1835 arched covered bridge is the only one of its kind in the U.S.

Critz
REYNOLDS HOMESTEAD Tobacco magnate R. J. Reynolds lived in this brick house as a boy. *Open Sat., Sun. June-Oct. Adults and children over 12 small charge.*

Culpepper
LITTLE FORK EPISCOPAL CHURCH *Rtes. 624 and 726* One of the few surviving Colonial churches in the area retains much of its original interior woodwork.

Danville
DANVILLE PUBLIC LIBRARY *975 Main St.* The former home of Major William T. Sutherlin is a fine example of Italianate architecture. *Open Mon.-Sat.*

Fairfax
FAIRFAX COUNTY COURTHOUSE *4000 Chain Bridge Rd.* The original wills of George and Martha Washington are displayed here.

Falls Church
FALLS CHURCH *115 E. Fairfax St.* The oldest church in northern Virginia has a baptismal font dating from Colonial days. *Open daily.*

Farmville
HILLSMAN HOUSE *Sayler's Creek Battlefield Historical State Park* The house served as a hospital during the last major battle of the Civil War. *Open daily late May-early Sept.*

Fort Eustis
MATTHEW JONES HOUSE *MacAuliffe Ave. and James River Rd.* This is one of the few surviving medieval-style houses in Virginia.
U.S. ARMY TRANSPORTATION MUSEUM Here are extensive collections of aircraft and vehicles. *Open daily.*

Fredericksburg
HUGH MERCER APOTHECARY SHOP *1020 Caroline St.* Eighteenth-century medical and pharmaceutical equipment are displayed here. *Open daily. Small charge.*
ST. GEORGE'S CHURCH *Princess Anne and George Sts.* This 1849 church stands where the original 1732 one once stood. *Open daily.*

Front Royal
WARREN RIFLES CONFEDERATE MUSEUM *95 Chester St.* Civil War relics are displayed here. *Open daily May-Oct. Adults small charge.*

Gloucester
WARE EPISCOPAL CHURCH *Rte. 14* This rectangular Colonial church was probably built in 1690.

Hague
YEOCOMICO CHURCH *Rte. 606* The 1706 church has both medieval and Georgian architectural elements.

Hampton
FORT WOOL *Offshore in Hampton Roads* Robert E. Lee supervised part of the construction of this coastal fortification, begun in 1819. It can be seen from the Hampton Roads Bridge-Tunnel.
ST. JOHN'S CHURCH *100 W. Queen St.* The 1728 church still serves a parish founded in 1610. *Open daily.*

Hanover
HANOVER COURT HOUSE *Rte. 301* Patrick Henry tried the Parson's Cause case here in 1763.

Hot Springs
WARWICK HOUSE *Hidden Valley* The house was built in 1858 for a plantation farmer.

Irvington
CHRIST CHURCH *Rte. 3* One of the finest and best-preserved Colonial churches in the state was built in 1732 by Robert "King" Carter. *Open daily except Dec. 25.*

King William
ELSING GREEN This unique Queen Anne-style house was built about 1720 in the shape of a U.

Lancaster
EPPING FOREST *Rte. 3* George Washington's mother, Mary Ball, was born here. Four original outbuildings remain. *Open daily Apr.-Nov. Adults $1.50, children small charge.*

Lexington
TIMBER RIDGE PRESBYTERIAN CHURCH *Rte. 11* The original 1756 sanctuary still is used. *Open Sun.*

Lorton
POHICK CHURCH *9301 Richmond Hwy.* George Washington was a vestryman for 27 years in this church, built in 1774. *Open daily.*

Luray
AVENTINE HALL *143 S. Court St.* This 1852 Greek Revival mansion has a two-story portico. *Open daily mid-June-Oct. Adults $1.50, children small charge.*
CAR AND CARRIAGE CARAVAN *Luray Caverns* Here are vehicles dating from 1625. *Open daily. Adults $4.00, children $2.00, including caverns.*
LURAY SINGING TOWER *Rte. 211* The carillon was made in England in 1937. *Recitals Sun., Tues., Thurs., Sat. mid-Mar.-mid-Nov.*

Lynchburg
MILLER-CLAYTOR HOUSE *Riverside Park* This 1791 house typifies the average life and domestic architecture of its time.
OLD COURT HOUSE *Court St.* Boars' heads project from the frieze of this classic Greek Revival structure, built in 1855.

Madison
HEBRON LUTHERAN CHURCH The oldest Lutheran church in continuous use in America dates from 1740. *Open daily.*

Manassas
MANASSAS NATIONAL BATTLEFIELD PARK *Rtes. 29 and 211* The Visitor Center has maps and relics of the two bloody Civil War battles fought here. *Open daily except Dec. 25.*

Meadows of Dan
MABRY MILL *Blue Ridge Pkwy., milepost 176.1* Pioneer industries are centered around the water-powered gristmill. *Mill open daily May-Oct., grounds open daily.*

Newport News
PENINSULA NATURE AND SCIENCE CENTER *524 J. Clyde Morris Blvd.* A large aquarium and live animals are among the exhibits. *Open daily except holidays. Small charge.*
WAR MEMORIAL MUSEUM OF VIRGINIA *9285 Warwick Blvd.* Relics of all American wars are displayed. *Open daily except Dec. 25.*

Norfolk
ST. PAUL'S EPISCOPAL CHURCH *201 St. Paul's Blvd.* A British cannonball is still embedded in a wall of this 1739 church. *Open Tues.-Sun.*

U.S. CUSTOMHOUSE *101 E. Main St.* The American architect Ammi B. Young designed this classic structure built in 1858. *Open daily.*

Petersburg

OLD BLANDFORD CHURCH *S. Crater Rd.* The church's 15 Tiffany windows are memorials donated by the Confederate States. *Open daily.*

Portsmouth

BALL HOUSE *417 Middle St.* The mid-1700s two-story house appears to be only a story-and-a-half and is known as a tax dodger.

EMANUEL AFRICAN METHODIST EPISCOPAL CHURCH *637 North St.* A congregation of slaves built this church in 1857. *Open daily.*

HILL HOUSE *221 North St.* One family occupied the English basement-type house for over 150 years. *Open Tues.-Sun. Small charge.*

LIGHTSHIP MUSEUM *London St.* A former Coast Guard lightship is now a museum with realistic fittings and equipment. *Open Tues.-Sun.*

PORTSMOUTH NAVAL SHIPYARD MUSEUM *2 High St.* Exhibits of ship models and other mementos trace U.S. naval history. *Open Tues.-Sun.*

Quantico

U.S. MARINE CORPS MUSEUM *Marine Corps Base* Exhibits trace the history of the Marine Corps from 1775 to the present. *Open daily.*

Richmond

CARILLON *William Byrd Park Blvd. and Idlewood Ave.* The carillon is a memorial to Virginia's World War I dead. *Open Mon.-Fri.*

CITY HALL *900 E. Broad St.* This modern white marble building is the tallest in the state. *Open Mon.-Fri.*

COURTS BUILDING *11th and Broad Sts.* The ornate, late 19th-century building was designed by Elijah E. Myers. *Open daily.*

EGYPTIAN BUILDING *312 N. College St.* The magnificent Egyptian-style building was completed in 1845. *Open Mon.-Fri.*

MALVERN HILL FARM *S.E. of intersection of Rtes. 5 and 156* Here are the ruins of one of Virginia's few cruciform houses. *Open daily.*

MONUMENTAL CHURCH OF RICHMOND *1226 E. Broad St.* The church was built as a memorial to 72 people who perished in a fire on this site in 1811. *Open Mon.-Fri.*

RICHMOND NATIONAL BATTLEFIELD PARK VISITOR CENTER *3215 E. Broad St.* An audio-visual program and exhibits tell the story of the Civil War battles around Richmond. *Open daily except Jan. 1 and Dec. 25.*

ST. JOHN'S EPISCOPAL CHURCH *E. Broad and 24th Sts.* Patrick Henry gave his "Liberty or Death" speech here in 1775. *Open daily Feb.-Nov.*

ST. PAUL'S EPISCOPAL CHURCH *815 E. Grace St.* Unusually lovely ornamentation, including a Last Supper of Tiffany tiles, marks this Greek Revival church. *Open daily.*

ST. PETER'S CATHOLIC CHURCH *808 E. Grace St.* The oldest (1834) Roman Catholic church in the city is Roman in style. *Open daily.*

VIRGINIA STATE LIBRARY *12th and Capitol Sts.* Maps, documents and printed matter relating to the state are exhibited here. *Open Mon.-Sat. except holidays.*

VIRGINIA WAR MEMORIAL *621 S. Belvidere St.* The shrine is dedicated to Virginia's World War II and Korean War dead. *Open daily.*

Smithfield

HISTORIC ST. LUKE'S CHURCH *Rte. 10* The 1632 church was built in the Gothic style of English parish churches. *Open daily Feb.-Dec.*

OLD ISLE OF WIGHT COUNTY COURT HOUSE *Main and Mason Sts.* This 1750 courthouse has a T-shaped plan and a rotunda courtroom.

Spring Grove

BRANDON PLANTATION *Rte. 611* Beautiful gardens bloom around this 18th-century manor house designed by Thomas Jefferson. *Small charge.*

Staunton

TRINITY EPISCOPAL CHURCH *214 W. Beverley St.* The church is built on the site of a church where the Virginia General Assembly met during the Revolution. *Open daily.*

Surry

ROLFE-WARREN HOUSE *Rte. 31* One of the state's oldest (1652) houses stands on Smith's Fort Plantation, which originally belonged to John Rolfe and Pocahontas. *Open daily Apr.-Oct. Small charge.*

Talleysville

ST. PETER'S EPISCOPAL CHURCH *Rte. 609* Martha and George Washington were married here Jan. 6, 1759. *Open Sun.*

Virginia Beach

CAPE HENRY LIGHTHOUSE *Atlantic Ave. and Rte. 60* The first Federal lighthouse, whose lamps were lighted in 1792, stands near a cross marking the landing place of the Jamestown settlers. *Open daily.*

WISHART-BOUSH HOUSE *E., off Absalom Rd.* Here is one of the oldest brick houses in the U.S.

West Point

CHELSEA PLANTATION *6 mi. N.E.* Augustine Moore built this house in 1709. *Open Mon.-Fri. Adults $1.50, children small charge.*

White Marsh

ABINGDON EPISCOPAL CHURCH *4 mi. S. of intersection of Rtes. 17 and 614* The historic 1755 church still uses Communion silver made in the early 18th century. *Open daily.*

Winchester

ABRAM'S DELIGHT *Rouss Spring Dr.* This 1754 house and an earlier log cabin have authentic furnishings. *Open daily May-Oct. Small charge.*

GEORGE WASHINGTON'S OFFICE *Cork and Braddock Sts.* Washington worked here as a surveyor. *Open daily May-Oct. Small charge.*

STONEWALL JACKSON HEADQUARTERS *415 N. Braddock St.* Jackson memorabilia are displayed in his Shenandoah Valley headquarters. *Open daily. Small charge.*

Yorktown

MOORE HOUSE The terms of Cornwallis's surrender were drafted here in 1781. *Open daily mid-June-early Sept. Small charge.*

SWAN TAVERN *Main and Ballard Sts.* The tavern and stable are authentic replicas of the original 1722 tavern group. *Open Mon.-Sat.*

Washington, D.C.

See District of Columbia.

West Virginia

Barrackville

BUFFALO CREEK COVERED BRIDGE *Pike St.* This wide-arched bridge was built in 1852.

Cass

CASS SCENIC RAILROAD Rides on old logging trains are offered. *Open daily late May-early Sept., Sat., Sun. early Sept.-Oct. Adults $2.00, $4.00, children $1.00, $2.00.*

Charles Town

CLAYMONT COURT *Huyett Rd.* A grandnephew of George Washington rebuilt his original 1820 mansion after it burned down in 1838.

HAREWOOD *3 mi. W. on Rte. 51* Beautiful paneling decorates the drawing room of the 1770 stone house, built by Washington's brother.

JEFFERSON COUNTY COURT HOUSE *George and Washington Sts.* In 1859 John Brown was tried for treason in this red brick Georgian Colonial building. *Open Mon.-Sat.*

JEFFERSON COUNTY MUSEUM *200 E. Washington St.* Artifacts relating to the county, John Brown and the Washington family are displayed. *Open Tues.-Sat. Apr.-Oct.*

Fort Ashby

FORT ASHBY *Rte. 46* This Indian fort was built in 1755 under the orders of Colonel George Washington. *Open daily June-Aug.*

Grafton

INTERNATIONAL MOTHER'S DAY SHRINE *Main St.* Mother's Day was first officially observed in Andrews Methodist Church on May 10, 1908. *Open daily mid-Apr.-mid-Nov.*

Hillsboro

LOCUST CREEK COVERED BRIDGE *Locust Creek Rd.* The only surviving covered bridge in the county was built in the early 1890s.

Lewisburg

GREENBRIER COUNTY COURTHOUSE *Court St.* Bricks made on the premises were used for the construction of this building in 1837. *Open Mon.-Fri.*

GREENBRIER COUNTY LIBRARY AND MUSEUM *Rte. 60* Items of local history are shown. *Open Tues.-Sat.*

OLD STONE PRESBYTERIAN CHURCH *200 Church St.* The original slave balcony and hand-hewn woodwork remain in the 1796 church. *Open daily.*

Lost Creek

WATTERS SMITH MEMORIAL STATE PARK *Off Rte. 19* A pioneer farm of the late 1700s and family heirlooms are included here. *Open daily late May-early Sept.*

Marlinton

POCAHONTAS COUNTY HISTORICAL MUSEUM *Rte. 219* Historical items of the county are displayed. *Open daily mid-June-early Sept. Small charge.*

Mathias

LEE CABIN *Lost River State Park* Household items are displayed in the summer home of "Lighthouse Harry" Lee. *Open daily late Apr.-Oct.*

Morgantown

ARCHEOLOGY MUSEUM *White Hall, Willey St.* Samples of artifacts of the state's pre-historic cultures are displayed. *Open Mon.-Fri.*

Philippi

PHILIPPI COVERED BRIDGE *Rte. 250* Lemuel Chenoweth designed this twin-barreled bridge in 1852.

Romney

MYTINGER HOUSE *Main St.* The oldest building in Romney is believed to date from about 1770. *Open daily.*

Shepherdstown

MCMURRAN HALL *Shepherd College* Now housing the music department, it was once the Jefferson County Courthouse (1865-71). *Open Mon.-Fri. during college sessions.*

ST. PETER'S LUTHERAN CHURCH *King and High Sts.* The tower door of this 1906 church bears the escutcheon from the original 1795 church. *Open daily.*

THOMAS SHEPHERD'S GRIST MILL AND MILL HOUSE *High St.* Near the restored 18th-century home is the world's largest water wheel.

Weston

JACKSON'S MILL MUSEUM *Off Rte. 19* Historical artifacts are displayed in a mill built on the boyhood homestead of "Stonewall" Jackson. *Open daily June-Sept.*

White Sulphur Springs

PRESIDENTS' COTTAGE MUSEUM *Greenbrier* Several 19th-century Presidents made this their summer White House. *Open daily Apr.-mid-Nov.*

REGION 4 [map page 244]

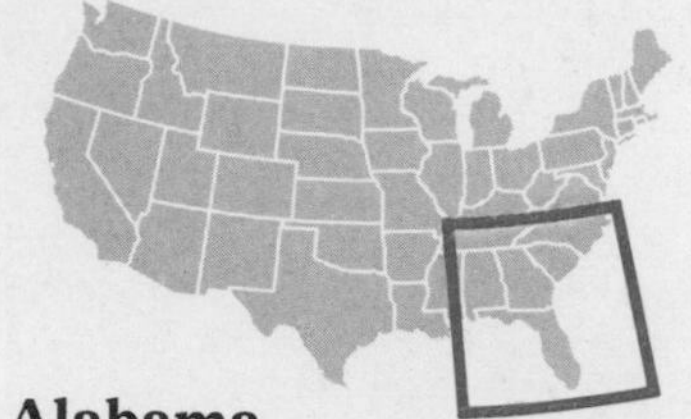

Alabama

Anniston

REGAR MUSEUM OF NATURAL HISTORY *1411 Gurnee Ave.* Exhibits here feature the first dioramas of birds ever displayed in the U.S. *Open Tues.-Sun. except holidays.*

Dauphin Island

FORT GAINES *Rte. 163* Relics are displayed inside this mid-19th-century fort. *Open daily. Small charge.*

Eufaula

FENDALL HALL *917 W. Barbour St.* The fine 1854 mansion harbored wounded soldiers during the Civil War.

TAVERN *Front St.* The 1836 frame house has served as a hospital and a church. *Open Mon.-Sat.*

Florence

KARSNER-KENNEDY HOUSE *303 N. Pine St.* This small 1828 town house has been faithfully restored. *Open Mon.-Fri.*

ROSENBAUM RESIDENCE *117 Riverview Dr.* The house was designed by Frank Lloyd Wright.

Mobile

BRAGG-MITCHELL HOUSE *1906 Springhill Ave.* The lovely antebellum house was once the home of Confederate General Braxton Bragg.

CARLEN HOUSE *High School Dr.* Heirlooms of Mobile families furnish the home. *Open Tues.-Sun.*

CATHEDRAL OF THE IMMACULATE CONCEPTION *Dauphin and Claiborne Sts.* Symmetrical towers flank the pillared facade. *Open daily.*

DE TONTI SQUARE HISTORIC DISTRICT A 12-block area includes 40 restored 19th-century buildings.

LONG GARDENS *250 Tuthill Lane* Ten acres of gardens are filled with azaleas and camellias. *Open daily mid-Feb.-mid-Apr. Adults $1.25.*

MOBILE CITY HALL *111 S. Royal St.* This 1858 building represents a rare fusion of West Indian and Palladian architectural styles. *Open Mon.-Fri. except holidays.*

SOLDIERS' AND SAILORS' MEMORIAL *Memorial Park* The classical-style monument honors American war casualties.

Montgomery

DEXTER AVENUE BAPTIST CHURCH *454 Dexter Ave.* The church was a center for civil rights activity in the 1950s when Martin Luther King, Jr., was pastor. *Open daily.*

EXECUTIVE (GOVERNOR'S) MANSION *1142 S. Perry St.* This 1907 Greek Revival mansion has been used by Alabama's governors since 1950. *Open daily.*

GRIEL MANSION *305 S. Lawrence St.* The Alabama Historical Comission is housed in this 1854 Greek Revival mansion. *Open Mon.-Fri.*

MONTGOMERY MUSEUM OF FINE ARTS *440 S. McDonough St.* Nineteenth- and 20th-century American art can be seen here. *Open Tues.-Sun. except holidays.*

ST. JOHN'S EPISCOPAL CHURCH *113 Madison Ave.* The pew used by Jefferson Davis remains in this 1855 Gothic-style church. *Open daily.*

WEBBER COMPANY *39 N. Perry St.* This department store was a theater during the Civil War. *Open Mon.-Sat.*

Tuscaloosa

CAPITOL SQUARE Here are an 1820 house and an 1827 stagecoach inn. *Inn open Tues.-Sun. Small charge.*

FRIEDMAN HOME *1010 Greensboro Ave.* A Negro slave painted the delicate frescos inside this 1835 Greek Revival house. *Open Sun.*

FRIEDMAN MEMORIAL LIBRARY *1305 Greensboro Ave.* The 1860-2 Italian villa-style house was built as a private residence. *Open Mon.-Sat.*

University

WOODS HALL *University of Alabama* Once quarters for cadets of the original military school, this Gothic-style edifice now houses classrooms.

Florida

Apalachicola

DR. JOHN GORRIE HISTORICAL MUSEUM *Sixth St.* Exhibits here honor the inventor of the first ice-making machine. *Open daily. Small charge.*

TRINITY CHURCH *Sixth St.* The 1838 Episcopal church is said to be the oldest prefabricated building in Florida. *Open daily.*

Bradenton

SOUTH FLORIDA MUSEUM AND BISHOP PLANETARIUM *201 10th St. W.* Exhibits portray Florida's history; the planetarium features daily shows. *Open Tues.-Sun. Adults $1.50, children small charge.*

Clearwater

PINELLAS COUNTY COURTHOUSE *315 Haven St.* The building houses a historical museum devoted to pioneer articles. *Open Mon.-Fri.*

Coral Gables

CORAL GABLES CITY HALL *405 Biltmore Way* This building incorporates Spanish, Italian and Moorish elements. *Open Mon.-Fri.*

LOWE ART MUSEUM *1301 Miller Dr., University of Miami* Exhibitions stress American art, but also include Indian, Oriental and Renaissance works. *Open daily.*

Key: Historic Place · Historic House · Old Mill or Works · Museum or Collection · Significant Buildir

DeBary

DEBARY HALL *210 Sunrise Blvd.* This 1871 mansion serves as an art gallery, museum and cultural center. *Open Tues.-Sun.*

DeLand

GILLESPIE MUSEUM OF MINERALS *Stetson University* Fluorescent minerals are among the items featured here. *Open Mon.-Fri. during academic year.*

Ellenton

GAMBLE MANSION STATE MUSEUM Civil War relics are displayed in this 1840s plantation house. *Open daily. Small charge.*

MADIRA BICKEL MOUND STATE ARCHAEOLOGICAL SITE *Terra Ceia Island* The Indian ceremonial mound is 170 feet long. *Open daily.*

Fort Lauderdale

FORT LAUDERDALE MUSEUM OF THE ARTS *426 Las Olas Blvd.* There is an excellent collection of primitive art here. *Open Tues.-Sun. Sept.-June except holidays.*

Gainesville

UNIVERSITY GALLERY *Rte. 441, University of Florida* Monthly exhibits here range from East Indian to faculty works. *Open Sun.-Fri. Sept.-July except holidays.*

Hawthorne

MARJORIE KINNAN RAWLINGS HOME *Rte. 325* The Pulitzer Prize-winning author of *The Yearling* lived in this rambling farmhouse. *Open Tues.-Sun. Adults small charge.*

Homosassa

HOMOSASSA DOLL MUSEUM *Rte. 490* More than 1000 dolls are exhibited, most in period room settings. *Open daily.*

Jacksonville

JACKSONVILLE ART MUSEUM *4160 Boulevard Center Dr.* Oriental and modern art is displayed. *Open daily Sept.-July except holidays.*

JACKSONVILLE CHILDREN'S MUSEUM *1025 Gulf Life Dr.* Here are environmental and historical displays for children. *Open Tues.-Sun. Oct.-Aug. except holidays.*

Key West

LIGHTHOUSE MILITARY MUSEUM *Whitehead St. and Truman Ave.* A former lighthouse keeper's dwelling contains military relics. *Open daily except Dec. 25. Small charge.*

Madison

WARDLAW-SMITH HOUSE *103 N. Washington St.* The classic trim and columned porches were added in 1900 to this antebellum mansion.

Miami

HISTORICAL MUSEUM OF SOUTHERN FLORIDA *3280 S. Miami Ave., Bldg. B* Here are artifacts covering 25 centuries of mankind's activities in southern Florida. *Open daily.*

MIAMI MUSEUM OF MODERN ART *381 N.E. 20th St.* Exhibits include contemporary, primitive and Oriental art. *Open Tues.-Sat. Sept.-June. Adults $1.25, students small charge.*

MUSEUM OF SCIENCE *3280 S. Miami Ave.* Exhibits of Florida natural history, a coral reef and the Everglades as well as a major planetarium are here. *Open daily.*

ST. MARY'S CATHEDRAL *7506 N.W. Second Ave.* Mosaic domes top this mission-style cathedral. *Open daily.*

ST. RAPHAEL CHAPEL *St. John Vianney Seminary 2900 S.W. 87th St.* This cruciform chapel was built in 1966. *Open daily.*

Monticello

WIRICK-SIMMONS HOUSE *Jefferson and Pearl Sts.* The Greek Revival mansion is the home of the local historical society.

Orlando

JOHN YOUNG MUSEUM AND PLANETARIUM *810 E. Rollins Ave.* Natural history, space and other science exhibits are shown. *Open daily. Small charge for planetarium.*

Ormond Beach

ORMOND WAR MEMORIAL ART GALLERY AND GARDEN *78 E. Granada Ave.* Lush gardens surround this art gallery. *Open daily.*

Pensacola

DOROTHY WALTON HOUSE *221 E. Zarragossa St.* The wife of a signer of the Declaration of Independence once lived here. *Open daily mid-May-mid-Oct. Small charge.*

DORR HOUSE *311 S. Adams St.* The 1871 house reflects the city's lumber boom era. *Open Tues.-Sun.*

FORT SAN CARLOS DE BARRANCAS *U.S. Naval Air Station* Visitors may walk around and on top of the 1850 brick fort.

PENSACOLA HISTORICAL MUSEUM *405 S. Adams St.* Local memorabilia are housed in an 1832 church. *Open Tues.-Sun. except holidays.*

T. T. WENTWORTH, JR., MUSEUM *Palafox Hwy.* The collection features many items of local and regional significance. *Open Sat., Sun.*

Plantation Key

SAN PEDRO CHURCH The church was built in 1954 in the Spanish style. *Open daily.*

St. Augustine

BENET STORE *62 St. George St.* This mid-19th-century general store was reconstructed on the site of the original structure. *Open daily.*

CASA DEL HIDALGO *Hypolita and St. George Sts.* This replica of a 16th-century Spanish nobleman's home is authentically furnished. *Open Tues.-Sat.*

DR. PECK HOUSE *143 St. George St.* The original wooden building was replaced by a stone one about 1750. *Open Mon.-Sat. Small charge.*

FORT MATANZAS NATIONAL MONUMENT *14 mi. S. off Rte. A1A* The Spanish built this bleak fort in 1742. *Open daily except Dec. 25.*

GALLEGOS HOUSE *21 St. George St.* This reconstructed 1720 home is an example of everyday life in the Spanish period. *Open daily.*

GOMEZ HOUSE *27 St. George St.* This simple wooden house is a replica of a typical early Spanish Colonial home. *Open daily.*

SANCHEZ HOUSE *105 St. George St.* The 1809 home has been faithfully restored. *Open Fri.-Wed.*

SPANISH MILITARY HOSPITAL *Aviles St.* The rebuilt hospital contains an apothecary, doctor's office and wards. *Open daily.*

STATE ARSENAL *82 Marine St.* This former barracks has housed English, Spanish and U.S. troops. *Open Mon.-Fri.*

WILLIAM WELLS PRINT SHOP *27 Cuna St.* Early printing and binding arts are demonstrated in a facsimile of the 1783 printshop. *Open daily.*

WILLIAM SIMS SILVERSMITH SHOP *12 Charlotte St.* This is a replica of a 1780s home-shop. *Open daily.*

St. Leo

ST. LEO ABBEY The Abbey Church, Lombardic-Romanesque in design, was built by the Benedictine Brothers and the townspeople between 1937 and 1945. *Open daily.*

St. Marks

SAN MARCOS DE APALACHE MUSEUM *Canal St.* Indian and Spanish artifacts are displayed here. *Open daily. Small charge.*

Stuart

HOUSE OF REFUGE MUSEUM *Hutchinson Island* The last such refuge for shipwrecked sailors is now a marine museum. *Open Tues.-Sun. Small charge.*

Tallahassee

FLORIDA STATE CAPITOL *Monroe St. and Apalachee Pkwy.* The original 1845 capitol is now the building's central portion. *Open Mon.-Fri.*

Tampa

HENRY B. PLANT MUSEUM *Plant Park* Oriental, European and American period furnishings and objets d'art are housed in a former hotel. *Open Tues.-Sat.*

Tarpon Springs

ST. NICHOLAS GREEK ORTHODOX CHURCH *36 Pinellas St.* The altar in this Byzantine-style church is of Greek marble. *Open daily.*

West Palm Beach

SCIENCE MUSEUM AND PLANETARIUM OF PALM BEACH COUNTY *1141 W. Lakewood Rd.* Among the exhibits is a complete juvenile mastodon skeleton. *Open Tues.-Sun.*

White Springs

STEPHEN FOSTER MEMORIAL *Rte. 41* Mementos of the noted composer are displayed. *Open daily. Adults $1.50, children small charge.*

Georgia

Albany

BANKS HALEY GALLERY *813 N. Slappey Blvd.* Here are changing exhibitions of the work of local artists. *Open daily.*

Atlanta

ATLANTA ZOOLOGICAL PARK *518 Atlanta Ave.* The largest family group of orangutans in the U.S. lives here. *Open daily. Small charge.*

CATHEDRAL OF CHRIST THE KING *2699 Peachtree Rd., N.E.* This Gothic-style cathedral was completed in 1937. *Open daily.*

CHURCH OF ST. JUDE THE APOSTLE *7171 Glenridge Dr., N.E.* The 1966 church is shaped like a blunted arrowhead. *Open daily.*

EBENEZER BAPTIST CHURCH *413 Auburn Ave., N.E.* The grave of Dr. Martin Luther King is located on the grounds of the church where he once preached. *Grounds open daily.*

MARGARET MITCHELL ROOM *Atlanta Public Library, 126 Carnegie Way, N.W.* Mementos of the author of *Gone With the Wind* are on display. *Open daily.*

"PHOENIX" *Hunter and Spring Sts.* The bronze statue by Gamba Quirino portrays a graceful female figure holding high the city's official symbol, the phoenix.

"RENAISSANCE OF THE CITY" *230 Peachtree St.* The 21-ton, 33-foot-high structure is thought to be the world's largest fiber glass sculpture.

TULLIE-SMITH HOUSE RESTORATION *3099 Andrews Dr., N.W.* Here is one of the last pre-Civil War houses in the area. *Open Tues.-Sun. except holidays. Small charge.*

Augusta

BELLEVUE HALL *Augusta College* The oldest (1805) building on campus is the former home of Freeman Walker. *Open Mon.-Fri.*

MEADOW GARDEN *1320 Nelson St.* The home of George Walton is filled with Colonial treasures. *Open Tues., Thurs., Sat. Small charge.*

MONTROSE *2249 Walton Way* This fine example of Greek Revival architecture was built in 1849.

Carrollton

BONNER HOUSE *West Georgia College* This farmhouse, with its Greek Revival facade, is a link between the state's frontier and antebellum homes. *Open Mon.-Fri.*

Columbus

COLUMBUS MUSEUM OF ARTS AND CRAFTS *1251 Wynnton Rd.* Fine and decorative arts and American Indian collections are featured here. *Open Tues.-Sun. except holidays.*

FIRST NATIONAL BANK BUILDING *1048 Broadway* This early prefabricated building has walls made of cast-iron sections fashioned in the Greek Revival style. *Open daily.*

MUSEUM OF CONFEDERATE NAVAL HISTORY *Fourth St. and Rte. 27* Sections of two Confederate ships and other naval relics are preserved here. *Open Tues.-Sun. except Thanksgiving Day and Dec. 25.*

Cordele

WORLD WAR I AND II MUSEUM *Georgia Veterans Memorial State Park* Here are relics of both wars. *Open Tues.-Sun. Small charge.*

Dahlonega

PRICE MEMORIAL HALL *North Georgia College, College Ave.* The building stands on the foundation of the original U.S. Branch Mint. *Open Mon.-Fri.*

Darien

FORT KING GEORGE MUSEUM *1 mi. E. of Rte. 17* Displays here depict the area's occupation by Indians, the Spanish and the English. *Open Tues.-Sun.*

Eatonton

ROCK EAGLE EFFIGY MOUND *6 mi. N. on Rte. 441* The huge bird-shaped rock mound was built by prehistoric Indians. *Open daily.*

UNCLE REMUS MUSEUM *Turner Park* The setting for Joel Chandler Harris's stories is reconstructed here near his birthplace. *Open Wed.-Mon. Small charge.*

Jefferson

CRAWFORD W. LONG MEDICAL MUSEUM *On the Square* Displays here trace the development of anesthesia. *Open Tues.-Sun. except holidays.*

Louisville

OLD MARKET HOUSE *Broad St.* The original 1758 public market is still intact. *Open daily.*

Macon

BIRTHPLACE OF SIDNEY LANIER *935 High St.* The cottage where the South's beloved poet was born is maintained as a public shrine.

NAPIER-SMALL HOUSE *156 Rogers Ave.* This outstanding example of Greek Revival architecture was completed in 1846.

OLD CANNONBALL HOUSE *856 Mulberry St.* This 1853 house contains antebellum furnishings. *Open Tues.-Sun. Small charge.*

Marietta

JOHN KNOX PRESBYTERIAN CHURCH *2041 Powers Ferry Rd., S.E.* This modern church is built of native materials. *Open Sun.*

KENNESAW MOUNTAIN NATIONAL BATTLEFIELD PARK *2 mi. N. off Rte. 41* Here are a visitor center and preserved earthworks of the Civil War battle. *Open daily except Dec. 25.*

Midway

MIDWAY CHURCH *Rtes. 17 and 38* This well-preserved church was built of cypress in 1792.

MIDWAY MUSEUM *Rte. 17* A replica of a raised cottage-style house contains historical exhibits of the Midway community. *Open Tues.-Sun. except Thanksgiving Day and Dec. 25.*

Milledgeville

ST. STEPHEN'S EPISCOPAL CHURCH *220 S. Wayne St.* The original pews remain in this Gothic-style church, completed in 1843. *Open daily.*

Oxford

SENEY HALL *Oxford College of Emory University* The bell in the tower of this 1880s building was a gift of Queen Victoria. *Open Mon.-Sat.*

Richmond Hill

FORT MCALLISTER *10 mi. E. of Rte. 17* Here is an outstanding example of Confederate earthwork fortifications. *Open Tues.-Sun.*

Savannah

CITY HALL *Bull and W. Bay Sts.* A model of the *Savannah,* the first steam-propelled ship to cross an ocean, is displayed in this 1905 building. *Open Mon.-Fri.*

FORT JACKSON MARITIME MUSEUM *Off President St. Ext.* The 1840s masonry fort contains exhibits of the state's maritime history. *Open daily.*

HODGSON HALL *501 Whitaker St.* Historical material is housed in the headquarters of the Georgia Historical Society. *Open Mon.-Sat.*

OLDE PINK HOUSE *23 Abercorn St.* Originally a Georgia patriot's home, this 1771 mansion is now a restaurant and tavern. *Open Mon.-Sat.*

ST. JOHN'S CHURCH *1 W. Macon St.* Here is an 1852 Gothic-style church and its parish house, the Green-Meldrim House. *Church open Sun., house open Tues.-Thurs.*

SHIPS OF THE SEA MUSEUM *503 E. River St.* A large collection of ship models and marine artifacts is housed in an 1853 cotton warehouse. *Open daily. Small charge.*

TRUSTEES GARDEN VILLAGE *Bishop's Ct.* A number of 19th-century homes have been restored on the site of what is said to be the country's first experimental garden.

Mississippi

Biloxi

BILOXI LIGHTHOUSE *Fred Haise Blvd.* Electricity now operates this 1848 mariners' guide.

CHURCH OF THE REDEEMER *E. Beach, Bellman and Water Sts.* Jefferson Davis was a member and vestryman of this church. *Open Wed., Fri.-Sun.*

Columbus

GALLERY MUSEUM *Fine Arts Bldg., Mississippi State College for Women* Contemporary American paintings are shown here. *Open Sun.-Fri.*

Meridian

SCOTTISH RITE TEMPLE *11th St. and 23rd Ave.* The 1915 building is

Key: Historic Place · Historic House · Old Mill or Works · Museum or Collection · Significant Buildir

a replica of an Egyptian temple. *Open Mon.-Sat.*

Ship Island

FORT MASSACHUSETTS *12 mi. offshore from Gulfport and Biloxi* This fort was occupied alternately by Confederate and Union forces. *Open daily.*

North Carolina

Asheville

COLBURN MINERAL MUSEUM *170 Coxe Ave.* Here are displays of rocks, minerals and gems indigenous to the state. *Open Mon.-Fri.*

Bath

GLEBE HOUSE *Rte. 264* The restored and furnished rectory was built in 1762 by Reverend Alexander Stewart. *Open daily. Small charge.*

ST. THOMAS EPISCOPAL CHURCH *Craven St.* This is the oldest (1734) church in the state. *Open daily.*

Beaufort

ALPHONSO WHALING MUSEUM *Polock and Front Sts.* Relics of a nearby whaling fishery are displayed in a ship, the *Alphonso. Open daily June-early Sept. Small charge.*

HAMPTON MARINE MUSEUM *120 Turner St.* Here are collections of mounted fish and seashells of the area. *Open Tues.-Sun.*

JOSEPH BELL HOUSE *127 Turner St.* West Indian styling highlights the 1767 house. *Open Tues.-Sun. Small charge.*

OLD JAIL *Courthouse Sq.* The 1836 jail, used for 120 years, now houses items of local history. *Open Tues.-Sun. June-Aug. Small charge.*

Belhaven

BELHAVEN MEMORIAL MUSEUM *City Hall, Rte. 264* A collection of historic and scientific artifacts is displayed. *Open daily except Dec. 25.*

Belmont

BELMONT ABBEY CATHEDRAL *Belmont Abbey College* The cathedral's baptismal font was once used as a slave auction block. *Open daily.*

Burlington

ALAMANCE BATTLEGROUND STATE HISTORIC SITE *Off Rte. 85* A visitor center and the Allen House, a 1782 log cabin, are here. *Open Tues.-Sun.*

Carolina Beach

BLOCKADE RUNNER MUSEUM *N. on Rte. 421* The story of Civil War blockade running is told through audio-visual displays. *Open daily. Adults $1.50, children small charge.*

Carthage

HOUSE IN THE HORSESHOE *Off Rte. 15-501* This 1772 house was built by Whig leader Phillip Alston. *Open Tues.-Sun.*

Charlotte

CHARLOTTE NATURE MUSEUM *1658 Sterling Rd.* Here are live animal and ecology exhibits, nature films and a planetarium. *Open daily.*

HEZEKIAH ALEXANDER HOUSE *Shamrock Dr.* The oldest (1774) house in the county was built by a framer of the state's first constitution. *Open Tues.-Sun. Small charge.*

Claremont

BUNKER HILL COVERED BRIDGE *2 mi. E. near Rte. 64-70* This Haupt truss-type bridge was built in 1895.

Durham

BENNETT PLACE *Hillsboro Rd.* Here Joseph E. Johnston surrendered to William T. Sherman on Apr. 26, 1865, ending the Civil War in the Carolinas, Georgia and Florida. *Open Tues.-Sun.*

Fletcher

CALVARY EPISCOPAL CHURCH *Rte. 25* In the churchyard markers commemorate Southern poets, musicians and composers. *Open daily.*

Fremont

AYCOCK BIRTHPLACE *1 mi. S. off Rte. 117* Here is the restored birthplace of Governor Charles B. Aycock, crusader for statewide public education. *Open Tues.-Sun.*

Gastonia

SCHIELE MUSEUM OF NATURAL HISTORY *1500 E. Garrison Blvd.* Indian artifacts, mounted animals and rocks and minerals are shown. *Open Tues.-Sun.*

Gillespie Gap

MINERALS MUSEUM OF NORTH CAROLINA *Blue Ridge Pkwy., milepost 331* Local minerals, gemstones and precious metals are on display. *Open daily early May-late Oct.*

Greensboro

MASONIC MUSEUM *426 W. Market St.* An extensive collection of Masonic relics is featured.

NATURAL SCIENCE CENTER AND ZOO *4301 Lawndale Dr.* The nature museum and zoo is in an 83-acre wildlife sanctuary. *Open daily.*

TEMPLE EMANUEL *713 N. Greene St.* This 1925 temple was designed by Hobart B. Upjohn in the American Colonial tradition. *Open daily.*

High Point

JOHN HALEY HOUSE *1805 E. Lexington Ave.* This is a restored 1786 Quaker home, furnished in the period, with an operating blacksmith shop. *Open Tues.-Sun. Small charge.*

Hillsborough

FIRST BAPTIST CHURCH *Wake and W. King Sts.* Built between 1860 and 1870, this church is Romanesque in design. *Open daily.*

Jackson

NORTHAMPTON COUNTY COURTHOUSE *Jefferson St.* The Greek Revival courthouse was constructed in 1853. *Open Mon.-Fri.*

Kure Beach

FORT FISHER STATE HISTORIC SITE *Rte. 421* The remains of a Confederate earthwork fortification are here. *Open Tues.-Sun.*

Lake Junaluska

COMMISSION ON ARCHIVES AND HISTORY: UNITED METHODIST CHURCH *Lakeshore Dr.* Collected here are documents and mementos relating to Methodist history. *Open Mon.-Fri.*

Laurel Springs

BRINEGAR CABIN *Blue Ridge Pkwy., milepost 238.5* A pioneer built this log cabin for his family in 1877. *Open daily May-Oct.*

New Bern

MASONIC TEMPLE *514 Hancock St.* This interesting building was erected in 1801.

NEW BERN CITY HALL *Pollock and Craven Sts.* This is modeled after the clock tower of Bern, Switzerland.

Newton Grove

BENTONVILLE BATTLEGROUND STATE HISTORIC SITE *3 mi. N. off Rte. 70* On the site is the Harper House, which was used as a hospital during the 1865 battle. *Open Tues.-Sun.*

Pinehurst

CLARENDON GARDENS *Linden Rd.* The nation's largest collection of varieties of holly grows in this 20-acre garden. *Open daily. $1.50.*

Robbinsville

BEAR CREEK SCENIC RAILROAD *5 mi. E. on Rte. 129* Here are operating Shay locomotives, an 1890 depot and logging exhibits. *Open Sat., Sun. and holidays late May-Oct. Adults $2.50, children small charge.*

Salisbury

MUSEUM OF ANTHROPOLOGY *Catawba College* Exhibits here emphasize southeastern North America. *Open Mon.-Fri.*

OLD STONE HOUSE *3 mi. E. off Rte. 52* This restored 1766 house is furnished in the style of the period. *Open Sat., Sun. Small charge.*

ROWAN MUSEUM *114 S. Jackson St.* Federal furniture is displayed in this 1819 house. *Open Wed., Sat.-Sun. June-Sept., Tues.-Sun. Oct.-May.*

Statesville

VANCE HOUSE *W. Sharpe St.* Governor Zebulon Vance lived here temporarily after the Union capture of Raleigh in April 1865.

Tarboro

CALVARY EPISCOPAL CHURCH AND CHURCHYARD *401 E. Church St.* Rare plantings grace the churchyard of this 1868 church. *Open daily.*

PENDER MUSEUM *St. Andrew St.* Local artifacts are displayed in an 1810 farmhouse. *Open Sun.*

Wadesboro

BOGGAN-HAMMOND HOUSE *210 E. Wade St.* Colonial furniture is exhibited in this 18th-century house.

Wilmington

LOWER CAPE FEAR HISTORICAL SOCIETY *126 S. Third St.* This 1850 double town house is also known as Latimer House.

South Carolina

Abbeville

OPERA HOUSE *Court Sq.* The 1906 structure is noted for its elaborate styling. *Open Mon.-Fri.*

TRINITY EPISCOPAL CHURCH *101 Church St.* The steeple on this 1850s Gothic-style church rises to a height of 10 stories. *Open daily.*

Camden

HISTORIC CAMDEN This area features the restored foundations of Revolutionary War structures. *Open Tues.-Sun. Small charge.*

Central

MONTPELIER *Rte. 88* When the house was rebuilt about 1848 after a fire, double doors replaced all the ground-floor windows.

Charleston

ARCHIVES MUSEUM *The Citadel* Materials relating to the military college's and the state's history are exhibited. *Open daily except Dec. 25.*

BATTERY *E. Bay St. and Murray Blvd.* Now a park with monuments and relics, this was the 1735 site of Fort Broughton. *Open daily.*

BETHEL UNITED METHODIST CHURCH *215 Calhoun St.* A fine portico graces the facade of the Greek Revival church. *Open daily.*

CHARLESTON TRIDENT CHAMBER OF COMMERCE *Lockwood Blvd. and Municipal Marina* The building once housed the oldest steam-operated rice mill in the U.S. *Open Mon.-Fri.*

CHARLES TOWNE LANDING *1500 Old Town Rd.* Exhibits, gardens and an animal forest are in the park on the site of the state's first English settlement. *Open daily Feb.-Dec. except Dec. 25. Small charge.*

CIRCULAR CHURCH *150 Meeting St.* The brick Romanesque-style church serves the second oldest congregation in Charleston. *Open daily.*

COLLEGE OF CHARLESTON *66 George St.* Several distinguished buildings are on the campus of the college, which was founded in 1770. *Open Mon.-Fri. except holidays.*

CONFEDERATE MUSEUM *188 Market St.* Market Hall, built in 1841, contains Confederate memorabilia. *Open Tues.-Sat. Small charge.*

EXCHANGE BUILDING *E. Bay and Broad Sts.* In the basement is the Provost, once a dungeon and now a museum. *Open daily Feb.-Nov. Small charge.*

FIREPROOF BUILDING *100 Meeting St.* The first fireproof building in the U.S. (1822-6) was designed by Robert Mills. It is now the home of the South Carolina Historical Society. *Open Mon.-Sat.*

FIRST BAPTIST CHURCH *61-3 Church St.* Robert Mills designed this 1822 colonnaded church to replace a 1699 structure. *Open daily.*

FIRST (SCOTS) PRESBYTERIAN CHURCH *53 Meeting St.* The seal of the Church of Scotland is above the main entrance of this 1814 building. *Open daily.*

GRACE PROTESTANT EPISCOPAL CHURCH *98 Wentworth St.* Charleston architect Edward Brickell White designed this Gothic-style structure, completed in 1848. *Open daily.*

OLD CITADEL *Marion Sq.* This impressive structure was built as a refuge for white women and children in case of a slave rebellion.

POWDER MAGAZINE MUSEUM *79 Cumberland St.* Exhibits of Colonial Carolina items are housed in a 1713 structure. *Open Mon.-Fri. Sept.-July. Small charge.*

ST. JOHANNES LUTHERAN CHURCH *48 Hasell St.* The classical Tuscan-style structure was built in 1841 from plans by E. B. White. *Open daily.*

ST. JOHN'S EVANGELICAL LUTHERAN CHURCH *Archdale and Clifford Sts.* Dedicated in 1817, the building is noted for its steeple, wrought iron gates and rail fence. *Open Mon.-Wed., Fri.*

TRINITY UNITED METHODIST CHURCH *273 Meeting St.* The lovely structure was patterned after the Church of the Madeleine in Paris. *Open daily.*

Cheraw

ST. DAVID'S EPISCOPAL CHURCH *First and Church Sts.* Begun in 1768, this was the last Colonial Anglican church erected in South Carolina.

Columbia

FIRST PRESBYTERIAN CHURCH *1324 Marion St.* Woodrow Wilson's father once was minister here. *Open daily.*

PICRICCORN HOUSE *1601 Richland St.* The 1796 house may be the oldest in the city. *Open Mon.-Fri. except holidays.*

Conway

CONWAY CITY HALL *227 Main St.* Designed by Robert Mills, this brick, four-columned structure was completed in 1824. *Open Mon.-Fri.*

Drayton Hall

DRAYTON HALL *5 mi. N.W. on Rte. 61* This 1738-42 house is considered one of the finest examples of Georgian architecture in the U.S.

Georgetown

CHURCH OF PRINCE GEORGE, WINYAH *Broad and Highmarket Sts.* Colonial citizens are buried in the graveyard of this 1734-50 church.

Greenville

CHRIST CHURCH *10 N. Church St.* The oldest church building in the city has notable stained-glass windows. *Open daily.*

GREENVILLE COUNTY MUSEUM OF ART *106 DuPont Dr.* The collections emphasize contemporary American art. *Open daily.*

Greenwood

CALLIE SELF MEMORIAL BAPTIST CHURCH *509 Kirksey Dr.* The carillon tower contains 37 bells from the Netherlands. *Open Sun.*

Kingstree

THORNTREE HOUSE *Fluitt-Nelson Memorial Park* This 1749 plantation house is the oldest residence in the area. *Open Sun. Adults $2.00, students small charge.*

Myrtle Beach

BROOKGREEN GARDENS *18 mi. S. on Rte. 17* A collection of American sculpture is set in a park. *Open daily except Dec. 25. Small charge.*

Pendleton

ASHTABULA *3½ mi. N.E. on Rte. 88* Typical of the early 19th-century plantation homes in the Pendleton area (one of the country's largest historic districts), the house has large, airy rooms and verandas. *Open Sun. May-Sept. Small charge.*

FARMER'S SOCIETY HALL *On the Green* This 1820s building is the oldest Farmer's Society Hall in the country. *Open Mon.-Fri.*

Ridgeway

CENTURY HOUSE Built in 1853, this brick mansion was used briefly by Confederate General P.G.T. Beauregard. *Open Mon.-Fri.*

Seneca

LUNNEY MUSEUM *211 W.S. First St.* The commodious 1909 residence is furnished with antiques and contains historical exhibits. *Open Sun.*

Spartanburg

REGIONAL MUSEUM OF SPARTANBURG *501 Otis Blvd.* Regional history exhibits are featured here. *Open Tues.-Sat. June-Aug., Tues.-Sun. Sept.-May.*

Switzer

PRICE HOUSE RESTORATION *4 mi. S.E. of Rte. 221* This 1795 furnished brick house has a gambrel roof and inside chimneys. *Open Tues.-Sun. Adults $2.00, children small charge.*

Winnsboro

FAIRFIELD COUNTY HISTORICAL MUSEUM *S. Congress St.* This Federal-style 1830s structure has a brick facade in Flemish bond.

Tennessee

Dover

FORT DONELSON NATIONAL MILITARY PARK The Battle of Fort Donelson was fought here. Historical and military artifacts are exhibited. *Open daily except Dec. 25.*

Elizabethton

COVERED BRIDGE This covered wooden bridge was first opened for traffic in 1882.

Franklin

CARTER HOUSE *Rte. 31* The 1830 home, still marked with bullets from the Civil War, holds period furnishings. *Open daily. Small charge.*

WILLIAMSON COUNTY COURTHOUSE *On the Square* This is one of the nation's few antebellum Greek Revival courthouses. *Open Mon.-Sat.*

Gallatin

TROUSDALE HOUSE *W. Main St.* Dating from 1820, this was the home of Governor William Trousdale. *Open Sat., May-Oct. Small charge.*

Greeneville

ST. JAMES EPISCOPAL CHURCH *105 W. Church St.* This 1850 church has the original pipe organ and hand-planed walnut pews. *Open daily.*

Hohenwald

MERIWETHER LEWIS PARK *7 mi. E. on Natchez Trace Pkwy.* Here are the explorer's grave site and a small museum. *Open daily.*

Johnson City

CARROLL REECE MUSEUM *East Tennessee State University* Exhibits relate to frontier life in Tennessee and the Appalachians. *Open daily.*

Kingston

ROANE COUNTY COURT HOUSE This three-story Greek Revival structure, built of brick, dates from the 1850s. *Open Mon.-Sat.*

Knoxville

CONFEDERATE MEMORIAL HALL *3148 Kingston Pike* This museum was Confederate headquarters during the 1863 siege of Knoxville. *Open daily June-Aug. Small charge.*

FIRST PRESBYTERIAN CHURCH *620 State St.* Several prominent Tennesseans are buried in the cemetery adjoining the handsome classical-style church. *Open daily.*

LAWSON-MCGHEE LIBRARY *500 W. Church Ave.* The collection includes thousands of books and documents on Southern history. *Open Mon.-Fri. late May-early Sept., Mon.-Sat. early Sept.-late May except Memorial Day.*

Limestone

DAVY CROCKETT BIRTHPLACE PARK *Off Rte. 411* A replica of the cabin where Crockett was born stands in this five-acre park. *Open daily.*

Manchester

OLD STONE FORT STATE PARK *Rte. 41* Massive earth and stone walls here were built by prehistoric Indians. *Open daily.*

Maryville

SAM HOUSTON SCHOOLHOUSE *6 mi. N.E. off Rte. 129* Houston once taught in the state's oldest schoolhouse. *Open daily except Dec. 25.*

Morristown

DAVY CROCKETT TAVERN AND MUSEUM *E. Main St.* The frontiersman's reconstructed boyhood home contains pioneer relics. *Open daily May-Oct. Small charge.*

Nashville

"BELLE CAROL OF THE CUMBERLAND" *Foot of Broadway* River tours are offered on the old stern-wheeler. *Cruises Fri.-Sun. May, mid-Sept.-Oct., daily June-mid-Sept. Adults $3.50, children $2.00.*

COUNTRY MUSIC HALL OF FAME AND MUSEUM *700 16th Ave. S.* Exhibits honor country music greats. *Open daily except Jan. 1 and Dec. 25. Adults $1.25, children small charge.*

FORT NASHBOROUGH *170 First Ave. N.* A stockade surrounds log cabins in this reconstruction of the 1799 fort. *Open Tues.-Sat.*

STATE OFFICE BUILDING *500 Charlotte Ave.* Murals by Dean Cornwell in the lobby depict outstanding Tennesseans. *Open Mon.-Fri. except holidays.*

TENNESSEE STATE MUSEUM *War Memorial Bldg., Capitol Blvd.* Varied exhibits relate mainly to the history of Tennessee. *Open Mon.-Sat. except holidays.*

Oak Ridge

AMERICAN MUSEUM OF ATOMIC ENERGY *Oak Ridge Tpke.* Exhibits portray the peaceful uses of nuclear energy. *Open daily except holidays.*

Shiloh

SHILOH NATIONAL MILITARY PARK AND CEMETERY *Rte. 22* A bloody struggle waged here in April 1862 was the Civil War's first great western battle. *Open daily except Dec. 25.*

Vonore

FORT LOUDOUN *Off Rte. 411* The first (1756) English garrison in Tennessee is reconstructed here. *Open daily except Thanksgiving Day and Dec. 25. Small charge.*

Region 5 [map page 306]

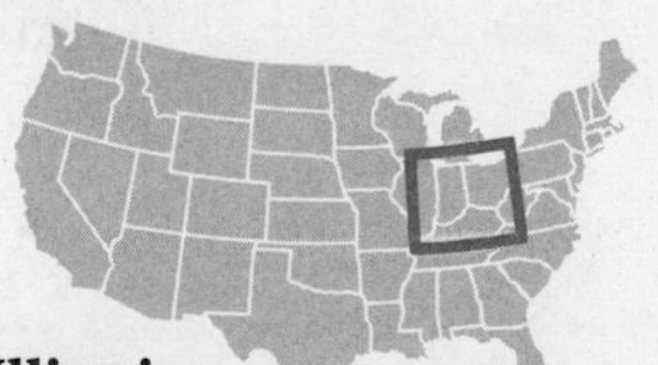

Illinois

Bement

BRYANT COTTAGE STATE MEMORIAL *146 E. Wilson Ave.* Senatorial contestants Abraham Lincoln and Stephen A. Douglas were guests here in 1858. *Open daily except holidays.*

Carmi

RATCLIFF INN *216 E. Main St.* The 1828 stagecoach inn houses a museum featuring items of famous politicians. *Open daily June-Aug.*

ROBINSON-STEWART HOUSE *110 S. Main Cross St.* The 1814 dwelling, furnished in period style, was the home of Senator John M. Robinson. *Open daily June-Aug., Sat., Sun. Sept.-May. Small charge.*

Charleston

LINCOLN LOG CABIN STATE PARK *7 mi. S.* Lincoln's father and stepmother settled on a farm here in 1837. *Open daily.*

Chicago

ALBERT F. MADLENER HOUSE *4 W. Burton Pl.* This 1902 cube-shaped structure was architecturally ahead of its time.

BALZEKAS MUSEUM OF LITHUANIAN CULTURE *4012 S. Archer Ave.* Exhibits trace 800 years of Lithuanian culture. *Open daily.*

CHRIST THE KING CHURCH *9235 S. Hamilton Ave.* The church's stained-glass facade dominates a campanile, library and rectory. *Open daily.*

CROWN HALL *Illinois Institute of Technology, 3360 S. State St.* The building is among the finest works of architect Mies van der Rohe. *Open Mon.-Fri.*

DOUGLAS TOMB STATE MEMORIAL *636 E. 35th St.* A tall column crowned by a statue of Stephen A. Douglas surmounts his tomb.

ELKS NATIONAL MEMORIAL BUILDING *2750 N. Lakeview Ave.* Murals and statues honor Elks servicemen. *Open daily except Thanksgiving Day and Dec. 25.*

FIRST NATIONAL BANK OF CHICAGO *1 First National Plaza* The glass and granite tower holds a fine art collection. A monumental Chagall mosaic is on the plaza. *Open Mon.-Fri.*

FOURTH PRESBYTERIAN CHURCH OF CHICAGO *126 E. Chestnut St.* Built in 1912, the majestic church features classically Gothic design details. *Open daily except holidays.*

HALL OF FAME OF THE INTERNATIONAL COLLEGE OF SURGEONS *1524 N. Lake Shore Dr.* Bizarre cures and equipment highlight the early history of surgery throughout the world. *Open daily except holidays.*

MARINA CITY *Dearborn and State Sts.* This urban complex is a city within a city.

Danville

COVENANT UNITED PRESBYTERIAN CHURCH *Bowman and Voorhees Sts.* Triangle motifs and sleek cedarwood hallmark the church. *Open Sun.*

East Dundee

HAEGER POTTERIES *7 Maiden Lane* A museum holds ceramic pieces from 3000 B.C. to the present. *Open daily.*

Junction

OLD SLAVE HOUSE *Rtes. 1 and 13* Kidnapped slaves were once confined in the 1838 house. *Open daily.*

Lawrenceville

LINCOLN TRAIL STATE MEMORIAL *9 mi. E. off Rte. 50* Here is the place where the Lincoln family first entered Illinois from Indiana in 1830.

Lerna

MOORE HOME *Lincoln Log Cabin State Park* Period furnishings are displayed in the former home of Lincoln's stepsister.

Lockport

ILLINOIS AND MICHIGAN CANAL MUSEUM *803 S. State St.* Memorabilia relating to the canal are exhibited. *Open daily except holidays.*

Rantoul

DISPLAY CENTER *Chanute Air Force Base* Exhibits show the installation's role in training technicians. *Open Wed.-Sun.*

Indiana

Berne

FIRST MENNONITE CHURCH The structure serves a community founded by Swiss Mennonites. *Open daily.*

Bluffton

WELLS COUNTY HISTORICAL MUSEUM *211 W. Washington St.* Objects of local significance are displayed. *Open Sun. Apr.-Sept.*

Bristol

ELKHART COUNTY HISTORICAL MUSEUM *Rush Memorial Center* Period rooms and pioneer artifacts can be seen here. *Open Sat., Sun.*

OPERA HOUSE The 1897 theater is decorated in Gay Nineties style. *Open Thurs.-Sat. for performances.*

Brook

GEORGE ADE HOME *E. on Rte. 16* The Hoosier author-humorist lived in this English manor-style house.

Centerville

Once the county seat and an important railroad town, Centerville has many fine old Federal town houses.

Columbus

BARTHOLOMEW COUNTY HISTORICAL MUSEUM *524 Third St.* Victorian items are on view in the stately 1865 brick house. *Open Tues.-Sun.*

IRWIN GARDENS *608 Fifth St.* A pergola, fountains and pools resemble a classic Pompeiian garden. *Open Sat., Sun. and holidays.*

Corydon

CORYDON CAPITOL STATE MEMORIAL This 1813 stone structure was Indiana's first capitol. *Open Thurs.-Tues. Oct.-May except holidays. Small charge.*

Crawfordsville

CENTER HALL *Wabash College* Work began in 1853 on the Italian villa-style structure. *Open Mon.-Fri.*

Culver

CULVER MEMORIAL CHAPEL *Culver Military Academy* The spire contains an inspirational carillon. *Open daily during academic year.*

Fort Wayne

CATHEDRAL OF THE IMMACULATE CONCEPTION *1121 S. Calhoun St.* Bavarian stained-glass windows and a carved main altar distinguish this stone edifice. *Open daily.*

JACK D. DIEHM MUSEUM OF NATURAL HISTORY *Franke Park* Animals are shown in simulated natural settings. *Open Tues.-Sun. Small charge.*

Geneva

LIMBERLOST STATE MEMORIAL Novelist Gene Stratton Porter completed this log house in 1895. *Open Tues.-Sat. except holidays. Adults and children over 12 small charge.*

Greenfield

JAMES WHITCOMB RILEY HOME *250 W. Main St.* Many of the poet's manuscripts are displayed. *Open daily May-Oct. Small charge.*

OLD LOG JAIL MUSEUM *Riley Park* Hancock County history unfolds in this building. *Open Sat., Sun. May-Oct. Small charge.*

Greensburg

DECATUR COUNTY COURTHOUSE Aspens grow from the tower of this Romanesque structure. *Open daily.*

Indianapolis

CHRIST CHURCH CATHEDRAL *Monument Circle* Completed in 1859, the church contains fine stained-glass windows. *Open daily.*

INDIANAPOLIS MOTOR SPEEDWAY MUSEUM *4790 W. 16th St.* Famous race cars and photographs of racing can be seen here. *Open daily except Race Day and Dec. 25.*

KEMPER HOUSE *1028 N. Delaware St.* The antiques in this ornate 1873 "wedding cake house" are all in use.

MORRIS-BUTLER MUSEUM *1204 N. Park Ave.* Victorian furnishings grace an 1870s home. *Open Sun., Thurs. Sept.-July except holidays.*

STATE OFFICE BUILDING *100 N. Senate Ave.* A mosaic in the lobby portrays Lincoln's Hoosier years. *Open Mon.-Fri. except holidays.*

Jeffersonville

HOWARD STEAMBOAT MUSEUM *1101 E. Market St.* Early Ohio River boats are the theme of the 1892 mansion. *Open daily June-Dec. Small charge.*

Kokomo

ELWOOD HAYNES MUSEUM *1915 S. Webster St.* Displays relate to the designer of the first U.S. commercially successful gasoline-engine automobile. *Open Tues.-Sun.*

La Crosse

MILLER'S MUSEUM *3½ mi. S. on Rte. 421* Here is vintage machinery, including tractors and steam engines. *Open Sat., Sun. May-Oct.*

Lafayette

LAFAYETTE ART CENTER *101 S. Ninth St.* Works of Midwest artists are emphasized. *Open Tues.-Sun. Sept.-July except holidays.*

ST. MARY'S CATHEDRAL CHURCH *1207 Columbia St.* The Victorian Gothic Catholic church was completed in 1866. *Open daily.*

TIPPECANOE COUNTY HISTORICAL MUSEUM *909 South St.* An English Gothic mansion has an extensive fine arts collection. *Open Tues.-Sun.*

La Porte

LA PORTE COUNTY HISTORICAL MUSEUM *Court House* Antique guns and pioneer and Indian relics are shown here. *Open Mon.-Fri.*

Madison

DR. WILLIAM HUTCHINGS MEMORIAL *120 W. Third St.* A turn-of-the-century doctor's office contains the original equipment and furnishings. *Open Sun., Thurs., Sat. May-Oct. Adults small charge.*

TALBOTT-HYATT PIONEER FRONTIER GARDEN AND KITCHEN *301 W. Second St.* Early 18th-century plantings grow near a Federal-style house with a separate kitchen and a carriage house. *Open daily.*

Mitchell

VIRGIL I. GRISSOM STATE MEMORIAL *Spring Mill State Park* The astronaut's space suit and Mercury backup capsule are highlights. *Open daily. Park admission $1.25.*

Nappanee

AMISH ACRES *1 mi. W. on Rte. 6* This Amish farm includes restored buildings. *Open daily May-Oct., Sat., Sun. Nov.-Apr. Adults $1.50, children over 6 small charge.*

Peru

CIRCUS MUSEUM *N. Broadway and Seventh St.* Many circus relics are on display. *Open Mon.-Fri.*

Plymouth

CHIEF MENOMINEE MONUMENT *5 mi. S.W. on Rte. 30* This statue honors a Potawatomi chief who resisted the removal of his tribe to Kansas.

Richmond

ART ASSOCIATION OF RICHMOND GALLERY *McGuire Hall, Whitewater Blvd.* This varied collection excels in early 20th-century American art. *Open Sun.-Fri. Sept.-May except holidays.*

JULIA MEEK GAAR WAYNE COUNTY HISTORICAL MUSEUM *1150 N. "A" St.* Period rooms are featured here. *Open Tues.-Sun. mid-Feb.-mid-Dec. Small charge.*

Rockville

BILLIE CREEK VILLAGE *1 mi. E. on Rte. 36* Old buildings have been gathered to re-create a turn-of-the-century hamlet. *Open daily late May-late Oct. Small charge.*

PARKE COUNTY COVERED BRIDGES This area has more covered bridges than any other county in the U.S.

Rome City

GENE STRATTON PORTER STATE MEMORIAL *Off Rte. 9* The famous novelist built this rustic home in 1913 in a woodland. *Open Tues.-Sun. except holidays. Small charge.*

Seymour

H. VANCE SWOPE MEMORIAL ART GALLERY *Second and Walnut Sts.* Many fine paintings by Swope are here. *Open Mon.-Sat.*

Shelbyville

THOMAS A. HENDRICKS HOMESTEAD *Shelby County Fair Grounds* Grover Cleveland's Vice President lived in this log cabin.

South Bend

NORTHERN INDIANA HISTORICAL SOCIETY MUSEUM *112 S. Lafayette Blvd.* Indian and pioneer relics are on view in a former courthouse. *Open Tues.-Sat.*

Terre Haute

PAUL DRESSER BIRTHPLACE *Fairbanks Park* The Gay Nineties composer of "My Gal Sal" was born here in 1858. *Open Sun.-Fri. Apr.-Oct.*

Valparaiso

PORTER COUNTY HISTORICAL SOCIETY MUSEUM *Old County Jail* Locally found mastodon bones are featured. *Open Tues., Wed., Fri.*

Versailles

RIPLEY COUNTY HISTORICAL MUSEUM Old tools, weapons and other antiques are on display. *Open Sat., Sun. late May-early Sept.*

Vincennes

INDIANA TERRITORY STATE MEMORIAL *First and Harrison Sts., Harrison Park* The territory's first capitol and a replica of its first newspaper printshop are here. *Open daily except Thanksgiving Day and Dec. 25. Small charge.*

KNOX COUNTY COURTHOUSE *Seventh St.* This Victorian edifice was built to honor Knox County soldiers and pioneers. *Open Mon.-Fri.*

OLD STATE BANK STATE MEMORIAL *Second St.* A sturdy Classic Revival bank dating from 1838 now houses an art gallery. *Open Tues.-Sun.*

Wabash

LINCOLN MEMORIAL *Courthouse Sq.* The seated bronze statue is known as the *Lincoln of the People.*

Zionsville

COLONIAL VILLAGE *Rte. 334* The remodeled district resembles a 19th-century New England village.

Kentucky

Bardstown

BARTON MUSEUM OF WHISKEY HISTORY *Barton Rd.* Displays tell of the U.S. liquor industry up to Prohibition (1920). *Open daily.*

Frankfort

FIRST PRESBYTERIAN CHURCH *416 W. Main St.* The dignified 1848 structure is English Gothic in style. *Open daily.*

La Grange

ROB MORRIS MEMORIAL *110 Washington St.* This was the home of the famous Mason who founded the Order of the Eastern Star. *Open Fri.-Wed.*

Lexington

ART GALLERY *Fine Arts Bldg., University of Kentucky* The gallery features exhibitions of contemporary and historical works. *Open daily Sept.-May.*

MUSEUM OF ANTHROPOLOGY *University of Kentucky* General anthropology and Kentucky prehistory are represented. *Open daily.*

London

MOUNTAIN LIFE MUSEUM *Levi Jackson State Park* Pioneer tools and artifacts are displayed in seven buildings. *Open daily mid-May-mid-Oct. Small charge.*

Louisville

FILSON CLUB MUSEUM *118 W. Breckinridge St.* Indian artifacts and portraits by early Kentucky artists are shown. *Open Mon.-Fri. July-Sept., Mon.-Sat. Oct.-June.*

FOUNDERS SQUARE *501 W. Walnut St.* The founding of the city in 1778 is commemorated at this modern visitor center. *Open daily June-early Sept., Mon.-Sat. early Sept.-May.*

Middlesboro

CUMBERLAND GAP NATIONAL HISTORICAL PARK *Rte. 25E* An iron furnace dating from about 1815, some 28 restored buildings and a museum mark the historic passage west across the mountains. *Open daily.*

Owensboro

OWENSBORO AREA MUSEUM *901 Frederica St.* The features include live reptiles that may be held and a planetarium. *Open Sun.-Fri. except Thanksgiving Day and Dec. 25.*

Paris

CANE RIDGE SHRINE *8 mi. E. on Rte. 537* A modern limestone structure shelters the old log meetinghouse where the Christian Church (Disciples of Christ) was formed in 1804. *Open daily Apr.-Nov.*

Springfield

LINCOLN HOMESTEAD STATE PARK *Lincoln Park Rd.* The homes of Lincoln's parents are re-created here. *Open daily May-Sept. Small charge.*

Michigan

Albion

VISUAL ARTS BUILDING *Albion College* Decorative arts, paintings, sculpture and a print collection are on display. *Open daily Sept.-mid-May except holidays.*

Allegan

ALLEGAN COUNTY HISTORICAL MUSEUM *113 Walnut St.* Period rooms portray styles of living since pioneer days. *Open Fri.-Sun. June-Sept. Small charge.*

Battle Creek

KIMBALL HOUSE MUSEUM *196 Capital Ave., N.E.* Period furnishings fill this doctor's Victorian home and office. *Open Sun., Tues., Thurs. except holidays.*

Delton

BERNARD HISTORICAL SOCIETY AND MUSEUM *7135 W. Delton Rd.* Pioneer rooms and buildings illustrate local history. *Open Sun. May-June, Sept.-Oct., daily July-Aug.*

Detroit

ANNA SCRIPPS WHITCOMB CONSERVATORY *Belle Isle Park* Lush plants fill this large conservatory set in landscaped gardens. *Open daily.*

CATHEDRAL OF THE MOST BLESSED SACRAMENT *9844 Woodward Ave.* This Gothic-style cathedral has fine stained-glass windows. *Open daily.*

CECILIAVILLE, U.S.A. *10400 Stoepel Ave.* This church is famous for the *Black Christ* mural and the Shrine of the Black Madonna.

CHILDREN'S MUSEUM *67 E. Kirby St.* Exhibits of science, history and ethnology are geared to children. *Open Mon.-Fri. June-Sept., Mon.-Sat. Oct.-May, except holidays.*

DETROIT HISTORICAL MUSEUM *5401 Woodward Ave.* Exhibits here cover Detroit's history from 1701 to the present. *Open Tues.-Sun. except holidays.*

FORT WAYNE MILITARY MUSEUM *6053 W. Jefferson Ave.* Military uniforms and Indian artifacts are displayed in the Civil War fort. *Open Wed.-Sun.*

GESU CHURCH *Livernois and McNichols Sts.* The Spanish-style church was built in 1937. *Open daily.*

PRECIOUS BLOOD CHURCH *13305 Grove Ave.* Lavish decorations enhance the interior of the church, modeled after one in Rome. *Open daily.*

ST. MARY'S CHURCH *646 Monroe Ave.* A magnificent main altar, ornately patterned walls and stained-glass windows attract visitors to this 1884 church. *Open daily.*

Grosse Ile

ST. JAMES CHAPEL OF ST. JAMES EPISCOPAL CHURCH *25150 E. River Rd.* This charming 1867 Gothic Revival chapel was started with funds left by a former slave. *Open daily.*

South Haven

LIBERTY HYDE BAILEY MEMORIAL MUSEUM *903 Bailey Ave.* The noted botanist and horticulturist was born here in 1858. *Open Tues., Fri.*

Ohio

Akron

JOHN BROWN HOME *514 Diagonal Rd.* Papers and belongings of the famous abolitionist are shown. *Open Tues.-Sun. except holidays.*

Bainbridge

DR. JOHN HARRIS FOUNDATION OF DENTISTRY *Main St.* Old-time dental equipment can be seen in America's first school of dentistry. *Open Fri.-Sun. mid-Apr.-Oct.*

Berea

RIEMENSCHNEIDER MEMORIAL BACH LIBRARY *57 E. Bagley Rd.* More than 5000 rare volumes and manuscripts deal principally with the music of Bach. *Open Mon.-Fri. mid-Sept.-mid-June.*

Canal Fulton

OLD CANAL DAYS MUSEUM *Walnut St.* Relics in this museum tell the story of the Ohio-Erie Canal. *Open daily June-Oct.*

"ST. HELENA II" *Canal Fulton Park* The replica of a mule-drawn canal boat carries passengers along the canal. *Trips Tues.-Sun. May-Oct. Adults $1.50, children small charge.*

Canton

MCKINLEY TOMB *Seventh St., N.W.* The 25th President and his wife are entombed in this impressive monument.

PROFESSIONAL FOOTBALL HALL OF FAME *2121 Harrison Ave., N.W.* The history and great players of professional football are honored. *Open daily. Adults $1.50, children small charge.*

STARK COUNTY HISTORICAL CENTER *749 Hazlett Ave., N.W.* Memorabilia of President McKinley are featured among the science and history collections and a planetarium. *Open Tues.-Sun. Small charge.*

Carey

BASILICA OF OUR LADY OF CONSOLATION *315 Clay St.* This shrine is dedicated to Mary as Consoler of the Afflicted. *Open daily.*

Chillicothe

ADENA STATE MEMORIAL *W. Allen Ave. Ext.* Ohio's sixth governor completed this elegant stone mansion in 1807. *Open Tues.-Sun. Apr.-Oct. Small charge.*

ROSS COUNTY COURTHOUSE *Main St.* On the floor of the 1856 modified Greek Revival building is a mosaic of the state seal. *Open Mon.-Fri.*

ROSS COUNTY HISTORICAL SOCIETY MUSEUM *45 W. Fifth St.* Ohio's Constitution Table is among the items on view. *Open Tues.-Sun. Feb.-Nov. Small charge.*

Cincinnati

CINCINNATI FIRE DEPARTMENT HISTORICAL MUSEUM *329 E. Ninth St.* Antique fire-fighting equipment is featured. *Open daily.*

FLEISCHMANN GARDENS *Forest and Washington Aves.* Thousands of tulips and other flowers bloom in this oasis of beauty. *Open daily.*

ST. FRANCIS DE SALES ROMAN CATHOLIC CHURCH *Woodburn Ave. and Madison Rd.* The huge bell in this Gothic-style church's steeple may be the world's largest swinging bell. *Open daily.*

STOWE HOUSE *2950 Gilbert Ave.* The home of Harriet Beecher Stowe's father is a museum devoted to American Negro history. *Open Sat., Sun. and holidays June-mid-Sept. Small charge.*

WILLIAM HOWARD TAFT NATIONAL HISTORIC SITE *2038 Auburn Ave.* The nation's 27th President was born in this stately home in 1857.

Claridon

CONGREGATIONAL CHURCH The Classic Revival church has a nicely restored interior. *Open daily.*

Cleveland

ABRAHAM LINCOLN STATUE *Mall side of Board of Education Bldg.* Donations from schoolchildren paid for the fine statue of Lincoln.

CLEVELAND CITY HALL *601 Lakeside Ave.* Archibald Willard's famous painting *The Spirit of '76* hangs in the rotunda of this dignified building. *Open Mon.-Fri. except holidays.*

CLEVELAND HEALTH MUSEUM AND EDUCATION CENTER *8911 Euclid Ave.* Imaginative exhibits reveal the intricate workings of the human body. *Open daily. Small charge.*

DUNHAM TAVERN MUSEUM *6709 Euclid Ave.* The former stagecoach inn is furnished with antiques. *Open Tues.-Sun. except holidays. Adults and children over 11 small charge.*

HOWARD DITTRICK MUSEUM OF HISTORICAL MEDICINE *11000 Euclid Ave.* Thousands of items trace the history of medicine. *Open Mon.-Sat. except holidays.*

ROMANIAN FOLK MUSEUM OF ST. MARY'S ROMANIAN ORTHODOX CHURCH *3256 Warren Rd.* Romanian costumes, handcrafts and artworks are shown. *Open daily.*

SOCIETY NATIONAL BANK BUILDING *127 Public Sq.* Handsome stone- and metalwork adorn one of Cleveland's first skyscrapers. *Open Mon.-Fri. except holidays.*

TERMINAL TOWER *Public Sq.* Broad panorama is visible from the 42nd-floor observatory of this 1928 structure. *Open daily. Small charge.*

Clifton

CLIFTON MILL *75 Water St.* The 1869 gristmill is still in operation. *Open daily. Small charge.*

Columbus

CENTER OF SCIENCE AND INDUSTRY *280 E. Broad St.* Exhibits deal with history, science and industry. *Open daily except holidays. Small charge.*

COLUMBUS PARK OF ROSES *4015 N. High St.* More than 400 varieties of roses are found in this enormous park. *Open daily June-mid-Oct.*

FRANKLIN PARK CONSERVATORY *1500 E. Broad St.* Exotic flowers, shrubs and trees form a year-round display. *Open daily.*

ORTON MUSEUM *Ohio State University, 155 S. Oval Dr.* Here are fossil and mineral collections. *Open Mon.-Sat. except holidays.*

Dayton

DUNBAR HOUSE STATE MEMORIAL *219 N. Summit St.* The home of the eminent black poet Paul Laurence Dunbar appears much as it did when he died in 1906. *Open Wed.-Sun. June-Sept. Small charge.*

Defiance

AUGLAIZE VILLAGE *Krouse Rd.* Restored, reconstructed and relocated buildings make up a community of the 1860-90 era. *Open Wed.-Sun. June-Nov. Small charge.*

Delaware

WESLEYAN UNIVERSITY ARCHIVES AND SPECIAL COLLECTIONS *Beeghley Library* Rare books and manuscripts are the impressive focus. *Open daily during academic year.*

Dover

WARTHER MUSEUM *331 Karl Ave.* Exquisitely carved models of locomotives tell the history of steam power. *Open daily. Adults $1.50.*

Fort Recovery

FORT RECOVERY HISTORICAL MUSEUM *Old Fort St.* Exhibits illustrate aspects of the late 18th-century Indian wars. *Open Tues.-Sun. Mar.-Nov. Small charge.*

Georgetown

GRANT SCHOOLHOUSE *Water St.* As a boy Ulysses S. Grant attended classes in this picturesque schoolhouse. *Open Wed.-Sun. June-Sept.*

ULYSSES S. GRANT HOMESTEAD *219 E. Grant Ave.* In 1825 Grant's father built the sturdy brick home. At the age of 17 young Grant left here for West Point. *Open holidays.*

Germantown

MUD-LICK MILL AND MUSEUM *Astoria and Sigal Rds.* Early tools and household appliances are among the extensive exhibits in the old mill. *Open Sat., Sun. and holidays.*

Greenville

GARST MUSEUM *205 N. Broadway* The most popular exhibits tell of two local notables: sharpshooter Annie Oakley and broadcaster Lowell Thomas. *Open Sun.-Tues., Fri.*

Kelleys Island

INSCRIPTION ROCK Ancient carvings on a boulder reveal figures of animals and men. *Open daily.*

Lakewood

OLD STONE HOUSE *14710 Lake Ave.* The 1838 home has been restored and furnished with pioneer relics. *Open Sun., Wed. Feb.-Nov. Small charge.*

Lebanon

FORT ANCIENT STATE MEMORIAL MUSEUM *7 mi. S.E. on Rte. 350* Implements and ornaments tell of the area's prehistoric Indians. *Open Tues.-Sun. Mar.-Nov. Small charge.*

GOLDEN LAMB INN *27-31 S. Broadway* Ohio's oldest inn (1803) still offers hospitality to wayfarers. *Open daily except Dec. 25.*

Lima

MACDONELL HOUSE *632 W. Market St.* Grand Victorian architecture and furnishings recall the late 19th century. *Open Tues.-Sun. except holidays. Small charge.*

Lisbon

OLD STONE HOUSE MUSEUM *100 E. Washington St.* The former tavern, built in 1805, houses pioneer items. *Open Tues.-Sat. June-Aug., Sun. Sept.-mid-Oct. Small charge.*

Marietta

MOUND CEMETERY *400 Fifth St.* Ancient farming Indians buried their chieftains here; nearby are graves of pioneer settlers. *Open daily.*

STEAMER "W. P. SNYDER, JR." *Foot of Washington St.* Everything appears in mint condition in this 1918 stern-wheeler. *Open daily Apr.-Nov. Small charge.*

Marion

HARDING HOME AND MUSEUM *380 Mt. Vernon Ave.* Warren G. Harding lived here before he moved to the White House. The museum holds mementos of the President. *Open daily June-Aug., Tues.-Sat. Oct.-May. Small charge.*

Mentor

LAWNFIELD *8095 Mentor Ave.* James A. Garfield's clapboard home still holds family furnishings. *Open Tues.-Sun. May-Oct. Small charge.*

Metals Park

AMERICAN SOCIETY FOR METALS WORLD HEADQUARTERS An 11-story geodesic dome powerfully symbolizes metal engineering. *Open daily.*

Mount Pleasant

FRIENDS MEETING HOUSE *Off Rte. 150* In 1814 Quakers built the huge house and engineered a movable partition for men's and women's sections when needed. *Open Wed.-Sun. May-Oct. Small charge.*

New Philadelphia

SCHOENBRUNN VILLAGE STATE MEMORIAL *3 mi. E.* In 1772 missionaries built Ohio's first village, school and church here. *Open daily Mar.-Nov. Small charge.*

Norwalk

FIRELANDS HISTORICAL MUSEUM *4 Case Ave.* Indian artifacts and pioneer possessions are the specialties. *Open Sat., Sun. Apr., Nov., Tues.-Sun. May-June, Sept.-Oct., daily July-Aug. Small charge.*

Point Pleasant

GRANT BIRTHPLACE Ulysses S. Grant was born here in 1822. *Open Tues.-Sun. Apr.-Oct. Small charge.*

Port Clinton

"TIN GOOSE" *Airport* The versatile 1928 Ford trimotor plane is still in service here. *Trips daily. Adults and children over 10 $6.00, children 3-9 $3.00.*

Powell

COLUMBUS ZOOLOGICAL GARDENS *9990 Riverside Dr.* Gorillas and reptiles are the prize residents. *Open daily. Adults $1.25, children small charge.*

Put-in-Bay

PERRY'S VICTORY AND INTERNATIONAL PEACE MEMORIAL NATIONAL MONUMENT The 352-foot shaft honors Commodore Oliver Perry's 1813 naval victory and the ensuing peace with Canada. *Open daily Apr.-Oct. Small charge for elevator.*

Ripley

RANKIN HOUSE STATE MEMORIAL The home of the Reverend John Rankin was one of Ohio's most famous "Underground Railroad" stations. *Open Tues.-Sun. Apr.-Oct.*

Springfield

CLARK COUNTY HISTORICAL SOCIETY MUSEUM *300 W. Main St.* Countless relics here bring history to life. *Open Mon., Thurs., Sat. and 2nd and 4th Sun. except holidays.*

Steubenville

FEDERAL LAND OFFICE *Rtes. 22 and 7* This was the Northwest Territory's first federal land office. *Open Tues.-Sun. late May-early Sept.*

Strongsville

GARDENVIEW HORTICULTURAL PARK *16711 Pearl Rd.* Some 500 varieties of flowering crabapples and other rare plants grow in this lovely park. *Open Sat., Sun. Small charge.*

Twinsburg

TWINSBURG FIRST CONGREGATIONAL CHURCH *Public Sq.* This beautifully proportioned Greek Revival church was built in 1848. *Open daily.*

Upper Sandusky

INDIAN MILL STATE MEMORIAL *Rte. 47* Exhibits in this 1861 gristmill explain old-time milling methods. *Open Wed.-Sun. May-Oct.*

WYANDOT COUNTY MUSEUM *130 S. Seventh St.* The 1852 mansion contains Indian and pioneer relics. *Open Tues.-Sun.*

Van Wert

COUNTY COURTHOUSE *E. Main St.* Fanciful ornamentation enlivens this elaborate Victorian 1876 building. *Open Mon.-Fri.*

Wooster

COLLEGE OF WOOSTER MUSEUM OF ART *University St.* A fine collection of 5000 prints includes works by major printmakers from Dürer to Dali. *Open Sun.-Fri. Sept.-June.*

Youngstown

FORD NATURE EDUCATION CENTER *Old Furnace Rd., Mill Creek Park* Natural history exhibits are on display. *Open Tues.-Sun.*

OLD MILL *Canfield Rd., Mill Creek Park* The building dates from 1845-6. *Open daily June-Aug.*

Virginia

Abingdon

ABINGDON HISTORIC DISTRICT *Main St.* An 18th-century rural Virginia town is exemplified by these authentic buildings. *Open daily.*

Austinville

SHOT TOWER Lead shot was made in this 1820s limestone structure. *Open Tues.-Sun. June-early Sept.*

Big Stone Gap

JOHN FOX, JR., HOME Mementos of the author of *The Trail of the Lonesome Pine* can be seen. *Open Tues.-Sun. Apr.-Dec. Small charge.*

JUNE TOLLIVER CRAFT HOUSE Traditional arts and crafts are taught in the house where Fox's heroine lived. *Open Tues.-Sun. Apr.-Dec.*

Wytheville

ROCK HOUSE MUSEUM OF THE WYTHE COUNTY HISTORICAL SOCIETY *Monroe and Tazewell Sts.* This handsome Pennsylvania Dutch stone structure was built in 1823.

West Virginia

Ansted

FAYETTE COUNTY HISTORICAL SOCIETY COMPLEX *Rte. 60* An antebellum house, a museum with 19th-century memorabilia and a one-room schoolhouse can be visited. *Open Sun. May, Sun.-Thurs. June-Sept. Small charge.*

Charleston

SUNRISE *746 Myrtle Rd.* A children's museum, planetarium, art gallery and garden are part of this cultural center. *Open Tues.-Sun. except holidays.*

Hinton

GREENBRIER FORT *11½ mi. E. on Rte. 3* Constructed in 1772, this is one of the best-preserved 18th-century log structures in the state.

Kesler's Cross Lanes

CARNIFEX FERRY BATTLEFIELD STATE PARK MUSEUM *1 mi. S.* Weapons help relate the story of the Civil War battle fought here in 1861. *Open daily May-Oct.*

Milton

BLENKO GLASS COMPANY *Off Rte. 60* Observation tours of the plant can be made. *Visitor Center open daily, tours Mon.-Fri.*

Moundsville

GRAVE CREEK MOUND *700-800 Ninth St.* This prehistoric burial mound unfolds in the adjacent museum. *Open daily May-Nov. Adults and children over 12 small charge.*

Point Pleasant

MANSION HOUSE *Tu-Endie-Wei Park, 105 Main St.* This 1796 former tavern houses Colonial furniture. *Open daily Apr.-Oct.*

Union

REHOBOTH CHURCH *2 mi. E.* Dedicated in 1786, this is the oldest Methodist church west of the Allegheny Mountains. *Open daily.*

Zenith

MCCLUNG'S MILL A 25-foot gristmill in a mountain setting provides opportunities for photographers. *Open Sat., Sun. Apr.-Oct.*

REGION 6 [map page 356]

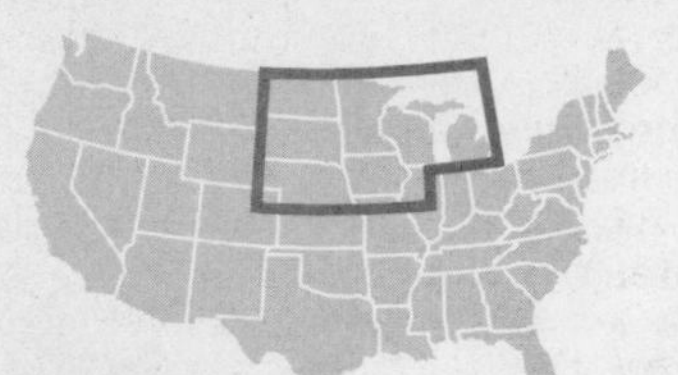

Illinois

Bishop Hill

BISHOP HILL STATE MEMORIAL Religious dissenters founded the Midwest's first large Swedish settlement in 1846. Some of the original structures still stand. *Open daily except holidays.*

Bloomington

MILLER PARK ZOO *Morris Ave.* Here is one of the best collections of exotic cats in the U.S. *Open daily.*

Carthage

OLD CARTHAGE JAIL *307 Walnut St.* Mormons Joseph and Hyrum Smith were slain here in 1844. *Open daily.*

Lincoln

POSTVILLE COURT HOUSE *914 Fifth St.* Abraham Lincoln practiced law in a building similar to this. *Open daily except holidays.*

Metamora

METAMORA COURT HOUSE STATE MEMORIAL Lincoln argued cases here. *Open daily except holidays.*

Mount Pulaski

MOUNT PULASKI COURT HOUSE STATE MEMORIAL This courthouse was another stop on lawyer Lincoln's circuit. *Open daily except holidays.*

Peoria

GLEN OAK PARK CONSERVATORY *2602 Prospect Rd.* A rose garden, tulip beds, floral displays and three greenhouses are here. *Open daily.*

GLEN OAK PARK ZOO *Glen Oak Park* There are birds, reptiles, tropical fish and mammals. *Open daily late May-early Sept., Sat., Sun. early Sept.-Nov. Small charge.*

LAKEVIEW CENTER FOR THE ARTS AND SCIENCES *1125 W. Lake Ave.* This cultural center has exhibits of art, history and natural science. *Open Tues.-Sun. except holidays.*

ST. MARY'S CATHEDRAL *607 N.E. Madison Ave.* Twin spires tower over the church. *Open daily.*

Rockford

BURPEE ART MUSEUM *737 N. Main St.* Contemporary American art is stressed at this small museum. *Open Tues.-Sun. except holidays.*

BURPEE NATURAL HISTORY MUSEUM *813 N. Main St.* Displays focus on local flora and fauna. *Open Tues.-Sun. except holidays.*

MEMORIAL HALL *211 N. Main St.* American war relics are exhibited in the 1902 building. *Open Mon.-Fri.*

SINNISSIPPI SUNKEN GARDENS *1301 N. Second St.* Formal plantings include thousands of roses, perennials and annuals. *Open daily.*

TIME MUSEUM *7801 E. State St.* Antique and modern instruments trace the history of timekeeping. *Open Tues.-Sun. except holidays. Small charge.*

Rock Island

BLACK HAWK MUSEUM *Black Hawk State Park, 1500 47th Ave.* Indian artifacts include relics from the 1832 Black Hawk War. *Open Wed.-Sun. except Thanksgiving Day and Dec. 25.*

JOHN M. BROWNING MUSEUM *Rock Island Arsenal* There is an extensive collection of antique and modern firearms. *Open Wed.-Sun.*

Utica

LaSALLE COUNTY HISTORICAL MUSEUM *Rte. 178* Local historical items are well displayed in this pre-Civil War warehouse. *Open Sat., Sun.*

Iowa

Ames

ST. THOMAS AQUINAS CHURCH *2210 Lincoln Way* This church, built of redwood and stone, has an all-glass front. *Open daily.*

Cedar Rapids

ALL SAINTS CHURCH *720 29th St., S.E.* Dedicated in 1965, the church was built to resemble a crown. *Open daily.*

ST. PIUS X CHURCH *Council and Collins Rds.* The stone church contains fine wood paneling. *Open daily.*

Cherokee

SANFORD MUSEUM AND PLANETARIUM *117 E. Willow St.* Exhibits stress local history and natural science. *Open daily except holidays.*

Clinton

SHOWBOAT MUSEUM *Riverfront Dr.* In this stern-wheel steamboat are a theater and a museum. *Open daily June-Sept. Small charge.*

Davenport

CHILDREN'S ZOO *Fejervary Park* Real animals illustrate "Mother Goose" nursery rhymes. *Open daily May-Sept. Small charge.*

Des Moines

ST. AUGUSTIN'S CHURCH *42nd St. and Grand Ave.* This church has hand-carved oak panel walls and a marble altar. *Open daily.*

Fayette

ST. FRANCIS CHURCH *205 Lovers Lane* The church's roof is sloped to represent Noah's Ark. *Open daily.*

Fort Dodge

FORT-MUSEUM *Museum Rd.* Displays relate to pioneer-Indian conflicts. *Open daily mid-May-mid-Oct. Small charge.*

Iowa City

OLD CAPITOL *Clinton St. and Iowa Ave., University of Iowa* The Greek Revival building was Iowa's first seat of state government. *Open daily.*

Jefferson

TELEPHONE MUSEUM *105 W. Harrison St.* Early telephones, switchboards and directories are displayed. *Open Mon.-Fri.*

Keosauqua

PEARSON HOUSE Used as an Underground Railroad station before the Civil War, the 1845 house contains historical artifacts. *Open Sun. June-Aug.*

VAN BUREN COUNTY COURT HOUSE The 1843 building is the state's oldest courthouse still in use. *Open Mon.-Fri.*

Le Claire

BUFFALO BILL MUSEUM *Jones and River Dr.* Memorabilia of "Buffalo Bill" Cody are on view. *Open daily May-Oct., Sat., Sun. Nov.-Apr. Adults and children over 12 small charge.*

Mason City

CHARLES H. MacNIDER MUSEUM *303 Second St., S.E.* Collections of American art include pottery, paintings and prints. *Open Tues.-Sun. except holidays.*

Nashua

LITTLE BROWN CHURCH IN THE VALE *2 mi. N.E. on Rte. 346* The song "The Church in the Wildwood" was first sung in this 1864 frame edifice. *Open daily.*

Sioux City

SERGEANT CHARLES FLOYD MONUMENT *Rte. 75 S.* A granite shaft marks the grave of Floyd, a member of Lewis and Clark's expedition (1804).

Spillville

ST. WENCESLAUS CHURCH Antonín Dvořák played the organ here in 1893. *Open daily.*

Wapello

TOOLESBORO HISTORICAL MUSEUM Six dioramas depict Indian cultures and the coming of the white man. *Open Tues.-Sun. May-Oct.*

Waterloo

MUSEUM OF HISTORY AND SCIENCE *Park Ave. and South St.* Regional history is emphasized here. *Open Tues.-Sun. except holidays.*

Winterset

CUTLER-DONAHOE BRIDGE *Winterset City Park* The covered bridge was moved here for pedestrian use.

Michigan

Ada

ADA COVERED BRIDGE *Rte. 21* The 1867 span is 125 feet long.

Au Train

PAULSON HOUSE *Forest Lake Rd.* This house of cedar logs was built in 1883. *Open daily May-mid-Dec.*

Bay City

MUSEUM OF THE GREAT LAKES

Key: Historic Place · Historic House · Old Mill or Works · Museum or Collection · Significant Buil

1700 Center Ave. Exhibits on state and Great Lakes history are featured. *Open Tues.-Sun. except holidays.*

Bloomfield Hills

ST. HUGO OF THE HILLS CHURCH *2215 Opdyke Rd.* Norman Gothic styling marks this handsome Catholic church. *Open daily.*

Charlevoix

GREENSKY HILL INDIAN CHURCH *Old Rte. 31 N.* Hymns in Ojibwa are still sung here. *Open Sun.*

Coopersville

CHURCH OF THE SAVIOUR *180 68th Ave.* On the roof of the 1970 church are symbols of the Word and Sacraments. *Open daily.*

Copper Harbor

FORT WILKINS *Fort Wilkins State Park, Rte. 41* Restored buildings and museums are at the 1840s army post. *Open daily June-Oct. Small charge each car.*

East Lansing

BEAUMONT TOWER *Michigan State University* The tower with its 47-bell carillon stands in the center of the main campus. *Open daily.*

MUSEUM *W. Circle Dr., Michigan State University* Archaeological and historical items can be seen here. *Open daily except holidays.*

Escanaba

DELTA COUNTY HISTORICAL MUSEUM *Ludington Park* Early regional industry is the theme of the displays. *Open daily late May-early Sept.*

Fremont

WINDMILL GARDENS AND OLD TOWER VILLAGE *4634 S. Luce Ave.* Early American windmills and a museum village are here. *Open Wed.-Sun. late May-early Sept. Small charge.*

Grayling

LUMBERMAN'S MUSEUM *Hartwick Pines State Park* An old lumber camp has been re-created. *Open daily mid-May-mid-Oct., Sat., Sun. Nov.-mid-May. Small charge each car.*

Hastings

CHARLTON PARK VILLAGE AND MUSEUM *Charlton Park Rd.* The reconstructed 19th-century village features craft demonstrations and early farm tools. *Park open daily, museum open daily June-Sept., Mon.-Fri. Oct.-May. Small charge each car.*

Holland

NETHERLANDS MUSEUM *8 E. 12th St.* The 1889 brick and stone house has a fine collection of old Delftware. *Open daily. Small charge.*

POLL MUSEUM *Rte. 31 and New Holland St.* Old cars, trucks, model trains and carriages are displayed. *Open Mon.-Sat. May-Sept. Small charge.*

WINDMILL ISLAND *Seventh St. and Lincoln Ave.* A miniature Dutch village surrounds a windmill from Holland. *Open daily May-Sept. Adults $1.50, children small charge.*

Houghton

A. E. SEAMAN MINERALOGICAL MUSEUM *Michigan Technological University* A fine mineral collection is here. *Open Mon.-Sat. except holidays.*

Ionia

HALL-FOWLER MEMORIAL LIBRARY *126 E. Main St.* This building is an example of the Italian villa style. *Open Tues.-Sat.*

Lake Linden

HOUGHTON COUNTY HISTORICAL MUSEUM *Rte. 26* Period rooms tell the story of life in the copper country from the 1840s. *Open daily June-early Sept. Small charge.*

Lansing

MICHIGAN STATE CAPITOL *Capitol Ave.* There are displays of Michigan heritage in this Greco-Roman building. *Open daily.*

MICHIGAN STATE HISTORICAL MUSEUM *505 N. Washington Ave.* Michigan Indian, French and 19th-century history is highlighted. *Open daily except holidays.*

Lapeer

LAPEER COUNTY COURTHOUSE *Nepessing St.* This is Michigan's oldest courthouse still in use. *Open Mon.-Fri.*

Ludington

GHOST TOWN OF HAMLIN *Ludington State Park* A marker and the ruins of the dam that broke and destroyed the town in 1888 remain.

ROSE HAWLEY MUSEUM *305 E. Filer St.* Indian artifacts and marine equipment are displayed. *Open Wed., Fri. mid-Mar.-June, Mon.-Sat. July-Aug., Wed., Fri. Sept.-Nov.*

Mackinac Island

ROBERT STUART HOUSE *Market St.* Fur-trade exhibits can be seen in this 1817 house. *Open daily June-mid-Sept. Small charge.*

Mackinaw City

TEYSEN'S TALKING BEAR MUSEUM *416 S. Huron Ave.* Indian, lumbering and maritime artifacts illustrate the area's history. *Open daily mid-May-mid-Oct. Small charge.*

Manistee

MANISTEE COUNTY HISTORICAL MUSEUM *425 River St.* Manistee's lumbering days are recalled in exhibits here. *Open Mon.-Sat. Apr.-Oct., Tues.-Sat. Nov.-Mar.*

OLD HOLLY WATERWORKS BUILDING MUSEUM *W. First St.* An 1881 structure houses articles of local historical interest. *Open Mon.-Sat. July-Aug.*

Manistique

IMOGENE HERBERT HISTORICAL MUSEUM *Deer St.* A small house contains items of local history. *Open Mon.-Fri. July-Aug. Small charge.*

Marquette

MARQUETTE COUNTY HISTORICAL SOCIETY MUSEUM *213 N. Front St.* Interesting displays tell the county's history. *Open Mon.-Fri. except holidays. Small charge.*

Menominee

MYSTERY SHIP SEAPORT *River Park* A Great Lakes schooner that sank in 1864 has been refloated. *Open daily May-Oct. Adults $1.75, children small charge.*

Midland

DOW GARDENS *St. Andrew's and Eastman Rds.* Seasonal floral attractions are displayed. *Open daily.*

MIDLAND COUNTY HISTORICAL SOCIETY OF THE CENTER FOR THE ARTS *1801 St. Andrews Dr.* This museum has various craft demonstrations. *Open Mon.-Fri.*

Muskegon

MUSKEGON COUNTY MUSEUM *30 W. Muskegon Ave.* Items illustrate the state's lumbering and fur-trading days. *Open Tues.-Sat.*

ST. FRANCIS DE SALES CATHOLIC CHURCH *2929 McCracken St.* Marcel Breuer designed this massive modern church. *Open daily.*

Ontonagon

ONTONAGON COUNTY HISTORICAL SOCIETY MUSEUM *River St.* Mining and logging items are featured. *Open daily June-Aug.*

Pontiac

FIRST BAPTIST CHURCH *34 Oakland Ave.* The contemporary structure serves the state's oldest Baptist congregation. *Open Sun.-Fri.*

PINE GROVE *405 Oakland Ave.* The 19th-century home contains period furnishings. *Open Tues.-Sat. July-Aug. Small charge.*

Port Huron

FORT GRATIOT LIGHT *Foot of Garfield St.* This 86-foot-high tower offers fine views. *Open daily.*

MUSEUM OF ARTS AND HISTORY *1115 Sixth St.* Local historical and marine artifacts are displayed. *Open Wed.-Sun. except holidays.*

Port Sanilac

SANILAC COUNTY HISTORIC MUSEUM *228 S. Ridge St.* This 1872 mansion is furnished in the period. *Open Tues.-Sun. late June-early Sept., Sat.-Sun. early Sept.-mid-Oct. Small charge.*

Presque Isle

OLD PRESQUE ISLE LIGHTHOUSE The lighthouse was built in 1840. *Open daily. Small charge.*

St. Ignace

FATHER MARQUETTE MUSEUM *N. State St.* Historical items are featured near the grave of Father Marquette. *Open Mon.-Sat. late June-Sept.*

STRAITS OF MACKINAC BRIDGE *Rte. 75* The five-mile suspension bridge

St. Ignace (*continued*)
connects Michigan's Upper and Lower Peninsulas. *$1.50 each car.*
TREASURE ISLAND MUSEUM *587 N. State St.* Indian artifacts and pirate treasures are exhibited. *Open daily May-mid-Oct. Small charge.*

Sault Ste. Marie
BISHOP BARAGA MUSEUM *315 E. Portage Ave.* The small frame house was the home of the first bishop of the diocese. *Open daily June-Sept.*
FORT BRADY *Lake Superior State College* The 1890s officers' quarters of an 1822 fort now house the college faculty. *Open Mon.-Fri.*
JOHN JOHNSTON HOUSE *415 Park Pl.* The clapboard-covered log house was built in the early 1800s by a local fur trader. *Open daily mid-Apr.-early Sept. Small charge.*
TOWER OF HISTORY *326 E. Portage Ave.* This three-towered structure offers breathtaking views. *Open daily Apr.-Oct. Small charge.*

Minnesota

Aitkin
AK-SAR-BEN GARDENS *Tame Fish Rd.* Here are rock and floral gardens, tame fish and animals. *Open daily late May-Sept. Small charge.*

Anoka
CHURCH OF ST. STEPHEN *516 School St.* The contemporary church is topped by a bell tower holding the bell from the original 1888 church building. *Open daily.*

Argyle
OLD MILL STATE PARK An 1888 water-powered flour mill is here. *Open daily May-early Sept. Small charge each car.*

Bemidji
HISTORICAL-WILDLIFE MUSEUM *Third St. and Bemidji Ave.* Pioneer-day relics and mounted animals are displayed. *Open daily late May-early Sept. Small charge.*

Carver
CARVER-ON-THE-MINNESOTA This typical 19th-century river town contains many restored buildings.

Crookston
POLK COUNTY HISTORICAL SOCIETY PIONEER MUSEUM *Washington Ave. and Jerome St.* Items of local history are on view. *Open daily June-Sept. Small charge.*

Crystal
BRUNSWICK UNITED METHODIST CHURCH *42nd and Brunswick Aves.* The brick church is noted for its simple, clean lines. *Open Tues.-Sun.*

Detroit Lakes
BECKER COUNTY HISTORICAL SOCIETY MUSEUM *915 Lake Ave.* Indian and pioneer relics are displayed. *Open Mon.-Fri. except holidays.*

Duluth
NORTHERN BIBLE SOCIETY BIBLE HOUSE *715 W. Superior St.* Bibles and Hebrew scrolls are featured. *Open Mon.-Fri. Mar.-Oct.*

Fairmont
MARTIN COUNTY HISTORICAL SOCIETY MUSEUM *304 E. Blue Earth Ave.* The old brick schoolhouse contains historical artifacts. *Open Tues.-Fri. May-Sept.*

Frontenac
OLD FRONTENAC The 1857 river community contains Colonial-style mansions and the Lakeside Hotel.

Glenwood
POPE COUNTY HISTORICAL SOCIETY MUSEUM *Rte. 104* The museum has a fine collection of Indian arts and crafts. *Open daily May-Sept., Mon.-Fri. Oct.-Apr. Small charge.*

Granite Falls
YELLOW MEDICINE COUNTY HISTORICAL MUSEUM *Rte. 2* This is a museum of history, geology and archaeology. *Open Tues.-Sun. May-mid-Oct.*

Hibbing
VILLAGE HALL *21st St. and Fourth Ave. E.* The brick town office building was patterned after Boston's historic Faneuil Hall. *Open Mon.-Fri.*

Little Falls
CHARLES A. LINDBERGH STATE MEMORIAL PARK The boyhood home of the famous aviator is here. *Open daily May-Oct.*

Mankato
BLUE EARTH COUNTY HISTORICAL MUSEUM *606 S. Broad St.* The Victorian-style mansion contains Indian and pioneer artifacts. *Open Tues.-Sun. except holidays.*

Mantorville
DODGE COUNTY COURTHOUSE Gas street lights enhance the 19th-century atmosphere of this small town. The pillared courthouse of native limestone was completed in 1865. *Open Mon.-Sat.*
DODGE COUNTY MUSEUM Once a church, the edifice now serves as a museum. *Open Sun. mid-May-Oct.*
HUBBELL HOUSE The opening walls of this hotel sheltered people from Indian attack. *Open Tues.-Sun.*
RESTORATION HOUSE This courthouse has a basement jail cell. *Open Sat., Sun.*

Mendota
FARIBAULT HOUSE *Rte. 113* An 1836 fur trader's home contains antiques and Indian relics. *Open Tues.-Sun. May-Oct. Small charge.*

Minneapolis
JAMES FORD BELL MUSEUM OF NATURAL HISTORY *17th St. and University Ave., S.E., University of Minnesota* Minnesota wildlife is featured here. *Open daily except holidays.*

Montevideo
CHIPPEWA CITY PIONEER VILLAGE *Rtes. 59 and 7* Restored buildings are grouped around a village square. *Open daily May-Sept. Small charge.*

Moorhead
CLAY COUNTY HISTORICAL SOCIETY MUSEUM *22 Eighth St., N.* Varied local historical artifacts include a Viking sword. *Open Mon.-Fri.*

New Ulm
BROWN COUNTY HISTORICAL MUSEUM *Broadway and First St., N.* The regional museum contains pioneer and Indian relics. *Open Mon.-Sat.*

Pine City
CONNOR'S FUR POST *Pine County Rd.* A reconstructed 1804 post tells of fur-trading days. *Open daily May-Sept. Small charge.*

Pipestone
PIPESTONE NATIONAL MONUMENT VISITOR CENTER *Off Rte. 75* The story of Indian ceremonial pipes made of red stone still quarried here is presented. *Open daily.*

Redwood Falls
LOWER SIOUX AGENCY INTERPRETIVE CENTER *9 mi. E. on County Rd. 2* This is the site of the original Lower Sioux Agency. *Open daily.*

Rochester
MAYO MEDICAL MUSEUM *217 First St. S.W.* Many excellent exhibits illustrate the human body and its treatment. *Open daily.*
PAUL L. HEMP OLD VEHICLE MUSEUM *Country Club Rd.* Antique cars, farm machinery and musical instruments are featured. *Open daily Apr.-Nov. Small charge.*

Roseau
ROSEAU COUNTY HISTORICAL SOCIETY MUSEUM *City Hall, Center St. and Second Ave., N.E.* Mounted birds and animals and 1300 eggs are here. *Open Mon.-Fri.*

St. Paul
INDIAN MOUNDS PARK *Mounds Blvd. and Earl St.* Six of the original burial mounds remain. *Open daily.*
MINNESOTA HISTORICAL SOCIETY MUSEUM *690 Cedar St.* The displays reflect regional history. *Open daily.*

Soudan
TOWER-SOUDAN HISTORICAL SOCIETY MUSEUM *Rte. 169* Mining exhibits are housed in a railroad coach. *Open daily late May-early Sept.*

Stewartville
FUGLE'S MILL AND MUSEUM *Rte. 1* The 1868 stone mill in its picturesque setting contains over 1000 historical exhibits.

Stillwater
WASHINGTON COUNTY HISTORICAL MUSEUM *602 N. Main St.* Lumbering mementos are displayed in an 1850s house. *Open Sun., Tues., Thurs., Sat. May-Oct. Small charge.*

Walker
WALKER MUSEUMS *E. on Rte. 371* Here are a wildlife museum, a history museum and a rural school. *Open daily mid-June-early Sept. Small charge for wildlife museum.*

Key: Historic Place · Historic House · Old Mill or Works · Museum or Collection · Significant Build

Winona

WINONA COUNTY HISTORICAL SOCIETY MUSEUM *160 Johnson St.* Pioneer and Indian relics are shown. *Open Sun.-Fri. Sept.-July. Small charge.*

Zumbrota

ZUMBROTA COVERED BRIDGE *Covered Bridge Park* This is the state's only surviving covered bridge.

Missouri

Maryville

PERCIVAL DeLUCE MEMORIAL COLLECTION *Olive DeLuce Fine Arts Bldg., Northwest Missouri State University* Paintings, drawings and prints by DeLuce and others are on view. *Open Mon.-Fri. during academic sessions.*

Nebraska

Bellevue

OLD PRESBYTERIAN CHURCH *20th and Franklin Sts.* This is the oldest (1856) church building in the state. *Open daily.*

Chadron

MUSEUM OF THE FUR TRADE *4 mi. E. on Rte. 20* On the grounds is a reconstructed trading post. *Open daily June-early Sept. Small charge.*

Champion

CHASE COUNTY HISTORICAL SOCIETY MUSEUM Changing exhibits are featured at this local museum. *Open Sun. mid-May-mid-Sept.*

Chappell

CHAPPELL MEMORIAL LIBRARY AND ART GALLERY *289 Babcock Ave.* Indian and Oriental paintings are here. *Open Mon., Wed., Sat.*

Gothenburg

PONY EXPRESS STATION *Ehmens Park* The 1854 log cabin was moved to this site. *Open daily May-Sept.*

Grand Island

CATHEDRAL OF THE NATIVITY OF ST. MARY THE VIRGIN *204 S. Cedar* The beautiful Gothic-style cathedral was consecrated in 1928. *Open daily.*

Lincoln

NEBRASKA STATE HISTORICAL SOCIETY MUSEUM *1500 R St.* Here are collections of Indian and pioneer life. *Open daily except holidays.*

UNIVERSITY OF NEBRASKA STATE MUSEUM *14th and U Sts.* This is a museum of natural history. *Open daily.*

McCook

MUSEUM OF THE HIGH PLAINS *423 Norris Ave.* Visitors may touch the exhibits of local history. *Open daily.*

Minden

HAROLD WARP PIONEER VILLAGE *Rtes. 6 and 10* The complex shows American progress from 1830 to the present. *Open daily. Adults $1.50, children small charge.*

Neligh

NELIGH MILLS *N St. and Wylie Dr.* Milling history exhibits are housed in the 1874 mill. *Open daily June-Aug.*

Omaha

UNION PACIFIC HISTORICAL MUSEUM *1416 Dodge St.* Among the railroad exhibits is a large collection of Abraham Lincoln mementos. *Open Mon.-Sat.*

Osceola

POLK COUNTY HISTORICAL MUSEUM *S. State St.* Here are an 1884 mansion, log house and old school. *Open Sun. late May-early Oct.*

Red Cloud

WEBSTER COUNTY HISTORICAL MUSEUM *721 W. Fourth Ave.* Local pioneer items are on display. *Open daily May-Sept. Small charge.*

Sidney

FORT SIDNEY POST COMMANDER'S HOME *1108 Sixth Ave.* This 1870 house is furnished in the period. *Open daily late May-early Sept.*

Trenton

HITCHCOCK COUNTY MUSEUM *Off Main St.* Here are local antiques and Indian artifacts. *Open Sun. June-Aug.*

Wilber

WILBER CZECH MUSEUM *102 W. Third St.* Local pioneers' Czech heritage is preserved. *Open Sun.*

North Dakota

Abercrombie

FORT ABERCROMBIE HISTORIC SITE *Off Rte. 81* The 1858 army post has an original guardhouse, reconstructed blockhouses and a military museum. *Open daily May-Aug. Small charge.*

Belfield

FORT HOUSTON MUSEUM Displays include a Ukrainian Eastern Rite altar and a carved Austrian altar. *Open daily Apr.-Oct. Small charge.*

Bismarck

CAMP HANCOCK HISTORIC SITE *First and Main Sts.* The 1873 frame building houses relics of Dakota pioneers and Indians. *Open Mon.-Fri. mid-May-mid-Sept.*

STATE HISTORICAL SOCIETY MUSEUM *Liberty Memorial Bldg.* The classic-style building contains a Plains Indian collection. *Open daily June-Aug., Mon.-Sat. Sept.-May.*

Cando

TOWNER COUNTY SCHOOL MUSEUM *Court House grounds* The rural school has original furnishings and old photographs. *Open Tues.*

Fort Rice

FORT RICE STATE HISTORIC SITE There are restored blockhouses at the military post. *Open daily.*

Hettinger

HETTINGER SOD HOUSE AND MUSEUM *City Park* The authentic sod house exhibits relics used in the late 1800s. *Open daily June-Aug.*

Hillsboro

TRAIL COUNTY MUSEUM *Caledonia Ave.* The 1895 native brick Victorian building contains historical items. *Open Sun. late May-Sept.*

Larimore

LARIMORE COMMUNITY MUSEUM *Town Sq.* There are Indian artifacts and native bird eggs dating from 1893. *Open Sun. June-Aug.*

Medora

MALTESE CROSS CABIN *Theodore Roosevelt National Memorial Park* Roosevelt lived here in 1884, after he bought the Maltese Cross Ranch. *Open daily mid-June-early Sept.*

MEDORA DOLL HOUSE The 1884 building contains a collection of antique dolls and toys. *Open daily mid-May-Sept. Small charge.*

MEDORA MUSEUM Displays include Indian costumes and artifacts, furs and wildlife. *Open daily mid-May-early Sept. Small charge.*

Niagara

NIAGARA LOG CABIN The 1881 hand-hewn cabin contains period furnishings. *Open daily.*

Pembina

PEMBINA STATE MUSEUM *Pembina State Park* Exhibits trace the development of the 1797 fur-trading post. *Open daily late May-Sept.*

Walhalla

KITTSON TRADING POST The 1844 oak log cabin is the oldest surviving building in North Dakota.

Williston

WILLIAMS COUNTY HISTORICAL SOCIETY FRONTIER MUSEUM *N. off Rtes. 2 and 85* The 11-building complex has displays from the Dakota homesteading period. *Open daily June-Aug. Adults $2.00, children small charge.*

South Dakota

Armour

DOUGLAS COUNTY HISTORICAL SOCIETY MUSEUM *Rte. 281* The building houses historical items from the county. *Open Sun. June-Aug.*

Belle Fourche

TRI-STATE MUSEUM *831 State St.* Various items trace the area's history. *Open Sun.-Fri. mid-May-mid-Sept.*

Britton

PRAYER ROCK MUSEUM *Main St.* On display is the 4500-year-old Prayer Rock used by the Sioux. *Open daily late May-Aug.*

Custer

GAME LODGE DOLL HOUSE *Custer State Game Lodge* More than 1000 antique dolls are displayed. *Open daily mid-May-Sept. Small charge.*

HOW THE WEST WAS WON MEMORIAL MUSEUM *624 Crook St.* Exhibits include a fine gun collection. *Open daily May-Oct. Adults $1.25, children small charge.*

Custer (*continued*)

WESTERN WOODCARVING *Rte. 16 W.* These carvings by master craftsman H. D. Niblack range from miniature animals to life-size Indians. *Open daily May–Oct. Small charge.*

Deadwood

DEADWOOD GULCH ART GALLERY *665½ Main St.* A main attraction is the Chinese Museum in the tunnel under the 1888 building. *Open daily Apr.–mid-Dec. Small charge.*

THEODORE ROOSEVELT NATIONAL MONUMENT *Mount Theodore Roosevelt* This tower was the first memorial in the U.S. dedicated to the "Rough Rider" President. *Open daily.*

Fort Pierre

VERENDRYE MONUMENT *Verendrye Hill* The stone tablet marks the spot of a 1743 marker claiming all of the region for France. *Open daily.*

VERENDRYE MUSEUM Historical objects trace the history of the Dakota Territory. *Open daily June–early Sept. Small charge.*

Hill City

1880 TRAIN *Rtes. 16 and 385* A steam train travels a scenic 32-mile route. *Trips daily mid-June–Aug. Adults $4.50, children $2.50.*

Huron

STATE FAIR PIONEER MUSEUM *Fair Grounds* Displays include articles from South Dakota's homesteading era. *Open daily June–Aug.*

Interior

CEDAR PASS VISITOR CENTER *Badlands National Monument* On view are regional prairie fossils and wildlife. *Open daily.*

Lemmon

PETRIFIED WOOD PARK MUSEUM *Petrified Wood Park* The museum, made of petrified wood, houses fossils. *Open daily mid-May–mid-Sept.*

Mobridge

SITTING BULL MEMORIAL *Rte. 12* A six-ton statue of the famous Sioux marks his grave. *Open daily.*

Pickstown

FORT RANDALL CHAPEL RUINS *Lake Francis Case Area* The walls of the chalkstone chapel are all that remain of the 1856 fort. *Open daily.*

Presho

LYMAN COUNTY HISTORICAL SOCIETY MUSEUM *Rte. 16* The complex houses displays of pioneer artifacts. *Open daily June–Aug.*

Sioux Falls

MINNEHAHA MUSEUM *200 W. Sixth St.* Relics of pioneer days are found here. *Open daily.*

ST. JOSEPH CATHEDRAL *Fifth St. and Duluth Ave.* Fine windows adorn this church. *Open daily.*

Sisseton

POHLEN CULTURAL CENTER Sioux Indian artifacts and interesting murals can be seen here. *Open daily.*

Wall

SIOUX INDIAN VILLAGE *Rte. 16A* Indians in full dress demonstrate native crafts. *Open daily May–Sept. Small charge.*

Wisconsin

Appleton

DARD HUNTER PAPER MUSEUM OF THE INSTITUTE OF PAPER CHEMISTRY *1043 E. South River St.* Exhibits cover the history of papermaking. *Open Mon.–Fri.*

WORCESTER ART CENTER *Lawrence University, S. Union and Alton Sts.* Student and faculty work is exhibited here. *Open Mon.–Sat. Sept.–May.*

Baraboo

MAN MOUND PARK *E. off Rte. 33* This unusual effigy mound resembles a human figure. *Open daily.*

SAUK COUNTY HISTORICAL SOCIETY MUSEUM *531 Fourth Ave.* Collections are housed in a 1906 English Tudor-style home. *Open Tues.–Sun. late May–Sept. Small charge.*

Beaver Dam

DODGE COUNTY HISTORICAL SOCIETY MUSEUM *127 S. Spring St.* Here are 4000 items relating to the history of the county. *Open Mon.–Sat.*

Dickeyville

DICKEYVILLE GROTTO One priest made the grotto from stone, glass and shells. *Open daily.*

Ephraim

ANDERSON STORE *Anderson Dock, Rte. 42* Local relics are displayed in this authentically restored 1858 general store. *Open Fri., Sat. mid-late June, Mon.–Sat. July–Aug., Fri., Sat. Sept.–mid-Oct.*

Fort Atkinson

HOARD HISTORICAL MUSEUM *409 Merchant Ave.* A large collection of local history relics is featured. *Open Tues.–Sat.*

Green Bay

CHRIST CHURCH *421 Cherry St.* This is an English Gothic-style church. *Open daily.*

FORT HOWARD HOSPITAL MUSEUM *402 N. Chestnut St.* Relics of the fort are displayed in the 1816 hospital and ward. *Open Tues.–Sun. May–Oct. Small charge.*

Hayward

HISTORYLAND *E. on Rte. B* An Indian village and a logging camp have been reconstructed. *Open daily late June–early Sept. Adults $2.00, children small charge.*

Kenosha

CIVIL WAR MUSEUM *Lentz Hall, Carthage College* This is a fine assembly of uniforms, weapons and documents. *Open Mon.–Sat.*

Kohler

WAELDERHAUS *W. Riverside Dr.* The memorial to John Michael Kohler is a replica of his Austrian home. *Open daily except holidays.*

Lake Mills

LAKE MILLS-AZTALAN HISTORICAL SOCIETY MUSEUM *3 mi. E. on Rte. B* Relics from an ancient Indian town nearby can be seen here. *Open daily May–Oct.*

La Pointe

MADELINE ISLAND MUSEUM Fur-trade era relics are displayed. *Open daily mid-June–mid-Sept. Small charge.*

Madison

GREAT BIRD MOUND *Mendota State Hospital grounds* This effigy mound is in the form of a bird with a 624-foot wingspan. *Open daily.*

MADISON ART CENTER *720 E. Gorham St.* Modern graphics, paintings and sculpture are featured. *Open Tues.–Sun. Sept.–July.*

Manitowoc

MANITOWOC MARITIME MUSEUM *402 N. Eighth St.* A U.S. submarine, ship models and equipment illustrate maritime history. *Open daily except Jan. 1 and Dec. 25. Small charge.*

RAHR CIVIC CENTER AND PUBLIC MUSEUM *610 N. Eighth St.* American art exhibits change monthly. *Open daily except holidays.*

Marinette

MARINETTE COUNTY HISTORICAL MUSEUM *Stephenson Island* Miniature carved lumberjacks depict their daily routine. *Open daily late May–mid-Oct. Small charge.*

Milton

MILTON HOUSE MUSEUM *Rtes. 59 and 26* This hexagonal building may be the oldest grout structure in the U.S. *Open daily May–Oct. Small charge.*

Milwaukee

ST. JOAN OF ARC CHAPEL *Marquette University* The rebuilt 15th-century French chapel is decorated in the period. *Open daily.*

Mineral Point

MINERAL POINT HISTORICAL SOCIETY MUSEUM *Pine and Davis Sts.* Regional historical items and a mineral collection are featured. *Open daily June–Sept. Small charge.*

PENDARVIS HISTORICAL SITE *Shakerag St.* Several 1830s stone houses built by Cornish miners have been painstakingly restored. *Open daily May–Oct. Small charge.*

Nashotah

CHAPEL OF ST. MARY THE VIRGIN *Nashotah House* The Victorian Gothic-style chapel has fine interior details of carved walnut. *Open daily.*

New Glarus

CHALET OF THE GOLDEN FLEECE *618 Second St.* The chalet contains many items of Swiss origin. *Open daily Apr.–Oct. Small charge.*

SWISS MUSEUM VILLAGE *Sixth Ave. and Seventh St.* Ten buildings of the 1845 Swiss settlement have

Key: Historic Place · Historic House · Old Mill or Works · Museum or Collection · Significant Building

been reconstructed here. *Open daily May-Oct. Small charge.*

Oshkosh

OSHKOSH PUBLIC MUSEUM *1331 Algoma Blvd.* An Apostles clock is a prime attraction. *Open Tues.-Sun.*

Platteville

MITCHELL-ROUNTREE STONE COTTAGE *W. Madison St. and Rte. 81* This restored 1837 cottage has many of its original furnishings. *Open Tues.-Sun. June-Aug. Small charge.*

Portage

FORT WINNEBAGO SURGEONS QUARTERS *1½ mi. E. on Rte. 33* The 1828 log house is furnished in the period. *Open daily May-Oct. Small charge.*

Prairie du Chien

BRISBOIS HOUSE *Water St.* Household items of the former owners are in the 1808 brick and stone house. *Open daily May-Oct.*

SECOND FORT CRAWFORD *Rice St.* The fort's only remaining building is now a medical museum. *Open daily mid-Apr.-Oct. Small charge.*

Racine

CHARLES A. WUSTUM MUSEUM OF FINE ARTS *2519 Northwestern Ave.* Contemporary American art is on display. *Open daily except holidays.*

Ripon

LITTLE WHITE SCHOOLHOUSE *Blackburn St.* The Republican Party was organized here. *Open daily late May-Aug. Small charge.*

Rudolph

GROTTO SHRINE AND WONDER CAVE *8 mi. S. on Rte. 34* The grotto is set among rock and floral displays. *Open daily Apr.-Oct. Small charge.*

Sheboygan

SHEBOYGAN COUNTY HISTORICAL SOCIETY MUSEUM *3110 Erie Ave.* Local artifacts are displayed in the 1850 Taylor Homestead. *Open Tues.-Sun. Apr.-Sept. Small charge.*

SHEBOYGAN INDIAN MOUND PARK *Ninth St.* The 33 burial mounds have various shapes. *Open daily.*

Spooner

MUSEUM OF WOOD CARVING *1 mi. S. on Rte. 63* Wood carvings depict the life of Christ. *Open daily May-Oct. Small charge.*

Spring Green

TALIESIN Architect Frank Lloyd Wright designed and lived in this Prairie-style house.

Sturgeon Bay

FARM *3 mi. N. on Rte. 57* A model turn-of-the-century farm has many early farm implements. *Open daily late May-Aug. Small charge.*

Superior

DOUGLAS COUNTY HISTORICAL MUSEUM *906 E. Second St.* Indian relics and historical items are displayed in this 1890 mansion. *Open daily June-Aug., Tues.-Sun. Sept.-May.*

Wausau

MARATHON COUNTY HISTORICAL MUSEUM *403 McIndoe St.* Exhibits relating to Marathon County's lumbering days are housed in this 1901 lumber baron's house. *Open Sun.-Fri. except holidays.*

Wauzeka

PHETTEPLACE MUSEUM *Rte. 60* A large collection of gemstone inlays is displayed here. *Open daily mid-May-mid-Oct. Small charge.*

REGION 7 [map page 400]

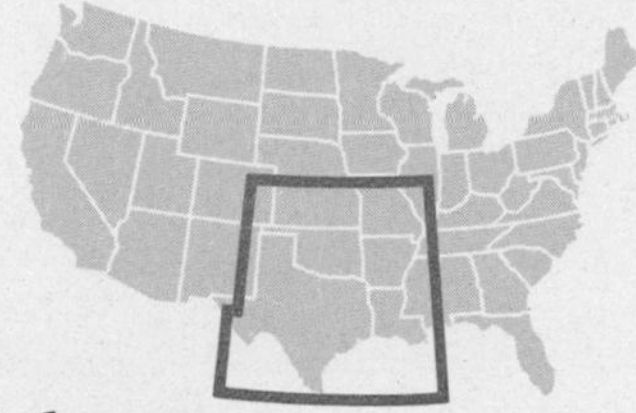

Arkansas

Arkadelphia

HENDERSON STATE COLLEGE MUSEUM Caddoan Indian relics and the history of lighting are shown. *Open Sun., Mon., Wed.*

Eureka Springs

CHRIST ONLY ART GALLERY *3 mi. E. off Rte. 62* Christ is the subject of every artwork in this unusual collection. *Open daily. Small charge.*

CHURCH IN THE WILDWOOD BIBLE MUSEUM *E. on Rte. 62* Bibles and manuscripts in 625 languages are here. *Open daily except Easter Day and Thanksgiving Day. Small charge.*

Fayetteville

FINE ARTS CENTER *University of Arkansas* Edward Durell Stone designed this ultramodern cultural center. *Open daily except holidays.*

UNIVERSITY OF ARKANSAS MUSEUM *Old Student Union* Indian artifacts and American pressed glass are highlights. *Open daily except Dec. 25.*

Little Rock

ST. ANDREW'S CATHOLIC CATHEDRAL *623 Louisiana St.* This native granite Gothic-style church is a copy of one in Germany. *Open daily.*

VILLA MARRE *1321 Scott* A saloon owner built this Italianate Victorian-style house in 1881. *Open Tues., Thurs., Sat., Sun. Small charge.*

Murfreesboro

ANCIENT BURIAL MOUNDS *1½ mi. W. off Rte. 27* Indian burial mounds and artifacts can be seen here. *Open daily Apr.-Oct. Adults $1.50, children small charge.*

Pea Ridge

PEA RIDGE NATIONAL MILITARY PARK *Rte. 62* A major Civil War battle erupted here in 1862. *Open daily.*

Washington

AUGUSTUS H. GARLAND HOME This 1830 home of an Arkansas governor is furnished with antiques. *Open daily. Adults $2.00, children 6-15 small charge.* (*Fee includes buildings below.*)

BLACKSMITH SHOP Here is a replica of the shop where James Black fashioned the original Bowie knife.

CONFEDERATE STATE CAPITOL This one-time county courthouse was Arkansas's capitol for two years during the Civil War.

TAVERN Davey Crockett and Sam Houston once visited this 1824 inn.

Colorado

La Junta

KOSHARE INDIAN MUSEUM *18th St. and Colorado Ave.* Indian art and crafts are displayed. *Open daily.*

Illinois

Alton

LOVEJOY MEMORIAL *Alton Cemetery, Fifth and Monument Sts.* This monument honors a pioneering abolitionist newspaper editor.

Belleville

NATIONAL SHRINE OF OUR LADY OF THE SNOWS *Rte. 460* A dramatic contemporary altar is the focal point here. *Open daily.*

Cahokia

CHURCH OF THE HOLY FAMILY *116 Church St.* This 1799 church is the oldest one in continuous use in the old Northwest Territory.

Collinsville

CAHOKIA MOUNDS STATE PARK *Rte. 40* The Indian mound here known as Monk's Mound is the largest in North America. *Open daily.*

Edwardsville

MADISON COUNTY HISTORICAL MUSEUM *715 N. Main St.* Period rooms and historic items are on view in this 1836 Federal-style house. *Open Wed., Fri.-Sun. except holidays.*

Elsah

DOLL MUSEUM All types of dolls are displayed in this quaint stone cottage. *Open daily. Small charge.*

GLENN FELCH ART PROJECT *Principia College* A student's drawings and models portray many of the town's old buildings. *Open Mon.-Fri. during college sessions.*

SPATZ FILLING STATION Perhaps the country's first truly decorative gas station, this stone building was designed by architect Bernard Maybeck to harmonize with the beauty of the rest of the town.

VILLAGE INN *Principia College* In the 1880s Italianate features were added to the pre-Civil War structure, the home of a wealthy merchant.

Jacksonville

GOVERNOR DUNCAN MANSION *4 Duncan Park* Illinois' fifth governor owned this 1834 Georgian dwelling. *Open Thurs. Apr.-Oct. Small charge.*

Springfield

FIRST PRESBYTERIAN CHURCH *321 S. Seventh St.* This 1868 edifice contains a pew used by Lincoln. *Open daily.*

LINCOLN MEMORIAL GARDEN NATURE CENTER *2301 E. Lake Dr.* Native plants are used to beautiful effect. *Open daily.*

LINCOLN'S DEPOT *10th and Monroe Sts.* In 1861 Lincoln left from this station for his inauguration. *Open daily Apr.-Nov. Small charge.*

Vandalia

VANDALIA STATE HOUSE *315 N. Gallatin St.* Lincoln attended the legislature here before the state government was moved in 1839. *Open daily except holidays.*

Kansas

Ashland

PIONEER MUSEUM *Rte. 160* Contrasting exhibits include a pioneer collection and an airplane aerobatics museum. *Open daily except Dec. 25.*

Atchison

ATCHISON POST OFFICE *621 Kansas Ave.* Ornate turrets and entryways decorate this 1890s stone building. *Open daily.*

Athol

HOME ON THE RANGE CABIN The words to Kansas's state song were written here in 1873. *Open daily.*

Bonner Springs

AGRICULTURAL HALL OF FAME AND NATIONAL CENTER *630 N. 126th St.* Farming through the years is the museum's theme. *Open daily except holidays. Small charge.*

Chanute

MARTIN AND OSA JOHNSON SAFARI MUSEUM *16 S. Grant Ave.* Africa and the South Seas are the themes here. *Open daily. Small charge.*

Coffeyville

COFFEYVILLE HISTORICAL MUSEUM (DALTON MUSEUM) *113 E. Eighth St.* Objects relating to the notorious 1890s Dalton Gang are on display. *Open daily. Adults small charge.*

Colby

SOD TOWN MUSEUM *2 mi. E. on Rte. 24* Once-common prairie sod houses hold pioneer furnishings. *Open daily May-Oct. Adults and children over 12 small charge.*

Cottonwood Falls

RONIGER MEMORIAL MUSEUM Arrowheads and other regional Indian artifacts are a major part of this collection. *Open Tues., Wed., Fri.-Sun.*

Council Grove

FARMERS AND DROVERS BANK *201 W. Main St.* Limestone trim adorns this 1893 brick building. *Open Mon.-Sat.*

OLD KAW MISSION *500 N. Mission* The old school keeps the Santa Fe Trail days alive through pioneer and Indian artifacts. *Open Tues.-Sun.*

Dodge City

HOME OF STONE *112 E. Vine St.* Thick native stone walls are of interest in this furnished 1881 residence. *Open daily June-early Sept.*

Ellsworth

HODGDEN HOUSE *104 S.W. Main St.* Indian and pioneer artifacts are on view. *Open Tues.-Sun.*

Hanover

HOLLENBERG PONY EXPRESS STATION MUSEUM *2 mi. N.E.* Pioneer items can be seen in this unaltered Pony Express stop. *Open Tues.-Sun.*

Hays

STERNBERG MEMORIAL MUSEUM *Fort Hays Kansas State College* Fossils, guns and geological specimens are on display. *Open daily.*

Hill City

OIL MUSEUM *W. on Rte. 24* The full story of oil production is presented here. *Open Tues.-Sun. Mar.-Oct.*

Iola

GENERAL FUNSTON BOYHOOD HOME *4½ mi. N. on Rte. 169* General Frederick Funston, hero of the 1901 Philippine campaign, lived in this frame house. *Open daily.*

La Crosse

POST ROCK MUSEUM Early limestone farm posts and related tools are displayed here. *Open daily Apr.-Sept.*

Lawrence

TENNESSEE STREET Imposing old homes of varying architectural styles make this street worth a visit.

Leavenworth

LEAVENWORTH HISTORICAL MUSEUM *334 Fifth Ave.* The woodwork is notable in this Gilded Age mansion. *Open Tues.-Sun. Small charge.*

Lebanon

GEOGRAPHIC CENTER OF THE CONTINENTAL 48 STATES *2½ mi. N.W.* The gravity method was used to accurately place this marker.

Lyons

RICE COUNTY HISTORICAL MUSEUM *221 East Ave. S.* Coronado and Quivirian Indian cultures are emphasized. *Open Tues.-Sun.*

Meade

DALTON GANG HIDEOUT A tunnel once used by the outlaw Daltons connects a house and barn (now a museum) owned in the 1880s by their sister. *Open daily. Small charge.*

Medicine Lodge

CARRIE NATION HOME *211 W. Fowler* Period furniture and pictures of Mrs. Nation destroying saloons are exhibited. *Open daily.*

MEDICINE LODGE STOCKADE MUSEUM *209 W. Flower* Indian artifacts and a furnished 1877 log house are featured attractions. *Open daily Apr.-Oct. Small charge.*

Muncie

GRINTER PLACE MUSEUM *1420 S. 78th St.* This handsome brick house was built in 1857 by a ferry operator. *Open Tues.-Sun.*

Oberlin

LAST INDIAN RAID IN KANSAS MUSEUM *258 S. Penn St.* Objects associated with an 1878 Indian raid, period rooms, a library and an authentic sod house attract visitors. *Open daily Apr.-Dec. Small charge.*

Osawatomie

JOHN BROWN MUSEUM *John Brown Memorial Park, 10th and Main Sts.* This 1854 cabin holds memorabilia of the abolitionist. *Open Tues.-Sun. except holidays.*

OLD STONE CHURCH *Sixth and Parker Sts.* Completed in 1861, the state's oldest church is still in use.

Phillipsburg

OLD FORT BISSELL *Rte. 36* This is a replica of an enclosure used for defense against Apaches. *Open daily late May-early Sept.*

Pleasanton

MARAIS DES CYGNES MASSACRE MEMORIAL PARK *5 mi. N.E. on Rte. 69* This park contains a museum and is rich in the history of John Brown. *Park open daily; museum open Tues.-Sun.*

Smith Center

OLD DUTCH MILL *Wagner Park* This wind-powered gristmill was built about 1882. *Open daily May-Sept.*

Topeka

MUNN MEMORIAL *Gage Park, 10th St.* Kansas pioneers are memorialized in stone in a landscaped setting.

Wallace

FORT WALLACE MEMORIAL ASSOCIATION MUSEUM *½ mi. E. on Rte. 40* Military and pioneer relics are on display. *Open daily mid-May-early Sept., Sun. mid-Sept.-early May except holidays.*

Wichita

HISTORIC WICHITA COW TOWN *1717 Sim Park Dr.* Thirty buildings dating from 1868-85 include Billy the Kid's boyhood home. *Open daily mid-Mar.-Nov. Small charge.*

WICHITA CITY HALL *204 S. Main St.* A tall clock tower rises above this ornate French Romanesque stone building. *Open Mon.-Fri.*

Louisiana

Alexandria

KENT PLANTATION HOUSE *Rapides Ave.* This is one of Louisiana's oldest homes. *Open daily. Small charge.*

Baton Rouge

MUSEUM OF GEOSCIENCE *Louisiana State University* Exhibits of Indian culture, fossils, bones, minerals and artifacts make up this collection. *Open daily.*

Bermuda

OAKLAND PLANTATION *Rte. 119* Antique furniture and tools are displayed in this 1821 cypress dwelling.

Darrow

HERMITAGE PLANTATION This 1812 Greek Revival brick mansion is surrounded by 24 Doric columns.

Destrehan

DESTREHAN MANOR HOUSE The great Colonial plantation house was built in 1787 by a free black artisan. *Open Sat., Sun. Small charge.*

Jackson

ASPHODEL PLANTATION *4 mi. S. on Rte. 68* Audubon was often a guest in this 1820 Greek Revival home. *Open daily. Small charge.*

Lafayette

UNION ART GALLERY *University of Southwestern Louisiana* The work of local artists is stressed, but famous American and foreign artwork is also exhibited. *Open Mon.-Fri.*

Lake Charles

IMPERIAL CALCASIEU MUSEUM *204 W. Sallier St.* Many items here relate to Louisiana's past. *Open Wed.-Sun. except Christmas week.*

Loreauville

LOREAUVILLE HERITAGE MUSEUM Replicas of antebellum buildings reveal the life-style of southern Louisiana's French settlers. *Open daily.*

Mansfield

MANSFIELD BATTLE PARK AND MUSEUM *4 mi. S. on Rte. 175* A museum tells the story of the last Confederate victory, won here in 1864. *Open Tues.-Sun. Small charge.*

Many

FORT JESUP STATE MONUMENT *6 mi. N.E.* The original army kitchen, now restored, can be seen in this 1822 fort. A museum is in the reconstructed officers' quarters. *Open Tues.-Sat. Museum small charge.*

New Orleans

BANK OF LOUISIANA *334 Royal St.* This elegant old bank is now a visitor information center. *Open daily.*

BEAUREGARD HOUSE *1113 Chartres St.* Civil War General Pierre Beauregard lived in this house, later restored by novelist Frances Parkinson Keyes. *Open daily.*

CONFEDERATE MUSEUM OF THE LOUISIANA HISTORICAL ASSOCIATION *929 Camp St.* Jefferson Davis memorabilia, portraits of Confederate leaders and Civil War relics abound here. *Open Mon.-Fri. Small charge.*

CUSTOMS HOUSE *423 Canal St.* Begun in 1848, this imposing Egyptian-style granite structure was not completed until 1913. *Open daily.*

FORT PIKE STATE MONUMENT *E. on Rte. 90* Surrounded by water, this 1821 military installation was once considered impregnable. *Open Tues.-Sun. Adults and children over 12 small charge.*

INTERNATIONAL TRADE MART *2 Canal St.* Good views of the city and the Mississippi River can be enjoyed from atop this modern building. *Open Mon.-Fri.; observation deck open daily. Small charge for deck.*

LABRANCHE BUILDINGS *Royal and St. Peter Sts.* Wrought-iron balconies decorate these 11 brick row houses which were built in 1840.

LOYOLA UNIVERSITY *6363 St. Charles Ave.* The Holy Name of Jesus Church and Marquette Hall are both Tudor Gothic structures. *Church open daily; hall open during academic sessions.*

MANHEIM GALLERIES *401 Royal St.* Designed by Benjamin Latrobe in 1820, this building is now an antique shop. *Open Mon.-Sat.*

NEW ORLEANS HISTORICAL PHARMACY MUSEUM *514 Chartres St.* Objects from 19th-century apothecary shops are displayed here. *Open Tues.-Sat.*

ST. ALPHONSUS CATHOLIC CHURCH *Constance St.* Windows and statues depict international religious symbols in this richly decorated 1855 edifice. *Open daily.*

ST. FRANCES CABRINI CHURCH *5500 Paris Ave.* In this bold modern church, a canopy soars over an enormous marble altar. *Open daily.*

Opelousas

JIM BOWIE MUSEUM *153 W. Landry St.* Mementos (including the knife) are here. *Open Tues.-Sat. Small charge.*

Plaquemine

CARRIAGE HOUSE MUSEUM *712 Eden St.* Farm tools are exhibited in an authentic Creole kitchen and Cajun barn. *Open Mon.-Sat.*

St. Francisville

CATALPA PLANTATION *N. on Rte. 61* This Victorian residence is furnished with antiques and surrounded by a 30-acre garden of native plants. *Open daily Mar.-Nov. $1.50.*

St. Joseph

DAVIDSON HOME This old plantation house is furnished with heirlooms. *Adults $1.50.*

Shreveport

LOUISIANA STATE EXHIBIT MUSEUM *3015 Greenwood Rd.* Imaginative dioramas and murals illustrate the state's history and resources. *Open daily except Dec. 25.*

Tangipahoa

CAMP MOORE CONFEDERATE CEMETERY AND MUSEUM About 500 Confederate soldiers are buried on the grounds; a museum contains Civil War relics. *Open Sun.-Fri.*

Thibodaux

EDWARD DOUGLAS WHITE MEMORIAL *6 mi. N.* The state's only chief justice was born in this house, built in 1790 of pegged cypress wood. *Open Tues.-Sun. Small charge.*

Vacherie

OAK ALLEY PLANTATION *3 mi. W.* This Greek Revival mansion was built in the 1830s. *Open daily except Dec. 25. Small charge.*

Washington

ARLINGTON The restored brick and clapboard house is stylishly furnished. *Open daily. $2.00.*

Waterproof

MYRTLE GROVE *1 mi. N.* One of the earliest prefabricated homes in the South, this 1810 plantation house is beautifully furnished.

Mississippi

Greenville

WINTERVILLE MOUNDS STATE PARK AND MUSEUM *5 mi. N. on Rte. 1* On a ceremonial site of prehistoric Indians, the museum contains rare artifacts. *Open Tues.-Sun. Small charge.*

Holly Springs

WALTER PLACE *331 W. Chulahoma Ave.* During the Civil War General and Mrs. U. S. Grant lived briefly in this turreted brick mansion.

Jackson

MYNELLE GARDENS *4738 Clinton Blvd.* The floral eden offers lovely vistas at every season of the year. *Open daily. Small charge Mar.-Dec.*

Lorman

OLD COUNTRY STORE *Rte. 61* Outfitted much as it was in the 1890s, this is among the few general stores still operating in the U.S. *Open daily except Easter Day and Dec. 25.*

Mannsdale

CHAPEL OF THE CROSS This Gothic Revival church dates from 1852. *Open 2nd Sun. each month.*

Natchez

EVANSVIEW *107 S. Broadway* Finished in 1830, the Creole-style house is richly furnished with period pieces. *Open Wed. Small charge.*

KING'S TAVERN *611 Jefferson St.* Considered the oldest Natchez structure, it once served as a stagecoach and mail station. *Open daily except holidays. Small charge.*

MOUNT LOCUST *Natchez Trace Pkwy., 20 mi. N.E.* The 1780s farmstead is among the oldest in the state. *Open daily Mar., June-Aug., Sat., Sun. Sept.*

ST. MARY'S CATHEDRAL *107 S. Union St.* The multispired Gothic-style cathedral was started in 1842. *Open daily.*

Oxford

MARY BUIE MUSEUM *510 University Ave.* Here are Revolutionary War documents, Civil War memorabilia and dozens of rare dolls. *Open Tues.-Sun. Sept.-July.*

ROWAN OAK, WILLIAM FAULKNER HOME *Old Taylor Rd.* After 1930 the great novelist lived in this Greek

Revival house. *Open Mon.-Sat. during academic year.*

Port Gibson

GRAND GULF MILITARY STATE PARK *7 mi. N.W.* The remains of two forts and a museum of Civil War relics stand here. *Open daily.*

PRESBYTERIAN CHURCH *Church and Walnut Sts.* Atop the tall steeple is an iron hand with its forefinger pointing heavenward.

Sandy Hook

JOHN FORD HOUSE Part brick, part pine timber, the three-story home was hand-built in the early 1800s. *Open Sat., Sun. Small charge.*

Vicksburg

U.S. ARMY ENGINEER WATERWAYS EXPERIMENT STATION *Halls Ferry Rd.* Among the absorbing installations here are working models of many U.S. harbors and waterways. *Open Mon.-Fri.*

Washington

JEFFERSON COLLEGE The buildings at this attractive college, incorporated (1802) by the territorial legislature, are in the process of being restored. *Open daily except holidays.*

Missouri

Affton

OAKLAND *7802 Genesta St.* Built about 1850, the house is an intriguing mixture of styles. The roof has Greek pediments, the windows, Romanesque arches and the four-story tower is Italianate.

Branson

SHEPHERD OF THE HILLS MEMORIAL MUSEUM *7 mi. W. on Rte. 76* Antiques, artwork, dolls and Ozark crafts are among the displays. *Open daily late Mar.-late Nov.*

SILVER DOLLAR CITY *9 mi. W. on Rte. 76* Artisans demonstrate their crafts at this re-created Ozark settlement of the 1880s. *Open Wed.-Sun. early May-late May, early Sept.-Oct., daily late May-early Sept. Adults $3.00, children 6-11 $1.50.*

Burfordville

BOLLINGER MILL *Off Rte. 34* This three-story brick gristmill is one of the few remaining in the state.

Camdenton

KELSEY'S ANTIQUE CARS *Rte. 54* A rare Stutz Bearcat and an Auburn are among the prize vehicles. *Open daily. Small charge.*

Centralia

CHANCE GARDENS The beautifully planted grounds are enhanced by a rock grotto and a winding brook. *Open daily May-Sept.*

Independence

HERITAGE HALL MUSEUM *1001 W. Walnut St.* Historic Mormon documents are on display here. *Open daily except holidays.*

JAIL MUSEUM *217 N. Main St.* The 1859 jail and marshal's home both have period memorabilia. *Open daily June-Aug., Tues.-Sun. Sept.-May. Small charge.*

Kansas City

INDIAN SCOUT AND PIONEER MOTHER STATUES *Penn Valley Park* The Sioux hunter and pioneer family honor early American settlers.

KANSAS CITY ART INSTITUTE *4415 Warwick Blvd.* The new Ceramics Building is an architectural prize-winner, and the Charlotte Crosby Kemper Gallery has rotating exhibits of works by students, faculty and guest artists. *Open daily.*

KANSAS CITY MUSEUM OF HISTORY AND SCIENCE *3218 Gladstone Blvd.* Thousands of items tell of the region's history, anthropology and wildlife. *Open daily except holidays.*

SWOPE PARK AND ZOO *Swope Pkwy. and Meyer Blvd.* The enormous playground features sports areas, nature trails, a theater and a zoo with an outstanding children's section. *Open daily. Small charge for zoo.*

Lamar

HARRY S. TRUMAN BIRTHPLACE *1009 Truman Ave.* In 1884 the late President was born in this modest six-room frame house. *Open daily.*

Lexington

MUSEUM OF THE YESTURYEARS *Rtes. 13 and 24* Early vehicles, old-time shops and household items are among the frontier Americana here. *Open daily Mar.-Nov. Small charge.*

Liberty

CHARLES F. CURRY LIBRARY *William Jewell College* Rare books and Victorian glass are the specialties. *Open Mon.-Fri.*

HISTORIC LIBERTY JAIL *216 N. Main St.* Housed in a museum, the reconstructed jail once held Mormon leader Joseph Smith. *Open daily.*

Mansfield

LAURA INGALLS WILDER HOME AND MUSEUM *Rocky Ridge Farm* The home honors the noted author of children's books. *Open May-mid-Oct. Small charge.*

Paris

UNION COVERED BRIDGE *8 mi. S.W.* The last of the county's covered bridges was built in 1870.

Republic

WILSON'S CREEK NATIONAL BATTLEFIELD *3 mi. E.* More than 2500 soldiers were killed or wounded here in a fierce Civil War battle on Aug. 10, 1861. *Open daily.*

Rolla

UNIVERSITY OF MISSOURI-ROLLA GEOLOGY MUSEUM *Norwood Hall* Rare and familiar minerals from all parts of the world dazzle rock hounds and others. *Open Mon.-Sat.*

Ste. Genevieve

BOLDUC HOUSE *125 S. Main St.* Built about 1770, Bolduc House is probably the finest restoration of a Creole structure in the Mississippi Valley. *Open Apr.-Oct. Small charge.*

CHURCH OF STE. GENEVIEVE *49 DuBourg Pl.* This Gothic-style church was built in 1880. *Open daily.*

FUR TRADING POST AND DR. SHAW HOME *Second and Merchant Sts.* These adjoining structures probably were built before 1785. *Open daily Apr.-Oct. Small charge.*

GREEN TREE TAVERN *244 S. Main St.* French antiques are among the furnishings in this former inn. *Open daily except Dec. 25. Small charge.*

MUSEUM *Merchant St.* Local items on view here include bird specimens stuffed by John James Audubon. *Open daily. Small charge.*

ST. GEMME-AMOUREAUX HOUSE *St. Marys Rd.* This charming Creole home was built about 1770. *Open daily Apr.-early Jan. Small charge.*

ST. GEMME BEAUVAIS HOUSE *20 S. Main St.* This 200-year-old house has distinctive post-in-ground type of construction. *Open daily. Small charge.*

St. James

MARAMEC IRON WORKS DISTRICT *7 mi. S. on Rte. 8* Furnace and forge stacks are among the remains of an iron refinery that flourished from 1863 to 1872.

St. Louis

B'NAI AMOONA CONGREGATION *524 Trinity Ave., University City* The modern synagogue is shaped by the parabolic sweep of its roof. *Open daily.*

CITY HALL *12th Blvd. and Market St.* The imposing four-story building is modeled on the Hôtel de Ville in Paris. *Open Mon.-Fri.*

GRAND AVENUE WATER TOWER *N. Grand Blvd. and 20th St.* No longer used to store water, the 154-foot Corinthian column is a city landmark.

GRANT'S FARM *Gravois and Grant Rd.* Ulysses S. Grant's 1854 log cabin stands here on land he once farmed. A small zoo and a game reserve are other attractions. *Open Tues.-Sat. Apr.-Oct. except holidays.*

SOLDIERS MEMORIAL *13th and Chestnut Sts.* Military relics from past wars are on view in this memorial dedicated to local men who died in World War I. *Open daily.*

TERMINAL BUILDING *Lambert-St. Louis International Airport* Soaring arches capture the spirit of flight in this stunning building by Minoru Yamasaki. *Open daily.*

UNION STATION-ALOE PLAZA *Market, 18th to 20th Sts.* The colossal 1896 stone terminal is a monument to the railroading era.

WAINWRIGHT TOMB *Bellefontaine Cemetery* This elegantly simple tomb was designed by Louis Sullivan.

Sibley

FORT OSAGE This frontier outpost was built in 1808. *Open daily except holidays.*

Weston

GATEWAY TO THE WEST MUSEUM *500 Welt St.* The world's largest ball of string, weighing over 3000 pounds, is one of the many items included in this large collection. *Open daily. Small charge.*

New Mexico

Hobbs

CONFEDERATE AIR FORCE FLYING MUSEUM (NEW MEXICO WING) Examples of the fabled aircraft that helped win World War II can be seen here. *Open Mon.-Fri. Small charge.*

Portales

BLACKWATER DRAW MUSEUM *7 mi. N.E. on Rte. 70* Artifacts from a nearby site tell the story of the Paleo-Indian. *Open Sat., Sun.*

GENERAL ANTHROPOLOGY MUSEUM *Eastern New Mexico University* Displays emphasize artifacts of the Paleo-Indian. *Open Mon.-Fri.*

MILES MUSEUM *Eastern New Mexico University* Local Indian artifacts and area gems and minerals are exhibited. *Open Mon., Wed., Fri.*

Tucumcari

TUCUMCARI HISTORICAL MUSEUM *416 S. Adams St.* Mementos here recall pioneer days in the Southwest. *Open daily mid-May-early Sept., Tues.-Sun. early Sept.-mid-May. Small charge.*

Oklahoma

Altus

MUSEUM OF THE WESTERN PRAIRIE *Falcon Rd.* Artifacts and old photos here portray all phases of man's life on the prairie. *Open Tues.-Sun.*

Alva

NORTHWESTERN STATE COLLEGE MUSEUM *Jesse Dunn Hall* Two whooping cranes highlight this natural history museum's collection of mounted birds. *Open Mon.-Fri. Sept.-July except college holidays.*

Anadarko

INDIAN CITY U.S.A. *2 mi. S. on Rte. 8* Members of seven Indian tribes have re-created their traditional ways of life. *Open daily. Adults $2.00, children small charge.*

SOUTHERN PLAINS INDIAN MUSEUM AND CRAFTS CENTER Intricate handcrafts are shown. *Open daily June-Sept., Tues.-Sun. Oct.-May except holidays.*

Bacone

ATALOA LODGE *Bacone College* American Indian artifacts are on view. *Open Mon.-Fri.*

Beaver

BEAVER CITY MUSEUM *Main St.* In this authentic sod house are local antiques, historical photographs and a huge and unusual collection of strings of beads. *Open daily.*

Broken Bow

MEMORIAL INDIAN MUSEUM *Second and Allen Sts.* Caddo Indian pottery and other local Indian artifacts are on display. *Open daily.*

Cayuga

SPLITLOG CHURCH This 1896 stone edifice is named for its Cayuga Indian builder.

Chandler

LINCOLN COUNTY MUSEUM OF PIONEER HISTORY *717 Manvel Ave.* Homesteaders' furniture and tools are shown. *Open Tues.-Sat.*

Clinton

WESTERN TRAILS MUSEUM *2929 Gary Frwy.* Collections of Indian and pioneer artifacts are on display here. *Open daily.*

Dewey

DEWEY HOTEL *801 Delaware St.* This 1899 Victorian structure was the town's first major building. *Open Tues.-Sun. mid-Mar.-mid-Dec.*

El Reno

CANADIAN COUNTY HISTORICAL MUSEUM *Wade and Grand Sts.* Local items, including railroad memorabilia and Indian artifacts, are shown in a 1906 depot. *Open Sun., Tues., Fri.*

Fort Gibson

OLD FORT STOCKADE Jefferson Davis and Robert E. Lee served at this 1824 fort which now includes a museum. *Open daily.*

Foyil

WORLD'S LARGEST TOTEM POLE *E. on Rte. 28A* There are windows in this 65-foot concrete design. *Open daily.*

Goodwell

NO MAN'S LAND HISTORICAL MUSEUM *Panhandle State College* Archaeological, geological and historical objects tell the story of this part of the state. *Open Sun.-Fri. Sept.-July.*

Heavener

PETER CONSER HOUSE A Choctaw Indian built this dwelling. *Open Tues.-Sun. except holidays.*

RUNESTONE The date Nov. 11, 1012, appears in eight runes on this sandstone slab. Were they carved by Vikings? *Open daily.*

Kingfisher

CHISHOLM TRAIL MUSEUM *605 Zellers Ave.* Exhibits feature relics of the old cattle trail. *Open daily except holidays.*

GOVERNOR A. J. SEAY MANSION *11th and Overstreet* The Oklahoma Territory's second governor completed this frame structure in 1892. *Open daily except holidays.*

Norman

UNIVERSITY OF OKLAHOMA Books on the Southwest are held in the W. B. Bizzell Memorial Library. Life and social science displays can be seen in the Stovall Museum of Science and History. *Library open Mon.-Sat. June-Sept., daily Oct.-May; museum open daily except Jan. 1 and Dec. 25.*

Okemah

TERRITORY TOWN, U.S.A. *5 mi. W. on Rte. 40* This village recalls the 1880s and includes a museum. *Open daily Apr.-Nov. Adults and children over 12 small charge for museum.*

Oklahoma City

CONFEDERATE SOLDIERS' MEMORIAL HALL *Wiley Post-Historical Bldg.* Exhibits and films explain aspects of the Civil War in Oklahoma. *Open daily except holidays.*

OKLAHOMA FIREFIGHTERS MUSEUM *2716 N.E. 50th St.* The state's first automotive fire "wagon" stands near an array of other varied equipment. *Open daily except holidays.*

OKLAHOMA MUSEUM OF ART AT REDRIDGE *5500 Lincoln Blvd.* A superb Florentine table of about 1800 is a prime treasure. *Open Tues.-Sun. Sept.-July. Small charge.*

ST. LUKE'S UNITED METHODIST CHURCH *15th and N. Robinson Sts.* Vertical stained-glass windows surround the sanctuary of this striking structure. *Open daily except holidays.*

Perry

CHEROKEE STRIP HISTORICAL MUSEUM *Off Rte. 35* Sodbuster utensils are from the 1893 claims run. *Open daily except holidays.*

Ponca City

PIONEER WOMAN MUSEUM *701 Monument Rd.* Displays feature homestead relics. Bryant Baker's bronze *Pioneer Woman* stands near the entrance. *Open daily.*

Sallisaw

SEQUOYAH'S HOME *11 mi. N.E. on Rte. 101* The inventor of the Cherokee alphabet lived in this log cabin. *Open Tues.-Sun.*

Stillwater

OLD TIMERS BANK *First National Bank and Trust Company, 808 Main St.* This replicated setting contains 1890s banking equipment and furnishings. *Open Mon.-Fri.*

Stilwell

GOLDA'S OLD STONE MILL *9 mi. N.W. on Rte. 51* Corn is still ground at this 1838 mill. *Open daily. Adults and children over 6 small charge.*

Tahlequah

CHEROKEE NATIONAL CAPITOL *Muskogee Ave.* The courthouse of Cherokee County is a two-story Victorian structure built in 1867 by Cherokees. *Open Mon.-Fri.*

NORTHEASTERN STATE COLLEGE Cherokee artifacts and college history are stressed in the museum. *Open daily during academic year.*

Tulsa

REBECCA AND GERSHON FENSTER

Tulsa (*continued*)
GALLERY OF JEWISH ART *1719 S. Owasso Ave.* Judaic religious ceremonial objects date from 8000 B.C. to the present. *Open Sun.*
TULSA MUNICIPAL ROSE GARDEN *Woodward Park* More than 230 rose varieties bloom here. *Open daily.*

Tuskahoma
CHOCTAW COUNCIL HOUSE *Rte. 271* Artifacts trace Choctaw Indian history. The house was built in 1884 by Choctaws.

Waurika
CHISHOLM TRAIL HISTORICAL MUSEUM *Rte. 70* Items here pertain to Spanish explorations of this area and the early big cattle drives. *Open Tues.-Sun.*

Yale
HOME OF JIM THORPE *704 E. Boston* The great Indian athlete lived in this bungalow from 1917 to 1923. *Open Tues.-Sun.*

Texas

Alamo
LIVE STEAM MUSEUM *1¾ mi. N. on Alamo Rd.* Equipment includes an 1896 Peerless portable engine. *Open daily except holidays.*

Austin
BREMOND BLOCK *Between Seventh, Eighth, San Antonio and Guadalupe Sts.* Victorian dwellings here were built by members of the same family.
ELISABET NEY MUSEUM *304 E. 44th St.* Original works by sculptor Elisabet Ney (1833-1907) are exhibited in her studio. *Open daily.*
O. HENRY MUSEUM *409 E. Fifth St.* Several of the author's belongings are shown in this frame house where he lived from 1893 to 1895. *Open daily.*
ST. DAVID'S EPISCOPAL CHURCH *Seventh and San Jacinto Sts.* This castellated limestone church was consecrated in 1855. *Open daily.*
TEXAS MEMORIAL MUSEUM *24th and Trinity Sts.* Subjects range from state and natural history to geology and the American Indian. *Open daily except holidays.*
ZILKER PARK *2200 Bee Caves Rd.* Nature trails and lovely flower gardens are attractions. *Open daily.*

Bonham
SAM RAYBURN LIBRARY Here are mementos of the great Speaker of the House. *Open Mon.-Sat.*

Brackettville
ALAMO VILLAGE *7 mi. N. on Rte. 674* The huge movie set for *The Alamo* even has mock gunfights. *Open daily. Adults $2.00 June-Aug., $1.50 Sept.-May, children 6-12 $1.25 June-Aug., small charge Sept.-May.*

Brazosport
"MYSTERY" MONUMENT *400 Brazosport Blvd.* A retired shrimp trawler, the *Mystery,* stands on land now, a monument to the Gulf Coast shrimp industry.

Brownsville
STILLMAN HOUSE MUSEUM *1305 E. Washington St.* In 1850 the founder of Brownsville built the home, which holds Colonial furnishings and other period mementos. *Open Sun.-Fri. Small charge.*

Corsicana
PIONEER VILLAGE *912 W. Park* Authentic log cabins have been moved here and furnished with period pieces. *Open daily. Small charge.*

Dallas
MILLERMORE *City Park* This 1855 house is furnished with antiques. *Open Sun., Tues.-Fri. Oct.-June except holidays. Small charge.*

Denton
NORTH TEXAS STATE HISTORICAL COLLECTION *North Texas State University* Displays include antique firearms and Eskimo objects. *Open Mon.-Sat. during academic year.*

Fort Stockton
ANNIE RIGGS MUSEUM *S. Main and Callaghan Sts.* Displays in an 1899 hotel focus on turn-of-the-century life. *Open Thurs.-Tues.*
HISTORIC DISTRICT Markers point out an array of 19th-century buildings, including the town's first school.

Fort Worth
FORT WORTH ZOOLOGICAL PARK *2727 Zoological Park Dr.* Performing porpoises are a star attraction at this multifaceted zoo. *Open daily. Adults and children over 11 small charge.*

Fredericksburg
KAMMLAH HOUSE PIONEER MUSEUM *307 W. Main St.* Pioneer memorabilia are displayed in this old stone house and store. *Open daily May-Oct., Sat., Sun. Nov.-Apr. Small charge.*
PIONEER MEMORIAL LIBRARY *115 W. Main St.* This handsome stone building was once the country courthouse. *Open Mon.-Sat.*

Gainesville
MORTON MUSEUM OF COOKE COUNTY *Dixon and Pecan Sts.* A stained-glass skylight and windows from a 19th-century home can be seen in this renovated building. *Open Fri.-Sun.*

Galveston
ST. JOSEPH'S CATHOLIC CHURCH *2206 Ave. K* This beautiful historic church contains a museum of the city's religious history. *Open Fri. June-Aug. Small charge.*
SAMUEL MAY WILLIAMS HOUSE *3601 Ave. P* The city's oldest house was precut in Maine and the numbered pieces were then shipped to Texas. *Open daily June-Aug. Small charge.*
STRAND HISTORIC DISTRICT *20th to 25th Sts. on The Strand* Many fine 1800s buildings are being restored in the city's main business district.

Houston
NASA LYNDON B. JOHNSON SPACE CENTER *25 mi. S. off Rte. 45* Spacecraft and mementos of space flights can be seen at this vast complex. *Open daily except holidays.*

Jefferson
MANSE *Delta St.* This Greek Revival house was begun about 1839. *Open daily. Small charge.*

Langtry
JUDGE ROY BEAN VISITOR CENTER Here is the combination courtroom/saloon/billiard hall of the legendary judge. *Open daily except Dec. 24-6.*

McKinney
HEARD NATURAL SCIENCE MUSEUM AND WILDLIFE SANCTUARY *1 mi E. off Rte. 5 S.* Trails through a 266-acre sanctuary supplement the modern museum's exhibits. *Open Tues.-Sun.*

Nacogdoches
STONE FORT MUSEUM *College Dr. and Griffith Blvd.* Local historical relics are displayed. *Open Sun.-Fri.*

Odessa
PRESIDENTIAL MUSEUM *Ector County Library, 622 N. Lee St.* This unique collection honors all U.S. Presidents. *Open Mon.-Sat. except holidays.*

Quitman
GOVERNOR HOGG SHRINE *518 S. Main St.* Mementos of Governor James Hogg are shown in his home. *Open Thurs.-Mon. except Dec. 25.*

San Antonio
FORT SAM HOUSTON The main quadrangle and military museum are highlights at the Fifth Army's 3300-acre headquarters. *Open daily except holidays.*
HEMISFAIR PLAZA An observation tower, revolving restaurant and several exhibits from the 1968 World's Fair are here. *Open daily.*
HERTZBERG CIRCUS COLLECTION *Public Library, 210 W. Market St.* A complete miniature circus and thousands of mementos trace the history of the Big Top. *Open Mon.-Sat.*
LA VILLITA *416 Villita St.* The "Little Village" is an echo of the past. *Open daily except Jan. 1 and Dec. 25.*

Teague
BURLINGTON-ROCK ISLAND RAILROAD MUSEUM *208 S. Third Ave.* Railroad memorabilia and historical relics are displayed in a 1906 rail depot. *Open Sat., Sun. Small charge.*

Tyler
TYLER MUNICIPAL ROSE GARDEN More than 36,000 roses bloom in this attractive 22-acre garden. *Open daily.*

Vernon

PRIVATE BIRD EGG COLLECTION OF ROBERT L. MORE, SR. *1907 Wilbarger St.* More than 10,000 bird eggs are on view here. *Open Mon.-Sat.*

Waco

BAYLOR ART MUSEUM *Baylor University* Prints, paintings and New Guinean sculpture are shown. *Open Mon.-Fri. except academic vacations.*

FORT FISHER AND HOMER GARRISON MEMORIAL MUSEUM *University-Parks Dr. and Rte. 35* Memorabilia of the famed Texas Rangers can be seen here. *Open daily except Jan. 1 and Dec. 25. Small charge.*

JOHN K. STRECKER MUSEUM *Baylor University* This natural history museum also exhibits some live reptiles and amphibians. *Open Mon.-Sat. except holidays.*

REGION 8 [map page 454]

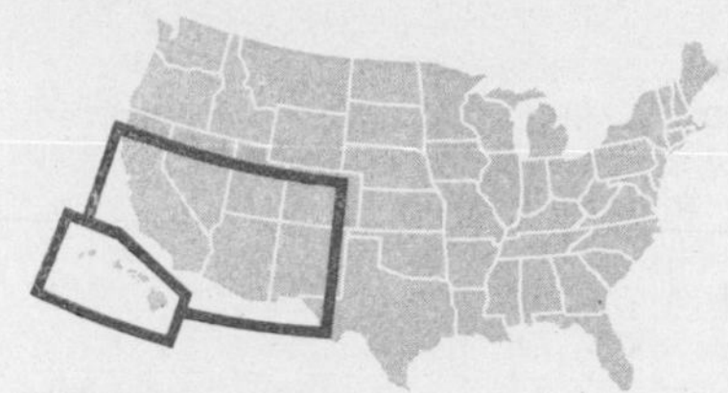

Arizona

Bisbee

BREWERY GULCH There are many restored 1900s buildings in this former mining camp. *Open daily.*

Camp Verde

FORT VERDE STATE HISTORIC PARK Three of the structures in this 1870-90s military post contain period furniture and guns. *Open daily except Dec. 25. Small charge each car.*

Flagstaff

PIONEERS' HISTORICAL MUSEUM *Fort Valley Rd.* Early movie equipment and pioneer artifacts are housed in this former hospital. *Open daily mid-Apr.-mid-Oct.*

Florence

PINAL COUNTY COURTHOUSE *Pinal and 12th Sts.* An ornate clock tower crowns this Victorian building.

Oraibi

HOPI INDIAN RESERVATION *2 mi. W. on Rte. 264* Several multidwelling adobe structures stand in Old Oraibi, where the Hopis have lived since the 12th century. *Open daily.*

Phoenix

A. J. BAYLESS COUNTRY STORE MUSEUM *118 W. Indian School Rd.* Cracker barrels and a pot-bellied stove are in this 1890s general store. *Open Tues.-Sun.*

ARIZONA MINERAL MUSEUM *State Fairgrounds* The collection features gemstone bowls and fluorescent minerals. *Open daily except holidays.*

PHOENIX CIVIC PLAZA COLLECTION OF ART TREASURES Contemporary works in the civic center include glass and bronze sculpture and colorful Indian tapestries. *Open Mon.-Fri.*

Pima

EASTERN ARIZONA MUSEUM *2 N. Main St.* Painted Indian pottery is displayed with pioneer farm and household items. *Open Mon.-Fri.*

Prescott

SHARLOT HALL HISTORICAL MUSEUM OF ARIZONA *W. Gurley St.* The Old Governor's Mansion (1864), a log building, contains period guns, clothing and furniture. *Open Tues.-Sun. except holidays.*

SMOKI MUSEUM *N. Arizona Ave.* Artifacts of prehistoric Indians are on display. *Open daily June-Aug.*

Scottsdale

MCGEE'S INDIAN DEN *7239 First Ave.* Although a retail store, this is a place to see outstanding Indian artwork. *Open Mon.-Sat.*

Sedona

SHRINE OF THE RED ROCKS The Masonic landmark atop Table Mountain offers a sweeping vista of the surrounding area. *Open daily.*

Snowflake

SNOWFLAKE HISTORIC DISTRICT Outstanding among the buildings in this Mormon community is the 1889 James M. Flake Home. In the 1906 Smith Pioneer Memorial Home Museum are original furniture and artifacts. *Museum open Mon.-Sat. late June-late Sept.*

Tombstone

Marshall Wyatt Earp and Doc Holliday tried to keep order here, but Boothill Graveyard is filled with reminders of murders and hangings. Tombstone Courthouse State Historic Monument and Museum has interesting relics. *Open daily. Small charge for each of five museums.*

Tubac

TUBAC PRESIDIO STATE HISTORIC PARK Ruins of a 1750s Spanish fort and dioramas in a museum explain Tubac's heritage—Indian, Spanish, Mexican and American. *Open daily except Dec. 25. Small charge.*

Tucson

ARIZONA HISTORICAL SOCIETY MUSEUM *949 E. Second St.* A casino, hotel lobby and other period rooms capture the color of territorial days. *Open daily except holidays.*

FORT LOWELL MUSEUM *2900 N. Craycroft Rd.* The commandant's house reflects military life during the 1880s Geronimo campaigns. *Open Tues.-Sat. except holidays.*

OLD TUCSON *201 S. Kinney Rd.* Live action gunfights erupt in this late 1800s-style TV and movie location site. *Open daily. Adults $2.50, children over 6 small charge.*

Yarnell

SHRINE OF ST. JOSEPH OF THE MOUNTAINS *W. on Rte. 89* Episodes in the lives of Joseph, Mary and Jesus are portrayed in life-size statues and plaques. *Open daily.*

Yuma

CENTURY HOUSE *240 Madison Ave.* This 1870s adobe home, converted to a museum, reflects the history of the lower Colorado River region. *Open Tues.-Sat.*

California

Bakersfield

KERN COUNTY MUSEUM AND PIONEER VILLAGE *3801 Chester Ave.* Indian and pioneer items and natural history lore fill the museum. Next door stands a late 1800s Western village. *Open daily.*

Barstow

CALICO DIG *E. off Rte. 15* Visitors can observe progress at this site where stone tools that may have been made 80,000 years ago are being recovered. *Open daily.*

Belmont

RALSTON HALL *College of Notre Dame* This 1860s Italian villa-style former residence has a lavish mirrored ballroom.

Ben Lomond

WEATHERLEY'S CASTLE The small-scale replica of a Scottish castle is furnished with unusual pieces.

Berkeley

BERKELEY MUNICIPAL ROSE GARDEN *Euclid Ave. and Bayview Pl.* Over 4000 rose bushes are planted in a terraced setting with a fine view of the Bay Area. *Open daily.*

Bishop

INDIAN PETROGLYPHS *Fish Slough Rd., N. off Rte. 6* Many geometric and naturalistic designs etched on limestone by early Indians can be seen on a "petroglyph loop" trip. *Open daily.*

Buena Park

KNOTT'S BERRY FARM AND GHOST TOWN *2 mi. S. on Beach Blvd.* The deserted village and historical displays are popular. *Open daily except Dec. 25. Ghost Town: adults $1.50, children over 5 small charge.*

Claremont

RANCHO SANTA ANA BOTANIC GARDEN *1500 N. College Ave.* Eighty-three acres are devoted to native California plants. *Open daily except holidays.*

Coalinga

R. C. BAKER MEMORIAL MUSEUM *297 W. Elm St.* Early oil field drilling equipment, fossils and Indian artifacts are exhibited. *Open daily.*

Death Valley Junction

MARTA BECKET'S AMARGOSA OPERA HOUSE Ballet-pantomimes are presented in a muraled setting depicting a 16th-century Spanish audience.

Open for performances Sat. mid-May–mid-Oct., Mon., Fri., Sat. mid-Oct.–mid-May.

Eureka

CLARKE MEMORIAL MUSEUM *240 E St.* A pioneer gun collection and 1300 mounted California birds are the major attractions. *Open Tues.–Sun. except holidays.*

FORT HUMBOLDT STATE HISTORIC PARK *3431 Fort Ave.* Redwood logging history is shown in an outdoor exhibit. There is also a museum. *Open daily.*

Fort Bragg

MENDOCINO COAST BOTANICAL GARDENS *2 mi. S. on Rte. 1* Acres of gardens open onto a grassy cliff. *Open daily. Adults $1.75, children 13–18 $1.25, 6–12 small charge.*

Fremont

MISSION OF SAN JOSÉ DE LA GUADALUPE *Mission Blvd.* Early mission artifacts are on display. *Open daily.*

Fresno

M. THEO. KEARNEY MANSION *7160 W. Kearney Blvd.* The 1900 Victorian-style house contains furniture from the 1800s. *Open Wed.–Sun. Mar.–Dec. Small charge.*

Independence

EASTERN CALIFORNIA MUSEUM *155 Grant St.* An excellent display of Indian artifacts includes a children's "touch table." *Open daily.*

Lakeport

LAKE COUNTY MUSEUM *175 Third St.* Pomo Indian baskets are shown. *Open Mon.–Sat. except holidays.*

Lomita

LOMITA RAILROAD MUSEUM *250th St. and Woodward Ave.* The museum is a replica of a 19th-century depot; a 1902 locomotive stands on the tracks outside. *Open Wed.–Sun. except Dec. 25. Small charge.*

Lompoc

LOMPOC MUSEUM *200 S. H St.* The main attractions are Chumash Indian stone bowls and obsidian blades. *Open Sat., Sun.*

Long Beach

"QUEEN MARY" *End of Long Beach Frwy.* Visitors can tour the historic ship and, belowdecks, see Jacques Cousteau's "Living Sea" exhibit. *Open daily. Adults $3.50, children 12–17 $2.50, 5–11 $1.25.*

RANCHO LOS CERRITOS *4600 Virginia Rd.* This 1844 adobe ranch house is furnished with antiques. *Open Wed.–Sun. except holidays.*

Los Angeles

CITY HALL *200 N. Spring St.* The marble and tile rotunda and city council chambers are features of this imposing building. *Open Mon.–Sat.*

LA CASA DEL RANCHO AGUAJE DEL CENTINELA *7634 Midfield Ave.* This excellently preserved adobe house was built in 1834 and contains Victorian furnishings. *Open Sun., Wed.*

LOS ANGELES PUBLIC LIBRARY *630 W. Fifth St.* Apart from notable books and graphics, the massive building features sculptures, murals and frescos. *Open Mon.–Sat.*

ST. VINCENT'S CHURCH *Adams Blvd. and Figueroa St.* This 1925 church exemplifies Spanish Colonial styling. *Open daily.*

Marysville

MARY AARON MUSEUM *704 D St.* Period rooms and historical relics can be seen in this 1856 brick house. *Open Tues.–Sat.*

Modesto

MILLER'S CALIFORNIA RANCH HORSE AND BUGGY DISPLAY *9425 Yosemite Blvd.* This collection includes antique buggies, cars and vintage bicycles. *Open Wed.–Sun. Small charge.*

Monterey

COLTON HALL MUSEUM *Pacific St.* The state's first Constitution was written (1849) in this dignified building. *Open daily except holidays.*

LARKIN HOUSE *Calle Principal and Jefferson St.* Built in the 1830s, the adobe dwelling became the prototype of fashionable local architecture. *Open Wed.–Mon.*

Murphys

OLD TIMERS MUSEUM This local history museum, built in 1856, emphasizes mining days and Indian craftsmanship. *Open Wed.–Sun. June–Sept., Sat., Sun. Oct.–May.*

National City

MUSEUM OF AMERICAN TREASURES *1315 E. Fourth St.* Much of this unusual collection relates to American history. *Open Sun.*

Newhall

WILLIAM S. HART COUNTY PARK AND MUSEUM *24151 N. Newhall Ave.* In the actor's Spanish-style ranch house are works by Russell and Remington. *Park open daily except holidays, museum open Tues.–Sun.*

Oakland

MILLS COLLEGE ART GALLERY The outstanding print collection includes the work of Marsh, Feininger and Léger. *Open Wed.–Sun. during academic year.*

MORCOM AMPHITHEATER OF ROSES *Jean St.* Numerous varieties of roses bloom in this magnificently landscaped garden. *Open daily.*

Perris

ORANGE EMPIRE TROLLEY MUSEUM *2201 S. A St.* More than 60 trolleys lure visitors to this outdoor museum. *Open daily; rides Sat., Sun. Small charge for trolley rides.*

Petaluma

PETALUMA ADOBE STATE HISTORIC PARK *3325 Old Adobe Rd.* This adobe structure, built about 1836, served as the hub of a huge ranch. *Open daily except holidays. Small charge.*

Randsburg

DESERT MUSEUM *Butte Ave.* Relics evoke the boom and bust days of the district, where first gold, then tungsten and silver were discovered. *Open Sat., Sun. except holidays.*

Red Bluff

WILLIAM B. IDE ADOBE STATE HISTORIC PARK *Adobe Rd.* This adobe house in a riverside park was built about 1850 by the only president of the California Republic. *Open daily.*

Redding

SHASTA DAM *9 mi. N. on Lake Blvd.* The spillway waterfall here is three times higher than Niagara Falls. *Open daily.*

Sacramento

STATE INDIAN MUSEUM *2618 K St.* Feathered robes and reed boats are some of the thousands of Indian-made objects displayed. *Open daily except holidays. Small charge.*

STATE LIBRARY *On Capitol Mall between 9th and 10th Sts.* Vast murals here trace the state's history. *Open Mon.–Fri. except holidays.*

SUTTER'S FORT STATE HISTORICAL MONUMENT *2701 L St.* Workshops, offices and living quarters have been restored in this pioneer fort. *Open daily except holidays. Small charge.*

San Diego

CABRILLO NATIONAL MONUMENT *Point Loma* An old lighthouse has been restored at this memorial to Juan Rodriguez Cabrillo, the first European to explore the California coast, in 1542. *Open daily.*

CUYAMACA INDIAN EXHIBIT *Cuyamaca Rancho State Park* Diegueño Indian artifacts are exhibited in the park headquarters. *Open daily.*

MISSION SAN DIEGO DE ALCALA *10818 San Diego Mission Rd.* This was the first Spanish mission established in the U.S. *Open daily except Dec. 25. Small charge.*

San Francisco

FIRE DEPARTMENT PIONEER MEMORIAL MUSEUM *655 Presidio Ave.* The array of fire-fighting equipment here dates from the mid-19th century. *Open daily.*

LOMBARD STREET SERPENTINE Designed to reduce the grade for horse-drawn drays, the steep, hydrangea-banked street lined with handsome homes has 10 switchbacks.

MISSION DOLORES *16th and Dolores Sts.* Built nearly 200 years ago, this is one of the city's oldest buildings. *Open daily except Thanksgiving Day and Dec. 25. Small charge.*

PRESIDIO OF SAN FRANCISCO *W. end of Lombard St.* Miles of tree-lined trails and roads wind through this parklike military reservation. *Open daily.*

SS. PETER AND PAUL CHURCH *666 Filbert St.* Salesian fathers built the stately Romanesque church for the city's Italian community in 1924. *Open daily.*

SAN FRANCISCO MUSEUM OF ART *McAllister St. and Van Ness Ave.* Painting, sculpture, graphics and photography spotlight 20th-century artists. *Open Tues.-Sun.*

WELLS FARGO BANK HISTORY ROOM *420 Montgomery St.* A Concord coach is the highlight of this collection of Wells Fargo mementos. *Open Mon.-Fri. except holidays.*

San Gabriel

MISSION SAN GABRIEL ARCANGEL *537 W. Mission Dr.* Extraordinarily well preserved, the huge mission complex recalls Spanish Colonial days of around 1800. *Open daily except holidays. Small charge.*

San Jose

JAPANESE FRIENDSHIP TEA GARDEN *1490 Senter Rd.* Paths wend among lakes to a teahouse in this serene Japanese-style garden. *Open daily.*

SAN JOSE HISTORICAL MUSEUM *635 Phelan Ave.* Indian relics, mining tools and other items outline the history of the Santa Clara Valley. *Open daily. Small charge.*

San Luis Rey

MISSION SAN LUIS REY DE FRANCIA *4050 Mission Ave.* The 1798 mission, still in use, is a masterpiece of design and decorative art. *Open daily. Small charge for tour.*

San Mateo

SAN MATEO COUNTY HISTORICAL MUSEUM *1700 W. Hillsdale Blvd.* An 1801 Russian cannon and the county's first fire engine (1862) help illustrate local history. *Open Mon.-Sat. except holidays.*

San Pedro

CABRILLO BEACH MARINE MUSEUM *3720 Stephen White Dr.* Sea life, ship models and seafaring gear are on display. *Open daily.*

San Rafael

MISSION SAN RAFAEL ARCANGEL *1104 Fifth Ave.* Services are still offered in a picturesque chapel of this 1817 mission. *Open daily.*

Santa Barbara

ART GALLERIES *University of California* Renaissance and Baroque medals, plaquettes and paintings as well as regional architectural drawings are featured here. *Open Tues.-Sun.*

COUNTY COURT HOUSE *1120 Anacapa St.* The rambling 1929 building epitomizes traditional Spanish-Moorish design. *Open Mon.-Fri.*

EL CUARTEL ADOBE *122 E. Canon Perdido St.* The late 18th-century building is what remains of a Spanish fortress. *Open Mon.-Fri.*

FERNALD HOUSE AND TRUSSELL-WINCHESTER ADOBE *414 W. Montecito St.* The Fernald home exemplifies the Victorian period, while the adobe house (built in 1854) represents the period between Spanish and American rule. *Open Sun.*

HILL-CARRILLO ADOBE *11 E. Carrillo St.* This was the first adobe dwelling in Santa Barbara to have a wooden floor. *Open Mon.-Fri.*

SANTA BARBARA HISTORICAL SOCIETY MUSEUM *136 E. De la Guerra St.* Exhibits span the Spanish, Mexican and American eras of local history. *Open Tues.-Sun.*

SANTA BARBARA MUSEUM OF ART *1130 State St.* Just about every notable American painter is represented here. *Open Tues.-Sun.*

Santa Rosa

LUTHER BURBANK MEMORIAL HOUSE AND GARDENS *200 Block of Santa Rosa Ave.* The great horticulturist lived here and conducted his botanical experiments. *Gardens open daily.*

Susanville

ROOPS FORT *75 N. Weatherlow St.* In Lassen County's first log structure are items relating to the area's past. The nearby H. Pratt Memorial Museum contains Indian artifacts. *Open Tues.-Sun. mid-May-mid-Oct.*

Truckee

DONNER MEMORIAL STATE PARK *3 mi. W. on Rte. 80* A monument and museum recall the ordeal of the Donner party and the building of the transcontinental railroad. *Open daily. Small charge each car.*

Ventura

VENTURA COUNTY PIONEER MUSEUM *77 N. California St.* Local history is reflected in exhibits of pioneer and Indian artifacts. *Open Mon.-Sat.*

Weaverville

J. J. JACKSON MEMORIAL MUSEUM *Main St.* Mining relics and a blacksmith's shop are among the exhibits. *Open daily May-Nov.*

Whittier

PIO PICO STATE HISTORIC MONUMENT *6003 Pioneer Blvd.* The 1885 adobe house was the home of California's Mexican governor. *Open daily except holidays.*

Williams

SACRAMENTO VALLEY MUSEUM *1491 Williams Ave.* Blacksmith, barber and apothecary shops and three rooms of an early home portray pioneer life. *Open Fri.-Wed. except Dec. 25. Small charge.*

Colorado

Cimarron

MORROW POINT DAM *Off Rte. 50* The double curvature dam—it arches from side to side and top to bottom—has a free-fall spillway and underground power plant. *Open daily May-Sept.*

Colorado Springs

CHEYENNE MOUNTAIN ZOOLOGICAL PARK *Broadmoor-Cheyenne Mountain Hwy.* The zoo is perched on a lovely mountainside site. *Open daily. Adults and children over 11 $1.25, children 6-11 small charge.*

Craig

DAVID H. MOFFAT PRIVATE BUSINESS CAR *341 E. Victory Way* The sumptuous 1906 Pullman car was built for rail tycoon Moffat. *Open Mon.-Fri.*

Denver

DENVER MUSEUM OF NATURAL HISTORY *City Park* The displays include animal habitat groups, prehistoric fossils, Indian relics, meteorites and mineral samples. *Open daily.*

Greeley

GREELEY MUNICIPAL MUSEUM *919 Seventh St.* Local history is recalled through an array of items dating from the early 1800s. *Open Mon.-Sat.*

Montrose

UTE INDIAN MUSEUM *4 mi. S. on Rte. 550* Weapons, utensils, clothing, arts and crafts tell the story of the Ute tribe from earliest times. *Open daily mid-Apr.-late Oct.*

Pueblo

EL PUEBLO STATE HISTORICAL MUSEUM *905 S. Prairie Ave.* Highlight of the displays is a full-scale reproduction of 1842 Fort Pueblo. *Open daily except holidays.*

Hawaii

HAWAII

Kailua-Kona

ST. PETER'S BLUE CHURCH *4 mi. S. on Alii Dr.* Set by the ocean on former royal land, the tiny church holds only 20 people. *Open daily.*

Kau District

THOMAS A. JAGGAR MEMORIAL MUSEUM *Hawaii Volcanoes National Park, off Rte. 11* Models, paintings and other exhibits tell the story of volcanoes. *Open daily.*

Upolu Point

MOOKINI HEIAU *Off Rte. 270* Impressive even in ruins, the huge temple was an ancient sacrificial site. *Open daily.*

KAUAI

Kekaha

KOKEE NATURAL HISTORY MUSEUM *Kokee State Park, 16 mi. N. on Rte. 550* Exotic shells, plants and birds highlight the exhibits here. *Open daily.*

Lihue

WAILUA COMPLEX OF HEIAUS *Wailua River State Park, 6 mi. N. on Rte. 56* The ancient, once-sacred spot held a city of refuge, temples and royal birthstones. *Open daily.*

MAUI

Wailuku

HALE HOIKEIKE *2375A Main St.* The collection includes relics of missionaries and Hawaiian artifacts. *Open Mon.-Sat. Small charge.*

MOLOKAI
Ualapue
HOKUKANO-UALAPUE COMPLEX *Rte. 450* The site holds six ancient temples and two ponds once used by Hawaiian royalty to store fish for eating.
OAHU
Haleiwa
PUU O MAHUKA HEIAU *4 mi. N.E. on Rte. 83* Ruins of the island's largest ancient temple stand here, grandly overlooking the sea. *Open daily.*
Honolulu
FIRST CHINESE CHURCH OF CHRIST *1054 S. King St.* Although the church has Christian motifs inside, the facade is dominated by a pagodalike tower. *Open daily.*
HAWAII STATE CAPITOL *S. Beretania and Punchbowl Sts.* Hawaii's volcanoes are symbolized in the cone-shaped legislative chambers, its graceful coconut palms in the exterior columns. *Open daily.*
HONOLULU ZOO *Kapiolani Park* Tropical birds upstage this zoo's other denizens. *Open daily.*
IZUMO TAISHAKYO MISSION *215 N. Kukui St.* A graceful concrete torii, or gateway, leads to the classic Japanese Shinto shrine. *Open daily.*
KAWAIAHAO CHURCH *957 Punchbowl St.* Solidly built of coral stone in 1842, the church is Honolulu's oldest. *Open daily.*
LA PIETRA *2933 Poni Moi Rd.* Diamond Head, Honolulu and the sea unfold from the site of this former home, now a girls' school. *Open daily.*
MOILIILI INARI TEMPLE *2132 S. King St.* The small windowless shrine is approached through an archway in a lavishly decorated garden. *Open daily.*
PARADISE PARK *3737 Manoa Rd.* Free-flight aviaries, a flamingo lagoon and jungle trails offer an instant Shangri-la. *Open daily. Adults $3.00, children 6-12 $1.75.*
ROYAL MAUSOLEUM OF HAWAII *2261 Nuuanu Ave.* Members of two royal Hawaiian families are buried here. *Open Mon.-Sat.*
TENNENT ART FOUNDATION GALLERY *203 Prospect St.* Madge Tennent's Impressionist paintings of Hawaiians hang here. *Open Tues.-Sun.*
Y.W.C.A. BUILDING *1040 Richards St.* Built in 1926 in the Italian Renaissance style, the building features an arcaded patio. *Open daily.*

Nevada

Berlin
BERLIN-ICHTHYOSAUR STATE PARK The area preserves fossils of giant sea reptiles that lived more than 185 million years ago. *Open daily mid-June-early Sept., Thurs.-Mon. early Sept.-mid-June.*
Ely
WARD CHARCOAL OVENS HISTORIC STATE MONUMENT *15 mi. S. on Rtes. 50 and 93* The superbly crafted beehive ovens served the local mining boom in the late 1800s. *Open daily.*
Eureka
OLD MINING CAMP Lead and silver ore created a fabulous boomtown here. A wealth of the original buildings still remainins, including a courthouse and an opera house.
Genoa
MORMON STATION STATE HISTORIC MONUMENT The 1851 structure was originally a trading post in the state's first settlement. *Open daily May-Sept.*
Las Vegas
MUSEUM OF NATURAL HISTORY *University of Nevada, 1310 Ascot Dr. #5* Highlights include live desert reptiles. *Open daily.*
Overton
LOST CITY MUSEUM OF ARCHAEOLOGY Rare artifacts highlight ancient pueblo Indian cultures. *Open daily.*
Rhyolite
BOTTLE HOUSE Built about 1906 of thousands of beer bottles, this dwelling is still occupied. It is located at the edge of Death Valley, in a once-rich gold camp full of memories.
Silver Springs
FORT CHURCHILL HISTORIC STATE MONUMENT *Rte. 2B* This adobe fort and Pony Express station was begun in 1860. *Open daily.*

New Mexico

Albuquerque
OLD TOWN *Rio Grande Blvd.* Craft shops and art galleries abound on the city's original site, with its early 18th-century church and other historic buildings.
Capitan
SMOKEY BEAR MUSEUM Photographs show the national fire-prevention symbol as a cub and adult bear. *Open daily May-Aug.*
Cimarron
CIMARRON HISTORIC DISTRICT Many interesting structures dating from 1847 can be seen in this once-important Santa Fe Trail stop.
Espanola
SAN ILDEFONSO PUEBLO *13 mi. S. on Rte. 4* This is the home of Maria Martinez, the renowned Indian creator of exquisite black pottery. *Open daily.*
Gallup
MUSEUM OF INDIAN ARTS AND CRAFTS *103 W. 66th Ave.* The differences between Hopi, Navaho and Zuni silver jewelry are explained. *Open Mon.-Sat.*
Las Cruces
MESILLA PLAZA Thick-walled adobe buildings cluster around the old church of San Albino and the Spanish-style plaza, interspersed with craft shops and restaurants.
Las Trampas
HISTORIC DISTRICT The Spanish-American agricultural community retains much of the appearance of the Colonial 18th century.
Los Alamos
NORRIS E. BRADBURY SCIENCE HALL *Diamond Dr.* Exhibits demonstrate the work done at the Los Alamos Scientific Laboratory in the harnessing of nuclear energy. *Open daily except holidays.*
Mogollon
In the 1880s Mogollon was a boomtown, thanks to gold and silver discovered here. Old stores, houses and mine buildings stand as relics of the bonanza days.
Moriarty
LONGHORN RANCH AND MUSEUM OF THE OLD WEST *6 mi. E. on Rte. 66* Visitors here enter an Old West town. *Open daily except Jan. 1 and Dec. 25. Small charge.*
Raton
DORSEY MANSION *Off Rte. 64* Senator Stephen W. Dorsey built this ambitious house in the mid-1800s of both logs and sandstone. *Open daily. Small charge.*
RATON MUSEUM *Rio Grande Ave. and S. Fifth St.* A late 19th-century house contains items that recall turn-of-the-century local history. *Open daily late June-early Sept.*
Santa Fe
SETON VILLAGE *6 mi. S. off Rte. 84-5* The home of writer-artist-naturalist Ernest Thompson Seton contains many of his books and paintings.
Taos
RIO GRANDE GORGE BRIDGE *10 mi. N.W. on Rte. 64* At 650 feet above the Rio Grande, this spectacular steel span is the second highest in the U.S.
Zuni
OLD MISSION OF ZUNI *Rte. 53* The 1629 mission church is located in the center of Zuni Pueblo where the Zuni Indians have lived since prehistoric times. *Open Mon.-Fri.*

Texas

San Elizario
SAN ELIZARIO MISSION This lovely old adobe church was built by early Spanish settlers. *Open daily.*

Utah

Alpine
MOUNTAINVILLE RELIC HALL *115 N. Main St.* The 1863 structure has been a Mormon church (dedicated by Brigham Young), a school and a community center. It now holds pioneer relics. *Open Mon.-Sat.*
Cedar City
OLD IRONTOWN *22 mi. W. on Rte.*

56 Abandoned mines, a beehive stone oven and brick ruins mark this iron industry site dating from 1868.
SOUTHERN UTAH MUSEUM OF NATURAL HISTORY *Southern Utah State College* Wildlife exhibits are featured, but the showpieces are ancient Indian clay figurines. *Open daily.*

Fairfield
CAMP FLOYD STATE HISTORIC SITE *Off Rte. 73* The restored Stagecoach Inn can be seen on what was an important military post (1858-61). *Open daily mid-Mar.-mid-Nov.*

Frisco
Dilapidated shacks and equipment still stand in this deserted 1870s silver-mining camp.

Heber City
WASATCH STAKE TABERNACLE Built of sandstone in 1887, the building (now a theater) served Mormons as a church and civic center. *Open for performances Mon.-Sat. June-Sept.*

Midway
WATKINS-COLEMAN HOME *5 E. Main St.* Sandstone quoins and "gingerbread" woodwork adorn this 1868 adobe brick dwelling.

Orderville
ORDERVILLE CHAPTER DAUGHTERS OF UTAH PIONEERS RELIC HALL *Rte. 89* Relics of the area's pioneer days are housed in a reconstructed school and church building.

Price
PREHISTORIC MUSEUM *Municipal Bldg.* Displays include the skeleton of a 140-million-year-old Allosaurus quarried nearby. *Open daily May-Aug., Mon.-Fri. Sept.-Apr.*

St. George
BRIGHAM YOUNG WINTER HOME *89 W. Second N.* The great Mormon leader's winter retreat has been fully restored. *Open daily except Thanksgiving Day and Dec. 25.*

Salt Lake City
EAGLE GATE *State and S. Temple Sts.* A copper eagle stands atop this arch, built in 1859 to mark the entrance to Brigham Young's estate.
FORT DOUGLAS The officers' quarters here date from 1876. *Open daily.*
INTERNATIONAL PEACE GARDENS *Jordan Park, 10th S. 900 W.* The cultural heritage of 19 nations is symbolized in formal plantings. *Open daily May-Sept.*
LOCKERBIE COLLECTION *Science Bldg., Westminster College* Utah agates highlight an exhibit of rocks, minerals and fossils. *Open Mon.-Fri. except holidays during academic year.*
PIONEER CRAFT HOUSE *3271 S. Fifth St. E.* The international crafts exhibits feature one of Gandhi's spinning wheels. *Open daily.*
PIONEER VILLAGE MUSEUM *2998 S. Conner St.* Buildings dating from 1847 to 1900 are furnished in period style. *Open Apr.-Oct. Small charge.*
ST. MARK'S CATHEDRAL *231 E. First St. S.* Huge wood roof trusses and fine stained-glass windows distinguish this small 1870 Episcopal church, designed by Richard Upjohn. *Open daily.*

Spring City
PETER MONSON HOUSE *First East and First North Sts.* A cattleman from Sweden completed this large stone dwelling in 1883. Its double front entrance doors are noteworthy.

REGION 9 [map page 506]

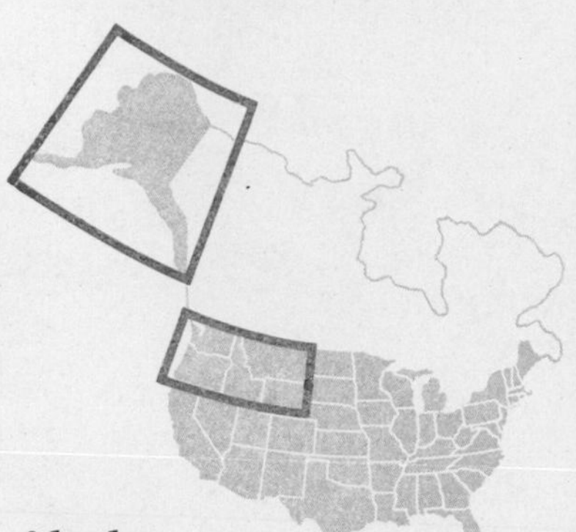

Alaska

Anchorage
WILDLIFE MUSEUM *12th and H Sts., Elmendorf Air Force Base* An array of mounted animals reflects Alaska's wildlife riches. *Open Mon.-Fri.*

Haines
TOTEM VILLAGE Chilkat Indians practice traditional crafts in a community that includes a replica tribal house and totem poles. *Village open daily; craft shops open Mon.-Fri.*

Homer
HOMER MUSEUM *Bartlett St.* The area's natural history is featured. *Open daily late May-early Sept.*

Juneau
ALASKA STATE CAPITOL *120 Fourth St.* Alaska marble columns decorate the 1931 structure's facade. *Open Mon.-Fri. mid-May-mid-Sept.*
HOUSE OF WICKERSHAM *213 Seventh St.* A living history tour and native artifacts can be enjoyed in this home of an early judge. *Tour $3.50.*

Petersburg
CLAUSEN MEMORIAL MUSEUM *F and Second Sts.* A 126½-pound king salmon upstages other regional exhibits here. *Open daily May-Sept.*

Sitka
CASTLE HILL This was the scene of the transference of Alaska from Russian to U.S. control. *Open daily.*

Skagway
TRAIL OF '98 MUSEUM *Spring St.* The museum, in the midst of the frontier buildings that comprise the Skagway Historic District, holds colorful relics of gold-rush days. *Open daily May-Sept. Small charge.*

California

Dorris
HERMAN'S HOUSE OF GUNS *Second and Oregon Sts.* More than 1300 firearms make up the extraordinary private collection. Other antique items include clocks and tankards.

Idaho

Atlanta
Picturesque Atlanta saw its heyday about 100 years ago when gold mines prospered.

Blue Dome
CHARCOAL KILNS RUINS *Targhee National Forest, 15 mi. N. off Rte. 28* These beehive brick structures were used from 1883 to 1889. *Open daily.*

Boise
JULIA DAVIS PARK ZOO *Julia Davis Park* The emphasis is on native birds and animals. *Open daily. Small charge.*
SIMPLOT BUILDING *Eighth and Idaho Sts.* Completed in 1892 this building reflects Romanesque design in its round arches and rough stone walls. *Open Mon.-Sat.*

Bonanza
This 1870s boomtown today consists of a few weathered buildings, a gold dredge and a cemetery.

Florence
Remains of the fabulous gold days are a decrepit jail, a boot-hill cemetery and old mining sites.

Gilmore
Among the ruins in this old mining town is a ramshackle frame hotel.

Hansen
HANSEN BRIDGE *Rte. 50* The piers supporting this steel span are more than 300 feet tall.

Idaho City
The residents of the once-rich mining camp have preserved some of the old buildings. In the ancient post office are museum relics of bonanza days. *Museum open daily mid-May-mid-Oct. Small charge.*

Idaho Falls
MORMON TEMPLE *1000 Memorial Dr.* The grounds spectacularly complement the gleaming edifice. *Grounds open daily.*

Lewiston
LUNA HOUSE MUSEUM *0310 Third St.* A wide range of Indian artifacts is exhibited in the 19th-century residence. *Open Tues.-Sun.*

McCammon
MCCAMMON PETROGLYPHS *N. on Rte. 15 at rest area* Prehistoric Indians chipped the pictures on these boulders. *Open daily.*

Murray
Gold and silver brought great riches to the 1880s settlement.

Orofino
CLEARWATER HISTORICAL MUSEUM Nez Perce Indian and pioneer relics are exhibited. Artwork can be admired in the Te-Wap-Poo Art Gallery. *Open Mon.-Sat.*

Orogrande
This mining community never lived up to the promise of its name, and is now a ghost town.

Pioneerville
Some weathered buildings and evidence of mining activities recall the days of gold-rush glory.

Salmon
LEMHI COUNTY HISTORICAL SOCIETY MUSEUM Pioneer and Indian relics highlight this regional collection. *Open Mon.-Sat. Apr.-Oct.*

Tendoy
SACAJAWEA MONUMENT *4 mi. N. on Rte. 28* A plaque and stone marker honor the Shoshoni woman who helped guide Lewis and Clark.

Montana

Billings
PICTOGRAPH CAVES STATE MONUMENT *7 mi. S.E. off Rte. 87* Wall paintings attest to ancient Indian occupation of these two caves. *Open daily.*

Chester
LIBERTY COUNTY MUSEUM Homesteading days are vividly recalled in the displays here. *Open daily June-mid-Sept.*

Circle
MCCONE COUNTY MUSEUM Indian relics and homesteaders' possessions are among the collections. *Open Tues.-Sat. June-Sept.*

Gallatin Gateway
LORENE'S ANTIQUE MANSION *Rte. 191* Old-fashioned furniture and cars are the specialty. *Open daily. Small charge.*

Glendive
FRONTIER GATEWAY MUSEUM *E. off Rte. 90* Items used by homesteaders and a restored schoolhouse are featured. *Open daily mid-May-mid-Sept.*

Havre
NORTH MONTANA COLLEGE COLLECTIONS *Math-Science Bldg.* Indian items, fossils and birds are of interest. *Open Mon.-Fri.*

Helena
FRONTIER TOWN *15 mi. W. on Rte. 12* A stockade, jail and museum form part of this replica pioneer log village. *Open daily Apr.-Sept. Small charge.*

Lewistown
CENTRAL MONTANA HISTORICAL ASSOCIATION MUSEUM *E. Main St.* The main emphasis is on Indian artifacts. *Open Mon.-Fri.*

Livingston
PARK COUNTY MUSEUM *Fifth and Callender Sts.* Early schoolbooks are among the pioneer objects here. *Open Mon.-Sat. mid-May-mid-Sept.*

Logan
MADISON BUFFALO JUMP MONUMENT *7 mi. S. off Rte. 90* For more than 2000 years local Indians killed buffalo by driving them over these cliffs. *Open daily May-Nov.*

Shelby
MARIAS MUSEUM OF HISTORY AND ART *229 Maple Ave.* An ancient treadle sewing machine is one of many pioneer items shown. *Open Mon., Thurs. June-Sept.*

Stevensville
FORT OWEN NATIONAL HISTORIC SITE *Off Rte. 93* Montana's first town developed around this partially restored 1852 trading post. *Open daily.*

Wisdom
BIG HOLE NATIONAL BATTLEFIELD *12 mi. W. on Rte. 43* Nez Perce Chief Joseph fought a battle here in 1877. *Open daily May-Oct.*

Oregon

Baker
U.S. NATIONAL BANK OF OREGON GOLD DISPLAY *2000 Main St.* The collection includes a seven-pound gold nugget. *Open Mon.-Fri.*

Barton Lake
ROUND BARN A cattle baron built this distinctive winter horse-breaking structure in the 1870s. *Open daily.*

Corvallis
CORVALLIS ARTS CENTER *700 S.W. Madison St.* Changing art exhibits are shown. *Open Tues.-Sun.*

Florence
INDIAN FOREST *4 mi. N. on Rte. 101* An earth lodge is one of many replica Indian dwellings. *Open daily mid-Mar.-Oct. Small charge.*

Fossil
CITY OF FOSSIL MUSEUM Local history unfolds in a 1930s saloon. *Open daily May-Sept.*

Hammond
FORT STEVENS STATE PARK Gun emplacements recall the fort's role as guardian of the mouth of the Columbia River. *Open daily.*

Hood River
HOOD RIVER COUNTY HISTORICAL MUSEUM *County Courthouse, State St.* Items relating to the area include Indian handicrafts. *Open Mon.-Fri.*

Newport
LINCOLN COUNTY HISTORICAL MUSEUM *579 S.W. Ninth St.* Beads, baskets, furniture and tools depict the region's varied cultures. *Open Tues.-Sun. except holidays.*

Oregon City
CLACKAMAS COUNTY HISTORICAL SOCIETY MUSEUM *603 Sixth St.* Regional artifacts are displayed in a 1908 house. *Open Sun., Thurs.*

Portland
LIBRARY ASSOCIATION OF PORTLAND COLLECTIONS *Central Library, 801 S.W. 10th Ave.* Artwork and folios are the highlights. *Open Tues.-Sat.*

PENINSULA PARK SUNKEN ROSE GARDEN *6400 N. Albina St.* The gardens are formally arranged. *Open daily.*

PIONEER POST OFFICE *520 S.W. Morrison St.* Greek Revival styling is embellished by a handsome octagonal cupola. *Open Mon.-Fri.*

ST. JOHN'S EPISCOPAL CHURCH *S.E. Grand Ave. and Spokane St.* This 1851 frame edifice resembles New England churches.

SKIDMORE FOUNTAIN *S.W. First Ave. and Ankeny St.* Two bronze figures stand in the fountain.

Prineville
A. R. BOWMAN MEMORIAL MUSEUM *242 N. Main St.* Old photographs and documents relate to county history. *Open Wed.-Sun. mid-Apr.-mid-Oct.*

The Dalles
WINQUATT MUSEUM *Seufert Cannery Bldg., Seufert Park* Ancient and modern Indian artifacts are featured. *Open Tues.-Sun. May-Sept., Wed.-Sun. Oct.-Apr.*

Vernonia
COLUMBIA COUNTY MUSEUM *511 E. Bridge St.* Logging equipment and pioneer artifacts are displayed in a former lumbermill office. *Open Tues.-Sun.*

Wolf Creek
WOLF CREEK INN Still open to travelers, this 1857 structure is Oregon's oldest hotel. *Open daily.*

Utah

Logan
L.D.S. TEMPLE *175 N. Third E. St.* Mormons completed the massive spired building in 1884. *Grounds open daily.*

UNION PACIFIC RAILROAD STATION *600 W. Center St.* The building is a fine example of 1890s station architecture. *Open Mon.-Fri.*

UTAH STATE UNIVERSITY The Ronald V. Jensen Historical Farm and Man and His Bread Museum tell of early agriculture in the arid West.

Ogden
DAUGHTERS OF UTAH PIONEERS RELIC HALL *2148 Grant Ave.* Pioneer belongings include musical instruments. *Open daily June-Sept.*

JOHN M. BROWNING ARMORY *4 mi. S. on Rte. 89* A special room displays models of guns by inventor John Browning. *Open Mon.-Fri.*

Washington

Bellingham
PICKETT HOUSE *910 Bancroft St.* Civil War general George E. Pickett built this home in 1856.

Blaine
PEACE ARCH On the Canada-U.S.

Key: Historic Place · Historic House · Old Mill or Works · Museum or Collection · Significant Building

boundary, the portal celebrates the two nations' peaceful relations.

Brewster

FORT OKANOGAN *5 mi. E. on Rte. 97* The 1811 Astor fur-trading post here was the state's first American settlement. *Open daily June-Sept.*

Cathlamet

WAHKIAKUM COUNTY HISTORICAL SOCIETY MUSEUM *Division and River Sts.* Items here emphasize local history. *Open Tues.-Sun. June-Aug., Thurs.-Sun. Sept.-May.*

Centralia

FORT BORST BLOCKHOUSE *Fort Borst Park* The log building was a grain depot during Indian wars.

Kettle Falls

ST. PAUL'S MISSION *W. off Rte. 395* The small log chapel, built by Jesuit missionaries, served the region from 1847 to 1869. *Open daily.*

Maryhill

STONEHENGE WAR MEMORIAL A replica of England's ancient Stonehenge honors World War I dead.

Miles

FORT SPOKANE Four buildings of the late 1800s garrison tell of frontier military life. *Open daily.*

Moses Lake

ADAM EAST MUSEUM *Fifth and Balsam Sts.* Columbia River Indian artifacts are shown. *Open Tues.-Sun. Mar.-Oct. except holidays.*

Pasco

SACAJAWEA STATE PARK *6 mi. S.E. on Rte. 395* In 1805 Lewis and Clark made their camp here. An Interpretive Center features Indian artifacts. *Open daily May-early Sept.*

Puyallup

PIONEER PARK *S. Meridian and Fourth Ave.* The large park honors the town's founder, Ezra Meeker, whose statue symbolizes the pioneer spirit. *Open daily.*

Seattle

ALKI POINT LIGHT STATION *3201 Alki Point S.W.* The lighthouse overlooks the point where Seattle's first settlers landed in 1851. *Open daily.*

CHIEF SEATTLE STATUE *Fifth Ave. and Denny Way* Chief Seattle is honored as a leader and peacemaker.

HIRAM M. CHITTENDEN LOCKS *W. end of Salmon Bay* Active locks and exotic gardens make this a popular site. *Open daily.*

ST. JAMES CATHEDRAL *804 Ninth Ave.* Twin towers flank the Renaissance-style edifice. *Open daily.*

Spokane

CROSBY LIBRARY *Gonzaga University, E. 502 Boone Ave.* Items associated with alumnus Bing Crosby are highlights. *Open daily.*

INDIAN PAINTED ROCKS *9 mi. N.W. near Rutter Pkwy. Bridge* Ancient Indians decorated rocks here.

SPOKANE HOUSE *Riverside State Park* Exhibits focus on the fur-trading post located here from 1810 to 1826. *Open daily mid-Apr.-mid-Sept.*

Tacoma

JOB CARR'S HOUSE *Point Defiance Park* Tacoma's first settler used this log cabin as a combined home-post office. *Open daily.*

Vancouver

COVINGTON HOUSE *4208 Main St.* The 1846 log house was the home of an employee of the Hudson's Bay Company. *Open Tues., Thurs. June-Aug.*

OLD SLOCUM HOUSE *605 Esther St.* The 1867 New England-style mansion has been converted into an amateur playhouse.

PIONEER MOTHERS STATUE *Eighth and Columbia Sts., Esther Short Park* The sculpture of a woman and three children honors all frontier women.

Woodland

CEDAR CREEK GRIST MILL *10 mi. E.* The picturesque 1876 mill is built of cedar. *Open daily.*

Wyoming

Casper

NATRONA COUNTY PIONEER MUSEUM *Fairgrounds* An 1891 church holds local pioneer artifacts. *Open Wed.-Mon. mid-May-mid.-Sept.*

Cheyenne

WARREN MILITARY MUSEUM *F. E. Warren Air Force Base* Exhibits depict its history from cavalry post to missile station. *Open daily July-Aug., Sun. and holidays Sept.-June.*

Douglas

FORT FETTERMAN *11 mi. N.W. on Orpha Rd.* The 1867 military post has historical exhibits in the old officers' quarters. *Open daily May-Sept.*

WYOMING PIONEERS' MEMORIAL MUSEUM *State Fairgrounds* Relics of pioneers and Indians are the major attractions. *Open Tues.-Sun. mid-Apr.-Oct.*

Fort Washakie

FORT WASHAKIE *Wind River Indian Reservation* Several buildings remain at the old fort. *Open daily.*

Gillette

WELTNER WONDER MUSEUM *S. on Rte. 59* Peace pipes are among the collections. *Open daily Apr.-Oct. Small charge.*

Green River

SWEETWATER COUNTY MUSEUM Artifacts used by Chinese workers in the coal-mining days are the feature. *Open Mon.-Fri. except holidays.*

Greybull

GREYBULL MUSEUM *325 Greybull Ave.* The museum has an outstanding fossil collection. *Open daily June-mid-Sept., Mon.-Sat. mid-Sept.-May.*

Jackson

JACKSON HOLE MUSEUM Ancient Indian bowls, fur trappers' guns and a pioneer piano recall local history. *Open daily May-Sept. Small charge.*

Lander

FREMONT COUNTY PIONEER MUSEUM *630 Lincoln St.* Bygone lifestyles are seen in tools, utensils and wagons. *Open daily May-Oct.*

Laramie

LARAMIE PLAINS MUSEUM *603 Ivinson Ave.* Memorabilia from pioneer days comprise a choice collection. *Open Mon.-Fri. Small charge.*

WESTERN HISTORY RESEARCH CENTER *Coe Library, University of Wyoming* The center, devoted to Western materials, offers occasional special displays. *Open Mon.-Fri.*

Lusk

STAGE COACH MUSEUM *342 Main St.* Star attraction of the frontier items is an 1850s Concord stagecoach. *Open daily mid-May-late Oct. Small charge.*

Mammoth Hot Springs

MAMMOTH HOT SPRINGS VISITOR CENTER *Yellowstone National Park* Five exhibits tell of Indians, early explorers and local wildlife. *Open daily. Park admission $2.00 each car.*

Moose

MOOSE VISITOR CENTER AND FUR TRADE MUSEUM *Grand Teton National Park* Exhibits dramatize fur-trading days of the 1820s and '30s. *Open daily except Dec. 25.*

Newcastle

ACCIDENTAL OIL COMPANY EXHIBITS *4 mi. E. on Rte. 16* Oil oozing from the earth in an underground room relates to the antique oil rigs and the refinery. *Open daily. Guided tour small charge.*

ANNA MILLER MUSEUM Tools, machinery and furnishings reveal homesteading days. *Open Sun.-Fri. June-Aug., Fri. Sept.-May.*

Rawlins

CARBON COUNTY MUSEUM *Courthouse, Fifth and Pine* Indian and pioneer items of the area are featured. *Open Mon.-Fri. June-Sept., Fri. Sept.-June.*

Rock River

FOSSIL CABIN *Rte. 30* The extraordinary structure was built from hundreds of dinosaur bones. *Small charge.*

South Pass City

Untouched and restored buildings stand together as a testament to the community's gold-mining era.

Story

FORT PHIL KEARNY *Off Rte. 87* A replica officers' quarters and a stockade stand at the post. *Open daily.*

Thermopolis

HOT SPRINGS COUNTY PIONEER MUSEUM *235 Springview* Diverse exhibits include Indian artifacts, guns, a stagecoach and a sheepherder's wagon. *Open daily Mar.-Oct.*

Topical Directory

If you have any particular interest in any of the following 17 subjects, this directory will help you find the places where the most outstanding collections can be seen. The states are in alphabetical order, as are the entries within a state. The first number indicates the page, the second—in brackets—is the entry number on the page and on the regional maps.

Arms and Armament

Costume

Furniture

Glass and Glassware

Indian Artifacts and Arts

The first number indicates the page. The bracketed number indicates the entry on that page.

Marine Museums and Collections

Museum Towns

Oriental Arts

Painting: Old Masters

Painting: Early American 19th- and 20th-Century American Realist

* Exceptional collections of early American paintings

The first number indicates the page. The bracketed number indicates the entry on that page.

Painting: Impressionist, Post-Impressionist, Cubist and Early Modern

Painting: Late Modern and Contemporary

Sculpture

Silver and Pewter Ware

Tools and Implements

Toys and Dolls

Transportation: Planes, Trains, Carriages and Cars

The first number indicates the page. The bracketed number indicates the entry on that page.

Index

The first number indicates the page (boldface for illustrations). Bracketed number indicates the entry on that page.

The first number indicates the page (boldface for illustrations). Bracketed number indicates the entry on that page.

The first number indicates the page (boldface for illustrations). Bracketed number indicates the entry on that page.

The first number indicates the page (boldface for illustrations). Bracketed number indicates the entry on that page.

The first number indicates the page (boldface for illustrations). Bracketed number indicates the entry on that page.

The first number indicates the page (boldface for illustrations). Bracketed number indicates the entry on that page.

The first number indicates the page (boldface for illustrations). Bracketed number indicates the entry on that page.

The first number indicates the page (boldface for illustrations). Bracketed number indicates the entry on that page.

The first number indicates the page (boldface for illustrations). Bracketed number indicates the entry on that page.

The first number indicates the page (boldface for illustrations). Bracketed number indicates the entry on that page.

The first number indicates the page (boldface for illustrations). Bracketed number indicates the entry on that page.

The first number indicates the page (boldface for illustrations). Bracketed number indicates the entry on that page.

The first number indicates the page (boldface for illustrations). Bracketed number indicates the entry on that page.

Picture Credits

Cover stamping design, James Alexander. Title page drawing, Cal Sachs.

Drawings **5, 18, 20, 21, 22** *bottom,* **23, 25, 27, 28, 29, 30, 31, 32** *top,* **33, 34, 35, 36, 38** *top,* **39** *left,* **40, 41, 42, 43, 44, 45, 47, 48,** Howard Berelson.

Architectural renderings **77–9, 158–9, 224–5, 256–7, 330–1, 396–7, 450–1,** Peter Rahill.

All maps by H. M. GOUSHĀ COMPANY
A SUBSIDIARY OF TIMES MIRROR COMPANY.

Photographs

8 Worcester Art Museum. **9** Museum of Fine Arts, Boston. **10** *top* Cleveland Museum of Art, Gift of the John Huntington Art and Polytechnic Trust; *bottom* Smithsonian Institution. **11** The Granger Collection. **12** New York Public Library. **13** *top* Museum of Fine Arts, Boston; *bottom* National Gallery of Art/Harris Whittemore Collection. **14** *top* Metropolitan Museum of Art, Bequest of Jacob Ruppert; *bottom* Philadelphia Museum of Art. **15** Philadelphia Museum of Art/Louise and Walter Arensberg Collection. **16** Whitney Museum of American Art. **17** Metropolitan Museum of Art, Bequest of Adelaide Milton de Groot. **22** *top* Dover Publications, Inc. **24** New York Public Library. **32** *bottom* Culver Pictures. **37** *top* International Museum of Photography at George Eastman House; *bottom* Brown Brothers. **38** *bottom* Culver Pictures. **39** *right* Brown Brothers. **54, 55** Douglas Armsden. **56** *left* Douglas Armsden; *right* International Museum of Photography at George Eastman House. **57** International Museum of Photography at George Eastman House. **58** Memorial Art Gallery of the University of Rochester. **59** Douglas Armsden. **60** *left* Steuben Glass; *right* Corning Glass Center. **61** Editorial Photocolor Archives, Inc. **62, 63** Remington Art Museum, Ogdensburg, N.Y. **64** Douglas Armsden. **65** Holy Trinity Monastery. **66** *left* Canajoharie Library and Art Gallery, Canajoharie, N.Y.; *right* Douglas Armsden. **67** Adirondack Museum. **68** Fort Ticonderoga. **69** National Museum of Racing. **70, 71, 72,** Shelburne Museum, Inc., Shelburne, Vt. **73** *top* Shelburne Museum, Inc., Shelburne, Vt.; *bottom* © Grandma Moses Properties, Inc., New York, N.Y. **74** *left* Frank L. Forward; *right* Douglas Armsden. **75** The Elizabeth McCullough Johnson Collection/Bennington Museum, Bennington, Vt. **76** Vermont Council on the Arts, Inc. **80** Adrian Bouchard. **81, 82** Vermont Development Agency. **83** Steamtown Foundation. **84** Vermont Development Agency. **85** *left* Million Dollar Schuller Museum; *right* Carroll C. Calkins. **86** Bill Finney. **87** Currier Gallery of Art. **89** Ned Bullock Studio/Clark House. **90** Douglas Armsden. **91** Louis H. Frohman. **92** Douglas Armsden. **93** *top* Douglas Armsden; *bottom* Louis H. Frohman. **94** Maine Department of Commerce and Industry. **95** *top* Augustus D. Phillips; *middle* Oscar Keller; *bottom* Lucille Johnston/Maine Historical Society. **96** Lyman Owen. **97** Carroll C. Calkins. **98** Louis H. Frohman. **99** *top* Carroll C. Calkins; *bottom* Louis H. Frohman. **100** University of Maine at Orono. **101** Augustus D. Phillips. **104** *left* New York State Historical Association; *right* National Baseball Hall of Fame and Museum. **105** New York State Office of General Services. **106** Huguenot Historical Society. **107** Donna Harris. **108** Curt Teich & Co., Inc. **109** Duke Gardens Foundation, Inc. **110** George A. Tice. **111** Metropolitan Museum of Art, Gift of John S. Kennedy. **112** Roosevelt-Vanderbilt National Historic Sites. **113** *top* Richard Watherwax; *bottom, left* Carroll C. Calkins; *bottom, right* Boscobel Restoration, Inc. **114** Frank Moscati/Reader's Digest. **115** Robert Phillips/Reader's Digest. **116** *left* Tony Linck; *right* American Museum of Natural History. **117** © Dexter Press, Inc. **118** *top, left and bottom* Metropolitan Museum of Art/The Cloisters Collection; *top, right* Metropolitan Museum of Art/The Cloisters Collection, Fletcher Fund. **119** Metropolitan Museum of Art/The Cloisters Collection, Gift of John D. Rockefeller. **120** Empire State Building. **121** Manhattan Post Card Publishing Co., Inc. **122** *top* Metropolitan Museum of Art, Gift of Edgar William and Bernice Chrysler Garbisch; *bottom* Metropolitan Museum of Art, Gift of Henry G. Marquand. **123** *top* Metropolitan Museum of Art, Gift of Mrs. David M. Levy; *bottom* Metropolitan Museum of Art. **124** *top, left* Metropolitan Museum of Art, Fletcher Fund; *top, right* Metropolitan Museum of Art, Gift of Mrs. Henry McSweeney; *bottom, left* Metropolitan Museum of Art/The Carnarvon Collection, Gift of Edward S. Harkness; *bottom, center* Metropolitan Museum of Art, Munsey Fund; *bottom, right* Metropolitan Museum of Art, Rogers Fund. **125** *top* Metropolitan Museum of Art; *bottom* Metropolitan Museum of Art, Rogers Fund. **126** Museum of Modern Art. **127** Pierpont Morgan Library. **128** *left* Donna Harris; *right* St. Patrick's Cathedral. **129** United Nations. **130** Whitney Museum of American Art. **131** © Arnold Newman. **132** First Presbyterian Church. **133** *left* John King; *right* Carroll C. Calkins. **134** Winchester Gun Museum. **135** *left* Yale University Art Museum; *right* Henry Whitfield State Historical Museum. **136** Mystic Seaport, Mystic, Conn. **137** *top* Donna Harris; *bottom* Mystic Seaport, Mystic, Conn. **138** Chesterwood/National Trust for Historic Preservation. **139** Hitchcock Chair Company. **141** © Arnold Newman. **142** Museum of Fine Arts, Springfield, Mass. **143** Mark Twain Memorial. **144, 145** Wadsworth Atheneum. **146** Goodspeed Opera House. **147** *left* Kurklen Studio; *right* Worchester Art Museum, Gift of Richard K. Thorndike. **148** *top and bottom, left* Old Sturbridge Village, *middle and bottom, right* Walter H. Miller. **149** Old Sturbridge Village. **151** *top and bottom, left* Lexington Historical Society, Inc.; *bottom, right* Keith Martin. **152** *left* Bromley & Company, Inc.; *right* Donna Harris. **153** First Baptist Church in America. **154, 155** © John T. Hopf. **156** Whaling Museum, New Bedford, Mass. **157** Peabody Museum of Salem. **161, 162** Angelo Hornak. **163** First Church of Christ, Scientist. **164, 165** Museum of Fine Arts, Boston. **166** Editorial Photocolor Archives, Inc. **167** Angelo Hornak. **168** P. W. Grace/Photo Researchers. **172** Old Economy Village. **173** *top and middle* Museum of Art/Carnegie Institute, Pittsburgh; *bottom* Carnegie Museum/Carnegie Institute, Pittsburgh. **174** Fallingwater. **175** Richard Frear/National Park Service. **176** Hershey Estates. **177** Automobilorama. **178** *top* Jacques Jangoux/Photo Researchers; *bottom* Frank Moscati/Reader's Digest. **179** *left and bottom, right* Frank Moscati/Reader's Digest; *top, right* Dick Durrance/Photo Researchers. **180** Historical Society of York County. **181** *top* Thomas J. Harrison/National Park Service; *bottom* Colourpicture Publishers. **182** Arnout Hyde, Jr. **183** U.S. Department of Transportation/Federal Aviation Administration. **184** Photri. **185** *left* Corcoran Gallery of Art; *right* Fred J. Maroon. **186, 187** Photri. **188** Lee Boltin. **189** *top* Gabor Kiss; *middle and bottom* Lee Boltin. **190-1** Arnold Newman/ © 1965 Smithsonian Institution. **190** *bottom* Freer Gallery of Art/Smithsonian Institution. **191** *top, right* National Gallery of Art; *bottom* Donna Harris. **192** *left* Stan Wayman; *right* Lee Boltin. **193** *top* Arnold Newman/ © 1965 Smithsonian Institution; *bottom* Lee Boltin. **194** *top, left* Robert C. Lautman; *top, right* National Portrait Gallery/Smithsonian Institution, Washington, D.C.; *bottom* Lee Boltin. **195** *top* Donna Harris; *bottom* Stan Wayman. **196** J. D. Barnell. **197** Photri. **198** *left* Fred J. Maroon; *right* Phillips Collection. **199** Angelo Hornak. **200** M. E. Warren. **201** Photri. **202** Clare Clement. **203** Marler/National Trust for Historic Preservation. **204** Mount Vernon Ladies' Association. **205** *top* Jacques Jangoux; *middle and bottom* Mount Vernon Ladies' Association. **206** Photri. **207** *left* Louis H. Frohman; *right* Jacques Jangoux. **208** Virginia State Travel Service. **209** Virginia Museum of Fine Arts. **210** *left* Angelo Hornak; *right* Thomas L. Williams. **211** Beckwith Studios. **212, 213, 214, 215** Colonial Williamsburg Foundation. **216** Photri. **217** *left* M. E. Warren; *right* Hermitage Foundation Museum. **218** Photri. **219, 220** M. E. Warren. **221** Star-Spangled Banner Flag House. **222** Walters Art Gallery. **223** M. E. Warren. **227** Longwood Gardens. **228** Colourpicture Publishers. **229** R.C.A. Records. **230** The Henry Francis du Pont Winterthur Museum. **231** *top* Gottlieb and Hilda Hampfler; *bottom* The Henry Francis du Pont Winterthur Museum. **232** Edgar William and Bernice Chrysler Garbisch. **233** Samuel H. Kress Memorial Collection/Allentown Art Museum. **234** *top* Photri; *bottom* Bucks County Historical Society. **235** Joseph F. Morsello/Buten Museum of Wedgwood. **236** Editorial Photocolor Archives, Inc. **237** Angelo Hornak. **238** Office of the City Representative and Director of Commerce. **239** *left* Editorial Photocolor Archives, Inc.; *right* Pennsylvania Academy of the Fine Arts. **240** Office of the City

Representative and Director of Commerce. **241** Photri. **242** *left* University Museum; *right* Pendor Natural Color. **243** George A. Tice. **247** Beauvoir/Jefferson Davis Shrine. **248** Fred W. Holder/Bellingrath Gardens. **249** *left* © Dexter Press, Inc.; *right* Historic Mobile Preservation. **250** Naval Aviation Museum. **251** *left* James K. Polk Memorial Auxiliary; *right* Keily Studio. **252** Polk Studio. **253** Dan Quest & Associates. **255** Tennessee Tourism Development Division. **258** *left* Houston Antique Museum; *right* Siskin Memorial Foundation. **259** Russell Cave National Monument. **260** *left* Stone Mountain Memorial Association; *right* Governor's Mansion. **261** Atlanta Historical Society. **263** Westville Historic Handicrafts. **264** Early American Museum. **265** Frank Hutchins. **266** The American Foundation, Inc. **267** Lincoln Memorial University. **268, 269** Ringling Museum of Art. **270** National Park Service. **271** Buckhorn Press. **272** Biltmore House and Gardens. **273** Bob Jones University/Gallery of Sacred Art. **274** Georgia Museum of Art, Gift of Alfred H. Holbrook. **276** The Grand Opera House. **277** Reynolda House, Inc. **278, 279** Old Salem, Inc. **281** Mint Museum of Art. **282** University of South Carolina. **283** Santee Exhibitions. **284, 285** Paul Jensen. **287** State of North Carolina Department of Art, Culture and History/Office of Archives and History. **288** Arnout Hyde, Jr. **289** Hugh Morton. **290** *top, left and bottom* Tryon Palace. **290-1** North Carolina Dept. of Natural and Economic Resources. **291** *middle and bottom* J. D. Barnell. **292** Photo Arts. **293** Middleton Place. **294** Historic Charleston Foundation. **295** Arnout Hyde, Jr. **296** *left* Jack Zehrt; *right* Savannah Area Chamber of Commerce. **297** Walter H. Miller. **299** Telfair Academy of Arts and Sciences. **300** Jack Zehrt. **301** *left* Arnout Hyde, Jr.; *right* Jack Zehrt. **302** Hugh and Jeannette McKean. **303** Real Eight Co., Inc. **304** Metropolitan Dade County Park and Recreation Dept. **305** Audubon House, Key West, Fla. **308** *left* Art Institute of Chicago/Friends of American Art Collection; *right* Art Institute of Chicago/Helen Birch Bartlett Memorial Collection. **309** Carson Pirie Scott & Co. **310** Chicago Dept. of Water and Sewers. **311** *left* Chicago Convention and Tourism Bureau; *right* Field Museum of Natural History, Chicago. **312, 313** Museum of Science and Industry, Chicago. **314** University of Chicago. **316** Don Blair. **317** Indiana Dept. of Natural Resources. **318** Kentucky Dept. of Public Information. **319** Kalamazoo Public Museum. **320** Detroit Zoological Park. **321** Detroit Institute of Art. **322, 323, 324, 325** Collections of Greenfield Village and Henry Ford Museum. **326** University of Notre Dame. **327** Gene Pickett. **328** © Indy Images, Inc. **329** Indiana University. **333** Lincoln Boyhood National Memorial. **334** Lin Caufield Photographers. **335** J. B. Speed Art Museum. **336** Kentucky Dept. of Public Information. **337** *left* Toledo Museum of Art; *right* Curt Teich & Co., Inc. **338** U.S. Air Force Museum. **339** McGuffey Museum. **340** Cincinnati Art Museum. **341** Ralph Clyburn. **342** Taft Museum. **343** *left* Lawrence Zink; *right* Headley Museum. **344** Berea College. **345** Curt Teich & Co., Inc. **346** Columbus Gallery of Fine Arts. **347** Tony Linck. **348** Cleveland Museum of Art, Leonard C. Hanna, Jr. Bequest. **349** *top* Cleveland Museum of Art, Gift of Hanna Fund; *middle* Cleveland Museum of Art, Hinman B. Hurlbut Collection; *bottom* Cleveland Museum of Art, Gift of John Huntington Art and Polytechnic Trust. **350** Western Reserve Historical Society. **351** Hale Farm and Village. **352** Walter A. Long. **353** Ohio Historical Society. **354** Butler Institute of American Art. **355** Oglebay Institute. **359** National Park Service/Mount Rushmore Memorial. **360** Rushmore Photo. **361** National Park Service/Scotts Bluff National Monument, Nebr. **363** North Dakota Highway Dept. **364-5** Stuhr Museum of the Prairie Pioneer. **367** Dacotah Prairie Museum. **368** South Dakota Memorial Art Center. **369** Clyde H. Goin. **370** *top* Joslyn Art Museum; *bottom* Northern Natural Gas Company Collection/Joslyn Art Museum. **371** *top and bottom, right* Joslyn Art Museum; *bottom, left* Northern Natural Gas Company Collection/Joslyn Art Museum. **372, 373** Nebraska Game and Parks Commission. **374** National Park Service/Homestead National Monument. **375** St. John's. **376** Iowa State Education Association. **377** St. Louis County Historical Society. **378** The Minneapolis Institute of Arts. **380** Warren Reynolds & Associates. **381** Norwegian-American Museum, Decorah, Iowa. **382** The Telegraph-Herald. **383** University of Iowa Museum of Natural History. **384-5** Deere & Company. **386** Circus World Museum, Baraboo, Wis. **387** Little Norway. **389** City of Neenah Municipal Museum Foundation/John Nelson Bergstrom Art Center and Museum. **390** Paine Art Center and Arboretum. **391** Watertown Historical Society. **392** Marquette University. **393** *top* Milwaukee Public Museum; *bottom* Kenosha Public Museum. **394** Jack Zehrt. **395** Hackley Art Gallery. **399** Mary Riordan/Cranbrook Academy of Art. **402** Museum of Texas Tech University. **403** National Park Service. **404** Renee Studio. **405** Wichita Art Museum. **406** Fred W. Marvel/Oklahoma Tourism and Recreation Dept. **407** Fort Sill Museum. **408-9** Courtesy Amon Carter Museum of Western Art, Fort Worth, Tex. **410** Fort Worth Art Center Museum. **411** Fort Worth Museum of Science and History. **412, 413** Texas Highway Dept. **414** *left* The Alamo; *right* Lee Boltin. **416, 417** St. Joseph Museum. **418** Harry S. Truman Library. **419** Country Club Plaza Association. **420** Woolaroc Museum. **422, 423** Thomas Gilcrease Institute of American History and Art. **424** Kerr Museum. **425** R. W. Norton Art Gallery, Shreveport, La. **426, 427** Bayou Bend Collection/Museum of Fine Arts, Houston. **428** Missouri Tourism Commission. **429** Ronald G. Marquette/Museum of Art and Archaeology, University of Missouri-Columbia. **430** Winston Churchill Memorial and Library. **431** The Museum of Automobiles. **432** Josef Muench. **434** Arnout Hyde, Jr. **435** Illinois State Museum. **436, 437, 438, 439, 440** Jack Zehrt. **442** William R. Ellis, Jr. **443** Helga Studio/Courtesy of *Antiques* Magazine. **444** Jack Zehrt. **445** Pilgrimage Garden Club. **446** Rosedown Plantation and Gardens. **448** Jack Zehrt. **449** *top* Jack Zehrt; *bottom* Lee Boltin. **453** Lee Boltin. **456** Camera Hawaii. **457** Bernice P. Bishop Museum. **458** Honolulu Academy of Arts, Gift of the Charles M. and Anna C. Cooke Trust. **459** Camera Hawaii. **460** Jack Zehrt. **461** The Fine Arts Museum of San Francisco/California Palace of the Legion of Honor. **462** Jack Zehrt. **463** San Francisco Convention and Visitors Bureau/Courtesy Ghirardelli Square. **464** Theodore Osmundson. **465** Stanford University. **466** Rosicrucian Egyptian Museum. **467** Mission San Carlos Borromeo. **468, 469, 470, 471** State of California Dept. of Parks and Recreation/Hearst San Simeon State Historical Monument. **473** Steve Jost Co. **474** Los Angeles County Museum of Art. **475** Southern California Visitors Council. **476** Mission Inn. **477** Riverside County Art and Culture Center/Edward-Dean Museum of Decorative Arts. **478, 479** Huntington Library, Art Gallery and Botanical Gardens. **480** Hale Observatories. **481** Edmund F. White/San Diego Maritime Museum. **482** Tom Myers. **483** *left* David Muench; *right* Tom Myers. **484, 485** Harrah's Automobile Collection, Reno, Nev. **486** Jack Zehrt. **487** Bureau of Reclamation. **488** Jack Zehrt. **491** David Muench. **492** Robert J. Woodward. **493** Willis Peterson. **494** Arizona State Museum. **495** National Park Service/Dinosaur National Monument. **496** Josef Muench. **497** Donna Harris. **498** *top* Denver Art Museum; *bottom* Forney Transportation Museum. **499** O. A. Sealy. **500** Dept. of the Air Force. **502** M. E. Warren. **503** Museum of Navaho Ceremonial Art. **504** Harvey Caplin. **505** Maxwell Museum of Anthropology. **508** John F. Hermle. **509** Alaska Division of Tourism. **510** Bob and Ira Spring. **511** *top* Columbia River Maritime Museum; *bottom* Jack Zehrt. **512** *top* Whatcom Museum of History and Art; *bottom* Kitsap County Historical Society. **513** Josephus Daniels. **514** *top* Seattle Art Museum/Samuel H. Kress Collection; *bottom* Seattle Art Museum, Gift of Mark Tobey and the Otto Seligman Gallery. **515** Seattle Art Museum/Eugene Fuller Memorial Collection. **516** Permanent Collection of the Tacoma Art Museum. **517** Ellis Post Card Co. **518** Cascade Locks Historical Museum. **519** *top* Sweeney, Krist & Dimm; *bottom* Larry J. Van Winkle. **520** Portland Art Museum, Portland, Ore. **521** Japanese Garden Society of Oregon. **523** University of Oregon. **524, 525** Southern Oregon Historical Society. **526** *left* Ray Atkeson; *right* Maryhill Museum of Fine Arts. **527** Gladys Seufert. **528** Schminck Memorial Museum. **529** *top* Ray Atkeson; *bottom* Eastern Washington State Historical Society. **530** Bob and Ira Spring. **531** Boise Gallery of Art. **532** *left* Greater Boise Chamber of Commerce; *right* Museum of the Plains Indian. **533** Ross Hall Scenics. **534** Tom Myers. **535** Copper King Mansion. **536** Dick Ellis. **537** Box Elder Tabernacle. **538-9** Gallery '85. **540** Bradford Brinton Memorial. **541** Fort Laramie Historical Association. **542, 543** Buffalo Bill Historical Center. **544** University of Wyoming Geological Museum.

PICTURE EDITOR: Robert J. Woodward.